SEEDER WARS

The Complete Trilogy

J. Houser

Painted Wings Publishing

Note from the Author

When I decided to make a *Seeder Wars* trilogy omnibus, I chose to go all-in on the extra touches. This thick beauty not only holds the full trilogy, but also contains annotations, a few bonus scenes found in *Seeder Stories*, and more. I hope you enjoy the extra touches, and the exciting stories!

*Annotations are designated by a small coordinating symbol such as (a) which can be matched up to commentary in the back of the book.

**Find extra books, merch, and more on my site!

Table of Contents

Content & Trigger Warnings...i
Pronunciation Guide...ii
Map...iii
Seeder Shadow Wars (Book 1)...1
The Return & Question (Bonus Scenes)..245
Trouble in the Green Lands (Book 2)...253
Kaylah's Chronicles (Bonus Scenes)..547
Unitas: Trio (Book 3)...573
Annotation Guide...1003
Character Art..1008
Connect with the author..1009
More by J. Houser...1010

Content & Trigger Warnings

While this series is not particularly dark or graphic, some topics and scenes may be hard for some readers or inappropriate for younger audiences. While it's impossible to list every possible concern, I've included a list of some of the most common or serious concerns.

Swearing: Minor

Romantic heat level: Includes fade-to-black scenes and discussions of sex

Violence: Involves war & assassins, but is not graphic/gratuitous

Possible triggers: manipulation, mental health struggles, self-harm, death/grief, assault and thwarted sexual assault, discrimination, racism, ableism, and mentions of abuse and suicide

I love a good adventure and romance, but I also bring up meaningful topics in a fantasy setting that can spark conversation and help readers feel less alone in their struggles.

I aim to tactfully include sensitive topics, and have had positive feedback from beta readers and editors about the way they're approached here. My intention is never to glorify or justify harmful behavior, even if a fictional character doesn't get it quite right. If you find yourself struggling with any of these issues in real life, please know you're not alone, not past hope, and not beyond help from professionals, friends, and family.

~J. Houser

Pronunciation Guide

People

Beata: bay-AH-tuh

Boman/Bomen: BOW-man

Dahlia: DAH-lee-uh

Elonta: ee-LAWN-tuh

Guillen: GUY-en

Kaylah: KAY-luh

Kyas: KAI-us

Lyza: LIZ-uh

Magda: MAWG-duh

Marigold: MARE-ih-gold

    (**Mari:** mah-ree)

Murial: MYUR-ee-ul

Nuren: NYUR-en

Rian: ree-ann

Saffrona: suh-FRONE-uh

    (**Saff:** saff)

Sanath: SAN-uth

Teagan: TEE-gun

Thod: thawed

Tobias: toe-BYE-us

    (**Toby:** TOE-bee)

Places & Things

Arcadia: are-KAY-dee-uh

Cassa: CASS-uh

Domiten: dome-IDE-en

Fortinda: for-TIN-da

Guenjalis: gwen-YAWL-iss

Siqendra: sick-EN-druh

Tonoru: TONE-oh-roo

Unitas: OO-knee-tas

*To hear an audio clip by the author, go to JHouserWrites.com/swpronunciation

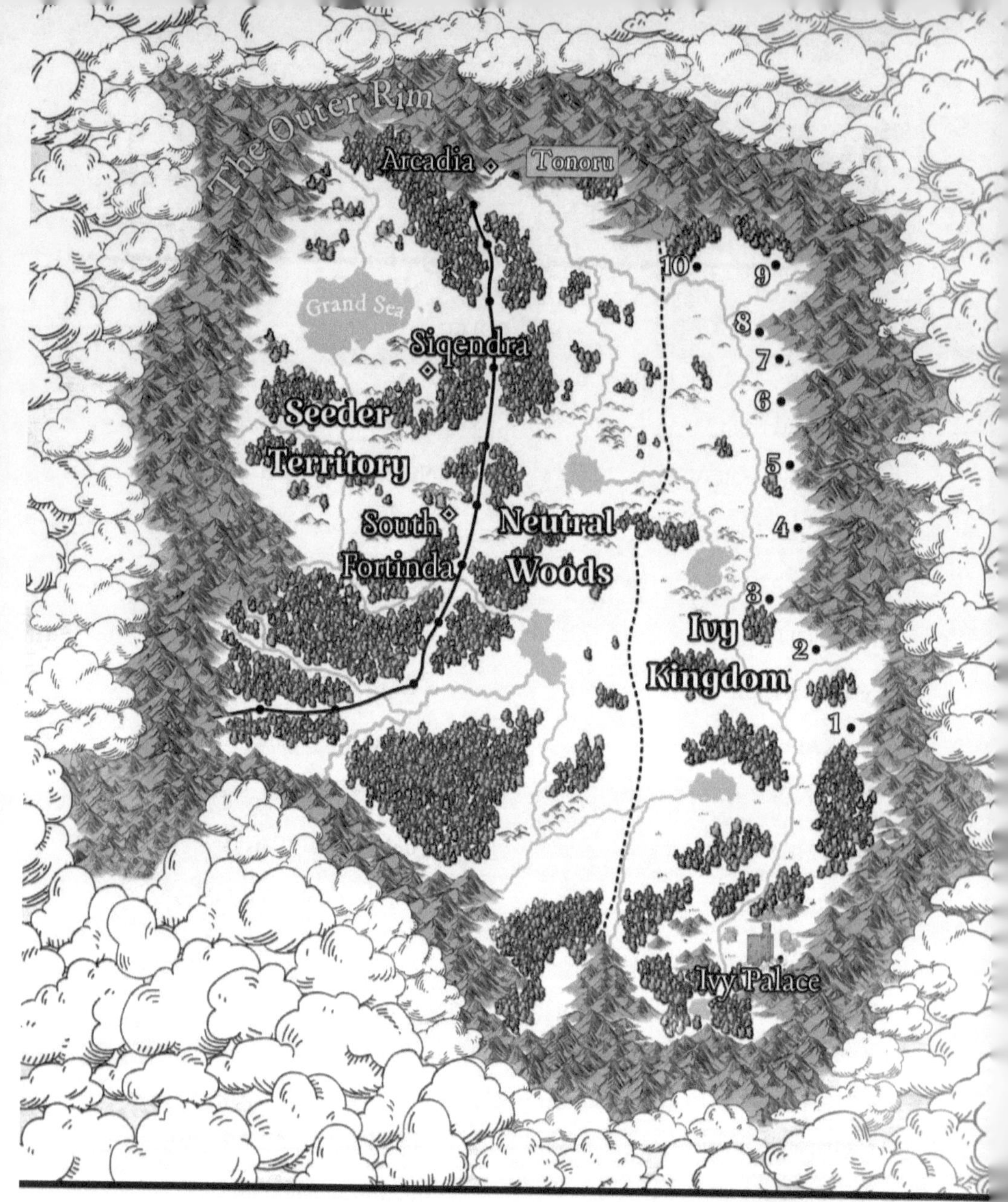

The Green Lands

SEEDER SHADOW WARS

BOOK 1

Prologue

Bordered by impassable mountains, a pocket realm tucked away on Earth was safely shrouded from human knowledge and interference. The hidden paradise was a land of beauty and lush plant growth, filled with an energy that coursed through the very veins of the people who lived there. The inhabitants could sense the cyclical energy shifts associated with the human world, though their own realm lacked any true change in season.

On the western front, people lived simple lives in quaint communities. As simple and quaint as they could be, in the midst of a never-ending war.

Murial[a] stared down at her clutch of seedlings, her children. She wore a faint smile, her joy tainted by the vicious aching in her heart. Today would be the hardest day of her life.

Thod walked up behind Murial, wrapping his arms around her. He moved her auburn hair to the side and placed a sweet kiss on her cheek. "Are you going to be okay?"

She swallowed hard, reminding herself that she'd signed up for this. She wanted kids. Murial turned to face her husband, giving him the best smile she could muster. "I'll be great."

She looked around at the new home they'd just moved into. Like others lining their lane, it was much bigger than the tiny cottage they'd moved out of. It was beautifully simplistic with raw, natural wood. Books and potted flowers covered the shelves in the corner. The extra space and larger garden out back would be just enough for this next phase of their lives.

Thod gazed into her eyes. "I couldn't have picked a better woman to raise my boys."

Murial drew a deep breath, her smile warming. "I'll make you proud. And I know you'll take good care of the girls."

He nodded, then patted his pants pocket. "I've got the letter for your dad. Anything else?"

She pursed her lips, thinking of the human dad that had helped raise her. Letters were all they had now. Having reached maturity, which allowed her to have a clutch, she wasn't capable of leaving the Green Lands anymore. She scanned Thod, then glanced back at their seedlings.

"I think we're all set." Murial pulled him in closer. "There's just one last thing."

They shared a smile and she leaned in, giving him a kiss. The kind of kiss only a Seeder woman could give. The kind that imbued him with a portion of her energy, both expressing her love, and bolstering him for the long and difficult journey ahead.

It being the first day of spring, Murial and Thod gathered their seedling hopefuls and stepped outside. Walking a few feet from the door, they placed the glistening, round seeds on the dirt in the middle of the lane. A handful of neighbors were proudly doing the same with their own clutches for this year's sprout reveal. Murial breathed deeply, tightly gripping Thod's hand and forcing herself to soak in the wonder and beauty of the moment.

As the sun rose, it peeked over the wooden homes and bathed the eager parents waiting in anticipation. Shortly after the rays reached the seeds, they began to wiggle. Next door, a shout of glee rang out; someone's first seedling had sprouted. Murial and Thod glanced over for just a moment to check it out, then returned to watching their own clutch.

Puff.

"There's one!" Thod rejoiced, squeezing her hand.

Puff. Puff. Puff.

"Come on, girls, show yourselves," Murial cheered in a whispered tone.

Twelve in total sprouted. The other twelve remained unchanged.

The breeze blew, and the palm-sized sprouted balls of fluff began to sway. Murial and Thod knew their time was short. They embraced, and then Thod stood next to the seedlings, like the other men in the street were starting to do. A gust rushed past—this was the one![b]

The wind swept up the balls of fluff—resembling dandelion seeds floating in the wind, but much more fluffy, like a bichon frise puppy.[c] As soon as they lifted up, Thod sprang into the air, leaping forward into a somersault, transforming into his botanical form. His hair took on a purple hue, spiked like a thistle. A spiny leaf extended from each forearm between his wrist and elbow. His legs were now wrapped in taproots to his ankles.

Thod gathered their twelve sprouted seedlings in his arms and gave a reassuring, loving look to his wife down on the ground. The breeze blew them higher and higher, further from their village.

Murial watched on as he disappeared from sight past the lush hills in the distance. The knots in her stomach took over as she imagined the journey ahead of him and the time and space soon to be between them.

Years. In a completely different realm.

And there was no other choice.

Wiping tears from her face, Murial followed the example of the other women, taking her remaining seedlings back inside. She carefully laid them in a basin filled with earth. Sitting down, she gazed lovingly at her little boys, her heart swirling with a mix of emotions. Delighted to see her family grow. Gutted by her mate's departure. And indignant at the other occupants of the Green Lands, the Ivies...

The Ivies considered themselves superior and insisted they'd been cheated out of prime land centuries ago, which was far from the truth. They'd deserted their claim to those lands and devastated the new region they now resided in. Not that truth held much weight in old feuds littered with propaganda.

Murial's eyes glowed green, as she no longer tried to hide the change. This was the only way their species could survive anymore—by tearing their families apart.

Over a century ago, the Ivies had poisoned Seeder territories. Ivy poison, produced by their females, was strong enough to kill a human, but not a Seeder. The Seeder males were barely even affected by the attack. Future generations of females exhibited less power. Most devastating was the effect it had on the young Seeder daughters. Not having their powers yet, they were essentially human, defenseless. Every last one of them perished within a week of the Great Poisoning. After girls in new clutches also failed to survive, the true and lasting effects were realized and drastic measures had to be taken to protect their young.

A knock at the door broke Murial from her trance. She wiped away more tears and centered her energy, her eyes changing back to a deep shade of brown. She opened the door with a smile. "Hey! Come in!"

Sandra, her new neighbor, a short woman with light brown hair who was also in her late twenties, entered, giving Murial a long hug. "Just wanted to see how you're doing."

Murial pulled back, gesturing for her to sit down. "I expect we're feeling about the same."

Sandra gave her an understanding frown. "They'll be okay."

Murial nodded. "I know." She picked at her fingernails. "It's just different when it's your own."

Sandra crossed her legs, resting her hands on her knees. "How old were you at the time of your bloom?"

"Sixteen."

"Right. I forgot. I was seventeen."

So many years of waiting. Of separation.

Murial glanced down at her remaining seedlings. The boys always took longer to sprout, but by nightfall, they would start to form roots. She vowed to enjoy every moment she had with them before their childhood would be replaced with training. Whether protecting their homeland borders against Ivy attacks, or crossing over into the human world, the boys all shared one thing: they would be soldiers. Looking up with a forced smile, Murial added, "I'll feel so much better once the first one is old enough to go over for protection duty."

Sandra sighed. "We've got this." She gave Murial a calm smile, standing back up. "I just wanted to pop in real quick, but I better get back to my own boys. You know where to find me."

Murial walked Sandra to the door, giving her another hug. "I'm glad we're neighbors."

❖

Murial spent the rest of the day preparing a vegetable stew and coconut-almond biscuits. She constantly looked over at her boys. Not that anything had changed about them yet—they were still little glistening seedlings, full of potential. It would be a couple of weeks before their roots developed enough to shed their seedling forms, rapidly growing to appear like any regular human.

Sitting down after sunset, Murial grabbed her journal from the shelf. *Day One.* She processed her thoughts and feelings before she began to write.

Human teenagers have it so easy. Then again, when she'd been a teenager, before her bloom, she'd thought she was an average human, too.

It wasn't enough for the Ivies to attempt genocide and lay siege to Seeder borders. Fully-rooted female Seeders were twice as powerful as the males—their energy was used to charge the border walls that kept their lands relatively safe from further Ivy attacks. With these girls being the only thing that kept the Ivies from their goal of Seeder annihilation, their safety was paramount. When the Ivy Kingdom had discovered that Seeders were hiding their daughters away in the human world, it became their new hunting ground.

The Ivies knew their enemies well. They focused on finding the girls during the vulnerable bloom-to-root period when their powers came in. Ivy assassins lay in wait, always watching for a hint of a bloom.

Murial put her pen to paper.

I miss him already. And our girls. I look forward to seeing each one of their faces some day.

She grinned, thinking of her boys.

This is going to be quite the adventure. Things will work out. I know they will. I have to believe it.

Murial tried to imagine the faces of each of her girls—what interests and personalities they would have. Each day without them, without Thod, would be a battle. But she was confident in her husband; he had done so much work ahead of time, planning and preparing, to keep them safe for the coming years.

The fate of the Seeder girls relied on one thing—who was in the know. In the mix of it all were humans, oblivious to the hunt happening around them—the two enemies constantly trying to sniff and snuff each other out.

In their own realm, Seeders had no need to be on the offensive. In the human world, they watched over their daughters and sisters, always observing for signs of the Ivies. Once the girls were old enough, they would show signs of budding, and then bloom, gaining their full powers. Their family just needed to keep them safe and guide them home, without being discovered. And so the game went.

As if high school wasn't already enough of a jungle.

Chapter 1

A chiming sound announced an incoming text.

<You ready for this?> Zach asked, sending a silly selfie, a tradition of theirs on the first day of school every year. The selfie showed off his sharp new haircut and friendly hazel eyes.

Mel shook her head and couldn't help but smile. She'd been bugging him all summer about looking like a caveman by letting his hair grow wild. He said it was his 'new aesthetic,' though she figured he just didn't bother, seeing as he went camping every weekend.

She drew a deep breath and texted back.

<You know it! The real question is, are they going to be ready for our level of awesomeness? ;) lol>

She took her own selfie, having just finished curling her strawberry blonde hair. Her fuchsia polo shirt made her blue eyes stand out, and she finished her look with a touch of mascara before heading out for the first day of their junior year.

She half-expected another chime to sound, a third picture. But it didn't. The trio was now only a duo. She leaned back against the bathroom counter and frowned while pulling up a picture of the three of them. Mel was in the middle, a shorter Tabatha to her left, a taller Zach to the right. There were so many great memories there. Tabatha hadn't made them a trio until the fifth grade, but after that, they had been inseparable. Now, all Mel was left with was a twinge of abandonment. She knew she wouldn't get another text. Pulling up Tabatha's last known number, she read the final message.

<I know it's crazy, but my mom got a new job and we moved. So sorry I wasn't able to give you more of a heads-up! Love ya!>

No follow-up text ever arrived. She completely ghosted Mel and Zach. Mel wasn't sure if Tabatha had blocked them, or took a permanent social media break, but they lost touch completely. That actually happened a lot in their high school. Not the ghosting necessarily, but the constant shuffling of kids. People were always moving in and out; it was a revolving door of new characters.

Luckily, Mel still had Zach; they'd been friends since the fourth grade when another boy was chasing her relentlessly on the playground and Zach punched him. Not that she needed saving—she could handle herself. But he was a true friend she could always count on. He even offered to stay home and hang out with her, instead of camping with his family, after Tabatha deserted them both. But Mel hadn't taken him up on the offer; it wouldn't have been fair to him. It wasn't right for him to miss out on one of his favorite activities, just to bum around with Mel, playing prisoner to her parents' strict rules.

Mel finished getting ready and headed downstairs. Her mom was already up for the day, in the kitchen, baking.

Mel smiled, the aroma of chocolate cake wafting past her. "If only that had been ready an hour ago, we could call it a muffin and have it for breakfast."

Her mom chuckled as she cleaned the kitchen island. "Sorry. It's only a muffin until it's frosted. Such poor timing on my part, and it'll be frosted before you get home." She rounded the island and gave Mel a hug. "Thought it would be nice to come home to something sweet on the first day of school."

Mel gave her an extra squeeze. "You speak my language. Love you."

Heading down the hall, she snagged her already-packed backpack and closed the front door behind her. Mel surveyed the quiet suburban neighborhood and breathed in the fresh air. Passing that one oddball turquoise house(d) with the half-dead lawn and a thriving patch of dandelions, she turned and made her way to Franklin High, just a few blocks away. Its most notable feature being how old it was, past due for renovation or replacement, it was otherwise a rather unremarkable American high school.

The closer she walked to the aging brick building, the tighter the knots in her stomach twisted. The roar of excited teenage chatter became deafening. Approaching the front door, her first-day jitters melted away once she got a warm hug from Zach.

"You look great. Even better without the cross-eyes in your selfie." He pulled back, smiling.

Mel reached up, rubbing his silky-smooth face. "Oooh. I almost forgot what you looked like under your fur."

Zach rolled his eyes. "Beards are manly."

She cleared her throat and grinned. "Yeah. Sure. I'm just glad you finally took my advice. The ladies won't be able to resist you now." She poked him in the arm.

He tugged on his backpack straps, his cheeks a smidge pink. "Right. So, um ... classes?"

Mel pulled out her phone, double-checking the time. "I suppose if I don't have anything else on my to-do list, I could manage some classes today."

He shook his head with a smile.

They approached the busy front door, prepared to tackle the day head-on, happy to have a couple of classes and their lunch break together. As expected, there were some fresh faces Mel didn't recognize, including several new guys—which she was not mad about in the slightest.

Mr. Colburn, the principal, and his vice principal, Mr. Simons, were there as usual, monitoring the halls as students poured in. Mel wasn't sure if it was a tactic to instill fear or show dominance, but it was a tradition on the first day to be stared down like they were interrogating you with their piercing eyes. At least for most students. Mel got a welcoming wink from Mr. Colburn, which would have been absolutely creepy for the average student, but the principal was a close family friend; an unofficial uncle.

She smiled in response to his wink, but her smile faded a tad when she remembered how she'd hurt his feelings once, when she'd told him over a Sunday dinner that she would rather they pretend to not know each other when she entered high school. She didn't want to get teased for knowing the principal. He'd tried to hide his disappointment, but she'd seen an inkling of it in his expression. Despite being hurt by her request, he did a good job of treating her like any other student and keeping his distance at school.

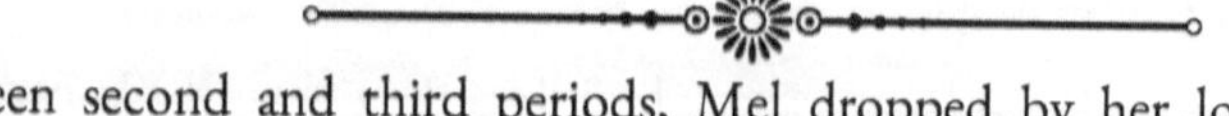

Between second and third periods, Mel dropped by her locker to swap out textbooks. Before heading off to American History, she took a moment to touch-up her lipstick in a small mirror. She was lost in thought, planning out her approach for the onslaught of homework, when the slam of a locker behind her made her jump.

"Sorry about that. It kind of jams," a male voice said.

Mel turned around, pleasantly surprised with the owner of the voice. His sandy blond hair was brushed with a wave to the side, very smooth. He wore an open button-up shirt over a plain t-shirt and flashed a confident smile. His dark brown eyes focused on hers.

"I'm Devin. I'm new here. It's Melody, right?"

"Yeah, that's me." She capped her lipstick and tucked it into her pocket. "Well, I go by Mel." She squinted and tilted her head to the side. "How did you know my name?"

"We just had Trigonometry together." He raised an eyebrow. "The teacher called your full name going over the roll."

"Oh, gotcha."

His brow furrowed as he looked past her.

Someone jabbed her in both sides and Mel jumped, letting out a sharp squeal.

"Never fails!" Zach laughed. "Have I told you yet today, how much I love that you're so ticklish?"

"That's not funny!" she protested through clenched teeth.

"That's a matter of perspective." Zach shrugged playfully. "Don't be late for class. I'm not holding a seat for you if a hot new girl wants to sit next to..." He gestured with an open palm along his body like a car salesman showing off his finest exhibit. "All of this."

"Then it's your loss. I'm not arm wrestling over you." She stuck out her tongue and chuckled as he walked away.

Zach and Mel always knew how to push each other's buttons. She loved their playful banter and how drama-free their friendship was. Honestly, he would make an ideal boyfriend for some girl if he would actually try. He just spent most of his time hanging out with Mel (and Tabatha, back in the day...) or enjoying the great outdoors. Dating didn't seem to be at the top of his list.

"You guys together?" Devin asked with quizzical eyebrows.

First day of school and a cute guy wants to know my relationship status? Not bad...

"No. Zach and I are just friends."

"Gotcha." He smiled. "I look forward to seeing you around." He took off in the opposite direction of her next class.

"Hey!" she called after him. "Do you need any help finding your classes?"

He turned around and grinned. "Wouldn't want to make you late. But thanks."

She slowly closed her locker door and smiled. Cute? *Check.* Confident? *Check.*

Maybe, just maybe, she could get her parents to relax on their dating rules this year.

Zach and Mel sat across from each other at a long table in the cafeteria.

"So, who's the looker?" Zach asked as Mel eyed Devin from across the room while he paid for his lunch.

"What?" She blinked and met Zach's eyes. "Just a nice guy." Her cheeks warmed as she took a sip of water. "He's my new locker neighbor."

She and Zach never talked about each other's crushes or dating, at least not seriously. Granted, she hadn't ever had a real boyfriend, and Zach's previous two relationships were both short-lived. In the past, if Mel had wanted to talk about a guy, she had Tabatha. It felt weird to put Zach in that position now.

Devin caught her watching him. He waved and made his way across the crowded room.

"This seat taken?" He gestured with his chin at the spot next to Mel.

Mel smiled. "It is now."

Devin sat down and peeled a mandarin orange.

Mel glanced at Zach, who was eyeing Devin. "Oh, yeah. Devin, meet Zach. Zach, meet Devin."

The two guys gave each other a 'Hi' and a polite nod.

Zach stabbed at his salad, looking down. "You and me—still on for later, right, Mel?"

She dipped her pizza in a small cup of ranch. "Yeah, of course."

Mel arrived home after a long day filled with rules and introductions. She grabbed the mail before walking inside. Her mom was watering the houseplants in the living room bay window.

Mel sorted through the mail. "Hmm. Two for Pam Walters. Two for George Walters." She pulled out a postcard with coupons for an oil change. "And one for Resident. Are you and Dad going to fight over it? Who gets to be the lucky resident?"

Her mom chuckled. "I'd like to say we could make a civil decision over that one. But today, maybe we'll generously donate it to the recycle bin."

Mel handed the rest of the envelopes to her mom before heading down the hall to the kitchen. While tossing the postcard in the recycle bin, she spotted the frosted cake her mom had been baking that morning. She sliced a large piece, bringing it and two forks back to the living room on a white saucer. Mel plopped down next to her mom on the settee and dug in while her mom finished looking over the bills.

Her mom shifted her focus after putting the papers on a side table, and picked up the spare fork. "Tell me about today."

Leaning against her mom, Mel pursed her lips in thought about the entire day. "Oh, ya know... No eating in class. Don't be tardy. Plenty of homework to be had." She took a bite of the cake.

"Any new friends?"

Mel fought a frown. How much better would the day have been if Tabatha had been there? "Um... I don't know." She smiled, remembering her new locker neighbor. "I met a new guy."

Her mom nodded, finishing a bite of cake. "Guy friends are nice. Sounds like a new candidate for movie nights."

Taking a deep breath, Mel set the cake down on the closest side table. "Guy friends are nice. So are *boy*friends. There's this novel concept; it's called dating. It's like movie night. But you *leave* the house. Just two people who share a mutual interest in each other."

Her mom pressed her lips together, narrowing her eyes. "I think I've heard of this concept. I also heard it's not a requirement for high school or a satisfactory youth." She raised an eyebrow. "Believe it or not, your dad and I were young once."

Mel frowned dramatically. "I know. But things change. We have electricity now, and the dinosaurs are gone and everything."(e)

Her mom busted out laughing while Mel picked up the saucer with a good portion of cake still on it. "Can I bribe you?"

"Are you trying to bribe me with my own cake?"

Mel bit her lip. "I can bake you a different one?"

Sighing, her mom stood. "We love you. You know that, sweetheart."

Mel looked down. "Yeah. I love you, too. Anyway, Zach's coming over soon to study."

"Okay. Remember, your dad started his new office hours this week, so dinner will be an hour later."

Mel nodded as her mom left the room. Annoyed, she considered getting changed and going for a jog. Instead, she looked at the remaining cake in her hands and shoved half of it in her mouth.

An hour later, Mel and Zach sat in the family room, poring over trees that had been killed in the name of teenage torture and learning. Family pictures covered the walls. There were no windows to allow in natural light, but the lamps lit the area well enough.

"Chemistry is going to kill me." Mel's head slumped to the side, her eyes wide open, lips pouting.

Zach scoffed. "Says the girl that always has one of the highest grades in class."

"Yeah, you know me." She widened her eyes. "Why have lots of friends and go hang out, when you can stay home and do homework all the time?"

He cringed. "Eww, gross. Make more friends? And do things that don't consist of hanging out at your house? *So* overrated."

"You dare mock me in my plight?" She chucked a throw pillow at him.

He ducked and the pillow knocked his water bottle to the floor; luckily the lid had been closed. "Never!" He smiled. "I have sat on *many* a couch in my lifetime, and yours is by *far* my favorite." He winked, then said more sincerely, "I've never minded coming over here and having it be just us."

She sighed; he was always so sweet. "So, *now* I see why you come over all the time. And here I thought people our age valued hygiene, good looks, and a sense of humor. I'll make sure my parents never get rid of this couch, so I don't lose you!"

They both chuckled. "You know..." His face got more serious. "I—"

Mel's mom peeked her head into the room. "Dinner in ten."

"Okay, Mom."

"Mrs. Walters?" Zach called, causing her head to pop back in. "We're having a back-to-school party at my house." He quickly added, "My parents will be there the entire time."

Mrs. Walters wasn't that intimidating physically, reaching a mere five-foot-three with a few extra pounds, but she knew how to wield a mother's stern look and tone. "Sorry, Zach. You know our rules."

Mel had known her mom would say no. She was well aware of the rules, and there were a lot of them. Mel was an only child and her parents were overprotective. Well, *kind of* an only child. They'd fostered a few kids over the years, but half of them were before Mel was born or old enough to even remember. They ended up having Mel when they were older. She always wondered if she was an 'oops' baby, though her parents denied it.

"Please, Mom. Just this once?" Mel pleaded. "Seriously, don't you think I'm old enough?" Their rules were so convoluted. With Tabatha out of the equation, they had become even more strict. Somehow, Mel and Zach being left alone without her parents as chaperones was some great sin.

"No," her mom repeated while walking back to the kitchen.

Mel hollered down the hallway, "You know, this is why some kids sneak out of the house at night."

Her parents wouldn't budge. And she wouldn't sneak out. That's just the way things worked.

Zach always had to go over to Mel's house to hang out. She was never allowed to go to a boy's house. She couldn't date. Couldn't babysit. It was like they thought she was a fragile porcelain doll. The only time they ever gave in on anything big was this last summer when Mr. Colburn spoke up at a Sunday dinner, saying he thought she could handle a part-time job for the summer, since she wanted it so badly. Her parents respected Mr. Colburn, being a principal and all—his advice carried some weight. Even then, she still wasn't allowed to apply to the jobs her peers could; she went to work as a receptionist at her dad's chiropractic office.

A lot of kids probably would have rebelled a long time ago, being that cooped up. But Mel generally had a good relationship with her parents. She wasn't exactly a homebody, but she was fairly content with her hobbies and small group of friends. Though, lately, the more she saw her peers enjoying activities she couldn't, the more a sliver of resentment began to fester.

Chapter 2

After her third day in the new school year, Mel was helping set the dinner table. The mouthwatering smell of steak on the grill wafted through the open kitchen window. Her parents, in their old-fashioned style, always insisted on family dinner at the table—and no electronics.

"Set an extra place setting," her mom instructed. "Tom's coming for dinner tonight."

Tom was Mr. Colburn's first name. When not at school, he was fine with everyone addressing him less formally.

Mel stopped and looked at her mom in confusion. "What's so special about today?"

"Does there need to be something special happening, to have friends come over?" Her mom casually brushed away the question.

Not much later, Tom arrived with a smile and side-hug for Mel.

Despite being a weekday night with no special occasion to warrant Tom's presence, the dinner and conversation started out normal.

"So, how are you doing with all the new student interviews?" Mel's dad asked, adjusting his glasses.

Tom let out a long sigh. "We've got a lot of them this year."

After swallowing a mouthful of garlic mashed potatoes, Mel asked, "Why do you guys always drill the newbies so much? I swear they come out of your offices terrified and wanting to transfer."

Tom chuckled. Even sitting down, his broad shoulders helped with the intimidation factor as a high school principal, but unless you were in trouble, his kind face softened his presence. "Gotta keep out the riffraff." He cut into his steak. "We just feel it's important to know who we have in our school, that's all."

Mel's dad cleared his throat. "Speaking of new arrivals, there will be another young man at your school next week."

Mel scrunched her face, perplexed. That was an odd announcement, coming from him of all people.

Her dad continued, "And here." He looked down, focusing on his plate.

Mel glanced over to her mom for more of an explanation.

"It's been a while, but we felt like it was right." The cryptic explanation didn't help. "We're going to be fostering a nice boy." Her mom paused. "He's a senior."

Mel's jaw dropped. "Wait, *what?*" she shrieked. "Are you crazy? Did you just use 'boy' and 'senior' in the same sentence? Living *here?*" Her eyes darted between her parents while Tom awkwardly stabbed at the mashed potatoes on his plate. "I don't get a say in this?"

Her dad scolded her with his eyes. His voice was firm but calm. "Don't be selfish. He needs a place to stay. You could stand to think of others more, kids in need of a good home."

Mel dropped her utensils and pushed her plate forward, excusing herself from the table and heading up to her room. It just didn't make any sense. If they wanted to foster again, couldn't they pick a younger kid, or wait a couple of years until she was in college?

"Isn't that ... kind of weird?" Zach said over lunch the next day, cringing. "I'm surprised it's even allowed."

"I don't know. But it's stupid," Mel said while murdering her fries with a fork. She resented her dad calling her selfish. It wasn't like she was some stereotypical only child demanding attention. But bringing a teenage boy into the house just felt ... weird. He could be a creepy perv, for all she knew.

"Maybe it's not such a bad thing?" suggested Devin, who was now eating lunch with them daily.

Mel fought to hide a smirk. Since meeting him, she hadn't heard him say anything negative about another person, or thing, really.

"But, what if he ... hits on you?" Zach asked.

Her eyes shot up from her lunch tray. "Then I'll kick him in the balls."

Both guys flinched at the idea.

Saturday rolled around and Mel was forced to wait in the living room with her mom, ready to meet the foster boy when her dad brought him home. They sat on the settee as light flooded the room.

It was painfully quiet. Mel had been warned the night before to be friendly and welcoming. The life of a foster kid was hard enough, and moving in right after the school year started was just another hurdle.

The familiar hum of her dad's car pulling into the driveway announced their arrival, and Mel let out a long sigh, mustering the best smile she could, which wasn't all that convincing.

When the door opened, she was surprised to see a tall, buff, clean-cut guy following her dad. He carried himself with confidence and didn't appear menacing or troubled—no tats, piercings, wild hair, or death metal t-shirts.

"Melody, this is Ben." Her dad took the lead. "Ben, this is our daughter, Melody."

Ben smiled and extended his hand for a handshake. "Nice to meet you, Melody."

She took a deep breath, the scent of a lavender candle in the room calming her. She accepted his outstretched hand. "Call me Mel."

After introducing his wife, Mel's dad offered to show Ben to his new room upstairs.

Shortly after the meet and greet, Mel sat down at the kitchen table with her watercolors. Painting was therapeutic for her. She'd watched every online tutorial she could find, though she favored nature scenes.

"Wow. That's really good." Ben's voice came from behind her.

She glanced over her shoulder, startled to see him towering above her, watching.

She shifted uncomfortably in her seat. "Thanks... All settled in up there?"

"Yeah. I didn't bring much with me."

Mel frowned, humbled by his situation. He sat down at the other end of the table.

She went back to painting, distracted by his awkward gaze, not sure what kind of conversation to start.

He tapped his fingers on the table. "Sorry if this is weird."

She didn't look up right away, considering her response while adding a few more brush-strokes to her tropical scene. At least his room was at the end of the hallway upstairs. Between their rooms was her parents' room and her bathroom. She felt better having a barrier between them, even *if* he was a nice guy.

Swishing the brush in a cup of water, she met his gaze. "I just want to have a normal school year, that's all."

A hint of a grin grew on his face. "You know, they say normal is overrated. But I'll try not to get in your way."

After a little more conversation about school and what there was to do around town, Mel decided Ben wasn't such a bad guy. He wasn't coming across as creepy, or pervy, or weird. He was actually really nice and well-adjusted for a teenager in the foster care system. But maybe that wasn't a fair generalization for foster kids; it wasn't like all of them were troublemakers. Mel figured it would be impolite to ask about his family, and his silence on the topic confirmed she'd made the right choice by not bringing it up. As long as he stayed out of her way, Mel expected they wouldn't have any problems.

Regardless of her truce with the foster boy, Mel couldn't help but wonder why her parents felt like *now* was a good time to rock the boat.

It had been five days since Ben moved in. And the last four of those nights involved him leaving the house in the early evening and not coming back for hours. Mel stood at her bedroom window, peering through the blinds at the street below, as if he would materialize and his reappearance would somehow mean something.

Great. Now I'm the creepy stalker. She huffed. But she knew the truth about why he was always gone—her parents were giving him more freedom than they had ever given Mel—and it wasn't fair. She left her room and headed down the hall to her parents' bedroom. Their door was slightly ajar.

"She'll get over the disappointment," her dad said.

Mel stopped and listened. They had to be talking about her.

"I know," her mom replied.

"It's not like they *have* to murder them, to obtain their goal."

Or maybe not about me.

He continued. "Kidnapping or manipulating them into staying for some other reason is just as good."

Mel realized it was senseless to eavesdrop on her parents talking about what was probably some true-crime documentary series they'd been watching. She knocked on their door.

Her dad opened it, his brown hair a tousled mess. "Um, hi. What, uh... Come on in, sweetheart."

Mel stepped forward, crossing her arms and leaning against the doorframe. "Is Ben taking driver's ed?"

"No," her mom replied, closing a dresser drawer. "He already has his license."

Mel nodded. "Is he getting tutoring? Or maybe he has a job?"

Her mom cocked her head to the side. "No. What's this about?"

"I'm just curious why he's never around. I guess we didn't talk about *all* the rules. Does he get to go to parties? Or date? Or maybe there's a more reasonable explanation, like he's in a gang."

Her mom scoffed. "A gang? Really? He's a good kid."

Mel stood up straight, placing her hands on her hips. "How do you even know what kind of person he is, if he's hardly here? You didn't answer me. Does he get to go to parties and date? And have, you know, a social life?"

Her dad raised his eyebrows, unamused. "You have *absolutely no* social life? You can invite over anyone you want. Zach's over often enough."

Mel clenched her jaw. "Does Ben get to do things I don't? Yes or no?"

Her mom sighed. "It's not the same."

Mel was astounded at the double standard. "Because I'm a girl? I took those self-defense classes you wanted me to a couple years ago. I have mace."

Her mom clarified, "It's not the same because he's in the foster care system, and almost eighteen, sweetheart."

"Right. He's a foster kid. I get that it might be hard for him. But I'm your own flesh and blood! And you say he's a good kid." She looked between them, pointing to herself. "I follow the rules. I get good grades. When other kids get in trouble, they have privileges taken from them. I don't even get them to begin with!"

Her dad let out a heavy sigh. "Maybe we should..."

"George." Mel's mom flashed a look of disagreement. "I think," she turned her focus to Mel, "you need to calm down, and we'll discuss this another time."

George pursed his lips and nodded.

Mel scowled and left the room, heading back to her own. Just minutes later, the front door squeaked open. She went downstairs, meeting Ben. "What have you been up to?"

Ben raised his eyebrows. "Didn't realize I answered to you."

She read his face, trying to remain civil. "Are my parents allowing you to date?"

His eyes focused on hers, his lip curling slightly in disgust. "You're not really my type."

Her eyes narrowed with revulsion. "Seriously? Don't flatter yourself." She bounded up the stairs back to her room.

Chapter 3

The Saturday after Ben and Mel's misunderstanding, her parents hosted a backyard barbeque with neighbors and friends. Like her mom had suggested, Mel had calmed down. Dating wasn't the end-all, be-all. Not that she didn't still want to.

Adding to the annoyance, however, Ben had taken a liking to Stacy, a cheerleader Mel had been friends with in elementary school. As childhood friendships often go, they grew apart and ended up in different crowds. Mel didn't much care for Stacy's constant need for attention. Honestly, she was probably the main influence that had led to Mel mostly hanging out with guys. Too much gossip, drama, and Stacy's chase after popularity, forced a wedge between the two.

Mel's parents were over at the barbeque, flipping burgers and chatting with Tom and a couple of their neighbors—including Mr. Rasmussen, a biology teacher at her school.

"You're wasting your time with that one," Mel warned Ben about Stacy. "She's really stuck up. It's cliché, but she goes for the jocks, the troublemakers, the models. Pretty much every type but yours." She crunched into a carrot stick, her eyebrows lifted in mockery. It wasn't completely true. Ben wasn't ugly, and he definitely worked out. He was just too uptight to be the popular type.

She'd never admit as much, but it drove Mel beyond crazy that he was interested in Stacy. She remembered well how Stacy had teased her, had turned on her, during a particular sleepover a few years back. And it had all happened to Mel at her own house.

Ben gave her a death glare. "I'm not trying to date her. I just want to get to know her better."

"Right, you and every other guy." Mel sang with flippant sarcasm, "Fri-ends. That's how it wo-orks."

Zach plopped down on the empty patio chair between Mel and Ben. "What's this I hear? Girls and guys can't be friends?" He wiggled his eyebrows at Mel as he placed the top of the sesame bun on his burger.

She grinned in response. "You and I don't count. We're outliers."

Zach feigned being hurt, putting a hand to his chest, and turned to Ben. "I'd either say she shot me down with vocabulary from math class, or she's questioning my integrity. You know, out-LIAR?"

Ben stared at Zach, unamused. Despite Zach's attempts to win Ben over, they didn't exactly mesh. And not for a lack of Zach trying—he'd made a valiant attempt earlier in the week when doing homework, and a couple of times already at the barbeque.

Mel's initial assessment of Ben had *definitely* changed. Chasing a girl in the wrong crowd? Stiff and surly? He might not have been a creeper trying to hit on Mel, but he definitely *wasn't* normal.

Mr. Rasmussen wandered over to where the teens were sitting. Mel couldn't help but wonder if the balding man ever dressed casually—he was wearing the same attire at a backyard barbeque as she'd seen him in at school.

"Mel." He nodded. "And this is Ben?"

"Yes, sir." Ben offered a hand to shake.

Mr. Rasmussen shook Ben's hand then turned again to Mel. "I hope you're making your brother feel welcome."

Mel scowled. "He's not my *brother*."

"Sorry," he corrected himself, "your foster brother."

She rolled her eyes. Ben might not have been a *complete* nightmare, but she was far from being sold on the idea of having him around.

Ben shook his head and went inside, clearly annoyed.

"Right..." Mr. Rasmussen pursed his lips awkwardly and walked back to the grill.

"Don't worry about it," Zach said. "You only have to put up with Ben for a year, right?"

A year felt like it was going to be forever. She had to share a bathroom with the guy, and he didn't even clean up his toothpaste in the sink.

The next Monday before class, Devin came up to his locker just as Mel was opening hers.

"Hey, favorite locker neighbor," he said.

She chuckled. His locker was on the end—she was his *only* locker neighbor. "How was your weekend?"

Mel found herself dropping by her locker more often than she'd normally have done, just to catch him swinging by to have a quick chat. She hadn't invited him to her house yet, but she'd been considering it, wanting to make him a more official member of the posse. He would add a fun dynamic, and ... she was beginning to see him less and less as just a friend.

He didn't even try to hide his interest—the boy knew how to flirt. After their initial meeting, she'd caught him glancing her way in class. The first time, he'd blushed and looked away. After that, he'd gotten bolder, acknowledging her with a smile. That smile, complete with dimples... She was starting to look forward to seeing it each school day. She didn't specifically save him a seat, but when possible, she picked a desk with an empty one next to her, and he always took that opening.

As they were finishing up their chat to head to class, Devin rummaged through his locker, looking for one last thing. An arm wrapped around Mel's shoulders.

"Hey, Walters, how was your summer? We haven't talked in forever!" Blake was the last person she expected to approach her. They'd been lab partners in science last year and she admired his good looks, as did every girl, but they were hardly friends.

"Hey, yeah. Good. You?" She stumbled to make casual conversation, even blushing at having his arm around her.

"It was great! Got to hang out with the guys a lot. Worked as a camp counselor. But now I'm all geared up for the best year yet." He still had his arm around her shoulder.

Devin closed his locker and stood there in silence as the first bell rang.

Blake aimed his attention at Devin. "Can't build up the tardies this early in the year, right?" He turned back to Mel. "You coming to watch the game on Friday?" He was, of course, a jock—but not a mindless meathead. He was pretty funny in class. And it was sweet, imagining him leading younger kids as a camp counselor over the summer.

"We'll see." Mel smiled as he walked away, knowing it wasn't likely she'd make it to the game.

"What do you see in a guy like that?" Devin scowled.

Mel lifted her eyebrows. "Is that jealousy?"

"What do I have to be jealous of? Jocks have stereotypes for a reason. His muscles try to make up for the air between his ears," Devin mocked.

She furrowed her brow. "That's harsh. How would you like to be treated based on a stereotype?"

"What kind of stereotype is that?" he asked. "Dashing looks, yet still humble?" he kidded with a seductive grin.

His attempt at levity fell flat.

"Would you want people making assumptions about you coming to live here?" She thought of a prior conversation they'd had at one of their locker rendezvous. "Who transfers in the middle of high school to go live with their uncle? That sort of thing could start a rumor. About someone that caused trouble, that maybe got expelled and sent away."

She cocked her head to the side, lips pursed, waiting for a response. He'd deflected most questions about his family and previous high school, which she'd respected, and in some ways almost even liked; it gave him an air of mystery.

It surprised her to see his demeanor change; she'd hit a nerve.

Devin was now looking down at his fidgeting hands, as if choosing his words carefully. "It's not like that." He shook his head. "I'll see you later."

Mel's stomach was in knots after watching Devin walk away, guilt weighing her down for bringing up what was clearly a sensitive subject. She thoroughly apologized at lunch and he forgave her, but was still acting a bit put out.

They were at their lockers, sorting out their backpacks at the end of the day, when she decided it was a good time to take the plunge and invite him over.

"Are you doing anything this weekend?"

He perked up, eyebrows raised.

"Zach and I are going to have a movie night. Ben will probably be there, too, I'm not sure if you've met him. And my parents... It's not exactly the hippest joint, but if you're not doing anything?"

"I'll pencil you in," he said coolly.

"Oh, just a pencil?" she challenged playfully.

He narrowed his eyes while zipping his backpack. "I'll be there."

A couple of days flew by and Mel was walking back to her locker at the end of the school day when the warmth of an arm linking through her own startled her. She whipped her head to the left to see who had joined her.

"Hey." Blake flashed her a warm smile, towering over her like a bulky skyscraper.

"Hi," she replied awkwardly, utterly confused at having him seek her out twice in one week. She stopped walking, freed her arm, and leaned back against the brick wall. "What's up?"

"I, uh..." He shrugged. "I know this seems like it's coming from left field, but I was wondering if you're busy this weekend?"

Her cheeks warmed. "I don't think I'll be able to make it to your game, sorry."

He grinned. "I didn't mean to come watch the game. I meant like ... a date..."

"Oh." She swallowed. "I ... can't..."

"You can't?" he asked, squinting like a detective. "Like, you're busy? Or seeing someone? Or you just don't know how to tell me I'm not your type?"

She chuckled. "None of the above. My parents just have weird rules." She scrunched her face. "But thanks for asking."

He sighed. "That sucks. I'd go ballistic if I had overprotective parents like that."

"Yeah." She frowned. *This does suck!*

"Well, think about it. Maybe you just need to give them a piece of your mind." He lifted an eyebrow. "We're only young once." He winked. "I've got to get going. Just think about it."

She watched him as he walked away in the direction of her locker. Shaking her head, Mel couldn't help but smile. He wanted to go out? Guys with letterman jackets prowled the popular crowds. They went out with girls like Stacy, not Mel.

Reaching her locker, she dialed the combination.

"Has anyone told you that you have a beautiful smile?" Devin asked as he approached his own locker.

She bit her lip. Feeling his gaze, she looked over at him. "You have a handsome smile, as well."

Her compliment made his grin widen. "We're still on for this movie night?"

"Yes," she confirmed with a firm nod.

"Hey, um..." He closed his locker and leaned against it to face her. "I never really apologized for the whole Blake argument we had the other day. I hope you're not still mad about that?"

She hadn't been dwelling on it, but it was sweet that it still bothered him. "It surprised me. It just kinda came out of nowhere. I know we haven't known each other that long, but at first you came across as a really nice guy."

He frowned. "I *am* a nice guy."

He really *was* usually positive about everything. The weather, the cafeteria food, everything. Not quite to the point that he was *annoyingly* positive, but within a safe distance. She tilted her head to the side. "Then let's start over."

He gave her a half-smile. "Deal." His eyes moved from her face to her open locker door. "So, what does one have to do to get a custom painting done?"

She lifted her eyebrows with intrigue. "Ask nicely?"

"Sweet. I'll think about what I want. I really like your style."

She blushed. Not that she hid her art—she had it on display, hanging in her locker. But she'd never had anyone ask her to paint for them before. Other than her parents, of course, but family didn't count.

He adjusted his backpack strap. "And how would you feel about going over notes for next week's test before movie night?"

"Oh." She thought about it. "Zach is coming over before the movie. Maybe afterward?"

He read her face. "Yeah, sure. You spend a lot of time with him, don't you?"

She shrugged. "We're friends, we have classes together, so ... I'd say that's a fair assessment. Why?"

He shook his head. "Just asking. Nothing big." He paused and then pointed at her. "It's not jealousy. I remember last time we had this conversation. It didn't end well."

She sucked in a breath. "Right. Well, I'll see you around tomorrow? I'll text you my address."

He smiled. "Sounds good. I look forward to it."

Saturday night rolled around and Zach came an hour early to study. He was his usual friendly self, though he acted a bit off once it got closer to movie time. Mel left the family room to grab them each a drink.

"You get to choose: root beer or orange soda," she offered, returning to the room.

He looked up from his laptop, turning it ever so slightly so she couldn't see the screen. He'd done it subtly, but she noticed.

"I'll take the root beer," he answered with a smile, holding out his hand.

She passed him the can while playfully craning her neck to see what he was hiding. "What's this?"

Clearing his throat, he closed his laptop, setting it to the side. "Nothing."

That piqued her interest even more. "Really?" She grinned.

He raised his eyebrows in protest. "Nothing you need to worry about."

Her eyes grew wide after considering why he'd be keeping a secret from her. "Oh ... um ... I really shouldn't ask a guy what he's hiding on his laptop, should I?" She couldn't look him in the eyes. They didn't talk about dating, and they *definitely* never talked about *that*!

He laughed. "Gosh, Mel. Your face is hilarious. No, I'm not into that."

She bit her lip. *This is just getting awkward.* "Right." She cleared her throat and opened her drink, allowing the hiss of the soda can to fill the uncomfortable silence before taking a swig. She desperately wanted to move on to another topic. "So ... um..." She couldn't think of anything else now...

Luckily, Ben saved her, entering the family room and dropping into the recliner. Sorting through a stack of DVDs on the coffee table, he stopped for a second to look up. "Sorry, am I interrupting anything?"

Mel choked back a laugh and looked over at Zach, who wore a slight scowl. Apparently, Zach was done trying to make friends with tactless Ben.

Chapter 4

Devin was the last person they were waiting on. He texted he'd be there for movie night any moment. Mel was grateful when Zach started up a more normal discussion after their briefly mortifying conversation.

Shortly after Ben joined them, Mel's mom called for her from the other room. Before leaving to find out what she was being summoned for, Mel pointed to Zach, and then Ben. "I get veto power."

Mel's mom was waiting for her in the kitchen. "Honey, can you give me a hand with cleaning up real quick? I hate for it to be a mess with your friends here."

"Right now?" Mel whined. "Can't I clean it up when they're gone? We're already getting started."

"It won't take more than five minutes. You're waiting for that other boy anyway, right?"

"Yeah. Fine." Mel started to unload the dishwasher.

"So, tell me about this boy." Her mom scrubbed at a large serving platter in the sink full of suds.

Mel placed a couple of coffee mugs in the cupboard. "There's not a lot to say. He's a nice guy. Just like Zach."

"That's all you have to say about him? Does this happen to be the one you mentioned the first day of school?"

"Why are we having this conversation?" Mel stopped and leaned back against the counter, crossing her arms. She thought about what Blake had said, and she agreed. She'd had enough of their overprotective crap. "It doesn't matter if I like him, or any other guy, if I can't date. And it's not like you guys told me about Ben before bringing *him* into our lives. I'm old enough to be trusted. With dating. With information about what goes on in this house." She huffed and went back to putting away dishes. *This is stupid. This year was supposed to be different. In a good way.*

This time it was her mom's turn to stop what she was doing. "What's gotten into you lately? Ben isn't doing you any harm. I didn't think we raised you to be so spoiled."

"It's not just about him!" Mel snapped back. Her face warmed with anger to match her raised voice. "It's everything. When are you going to realize I'm growing up? Every single girl my age can date. But I can't. I can't even go hang out at Zach's house, and you and Dad have known him for *years*! Do I have to wait until I'm eighteen? Does that much really change in two years? I'm somehow going to be mature enough to handle myself and make my own choices?" The chime of the doorbell stopped her tirade.

Her mom pointed at her with the sudsy scrub brush. "Stay! We're going to finish this discussion." She called down the hall, asking Ben to get the door. "Again, it's not about you. It's not that we don't trust you. It's about us asking you to trust our judgment, that we know what's best for you. And yes, two years can make a big difference. Two *seconds* can make a big difference, if the choice is the wrong one."

Mel stood with her mouth agape, flabbergasted. "Really, Mom?! What exactly are you so worried about? It's not like I'm planning on running around and getting knocked up!" Out of the corner of her eye, she noticed Devin standing sheepishly at the entrance to the kitchen.

How long has he been standing there? Of course, he would walk in at this very moment. Tears welled up in her eyes, a mixture of anger and now embarrassment. She shoved the empty top rack of the dishwasher into place and rushed out of the room, avoiding eye contact with Devin as she passed by.

Mel overheard Devin as she made her way to the upstairs bathroom. "I, uh ... brought ice cream for movie night, Mrs. Walters. Just wanted to put it in the freezer."

The argument had probably been loud enough for everyone to hear. Mel was mortified. And just ... pissed. And also really grateful no one came knocking on the bathroom door to console her, or try to get her to come down. She just needed a few minutes to be mad and then clean herself up before heading down and pretending everything was normal.

Her mom was no longer in the kitchen when she came down, but the dishes had all been taken care of. Mel returned to the family room and the guys stopped talking, all sporting some expression of pity in her direction.

Oh gosh, not that 'poor little lost lamb' look.

She drew in a deep breath and sighed. "Can we please just watch a movie?"

They took the hint and each presented a movie of their choosing for her to make the final decision.

"You can tell there's a lot of testosterone in the room," she said. "Superheroes and a slasher?" Her eyebrows lifted in disapproval.

"You *do* spend a lot of time around guys," Ben said. "Maybe you should make some girl friends. And then Zach might actually have a chance of finding a girl to go out with him before he graduates." He snickered, and Devin followed suit.

Zach scowled. "I don't see either of you two with girlfriends."

"Meh." Ben brushed him off with a wave of the hand. "Plus, we're both new here. You've had *years* to woo the ladies."

Devin changed the topic, addressing Mel. "I suggested we let you pick whatever movie you wanted."

Ben busted out laughing and threw a package of M&M's from the coffee table candy dish at Devin's head. "Yeah right, you liar!"

"You know what?" Mel spoke up. "I've had a rough night, and you are being idiots. So, we're watching a rom-com, and you will all love it."

Devin grinned.

Mel picked out one of her favorite go-to rom-coms. Ben seemed annoyed at the choice but didn't leave the room. Mel and Zach usually alternated between their favorites, so he was used to being subjected to chick-flicks.

Mel sat on the couch, cross-legged between Zach and Devin, after picking the movie.

Not long into it, Devin adjusted so his right leg was up on the couch, his foot tucked under the other leg. His right leg touched Mel.

And he let it linger there, not adjusting or apologizing for bumping into her. A few minutes later he leaned over and whispered playfully, "You said we had to love this. What happens if we don't?"

She whispered back, "There will be severe consequences."

They both snickered.

His whisper did more than bring a smile to her face. He was now conveniently even closer to her. This boy was smooth. His hand moved over, barely brushing against her leg, just sitting there. She glanced down. *There's no way a guy does that without wanting to hold hands, right?* Her heart beat faster. She glanced over at his face. He met her gaze with a knowing look and then rolled his hand over, subtly offering it up. She desperately wanted to move her hand into his. Maybe it was nerves or perhaps it was something else, but she wasn't ready.

Of course, her parents always checked in on her constantly when she had Zach over. This would be an opportune time for them to burst in. But after no parental intervention, she stood up and offered to go scoop ice cream for everyone.

Mel leaned against the kitchen counter, face in her hands. Why didn't she want to hold Devin's hand? She did. But she didn't. Why was everything so confusing all of a sudden? Why was everything so weird this year? Zach was acting odd. She still didn't know much about Devin. Ben was a rando addition. And she hadn't admitted to anyone that she'd been texting with Blake the last few days. He'd even invited her to sit with him at lunch, but she'd turned him down, knowing the invite didn't extend to Zach and Devin.

Her mental torture in solitude was interrupted.

"Hey, you alright?" It was Devin's voice.

She moved a finger and peeked out with one eye. Mel drew in a deep breath and forced a cheesy, tight-lipped smile while dropping her hands.

"Yeah." She shook her head. "I'm sorry. I'm being weird. This whole night is weird."

"You don't have to apologize for anything." He gave her a warm smile. "If anything, *I* should be apologizing."

That comforted her. *He really is a good guy.*

"I'm not going anywhere," he said. "I'm not trying to rush anything."

"Thought I'd come help scoop that ice cream," Zach announced as he butted into the conversation, appearing out of nowhere at the kitchen entrance.

Devin threw him a look of obvious frustration for the intrusion. "I don't think it takes more than two people to scoop ice cream. We can handle it."

Zach surveyed the empty counters. "And yet I don't see anything scooped." He rubbed his wrist and smiled disingenuously at Devin. "I wouldn't want you to sprain your wrist with all of that effort."

Mel stood there, perplexed at the exchange. "Oh, gosh!" She rolled her eyes. "Maybe I *do* need to find some girl friends. Then it wouldn't be a pissing match. I'm going to let the two of you work out that ice cream by yourselves." She left them to it, returning to the family room.

Zach called down the hallway, "We'll be right back." And then much quieter, "But not too fast, we don't want to ... *rush anything*."

Escaping the awkward kitchen mini-drama, Mel glanced at the couch. Instead of taking her spot in the middle again, she sat on the floor in front of it. She considered what the guys had said earlier, about not having any girl friends. She frowned, thinking of Tabatha again. Sure, Mel had other friends, but they were really more of acquaintances. With her parents' strict rules, and her extreme aversion to gossip and drama, she didn't have a lot of people in her close circle. And she'd been fine with that for a long time. But then Tabatha ditched her. Not that Mel had really minded it just being her and Zach over the summer, but it still hurt.

Zach... She shook her head. He was the one that just showed up in the kitchen, acting all weird. Had he noticed Devin's flirting? Was that supposed to be him acting protective? This wasn't the fourth grade, and she certainly didn't need Zach, or anyone else, protecting her from Devin.

Devin was being sweet. Mel glanced at Ben. He was oblivious, messing around on his phone while the movie was paused. Why couldn't they have fostered a girl her age, instead of a guy? Then she'd have another girl around to balance things out. She frowned. That was selfish. And it didn't even matter. *Why does it matter if you have more friends of one gender than another?*

Zach and Devin returned, Zach handing her a bowl of cookie dough ice cream as they sat down and resumed the movie. Thankfully, the guys played nice and kept to themselves for the rest of the evening. It only got weird again as they were wrapping up for the night.

Zach gave Mel a goodnight hug in the hallway. "Hey, could we chat for a second?"

She scrunched her nose. "Tomorrow?"

His eyes wandered through the doorway, glancing at Devin, who wasn't getting up to leave yet. "Yeah, sure."

After the room cleared out, Devin helped Mel straighten up the family room.

"Is Zach always like that?" Devin asked, picking up candy wrappers.

"Like what?"

"You're kidding me, right? He's a bit aggressive. Have you guys ever...?"

"Ever what?" she asked while gathering dishes to take to the kitchen.

He followed her down the hallway. "I don't know. Ever dated?"

She gave a half-hearted chuckle. "No. I have no idea what all that was about. I figured you could shed some light on it." She raised her eyebrows in question.

He stood tight-lipped, shrugging his shoulders.

She continued, "As for dating... I guess I haven't done a good job at explaining my parents' Ten Commandments. We haven't dated. I've never dated at all. I'm not *allowed* to date."

"That's a shame, because I was hoping to go out and spend some time together, one-on-one."

Mel looked up, pulling her attention from the ice cream bowls in the dishwasher. She smirked. "I think I figured that out."

He wore a charming, dimpled smile. "Oh, good. I was afraid I was being too subtle." He laughed, running his hand across the countertop. "I don't know, do you think they'd budge if *I* asked their permission? Your mom seemed to like me."

Mel scoffed at the suggestion. "Will you be negotiating how much I'm worth for my dowry, too?"

He seemed confused by the reference.

"If they're not going to budge for me, they're not going to budge for a guy they just met."

He nodded. "Right. Well... Studying?"

"Yes, let's do that."

They went back to the family room, where Devin claimed a spot on the floor, lying down on his stomach and opening his book. "So..." He craned his neck up to look at Mel on the couch. "Trig." He pretended to gag, garnering another chuckle from her.

She joined him on the floor, also lying down on her stomach and spreading out her books. "Okay." She looked up at him, noticing his eyes dart from her direction back to his book with a blush. Looking down, she realized her neckline was ... a little low ... in that position. She bit her lip and tugged on the back of her shirt to fix things before continuing.

"Right." She cleared her throat.

He cautiously glanced back up. "Yes. So ... I kind of hate math."

They quizzed each other for a while. Mel felt bad, realizing he had to be struggling in class.

He let out a loud sigh. "Honestly, this is such a stupid subject." He rolled onto his back, yawning at the ceiling.

She frowned. "Let me show you. Maybe you just need it to be more visual." She picked up her stuff and scooted next to him, lying on the floor in the same direction.

He rolled back over, his arm now touching hers. "Teach me your ways." He nudged her playfully.

She turned to a new page in her notebook and drew some examples. Her heart fluttered each time their hands touched, as they took turns using her pencil to work through the problems.

While she was in the middle of trying to explain an equation to him again, she looked over and caught him staring at her with a smile, instead of looking down at the paper where she was trying to demonstrate her point. "Hey!" Her cheeks warmed. "Do you want to pass this test?"

He shifted onto his side and reached over to tuck a strand of hair behind her ear. He frowned dramatically. "I guess I don't care that much. But I think it's cool that you're really smart."

She shifted a little to face him more. "I don't know about that. I think with math, you just have to find the right way for it to click with how your individual brain works."

He grinned. "But you get good grades in all of your classes, don't you?"

She looked down at the carpet; they hadn't discussed grades before. It was kind of awkward to do it now, knowing she was almost a straight-A student, and he ... obviously wasn't. At least not with math.

She glanced back at him. "What are your favorite classes?"

He twisted his lips in thought. "Lunch?"

She laughed louder than intended and he gave her a big smile.

He answered more seriously, "Gym is cool, and I like English most of the time. History is pretty interesting."

She smiled.

"Oh," he added, "Trigonometry has its perks."

She arched an eyebrow. "The last half-hour has looked like pure torture for you. Explain to me how it makes the list?"

His expression soft, he read her face. "I get to study with you, don't I?"

Her heart skipped a beat, realizing this whole study session might not have been about him wanting a decent grade at all. He kept his eyes trained on Mel as her breathing became heavier. She knew she needed to say something, but she wasn't sure what.

"You guys wrapping it up?" Her dad peeked in the doorway.

Devin quickly sat up and shuffled around his school supplies. "Yeah. We were just finishing up."

Mel's dad tilted his head and glanced at her as if he disapproved.

She rolled her eyes and also sat up. "We're done." She huffed in frustration as he vacated the doorway. They hadn't been doing anything wrong. She half-expected her parents to come up with a new rule that she had to be a few feet away from the opposite sex at all times, or something equally annoying.

As Devin was leaving for the night, she offered a hug. *Gosh! Why does it feel like his arms were molded perfectly to embrace me?* She melted like butter as he held her close.

"I think you're pretty amazing," he whispered into her ear before letting go and heading home.

Chapter 5

By the time Mel looked at her phone after Devin left, she already had a few texts, from both Blake and Zach. She stayed up late texting with Zach. He wouldn't say why he and Devin had acted weird in the kitchen, being as vague as Devin had been. She figured the two guys just needed to duke it out or get over themselves.

Luckily, they had some sort of truce when it came to hanging out at school the next week. It mostly involved ignoring each other, but it got the job done.

Blake, however, was continuing his attention toward Mel, even approaching her a couple more times at school, along with his consistent texting. He was waiting for her outside of her last class one day.

"Walters, c'mon. Just give me *one* chance. It'll be a great date. Cross my heart." He leaned against the wall, armed with his letterman jacket and a pouty face.

From their chatting, she was definitely starting to warm up to him. He wouldn't just text randomly, as if she were a backup option when he was bored. She still couldn't date, but if she could, she might consider it with Blake. She wouldn't have pegged him as her type, but there was a certain appeal to considering someone so different from what you'd normally turn to.

"It even comes with a money-back guarantee if you're not satisfied." He smiled.

She raised her eyebrows. "First of all, I told you: I can't. Second, what does that even mean, 'money-back guarantee?'"

He cocked his head to the side. "You know what I mean. It'll be fun."

Both flattered and annoyed, she sighed and walked away. "Bye, Blake."

A couple of nights later, Mel's parents took her out to her favorite restaurant for a family night. Ben was out with friends, so it was just the three of them. It was nice to get out of the house and have her parents to herself for the night. Things had even been less tense lately.

The waitress delivered their appetizers and Mel happily dug in. She chomped down on a mozzarella stick and then wiped her greasy hands on a napkin.

"We wanted to talk," her dad said.

She finished chewing her mouthful with wide eyes. The last time they had any sort of 'special dinner,' they'd announced Ben was joining them. She dreaded what might come next.

He continued, "The argument you had with your mom a couple of weeks ago. About dating?" His eyebrows lifted.

Mel met her mom's eyes before looking down at her plate. She'd apologized to her mom; perhaps it hadn't been a very sincere apology, but she thought they'd gotten over it. "Yeah…?"

"Pumpkin, we just want what's best for you," he said.

Great, another lecture.

Her mom spoke up. "That being said, we've agreed you're old enough to *consider* relaxing some rules."

Mel perked up with a huge smile, looking between them. "Really?!"

Her dad gave a hesitant smile. "Yes. With rules."

"I promise, I won't go anywhere sketchy. I'll take pepper spray. Whatever you want!"

His smile warmed, though his tone was authoritative. "This is what we've agreed on: Dates are to pick you up from home. We have to get to know them. You let us know everywhere you plan to go. Check in with us and be back by curfew. Dates have to be in public places."

"I can do that!" she squealed, wanting to leap over the table and hug them both. "Thank you!"

The rest of dinner was absolutely perfect—the food, the company. Her dad regaled them with stories of amusing mishaps at work from earlier in the week and her mom gave them updates on one of Mel's older cousins who had recently had a baby.

Mel's phone vibrated in her pocket a couple of times while they finished eating. On the drive home she opened her messages, smiling at the contents and the thought of her newfound freedom. Zach had sent a funny meme. Devin a random hello. And Blake, another text about going on a date. She was torn; there was definitely more chemistry with Devin, but that might increase the tension between him and Zach. She closed her eyes. Of course, Devin had made it pretty clear he wanted a date. He was sweet and had the best smile. But no ... Zach. He still wouldn't talk about why he disliked Devin. And he always had good judgment, facial hair choices excluded.

She shook her head, thinking more about Blake. Here his text was, right in front of her, a direct question. And his encouragement *was* what had given her the opportunity in the first place, helping her to stand up to her mom. And ... Blake could be a 'starter' date... She could see if maybe he really was her type, how she felt about him once they were in a different setting. And if it didn't go well, she would at least know and be able to get him out of her hair.

She shot off a text and got a quick response.

<Saturday?>

<It's a date!>

It took Mel quite a while to get ready for her afternoon date. They were only going to grab a bite and go mini-golfing, but she wanted to look nice. Her makeup was usually pretty basic, and she didn't fuss over her hair much on the daily. She ran down the stairs as soon as the doorbell rang.

Blake looked sharper than usual. Wearing dark jeans and a plaid button-up shirt with the sleeves rolled up, he gave her a huge smile. "Walters!"

"Hey, come inside. I'm almost ready." She beckoned him in.

He stepped inside and from around the corner they could hear Ben.

"Heyyyyyyy..." Ben's voice trailed off, going from casually welcoming to awkward confusion once he saw who was at the door. "Blake, what are you doing here?"

"Ben, right?"

Reading the room, Mel threw a glare at Ben and ushered Blake to the family room before she went upstairs to finish getting ready. Ben followed right after her and blocked the bathroom doorway while she spritzed some perfume.

"What was that about?" she asked.

"Why are you going out with *him*?" He paused a moment. "I thought your parents said you had to go out with someone they knew."

Her jaw dropped. "How is that any of your business?" She thought of their encounter shortly after he moved in. "What was it *you* said? 'I didn't know I answered to you?'"

He didn't respond; instead, he just crossed his arms.

"My dad said he'd have to pick me up and they would get to know him before we head out. That's exactly what's happening right now." She huffed. "Plus, you're the one chasing after Stacy. They're in the same crowd. A bit hypocritical of you, don't you think?"

He narrowed his eyes. "He has a reputation, you know."

She pursed her lips and avoided eye contact. She might have heard rumors that Blake dated a lot. But she didn't like judging people based on rumors. She wouldn't be alone with him anywhere, and he hadn't been aggressive about anything. "You know, when you first came here, you didn't seem all that bad. But you're getting on my nerves."

He frowned. "I'm sorry. I just ... don't want you getting hurt."

"I appreciate the gesture, okay? I can take care of myself. Can you get out of my way now?"

Ben stepped aside and Mel grabbed her purse from her room before going downstairs. By the time she reached the family room, her parents were already in there, grilling Blake.

"Cool, you've met, you know the particulars. Can we go now?"

Her dad looked at his watch. "We'll see you in three hours, not a minute later."

Mel teased Blake as he drove his pickup. "So, you want to risk me beating you and hurting your pride, eh?"

"Dinner and a movie is how you make out, with bad breath." He laughed. "Lunch and mini-golf is how you actually get to know someone."

Okay, that earned some points. Who talks like that?

They dropped by a local Mexican mom-and-pop restaurant first. The air carried the scent of chilis and refried beans. Latin music drifted down from overhead speakers, not quite loud enough to muffle the sizzle of fajitas.

"So, what's your thing, Blake?" she asked, scooping some fiery salsa with a chip. "I thought for a while that you and Stacy were an item. And you've never shown any interest in me before now."

"No, no. Stacy and I aren't exclusive or anything like that. We just spend a lot of time in the same crowd." He took a sip of his horchata. "As for you, Walters, I think it's good to branch out sometimes. Meet new people." He smirked. "Is it corny to say you blossomed over the summer?"

She grinned. *Yes, that was corny.* Mel didn't have a false sense of modesty. She knew she wasn't ugly, but she wasn't exactly used to guys lining up to date her.

Stacy was more the type to let her curves do the talking for her. Then again, Mel reasoned, maybe she *had* matured a little herself over the summer break—why else would two guys be so interested in her this early in the school year?

When she didn't answer, he carried on. "I saw that new painting of the field of sunflowers hanging inside your locker door. Did you make that?"

She smiled. "Yeah. I love to paint. That one's a mix of acrylic and watercolor."

He took another sip of his drink. "I've noticed people's locker decorations almost always say something about them."

"Oh really? And what does mine say about me?"

He gazed into her eyes. "Like the artist, the painting is beautiful."

Her cheeks flushed red hot.

The rest of their lunch was filled with good conversation. He was genuinely interested in her and her family, asking lots of questions about how her summer went.

"And that foster—Ben, right?" he asked.

"Yeah. That's his name."

"I didn't know your parents fostered. Is that a new thing?"

She shook her head, setting her plate to the side. "Not really. They've fostered a little over the years. But he's definitely the weirdest I can remember."

"Hmm." Blake nodded. "What's so weird about him?"

She was getting annoyed. Why were they talking about Ben on a date? "I don't know. I'm sure it's just how close we are in age. The last fosters were a brother and sister, seven and nine." She squinted while trying to remember. "I think I was eleven or twelve at the time?"

"Gotcha. Before my time." Blake had moved there a couple of years earlier. She'd first met him as a freshman. "It's cool they help out like that."

While waiting for their check, Mel excused herself to use the restroom. As she stood up, she recognized someone staring at her from across the room.

You've got to be kidding me. "I'll be right back, you stay here."

Before she even got to the bathroom, she sent off a text.

<WHAT RU DOING HERE?! GO HOME!>

By the time she came back out, the spy was gone. But Mel was still livid.

She was so flustered, she knew she wouldn't be able to enjoy the rest of the date. "I hope you don't hate me; I'm not feeling so great. Could we take a rain check for golf?"

"Yeah, sure." Blake raised his eyebrows. "Everything alright?"

Coming out from the bathroom and telling your date you weren't feeling well? Yeah ... that wasn't embarrassing at all. But at that point, she really didn't care. She was too angry to care. "I'll be fine. I just want to go home."

He seemed a bit put out. She didn't think he'd seen that Ben had followed them to the restaurant. But he *did* shift his questions to Ben again, and Ben's friends, on the ride home; so maybe he had, after all.

"Why do you think they put someone so close to your age as a foster?" he asked.

If Ben wasn't ruining the date, Blake was.

"I don't know." She stared out the window, wishing there was a redo button for her first-ever real date.

Once they got back to her house, Blake walked Mel to the front door and offered a hug. "Let me know if you need anything, okay?" He sounded really sweet, until his arms slithered down her back and to her hips. "Kinda sucks we didn't get to finish. But that doesn't mean it can't end on a good note."

He pulled her closer while leaning in for a kiss. Her heart was beating fast as her eyes grew wide, taken completely by surprise.

"Um..." She turned her head last minute, cringing. "I, uh..."

Luckily, her mom opened the door and saved her from having to finish the conversation.

"Melody. You're back early." Her mom stared them both down.

Blake was quick to take the cue. "Hey, I'll text you." He gave her one last grin before turning and heading back to his truck.

Mel followed her mom through the door, shutting it with a breath of relief.

"That's a first date?" her mom chided.

Mel's mouth hung open. She'd just been grateful for the rescue, but was now being scolded for having someone try to kiss her? "I didn't ask for that!"

Her mom sighed and shook her head. "Well, that's not what it looked like." She paused while Mel grappled for words. "Do you plan to see that boy again?"

"No!" Mel's brow furrowed.

"Good," her mom replied curtly. "Why are you back so early, anyway?"

Mel narrowed her eyes. "Do you know who followed me on my date?"

"What do you mean?"

"Ben. Ben was at the restaurant. That creep followed me!"

Her mom frowned skeptically. "That doesn't seem right."

"No. It doesn't." Mel glared, half-accusing. "That was humiliating, like I needed a chaperone."

Her mom shrugged innocently. "He just wants what's best for you. It's probably a coincidence, anyway, honey. I'm sure he meant nothing by it."

Right. An astounding coincidence. By sheer happenstance, he showed up at the same place, at the same time, during my first date with a guy he seemed annoyed about, when my parents were the only ones I gave the location to. Coincidence.

"A 'coincidence,' Mom? 'That's not what it looked like,'" Mel shot back before heading to her room, fuming.

Before shutting her door, she made out her mom's voice from down the stairs. "I'll talk to him."

Ben hadn't returned to their house yet, so Mel couldn't confront him in person like she wanted to. And he conveniently remained missing the rest of the day, returning home after Mel went to bed.

He either stayed in his room or snuck out before she woke up on Sunday. She stared at his closed door, wanting to knock on it and give him a piece of her mind, but she knew she'd lose it. In the end, she didn't have any concrete proof, but ... she knew something was off. And she couldn't figure out why her mom would protect him.

For the rest of the weekend, Mel barely spoke two words to her mom and dad. From what she'd gathered from other friends growing up, she had pretty amazing parents—ones that would actually apologize when they realized they were in the wrong. But they didn't this time; maybe they hadn't realized they'd stepped over the line, or maybe they genuinely hadn't been involved and Ben had acted alone. Along with relative silence between herself and her parents over the weekend, Mel ignored Blake's texts, and even Devin's. The only person she replied to was Zach. He came over Sunday night to go for a walk.

Mel's parents were out of the house, off visiting a friend in the hospital. She forgot to tell Zach not to knock, and she regretted it when Ben got to the door before she did.

"We're just going for a walk," she barked. "And if you ever stalk me again, I'm going to murder you in your sleep."

She slammed the door behind her and turned around. Zach's eyes were wide in shock.

"Let's go," she ordered.

They walked half a block without saying anything.

"So ... haven't ever heard you threaten to kill anyone before." He nodded thoughtfully. "Does that mean I should invest in a shovel?"

She took a deep breath. "I feel like I'm going crazy. It's not just me, right?"

He didn't answer.

"Everyone's being so weird, right?"

"Well, I was going to say something after our last movie night." He cleared his throat. "But Romeo wanted to steal more of your time." He glanced over at her.

She met his gaze, but said nothing.

"When you and your mom were in the kitchen, Ben was acting weird. He was grilling me the whole time."

"About me?"

"Not directly. Some about your friends in general. All sorts of personal questions about me and my family. He only asked about you when he asked about our friendship." Zach laughed awkwardly. "I felt like it was the talk I never had with your dad. 'What are your intentions with my little girl?'" he said in a deep voice, trying to imitate her dad.

She smiled at his impression. "I don't get why my mom comes to his defense, or why they would put him up to spying on me. I feel like he's brainwashed them or something. I think I'm going to talk to Tom—er, Mr. Colburn—about it."

"That's probably a good idea. But until then, you sleep with your door locked, right?" He looked at her, both eyebrows raised. "I'm serious."

She acknowledged the crazy of the situation with a nervous chuckle. "Yeah. And I'll have my mace closer to me, too."

They walked a bit further as the sun set in the sky.

"Got a rash or something?" Zach asked.

"What?"

"Just, you've been scratching your arms this whole time."

She looked down and stopped scratching. It was the weirdest thing; she hadn't even realized she was doing it again. She'd woken up that day with both arms itching, the exact same spot on each forearm, between her wrist and elbow. She crossed her arms. "I'm fine."

"And what about your choice of a first date?" he casually asked.

Mel rolled her eyes. "Such a creep. I can't believe he thought I'd want to kiss him after half of a date. And when I said I wasn't feeling well!" She wanted to reassure her best friend. "I'm not going out with him again. You have my word on that."

He looked relieved. "Why go out with some bozo like that when you've got me?"

She managed a faint smile. Zach always had her back.

They turned around and started walking back to her house. Her mind replayed the botched date as a breeze stirred the wind chimes on a neighbor's front porch.

"I blame this all on Tabatha, you know," Zach joked. "She left us and these creeps all came to fill her place."

Mel laughed. "Such a jerk, I can't believe her!" She got a little more serious. "I mean, it *does* suck that she dropped us like a sack of potatoes. But we can hardly blame her for Blake, I'm sure he's been the same since he moved here. And Ben, I think he's just a freak of nature."

Zach shoved his hands in his pockets. "Don't forget Mr. Ice Cream trying to put the moves on you."

She tilted her head to the side. "That's not fair. He's never done anything to you." She looked at Zach, waiting for a response. "Why don't you like him?"

He stared down at the sidewalk. "Well … I … maybe I'm just not a fan." He looked back at her, squinting. "Do you like him?"

She paused a moment. Why the sudden interest? They never talked about crushes. Why did he care so much? And why did Blake or Ben care about *anything* she did?

Mel shrugged, continuing to walk. "He's nice."

"Right. But there are a lot of nice guys out there that might be better for you. I mean, the fact that you're able to date now … I think that's great."

Mel huffed. She'd been forced to wait to date, and *this* was what all of that hopeful anticipation had led to. "I don't know how much I care about dating right now, if this is how it's going to go. Calling what just happened a date, is like calling a dumpster a five-star hotel." She kicked a pebble off of the sidewalk, into her neighbor's yard.

Zach pressed his lips together and nodded, not saying another word on the topic.

Reaching her house, they ended their stroll with a longer and tighter hug than usual.

Chapter 6

Devin was waiting for Mel at their lockers first thing the next morning.

"Blake?" he asked in shock. "You tell me you can't date, and then you go out with *Blake*?"

"Can we please not start the week this way?" She moaned. "I get it. Everyone realizes he's a creep. I was stupid. I vote we move on." It was a bad memory she wanted to wash away. Blake had even texted her a couple of times already to ask her when they were going to go out again. He said she 'owed' him a date because they ended their first one early. She resented that. No one ever 'owed' anyone else a date. She couldn't for the life of her figure out why she'd gone out with him in the first place. Any charm he'd held was now long gone.

"Okay, no more talk about Blake. But ... I kind of thought we had a thing, that maybe..." He rocked his head back and forth.

She blushed. "Devin, I like you. But can we just dial things back for now? Have a movie night without a soap opera? You, me, Zach." Rolling her eyes, she added, "We'll make sure Ben is out of the house."

Devin raised an eyebrow.

"I didn't mention that part? He's practically a stalker. I'll tell you more at lunch." The bell rang. "Are we cool?"

He forced a smile. "We're cool."

Before she turned to go to class, she thought to ask, "How did you hear about Blake, anyway?"

He gave a delayed response, first scanning her face, then shrugging. "People talk."

"Greaaat..." She let the word drip with sarcasm while walking away, only imagining the kinds of rumors she might be part of if Blake hadn't taken kindly to her rejection.

Tom could always be found in his office after school. Mel headed down there to chat about the Ben situation. She could have talked to a guidance counselor, but Tom was like family. He understood what her parents were like and usually gave solid advice.

She made her way through the busy office and tapped on his partially open door.

He grinned and stacked some papers when he spotted her. "Come on in! Not in trouble, are we?"

"No. Nothing like that." She smiled, sitting down across from him at his desk.

Mel went on to explain how Ben was acting, and how her parents weren't taking her seriously regarding him. "Parents are supposed to trust their own kids more than a stranger off the streets, right?"

He assured Mel that her parents had her best interests at heart and, while it wasn't technically legal for him to disclose anything about Ben, he divulged that everything on Ben's school record was squeaky clean from his past. "I'll talk to your parents, okay? We'll get it sorted out."

She hoped it wasn't just a platitude. It wasn't like her parents, or Tom, to be so dismissive. But he seemed sincere, and he had never steered her wrong before.

Mel picked up her backpack and was heading out when she heard a familiar voice coming from another room in the school office. She snooped and peeked in the half-opened door.

"I'm telling you; he *has* to be one of them!" Devin hissed.

"Miss Walters, how can I help you?" Vice Principal Simons spoke up as soon as he saw her, calmly sitting up straight in his chair.

She fidgeted with her hands guiltily. "Nothing. I was just chatting with Principal Colburn for a second."

"Great. Was there anything else I can help you with, Devin?" Mr. Simons smiled.

"No, sir, thanks." Devin picked his backpack up off the floor and exited with Mel.

Devin looked at a text that chimed in right after they left the office. "Fancy walking home?"

Mel often walked to school, while Devin usually had a car he borrowed from his uncle.

"You sure you want to walk? Is your place far from mine?" she asked as they left the building.

"Your place is actually along the way," he said.

"It's kind of stupid I didn't know that, right? But I guess it doesn't come up much when everyone always has to come to me." She gave him a faint smile. "You could live with a family of killer clowns and I wouldn't know it."

"We try to keep the killer clown part quiet, so we'd appreciate you respecting our privacy." He tried to keep a straight face and successfully earned a giggle.

"What was that about back there?" she asked. "Did you get in trouble for something?"

"Okay, if we're being serious about secrets..." He looked at her with a raised eyebrow. "Mr. Simons is my uncle."

"No way!" Her jaw dropped. "Why didn't you tell us? That's who you came here to live with?"

"I've got a reputation to uphold." He brushed off his shoulder coolly. "Okay, I don't know that I actually *have* a reputation." He sniggered. "But it's like you and Mr. C. I know you guys are chummy, but you don't act like it at school. No one wants to be friends with someone that has an authority figure breathing down their neck."

"Touché. I fully understand that." She playfully nudged his arm. "But look at us. We have friends in high places." She tapped her fingertips together and let out a villainous laugh.

It garnered the handsome smile and laugh she was looking for.

"I told you we make a nice duo." He returned the nudge.

Whatever Tom did, it seemed to work. The next few weeks were peacefully mundane. And somehow, no rumors about Mel and Blake circulated, at least not that she'd heard about.

Her parents didn't nag her about anything, and Mel barely even saw Ben around the house. She would have continued to be frustrated at the hypocrisy of how few rules they seemed to have with him, if she wasn't happy to not have to be around him. She was even a little worried about him being out at all hours, possibly getting into trouble. Then she noticed he was sitting next to Stacy every lunch at school. Of course, a girl like that might cause her own problems. Mel was both impressed and annoyed that he'd actually caught Stacy's attention.

That is, until one random day at lunch. Stacy literally bumped into Mel in the lunch line, almost spilling her tray.

"Gosh! Sorry, Melody!"

Mel struggled to not show her annoyance while straightening the food on her tray. "I've gone by Mel for a long time."

"Right." Stacy frowned. "Mel. I should have known that. I, uh... I just wanted to say I'm sorry for the way I treated you, for the way things ended between us."

Mel stood there, stewing in the awkwardness of the situation, as they had to wait for their turns to pay for their food. "No problem. Life happens."

Stacy handed the lunch lady some cash and turned around again. "I'm glad we could talk." She gave a weak smile.

Ben was impatiently waiting for her at the end of the line. "Come on, Stacy."

She followed him and they sat at Stacy's usual table, but at the far end. Away from Blake and some of his closer buddies. Maybe Ben was a good influence on her? She had hardly spoken to Mel in years, and when she had, it was never anything kind or ... like whatever that just was. Mel couldn't help but wonder if she'd been wrong about them. Perhaps they really did make a good couple. And Ben didn't even have his hands all over her like some guys were happy to.

Mel still couldn't resist the urge to roll her eyes, noting that Ben and Blake were now in the same crowd, even if they sat at opposite ends of the group.

"Your account number?" the lunch lady drawled with impatience.

Mel snapped back from her musings. "Yeah, sorry."

⁎

The next movie night, Devin asked if he could bring a new friend. He brought a girl named Heather. She was a super-friendly, cute little blonde thing with a slightly nasal voice.

"Thanks so much for having me over!" She pulled Mel in for a hug.

"Sure thing." Mel smiled.

Heather was a little spunky compared to Mel's normal crowd, but she seemed like a sweet girl. And frankly, it was nice to balance out the hormones of the group. Mel grinned as they watched the movie. Heather and Zach seemed to get along well enough, and things hadn't been too awkward between Zach and Devin lately. She noticed some scrutinizing glances, perhaps, between them, but no open animosity.

It was nice to consider more options than just staying at home, now that their group was expanding more, and included a girl her parents could feel better about.

Halfway through the movie, Mel accidentally spilled soda and cleaned it up. She returned the soiled rag to the kitchen, Devin following her.

"Hey, flashbacks to our first hang-out. Hiding away in the kitchen." He smiled as he leaned against the island between them.

She shook her head with a smirk, turning on the water to rinse out the rag. "Heather seems really nice. It took me a while to recognize her, but I think we've had some classes together. I guess she's pretty quiet in class, but a chatterbox in smaller groups, huh?"

Devin chuckled. "Yeah, that's a good way of describing her."

Mel wrung out the cloth and faced him. "She's really pretty."

He looked over his shoulder to the doorway that led to the main hall. "Yeah. I guess you could say that. She's a new friend. Not really my type."

Mel's heart calmed a degree. She'd felt a hint of jealousy at first, when she saw Heather and Devin arrive together. He hadn't told Mel he was bringing a girl. She pressed her lips together, not sure if she should ask... "So, what is your type?"

He glanced over his shoulder again, then went back to looking at Mel. Charming as ever, he raised an eyebrow. "The kind who secretly thinks the best of everyone, even when she's wrong. And loves her family, even when she's frustrated."

She looked down at the floor, biting the insides of her cheeks.

"It also doesn't hurt when she's beautiful and smart. Oh, and the creative type—I like that."

She glanced at his face, matching his grin.

He looked over his shoulder again.

"Why do you keep doing that?"

He chuckled. "Waiting for someone to burst into the room and ruin our chat like last time."

She smiled. She'd put Blake behind her and wanted to give it some time before dating again. But if Devin had asked her out, right then and there, she knew she wouldn't turn him down.

"C'mon." He gestured with his head. "Let's get back to the movie."

Chapter 7

As Christmas approached, the topic of Winter Formal came up. They decided to go together as a group—Mel, Devin, Zach, and Heather—no formal dates.

Mel pulled her new dress out of the closet, talking on speakerphone with Zach.

"You really went all out? Cummerbund and all?" she asked.

"Yeah. Figured, why not?"

Mel searched her closet, trying to remember where she'd placed her dress shoes.

"So, if four of us are going stag, but together, does that make us a herd?" he asked.

She chuckled. "These are the reasons I keep you around."

"I really look forward to seeing you tonight."

Mel put her shoes next to the dress on the bed. She looked in the full-size mirror in her room, deciding which makeup she'd pull out. She squinted, taken aback at the color of her eyes. They'd taken on an almost greenish hue. She blinked a couple of times. No—blue—like they always were. Shaking her head, she grabbed her water bottle and sipped.

"I guess maybe I should let you go to finish getting ready," Zach said.

"Yeah, sorry. A little distracted. Just lining everything up. I'm sure tonight will be one to remember. See you there."

After ending the call, Mel curled her hair, then slid into the teal satin dress she'd bought on a special shopping trip with her mom. She then turned to applying makeup. After getting dolled up, she stood for a moment, admiring the girl looking back in the mirror. She smirked and traced the neckline, a deeper V than she'd ever worn before. This was her first formal, and she had Devin on her mind. Unlike Blake after being turned down, Devin was patient, continually building their friendship. She figured she'd see how the night panned out. Maybe *she* would be the one to ask *him* out.

Mel and Ben drove to the dance together, being relatively civil with each other these days. She wondered if Stacy's influence was equally good for him, helping calm him down. Unfortunately, Stacy was sick and had missed a few days of school. She wouldn't be at the dance so Ben was also going stag, meeting up with friends.

Despite the dance being held in the main school gym, it was decently decked out for the occasion. Snowflakes sparkled, hanging from the ceiling on fishing line. A winter village backdrop was set up for couples and groups to get pictures. The music was fairly good and their group was all smiles. Ben even dropped by and asked Heather to dance a couple of times.

Devin was the first to ask Mel for a turn on the floor. He was an amazing dancer—able to do all the spins, dips, and everything in between. He was a great leader as well, which was good because Mel had one-and-a-half left feet.

"I dare say, you do look rather dapper tonight." She smiled while dancing. "And how did you learn to dance like this?"

He spun her and pulled her in close. "Lots of practice," he whispered in her ear. After another spin, he brought her in again and whispered in the other ear, "Or maybe it's all natural." He held her out at arm's length and bit his lip seductively; she giggled. At the end of the song, he planted a sweet peck on her cheek and winked.

Before joining the others, his eyes wandered over her face and dress. "Do you realize how breathtaking you are?"

She'd already been feeling warm—now her cheeks were positively on fire. She locked eyes with him, feeling a new connection. Something had changed. It wasn't just his compliment. She couldn't put her finger on it, but she could get lost in his eyes. Her heart racing, she decided that sometime that night, she'd talk to him about going on a date. But she didn't have it in her quite yet. She averted her eyes, wringing her hands. "Thanks."

They rejoined the group to chat during a fast song.

"Gosh, it's hot in here," Mel complained, not ten minutes later. Truth be told, she'd been feeling a little off all day. She hadn't said anything, not wanting to miss out.

"Maybe it's time we brave the punch and see if it's been spiked." Zach laughed and gestured for Devin to come with him.

Mel and Heather stood in the corner, fanning themselves with their hands and talking about upcoming Christmas plans. Across the room, Mel noticed Devin leave Zach's side, following a guy she vaguely recognized as a sophomore out of the room.

She continued to people-watch. Vice Principal Simons was one of the chaperones. When their eyes met, he twitched slightly before glancing back at the door she'd seen Devin leave from. She realized she really didn't know much about Mr. Simons at all, especially for being Devin's uncle.

Her focus shifted back to Zach, and then Heather. They might make a cute couple. Mel mentally shelved that one, not too sure of the pairing, and even less sure of her ability as a matchmaker. She'd tried suggesting some girls to Zach before, but they never worked out.

Zach awkwardly carried three cups of punch back to the girls.

"What's that about?" Mel shouted over the music, motioning with her head to the door Devin went out of.

Zach shrugged. "I dunno, he just said he needed to talk to someone."

They drank their punch and chatted at a table to the side of the dance floor. Mel looked past the crowd of people, eyes fixed on the door, waiting for Devin to return. Another slow song came on.

"Hey, Mel." Zach turned, offering his hand to her.

A trained dancer, he was not. But she enjoyed the slower pace, simply swaying and talking about the dance décor and music. It was like hugging him, except with romantic lyrics in the background. And not *quite* like hugging him. She was acutely aware of his hands placed on her hips.

"I must say, madam, you look very magical tonight." He wiggled his eyebrows.

"I do, do I?" Her face got a little warmer. She teased back in an English accent, "Are you saying I require magic to make me look presentable, good fellow?"

He squinted. "You're not the kind of girl that needs to fish for a compliment." He smiled and brought her in a little closer. "To be honest, I've been lucky all of these years to have you to myself. I got in under the radar at a young age, before your parents realized they wanted you to be a nun."

Mel couldn't help but laugh at that.

His playful face and tone changed to a sincere one. "I'm just saying—it doesn't take much for my best friend to go from stunning to hot." And then he tried to backpedal, breaking eye contact. "Well, hot isn't very, um … just…"

She couldn't help but smirk at him struggling. And the fact that he'd just called her 'hot.' That was definitely a first.

"...just, you look great."

The song was ending as he added, "I've seen you that way for a long time ... I always thought we might ... become something more." He searched her eyes as though he were hoping for a response.

She was speechless, standing there with his arms around her, her heart beating fast as her breathing intensified. It's not like she'd never considered it. He was great. But she'd always thought he was joking ... not genuinely flirting.

Their magical moment melted away as Heather interrupted them, followed by Devin not much later.

Mel sat out the next two songs. Partially to take in what Zach had just said, and partially because she was starting to feel worse. Her throat was dry and her stomach ached. She noticed Blake looking in her direction. He had been cold in the hallways at school since her rejection, but he seemed to be getting over it, as he gave her a casual wave across the dance floor. Zach was chatting with Heather and Devin, but looked over at Mel longingly a couple of times, as though he wanted to go sit with her, but wasn't sure if he should give her some space.

Devin came to join her with a cup of water. "You okay?"

"Yeah, I'm sure it's just how hot it is in here. Is it hot to you?"

"It's warm, but not that bad." He felt her forehead and held her hands; they were clammy.

She loved the feeling of their hands touching, but felt guilty after Zach's declaration.

"Let's go outside for a bit, get some fresh air and see if that helps," Devin said.

She happily obliged.

It definitely did some good, feeling the cool air on her burning cheeks. A light coating of fresh snow crunched under their feet, a rare occurrence in these parts.

They walked a few yards down the sidewalk and approached a bench. Devin cleared the snow off of it and laid his suit jacket down for them to sit on. After sitting, Mel bent over, burying her face in her hands. He gently scratched her back.

"Thanks, this feels nice," she said. She'd meant that about his suggestion to take a walk outside, but she didn't at all hate the feeling of him scratching her back. Her mind wandered to Zach.

This doesn't actually happen to people. At least not girls like me. It wasn't like she hadn't ever seen Zach as potentially more than just a friend. Friends make the best partners. But it was high school, and she hadn't been able to date, and didn't want to risk changing their dynamic.

And then there was Devin. He always said the right thing, and was on a different level altogether. And the chemistry—that could power a steam engine. Devin had respected her request to not talk about dating after the Blake disaster, but his interest was still obvious, his charm as alluring as ever.

After a minute of trying to gather her thoughts and strength, Mel raised her head and leaned back. Devin moved from scratching her back to draping his arm around her shoulder. She looked over at him.

"And then ... Zach..."

He furrowed his brow.

"He just... He told me he likes me. You know...?"

His face relaxed into a dimpled grin.

"You knew? Of course, you would know. I'm apparently daft at this sort of thing."

He chuckled softly. "Daft, no." He pressed his lips together as though he were picking his words thoughtfully. "Fantastic at reading romantic cues? Also, no." He offered his free hand like he had on their first movie night.

She didn't feel the same hesitation this time. She put her right hand in his and Devin pulled her in tighter, his lips gently caressing her cheek for the second time.

Mel grinned. "I don't know. I did a good job at picking up *your* romantic cues." She glanced at him out of the corner of her eye. "Then again, you're not exactly subtle."

He bit his lip. "Maybe not."

She leaned against him, melting in his arms for a few minutes.

Only feeling mildly better after a while in the cold, she took in a deep breath and shook her head a little, closing her eyes.

"Still sick?" he asked. "How long have you been feeling like this?"

"Yeah, I'm still so hot, despite the cold. And just getting kind of dizzy. Um... I've been feeling kinda weird all day, to be honest."

He felt her forehead again. "You're burning up, maybe I should take you home."

"I don't know." She rubbed her forearms. "It's so crazy. It's like the same exact spot."

Devin looked at Mel's arms. "Are they hurting?"

She leaned away, nodding. "Yeah. Right here and here." She drew a line across each arm between her wrist and elbow. "I didn't even realize it before Zach pointed it out, but it was super itchy one day, in the same exact spots." She narrowed her eyes, examining her arms. She'd only noticed the aching at the beginning of the dance.

Devin squinted. "Zach knows your arms were itching? Does anyone else?"

What an odd question... She looked at him with a grin. "That I had dry skin for a day? No. I don't think I announced that one on social media."

He chuckled. "Let me take you home."

"I'm sure I'll be fine." She grimaced. "Maybe just a few more songs."

"*I'm* sure you'll feel better away from a huge crowd and blaring music," he countered. "You're not going to have any fun in there if you're feeling this way. Let me take you home."

He was right. She was getting increasingly nauseous and lightheaded, which became much more evident the moment she stood up again.

Devin steadied her with a hand on her back and escorted her to his car, pulling out his phone before heading out. "I'm letting the guys know I'm taking you home so they don't think I kidnapped you." He sent off the text and started the car, then held her hand on the ride back to her place.

She leaned her burning face against the cool glass of the car window. Halfway to her house she asked, "Do you think someone really did something to the punch?"

He quickly replied, "No, I doubt it."

"Did you have any?"

He glanced over at her and squeezed her hand. "No, but I'm sure more people would be sick if that was the problem."

She closed her eyes to keep everything from spinning, taking slow breaths. "That's right, you left to go talk to that guy. What did he want?"

"What? Oh, that's nothing. I've been doing a little tutoring."

"Really? What subject?"

"You like that, don't you? All this time and I'm still a man of mystery."

Mel managed a small smile. She knew, for sure, that he *definitely* wasn't tutoring Trigonometry.

Chapter 8

Mel felt a little better away from the crowds and noise, but her symptoms persisted the next day. Her mom doted on her while she napped most of the afternoon on the couch. Mel assured Zach she was fine, after waking up to texts from him, worried out of his mind that she'd left without telling him. Apparently, he hadn't gotten Devin's text. She felt crummy for not talking to Zach even once after his confession, and before going to bed.

"You're sure you'll be fine, honey?" her mom asked with a frown.

Mel moaned. "I'm pretty sure the only thing I'm in danger of is this couch swallowing me whole."

"Your dad and I will only be gone a couple of hours. Ben knows you're home alone. You can text him if you need something."

Mel internally scoffed at the thought of ever asking Ben to come to her rescue. Zach and Devin lived close enough. Either of them would be her go-to, even if she and Ben had been getting along lately.

A half hour later, Mel woke to the sound of the doorbell and stumbled over to answer it. It was Devin, with a small vase of daisies(f) and a dimpled smile.

"Checking to see how my favorite girl is doing. Can I come in?"

She thought about it for a second, her head cocking to the side. "If my parents catch you here, you might not live to see tomorrow."

He cracked a mischievous grin. "I like to live on the edge."

She let him inside and he followed her to the family room, where she flopped back on the couch, sprawling out and claiming every inch of it.

Devin crouched in front of her, setting the vase on the floor. He gingerly moved a few wisps of hair from her face, frowning. "You don't look much better."

She lifted a hand and flapped it at him. "Stop it, you're making me blush."

He grabbed her hand, kissing it. "Where should I put these flowers?"

She looked around the room for a good spot. But what would she say if her parents asked how flowers mysteriously appeared out of thin air while they were gone? She gestured with her hand again. "Upstairs, first door on the left. You can leave them on my dresser."

He wore a cat-that-ate-the-canary grin. "You're inviting me into your bedroom? You move quick. I'm not sure I'm that kind of guy." He batted his lashes.

She squinted, acknowledging his playful banter. "You're killing me."

He kissed her hand again. "No killing today." Standing up, he took the vase up to her room and returned with two glasses of water from the kitchen. "Hydration is important, drink up."

She sat up and accepted a glass as he took a seat next to her.

Mel downed three-fourths of the water and pointed to the TV. "If you stay, you have to watch a chick-flick with me."

He motioned his head to have her move closer to him. She set her glass down on the coffee table and obliged, being wrapped in his arms, laying her head on his shoulder. They'd barely even started anything between them, but it felt natural to be with him.

Ten minutes into watching the movie, he whispered in her ear, "You don't think it's anything contagious, right?"

She moved her head to look at him. "I don't know..."

He studied her eyes. "I'm going to assume it's not. I'd hate to catch something if you decided you wanted to kiss."

Her cheeks flushed red. "Is that your way of asking?"

"It depends, is that your way of saying yes?"

She glanced at his lips. Just lying there in his arms, for those few minutes, had helped calm her. She appreciated that he wasn't too shy to ask, and not so bold as to launch at her face without invitation. She gazed into his eyes, sharing a look of wanting.

Mel leaned in and closed her eyes. His soft lips caressed hers with a couple of sweet, slow kisses. He then nibbled her lower lip, drawing it in. She returned the nibble, following his example.

Her heart picked up the pace and his breathing quickened. He moved his hands to hold the back of her head, leaning in for something more than just a simple kiss.

He felt like the sun on a warm spring day, like every part of him was designed just for her.

He slowed down and pulled back, leaving her with the soft caresses that he had started with. Mel caught her breath and studied his face; Devin was beaming and gazing into her eyes.

"They're beautiful. Your eyes."

She smiled. He glanced up at her hair. The absolute maximum Mel could muster that day was to put on a bra and brush her teeth, both of which she was now immensely grateful for. Though she was in cute pajamas, they were still pajamas. And her hair had to be an embarrassing, disheveled mess. She moved her hand up to smooth out her hair, but Devin grabbed her hand.

"I brought more than the flowers to cheer you up." He reached into his pocket with his other hand.

She smirked. "I think you've already done a good job of that."

He pulled out what looked like a piece of jade stone carved into a triangle, hanging from a long chain. "Can I put it on you?"

"It's beautiful."

He went around to the back of the couch and fastened the chain around her neck, leaving a kiss there before sitting down again.

She held the pendant in her hands for a moment. "I'll have to get a shorter chain." It was far too long; it would hide under her shirt at its current length.

"No, it's meant to be that way," he said. "Then it's our secret. Turn it around."

The pendant had a sun carved into it. "It's supposed to be worn that way, too, with the sun facing you. It's like a permanent hug from me." He winked. "Will you wear it for me? All the time?"

She marveled at the workmanship. "Yes, definitely."

"That's exactly what I wanted to hear."

He gave her a peck on the lips and they went back to watching the movie. With his arms wrapped around her again, she felt comfortable, calmer, better.

She couldn't focus on the movie much, distracted by the moment they'd just shared. She smiled at the warmth of his body, at his assertiveness, at how natural it felt to be there in his arms.

An hour later the credits were rolling. Mel was nervous about what was going to happen next. She'd never kissed anyone, and that had been quite a doozy.

"Can I ask a favor?" She shifted from his embrace, turning to face him. "Can we keep this, what's between us, well ... between us?"

"Is this about the 'your parents would probably murder me' thing?"

"Well, yeah. But not just them." She wrinkled her nose. "It's not fair to Zach. I don't want to parade it around him now that I know how he feels. I just want us to be discreet."

Devin looked disappointed. "I get it. I would be ashamed of me, too."

"No, I swear, it's not..." She noticed he couldn't keep a straight face and lightly punched him in the shoulder. "Don't be a jerk."

"Sorry." He laughed, rubbing his shoulder. "I'm just kidding. I totally get it." He stood up and reached down to her, helping her up. He drew her in close, his hands on her lower back. "I'm good with secrets, they make things more fun."

Mel looked up at the ceiling, shaking her head and taking in a deep breath. She couldn't have wiped the smile off of her face if she had tried.

"Do I get to ask a favor, too?" he asked.

She looked back at him. "What?"

"One more kiss before I go?"

She put her arms around his neck and slowly, gently caressed his lips with hers.

The sound of the garage door opening startled them.

"Crap!" she yelled. "Take the kitchen door to the patio, then go around to the gate."

He stole one more kiss, like his life depended on it, before dashing down the hall and out the kitchen door. Mel lay back down on the couch, pretending to be asleep, making sure the necklace was tucked under her shirt.

"Hey, sweetie, we're home," her mom called. "How are you doing?"

Mel gave the best performance she could muster of opening her eyes and stretching. "Home already? I'm starting to feel better."

Mel was grateful Zach didn't bring up his feelings for her again. It seemed more natural for them to pretend he hadn't professed romantic feelings, to allow their friendship to continue as it had been. While things were unspoken and calm with Zach, and her parents had technically given her permission to date, she didn't want to do anything to jeopardize what she was starting with Devin. Under the radar, they didn't have to deal with Ben's date-stalking, or her parents' rigid dating rules.

She and Devin tried to be as discreet as possible around others. Pretending was harder than she thought it would be—her stomach fluttered at the very sight of him. But they did their best, holding hands under a blanket at movie night, resting hands on thighs under the cafeteria table. Her focus would flee every time he would slowly draw on the palms of her hands with his fingertips; the lighter his touch, the more distracted she became.

Once winter break started, they resorted to talking on the phone more. Her parents wanted to have family night more often than usual, so they weren't having group get-togethers at their place during the break. Still wanting to see each other, Devin and Mel knew they'd have to be sneaky. Right before Christmas, they planned to rendezvous at the mall to have a date, under the guise of Mel needing to do last-minute Christmas shopping.

"I just need to pick up a couple more things," she told her parents after dinner. "But is it okay if I'm back late? Heather and I talked about watching a movie." She swallowed the lump in her throat. She wasn't accustomed to lying, least of all to her parents. They'd given their permission to date, but after how the Blake disaster ended, with a near-kiss ... she knew they wouldn't approve of her relationship with Devin.

"That should be fine as long as it's not too late. You're sure you don't need the car?" her mom asked.

"No. She's picking me up." Starting to sweat, Mel looked down at her phone. "I better get going. Love you."

"Make good choices," her dad called out as she left through the front door.

She closed her eyes and breathed in the cool air. A text came in from Zach.

<What are you up to tonight?>

Mel sighed while trying to think of a lie. She didn't want to risk him showing up at the mall. Since she'd already used Heather as a cover with her parents, she figured she might as well double-down on it. <Girls' night at Heather's.>

Devin's text came in. <On my way.>

She walked to the end of the block and waited for his car to pull up. The lies were exhausting, but Devin's bright smile melted away some of the stress. She hopped in the car and he leaned over for a kiss.

"I've missed you!"

Her heart fluttered. "I missed you, too. Let's get out of here."

As they walked the mall hand-in-hand, Mel reminded Devin, "I really do need to do some shopping."

He was helping her pick out a gift for her dad when she decided to bring up the elephant in the room.

"Is this... Are we ... exclusive?" she asked. "Like I said, this is all new to me and I don't want to assume the wrong thing."

He raised an eyebrow. "Unless you're running around with some guy I don't know about, I thought that's what this was."

She chuckled. "Definitely not. Just making sure." She bit her lip. "I've been thinking about a present for you ... but ... wasn't sure, and don't know what you want."

His warm smile matched the cheery mood of the holiday music playing in the store. "I already have the perfect present. I get to spend time with you."

She cringed. "You know that's pretty much the cheesiest thing I've ever heard, right?"

He let out a breathy chuckle. "Maybe. I'm not sure what to get you, either."

She shrugged. "Let's not worry about it. I really don't need anything."

Minutes later, Mel was sorting through ties, trying to pick out one for her dad. She hated shopping for him; he was the hardest to shop for, of anyone she knew.

Devin stood behind her and wrapped his arms around her midriff. He rested his chin on her shoulder. "I like the yellow one."

She agreed. Though she feigned indecision for another minute, savoring the warmth of his embrace.

With some proper shopping under their belts and a couple of bags at their feet, they sat on a bench near the food court, sharing a large smoothie. Mel sat sideways, her legs bent over Devin's lap, her feet on the bench at his side.

"Guess what?" she said.

He smiled. "Mmm ... I got nothin'."

She leaned over and whispered in his ear, "I bought us some time to watch a movie if you want. I told my parents I was going to go watch one with Heather."

He laughed. "That's awesome. You know, you were such a good girl when I first met you."

The giddiness drained from her face. But he wasn't completely wrong... She had changed. She was now the kind of girl that lied to her parents, and snuck around, stealing kisses and even making out with a secret boyfriend. "Thanks." Mel twisted to set her feet on the floor, now facing the same direction as him. Fidgeting with her hands, she whispered, "That makes me feel like a two-dollar hooker."

He huffed in frustration. "I didn't mean it like that. C'mon. You're still a good girl, an amazing girl. I love..." He paused, before adding, "...spending time with you."

She looked over at him with a somber face. "I don't know. Every time we do something like this, I'm happy. But then I go home or see Zach, and I'm tired of lying. Maybe we should just tell people."

He rocked his head side to side. "I know we've kept this a secret because *you* wanted to, but I'll admit, I kind of like not having us under a microscope." He clasped his hands together, putting them under his chin. "But … I get it. It sucks having to lie to people you care about. How about … let's talk about it after school starts back up again?" He grinned. "I would rather your dad not kill me at Christmas time."

Her smile returned. "Deal." She slung her legs back up on the bench.

"Are you still wearing the necklace I gave you?" he asked.

"Every day, with the sun-side to my heart," she proudly reported.

"Mmm, that makes me happy." He reached over and kissed her, one hand holding her neck and hair, the other on her waist. He moved down to nuzzle her on the neck and she let out a giggle.

She looked up and realized they now had an audience. Her eyes grew wide. "Oh crap!" she whispered.

Devin immediately stopped. "What?" He turned to see what she was looking at.

Ben was standing a few yards away, staring at them. And rather livid by the looks of it.

"What if he tells my parents?" she panicked under her breath.

"I'll handle it." Devin cleared his throat as he got up, shoving his hands in his pockets. He approached Ben, who had been walking by with Heather.

Mel doubted Ben cared what Devin had to say. And it wasn't really his concern who, or if, she dated. They'd been over that before. Heather awkwardly backed up, allowing the guys to chat more privately. Mel wondered if Heather's presence there would help or hurt her alibi with her parents, assuming Devin could convince Ben not to blab.

They weren't that far away, but Mel still couldn't hear what they were saying. Whatever it was, it looked like a heated discussion.

Out of nowhere, Ben shoved Devin.

"Ben!" she yelled.

Ben looked over at Mel, still seething mad. He turned back to Devin, aggressively pointing at him, whispering what she could only assume by their behavior were threats.

Devin looked in Heather's direction, then back to Ben, and had the last word. He turned, stomping back to Mel and picking up their shopping bags. "Let's get you home."

Making their way to the parking garage, Mel grappled to understand why Ben was the way he was. Maybe she *should* have asked more about his biological family. Maybe they had violent tendencies. Why was he so mercurial, so spastic? Perhaps he'd been separated from siblings in the system and was taking this foster 'brother' thing a bit too seriously?

Devin and Mel hopped in his car and drove in silence for the first five minutes.

"He's a moron," she said. "He should be medicated."

"He's not going to cause problems with your parents. Just don't say anything to him." He kept his eyes on the road, puckering his lips in anger. "It'll just make things worse."

"You're sure?" She cocked her head. "Maybe I *should* say something to my parents, if he's going to be mental like this."

"No." He threw her a glance as they went over a speed bump. "I promise, he won't say anything."

She gnawed on her bottom lip. Ben didn't like Devin. He hadn't liked Blake, either. He'd always been moody with Zach. She shook her head. Ben hated all the guys that showed any interest in her. But he'd made it clear he didn't want to date her. And he was with Stacy, anyway.

"What did he say to you?"

Devin huffed. "I don't want to talk about it, okay? Let's just pretend this never happened."

They parked a few houses down from her place so her parents wouldn't see who she'd actually gone with.

He ruffled his hair. "I'm sorry, okay? I'm being stupid."

"What do you mean? You have nothing to apologize for." He wasn't making any sense.

"No, I'm not being smart. I just ... really like you. And ... this is just making things complicated."

She frowned and tried to say something, but it was hard with her heart being ripped out. She felt tears coming to her eyes. This was her first boyfriend, so she didn't know what it felt like to be dumped, but it sounded like he was thinking about it. "Are you... Do you want to break up?"

His head jerked over to look at her, frowning. "Do you?"

"No. But I get it. I wouldn't want to go out with me right now, either."

"Come here," he said, sliding to the edge of his seat. She moved to the center, and he put his hand up to her face, wiping away a tear as it tried to run away. "You are ... amazing. I'd be willing to risk a hell of a lot to keep you."

She gave him a hesitant smile.

"I'm placing my bet on you, okay?"

"Yeah," she whispered.

"But maybe let's just take a step back. I probably shouldn't see you until after winter break," he said, moving his hand away from her face.

"Yeah. Fine," she answered dejectedly. "You're sure he won't say anything?"

Devin gave her a soft smile. "Yes."

"I, uh, I'm still wondering if *we* should say something." She rubbed the back of her neck. "What if he tries something ... tries to hurt me?" He obviously had violent tendencies...

Devin raised his eyebrows. "Has he ever tried anything with you before?"

She shook her head.

He shrugged. "He won't hurt you. He's all bark, no bite." Devin must have sensed her continued hesitance, reaching out and holding her hand. "Let me handle this one, okay? I'll take care of Ben." He gave her hand a double squeeze. "And I'll take care of you."

"Okay." Mel forced a smile and grabbed her shopping bags, getting out of the car.

While lying in bed that night, she heard the door open downstairs—Ben had come home for the night. She resisted the urge to confront him, instead remaining in bed, not sure whether to be angry or sad about the way the night had ended. If she told her parents about Ben's crazy behavior, she'd have to fess up to lying to them and sneaking behind their backs. She double-checked her door lock and gave Devin the benefit of the doubt. Shortly before falling asleep, a text came in.

<Things will work out. <3 >

And then another.

<I'm not going anywhere.>

Chapter 9

Devin was right; things would work out. At least on paper. The next morning while Mel was eating cereal at the kitchen table, Ben joined her, sitting across from her, just looking at her.

Staring at her cereal bowl, uncomfortable about his gaze, she wondered what Devin would say about this. Mel looked up. "Do you have something you'd like to say?"

Ben looked intently into her eyes. "I would *never* hurt you."

She bit her lip, studying his face. Devin must have told him off, sharing that concern.

"That doesn't mean I have to like all of your friends. Or *secret* boyfriends."

She glared.

"Hey, sweetie," her mom's voice came from the hallway.

Ben stood up, putting a hand on the table. "I've said what I needed to say."

Mel's mom's cheery voice drew closer, and she appeared from the hallway. "Oh, hi, Ben. Good morning." She turned back to Mel as Ben took a couple of steps back. "I only have these two wrapping papers left. Which one do you want?"

Mel watched Ben, who was now standing behind her mom, out of her view. He shoved his hands in his pockets, ever so slightly raising his eyebrows. Was it a stand-off? Or a truce? He wasn't tattling on Mel.

She focused back on her mom. "I'll take either."

Pam looked the rolls of wrapping paper over once more. "Use up the rest of this red one. I'll take the blue."

"Sounds good." Mel glanced back up at Ben. *We'll call it a truce.* "No problem here." She smiled at her mom. "Red is much more festive and I think that'll be more than enough for what I need."

Out of the corner of her eye, she thought she saw Ben nod before he left the room. She hated this kind of drama, especially around Christmas. As Mel finished her cereal, she sported a small grin. Devin must've been pretty persuasive.

She and Ben never said a single word about the incident after that. Her parents never brought anything up. Devin kept a steady stream of texts and calls coming her way. Christmas was awesome—her mom and dad shocked her by gifting her a family trip to Costa Rica. They mentioned going for spring break, or at the start of summer; the reservations were flexible.

Ben was uncharacteristically happy on Christmas Day, which was only that much more humbling to Mel, reminding her that although he probably didn't want to be stuck at her house any more than she wanted him there, he didn't have any choice in the matter, and this was a safe, happy home and family. They even exchanged a smile as she hugged the gift he'd bought her—a new watercolor set. She'd only gotten him a basket of sweets and other junk food because that was what her mom had recommended, but he seemed to enjoy it.

New Year's Eve was also a quiet family event this year. Mel was bummed her parents insisted on not having friends over; she'd secretly hoped to rally the posse and sneak away at midnight for a smooch with Devin. But ... it was probably good to take time and work on her relationship with her parents after all the lies, even if they weren't aware of them.

On New Year's Day, Mel invited Zach over to hang out. She could hardly look him in the eye when she opened the door. Even their hug had some obvious hesitance from both sides.

"Come on in." She smiled and turned to the family room.

"Yeah. I'm glad we finally get to hang out." He followed her and they sat down on the couch.

She had tried to figure out what to say to him. About not responding to his declaration of feelings, about dating Devin. The only thing that came to her mind was 'Sorry, but I chose Devin instead.' And that just didn't feel right. She was at a loss for words.

"So, how's the new puppy?" she asked. Zach had been texting her pictures of the new golden retriever they'd gotten for Christmas.

His smile was warm. "Good. He's super cute."

She nodded. This was painful. At times in their friendship, she'd thought about him that way, in a more-than-friends kind of way. But she hadn't said anything, worried about ruining things between them. And now that *he* had brought it up, and things hadn't progressed, she was terrified things might be ruined between them anyway. She couldn't win.

"Costa Rica? Are you excited?" he asked.

"Yeah. Of course, it'll be awesome."

She noticed his hands fidgeting. His face was a bit whiskery. Was he not shaving because it was the holidays, or because she'd hurt him by not saying anything and he was having a hard time, or because he was trying to send a message—that he used to care about her opinion and didn't anymore? Then again, he could have just needed to buy a new razor, too.

The small talk was hard, the tension thick.

"So, uh, just you and me today?" he asked.

"Yeah." It wasn't like they hadn't talked, or been in each other's presence since the dance, but this was their first solo face-to-face hang-out since then. She read his face. "Just us. 'Cause I want to spend time with my best friend." She pursed her lips, hoping that's what they still were.

He smiled and nodded. "I like spending time with my best friend, too. Works for me."

Relief washed over her, but she didn't know if she could handle more of the small talk. "Movie?"

"Sounds good."

"Great. You get to pick this time. I'll go make some popcorn."

A few minutes later, Mel returned with a bag of microwave popcorn. "Sorry, we only had the low-salt stuff."

Zach quickly turned off his phone, tucking it away in his pocket. "Okay, sure."

She did her best to ignore it, but it wasn't like him to be secretive like that. Then again, she could hardly judge, after keeping him in the dark about her relationship with Devin. For all she knew, Zach had moved on and there was a girl he wasn't ready to tell her about.

"Cool." She set the popcorn on the coffee table and settled down on the couch. And shifted a little further away from Zach. And then back to be closer again. *When did our proximity matter?* If he still had feelings for her, would sitting too close give him the wrong idea? If she sat too far away, would it be insulting? *How close did we used to sit?* She tried to settle on a place. An inch closer might be too close, an inch further felt like it might as well be a mile.

"Mel?"

She looked over to meet his gaze.

Zach tilted his head to the right, looked down at the cushion between them, and then met her eyes again. "Don't be weird. I don't bite." And then he grinned and pelted her with a fistful of popcorn.

She laughed, scooching a bit closer while pulling kernels out of her hair.

Zach chose a scary movie. One of those that has you screaming 'No! Don't go into the basement alone!' It wasn't really to Mel's taste, but since he had let her choose the last time and it had been a Jane Austen, she was happy to go with anything that wasn't focused on romance.

By the end of his visit, what had been said—or what didn't need to be said, at least for the time being—was enough. Their goodbye hug was much more natural.

◦—————•—•◦❂◦•—•————◦

Once school started back up, Mel and Devin agreed to go much slower, but she was still beyond excited to see him. They gave each other a simple hug at their lockers and didn't even touch each other the rest of the day.

There was usually a buzz of excitement the first few days after coming back from winter break, but the school's mood was downcast on account of the news that Stacy had been diagnosed with leukemia and had to leave the state for treatment.

Mel felt a twinge of guilt that she hadn't made more of an effort to reconcile with her. She wondered if maybe Stacy's sudden humble apology in the lunch line stemmed from her already knowing something was wrong. And Mel felt sorry for Ben, who had obviously gotten pretty close to Stacy. Maybe that was part of why he'd been acting like such a jerk before—he probably knew about it a while ago and didn't know how to process it.

On the third morning back, between first and second period, Mel opened her locker to unload some books, only to cock her head in confusion at the item before her. She moved a hand up to her neck. *Huh ... I could've sworn I...* No. Obviously, she hadn't. She hadn't put on Devin's necklace that morning. She couldn't have. Because it was sitting right there. She didn't recall taking it off and leaving it in her locker. She vaguely remembered she'd taken it off the night before and put it on her nightstand. She shook off the weird feeling like the bad case of deja vu it was, then slipped on the necklace, smiling as the sun symbol touched her skin, sliding down her shirt.

Not more than a minute later, Devin strolled up to his locker. "Fancy meeting you here."

She grinned. "Coincidence? Or destiny that we're locker neighbors?"

Devin dialed the combination. "Whatever you call it, I know I'm not mad about it." He winked.

Mel unzipped her backpack and pulled out a thin, wrapped gift. She handed it to Devin.

"What's this?" He carefully opened it, smiling at the painting she'd made for him.

"I guess I should have asked for a request, but I also wanted it to be a surprise." It was a new watercolor of a seaside landscape.(g)

"I love it." He beamed. "But I thought we agreed on no presents."

She shrugged. "You told me a while ago you wanted a painting. We're well into the new year, anyway." She moved a thumb up, underneath the chain of her necklace. "We can call this an *early* Christmas present if we call mine a *late* Christmas present."

He carefully put the painting on the top shelf of his locker. "I can accept that." He glanced over at her neck. "Still calm on the home front? Ben didn't cause any more drama, right?"

She closed her locker, leaning up against it. "Nope. All good there. I still don't know how you did it."

"Isn't the answer obvious?" He put a book in his locker. "It's the power of that necklace. It's our good-luck charm." He closed his locker with a smile.

She opened her arms and they shared a hug.

"Mmm, you smell good. New perfume?" he asked.

Mel pulled back. "We girls call that 'shampoo.'"

He chuckled as the bell rang. "I'll see you later."

Mel had gym as her last class for the new semester. It was nice to take a long shower and not have to rush to get to the next class or be sweaty for the rest of the day. A week after returning from break, she was taking her time brushing her hair, straightening out her necklace, and even applying some mascara. She was in better spirits now that Devin was holding her hand again. Only under the table at lunch, but she'd take it. The locker room had cleared out. She swung her backpack over her shoulder and opened the door to the hallway.

"Walters." Blake was leaning against the painted brick wall, all alone.

She rolled her eyes at the thought of him waiting for her. "What do you want, Blake?"

"I just want to talk." He grinned. "You look different."

"Okaaay?"

He walked up to her. "I think you should give me another chance." He had his usual arrogant smile, the one she'd convinced herself was genuine, before realizing he was a handsy creep.

"Sorry, I'm seeing someone." She started to walk away.

"Really? Who's that?"

Everything about this exchange was rubbing her the wrong way. "That's none of your business." She scowled.

"I know your type." He stepped in front of her, blocking her path.

"What type is that?"

He moved closer. "You think you're better than everyone else. You think there's something special about you."

"You're crazy." She shook her head, trying to fathom why she had ever given him a chance. And why she'd stood up for him in the first place. As she turned to walk around him, he surprised Mel by grabbing her wrist and whipping her around.

"Maybe I'm just impatient." He furrowed his brow, twisting her arm painfully.

"What's wrong with you? Leave me alone!" She tried to yank her arm free, but he had a tight grip.

He twisted harder and she cried out in pain. He pushed her against the wall. "I bet your boyfriend thinks you're a great kisser. I can give a second opinion."

"You're sick, Blake. Let me go!" Her heart was racing, but her body just ... froze. He was peering into her eyes and leaning in.

"Leave her alone!"

It was like fourth grade all over again. Zach was at the end of the hallway, fists clenched at his sides, there to fight for her. He wasn't scrawny, but there was no way he could win in a fight against Blake.

Blake loosened his grip but didn't let go completely.

A deep shout roared down from the other end of the hallway. "BLAKE HUNTERS! MY OFFICE. NOW!" It was Tom.

Blake quickly let go and backed away, putting his hands up like it was all some kind of misunderstanding. He scowled at Zach and Mel, before marching down the hall as ordered.

Zach offered her a hug, and she started to cry in his arms.

"It's okay," he whispered. After a couple of minutes, he stepped back, wiping up her fresh mascara streaks. "Do you want me to call your parents for you? Or, um..." He cleared his throat. "Devin? Where is he?"

"I don't know, he's usually tutoring after school." She looked down.

"I know about you two," he confessed.

She looked up and frowned sheepishly.

He let out a small chuckle. "You suck at hiding how you feel about a guy as much as you suck at knowing how a guy feels about you."

Her heart was heavy with guilt, having kept it a secret from him. He was more understanding than she'd given him credit for. "I'm sorry. I should have said something. I was a jerk to leave you hanging."

He shrugged, though his eyes still showed disappointment.

"It's not like I've never thought about you like that before. Or that you're not attractive. It's just ... timing."

He rubbed his hands together uncomfortably at her confession. "That doesn't really make me feel better, but thanks." He tried to force a smile. "We don't really need to talk about that right now. Let me walk you home."

Once they got to her house, Zach led Mel into the family room.

"What are *you* doing here?" She was surprised to see Devin sitting on her couch.

"I'll ... leave you guys to it." Zach sounded just as confused. "Text me later?" He gave her another hug before leaving.

Devin got up and offered his arms. She buried herself in them as he set his chin on her head. "I should've been there for you."

After a minute, he invited Mel to sit together. He held her hands. "Is your arm okay?"

She wiggled it and furrowed her brow in confusion. "Yeah, actually. In all the chaos of everything, I kind of forgot about that."

He gave her a weak smile, something still clearly weighing heavily on him. "Blake," he paused, "is a problem. I can't really explain it, but I don't think he's going to just leave you alone. He's probably trying to provoke you." He paused again. "Or me."

She was understandably confused by his cryptic warning. Especially since Blake didn't seem to even know *who* she was dating.

Devin buried his face in his hands. "Why does this have to be so complicated?" He took a deep breath. "Just, try not to react. Ignore him. Find a way to keep your distance. I'm sure he'll be suspended for at least a few days, so that should help."

"It's not like I went looking for trouble," she said, defeated.

"No, I know. Cause you're a good girl, right?" He winked, gently lifting her chin with his hand.

He always knew how to make her grin.

"I see you're still wearing the necklace?" He glanced at the chain visible around her neck. "Well, it wasn't a very good luck charm today." He frowned dramatically. "I think it must be getting low on batteries."

"And how does one replace the batteries on a stone?" she asked, playing along.

He jerked his head back, dropping his jaw, as if she had insulted him. "No, no, no. One does not *replace* the batteries. One must *recharge* the batteries."

"Oh, so sorry." She smiled more sincerely, biting her lip. "How does one *recharge* the batteries?"

"Let me show you how." He pulled her in for a kiss. It was as sweet and wonderful as the first. Not as passionate, but...

"Wait a second," she whispered, pushing him away. "I saw my mom's car out there."

He grimaced. "Yeah. I, uh ... talked to your parents?" He squeaked like he was asking a question rather than making a statement. "I dropped by to see you, and then I decided to come clean about wanting to date you. And," he shrugged, "I lived to tell the tale."

She threw her arms around him, giving him a quick peck, and then a tight squeeze. For a split second she was annoyed that he'd gone behind her back to talk to them, but she was too happy to hold a grudge. Zach knew, her parents knew—there didn't have to be any more secrets.

She stepped back to look at him. "I don't know what spell you had to put on them, to make *that* miracle happen. But I'm sure they didn't give you carte blanche to make out in the family room. You should head out."

She saw him to the door, and he gave her one last tight squeeze before leaving.

"Love ya," he whispered in her ear.

She didn't know what to say to that, and luckily, he didn't linger awkwardly, expecting a response. Perhaps it was just a knee-jerk reaction, like when you accidentally tell a customer service stranger 'okay, love ya, bye' over the phone.

She slowly made her way to the stairs. When she looked up, Ben was sitting at the top, within hearing range. Her trigger response was to be annoyed at his eavesdropping, but he surprised her. He shifted to one side, leaving enough room for her, then patted the carpeted stair for her to come sit down.

"You alright?" He frowned.

"I'll be fine. How did everyone hear about it so quickly?" She plopped down next to him.

"The school called your mom."

She nodded, realizing she and Zach probably should have stopped by the office before leaving. "I'm sorry about Stacy. I know you guys are close."

He smiled. "It's fine. I'll see her soon enough." He looked down at his hands, speaking softly. "I know I sometimes act ... irrationally. You think I'm a jerk, and that I don't care. But I do, okay?"

"Thanks." She had to give him some credit—he'd spotted Blake as a perv from the start. *But ... he still doesn't like Zach or Devin.*

They sat for a second, each waiting to see if the other had anything else to add to the conversation.

"So," he broke the silence, "you really like Devin?"

Mel laughed. "We're not having this conversation, Ben." She stood to continue walking up the stairs, briefly looking down at him. "But I mean it, thanks for caring."

Mel went upstairs and washed her face, then headed to her room to grab her painting supplies. Her mom appeared in the doorway, frowning.

"I wasn't sure if you would want to talk about what happened, or if you needed some time to yourself."

Mel put her things down and gave her mom a big hug. She closed her eyes, processing what Blake had done. "I... I don't know."

"That's okay, sweetie. If you want to talk, you know your dad and I are always willing to listen."

"Thanks, Mom. You guys are the best." She was beyond grateful to not have another scolding about her poor judgment for her first date, and ... they were cool with Devin and her dating.

Her mom left the room as Mel picked her things back up and went downstairs to paint. With each brush stroke, she replayed her stupid mistake of a date with Blake. And then the events of that afternoon. He was so hot and cold; she couldn't make out what had prompted him to lash out, out of nowhere like that. In the end, his motivations didn't matter. She was mostly disappointed in herself. What was the purpose of her parents paying for self-defense classes, if she was just going to freeze up? It had been a couple of years since she'd taken them, but still...

By the time she sorted through her train of thought, a beautiful, thorned rose had emerged on the page.

Devin was right that Blake would be suspended for a few days. Tom called Mel into his office the next day to talk about the incident.

"How are you doing? I talked to your dad, he said you're alright, physically?"

"Yeah, he didn't hurt me that bad."

"It doesn't matter how much he hurt you, that behavior is unacceptable. I wanted you to know we're taking it seriously. If he approaches you again, or threatens you, in any way, let me know. Don't even waste your time talking to a teacher. I'm not too busy, alright?"

She nodded, wishing she could give him a hug. She was lucky to have someone like him watching out for her. But this wasn't her family friend after Sunday dinner; right now, he was the principal, in his office. "Thanks, I'll let you know if there are any more problems."

"Can you tell me what was said? What the discussion was about, from your side of things?"

She went over what had happened.

He squinted. "Do you know what would have caused him to react like that out of nowhere? He didn't say anything odd? You didn't do or say anything that he reacted to?"

She furrowed her brow in confusion; she'd just explained the whole situation, not leaving anything out. "No... I'm not sure what you're getting at... Are you trying to say this is somehow *my* fault?"

He straightened in his chair and shook his head with a frown. "No. Never. I would never blame the victim. I'm just trying to do a thorough review for our records."

He dismissed her back to class. Mel slowly meandered through the hallways and couldn't help but wonder why it felt like more than a simple interview about an incident. Tom's probing felt insulting. It was a pretty open-and-shut case. Blake was an egotistical, perverted jerk. She'd frozen up. That was ... it. She knew she was probably just overthinking it, but why would Tom doubt her, question her behavior and motives? She never did anything to deserve Blake's assault, or Tom's scrutiny.

Chapter 10

When Blake came back from suspension, he kept his distance, though his eyes threw daggers every time they met Mel's.

She did her best to move on, which wasn't too difficult with how over the moon she was about finally being able to be more public about her relationship with Devin. It was out in the open. Their hand-holding was 'above the table' now, but they tried to keep PDA to a minimum around Zach so things wouldn't be too awkward. And she was seriously grateful her parents didn't sit her down for another sex talk. They only stressed that their dating rules still applied. Curfews, expecting to know where she was going, etc.

While they could now date openly, Mel still tried to keep things fairly normal, under her parents' rules. Some days after school, Zach would come over and they'd study, hang out. Her parents allowed him to bring his new puppy over once it was better potty-trained.

More of her after-school time was spent with Devin, again, at her place. Aside from studying, he tried teaching her how to dance. She taught him to play several board and card games. She was astounded he hadn't played most of the standard games everyone knows.

"This isn't my favorite, but it's still a well-known one. We each get armies, and basically take over the world," she explained while setting it up on the kitchen table.

"Risk, huh?" He shrugged. "Let's give it a go."

He was doing really well for a first-time player, but didn't seem to actually enjoy it much. He was distracted, distant.

"Imagine if it were this simple," Devin mused. "To win or lose an actual war this way."

She glanced at him, perplexed. "I guess I've never really thought much about it."

She took her turn. When she finished and looked up, she caught him staring at her, grinning.

"What's on your mind?" she asked.

"I'm just happy." He picked up his dice and rolled them from his palm to his fingers, and back. "Where would you go, if you had no limitations?"

"Like on a trip?"

"Yeah."

She thought for a moment. "I actually have a whole list of places I want to go. My parents have always said I should take some time off before deciding what college I want to attend. They say people waste too much money getting degrees they don't use. So, I'm hoping to save up and travel a little while I figure it out. Somewhere warm would be nice. Honestly, I'd considered Costa Rica on my short list of fun places to visit. But I guess my parents beat me to that."

"You don't think it would be too weird to live in a different culture?"

"It's not like I'm planning on moving there permanently, it would just be a visit. I don't want to move anywhere too far away from my parents."

He nodded thoughtfully and started his turn.

"What about you, have you traveled much?" she asked.

"Not really, not compared to a lot of people."

He still never talked about his family. He'd get awkward every time she asked, so she'd stopped asking a while ago, figuring he'd get there when he was ready. But his uncharacteristically downcast mood prompted her to give it another go.

"So, if your family never plays board games, or goes on vacations, what did you guys do growing up?"

He rested his chin on his hand. "My parents—"

Ben walked into the kitchen to grab something from the fridge. Devin stopped talking, instead following Ben with his eyes. Only after he left, Devin continued, "My mom's a nurse and my dad's in the military. I came here to live with my uncle because they're gone so much."

She frowned. "I'm sorry. That sucks. But that's cool your dad's in the service. Tell him thank you next time you talk to him."

He smiled. "I'm sure he'll appreciate that."

She figured she wouldn't push things any further. He still seemed like he wasn't ready to open up more. "You know you can talk to me, right? I'd like to think I'm a good listener."

He gave her another half-hearted smile. "I know, and you are."

It killed her that he was struggling with something. But she promised herself she wouldn't be a clingy, or jealous, or needy, girlfriend.

Mel won the game, though she was certain Devin let her win.

"You changed your strategy, I'm sure you should have won." She put her hands on her hips in accusation.

"I don't know what you're talking about." He smirked.

She walked him out the front door, standing on the porch. She squinted playfully. "No letting me win. You only do that to little kids, and I'm pretty sure I haven't been one of those for a while."

He wrapped his thumbs through her belt loops and pulled her close. "No. You are *definitely* not a little kid. I'd say you're an amazing woman." He leaned in and gave her a sweet kiss.

She couldn't help but smile. "You're pretty amazing yourself."

He gazed lovingly into her eyes. "And I *didn't* just let you win. Sometimes, you have to change your strategy, to get the results you want. I'd say a slow death in the game gave me more time with you tonight."

She shook her head. Wrapping her arms around him, she gave him an appreciative kiss. And she *really* appreciated his sweetness.

His phone rang in his pocket, ruining their moment. She pulled back, and he looked at his phone, smiling. He pushed the ignore button and shoved it in his pocket. He picked up where they'd left off. His phone rang again. He pulled it out and turned it off.

"You're sure you don't need to answer that?"

"Yep." He grinned before meeting her lips once more.

Mel groaned when the front door opened behind her a couple of minutes later.

"Mel, I need to do some laundry. Will you move yours?" Ben asked, squinting at Devin.

She glared. "Seriously? I'm kind of busy right now."

Devin rubbed the back of his neck, looking at Ben with a menacing grin. "It's funny, isn't it? It's almost like he actually *is* your brother. They're meant to be annoying, aren't they?"

Ben scowled. "Maybe you should go home."

"I probably should." Devin gave her one last peck on the lips before taking off.

Mel followed Ben into the house. "What's your problem? We've gone over this."

"I just don't think you should be getting so serious with him."

"Why?" she challenged. "What do you know that I don't?"

He shrugged. "I'm just saying, you shouldn't."

"Wow. That's a pretty valid reason. I'll make sure to file that away." She grabbed her laundry from the dryer and went up to her room for the remainder of the night.

She couldn't help but wonder, though—who had been calling Devin? Was there something Ben knew that she didn't? Or was he only being his usual meddling, annoying, self? Her stomach knotted, thinking of how Ben had called it on Blake. Could he be right about Devin, too? No. The only thing Blake and Devin ever shared were their interest in her. Devin was a thousand times better.

She looked up to her ceiling, staring at the glow-in-the-dark stars. Devin had disliked Blake, too. She snorted out loud. *Devin probably doesn't object to himself, and I care about his opinion just a smidge more than Ben's.*

⁕

After a couple of months in a secret relationship, and then bumming around the house openly as a couple, they were finally going to go on a legitimate date. Valentine's was coming up and Mel insisted she didn't need any sort of elaborate plans, she just wanted to spend time with Devin away from the constant supervision at her house. Keeping her parents' rules, they decided on a basic dinner and movie.

After a nice Italian meal, avoiding anything too garlicky, they went to the theater for a new release they'd compromised on. Devin was more interested in it than Mel was, but she was plenty happy just to be with him.

The credits were starting, and he didn't waste any time pushing up the armrest separating them. She snuggled next to him as he put an arm around her. She kissed his cheek and smiled. He sweetly tickled her neck with his fingers and she guided his lips down to hers with a hand under his chin.

Their kiss didn't last long as he pulled back, brow furrowed. "You're not wearing your necklace?"

"Oh." She frowned. It was just a little piece of jewelry, but it was something special from him. She regretted not taking the time to put it on. And, of course, it would be on a romantic date that he'd notice. "The chain got a little tangled. After my run and shower this afternoon, I didn't get around to putting it back on."

"It's been a few hours?" he asked, reading her face.

"Yeah. Just a couple." He was overreacting ... showing a possessive side she hadn't seen before. She cleared her throat, feeling uneasy. "It's just a necklace."

He moved his arm down, no longer holding her. "It just means a lot to me. It's ... a family thing."

"Oh, you didn't tell me that." The guilt piled up, knowing he missed his parents. "I'll put it on as soon as I get home. You're not ... mad at me, are you?"

"No. Of course not." He shifted away from her. "I feel like snacks, after all. Any requests?"

She shook her head, then watched him walk away to get concessions. After a couple of minutes of him being gone, Blake walked into the theater and her stomach knotted. He was holding a girl's hand and glared at Mel once he realized she was in the theater. He slid his hand into the girl's back jeans pocket as he guided her to a seat just a few rows in front of Mel, then promptly started to make out.

Mel rolled her eyes, determined to not let him spoil her night.

Devin came back with a huge soda and popcorn, bringing the armrest down between them to put the drink in the holder. "There we go. Lots to share," he whispered.

She shook her head again. This was her first Valentine's with a boyfriend, and he was acting weird. She picked up the soda and moved it to the armrest on her side, putting the shared one back up. "You can let me know when you want a drink." She smirked, trying to bring back their romantic moment.

He shifted in his seat and munched on a handful of popcorn.

She frowned again. "Seriously, what's wrong? If it means that much to you, I need more of an explanation. I want to enjoy some time alone with you, and right now, this is as close as we get."

He sighed. "It's nothing. Honestly. I just want to watch the movie."

"Fine." She moved the armrest down and transferred the drink back, crossing her arms.

"Is that ... Blake?" he whispered.

"Yeah. Wonder if she knows what a winner she's with." Mel scowled.

Devin set the popcorn down in the empty seat next to him. "Let's go back to your place."

She furrowed her brow. "Why? I'm not leaving just because that jerk is here."

Someone in a nearby row shushed her.

"Please?" he pleaded. "For me?" He stood up and extended his hands.

Mel reluctantly got up.

He drove her home, parking his car and looking over at her. "I'm sorry. I'm just off today... Family stuff."

She frowned. "Fine."

Devin grabbed her hand and gave her a smile. "I promise, I'll make it up to you another time. As for tonight, we can head inside and play a game or something?"

"No. I'd rather just call it a night at this point."

He matched her frown, nodding. After walking her to the door, he left her with a tiny peck on the lips.

She went straight to her room and plopped down on her bed. Staring at the knotted chain on her nightstand, she scowled at the stupid thing. She was starting to feel pretty tired anyway, but this wasn't how she'd wanted this night to go.

Mel remembered how sweet he had been, taking care of her, when he first gave her the necklace. And how hard it was for him to be separated from his family. She sighed and unknotted it, putting it on and lying down. Even if he made it up to her, her first Valentine's with a boyfriend, like her first-ever date, would not be the kind of story worth telling her kids someday.

Luckily, he did make it up to her. The next day, he was right back to being his normal self—with a bounce in his step, a sincere apology, and plenty of affection when they could sneak it. They rescheduled their date, and he planned a fun surprise, taking her to a painting class.

Chapter 11

Before Mel knew it, it was mid-March. The drama seemed to calm down on all fronts. Mel tried to talk her parents into letting her go camping with Zach's family over spring break, but they weren't having it. Instead, she'd be staying home, and talked with Heather about possibly having a girls' night at some point. While Mel's parents originally had aimed for spring break in Costa Rica, her dad had a chiropractic convention, so they decided they'd move it to right after school ended.

The Friday before the break, Mel woke up feeling off. She'd started to feel pretty worn down the night before, and hoped to sleep it off. She wasn't any better in the morning, but hated missing school and having to play catch-up.

Before heading out for the day, Mel stopped by the kitchen for her usual morning hug with her mom or dad. Instead, she found them scrambling around the room with towels, sopping up the carnage of a burst pipe or leak of some sort.

"Do you guys need help?"

Her mom waved her off. "It's okay, sweetie. We'll be fine. Have a good day at school."

Devin was late to school, so she didn't get to see him before starting classes. After missing all of her morning hugs, and feeling cruddy, she sulked a little until she saw Zach, armed with a warm hug.

But she still felt off. By the last period, she *knew* she should have taken a sick day. Nauseous and overheating, she showed up at the gym and didn't even have to ask to sit it out.

"Are you alright?" Mr. Cress, her P.E. teacher, asked. Mel didn't know him that well, though P.E. teachers weren't all that chatty about their personal lives like classroom teachers could sometimes be. He looked down at her with concern in his brown eyes. "You're pretty pale. How long have you felt this way?"

She shook her head. "I'll be fine. Last time this happened, I got better the next day."

He furrowed his brow. "Sit today out."

She watched the class from the old gym's run-down bleachers, drinking some water. She was embarrassed every time Mr. Cress would glance over or check in on her. But she got to meet a nice girl, Emily, who also had to sit out, having recently broken her ankle.(h)

After class was dismissed, Mel returned to the locker room, getting dressed and folding up her practically unused gym clothes. Lightheaded, she realized she'd left her favorite water bottle in the gym—sipping during class had helped. She exited the locker room and crossed the hall to go grab it. The gym was empty, the doors open. She bent over into the bleachers and grabbed the bottle, right where she had forgotten it. A sudden dizzy spell forced her to sit down.

She started panicking, wondering if this was what it felt like to be drugged, or have a heart attack. She was sweating, her heart racing and breathing labored. Sure, she'd been a little off earlier in the day, but whatever was happening was coming on rather suddenly. The room spun as she felt an unsettling energy build up—like when a person is restless and can't sit still. The energy magnified by a thousand. She bent over, falling to her knees on the gym floor in pure agony. She wanted to call for help, but her voice betrayed her; her clarity of mind waned.

Mel wanted to curl into a ball until it all went away, but her body had other plans. Her muscles twisted, forcing her to hold her head up. Her face and arms were itching, as if dozens of spiders were crawling all over her.

The next thing Mel knew, her throat was closing—something had wrapped around it, strangling her. Gasping for air, she tore at the cords, fighting with every molecule of energy she could muster to free herself. She felt it tugging, pulling tighter, even stinging a little as if she were being cut.

Then a deep voice cut through the darkening haze. "I've got a weed, one of your girlfriends. Get to the gym. Let's take care of her."

As Mel was teetering on the edge of consciousness, a familiar voice lunged into the gathering darkness. "GET OFF HER, YOU LEECH!"

She heard footsteps running up behind her and a *slash*.

The cords around her neck slackened, and she finally ripped them from her throat.

Mel slumped onto her side, heaving and gasping for air. The excruciating pain from whatever was happening to her still coursed through every inch of her body.

Struggling to focus through blurred vision, Mel thought she saw Ben, of all people, and her assailant, brawling just a few feet away. They weren't just swinging punches, either. But Ben ... looked different. They both did.

Ben had some sort of growths on his arms. Were they green wings? No... And when did he dye his hair? He had also never given any indication that he knew how to fight at this caliber, but he was landing punches, agile on his feet—he even kicked the other guy in the head at one point.

The other guy was mostly attacking with ... dark rope? No, vines! They sprouted from his wrists and he seemed to be able to control them. If she wasn't completely incapacitated, she may have begun to question her sanity.

"Nice! Two weeds for the price of one," the backup called out as he arrived. The newest voice belonged to none other than Blake. His wrists also shot out those dark green vines, covered in small leaves. His odd ability matched his fighting partner, whom she now recognized as a kid from her English class.

"Nuren might want the female," Blake said.

Blake went after Mel with a set of vines. Ben lunged forward, using the green blades on his arms to slice them off before they reached her. Using the distraction, the other attacker wrapped a vine around Ben's leg and pulled it out from underneath him. Ben landed with a heavy *thud*.

Blake turned his attention to Ben; Mel still wasn't in any position to fight for herself. Blake wrapped vines around one of Ben's wrists. Ben grunted and kept slashing at their cords, time after time. But it was a numbers game, and they had four weapons to his two.

"I NEED YOU TO GET UP, MEL!" Ben yelled in her direction.

Did he know what he was asking?! She closed her eyes to summon every ounce of strength she could to stand up. She pushed herself to her hands and knees. A vine wrapped around her ankle and she reached back, grabbing it. She instinctually used the energy she had been fighting against to bend and crush it.

Blake swore.

"MEL! I NEED YOU TO GET UP!" Ben yelled again.

She lifted a knee and forced herself to stand, barely balancing.

Ben reached back. "Give me your hand!"

She stretched toward him and he managed to grasp her hand. A light transferred from her skin through to Ben's. With his free hand, he flicked his wrist at Blake, and something like stakes, or maybe spikes, impaled Blake in the throat. Blake fell back and didn't move.

Still holding her hand, Ben did the same maneuver against the other fighter and she saw at least one stake each find a place in his chest and shoulder, with one grazing his neck. He fell back and Ben let go of Mel.

On the verge of passing out, she closed her eyes and heard Ben slash off the remaining vines that had wrapped around him.

"We need to go," he barked, taking off his jacket and wrapping it around her.

She tried to walk, but he hastily swept her off of her feet, out of the building and to a car. Ben opened the passenger door and shoved her in.

"Buckle up!" He slammed the door and got in to drive. Jamming the keys in the ignition, he started the car and sped out of the school parking lot.

He pounded on the steering wheel. "Damn it!" Whipping out his phone, he made a call. "I've got Saffrona. Two Ivies in the gym. Tell Pam to be ready in five."

Through her haze, she made out her mom's name. Pam. It also registered that Ben was bleeding.

He started yelling at Mel. "You're such a pain in the ass! You know that? Everyone else was just fine! Tabatha was a breeze. Even Stacy made it out undiscovered. And she was a cheerleader, a flipping cheerleader with tons of eyes on her." He took a breath in the middle of his rant. "Where's your boyfriend's necklace?"

Her eyes widened as she recognized what he was saying, and asking. *He never even met Tabatha before she moved. And what about the necklace?* She moved a hand up to her neck. It wasn't there. When she returned her hand to her lap, her fingertips were coated in blood. Her own blood. And her hand was literally glowing.

He didn't stop for a moment to let her try to formulate a sentence. Even if she could have, he probably didn't care to hear what she had to say. "Why weren't you wearing it?! Never mind. It doesn't even matter now."

Mel closed her eyes and leaned against the passenger window, wincing and fighting back tears. Not just from the pain, but from the whirling confusion, and from ... whatever had just happened.

She heard the familiar sound of a garage door opening. They pulled in and it closed behind them. Ben got out of the car and slammed the door shut, going inside the house and leaving her behind. The door to the kitchen opened again and her mom came running out.

Ben opened the door. "We don't have time, Pam!"

She looked back at Mel, her face and voice full of concern. "Do you think you can make it inside, sweetie?"

Pam went back inside at Ben's insistence while Mel forced herself to move through the discomfort, opening the door and hanging onto the car to help her keep balance. As soon as she made it in the house, she saw her mom feverishly packing her clothes in a duffle bag.

"Help her to a chair!" Pam ordered Ben. "You could be a little nicer," she scolded. "There's only so much she can do about it."

Ben helped Mel to a chair at the kitchen table.

"Where's the charm?" Pam asked. "Sweetheart, where's your green necklace?"

Mel searched her foggy thoughts. She didn't know.

"Look at her," Ben said, pointing to Mel. "She's gone too far."

Pam frowned. "We could still try." She looked to Mel. "Do you know where it is?"

Beyond rattled, still in agony and the throes of confusion, trying to remember when she'd last seen or worn it wasn't Mel's top priority.

Ben's phone chimed and he stalked down the hallway to the front door. Pam resumed packing Mel's things when the front door opened and Mel heard Ben talking to someone. She heard Blake's name and the name of the other kid, Ken.

Ben returned to the kitchen, Devin close behind him.

Devin pulled a chair to her side, sitting down and grabbing her hands. "Gosh, Mel." He looked panicked. "What happened?"

Ben was still clearly frustrated. "What do you think happened? She lost it."

Devin ran his finger under her collar, where the necklace would normally sit. He looked up at Ben. "Can Thod help?"

Ben shook his head. "No, we've got one more, she'll be out any time now. We can't risk it."

Devin pursed his lips. "I'll take her. That means you have two of mine."

Ben rubbed his forehead. "Fine."

Devin looked back at Mel and smiled reassuringly. "It'll be okay. We're going on a road trip." He grinned. "I know, you're so excited, you're practically glowing."

She raised her eyebrows and glanced down again at her glowing skin. The joke wasn't lost on her, but she didn't have any energy to respond.

"Did you kill the leeches?" Devin asked Ben.

"I don't know." Ben ran his fingers through his hair while pacing.

"I texted my dad and," Devin paused, "someone else. They'll stop by the gym."

Pam zipped up the duffle bag and handed it to Ben. He left to take it out to Devin's car, returning with a blanket from the family room to wrap Mel in.

"You'll be fine, sweetie." Her mom's look of concern was less reassuring than her words. "You can trust Devin."

Devin picked Mel up, barely exerting himself. He carried her out to the car and buckled her in. Hopping in the driver's seat, he buckled up and rolled the window down.

"Take good care of her," Pam pleaded.

"Try to keep your hands off my sister," Ben threatened.

"I absolutely will, Mrs. Walters." Devin assured her, putting the car in gear.

"Devin..." Ben was giving him a death glare.

"Stay focused, Ben, we've got people counting on you," was all Devin said to Ben's challenge. Even in her current state, Mel could tell Devin's tone was playfully antagonizing.

Devin reached over to squeeze her hand and backed out of the driveway.

Soon after leaving the city limits, he pulled the car off to the side of the road and parked. He looked at Mel, whose eyes had been fixed on him since getting in the car; at least during the times she had her eyes open.

He wore a sympathetic frown. "It's pretty rough, isn't it?"

"What's going on?" A tear rolled down her face.

"What's going on, is you're going to be one-hundred-and-ten percent okay. I need you to trust me. Can you do that?"

She nodded.

He reached back and grabbed a bottle of water from the backseat. "You need to stay hydrated. It's a forty-five-minute drive and then we can get you more comfy. There will be plenty of time for questions."

She cracked the bottle open and drank. It helped a little.

They pulled into a long gravel driveway and Devin turned off the car. He carried Mel into a small, dark house. All the curtains were pulled, blackout style; the walls were white and the carpet brown. He sat her down on a stiff couch and turned on the lights, taking in a deep breath of the stale air. "Mmm. Home sweet ... not home."

The house was simply furnished; no care had been taken for décor. The walls were mostly bare, and everything looked plain and practical.

Devin disappeared into a room down the hallway only to emerge a couple of minutes later, scooping her up. He took her to the same room, a bedroom with two beds. After laying her down on one, she curled up in a ball. Devin went down the hall and came back with a first aid kit, breaking out rubbing alcohol and sterile pads.

He shook his head. "They did a number on you, didn't they?" The alcohol stung as he tended to her neck and ankle. "The great thing is, you are going to heal like a champ now." He smiled. "No scars for you. This is just an added precaution."

She still had no idea what the heck was going on. And somehow, she didn't even care. Whatever her body was going through was brutal, and she was barely keeping it together.

He took the bloodied supplies to the bathroom and washed up, returning with another bottle of water. "Let's have you drink some more. Can you sit up?"

She guzzled the water down after Devin helped her sit up. He took the empty bottle from her as she slipped back down into the fetal position. He crouched and gingerly brushed the hair from her face, smiling lovingly.

"This reminds me of the first time we kissed. Do you remember how sick you were that day? It's going to kind of fade back to that before you feel better. Unfortunately, there's not a lot we can do about how you're feeling right now, but you should be loads better in the morning." He gently rubbed the back of her hand. "I think the best thing we can have you do is try to sleep it off."

She whimpered in pain.

He winced. "I'm going to go hit the lights. I'll let you choose: I can sleep on that bed over there, or if you'd prefer, I can cuddle up next to you—maybe it'll help." He put his hands in the air. "Total gentleman, I promise."

She nodded ever so slightly.

"The second?" He kissed her forehead. "Okay."

After turning off the lights, he crawled into bed and wrapped his arms around her. It was a long night of agonizing pain, surging and draining energy, nausea—the whole package. She was grateful to have him there with her through it all.

Chapter 12

Mel woke the next morning to the sound of running tap water from down the hallway. Footsteps drew close and she pried her eyes open to see Devin standing at the other side of the room, brushing his teeth in nothing but boxers. He noticed her gaze and held up his pointer finger, mumbling with his mouth full of foam. He finished in the bathroom and came back to the bedroom.

He crouched next to Mel with a sympathetic smile. "Hey, gorgeous, you're awake. How are you feeling?"

She considered how to respond for a moment, looking him over. Even if it felt like she had a nasty hangover, his attractiveness registered. Mel looked down to see she was still in the clothes she'd worn to school the day before. He must have noticed her eyes wandering—he popped up to his feet.

"Oh, yeah." He started rifling through the closet and holding clothes up to himself to see if they would fit. "I, uh … I promise nothing happened. You were just really hot last night."

She managed a small grin.

He stopped and turned back to her. "That didn't come out right." Pulling a t-shirt off of a hanger, he tugged it over his head. "While I'm sure you are *very* hot in bed, what I mean is, you were *literally* very hot, like … emanating heat from your body during the change."

She lay still. Everything from the day before was rattling around in her head. She didn't even know where to start, what to ask.

He zipped up a pair of clean jeans and grabbed a fresh bottle of water, returning to her side. "Can I help you sit up?"

She shook her head, opting to force herself to slowly scoot up against the wall at the head of the bed.

He felt her forehead and looked her over. "It'll probably be a few more hours, but the worst is past. I've never actually heard of it happening like that; you had me pretty worried there."

She finished off the bottle of water. While feeling ten times better than the night before, she was still worn out.

"Absolutely no rush, but when you're ready to get cleaned up, there's plenty of hot water." He winced. "I, uh … probably should have waited for you to wake up, but I looked at the bag Pam packed for you. She forgot to pack you a toothbrush, but that's not a problem. We keep extras around here. I set one out for you on the counter."

He eased down on the edge of the other bed. "What can I do to help?"

The idea of a shower felt fantastic—she was drenched in sweat, not to mention the blood from the cuts on her neck, which had soaked into her shirt. But she didn't think she could stand yet. And she desperately needed some answers, anything, to help ground her.

"Where are we?" Her voice was froggy.

"We're at a safe house. Only a few people know where this place is. No close neighbors. We'll be okay here."

"Why do we need to be at a safe house?"

"I've never actually done this part of it, so I may not explain everything the best. Let's start with what you remember about yesterday."

She stared at the wall as if reading invisible ink, trying to make sense of what she could remember. "Why did they attack me?" Tears welled up from the blur of trauma.

He frowned. "Mel, there's a lot you don't know about yourself. So, it'll take some time to get through all of it. You were being protected, and," he swallowed, "we let you down. I had to take care of something, and Ben got held up, and it was just bad timing." He whispered, "I'm really so sorry."

Nothing made sense. "Why would I need to be protected? I never did anything to them."

"No, love, it's not like that. Do you remember who attacked you? I'm not sure what all you were able to see or hear while your body was going through … what it went through."

She adjusted herself to sit up a little straighter. "It was Blake, wasn't it? And another kid from our school? But there was something … not natural about them."

His lips twisted into an ironic grin. "Natural. Yeah… Yes, it was Blake, and you're right, the other leech was from our school."

"You guys said that a couple times, 'leeches.' They were like some kind of monster."

He winced at that. "I don't know that there's an easy way to tiptoe down this road. Let me just lay it all out there and you can ask questions as we go."

"Okay."

He squinted at her and rocked his head back and forth, as if formulating the best angle to start from. "They weren't human, Mel. And neither are you, and neither am I. We're not from here."

She pressed her lips together and furrowed her brow, but said nothing.

"I can only imagine it sounds crazy. *I've* known my whole life, but you haven't—that was to keep you safe, and to give you a normal life."

He kept pausing, reading her face.

"We call the jerks that tried to hurt you 'Ivies,' or more appropriately 'leeches,' because that's what they are. They cheat and steal and do anything to get an advantage. Including killing people like you."

She spoke up, the reality of what she'd seen and heard the day before still swirling in her head. "You said we're not people."

"No, no, no. We're people, we're just not *human* people. You saw them transform; you saw their vines?"

She nodded.

"That's where their name comes from. You and I, we're more like them than we are like humans. We're botanical beings. We have abilities that humans don't have and can't understand. Did you see how Ben looked when he was fighting? Did you get a look at yourself?"

She remembered that Ben had changed, and obviously *something* was happening to her.

"You and I, and Ben, and … several more people in town, we're called 'Seeders.' Our form is more floral. You really should see yourself when you change—you're breathtaking." He beamed. "Anyway, long story short, Seeders and Ivies are from the Green Lands. We live different lives, have large families, and unfortunately, fight a lot. The only reason you grew up in the human world and I didn't, is because we hide our daughters and sisters in the human world until they're old enough to fully mature, to bloom. That's what you just went through." He paused. "What questions do you have for me?"

Only about a million. "Did Ben kill Blake?"

He huffed. "I don't know for sure. By the time our guys got back, there weren't any bodies. So, either they got up from the fight, or one of their cronies or generals was nearby and picked up the bodies before we could get there." He quickly added, "But you won't see them again. Even if they survived, they've been made and know we would hunt them down."

"He... Did you guys know that's what he was?"

Devin frowned. "We suspected, obviously, after he first attacked you. But sometimes humans are just jerks like that. We couldn't be sure. We can't just go around taking out suspects or interrogating them and giving ourselves away. I just wish..." He closed his eyes and shook his head. "I wish one of us had been there. I feel horrible."

"I don't blame you."

"Thanks, Mel." His eyes frowned as though there was turmoil still hiding behind them.

So many questions ricocheted in her mind, and she knew some were more important than others. But she decided to go with an intriguing one, one that offered physical proof and validation. "So, you can look like Ben? Can I see?"

He beamed at the request and transformed before her. His arms each sprouted a long, sharp green leaf, flaring out at the wrist and ending at the elbow. The serrated edges were menacing, and perfect for cutting Ivy vines, as Ben had done. The tips of his hair turned purple. He lifted his pant legs to show almost flesh-colored roots wrapping around his ankles. "These are mostly good for armor."

As freaky as it was to see, it was also really impressive that Devin could change himself so drastically, with so little effort.

He reverted back to his human appearance. "Honestly, if I'm not fighting, I like this form—it's not as bulky. Even back home, this is how everyone walks around."

"So, you're saying I can look like you?" She was genuinely wondering if this all had to be some kind of hallucination.

"No. You look even better." He winked. "Your leaf blades are wider, softer, more rounded. Honestly, you're kinda sexy any form you take." He cleared his throat. "Anyway, um ... your eyes and hair change differently—if you want to see in a mirror, you still kinda look like that as you finish blooming."

Mel definitely wanted to see. She considered whether she trusted her body enough to stand yet. "I think I'm ready to get cleaned up."

"Your wish is my command. Let me draw you a bath. I don't want you getting dizzy and falling in the shower, alright?"

He left the room and popped back in as the water ran. "I, uh … put your stuff back in your bag and left it in there, so you can," he swallowed hard, blushing, "pick what you want to change into."

She managed a smirk at his discomfort. Served him right for rummaging through her things like that. Then she started to blush herself, wondering what her mom had hastily packed from her underwear drawer. He mentioned only the forgotten toothbrush, so she assumed at least the clothing basics were covered.

Devin offered a hand and helped steady her as she got up and walked to the bathroom. "Let me know if you need anything."

She sat down on the edge of the tub as he stood in the doorway.

"Um…" He broke eye contact. "There's one thing I need you to check."

She raised her eyebrows. "What?"

"Well, the roots that I showed you, you have them, too. But yours are still developing, and they'll continue to for a while, even after you feel better."

She nodded.

"Well, um…" He seemed even less comfortable with this topic than rummaging through her clothes. "Just, they start at your hips, and work their way down to your ankles. But we need to know how far down they are when you're done in here. So just," he cleared his throat again, "take a look and let me know?"

She nodded again, acknowledging the awkward in this whole situation.

After Devin closed the door, Mel soaked in the tub until it barely had any warmth left. The scene from the day before played through her mind. She considered everything she'd just experienced and what Devin had told her; it reframed her entire life. It took less than a day for her world to come crashing down around her. She wasn't human … she was a *creature*.

And people wanted her dead.

She drained the water and then crawled on her knees, turning the showerhead on. She stayed kneeling, letting the water run over her, muffling the sounds of her sobbing. Her life had been ripped from her without warning; the circumstances hazy, the consequences exhausting. And the dust hadn't even started to settle.

After there were no more tears to cry, she pulled herself to a standing position and finished cleaning up with the toiletries in the room. She dressed in clean clothes and brushed her teeth, gazing at the glowing green eyes staring back at her, slowly fading. Staring at herself in a near catatonic state, she picked up a brush and ran it through the hair that was fading from yellow back to her natural strawberry blonde. Curious, she plucked a hair out; it instantly faded to her regular, human coloring.

She was running her fingers over her neck when Devin's knock at the door pulled her from the abyss of her thoughts. "The door's unlocked."

Devin slowly cracked the door, then fully opened it, seeing she was decent. He walked up behind her and wrapped his arms around Mel's body, holding her close and standing cheek-to-cheek while looking in the mirror. "Are you okay?"

She didn't respond, fixated on her neck where the vines had dug into her. There were barely any signs of injury by now.

He grabbed her hand and pulled it down, replacing it with his lips. "All better."

Mel continued to stare blankly into the mirror. "I never asked for any of this."

He frowned. "No one asks to be what they are. It just ... is what it is. We are who we are."

"My life is a lie," she whispered.

He pressed his lips together, remaining silent.

After a moment, he kissed her on the cheek and whispered in her ear, "Your life is full of so much love, more than any human could ever have." He gave her hand a squeeze. "Let's go sit down."

He had her sit at the small round table in the kitchen area. "Do you feel up to more than water? Let's see if that'll help." He poured some apple juice, and she drank it while he rifled around in the fridge and pantry. "We're never really sure when we'll need this place, so we don't keep much around that's perishable. I could make you some oatmeal, or frozen waffles?"

She shook her head.

"Granola bar?" He raised an eyebrow.

She shook her head again.

"I need you to eat something. You need to get your strength back." He grabbed a bag of sliced bread from the freezer, toasting a couple of slices and smothering them in peanut butter and honey. "My specialty."

Chapter 13

Mel slowly risked eating the breakfast Devin had prepared for her, one small bite at a time while he watched. She polished off one piece of toast, ready to start the second. "I want to hear my story. Start at the beginning."

Devin explained how Seeder seedlings sprouted, how the girls were escorted by their fathers to the human world and placed with host families.

"You're saying my parents aren't really my parents, right?"

"Pam and George are just as much your parents as your biological parents are, if you ask me. Everything they've ever done was to protect you, from the moment they got you."

She furrowed her brow. "They lied to me my entire life."

He frowned, then continued by explaining the complex family dynamics they had to work with—Seeder mothers raising their sons in the Green Lands, preparing them for protection duty with their fathers in the human world. Seeder girls couldn't survive back home, not with their poisoned lands, not when they were trapped within their own borders by the enemy. He offered to let her call home, but she was too conflicted to broach the topic with her parents at the moment.

"So, Ben is legit my brother?" His annoyances instantly became more endearing. She'd always imagined what it was like to not be an only child. Foster-children excluded, of course.

"Yep, he is. And he's actually a great guy if you give him a chance." Devin shrugged. "He's one of my best friends back home. He's just hyper-focused on the work, so he comes off a little less than friendly sometimes."

Devin's explanation about Seeder families sending brothers to protect their sisters clicked, and she went wide-eyed. "Wait, you're not one of my brothers, right?!"

He grimaced in disgust. "No, Mel. No. Gross, no! We're not human but we're also not perverts! Your dad strategized with mine to join forces with their girls. We help each other out, watch each other's backs."

She let out a sigh of relief. "You said you're friends with Ben, but you two never hung out."

"Part of the plan is carefully controlling who's seen together. If one person's discovered, it could spread out like a web and jeopardize us all."

She narrowed her eyes. "What about at the mall? And that time at my house? Not friendly and not exactly neutral."

He laughed. "Really?" A mischievous grin was plastered on his face. "I was there to help keep his sister safe. Not fall for her. Our relationship hasn't exactly been G-rated." He laughed again. "He wasn't super excited to see us that close. I get it."

Blushing, she stood up from the table, her plate now empty. She remembered their first movie night, when Ben seemed ... uncharacteristically friendly, laughing and teasing, even teaming up with Devin against Zach... Devin and Ben *were* actually friends. "Keep going." She shoved her hands in her pockets, pacing the room.

"Well ... I trained up on the human world, took the place of one of my brothers that escorted a sister home, and Ben came in to take the place of the one that helped Tabatha get home."

She cut him off. "I still can't believe that. She completely ghosted me. She was one of my best friends."

"We don't have reliable communication between our worlds. No internet or phone lines. And she needed to move on with the next part of her life."

"Wait." Mel paused, sifting through her questions. "These Green Lands. Where are they? And what do you mean by 'next part of her life?'"

He slowly tipped his head to the side. "It's here. Like, on Earth ... I'm pretty sure. But you have to be one of us, green folk, someone from the Green Lands, to be able to open a rift to go between the realms. We're going to teach you how to do that."

Her eyes widened at the thought. Things were sinking in. She wasn't just some freak of nature, she could now magically go to some mysterious place no one had ever heard of. "When you say Tabatha moved on, is that what you mean? She's over there now? If she can't text, why couldn't she visit?"

He rubbed the back of his neck. "Yeah. She went home. So did Stacy. And ... there's just a lot to cover."

"Keep going."

"So, I was assigned to watch you, as well as others. Everything was planned out. Your mom and dad knew who I was, we played by their rules." He bobbed his head awkwardly, shoving his hands into his pockets. "I was actually the one that talked your parents into relaxing their dating rule in the first place."

She blushed again.

He elaborated. "I ... liked you. And after your fight with your mom, I figured I might be able to convince them. You were miserable. I wanted to date you. I figured it was a win-win. Of course, I didn't expect you to choose Blake over me..."

"Yeah, thanks for reminding me." She rolled her eyes. "I dated a guy that wants me dead. And there's nothing quite like having a guy walk in when you're shouting at your mom that you won't get knocked up."

He tried to stifle a laugh. "I mean ... on the topic ... well, this is kind of the birds and bees, but ... now that you've bloomed, you're considered an adult in our culture, and physically, you've changed. But you won't actually be able to have your own clutch for several years."

"Clutch meaning kids?"

He nodded.

"How absolutely refreshing." She feigned excitement. "I really *don't* have to worry about getting knocked up as a teen!" She stopped pacing and pointed down the hall. "There are *two* beds in there."

He put up his hands. "Trust me, I was *not* expecting anything." He grabbed her dishes and started to wash them. "Once I realized you were budding at the dance, we prepared the charm—the necklace, to help temper your changes. It helps to stretch out the process, so it's not as noticeable or excruciating. If you don't wear a charm, the process can be done in a few days, but it's so hard on you that you can slip into a pretty serious coma. It's rough."

He cringed. "There's so much raw power surging through you, the human body can't handle it." He started to dry the dishes. "If you hadn't forgotten to wear it, we might have been able to stretch it out until near the end of the school year. You could have stayed undetected."

She thought back to when she last remembered wearing it. It was probably a full day that she'd forgotten it. "Why didn't we get it from my gym locker before coming out here?"

"Once you reach a certain point, it's useless to put it back on; the process has to take its natural course."

Thinking about it, she remembered what were supposedly inconsequential conversations when her mom would hug her in the morning before school and ask where 'that pretty necklace' was, when Mel would forget to put it back on after a shower. And now their ruined Valentine's date made sense. Blake's presence ... not having the protection of the charm.

And then there was... She crossed her arms. "I'm guessing that necklace doesn't magically put itself into my locker?"

Devin pursed his lips, shaking his head.

She raised an eyebrow. "And who would have had access to my locker to put it there?"

He wore a soft smile. "Someone that cares about you?"

She still couldn't believe it. It had been around three months that she'd been going through this change and she hadn't known it.

He tilted his head to the side. "You must've been feeling pretty miserable, for a while, to go full-bloom. If you'd complained more to me or your parents, that would have given us a hint."

She let out a heavy sigh. She'd forgotten the necklace, she'd sucked it up when she felt sick, and it backfired. "So, all of this is my fault. That's awesome. Ben got hurt; I got hurt. We're out in the middle of nowhere." She continued her pacing. "But in my defense, it's not like anyone was honest with me about it. It's not my fault I didn't know a silly piece of jewelry was what stood between me and being murdered."

"No one's blaming you," he replied softly. "I'm just explaining how it works."

"Yeah, well, it's stupid." She scowled. "That no one told me. That this all could have been prevented ... by a stupid necklace."

He frowned. "The system's not perfect. I get that. We could have done a ring, or bracelet, something else. But the stone has to touch your skin to work. And honestly, everyone tried their best to make sure you were wearing it at all times. We just ... slipped." He looked into her eyes. "They wanted you to live a normal life. For the sake of the family network. For your own happiness." He huffed. "And I have to trust Ben's judgment about how things went down back at the school. I'm just ... we're just ... doing our jobs the best we can."

That stung. That's what she was to him, a job.

Devin shook his head. "Your parents were overwhelmed yesterday morning, and I slept in, so I didn't double-check that you were wearing it first thing." He looked down. "Not our finest work."

He paused.

She didn't know what to say, other than, "Go on."

"I suggested you'd be more likely to wear the charm faithfully if it came from me instead of your parents, with the way you'd been arguing with them about dating and Ben's arrival. And," a slight grin formed on his face, "we were pretty darn sure you were blooming, but I kinda wanted to see what your eyes would look like. And ... I hoped you felt the same about me, as I did you." He mused on the event. "Gosh, you are seriously an amazing kisser. And the way your eyes light up, the green is mesmerizing."

She scoffed at his fond memory. "The irony of my parents keeping me under lock and key just to set me up to have a fake boyfriend seduce me. Every girl's dream."

"It's not like that!" He startled Mel—Devin had never raised his voice at her before.

"It's not like what?" she yelled back. "You were *assigned* to me. Every aspect of our relationship was planned. You manipulated me and lied to me, every single day!"

He threw the dish towel on the ground. "No!"

She'd never seen him so angry. Her eyes grew wide in shock as he stomped over to her. Surprised, she stepped back against the wall. Her breathing was heavy.

He immediately stopped, just a couple of feet in front of her. He frowned, reading her face. "I'd never hurt you," he whispered. He looked down, shaking his head.

She steadied her breathing as he stood there, silent.

Devin balled his fists and held them up to his forehead. He finally said something, dropping his fists. "But I did what I had to do, to keep you and a *whole lot* of other people safe." His voice was firm. "Things went as far as they did, because I love you. I didn't *fake* that. I regret nothing. I'm not apologizing." He stayed in place, but his breathing calmed, his eyes softened. He glanced down at her lips, then back to her eyes with a frown. Barely above a whisper, he added, "I came here for my sisters. To meet and help my dad. I came for my family." He shook his head and walked away. "You need to realize it's not all about you."

Back in the kitchen, he picked up the towel and finished cleaning up. "By the way, go look in the mirror."

She headed to the bathroom and turned on the light. Her eyes were glistening green again, even more than they were before her shower. Her hands were glowing, like they had when Ben grabbed her hand during the fight. She'd been just about to ask if she could leave the house to go for a stroll, to clear her mind, but that was obviously out of the question now.

She walked back out, sitting next to him at the table. "What's this supposed to mean?"

He met her gaze. "This is exactly what Blake was trying to make happen. They know that as soon as you start the process, you have your powers, but you don't know how to control them. One moment of passion, one moment of rage, and they discover you. He tried to kiss you, hurt you. He was trying to get you to react, tip your hand.

"First, he'll fish around, dating lots of girls, asking questions, saying certain things to see if he can get a reaction. And then he'll try to get closer if he suspects you. It's just one of their tactics. Not all of them are jerks like him. Some are more suave, friendly, convincing."

She furrowed her brow. Yeah, he had a reputation... And apparently, he wasn't just a flirt because he was a jock.

"I still don't get it. He obviously knew. Why did they wait? And if we knew, that he knew, why didn't we stop them?"

Devin sighed. "He obviously *didn't* know. Otherwise, they would have come for you earlier. And they would never normally be stupid enough to take one of us on in the middle of a public place in broad daylight like that. If you were going through the change without the charm, you were an easy target, and a lucky find." He shook his head. "Anyway, it's pretty clear they suspected. But ... I think it just shows that they don't understand exactly how our changes work, and the jade. They don't go through that whole thing. It would take a lot more than what Blake did, for you to show with the charm on. If he had tried that on you a week from now, it would be a different story. And we *did* follow him. Though the other guy, Ken ... he wasn't even on our radar."

"But why would he be so stupid, to do something that would get him suspended? Just to fish for a reaction?"

"Well..." Devin smirked. "Honestly, I don't think he's too used to rejection, so he may have genuinely been pissed about that. Other than that, it's just speculation. You said something about him saying he was tired of waiting?"

She nodded. "Yeah, something like that."

He shrugged. "I don't know. We have different motives. Ours is preservation. Theirs is ... pride—personal and as a people. He might have gotten in trouble with their general about not doing a good enough job on his mission. Showing his cards like that, I'm sure he had his backside handed to him with a reprimand for being a pathetic soldier."

"You and Ben won't get in trouble, will you? For this?"

He smiled. "You're sweet. We'll be fine. Our guilt is enough punishment." He drew a deep breath. "Will we hear about it? Yes. But honestly, I was about ten times more terrified when I had to talk to Thod—your biological dad—after Ben spotted us at the mall."

She tried to suppress a grin. At least he had to do some suffering for his part in all the deceit. And the thought of this mystery dad coming down on him, it was kind of cute.

Though, it became less cute when she thought of all of their sneaking around, just to have her parents actually know about it and pretend they didn't. "They seriously knew we were dating the whole time? I, uh … I'm not sure how I feel about this, us, and being set up that way."

He furrowed his brow. "No." He pointed at her. "I see what you're thinking. You got *permission* to date because I asked for it. But none of our parents knew we were actually together until the run-in at the mall. They knew we were friends, and that you'd be safe as long as you were with me." He frowned. "I didn't lie about enjoying not being under a microscope with you. It felt kinda nice, to just be us."

She raised her eyebrows, still skeptical. "You didn't plan things with my parents at all? They didn't 'coincidentally' leave the house for you to come over to kiss me and give me the necklace?"

His face turned pink. "I was supposed to come over to hang out and check on you when they were home, but I knew they'd be gone, so, I … well…" He cleared his throat. "They were a bit annoyed that I did that, and that you let me in. But it got the job done." His deep brown eyes focused on hers. "I'd happily get in trouble, and risk anything, to be with you. And to keep you safe."

Mel looked down at her hands, processing everything. It was still shocking to see a slight glow to her skin. Her thoughts drifted back to the talk of concealment. "How do I control it?"

He managed a weak smile. "That's what we're here for. Despite the unfortunate timing of your bloom, at least it happened right before spring break. I'm going to teach you."

Everything about this change, this reveal, was an undeniable suck-fest. But at least there was something she could do about it; she was up to the challenge. "Alright."

He placed a hand on hers. "Mel ... I'm ... sorry, for getting so angry earlier. That was uncalled for. But I stand by what I said. I only lied to you because I had to, and because I care about you."

"It's okay," she whispered. "I know you care." The question bubbled up in her; she had to know. "When did you actually start to like me? When was anything between us real?"

He grinned. "Before we even met. When one of the girls whose profile I'd studied raised her hand more than once in Trigonometry. Great questions, right answers. And beautiful."

She looked down, drawing a pattern on the table with her finger.

"I know I've had to lie to you. And I meant it, too, when we were at the mall and I said I knew how much it sucks to lie to someone you care about." He raised his eyebrows. "But I've never had to fake an attraction to you. We're encouraged to keep you away from guys that aren't in the network, so you don't get too attached to a human or Ivy, but it's not like I was tasked with dating you."

He took his hand back and slumped down in his chair. "I'd understand if..." He whispered, "I was only supposed to be your friend. I promise. But I really..."

She sat up straighter, looking over at him, her heart aching.

"It's one more thing they take from us." He shook his head. "Everything got so convoluted. I had orders. I just..."

She watched him pick at his fingernails, frowning. That was almost exactly the same look he'd had when they were playing board games one night. That distant, regret-filled, hurting gaze. She remembered him asking how she'd feel, living in a different culture. How he'd reluctantly talked about his mom and dad ... which, his mom being a nurse could be true, if she had healing powers like Mel had just witnessed with her own injuries, and his dad *was* a military man ... just not the kind she'd thought.

Amidst Devin's passion, and confidence, and humor, he had his own heartache. Just like her parents' lies, she knew it was going to be hard sorting things out with Devin. But despite all of his flaws, all of what he'd had to do, she knew this side of him.

She gave him an encouraging smile. "We'll figure it out."

He wiped at the corners of his eyes. "Thanks. I promise, no more lies." He frowned. "I mean, I still have to follow orders. What our parents want ... stuff like that. But from now on, I'm one hundred percent me, you don't have to doubt any of that."

"Okay," she whispered with a nod.

They sat in silence for a moment. She didn't know how to feel about any of this. Everything was so big; so many questions remained unanswered. Mel plucked another from her mind. "You said no more lies. Can you tell me what you've already lied to me about? Like the charm. You once said you were recharging the batteries on the necklace you gave me. That's not a thing, right? I thought you were just flirting, but now I guess I don't really know."

He laughed, then stifled it with a hand over his mouth. "Sorry. I promise I'm not laughing at you. It's just cute. No, nothing either of us did or could do, affects the way it works." He cocked his head to the side. "As for other lies, I'll give you what I can..."

He didn't actually give her that much, explaining that he was hesitant and unsure as to whether or not he'd have permission to do so, if it might compromise the cover of a different family member. But he promised he'd share more with her as he could.

He sighed, sitting up straighter. "Want to see something neat with that light in your hands?" He reached out with one hand and she obliged. He grinned and waved his free hand in the air. A misty shower of lights rained down.

Her jaw dropped in amazement.

He smirked at her awe. "You have *so* much power in you."

"Ben grabbed my hand in the fight and then did something, that's how we got away."

"Yeah?"

She described the spikes that shot from Ben's hands, impaling the attackers.

"Gotcha, yeah. We call those darts. They're pretty handy. We can do those on our own, but they're a lot more impressive with your kind of power." He now held both of her hands, rubbing them tenderly with his thumbs. "Our people are so much stronger together, than we are alone. We're better when we fight side by side. I don't want to fight with you. I want you by my side."

She surveyed his face, knowing that, despite everything going on, she had fallen for him. "I want that, too."

Chapter 14

"How about I tell you more about your family?" Devin suggested at the kitchen table.

Mel raised her eyebrows high. "Not an only child anymore, right?"

He laughed. "I suppose that would be a bit of a shock. You have twenty-three brothers and sisters. Actually, I guess it's kind of like you're twenty-four-uplets? One more thing we have in common." He winked. "I can't tell you too much, because even if they've gone to live in the Green Lands already, we rely so heavily on anonymity. But Ben said he only let a couple of names slip?"

"Tabatha and Stacy? Sisters?"

He nodded.

"It's actually kind of cool, now that I realize Tabatha didn't just forget about me. And Stacy? That's a little hard to wrap my head around. How did she do when she learned all of this?"

"I'm not sure." Devin shrugged. "Ben did most of her detail and training." He lifted an eyebrow. "After school, when you thought he was off having a social life."

She nodded, another piece of the puzzle fitting into place.

"Him moving in with you guys was a last-minute change. That's probably why it didn't go as smoothly as it could have." Devin chuckled. "It was hard to keep a straight face when you all thought he was trying to date Stacy."

"Oh, gosh, yeah." Mel shuddered. "That's seriously weird. Like ... I may have had a crush on one of my brothers and not known it..."

"Yeah, it's complicated. But you have to remember that while all of your sisters came to this world, not nearly as many of your brothers have. And it doesn't mean you've even met all of them—they don't all necessarily go to the same school."

He had told her as much, that maybe only half of her brothers would come to the human world, over the years, for protection detail. The others continued their education back in the Green Lands, helped protect their borders against the Ivies, and contributed to society in other ways.

"Tabatha, Stacy, Ben, and I really don't look much alike ... I would never guess we were related," she said.

"In botanical appearance, all females take the same basic form—the yellow hair, green eyes. Same for the men, we look like our fathers with the purple hair tips. But in our more human forms, there's a lot of diversity in our genome. It's actually kind of weird to be over here and see families look so much like each other."

That was pretty cool. It made her more curious about how her people came to be.

More than once, in the blur of the reveals, a name and face had crossed her mind. "What about Zach?" She had been too afraid to ask where her closest friendship now stood in the mix of things.

Devin hesitated. "I can't give you an answer on everyone you want to know about right now. But I know he means a lot to you. He's not one of us. We don't know if he's Ivy or human. Our best guess is that he's just an ignorant human, but we have no way of knowing right now."

That answer didn't give her any sort of comfort. At least Zach wasn't trying to Luke and Leia it ... but to imagine that he could be an Ivy was impossible. She was sure Zach had to be human. He was so sweet and thoughtful.

She moved back to siblings. "So, I only get to know about Stacy, Tabatha, and Ben?"

He frowned. "Sorry, yeah. For now. But you'll get to meet them all when you come back to the Green Lands. The ones I've met are all really cool. I'm sure you'll recognize a few from your high school. But some attended private schools or homeschooled in the area."

Mel mused to herself. Her parents had tried to do that when she'd first started school, and had suggested it again later on, as she got older. But Mel thrived in public education, with the structure, opportunities, and social life. She realized how much more of a shut-in she could have been, if they'd not only denied her social outings and dating, but regular school, as well.

"Your mom back home is really awesome, too, Mel. You guys are going to be so excited to meet each other. Her name's Murial. She's an *amazing* cook. Our moms hang out a lot."

Mel fought a smile. She didn't even know these people, but she was somehow drawn to them... They were real, legitimate people. People like her. "Our families are really that close?"

He grinned. "You're *literally* the girl next door. We're neighbors. Honestly, if I'd known who you were, I probably would have gotten to know Tabatha better before coming over." He rubbed his hands together, wiggling his eyebrows. "Gotten some good dirt on you."

She smiled. "Then I'll consider myself lucky."

He hummed playfully. "Anyway. I've known your mom my whole life, but obviously your dad just since I got here. They're both pretty cool. Gosh, your dad..." He paused and took a breath in obvious admiration. "He took out two Ivies single-handedly last year, completely undiscovered."

That made her more than a little uneasy. "Did someone else in my family get attacked?"

He shook his head. "No. But they let it slip that they were Ivies. And they would have killed any of us, if it had been the other way around."

She scrunched her nose. "That's kinda weird ... hearing my biological dad is a murderer. Doesn't exactly bring warm, fuzzy feelings. It kind of ... creeps me out."

He furrowed his brow. "No, it's not like that. You still don't get it. He deserves a lot more respect than that."

She was taken aback by how adamant he was, defending her Seeder dad's character.

"Try to imagine leaving your mate, the love of your life, for sixteen, seventeen, eighteen years. Years without contact, other than a rare letter brought by a new son. And to spend all of those years focused on watching your daughters from afar. Every scraped knee, every breakup—you can't hug them. You can't let them know who you are. Worrying for their lives. Training and coordinating night and day to make sure your sons do what they need to. Falsifying documents. Even having to start from scratch to position yourself in a good place in the community, balancing a job with all of that. You need to give him a little more credit. Yeah, he can be deadly, he'll get the job done. But he's a family man."

She slumped in her seat. The pressure and guilt were growing. So many people were literally giving so much, risking so much, just for her. And she never knew it. Even if she hadn't been an only child, she conceded her existence had been pretty self-serving to that point. Memories flashed through her mind of yelling at her mom about being so strict, about hating Ben for his actions.

"Now the Ivies, on the other hand... Those bastards are one hundred percent assassins. They *literally* have no reason to come to the human world other than to hunt us down and kill us. Well, I mean you girls; taking out one of us guys is just icing on the cake. They don't come here to vacation or settle down."

Mel realized she needed deeper answers if she was in the middle of a war. "Why do they hate us so much? Why can't we just work things out?"

He sniggered and shook his head as though he were amused at the thought of ever being on good terms with the Ivies. "It's a core difference in who we are. Seeders, we spread out, we nourish, we focus on our families. They hate us for our diversity, consider themselves better than us. They blame us for things we never did. All they do is destroy. Ivies live in a wasteland, a place they decimated long ago, and now they try to take over our homes and resources. They even punch into the human world instead of respecting it the way we do." His mouth puckered with rage. "They don't have a single redeeming quality."

Devin was so passionate, goal-oriented, and clearly smart. Strong and tender at the same time. He had already expressed his love for Mel. She hadn't reached that point yet—she still needed to figure out who she was as a person, before she could figure out what they were as a couple. But she was starting to wonder if it was love. She looked down at her hands; the glowing had subsided.

"Do you think we could go for a walk?" she asked.

He decided they could risk a short stroll as long as they kept close to the house. They walked hand in hand down a dirt path on the safe house property, obscured from any neighbors or roads by trees. Mel soaked in the sunshine and savored the breeze. It was calming, it was cleansing, it was a much-needed breather from the crazy.

At her request, Devin told her what he could about his family. He shared fun childhood memories he had with his brothers and mom, Sandra.

"You know, all of you girls were given a name by our dads after sprouting. They're different from what your human host families gave you." He twirled a strand of her hair around his finger. "Yours is Saffrona.[i] I'd love to call you that in private, if you're okay with it."

"That's pretty." She smiled. "I remember hearing Ben say that when we were leaving the gym. We could try it out, or maybe Saff for short?"

He matched her smile. "Could I kiss you, Saff?"

She bit her lip. It was cute for him to ask, and fun having a secret name he could call her. "Yeah."

He leaned in, holding the nape of her neck. Her heart pounded like it always did when they kissed. His kiss took her away to another world altogether. His lips were soft and supple. And warm. Really warm.

"Oh crap." He backed away and held her at arm's length. "We can't do this out in the open, not until you learn to control yourself."

She was actually starting to recognize the cues, like a warmth in her eyes. They must have started to change again.

"We can't get distracted, we're not just here to hide. There's a lot of work to do." His smile faded. "A lot."

She nodded and took his hand as they turned to head back to the house.

"So, what's next? You said we have all spring break together, just you and me?" she asked.

He grinned. "Do you know how much I love that we get to spend an entire week alone? And how much it sucks that it's not just for fun?"

"Yeah, yeah, yeah. Says every guy after telling a girl he can only kiss her inside an empty, secluded house, but not out in the open." She winked and nudged him.

He pursed his lips, shaking his head. "You're not going to make this easy for me, are you?"

She laughed. "I feel like you enjoy a challenge."

After returning to the house, Devin offered to make some lunch. Only the slightest aching lingered from Mel's change and she had developed a healthy appetite. She sorted through her packed bag and made up her bed with fresh sheets from the linen closet while Devin took care of the cooking.

She came into the kitchen, leaning against the counter while he stirred a pot on the stove.

"So, I have a secret name. Do you have one, too?"

"Afraid not. Just boring Devin here."

"I'd say you're anything but boring. Though..." She reached out her hand for a handshake.

He looked at her hand in confusion.

She grinned. "Hi, my name is Saff, humans call me Mel. Nice to meet you."

He narrowed his eyes at her, not sure what she was getting at.

She shrugged. "I just figured, I'm not sure how much of the real you I know. I'm assuming some of your hobbies and responsibilities were covers. I'd like to get to know what you're really like."

He smiled and shook her hand, pulling it up for a kiss before letting it go. "Nice to meet you. My name is Devin. One of the top in my acting class." He put a hand over his heart and lifted his chin comically in pride. "As evidenced by my *amazingness* at blending in here. Pretty great marks in sparring, thus my *deployment* here." He flexed a bicep and threw her a seductive look.

She giggled at his silliness.

"And someone that appreciates beauty, as evidenced by my stolen heart." He gazed into her eyes. That look—it got her every time. His eyes, his dimples, just everything about him drew Saff in.

She bit her lip. "How about I help with cooking?"

"Are you trying to throw me out of the kitchen? I thought I made a pretty mean peanut butter toast this morning."

"Maybe I just want to cook with you." She raised her eyebrows in challenge.

"It's almost done, but please, be my guest." He stepped back, hands gesturing to the pots on the stove.

She moved over and began to stir. "I really don't cook much. Does it matter if it's clockwise or counter clockwise?" She looked over her shoulder with a grin.

"Oh, there's *definitely* a technique. Let me show you." He moved up behind her, wrapping his left hand around her waist and putting his right hand over hers to stir. "See, just like that. I know it's *immensely* difficult, but you might just learn."

She chuckled. "You're such a great teacher. I think I'll keep you."

He took the wooden spoon from her hand and set it down, then spun her around, starting to dance. "I wouldn't have it any other way."

She'd almost forgotten how skilled he was at dancing; it didn't matter that there wasn't any music playing. "You know, you still only told me how you did in school, with acting and sparring. What did you do in your free time back home?"

He cocked his head while thinking about it, not losing his rhythm while dancing. "Our lives are pretty simple, Saff. We don't get much choice in the schooling we do. You're trained to fight, no matter who you are. You take a lot of classes that would prepare you for life in this world."

"Like dancing?"

He chuckled. "That one's not exactly compulsory. Actually, it's quite hard to get into a dancing class. Imagine what it's like, not having a single girl your age or younger in the entire village until you turn fifteen. Absolutely every girl is older than you until those from your year start to trickle in."

"Wow ... yeah. That's crazy to imagine. And sad." Her contemplative look turned into a jovial one. "No wonder you fell for the first girl you saw when you came here."

He stopped dancing and gave her a frustrated look.

She frowned. "I'm kidding."

He shook his head and went back to stirring the food. "I don't think it's very funny. It's a pretty messed-up life compared to how Ivies and humans get to live. Remember that, when you get mad about everyone keeping it a secret. *You* got to live a normal life." He paused. "And I don't exactly appreciate you discounting my feelings like that, even if you don't feel the same way about me."

She touched his arm. "I'm sorry, I really didn't mean anything by it. And you know I feel the same way."

He turned to face her. "Do you?"

He had outright said he loved her, but that was a huge step for Saff. "I don't know if I'm ready to say what you want to hear. But that doesn't mean I don't care about you. I'm the one that never had to pretend, remember?"

He sighed, his shoulders dropping. "I'm not trying to rush you, I never have. Maybe it's just the Seeder culture in me, but I don't take relationships that casually." He still carried a tone of frustration in his voice. "And I want you to remember, just because I wasn't forced to live away from my homeland growing up, doesn't mean my childhood was all fun and games. And I didn't come here to vacation or date."

Shame stung her eyes as she looked at the ground. "I'm sorry," she whispered. "I'll go set the table."

After placing the dishes, she sat at the table while Devin finished up, watching as he stirred and added extra seasoning. They had lived vastly different lives. And, while she got the short end of the stick in some ways, maybe it wasn't such a raw deal after all, compared to the men of their kind.

He set out a hot pad and a pot of rice and beans, then started to dish them up. "I accept your apology. I know you're going through a lot. You have lots to take in."

She fidgeted with her fork. "Thank you."

He continued with a straight face, "I'm good in the garden. Love going on nature walks. I like reading, and swimming, and you'd be a fool to try and win a poker game against me." He cleared his throat. "And, uh, I never got into those dancing classes. My mom and aunt taught me."

She smiled and he grinned back.

"It's nice to meet you, Devin. I look forward to getting to know you better."

He gave her a nod and they dug in. It wasn't on his list, but he was not at all a bad cook, either.

Saff picked up a forkful of food, gazing upon the beans. "Is this cannibalism?" She glanced back at him.

Devin stared at her. "That's morbid."

She busted out laughing. "Come on. We're part plant!"

He cocked his head to the side. "We're more human than hydrangea. We're part mammal, too. I don't know about you, but I'll take bacon or a salad any day over dirt and sunshine."

She grinned. They were weird, but at least not *that* weird...

After eating, they sat together in the living room. It was still natural to be close to Devin. He put his arm around her and she leaned against him.

"So, let's recap here," she said, grabbing his free hand. "Not human. Being hunted by assassins. I have powers and family I never knew about. And I'm from a place called the Green Lands?"

"Good summary."

"You haven't talked much about the Green Lands." Her anxiety was building, her mind having rehashed some of the things he'd been saying. "All of my sisters are back there now?"

He nodded. "Unless they're back here secretly for a visit. But you still have one sister here."

Saff pursed her lips. "They all moved to some other world, or realm, or whatever you call it. And you've said things about me going there." She turned to face him. "That's the expectation of me, right? I'm expected to move?"

He wore a slight frown. "Yeah, Saff. This isn't our world. You never would have grown up here if it wasn't necessary."

It was a strange notion, and a sad one. That the parents she loved might not have been the ones to raise her, if things were different. And only Seeders and Ivies—'green folk,' as Devin had previously referred to the residents of the Green Lands—could travel between the worlds. She wasn't just leaving behind normalcy and safety, she was leaving behind her family.

"No one would force you to go," he added. "But... Well, that's the way it's supposed to be."

Saff gnawed on her lip, scanning his face. She still wasn't sold on the idea, and there was so much left to learn. She barely knew anything about this alternate home. But she tackled it one question at a time. "You said, what was it? We open a doorway?"

He nodded. "A rift."

"How much work does that take to learn? Could we go take a look now? That could help me feel better about all this."

His mouth hung open for a moment. "Not that easy, unfortunately. And forming a rift isn't the hard part. We'll be teaching you to catch a breeze to get to the nearest rifting location."

She raised an eyebrow. "Catch a breeze?"

He grinned. "Sorry, like I said, I've never explained it all before. Seeders can't just rift from the ground. 'Catch a breeze' is how we say 'fly.'"

Her eyes grew wide. "Wait, what? I can fly?"

He chuckled. "Yeah. But as you can imagine, that's not the easiest thing to master. And we won't have time to focus on it this week. Right now, we need to use our time to make sure you'll be safe when we go back into town, when spring break's over."

She nodded, eager to learn more about her new abilities.

He pulled one of her hands up to his lips. "So, let's get started on powers?"

She smiled. "Yes."

"The priorities for this week are to learn how to conceal your energy, defend yourself, and transform. Let's start off with concealing, masking. You don't see me change every time I have emotions, because I've learned to center my energy. It's even more important for you, because your energy is stronger." He handed her a small mirror. "Close your eyes for this exercise. I want you to think of Blake."

Her eyes snapped open. "I never want to think about that jerk again."

"Do it, Saff. Trust me."

She sighed and closed her eyes again.

"Think back to when he pissed you off the most. Can you envision it?"

"Oh yeah."

"Good. Think about what you'd have liked to do to him."

"If he hadn't pinned me by twisting my arm, I would have kicked him in the groin and punched him in the face!"

"That's my girl. Picture yourself doing that."

She had a smile on her face.

"Now open your eyes and look in the mirror."

The transformation was glaringly obvious. "Yeah, that's a problem."

"Close your eyes again. Visualize all of your energy coming from your heart. And when you feel emotion, it starts to spread to the other parts of your body. Imagine coaxing that energy back into your heart, extracting it from your mind, neck, arms; drain it all back and then seal it there."

She took a few deep breaths, envisioning it the way he'd explained.

"Good. Now open your eyes."

She looked in the mirror. "It worked!"

"The trick is learning to harness it before it gets away from you. It's better to prevent the physical changes in the first place."

She frowned. "That sounds like I have to walk around emotionless ... avoiding people... That's depressing."

"I don't know. I feel a heck of a lot of emotions whenever I'm with you." He grinned. "It's not too depressing when you've got it down."

She blushed. "Yeah, well, you've also had years of practice."

"Touché. But it's not like you can't have emotions. It's more like separating your emotions from your energy. Seeing the energy as an internal layer, so the emotions can reside by themselves in the outer layers, on the surface. Let's practice a little more."

Devin ran her through several visualizations—times in her life where she'd been excited, happy, sad, angry, afraid. She practiced trying to keep the energy contained and then bringing it back quickly whenever she let any spread.

"You're actually doing amazing for your first day! And I'm not just saying that." He was beaming at her progress. "Let's try this one. Close your eyes, take a deep breath, clear your mind..."

She expected to hear more instruction but instead felt his lips on hers, his hands moving to hold her head. He gently pulled her to standing and wrapped his thumbs through her belt loops. She enjoyed every moment of it.

He stopped and studied her face as she opened her eyes. He grinned. "Nope, going to need a lot more practice."

She looked at her hands. "That's not fair, you ambushed me!"

He chuckled and walked away. "That's the point, Saff. They're not going to wait for you to be mentally and emotionally prepared before they attack."

Returning from the bedroom with a book, he invited her to sit next to him on the couch again. She gave him the stink eye for his sneaky demonstration.

Devin shrugged. "Hey, there's a reason I'm good at poker, and probably the *only* reason Ben even let me bring you here—I'm a master at controlling my energy and emotions. I focused on it in my studies so I could better teach it."

She raised an eyebrow. "Is that a challenge? To see if I can spot green eyes? I'm willing to try kissing you until it happens. I can take one for the team."

He laughed. "As much as I love your willingness to sacrifice, there are two problems with that plan. One: My eyes can't glow green like yours, at least not yet." He leaned over and gave her a peck. "And two: we have a lot we need to get done. Let's go over some basic fighting and protection forms."

Chapter 15

Devin spent the next couple of hours showing Saff a book about the abilities of their people. One of the most notable differences between the genders amongst Seeders, was that the females of their race could heal others. Similar to the female Ivies, Seeder females' leaves were softer, less sharp than their male counterparts. That was part of why the Ivies rarely sent women to the human world—they weren't as lethal of assassins. But female Seeders weren't left without the ability to fight. Their blades could still cut Ivy vines, and they had a natural agility and lightness that aided them in various hand-to-hand fighting styles like humans had.

"Learning to fully transform, to catch a breeze back to the Green Lands, that's the end goal, and not easy. Part of that is mastering how to extend your blades properly," he explained.

She was still reeling from that reveal. 'Catch a breeze.' She could *literally* fly. Saff flipped the page back and forth. "Wait, it doesn't say anything about the dart things Ben did in here."

"Those are in the male chapters, they're not inherently a female ability."

She wrinkled her nose at the unfairness of it. "That sucks. Those seem like they would be really helpful..."

He shifted uncomfortably in his seat. "Well, there's a way for our girls to be able to do the darts, but it's not something you're going to be worrying about right now. We're focusing on basics."

Saff flipped through more of the book. It explained how the female form possessed more energy, and it could be shared, transferred to males if needed. "Like what Ben did. Can my energy be ... taken from me, or do I have to give it?"

"You have to give it, no one can take that from you without your willingness," he answered.

She sighed in relief. "Good. That would be so ... violating..."

"You're no damsel in distress." He nudged her arm.

Past the different chapters covering male and female abilities, there was a section titled 'Mixed Forms.' He took the book from her hands, closing it and setting it down. "That's something you'll learn about later. It's definitely beyond the basics. Right now, we keep you hidden, alive, and prepare you to go home."

He said it so casually. 'Go home.' Devin really didn't realize that *this* was her home. The only home she'd ever known.

He stood, holding out his hands. She obliged, joining him.

"Our abilities are all basically physical, transformative. They're not like magic tricks or silly potions. They come from your essence and relationship with nature; they're actually pretty intuitive once you understand and practice a little. Cup your hands together like you're holding something you don't want to get out."

She lifted her arms and followed his directions. It reminded her of when she would catch grasshoppers as a little girl and they would hop around between her palms without being harmed.(j)

"Close your eyes again. Now you're going to do the opposite of what we've been practicing. I want you to envision the light, the energy in your heart and let it spread, but only to your hands. Like you're using a squeegee to guide it there."

She opened her eyes and her hands; her hands were glowing.

"That's not enough. You got it to reach your hands, but you need to *contain* it there. Right now, it's like you're forming a channel from your heart to your hands. You need to clear out your arms and push it all into the gap between your palms. Try again: Open the channel from the heart. Reach to the hands. Concentrate it there."

She closed her eyes and tried once more.

A couple of deep breaths and a minute later, she looked again. She had successfully filled the space between her hands with a ball of light. She held it there like it was a handful of water. "Oh my gosh! What do I do with this?"

"Let me show you how you can help in a fight." He made a fist and flicked it open, spraying a handful of small darts into a corkboard on the wall that had seen some damage over the years. "If you'll allow me, I'm going to access that energy—is that alright?"

She nodded in consent.

He put one hand over hers, cradling the light between them. It surged through his hand as he tossed more darts into the cork. They were ejected with more speed and were three times as wide, and twice as long, as his original darts. Even he looked a little shocked and impressed. "That's a heck of a boost, right? The only reason Ben could use your energy earlier without you understanding it is because it was flowing from you unchecked during your bloom."

He squinted, calculating something. "Remind me to teach you another way to do this ... another time."

She made a mental note to remind him.

He walked over to the wall of darts. "There's not really a way around this. You need hands-on experience." Pulling one of the larger darts from the cork, he cringed while slicing a gash in his own arm.

Saff gasped. "Are you crazy?!"

"It hurts a lot." He sucked air in through clenched teeth. "What do you think you can do about it?"

She looked from his bleeding arm to her hands. She'd read about healing in the book, but not in depth. Closing her eyes, she envisioned more light forming as it had before. Successful, she cupped her hands on his wound. "This is it, right? How do I know when it's done?"

His squinting eyes relaxed. "Exactly. There are different techniques, but this is a pretty basic one. It takes practice to know when it's done the job." He looked down. "Honestly, I think you've already fixed it. Go ahead and take your hands off."

Removing her hands, the light dissipated; the wound had closed up. Though there was still residual blood on his arm and now on her hand. They went to the bathroom to wash up.

While drying her hands, Saff became lightheaded and almost took a spill before he caught her.

"Sorry, should have had you sit for a little while first. Shouldn't have had you do that right after a round of darts. Healing can take a lot out of you, especially when you're new at it, so it's not something you want to expend energy on for every bruise and scrape." He helped her back to the kitchen table.

"Noted." She sat down, laying her head on the table until she recovered. "Can we please not stab or maim you anymore? I'm not a fan."

He poured her some water to drink. They practiced more with controlling her energy and wrapped up for the afternoon when her energy was spent. Devin dug through the cabinets and freezer to find something to make for dinner. "It really zaps you when you're first learning, because you have to put so much into making your body do what you want. But after a while, it's as easy as breathing."

They sat down for a dinner of frozen pizza and canned peaches.

"When can I meet my birth mom and other family in the Green Lands?" She assumed it must be pretty amazing, if ten of her sisters had already chosen to leave this world behind. She was still conflicted, but more excited after learning more about her powers. "It sounds like I might be making changes to my summer plans!" She thought of her parents' gift—the trip to Costa Rica. To say things were now a little complicated would have been a serious understatement. "Or maybe some of them could find time to come here?"

She envisioned how fun it might be to get everyone together. "I mean, obviously it would have to be in secret, but I can just imagine what my mom and dad would do, having a barbeque with twenty-three of my siblings, together with my biological parents someday!"

Devin swallowed a couple of times and looked down at the table. "There's a lot that has to be taken care of, in a short amount of time. And your choices will have permanent consequences." He looked back up at her. "Saff, you have to choose."

Her eyes narrowed. "What do you mean, choose? Between my families?!"

He rubbed his hands together nervously. "That's part of it. Let me just explain how it works, okay?"

He had her full attention. She wondered how there could possibly be more to this big revelation.

"Your physiology is so unique. That's why you were raised in the human world, right? You couldn't survive the poison back there without your powers. But ... what's different about you doesn't stop there. There's a reason your mom isn't here like your dad is. Once you bloom, like you just did, you only have a short amount of time before you take root. That means you're *permanently* selecting a home, which world you'll live in. Our energy is stronger in the Green Lands.

"It's like..." He rocked his head back and forth. "So, the cool thing is, Seeder females are the most powerful beings in the Green Lands. You have a strong tie to the energy there. But with that ... comes the downsides." He bit his lower lip. "It's like a two-step tethering. When you go back, like Tabatha, you 'root'—you're connected to the realm. You can't just come back and visit whenever you want. Once you're mature enough, like our moms were when they had us, the final phase sets in, and you ... can't leave."

He paused, scanning her face. The chaos of the new restrictions in her life overwhelming her, she struggled to form a question.

He continued in his explanation. "After you take root over there, you have enough of a boost to get back here for a short visit, but that's all. Once a year, for maybe a week in the spring. That is, until you mature to the age where you can have a clutch of seedlings yourself, usually ten years down the road. Like I said, at that point, you're never able to return to the human world. Pam can't go to our world, and Murial can't make it back here. They'll never meet."

Her heart dropped. She stared at the table, running her fingernails across it. Asking her to move to another realm was bad enough. But it wasn't a simple road trip or flight away to come back and visit.

His voice carried guilt. It was obvious he disliked being the bearer of bad news as much as she disliked being the recipient of it. "Our roots aren't as deep, us guys. But we can still only go back and forth maybe, at most, a handful of times a year."

She looked down at her hands, trying to process. "That means if I go, I could only see my parents once a year? My friends. Zach. I... I wouldn't... College... I mean, I don't know what it's like over there ... what you guys do for education, careers." Her breath quickened, her heart thumping in her chest. Her vision blurred with a coating of tears. "That's horrible. What if I don't want to choose?"

He tilted his head with a sympathetic frown. "Not choosing between worlds means you choose the human world, and all that comes with it. If you don't learn what you need to, to catch a breeze by the time you root, you'll never see your homeland. You'll never meet your mom, or most of your family. Your energy is cut off from the Green Lands and dies out. You revert to human form for the rest of your life. Well ... mostly human. Technically, you can't have kids with a human, and if you root here, you couldn't have Seeder kids, either. In case that matters to you." He pursed his lips. "And, not to be selfish, Saff, but you and I couldn't be together."

Her chest ached as though she'd just had the wind knocked out of her. Rubbing her forehead, she looked at the table, trying to understand all that her choices meant. "You said I have a short amount of time to learn this and decide if I want to go back. How long is that?"

He frowned. "I asked you to check what your roots look like, in the shower. How, uh, far down do they reach?"

She moved a hand to her hip, then showed him with her thumb and pointer finger. It was probably two to three inches of these weird growths.

He nodded, biting his lip. "About what we expected." He took a deep breath. "I'm not saying this to make you feel bad."

Her heart sank further.

"If your change had been completed with the charm on, you'd have three, maybe four months. But ... your timeframe was accelerated. You only have maybe a month."

"A month? A month!" She covered her mouth with her hand and stared into Devin's eyes. Her eyes warmed—they were glowing bright green again, forming more tears.

She stood up from the table. "I need to go lie down."

Shock overwhelming her, she didn't even try to not cry. She wished he'd led with all the downsides first. She had powers—that was great! A new family she hadn't known about—exciting. Assassins lurking in the human world—less than ideal. Leaving her entire life behind, permanently, and only having a month to learn everything and decide—impossible.

She never came back out that night. As she sniffled into her pillow, she heard Devin cleaning up in the other room. Eventually, he joined her in the bedroom, lying down on the other bed.

"I'm sorry," he whispered once the lights were out. "Good night."

Saff woke in the morning to the smell of coffee wafting into the bedroom. The shower was running down the hall as she made her way to the kitchen and poured herself a cup of hot brew. She cringed at the bitterness, but needed the pick-me-up. Seeder energy and human energy were related, but not one and the same. She felt at 'full charge' in the Seeder department. Not so much in her human mind and body.

After plopping down onto a dining room chair, she laid her head down on the table. Shortly after the shower turned off, the bathroom door opened. Devin strode out with a towel wrapped around his waist.

"Hey beautiful." He smiled. "I'm seeing a pattern here. You keep catching me in compromising situations in the morning." He pointed at her. "You, ma'am, are scandalous."

She managed a weak smile, taking a sip of her drink.

After getting dressed, he joined her at the table. "I'll have you know that you are adorable when you're sleeping."

She certainly didn't feel adorable. Her eyes were puffy, her head ached, and she surmised being run over by an eighteen-wheeler might feel a bit like this.

He gently placed a hand on the table. "Before you say anything, I want to make a proposal. I know I threw a lot at you last night. And I'm not going to pretend like these are inconsequential decisions you need to make. But I think what we should focus on is your training. No matter what you choose, you're going to need to be able to protect yourself until you take root or return home—to our home, that is. You need to learn to harness your energy before we start back up at school. We're going to be back at Pam and George's house a week from tonight."

"They're my parents," she snapped. "They deserve to be called my parents, not just 'Pam and George.'"

Devin fixed his eyes on hers, speaking softly. "You're right, I'm sorry. We'll be going back to your *parents'* house a week from tonight. And I know they'll be excited to see you, and you'll have tons of catching up to do." He raised his eyebrows and smiled. "I'd even put money on grumpy ol' Ben being happy to see you."

She nodded ever so slightly.

"Do we have a deal? Focus on the short-term needs, sort out the other stuff as it comes up?"

"Is there anything else you haven't told me that I should know about? Anything you're keeping from me?"

He frowned. "I'm sorry. I told you I haven't done this part before. But, no. Nothing else big, I don't think. Not intentionally, anyway."

She studied his face. "Okay. We'll focus on training." She had a heck of a lot to figure out and not nearly enough time to do so, but trying to appear normal and keeping herself safe seemed like the logical place to start.

He gave her a half-smile. "And, you know, we can still enjoy our time together. I really love just being with you."

Her cheeks warmed as she looked down at her hands, thinking of him coming out in a towel, knowing how livid her parents would be. "Ditto."

He grabbed a granola bar for each of them and sat back down. A couple of questions nagged at her from the previous night.

"Why am I even going back to school? It's not like I'm going to graduate, or even finish up the rest of the school year, if I go to the Green Lands. And if the Ivies might know what I am, aren't I just making myself more of a target by going back?"

He raised an eyebrow. "Have you decided you're going home?"

She shook her head, opening the granola wrapper.

"Then you'll continue school. And even if you were going home, we don't know for sure that Blake or Ken survived. Whether or not they did, it's true, they still might have tipped off the others. If that's the case, they also know we'll be extra vigilant."

He motioned for her to join him in the living room to start practice for the day. "If we're lucky and the other Ivies don't know who you are, then we don't want to give them any reason to suspect you by changing your behavior. You might just be one of many names on their list of suspected Seeders. If we do something to confirm their suspicions, that implicates all of us. They'll wonder if your brother is a plant, if you're dating a Seeder; all eyes will be on us."

She stifled a laugh.

He wrinkled his forehead. "What?"

"Sorry, you said my brother is a plant. That's, you know ... true."

He pursed his lips to suppress a smile and shook his head. "You are a dork."

She wore a huge grin. "But you love me anyway."

He bit his lip. "I do." He took a deep breath. "Anyway ... you'll have plenty of eyes on you at school. I can't go into the details, but you'll be in good hands. Your dad texted to let me know they expect your last sister to leave in the next week or two, so you'll have even more of our focus."

She realized that most of the time he mentioned 'mom' and 'dad' he meant the Seeder ones. "When do I get to meet him?"

"Probably not until you're ready to leave, assuming he goes back with you. I'm not sure what he's worked out with my dad on who will stay, since I've got sisters that will be here longer."

She crossed her arms, still somewhat frustrated at being in the dark. "Why can't I know more about who's on our side? That would make me feel a heck of a lot safer at school. I would obviously keep it a secret."

He shook his head. "It's out of the question. It's not about whether or not we can trust you. You may give it away without knowing."

She scowled. "I'm not a gossip! What, only men are capable of keeping secrets? The fathers and sons of the Seeder networks?"

He rolled his eyes. "One of us in this room spent *years* preparing for this situation. And that person is not you. Think back to when you were oblivious to Ben, Tabatha, and Stacy being your siblings. Can you honestly tell me you wouldn't throw in an extra smile in the hallway if you knew? You wouldn't accidentally look over at Stacy and wonder how she was progressing with her training? You wouldn't have reacted differently at all to Ben getting caught spying on you?"

She thought it over and cocked her head to the side. A memory flashed through her mind. Stacy, being nice in the lunchroom. She wasn't making amends because she was sick; she was doing it because she knew she was leaving... If it was true that Stacy didn't even know she had this in common with Saff... she still gave away that something was off. "Fine. I see your point."

He smiled and pointed a finger at her. "Bingo."

Saff scrunched her nose. "Why is it that I love and hate everything that comes out of your mouth?"

Devin showed off a huge, toothy smile.

"That wasn't a compliment."

"You said you love me."

"I said I love *what you say*, but I also said I hate what you say."

He sat beside her on the couch, sliding an arm around her shoulders. "But you'll forgive me. I like to focus on the positive. You said something about love, and my mouth." He raised his eyebrows in challenge.

She pursed her lips and shook her head. "You think you're such a charmer."

He feigned taking offense. "How dare you! I *know* I'm charming."

She giggled. "Let me see if I remember how much I love those lips."

She drew him in, running her hands through his hair. His hands trailed along her legs, eventually resting on her hips.

Saff moved her lips to his neck, trailing the kisses higher until she reached his ear, whispering, "You said I'd be in good hands, and I guess you were right. I like being in your hands."

He let out a loud laugh. "So, this is how it's going to be all week? Flirting with the teacher?"

She didn't answer; instead, she focused on giving him a hickey.

Devin chuckled, leaning away and grabbing the small mirror. "Saff?"

She finished her handiwork with a smirk. "What?"

He held up the mirror. "If we're going to get distracted, we should at least work on your training so you don't look like *this* every time we kiss."

She frowned, spotting her green eyes. She took the mirror from his hands and set it down. "I'm insulted by that! I'm not distracted. I just needed something to heal." She flashed a mischievous grin, then put her hand up to his neck, pushing energy to it. The hickey faded. She planted a peck where the hickey had been. "A kiss to make it better, for added measure."

He smiled. "You're good."

Chapter 16

Getting more on task, Saff and Devin spent the rest of the morning and afternoon practicing what she'd learned the day before. It was grueling work, but they needed to push hard—time wasn't on their side.

While taking a much-needed break, Devin pulled out his phone. In the chaos of her discovery, Saff's had been left behind, though they agreed it was probably for the best.

"We need you to send a message to Zach and post on social media about our fun spring break getaway. Everyone needs to know you're alive and living a normal life." He handed her the phone. "Here, apologize to Zach and explain that I surprised you with a road trip to meet my parents. You dropped your phone and it didn't make it; that's why you've been out of touch."

She started to type a message. "You're going to have to teach me to be a convincing liar and how to come up with stories like this on the spot." She looked up and noticed he was visibly offended. "Sorry, I didn't mean it like that. I just mean ... I'm not used to this kind of stuff. Living in secrets and shadows is your thing." She finished typing up the message. "Here, come check it before I send it."

While he was reading it over, she smiled. "You know, you say you're amazing at poker and acting, but now that I look back, you gave yourself away a few times."

He looked up, raising his eyebrows. "Really? Give me an example."

"Mmm. When we had that argument about Blake and stereotypes. I said you could be judged as a troublemaker because you moved here in the middle of high school. I could tell for the rest of the day that I'd hurt your feelings."

He smirked. "Maybe I didn't expect the same girl who was stealing my heart, to hurt it. Plus, I'm only human, I'm not perfect."

She gently poked his arm. "But you're not human."

He threw his hands in the air with a hint of a smile. "It's a saying. The kind *you* learned growing up!"

She smiled wide. If everyone in the Green Lands either grew up over here, or trained to blend in ... it might not be so foreign after all.

He went back to reading her message to Zach, mumbling under his breath with a smile. Approving of the message, they sent it off. Devin returned his cell to his jeans pocket, then opened the living room coat closet. "Next on the list," he said, starting to pull out equipment. After grabbing a few things, he closed the door and began to set it up. He extended poles and popped open two lights with white umbrellas, like photographers use, then hung a green sheet on the wall. "Gotta make it look convincing. Let's get some pictures for social media. We've got a guy that edits us anywhere we want to be."

"Wow, you guys seriously think of everything." She joined him in front of the green screen.

"I know this is going to be tough," he said with a straight face. "But you'll have to pretend you enjoy spending time with me."

She frowned. "Dang it. This may be the hardest thing I've had to do in the last week!"

He poked and tickled her until she giggled and begged for mercy.

They took some standard cutesy couple pictures, changing shirts a few times, and then texted them to his contact. Later that night they'd get them back to post.

"So, handsome, we're visiting your parents? How long is the car ride? Do they like me? What kinds of things are we doing?"

He collected the photo shoot equipment, putting it back in its place. "It's a four-hour drive to get there. Of course, my parents love you, why wouldn't they? And we're spending our week hiking and playing board games."

"What if I don't want to go hiking?"

He raised his eyebrows. "We're hiking. Everyone that needs to know back home has the same story down."

"Fine. I hope I remember to wear sunscreen." She stuck out her tongue playfully. "What are our favorite road-trip snacks?"

He looked confused.

"You really didn't grow up in the human world, did you?" She grinned. "Finally, I get to be the teacher! This is a quintessential fact. You know what junk food is, but you really ought to know its place in road-trip culture. I think we should argue over Red Vines versus Twizzlers and both agree that *no* chocolate should have raisins in it."

He raised his hands. "I'll go with whatever you say. You're the expert on this one."

"Seriously though, I would never guess that you and Ben weren't from this world. It has to be pretty different from ours over there. You really blend in."

He nodded. "One appreciates when someone admires their hard work. Thank you. I mean, we learn really early how to talk like we're from here, what kinds of references to make, even if we've never been to a place or done the activity."

Her smile faded to a frown. "I would love to show you around, give you a real human experience. But I'm guessing we're not going to have time for that, are we?"

He squinted at the ceiling. "How about this... Promise me you'll try your hardest, and I promise I'll let you take me on an adventure before you leave."

Her smile returned.

"But I mean it. As much as I love getting lost in your glowing green gaze, I want to see a normal human looking back at me when we make out."

"Deal!" she said. "Should we practice that now?"

He laughed and shook his head. "This girl ... one-track mind. What am I supposed to do with you?"

She replied in a playfully sexy voice, "What do you want to do with me?"

He shook his head again. "You're killing me, Saff."

"Okay, okay, okay."

"Anyway..." He cleared his throat. "To finish answering your question, we also tutor new arrivals once they get here. Teach them things on the spot, like how to drive a car. How to use electronics. I wasn't completely lying about tutoring after school."

She put her hands on his waist, finding herself continually enamored with his dedication. "You guys are underrated. It's like you never have a free second to just enjoy life. You're always on the job. How do you even manage it? And go to school?"

He raised both eyebrows. "One of the secrets ... our 'parents' don't care that much if we skip class on occasion, and they don't give a crap about our Trigonometry grades. We don't use that nonsense in the Green Lands."

She sighed pensively. "You know what, I don't think we use Trigonometry here either." They both laughed.

After hours of more strenuous practice, they'd earned a solid night's sleep. They lay down, facing each other from their separate beds.

"Will you tell me more about the Green Lands? What's it like?"

She couldn't see his face in the dark, but she could hear his smile in the softness of his reply.

"You'll love it, Saff. In a lot of ways, it's not all that different from the human world. We have roads and houses. But life is simpler. Excuse the pun, but it's more 'down to earth.' We have gravel or dirt streets. No cars or pollution. Actually, no electricity at all, as you know it. But we have our own equivalent for a lot of things—lamps, solar showers, all that. More basic diets—we're generally vegetarians. Everyone, and I literally mean everyone, has a garden; we grow a lot of our own food. We don't have the same technology, but we do have entertainment."

She smiled. It sounded so primitive. But also idyllic and peaceful.

"Our society is more cooperative, family-centered. Couples live in fairly small cottages, until they have kids—then there are, I guess you'd consider them like apartments or dorms? Housing lots are shared amongst neighbors to accommodate a variety of needs. Property lines and ownership aren't like they are here. A family quickly goes from two to thirteen—then builds up to twenty-six—then shrinks as the kids grow up, move away, pair off. Our schools are tailored to the needs of war on the home front; how to be prepared for the human world, and also basics like history, art, literacy.

"Of course, this is all the Seeder side of things. I've never been to the Ivy side, but from what I understand, it's like Detroit. It's the armpit of the Green Lands."

She chuckled at his last description and then yawned. "It sounds so beautiful. Well, not the Detroit part, but the rest of it."

"It is, Saff. I wish I could be there to see your face when you first arrive."

She was exhausted, but stayed awake long enough to give it more thought. Devin assumed she would go back to the Green Lands, giving up her life here. She envisioned herself walking through the simple streets lined with cottages. Unique people, just like her, in family-centered communities.

She frowned. Family. Her parents. And kids ... the Seeder way of life was so wholly unhuman. And Zach. She was over the moon about getting to see Tabatha again, and sharing this exciting adventure they were both on. But Zach had already been hurt by losing one of his best friends.

A thousand other thoughts swirled in her mind, until she drifted, not-so-peacefully, off to sleep.

After some vigorous drilling of concealment exercises the next morning, Saff sat down at one end of the couch to take a break. Devin joined her. He grabbed a throw pillow, tossing it on her lap, and lay down.

He closed his eyes. "Mmm. Hard work. Nap time."

She chuckled. "Yes. It must be so tiring for *you*. The one whose job is mostly to talk."

He opened his eyes and smiled. "Hey, now." He laid a hand on his chest. "It's exhausting, seeing you so exhausted."

She rolled her eyes. Reaching a hand down, she held his and took a deep breath. She was ready to ask some harder questions.

"You expect me to go back."

He kissed her hand. "I hope you go back."

"I'm still trying to figure all that out. Why I should move to the Green Lands. Why me, or any of the other girls of our kind, would choose to go there. It's such a big change. And you have to admit it doesn't come without a huge sacrifice."

He squeezed her hand. "The energy, the abilities. How do you feel, now that you have them?"

She shrugged. "They're obviously amazing. But it feels superficial to give up my way of life for them."

He frowned. "No. It's more than that—it's a unique feeling. I immediately sensed the change when I first came here. The air here is ... thinner, more draining. Back home there's a warmth, a richness. And I don't just mean a warm temperature. It's ... different. You really don't feel a pull to go there? Something in your heart?"

She pondered his description. "It's hard to say. I don't have any way to compare like you do." She ran her fingers tenderly through his hair. "And my heart..." She smiled. "My heart is telling me a lot of different things."

He broke eye contact. "I hope you come home." He added with a small smirk, "Did I mention we live about ten years longer than humans?"

She nodded at the nice bonus, but her heart was still heavy. "If you were in my shoes, and lived a happy life, blissfully unaware of this war ... can you honestly say you'd choose to leave this behind and surround yourself with that? Just walk into a world at war?"

He looked her in the eyes, furrowing his brow. "No, love, it's not like that. If you can make it through this month, you'll be perfectly safe over there."

She was a bit skeptical about that. Having grown up there, he was bound to have a different perspective. "I'm in danger here, because of Ivy assassins. But half of my brothers stayed there, too, to protect Seeder territory? That sounds like a no-win situation."

He sighed. "Around the time of the poisoning, we erected *huge* border walls to protect our villages, powered by the excess energy of our women. With the wall and our regular patrols, the Ivies haven't actually gotten through to harm our communities in decades.

"It's a stale war. I don't even know if there's been a significant attempt at breaching our borders in our lifetime. They still keep us on our toes, though, every time we've tried to expand to unharmed neutral areas, to be able to keep our families together. But the shadow wars here, in the human world—that's the most dangerous part for you. If we lose our women ... by Ivy hands..." He looked at her knowingly. "Or by choice ... that weakens the safety of our borders."

The weight of the decision rested heavily on her shoulders. He wasn't trying to give her a guilt trip, but it still led down that alley.

"One person doesn't make that big of a difference, though, right?" she asked.

Devin took a deep breath. "Maybe not. Though, if everyone thought that way and stayed here..." He pursed his lips. "Our women used to be stronger. The poison doesn't kill our girls once their powers come in, but they're not able to store as much energy as they used to. The contributions required now are still comfortable, not too demanding, with our current population."

Saff mulled it over. "So, the powers make me able to survive, but I'll actually be able to do less than I can now?"

His look of confusion made it evident she'd misunderstood. "No. You actually get a boost once you root, and then when you reach full maturity."

"You just said we can't store as much energy because of the poison."

"Oh, that. What I mean is that the generations after the poisoning aren't as strong as they used to be. But what you have now won't go any lower." He raised his eyebrows. "And you're actually really powerful for your age. Not lying."

She blushed. "I have to ask. They poisoned our lands, breaking up our families ... and they obviously don't have qualms about killing us ... but we really don't do *anything* to provoke it?"

He scowled. "No! They used to live just like us, *with* us, even. They're the ones that moved away and set up a corrupt kingdom, and attacked us without provocation."

"Alright. I just ... needed to make sure."

His expression softened. "If anything, our people are pacifists to a fault. The Ivy Kingdom barely has a proper border, from what I've heard. We've boxed ourselves in with our walls, and never take the offensive. That's why this has gone on so long. We'd lose a lot of lives if we took them on, if we attacked, so the councils never do anything." He sighed. "It's like a hundred-year siege. Kinda..."

"Would you do things differently?" she asked, sensing his frustration.

He huffed. "I don't know what I'd do. I don't like any of it, but ... it's the life we were given. For now, I'm just happy I'm with you." He gave her a smile. "Meeting you makes it all worth it for me."

She bit her lip as her face warmed again.

He cleared his throat. "I mean, I'm glad I volunteered to come help my sisters and meet my dad. But..." He gazed lovingly into her eyes.

She grinned and shook her head. He was smitten, as was she. But she needed logistics, not just feelings. "What if we all stayed here? Just relocated?"

He lifted his eyebrows. "Aside from abandoning our homes, and giving up our culture and what makes us special?"

She wrinkled her nose, embarrassed for having oversimplified the situation. "I get it."

"Remember, too. Our moms literally can't come back. And ... when I said you were picking a permanent home, I meant it. Once you've rooted over there, you can't survive over here for more than a week."

She frowned. "Right. That was a stupid question."

He gave her a reassuring smile. "Not stupid. Maybe someday we can figure it out. We can end this crap and put those leeches in their place."

She smiled back, though it didn't reach her eyes. "I'd love to see that, end this craziness." She paused for a moment. "You and Ben, and Ken and Blake, you've used words like that, 'leeches.' Is that just a nickname?"

He squinted. "Well ... we're Seeders, but they sometimes call us 'weeds.' It's an extremely offensive term. And instead of Ivies, you could say our equivalent version for them is 'leeches.'"

She nodded. "Gotcha. I was pretty out of it, but I heard another one. 'Nuren,' I think? Is that a derogatory term for humans?"

He furrowed his brow and his mouth dropped open. "Wait, what? No ... all of us just call humans ... humans. What about Nuren?"

His drastic change in demeanor was startling.

"Well ... I... I don't know. Like I said, I was pretty out of it. Is that a bad word? I don't remember anything else. I just remember that word because it stood out at the time. I think it was Blake that said it."

He sat up and pulled out his phone, typing. "Bad word ... no. Bad news ... possibly."

He looked genuinely spooked.

"What's that supposed to mean?" she asked, growing more worried.

He put up a finger. "Just a second." His phone chimed and he groaned. "I was right."

"What?"

He turned to face her. "Nuren isn't just a nickname. Nuren is a person. That's a known identity of Ivy royalty."

He was clearly concerned. Her heart beat faster to match his mood. "Right, but what's that supposed to mean for me?"

His expression was calculating. After a moment, he bit his lip and shook his head. "Honestly, I don't know. It might mean nothing. But ... a connection like that to their palace... Nuren's *not* a lackey. It just kind of freaks me out to hear one of their names mentioned here."

He forced a smile. "I'm sure I'm overreacting. We'll look into it. If you remember anything else, let me know. For now—I think it just means we better get back to work."

Chapter 17

They worked hard all week. Saff could even form her blades, though not for long, and not nearly as rigid as they would need to be for catching a breeze or extended fighting. One of the hardest tasks for Saff was separating her emotions from her energy. But she had it down enough that they felt fairly comfortable she could get through a school day and be safe. They would, of course, avoid extreme emotions and circumstances as much as they could, just as a precaution.

"I'm really proud of you. I mean it," Devin praised her the night before they were to drive home. "Now, I told you a while ago that there was something else I could teach you, about energy transfer." He sat down on the sofa. "It goes against everything I've taught you so far. Want to spice things up?"

Still standing on the other side of the living room, she rubbed her chin. "With that introduction, how could I resist?"

"So," he said, blushing, "it's a tradition when sending off a male you love." He quickly added, "Nothing too scandalous. And no pressure, if you're not ready."

"Okay..." Her interest was sufficiently piqued.

He fidgeted awkwardly with his hands. "So, instead of channeling the energy to your hands to share, and instead of suppressing the energy when you kiss, you can actually imbue him with energy *while* you kiss."

"Oooh, that sounds like a challenge I'm willing to take on." She smirked, then dragged over a kitchen chair and sat directly in front of him. "Just like a regular kiss, right? But focus on where the energy is going?"

He nodded with a shy smile. "It's supposed to be pretty ... amazing."

"You don't say. I think what we've got already is pretty amazing."

His face turned a couple of different shades of pink.

Devin was Saff's first boyfriend, and while they hadn't talked about him possibly having a previous relationship, she realized it wasn't likely. Given the slim pickings back home... She felt a little more nervous.

"So you haven't, um..." she started to ask.

"Your first kiss was my first kiss."

She loved that. He could be confident and borderline cocky, and she wondered how much of that was his training. But at the heart of it, they were sharing this journey, these special moments together.

"I, uh," he paused, clearing his throat "well, you know, planned on kissing you to confirm your eyes would glow, when I suspected your change." He looked her dead in the eyes. "I got carried away, I ... really... Gosh, Saff."

She remembered it well, licking her lips. She'd never envisioned her first kiss being a full make-out session, French kiss and all. But she had zero regrets.

"Anyway." He let out a short breathy chuckle. "We kissed enough to make your hair change—that's indicative of more emotion than the simpler stuff that does just the eyes." He sat up straighter. "But ... if you're not ready, we can try this another time."

She smiled at his sweetness. "It's a kiss. I can handle a kiss. Let's give it a try."

Saff placed her hands on Devin's shoulders, pressing her lips against his. She kissed him softly as she tried to visualize her energy moving. The tingling warmth traveled up her chest, through her neck, and into her lips and tongue.

The moment her energy started to transfer to him, it ignited them both into a frenzied passion. She climbed into his lap, closing the gap between them. His hands caressed her back, moving up under her shirt. Saff's hands roamed to his belt buckle.

She said what she'd finally realized was in her heart. "Devin, I love you, too."

He slid his hands off her back and pushed her off of his lap. He covered his face with his hands. Even *he* had partially transformed this time, his hair tips now purple. "No, no, no. We can't do this."

Her eyes still glowing, her heart beating a mile a minute, she sat with her mouth open, confused. "I thought ... I just..." She swallowed. "Did I do something wrong, say something wrong?"

He stood up and started pacing the room. "No, Saff, of course not." He clenched his fists, then ran his hands through his hair. "You are ... gosh... Why do you have to make this so difficult?"

She bit her lip, devastated and embarrassed. "I just thought, we're going home, and then if I'm leaving, I might not see you for a year or two, and..."

"It's not that simple." He pleaded with his eyes. "You know I love you. You seriously have *no idea* what you do to me. I want you in every way possible." He closed his eyes and drew a deep breath. "This is not something we guys have to teach our sisters when we come over." He stood for a moment, pinching the bridge of his nose.

"It's just... Okay, let's first put aside the fact that every single member of your family would want to murder me. It's actually one of our highest laws." He shoved his hands into his pockets. "You've bloomed. You're an adult. Your physiology has changed. Our kind... Saff," he sighed, "we mate for life. That's a huge commitment I can't let you make, especially without understanding it." He looked down. "I guess ... I'm assuming that's what was about to happen. I just..."

Her eyes drifted down as she wrung her hands.

He sat back down in front of her and lifted her chin. "It's not a 'no,' it's a 'not right now.'"

She pressed her lips together, looking at the ceiling, trying to hold back tears. "No, I get it. Not a big deal."

"Hey, look at me."

She lowered her gaze to meet his and wiped away a tear.

"I'm sorry everything's so complicated. It sucks. There's so much you still need to learn about yourself. Remember when I said there's a way for our women to throw darts?"

She nodded.

"Well ... that's part of that beautiful, but complicated process. Once you mate, some of your abilities transfer. I told you once that we're stronger together, and that's one of the many ways. Your darts would fall somewhere between the plain ones I can throw on my own, and the kind I can do with your help. The green eyes, that's also a thing we only get from you."

She faintly smiled. "Humans worry about STIs and STDs, we get to have STPs—Sexually Transmitted Powers."

He gave her a small grin and chuckle. "I guess that's one way to put it."

She nodded again with a sniffle. "I should go to bed, anyway."

He looked down and pursed his lips. "Yeah. Okay."

She got ready for bed and turned in for the night. Devin chose to sleep on the couch in the living room. She was grateful, at first, that he stayed out of the bedroom. She was ashamed that she had allowed herself—allowed that kiss—to take her so close to such a serious step. But then she missed his presence, their nightly conversations in the dark. A familiar feeling ached in her gut. If he were a room closer, it might be too close. If he were a room further away, it would have been as if he were an entire realm away.

Devin came into the bedroom in the morning. "What's going on?" he asked groggily, squinting at Saff.

She barely spared him a glance before continuing to pack her bag. "I just don't want to wait to head home. I want to get on the road earlier so I can spend time with my family before going back to school tomorrow. Is that alright with you?"

"Yeah, if that's what you want."

"It is."

They tidied up everything to leave the house ready for the next time it would be needed. Saff was ice-cold and quiet all morning. After getting in the car, Devin tried to hold her hand, but she pulled back.

They rode in silence for several minutes.

"Saff, you're not being fair to me. It's not that I didn't want to be with you last night."

"You should go back to calling me Mel. That way you don't slip when we're around other people."

"Right," he said, his voice petering off to a whisper, "of course."

A few minutes passed before she spoke again. "If I don't have much time left here, I'm going to spend any time not in school or training how I want. I'm going to spend a lot of time with Zach—that's nonnegotiable."

His reply was far calmer than her mood. "I wouldn't stop you from seeing him. I know he means a lot to you. You just have to remember that he can't know anything."

"I'm not stupid, Devin!"

"Dammit, Saff! Mel ... don't take this out on me. I don't make the rules." He kept his eyes on the road, his jaw clenched.

She leaned her head against the car window, crossing her arms.

He continued, "And I know you're not exactly sunshine and rainbows about me right now, but you're going to need to remember the story, and pretend everything is normal. If you don't want to see me anymore," he paused, "then we'll have to make the breakup believable."

She glanced over at him and then went back to looking out the window with a frown. "I never said that's what I wanted." She took a deep breath. "I'm not as good of an actor as you are, but I'll do my best to be excited about returning from a fun vacation."

The rest of the forty-five-minute drive went by in complete silence.

They pulled up to the Walters residence and Mel hopped out. Her mom ran out to give her a big hug. "Sweetie, I'm so happy you're back! Come on in. I want to hear how everything went."

They entered the front door and were met by Ben, actually smiling, clearly excited to see her. "Hey, Mel, how did training go?"

She glared, put up one hand, lit up a ball of energy, and absorbed it back. "Send me a report card."

She turned to her mom. "Where's Dad? I want to give him a hug."

Pam stood with her mouth wide open. "Um ... he's in the garage."

Devin came in, carrying Mel's bag. Mel wouldn't even look at him, promptly heading down the hall to the garage.

"What did you do to my sister?" Ben demanded.

Mel lingered at the door to the garage, needing to know what Devin would share. Where he'd draw the line between his duties and their relationship.

"You know what, Ben? This one's not on me. I didn't do anything. If you want to know more, you can ask Mel."

He continued, "Mrs. Walters, you should be very proud of her—she's an amazing woman. I'll message everyone an update with where she is in training, and we can sort out the rest of it. I'm going to head home."

Devin didn't waste any time dawdling. By the time Mel emerged from the garage, he had already left.

"Do you want to talk?" her mom asked with a hesitant frown.

"I'll be fine. I just want to lie down for a while and get unpacked." Mel grabbed her bag from the hallway and headed upstairs.

She threw her bag on her bedroom floor and shut the door behind her. Her cell phone sat on the nightstand; her mom must have unpacked her things they'd retrieved from the gym. She flopped on the bed and picked her phone up to scroll through all of her missed texts and messages. As expected, there were several from Zach before she'd messaged him from Devin's phone. She returned the phone to her nightstand and lay on her back, looking up at the glow-in-the-dark stars on the ceiling. They weren't very noticeable in the daylight, but they gave her a focal point. She visualized moving her energy around within her body. Back and forth. Filling her entirely and shrinking down, concealed in her heart. Like the anger and sorrow and frustration also in her heart.

Someone knocked on her door.

"I don't want to talk," she hollered.

"I'm coming in either way, so you better be decent," Ben replied.

He opened the door and stood in the doorway. She glanced in his direction, then went back to focusing on her energy exercises.

"Devin was right, you're a natural," he said.

She found no comfort in his compliment. "I guess I better be, since I screwed everything up, right?"

He frowned. "Hey, I'm sorry I got so mad. It caught me off guard, that's all. No one blames you. That was actually a pretty brazen attack from them, right there at school."

"Doesn't change the facts though, right?"

He sighed. "What can I do to help you?"

She quietly scoffed. "I wish I knew. I just need to sort things out for myself."

"Let me know when you figure it out, okay? I'm guessing you don't want to talk about what's going on between you and Devin?"

She practiced flaring out her arm blades, looking them over. 'Blades'—like a wide blade of grass, and like a knife blade, when sharpened. "That's a hard pass."

"Right... Well, if you need me to pummel him, I'll do it." He leaned in, trying to make eye contact.

She smiled. "That kind of talk is a lot less creepy, now that I know you're my real brother."

He smiled back. "Would it be helpful if I took over the bulk of your training? It's good to have more than one teacher, anyway."

"Sure. Let's try that."

"Okay, I'll get the details sorted out. Sure there's nothing else I can do for you right now?"

She thought for a moment. "Can I have a hug?"

He came over and settled down on the end of her bed with his arms wide open. She sat up, leaning over, and he squeezed her tight.

It was sad, realizing this was actually her first hug with Ben, her real brother. "Sorry I almost got you killed," she mumbled into his shoulder. After pulling back, she looked down at his wrists—the bruises and cuts from the fight were still healing. She ran a finger over them to finish the job.

He gave her an appreciative smile. "Ditto. I'm sorry I wasn't there when you needed me. That won't happen again."

After another long, solid hug, he let her go. "You've been through a lot, and I'm sure you want to get caught up with Pam and George. But we're working within a pretty tight timeframe, and we really need to make sure you're okay with going back to school tomorrow. We'll need to practice today."

She nodded hesitantly. "Yeah, I know."

"Let's say an hour? I'll clear space in the garage."

"Sure." A faint smile formed on her face. A brother. Her real brother. He wasn't so bad. And she had a heck of a lot more of them waiting for her. If she gave up her life as she knew it...

The floorboards creaked as he stepped from the room, bringing her back to the present.

"Ben?"

He popped back in, leaning against the doorway. "What's up?"

"You're really close to Devin?"

He looked down, pursing his lips. "Have been for years." He raised his head. "If we stay friends, I guess that depends a lot on how he treats you."

Knowing Ben was actually her brother made her want *even less* to share anything about her dating life, but she needed more information. "Pretend he's dating someone else's sister. You think he can be trusted?"

Ben hesitated. "I trust him with my life. And I trust him with yours." He shrugged. "It's just, you know... You spend your whole life not only hearing about sisters, but preparing to meet them all, and protect them. And then you two are ... well..."

"I know you saved my life, and I'm grateful for that." She raised her eyebrows. "I'm all ears for anything you have to say about him, if you think there's something you should warn me about. But if you'd be equally protective of me with any other guy, then you're going to have to accept that I get to choose on this. I'm done being micromanaged."

He looked up, shaking his head. "I'd like to think I'm not friends with a complete jerk."

She grinned. "Such high praise."

He rolled his eyes.

She remembered a couple of remarks Devin had once made. "I understand you all think everyone needs to be super careful about our identities. But why would the Ivies suspect Devin of being a Seeder and protector, if it's normally just brothers taking care of sisters?"

Ben crossed his arms. "Just because it's not normal, doesn't mean it's never been done before. Each family chooses how they approach the protection of their own clutch. And tactics change, on both sides of the war."

She nodded in understanding.

Ben frowned. "I guess I was too distracted with the fighting. You really heard one of them mention Nuren?"

She matched his frown. Human life was definitely less complicated. "I think so. Why does it feel like things are even worse than they seem, when you and Devin ask about that?"

He shook his head dismissively. "It's okay. We've got you covered. It's just one of those things to take note of. Their network could be more complicated than we were expecting in this town. It means their tactics might be different than we've seen before."

"But in a hundred years of living like this, surely a member of their royal family has been seen or talked about in the human world."

He tilted his head to the side. "Communication between our villages may be limited and slow, but something that big ... I feel like we'd know." He gave a forced smile. "But I'm sure we'll be fine, alright? I'm going to get the garage ready. We can talk more later."

"Okay." Her heart was heavy as he left.

Because a *regular* network of assassins after her wasn't complicated enough...

Chapter 18

There obviously weren't any romantic distractions with Ben's training. But even putting that aside, he was a more militant teacher than Devin. They drilled over and over on what Mel had learned during her spring break, and he even introduced more direct fighting techniques.

Ben pushed her hard on forming her blades as they practiced in the garage. "If you can't get that down, then you can't protect yourself, or catch a breeze."

She shook her head, frustrated at the concentration it required. "Why don't we just call it flying? 'Catch a breeze' sounds pretentious."

He scowled. "That sounds stupid. Human airplanes fly. We catch breezes."

She chuckled. "Fine. Whatever."

Finding it too hard to practice defense techniques with both arms sporting blades, they focused on having her do just one, and working with that for now. Ben pulled out spools of rubbery cord and standard rope, each about as thick as one of her fingers.

"It's hard to find something that compares, but these do a decent enough job." He strung them up taut and she practiced cutting the cords with one of her blades.

"Come on, Mel," he drawled. "If you don't focus, your blades won't stay rigid. The leeches aren't going to stay still for you to slowly *saw* away at them."

She threw a scowl in his direction. Taking a deep breath, she attempted to deliver a swift slash to the rubbery cord. Not quite enough—her arm bounced off. It was such a weird sensation. She could feel her blades, but they weren't nearly as sensitive as her regular skin. She prepared for another round and sliced clean through, beaming.

Ben gave her a nod of approval as she moved over to the more traditional rope. Right as she went to try on it, her phone chimed with a text. Distracted, she lost control of her blade and instead gave herself a rope burn.

She sucked in air through clenched teeth.

"Focus!"

Mel had to keep reminding herself why she was putting up with this. She had to protect herself. And ... one month. No ... one of those four weeks had already been used at the safe house. Three weeks, and maybe some change, if she was lucky. She gritted her teeth, focused her frustration, and took another shot at the rope, easily slicing through it.

"Alright. Let's do that a few more times." He started to restring the ropes.

They practiced a couple of new techniques until after dark and every ounce of her energy had been used up. Ben explained more about what to expect in any possible future attacks. She was plenty familiar with the damage Ivy vines could do, though he explained she'd actually gotten off pretty easy.

"If they hook their leaves in right, if they get deep enough and then give it a good yank..." Ben winced. "They can do some serious damage." He ran a finger along his wrist. "This is where the vines come out. Their vines can regenerate, so don't let your guard down if you hack some off." He moved his finger up a little further on his wrist. "If you can manage a deep cut here, it severs the vine. They might be able to recuperate, but definitely not before you can take care of them." He looked into her eyes. "It's a narrow target. If you're fighting for your life, go for the obvious lethal moves when you can."

Mel swallowed hard, her mind replaying memories of the attack. In the school gym. The school she'd be back at the next day.

Going back to school while she sorted things out was less than appealing. But removing herself from society altogether wasn't an idea they could entertain, either. She'd have to break one of their covers, pulling them away from other duties. And she'd lose what little time she had left with her parents and friends. That is, assuming she planned to go back to the Green Lands.

She sat down for a minute on the cool garage floor, resting and thinking things over.

"I don't really get a choice in this, do I?"

Ben let out a slow exhale. "It's not really my place to say. But you *do* get to choose."

She took a swig of water, wondering how true that was. Questioning how much she owed him for saving her life. "You could have died, trying to keep me safe. I know everyone expects me to go. And maybe, if I had more time ... it wouldn't be such a hard decision."

He nodded thoughtfully. "Everyone back home *does* want you to come back. I won't sugarcoat it. Mom ... would take it hard. And your energy is the strongest I've seen from an unrooted girl—and we're not even in the Green Lands. Don't underestimate your potential."

She frowned, thinking about what Devin had said. That the female energy was what kept Seeder borders safe. So, her potential was ... what? It was like telling someone that has O-negative blood, *Congratulations, you're a universal blood donor. You're so useful!* She didn't want to just be 'useful' in that way. She wanted to do something with her life, she just wasn't sure what that was yet. All her life she'd been restricted. By her parents' rules. By school rules. Waiting to be old enough to figure out what she really wanted. The gut-wrenching thing now was that she *had* a choice. Too big of a choice. A permanent choice. And both options held pain and sacrifice.

In the absence of her reply, Ben added, "Don't worry about me. Any of us that come here, volunteer to do so. I signed up for this."

That comforted her a smidge. Her mind jumped back in the conversation. Her mom, the Seeder one. She would take it hard if Mel didn't return. But what about her human mom? It wasn't like it was going to be easy on her, either. "Tell me a little about our mom."

He smiled. "You don't look all that much like her, but I agree with Dad that you two have a lot of similarities. She loves to paint." His smile grew to a smirk. "And she can be stubborn."

Mel chuckled. "Sounds pretty awesome, if you ask me."

"She grew up here. In this town."

Mel cocked her head to the side. "Really?"

He nodded. "And our parents fell in love here."

"Wait. Devin said this isn't normal, for families to team up."

Ben straightened up the spools of cords and other training supplies. "No, they were in their twenties. He came back to ... work on a project. She was visiting her host dad for spring break. I shouldn't say too much. I just figured you'd think it was cool."

There was that feeling again—half-truths, edited stories. Now she was curious about her mom, and their story, and her mom's human host dad that might still be in this town. But the secrecy was souring the wonder.

"Do you have any human friends?" she asked, furrowing her brow.

He sat down next to her with a chastising expression. "I'm not a bigot. I've made human friends."

"Oh." She hadn't meant to imply that. "No. I was just wondering, 'cause ... you know... Everyone we hang out with, other than Zach of course, and ... maybe Heather?"

He lifted an eyebrow. "You know I won't give you names, right?"

Her cheeks warmed. She could really stand to have a girls' night. "Well ... I guess I just wanted to know if I'm safe to hang out with Heather, and, I don't know. This is all messed up, Ben."

"Hey." He frowned. "I'm sorry. Stacy's parents weren't as strict, right? But Pam and George did what they thought was best. And I know it seems like you're surrounded by us ... and you're not completely wrong. Seeders don't usually have two families team up this closely. But we *do* still maintain human relationships. Partially because we want to, and partially because it's smart to."

He cracked his knuckles. "As for Heather ... the reason your parents never restricted you from hanging out with girls is because it's pretty rare for them to send female assassins. They've got the poison thing, but like you and the other Seeder girls, their leaves aren't as sharp, and they're not as strong. I mean, I'm assuming that's why they don't send them. They're matriarchal like we are, but I don't really know their social dynamics other than that. I'm not saying it's impossible, but it's unlikely there are any here." He threw her a glance, eyebrows raised. "No matter who it is, just be careful, alright?"

She nodded thoughtfully. "Will do."

Thinking back to his mention of Stacy, she asked, "What was it like to train Stacy?"

He shrugged. "After she got over the shock, she was pretty dedicated. She was really excited about it all and getting to go home."

Mel scoffed. "I find that hard to believe."

He tilted his head. "Her process went smoothly, so she wasn't under the same stress you are. But even then, everyone has their reasons."

Mel shook her head. "She was popular. All the guys wanted to date her." Mel wanted to make sure Ben didn't think she was jealous. She never had been, at least not the way she remembered it. "Not that everyone wants that, but *she* sure did."

"People change, Mel."

She definitely knew that—that's why they'd stopped being friends. "I guess so. But I guess I really didn't know her anymore."

He wore a faint smile. "Funny, 'cause that's what she said about herself. That she barely knew herself anymore." He wrapped a frayed bit of rope around his hand. "There's lots of reasons to return home. The powers, culture, family. Some people don't get along with their host families as well as you do, or don't fit in at school. And some girls like the idea of a fresh start." He met Mel's gaze. "I, for one, hope she's able to have one. That people give her that chance."

Mel looked down, nodding. "Yeah. Me, too."

Mel showered and headed to her bedroom to pass out for the night. Her mom came in and sat on the end of her bed while Mel brushed out her wet hair.

"You may not be our biological daughter, but your dad and I want you to know that we've always considered you our own. We love you so much, honey. And it kills us you had to find out this way."

Her mom paused, frowning. "The reveal and change are usually a celebration. It's exciting to learn about this whole new side of you, about all the people that love you, about a future you never could have dreamed of. But you didn't get to have that experience."

She stood up and hugged her daughter. "We are so proud of you, and so happy for you. We've always known you weren't ours to keep forever. I hope you can forgive us."

"Of course, Mom. I love you." Mel squeezed tighter, aching at the thought of having to leave her parents, her home. When she pulled back, she scanned her mom's face. "Can I trust that you guys will actually be honest with me now? About everything?"

Her mom wore a deep frown. "Yes. Dad's already asleep for the night, but we want to sit down with you and talk more tomorrow about any questions you have."

Mel nodded, but didn't think she could wait on some things. "Devin—did you guys plan for us to date?"

Her mom's jaw dropped. "No. Why would you think that?"

Mel shrugged. "Because Seeders want girls to return to keep their lands safe."

Her mom raised an eyebrow. "We didn't let you date because we wanted to keep *you* safe." Her face softened. "But also because we were selfish about wanting you to ourselves. We would have been happy to let you live to your last day without dating anyone." She grinned. "But it's natural for most teenagers to want to date. And you were a smidge persistent."

Mel smiled.

"He asked if he could date you and he seemed like a nice enough guy. He was already one of your protectors." Mel's mom pursed her lips. "Didn't think my daughter would sneak behind my back to date a guy, especially when she already had permission to date."

Mel frowned. "I think we can call that a draw. Because there are a lot more lies in this family than I ever imagined, too."

Her mom pressed her lips together, nodding. "You really like him, don't you?"

Mel fought back tears, and her energy. "Yeah, well, it's not like I'm deciding to go back there just to chase a guy."

"I know." Her mom pulled her into another hug. "You'll make the right choice for the right reasons. We believe in you."

"Thanks," Mel whispered.

Her mom stopped at the doorway before leaving for the night. "I understand you have some big choices to make. We want you to do what you think is best for *you*. Your dad and I want you to know that we don't want you making any decisions based on concern for us. We'll always be proud of you."

"Thanks, Mom." Mel sighed. "You have no idea how hard this is."

Her mom gave her a sympathetic frown. "Get some good sleep. Love you."

"Love you, too."

The door clicked closed. Mel sat back down on her bed. Her mental pros and cons list was so skewed, so scattered. She thought back to what Ben had said, about different reasons for returning to the Green Lands. The problem was, she couldn't relate to some of those reasons. She didn't need a new start, or have a horrible family. Despite that, she had started to feel a pull there. And that scared her.

Mel struggled to find sleep, her mind forming a list of every family event she would give up by following everyone's expectation of moving to the Green Lands. She'd never have another Thanksgiving or Christmas with her parents. Had she done enough to savor last year's? No more opportunities to make her parents a special breakfast on Mother's or Father's Day. She imagined trying to feel happy celebrating those days with faceless strangers in a foreign place.

The word that plagued her the most, was 'enough.' What was *enough* of a reason to stay, or to go?

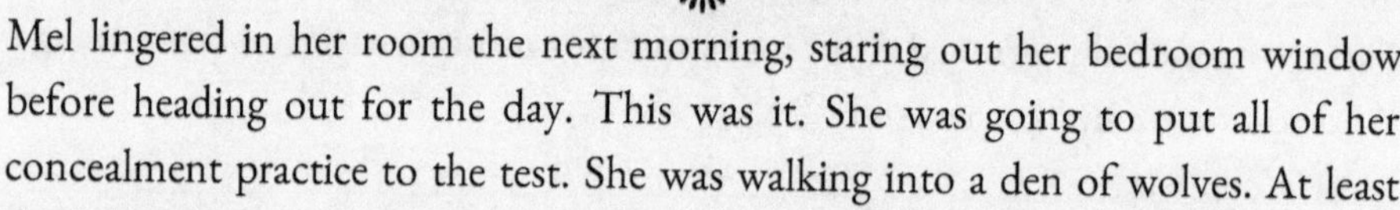

Mel lingered in her room the next morning, staring out her bedroom window before heading out for the day. This was it. She was going to put all of her concealment practice to the test. She was walking into a den of wolves. At least that's how it felt. *Maybe it's more of a nasty compost bin than a den of wolves, since we're part plant, and this definitely stinks...*

Devin, and now Ben, had reassured her daily that there hadn't been any chatter in their network about new Ivy activity after the attack. It looked good for them. Ken and Blake probably hadn't been able to share her identity before they died. But it was clear, by the missing bodies, that at least one Ivy remained in the area. And the likelihood that she was near the top of their list, after Blake's obvious suspicions ... made her stomach churn.

Forcing herself to leave the house, she walked through the neighborhood with a frown. Getting a root canal without numbing sounded like a more pleasant alternative to school.

The high school within her line of sight, Mel rolled her sore shoulders. Every muscle screamed at her. Ben walked several paces in front of her as her 'foster brother' and secret personal bodyguard. He had a spring in his step that Mel scowled at with jealousy. He was used to this kind of vigorous training.

And the elephant in the classroom? Just the earth-shattering revelation of her true nature; needing to conceal her identity and control her body; getting over the trauma of being attacked and knowing that she was walking into a place where assassins were after her. Don't forget having to remember an elaborate lie, and pretend she *wasn't* fighting with her boyfriend. No big deal.

Oh yeah, and Mr. Rasmussen's unrealistic expectation that they would have studied for his class during spring break.

Today is going to be a winner.

Chapter 19

Walking through the halls at school, it was surreal to think that so many people around her had no idea what was going on right under their noses. Locker doors squeaked and slammed. Teens chatted and laughed. Pen caps and papers littered the floors. It was like strolling through a museum of teenage normalcy, something from her past. Even if Mel chose to stay and be human, she wondered if she could ever really go back to who she had been, or planned to be.

Mel ached to be normal enough to only have to grapple with the simple decisions her human peers had to make. Everything that seemed regular, or even important, just a month ago, melted from the scope of her attention. Lost in her thoughts, she roamed listlessly to her locker with just enough time to sort out her books and get to class on time. Devin was waiting for her when she arrived. She gave him a hug and kiss before heading off. There was no spark. It was clinical, all for appearances. They hadn't so much as exchanged a text since he'd dropped her off the day before.

Zach hunted Mel down after first period and gave her a giant hug. She had a genuine smile plastered on her face. They hadn't ever had a wild, flashy romance like she'd had with Devin, but Zach felt like home—she knew he was always there for her.

"Gosh, Mel, I thought you were dead!"

His words gave her a traumatic flashback; she could almost even feel the vines still choking the life out of her. *If only he knew how close to the truth that was.*

"You could have messaged me sooner to let me know what was up."

She shook off her daze. "Sorry, I just got caught up in the fun of the trip. I promise it won't happen again."

She tried to hide it, but her heart sank as she realized that if she chose to return to the Green Lands, her promise would become a lie. She would go missing without warning. Like Tabatha, she would have to ghost him.

"You okay? Something looks different about you."

Wait, that's the kind of line Blake would use. Great. Now the paranoia is setting in. How was she expected to live a double life, pretend things were normal when the weight of the world was smothering her?

"Yeah, I slept like crap last night. Thanks for noticing." She laughed. "How did your camping trip go?"

The warning bell rang. "It was awesome. It involved a friendly muskrat and less-than-friendly mosquitos. I'll tell you more about it at lunch."

Her mind wandered all day, unable to focus on a single thing her teachers were saying or the homework they assigned. At lunch, Zach sat across from Mel at their usual table.

Devin was all smiles and wrapped his arm around Mel after sliding onto the bench. He kissed her on the cheek and whispered in her ear, "I hope you're doing alright."

She smiled and elbowed him as if he had said something flirty.

A couple of members of Blake's jock posse walked by. "Way to go, Devin! How was the honeymoon?"

The rage on Devin's face spelled out the horrible things he wanted to do to them, and Mel knew the actual extent of what that could be. Devin met their challenge. "Grow up, morons! Unless you want to end up like Blake."

Mel flashed a look of shock at Devin. What was he doing? He couldn't talk like that!

"Do you think it's true what they're saying? He got locked up in juvie?" Zach said.

She could relax. *The cover story must be out.* "He deserves worse than that if you ask me."

They took turns discussing the happenings of spring break. Mel let Devin do most of the talking, and he was pretty convincing. But Mel knew Zach recognized something was off. When Devin wrapped his arm around her again, Mel flinched. It was a split second, but she caught Zach's concerned glance the moment it happened.

Hoping to deflect any suspicion, she shook her head and shivered. "Gosh, I really need some caffeine. I'm so jumpy today." She hoped it would be enough.

"Hey, Mel, do you want to go over notes for history after school?" Zach offered.

Maybe it wasn't a good enough performance. Either way, she definitely needed some Zach time. "Let me check with my parents."

After texting with Ben about her training schedule, he agreed that she could have Zach over for a couple of hours after school the next day. He wanted to reserve that whole evening for training.

"How about tomorrow? My mom has about a thousand chores for me to do tonight." She rolled her eyes to lean into the lie. "A nice 'welcome home' gift for going on vacation, I guess."

Zach's eyes darted from her to Devin, then back. "Sure. If that's what you want."

Mel was dreading the last period of the day. Just walking down the hallway where Blake had pinned her against the wall made her feel dead inside. Her eyes were drawn to the gym door, her heartbeat racing, her palms getting sweaty. She considered excusing herself from class to go to the nurse's office, but decided against it last minute. Luckily, today they were holding P.E. on the outside track. Having had some time to recover from the exertion of the previous night's training gave her enough energy that she thought running laps might actually help her clear her mind and work out some aggression. She was right; it did her some good.

After showering, she grabbed for a hair tie from the bottom of her gym locker. Her hand brushed against Devin's necklace. Picking up the charm on its long chain, Mel cradled it in her hand, rubbing the little sun symbol. This tiny thing had made all the difference in her life. If only she had known. In a way, it had brought her and Devin together, and also symbolized what was tearing them apart. She stared at it for a couple of minutes, lost in her thoughts, before tucking it into the pocket of her jeans and closing the locker door.

Walking into the hallway, she couldn't resist the call of the gym. She found herself standing in the doorway, envisioning how it all must have played out, according to her limited point of view and hazy recollection. She imagined Ben running up, how she lay pathetically slumped over in agony. There were invisible footprints on the floor where her assailants stood. It was like she was there all over again. She looked at the path Ben had taken to get her out, and remembered where the bodies had fallen. Mel imagined them getting up and walking away to lick their wounds, or being dragged away by another Ivy. A faceless brother would have passed where she was currently standing, to collect her backpack and water bottle.

"Melody."

She gasped and jumped, turning to see Tom walking down the hall toward her. She realized her emotions were not in check and quickly turned back to the gym, closed her eyes, and reined her energy back in. She could only hope Tom hadn't seen any physical changes.

"Sorry, didn't mean to startle you," he said.

"Hi, Tom. I mean ... sorry, Principal Colburn."

"We'll let it slide this once." He winked. "I heard you had a fun adventure for spring break? You were missed at Sunday dinner."

"Yeah, my boyfriend took me to meet his parents. It was great."

"Devin's his name, right? He seems like a nice fellow."

"Yeah, he's ... he is."

"And that foster boy isn't giving you any more trouble, is he?"

"No, we've sorted it out." She didn't feel like another interview, already exhausted from a day filled with lies. "Anyway, I'd better run. Lots of homework and chores." She forced a smile. "The work of a teenager is never done."

"No problem, I was just passing by. Take care of yourself and tell your parents hi for me."

"Will do." Mel watched as he walked away. She liked Tom. He always gave great advice. What would *he* have to say about this doozy?

Her chest tightened. He could be Ivy, he could be Seeder, or he could just be a standard-grade human. He could be anyone. She wouldn't be stopping by his office for advice on this one.

Instead, she glanced one last time at the gym, swallowing hard.

Mel took her time walking home—delaying the inevitable pain of training, taking a breather, and sorting through her thoughts without the constant noise of public school assaulting her. Not that she was alone—Ben was with her, although almost a full block ahead.

Before starting on training, Mel's mom reminded her that she and her dad wanted to have a chat. Mel had been trying to sort through all of her feelings on her situation, but really wasn't sure where she stood, or what they were expecting.

"We love you, sweetie," her mom started, as they sat down together in the family room. "First, do you have any questions for us?"

Mel blinked a couple of times, not even sure where to start. "You don't think I could have handled knowing who I really was?"

Her parents frowned and held hands. "Some decisions were up to us, while others had to be agreed upon with your ... other ... dad," George said. "Even if we had permission to tell you when you were little, we wouldn't have." His eyes pleaded lovingly. "We didn't want you to have to worry about this your whole life. We knew they wouldn't come after you until your bloom, but who wants to live all their life with that hanging over their heads?"

Mel stared at her lap. "You could have at least told me when Devin found out about the change..." She would have taken the necklace more seriously.

"I'm sorry," her mom said. "You're right. We weren't ready to let you go. We ... just wanted more time with you before everything changed for good."

Mel looked up at her. "Like more game nights and Costa Rica?" She'd put that together the night before... An elaborate experience she'd never have (if she returned to the Green Lands), and their increased persistence in wanting to spend more time together. And now ... with three weeks or less left, they'd never go to Costa Rica together, unless she stayed here to be human.

They didn't respond, just nodding in confirmation of her suspicions.

She scanned their faces. Despite their explanation, she was still angry, hurt, confused.

Her dad's eyes welled up with tears. "We should have had *several* more months with you. Normal months. Happy months. But we failed you. And now..."

Mel swallowed hard, remembering how Devin had said she was allowed to live a 'normal life.' Her parents were good parents—she loved them. In a lot of ways, they had a healthy relationship. They would often be the ones to apologize after a disagreement, and confess that they weren't perfect, that even they, as the adults, were always learning. *What's done is done.* Dwelling on something they couldn't change wouldn't help.

"So ... family secrets... My biological dad?"

Her mom sighed. "That's one thing we can't budge on. He has dozens of Seeders and humans he coordinates. And it's not like he always lives within the confines of human laws, you know?"

"It's not like he's some outlaw, though," her dad added. "But creating and maintaining fake identities is just *one* aspect of his job. And everything is compartmentalized. I'm sorry. But his wish is to remain anonymous right now. And..." He looked down, rubbing his knee. "And I know it's selfish ... but this is still *our* time to enjoy with you while you're here. He'll, um, well, if you return like you're supposed to…" His voice faded. "You'll have time to get to know him and ask all the questions you want down the road."

Mel took a deep breath. "Fine. Fosters, other kids. Not all Seeders, right?"

"No." Her dad shook his head, wiping at his eyes. "A mix, over the years."

"How did you guys even get into this? With them being so secretive?"

"Well…" Her mom chimed in. "I knew some Seeders when I was younger. And we've kept in touch in one way or another."

Mel raised her eyebrows in surprise. Seeders obviously used to be more open. "How did that happen? That Seeders trusted you with their identities? With everything being so hush-hush?"

Her mom frowned, shaking her head. "Let's talk about that another time. Right now we want to talk about you and your future."

"I'm really honored, we both are, to be included in the network," her dad said. "Your people have always been kind."

It sounded so weird, so foreign, for her dad to address her that way. 'Your people.' Like she was something so completely different. She glanced at their family pictures on the wall. She wasn't her daddy's little girl. Not really. She hadn't expected something as harmless as his statement to bring tears to her eyes.

"Will you guys take in more kids? When I'm gone? If I go?"

"No," her mom said. "Well, there's a lot we're not sure of yet. But you'll be our last female Seeder." She gave Mel a loving smile. "And we couldn't be prouder."

After a couple more questions, they dug in deeper, explaining the whole Seeder picture. While neither of her parents had personally been to the Green Lands, they conveyed the general landscape as they'd had it described—how breathtaking the scenery and ambient energy were.

The hardest part to imagine was the lack of modern technology, but it didn't seem like such a deal breaker when framed by the idea of a calmer, simpler way of life. No noisy traffic, not having to work constantly to be able to afford the newest cell phone or gaming system. Also shocking, was the lack of larger animals, which explained why everyone in the Green Lands was a vegetarian. Mel thought of a life without bacon and her mouth watered. Also not a deal breaker, but something she'd definitely miss if she went. The Green Lands were home to a wide variety of birds, snakes, small rodents, and bugs. The flora and fauna were diverse, a mix of an unlikely variety of life, some seemingly never having been identified in the human world.

Most appealing for Mel was the talk about how their communities were run. Every village had a focus on family and community. With families that large, they didn't have much choice. People knew their neighbors well, and families were so much more intertwined than the regular American nuclear family. While she was usually the type to keep to a small group, she couldn't help but envision how friendly and open a place like that would be.

Not sure what all Devin had shared with her, or how much she'd retained, they went over details of culture and physiology. Mel squirmed in her seat when her mom briefly explained Seeder mating. She knew they were still talking about her behind her back, coordinating her training and protection detail, but at least they didn't know what had almost happened at the safe house.

And while it was uncomfortable, it was good to know they'd always intended to make her options clear. Devin had said her brothers wouldn't have normally come to the human world to tell her about Seeder mating, and she wondered if it was something they kept a secret until the girls returned, which would be a horrifying manipulation.

Once they finished laying it all out and she had plenty of answers, they asked if Mel had any more questions. She knew she'd have more, but she couldn't think of any at the moment.

"There's nothing else I should know?" she asked.

George looked to Pam, as if waiting for her to respond. She glanced back at him.

"I think that's pretty much it for now. We'll let Ben know you're ready to get back to work," her mom said.

Her dad sent off a text and his phone buzzed with the reply. "He'll probably be about a half hour or so. We'll give you some time to think?"

They all stood and exchanged long, tight hugs.

Mel was grateful for some time to mull things over. Despite the monumental decision before her, she found her mind focused on Devin. She knew it wasn't fair that she'd snapped at him when leaving the safe house. And that she hadn't said more than a handful of words to him over the last couple of days. It wasn't his fault. She wondered ... if that night, those things, had happened when she'd still had her charm on, or before her change had started... But it didn't matter. That wasn't the way it had happened. And she wouldn't have been ready for that step, anyway.

She lay down on the couch, tucking her hands under her head. She'd been lied to, and controlled, her entire life. Resentment mingled with guilt. She was still in the dark about so many things, and had now taken on the active role of being the liar, to the rest of the world. She'd moved from one prison to another.

Tears filled her eyes. She had really fallen for Devin. Whole-heartedly. She asked herself at first if it was just the heat of the moment, that she'd told him she loved him. But nothing was the same without him there, without his smile and reassurances. Without his dorky quips.

She frowned and wiped at her tears. Finding out that one last detail, that night—one more restriction, one more thing she couldn't control—that was what had thrown her over the edge. Knowing she wanted to be with Devin, it felt like she was cornered into giving up her human life. He'd said as much, that they couldn't be together if she chose to stay. And it had sunk in a little more that last night. It wasn't that they *couldn't* be together, it was that they *wouldn't*. He could physically survive here like their dads had, but just like he'd said—he had come for his own family. Asking him to abandon his way of life would be as cruel as the impossible decision she was being forced to make. She wanted to ask him to choose her, to reconsider staying in the human world. But it didn't feel right. She couldn't fault him for knowing and embracing what he was, *who* he was.

But who was Mel? Who was Saff? Devin was a Seeder because that's what he had sprouted as, and that's what he'd been raised as. Was Mel a human, because she'd been raised that way? Or was she a Seeder, because that's how she came into the world? The blessing, and curse, was that she even had a choice in the matter. She knew that she should be grateful to be able to choose her future. But it certainly didn't feel like much of a blessing at the moment.

Mel pulled out her phone and typed a message: <I'm sorry.> Devin didn't deserve her anger; he hadn't earned it. Mel stared at the phone's screen, her finger hovering over the send button. Instead, she deleted it. This was too much. She needed more time to mull it over. And this wasn't a conversation to have over text.

Ben arrived shortly thereafter, ready for more strenuous training. What he had put her through the night before had just been a warm-up for the beating she would take that night. Her energy was completely expended between exercises to try and lengthen the amount of time she could keep her blades out, and new fighting techniques.

Learning to channel her energy in hand-to-hand combat was on a whole new level, though. If she could move her focus to the right muscles, bones, and skin, letting the energy settle in, she could swing faster, punch harder, and stand up to more severe blows. He unapologetically beat the crap out of her. She took it, for the most part, without complaint.

Mel had just enough energy remaining to heal the cuts she was left with. She barely managed a shower and then promptly passed out, sleeping like a rock.

Chapter 20

Luckily, the next day at school was a little less stressful. Devin texted to say he wouldn't kiss Mel at all, unless she initiated it, that he didn't want her to feel uncomfortable. He assured her he was there for her in any way she needed, and understood she wanted her space. She was grateful for his understanding, giving him a brief hug and holding hands where appropriate.

Zach walked her home after school and they settled down in the family room to do homework. She came back from a bathroom break and he again hid his phone suspiciously.

Knowing this was the kind of thing she should probably report to Devin or Ben, she decided to nip it in the bud instead. They didn't think Zach could be trusted, but she knew she was safe with him.

"What's that about?" she demanded.

He furrowed his brow. "What?"

"You. Your laptop, and phone." She frowned. "Since when do you keep secrets from me?" She knew she was being a hypocrite, but still...

He shook his head. "Don't worry about it."

She crossed her arms, studying his face. "Please?" she pleaded. "Just tell me? I don't care what it is." She couldn't handle more secrets, least of all from him.

He sighed, pulling out his phone and holding it up for her to see. She took it from his hand and sat down next to him, looking it over. The screen displayed search results.

"Tabatha?" Her eyes grew wide, looking up at him. "What's this about?"

He shrugged. "It was just too weird, the way she left." He paused, looking down at his hands. "I just thought ... if I could find her, and get more answers..." He looked back up, pursing his lips. "I didn't want you to know I was looking. I know how much her leaving hurt you. And ... I've checked a lot of places. Even obituaries... It's like she vanished into thin air. And ... I didn't want to tell you until I actually figured out what was going on."

Mel bit her lip and started to cry. She knew Tabatha's sudden departure had bothered him, too. But she hadn't realized he'd been obsessing this way. She wanted to comfort him, assuring him that Tabatha was fine. But she couldn't.

He cocked his head to the side, frowning. "This is why I didn't tell you." He gently took his phone back.

She wiped away her tears. "No. I'm fine. I promise."

They sat in silence for a minute.

"Did you want to look over any more notes?" he offered.

"I'm really wiped out. Can we take a break and just chill for a minute?" she asked.

Mel scooted a little closer and leaned against him, resting her head on his shoulder.

He leaned his head against hers. "What's wrong?"

"Can we not talk? I just need this." The sheer magnitude of her daily existence was wearing her thin. She struggled to keep her composure; luckily, he couldn't see her face.

"Yeah, Mel, of course." He wrapped an arm around her.

After a few minutes, he spoke up. "You know, I noticed you've been tense the last couple of days. It's okay if you don't want to talk about it, but just know that you can." He then suggested, "Would a shoulder massage help?"

"Oh, gosh, I'd be an idiot to turn that down." She got off of the couch and sat in front of him. Mel had been so comfortable with Zach for years, that something like a simple shoulder massage wasn't loaded. It had taken her a while to realize that it might not be appropriate anymore, after she started dating Devin. But he had been understanding of their friendship, especially since Zach had backed down after Mel chose Devin. She frowned—Devin was being really patient while she was sorting through all of this. She still wasn't sure she could meet his expectations.

Zach's hands worked magic on all of her knots and tight muscles. "Seriously, what *have* you been up to?" He moved his hands from her neck and shoulders down to her upper arms and rubbed them reassuringly.

She flinched and recoiled at the pain in her right arm.

"Sorry, you alright?"

Before she could stop him, he lifted her sleeve to reveal a giant bruise from Ben's training the night before. She'd only had enough energy to heal injuries that broke the skin, or were visible when fully-clothed. The bruise had somewhat faded already, but didn't automatically heal as quickly as her cuts had when she was blooming.

"You're kidding me!" he exploded. "What the hell happened?"

Pulling her sleeve back down, she turned to him. "You're seriously overreacting. I got it in gym class."

Zach scowled. "Why would you lie to me? That jerk's not worth it!"

She furrowed her brow in confusion. "What are you talking about?"

"I saw the way you reacted the other day, when Devin touched you. It's insulting you chose a jerk like that over someone that genuinely cares for you."

"Don't you dare!" she snapped back. "You don't even know the half of it. Devin would *never* hurt me."

Ben appeared in the doorway. "Go home, Zach."

"Stay out of it, Ben," Mel ordered.

Zach looked between them. "If it's not your boyfriend, was it this psycho?"

"Don't!" Mel barked at Ben, who was clearly about to lose his temper. "Let's go for a walk, Zach." Mel got off the floor and walked up to Ben, who was blocking the doorway.

"I don't think that's the best idea," Ben advised forcefully.

"Get out of my way or I'll find a way to make you regret it," she threatened.

Ben didn't budge.

Knowing Zach couldn't see from behind her, she intentionally shifted energy to her eyes, briefly flashing them neon green. "Move."

Ben glared, whispering, "That's a stupid way to make a point right here and now." After another moment of their stare-down, he stepped aside.

Zach followed her as she charged out the front door and down the street.

"Seriously, Mel, what's going on? This is not normal behavior for you."

She kept silent as her frustration festered; she had to put all her effort into centering her energy.

"Have I ever lied to you?" she asked.

"I guess I don't really know, do I?"

She couldn't assert herself as being honest now... She actually *was* lying to him, at minimum a lie of omission. "Can we just rewind things? I don't want to lose you, and I don't want to waste any time fighting. If I tell you I'm fine, can you please just believe me?"

He pressed his lips together. "I don't know what you want me to say. I don't know if I can just drop it."

"If you can't drop it, then... I don't know. You're making things so much harder." She choked down her energy to bury it, but she couldn't keep from tearing up.

He sighed and pulled her into a tight hug. "I just want you to be okay," he whispered.

She nodded and then gently pulled away from his hug. "I..." It was ridiculous that she couldn't even say that, well ... she couldn't even say that there were things she couldn't say. She tried to think about it from a human perspective. What kind of normal drama could she make it sound like, but still convey the right feelings?

"Mel, I need you to know that I love you. Like, really love you." He searched her eyes for a reaction. "I know you haven't felt the same way about me, and you chose Devin. But my feelings haven't changed."

Her heart sank. "I thought we agreed to just be friends."

Zach shoved his hands into his pockets. "No. We never had that conversation. I just didn't push anything because I knew you were already with him." He frowned, staring into her eyes. "I really think we could be happy together. Things were less complicated and stressful for you before he came around, you can't deny that."

She closed her eyes and took a deep breath. "Zach, I love you, too. I don't *want* to live my life without you in it."

Cradling her head with his hands, he leaned in for a kiss. Mel's eyes shot open in surprise. She wasn't sure why, but she didn't stop him. He was sweet and tender. She found herself actively kissing back, being enveloped in the wealth of possibilities true friendship could offer. He'd never lied to her. Things were never complicated with him. There was something there that she hadn't ever allowed herself to feel about Zach before. She'd never needed to rush things with him, but everything felt so much more accelerated now. She might never get a chance to explore their possibilities if she continued her training.

And then thoughts of Devin consumed her mind.

She was about to pull back, but realized she hadn't been cautious enough to focus. She had to pull back emotionally for a moment while still kissing Zach, to concentrate on containing her energy before he could open his eyes and discover her secret. Once she felt her energy back in place, she stepped back.

"We can't be doing this," she said.

"Why not?"

She covered her face with her hands. "I ... am still with Devin."

"But are you going to stay with him?" His eyes burned incredulously.

"Zach, I ... have a thousand decisions to make. And I can't give you an answer right now." She shook her head. "You really shouldn't have kissed me."

His brow furrowed. "Maybe I shouldn't have. But I've waited *forever* for your parents to allow you to date. And then you don't even give me a chance. You date Blake, and Devin."

She was struggling to control her anger, and energy. "Maybe you would have had a chance, if you'd had the guts to ask me!"

He scowled. "I told you how I felt at the dance."

She frowned. He had. The night she started to bloom. The first night she finally gave Devin a chance. She looked down, hating every moment of this conversation.

He continued in her silence, "You can't tell me you didn't just feel something between us. Am I wrong?"

She hugged herself. "It's not fair to ask me that right now."

"That answers my question." He shrugged. "Ultimately, the choice is yours. But if he's hurting you, if he's not treating you right, I *won't* let him get away with that, no matter what your decision is."

"I told you, you don't have to worry about that."

He gently raised his eyebrows. "The problem is, I think I do. And you haven't given me anything to convince me otherwise. I'm serious. I'll go to the cops if I have to."

She shook her head, looking him in the eyes. "Thank you for caring. I mean it. No one in my life wants to hurt me. Not Devin, or Ben, or my parents. If I was being abused, I promise I would tell you, okay?"

"Fine." He scanned her face. "But I'll be watching. And ... hoping you'll seriously give it some thought, the possibility of me and you."

Mel looked down the street to her house. Ben was, of course, watching them from the front porch. And to add to her luck, there was an extra set of eyes on them. Mr. Rasmussen, her biology teacher that lived a couple of houses down, was out watering his front yard and glancing their direction from behind his chain-link fence.

"Can I bring your stuff to school in the morning?" she asked.

Zach looked over at Ben and nodded. "Sure. I don't have anything important due tomorrow."

"Okay. I'm going to go. Can we keep this between us for now, while I sort things out?"

"Yeah." He rubbed the back of his neck. "I think I'll spend lunch elsewhere, until you make a decision."

Even if Devin didn't know what just happened, things would never be the same in their little group now. She agreed it was a good idea.

As Mel returned to the house, she held up a hand to Ben. "I don't want to hear a thing."

"We need to get to work." He bypassed the obvious lecture she knew he wanted to give about wandering off unprotected.

"No, we don't. That's MY decision to make." She was fuming. "And what you just saw back there, that's *private*. So help me, if you breathe a word of it..." It wasn't Ben's fault. She was just mad at the situation, mad at the world ... or really, mad at the worlds—plural. Her eyes were glowing green, and she didn't care enough to stop it. Mel was at the end of her rope. Zach coming over was supposed to give her a comforting reprieve from the chaos in her life, not fan the flames.

Her voice trembled as her eyes moistened in frustration. "You have NO idea what this is like. If you back me into a corner, you *won't* get what you want!"

Ben didn't respond, instead letting her pass and go upstairs to her room. A whole evening, desperately needed for training, was about to be wasted.

Chapter 21

Mel lay in bed, scrolling through what must have been dozens, perhaps even hundreds of pictures on her phone. So many with Zach, or Zach and Tabatha. Tons now with Devin. Selfies with her parents on holidays. The saying 'best of both worlds' came to her mind, and 'have your cake and eat it, too.' Which ... really didn't make much sense, because why have cake if you can't eat it? But that was a tangent.

What did she want? Without the pressure, or the fear, or the unforgiving countdown. If she wasn't forced to make a choice, what path would she willingly take? If she had it her way, she would keep these cool new powers, and be with Devin, and not have to lose her mom and dad or Zach. But honestly, could a world with both Devin *and* Zach in it be what she wanted anymore? Would Zach be happy climbing back into the friend box? And would she want him to?

Whoever says it's a fantasy to be fought over by two guys, is an absolute idiot. She huffed. *Seriously though, can someone honestly even love two people? Friendship that blooms into love surely trumps passion, right?* But that wasn't fair to Devin. He wasn't just a handsome face with exceptional kissing skills. He'd dedicated his entire youth—more than any human really ever sacrifices for another—to coming here and helping his family *and* hers. And it was impossible to deny how much he cared for her.

When it came to love, she needed more information. What did the guys even have in mind? How serious was Devin, really? If she was willing to make a lifetime commitment to him, would he reciprocate? Was he just being a gentleman when he turned her down?

What was Zach's endgame? If she stayed here to be human, her lifelong expectations would still be in play. School, work, marriage, family—in whatever order they happened to occur. Did he want kids? Was he thinking that far ahead? What junior in high school is even considering that kind of commitment? Like Devin had mentioned, Mel wouldn't even be able to have human kids. She'd always imagined having a big family, though not as large as Seeders had...

And was she a fool to give up her powers, to turn down ever meeting her biological mother and other family, other people like her—knowing they also needed her powers—just for the faint possibility that a high school romance could work out? She scoffed at the questions running through her head. It wasn't just about who she would date or marry. It was about who she was choosing to become, the whole package.

Mel had less than three weeks to sort it out. The implications, the small details, the finality of it all was crushing her. She tossed her phone to the floor, put a pillow over her face, and screamed.

There was a knock at her door and it opened.

She removed the pillow from her face to see her mom standing there. Mel sat up in bed, hugging her pillow. "Sorry."

"You have a right to be frustrated, don't apologize." Her mom sat down next to Mel and smiled. "Your eyes are so stunning that way."

Mel had forgotten again. "Sorry." Regaining control, her eyes faded to their regular blue.

"Stop that. Never apologize for being who you are," her mom scolded. "It's time I gave you some advice."

Other than their conversation the day before, Mel's 'host parents' had stood back and let the Seeders take care of things. Her parents had said as much, that they knew it wasn't their place to demand or direct at this point; they trusted Mel was following the path prepared for her all along.

"I should have said something earlier. But I..." Her mom looked down. After a while she finally looked up and spoke again. "I understand your struggle more than you know. It's a hard decision. I know, because I had to make that judgment call myself at your age."

Mel's jaw dropped. "Wait, what do you mean?"

"I was a Seeder."

"What? No. But ... you're human, you live here."

"Well, I'm human *now*. Because I stayed."

Mel blinked repeatedly in shock. She needed to know every detail of her mom's story and how she came to her decision.

Her mom took a deep breath. "Most Seeder girls only find out about their identities once the change has been completed. Generally, their parents give them the charm, and then when the biggest danger is over, they have to face the music and allow the brothers to step in and train. That's how it happened for me. That's how it happened for Murial."

Mel ached, hearing about both of her moms—sharing a story, divided by the worlds.

"The change happened smoothly for me. I was informed about who I was, what my heritage was. What the expectations of me were. I trained, maybe not with all of my heart in it, but I trained, did what I needed to do to stay hidden and safe. But when the time came ... I decided not to go."

"But why? Do you ever regret your choice?"

"When it comes down to it, I think I was just too scared. I didn't want to leave my family and friends; I didn't want to face the unknown. I worried I wouldn't be enough, that I wouldn't fit in, and get along with my family there, like I do here."

She paused, tucking a strand of Mel's hair behind her ear. "Do I regret my choice? That's hard to say. If I hadn't made that choice, I never would have met and married your father, and I wouldn't give him up for the world. And I wouldn't have been able to have you or Ben in my life, or any of the others we've fostered. Being human affords me peace; I don't have to worry about Ivies coming after me. Their focus is stopping Seeders from coming home. Once my time passed—so did the threat."

She sat pensively for a minute. "But I missed out on so much. I'll never be able to get over the shame of turning down my true nature, what I feel my destiny might have been. I gave up amazing power. Not that there's anything wrong with an ordinary life—you can be happy in either world, with or without the extra abilities. There are so many people I never got to meet. And..." Her voice pitched higher as tears filled her eyes. "I never got to meet my mother. I'll never stop imagining the pain my choices caused. She sent me out and trusted I would come back, that we would be reunited. And when I didn't come back ... it wasn't because I couldn't. It's because I wouldn't."

Mel rarely ever saw her mom cry.

"Sweetie, now that I'm a mother, I can imagine how that would feel. I would never want to keep you from her. When we agreed to take you in, it was with a promise that we would be ready to let you go, when the time was right."

Mel wrapped her arms around her mom. After a minute, Mel dared to ask, "So, you think I should go?"

Her mom pulled back, wiping away tears. "I think you need to be careful and brave as you decide. You only have two or three weeks. Most girls might still have three months at this point in training—enough to learn, get there, and maybe turn around before rooting if they changed their mind. You don't have that luxury. And I think you need to devote every ounce of your energy to preparing to leave. It takes a second, when the time is right, to make a final decision. But if you don't do what you need to, right now, you'll only be robbing yourself of the ability to make that choice."

Mel nodded. Her mom was right. "I'll try harder. Can you tell me how it feels, when you take root in the human world?" It was nice to talk to someone that had been through all of this.

Her mom frowned. "Once your roots wrap around your ankles, you feel a heaviness in your energy, like gravity doubled. It takes about a month for your abilities to fade completely. You lose the ability to fly right away, but then transforming, extending blades, controlling the energy, and last of all, your eyes fade. The day I realized I couldn't do anything was a devastating day for me. That's when it really hit me that I had closed an important chapter in my life; I really doubted myself and my decision."

Mel sat in silence for a moment as her mom's haunting regrets hung in the air. "The Ivies really wouldn't care if they found out you were a Seeder, once you became human? Devin assured me you guys wouldn't get hurt, but I sometimes worry they would come after you guys, to get to me."

"We're fine." Her mom smiled. "It's rare for a human to get hurt in all of this. The Ivies think of humans like ... I don't know, houseflies, and Seeders like mosquitos. One is annoying, practically unworthy of their attention; the other, they want to eradicate. We've got Ben, and we take all the precautions we can to keep ourselves safe. Don't worry about us."

"Okay." Mel nodded.

Her mom cocked her head to the side. "I noticed Zach's backpack is still in the family room. He went home without it?"

Mel pressed her lips together; she could almost still feel Zach's lips on hers. "I... I don't want to talk about all that. I'll clean it up before going to bed."

"Okay. But I'm always here for you if you want to talk." She gave Mel one last reassuring smile and wished her good night before heading out.

'I'm always here for you if you want to talk.' Mel wished that could be true, but it wasn't. If she went to the Green Lands, she couldn't just text her mom or sit down for a chat like this. And she didn't know if she'd ever have the same kind of relationship with Murial.

She took a deep breath, finding strength in her mom's advice. That she needed to prepare herself now, and the final decision could be made later.

Mel grabbed workout clothes from her dresser and changed. She went to Ben's room and knocked on the door. He looked surprised to see her when he opened it.

"Let's get to work," she said, making sure to add, "But I need to be able to heal my bruises, unless you want an investigation."

<hr>

The next day, Ben agreed that Mel could take a couple of hours after training to have Heather over for a movie. In the spirit of keeping up appearances, she would've called the whole posse together, but things were hardly in the right place with either Devin or Zach.

She'd left just enough time to shower and heal up before Heather came over. Mel silently chuckled as she finished getting dressed. Her life was the epitome of a dumpster fire right now. As if the whole Seeder thing wasn't enough, she apparently needed to add *every* aspect of her life to the crazy.

The doorbell rang and Mel bounded down the stairs to answer the door, grinning from ear to ear at Heather's bubbly smile.

"Come on in! I've got like a thousand kinds of chocolate and I intend to eat them all." Mel nodded in the direction of the family room and Heather giggled. "Sorry we always have to do things over here."

"No worries. I like your place."

They sat down and flipped through DVDs in awkward silence. Nothing jumped out at Mel, and Heather didn't seem invested in picking one either. This *was* the first time it was just the two of them hanging out.

"Sorry again about bailing on you for spring break. And thanks for coming over." Mel sat back on the couch. "I seriously needed some girl time."

Heather sat cross-legged on the other end of the couch, facing her. "It's okay. Boy troubles? What's up with you and Devin?"

Mel shook her head. She knew she wanted to talk, but wasn't really sure what all about. Looking at Heather's neck, she searched for a chain, just out of curiosity. She gave up, remembering Devin's description. It could be a toe-ring for all she knew, if Heather even was a Seeder. And she'd only be wearing it during her bloom, not before or after. But Heather could be anything.

"I don't know. Guys are just complicated, aren't they?"

Heather made a silly face and nodded. "They certainly can be."

"Are you dating anyone?"

Heather hummed playfully. "I've got one I like. But I don't want to jinx anything."

Mel chuckled. Heather hung around a lot of other people outside of their little group. She had enough energy to be a cheerleader, and enough heart to make everyone love her. Mel was honestly surprised she wasn't already taken. Being short and cute didn't hurt, either.

"Well, anyway..." Mel moved on, deciding she wasn't ready to spill her guts about anything. "Let's pick out a solid chick-flick we can watch without the guys."

"Yes!" Heather pumped her fist in the air.

Halfway through the movie, Ben made an appearance.

"Hey, girls." He smiled.

"Hi, Ben!" Heather greeted him in her usual cheerful voice.

Although Mel finally understood Ben's weirdness, it felt like overkill to have him pop in on just her and Heather, like her parents had for years when it was just her and Zach. But then again, he'd warned that Ivy females were rare in the human world, but not impossible.

Ben lingered in the doorway.

Mel waved him away with her hand. "Shoo! Girls' night!"

"Whatever." He rolled his eyes. "Good night, both of you."

It was getting late for a school night by the time the movie ended. Heather helped Mel clean up their disaster of candy wrappers and gave her a hug on the way out. This was what Mel had needed from Zach's visit. No guilt trips, no confusion. Heather wasn't Tabatha, but... She shook her head, wishing she could *really* confide everything to just one person. But she and Heather weren't on that level, even if she felt she could be trusted.

Chapter 22

Devin deserved to know the truth about the kiss. They weren't officially broken up, after all. And Mel deserved to know where he wanted to be in her future. She texted to ask if they could train together the next night; they could chat then. He quickly responded, <We'll make it happen.>

They got in his car after school ended; it was quiet. They hadn't really even been trying to keep up appearances much at school.

"Ben said you want to focus solely on catching a breeze right now? Put fighting on the back burner?" he asked.

"Yeah, I think so. Where do you go for that?"

"Some of the basics we can do indoors. But the bulk of that training is best done outdoors, in the dark, away from prying eyes."

"Sure, let's do it." Knots were already forming in her stomach. "But can we talk first? Go on one of those nature walks you like?"

He agreed to take a little downtime and drove to a local park where they could stretch their legs and have privacy. The spring sunshine was invigorating, the fluffy clouds uplifting. The trickle of a nearby stream soothed her nerves. The walking path they were on was safe from unwanted attention.

She started, "I owe you a huge apology. I can only imagine what you think of me. I'm sorry I was such a jerk."

He kept silent but acknowledged with his expression how hurt he had been.

"I'm going through a lot, but that doesn't mean you deserve me taking it out on you."

He interrupted before she could continue, "Saff ... I ... or, Mel, whichever. It's not that I—"

"I know. You were a perfect gentleman." She shoved her hands in her pockets. "Honestly, you're kind of perfect in everything, and I take that for granted. I'm selfish."

"No," he interjected.

"Please, just let me get out what I need to say," she pleaded. "I need you to know where I'm at."

He motioned with a hand for her to proceed.

"I don't know if I'm ready to say it again, but I really did mean it when I said I loved you." Just saying it aloud again brought her butterflies. "My frustration after that night wasn't just about you turning me down. I mean, I think obviously a lot of it was my hurt pride. But I realized how much more that meant to me."

She frowned. "It was just one more thing that made me feel like I had no control over my life. That I have to make a huge and irreversible decision. I have to ask myself if I want to commit to that life. How do you know for certain that you're picking the right mate? Do we both want kids? In this world, you can have one at a time, pretty much whenever you're ready."

She threw her hands up in the air, exasperated. "In your world, we don't get to choose the timing. And if we do want kids, it's twenty-four at a time! And I wouldn't see you, or my daughters, for as long as I've been alive, and then I would be stuck there, forever, in a world at war.

"That's a lot of pressure, all decided in a moment of passion." She furrowed her brow. "Devin, I've never even dated anyone before you. I have a hard time just picking what to watch on movie night, for heaven's sake!"

He grinned at that; she was notoriously indecisive.

"And I don't know what you want out of life, what you want from me. It's not just fooling around and having fun in the human world. What if you fall for someone else while you're still here and I'm waiting for you back home? Or what if it's the other way around? I just... I needed to say I'm sorry. And I'm obviously considering all the factors involved, but I need to know what *you* want."

She paused for a moment.

"Can I call you Saff?" he asked.

She grinned, then it faded to a frown. "There's one more thing I need to tell you first. That is, assuming Ben didn't already tell you."

His face indicated he hadn't.

She closed her eyes, hating herself. "I don't want you to get mad, and I don't want you to hate me."

He grabbed her hand and gave it a squeeze. "Saff, I could never hate you."

"See." She took her hand back and shoved it into her pocket again. "This is you, being more amazing than I deserve." There wasn't an easy way to say it. "Zach kissed me." She looked for his reaction.

His lips pursed and nostrils flared, but he didn't completely lose it.

"And I think it's my fault—I said the wrong thing. And I kissed him back, and I'm not sure where I stand." She kept talking without hardly taking a breath. "He told me he loved me, and I told him I loved him. But it's not the way I love you. It's like, chemistry and friendship—you have more of one, he has more of the other. And I told him I didn't want to live my life without him, but, you know, I was thinking in a my-big-decision-ending-our-friendship kind of way, not in the standard human-pledging-loyalty kind of way. Either way, I said it, and he kissed me, and I'm more confused about what I want in life. And it's not fair to you, and I'm so, so, so, sorry."

He didn't respond, instead shoving his own hands into his pockets and reading her eyes. "You need to give me some time to think about it. Let's keep walking."

After what felt like an eternity, he began to talk. "I need to be practical, but I also need to be honest. Mel, I still love you. But the truth is, I can't get distracted by *your* feelings."

He frowned, his dark brown eyes showing his struggle. "That might sound like I don't care, but the fact is, I didn't come here to fall in love. I care about our world. I care about our people. Our survival and happiness. I care about my sisters, and my family. And I wouldn't trade any of that, or my powers, for you. And I know you wouldn't ask me to. And I'm not asking you to do that, either."

She swallowed the lump in her throat as he continued.

"If you choose to stay here and forfeit your heritage," he raised an eyebrow, "I hope you do it because you are *absolutely* sure you want the entire book, not just the next chapter that may or may not work out like you want."

His gentle eyes were piercing, pleading. "I want you to return home, not just because I love you, but because I know your family loves you, and *all* of our people will welcome you home with open arms. You were meant to be there—you would absolutely love it. You could be so happy, Mel."

She had to give it to him; he was even more mature than she had given him credit for. He was more than a flirt that could make her swoon. He had his priorities sorted out more than she had ever come close to with her own.

He glanced at her neck, then slowly reached over and pulled the long chain out from under her shirt. The charm faced in, like he had originally told her to wear it. He grinned and gently slipped it back in place. "You know this doesn't help you anymore, right?"

She blushed. "Yeah, I know."

He nodded. "About Zach... I'm not mad at you. You deserve to figure out what will make you happy." He rolled his eyes. "Doesn't exactly make me like the prick any more than I used to."

She wanted to say something in Zach's defense, but Devin had a right to his feelings.

"If you want to know the truth, what I want, what would be my ideal... I would pick you every day of the week. I've met plenty of girls in both worlds, and you're the only one I'm crazy about. Despite everything I've said, I'd be absolutely devastated if you didn't come back."

His eyes glistened with emotion.

"I could see us loving every day together. I really could see us having a family, taking on challenges together, just like we're taking on challenges together right now, Saff. I understand most human teenagers aren't even close to thinking about this kind of thing. But ... you're not human. You're different."

He stopped walking and took her hands. "Now you know, but I'm only one piece in your puzzle. You have a lot of other pieces to put in place." He looked her in the eyes. "You need to focus, and be free to explore, Saff. I'm here for you every day, until either one of us leaves. I'm here if you need to vent, or need a hug. And as much as I want to sweep you off of your feet this very moment and remind you how much I love every part of you..." He frowned and swallowed. "I'd also be willing to step back, and just do the job I came here to do. First and foremost, I'm one of your protectors. If you need to, spend some time with Zach."

He paused. "To be clear, I'm not saying I'm okay with him launching himself at you the way he did. And he can't distract you, either. And I think I really need to stress—we still have no way of knowing he's human like you're assuming." He lifted his eyebrows. "That's exactly what Blake tried to do, right? Kissing you while you're dating someone else? Pretty Ivy behavior."

"It's not the same thing." She wanted to explain how it all stemmed from Zach trying to protect her. It was nothing like Blake attempting to kiss her while twisting her arm. She decided it wasn't worth her time trying to hash it out. She knew how it compared and that was enough.

He sighed. "The leeches don't have to kill you. Remember that all they need to do is ensure you don't make it home. Not that you can't have human friends that would genuinely miss you... Either way, if you need to sort out your feelings, then," he paused again, like it took everything he had to complete his sentence, "then sort through your feelings with him. I'm assuming we're on the same page, that ... if you're going home, you're obviously going to have to give him up. And if you stay ... you and I could only be together for so long. Just... I don't know what I'm trying to say. I don't want you to choose me as a default. I want you to choose me because you love me, as much as I love you."

She nodded. "I don't know what I'm going to do with all of that, but I'll really give it some thought." She pursed her lips. "I'm starting to question whether or not I believe in karma. Because I've never done enough to earn someone like you in my life."

He blushed.

"Can I ask you one more thing?" she said.

"I think I have one more answer in me."

"Can I have a hug?"

He grinned. "I have an infinite supply, just for you."

She fell into his arms, breathing deeply. When she started to pull away, she couldn't help herself—she leaned forward and kissed him ever so sweetly. Soft, gentle, slow. Every memory of her feelings for him came flooding in. Their last night of passion, spending a week together in seclusion, their secret relationship, their first kiss, even the first time they sat next to each other, and she knew he wanted to hold her hand. More than that were the sacrifices, the jokes, the meaningful conversations, the way they were able to work through problems together. She quietly moaned and took a deep breath.

She loved him—she knew that. Zach was a different kind of love. But Devin... She knew who she wanted to be with, with every fiber of her being. He pulled her in tighter, echoing the magnetism she felt within their souls. She wondered if their supernatural energies had anything to do with their chemistry, and if it was fair. Even if it *was* a factor, she couldn't fault the advantage more than she could his handsome eyes or dimples.

As she released him and gazed at his face, his eyes darted around. Luckily, they were still alone. She realized she hadn't been careful about her changes. He focused back on her, locking eyes.

She wanted to tell him that she *did* love him. But she'd decided—her choices needed to be separate. She wasn't going home for him. And she wasn't choosing him just because she chose the Green Lands. She was teetering on the edge of decision, but fear held her back.

Time. More time.

Luckily, he didn't demand an answer. He smiled lovingly and asked, "Should we get back to flying practice?"

She wondered if his question held more weight to it than it sounded. "Yeah." She thought for a moment. "If I go home, to your home…"

"Our home?" he corrected with hopeful eyes.

"Back *there*… What am I supposed to do with my life? Other than exist … with energy?"

He smiled. "I guess we need to go over the brochure a little better, huh? But you, I could see you being a mentor. That's what I want to be, when I go back. Teaching the younger boys how to blend in over here, that kind of stuff."

He gently lifted her chin. "You care. You worry about your parents, and Zach, and hurting their feelings. And you're stressed and confused. When you get back, you'll have mentors to help you master your abilities, but they'll also help you find your way. I can't imagine anyone better suited to that kind of work than you, when the time comes." He rocked his head back and forth. "I mean, there's art classes, too." He grinned.

She pulled him in for another hug. "Thank you."

Chapter 23

To make good use of their time before dark, Devin and Mel went back to her house to practice in the garage, as they usually did for training now.

Mel went over the techniques Ben had recently taught her. Devin was able to give her extra tips on how to focus her energy to achieve what she wanted; he was a better teacher on the energy side of things, compared to Ben's focus and specialty on form.

As they took a short break, Devin's phone chimed. He read the message and couldn't contain his excitement. "Change of plans!"

They hopped in the car and started driving.

"I really want to focus on catching a breeze. What's so important?" she asked.

He still had a grin on his face. "We're going to practice. But we've got a bit of a drive to go to a location further out. We're meeting up with some people."

"Really?" Her excitement was growing to match his. "Who am I going to meet? Someone we don't have to keep our distance from?"

"We can make some exceptions when Seeders are leaving, as long as we're careful. Saff—Thod's eleventh daughter is taking off tonight." He reached over and squeezed her hand.

"Wait, Thod? My dad, right? Will he be there?"

"No, sorry. He only accompanies the last one back. Which is going to be you, so that's a special honor. But as long as we're discreet and aren't followed, you can see how it's done, and meet your sister, and your brother that's escorting her."

She beamed. "Oh my gosh, that's... How long till we get there?"

Mel and Devin drove far out of town. As the sun dipped below the horizon, the evergreens became taller, thicker. Leaving paved roads, they drove deeper into the woods, the car jostling them on the bumpy path. They slowed and creeped to a stop. There was already another car parked in the area. They hopped out and Devin guided Mel to a clearing on foot.

Under the glow of a full moon and stars, it was a breathtaking scene to behold. The clearing ended in a cliff. Looking beyond the cliff and past the sea of trees, the faintest glow of their hometown glimmered on the horizon.

They approached a group of three others, including Ben, excitedly chatting.

"Bonnie?" Mel said.

"Hey! Oh my gosh!" Bonnie ran up and hugged Mel as Devin left to go talk to the others. "As if I am not already nervous and excited enough, I'm so excited I get to meet you this way!"

Mel knew Bonnie mostly through her older sister. Bonnie was only a sophomore, but Devin had explained that it was planned that way to space everyone out, just like they made Ben a senior and Mel was a junior. Having massive attrition in just one grade in a given town would raise more red flags than was necessary.

"So ... you're Thod's daughter? What about your brother and sister?" Mel asked.

"Boring humans." Bonnie laughed. "Well, I mean, typical families, right? But everything got so exciting when I found out and started training. We only just got to tell my brother and sister last night. Can't trust them as far as we can throw them to keep a secret. Well, they understand how serious it is, so they won't blab, but still. Didn't want to risk anything until I was gone."

"I guess we haven't really talked a lot about my exit. I imagined your family would be here to see you off," Mel said.

Bonnie looked hesitant to answer. "We decided to say our goodbyes at home. If it was only my parents seeing me off, we could trust them with the location." She wore a warm smile. "But they told me I had a sister that could use some support."

Mel glanced at Devin, who was talking to Ben and another guy she only recognized as a new kid in school that year.

"For me?" Mel was touched Bonnie would give up a special moment with her host parents for her. "Aren't you nervous? That's a huge decision!"

Bonnie's smile widened. "You could travel the whole human world and it would never compare to this adventure. It's what we're meant to do, Mel."

A calmness swelled in Mel's heart. She looked Bonnie over. "No bags. I guess I hadn't thought about that. And what's your cover story?"

"I tucked away some photos in my pockets. I left my charm for my sister as a gift. Everything else ... it's not that big of a deal in the grand scheme of things." She leaned in and whispered, "I burned my school books last night just for fun."

She chuckled and continued, "It's kind of a rite of passage, if you want to do it. Get out of those annoying human public schools and transfer to one in the Green Lands. And my cover story is my dad got a job offer in Chicago. He has to start right away and we're moving. All our parents know when they take us in that they may have to uproot themselves. It'll be an adventure for my siblings here, anyway."

Mel turned her attention to the other guy who was now walking toward her with open arms.

"Melody! or Saffrona? Not sure what to call you." He gave her a big hug. "Back home, they call me Kyle."

"Either works. You're one of my brothers?"

He beamed with pride. "One of Thod's best."

"So, what's *your* cover story for leaving?" Mel asked. She realized he might not actually be leaving for good. Some brothers escorted sisters home and returned. But this was during the middle of the week and he definitely couldn't be back by the start of school the next morning.

He responded in a rather convincing Slavic accent, "My host parents dropped me off at the airport earlier today. Unfortunately, I'm having to cut my foreign exchange year short to return home, because of a death in the family." He went back to speaking normally. "You kinda feel bad for making people worry about you, but they'll get over it."

Mel's mouth hung open. "So, your host family never knew what you were?"

"No, definitely not. A lot of us guys, and I'm assuming the Ivies, too, are with hosts in the dark. Real foster parents and the like."

Ben reminded them they had to keep their reunion short. They needed to see Bonnie off, and Mel needed to get back to training.

"Okay!" Bonnie squealed with excitement, her eyes shifting from light brown to neon green. She turned back to Mel one last time. "I'll see you on the other side. Oh yeah, I think I'll be going by my other name over there. Call me Rose when you see me next!"

Rose and Kyle moved further out and talked in preparation. Ben walked over and put his arm around Mel. "This is going to be you soon."

They watched the brother-and-sister duo talking and gesturing, doing a preflight check.

"Make sure to pay attention to everything they do, especially Rose," Ben told Mel.

"So, we literally jump off a cliff?" Mel said with a gulp, realizing how badly it could go if she didn't master the right skills in time.

Devin answered, "Take-offs in the Green Lands are ten times easier, with the energy of the realm. And especially when you're so new at catching a breeze, having a running start in a location like this can make all the difference to get you going."

Her fears were trying to pry into her moment of happiness and wonder. "You say we 'catch a breeze.' What if the air is still? What if I don't learn in time?"

"You'll get it, Mel," Ben said. "We're going to make sure of it."

"And we don't actually need a gust of air," Devin said. "While it's helpful, we can fly without it. When you get back home, you'll be able to commune more with the energy in nature, not only what you have in your body. This is just the start of it. You can control your own breeze—your body working in tandem with nature."

His explanation was so poetic. Lifting her hand, she focused on the air around them. She tuned in and sensed the rhythmic motions surrounding her, the push and pull of tidal forces, the unheard song formed by the whisper of wind grazing leaves. Mel grinned, watching her new brother and sister intently.

Seeder girls always had a personal escort to get home. The escort would guide them, coach them if they were struggling on their journey, and help by opening the rift between the worlds. It would be the trip of a lifetime. Long and strenuous, but worth every ounce of energy, and every moment of preparation, that it consumed.

Rose transformed next to her brother. Her hair shifted from dark brown to a glowing yellow. Blades protruded from her arms. Legs covered in roots peeked out from her shorts. Mel noticed the roots extended to Rose's ankles, just barely starting to wrap around, but still having some time before they completed the final stage of rooting.

Rose faced her palms away from her body and they glowed. She sprinted and leapt from the cliff without hesitation. Her body took a small dip in the flight path and then soared higher. Her posture was somewhat precarious; it took a while to stop wobbling, to embrace the wind rather than trying to fight it.

Kyle walked up to the cliff and jumped forward, doing a somersault in the air and fully transforming, picking up speed quickly to coast by Rose's side. They aimed for the clouds and disappeared from sight.

Mel stood with her mouth open, dumbfounded at what she'd just witnessed. Devin looked at her and grinned. Ben gave her a side hug and announced it was time for him to go.

"I've got to take the car back to Bonnie's family. You two need to get to work."

Mel turned to Devin. "How am I supposed to learn to do that in enough time? I saw her ankles, she's about to take root any day!"

"It's a lot of hard work and focus, I won't lie about that. But don't freak out. Rose could have returned at least a couple of weeks ago; she practiced enough. She stayed longer to spend more time with people here. It's not impossible to learn by your deadline, not with how much raw energy and talent we've seen in you." Devin grinned again. "Plus, this is the cliff your mom first caught a breeze from. It's in your blood."

She smiled. Sometimes it was confusing, which 'mom' or 'dad' they were talking about. This time she knew—Murial once took her leap of faith from here. There was a rightness to this place.

An engine started in the distance and the crunch of wheels on gravel faded. Now it was just Mel, Devin, and the crickets in the woods. The breathtaking view in such a secluded space would make this a perfect getaway for lovers. But romance was the farthest thing from Mel's mind. She knew how much she needed to focus. It would take everything she had to try and replicate what she'd just witnessed, in the two to three weeks she had left.

"What's first?" she asked her trainer.

Chapter 24

They could only cover so much of their training at the cliffs. Different aspects could be better taught in other locations—more space to run, softer places to land.

Since they were already there, and energy was his forte, Devin ran Mel through meditation exercises focused on blade extension and simultaneously moving energy to all parts of her body, strongest in the hands and core. It was an insane amount of multitasking—a lot of things to focus on, and balance. She could concentrate and flare her blades to their full extent, but would struggle to keep them there when she shifted focus to moving energy to all parts of her body.

After a couple of hours in body-centered exercises, Devin let her take a break by working more on her relationship to the wind. She shifted the energy to her hand, raising it in the air. Mel could sense the smallest of movements, the currents that flowed around her. Waving her hand, she perceived the disruption she was capable of making as her gesture cut through the sea of oxygen, causing waves that dulled to ripples before continuing on their path.

There was something so profoundly rich about this experience. Something that had been awoken in her.

The gravel crunched under their tires late that night, hushing as they reached paved roads.

"I had no idea what all we're capable of. How big this all really is," Mel said in awe. "I wish we would've started earlier on flying."

He smirked. "You have to walk before you can run, and you have to glow before you can fly. One step at a time."

"How am I supposed to keep up appearances at school? I don't mean relationships or controlling emotions anymore. School eats up so much of my time. I'd rather be out here focusing on this. I really want to give this a chance."

Devin took a deep breath. "That's actually something we were going to talk about tonight. You know better than anyone—we're rushed. Thod and your parents agreed you don't need to do homework anymore. But we can't have teachers getting suspicious about your grades plummeting. We don't normally have to go this far, but we're going to have your work taken care of for you."

"What?" Mel could hardly believe what she heard. "I've never cheated in my life! Well, there was that one time in first grade I helped a friend on a spelling test. But we got caught, and Mrs. Goff tore up our tests." She shook her head. "I promised myself I'd never cheat again."[k]

"I know, and that's a great thing about you—you have integrity and a good work ethic." He added with a smile, "You're a good girl, right?"

She considered the course of action that had been decided on. Focusing on her priorities, cheating on homework seemed pretty trivial. She accepted it with a heavy heart. "I get it."

"We're only doing it because we feel it's necessary. It's risky even giving an excuse, like you started experiencing migraines or something like that. While we can use those kinds of covers to our advantage, we want to avoid suspicion at all costs. Every incident out of place adds to the list of an Ivy on the hunt."

"And still no news about Blake or Ken, about other Ivies identifying me? Or ... that one guy? I don't feel like I've had any extra eyes on me since I returned."

Devin shook his head. "No, there hasn't been any chatter. We're not sure how many Ivies are positioned in our neighborhoods and school. For all we know, they only had those two, plus a general—which we know for sure they always have, and we need to stay vigilant on that account. Most communities aren't as concentrated, so when our dads teamed up, it went against the norm. As long as they haven't figured that out, they may not have dedicated as many soldiers as they normally would for this large of a group of Seeders."

"But we really have no way of knowing? It could just be a general left, or half a dozen Ivies? What about back-ups, replacements?" she asked.

"Mid-year is highly suspicious. It's not impossible; even humans move mid-school-year sometimes, but it's less noticeable to move troops in the summer, like me showing up at the beginning of the year." He added, "We've got good intel to monitor that kind of thing."

Mel thought about it, trying to remember any instances where there may have been the tiniest hint of an Ivy, of something off. "I recall ... overhearing you talking to your 'uncle' a while back, in his office. He's obviously not a brother, but I get the impression he knows what's going on..."

He flashed her a stern look. "You know I can't give you a 'yes' or 'no' about anyone." He reached over and squeezed her hand. "Whether he's blissfully unaware of what's going on around him, or he's deeply entrenched in our lives, just know the Vice Principal is a good guy, alright?"

"Okay. I guess you can at least give me *one* person to feel good about. I'm assuming you would organize things so you knew for sure none of us were hosted by an Ivy," she conceded.

They pulled up to Mel's house and parked. "Do we know what my story will be? My parents and I haven't really talked about it... Will they need to move?"

Devin turned in his seat to face her. "There's a list of options. Your parents, Thod included, will narrow it down. But you normally get some say in it. Obviously, we try to avoid anything too tragic. Throwing a fake funeral is not only expensive, it's hard on everyone."

"Yeah ... well, if I jump off that cliff and I'm not ready, at least they won't need to fake one of those."

Devin frowned at the grim statement. "You'll make it."

They got out of the car back at her house and she gave him a hug. "You're not just a great boyfriend. You're a great teacher, and friend, too."

He tucked her hair behind her ears. "And you are not just a great girlfriend."

After going inside, Mel slowly climbed the stairs to the second floor, using the railing to pull her up. Her feet were heavy from exhaustion. But more than that, every step was intentionally taken, deep in thought.

Everyone else had turned in for the night. She changed into pajamas, then sat on her bed and focused on seeing her roots. They bulged out like thick veins and made their way down, twisting around her legs—only when she transformed, of course. She'd been disgusted with them at first; they reminded her of the Swamp Thing. But they came to be a unique part about her she didn't mind. Like fingerprints, no two Seeders had the same root growth pattern. She looked down, feeling them extending to her knee now. Her legs were like a calendar—each small extension was one more moment counting down to the inevitable rooting.

Devin had to explain it to her a couple of times back at the safe house. The complexities of their maturation process and limitation in their powers were pretty intense. All Seeder boys rooted around the time of their sprouting. Devin said their roots didn't run as deep, and that's why they could come and go more often, and even reside permanently in the human world, without harm and without losing their powers. Mel had come to understand that 'rooting' was really just another way of describing their connection, and even dependence, on the energy found in the Green Lands. The females were more connected—that explained the difference in energy they could harness, but also the physical limitations and requirements they had to live by.

Mel ran a finger across her lower roots. The growth was slow, but constant. Their path down to her ankles *literally* represented her ticking clock. Her physiology and permanent binding to whichever world she was in at the time, depended entirely on these things. Once they reached her ankles and wrapped around, forming a link on each one, the process would be complete.

Still staring at her roots, Mel mused on the events of the day. Something about that night had cleared her head. It wasn't just about comparing pros and cons. It wasn't what she wanted versus what others wanted, or about what she had perceived as being taken from her. She started to see this opportunity in a new light. A giant step in fulfilling her potential.

Mel thought about her mom's words, her regrets. She pondered on Devin's insistence that he wouldn't ask her to give up anything for him—it was a grand gesture considering his declaration of love.

She needed to stop fighting her decision. She needed to pick her path and face it without wavering.

Looking around her room, Mel saw things through a different lens. They were just that: things. Her painting supplies—if her biological mom liked to paint, she could get a new set there. Trinkets, clothes, even her oldest stuffed animals— replaceable, and the memories attached to them could stay with her.

What future was she really going to miss out on here? Art was a hobby. Travel was a fun goal. But she hadn't narrowed down what she would study in college; she still had a half dozen options she was considering. Mel shook her head with a slight smile. Her parents may have kept her true nature a secret, but they'd prepared her for this. They'd always told her to take time off after high school to consider her options. They'd known this day would come, and she loved them that much more for it. And the Green Lands, everything there was so ... simple, basic, compared to the modern world she'd grown up in. But simple didn't mean inferior. She now understood what Devin meant by there being a pull to the Green Lands. She'd felt that by the cliff.

Mel considered what pictures she would take, starting a to-do list for her remaining time. She'd need to print some photos, like Bonnie had done ... as she wouldn't be taking her cell phone where they were all currently stored. Devin had explained that electricity didn't work the same there—modern human electronics were useless. Mel asked herself what she would wear, and if she should pack things up to make it easier for her parents to donate. Would she take time to revel in a rite of passage like burning her school books, too? She still had a little while for those minor details. She could think about them while zoning out in classes.

But she'd made the most important decision. Mel was going home.

She took a deep, calming breath and closed her eyes, imagining what it would look like from the clouds. The weight of the decision melted away. This was the most at peace she'd been since the day of her attack.

The chime of her phone pulled her down from the clouds.

A text from Zach.

"Crap," she whispered.

Mel was itching for classes to pass by on Friday; each brought her closer to the weekend with free time to train. So naturally, each class felt hours longer than the one before.

Fourth period came with a surprise. A new lab partner was paired up with Mel. A new student, having transferred in the middle of the year. A boy. She focused more on controlling her energy as her mind ran through every scenario. Could he be a new Ivy, if her cover was compromised? Could he be another brother in their Seeder network, set up as extra protection?

Or is he just a normal human and you're completely losing it?

The Seeders were convinced Blake and Ken got lucky, that they hadn't actually known Mel's true identity before the attack. And it made sense. She'd been lit up like a Christmas tree, out in the open on the day of her botched bloom. Anyone, green folk or human, would have known something was up just by walking past the gym at the right moment that day.

Not so lucky for the Seeders, was the fact that at least one Ivy remained—and knew Seeders were around.

Ken and Blake's bodies were gone. And they'd been pierced by Seeder darts. No news reports ever spoke about them, no rumors circulated at school, and Seeder attempts to look into their cover stories for having gone missing turned up nothing—the lies about Blake and Ken's disappearances were just as reliable as any Seeder or Ivy fake identity or cover.

Mr. Rasmussen asked Mel to hang back after class. He waited until all the other students had filed out of the room, casting a glance at the cut-out window in the door.

"Ms. Walters. I wanted to chat. Is everything okay?"

"Yeah, of course," she lied. Things were less stressful now that she'd made her choice, but there was still a heck of a lot going on. *Especially* with a new concern popping up in his class in the form of her lab partner.

"It just seems like your mind has been wandering. You used to always be so active in class."

She kicked herself for not doing a better job at keeping up the facade. *Just a couple more weeks.* "No, sorry. Just family stuff."

"I always care about my students, especially the bright ones that show a love for learning. Is there anything I can help with? I'm here if you need someone to talk to."

"No. I'm fine, thanks. I'll swing by the guidance counselor if things don't settle down."

"Sounds good. Just remember the offer stands. I'd hate for your final grade to suffer because of a bump in the road."

The classroom door swung open. Tom stood at the door.

"Oh, hi, Melody," he addressed her once he noticed there was a student in the room. He turned to Mr. Rasmussen. "I was walking by when I remembered our need to talk about that suspension. Could you swing by my office at the end of the day?"

"No problem."

Tom nodded. "You've got a crowd lining up out there—make sure you give Ms. Walters a note if she's going to be late for her next class."

"Of course. We were just going to discuss our newest transfer. We were finishing up."

Tom raised an eyebrow. "Newest transfer?"

Mr. Rasmussen smiled. "New lab partner."

"Ah, gotcha." Tom nodded. "I think that would be great for them both. Anyway, sorry to interrupt you. I'll see you later." Tom threw Mel a smile and left the room.

Mr. Rasmussen turned his attention back to Mel. "Rick just transferred from Lakeside. I think you'd make a good partner to help him get caught up. He could really use a friend, transferring this late in the school year. That won't be a problem, will it?"

A month ago, this would have seemed like a regular conversation. 'How are you doing?' 'Get to know the new kid that showed up out of nowhere in the middle of the school year.' But now, everything was suspicious.

Mel focused on keeping her energy in check. Her emotions flowed over her heart, but under the surface enough so her body language didn't give her away, either. She realized this was the kind of training her brothers went through for years, but she was getting an immersive crash course, on-the-job training, in the middle of fighting to stay undetected.

"Yeah, sure. Why not?" she offered.

Mel grabbed her backpack and left the classroom. Mr. Rasmussen opened his door for students to find their seats. She pulled out her phone and texted Devin.

<Office. Now.>

Chapter 25

Devin arrived at the office only moments after Mel.

"I need to lie down for a minute in the sick room," she said. "The Vice Principal called you down here? You in trouble?"

He picked up the hint with a nod. Mel patted herself on the back. She was getting used to this working-undercover business. Knowing Mr. Simons was at worst benign, she hoped he could pull some strings and help.

Mel headed to the nurse's station and Devin pulled out his phone.

She put on her best act of a stomachache to garner pity and gain entrance to go lie down. Fortune shined on them; there was no one else in the sick room right then.

"Do you think you need to call home? Or do you want to wait awhile and see how you feel?" the nurse asked.

"I don't want to bug my parents. Can I just lie down for a little while?"

The nurse finished checking her temperature. "Sure. If it gets worse, let me know. There's a trash can right here next to the bed if you need it."

The phone on the wall rang, and the nurse answered. "Sure, I'll be right there."

After hanging up, she turned to her patient. "I'm just going to be a few doors over. I'll be back in a while to check on you."

As soon as she left the room, Devin slipped in and rushed to Mel's side.

"What's up? Are you actually sick?"

"I'm fine," she said.

He let out a sigh. "A bit of an elaborate plan for a make-out rendezvous in the middle of the day, don't you think?" He smirked.

She scolded him with her eyes. "I'm worried. I figured it's best to pass on this information in person, not in text, right?"

He motioned for her to continue.

"Mr. Rasmussen... He was being weird. He seemed pretty concerned about how I'm doing. Could he be an Ivy?"

Devin's face gave nothing away.

She continued, "Or, if he was worried, could he be..." She asked with her eyebrows, not daring to finish her question. Could he be her dad, or Devin's dad? Just checking on her, knowing she was going through a hard time?

It was Devin's turn to give the disapproving expression. "You know I can't tell you either way. We're not playing a guessing game. But it's good to hear observations I can pass on. He lives on your street, right? Was there anything else?"

"Yeah, I pass his house every day when I walk to school. And he just partnered me up with a guy that recently transferred," she added.

"The new kid didn't attack you in the middle of class, right?" he said matter-of-factly. "We're aware of any new transfers."

"So ... maybe I overreacted."

"No, it's good. This is the kind of observation that helps keep you safe. But maybe next time don't be quite as cryptic, just give me a smidge more to know you're not in imminent danger?"

Her face scrunched in embarrassment. "Sorry ... yeah..." She didn't want to sound crazy or waste any more time, but figured she might as well just throw it all out there. "One more thing." She lowered her voice. "Since there are two Seeders teamed up in our town, could there also be more than one Ivy general?"

Devin tilted his head ever so slightly. This time he gave away more. He looked curious. "Anything's possible."

"It's probably nothing... No, it's stupid."

"Mel, spit it out. We don't have a lot of time."

"Tom?" She waited a second. "I know. You can't say anything. He came by when Mr. Rasmussen was talking with me. It probably meant nothing. He thought it was good for me to help the new transfer. And then I thought about how he asked me weird questions after Blake first attacked me, and then he asked about you and Ben when he caught me looking in the gym after spring break. But no ... he couldn't be. I can't imagine an Ivy getting so close with my parents. I'm just being paranoid now. But ... then again ... Blake and Ken..." She rubbed her temples. "Gosh, I'm sorry. I'm losing it. Everyone seems suspicious. I was even starting to think my P.E. teacher could be one of them. I can't wait until I can put this all behind me."

She figured she might as well round off her explanation of suspicions. "Mr. Cress, my gym teacher. He was there and noticed how sick I was before the attack. He didn't insist I come down here to the sick room, so maybe he was keeping an eye on me. And ... I saw him jogging down our street the other day. Does he even live close to me?"

Devin shrugged. "We'll look into all of them, okay? I promise, we won't let you down."

She'd almost felt the tiniest bit calmer a couple of hours ago, working on her mental to-do list for leaving her human life behind. Now her heart wouldn't stop racing. Maybe the Ivies had moved on. If they knew who she was, why wouldn't they have come by her house to finish her off already? What was their plan?

"How do they even find us? My parents told me there's only a few million green folk back in the Green Lands. What's the likelihood they'd focus resources in the right places to find us? Or care enough to send more backup?"

Devin frowned. "I can't give you all the answers you want."

Mel huffed. The secrets were getting old.

"It's not what you think." He looked her squarely in the eyes. "We genuinely don't know some of those things. How they find us—sometimes ending up in the same places as we are in the human world. We don't know how all their powers work." He shrugged. "Or even how all of *ours* work." He frowned again. "Love, I don't know. I wish I did."

Her heart sank further, grasping at straws. "You've never met one other than Blake, right? It sounds like interactions between our people are rare. Maybe I'm not worth the bother?"

He held her hand. "No. I've never knowingly met one other than Blake. But you've seen their handiwork. We keep ourselves safe by staying within our borders and staying hidden when here. They could happily stay in their own kingdom. Not taking this threat seriously only risks your life."

She felt a headache coming on.

Devin must have sensed it, squeezing her hand. "I would kill for you and I would die for you. You know that, right?"

Mel swallowed hard. She understood that—he was a soldier, one of her assigned protectors. She wished he didn't have to be either of those things.

He flashed a comforting smile. "And so would Ben, and all of our brothers and dads. I understand the vast majority of human teens aren't really up to snuff on this kind of thing. But they don't grow up the way we do." His voice was soft, his face relaxed. "I know we dropped the ball. Epically. Unforgivably. Idiotically. That was once. We won't make that mistake again. Please try to trust the plan." He lifted her hand, giving it a gentle kiss. "I would have killed for you before I even knew you, before I loved you. If you can't trust our dads, please try to trust me."

She loved that he knew how to wash away her worries. How he could make sense in this chaos. "I'll do my best." She gazed into his eyes. "I really do lo—"

Their time was up; the nurse walked back in. "Excuse me, do you need some help?" she asked Devin.

He was still crouched down next to where Mel was sitting. "No, I just saw Mel come in here and wanted to make sure she was okay."

The nurse frowned. "This isn't a social club. Get back to class. Make sure to grab a tardy slip from the office."

"Yes, ma'am, sorry." He gave Mel a reassuring smile as she lay down.

They met at their lockers after school. "So, did you get a tardy, or did you get a pass from the Vice Principal?" she asked.

Devin raised his eyebrows. "I don't believe my attendance record is any of your concern."

Mel leaned in and whispered, "Just wanted to see if I was right about strings being pulled by a certain someone with power."

He whispered back, "I'm insulted you think my uncle would give me preferential treatment. Surely, that's what you're implying?" He straightened and asked at a normal volume, "By the way, who do you want to hang out with tonight?"

She stood up straight, rolling her eyes. "Fine."

His warning, the one that ended the conversation, was his way of asking if she wanted to train with him that night, or if she would be punished with Ben. Not that Ben was bad, but she and Devin were on better terms now, and she'd rather spend the time with him.

And he'd won their secretive battle of wills and wits. She wanted to find out if Mr. Simons was in the know; a helpful human, or perhaps even one of their dads. But she knew better. She needed to stop testing Devin. Though she *was* a little turned on by the thrill of the chase, and his competence as a covert operative was undeniably sexy.

They left directly from school for their nightly training.

"A warehouse? We have a whole warehouse?" Mel had assumed they would be doing more flight training outside.

"Our dads have had a long time to accumulate wealth here. It's not like they squander money on vacations," Devin explained before giving her the grand tour.

The warehouse was closed tight. Doors locked; windows covered. They would have total privacy with lots of space. There wasn't much to see in there, only the necessities.

"As you progress, we'll obviously need to work outside at night. But this is perfect when the sun is up, especially for flight basics."

They did a quick review of what they had gone over the night before. She still struggled the most with keeping her blades out, especially when focusing on other things she needed to do concurrently.

"Think of it like good posture," Devin coached, "the kind no one has anymore. If your shoulders are up and back, your neck and the rest of your body are in the right places and work better. Imagine your blades like that. Lock them in place."

She visualized it the way he explained, then smiled when it appeared to do the trick. They did more practice 'communing with the wind' as he called it. A warehouse wasn't the draftiest of places, but they had fans they would use at different speeds. Even then, she would need to learn to manipulate the air without a breeze.

The latter half of the night, they moved over to a stack of squishy foam mats. She realized things were getting serious when he mentioned next up was learning to hover.

"I don't expect you to fly around in here. We'll start with the fans. You'll focus with everything we've been doing, and you'll learn to balance yourself and get a small lift."

That was a huge leap from everything she had learned so far. They used different settings on the fans and changed up the direction of the air flow. For hours, she worked to balance the variables required for flight—mental concentration, proper posture, and centering energy in her core while carefully spreading enough out to the rest of her body. She felt defeated when she barely got the teeniest, tiniest lift at the end of the night, despite Devin's praises.

Mel lay face down on the padded mat.

"Do you have any more in you tonight?" he asked.

She moaned.

"I can't tell if that was a 'heck yes' moan, or a 'screw you' moan," he teased.

She rolled her head to the side. "I'm calling it."

She wanted to get home and shower. Her distracted mind was probably hampering her efforts, anyway.

Her phone chimed after she scraped up the wherewithal to stand. It was Zach. <Still on for midnight?>

She was grateful none of their recent practices had involved bruises. Zach wouldn't be fretting about her well-being that night.

She turned to Devin. "You promise, no one's noticed *anything* suspicious? No more Ivy movement out there?"

He gave her a reassuring smile. "I promise you. We're being extra careful."

Chapter 26

Zach had been texting Mel about wanting to spend time with her. She had been too tied up with her secrets to carve out time or attention for him like she'd hoped to. But when it came down to it, she'd made her decision, and he deserved to know where she stood. She agreed to meet him down the street from her house at midnight.

The only sound in the house was a box fan her dad always had on at night for white noise. Mel gave herself plenty of time to inch her way through the house, to sneak out undetected. Slipping out through the small garage door was her best bet to avoid the motion-sensor lights at the front and back doors. She power-walked to the edge of the street, glancing over her shoulder regularly. A figure approached from the shadows—Zach was on time. The irony wasn't lost on her that every part of her life had now become a clandestine affair; full of secret meetings, code words, fake identities.

She launched herself into his arms in a bear hug. It felt amazing. She lingered there, not wanting the moment to end. Once she pulled away, things were going to change, and there would be no undoing it.

"Hey, what's with all the mystery?" Zach asked.

"Things are just crazy, and busy."

"Okay... You're still acting weird. Are you alright?"

"You know, all things considered, I'm doing well."

He lifted his eyebrows; his curiosity was apparent under the faint glow of a nearby streetlamp. "All things considered?"

"This may sound weird, but can you tell me about your childhood before we met?" she asked, thinking this was the only way she might be able to suss out, for absolute certain, if he was somehow an Ivy. Of course, if he had convinced her of his ignorance thus far, he probably wouldn't skip a beat in continuing to keep his identity a secret.

"Umm..." He continued to look confused. "Well, what do you want to know? You know I was born in Dallas and moved here the summer before we met in school. That's ... all..."

She sighed. What did she really hope to learn from questioning him about his past?

"Is this about the other day? Do you need more time? Or..." He squinted as if trying to read her mind.

"Devin and I ... are... Things are complicated right now..."

He bit his lower lip. "'Complicated' isn't exactly synonymous with 'broken up.'"

"I need you to understand that he's not the reason for my decision. Neither are you." She realized she wasn't making sense. "Dating isn't my main focus right now..."

He was visibly disappointed, but not devastated—it wasn't an outright rejection.

Zach shook his head. "Okay, Mel. I understand. You're still my best friend. And I've waited this long; I can wait until you sort out whatever it is you're dealing with."

Her heart sank. Time—he didn't realize how finite hers was.

She'd been fighting a battle in her heart, ever since she'd found out she might need to leave. And she couldn't keep it inside anymore. Zach had been hurt by Tabatha leaving, too. It would be that much worse, knowing now how he felt about her, to just leave him without more of an explanation. She was certain he could be trusted.

"I need to tell you something, and doing so puts lives at risk, especially mine—which I know sounds like overkill, but hear me out." She had been working on how to word it just right all afternoon.

He looked understandably concerned by her ominous pronouncement.

"I'm not from here." She looked to see if there was a reaction.

Nothing that gave him away yet.

"And I'm going to be leaving." She waited to see what he would do. If he were an Ivy, surely vague hints such as this would be evidence enough to elicit a response.

"You're not really making any sense. From where? Going where?" he asked.

"I need you to promise to not freak out. Look into my eyes."

He cocked his head slightly. "Okay..."

She pushed energy to her eyes, gazing into his while hers changed.

His jaw dropped. "What's going on? How are you doing that?"

She suppressed the change, reverting to normal.

"I'm not from here."

He scoffed. "Are you trying to tell me you're an alien?"

She grinned at his guess. "No. Not quite that crazy... At least, I don't think so."

She cupped her hands, moving in closer, practically pressing herself against him to use their bodies as a shield. She looked down, and he followed her gaze. A small ball of light rested in her palms. She reabsorbed it. "It's not just a magic trick." She moved back a pace.

"But how do you do it?" he whispered. "Where are you from? How long have you known?"

"Even if I had the time, I couldn't explain everything to you." She frowned. "I'm moving away in less than two weeks; I ... might not ever see you again."

"Why? Why can't you stay? I can keep a secret!" Zach protested.

Mel started to get more emotional than she'd expected to. She'd worked it all out; she'd practiced her lines to avoid this.

"I believe you; I just don't have a choice." She knew that wasn't true, but it was an extremely watered-down version of the truth. She didn't have a choice in the *timing* of it...

He tilted his head, looking past her. "We have trouble."

She whipped around, ready to do whatever she needed to. It was Ben. Of course, it was Ben. It was *always* Ben.

She rattled off a warning. "I told you lives were in danger. Yours could be, mine absolutely is. You can't say anything, you have to pretend like you've never seen anything, or heard anything. Like nothing has changed. I'm serious, Zach."

He was breathing heavier and turned his gaze back to Ben, who was quickly closing in on them.

She looked back. "Ben won't hurt me. He's not the problem. Promise me, you know nothing."

"Yeah, yeah, of course." He nodded.

"Get back to the house, Mel!" Ben ordered from a few feet away, as loudly and forcefully as possible without being too loud for that time of night.

She gave Zach another quick squeeze. "You need to go."

He looked distressed, as if not wanting to let her leave, afraid for her after her ominous warning.

"Go. I'll be fine."

He started backing away down the street, keeping his eyes on them.

Ben scowled at Zach, then turned to follow Mel as she ran past him back to the house.

Ben caught up to her, entering through the front door right behind her.

"YOU ARE SO SELFISH!" he belted once the door was shut.

Mel wasn't sure if he was mad just because she'd snuck out, or if he had actually seen or heard anything.

"YOU KNOW WHAT? I AM!" she screamed back. "Sometimes we *get* to be selfish."

He glared. "I'm at least glad to know the new security cameras work."

She swallowed hard, feeling beyond stupid. They obviously would have added more security measures; she just hadn't noticed them.

Pam and George rushed out of their room at the commotion.

"What's going on?!" George demanded.

Ben was seething mad. "Zach. She revealed herself to Zach."

Pam and George looked at her disapprovingly.

She defended her choice, throwing her hands in the air. "Why does it matter? If he was an Ivy, we'd know now. You're welcome. Then you could kill him and stop worrying about it. Just another mark on your tally board. But he's NOT one of them."

Still clearly livid, but no longer shouting, Ben let Mel get under his skin. "You have absolutely no way of knowing for certain what he is. You're a horrible judge of character. You're a moron! You even think our dad is one of them."

Her eyebrows raised at the slip and he pursed his lips, obviously realizing he'd said too much.

She looked from Ben to her parents. Their eyes were wide. They shook their heads ever so slightly, remaining tight-lipped.

"You know what? I don't even care right now. You think I'm selfish. But I think Zach deserves closure about my leaving, just as much as my parents do. Even Bonnie got to tell her brother and sister."

Ben gave her a death glare. "Do you know what happens when a Seeder family gets compromised? Or were you and Devin too busy groping each other to discuss the risks?"

Mel clenched her teeth.

George spoke up. "That's enough, Ben!"

Ben turned his anger on George. "It's not even *close* to enough!" He glanced back at Mel before dropping his gaze with a guilty frown. "*We* all let you down, not realizing you hadn't been wearing your jade." Ben looked back up, meeting Mel's gaze. "But what you just did. That was *all* you."

Mel averted her eyes in shame.

"A few years ago, an entire family from a neighboring village was wiped out. *Every* daughter. The dad and *every* son sent to this world. Maybe you're too selfish to care, because you're the last daughter from our family left here. But Dad and I are still here, too. And maybe I thought you'd give a damn about Devin's safety, and that of his family."

"I'm sorry," Mel whispered with tears in her eyes.

Ben glanced at the ceiling, shaking his head. "We do the best we can with what we have. But when things go wrong for us, it can go from bad to unbelievably worse in a heartbeat." He turned his gaze back to Mel, his eyes scanning her face. "Or would you have preferred Dad to raise twelve daughters all alone, secluded their entire youth up in the mountains somewhere, to keep you safe? This isn't a game."

She frowned. "I know it's not a game."

Ben narrowed his eyes. "Go to bed. You have a whole day of training ahead of you." He stomped up the stairs.

Mel followed after him to her own room, unable to even look at her parents as she passed them. While she normally would have stayed up all night festering over what Ben had said, her mental, emotional, and physical capacities had met their limits. She was out cold the moment her head hit the pillow.

Chapter 27

Mel woke to a dozen texts from Zach. She kicked herself for not texting him before falling asleep—reminding him to keep his cool, and reassuring him she was fine. And of course, he was freaking out.

<Are you ok?>

<Mel?>

<I'm worried about you.>

<Please answer me.>

<Are you ok?>

<I promise I won't say anything. Please just respond.>

She sent off a reply. <I'm fine. Sorry. Went straight to bed.>

He immediately responded. <You scared the daylights out of me! Can we meet more to talk about this?>

<No. Don't text. Business as usual.> She couldn't risk her phone, or his, falling into the wrong hands. Written communication always had to be extremely limited and coded amongst the Seeder network in the human world.

Mel finally rolled out of bed at 10 a.m. Only her mom was still at home, doing breakfast dishes. Sitting down at the table, Mel looked at her mom sheepishly, waiting for her to speak first.

Her mom met her gaze and continued cleaning, eventually breaking the silence. "Ben's right. You can't be doing this."

Mel switched to staring at the table. "I don't mean to keep screwing things up. But I felt like it was a calculated risk worth taking."

"Maybe your calculations were off." This was not Pam's kind, nurturing voice. She was ticked. "You could have told him your cover story the night before you left. He'd have more closure than anyone else will, with you disappearing suddenly." She huffed. "You didn't have to give away the farm. He didn't have to learn about your true nature."

Pam and Ben had both made some extremely valid points. And Mel realized that. "But..." She still tried to defend her decision. "I *know* Zach is good. And I remember how hard it was for Zach and me when Tabatha left. I didn't want him to go through that again. It's not fair to him."

Pam sat down with her at the table. "You, of all people, know that life isn't fair. You didn't sign up for all of this. We don't always get what we want. Zach will learn that lesson himself, one way or another." Pam stood up again. "You know who *did* sign up for this? All those boys working so hard to keep you safe, giving you a chance at finding your way home. Is it fair to them?" She walked away. "I'll be in my sewing room."

Mel sat in silence, stewing in the shame of her constant mistakes. She was pulled from her solitude by the front door opening. Walking up to Ben, who'd just come in, she looked down at the floor. "I can be ready to start in five minutes."

He walked past her. "Good for you, you're not my problem right now."

She looked up as he rounded the corner to go upstairs. "Devin said you were taking the first half of today."

He gave no reply as he continued to his room. Her phone chimed. It was Devin. <Be ready in half an hour.>

Mel sighed, shoving her phone back in her pocket. *Time for damage control.*

Walking into her mom's sewing room, Mel sat quietly on a spare rolling chair. Pam glanced over out of the corner of her eye, sorting through an old shortbread tin filled with miscellaneous bits and bobs.

"If I'm going to leave, I don't want to waste any of the time I have left fighting with you and Dad."

Pam sighed, turning to give Mel her attention. "If? I thought you'd decided."

Mel bit her lip. "I did. I just... You said Ivies don't bother humans, right? Maybe it's safer if I stay? For me? For everyone? Give up being a Seeder?" It hurt, just saying that out loud.

Pam shook her head with a frown. "If they know you're a Seeder, they're not going to wait and ask if your rooting has taken place, just to leave you alone. Your dad and I are relatively safe because they know I'm too old to be a Seeder female in the human world. Despite their lack of apparent ethics, I think Ivies want to avoid problems with humans as much as they can. This whole war, being played out in the shadows of the human world, is only possible because of the cover humans afford green folk. Ivies seem to want to avoid public discovery as much as Seeders do."

Mel looked down, fidgeting with her hands. "I can't win. I'm sorry. And I'm sorry Ben was a jerk to Dad last night."

Pam's sniffling caused Mel to look up.

"Ben wasn't wrong to be mad. We could have done things differently. Your dad and I will never be able to forgive ourselves for that."

Mel's eyes teared up. "But I do."

Pam gave her an appreciative smile. "I agree that we should put these arguments behind us. How about you keep being the amazing student I know you are? Instead of math, get some straight A's in catching breezes."

Mel grinned. "I'll see what I can do."

"You look well rested," Devin said as Mel got in the car.

She actually was, for a change, but the small talk felt almost condescending, despite his friendly voice. "You don't have to patronize me. I'm sorry." She thought about it. "I'm sorry about *some* things. Not everything." No one could convince her Zach wasn't safe. But she could admit to herself that the way she'd revealed herself to him hadn't been the smartest thing she'd ever done.

Her phone chimed.

Devin glanced over. "Zach?"

"Yeah, he's texting me every half hour to make sure I'm still alive. It's going to be a long weekend."

"Maybe we should put it on silent," Devin suggested.

Halfway to the warehouse she asked, "Is Ben not working with me because he's pissed?"

Devin didn't answer.

She wasn't surprised. "Now I know what it feels like to be a pariah."

He spoke calmly. "Mel. I could go off on you. Trust me. I wanted to, when I found out. But I'm guessing you've already had that. You need to be more careful in your choices. Even in the Green Lands we know what Pandora's box is. You can't *fix* everything with an apology, and you can't just *unsay* something."

He sighed. "I told myself I wouldn't lecture you. Let's just focus on the work at hand. We don't even know if we have two more weekends. Let's make the most of this one."

After another five minutes of silence, he chuckled and rubbed his forehead. "Honestly, maybe we should be thanking you. Everything has gone so smoothly for our families up until this point. What's the purpose of all our training if we can't use it, right? You're keeping us on our toes."

Mel pursed her lips, shaking her head. He was always generous with her.

"I get that you guys don't trust my judgment. But I'm telling you, he's a good guy. Just like you. I know it."

Devin smirked. "While I appreciate the vote of confidence, you hated Ben and liked Blake..."

She wrinkled her nose. "Maybe I don't have the best track record... But," she raised a finger, "back then I didn't understand what was going on. I do now, and I'm still saying Zach's a good guy."

He sighed again. "I get it. He's your friend. You like him."

She frowned. "You guys don't understand why I told him. But you didn't see his face after he admitted to looking for Tabatha's obituary."

Devin furrowed his brow. "What?"

"He really misses her. I couldn't tell him what happened to her. But he confessed he's been looking into her disappearance."

Devin scratched his head. "Well, that's good to know. It didn't occur to you that an Ivy would be serious about tracing a returned Seeder's cover story?"

She scowled, annoyed she'd said anything. "It's not like that. We were both really close to her."

"Really?" He raised his eyebrows. "Equally close? Did he kiss her, too?"

"Never mind." Mel crossed her arms. "Just ... you guys need to do a better job with your cover stories if you don't want people digging."

He shook his head. "Yeah, we'll see what we can do. I mentioned your dad killed a couple of Ivies last year, right? It's not like anything that's happened with you, but we got kind of spooked. There were other circumstances; it wasn't great. She left earlier than she had to. I'll admit, it was rushed."

They pulled up to the warehouse. "Text him that you won't be responding for a few hours. We don't want him filling out a missing person's report."

They worked for two hours before breaking for a bite to eat.

"We're going on a field trip," he announced, grabbing his car keys. "Follow me."

Devin wouldn't say where they were going. It had to be important if they were taking time away from training.

Mel was confused when they finally pulled into a half-full parking lot on the other side of town, facing a brick building. "A library?"

"Wait here," he instructed.

After five minutes, he came back out. He was visibly unhappy, but he didn't take his mood out on her when he got back to the car.

"You get one chance, Mel. I mean it. And I want you to remember, with absolute clarity, what your priorities are, and what the effects of your choices are."

He spoke slowly, enunciating each word. "I want you to walk in there with one motto in mind, okay? 'Bare minimum.' You started this; you make this go away." He searched her face. "Room 12A. You have one hour, not a minute more."

Mel was still unclear what he was expecting her to do as she opened the car door. She stopped for a moment when he added, "And this never happened, do you understand?"

She nodded.

The silence in the library was punctuated by the soft beep of a barcode scanner, a printer busy at work in the back room, and the occasional whisper between patrons. Mel asked a librarian where she would find room 12A and made her way to it without much trouble. There was a hallway with several small rooms, private rooms with narrow windows in the doors. They could be used for quiet studying or meetings of perhaps four people each, max. She opened the door to see Zach. He sprang from his chair and pulled her into a hug.

"Are you really okay?" he asked.

"Yes, I told you. I'm fine."

They sat down, facing each other with the small table between them.

"Yeah, well, you'll have to forgive me for worrying after the bombshell you dropped last night."

She fidgeted with her hands and scrunched her face. "Sorry, that could have gone smoother."

He sighed. "You weren't kidding about this being life and death, were you?"

She shook her head. "Wish I was."

"That boyfriend of yours is a piece of work. This would be the first time I've been threatened with being murdered in my sleep. And trust me, he was convincing."

She pressed her fingers to her lips.

"Let's start with this. Just to get it out of the way. How much is *my* life in danger? And my family?"

She lowered her hands. "He would do it." She repeated Devin's advice to herself. 'Bare minimum.' But she felt the emphasis was necessary for Zach to realize the severity of the situation. They needed to rein it in before it got away from them. "And he would get away with it."

Zach looked uncomfortably surprised by her casual confirmation.

"But only if you did something to betray me. That would be the *only* reason he or anyone else would go after you. Same with your family."

He nodded. "That is ... good to know... Just so we're absolutely clear, what constitutes betraying you?"

She frowned. "I'm sorry, I never should have said anything. Ignorance is bliss, right?" She traced patterns with her finger on the table. "I guess I would say there are two ways you could betray me and it wouldn't end well. The first is to attack me."

His face contorted at the incredulous suggestion.

"I know, you would never hurt me. Zach, I get it. We're just laying it all out on the table, right?"

"Right. No hurting you. Twisting your arm or leaving you bruised isn't on my agenda."

That felt like a cheap shot. But ... fair enough, considering he always came to her aid. It had to be insulting to have his integrity questioned like that.

"Okay. The second way you can betray me is to let anyone know about me. My world. My people. And I know you can keep a secret, but it's not just that. There are..." She paused to be careful and concise, asking herself, *Does he need to know this? Will this put someone else at risk?* "There are people that want to hurt me. Think of it like the witness protection program. Yeah, that's a good comparison. They don't know who I am. But they want to."

She pondered, asking herself if she should tell him they had already tried. No, that would only make him more worried. He seemed to understand how serious this was now.

"Any behavior out of the norm could tip them off. Looking around anxiously, asking me a question about all of this. We really have to pretend like everything is normal. I've only known about this a couple weeks. Hopefully, I've concealed it well enough that you didn't notice a change?"

He bobbed his head, wrinkling his nose.

That's reassuring... "Okay, other than the bruise and my fight with Devin. Nothing else too weird?"

"Yeah. I guess you were normal-ish."

She rolled her eyes. "Thanks. Glad to hear I'm doing so well. I'm giving myself a pass because we're so close that you might notice more than the thugs out there."

"Alright. I think we're clear. I have a blip in my memory from last night, I refrain from trying to hurt you, and I don't have to look over my shoulder every waking moment? Or I guess even when I'm not awake, judging by what lover boy said."

Mel tried to keep a straight face. "That pretty much sums it up. See? Easy peasy."

He frowned. "And what about you? Why do people want to hurt you? How can I help keep you safe?"

She blushed. Always wanting to be the knight in shining armor. "Other than keeping my secret, there's nothing you can do. It's being handled. They want to hurt me because I'm different. They are ... specific people, with specific reasons."

"Wow, could you be any more vague?" he mocked.

She frowned. "The only reason I even told you was for your benefit. I didn't want..." She stopped herself. Would mentioning Tabatha's ghosting be giving too much information? "I didn't want you to worry about me when I suddenly disappear. Because I will. And I want you to know it doesn't have anything to do with you. And that I'll be safer, and happy. And I'm sorry, because I know it's bad timing, now that I know how you feel about me, about ... us."

He looked down at the table. "Why do you have to leave so soon? And if it's so important to leave quickly, why are you waiting?"

Her heart sank, thinking of their many years together, all of them filled with great memories. "Remember what you saw last night? I'm physically not normal. It's related to that. That's all you need to know. I don't get to choose the timing. No one does." She reached over, grabbing his hand, getting his full attention. "If I could delay it, I would risk hiding here longer. Things ... could have been different. I... I can't give you the chance you want. I'm sorry." She bit her lip. "You'll always be my best friend. I'm sorry."

They sat for a moment in silence. What more needed to be said? That was the bare minimum, right? She looked at the time on her phone—they still had half an hour left. They both stared at the desk between them. He, probably evaluating what he could ask. She, considering what else she could get away with telling him.

He braved the waters first, looking at their hands. "How many others are there involved in all of this? I'm guessing ... Ben, Devin, your parents?"

"My parents are normal. They're not my birth parents. Like you, they just want to protect me. I can't say anything about anyone else. Just know that Ben and Devin are good guys."

"How did this all start? How did you get wrapped up in all this?" he continued, laying out his curiosities.

"It's just a ... my people versus their people thing. I didn't do anything. I'm just lucky enough to be on the good side. Where I'm from, where I'm going back to, our people have been at war for a long time. I was sent here for my safety ... and I'll be safe again when I leave. It's complicated."

"And you're one hundred percent sure there's no other way to make this go away?" His eyes were sad. "You can't just leave for a little while and come back? We can't see each other ever again? Just losing another friend like Tabatha? Poof!"

She hoped her eyes hadn't given away anything when he mentioned Tabatha's name. "If I don't leave soon, I will ... miss out on very important parts of my future. I'm not able to go and just come back when I want."

She had thoroughly probed every possible loophole with Devin long ago. Why couldn't she just make the journey, form her roots, catch a breeze the next spring, and spend as much time in the human world as she wanted for the next decade, until she permanently rooted to the Green Lands? Completely logical, right? Nature was too cruel for that.

There was a reason she would only be able to visit once a year for a week in the spring, at least until she was old enough to have a clutch. If Seeder girls rooted in the Green Lands instead of the human world, they literally started dying when they came back for a visit. More than a week and necrosis set in. They rotted from the roots up with the lack of ambient energy. It would be painful, and there was no cure. There were a lot of lose-lose details in this package.

Was it fair to give him a speck of hope? Or risky? He deserved some honesty, and she wanted it personally, anyway. "There may be a chance—and I want to stress the word 'may'—that I can come back for a week each year to visit. But that's all. Don't ask how, don't ask when. But maybe we can set up something."

He perked up at the news. "And there's no possible way for me to visit you? Wherever you're going?"

Her heart ached as she shook her head. That was a resounding 'no.' Even if, somehow, miraculously, they found some kind of way to get him through a rift ... Zach would die. Seeder lands were still haunted by the poison that had forced them to send her to the human world in the first place.

She looked at her phone more frequently, monitoring the time. They had five minutes left, and she wasn't sure if Devin would come in to fetch her, or if he'd wait in the car. She didn't want to risk him coming in at the end.

"Can I give you a hug?" she asked, and Zach obliged. It gutted her, knowing they weren't going to have many more of these. There was so much more she wanted to say, to do. Instead, she leaned back from their hug, gave him a kiss on the cheek, and fashioned the least-sad smile she could muster.

Mel wanted to say more, but apparently, she wasn't very good at goodbyes. She didn't know if they would have another time to be so candid, but the sentimentality of the circumstance was getting to her. She wanted to dart out of there before she started to get choked up. Mel gave him one more quick hug. "See you at school on Monday. Business as usual." She left with two minutes to spare.

Devin was waiting in his car, listening to music on the radio. She wasn't sure if he'd been waiting there the whole time or if he'd left and come back, happening to get the same parking spot. She hopped in the car and buckled her seatbelt.

He handed her a smoothie; evidently, he *had* left. "Peace offering."

She smiled as the engine turned and they reversed, heading to the warehouse to get back to the perpetual grind of training. She took a sip of the orange-raspberry smoothie and glanced at Devin, grateful he'd given her the opportunity to work things out with Zach.

Devin didn't take his eyes off of the road. "If anyone asks, how did our afternoon workout go?"

She took a cleansing breath. "I'm exhausted from nonstop work, not even a single break."

"And you don't think we should have any problems?" he asked.

"We're set. Not a single lion, tiger, or bare ... minimum."

"Good."

It's not like the car was bugged, but ... plausible deniability.

Chapter 28

The entirety of Mel's weekend was consumed by training with Devin. They returned well past midnight both Saturday and Sunday. Her parents' lives were on hold for her; they focused on grabbing any moment where she could take a breather to reminisce over photo albums. They even cancelled Sunday dinner with Tom, which she felt was a bold move, something out of the ordinary that could give them away. She kind of wanted to say goodbye to him, granted ... he wouldn't know it was a goodbye. But she would still see him at school, and that would have to be enough.

Luckily, Zach got the hint and only texted her a couple of times a day to see how she was doing instead of twenty times.

That is, until Monday. He flooded her with texts Monday morning. He wasn't going to let her go that easily. Zach latched on to the little things that she had or had not said.

<This isn't your war to fight.>

<What happens if you stay?>

<Is not leaving an option?>

<I'm sure we can find another way.>

<It's not just me that will miss you.>

After the first one, all she replied was, <Business.>

After the second and third, she replied, <I don't know what you're talking about.>

She ignored him after the fourth.

After the fifth, she responded, <Lunch, doors by the tracks. STOP.>

She did her best to not throw him dirty looks that morning. And she didn't dare tell Devin their secret meeting hadn't gone off without a hitch after all.

Zach was waiting for her by the doors at the start of lunch. The gym hallway that led to the tracks was often pretty empty, which she definitely had the misfortune of knowing firsthand.

She ushered him out the door. "We can't talk about this. I told you. Especially in writing."

He pleaded, "Just give me some time to figure it out. I don't want to lose you. Even if it's just as a friend!"

She raised her voice, "You need to let it go."

"Everything okay here?"

They turned to look. Mr. Cress, her P.E. teacher, was walking past. "Shouldn't you two be in lunch or class? Care to explain?"

Mel tried her best, not sure if he had heard their conversation. "We just needed some fresh air; we'll head back to the lunchroom."

She and Zach put on the most genuine smiles they could manage and went back inside. She looked over her shoulder to see if Mr. Cress was observing them through the window, but she couldn't see him. Zach was practically knocked off of his feet as Mel shoved him to the side, into the closed gym door. She wasn't pulling any punches—she used her energy to boost that push. Mel had never expected to use her energy against Zach, and she hadn't fully intended to, but he was taking things too far.

She quietly nudged him through the door as he rubbed his shoulder in shock.

Pointing to the center of the room, she whispered in a threatening tone, "I was almost murdered, right there! If you want that to happen again, keep asking questions. If you want to be my friend, you'll accept that I have nothing else I can give you."

She promptly left the room, looking around the hall to make sure they weren't being followed. It took all she had to keep her energy locked away as she marched to the lunchroom. She regained her composure, opening the door to the bustling heart of the school full of ignorant human teenagers munching on highly questionable pizza and gossiping about normal things she no longer had time for.

She sat down next to Devin with a fake smile. "Chatting with Mr. Cress," she explained. It wasn't a lie. They'd spoken briefly, and it might or might not be important. But it gave her an excuse for being late. She gave Devin a kiss on the cheek and munched on one of his fries.

She glanced at the lunchroom door a couple of times, fighting back tears, trying to keep up her facade. It wasn't like Zach would be walking through them. He hadn't been eating with them, anyway. But this time, it wasn't because he'd kissed her and was hiding from Devin. *What did I just do?* He'd been taking things too far, but she had just crossed a line, too.

Zach didn't text her even once after that.

He didn't try to keep up pretenses, either. No locker drop-by, no hug, no anything. She hadn't even left, and their friendship was over. In her heart, she knew it.

The countdown to takeoff was merciless. That weekend, what might be their last full weekend by the looks of it, Ben finally agreed to instruct Mel again. His techniques helped round off everything Devin had been training her in. During daylight, they practiced in the warehouse. She was hovering successfully with different wind speeds and directions. At night, they drove to an old, abandoned speedway where she could get a running start to practice taking off.

Her first time at the old speedway, Ben explained the proper technique and pointed out a short ramp to help her get some lift. Mel stared at the ramp, rehearsing every instruction she'd received on catching a breeze. She focused the energy in her core and sprinted to the ramp. Right before running out of space at the end of it, she pushed energy to the muscles in her legs, kicking off and up. Before gravity called her back down, she rushed a portion of energy to her hands, balancing herself out. Almost simultaneously, with head-to-toe Seeder energy keeping her up, Mel focused on the wind. The breeze was barely there. Delicately reaching a smidge more into her core, she stretched extra energy to her hands and they glowed. Communing with the surrounding air, her hands stayed flat but tugged at the air and she rose higher.

Mel was flying. She was *actually* flying. Soaring to a few yards above the asphalt, she carefully turned her hands and body to veer to the left, hoping for a safe landing on the overgrown grass. The resistance of the surrounding air was like gently pushing against a trampoline; it had a little give. Aiming for the grass, Mel's eyes widened in preparation. She recalled Ben's advice about moving energy to her arms and legs last-minute to strengthen those muscles and bones so she wouldn't break anything on a rough landing. Unlike the soft pad keeping her safe in the warehouse, the ground outside was not so forgiving.

That first flight did not end gracefully. Nor did the first few after it. More than once, she had to pick a chunk of gravel out of an arm or leg before healing after a crash landing. But Ben was there to correct and cheer her through it.

In the end, the landing wouldn't be a concern. Once they crossed the Green Lands threshold, the energy would help balance her, and Thod could help guide her down. But if she couldn't nail a decent takeoff and sustain a breeze, she didn't have any hope. Not even two guides could carry her—Seeders weren't built to transport anyone but themselves. The act of taking seedling daughters between realms was only feasible on their first day, right after sprouting, because of how lightweight they were. Anything bigger or heavier, and it was too draining to make it.

It was decided that Saturday would be the day. They *might* be able to push it until Sunday, *maaaybe* Monday. But it was better to be safe, rather than sorry, when it came to unpredictable biology, and, heaven forbid, inclement weather that would make things more challenging.

Mel worried about Zach's radio silence. She messaged him a couple of times to ask how he was doing. He ignored her at school and via text. Her heart ached; so many years together, so many memories. Aside from her parents, she'd miss him the most. And her honesty had ruined everything between them. Honesty, and maybe a little temper.

Risking the potential red flags, Devin, along with Mel's family, made a last-resort grab at any time they could, to finish preparing her. A doctor's note was forged, excusing Mel from gym class, and instead of having to sit out in class and watch, they made it possible for her to leave school early, since gym was her last class of the day. That kind of exception, she assumed, could only be thanks to Devin's ties in the office. They wouldn't risk getting Devin or Ben out of class early, but she had the keys to her mom's car and the warehouse. She could get started on her own.

Friday arrived—still nothing from Zach. Mel typed up a dozen texts to ask him to come over one last time, only to erase each one. She couldn't risk screwing everything up now, just because he was throwing away their friendship. Or could she? How much risk did it really hold, when she knew he was human?

Each class she attended held special meaning. It was weird, studying the faces of those around her and knowing she might never see these people again. She actually liked school, but she was also excited to take courses in the Green Lands—lessons on culture, powers, history, all of it. She spent the freed-up gym hour organizing her room and pictures, setting out clothes, trying to keep it together.

Taking a quiet moment to think, she lay on her bed, staring at her ceiling and running through her checklist. It was still so crazy to imagine she was moving to another realm. Somewhere on the same planet so wholly different. The glow-in-the-dark stars on her ceiling made her smile. She could only really take with her what could fit in her pocket. Maybe she could take this part of the world, this part of her first home, with her. She stood up on her bed, grasping for a couple of stars. Pulling them off, she squished them together with the mounting putty on the backs. She blew out a long breath, setting the stars on top of her small stack of pictures to take when she left.

"How are you doing?" her mom asked, popping her head into Mel's room.

Mel took a deep breath. "I think ... that I don't even know how I feel." She shrugged.

Her mom leaned against the doorway. "Sometimes, there's no right or wrong answer."

Mel nodded pensively. "Yeah."

"Meals tomorrow, what do you want? Anything's on the table."

Mel smiled and thought about her list. "Surprise for breakfast, steak for lunch?"

"You got it! I'll need to do some shopping. Want to come with?"

"Could you actually drop me off at Dad's work? I'd love to spend a little time there."

Her mom nodded with a smile. "That's a great idea." She reached into her purse. "But first, a little something special. Doesn't quite make up for everything, but..." She handed Mel a chocolate bar. "From the World Market. Made in Costa Rica."

Mel beamed, giving her mom a giant hug. "You really do speak my language."

Fifteen minutes later, Mel arrived at her dad's chiropractic office.

"Hey, you!" the receptionist greeted her.

"Hi. Is he working with a client?"

"Yep, two more today. Want to use one of the massage chairs in the back room?"

The idea sounded like heaven after all the hard work she'd put in. It was a training-free night, a time to rest and recuperate. Ben and Devin felt confident she was up to snuff on her breeze-catching ability. "Yes, please!"

The woman guided Mel to a small back room and turned on a massage chair for her. Every muscle sighed in appreciation.

After a little while, her dad joined her. "Hey, stranger! I didn't expect to see you here." He shut the door behind him.

Her face lit up and she leapt out of the chair to give him a hug. "Just missed you."

They sat down on an adjustment table side by side.

"Hmm. Missing me? You're not even gone yet." He winked.

Mel frowned. "I know."

He took off his glasses, wiping them clean with the bottom of his shirt. "Well, I guess we're not on the same page, then. Because your mom and I are already making plans for all the fun things we'll do when you make your first trip back. It gives us something to look forward to, and we'll have a laundry list of all the things we'll want to hear about with your education and experiences." He replaced his glasses, giving her a smile.

She sighed, grateful they were both being so understanding about her choice to leave, or at least acting like it. "Are you guys being honest with me? Would you tell me if I was making the wrong choice?"

He put a hand on her knee. "Only *you* know the right choice. And yes, we're being honest with you."

Something had been nagging Mel since her talk with her mom weeks ago, when she'd learned her mom had passed on the Seeder life. "What are the conditions you had to agree to when you took me in? Is making sure I go back one of your responsibilities?" She looked down at her hands. "Devin and Ben say most girls choose to return and I wondered, you know..."

"Ah, I see. The conditions were to raise you safe, and give you a happy, normal life. I suppose we didn't hit the mark on some things." He frowned. "But no, it's not like we're censoring or lying about anything to coax you into going home. Your other dad knew our story before allowing us to take you in. He didn't ask us to hide anything." He shifted to face her more head-on. "When you're over there, your Seeder family will be there to help you, but they're different, and in their world, you're an adult already. You'll be expected to make your own decisions. I'm sorry we didn't do better at preparing you for that."

Mel hugged her dad. "I vote we agree to not apologize anymore. Me, for leaving and being a pain. You guys, for being a smidge imperfect."

He grinned. "A smidge, huh? I guess I'll take it."

There was a soft knock on the door.

"Come on in."

The receptionist opened it slightly. "Sorry. Just checking if it's okay that I take off?"

"Yep. Thanks for your hard work."

She smiled. "It was good to see you again, Mel. See you Monday, Dr. Walters."

Mel and her dad stayed silent for a while until they were sure she had left the building.

"So ... she doesn't know yet?" The guilt stabbed at Mel.

He took a deep breath. "That she's about to be out of a job? Not yet. Not until you're gone."

They'd decided it would be best to have George move his chiropractic practice across the state. Mid-school-year exits were always the worst to cover without a tragic ending. The Walters opted to move; they'd always known it was a possibility and had saved for it. Mel would 'transfer schools' and be with her dad while her mom stayed behind and packed up, meeting them later and allowing Ben to finish out his year at the same school.

Thinking of the receptionist, Mel frowned again. "That's not really fair to her, is it?"

He nodded thoughtfully. "Sometimes, you have to choose yourself. You can't make everyone happy." He nudged her arm. "Plus, I've got a friend across town needing a new receptionist. It'll be less of a drive for her. She'll be taken care of."

Mel took a deep breath and let it out. *Sometimes you have to choose yourself.*

Smiling, Mel looked at her dad. "This would have been a lot easier of a decision to make if you guys were horrible parents."

He grinned. "Ditto, kiddo." He slid closer, giving her a side hug. "Well, I imagine your mom is waiting for us, and we have things to do, don't we? Want me to crack a few bones first?"

Mel almost laughed. He hated people calling chiropractors 'bone-crackers,' but he used it jokingly with Mel and her mom in private. She glanced down at the padded adjustment table they were sitting on. "Let's do it. I want to be in tip-top shape for tomorrow."

After a quick adjustment, Mel and her dad headed home and took family pictures with her mom in front of a green screen, including a few outfit changes. As was common for Seeders, they would edit them and post them on social media after a daughter left. The frequency of posts would trickle off until 'she' would post that she was going to take a social media break.

And then she'd never come back from that break.

Mel set the table for their last family dinner. "Why only three plates? Is Ben not eating with us?"

"You'll see." Her mom hinted at a surprise.

Devin showed up to take Mel away on a last date. It would be only Ben and her parents eating at home. Mel hesitated at first, but her parents reminded her they'd spend all morning and afternoon together the next day before she left. Devin's hopeful smile won her over in the end, knowing she might not see him for a couple of years as he continued to watch over his remaining sisters.

She was all smiles in the car. They'd snuck a few kisses over the last week and a half, but not much had been said about their relationship. They knew they were on the same page from the time she'd made her decision to leave, and officially let Zach know.

Devin held her hand as he drove to a secret location. It was at least a half-hour drive and her stomach was protesting. But he insisted he wanted to get out of the city. Have it be private, secluded, special. They pulled into some camping grounds, not officially open for the season yet, but affording a beautiful view of nature. He grabbed a blanket from the car and laid it down in a clearing, along with some takeout boxes.

"Chinese, bold choice for a picnic." She nodded.

"I figured it would travel well, and I know it's one of your favorites."

She loved that he remembered little details like that.

They sat, chatting and enjoying their food, reminiscing, and talking about what it would be like for her when she arrived in the Green Lands.

"I'm sorry we never got around to having a full-day human adventure." He frowned.

Mel shrugged. "Yeah, I guess it just wasn't meant to be." Visiting Zach, giving Devin a better human experience—these could all be done on future visits. But with such limitations on her time when she'd come back to visit her parents, she couldn't be certain what that would really look like down the road.

"How about this? I'll make time while I'm still stuck here to take an entire day and go do any one human experience you think I should try; I'll do it in your honor."

She looked down at their dinner with a smile. "Mmm. Great Wall of China."

He poked her in the ribs, making her squirm. "Maybe something just a little closer?"

"Okay, fine. Have you been to a theme park?"

He shook his head.

"Then that's it. I declare you must ride at least one roller coaster and eat lots of cotton candy. Oooh, and an elephant ear."

He raised an eyebrow. "The ear of one of those giant animals?"

She smiled, remembering they didn't have anything nearly that large in the Green Lands. "It's the name of a dessert."

He nodded with a smile of his own.

"Take one of your sisters. Heck, take Ben along. Heaven knows he needs to learn to relax now and then."

Devin took another bite of food. "Deal. And in return, I promise to show you all my favorite places when I get back home."

She held out her hand and they shook on it. She looked forward to finally seeing the Green Lands for herself. And the thought of exploring them with Devin by her side, filled her heart.

"Fortune cookie time," she announced while handing him one. "You first."

He cracked it open. "It reads: 'You are the luckiest guy in the world and should kiss the girl next to you.'" He grinned and looked up at her.

She giggled. "I mean, you've got to listen to what the cookie says." She leaned over and kissed him. She then took it from his hands and read the real message. "Seek out the things you most want in life."

"I'm good." He winked.

"Well, I'm offended. You lied about what it said," she kidded.

"I'm sorry." He pouted dramatically. "Do you think you could forgive me? We could kiss and make up?"

She let out a melodramatic sigh. "I mean, I guess so."

Devin grabbed her hands, inching closer. He kissed the backs of her hands, the palms of her hands, her forehead and cheeks. He nuzzled her neck and whispered, "I love you." And then he moved in for the real deal. It was good they were in an uninhabited area. The glow between the two of them might have been brighter than a bonfire. Luckily, Seeder energy couldn't actually burn.

As they caught their breath and watched the light fade, they stared into each other's eyes. "I love you, too," Mel confessed. "I always will."

Devin sat for a moment, running his fingers up and down her calves. "How are they looking?"

She revealed her Seeder legs. There was barely enough of a gap in the roots wrapped around her ankles to place a pointer finger where it would finally close, sealing her fate. She prodded at the ends that were the bane of her existence. "What if we surgically implant something between them, so they can't join? No rooting in either world. Free as a bird to go between both? Problem solved! Voila!"

He shook his head. "But honestly, no cold feet, no last-minute doubts?"

She shook her head as well, a little unconvincingly. "No, I really don't. I just wish it hadn't ended this way with Zach. If I hadn't screwed that up, I wouldn't leave with any regrets."

"You did your best. That's all any of us can do."

"Yeah, I guess so." She frowned.

Thinking of something she'd been considering, Mel took a deep breath. "Do you know what I think?"

He raised his eyebrows. "I suppose I don't."

She narrowed her eyes. "I think you've known for a long time that Zach is human."

He cocked his head to the side. "Why's that?"

She poked his arm. "Because you left me alone with him for an hour in the library. After Ben's tirade, that was pretty ballsy."

"It's true I got an earful from Ben after what you did. That's why we kept your visit a secret." He pursed his lips. "How would you feel if I told you I'd bugged that room?"

Her smile dropped. "I'd be pretty upset..."

He looked her squarely in the eye. "Well, I didn't. Though I thought about *telling* Zach I did. But that would have been a hollow threat. And if you needed a goodbye with him, I figured it might as well be a sincere one. I wanted you to both be able to speak your mind."

She nodded. "Thank you."

He wore a faint smile. "There's a balance somewhere in there. Safety and happiness. If I'm being completely honest ... I did have one of our family members walk past and glance through the little window in the door a few times. Just to make sure he wasn't hurting you."

Mel sighed.

Devin reached forward to hold her hand. "You can't fault me for being protective when I'm *literally* one of your assigned protectors. And it's not like you've had all that much training for an attack. This isn't just me being some jealous boyfriend."

She had to concede the point. She'd thought it was a little reckless, no matter how much she appreciated being given the opportunity to chat with Zach. "But didn't he prove himself by sticking up for me when Blake was all over me in the hallway?"

Devin shrugged. "He could be a better actor than Blake. It wouldn't take much—we didn't suspect Ken. Or it could have been part of Zach and Blake's plan all along, to pull any suspicion away from Zach."

She raised her eyebrows in challenge. "Okay. What else do you have against him that makes you suspect he's an Ivy?"

"He pointed out your budding, when your arms were itching."

She'd given that some thought, but who *wouldn't* take note of their friend scratching their arms for the entirety of a conversation? "Yeah, well he's pointed out spinach in my teeth before, too. And I don't think he was somehow implying I was part plant by mentioning it."

Devin chuckled. "Add that to him looking into Tabatha's disappearance."

"We agree to disagree on the importance of that one." She lifted her eyebrows in challenge once more. "Anything else? How about the big thing in his favor? I've known him since the *fourth* grade."

Devin scratched his chin. "Why should that matter?"

"Because that's a lot of years in the human world when they know they can't even spot us blooming until we're teenagers?"

He shook his head. "That doesn't matter. Seeders send boys over that young, why shouldn't Ivies?"

Mel furrowed her brow. "Really?"

He nodded. "Deep covers. Every Seeder family sends one. As young as possible to make the journey and be embedded into daily life in their respective community."

Mel gulped, hating herself for having done something else she couldn't take back—sending a letter to Zach.

That was the one thing she couldn't resist doing—making one last effort with him. They'd been friends for too many years to allow their friendship to just slip away at the end so unceremoniously.

If she was right about the timing and he followed the instructions on the envelope, he'd open it after she was already gone. She wasn't going to screw things up, not again. She hadn't divulged the exact date or time of her departure (though she'd already told him an approximate deadline previously); she hadn't given anything else away. Just a heartfelt goodbye.

That was the compromise she'd settled on instead of texting to ask for a visit. The day before, she'd slipped it in the mailbox as the mailman approached, taking a deep breath, and slowly letting it go. She'd patted herself on the back, thinking how that chapter was being closed. The last box on her to-do list had been checked.

"Anyway." She wanted to change the subject, realizing she couldn't do anything about it now. And all of Devin's objections were still just conjecture. "My fortune. I'm assuming this is the most important piece of advice I will ever read in all of my existence."

She snapped the cookie in half and pulled out the little piece of paper. "'You will soon find something you have lost.' Well, that was anticlimactic. It couldn't say 'spread your wings and fly' or something like that? Anything about my future? I vote we swap."

He nudged her arm. "I vote we share mine. Our futures, our fortunes. I like the idea."

She stole a smooch. "I like that, too."

After the sun set, they lay down on the blanket, staring at the sky as the stars began to appear, cuddled up next to each other.

"Twenty-four hours," Devin announced with a melancholy voice.

"Do the Green Lands share the same stars?" she asked wistfully.

"I think so."

"Will you think of me each time you see the stars?"

"Every night, Saff."

She sat up and rolled over, pinning him down. "I have something I plan to take with me to remember you by." She pulled out the charm that had been hanging around her neck. "This is where it belongs, sun-side facing in."

They shared a warm smile.

"But I never really gave you anything special in return. As a thank you for the gift. For everything you've done to keep me safe," she said.

"I love the painting you made me. I—"

"No. I mean *really* special."

He tilted his head to the side.

She rolled off of him and sat cross-legged. "Come here."

He sat in front of her, also crossing his legs.

"There are rules that come with this gift," she said.

"Okay..." He smiled.

"We stay sitting just like this," she explained.

"I can handle that."

She leaned in. He followed her lead, meeting her lips. It was soft, slow, intentional. The energy flowed from her heart to her lips, imparting Devin with something special, something that was often given as a token when Seeder women were seeing off the men they loved. A human teenager might still be a bit young to know what they wanted. But they weren't human. She knew she had met her match, her mate.

They went back to cuddling and gazing at the stars.

"Is there only one match for a Seeder? Like soulmates?" Mel asked.

He kissed her on the forehead. "You know about the mating for life thing. So, yeah, after you ... get married—'cause that's extremely important to Seeders, even if it's not for all humans—then I guess you're soulmates."

She nuzzled closer. "I mean before that. Could you be equally as happy with option A as option B? Or is there some kind of energy thing that makes you destined to pick just one person in particular?" With so much still left to learn, she wanted to know how much free will she really had in the matter. She didn't just want her physiology telling her Devin was the right one for her.

Devin tickled her arm, barely grazing his fingertips across her skin. "No. It doesn't work that way. Seeders date and choose just like humans do." He whispered in her ear, "But I know you're the one for me. If you'll have me. You know ... someday, after we're both home."

Mel smiled wide. "I love you."

Not much later, she was falling asleep on Devin's shoulder when he decided to call it a night. He took her to the car and packed up their picnic.

"I suppose keeping you out all night before the big day is not the best way to get either of your dads' blessings," he whispered, grabbing her hand as she nodded off against the car window while he drove them back to the city.

Chapter 29

This was the last day Mel claimed permanent residency in the human world. Waking up, it felt like a day of celebration, like Christmas, or a birthday, but somehow more somber. It was a day of dichotomies.

Mel's parents surprised her with chocolate chip pancakes, bacon, and eggs for breakfast. There was an unspoken pact to stay positive. Mel smiled while watching them cook together in the kitchen. Her mind wandered to her Seeder parents, and how they would finally be reunited and get opportunities like this again. She surveyed the dining room and kitchen. This was the home she'd grown up in, the one she would be leaving for good. Like the chocolate chips that morning, it was all a little bittersweet.

As they sat down and ate together, Mel couldn't help but continue to smile. All of the practice, hard work, and stress had been worth it. No one dared say anything, not wanting to jinx it, but she'd made it to the end of her time there—still safe. The Ivies hadn't come for her. A small knot in her stomach reminded her she couldn't pat herself on the back yet. Not until her feet left the ground that night.

After breakfast, she considered texting some of her more casual friends. She couldn't say goodbye, but perhaps something like she hoped they were having a good weekend. But at that point, it was better to stay silent or they might wonder why she didn't give them her cover story then, before disappearing into thin air. She was more the type to keep to her small, closer group of friends anyway. She thought of Heather. Maybe she and Zach ... probably not. But it would be nice— hopefully they would still hang out and it could help with Mel's absence.

In the early evening, Mel was pacing unrelentingly across the living room, checking the bay window every minute or two.

"Cool it, Mel. You're going to wear a hole in the carpet," Ben teased. "Pam and George will have to replace it to sell the place."

Knowing they were going to have to part ways for some time to keep up their ruse, Pam and George went out for a date night, allowing Mel to meet her dad, Thod, at the house in private. They planned to rendezvous at her departure point. They would say their final goodbyes there.

They'd ordered pizza as Mel had requested for her 'final meal.' Just the thought of calling it that made her nauseous. She picked off a couple of pieces of pepperoni, but that was all.

Ben and Devin sat on the settee, refusing to spoil the surprise. She was a jumble of excitement and nerves. Based on Ben's previous outburst, she'd narrowed her guesses down to Mr. Rasmussen, the teacher that lived on their street; Mr. Colburn—Tom; or Mr. Cress, her P.E. teacher. Ben had said Thod was someone she'd suspected of being 'one of them,' which she assumed meant an Ivy, but they'd been talking about Zach, so it could have meant she had pegged him as a human? But it wasn't like she went around labelling humans; they were kind of the default assumption. 'Human until proven Ivy.' The only time she recalled sharing suspicions about an Ivy general was that day in the nurse's office.

The fact that Thod texted to say he was running late just added to the torture. But the man had a lot to do; he had nearly twenty years invested in the human world. Money in bank accounts, a house to sort out, a job to resign from, and a convincing cover to enact for his personal disappearance. He wasn't just leaving the human world willy-nilly. Thod's cover story had to be as convincing as Mel's, if not more, to ensure no disruption to the Seeder network left behind.

Ben would stay through the summer. As part of their agreement to help Devin's dad with his last two girls, Ben would help train and hopefully escort one back before school started up again in the fall. He was set to graduate in just a couple of months anyway and was limited on how much help he could give in a high school he would no longer be welcomed at.

Every time Mel saw movement of someone driving or walking by, she would jump to the window. She was ecstatic when a figure actually approached their house, finally. She squinted to see his face. Not Tom. It would have been a perfect fit; he'd always felt like an uncle. She felt bad for being disappointed to see Mr. Rasmussen walking up. They'd never had any real rapport between them, though he did show, at least a couple of times this school year, that he cared about her well-being. And he probably intentionally kept his distance from all of his daughters. It made sense. They would have time to really get to know each other and grow their relationship.

Ben stood up next to Mel, looking out the window as she prepared to go to the door, able to finally greet him as her birth father, the orchestrator of her journey here.

"Take her to the family room," Ben ordered. "He shouldn't be here."

"What? Who is it?" Devin asked, while grabbing Mel's hand and pulling her past the front door.

"Just stay quiet. If we're compromised, they may still not know about you."

After Devin whisked Mel into the family room, they remained quiet, listening carefully. "What's going on?" she whispered. "Is Thod not Rasmussen?"

Devin shook his head, his eyes growing wide. Mel recognized the fear in his expression, and Ben's concern. There was a zero percent chance he was coming over as a neighbor needing a cup of sugar. Mr. Rasmussen had no reason to be there that night.

The door creaked open. "Mr. Rasmussen, I'm afraid you've caught me home alone. Were you looking for my foster parents?" Ben's voice was cool as a cucumber.

"Ben, right?" the older gentleman asked.

"Yes, sir."

"Might I come in for a moment, give your foster parents a call? They were expecting me but must have forgotten."

That was a load of bull.

"Sorry, they're really strict about—"

Ben stopped talking, his voice muffled amidst shuffling in the hallway. The door slammed closed.

Devin peeked around the corner and swore under his breath. "He can't take a general alone," he whispered. "Let's have you go out the back while we take care of him."

Mel swallowed hard. She didn't want to just run like a coward. But it was time she followed orders.

She snuck down the hall to the kitchen. Twisting the handle, she glanced back. Devin, Ben, and Rasmussen had taken the fight into the living room; she couldn't see them.

Hesitating, she opened the door, ready to do as Devin had asked.

Ivy vines wrapped around her arm, yanking her into the back yard.

"Devin!" she screamed.

A hand covered her mouth while more vines began to wrap around her other arm. Before the sharp leaves could puncture her free arm, immobilizing her blade, she forced her energy into it.

Her Seeder blade sliced clean through the vine wrapped around her forearm. The portion of the vine around her upper arm remained. She tried to yank her wrapped arm away, gasping in pain as the embedded leaves tore through flesh.

Mel pushed more energy to that arm, strengthening her elbow and damaged flesh. With all her strength, she jammed her elbow into the ribs of the Ivy holding her hostage. Knocking him off balance, they landed on the grass.

Just one more quick tug freed her arm. She rolled over, using her free blade to hack the vine off of her other arm. With two hands free and new vines emerging, she tussled to keep the Ivy from wrapping her again.

She clenched her jaw, staring down into her attacker's eyes—just another teenage guy, one she didn't recognize.

Their bodies lurched to the side and Mel tumbled off of him. She looked up to see Devin extending a hand. The Ivy was unresponsive after the swift kick to the head Devin had given him.

"C'mon. Let's get you inside while I help Ben," Devin said.

She took his hand, leaping up. They ran inside together.

Devin pointed to the family room. "Stay here, hide, and be silent."

Mel glanced toward the backyard as she followed orders. "There's another one!"

"Stay," Devin repeated as he turned to the back door again.

The Ivy beat him to the door, entering and extending vines. Devin jumped into the air, kicking the Ivy's chest with both feet. The Ivy was hurled backward into a large glass window. The glass shattered and he landed in the backyard.

Devin used his blades to balance himself and land upright.

He ran back to the family room. "Get back. You're supposed to be hiding." He handed her his cell. "In contacts, under Emergency Two. Call my dad."

Mel took the phone from him, nodding. Glancing over Devin's shoulder, she spotted the Ivy who'd crashed through the window. Bloody, he climbed back inside.

Mel didn't want Devin and Ben both risking their lives for her while she cowered in the background. But she knew she wouldn't be much help, either. Her fighting lessons had only covered defensive strategies. They'd been forced to spend more time on flight training.

She extended her hand to Devin, offering a portion of her energy. "Behind you. Let me help."

He shook his head. "No, you *need* that tonight. Make the call and get back!"

Her stomach knotted as she stepped back and eyed the phone. Her hands shook as she clicked the on button.

Only to find a password screen.

She flinched with each *thud*, *slash*, and *crash*. Plenty of noise coming from the living room meant Ben and Rasmussen were still alive and at it. Another loud smash of glass in the kitchen made her jump.

Mel peeked around the corner.

It was Ken, one of her original attackers.

And the one Devin had kicked in the head was on the approach from the backyard.

She couldn't just stand there. A highly trained general was bad enough, but now her protectors were outnumbered.

Mel wrung her hands. Seeder or Ivy, these boys had trained for *years*. She only had a couple of weeks under her belt.

There's one thing I can do.

"Devin!" she called out, drawing his attention, and Ken's.

"She's down the hallway," Ken announced to the other Ivy.

"Dammit, Saff!" Devin slashed through a vine wrapping around his wrist, shoving Ken back and lunging to intercept the other Ivy on his way to the family room.

She held out her hand, cradling a ball of light. "Take it!"

"I said no!"

No one else was getting hurt on her account. She couldn't lose Ben or Devin, and she couldn't just wait for their dads.

Even if she didn't have enough energy to make it to the Green Lands before rooting, as long as they all made it out of this, she could live with her fate.

"It's *my* choice!"

They locked eyes.

Devin understood what that meant.

He stretched out a hand, accepting the energy. Balling his other fist, he flicked it at the closest Ivy.

Three large darts sunk into the Ivy's chest with instant success. He keeled over. Ken looked down on his fallen comrade, his face turning a fierce shade of red.

Mel's heart was racing. This time, she was seeing the action up close, and she was *fully* aware of her surroundings.

"That's enough. Get back!" Devin ordered before tackling Ken.

About to follow his orders, she froze in place. Another kid was approaching from the backyard.

That makes five of them.

And right behind him ... was Tom. They both held their human form.

That is, until the teenager extended his vines at the open door.

Tom yanked him back. Baring his Seeder blades, he slit the boy's throat.

Mel's eyes grew wide. Devin wasn't wrong to admire her dad. He had some serious brute strength.

Tom's eyes now glowed green, meeting her gaze for just a moment. "Get back!"

"Ben's got a general in the living room!" Devin called out. "This one's mine."

Mel was slowly stepping back to follow Tom's orders, but instead, leapt back into the family room as Ben and Rasmussen rushed past, taking the fight to the kitchen.

The doorbell rang.

SERIOUSLY?! If that was a Jehovah's Witness, they were going to be sorely disappointed, because *no one* was going to open that door.

Mel peeked out to look at the closed front door and then turned her head to witness the brawl raging in the kitchen and dining room.

Rasmussen and Tom dripped with disdain and loathing once they each recognized the other for what they were. Rasmussen threw Ben against the wall with a huge *thud*, opting to focus on the leader instead.

Ben blinked, disoriented and twice as bloody as Devin, who ran to his side. Mel craned her neck to see Ken lying on the floor behind the two leaders, Devin having taken care of him.

Her stomach churned at the sight of all the blood.

"What are *you* doing here?!" Devin sized up the newest addition to the fight as the front door opened.

"Where's Mel?!" The panicked voice belonged to Zach.

She stepped through the doorway to see Zach standing still, his wide eyes darting around in horror at the blood-smeared walls and corpse legs sticking out from the kitchen.

"Don't hurt him!" Mel screamed.

Devin looked at her in disbelief. She was drawing a line in the sand.

"He's not here to fight!" she yelled.

Zach was holding an envelope—no vines poking out anywhere.

Devin eyed Zach, then yelled for Mel to get back again as he helped Ben up.

Tom hacked at each vine thrown his way by the Ivy General. Devin and Ben approached from either side of Tom, each grabbing a vine and tugging it back. Tom shoved Rasmussen against the wall, moving one of his blades up to his throat.

The boys took their blades and slit deep into Rasmussen's wrists. He grunted as his extended vines went limp, disconnected. No replacement vines made an appearance.

"Take her. We can handle this!" Devin told Tom as they held Rasmussen against the wall.

Tom surveyed the room and ordered his troops, "Get what you can. Don't take too long."

He charged down the hallway, grabbing Mel's wrist, heading right toward Zach.

Zach had his hands up in surrender, eyes bulging. "I'm just normal!"

Tom grabbed Zach by the shirt and tugged him along, fully transforming into his human form seamlessly before exiting the door and heading to his car parked on the street. He looked Zach over. "Front seat." He turned to Mel. "Back seat. Now."

Mel stopped. "Ben didn't look so great. I can help." She looked into Tom's eyes, pleading.

He looked down, stern. "You think I didn't see that? Backup is on the way. We need to not make a scene. Get in the car."

Mel swallowed a lump in her throat. "Okay."

She and Zach scurried to their assigned places as Tom took the driver's seat and nudged the car into drive.

They left the bloodbath, not peeling out—but casually, quietly, unassumingly going along their way.

Chapter 30

Just before leaving her neighborhood, Mel spotted Vice Principal Simons driving by, heading toward her house. He and Tom gave each other a nod.

"Devin's dad, right? Kind of obvious," Mel said.

Tom shook his head. "Maybe obvious if you know what Devin really is."

She glanced at Zach; he was pale with shock. "Zach, I'd like to introduce you to my biological dad."

"Principal Colburn?!" Zach's whole face was lined with surprise.

Tom kept his attention on the road while wiping blood from his face. "I've had my eye on you. My daughter's insistence that you deserve to live is somewhat compelling."

She knew the situation was still grave, but she couldn't fight a small smile. Tom spoke like a true father. *Her* true father. One of them.

Mel looked down at her arm. A vine still dangled from it, the leaves embedded in her skin. She winced, carefully tugging each leaf free.

"Yes, sir, I ... um..." Zach stuttered at yet another mention of his demise.

"Tom, I swear it was just bad timing. He was coming by to see me about the letter in his hand." She tossed the vine remnant on the car floor with a look of disgust.

"Saffrona." Tom shook his head in exasperation.

She frowned. She genuinely hadn't thought a tiny letter would have hurt. "I'm sorry, I know. I suck at this." Either way, the damage was done ... and in a way ... she didn't hate that Zach could now be part of the most important moment of her life.

"Sir, I promise I've never meant to hurt anyone, least of all Mel. And I'll keep your secret, and do anything you want." Zach bargained for his life, adding that he hadn't told anyone anything, hadn't let anything slip. He'd just barely read the letter and drove right over.

Tom waited to reply. "I'm under the impression you understand how serious this is to us. And that you know you're being watched. You'll need to be convincing that you know nothing about my people, and about what you just saw."

Zach nodded vigorously.

"You'll report to Ben when I'm gone—he'll let you know our expectations. For now, you can prepare to make both of our disappearances convincing; you can be a witness to our cover stories."

"Yes, sir."

An enormous weight lifted from Mel's shoulders. But something was tapping her in the back of her mind. "How did they find out ... Dad?"

"Obviously, Ken made it out, so they've had you and Ben pegged for a long time. For all I know, Rasmussen heard or saw the wrong thing that pointed him to tonight." He ran his fingers through his hair. "I had a lot to take care of. I might have let something slip."

She felt a smidgen better; but they didn't really know the truth of it all.

Tom shook his head in frustration. "It doesn't make sense. If they knew ... why would they wait? Nuren, right? That's what they said? You're absolutely sure?"

That stupid name. "Yes, that's what I heard." She wished she remembered more. But even if she had, it wasn't like Blake had monologued about some terrible plan.

Tom sighed. "The network will keep an eye open. If royalty is closely involved, that must have something to do with their tactics."

Zach kept quiet, his eyes darting constantly between Tom and Mel as if trying to make out what they were talking about.

Mel's mind wandered back to the home she'd grown up in, worrying about Ben and Devin. She allowed a sigh of relief to escape now that Devin's dad was there for backup. She thought back to all of her attackers and frowned. "I warned Devin about Mr. Rasmussen."

"I know," Tom said with regret in his voice. "And I'm sorry. Human laws, public school politics—it's messy. And..." He huffed. "Simon and I hatched this plan to team up before we'd ever even met your mothers. We can get fake identities, but we still had to work our way up the system to place ourselves in a position that high up at your school. Fat lot of good that did us in spotting their covers." He gripped the steering wheel tighter. "Someday, I hope you'll understand what we tried to do, and how we had to do it. At least you'll make it back home safe."

Mel's heart sank as the reality set in. She hadn't conserved her energy the way she'd needed for her trip. And time was in short supply.

"I ... helped in the fight," she confessed, knowing they might be wasting their time driving out to the cliff.

Tom blew out a puff of air. "How much?"

She swallowed hard. "Just some hand-to-hand stuff and one round of darts." She intentionally didn't mention *who* she'd helped, not wanting to get Devin in trouble.

"We'll see."

Mel frowned. She could feel the energy that had drained from her. Zach glanced her direction, as if asking for an explanation. She couldn't give it to him. She couldn't explain to him that her decision would be final that night, and it might not be what she'd originally planned on.

"Mel, you're bleeding," Zach said, mirroring Mel's frown.

She surveyed her right arm. It was already healing a smidge where she'd just plucked out the Ivy leaves. Glancing at her left arm, she recognized the source of Zach's concern. She still had chunks of skin dangling from when she'd first yanked to free herself from the vines. Her upper sleeve and part of her chest were soaked with blood, but upon closer inspection, the actual bleeding had stopped. "If I heal myself, does it use up my energy?"

"Don't do it," Tom blurted. "Unless it's life or death, at this point." He looked back at her in the rearview mirror.

"It's not pretty, but I'm not bleeding anymore..."

He nodded. "Good. We can check it out when we get there." Tom craned his neck around, ensuring they still weren't being followed. "Your body will naturally heal some on its own. You can't really control that. But the energy you channel to your hands is expended once it leaves your hands. Even if it's back into your own body. It changes. It's not infinite."

Mel nodded. She'd probably learned that at some point and forgotten. One month was *definitely* not enough time to learn and retain it all. She wanted to draw a breath of relief at having escaped the attack, but Ben and Devin were still back there. "Are you sure they'll be okay?"

"How about you try trusting me for once?" Tom asked.

She pressed her lips together, nodding.

Tom kept scanning the area to make sure they weren't being followed. Taking a brief detour, he drove them to a warehouse Mel hadn't seen before. After parking the car, they got out and switched vehicles before proceeding on their way.

"Are we still going to be able to make it to the cliff my parents are meeting us at?" Mel asked.

Tom glanced at a message on his phone. "Yes. Not a lot of cliffs in the area. And it's still the best option. We really don't need to add more humans to this mess by having any see you jump off a building."

"You're what?!" Zach's eyes shot to Mel for an explanation.

She grinned. "Oh. That. Yeah ... I can fly now."

He pursed his lips, nodding. "Why not, right?"

Not much later, their car crept to a stop. George's car was already there.

"Stay," Tom ordered. He popped the trunk and got out. After closing it, he opened Mel's door and gave her a bottle of water. Crouching down, he looked at her injuries with a frown. She wasn't all that thirsty, but she knew it helped speed up recuperation, so she cracked the seal and began to drink.

Tom grabbed a first aid kit from the trunk, wrapping gauze around her injuries. "We'll see how these look in a few minutes." He glanced down. "Let's see your ankles."

Mel felt self-conscious, with Zach peering over to look. Of course, he'd just seen the others in full-on Seeder transformations, though their roots had been hidden.

She focused and revealed them. Tom looked to see how close they were to finishing the change. She was crushed, seeing his reaction. They were cutting things close, maybe too close.

He shook his head. "We should have done this yesterday. But we still have time." His eyes focused on hers. "If you have enough energy in you. It's not an easy journey."

She drank more water, not sure what to say. There wasn't a precise answer. This wasn't Trigonometry. Even if she could catch a breeze, which she felt she definitely had enough still left in her to do, just making their way to the rifting space was supposed to be grueling.

Tom studied her face. "Both Ben and Devin say you're pretty impressive in the energy department. Can you channel it to your hand so I can see? It'll give me a better idea of where we're at."

She curled her hand into a cupping shape, pushing more energy down. She smirked a little, looking over her shoulder to see Zach in awe, witnessing this particular ability for the second time.

Turning back to face Tom, she was surprised to see him wearing a wide smile.

"That's good. That's actually ... great." He raised his eyebrows. "Your mother didn't have that much power when we met, and she was rooted."

Mel pressed her lips together, tears filling her eyes. Her mom, Murial. She desperately wanted to meet this woman. And ... this was giving her hope that she could. "You think I can still do it?"

He nodded. "Finish the water. Take a breather while we wait for the guys to finish up." He tucked a wisp of hair behind her ear. "In the end, it's your choice. And you're the one that needs to listen to your body. But ... if you have it in you ... it would mean the world to your mother and I, having you back home."

She nodded. Clashing with the sweeping relief was the pang of guilt. Zach had just heard that—this was *her* choice.

"Speaking of parents," Tom said. "How about a hug and then we go meet up with Pam and George? They've got to be worried."

She smiled and stood up, giving Tom a tight squeeze. Her mind replayed her mental checklist of trying to figure out who her biological dad was. Tom had seemed like an easy answer, spending lots of time with different families in the school district. Though an Ivy on the hunt could've easily done that too, or just a lonely human principal...

Tom bent down before shutting Mel's car door. "Come on, Zach. You've already seen enough at this point, you might as well join us."

Passing the trees into the clearing at the top of the cliff, Mel was instantly on edge. Next to her human parents was another teenage boy, one she didn't recognize.

Tom leaned over. "Your brother."

Her nerves calmed. "I thought it was just Ben left."

Tom grinned. "You think I wouldn't send a son to get backup after one of my girls was attacked? And that I wouldn't do my best to look after Pam and George?"

Her heart melted. Though she kind of wished this new brother was back at her parents' house, helping Ben and Devin, Mel was grateful her parents had been kept safe.

"We were starting to wonder..." Pam began; her eyes widened as they approached. "Good heavens, what happened?! Is everyone okay?"

Mel ran up and hugged both her and George.

"A couple of troublemakers," Tom said. "We've got our people finishing things. But I'm sorry to say your house will need a good deal of cleaning."

"Right," Pam acknowledged in a daze, fixated on the blood that covered his arms and shirt.

Mel pictured the bodies now overlapping on the kitchen floor. That was *not* what they'd bargained for when they'd offered their house for a meet and greet.

She gave her new brother a hug and thanked him. He smiled and briefly introduced himself.

Mel then pulled Zach to the side. "I don't even know what to say at this point."

He furrowed his brow. "You ... um... He said you get to choose?"

She frowned. "It's more complicated than I explained. But ... yeah."

"Is it because of *him*?"

She knew he meant Devin. "No." She pressed her lips together. "I tried to tell you ... but it didn't come out right. Both choices had sacrifices. I'm sorry." Her heart ached, knowing Zach wasn't getting a fair chance. If she'd never met Devin, if she'd just been a regular human, they could have had something. But that wasn't who she was—she was invested in the next phase of her life.

He looked at the letter still clutched in his hand. His head bobbed in thought. "You said you can't give me what I want. But what I want ... is for you to be happy. Otherwise ... what kind of friend am I?"

She hugged him to within an inch of his life. "I promise, next spring, I'm going to come visit you, and Devin and my parents, for an entire week. Pencil me in!"

He nodded in agreement and looked her in the eyes. "You're *sure* this is what you want? Whatever you're leaving for?"

"I'm sure of it." She kissed him on the cheek, grabbing his hand and holding it while they waited for the rest of their party to arrive.

Chapter 31

After talking more privately with Pam and George, Tom—or Thod ... Mr. Colburn ... her dad—came over to Mel.

"I was kind of hoping it was you." She smiled.

"I'm glad you get to be the one I go back with." His smile softened his intimidating features. "It's been a long time coming. I'm really proud of you. Do you feel ready?"

"I don't know. I think so." She was bouncing with nerves. "Tom, I mean ... Dad?" She looked over at George. "I don't really know what to call you..."

"As long as it's not Mr. or Principal Colburn, I'll be happy." He reassuringly rested his hand on her shoulder.

Mel went back and forth between holding Zach's hand, and fidgeting with her own hands while pacing. The five of them stood around, chatting.

"We can wait a little longer, but we don't have all night," Tom said.

"I can't leave without saying goodbye. They're coming, right? You're sure they're alright?"

"They can handle themselves." Tom tried to calm her down. "But we need to get you out of here sooner than later. Your rooting is close."

Mel swallowed hard. Each moment that passed was one of agony.

She gave a sigh of relief once Pam and Tom finally got a text from Ben that they were on their way.

The stars and moon were out, and the only thing holding Mel back from the biggest leap in her life was waiting for the crunch of gravel under approaching tires. They heard the expected noise in the distance. Tom was cautious, just in case they may have been duped or followed. Mel was practically breaking Zach's hand, with energy magnifying her anxious squeezing.

But it was going to be okay. Devin emerged from the trees, a sight for sore eyes. His eyes lingered on Mel holding Zach's hand as he approached. She released it and ran to give Devin a hug. Zach stood there, rubbing his aching hand.

She quickly stepped back, panicking. "Where's Ben? Is he okay?"

Two recognizable voices came through the trees, even laughing. Ben was quite a sight to behold, his light tan t-shirt darkened with blood. Walking next to him was a blonde.

Mel turned her focus back to Devin with a smirk. "Heather? Your sister?"

He grinned. "Yeah."

Ben approached Tom, giving him a manly hug. Heather shyly greeted Tom with a handshake.

Devin held Mel's hand and had her hang back as the others chatted. He looked into her eyes, worried.

"It's okay," she reassured him. "He thinks I can still make it. And I do, too."

His eyes stayed fixed on hers. He cautiously nodded. "Okay." He scooped her up into his arms, squeezing tight, her feet no longer touching the ground. "I couldn't lose you. I don't want to ever lose you."

She soaked in the warmth of his embrace. "I couldn't lose you, either."

Devin put Mel back down on the ground and wrapped his arm around her shoulder, turning to join their audience.

Ben grinned with a glance at Zach, who was still clearly in shock from the events of the evening. "Seriously? Who invited a human to the show?"

Mel threw daggers with her eyes and Ben raised his eyebrows playfully. "They'll let any ol' riffraff in around here." He laughed, Devin joining him.

Mel rolled her eyes.

Pam responded to a look Tom was giving her. "Speaking of, Zach, why don't you come join George and I for an all-human chat and let them get caught up."

After they stepped away, the Seeders could talk more freely. Mel was grateful to *finally* be let into the inner circle. Minutes away from leaving this world, they no longer needed to keep secrets from her.

Her new brother left to patrol the area while the others had their debriefing.

"You're sure it's taken care of?" Tom asked the boys.

"Yes, sir. We've already got our people on clean-up." Devin reported. "We had a few more show up after you left."

Tom furrowed his brow. "Few?"

Devin glanced at Mel before turning his focus back to Tom. "Five more."

Tom looked to be as shocked as Mel. "That's ... a lot. I don't get it." He shook his head. "Anything useful?"

Ben spoke up. "We got the impression Blake didn't make it. The leech wouldn't give us much. I'm pretty sure Rasmussen *wasn't* Nuren, but he did make some vague threats once we brought Nuren up. We'll keep our eyes peeled." A mischievous grin overtook Ben's face. "Rasmussen really didn't have nice things to say about you, Principal Colburn. But you'll be pleased to know he 'handed in his resignation' before we left."

Tom smiled. "And no cops?"

Devin shook his head. "That hedge did us some good, covering up the backyard, and we reached out to our human connection in case any disturbance reports came in."

Tom surveyed the group. "You've done a great job." His phone rang and he excused himself.

Mel looked over the guys, checking out their injuries. They had both taken a beating, but Ben barely had an inch of him not covered in blood. "How much of that is yours?"

He shrugged. "I'll be fine." He glanced down at Heather. "Heather wants to specialize in healing after she comes home."

Heather met his eyes. "Heather can speak for herself."

Ben grinned.

Heather turned her focus to Mel. "But I do. I'm excited to learn all the different techniques."

Mel studied Ben and Devin again; they still had a lot of injuries. Though it was astonishing they made it out at all, with that many Ivies showing up.

Heather must have understood her concern. "I'll finish them up. I just needed to make sure the two of you didn't need my help before your journey."

"You're not returning tonight, too?"

Heather shook her head. "I don't know how to catch a breeze yet. This is still all pretty new to me."

The girls unwrapped Mel's injuries at Heather's urging. A lot of it had already started to heal itself without extra effort—they figured they could make it work. Heather focused her attention on Mel's upper arm. Mel winced as she poked and nudged ripped skin together, giving it a healing touch.

"Just make sure you're not doing too much," Ben coached. "If you get too dizzy, take a break." He slipped his arm around Heather's waist.

Mel glanced between the two of them with a smirk. "So ... Heather... You told me you liked hanging out at my house. I guess I see why."

Heather continued to focus on Mel's arm, grinning wide. "A person's allowed to have more than one motive for being somewhere."

Devin chimed in. "The irony of these two dating, after all the grief he gave us!"

"It's new." Ben glared at Devin. "And *we* know what it means to take things slow and be *discreet*."

Devin pursed his lips, raising his eyebrows, and looked at Mel as she stifled a laugh.

Tom returned as Heather finished healing the worst of Mel's injuries. "Alright, that was Simon." He glanced at Mel and Heather. "Simon is actually his first name back home." He cleared his throat. Anyway, we discussed a lot, but he's going to have to mull over some things and make the final call." He focused his eyes on Heather again. "*When* you return, and if you and your host family should leave the area now, are things you're going to need to have a conversation about. I'm sorry it might not go the way you planned."

Heather frowned and nodded.

A wave of guilt washed over Mel. "I'm sorry."

Heather gave her a smile. "Both of my human parents are nurses. They're really supportive of what I want to do. We'll... We'll sort it out."

Mel nodded, still feeling immensely guilty. If Heather had just finished her bloom, a normal bloom, she still had months left. Mel would've given anything for that extra time with her parents. And she'd potentially just robbed Heather of that.

Tom turned to Devin and Ben. "As for you two, you're staying for now. Unlike what I had to do last year ... well... Ten bodies have to go missing. It's up to Simon who stays and who gets sent home, and when. For all I know, the two of you will be back tomorrow. That's all his call." The boys both nodded.

Tom recommended Mel say her last goodbyes with her parents and Zach as they finished up their briefing, leaving his last orders with the boys.

Heather gave Mel a quick hug. "I'm excited to be neighbors. Those boys or not, I still want to be your friend."

The Walters cried, not wanting to end their hugs. Pam slipped Mel a piece of paper with their new address and contact information for next spring. They would leave their plans open. Mel tucked it safely into her pocket alongside her photographs.

She wiped tears from her eyes. "I'll make you guys proud."

George put his arm around Pam, rubbing her shoulder. "We're already proud of you, sweetheart."

Zach obviously tried his best to be brave and friendly, but the reality of losing her forever was sinking in. Heartbreak mingled with shock from the night's events showed through sad eyes and a forced smile.

After all Zach had just witnessed, Mel was confident she could soothe him a bit. "You can stop looking for Tabatha." She gave him a half-smile.

He looked down, slowly nodding in realization. "One of your kind, too?"

She leaned over to make eye contact. "Turns out she's my sister."

He smiled and shook his head. "I really never stood a chance, did I? I can't compete with both her *and* Devin."

She frowned. "Please don't look at it that way." She thought of her dad's words. *Sometimes you have to choose yourself.* "I'm not choosing between people. I couldn't. It's not between you and Tabatha or Devin. Or between my sets of parents. The only person I'm choosing is me, okay?" She considered how she'd decided to start going by Saff permanently after returning to the Green Lands. "I'm choosing who *I* want to be."

He pulled her into one last hug. "I think I get it. And I'm here to support you. I'm glad you'll have a friend waiting for you on that side. Tell her hi for me."

Mel leaned back, smiling. She hadn't planned for him to be there for her final goodbye, but she realized she had one more thing she wanted to do. Reaching into her pocket, Mel felt for two glow-in-the-dark stars, smooshed together with mounting putty. She blushed, showing them to Zach. "Maybe it's silly. I only took two down so the sticky stuff wouldn't mess up anything in my pocket." She bit her lip. "But these are from my first home. And, um, you'll always be a part of that." She pulled them apart, offering one.

Zach took it with a grin.

"Just know you have a friend thinking of you." She smiled as she carefully put one back in her pocket, the sticky side facing the back of a photograph.

They were interrupted as the Seeder group approached. Tom spoke with her parents and Ben took Mel to the side. She looked back to see Devin and Zach awkwardly shake hands. Heather watched on with a smile.

"Thank you so much for being there for me. And sorry for being such a pain," Mel apologized to her battered brother. "I'll find a way to make it up to you when you get home."

He smiled warmly. "Just do me a favor and try to follow some rules for a change."

She twisted her face in guilt as she opened her arms. He looked down at the fresh blood all over his clothes.

"I don't even care right now," she said.

He opened his arms and she nestled into his embrace. They may have been the same age, but she'd always see Ben as a big brother.

He spoke softly into her ear, "You know, Mel. I have a lot of sisters, so I can't pick a favorite. But I can comfortably say you were the biggest thorn in my side."

She backed up and punched him in the arm.

"But..." he added with a chuckle, "you're the only one I ever had to share a bathroom with, so that gives you a special place in my heart." He winked and she gave him a reluctant smile. "You'll do great." His eyes wandered past her.

Looking over her shoulder, she saw Devin and Zach watching them.

"Devin and I will take care of each other. We'll be back before you know it." Ben let out a loud sigh. "And your little friend, we'll watch out for him, too, as long as he knows how to keep his mouth shut."

Ben gave her one last quick hug and left her side, allowing Devin to approach.

Devin took her by the hands. "Have I told you recently how much I love you, and how much I'll miss you?"

She bit her quivering lip and nodded.

He gave a soft smile. "Hey now, you're going to be too busy getting to know everyone back home, and absolutely falling in love with everything there, to waste any time worrying about us on this side of things."

Mel wanted more than anything for Simon to send Devin home right away. But that wasn't fair of her to wish that. He'd made it clear he wanted to be there for his sisters. And creating convincing covers couldn't be that easy.

Her trembling voice betrayed her as she tried to hide her feelings. "It'll be great. Stay safe. And tell that last sister to hurry home?" She added with a small chuckle, "I'd tell you to rip off the proverbial bandage and get it over with, maybe lose her jade charm ... if I didn't know firsthand how traumatizing that is. Is she somewhere in her blooming already?"

Devin shook his head with a frown. "Not yet. We never know the timing of these things. But girls generally bloom around the time their moms did. So, hopefully not too long now."

She nodded, finding hope that it would be sooner rather than later.

Devin swallowed, looking into her eyes. "Like your dad said... I might be back tomorrow. Or it could be a couple of years. It's not fair for me to ask you to wait for me."

"But I'm going to, anyway."

"Then I'm the luckiest guy in either world." He smiled. "I'm not going to ask if you're ready. You are." He peered into her eyes and then pulled her in tight, whispering, "I'm so excited for you. Tell everyone hi for me." Devin released her from his grip and glanced over his shoulder. Their time was up; everyone was ready and waiting. "The stars. Every night, right?"

She nodded and he gave her one last, tender kiss.

They turned to rejoin the rest of the group. Rustling came from the trees to Mel's right. She gasped, gripping Devin's hand tighter and freezing in place.

Five more teenage boys stalked into the clearing, spreading out and forming a line between the farewell group and the parking area.

Seriously? Her heart raced—they were now cut off.

Devin squeezed her hand, whispering into her ear. "It's okay. All family."

Her eyes darted between the guys, doing a double-take, recognizing one. Kyle, the brother whose cover had been burned as a foreign exchange student, had returned from the Green Lands. He stood there, grinning as he crossed his arms.

She looked back to Devin, reading his face. "But... You said... All of those are mine? You guys said only half of Seeder boys ever come over for protection detail over the years. Half stay to protect the border walls."

He smirked, putting his hands on her waist. "Four of those are yours. One is mine. I have more back at your house still cleaning things up, and watching over Heather's family, and my other sister. We didn't have to enroll them all in school to keep more eyes on you." He spoke softly, confidently. "I guess it goes to show our dads had a decent strategy, after all." He furrowed his brow, looking down. "And with all those eyes on the threat, this still happened. It proves we can't really underestimate the enemy, either."

"Hey." She caught his attention with a smile. "I can't even begin to say how touched I am. And I know this wasn't all just for me. But..." She swallowed, her heart swelling.

He looked her squarely in the eyes. "*Nothing* is more important to Seeders than family." Devin glanced around at their large audience, a smile growing on his face. He removed his hands from her waist, shoving them into his pockets. "And speaking of family. We have a half-dozen of your brothers, your best friend, and both of your dads watching us right now. Not to mention Pam. I think I'll take Thod's advice to 'keep my damn hands off his daughter' and, uh ... let you leave with him now. The location's secured. You need to go home. Go start your new adventure."

She beamed, nodding and turning to Tom.

"It's time," Tom announced as she drew close.

Mel took a few deep breaths, walking up to her starting point. Closing her eyes, she focused every ounce of energy into the various techniques they'd been drilling into her. Her jitters were suppressed by the warmth of the energy actively flowing, covering her like a tight sleeve. She was a bit more nervous, having such a large audience for her first leap from a cliff, but their support balanced it all out.

Opening her neon green eyes, she knew this was the most ready she was ever going to be. Tom stood to her side, giving her a nod of encouragement. She looked over her shoulder one last time. George held Pam in his arms. Zach stood still, looking mildly terrified with Ben and Devin planted on either side of him, their arms slung threateningly around his shoulders. She raised her eyebrows with a look of warning to remind them to play nice.

One deep breath later and she bent down to get a good stance for her running start off of the familiar cliff. Without hesitation, she sprinted, tuning out the world behind her to focus on her balance, her communion with the surrounding wind.

Squinting, as if reminding the elements that *she* was in control, Mel felt a gust of wind push her forward as she kicked off with one foot.

This was it. She was airborne.

She wobbled a little, like Bonnie had, correcting her balance to match the air around her. She shifted her energy around her body as needed to compensate for any changes in the wind. Mel didn't dare look back; she couldn't split her focus, couldn't jeopardize her trajectory. After flying for several yards and gradually rising, she caught sight of Tom passing her on her right. He nodded to indicate the direction they would go. She followed, and they climbed. There wasn't much cloud cover that night, but as they flew past the few wisps in the sky, the landscape below grew smaller, darker.

Time passed slowly, though she wasn't sure if it was from the strain of constant focus, or if they were actually flying for as many hours as it seemed. While her energy usually kept her body warm, the wind chill at this elevation licked unforgivingly cold against her face. It was especially frigid when they hit larger patches of clouds. She hardly noticed the flock of birds flying nearby, but she smiled once she recognized them.

Her tank was running close to empty, the sun starting to rise from the east behind them. Tom looked over and offered his hand. She happily grabbed it, grateful for the guidance and warmth. With his free hand, he gestured at the air before them. The sky rippled as a rift formed, only perceptible through their trained Seeder eyes.

Chapter 32

Thod led Mel through the rift he'd created. Once they passed through, she felt a surge of renewed energy. He released her hand, allowing her to rebalance herself. The air was warmer, easier to coast on. The energy of the Green Lands welcomed her upon her arrival. On this side of the rift, the sun was rising to their left and much further along in the sky.

Thod slowed his speed to match hers and raised his voice to give instructions on landing; she hadn't exactly mastered that part. As they coasted over hills and forests, not unlike those in the human world, she began to see signs of civilization—dirt roads, a variety of rustic buildings. She couldn't help but smile. It was real. It satisfied an intense curiosity that had pulled at her from the moment she'd learned her true identity. It filled a place in her heart she'd never realized was empty.

As they started to descend, she saw groups of people watching the sky. They pointed, looking on in anticipation. She wasn't sure if they knew who she was, or if they were perhaps hoping it was one of their own returning. Finally, after all the waiting, Thod gestured to a house—it was theirs. Behind the modest cottage, she could see what looked like a jungle of a garden, and another building on the same plot in the back. Near it was a clearing with a pile of straw, kept ready for new learners needing a softer place to land.

Thod went first, somersaulting in midair to slow his speed and find his footing, landing with both feet squarely on the ground to absorb his momentum. For the first time since her journey began, Mel felt a pang of nerves. She took a deep breath and aimed for the soft landing. Moving her focus from her arms to her feet, she tried to keep her balance and prepare for the impact. Faltering a little, she crashed into the pile at an angle. It was far from graceful, but she arrived home safely, without another scratch.

Having been hyper-focused on a safe landing, she hadn't noticed the crowd of people running to join them. Several young men and women her age approached Thod to welcome him home. First alarmed by his bloody appearance, they happily greeted him once he assured them all was well. Daughters, many of which had known him from his position in the human world, but never as their father, until after their departure. Sons, one of which she recognized from his time of deployment at her school. A couple of the guys hung back, having never met either their father or Mel, waiting for the crowd to clear to get an introduction. Three familiar faces ran to Mel first: Bonnie (now Rose), Tabatha (who was still keeping her human name for now), and Stacy (now going by Dahlia).

It was a warm homecoming, with tons of hugs and congratulations, squeals of excitement. Even if there were a lot of them, each Seeder to come home was cause for celebration.

Someone yelled from beyond the garden. A tall woman with shoulder-length auburn locks ran toward them, calling Thod's name. Matching the description Devin had given her, Mel recognized this woman—her mother, Murial. The kids made space as Murial approached, her eyes growing wide at the dried blood Thod and Mel were covered in.

Murial gasped. "Are you okay? Is everyone okay?"

Thod grabbed her hands. "Yes. We're all safe. Everyone." He pulled her in and squeezed like he'd never let go. She wept audibly, while a stream of silent tears cascaded down his face. Thod kissed Murial passionately, something he'd been unable to share with the love of his life for almost two decades. They might live longer than the average human, but every day apart was a battle. He held his wife's face, examining it.

Mel, who had decided it was time to go by Saff now, stood in place, shyly waiting for her turn to meet Murial. She clasped her hands in front of her mouth, smiling, touched by their love, their unity and sacrifice. She barely knew these people, but Saff knew she wanted that kind of love. Her excitement wavered for a moment as she reflected on Devin. She imagined this being their story, feeling a hint of homesickness. Each day without him would be one with worry, would be torture as she waited. Saff rubbed her charm and watched on.

Murial's eyes turned to her and she broke free from her husband. She moved past him, opening her arms to Saff. "Sweetheart. We're so happy to finally have you back!"

Saff ran into her arms; there was an instant feeling of familiarity. They had a lot of catching up to do; she wanted to learn so much about this woman. Murial stepped back, insisting on finishing up the healing Heather had started.

Excited whispering came from Thod's direction. A handful of kids Saff's age, neighbors, had joined the group after seeing Thod's return. She recognized some of them, and assumed the smaller woman trailing behind them was Sandra, Devin's mom. His family also wanted an update on their loved ones, the situation back in the human world.

Saff had a chance to meet everyone. Each hug helped replenish her energy, which had been exhausted by the journey. After a long reunion, many departed to continue their activities of the day. Her closest sisters led her to the kids' home in the backyard and showed her the space they'd prepared for her, leaving her to clean up. They scheduled a big family dinner that night to welcome her and Thod home.

She sat on her new bed, trying to take it all in. This was it, no going back. Saff looked at her roots. They had, at most, hours before her rooting would happen, and she would feel the irreversible tie to this new place.

Her true nature had been thrust upon her. Her future, however, had been a choice—and in that decision, she was confident.

Saff removed the paper Pam had given her with contact information from her pocket, along with the photos she had chosen. She glanced at them and set them on her wooden nightstand. She removed her chain, setting it aside as well. Remembering one of the photos had a bonus on the back, Saff carefully freed the glow-in-the-dark star. She smiled and stood on her new bed, sticking it up on her new ceiling.

A knock at the door claimed her attention.

"Yeah, come in." She got down from the bed.

Tabatha peeked in. "Hey ... sis. Just wanted to chat some more. Unless you'd rather get cleaned up first."

Saff looked down at all the dried blood on her clothes and sat on the bed. "It can wait."

Tabatha sat down next to her. "I missed you." She glanced at the pictures Saff had laid down. "Aw. I miss Zach, too." She smiled. "I think he had a bit of a crush on you."

Saff blushed, looking down into her lap. "Well ... Yeah. Guess he did. But that wouldn't have really worked out, right?"

Tabatha nodded with a frown.

"But I think he'll be okay. He knows about us. He was at the cliff when I left. He says hi."

Tabatha beamed. "That's awesome." Her eyes wandered to Saff's shirt again. "Sounds like you have one heck of a story to share."

"You could *definitely* say that."

"Well ... I really should let you get cleaned up and settled in." Tabatha stood, reaching into a dresser drawer. "I helped pick out a few outfits for you." She set some clothes on the bed. "Oh, yeah. Let me show you how the lightkeeper works. This was my favorite thing when I first got here." She reached past Saff, picking up what looked to be a paperweight.

Saff was mesmerized once Tabatha explained how it worked. The bottom was dark, a thin disk of jade. The upper portion was a dome of clear quartz. "Give it a try," Tabatha encouraged.

Saff held it in her hand. Following her sister's instructions, she put a finger to the top of the quartz and transferred the smallest amount of energy into it. She covered the dome with her hand and the energy spread evenly throughout it, creating a soft glow. "A lamp." Saff grinned. Something as simple as learning to use a Seeder lamp was exciting, and this was just the beginning.

"And then touch the base to draw it into the stone. It keeps it there when you're not using it," Tabatha said. "Maybe every month or so, it might dim and you just zap it back to full strength."

Tabatha gave her one more smile before leaving. "I'm sorry I didn't get to give you more of a goodbye. I'll have to tell you all about that chaos. But I'm glad you're here now. You always felt like a sister. I'm excited to show you everything."

With a smile on her face, Saff headed for the solar-heated shower to clean up. She took her time getting there, and back to her room, admiring their humble abode. The house was beautiful—all raw, unpainted wood. Hand-crafted rugs and furniture using natural fibers. Stone tile and metal for fixtures. Not a hint of plastic anywhere, other than the piece of home now stuck to the ceiling of her room. A piece of her *old* home.

After the grueling events of that day and night, all her body and mind wanted was a good rest. But she wouldn't get a nap. There was too much to learn, too many people to meet, too few hours to see it all. Saff got a tour of the property and surrounding areas. She particularly enjoyed getting to know Devin's mom a little better and giving her an update on how he was doing. Few knew the extent of

Devin and Saff's relationship, or that Ben and Heather were an item back with the humans, but Rose gave her a reassuring wink as they left Devin's house.

A huge chapter of Saff's life had been closed. An adventure larger than she had ever imagined was now opening up to her.

After a long day of sights and learning about this foreign way of life, Saff was finally ready to drift into a deep sleep. Before she allowed her bed to claim her for the night, she sat on a chair in front of her new house, looking into the sky. She pensively rubbed her charm as the vibrant sunset gave way to darkness and brilliant stars. Nearby, eucalyptus trees rustled in a gentle breeze and filled the air with a refreshing scent.

She thought of what her human mom had said, how she'd described rooting in the human world. It wasn't like that here, at least not for Saff. It was like the comfort of a weighted blanket, a peace in her soul.

Keeping her from perfect joy was her guilt about the disaster left in her wake, knowing her parents and Zach would be having a hard time, and the fact that so many questions were left unanswered. Why had the Ivies handled things the way they did? And who was Nuren?

Saff studied the sun carved in her jade, thinking lovingly of Devin. Looking back up at the dazzling display in the heavens, she whispered, "Every night."

The Return & Question

Saff peered into the windows of the central marketplace found in her home village of South Fortinda.(1) It was a bit of a windy day, and the central shopping lane was muddy from the morning's showers, but she loved the smell of the Green Lands after it rained. And she desperately needed a distraction.

"Now *that* is a cute hair clip," Dahlia said as they slowed to look at a vendor selling all sorts of ribbons and accessories.

Tabatha grinned at Saff. Dahlia was still the frillier of the three of them. Possibly of all twelve of the girls in their family.

"Definitely cute. But Murial asked for us to bring home lemons." Saff raised an eyebrow and a basket of apples. Their primary purpose in this excursion was for trade.

Dahlia met her challenge with a smirk. "With how crazy you've been acting all week, I'd think you'd be grateful to spend all day shopping."

Saff couldn't help but blush. "I don't know what you're talking about." She averted her gaze and continued walking.

"Uh-huh..." Dahlia replied playfully, and Tabatha giggled.

Biting her lip, Saff tried her best to ignore them. They were both right. She'd been pacing, and sleepless, and excited, and terrified for days. Devin was expected to return home this week. Finally.

It had been almost a year since Saff had left the human world, since she'd seen Devin. Luckily, she'd gotten a few letters from him, courtesy of several of her brothers—and his—who had trickled home before him. But his last sister had finally bloomed and was fully trained, set to catch a breeze and rift home any day now. Saff had hardly even eaten that week with her stomach in knots. They'd only dated a few months, and now they'd been apart, in completely different realms, for more than twice as long. What if they didn't feel the same way about each other once he got back?

Taking a deep breath, Saff tried to stop obsessing. He'd return safely. They'd see how things went. Stressing over it all did her no good.

"So..." Tabatha linked her arm through Saff's. "What are your plans for tonight?"

Saff smiled. "Ben and I talked about going out to Glass Lake and skipping rocks." It was one of their favorite brother-sister hangouts. They would just go and chat, and he would identify flora and fauna for her. Parts of her surroundings were familiar—butterflies or apple trees just like in the human world—but sometimes there were things she didn't recognize, and she genuinely didn't know if they were from the human world and she just hadn't ever seen them over there, or if they were exclusively found in the Green Lands.

"Hmm. Mind if I tag along?" Tabatha asked.

Saff nudged her. "Of course not."

They continued their stroll, passing carts piled high with rhubarb, onions, several kinds of melons, and so much more.(m) Little boys ran through the streets, sometimes being chased and scolded by an aunt, sometimes catching a breeze overhead. Seeder life was interesting.

"Oooh, I was hungry!" A large hand grabbed an apple from Saff's basket.

She spun to see Ben, right as he crunched into the crisp apple. "Excuse you. Mom wanted us to swap that. Not eat it."

Ben beamed, chewing away.

Saff just rolled her eyes.

"Saff said we're headed out to Glass Lake tonight?" Tabatha said.

Ben wrinkled his nose and finished his bite. "Nah. Well... Heather and I are going, and you can join if you want. But Saff's not invited anymore." His lips spread into a mischievous grin.

Saff's jaw dropped. "Why? You're an apple thief, and I'm suddenly disinvited to hang out because I called you out on it?"

He shook his head. "Nah." He took another huge bite of apple. "I just figure you'll be busy."

Furrowing her brow, Saff tried to think of anything she might have forgotten. But she didn't have any classes or trainings or other obligations she could remember.

Tabatha took in a sharp breath. "Saff."

"What?"

Ben cleared his throat, still grinning, then nodded at a figure standing across the lane.

Saff's heart stopped, as did her ability to breathe, as she spotted Devin. He leaned against a tree, crossing his arms, his lips curved in a gentle smile. Saff shoved the basket of apples into Ben's arms and ran across the lane.

Without hesitation, Devin opened his arms, and she launched herself into them. All of her pent-up nerves washed away in his embrace. *This* was the last thing she'd needed to feel fully at home. Devin was what made it complete.

"I missed you," he whispered, squeezing her even tighter.

"You too. But you're really home. Safe and sound."

He released her, but held her hands between them. They studied each other. He'd grown a little, and was somehow even cuter.

"Ben said..." he started. "Well, when you left you said... Just, you know. That you and I..."

She gazed into his deep-brown eyes. "I said I'd wait for you, and I did."

His smile widened.

Her heart was racing, but he still hesitated. She bit her lip. "Why aren't you kissing me right now?"

Without skipping a beat, he leaned in and did just that. Starting with a couple of short, sweet kisses, he soon pulled her in tight, laying a proper reunion kiss on her. It was a busy lane, and three of her siblings were watching, but it didn't matter.

And then Tabatha started clapping and cheering for them, and Saff had to step back and laugh. Tabatha had always been a dork Saff could count on.

With Devin's arm wrapped around her, they approached her siblings.

"So, Saff, did you still want to hang out with me tonight?" Ben casually asked, before taking another bite of his apple.

She grinned in response. "I was disinvited, so I guess I'll have to figure out some other plans, won't I?"

Months later, Saff laid down a picnic blanket while Devin filled their water canteens from a nearby stream. She loved this park—it was one of their favorites, a little out of the way and less trafficked. Pulling the picnic basket onto the blanket, she sat, crossing her legs.

"Here you go." Devin handed her some water, joining her on the blanket.

Saff took a swig. "Thanks." As she went to open the basket, Devin stopped her, moving it just out of reach.

"I, uh ... just wanted to talk a minute," he said.

She tilted her head to the side. "Okay." She hid a smile, knowing full well why he had picked this day to go on a special picnic. It was the two-year anniversary of their first kiss.

"Well, I just thought, you know. Well... I love you." He cleared his throat.

She smiled at his obvious anxiety. "I love you, too."

"Yeah. I love you, too." He shook his head. "I said that already. I just, um, well, happy anniversary."

She searched his face, knowing he wasn't one to stutter without something more to say than a simple 'happy anniversary.' "You too."

A breeze rustled the leaves on the tree above them, and she was brought back to the day he'd returned home. They'd come to this park that night. Their lips would have been raw if she hadn't been able to heal them as they'd kissed.

Reaching for his pocket, Devin confirmed her suspicions. His hands shook as he pulled out a ring. A beautiful diamond ring. His eyes focused on hers. "Build a life with me. Marry me."

She gave him a soft smile. "You're sure that's what you want?"

He furrowed his brow. "Of course it is."

She slowly, pensively nodded.

He looked into her eyes with desperation. "Most girls say yes or no at this point."

Grinning wide, she reached into her own pocket, pulling out her own ring. It was an intricately carved dark wooden ring she'd bartered for with an elderly craftsman in their village.

Devin's eyes darted between her face and the ring. "You got me one?"

Saff sighed. "I pay attention in culture classes. I'd get A's in them if they were graded that way. I know it's Seeder tradition for the woman to ask. You take on my family sash at the ceremony—I should be the one asking."(n)

He cocked his head, smiling. "Come on. Most people still do the traditional ceremonies, but hardly anyone has the girl ask anymore. All of you come back with a human mindset about the guy asking."

She bit her lip in thought. This had become her home. Her people. "I think heritage is important. I love it here. As much as I love you. So, yes. I'll marry you, if you'll marry me."

His smile widened, until he looked down at the ring he'd gotten her. It was obviously a human design, nothing like Seeder jewelry. "I should have known that. I can get you something different."

She shook her head. "When did you even get it for me?"

His face turned pink as he ran a finger over the diamond. "Not long after you left. I guess it gave me something to look forward to, hoping you were waiting for me."

If he'd really bought it for her right after she'd left, that meant he'd been holding onto it for well over a year already. Her heart melted at his sweetness. "Then I love it even more."

He looked up, beaming. "You're sure?"

Nodding, she leaned in for a kiss. After pulling back, they exchanged rings. She instantly loved the feeling of it on her hand.

"Okay, then," he said with a sigh and a perma-smile. "Now the question is when. Obviously, spring is pretty popular, but that doesn't give us a lot of time to prepare."

With spring being the best time for female Seeders to make their yearly journey to the human world, it was common for those getting married to do it then. They could have a ceremony with human family and friends, and then a second ceremony back in the Green Lands.

Saff shrugged. "I don't need some huge to-do. You. Me. It's not like we don't have family nearby. When do *you* want to have the ceremony?"

His eyes roamed over her body, his mouth forming a mischievous grin. "Yesterday."

She smirked, leaning back on her elbows. "If we were married yesterday, we'd be doing *scandalous* things right now."

Devin inched forward, kneeling next to her. He bent down, caressing her neck with his lips. "They're not scandalous once you're married." He reached for her sides, tickling her.

Saff giggled and squirmed, shifting energy into her arms and legs to pin him down. She scrunched her nose. "No tickling!"

He grinned with defiance. "So, what will it be? What day are we aiming for?"

She sighed. "Would you hate it if we did spring?"

He shook his head with a soft smile. "I'd wait forever for you. I can manage spring."

She grinned back, letting his arms go but staying on top of him. "Forever? Then maybe we should push it back a couple years."

Narrowing his eyes, he moved his hands to her waist and hooked his fingers through the loops of her human-crafted jeans. "You think you are *sooo* funny."

She bit her lip.

"If you want spring, I vote first day of spring," he continued.

She raised her eyebrows in disbelief. "On sprout reveal day?"(o)

"Fine." He playfully stuck out his tongue. "The week after?"

She nodded. "Sounds like a plan." She looked down at his shirt more pensively. "You're still thinking you want a clutch?"

"I do. I thought you did, too."

"I think I do." She ran her fingertips over the fabric of his shirt. "Kind of a huge decision to make, though."

He frowned. "But it's years before that's even an option. And if we decided to not have one in the end, I'd still have you. And be the luckiest husband and uncle in the world."

She swallowed hard, having heard her Seeder parents' love story and knowing how difficult it had been for them to make the decision to have kids. The Seeder way of family life was far from easy.(p)

Saff drew a deep breath. "You. Me. Marriage. Spring. Then forever. We'll sort out the in-between as it comes."

He gave her a dimpled smile.

Saff's stomach growled, and she chuckled. "Now, about that picnic basket. I'm starving."

Devin kept his hands on her waist as she straddled him. "I vote we start with some dessert."

She grinned, but halted her approach when she spotted a mother walking by with her dozen little boys. Some of the boys gawked; the mother's disapproving glance was obvious. Saff cleared her throat and removed Devin's hands, getting off of him with a blush. "Maybe a little more of that later."

Sitting up and following Saff's gaze, Devin realized the cause of her behavior change, and smiled and waved at the little boys. "Maybe we should dig into that basket after all." He pulled the basket open. "And let's talk about what we want in a cottage together."

Just the idea of sharing a cottage almost made her want to change her mind and move up the wedding. But they'd been this patient; they could wait a few more months. As Devin pulled item after item out of the picnic basket, she watched him with admiration.

This was what it meant to have it all.(q)

TROUBLE IN THE GREEN LANDS

BOOK 2

Prologue

The Green Lands were divided into two peoples—the Seeders and the Ivies. They once lived and associated with each other, free to share the land, nurturing growth and community. But something changed over two centuries ago; a rising regime put an end to that. Where there was once community and cooperation, there was now conflict and contempt.

Seeder communities embraced the differences amongst their people. They found joy in simple comforts, honest work, and most of all, nurturing families and being wise stewards of nature. Each village would elect leadership to coordinate with neighboring communities, but any sort of formalities and laws were minimal. A code of ethics was deeply ingrained into Seeder society; it was rare to have a truly bad seed.

The Ivies turned to centralized leadership; they rallied around those who flattered them most. Pride swept through their kind like a whisper in the dark. A monarchy was established in the far mountains; the subjects withdrew from shared communities to start anew in their own kingdom. They were not without their own talents and skills, but their disdain for Seeders—and all that they stood for— grew. The Ivies claimed their lands had been usurped, those very communities they had deserted in favor of relocating to start a new nation. Their leadership demanded the best, and would settle for no less than unwavering respect. It needn't be earned when it could be taken.

The Green Lands stretched from the majestic Ivy palace in the mountains to the humble, bustling streets of the Seeder lands, with a great divide between. The Ivy side of the Green Lands was much more barren and desolate, a wasteland. The Seeder side was lush, green, well cared for. In the middle were the Neutral Woods.

At the edge of the Seeder side of the woods was a tall thicket, the Outer Wall, a heavily patrolled line of defense. Just miles further in was the Inner Wall, a thicket three times as tall, and the final line of defense against invasion and attack.

Ben donned a crisp uniform, walking down a quiet path through his home village to report for duty. Most people were still sound asleep; few lightkeepers glowed behind the windowpanes he passed. Happy cottages lined the dirt lane, the gardens on each property loosely resembling a vibrant jungle. The air, as always, was fresh and invigorating. He confidently squared his shoulders as he approached his new assignment.

Walking further from the center of the village, he became more aware of the thump and crunch of his footsteps on gravel, dirt, and twigs, all the while taking in the beauty of the sun rising behind the Inner Wall in the distance. Approaching the temple depositories, he nodded at the few women he passed, as was polite. They would acknowledge with a nod and a quick flash of neon-green eyes; he in turn extended his purple hair tips. Such was protocol in the border zones, as proof of identity that you were, indeed, a Seeder. Of course, some males could flash green eyes too, but that was hardly polite, as it was an ability only a mated male could possess.

He stopped to admire one attractive short blonde in particular as she fulfilled her duties at the temple depository. She stood at the carved jade well, her hands grasping an emerging root system. Closing her eyes, she breathed deeply, her chest rising. Her hands glowed a soft yellow, transferring energy to the roots—the roots that led to the border walls. The walls were that much stronger, more capable of protecting their people from harm, thanks to her contribution.

When she opened her eyes, Heather must have noticed Ben's gaze fixed on her—she blushed. She quickly finished, then walked toward her admirer, meeting him near the Inner Wall security point. She flashed green eyes; he responded with a wink.

He started the conversation with a smile. "Excuse me, ma'am. I must say that your eyes are *absolutely* stunning."

"Oh please, that's what all the guys say," she replied in her usual slightly nasal voice.

They shared a laugh, and he offered his arms for a hug. She accepted, squeezing him tight.

"You know, I think I might just marry you someday," he whispered into her ear.

"I might be okay with that. I'll pencil you in," she whispered back, still in his embrace.

Ben released her, they gave each other a knowing smile, and she snuck a quick kiss.

"I want to hear all about your day when you get back," she said, before leaving to return to the village.

He watched her walk away with a grin on his face. She was the most beautiful girl he knew—heart, body, soul. Someday, she'd be the mother of his children. Remembering their short exchange wasn't the reason he was there, and fully aware he had an audience, Ben shook his head and forced himself to focus on his responsibilities.

"Hey now, don't let a pretty face like that distract you from your important new duties," his colleague teased, standing by the large stone doorway at the security point.

"I don't understand why *any* girl would go for this loser. She falls for him just because he spends a year on human detail?" another poked fun at him.

Ben went along with the razzing from his friends, tucking his hands in his pockets and cocking his head to the side. "I don't know, guys, I got a girl *and* a promotion, and you've got what? Your sarcasm?"

"Ooooh, ouch!" one replied, while the other just laughed.

The friends playfully swung and blocked their blunted arm blades before letting him pass through.

Much more alert to his surroundings, he made his way through the forested safety zone to the Outer Wall. The giant Inner Wall cut off any residual sound from the villages. Out here eerie silence persisted, only punctuated by the soft buzzing of a passing dragonfly, a chatterbird scolding him from an apple tree that he snagged a ripe snack from, and the rustle of his own shoes marching forward. Once closer to the Outer Wall, he tucked the apple in his pocket and found a familiar clearing in the trees—a good launching point. He shifted his Seeder energy to his calves, communing with the wind around him. Taking a couple of steps, he launched himself up and forward, somersaulting and balancing in the breeze as he shot toward the wall. Gaining speed, he angled up toward the top of the thicket. With another somersault to slow his descent and get sound footing, he landed on the large platform at the top of the thicket wall.

Taking a left on the narrow walkway, he headed for his commander's platform station. "Reporting for duty," he announced on his approach.

"Ben, right?"

"Yes, sir."

"Murialson?"(r)

"That's the one."

"You know your way around by now?" the commander asked. "Go relieve Caleb."

"Yes, sir."

Ben found Caleb, a soldier nine years his senior, who was more than happy to see him, ready to head home for some well-deserved sleep.

"Any news?" Ben asked.

"It doesn't look good," Caleb reported. "Several more vines have made their way across the Neutral Woods." He shook his head, his frown conveying the severity of the problem. "I don't know how they're doing it. But these are just like the others. Fast-growing, thick, nearly impenetrable."

Why do we even call them that—'Neutral Woods'? Sure, they'd been named that after the old treaties were formed, around the time of the Great Division. But the Ivies had never respected those boundaries, constantly crossing them to ensure no Seeders could leave the confines of their own borders.

He stared at the massive bundle of vines below, which was easily six feet wide. A crew of a dozen men and women were hacking and sawing away at them, with minimal success. "You've got to give it to the leeches. These bastards know how to get creative," Ben said.

"Yeah." Caleb rubbed his chin and winced. "I might admire it more if I wasn't so worried about how we're going to stop it."

The news of this never-before-seen tactic still hadn't been widely shared throughout the Seeder nation. But that wouldn't last forever. And neither would their border walls if they couldn't find a solution. Ben's gut twisted with dread.

There was trouble brewing in the Green Lands.

Chapter 1

Saff woke to the sun peeking through the open screened bedroom window. Cherry blossoms just outside perfumed the room. The pendulum clock in the corner quietly ticked away. Sometimes when she was exhausted, the clock woke her a little later, but after three years in the Green Lands, her body had become used to the energy shifts in the seasons, and even in the days. The sun was up, and so was she. But she stayed in her cozy, warm bed for a while longer, soaking up the peace and serenity of the morning.

She glanced at the intricate cream tatted(s) curtains above the bed—a gift from one of many aunts. A wood dresser dominated the far wall, handcrafted by Devin's grandfather. She smiled, basking in the love and community embodied by each item in their cottage, most of which were gifts from their wedding.

One item hanging on the wall in the bedroom hadn't been gifted for their wedding—a painting Devin had insisted they keep. It was no Monet, but it was something he treasured—a seaside landscape she'd once painted for him in the human world, complete with creases from being folded in his pocket as he'd caught a breeze home.

Her gaze rested on Devin peacefully sleeping next to her. It wasn't possible to be happier. After the chaos and rush of the time they'd shared in the human world, they'd taken things slower when he got back. He'd ended up staying in the human world to help protect his last two sisters, returning just shy of a year after Saff had left. That year had given her ample time to meet people, take courses, grow closer to her Seeder family, and really find herself. Despite her love of the Green Lands, there hadn't been a day that went by that she hadn't thought of Devin, worried about him, and waited for him.

But he'd come back to her. They'd taken their time touring Seeder territory together and getting to know each other on a whole new level. Marriages in Seeder culture were serious and permanent. Not that divorces never happened, but the Seeder mating bond was for life. They'd known in high school they wanted to be together, but had agreed to take their time to ensure they weren't rushing into anything. Their wedding, just a few months prior—in the early spring—had been as simple as Seeder ceremonies got, and absolutely perfect.

Devin stirred in bed, opening his eyes with a gentle moan. Saff beamed and snuck a kiss.

Sliding his arms around her, he pulled her close. "Mmm, my favorite person."

"Yeah?" She studied his face.

He nodded.

"Ditto."

He raised his eyebrows. "You're your favorite person, too?"

She rolled her eyes, grinning and wrapping a leg around him. "Maybe I am now, after a ridiculous joke like that."

He frowned. "I thought it was a good joke. And if it didn't earn me a laugh, I know another way to get one." His smirk was mischievous.

Saff glared playfully as he inched his fingers to her sides, beginning his attack. She squirmed and giggled at his tickling. With the boost of energy that had accompanied her rooting in the Green Lands, and with three years of training under her belt, she could easily win this skirmish. But this time, she let him win. Devin pinned her down, getting lost in her eyes, sneaking a peck on the lips.

"I love you," she said.

"Ditto."

She bit her lip. "You love you, too?"

He busted out laughing, rolling off and snuggling up to her. "Touché." He ever so gently moved the sleeve of her nightgown to expose her shoulder, placing a sweet kiss there. "How much time do we have?"

"Hmm. I don't know." She reached her hand up and ran her fingers through his bedhead of sandy blond hair. "I was thinking about baking some muffins before work."

He wore a crooked, dimpled smile. "Liar. When was the last time you baked anything?"

She adopted a far-off look, as if calculating the days. "Baked? Or burned?"

Devin leaned forward, giving Saff a sweet, lingering kiss, the kind that always took her breath away. The clock chimed.

Lifting her head slightly, she pulled her strawberry blond hair to the side. She fixed her gaze on his dark brown eyes, now flickering with a hint of green. A neon, glowing green that he'd only had since their wedding. The warmth in her own blue eyes told her they were also shifting. The clock chimed once more. "I guess we have *that* much time."

"Mmm. You don't say. I can work with that."

Saff stood at the front of her log-hut classroom, a board of slate mounted behind her scribbled with chalk bullet points for the day's lesson. "Who can tell me why you have to be extra careful when playing sports with the humans?" she asked her classroom of two dozen eight-year-old boys.

A dark-haired boy named Dennis shot his hand up. "Because you can accidentally cut someone with your blades, or hurt them with your strength."

"Yes." She lifted her chin. "Any other reasons?"

Skyler, one of the shyer ones, raised his hand. "Because a human or Ivy might notice that you're too strong, or that you've transformed."

"Good job." She smiled, sitting on the edge of her wooden desk. "We have to be safe, and we have to be careful about detection over there. And," she held up a finger, "it's really not fair to use your powers when matching up against a human. We want good sportsmanship in either world."

"Not like Christopher in afternoon sparring yesterday," another boy chided.

Christopher glared at the other boy while several of their peers snickered. Movement at the open door caught Saff's attention. Devin stood there, lunch basket in hand. Saff glanced at the clock; he was ten minutes early.

"Hey! Your husband's here!" One of her boys had apparently also noticed. "That means lunch!"

"Nope." She slightly narrowed her eyes at Devin and he flashed a guilty frown. "Speaking of entertainment and games today, guys," she continued. "Let's revisit our discussion from earlier this morning—board games. I wouldn't want you to give away your lack of knowledge about something like that."

Devin let out a short laugh, then tried to disguise it as a cough. They shared a grin, knowing that was one of the things he hadn't been as well-versed on when he'd been trying to blend in as a human, back when he'd been one of her protectors.

"Someone asks you what your favorite board or card game is," she said. "I want to hear what you'd say if you forgot the names of the ones we've talked about."

"I think they're boring. I prefer video games!" one boy said.

"Very good. And believable. Any other ideas?"

"I can't pick a favorite. What's yours?" another boy offered.

She beamed. While she disliked lies, these would be the kind of lies that saved lives. "Brilliant deflection. Best when said with full confidence."

Devin winked at her.

Her stomach growled, and she decided to give in. "Alright. While at lunch, I want you to discuss what you've learned about games from your moms and aunts and uncles, okay? Board, card, video—all of them."

They all sat on the edge of their seats, barely listening anymore.

"Dismissed."

Devin backed away as the room erupted into a storm of little boys snatching their lunch satchels and bolting out the door.

Saff sighed and sauntered up to Devin, taking his free hand. "You are such a troublemaker. You know that?"

He squeezed her hand and pulled her outside. "I thought you liked that about me."

She chuckled as they walked across the grass to their usual path. One of Devin's sisters caught their attention from a nearby sparring field and waved. They returned the wave.

"Roasting me like that, though, ouch!" Devin continued.

Saff grinned. "Serves you right for barging into my classroom."

"Fair enough."

"Want to know what we're going to discuss next week in our unit on foods?" she asked as they turned onto a gravel path, waving at her brother Kyle.

"I'm scared to ask now." Devin arched an eyebrow, his tone playful.

She considered the other deficiencies in his Seeder network training before his assignment in the human world. "Road-trip snacks and elephant ears."

He let out a breathy laugh. "Alright. I need to see the list of all my shortcomings and deep, dark secrets that you're sharing with these boys. I thought I was a decent covert ops agent."

Releasing his hand, Saff wrapped her arm around his waist. "You were fantastic, love."

Ten minutes later, they sat on their favorite park bench, unpacking their lunch. Just yards away rested a peaceful little pond surrounded by cattails. Bright red-and-white butterflies danced from flower to flower. They made Saff think of her Seeder mom, Murial. She and Murial had spent countless outings painting nature scenes together, and Murial would always happily point out which plants and wildlife were unique to the Green Lands. These particular butterflies were also found in the human world, though the flowers they hovered between were a Green Lands exclusive.

Devin handed Saff a cloth napkin.

"So how has your day been?" she asked.

He shrugged. "Good. Like most days."

Devin worked mostly with the teens and preteens, with particular focus on covert operations—the kind he'd been part of, working protection detail for Saff and his sisters when they were in high school.

She took a sip of juice and smiled. "I'm glad you're back. And thanks for the letters."

He grinned. "Happy to do it."

His teaching position afforded him the special privilege of occasionally being chosen to deliver deep-cover boys to their fathers. Seeder families trained up their boys at an early age, selecting the most promising one of each family to leave as young as possible. Devin described escorting the boys as one of the most touching things he'd ever experienced, a great honor to be a part of. The journey was so difficult for each little boy, but the payoff was equally rewarding. Seeder fathers and husbands had been in the human world for years—working on their covers, keeping their distance while coordinating their daughters, and missing their wives and the sons they'd yet to meet.

That meeting—the first time a Seeder father got to meet one of his children, and they knew him for who he really was—was tender. From that point on, he placed them under the care of someone trusted, and continued their training in secret.[t]

"They looked like they're doing alright?" Saff frowned, thinking of her human parents, Pam and George.

"Yeah. They're doing great."

It was a complicated subject, that Devin was physically able to go between the worlds more easily, more often. But he only did it for work and for the week each spring he joined Saff for her visit. She'd accepted the limitation as best she could.

Whenever possible, if the boy he was dropping off was within a reasonable distance of her parents' current location, he'd take a letter from Saff to swap with her parents. She appreciated that extra line of connection, as rare as it was.

Three years prior, it had been a rude awakening to learn of her true nature and the dangers and limitations that came with being a Seeder. But to be a botanical being, having powers and abilities no human could fathom, enriched her life beyond compare and validated her decision to leave behind the world she was raised in.

While she never lacked for company, having twenty-three siblings, and having gained twenty-three siblings-in-law when she and Devin had married, she'd still exerted the effort to make the grueling journey back the last three springs to see her human host parents. She cherished the short amount of time she could spend with them. And with only a few years left where she would be able to make that journey, she vowed to not waste a moment, and never miss the opportunity when it arose. Seeder women generally only had ten years between their initial rooting and becoming fully-rooted, making them incapable of leaving the Green Lands.

"And thanks for Zach's letter." She smiled again, thinking of her human best friend. She'd only been able to coordinate seeing him once since she'd left, but he sometimes sent letters to her parents to pass along.

Devin popped a raspberry in his mouth. "No prob. How's he doing?"

"He's good. Questioning his major. Dating a new girl."

Devin grabbed a handful of grape tomatoes. "Hmm. Indecisive. Not the same girl as this spring?"

"Nope." She picked out a couple of tomatoes for herself. "But he sounds happy."

Devin wore a warm smile. "Good."

She pulled a fork and a glass jar of carrot slaw from the basket. While happily munching in silence, she mentally planned the rest of her day. Just one more hour with the little boys, then she had three hours at the healing station of their learning institution.

After they finished up their food, Saff leaned against Devin as he wrapped his arms around her. He planted a kiss on her cheek. "So... Are you nervous? Or excited? About next week."

She blushed. "Yes."

She'd accepted a new position at the school. She would miss working with the boys, and also helping at the healing station, but she was moving on to something she wanted even more.

"You'll be amazing." He nuzzled her neck.

She beamed, sneaking a kiss. "We don't make a horrible team."

He narrowed his eyes, stealing a peck on the lips in return. "Not at all."

She blew out a puff of air. "We'd better head back. Last time I took a longer lunch than my class, it was a madhouse when I got there."

He chuckled as they stood up. "Isn't it a fun glimpse into my childhood?"

They started to walk the weeping-willow-lined trail back to the school, hand in hand. Devin swung the woven basket in his free hand.

"Heather and Ben are still coming over for dinner tonight, right?" Saff said.

"Yes, ma'am. But Ben and I might be a little late."

She scrunched her eyebrows.

Devin shrugged. "I don't know. He asked me to drop by his station after work."

"Okay... Well, I guess I'll see you then. Love you."

Just short of being in sight of the school, he stopped her, giving her a hug. "I love you, too."

❄

Saff made it home to their cottage first, as expected. The tiny little thing was the perfect size for a married couple like Saff and Devin, too young to have a clutch yet, or for those who'd decided not to. It was as quaint as any of the cottages in this part of the village. The thatched roof sat atop a sturdy frame of raw wood with a charming pattern to it. Before opening the front door, she snapped off a handful of fresh pea pods from the front garden box.

Once inside, she set out a few juicy peaches on the round wooden dining table, then surveyed the living area to make sure it was all tidy. Their small kitchen and dining area connected to the living room. A wood-and-cotton sofa accompanied matching chairs. On the wall hung several pictures. Saff walked up to them, smiling wide. This wall of pictures was something she treasured as much as her own wedding ring or jade necklace—photos from her childhood and from visits to the human world. She lifted a hand, rubbing the bend from one photo. She'd always loved that one—Devin, Zach, Ben, and Heather on a roller coaster in the human world after she'd left. Devin wore a goofy expression for the camera, just for Saff. He'd said it was fun, but hadn't really seemed that impressed—he could fly, after all, so a little roller coaster plunge hadn't been that remarkable. Cotton candy and elephant ears had been the highlight of that day for him. Next to that photo, a small glow-in-the-dark star clung to the wall, a little piece of her first home.

A knock sounded on the door and Saff opened it, happy to see her sister-in-law, Heather.

After a big hug and swapping a jar of honey from Heather for a basket of peaches, they settled down for a chat.

"So, have you guys been looking for a place of your own?" Saff asked.

Heather sighed with a frown. "I wish. I'm afraid we might have to push back the wedding."

Saff matched her frown. "Why?"

Heather shrugged. "He's going to be so busy with his promotion. I don't know... Maybe I'm just overthinking things."

Saff gave her a reassuring smile. "We might have simpler ceremonies than some humans, but we sure have a lot more family to coordinate, don't we?"

Heather laughed. "Yep!"

"Either way, it'll be perfect." Saff mused about her wedding day. Her heart had swelled, not only at marrying Devin, but at all the family support they'd enjoyed. The exact same family members would be attending Heather and Ben's wedding, seeing as Heather was Devin's sister, and Ben, Saff's brother.

Saff had returned to the Green Lands filled with both curiosity and fear of the drastic changes that faced her upon leaving the human world. But this huge family, all of these built-in friendships, had made all the difference in the world. The energy of the realm was almost addictive, but more than anything, the people here made it home. Giving up the internet and a lot of modern comforts had been a token sacrifice for the free time and community she'd gained here.

"Did you hear Tabatha went out with Greg again?" Heather grinned.

"What?! I just talked to her a couple days ago. She didn't tell me that."

"Yeah." Heather fidgeted with a loose thread on her shirt. "I think she doesn't want people judging her and assuming he's the reason she's changing positions."

"Hmm..." Tabatha had recently stopped taking optional courses provided by the community, instead moving to full-time work at a local grain mill. The mill where this guy, Greg, worked. It was hard for Saff to keep up with all of her family, but Tabatha wasn't only her sister, she had also been one of her best friends back in the human world. "Well, I'll try my best to not draw that conclusion." Saff snickered. "Are *you* still going to join me for more classes?"

Heather wrinkled her nose. "I don't know."

Saff frowned again. They'd taken a lot of classes together, having returned from the human world within a few months of each other. There were mandatory classes upon Seeder girls' returns—courses on mastering their powers, basic history and cultural lessons. But several more courses were offered as optional. Having been a nearly straight-A student in human high school, and being enthralled with her home realm, Saff was trying to take them all.

"I get it. Not everyone's thrilled with the idea of school when it's not mandatory."

Heather fidgeted with her engagement ring. "Well... Maybe it's hypocritical of me to mention Tabatha ... but if Ben's going to be so busy with work soon..."

Saff raised her eyebrows.

"Well," Heather continued with rosy cheeks. "I've applied to work at a healing station just inside the Inner Wall."

"Gotcha. And I really don't judge you for it. Devin and I both love our work, and it's an awesome perk to work so close to each other. Ben's a great soldier. You're a great healer. It makes sense." Both of Heather's human parents were nurses.

Heather smiled. Saff swallowed hard, trying to stay positive. Ben really *was* a great soldier. He'd saved her life back in her human high school. But it still gave her a lot to worry about, having him positioned at the Outer Wall. That wall hadn't come close to falling from Ivy attacks in decades. But that didn't mean casualties didn't happen. Their border walls were charged by a massive root system running the length of the entire Seeder territory. Any regular thicket would be relatively useless as a defense, but this one was not only massive, it harnessed the energy given by Seeder women, making it near impervious, and every village contributed. The energy imparted to the thicket made it fire- and cut-resistant. Resistant, not proof. The Ivy Kingdom only seemed to care about one thing—Seeder annihilation. Seeders still had to patrol the border walls to stop Ivies from converging on a single point to weaken it and break through. If it wasn't the Ivy assassins sent after her kind in the human world, it was their soldiers constantly patrolling Seeder borders.

After another half hour of chatting, Devin and Ben arrived. Ben settled down on an armchair and wrapped his arms tight around Heather as she sat on his lap. Devin claimed a spot next to Saff on the sofa.

"So, what made you two late?" Saff asked.

Devin and Ben passed a look between one another, frowning. "Well, um..." Devin started.

"I'm sure we'll figure it out," Ben chimed in. "Just the leeches, as usual. But their approach is ... not usual." He cleared his throat, shifting in his seat. "Don't worry about it. The elders are saying they don't remember hearing about this tactic, but they're searching the archives."

Anxiety settled into the pit of Saff's stomach. She loved her life here. Nearly every part of it. The uncertainty of a new kind of attack reminded her of something she'd struggled to put behind her—the fact that they never figured out how the attacks on her and her family in the human world were connected to Ivy royalty. Attacks that had left ten Ivies dead at her childhood home. Attacks that had something to do with an Ivy royal named Nuren.(u)

Chapter 2

Samantha grew up with a cousin her same age next door. They were like two peas in a pod. That is, until Samantha's cousin, Lyza, turned seventeen. Lyza became distant, too busy to spend time with Samantha; and then she left. Lyza, as it turns out, wasn't human.

As much as she missed her best friend, Samantha looked forward to the few moments she would spend with her cousin during spring break each year. The last year Lyza would ever be able to visit her in the human world, she asked Samantha for a favor. Samantha happily accepted the request. She was unmarried, but willing to take on the challenge of adopting a little girl. Lyza's little girl. Or at least one of them. The day after Samantha received her cousin's daughter, the sweet baby molted her birth wisps, transforming into a tiny little human. Promising to do everything in her power to make this child happy and safe, she gave her a human name for the time she would be hers. She would be known as Rachel.(v)

Rachel lay in bed, snuggling the teddy bear she figured she was probably too old for, but she didn't really care. She stared at her bedside table, eyes fixed on a folded letter.

She knew, statistically, that she was loved. Being confident about that, however, wasn't always easy. Rachel grew up with three father figures in her life. She was aware from a young age that she was adopted. As it was a partially open adoption, her birth father—father-figure number one—would sometimes send her letters. Usually on birthdays, but sometimes for holidays, or at random. This letter was from father-figure number one, Garrett. He'd sent her a letter to wish her a good school year. It wasn't that her mom wasn't enough, or that Garrett wasn't caring in his letters, but Rachel always asked herself why he even tried to maintain a relationship with her after all these years, if he had been willing to give her up when she was a baby.

Rachel sighed, squeezing the bear tighter. That wasn't fair. Parents gave up their kids for a large variety of reasons, and she knew it was usually in the best interest of the children.

She frowned a little, thinking of father-figure number two, Brad. Brad had given this stuffed animal to her when he adopted her. He'd come into her life when she was five years old. He was kind and loving to both Rachel and her mom. They were husband, wife, and daughter—the whole package. But then Brad only stayed for two years. Like many children, Rachel was assured his decision to leave had nothing to do with her, but it didn't make it any easier. He never even said goodbye. He never once visited or reached out after leaving. It had been devastating for both Rachel and her mom.

But her mom had learned to love again. Less than a year later, a new man came into their lives—Rob. He took to Rachel quickly and treated her like his own. And he treated her mom right. Despite the pain of previous rejection, Rachel was grateful to have a good man in their lives. But she'd never been able to call her mom's new husband 'Dad.' It hurt too much to use that title again. And the older she became, the more she appreciated her mom and stepdad for not pushing that on her.

The shower turning off downstairs announced she had to stop dawdling. Rob was up, and that meant Rachel needed to get ready for school. She groaned, throwing off the covers. After a quick shower of her own, she blow-dried her hair and put on a full face of makeup. She pulled out her favorite pair of jeans and a cute button-up shirt. Smirking, she left one more button open than she normally would have.

Downstairs, she poured a bowl of sweetened puffed rice cereal. After eating in solitude and leaving the bowl in the sink, she grabbed her backpack, slinging it over her shoulder. Her mom, a curly-haired brunette of medium build, came down the hallway, offering a bright smile and a hug.

"Are you ready for today?" Her mom squeezed tighter.

Rachel smiled. "You're not getting too sentimental, are you?"

Her mom pulled back, holding Rachel's shoulders. "It comes with old age." She winked.

Rachel rolled her eyes. "Not old. *Aged.*"

Chuckling, her mom reached over and buttoned up a couple of Rachel's buttons. "Aged sounds so much worse. Unless you're wine or cheese, and I am neither."

Rachel shrugged. "I tried." She gave her mom another quick hug before heading out the front door, undoing the buttons her mom had just done up.

"Dang! Why do you look so sexy now that you're a senior?" David greeted Rachel from his shiny red car, picking her up for school. She often felt a little plain with her brown hair and brown eyes, but he never failed to remind her exactly how much he liked everything about her.

"You don't say." She grinned, throwing her backpack in the back seat and getting in. "That much difference between the summer-me of yesterday and the senior-me of today, huh?"

"You've definitely matured." He looked her over from top to bottom. "Yep, I'd definitely say you've matured." He wiggled his eyebrows.

Rachel squinted. He was tall, in great shape, and had dark brown hair and stunning green eyes. "Hmm..." She shook her head. "Nope, don't think I see it in you. That's too bad."

His jaw dropped. "You did not just say that."

She winked at him, and he stretched over the center console to greet her with a kiss. And it was *not* a little peck on the cheek.

"Ahem." Someone clearing their throat broke them from their mini make-out session.

David wore an awkward smile. "Hi, Mr. Samuels."

Rachel sheepishly wiped off her lips. "Have a good day at work, Rob."

"I intend to, thanks. One small problem—Romeo here is blocking my car." Rob furrowed his brow, holding a coffee cup with his company's logo on it. He had a kind face, but knew how to show when he meant business. Right now, he was somewhere in the middle, though his trimmed beard had a way of pushing it more toward the intimidating side.

"Sorry, sir," David said. "I'll make sure to pull forward more next time."

"I'd appreciate that. And perhaps you can save some of that energy and concentration for school and driving, instead of expending it all on my girl."

Rachel pressed her lips together, turning beet red. "K, bye, Rob!" She gave David a look begging him to floor it. Not that she disliked Rob; he really was a nice stepdad. And he obviously cared for her well-being. And Rob generally liked

David, but ... getting handsy with his stepdaughter was not on his list of approved activities.

David and Rachel had been an item for two years now. He enjoyed basketball and his time with the guys, but he always carved out time for what mattered to her. He came to most of her volleyball games and made a point of having special date nights.

After a short drive to school and the nightmare of finding parking, they walked hand in hand to the benches near the front entrance. Sliding onto a metal bench, they waited for their friends.

They didn't have to wait long; her best friend Meg strolled up with her boyfriend, Eric.

Rachel had met Meg the summer after her dad had left them. Meg had moved in down the street and they became instant friends. They always had each other's backs, no matter what. They'd enjoyed countless slumber parties and hiking adventures over the years. Rachel's mom had tried to teach her how to wear makeup when she'd wanted to learn, but Meg had been the real teacher—she could nail a winged eyeliner better than a winged bird could fly.

Unlike Rachel, Meg never struggled with self-confidence. Rachel was cute, but Meg was a bombshell, and had the kindest heart of anyone Rachel knew. But there wasn't any jealousy or rivalry between them. If anything, they were practically sisters. Meg was the one who had helped Rachel build up the courage to ask David on a date in the first place; Rachel had been drooling over him for weeks.

Meg's messy bun of jet-black hair bounced as she and Eric approached Rachel and David. She was wearing bright-red lipstick and an adorable top she'd bought when she and Rachel last went shopping. Her jeans hugged her curves in the right places, and Eric smiled with his arm around her.

Eric was a newer addition to their posse; he and Meg had just started dating over the summer. But he fit in well. He and Meg made a great pair; just like her, he was easy on the eyes and had a huge heart. He dressed sharp for the first day of school—he'd have fit right in on the cover of a magazine, or in a country club. Paired with his outfit, his blond hair and strong jawline made it easy for people to misjudge him as a stuck-up preppy kid. But the way he'd met Meg in the first place—at an animal shelter—was so sickeningly sweet, and so absolutely them.

Meg held two coffee cups and Eric had another in his hand. Rachel moved onto David's lap to make more room on the bench, but their friends stayed standing.

"I bring *good* beverage for *good* luck," Meg announced while handing one of her cups to Rachel.

Rachel savored the warmth in her hands, taking a swig. The piping hot liquid had a hint of hazelnut and French vanilla. "Mmm. Have I told you how much I love that you're a barista? Crappy hours, great perks."

"I can't help but notice you forgot one for yours truly," David said, eyebrows raised. "You know, they *do* make drink holders for four cups, right?"

"Yeah. I mean, I considered it. But," Meg pointed to Eric, "boyfriend," she then pointed to Rachel, "best friend." She shrugged. "And you're just ... David."

"You wound me," he replied wryly.

"It is okay. I shall share my spoils with you," Rachel said, taking another sip before handing it to him.

"So, Meg, how was your fun adventure this summer?" David asked before taking a drink.

"Paris is *not* overrated. Nor are the hot French guys." She winked at Rachel.

"Hey! Right here," Eric complained lightheartedly.

"I kid. I only have eyes for you!" Meg nudged him. "I mean, you're lucky we met *before* my trip, 'cause..."

Eric challenged her with a smirk, clearly knowing she was joking just to get a rise out of him. "If you need some time alone with your fantasies, I can head inside now." He pointed to the front doors of their high school.

She chuckled and gently rubbed noses with him.

Rachel extricated her drink from David's hands, taking another swig. She lifted the mostly full cup of coffee over her head, looking to see the bottom where Meg made a habit of writing her a little message each time she brought her a drink from work.

"Seriously?" David snatched it from her hands.

"Hey! I was looking at my love note," Rachel protested with a slight pout. "It's like a fortune cookie—it may be vital for a good start to my day."

"Yeah, well, fortune cookies don't give you second-degree burns. I like your face the way it is," he chided. "And mine as well, thank you very much."

She rolled her eyes. "I was being careful."

He gave her a disapproving look.

"Fine, whatever. Maybe you need the caffeine more than me if you're going to be grumpy." She got off of his lap, moving back onto the bench next to him.

Meg and Eric glanced at each other with wide eyes. "Yeah, we're going to head inside. We'll see you guys later." Eric wrapped his arm around her again, and they left.

Rachel let out a sigh, taking her coffee back. "Wait to read the bottom until the scalding hot liquid is all gone—noted."

"Thank you."

She sipped her coffee with a scowl.

David's lips formed a mischievous grin. "I know how we can make that coffee better."

She waited a moment, then took the olive branch. "How's that?"

"It's a little black for my liking, maybe it needs more sugar." He winked.

She laughed. "You think you can sweeten things up for me, do you?"

"It's my forte." He leaned in for a kiss.

Rachel recoiled after a small peck. "Ouch!"

"What?" He scanned her face with concern.

"My boyfriend warned me about being burned, and you're pretty hot." She smirked.

Rolling his eyes, David stood, offering his hand. "Let's get to class, dork."

Chapter 3

Saff sat on the ground, weeding in their garden, lost in thought. She'd recently started working as a welcoming apprentice. Once Seeder girls returned to their homeland, they still had so much to learn. They received minimal training in the human world to keep them safe and get them home to the Green Lands, but their education was far from over once they rooted in their ancestral lands.

Saff had an undeniable natural aptitude and strength when it came to harnessing Seeder energy. Devin had told her it was because she was stubborn and determined, and just naturally gifted. But Saff sometimes wondered if it was something else. There had to be an explanation for her ability to harness nearly as much energy as a fully-rooted matriarch. Before the Great Poisoning, Seeder women had actually been more powerful, but the lingering Ivy poison in their soil must have affected them, even if it didn't kill them like it did their young daughters before their powers came in. Saff must be immune—no one could offer a different explanation for why she could harness more energy than other girls her age.

She dug deep into the soil, trying to get to the bottom of the bindweed root system attempting to choke out their beets. This had been a recent discovery for Saff, that she might be immune to the poison that had forced her to grow up in the human world. She hadn't met anyone else immune, not that they made it a practice of testing those waters. Seeder girls were swept away to the human world the same morning they sprouted. Taking a risk to see if one was immune wasn't something any caring parent would do—it meant certain death if they weren't. From unfortunate and rare experiences, Seeders knew their lands were still poisoned; daughters who weren't taken away at the seedling reveals always died. *Always.* Saff couldn't imagine her Seeder parents gambling the lives of their twelve daughters to discover one of them held an immunity no one else had heard of.

Either way, the reason for Saff's extra capacity to wield energy didn't matter—she was still embarrassed by the attention. It had taken her some time to accept the offer to apprentice in a welcoming position, but she found it immensely rewarding. Girls were often confused, unsure, and even overwhelmed when they first returned.

It gave Saff a deep sense of fulfillment, being able to guide girls just like her in the wonder of their abilities. Equally rewarding was helping in the more emotional aspects of their transition to a new way of life.

As she finished weeding a row in the garden, a pair of hands slid onto her shoulders. "Mmm, that feels nice." She moaned as the hands worked on her knots. "But we need to be careful, my husband will be home any time now."

Her masseuse crouched down and whispered in her ear, "Mi amor, take me now before we're caught!"

She giggled like a giddy schoolgirl. "Hey, you, how was your visit?"

Devin ruffled his hair, sitting down next to her. "It was ... a visit."

"Hmm... That good, huh?"

"Not as good as this part of my day." He smiled warmly, giving her a peck on the cheek.

She let out a frustrated sigh, surveying the garden. The row of beets she'd just finished with had been planted wonky from the start. "You know, for being *green* folk, in the *Green* Lands, I really don't have much of a *green* thumb."

He scrunched his face, shaking his head. "Yeah, I guess there's a reason we take our parents up on their offers for Sunday dinners."

"Rude!" she protested, her jaw dropping.

"I'm kidding, you know that." He held out his hand for the trowel she'd been using. "I've always said we're better together, right?" He nudged her arm.

After some time working in the garden together, they stood and put the hand tools away for the day. Devin reached over and wiped at a smudge of dirt on Saff's forehead.

"Dirty work," she commented, dusting herself off.

"I like you when you're dirty." He puckered his lips.

"That's a shame, I was going to hit the shower." She raised her eyebrows and flashed neon-green eyes before heading into their cottage.

"Well, I mean, I like dirty. Or showers. Or being dirty in showers." He followed after her. "I'm not picky."

"So, tell me about the meeting," Saff said while brushing out her wet hair. "What's the bad news? I saw Ben's face earlier. It can't be good."

"Yeah, it's not great." Devin frowned. "There's been another surge. They breached the Outer Wall again last night."

Saff stopped, swallowing hard. "That's ... *really* not good." She hoped she was overreacting, but that hadn't happened even in her parents' lifetimes. "We still don't know how they're doing it?"

"There's ... a theory." He shook his head in despair. "It's probably unrelated. We're just kinda grasping at straws at this point. But, if it's what the neighboring council suspects..." His voice trailed off. "It's unimaginable," he whispered.

She put the brush down and wrapped her arms around him. "We'll figure it out."

"Yeah." He failed at sounding as though he believed her assertion. "Either way, I'm taking my class to the Inner Wall tomorrow; they're going to get a hands-on lesson in defense."

Saff nodded, sick to her stomach. Word had crossed the entire nation, from village to village on the borders, and even in the back territories. *No one* could explain what the Ivies were doing, or how they were accomplishing it. Elders had been consulted, as had old archives. But Saff had known from the start that the archives would be useless, or at least she'd feared they would be.

Devin had been right all those years ago when he'd first explained the threat to her. Ivies were clever liars, thieves, and murderers. Something they'd stolen in their exodus during the 'years of parting' and in raids during the following years of escalated fighting, were books packed with knowledge of their history. Barely any books remained in Seeder possession about the Ivies. Elders swore up and down that the Ivies had taken even more than that.

Very few Seeders were assigned to spy duty, which involved quick flybys to check on the state of the Ivy Kingdom. But they still did it from time to time. This new form of attack at first sounded like something the elders had called the 'Mother Vines,' and they'd wondered if the Mother Vines had mutated. But this was different, something altogether new. Something that crossed the Neutral Woods and led right to the Ivy palace.

Chapter 4

Rachel and Meg loved double dates with their men, but the guys didn't much care for the idea. Eric and David got along fine, but they didn't exactly have a blossoming bromance. The four of them would hang out on occasion; usually a movie or game night a couple of times a month.

Three weeks into school, they gathered for a movie night at Rachel's place. They'd planned to stream a much-anticipated new release and Rachel's place was always the go-to location. Her mom and stepdad weren't helicopter parents, but they understood how teenagers worked. Their door was always open, and Rob's income as a regional sales director gave them a nice house with an amazing theater room.

Meg was cuddled up next to Eric on the love seat, chatting away. Rachel and David arrived with fresh popcorn and licorice. After setting the popcorn down on the coffee table, Rachel crawled into his lap on the leather sofa.

"You know, I think I'm going to try out for the hockey team this year," David said while yanking off a piece of licorice with his teeth.

Meg lifted one eyebrow in disbelief. "We don't have a hockey team."

"What?" David furrowed his brow. "But I love hockey."

Rachel shook her head in confusion. "Do you even know how to play hockey?"

He grinned. "I think I'm pretty good at the tonsil variety."

She let out an exasperated sigh.

"Dude, get a room," Eric said. He was never afraid of sharing his opinions, especially when annoyed.

"That's what I keep suggesting." David shrugged.

Rachel punched him hard in the arm. "That's not funny!"

"TMI." Eric rolled his eyes.

Meg covered her ears with her hands. "Nah-nah-nah-nah. I'm not hearing this."

"Can we just get the movie started?" Eric asked, clearly irritated.

"We're actually waiting for someone else," Rachel announced with a forced smile.

Meg and Eric were visibly surprised, but David looked rather put out, having already heard the news.

"Jeff is coming over to watch," Rachel said.

Meg frowned, reaching for a drink on a side table. "The junior that comes over for piano lessons with your mom?"

"That's the one," David said, gnawing off another piece of licorice.

"Why?" Meg asked.

Rachel sighed again. "My parents think it would be good for him. I guess he's had a hard time adjusting after moving here over the summer."

"Yeah, that's 'cause he's awkward," Eric added, adjusting in his seat before taking Meg's hand again.

"And he's already over here all the time," David complained. "I swear he's been over here every other day since school started, doing one thing or another."

Rachel glared at David. "Don't be a jerk. He needs money to save up for college. Rob's happy to give him some yardwork to do." She stood, grabbing the bowl of popcorn, then sat on the opposite end of the couch. "Speaking of not being rude, I don't want to make him feel like a fifth wheel." She munched on popcorn, making it clear with her gaze that the distance between herself and David was intentional.

He tilted his head to the side. "I don't see why this charity case means *I* have to suffer."

Rachel scowled. "Don't be a dick. Go take a cold shower or something."

He winked. "I'll take *any* temperature of shower, if you'll join me."

Rachel's face didn't budge. She could admit she was flattered by how much he flirted. But sometimes, he took things too far, and she didn't always speak up.

"David," Meg said in warning.

David sighed. "Fine. I can play nice." He placed a hand over his heart. "I will be on *my* side of the couch. Contemplating a sad, lonely existence." He melodramatically sniffled while wiping away a fake tear.

Rachel grinned. "You're so giving." Sarcasm was one of their love languages.

The doorbell rang and Rachel stood to go get it. Leaning down as she passed David, she whispered in his ear, "If you can behave, I can make it up to you."

"I will be an A-plus student," he hollered down the hall as she walked away.

Jeff joined them and quietly watched the movie from the comfort of a recliner. Rachel and Meg tried their best to make him feel included in the conversation after the movie, but he ended up leaving before everyone else; it was still awkward. The poor guy was an underclassman, had just moved to a new area, and was ... not ugly, but also not the kind of guy girls were swooning over. Rachel couldn't help but feel bad for him. He was physically fit, but his hair was a bit unruly, and his parents obviously couldn't afford as nice of clothing as hers could. And like Eric had said, he was just ... awkward. He'd sometimes make odd references, or would be confused by normal ones. And he had very little filter. While she wouldn't have chosen to do it on her own, Rachel had agreed to her parents' request to try and incorporate him into their group activities until he found his place in school.

Not long after Jeff had left, Rachel ended up sending everyone else home, too. Meg had wanted to hang out longer, and David would have been more than happy to spend some time alone with Rachel making out, but Rachel had started to feel under the weather.

Nauseous and tired, Rachel took some antacids and went to bed early. But she was restless the entire night—tossing and turning, overheating, then shivering. Eventually she found sleep, only to be woken by a text from David. She cancelled their plans for the day.

Too drained to get out of bed, she pulled the covers over her head to block out the sunlight shining through her window. The next thing to wake her was a knock on her bedroom door.

"Come in," she muttered, forcing herself to raise her voice.

The door clicked open. "You okay?" her mom asked.

Rachel pulled back the covers and scratched her arm where it tingled—between her wrist and elbow. "Just feeling like crap."

Her mom surveyed her with slightly narrowed eyes. "Yeah? What's wrong?"

It was probably just a twenty-four-hour flu, but Rachel shared her symptoms.

Nodding, her mom stayed silent for a moment. "Well, rest up. We'll see how you feel in a little while? Want me to bring you something to eat?"

Rachel declined breakfast but guzzled the water her mom brought her. The water at least seemed to help.

A couple of hours later, her mom came back to check on her. "Alright, you and me. Movie and chicken noodle soup." She wore a forced smile.

After significant coaxing, Rachel finally rolled out of bed, throwing her hair into a messy bun and planting herself on the couch of the theater room. The soup was perfectly salty, with the right mix of egg noodles, chicken, and vegetables. It was one of her mom's few signature dishes, and it always helped in one way or another.

As they slurped down their soup, they watched an old DVD of *The Inn of the Sixth Happiness*. That had always been one of the classics they watched together when one of them was sick. Sometimes it was *Dancing in the Rain* or *The Sound of Music*—Rachel's mom loved the older stuff.

Without fail, Rachel cried when the older lady died in the movie. While trying to inconspicuously wipe away tears, she noticed her mom watching her.

"What?" Rachel chuckled. "You always cry in this one, too."

"Yeah," her mom whispered, frowning and turning to look at the screen.

For the rest of the movie, Rachel kept feeling her mom's eyes on her, but every time she looked, her mom would get up to grab something else to drink or snack on, or turn to watch the screen again.

By the time the end credits were rolling, Rachel was ready for a nap. If anything, she was feeling worse. Her mom grabbed her a blanket as Rachel lay down on the couch.

"Are you getting sick, too?" Rachel asked, her brow furrowed. Her mom's agitation was plastered on her face and spelled out in every action. She often doted on Rachel when she was sick, but not normally to this extent.

"No, I'm fine." Her hesitant smile and tone were far from matching her words. "And you'll feel better in no time." She kissed Rachel on the forehead and turned off the lights, heading out of the room.

Hours later, Rachel joined her mom for dinner and then in the living room once Rob got home from work.

"We need to tell you something, sweetheart," her mom said, sitting next to Rob on the sofa.

Rachel glanced between the two. Rob showed a hint of a frown, her mom a much more grim expression. Samantha gripped Rob's hand tightly.

"What's wrong?" Rachel's heart rate skyrocketed. "Did someone die?"

Her mom took a deep breath. "No, sweetie. It's just—" She pursed her lips, fighting back tears.

Rachel looked to Rob.

"There's no easy way to say this," he began. "You know you're adopted."

"Yeah..."

"Here's a letter from your biological father. It'll explain what's going on. We can help fill in any of the gaps."

Rachel hesitantly stood and took the envelope from her mom's hand. It was odd to get another letter so soon after the surprise back-to-school one.

This new letter was nothing like the others she'd gotten from her biological father over the years. While the penmanship was recognizable as his, this one *had* to have been written by a madman. It told her she wasn't human, of all things. It warned she was in danger. And worst of all, it said she'd be leaving behind the world as she knew it. She read the letter twice to try and grasp what he was getting at.

Rachel lowered the letter, gazing into her parents' eyes. "This has to be a really bad joke. You've read this?"

They nodded. Samantha found her voice. "It's not a joke. I grew up with your mom. I know what you are." She grimaced, fighting back more tears. "I, uh... Your arms hurt, don't they?"

Nodding, Rachel gently rubbed them. Where they'd been itching earlier in the day, they now ached a bit.

"Yeah, your blades," her mom said. "And your eyes ... during the movie. We have something for you that you'll need to wear at all times. It'll help you feel better, stay safe, and give us more time together."

Rachel shook her head in disbelief. "No. What are you talking about? I've never even met this man. *This* is my home."

"You know we love you," Rob said. "But it's time for you to go live with your people."

Rachel's eyes filled with tears, and she appealed to her mom. "You both think I should go?"

A tear rolled down Samantha's cheek. "Yes."

And just like that, Rachel knew her life would never be the same. She sniffled, looking down at her fidgeting hands.

Rob stood and approached Rachel with a small white box, handing it to her. "This is from your biological dad. It should make you feel better."

Opening the box, Rachel eyed the contents—a necklace, a long chain with a green stone pendant.

"You need to wear it with the carving next to your skin," Samantha added.

Rachel lifted the necklace from the box, running her thumb over the sun symbol carved into the rock. Rob continued to explain what it could do for her.

The charm would temper the change she was going through, letting it remain undetected and allowing them more time together.

She slipped on the necklace, tucking the pendant under her shirt, and all of the aches and pains and nausea Rachel had been dealing with shrank away within a matter of minutes. It didn't, however, do anything for her struggle to grasp her new reality.

Samantha cleared her throat, wiping away tears and putting on a brave face. "Your blooming will probably take three or four months to progress, and then you'll have another three to four months to train with your powers. For Seeders, it's customary to wait longer to break the news to you girls, but we agreed," she looked at Rob, squeezing his hand before turning to face Rachel again, "that this would be better for you. Knowing earlier will give you a better chance to prepare for training. And you'll be able to enjoy the time you have left here."

Rachel nodded, her mind lost in a sea of confusion and hurt and shock.

"There's a lot you can still enjoy over the next few months," Rob encouraged. "Especially before your formal training starts. You'll be doing that with Jeff—he's one of your brothers."

Rachel blinked, shocked at the additional revelation. The letter had said she had a ton of siblings. "Okay," she said in a daze. "Can I go lie down?"

Samantha frowned. "Yeah, sweetheart. If you want to. We can talk about the rest later."

After ambling upstairs to her bedroom, Rachel set the letter from Garrett down on her bedside table. Before plopping down in bed, she stared at herself in the mirror. She was ... a Seeder. She wasn't from this world.

She removed her necklace for just a moment. Her shock grew as a flicker of bright green rose in her own eyes. Eyes that had only ever been brown before. She lifted a hand to the mirror. The more freaked out she became, the brighter the green glowed.

Swallowing hard, Rachel forced herself to look away, put the necklace back on, and lay back down in bed.

<hr>

Rachel was already standing in front of her house the next Monday morning when David rolled up, not blocking the driveway. She wore a blank expression, the events of the weekend weighing on her mind as she got into the car.

"Everything okay?" David asked with a concerned frown.

"Yeah, just tired," she lied.

"You sure you're feeling better? You sounded pretty sick."

"Yeah. I just want to get to school, okay?"

He reached over for her hand, giving it a squeeze. "Let me know if you need anything."

She forced a small smile. "Thanks."

Their car ride to school was quieter than usual. David made sure she knew he had missed seeing her all weekend.

After going their separate ways at school, Rachel continued to be in poor spirits all day, processing her news and barely even responding to any texts between classes.

As she meandered back to their parking spot at the end of the day, she was greeted by a smiling David. Sitting on the hood of his car, he opened his arms as she approached, and she melted into his comforting embrace.

Moving her hair to the side, his finger brushed across the chain clasp of her new necklace. David planted a soft kiss on her neck. "Still not feeling great?"

She didn't respond, just shaking her head slightly.

"Would it cheer you up if I took you out to dinner, or something else fun?" he offered.

She shook her head again.

He held her at arm's length, then kissed her sweetly on the forehead. "I hate seeing you like this. Do you want to talk?"

"I'll be fine," she responded unconvincingly.

"It's not guilt weighing you down, is it?" he asked with raised eyebrows.

She scrunched her forehead in confusion. "No."

"You don't usually wear necklaces."

She took a step back, eyeing him with suspicion. "Why should that matter?" Supposedly, the enemy looking for her kind didn't know about the jade charm helping her stay safe and feel better. But the mention of it put her on edge.

"I'm just wondering if there's a handsome gifter I should be jealous of." He winked.

Her muscles relaxed. "You know I wouldn't do that to you."

Looking her in the eyes, he frowned again. "I know, sorry. I'm just trying to cheer you up. Let's get you home, okay?"

The ride was just as silent and depressing on the way back from school as it had been on the way there in the morning. Rachel gave David a small peck on the lips before going inside.

It took a couple of days for her mood to improve as she tried to reconcile the lost future she'd always envisioned, and the nebulous one now in front of her, if she met the unfathomable expectation to leave her human life behind.

Rachel imagined some host parents had a harder time than others in letting go of their Seeder charges. Not that it wasn't hard for them, but Rachel's mom and stepdad were adamant about her returning to the Green Lands, like the expectation of attending a parents' alma mater—Rachel was informed of her impending plans, not really having much say in the matter. At least that was how it felt when she'd dared to bring up the topic again.

Though they were more focused on Eric, being the newest addition to her circle, Rachel's parents reminded her that no one was above suspicion of being an Ivy, not even David. They discussed having her break up with David sooner rather than later so she wouldn't get distracted, and just in case he wasn't what he seemed to be. Rachel wouldn't have it, and luckily Rob ended up agreeing that she should be allowed to still spend time with him until she had to leave, as long as she was careful, and David didn't get in the way of her training goals.

Just as they had done their best to allow Rachel a normal, happy human life, they wanted these last few months to be something she could look back on with fond memories. She had been warned to always be alert, always remember her jade charm, and always have something on her for self-defense, especially until her powers came in. She would need to let her parents know where she was at all times. Realizing the severity of the situation, she agreed to follow all of their rules to the letter. She desperately wanted to share her struggle with Meg and David, even Eric. But she wrestled through it in silence.

Jeff was fine, but they didn't have an instant bond by any means. It was more of a casual mentor-mentee relationship than a joyful sibling reunion. He was around often to 'take piano lessons' and 'help around the house for college money.' She'd greet him as they passed, and regularly texted him her whereabouts. For the first few months, there were opportunities to learn about her people and how their powers worked. She just didn't have her powers to perform her unique abilities yet.

It was helpful they'd made an attempt to integrate Jeff into her circle of friends *before* the change had started—it had made it a smoother introduction. He found his place with them; not that they were exactly thick as thieves, but the group didn't grunt and groan anymore when he would butt in on movie and game nights, or join them for outings.

Rachel took every opportunity to savor her time left in the human world. She played on the school volleyball team and went to homecoming and winter formal. Every available moment was spent with David or Meg. The clock was ticking, and Rachel's focus would soon be divided between maintaining a normal life and training for her new one. She was fairly apt at observing, concealing the truth, being discreet. She was even happy most of the time. Until she had to lie to David about submitting college applications.

"It's okay, we don't have to talk about it," he said, when the spark of joy left her eyes at his mention of plans after graduation. "If we don't go to the same college, we can still make things work. We'll cross that bridge when we come to it."

In a lot of ways, she wished that 'bridge' would burn to the ground.

Chapter 5

During winter break, they tested to see how Rachel's blooming was coming along—taking off the charm, waiting a few hours to see if she would feel ill, checking to see if she could control any Seeder energy. Eventually, the time came when the charm had fulfilled its purpose and she was ready to move on to the next step.

Jeff had already helped her prepare for energy control by going through visualizations, so it was exciting to finally be able to put it into practice with her full powers. In awe at the amazing new energy coursing through her body, Rachel warmed up to her expected future. They worked on concealing her change and separating emotions from energy, before heading back to school after winter break. Even though she was fairly confident in her ability to do it right, she planned to keep a bit of distance from David for a few days. At least until she felt absolutely sure she could continue their relationship without giving herself away. As much as she trusted David and her friends, Rachel wasn't too keen on the idea of humans discovering she was different.

Perhaps it was a little paranoid of her, but every time she imagined letting her identity slip, she thought of the old *E.T.* movie where the government kidnapped and studied the friendly little alien—it sent a shiver down her spine.

Rachel and David sat next to each other on a bench in the school's enclosed courtyard, waiting for Meg and Eric before classes. She held his hand, but turned down other affection. Meg and Eric approached right on schedule.

"Give this girl a hot beverage, stat!" David called to Meg. "She's icing me out over here."

Rachel shook her head, smiling. Meg handed her a latte, pulling one out of a drink carrier for herself and another for Eric, and even handed one to David.

David's eyes lit up. "For moi? You are too kind."

Meg smirked. "Consider it a belated Christmas gift. Don't get your hopes up."

"I shall savor every last drop of it and take a picture of this momentous occasion, to remember it always." David laughed and took a selfie with his cup of coffee.

"Speaking of selfies..." Rachel said, tapping Meg's shoe with her own. "How is it possible you go on an amazing Caribbean cruise for Christmas and lose every single picture of it?" She raised her eyebrows. "I need to live my life vicariously through you, you know. My mom and Rob don't ever take me on lavish vacations like your parents do."

"You think *you're* the one that's upset? That was a brand-new phone, too!" Meg whined.

"So, what happened?" David inquired.

"Let's just say butterfingers and breathtaking views from the railings don't go together." Meg frowned. "I would like to ask for a moment of silence for my phone, please."

They all lowered their heads respectfully before laughing.

"Yeah, this *new* new phone is going to be synced up." Eric smiled, squeezing her hand. "So next time a body of water claims your phone, you don't lose everything."

"My hero." Meg sighed dramatically before planting a kiss on him.

"You don't even really look all that tan," Rachel noted. "Didn't you take time to enjoy that cute new bikini you showed me?"

"Girl, you know I'm not going to be the broad who looks twenty years older than I really am, with wrinkly, leathery skin." Meg puckered her lips with attitude. "I know how to SPF."

"What is this about a new bikini? Now I don't get to see pictures of the bikini? I want to see the bikini," Eric added with puppy eyes before growing a mischievous grin.

Meg blushed and whispered something into his ear. He whispered back, pulling her in tight and starting to lip wrestle.

"Oh brother." David rolled his eyes. "Can we change the topic?"

Rachel smiled at Meg and Eric. She was really going to miss this dynamic, these friends, more than any other friends. Swallowing hard, she tried to remind herself of all the positive things her parents and Jeff had been telling her. Things about heritage, about discovering her true nature. She'd be learning to heal and even fly!

David slid an arm around Rachel and she smiled again, trying to focus on the here and now. She glanced over at his coffee cup. "French vanilla. Mmm."

David raised an eyebrow. "Wanna try it?" He offered his cup, and she took a sip. Rachel reciprocated the offer with her drink. David read the side. "Hmm. Chai latte? Not feeling it, but thanks." He pulled Rachel in closer, nuzzling her neck.

She grinned until she felt the telltale signs of her emotions and Seeder energy mingling. She leaned away from David. "Not today."

He gave her pouty lips. "Are you mad at me?"

She huffed. "We're capable of keeping our hands and lips off of each other for more than two minutes, right?"

David shrugged. "Capable? Yes. But it's not nearly as fun."

Rachel rolled her eyes as the bell rang.

Despite her best efforts over the next couple of weeks, Rachel's emotions were taking a turn for the worse. Spending more time in training was stressful; trying to keep up her grades, and not making any noticeable changes in her daily pattern—it was all weighing her down.

And things were coming along slower than she had anticipated with her abilities. Slower than *any of them* had anticipated. While the first few days after her powers came in had been invigorating, that boost of energy had seemingly died off, and it became exponentially harder for Rachel to complete the tasks and exercises asked of her. It wasn't as though she couldn't keep her Seeder energy in check—she was even comfortable being around David more—but it was like she couldn't tap into the energy like Jeff expected of her, not to the level she needed.

Rachel and Jeff practiced in the basement family room with the furniture lined up against the walls. Jeff set up a target for practice with darts.

"Alright, like we've done before, channel your energy down to your hand," Jeff instructed.

Rachel followed the ample coaching he'd already given. The warmth of Seeder energy resided in her heart, and she envisioned moving it through her arm, down to her hand. Her hand glowed, but no excess energy pooled into a ball of light as she'd expected it to. She'd slept well. She'd even had a special coffee from Meg earlier. She was plenty energized...

"Come on," he said. "I know you're capable of more."

Rachel took a deep breath, focusing harder. Eventually, a tiny little ball of light formed above her palm.

Jeff looked thoroughly unimpressed. "That's really all you've got today?"

Rachel reabsorbed her energy, crossing her arms. She glared at his condescension. "Maybe I'm just too worn-out from yesterday's practice."

He shook his head. "I told you: it doesn't work that way. It might take a few hours if you're depleted, but you should be up to full-charge by now. Unless you've been doing practices in your own time?" He raised an eyebrow.

She stared at him, perturbed. He'd grown up with his powers, in their home realm. He didn't know how this felt for her.

"Yeah. Maybe I've been practicing too much," she lied.

"Doing what?" His head tilted to the side in challenge.

Her jaw clenched as she tried to remain calm. "That's the best you're getting out of me today. Maybe we should do something that doesn't demand so much energy."

Jeff sighed. "We can only *talk* about your abilities for so long. Theory only gets us so far. I need you to step it up."

Rachel's gaze dropped, and she swept her bare foot over the soft carpet. One of the most annoying things about Jeff was his inability to pick up on social cues. She'd come to realize some of his 'weirdness' stemmed from not being human and not blending in perfectly, but at times like this... He genuinely didn't seem to recognize when he ought not to be so blunt with her. He wasn't trying to be mean, so she couldn't fault him for it.

"Then let's... I don't know. Maybe go out back and work on practicing communing with the wind?"

Jeff shrugged. "Fine. Won't do you much good down the road if you can't focus enough to extend your blades and learn to catch a breeze. But I guess it's ... *something*..."

Rachel followed after him, wiping at a runaway tear. She'd asked him already about where she landed on the spectrum of Seeder girls with regards to powers. As he had explained it, there wasn't really a 'spectrum of powers' amongst Seeders. Some specialized more in one power than another, or had a *slight* difference in harnessing energy. But it wasn't that Rachel was low on energy or bad at energy-harnessing like she'd thought, that she had been born that way. To Jeff, she was a lazy disappointment. To herself, she was ... just a disappointment.

Rachel's parents and Jeff had promised her the training wouldn't be too exhausting, and that she'd be able to have a seminormal extracurricular life, to keep up appearances and enjoy what time she had left in the human world. But the practices were more draining than she'd expected, and they were starting to ask for more and more time. Rachel demanded a free afternoon the next day after school to hang out at Meg's house. She *desperately* needed this break.

After ambling to Meg's place, two houses down the street, Rachel rang the doorbell. Meg greeted her with a huge smile. "Come on in!"

They walked upstairs from the split entryway and headed to the kitchen to raid for snacks. Meg's tutor, Michael, popped his head in to wish Meg a good night. Meg was dyslexic and her parents had paid for tutors for as long as Rachel could remember.

Rachel leaned back against the kitchen counter as Meg stuck her head in the fridge, and then freezer.

"We've got like five kinds of ice cream in the downstairs freezer, but it looks like just mint chocolate chip up here," Meg reported.

Rachel shrugged. "Meh. Whatever."

Meg closed the freezer door and gave Rachel a calculating look. "Hmm. I'll be right back."

Meg's mom came into the kitchen before she returned.

"Hi, Ginger." Rachel smiled. Meg's parents were always welcoming, which made sense with how Meg had turned out. And they were pretty cool, wanting to be called by their first names.

Ginger's full lips turned up in greeting as she filled a glass of water from the fridge door. "Hey, Rach! Glad to see you again. I forgot Meg said you were coming over." Ginger was trim, tall, and her wavy red hair was true to her name.

Meg walked back in, clutching a container of ice cream. She stopped when she spotted her mom, giving her a humorous 'caught-in-the-act' side-glance.

"Hey!" Ginger protested. "That's *my* special ice cream. There's a reason I hide that!"

Meg laughed. "Yeah, but Rachel is having a 'meh' kind of day. It's an *emergency*."

Rachel grinned at the comedic duo.

"Yeah, whatever." Ginger rolled her eyes. "Since it's for Rachel." She winked.

Meg set it on the counter. "Yup, we know who your favorite is." She playfully narrowed her eyes at her mom.

Ginger smirked. "You girls have fun." She pulled the scoop from a drawer, handing it to Meg. "Don't forget to write it on the shopping list!"

They scooped some ice cream and took the bowls to Meg's room to hang out.

Meg sat on her bed, while Rachel claimed the purple reading-nook chair in the corner.

"So, what's up?" Meg asked.

Rachel looked down, poking at the raspberry-and-cheesecake ice cream with her spoon. "Things are just weird lately at home."

Meg frowned. "Like parental-problem weird?"

"No." Rachel shook her head. "No big problems there. I guess maybe it's not really home stuff. I've just been off, is all."

Meg lifted an eyebrow. "Off?"

Rachel took a deep breath. "You know what? It's nothing. I didn't come over to be a downer." She forced a smile.

Meg pursed her lips, clearly unconvinced. "Whatever it is, just remember things get better, okay?" She gave a reassuring smile.

Wanting to move on, Rachel nodded. "So... This year's prom theme, am I right?"

Meg pointed her spoon at Rachel. "Seriously. *So* cliché."

They chatted for over an hour before someone knocked on the bedroom door.

"It's unlocked," Meg called out.

Her dad opened the door. "He's here."

"Oh." Meg scrunched her eyebrows, grabbing her phone.

"Hi, Rachel." Meg's dad nodded.

"Hi, Nathan." She smiled and waved before he took off. Nathan had dark hair like Meg and was a bit shorter and quieter than his wife.

"Well, crap," Meg said. "I had my phone on silent. Eric's here."

Rachel picked up her empty ice cream bowl. "Let's go say hi."

As they walked down the stairs to the living room, Rachel smirked to herself. She followed the Seeder family network and her parents' rules, but they could sometimes be a smidge overreaching. Jeff had sounded a bit paranoid when he'd described the kinds of activities he thought Rachel should report. Something like this—Eric showing up at his own girlfriend's house earlier than expected, coincidentally while Rachel was there—was something Jeff would probably want to hear about. Rachel shook her head. Eric was a solid guy, and had shown no increase in attention toward her at all.

She followed Meg into the living room. Eric got up from the couch and Meg launched herself into his arms.

"I'm sorry. I didn't see any of your texts," Meg said, standing tall for a smooch.

"No worries. I just got off early and wanted to see you." He squeezed her tight, rocking them both side to side.

"Problem is, I'm still hanging out with Rachel." Meg pouted. "Girl time and all."

Rachel didn't want to intrude on their time. "Honestly, I should be getting home, anyway."

Meg frowned. "You're sure? Eric wouldn't mind hanging out in the car for a couple of hours while we keep chatting." She winked.

He leaned forward, tickling her sides while she giggled. "A couple hours, huh?"

Rachel shook her head while she grinned. "I'm good. Thanks for the hangout."

"Okay." Meg walked up to Rachel and gave her a hug, then held her at arm's length. "Remember: the glass isn't just half full, it's three quarters full. And you get to be the one that fills it up." She smiled.

Rachel strolled home, musing on her best friend's cheesy and well-intentioned advice. She wanted to think that way. And it would have been easier to do so had things not gotten so complicated.

Taking a deep breath, she prepared to text Jeff to let him know she was free for training. She was going to try to be more positive.

Chapter 6

Saff returned home from a long day of working as a welcoming apprentice. There was an influx of new girls returning. They were being rushed home as soon as their powers were sufficiently up to snuff to make the journey. Their energy was in high demand back home, their safety still more guaranteed in the Green Lands. Their hastened return also freed up brothers and fathers needing to take on other tasks.

Saff gazed out of the window at her sad patch of a garden, now wilted and neglected. She didn't have the energy to put into it today. The last time she'd felt this drained was right after her bloom in high school. Plopping down at the kitchen table, she laid her head down to rest for just a moment.

The front door squeaked open, and she moved her head to the side to see Devin coming in.

"You've never looked more beautiful." He smiled at her limp frame.

"Lies," she mumbled, forcing herself to sit up in the chair.

He walked over to greet her, pulling her up into a tight embrace as though he would never let her go.

"Any updates?" she asked, wary.

His chest shuddered with a heavy exhale. "We think there's been another one."

She stepped back and cupped a hand over her mouth. "No," she whispered. There were rumors and all sorts of speculation surrounding the new tactic being used by the Ivies to breach Seeder border walls. But official, reliable communication between Seeder communities traveled slowly. Scouting groups had taken to the Neutral Woods in an attempt to find answers. Most of those groups never came back, or returned with heavy casualties and no helpful information.

"Yeah," Devin whispered in defeat. "I'm going to go get cleaned up."

Devin took off his shirt, heading into the bathroom. He slammed the door behind him, causing Saff to jump. The door only slightly muffled his swearing. A jarring thud was promptly followed by the crash of glass. Saff ran to the bathroom and opened the door. Devin sat crumpled on the floor, surrounded by glass shards from the full-length mirror. His hands were balled up in fists pressed against his forehead, one of them bleeding.

Ripping a pair of towels off of the rack, she laid them over the glass so she could walk across safely. She crouched in front of him and grabbed the bleeding hand, picking a few small pieces of glass out of it and holding it between her hands to heal. She looked into his eyes with compassion.

He shook his head and pulled his hand back. "You shouldn't be wasting energy on an idiot like me. I can heal the human way."

She grabbed it again. "I get some say in this. I take care of my family."

He looked down, frowning. "Thanks."

"Are you going to be okay?" she asked.

"Yeah, it feels better."

She bit her lip, knowing how much of a toll this new surge in the war was taking on him, on all of them. Instead of full-time teaching and supplemental border duty, he was working full-time on border duty, and also almost full-time at the school. "No, I mean are *you* going to be okay?"

He took in a deep breath while squeezing her hand. "It's divide and conquer, Saff. If we pull more from the wall for protection detail, the wall will fall. But our girls in the human world are more vulnerable now than ever. We never saw this coming. Never. And we're stretched too thin to mount an offensive to stop it. How are we supposed to end this?" He shook his head. "Damn leeches. Damn every last one of them."

She glanced down at the stone floor. "I'm going to swing by the temple."

He looked up. "Saff..."

Her gaze stopped his protest. They both knew she was tired. She had been making *several* times more energy deposits a week than would normally be necessary. All of the women were. It was taking everything they had. She was worn down, but it was needed. Without the extra energy deposits, these enormous mystery vines were ripping up their border thickets like a can opener to a tin of tuna.

"I love you," he said. "There and back as quick as you can. Stay as far away from the wall as possible. They're sending out more and more soldiers on foot. The woods are crawling with them at night."

She nodded, and he released her hand. "I'll be careful," she reassured him with a weak smile.

He surveyed the mess of broken mirror around him. "I'll clean this up."

Saff left their cottage, hands washed free from blood and now hugging herself. She pondered their dilemma as her feet shuffled down the dirt lane toward the moss-covered temple. They still didn't understand how the Ivies were commanding vines strong enough to pierce the Seeders' borders. And their attacks on foot at the walls had become much more aggressive. This didn't feel like the two-hundred-year war she'd read about in her courses. There was something more to it. Sightings and attacks by Ivy assassins in the human world were also skyrocketing. The numbers didn't add up.

It felt like her high school days all over again—the nightmare she'd lived through, that her whole family and Devin's had been through, just to keep her and the other girls safe. Something hadn't made sense about the enemy tactics then, either. By the time both of their families had returned, they hadn't learned anything new. And she hadn't dwelt on it. She'd just been elated to have everyone home, safe and sound.

Until now.

Approaching the nearest temple depository, Saff frowned at the line of women waiting for their turn at the well. It was sickening. It was somber. She wished she could do more.

Saff watched on as other women took turns, giving a part of themselves to help bolster the border walls. Her heart dropped when she recognized one of them—the mother of one of Devin's former students. The boy had died a month ago on duty during a breach. He was only fourteen.

Pursing her lips, Saff fought tears. Things had changed so quickly. She looked away, studying the temple walls. Beautiful carvings decorated the stone, framing the entrances to several inner rooms most people never entered. She'd once painted some of this artwork, back when she'd had more time and energy.

People really only ever came to the temples for the energy wells anymore. She gritted her teeth in anger. It was one more thing the Ivy Kingdom had stripped from them. Seeders used to have a much richer culture, including nature-based worship. But their entire society had become overshadowed by human customs. She still loved humans and their world, but it hadn't been this way until Seeder families were forced to raise their daughters in the human world. An Ivy biological attack, dubbed 'The Great Poisoning,' had torn their society to shreds.

She had to admit that Devin was right to describe the Seeders as 'pacifists to a fault,' as he'd once said. Ivies had stirred up problems, ransacked Seeder temples, and then attacked in open war. In the midst of brutal battles, Seeders had channeled everything they had to create their border walls, giving them hope. But with their lands protected, they'd taken a breath instead of pushing back. And then the poison had somehow been snuck in and released. Seeders had never been sure if that had somehow been part of Ivy strategy, that the Seeders would box themselves in—their main protection becoming their prison. Her heart ached—what would the history books say of this current attack another hundred years down the road? If they made it that long.

Looking down at her wedding ring, Saff allowed a small smile to surface. Devin had brought back a traditional human engagement ring for her, though she'd given him a traditional Seeder one, an intricately carved wooden ring she'd bartered for, made by a local craftsman. And their ceremony had been as traditional as any Seeder wedding. She wanted to spend the rest of her life with him, and they'd discussed having kids when the time arrived. She suddenly frowned again. Plans for their first-year wedding anniversary were on hold. Sometimes she feared, when he was on wall duty, that Devin might not even make it to that anniversary.

And the yearly sprout reveal... What would that look like this year? How many Seeders would actually choose to bring new life into this mess? Taking a matriarch's focus away from defense, instead raising little boys. Sending away a soldier to defend his own girls in the human world. Her chest hurt thinking of it. *If the Ivies keep this up long enough, maybe we'll just die out because everyone chooses to not have kids anymore.* Her stomach knotted. *As if we could last long enough for that strategy to come to fruition.*

Once Saff's turn came up, she approached the well to deposit as much energy as she felt her body could spare. Like all the other times before, a warmth flowed from her heart down through her arms. With glowing hands grasping an emerging root system, she pushed her energy into it, coaxing as much out of her reserve as she could. She left once dizzy, and headed straight home, speaking to no one.

Something has to change.

Chapter 7

One Saturday afternoon, Rachel sat on her bed, sinking into a deep depression. She'd walked out on a training session with Jeff that morning. She couldn't handle his condescension that day. Then again, it wasn't really *him* that was the problem.

Rachel was the failure. She should have been a lot further along in her training than she was. She was useless, weak, unworthy. In her isolation, she stewed in her disgrace, disappointed in herself more than her parents and the Seeders claimed to be, but she couldn't shake the self-criticism.

Her eyes glazed over with tears as she rolled a sewing needle back and forth on her palm.

The doubt had become crippling. The training futile. The expectations unrealistic.

She grasped the needle between her thumb and pointer finger, and sank it into her forearm, pushing past the stinging pain. She pulled it out; a drop of blood pooled at the puncture site. Putting her middle finger on the wound, Rachel healed it. It was practice, that was all. She just needed to practice her healing. This much she could do.

But then she plunged the needle in again, pulling it out, then quickly healing her arm with a touch.

And again.

And again.

She found the self-torture cathartic. She stared at her arm, repeating the process time and time again, her mind playing her worst failures on a loop. Birth parents she'd never met, who were likely disappointed in her progress. A dad who'd left her as a five-year-old little girl because she wasn't enough. Her grades dropping. No time to play volleyball or even attend David's basketball games. Her inability to do even the *simplest* of things in Seeder training. The knowledge that she was going to have to leave behind and hurt the people she loved.

Despite her healing, smashed droplets of blood coated her finger and the injury site.

She dug in once more for good measure, twisting it and starting to pull it out slowly.

"What are you doing!" Meg gasped from the now-open door.

Rachel yanked the needle out, wide-eyed and panicked at seeing her best friend in the doorway. She breathed hard as a drop of blood rolled down her arm and fell on the white comforter. Releasing the needle, Rachel applied pressure to the wound.

"Nothing. Just..." She swallowed the lump in her throat as the floodgates released tears.

Meg set down the drink she'd brought and rushed to her friend's side, hugging Rachel until she stopped shaking and whimpering.

"You can't do this to yourself," Meg whispered. She pushed Rachel's bangs to the side. "Let's get you cleaned up."

They got up from the bed and headed to the bathroom. Rachel turned on the faucet, washing off the blood. The wound had stopped bleeding due to the pressure she'd applied; it looked much worse than it really was from the blood buildup. She left it unhealed since she'd been caught in the act.

"Where are your bandages?" Meg asked.

Rachel examined her arm again. "It's really not all that bad, look." She held up her arm.

Meg locked eyes with her, sporting an indiscernible expression. Likely a mix of concern, frustration, and fear. "It's not the size of the wound that concerns me, Rachel. It's the fact you were doing that to yourself in the first place. Where are your bandages?"

Rachel frowned in shame. "The hallway closet on the left. There's a first aid kit."

Meg left the room, returning with a small bandage, handing it over. She disappeared again while Rachel put it on herself.

Meg reappeared with the drink she had brought. Instead of handing it to Rachel, Meg took off the lid and poured it down the sink, setting the cup on the counter upside down. She pointed to the permanent marker on the bottom of the cup, a love note of sorts, like she always did for her friend. This time it had a picture of a sun with a smiley face on it. "I love you, and this is not okay." Meg hugged Rachel from behind. "Let's get out of here and talk," she suggested.

"What if I wanted to drink that?" Rachel asked with an ironic frown while looking at the dregs of caffeine lingering in the sink.

"I think you need something a little different to drink. Come on. I'm driving."

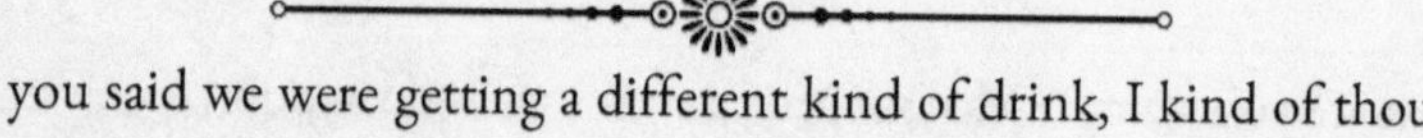

"When you said we were getting a different kind of drink, I kind of thought you meant the hard kind," Rachel confessed, holding a triple-chocolate milkshake. She pressed a fingernail into the styrofoam cup, drawing an indented line.

Meg winced. "I think you've done enough harm today."

"Yeah." Rachel looked down at the restaurant table between them.

"Have you ever even had alcohol?" Meg asked.

Rachel rocked her head side to side. "Two Christmases ago David and I tried a wine cooler."

"That boy." Meg rolled her eyes. "Sometimes I wonder about him."

They sat in silence, the slurping of their straws and the music overhead filling the blank spaces.

"Do you want to talk about what just happened?" Meg asked cautiously.

Rachel closed her eyes and swallowed before shaking her head.

"Okay. But you need to talk to someone. I'm seriously worried about you."

Rachel nodded, unable to make eye contact.

Meg narrowed her eyes. "Have you ever done something like that before?"

Biting the insides of her cheeks, Rachel shook her head again.

"Is it something about David? Or your parents? Is there something I can help with?"

Rachel rubbed her forehead. "No. I'm just," she searched for the right words, "a screwup."

"No!" Meg scolded. "You're better and stronger than you're giving yourself credit for. I understand if you don't want to talk about what's going on with you lately, but the Rachel I know can overcome anything she sets her mind to."

Rachel gave her a weak smile.

"And I'm not taking you home until you promise me you won't do that kind of thing to yourself again."

Rachel fidgeted with her hands, nodding again.

Meg stared at her unblinkingly.

"I promise."

Later that night, Meg drove Rachel home and left her with a long hug. "Twenty-four seven, any time, day or night, I don't care when. I'm a call or text away. Okay?"

"Thank you."

Rachel went straight to bed, drained from repeated healing and the emotional buildup. She cried herself to sleep, desperately wishing she knew what to do.

After a solid night's sleep, Rachel woke up in a much healthier headspace. She told Jeff she needed to take the day off to rest up. He protested, but she insisted she would work twice as hard the next week.

And she did. She was really starting to feel a lot better. As early as Monday morning, her spirits were up and her Seeder energy even felt like it was stronger, almost like when it first came in. She hadn't realized how much her emotions must have been hampering her efforts. She thanked Meg profusely for taking care of her and for a life-saving pep talk.

"I'm glad to see you smiling," David said on Thursday morning. He pulled Rachel in for a hug and cheered her up with a little more PDA than most would prefer to see.

"Hey, now, break it up. Break it up," Eric chimed as he and Meg walked up.

Rachel bit her lip and gave Meg a warm knowing smile of gratitude.

"Even one for David this time," Meg announced while handing out their ritual drinks.

"Ooh, what did I do to get in your good graces?" he asked with a grin.

"Oh, nothing," she replied with a disingenuous smile. "In my goodness, I try to make the little people and knuckleheads feel worthwhile sometimes."

That garnered a look between Rachel and Eric. Meg and David would sometimes throw quips at each other, but it didn't usually rise to this level of veiled hostility.

As they headed off to class, Rachel asked David what the awkward interaction had been about.

"I don't know," he replied with a shrug. "She's probably just PMSing."

Rachel scowled at him. "Sometimes, you have the sensitivity of a jackhammer."

Meg came over for an hour after school, before Rachel would have to kick her out to train.

"How are you doing?" Meg asked, taking a seat on the family room sofa.

"I'm better," Rachel said, joining her. "A bit tired today, but this week has been a lot better than last week."

Meg beamed. "I love it."

"So, did something happen between you and David?" Rachel lifted an eyebrow. "You seemed a little ... off ... this morning."

Meg gingerly set her purse on the coffee table. "How are the two of you doing? Are you guys good?"

"Yeah... Why?" Rachel asked.

Meg shrugged. "I don't know. I just wonder sometimes if you're too serious with him, not getting to know other guys."

Rachel furrowed her brow. "Isn't the point of dating to be with someone you like? Not just date around because you can? He can be an idiot sometimes, but you know how much he means to me."

Meg huffed. "Maybe I'm overthinking things. Maybe part of me wondered if you were in such a bad place last weekend because you guys ... did something you regretted."

Rachel's eyes grew wide. "Oh... I see. No. He knows I'm not there yet. He may be an annoyingly horny flirt sometimes, but he's never really pushed me. I promise, he's a good guy."

Meg nodded, not appearing convinced, pressing her lips together.

"Plus. You know I'd tell you." The two had made a pact years ago, that they'd let the other know if they'd ever gone all the way with a boyfriend. Not in a silly, gossipy kind of way. But just to help each other out, perhaps motivated by a touch of curiosity.

"Okay," Meg said.

"Though I do wonder..." Rachel smirked. "Are you and Eric taking things to the next level?" She hummed playfully. "You're not usually a scarf kind of girl. Are we hiding something behind that?" she teased while moving her hand to pull on Meg's scarf.

Meg slapped her hand away; Rachel practically jumped back in surprise.

"Sorry!" Meg said reflexively, her eyes wide.

"What's that about?" Rachel asked, fully confused at Meg's dramatic reaction.

"Sorry. Just drop it." Meg begged with her eyes.

Rachel sat perplexed, searching her friend's face for answers.

"I mean it, Rachel. It's nothing. Please, just don't say anything. Not to Eric, or anyone, okay?" Meg pleaded.

Rachel frowned. "Now you're worrying me."

"I should go." Meg gathered her purse and keys. "Promise me you won't say anything."

"Yeah... Sure..." Rachel agreed hesitantly, still stunned. Of course, she didn't even know what she was promising not to talk about. Was Meg ... cheating on Eric? No, Meg wasn't like that. She really seemed to be falling for him. And Eric seemed like a genuinely nice guy; he wouldn't do anything to Meg. Nor would her parents. The mystery started to eat at Rachel. She thought about the Seeder and Ivy dilemma—things were rarely as simple as they seemed.

Right after Meg left, Rachel shot her a text.

<I'm here for you, too. Remember these phones go both ways. Love you. <3 >

She then sent Jeff a text.

<Ready to start early if you want. Head over when you're ready.>

Chapter 8

Rachel's energy was waning again. She started to feel easily worn out. Too ashamed to bring it up to anyone, she wondered if Seeders struggled with a chemical depression of sorts, like humans. Something as simple as an off conversation or two affecting her mood, to the point that she was useless in training, didn't seem right.

Rachel's gaze acknowledged Meg's silent plea the next morning at school as Meg wore another scarf around her neck. It was just one more thing eating at Rachel. Keeping secrets. Having secrets kept from her. Eric and David both seemed oblivious to either girl's struggle.

As he would sometimes do, David came to the rescue of Rachel's mental health by whisking her away on a romantic date Saturday night. She'd been better at keeping up appearances with her parents, not wanting to disappoint them further, but David had commented more than once on her downcast mood. He knew she needed cheering up, and they were approaching the anniversary of their first date—this time would be extra special.

He said it would be a surprise, but she demanded to know where they were going, as it was her parents' rule (especially given her vulnerable position as a Seeder, not that he needed to know that part). He finally agreed to give up the secret location if he could tell only Rob—that way it would still be a fun surprise for Rachel. They agreed on the compromise.

"You're really not going to give me *any* hints about what we're doing? Or where we're going?" she asked as they drove out of town.

"Nope." He enjoyed torturing her too much.

"Not even a teeny, tiny one?" She smiled at his hand resting on her knee, right above the hem of her little black dress.

Smiling, he shook his head. "If you must know—I plan to take you far from town and have my way with you." He threw her a smoldering look.

She glared at him.

"In any consensual way you will allow me to."

She let out a heavy sigh, her reply dripping with sarcasm. "That is just ... *the* most romantic thing any girl has ever heard."

"Okay, fine. But that's what you get for trying to force my hand on the surprise." He crept his hand from her knee up her thigh before she intercepted it, moving it back down.

"Down, boy. I haven't been lying about taking self-defense classes after school." Most of all, she and David disagreed on how far they were willing to allow themselves to go. Rachel wanted to wait until she turned eighteen, or until after graduation. David was always chomping at the bit.

"I like you feisty." He removed his hand from her leg altogether, placing it on the steering wheel. "But seriously, I always want you to feel safe around me, okay? I respect you enough to wait."

"Thank you."

They turned off of the main road and drove through a wooded area, finally stopping at a cabin in the middle of nowhere.

He parked the car and turned to her. "Surprise. Romantic getaway. And I promise you'll be back by curfew."

She lifted her eyebrows, her heart beating faster. "I have a hard time imagining my parents being okay with this."

He frowned. "I know something's been bothering you, but it's not something I've done, is it? I just ... sometimes feel like you're taking it out on me. And I'm just trying to help, and enjoy our time together."

She matched his frown. He was right. He hadn't done anything out of the ordinary; it was all her subpar acting job and heightened suspicion of everyone around her. David had planned plenty of sweet and elaborate dates over their time together; his parents had always given him a healthy allowance.

"Cross my heart. I'll be good, and you'll see I didn't even plan this alone," he reassured her. "Plus, here—let me ping our location, as promised. They can send the cavalry if I'm lying." He sent a ping on his phone and showed her.

She considered it and decided to enjoy the gesture. He had never forced anything before, and she had more self-defense training under her belt by now. It was probably just hormonal nerves driving her crazy.

"Okay. Don't betray my trust," she warned as they got out of the car.

David led Rachel into the snug, romantic cabin, turning on the lights as he entered. It was clean and cozy, adorned with rustic and tasteful Americana-style decor. Just being away from the buzz of the suburbs and the demands at her house helped to melt away some of Rachel's nerves.

He gave her the short grand tour. "This here, of course, is the living room, opening to the kitchen and dining room. To the right is the bathroom, to the left the bedroom."

She glanced at him suspiciously when he mentioned the bedroom. He matched it by raising his hands, signifying he'd be a gentleman.

"Oh yeah, and out those sliding glass doors is the deck." He pointed past the dining room table.

She lifted her chin to look out. "Is that a hot tub?"

"Yes, ma'am." He grinned. "To soak away your worries."

She looked down at her dress, then crossed her arms. "Well, I'm not going in with these clothes, and I'm not going in without them, either."

"Everything has been prepared ahead of time. I've been planning this for a while." He gave her an innocent smile. "Go check out the bedroom. I won't move a muscle."

She scrunched her nose in curiosity and headed down the hallway, glancing behind her to see that he had crossed his arms and was leaning against the wall, watching her.

A towel and a small bag sat on the end of the bed.

She unzipped the bag. *Meg.* She must have smuggled the swimsuit from Rachel's room on a recent visit. *Thanks a lot for picking the skimpiest one... Let's make this as hard as possible for me.* She smirked.

Rachel sometimes questioned how much she could trust herself with David, despite her goal of wanting to wait. They had grown close; not many couples in high school made it as long as they had. She had even let her persistent frustrations in the Seeder energy department allow her to consider giving up on training altogether and taking root in the human world. She was perfectly happy with

David, Meg, her mom, and Rob. No one could physically *force* her to catch a breeze and rift to the Green Lands.

After her mom and Rob had gone over the Seeder version of the birds and the bees, Rachel felt confident that intimacy with a human could still be safe. And it was only Seeders that mated for life with each other. She was trying to decide if she would cave and go further with David, knowing she was going to have to leave him. Or if it would be better to avoid it altogether, saving that experience for a Seeder someday, in her unknown future.

But maybe tonight would be the night. For them, and for her, to make up her mind on what her final decision would be, which world she'd claim. She'd never told David she loved him. She felt like it would flow naturally when the time was right, and was kind of also waiting for him to say it first.

Leaving the bedroom and bikini behind, she sauntered up to him in the hallway. She leaned up against him, teasing him with a couple of kisses.

"Is that a yes for the hot tub?" he asked with a smile.

Her cheeks warmed. "That's a maybe."

He invited her into the dining room and pulled out a packed meal that had been brought there ahead of time, complete with chocolate-dipped strawberries. He was pulling out all the stops. They enjoyed reminiscing over the times they'd shared together, laughing, poking fun, smiling.

After dessert, he excused himself to go to the bathroom, where he changed into navy-blue swim trunks. He emerged with a towel over his shoulder and a lighter.

"You're free to do what you want. I'm going to be out there." He winked.

By the time she came out of the bedroom in her black-and-white polka-dot suit, he was soaking in the jetted tub with his eyes closed; candles were lit around the place, and the scent of pine from the woods filled the air. She stepped inside and tried to not move her hands or arms to cover more skin.

David opened his eyes with a giant smile, and held out his arms. Rachel studied the tub, considering her options as hot bubbles collided with her calves.

"I promise I can be a perfect gentleman."

"Hmmm..." She narrowed her eyes. "I think *this* side of the hot tub looks pretty comfy."

"You look stunning," he said in a measured tone. "Which means nothing compared to your mind, which I admire so much."

She blushed again, sitting down in the tub. Amidst his sometimes-crude hints and declarations, he could be sweet.

"I wanted to make this something special; you deserve it for putting up with me for so long."

She smiled.

He tilted his head slightly. "And, I wanted to bring you here to tell you two important things."

Her heartbeat quickened as the tension rose.

"I love you, Rachel." He searched her eyes. His face had a vulnerability to it she hadn't seen in him before.

Her heart was likely to pound out of her chest, as the butterflies in her stomach viciously multiplied.

She gazed into his handsome green eyes. "I love you, too, David."

Rachel scooted across the hot tub onto his lap, caressing his lips with her own. Even though they were both still clothed, she was acutely aware of how much of their skin was touching.

Her frustration grew at their special moment having to be weighed down by her caution to keep her energy under control. David would *definitely* notice if her brown eyes and hair changed to neon-green eyes and glowing yellow hair. But as it had been lately, her Seeder energy was pretty sparse and hidden anyway. Rachel considered giving in and not even trying to conceal it—it may not surface at all. And if it did, she could probably reel it back in before he noticed. Or perhaps it was time to tell him? All of her thoughts were playing ping-pong, distracting her from what she really wanted.

Luckily, he was leading things, as she was only partially in the moment with her thoughts. He kissed her more passionately, moving her hands down to his sides, then rested one of his arms on the middle of her back. The other slid up to the nape of her neck. His lips changed course to her neck as well.

Before she realized what was happening, her arms were tight against her body, his hand over her mouth. Her eyes shot open, now emanating a bright green glow, filled with terror. Adding to David's strong arms and hands restraining her, his *vines* were pulling tighter and tighter, keeping her from being able to move her arms or even extend her Seeder blades.

"I promise I won't hurt you. You have to believe me. I won't hurt you. I promise. I won't do anything to you," he rattled off, his voice and eyes almost as frightened as hers.

She struggled with everything she had to get loose, thrashing and even landing a kick in his swim trunks that made him curse and bend over. It loosened his grip enough for her to get off of his lap and let out a small scream before he wrapped a vine around her head, covering her mouth.

"Rachel, I'm not going to hurt you!"

Her whole body was heaving with rapid breathing and exertion in the struggle.

He spoke in a soothing voice. "I need you to stop. I'm not letting you go until you calm down. I could have hurt you by now—you know that. But I haven't. And I'm not going to. I just need you to calm down."

Determined not to let this be how she lost to an Ivy assassin, she continued trying to free herself. The water sloshed around unforgivingly.

"Please," he pleaded, looking as though he might cry. "I love you. I just want to talk to you. We can sort this out. Please stop struggling."

She sat still, catching her breath, realizing she wasn't going to be able to get out of his grip. Her rage turned to despair as she began to cry. He leaned over to wipe away a tear, and she jerked her head away.

"Rachel. Please. This is the only way I could bring this up."

Her eyes faded to their natural brown as her breathing slowly returned to normal.

"Before I release you, I need you to promise you won't run or scream. Just remember that I haven't hurt you, and I love you. And we're out in the middle of nowhere. I just want to talk. Okay?"

Her eyes were hot with rage, but she nodded in agreement.

He released her mouth; she didn't say anything. He loosened his grip on her arms and she stayed still.

"We can talk about this calmly," he said.

Her voice shook through clenched teeth. "I hate you."

He frowned. "You don't mean that."

"I hate you!" she yelled and lunged at him, punching him in the chest with what little strength she had left until he wrapped his arms around her, pulling her in tight. She sobbed in his arms. "Why did you have to ruin everything?"

"It'll be okay," he whispered reassuringly.

She pushed off of him and he let her go. "You don't get to do that! You don't get to talk like that after what you just did." Neither of them moved for a moment. "I'm going inside and you're taking me home."

Rachel grabbed her towel, wrapping it around herself. She marched inside and slammed the bedroom door behind her, locking it.

Sitting down on the end of the bed, she again sobbed. This couldn't be happening. Two and a half years together, and he was one of the enemy. An Ivy. A leech. The race that hunted down her kind. Her boyfriend was an assassin, and she was stupid enough to have never noticed.

She looked at her dress, neatly folded on the bed. Next to it sat her clutch purse, the smaller purse she'd picked out to match her date outfit. The one that was too small for the Taser she'd promised her parents she'd carry for protection. *You're the smartest girl ever. Sacrificing safety in the name of fashion. Great job.* Grabbing the purse, she yanked out her phone, wanting nothing more than to talk to her mom. To even talk to Meg and confess everything. One of them would show up and take her away.

No service... *Brilliant.* She dropped it on the bed in defeat.

Rubbing her arms, she acknowledged the truth. He hadn't really hurt her. He could have. He hadn't sharpened any of his leaves. At most, she might find some bruising from their tussle. But he could have easily killed her.

She frowned. Just before it had all happened ... he'd said there were two things he needed to tell her. The first was welcome; the second, not so much. Rachel pinched the bridge of her nose. At least he'd been honest about it. Either way, they were going to have to find a way to end it, and keep this all a secret. She couldn't endanger her family. And she couldn't imagine killing David, or having Jeff kill him. Even if he was an Ivy.

Rachel closed her eyes, deciding how to handle this. She had to ask herself if she'd really meant what she'd said. Did she genuinely love him? Moments like this made her wonder if they were only still together because she was afraid of being alone after having a boyfriend for so long. She wanted to think she was strong. *But my training proves just the opposite.*

Maybe it wasn't love. But just thinking that hurt, like she was betraying him, them, their two-plus years together. Either way, the fact remained: the Ivy Kingdom only sent *assassins* to the human world. She'd have to find a way to convince David to let her live.

Chapter 9

Rachel sat on the edge of the cabin bed, putting her hair up in a ponytail, then changed back into her dress. She threw her bikini in the trash can with a scowl. She'd never wear that thing again. Not after what had just happened.

When she came out, David was sitting on the couch in the living room, still in his swim trunks, wrapped in a towel.

"Let's go," she ordered.

"Not until we talk."

She glanced at the clock on the wall. "They're expecting me soon. Take me home."

He looked down, biting his lip. "I begged your parents for an extra hour for your surprise."

She shook her head, glaring. "The one time in my life I wish they were more strict."

"Come sit down. Let's talk." He gestured to the open spot next to him.

Rachel sat as far away as possible on the couch. "Okay. Talk."

"You have to believe me that I *do* love you." He pleaded with his eyes.

She crossed her arms. "Get to the point."

"Rachel, that *is* the point! I came here to tell you that, and come clean with you."

"What do you want from me?"

"I just want us to be happy." He raised his eyebrows.

She glowered. "How could I be happy with an asshole leech?!"

"Hey, watch your language." He scowled.

"That's what you are, David."

He looked away with a frown. "It's not like I'm going around calling you a weed."

She busted out laughing. "That's what you got from that? That I called you a leech?" Jeff had told her the term 'leech' was fairly synonymous with 'Ivy,' but that it had a more negative connotation. The same went for 'weed' in regards to Seeders.

David looked back at her, scratching his arm. "Yeah, well, I probably earned the other part."

"Probably?"

He pursed his lips. "Pretty certain."

"Who kidnaps their girlfriend and takes her to a cabin like an axe murderer, and then lures her into a hot tub before attacking and restraining her?" She threw daggers with her eyes.

"Okay, definitely." He picked at his fingernails. "I maybe should have done things differently. I just … got caught up in the moment."

"Why? Why now? How did you even know?"

"I realized last week." He winced. "Your eyes gave you away."

She frowned; more evidence she was a failure.

"I wanted to come clean because I know that means we don't have much time together here. How long until you leave?"

She shook her head. *At this rate, never.* "I don't have to answer all your questions."

"Fine. I … just didn't want things to end. We could be together, on the other side."

Flabbergasted, Rachel furrowed her brow. "So, you are insane, then? How would that ever work? Our people hate each other."

"You can't judge a whole race by the same standards. You didn't get to choose what you are or that you came to the human world, and neither did I."

Her mouth hung open at the audacious comparison. "You have got to be kidding me. *My* people come here to try not to be murdered. *Your* people come here to do the murdering. It's not the same!"

He nodded ever so slightly. "But we're not all like that, you have to believe me. There's a growing faction amongst our people that want things to go back to the old ways. There's a rebellion. We could find a place, make things work."

She narrowed her eyes in disbelief. "Really? Who are these good guys? Anyone I know? Eric? One of your basketball friends?"

He crossed his arms. "I'm not going to betray my network, just like I won't ask you to betray yours."

"Who all knows about me, then?"

"No one. I'm the only one that really knows what you are."

She tilted her head to the side. "What about the ping you sent of our location? How can I believe you don't have others on the way?"

A flash of guilt crossed his face. "That was a fake. I needed you to trust me."

She scoffed. "Yeah. Trust."

He looked down into his lap. "I'm sorry."

Sitting in silence, she fidgeted with her hands. "That's the first time you even apologized for this."

"I'm sorry. I can be a jerk sometimes."

She rolled her eyes. "Let's say I believe you that none of your people know—how highly do they suspect me?"

David shrugged. "We suspect everyone."

That wasn't nearly good enough of an answer. "Have you identified any more of my people here? Is someone I know in danger?"

He shook his head. "No. Not that I know of. But I don't know how much they trust me. I should have moved on to a new girlfriend a long time ago. I convinced my general that I've stayed with you to get close to Meg."

Rachel gave him a death stare. Meg had been acting weird... What if... "If you hurt her, I will kill you myself."

His eyes grew wide. "I wouldn't! I don't even know that she is—it's just my story." He sighed. "Can you please try to see this from my perspective? I didn't have to expose myself. I could have hurt you, or I could have let you go on your way. I'm risking a lot by hoping you really *do* love me, and you'll keep my secret as much as I keep yours."

"I hear what you're saying, but have you really thought it through, David? What happens when we break up? What stops you from killing me when you decide you're tired of me, or the other way around?"

David looked at Rachel sheepishly, not having an answer.

She scowled. "Right. I didn't think so. You threw everything away by being selfish."

"Do you want to break up with me? Do you want to kill me? Nothing has changed—I've always been me."

His face was vulnerable, but the facts remained. "Listen to the words that are coming out of my mouth. You. Are. An. Assassin. You were *literally* sent to this world to kill me and my family. And you want me to get weak in the knees at that? I don't have bloody Stockholm syndrome!"

He furrowed his brow, raising his voice. "Well, I can't undo this now, can I?"

She rubbed her temples. "I don't even know if I'm going back to the Green Lands. What if I forfeit my powers and stay here? Will your people leave me alone? Or now that I've been identified, will I always be a target?"

"Really?" His voice was soft. "But you have so much potential."

She scoffed. If only he knew how much she was struggling. If she was even a half-decent Seeder, she could have put up a much better fight just now. "Hypothetically."

"Well, we don't really care about humans. We just let them be. And that's what you'd become." He frowned. "But that's why I've stayed with you all this time. You're special. Something about you helped me to become better and really want to do things differently."

Rachel swallowed a lump in her throat, her eyes threatening to mist. That wasn't fair. He wasn't allowed to compliment her after betraying her. He was supposed to be a villain she could properly hate.

"Special. Yeah. So special," she whispered.

He reached his hand out toward hers; she pulled away.

"No matter what you decide, I'm making a promise to you, right now," he said. "Your secret is safe with me. And I only want the best for you. Even if it means not being with me, I want to see you fulfill your full potential back home."

She looked at him in disbelief. "I'd be your enemy. You want me to believe you're okay with that?" Jeff had taught her the number one rule in Seeder-Ivy relations: Ivies don't want Seeder girls to return home. Convince them to stay and become human, or kill them—*anything* that weakens Seeder border walls.

"Like I said, there's a rebellion. Change is coming. But yes. I want you to be happy, no matter what you choose."

She bent over, cradling her face with her hands. "When am I going to wake up from this nightmare?"

"Will you tell me how long you have left?" he asked again.

"I don't know. Let's just say a couple of months."

"Okay. How about this—we can agree to keep each other's identities safe until you leave. No matter what we decide with our relationship. But I don't want to waste a minute while we're both on this side of things. Don't think of me as an Ivy. Think of me as ... a foreign exchange student. And either way, if you decide you don't want to see me anymore, we have to be careful. Weird behavior from either of us could blow both our covers."

Sitting up, she studied his face. The face she had come to know and love, the one she looked forward to seeing every day. All of the fond memories welled up in her eyes. "Yeah, we can see how things go. You can trust me, as long as you promise I'm safe."

"You will be." He spoke softly, confidently. "Think of me as one of your brothers right now—I'm on your protection detail, too." He wrinkled his nose, shaking his head. "Wait, no. Don't think of me as your brother... That's all kinds of wrong. But you know what I mean."

She sniffled and chuckled. "Yeah. Not my brother."

"Do you have any more questions for me before we go? Obviously, we can talk more later."

She chewed on her lip and thought about it. She hated herself for what she wanted to ask. No, she couldn't do it. You can't ask for a hug from the person that hurt you. That's like asking to cuddle with a cobra while the venom takes hold. David had given up his right to any affection.

But no one else could do what he did for her. And no one else would know the agony she was in. She couldn't tell Meg about this, or her mom, Rob, or Jeff. "Would you hold me for a little while?"

He smiled. "Always."

She crawled onto his lap, and he enveloped her in his arms.

The next thing Rachel knew, she woke up to a kiss on the forehead. Taking a moment to get her bearings, she was taken aback by the wood-paneled walls. She was still in the cabin and must have nodded off. Looking up at David with suspicion, she moved to the other side of the couch. "What time is it?"

"We'll be late. But I'll call Rob and text him a picture of our flat tire as soon as we get to the car. It'll buy us enough time to get you home." He stood. "I made sure to have backup plans for my backup plans."

Looking at the floor, she remembered their conversation and agreement. "Yeah, you're an Ivy. Always planning and plotting."

"That's not fair," he said softly, but defensively.

"Maybe not," she admitted. "Sorry."

"I'm going to get changed, okay?" He left for the bathroom after she nodded.

David turned off the lights before locking up the cabin. He opened the car door for Rachel and they drove off. The wedge between them was palpable, the silence deafening.

Finally cutting through the stillness, the ping of her cell phone announced they'd gotten back in tower range. She opened it to a text from Meg.

<I won't pry, but I hope it was as special as David told me it would be. Happy Anniversary, I'm excited for you guys! :) >

The final approach to Rachel's house made the tension peak.

"So." He shifted the car into park. "Maybe we can talk more tomorrow after you've rested and had a chance to think about things?"

"Maybe." She looked down at her hands. As if finding out she was a Seeder, and a weak one at that, hadn't been enough, now her boyfriend had turned out to be one of the enemy. *You really know how to screw things up, don't you?*

"Okay," he whispered. "Let me know? Just remember—I'm going to keep you safe. And I hope I can trust you, too."

She nodded and got out of the car. Entering the house, Rachel put on her best possible smile to let her mom and Rob know she was back.

"How did the surprise party go?" her mom asked with a bright smile.

"No booze, right?" Rob asked with raised eyebrows. "David promised it would all be on the up-and-up."

Party? *The lying bastard.* She hated doing this to them, of all people. "It was great. You know me—no drinks or drugs. Do a lie detector or a drug test if you want," she said convincingly with a casual shrug.

They each gave her a hug, and she excused herself to go to sleep.

As Rachel sat on her bed in her fleece pajamas, she looked around the room. She wanted to scream. She wanted to throw things, smash anything she could. She wanted to punch the wall. Her skin was crawling with pent-up aggression, but she was impotent. She was trapped in her own head as much as she had been in David's vines just earlier that night.

Lying down, she stared at the corkboard on her wall, wondering what the pushpins would feel like compared to a sewing needle. She fought the urge, her promise to Meg the only thing that held her back.

Chapter 10

The next day, Rachel turned down David's offer to talk. It was too soon; she needed more time to think things through. She worked with Jeff all day in the basement family room, and despite her energy abilities being low, she wasn't pulling any punches with hand-to-hand defense training. He seemed to at least approve of her efforts in that regard, but it still wasn't enough.

"Rachel, I have to be honest. I'm worried about you," he said at the end of practice.

She frowned. He'd never said, in so many words, that he was outright disappointed in her abilities, but she'd known it was coming.

"I need you to give everything you have. I don't understand why you're holding back."

She resented that; she wasn't intentionally holding anything back. She was giving a good, honest effort. "I'm not. I'm trying my best!" She tried to ignore the sting of tears in her eyes.

He was never one to coddle. "I know you don't want to hear this, but I don't think you'll make it back in time if we keep going at this pace. And I haven't wanted to worry you, but things are getting really bad back home. They need as many of us to return as possible, and as soon as possible. The Ivies are actively pursuing war; they need both of us."

She couldn't look him in the eye. "I promise I'm trying. I really am. I'm just not good at this."

He took a deep breath. "I'm sure you can get it down; you just have to figure out what's holding you back. I know a girl that had only a month to get home from the time she bloomed, and she mastered it. You can too, with the time you have left."

Jeff had obviously meant it as a pep talk, but being compared to someone more talented didn't exactly boost Rachel's morale.

He continued, "And ... we never do this, but you could say we're short-staffed. I can't afford to dedicate all my time to training just you. So, we're going to introduce you to one of our sisters that's also learning."

Rachel looked at the ground, considering his words. "Okay. We'll see how that goes." That might be exactly what she needed—more support from someone like her.

But it wasn't. The next couple of days, Rachel trained after school with Jeff and her new sister, Emma. Emma had bloomed after Rachel, but was *much* further along in training. She attended a different local high school; she and Rachel had never met before that day. It took everything Rachel had to not just sit it out while Jeff focused on Emma. Rachel was wasting his time.

Tuesday night, she overheard her mom and Rob having a conversation about her.

"But would it really be all that bad if she stayed here with us?" Rob asked Samantha. "I know how much it hurts you to see her struggling so much. She was so much happier before this."

"You know I'd love it if she stayed, but I can't do that to my cousin. I can't take her daughter from her like that."

"I get that you made a promise. But Rachel's an adult in their world. She should have some say in her decision. She deserves to pick what would make her happy."

After a long pause, her mom added, "I love her. But I love my cousin, too. And they need *every* female Seeder back right now. Lives are on the line, Rob. I can't be selfish."

It gutted Rachel to be talked about in that way. To cause contention in their marriage. To know that people in her home realm could die if she didn't suck it up and return to contribute. And to not even know anymore *what* would make her happy.

<hr>

Wednesday morning, David pulled up to Rachel's house as usual, picking her up for school. He didn't lean over for a smooch. They still had a long way to go, figuring out where they stood with everything.

"How are you doing?" she asked.

"I'm fantastic," he drawled, staring straight forward.

Okay, so we're starting off in a bad mood. Grumpy and won't make eye contact... "Sounds like it. Why won't you even look at me?"

He turned his head to face her, revealing a nasty black eye.

Her eyes grew wide. "What the heck happened?"

"Basketball," he muttered, turning off the radio. "Some morons don't know where their elbows belong."

Rachel frowned. While she felt bad for him, she still wasn't completely sold that he could be trusted. "Basketball? Not assassin network problems? Nothing about me?"

He sighed forcefully, clearly frustrated. "You know the world doesn't revolve around you, right? Why would this have anything to do with you?"

She scowled. "I think I grasp the concept of it not revolving around me. Never said it did. But you'll have to forgive me if I get worried when my boyfriend hangs out with a rough crowd. I need to make sure our secret is safe."

David rolled his eyes. "Your secret is safe. I'll say it again: basketball, elbow."

She frowned. "Does it hurt?"

He narrowed his eyes. "What do you think, Rachel?"

Crossing her arms, she pursed her lips. "I think you're taking it out on me, and I did nothing wrong."

Gripping his hands tightly on the steering wheel, he closed his eyes. "You're right. Sorry."

"Do you still want to meet up today after school?" She'd decided it would be good to go over her thoughts about where they stood, now that she'd had a little time to process. She'd told Jeff she needed the night off. He was going to be working on catching a breeze with Emma anyway, and Rachel was nowhere near that level.

David reached over, squeezing her hand. "Of course."

After driving to school, they waited at their usual bench for Meg and Eric. Rachel was happy to see Meg was no longer wearing a scarf, and she was even smiling.

"Oooh. Ouch!" Meg wore a pained expression on their approach. "Nice shiner!" She put a hand to her head, closing her eyes as if divining something. "Hmm, let me guess. Biker bar?" She opened her eyes, grinning. "No. Defending some dame's honor?"

Eric joined in the fun as David glared. "No." He pointed at David. "Saving a cat?"

"I've got it! Saving a cat from a biker?" Meg added.

Eric snickered. "Even better, saving a biker from a cat."

"You're truly a pair of asshats," David replied wryly.

Rachel tried with every ounce of her being to not join in on the razzing. Their jokes were much more fun than the boring truth. But he was still in such a sour mood. And he had to be going through a lot, keeping secrets from other Ivies, from everyone close to him. Rachel frowned. "Be nice, guys."

"Okay, fine." Eric cleared his throat. "But some guys wear makeup. Do you think your foundation would match?" He turned to Meg, smiling triumphantly.

Meg did a poor job of stifling a laugh, pushing Eric along to go inside. She winked at Rachel before turning around.

Rachel rubbed David's back. His face was red with anger. She glanced around, making sure no one was within earshot. "I could try to heal it."

He glared again. "Really? And how would I explain to everyone that it magically disappeared? I'll just heal normally like a stupid human."

She pulled her arm back. "Is that really what you think of humans?"

He rubbed his temples. "Sometimes you are so dense. Humans are fine. Seeders are fine. Ivies are fine. We're all fine."

Rachel stood up, scowling. "I get that you're hurt. And I don't know how much of it is your face, and how much of this is your stupid pride. But you're being a real jerk. Maybe we shouldn't waste our time talking tonight."

David frowned, grabbing her hand. "Please. Just..." He sighed. "We're all allowed a bad day now and then, right?"

Rachel took a deep breath, looking at the hurt in his eyes. If only Meg and Eric had known who he really was—a trained assassin—they wouldn't have done that. "Fine."

David started up the car after school. "Thanks for meeting with me."

"Sure." Rachel wrung her hands. No one had come for her or her family—David was keeping his word. And now that school was over for the day, she had time to ask her questions—she'd prepared a list after a warning Jeff had recently shared. "Where are we going?"

"Somewhere we can talk and not be disturbed."

She raised her eyebrows. "Can you be more specific? The last time I went somewhere with you matching that description, it didn't end well."

He sighed. "Fair enough. But your family isn't going to be very happy with you being alone with me anywhere, are they? How about I take you there, and if you don't feel safe, we can go somewhere else. You can tell them whatever you want to tell them."

She rolled her eyes. "Thanks. No pressure, right? *I* get to choose the lies I tell my mom and Rob? Like you made me lie to them Saturday night?"

He cocked his head to the side. "C'mon. Don't be like that. We both have to lie all the time. That's just part of the package of being green folk in the human world. You know that. You lie constantly. You lied to me about plans after graduation, didn't you?"

Twisting her lips, she fiddled with the zipper on her backpack. "Fine. Whatever."

They drove through a residential area and parked on the street.

"This is my place; we can talk in privacy." He gestured to an apartment building.

She furrowed her brow. "What do you mean, 'your place'? I know it's been a long time since I've come over, but this is not your house."

"That couple moved. I've been living on my own for a little while. It wasn't hard, with us always spending time at your place."

"That couple? Obviously not your parents, right? Who were they to you?"

With a hesitant pause, he tapped his fingers on the steering wheel. "No talk about our networks, right?"

She let out a heavy sigh. "Fine."

They entered the studio apartment, and she looked around. Did this place represent the 'real' David? It was tidy and minimalistic, which made sense with him being there on a military mission. He hung back after shutting the door, letting her peruse the room. There was a small bathroom and a tiny kitchenette. Next to the bed were a closet, laundry hamper, and dresser. Rachel noticed a framed picture on the dresser and picked it up—a photo of them where they both wore mile-wide smiles at homecoming. Knives twisted in her stomach. They'd shared a lot of happy memories. Even if he *was* being honest about loving her, how many of those memories were tainted by who he was before he came to that conclusion? Before he'd discovered her real identity?

Was it really possible he loved the human Rachel, *and* the Seeder Rachel?

David stepped up behind her, wrapping his arms around her waist. "That's my favorite picture of us," he whispered.

She set it down and removed his hands, walking across the room. The only furniture for sitting was the bed, and she knew good and well she was not going anywhere near that. Instead, she sat on the floor, against the wall on the other side of the room. He took the cue to sit on his bed so they could talk.

"How much do you know about what's going on in the Green Lands right now?" she asked.

"I know things aren't good," he said.

She shared what she'd concluded over their time apart. "If there was ever a time to be careful about our choices, with the state of our people, it would be right now. I think maybe ... if things were calmer, we'd have more of a chance of working things out."

"But that's the thing. I mentioned the rebellion, right? If there was ever a time our people could come together for change, it's right now. It's more of an opportunity than you realize."

She hesitantly rocked her head back and forth. "Then tell me more about this rebellion. What's the purpose? How is it going? How does it work? What part would you and I play?"

Pulling his legs up, David sat cross-legged on the bed. "Right now, we're working on building up our numbers to petition the Ivy government. People are tired of the feud. And ... I'm sure we could find a way to include you and keep you safe." He shrugged. "And I don't see why you wouldn't still be able to be with your Seeder family over there."

She loved the sound of it. Jeff had confessed he'd been keeping details of the raging war a secret, that he hadn't wanted to dissuade her from returning to the Green Lands out of fear. But it actually made Rachel want to go more, once she'd heard how much they needed her, as did this—she wanted to help, she wanted to be part of the solution. But... "That sounds too good to be true."

David raised his eyebrows in acknowledgement. "Sometimes *any* hope in a war seems too good to be true."

"Maybe so, but I don't understand it. How does your people fighting against one another have anything to do with them also fighting us? Why would they spend their time attacking my people when they already have trouble to deal with?"

His voice carried hope. "The faction is growing rapidly in strength, as a *result* of the recent aggression. We want it to end."

Nodding thoughtfully, she considered something else Jeff had warned her to keep her ears open for. "Do you know any Ivy royalty?"

David chuckled, shifting positions on the bed. "That's cute. No. Regular soldiers might be a dime a dozen, but trained assassins are, what? A quarter a dozen? I'm not important enough to meet or report to the royal family."

She tucked her knees under her chin. "Who is Nuren?"

David's brow furrowed as he tilted his head. "How would you even know that name? I'm surprised you'd learn that kind of thing when you have all of your powers to learn, still."

Rachel shrugged. "Who is that? We think he has something to do with recent war tactics."

David took a deep breath, lightly scratching his comforter. "We said no talk about networks, but since I don't actually deal with Nuren, I'll throw you a bone." He arched an eyebrow. "Nuren is a member of the royal family and a consultant to the queen and king."

"Do you know where he is?"

David shook his head. "No. And like I said, it's not like I'm chummy with the royal family. You know Nuren just as well as I do."

The reality of how big this all was sank in a bit. Her emotions, hopes, and concerns ricocheted around in her heart. She felt like a coward for being on the fence, for being so wishy-washy. "I'm not sure if I'm even going back. I've seriously thought at times about staying here."

"But why?" David asked with a frown. "Why would you want to stay here?"

Rachel huffed. Was he ignorant, or just selfish? "You and I have very different options. Your people can practically come and go whenever they want. Mine can't do that. We're a lot more limited in how often and when we can go between the worlds. Especially us women. It's not that big of a choice for you, but it is for me."

He bit his lip. "You're right. That sucks. I'm sorry."

"Plus." She frowned in disgust. She couldn't just *hope* things into existence. "I don't think I could go back even if I wanted to."

He was visibly confused. "What do you mean?"

Finally, she had someone she could say it to out loud. "I'm pretty sure I'm the biggest disappointment in the history of my people. I'm doing horrible in training."

He cocked his head to the side. "I'm sure it's not all that bad."

"Yeah." She fidgeted with her hands. "You should have heard what my mom and Rob were saying the other day. And..." She almost slipped on Jeff's identity.

"My brother, too. None of them think I can do it. It's so frustrating. I just want to give up."

David scowled. "Well, screw them. You can do it if you put your mind to it, I know you can."

His words of encouragement gave her the slightest reason to smile. "Thanks. I mean it. That means a lot to me."

"Is there any way I can help?" he asked.

"I don't know. I think some of it is just stress."

He pursed his lips with obvious guilt. "So, I guess I'm not helping with that."

She quietly chuckled. "I don't even know how you could help. It's not like you guys fly or manipulate energy the same way we do, right? Or heal? Honestly, I really don't feel like I know all of the differences between us; I just know to watch out for your vines."

"I could teach you about us. About my people. *Anything* you want to know."

His support and willingness to help was uplifting. Ever so slowly, the wall between them was crumbling.

Rachel found herself forming a genuine smile. "Yeah, tell me about your people."

"Can I come sit next to you?" he asked.

Chapter 11

For the next couple of hours, David sat on the floor by Rachel and told his people's history from their perspective, including the Great Division that led to the Ivies moving across the Green Lands. Of course, a major difference in their beliefs was that the Seeders were the conceited race, thinking themselves morally superior, as well as physically more able.

"You guys have healing, and blades, and darts, and flying, and *way* more energy. You're the real deal. We're taught as kids that your people were starting to oppress ours because we don't have as many bells and whistles."

"No, we're not like that at all!" Rachel defended.

He raised his eyebrows. "Okay, first of all... We're talking mostly about people from well over two centuries ago who thought this way. Second of all, you're not the most qualified to vouch for your people or the state of things. You've never even been over there."

She sighed in frustration. He was right. "What all can you guys do? Obviously, the vines."

"Yeah, that's obviously our main thing. Good for," he cleared his throat, "restraining." He avoided her gaze. "And when they're flexed, the leaves become sharp. We can't heal like you guys can. Our healing is more accelerated than humans, of course, but we can't actively control our energy to speed it up the way you do."

She felt a little better, knowing his black eye would fade sooner rather than later, even without her help.

"And of course, rifts to go between the worlds. Yours do it in the air, ours through the trees.(w) I'm terrified of heights, so I can't even imagine how your people get used to that."

325

"C'mon, doesn't everyone want to fly?" She smiled.

He shook his head vigorously. "No, thank you."

She laughed. "How does that work, with the rifts?"

"Maybe I could show you some day." He smiled sweetly. "I really love being able to share this side of my life with you. Isn't this nice? Maybe someday you'll learn to forgive me." He offered his hand.

She accepted, slipping her hand into his.

He gave a reassuring squeeze. "I meant it when I said I love you. And I'm going to keep you safe." He opened his mouth, pausing as though hesitant. "Can I kiss you?"

She stroked the back of his hand. "Yeah."

He leaned toward her, his lips pressing against hers. The kiss was sweet and gentle. He was the same David she'd known this whole time. And maybe ... maybe even something more, now that they had this intimate secret between them.

"Can I see your vines?" she asked, gazing into his stunning green eyes.

He extended a short tendril from his wrist, and she ran her fingers over it. It was a sinewy, strong green cord. The short length he was demonstrating had a pair of small leaves on it. She rubbed them between her fingers. His leaves were soft and papery, not that different from how a normal leaf would feel.

"They get sharp when you flex?"

"Yeah, here, don't want to cut you." He moved her hand away and then the leaves became rigid.

She carefully felt the side of a leaf. It was as stiff as metal, as sharp as a razorblade. She ran her finger over it. "Ouch. You weren't kidding!" She pinched another finger against the cut to heal it.

He shook his head. "To live in a world where you don't have to suffer through paper cuts." He laughed, and she smiled.

"So, is there anything else about your people?" she asked. "Oh yeah, don't forget the poison."

He nodded guiltily. "Yeah, that about sums it up. But if we're looking for a silver lining, we probably never would have met if it weren't for that poison."

She scoffed. "Right. I can see it now, at our wedding reception. 'These two love birds were brought together thanks to his kind attempting genocide against hers.' And then everyone lets out a big 'Aww' in unison."

He sighed heavily. "You're being a little 'glass is half empty.' I'm just trying to stay positive, okay?"

"How does that even work, David? Relationships between our people?" She ran her fingers across the soft cream carpet they were sitting on.

"Ideally, like this." He winked.

"No. I mean ... like, physically..." Her cheeks warmed. "My kind mate for life. So ... there's something different there. It's not like we teach about mixing green folk races."

"Why do you want to know?" He wiggled his eyebrows suggestively.

"Stop it." She elbowed him in the ribs.

"Ouch! Okay, fine. I mean, we're not all that different. In the basics, we're all human. That's why we blend in so well here. Green folk have additional unique traits, so we may not be able to have kids together, but I don't see why we couldn't still have completely fulfilling lives and relationships."

"That's a nice perspective. I'd love for that to be true." She moved in closer, leaning her head against his chest. "Do you think there are ways for our abilities to be used together?"

"Hmm, that's a good question. I'm sure books on that haven't been around for a long time. But we draw our abilities from the same place, so maybe? Let's see."

He pricked his finger with one of his leaves, and she moved her hand up to heal it. It healed even quicker than she'd expected.

"That's cool; it really did work," she whispered. "I learned I can heal humans, too. But yours was so fast..."

He planted a kiss on her head. "We're not all that different. We could complement each other well."

Rachel smiled.

"I'd love to learn more about your people," he said. "You haven't been back there, but I'm guessing you've learned a lot."

She hesitated. "I... I want to believe that this is the real you..." Her mind recalled the lessons Jeff had been giving her about their people, their conflicts with the Ivies. She sat up straighter to get a good view of David's face. Feeling stupid for not having led with this question, she dared to ask, "Have you ever killed a Seeder?"

"No!" he replied emphatically and without hesitation. "I promise. I'd been prepared to..." He looked down. "It's actually pretty rare for an assassin to return successfully, having taken out a Seeder here. It gains you a lot of honor, career choices, and money back home."

That was nauseating to hear. But she also realized how much more he was giving up by not turning her in. By not hurting her. By not *killing* her.

"I'd say I'm sorry you're losing your prize, but..." she said lightheartedly.

He smiled warmly. "The better prize is that you're giving me a chance."

"How did it happen that you became an assassin?"

David puffed up his cheeks, then blew the air out. "Pretty much every male Ivy is trained to be a soldier. Those who can prove their worth and ability to blend in over here are picked for extra training." He softly glided a hand across her calf. "It used to be a point of personal pride for me, that I was chosen for an assassin network."

It made her even more sick to her stomach. Her own brothers were soldiers, but not assassins...

David studied her face. "It's easy to paint the enemy as monsters or savages. But then I met you. Guess I'm not a very successful assassin."

Rachel grinned. "I'm still kinda grateful for that."

He held her hand again. "So, tell me something fun about your people that I don't already know."

"Um..." She searched his eyes, still nervous to divulge anything. "What do you already know about? Other than what we've already discussed?"

David shrugged. "How about the necklace you were wearing a while back? Do you guys use any other tools like that?"

"Wait, what?" She slowly leaned away. "I thought you guys didn't know about those. And you told me you just barely found out I was a Seeder because of my eyes."

He smiled. "Your eyes gave you away, but I remember when you started to wear a necklace, after you were sick." He took a deep breath. "What the necklace does is actually newer intel."

Frowning, she toyed with her necklace. How had the Ivies gotten that intel? How could it be anything other than torturing it out of someone?

"Hey." He met her gaze. "No pressure. I just think it's cool to learn more about each other." He pulled her in tight.

They sat on the floor for some time. She loved being in his arms.

"So, where do we go from here?" David asked.

That was the pressing question that made Rachel's heart sink. "I really don't know. I'm still not sure if I'll make it back. How long are you supposed to be here?"

"No idea; we don't always know ahead of time. Sometimes it's till we graduate, or our cover is blown, or we ... complete a mission... It also depends on how things go back home. I imagine I'll be here until graduation. But I'd leave early, in a heartbeat, to follow you over there."

She glanced down at their hands, which fit perfectly together. "But let's say I don't make it over?"

He kissed her forehead. "I don't see why we can't plan for both options. Put your heart into your training to see if you can go back. But let's also enjoy every minute we have together, knowing we may only have a couple of months left."

She agreed to his proposal. Ultimately, even before his big reveal, that had been her plan—learn how to go home to the Green Lands, enjoy the last of her time with David, break up when she had to leave. His being an Ivy added stress in some ways, but in the end, the gut-wrenching decision of having to break up with him was now possibly off the table.

Rachel could breathe a sigh of relief. David's reveal as an Ivy was something new and exciting in some ways. He was showing a more vulnerable, sensitive side than she had ever seen in him. Their relationship grew stronger. Between practices and carving out some time for them and for Meg, Rachel was doing much better than she had in a while. Emotionally, things were finally on the mend.

Jeff was also really encouraging at her practices. When she was finally able to sustain a decent hover, she let David know. He beamed and took her out for ice cream to celebrate. They didn't talk too much about any green folk things, needing to be discreet, and promising to enjoy their time together in the human world. But they'd share a knowing wink now and then, and he'd text her words of encouragement.

Things had been going great for a solid month. Maybe, just maybe, she could pull this off.

Without warning, Rachel grew weak again. She was physically drained of energy, and it felt at times like there were barely any wisps of Seeder energy residing in her heart.

Nothing had been bothering her. She did everything she could to not start on a downslide. David was a huge support through it all. It was hard for her on nights he was unavailable because he had to keep up appearances with the other Ivies. Spring break was even more difficult because Meg's parents took her out of town to go visit extended family. Meg still wouldn't talk about acting weird earlier in the year, but she seemed to be more her normal self.

Rachel accompanied Jeff and Emma in training, watching Emma practice catching a breeze in preparation for her return to the Green Lands the next week. It was majestic, and beautiful, and inspiring. And also overwhelming to imagine Rachel could even come close to that by her rooting deadline. The next day, she met yet another sister who needed help training. Rachel wondered how few brothers she must have in the area if Jeff needed to divide his attention so much between them.

One particularly hard night, Rob invited Rachel into his home office. His beard was neatly trimmed, his hair parted and combed to the side. "I just wanted to chat before I leave." He traveled a lot for work. "I've noticed you're having a hard time. And I know I told your mom it would be good for you to keep dating David, but now I'm wondering if he's too much of a distraction."

"No! I'm not breaking up with him." She frowned. "He's really helpful, getting me through ... whatever this is ... that I'm having a hard time with in training."

Rob furrowed his brow. "You haven't told him anything, have you?"

"Of course not! David just helps me feel better. I promise, seeing him isn't distracting or harming my training, okay?"

He hesitantly nodded. "Alright. We just want what's best for you."

"I appreciate that." She hated lying to Rob. Though ... technically, her stupid eyes were the ones that had given away her secret; she hadn't initially done any blabbing...

One Friday night, Rachel was lying in David's arms, back at his place, crying.

"I'm never going to get this down." She whimpered.

He held her tight, showering her with encouraging words and comforting kisses. "You will. I know you will."

After a few more minutes without talking, he spoke up. "I have an idea." He rubbed her arm. "How about you turn in early tonight? Don't expend any of your energy tonight or tomorrow. I have a theory. I'll pick you up at two."

Two in the afternoon rolled around the next day and Rachel met David out at his car. "What's this theory of yours?" She was desperate; she needed something to get her over this hurdle. He'd hinted at it being something their powers could possibly do together.

"Mmm, a surprise," he answered cheerfully. "I promise you'll like this one." He smiled. "We're going on a field trip."

They drove out of the city and toward the woods.

"While I like surprises, I'm not too fond of ever seeing that cabin again," she warned with a side glance. The grapefruit-scented air freshener in his car drove the memory home; that had been the smell in his car the night of their hot tub fiasco.

David shook his head. "No, we're putting that behind us. And we won't be going out that far."

They turned down a small dirt road and parked just out of sight of the highway.

Rachel raised her eyebrows quizzically.

He asked with a grin, "How would you like to see the Green Lands for yourself?"

Chapter 12

Rachel's eyes grew wide. "What do you mean, see the Green Lands?"

David grabbed her hands in excitement. "I told you once that I could show you how we travel through rifts. But I think this could be more than a show-and-tell. I think I might be able to take you with me."

She searched his face. "How? How would that work?"

He squeezed her hands. "It's just a theory. But I was thinking about how you were able to heal my cut. That we could combine my method with a boost from your energy. I'm pretty sure the rift could let us both through."

Her jaw dropped. "You really think it would work? Is it dangerous?"

"I don't see how it could be. I've never heard of anyone getting hurt by a rift. Green folk use them all the time. We'd just use your energy to make it open more, for two of us to go through."

"What if we get stuck over there?" she asked. He sounded and appeared completely sincere, and even if he was, and it worked, she wasn't ready to say goodbye to her parents and Meg yet.

He shook his head. "Oh, no. That's never the problem. We draw strength from the realm on that side. It's at least twice as easy to get back."

She considered his proposal. He hadn't done anything to betray her trust, not even a hint of deception since that night at the cabin. "Where would we be arriving on the other side?"

He lifted his eyebrows. "Neutral territory. We'll be far from any dangerous action or prying eyes. When I was a kid, my sister and I stumbled upon the place— it's an old deserted area."

She smiled at his mention of having a sister. Like with his network, he hadn't discussed any family. It was endearing; she envisioned little David playing with a kid sister. "How about I watch you go through the first time, and then we try together the second time?"

"Sorry." He shook his head. "Even with your help, I wouldn't be able to make it through twice in one day. It's not that easy. That's one of the limitations of our powers."

Rachel took a deep breath, knowing she should be more patient. She studied his face, both nervous and excited. "Let's do it. What do I need to do?"

Their portal tree was selected, a nice healthy pine with a trunk a smidge wider than his hand from wrist to fingertip. With her permission, he held one of her hands, wrapping a short length of vine around her wrist to keep them together. Using his free wrist, he extended another short vine and ran it down the spine of the tree—it cracked under the pressure. A mesmerizing, shifting glow surrounded the crack.

"I think this is where I need you to focus your energy on my hand and vine. I'll go first and bring you through."

She closed her eyes and opened the energy pooled in her heart, willing it to head to her fingertips. He started to pull her through the rift. It felt like a warm hug, as easy to pass through as walking through a light breeze.

"Dammit! Ouch." She grimaced, clutching her wrist where his now rigid and sharp leaves were digging in.

"I'm so sorry! I didn't know that would happen. Are you alright?" He released her and tried to get a good look at the cuts as she healed her wrist.

"It's okay. No big deal." She smiled, showing him it was all better. There was barely any blood. She didn't have anything to clean it up with, so she cringed a bit while wiping it on her jeans, reminding herself to clean them properly when she got home.

He pulled her wrist up and kissed it. "I'm really sorry. I don't think there's a danger of that happening on the return."

"It's fine. Really."

With her injury tended to, she could seize the moment and survey the area. The air was somehow more refreshing, the energy that flowed through her invigorating. The woods even seemed greener. The forest floor was covered in pine needles and cones, leaves from other trees, mushrooms, and a scattering of vibrant wildflowers. While it was probably similar to some forests in the human world, this place felt ... different.

"This is amazing!"

He smiled and pulled her in close. "You're here. It's where you belong. I'm ecstatic we could share this, just you and me."

He met her contented smile with a gentle caress of the lips. She pulled him in closer, holding the nape of his neck, daring herself to be more carefree than she had ever been with him since her bloom.

Taking a moment to catch her breath, she leaned back to search his eyes.

He bit his lip. "You're amazing. I could lose myself in those eyes."

She felt the signature warmth accompanying her Seeder change—glowing green eyes. He'd said exactly what she was hoping to hear, confirming that Seeders and Ivies really did stand a chance of working things out. "I love you," she confessed.

He pulled her back in, their lips and hearts becoming one in this special moment.

Neither Jeff nor David had exaggerated the invigorating feeling of being in this realm. It made perfect sense why the Ivies preferred their home realm over the human world. Rachel sensed the energy building in her heart: The energy of the Green Lands. The rush of being in an entirely different realm. Something made possible thanks to David.

Her heart beating a mile a minute, Rachel pulled back and gazed into his bright green eyes. "I think I'm ready," she whispered. "If you want to."

Grinning and still catching his breath, David slid his hands down to the button on her jeans. "Really?"

She smiled, wanting nothing more in this magical place, in this magical moment. "Yeah."

He looked her squarely in the eyes, his expression dropping. "No. Not yet." He removed his hands from her waistband.

Her brow furrowed in confusion.

"I don't want to take advantage of you. I don't want you to ever worry if that's why I brought you here," he said.

"You're not the one asking." She gently took his hands, moving them back to her jeans.

Without hesitation, he removed his hands again, tucking them into his pockets. "No. And after all this time, it's killing me. But I can wait longer." He tenderly kissed her forehead. "This is your first time feeling the energy here—I don't want it messing with your head and leaving you with any regrets." He then kissed her hand. "I have something else in mind. Follow me."

He motioned with a nod of the head in the direction they were going to walk. After several minutes of exploring, weaving through a sea of trees, passing a lovely spotted frog and a half dozen blue-and-yellow butterflies, they found a rundown log cabin.

"I hope not all cabins are tainted for you. This is an old abandoned one I found. We can sit down and relax. I think you'd benefit from energy-bathing. Or at least that's what I'm calling it." He smiled. "Like sunbathing, but relaxing and soaking up the energy here before heading back."

"Let's give it a go."

The cabin door barely opened, the wood swollen from years of neglect. David pulled dust covers off of a wooden table, chairs, and a couch. They sat, wrapped up in each other, and just took it all in. It gave Rachel a couple of carefree hours to think, ponder, and heal.

"Do you know where you'll be leaving the human world from?" he asked after a while.

Rachel drew a deep breath. "I'm not sure. I don't think I actually find out until it's time."

He offered a sweet smile. "It would be awesome to see you off."

She frowned. "You know that couldn't work. They don't exactly allow many humans into our circle. And definitely not Ivies." Shifting, she lay down with her head in his lap.

He studied her face. "I know. Maybe I could sneak there and hide or something."

She smiled softly. "I'd rather keep you out of harm's way." She gazed into his mesmerizing green eyes. "You're not lying about being part of this rebellion?"

He shook his head. "I wouldn't lie about that. I was initiated a few months ago. I'm trying to think of the right way to get you involved, assuming you really want to."

"Of course I want to!"

He grinned. "I knew you'd be up for it. I *definitely* look forward to you meeting people in the movement. I just need to make sure we do it in a safe way. That we have all our bases covered."

Rachel closed her eyes, breathing in the energy, the hope, the peace. "I could get used to this feeling," she mused.

He lovingly tickled her face with his fingertips. "Ditto." He blew out a long exhale. "But we should get you back. Without cell service over here, I don't want anyone to get worried."

Sighing, Rachel sat up. He was right.

They threw the dust covers back on the furniture and fought to close the door tight.

"So, you just pick any tree, right?" she asked.

"Not quite *any* tree—there's an ideal size, and some other details. But most of these would do. Would you like the honor of picking one?"

She tapped a pointer finger against her lips and glanced around. Squinting, she walked up to one. "Maybe this one, let me see." She grabbed his hand and backed him up against the tree, playfully stealing kisses.

Pulling back, she bit her lip. "Nope, not this one." Looking around, she spotted another target, leading him by the hand, and again pressed herself against him, gently nibbling on his earlobe and caressing his neck with her lips.

He chuckled. "Okay, down, girl."

She grinned mischievously. "Alright, fine. I think this one will do."

Sizing up the tree, he extended a vine to make the rift. Without any extra effort, they both walked through, David again going first and holding Rachel's hand. His leaves barely broke her skin on the return; it was a quick heal. She didn't draw any attention to it so he wouldn't feel bad.

The difference between the realms was palpable. The air was cooler, more stale on this side. But it was still home. Before getting in the car, Rachel stopped and studied the tree they had chosen to take them to the Green Lands earlier. The area around where the rift had opened was discolored, the bark peeling. Yellow needles were falling to the ground.

She frowned. "Does this always happen?"

"Yeah. That's just a byproduct. We can always plant more trees."

David had been right about what Rachel needed—it was perfect. Perhaps taking a quick trip to the Green Lands now and then for a refresher was what she could use to get her through training. Of course, she had to dial things down so Jeff and the others didn't notice she went from ten to a hundred overnight.

On a beautiful star-filled night, Rachel and David talked about their future, how their plans might unfold. She was going to try and master flying to return on her own, and then find a way to meet up in the Green Lands when he returned. He couldn't safely make it past the Seeder border walls to sneak in and visit, but she'd be capable of flying over the walls to rendezvous in the Neutral Woods. And if for some reason she couldn't quite get back to the Green Lands by catching a breeze, he'd be able to help her get there in time to root. He'd then guide her to Seeder territory. And unlike Seeders normally did, he could help her come back to the human world and visit her mom and Rob, and Meg, as often as she wanted. There weren't a whole lot of negatives.

Other than the lies. How would she explain it to her family? 'Oh, no big deal. I'm not up to snuff with flying, but I'm also not worried because I'm finding alternate transportation. What's that? Oh yeah, dating the enemy. No biggie.' That was the sole concern right now, so she was putting her all into breeze-catching practice to avoid the topic at all costs.

"And no one on your side suspects me yet?" she asked as they cuddled under the moonlight in her backyard. "What would happen to you if they found out you're helping me?"

"We've done a good job. I haven't spotted any hint of suspicion. And don't worry about me. I know what I'm doing. I can take care of myself." He kissed her on the head. "And you, too."

"You're sure I can't meet someone else from the rebellion? We'd be on the same side, right?"

He shook his head. "No, we can't risk that yet. I've only got one guy on this side with me for sure."

Rachel sighed wistfully. "My brother doesn't seem to think there even is a rebellion."

David sat up, visibly frustrated and concerned. "You've talked to him about it? That's not very smart! Where do you think he'll assume you're getting that information from?"

"I'm being smart about it. I'm not stupid." She scowled. "All I did was ask him if he thought anyone from your side would feel like we do, and want to help."

His muscles relaxed.

"Why can't you just meet with him?" she asked. "If my people knew about the cause, couldn't we work together?"

"Frankly," he spoke softly, "I'm not high enough in the network to make the introduction. And I'm guessing your brother isn't either. Things will work out; we just have to be careful as we approach your departure. And be patient, and ready when everything falls into place. Okay?"

She nodded, and he went back to holding her.

A star fell from the sky and Rachel made a silent wish. If things could just slow down, smooth out, go undetected—she could be perfectly happy and up to the challenge.(x)

The countdown to rooting day continued. They estimated two and a half to three weeks. Prom was in two weeks. Rachel's mom asked her to sit down for a chat in the living room. Her short curly brown hair framed a concerned face.

"You know we're proud of you and love you, right?"

Rachel glanced at the family pictures on the wall. "Of course, Mom."

"You've made a lot of progress. Do you feel like you're going to be able to do it?" she asked, clearly worried.

"It's okay. I know I've been a little hot and cold. But I'll have it down. I'm not worried, and I don't want you guys to be either, okay?"

"Alright. If you're sure about it." Her mom frowned, evidently not sharing her daughter's cavalier attitude. "We've talked about pulling you from school for extra practice. Is that something you want to risk doing?"

"I'm fine with that, but can we wait until after prom? I really still want to go to prom before I leave, and then I'll give one hundred percent of my time to flight practice." Realizing she was being too casual, she tried to frown convincingly. "I really want to go to prom with David. And then I'll break up with him, and dedicate every last second I have to training."

Chapter 13

The next morning, Rachel and David were canoodling on their usual bench in front of the high school, waiting for Meg and Eric. She was ecstatic to share with David that they were definitely going to be able to attend prom together. They were midsmooch when Rachel spotted Meg approaching. Meg handed Rachel her signature drink and then handed one to David.

Rachel took a sip. "Where's Eric?"

Meg averted her gaze, but not before Rachel caught the turmoil in her eyes.

"He's not coming." She wouldn't make eye contact.

Rachel's face twisted with curiosity. "Is he sick?"

Meg pressed her lips together. "I'm going to go. We can talk later." She walked away at a brisk pace.

Rachel turned to David, who also wore a look of confusion.

"Go check on her," he said.

Meg ducked into a small bathroom. By the time Rachel went in, Meg was sitting on the tile floor, back to the wall, bawling into her knees.

Rachel crouched down next to her. "Hey, what's wrong?" She tried to move Meg's hair away from her face. "Are you and Eric fighting?"

Meg let out a whimper.

"Did you guys ... break up?"

Meg's shoulders shook as she sobbed, nodding, still staring into her lap.

Rachel sat on the cold tile floor next to her and shooed away a pair of girls that opened the bathroom door.

"Do you want to talk about it?"

Meg shook her head.

The first bell rang. Meg lifted her head, leaning it against the wall. She sniffled, wiping off her face with the back of her hands. "You should go to class."

"To hell with class, I'm staying here with you," Rachel said, standing and grabbing some tissues for her.

Meg dabbed her face, still sniffling.

Rachel frowned. "What happened? Did he do something? I've never even seen you guys fight."

"I don't want to talk about it," Meg squeaked.

"Okay. No pressure." Rachel leaned shoulder to shoulder with her friend, just being there for her.

She was a little worried her mom and Rob might get a truancy call for her skipping first period. But why did it even matter? Twelve years in the public education system and her Seeder nature was stealing the validation of walking at graduation. She couldn't care less about her attendance record at this point.

Right now, Meg was the priority. It already killed Rachel that she had to lie to her best friend, and that she'd be abandoning her. Rachel had felt more optimistic lately, now that she knew she could return more often with David's help. But leaving Meg right now, with a broken heart, wasn't going to make any of this easier.

David asked about Meg at lunch. "So, what's that about? What happened?"

Rachel scowled at him, remembering his 'cover story' amongst the assassins, that he was still dating Rachel to get close to Meg. "Is that a recon question?"

He rolled his eyes. "I can't ask about a friend's well-being?"

"Yes. You can ask her directly. I'm not your spy."

He narrowed his eyes. "Why are you pissed at me? I didn't do anything. Grow up." He stood up from their table, taking his food and leaving her alone.

She was angry on her friend's behalf. And she knew it wasn't David's fault, and felt a little guilty about questioning his motives. Near the end of lunch, Rachel spotted Eric walking in a nearby hallway and chased him down.

"What happened?" she barked. "What did you do?"

Eric's face spelled contempt. "You're kidding me, right? She's the one that broke up with me and wouldn't even tell me why!"

Rachel was able to smooth things over with David pretty quickly. She tried to coax information out of Meg about the breakup, but Meg refused to talk about it. They had planned to double to prom; Meg now told her to go without her, that she wanted to stay home instead. It ate Rachel up. She felt like Meg and Eric had enjoyed a really healthy, happy relationship. And to end it so abruptly, and right before prom...

Rachel was starting to wonder more if maybe, perhaps ... Meg was a Seeder, too? Breaking up abruptly before leaving was what Rachel was going to have to do, before she'd found out David's true identity. As much as she wanted to broach the topic, she knew it wasn't wise. If Meg was really a Seeder, she could look her up soon enough over in the Green Lands. If she wasn't, Rachel might give away too much by asking. She did love the idea, though, that Meg might even secretly be one of her sisters. Neither of the sisters she'd met thus far even went to their high school.

For now, Rachel planned to be there for Meg, and enjoy as much time as they could together, until Rachel had to leave. She hoped to visit often once things calmed down in the Green Lands and she and David could spend time together. Ivy rifting was so much more accessible compared to the grueling journey and limited capabilities of Seeders to go between the worlds. And by his description of things, the rebellion was growing rapidly; she was holding out hope that there could someday be peace.

With how busy things had been, Rachel hadn't gotten around to prom dress shopping yet. She'd kept putting it off, despite Meg's frequent prodding before her breakup with Eric. But it turned out to not be all horrible; Rachel was able to spend one-on-one time together with her mom, something she hadn't really been able to find time to do lately. Everything about Rachel's future was up in the air. She wasn't sure if she would ever marry, and if she did, if it would be her biological Seeder mom, or Samantha, that she would wedding dress shop with. But this felt like that special kind of moment, something equally sentimental.

Rob told her to spare no expense, his going-away gift to Rachel. She still felt guilty about spending too much, so she picked one that was midpriced. She settled on a wine-red dress with a rhinestone empire waist. It had thick straps and perfectly matching heels. Wanting to at least share something of prom with Meg, Rachel texted, offering to pay for Meg to get dolled up with her at the salon, just for fun. Meg declined.

An hour before David was set to pick her up, Rachel sat on her bed, a bundle of nerves. Her mom peeked in after softly knocking on the door.

"How are you doing? Need help zipping up?"

Rachel pulled her hair to the side. "Yeah. Thanks." She wrung her hands while her mom came around and zipped up the dress, then sat beside her.

"What's going through your mind?" her mom asked.

Rachel took a deep breath. *Too much.* "Just prom, and, you know, leaving..." Her room was untouched, as the cover story for her impending disappearance wouldn't require her parents to move.

Her mom frowned. "If you can't make it, or choose not to in the end ... we wouldn't be disappointed."

Rachel bit her lip, catching an unexpected stray tear with her hand. "The moment this all started ... it just felt like you guys wanted to ship me off."

Her mom threw her arms around Rachel. "No! Never. I'm sorry if it came across that way. I just..." She pulled back, wiping away a few tears of her own. "We wanted to be encouraging. We felt like you should embrace your heritage. And I promised your mother we'd get you back to your biological family." She wiped up a couple of Rachel's tears as well. "Who was right about waterproof mascara, huh?"

Rachel laughed and sniffled.

Her mom sighed. "I'm sure it's that much harder, saying goodbye to your friends and David. And it's probably the last thing you want to hear, but I know you'll make a lot of new friends over there."

Rachel frowned. As if giving up her human life wasn't bad enough, there had to be the lies. She didn't have the tiniest of hopes her family would understand her relationship with an Ivy. "Thanks. I'm nervous, but I've made my decision. Things will work out."

Her mom smiled. "They will. I'm sure of it. You've got a lot going for you." She grabbed Rachel's hand. "No matter what ... you will always have a place in our home and hearts. Okay?"

Rachel's heart swelled as she realized how much she'd really miss her mom. The two of them had started this journey together, and had gotten through it all. "Thanks. I love you."

"Love you, too." Her mom got up to leave, stopping with her hand on the doorknob. "I understand David means a lot to you and it's prom night. But I'm assuming you guys aren't going to... 'Cause of the whole energy and emotion thing, right?"

Rachel buried her face in her hands. "Seriously?"

"Hey, I wouldn't be a half-decent parent if I didn't check. You've worked hard. Things are different now."

Rachel looked up, smiling. "We'll be fine. Thanks for watching out for me."

Rachel was pacing around with nerves, waiting for David to arrive. Par for the course, she had been taking a dip on the energy roller coaster lately—she needed this kind of pick-me-up.

He arrived, looking sharp in a tux, wearing the biggest smile she'd ever seen on him. He brought her a wrist corsage with a yellow rose, ivy used as the greenery. He winked and whispered how it represented them as a couple—the ivy being an obvious nod to him, the yellow rose representing her hair when she transformed.

David even rented a limo, sparing no expense, just like he'd gone all-out for their anniversary-gone-wrong. In part, she guessed it was his way of trying to make up for the botched event. They made sure the divider was up so they could talk in private and ... get a little frisky without peeping eyes. But not so heated as to mess up her hair. They hadn't discussed it, but Rachel wondered if they'd revisit the topic of sex later that night. She wasn't nervous about that part of their relationship anymore.

"What restaurant are we going to?" she asked as they headed to the city limits.

"We're going to make a stop before dinner, if that's okay. I think you could use a little something magical to give you energy to dance the night away." He winked.

She didn't protest his idea. Rachel had considered asking him if he thought a second visit would do her some good, give her that burst of energy to really put her all into the last days of training before heading out. She genuinely didn't think she would be able to make the flight without it in her current state.

"I've already paid the driver to drop us off and come back a half hour later, so we won't be too late to everything else tonight." He smiled.

He always had a plan.

Her mind wandered to worries on the long drive. "What are we going to do if I realize last minute I can't make the flight?"

He squeezed her hand reassuringly. "First of all, you'll make it just fine. But if, for some reason, you realize you're not ready, then hold off. I think it would be a good idea to have a letter ready. That way I can get you home in time before you root here, and they won't be worried about you. That way you can let them know you found a way to the Green Lands and you'll be in touch."

"Yeah, that's a good idea." She rubbed one of her temples. "I don't know why I didn't think of that. My brain is all muddled."

He frowned. "You've got a lot on your mind. And I know with us officially 'breaking up' tomorrow, even if it's only for show—I'm going to be sad I can't be there with you." He gave her a half-smile. "Just remember I'm a text away. I'll be waiting to hear from you."

"Thank you." She glanced down at her fresh manicure. "What are we going to do to meet up on the other side?"

"Ah, yes." He smiled wide. "Part of the surprise tonight... I have a map over there. I'm going to show you where we have our meetups and I can briefly go over my plans to get in touch, assuming you catch a breeze home."

Things were starting to line up like they ought to. Except for Meg. "Do you think Meg could keep it a secret if I told her about being a Seeder? I've kinda been thinking about it lately." Leaving Meg with a broken heart, and so emotionally distant, was still killing Rachel.

"You really haven't told her, huh?"

Rachel shook her head. "I've been following the rules. Well," she grinned, "minus the 'dating an assassin' part."

He shared her smile.

"But no. Meg doesn't know yet. Whether or not you can help me visit more than the once-a-year that Seeders normally can, I feel like she deserves to know."

Looking down pensively, David shrugged. "I don't see why not. If you think she can keep a secret."

Rachel's tension about leaving eased. "Yeah. I think I will. Maybe the night before I leave."

He kissed her on the forehead as the limo pulled to a stop. They got out and waved the limo on.

"He has *seriously* got to be wondering what the heck we're doing out here," she said.

"I don't know about that. I'd think it's obvious I want a romantic stroll with the most beautiful girl in school." He pulled her in close, nuzzling her neck.

She giggled, until she realized he was giving her a hickey. "Seriously, David? Before prom?" She punched him lightly in the shoulder and moved her hand up to heal it.

He flashed an apologetic pouty face. "Sorry." He chuckled. "I'll admit I'm spoiled having a girl who can clean that sort of thing up so quickly."

She rolled her eyes. "I'm already drained, remember? And you need my help to get us both through, right?"

He sighed. "Yes. I'm sorry. That really was stupid. Speaking of, I know it hurt you last time. I hope it doesn't this time, but are you going to be okay if it does?"

She nodded confidently. "I can handle it. Especially once I get to the other side."

They picked a tree and followed the same procedure as the first time; he wrapped a vine around her wrist that didn't have the corsage.

"Dang it! Yeah, that definitely hurt worse this time!" She was bleeding a decent amount, with deeper gashes than on the previous visit.

"Shoot! Well, we'll figure it out eventually. Sorry." He pulled out a tissue. "I brought this just in case." He wiped up the blood before she healed it.

She calmed again with the pain now gone. "No harm, no foul." She inhaled deeply, the wonderful charm of this realm rushing into every cell of her body. With the time difference, it was already much darker in the Green Lands than back home in the human world. A few fireflies danced in the sky nearby.

Holding her hands, David looked lovingly into her eyes. "I can never thank you enough for giving me a chance, knowing who I am. I know not everyone would do that."

She smiled. "You're worth it. I love you."

He gave her a peck on the lips and then reached into his pocket. "Now, to add to the surprise, I want you to see what I've done with the dusty old place on a recent visit." He held up a blindfold.

She raised her eyebrows in curiosity.

He tilted his head. "All your training leaves me with some free time. I wanted to plan something as special as you are."

She bit her lip, and he covered her eyes, guiding her through the woods by the hand. Pine cones crunched under her feet along the way. He let her hand go for a moment while he yanked the tight wooden door open, then brought her inside. David moved one of his hands to her waist, standing close behind her. He gently kissed her neck.

And then it happened again. David's hand over her mouth, his other arm restraining her. But this time there were *several* vines wrapping her arms and legs. David released her from his grip and stepped away, but the vines only tightened.

"What the hell are you doing!" she screamed, struggling against the restraints, still unable to see anything. "David, please! Don't do this!"

"Get her out of here. But don't hurt her more than you have to," David's voice ordered coolly.

"Yes, Your Highness," came a female voice she didn't recognize.

New vines wrapped around Rachel's throat, the leaves sinking into her flesh. Searing pain emanated from the leaves as she fought for air. Weakness and nausea crippled her. She would have fallen to the floor had the vines around her not intentionally guided her down. With her sight still obscured by the blindfold, her mind joined in the darkness, her body unconscious on the floor.

Chapter 14

Saff tried not to cry as she walked home from work. She was beyond worn down. They'd announced just before classes ended for the day that her village had lost several people to the war the night before. She recognized two of the names this time. While grateful neither victim belonged to her immediate family, it gutted her nonetheless. She wished there was more she could do. All the Ivies ever did was murder—here at Seeder borders, and back in the human world, as she'd so personally experienced, thanks to their assassin networks.

She kicked a stone in the lane, barely missing someone. "Sorry." She frowned. This path hadn't always been this busy, but *all* lanes in her village were busy at this point. Before this newest surge in the war, the western villages had done their part in keeping the border safe through their own temple wells, depositing energy. They'd also sent regular volunteers over for patrol duty. But more and more help was needed, and the burden of keeping their lands safe weighed too heavily on the border villages, like Saff's home, South Fortinda. Full-time troops from the inner villages were now stationed in the border communities. While they were needed assistance, it strained resources. Fields where Seeder boys used to play were now filled with soldiers' tents. Housing was full. Food supplies taxed. The walls that had protected them for the last century were failing, no longer enough.

Saff entered their cottage only to find a letter on the kitchen table. It was a note from Devin asking her to meet him at her parents' house. She hadn't been able to spend much time visiting family lately anyway, so she was more than willing to walk over, though afraid of what might be prompting the visit.

Her fear of impending bad news was quickly realized after she entered the house. The kitchen had food laid out everywhere, cooking being one of her Seeder mother, Murial's, coping mechanisms.(y) The major players in their family Seeder network gathered around the table. Her Seeder father, Thod—who was looking increasingly gaunt from the stress; Devin's dad, Simon; her brother, Ben; and a couple of other brothers. Their expressions were grim. Devin sat with them, glancing over his shoulder when the door opened.

"What happened?" she demanded. "What's wrong?!"

Devin jumped up from his seat and hugged her. "The family's okay."

She was still braced for more bad news when he had her sit down.

"They got another one, Saff."

She twisted her face, trying to hold back tears. "How is this happening? How can we be letting down our girls so much?"

This was the sixth known kidnapping of a bloomed Seeder from the human world in the last year. Six wasn't really a huge number—that many female Seeders or more died in the human world in car accidents each year. But these weren't accidents. No bodies had been found, so they weren't typical assassinations, either. A disturbing trend had been recognized. With each girl's disappearance, the Ivy attack grew stronger. These menacing gigantic vines were crossing the Neutral Woods and ripping through the Seeders' protective walls, forcing more hand-to-hand combat. Saff's heart ached for the girl and her family, and the hopelessness of knowing things were only going to get worse.

Devin swallowed hard. It was obvious by his expression he wasn't done delivering the intel. "She's one of ours. She's from home." He frowned, defeated.

"What do you mean? From our village? Or do you mean my hometown back on the human side?"

He wouldn't look her in the eyes. "Yes. Both."

She bit the insides of her cheeks, wringing her hands, trying in vain to hold back the tears.

While rubbing her back, he glanced at the men seated at the table. "We're going to take care of it. Her dad is investigating now, and ... my dad and I are going to see what we can do on that side of things."

She sniffled. "I'm coming with you."

Devin shook his head, and Simon spoke up behind her. "We'll be okay. We don't need you to come."

"I'm going, Simon!" she snapped. Her outburst triggered looks of shock from everyone in the room. She had a great relationship with her in-laws and had never once raised her voice at either of them.

Devin pressed his lips together, surveying the room. "Let's go for a walk." He took her hand, leading her outside.

Just a couple of houses down the dirt lane, he dared to try to talk her out of her decision.

"I don't even know that *our* going will make a difference. It's not worth the risk to have you gone. You're needed here. And you know you don't have it in you to make it all the way there and back."

She dropped his hand and crossed her arms. "I don't need your permission."

He huffed. "No, but I think as your husband you'd at least care what I have to say."

"Don't talk to me like that; I'm not a child," she snapped back.

"Then don't act like one, Saff," he scolded. "I knew you'd do this."

She stopped walking and turned to face him, desperation taking over. "I *need* to do something different. I can only do so much here, and I'm losing it! Maybe I just need to give that poor girl's mom a hug. Just go for a day or two. Let my parents know I'm okay—they have to be worried that I haven't contacted them; it's so late in the season." Her voice betrayed her. "Please, just let me join you. I can't live like this, without hope. I want to try."

He drew a deep breath, moving a hand up to gently caress her cheek. "I'll talk to my dad. But you're going to have to rest up for an entire day, at minimum, to regain your strength. And then two days max over there. We can't be selfish with how much you're needed here."

She nodded. "Yes, I can do that."

The next day, Ben dropped by their cottage while Devin was at work.

"The door's open."

He entered and glanced at Saff in disapproval. "I don't think doing chores is considered 'resting up' in the strictest of meanings."

She kept drying dishes. "I'm not at work and I'm not at the temple. But you can't keep me from doing everything. I feel calmer with a clean house."

He hummed playfully. "Then by all means, want to go clean up my place, too?"

She threw a dish towel at him, and he caught it.

They sat on the couch to chat.

"Are you here to talk me out of going?" she asked, tucking her legs up underneath her.

He laughed. "You? I thought we learned a long time ago that you never listen to what I say."

She pursed her lips, remembering when he was her trainer just a few short years ago and she'd defied his orders time and time again.

He sighed. "Actually, Heather's kind of jealous you're going."

Saff raised her eyebrows. "Get me her parents' phone number. I'll call them when I'm over there; I'll let them know she's okay."

"While I'm sure she'll appreciate that, it's not what I meant. You know we got you home by the skin of our teeth, right? Back when our people had to start sending our daughters over to survive, we realized right away we needed to find a way to temper the changes."

"The jade charms." She reached up, feeling her own.

He nodded. "Yeah, the charms. Not only is the change more violent over there, they just didn't have the same amount of time to learn everything, with the accelerated rooting. The fact that you learned so quickly and made it home in time—I really don't think you give yourself enough credit for the power you possess."

She blushed. "I wish I could say it made more of a difference now, with everything going on."

He pointed at her. "You make a difference. Stop selling yourself short."

"Thanks." She rested a hand on his shoulder. "You always were my favorite brother that left his toothpaste in the bathroom sink." She smiled.

"Yeah, well, you're still my favorite sister that made me want to strangle her every other week as a teenager." He jutted out his chin sarcastically.

She laughed.

"What I wanted to tell you is that I think you have a lot of opportunity to do some good over there. Even if it's Devin and Simon doing the tracking and investigating, you could do even more good by giving some personal lessons to Rachel's sisters. Make sure to set it up as soon as you get there. They need a strong role model right now."

"Yeah, I'll absolutely do that." She loved Ben that much more for giving her a hint of hope, a purpose amidst all that was happening around them.

"I'm glad to hear it." He stood, offering her a hug.

Saff readily accepted it. "You know, I promised you a long time ago that I'd try to make up for the whole almost-getting-you-killed thing. I'm going to do everything I can to help with this war, so we can move on and you guys can stop pushing back the wedding."

He squeezed her tighter. "You're the best. It'll happen."

She reminded him as he left the cottage, "Make sure to get me Heather's parents' phone number. And stay safe. Love you, Ben."

"Love you too, little sis."

She smiled again as he closed the door. 'Little sis'—all of her brothers called her that. Sure, they were technically all the same age, and none of the twelve boys had even sprouted until two weeks after the girls, but she'd earned that title in their family as the last to return home. At times, it was annoying. But mostly, it was endearing.

She gazed at the main focal point of the living room, sitting back down on the sofa. Hanging on the wall was a large painting that her Seeder mom, Murial, had painted for Saff and Devin—a portrait of their wedding day. Heather had giddily talked about how much she was looking forward to theirs someday, back when they first got engaged. But no one was giddy right now. Seeder weddings continued, but in border villages like theirs, they could maybe manage the equivalent of a rushed courthouse wedding, at best.

Saff took a deep breath, standing up and getting back to cleaning the kitchen. She'd meant what she'd told Ben. She was going to do everything in her power so they could have a proper wedding, sooner rather than later. Every bride and groom deserved a special day. And *everyone* deserved to feel safe in their own home.

Chapter 15

Rachel woke to the quiet clink of glass against metal and a muted rustling sound. Her body was half-numb. Her head screamed, and her eyes were puffy, almost swollen shut. She pried her eyelids open to check her surroundings. A brunette woman in her early to midtwenties tidied up a tray across the room. She wore a simple long tan dress with a dark belt. The room itself ... was breathtakingly ornate. The walls had striped wainscoting, and above that, nature-themed murals.

Rachel shifted her body to be more comfortable, unintentionally alerting the woman to her conscious state when the clang of handcuffs rattled against the metal headboard of the bed she was on. The woman opened the door and poked her head out.

"Alert Prince Soren. She's awake."

A male's voice responded, "Yes, ma'am."

Closing the door, the woman turned to face Rachel, frowning. "You must be feeling miserable. I'm so sorry."

"Where am I? What happened?" Rachel asked. She glanced back up at the ceiling, more closely scrutinizing the painted mural above her. Her stomach dropped—a plethora of ivy vines were featured in the design.

The woman wore a forced smile. "You're at the palace. You'll have more answers soon enough. Just focus on healing yourself and building up your strength, okay?"

Rachel looked down—she was still in her prom dress; one of her ankles was strapped to the railing at the end of the bed with vines. Her immobilized foot had an IV in it. She glanced at her hands, both secured to the headboard with handcuffs. Her arms had faint bruising where vines had wrapped tight during the attack.

"How long have I been here?" she asked.

The woman still stood across the room, holding her hands casually in front of her. "Two days."

Rachel's heart sank. Everyone back home had to be panicked. She imagined her mom crying, Rob trying to comfort her. Meg pacing the floor with Eric. Wait, no Eric. *Poor Meg.* And... Well, David certainly didn't seem like he would be at home or worried about her in the slightest.

The door opened, and the devil himself walked in. The woman nervously curtsied. Gone was the prom tuxedo; he now wore tailored black slacks and a long-sleeved silky black button-up shirt. The only color in his ensemble was a green ombre stripe around one of his upper sleeves and grass-green decorative stitching around the hem.

The door closed behind him, and he gave Rachel a sympathetic frown. "Gosh, look at you." He walked to her side and sat next to her on the bed. "How are you doing? It looks like they were a little rough on you." Reaching up, he gingerly moved a wisp of bangs from her face, and she jerked her head away.

"It's okay. I know I betrayed your trust ... again." He looked her over. "And the dress got torn. That's probably not easy to fix, is it?"

She didn't say a word, breathing slowly, trying to figure out his game.

"You couldn't even clean her up?" he barked over his shoulder, causing both the woman in tan and Rachel to flinch. "Bring me a wet cloth."

The woman scurried to the tray she'd been tidying when Rachel woke up, and dipped a white washcloth into a bowl of water before wringing it out. She handed it to David with a bow, avoiding eye contact with him, but catching Rachel's eyes for just a moment.

He was aiming the cloth at Rachel's neck when she tried to dodge him again. "Really? What am I going to do to hurt you with a wet cloth?"

She sat tight-lipped, glaring and remaining silent.

He raised his eyebrows and spoke softly. "Just let me clean it up, okay?"

As he moved his hand again, she stayed still. Her body involuntarily shuddered at his touch, but calmed more as he wiped around her neck. Luckily, it didn't sting anymore, but there was a decent amount of blood staining the rag when he pulled it back. Folding it over revealed a clean spot, and he finished scrubbing off the dried blood where sharpened leaves had pierced her in the ambush.

Putting a hand under her chin, he caressed her cheek while gazing into her eyes. "There you go. That's my girl."

Rachel clenched her teeth. She was not now, nor would she ever again be, *his* girl.

"Was that so hard?" he snapped at the woman again.

She rushed over, bowing and taking the soiled cloth from his hands, giving him a new one to wipe his hands clean. "My apologies, Your Highness."

He threw the second cloth at the woman after he was done with it. David looked Rachel over again. "I bet you'd like... Yeah, let's..." He snapped his fingers at the woman. "A glass of water for her, and take out the IV." He smiled at Rachel. "I bet you'll like that."

The woman brought the water over and then went to Rachel's immobilized leg, removing the needle.

With her hands still secured above her head, Rachel had to rely on David to tip the glass up to her lips. She only realized how parched she really was once she started to guzzle it down.

He took the empty glass and got up, refilling it for her. "I hope you can understand it had to be done this way. We couldn't risk you not coming." He returned to the bed and sat down again. "Come on. You're perfectly capable of holding a conversation. I'm sure you have something you want to say."

She squinted at him in loathing. "So this is who you really are? A psychotic, self-important jackass?"

He again surprised her as his hand shot to her face, painfully grasping her jaw. He stared into her eyes. "I am a *prince*. And I deserve more respect than that from a stupid—peasant—weed." He enunciated each word. His fingers dug into her skin painfully, only releasing when her eyes teared up.

He inhaled deeply, then exhaled slowly. "Plus, there's a difference between psychotic, psychopathic, and sociopathic. Your human public education system is *grossly* insufficient."

His eyes moved from her face down to her restrained ankle. "Nurse, when did you last check her progress?"

"This morning, Your Highness."

"Show me."

The woman approached Rachel's immobile foot, holding a short tool with a rounded metal tip. She looked Rachel in the eyes apologetically before putting it against the arch of her foot and clicking a button.

The instant surge of pain caused Rachel to scream and writhe. David set the glass of water down and casually leaned over, studying her ankles, which were now exposing her Seeder roots.

"Okay, that's enough," he said. "Any time now," he reassuringly reported to Rachel while rubbing her calf, as if to comfort her or wipe away the pain from the stun gun. "And then, we can get you out of this room. That'll be a refreshing change of scenery!"

She scowled, still shaking, her breath and heartbeat racing. "I prefer the scenery back home. Please, just let me go." Her voice squeaked.

He pursed his lips. "Oh, that's cute. No. Sorry. We can't do that. That would mean a lot of wasted time. And my time is worth a lot." He adjusted his seat on the bed. "You should consider yourself extremely lucky. How many girls get to date a prince?"

She bit her tongue, wanting to say a few choice words, but not wanting him to hurt her again.

He looked her over with a lusty smile. "I really should have waited until *after* prom night. Then again, only one person stood between me and getting what I wanted out of you. And they're not here right now." He started to slide his hand up her leg, under her dress.

She struggled as much as she could to get his filthy hand off of her, but she wasn't able to move much. He tightened his grip.

"I should be repulsed by you." He stared into her eyes with a cold gaze. "Sleeping with a human was boring. But a Seeder... That's gotta be interesting. Why don't we check that box?"

His hand was halfway up her thigh.

"Your Highness..." the nurse interrupted.

His entire countenance changed to livid at the interruption, but he stopped moving his hand. "Get out!"

Rachel's breathing intensified as she focused on the nurse. Begging, pleading with her eyes for her to stay, to help.

The woman frowned and looked down. "Your Highness, your uncle..."

His eyes narrowed. "Did I stutter?"

The door swung open, catching everyone off guard. "Your Highness, we have an update."

David huffed and pulled his hand away, then straightened the hemline of Rachel's dress. He shook his head. "It's never the right time for us, is it?" He stood and glanced down at her. "It's okay. I always knew I'd get you in bed." He winked and gestured at the bed with open palms, smiling in grotesque mockery of her current place of captivity.

Before leaving the room, he turned to the nurse. "Next time you interrupt me or disobey one of my orders, you're going to *wish* you were in her position."

The woman kept her eyes trained on the floor. "My apologies, Your Highness."

He scowled. "Keep her hydrated and send for me once the rooting is completed."

Rachel was determined to have the last word as the door was shutting. "GO TO HELL!" she screamed at the top of her lungs.

The door closed without any hesitation at her outburst.

The nurse glanced at the door nervously before walking over to Rachel. "Let me help you drink some more. I promise you—you'll need everything you have, to heal up."

After draining another glass, Rachel met the woman's hazel eyes. "Thank you. What's your name?"

"Olivia. And they said your name is Rachel?"

She nodded.

"I'm so sorry, Rachel," Olivia whispered.

"Thanks."

Olivia returned to her position, holding her hands in front of her, standing in the corner of the room. After a couple of hours, she approached Rachel with another glass of water. She looked over her shoulder at the door before whispering, "Don't fight in here. Once they move you to the next phase, that's when you need to resist." She then stood and went back to her position in the room. An hour later, another nurse took her place, her expressions decidedly much less compassionate than Olivia's.

Chapter 16

Rachel learned quickly over the next couple of days to voluntarily reveal her Seeder roots when she saw the nurses approaching with the stun gun. They wouldn't even bother to ask her to do it; they would just force the transformation. Though she would get no warning when she had fallen asleep and they decided to prod her, sending her into a state of panic and agony, the high voltage surging through her body.

She had no other visitors over that time. Granted, after David's last visit, she wasn't that keen on having any. Rachel knew for certain she was still in the Green Lands—the energy helped her heal, and she could feel it coursing through her just as much as the first time David had brought her through a rift. She was still unsure as to what his plan was; the nurses were tight-lipped, and she was sad to not see Olivia report for duty.

Rachel didn't need a nurse to confirm when her rooting had finalized. She could feel the pull to this realm. Like every Seeder teenage girl, her legs—when transformed—were covered in a web of nearly-flesh-colored roots. The pattern was as unique to each Seeder as their fingerprints. At the onset of her bloom, they'd begun at her hips, and with each passing day, had inched down her legs. Once they reached her ankles and wrapped around, the rooting was complete—she was forever tied to the realm she was currently located in. Having rooted in the Green Lands, Rachel experienced a surge in her capacity to wield energy. It also meant she could never call the human world home again.

It was more emotional for her than she had expected it to be. It was a disgraceful and isolated way of leaving behind the world and family she loved. She didn't have a single hope anyone would come for her after the way she'd disappeared into thin air.

Nonetheless, a nurse checked and confirmed her rooting, and to Rachel's dismay, that meant she would be seeing David again.

"As lovely as ever!" He beamed upon entering the room. He confirmed the rooting for himself and ordered guards to escort her out. They first restrained her with vines, then unlocked the handcuffs and sliced off the vines restraining her foot. "Not even weed blades can cut through metal cuffs." He smiled again.

They led her through a series of hallways and into a small room. The only furniture in the room was a tall chair. Like the hallways in the palace, this room was completely built out of marbled stone. Despite her attempts to avoid their demands, she was easily overpowered. Guards strapped her into the chair with vines, and a nurse appeared. Rachel kept wondering what Olivia had meant about struggling in the 'next phase.' Maybe she should have tried to escape while being transferred between rooms? There had been far too many guards for her to have any hope.

"Just enough to numb for now," David instructed. "I want her lucid enough to chat once it's done."

The nurse bowed and approached, extending a vine and wrapping it around one of Rachel's wrists. Rachel winced as the leaf blades dug in, but quickly succumbed to a haze that clouded her mind, weakening her. She remembered blinking a lot, and her head bobbing, and the shuffling of feet, something about 'Your Majesty.' David's voice said 'Mother.' And then Rachel was aware of a new set of razor-sharp vines digging into her flesh. The searing sensation lasted just a moment before a new frightening horror took center stage.

It was as if someone had opened a black hole in the center of her heart. Whatever they were doing, it was siphoning off her Seeder energy. Soon thereafter, there was more shuffling of feet, mumbling, and the door clicked closed.

It could have been minutes or hours for all Rachel knew, but her clarity of mind returned as the pain of the vines puncturing her skin grew. She opened her eyes. David stood in front of her, leaning back against the wall, his arms crossed.

"And she's back! Modern human medicine is so overrated when you can go with something as natural as our poison, right?" He gave her a smile teeming with genuine pride. "And it's a shame you didn't get to properly meet my mother." He shrugged. "I mean, not that she cares to meet someone like you, but it would have been a great honor for you if you hadn't been drugged up."

He silently nodded, as if waiting for Rachel to say something. "Okay, so this isn't just going to be a one-way conversation. But to start it off, I would like to apologize for my rudeness the other day. I don't think I properly introduced myself. The name is Soren; I believe I mentioned the 'Prince' part. Commoner Ivies, or even your Seeder brothers, like Jeff—"

Her eyes grew wide at hearing Jeff's name. It probably hadn't been that hard to guess, given their relationship back home, but she had never betrayed him.

"Well, they can go with boring names like that," David continued. "Royalty needs a little more anonymity when we're in the field, if you know what I mean.

"Anyway, I asked myself if I went over the line when I brought you here earlier than necessary, depriving you of prom. It was kind of poetic, but maybe not in the best of taste. I'm not a savage, after all. So, I've decided to let you ask me any five questions you'd like. I'm sure this is all very confusing for you." He lifted his eyebrows in anticipation.

She frowned. "What are you doing to me? Why am I here?"

"That's two questions." He raised a finger. "Just to be clear, I'm counting. We are ... using your innate abilities as ... green energy." He busted out laughing, slapping his leg. "Come on. Don't you get it? I don't know why I didn't think of that one earlier. But, you know, back in the human world, it's considered 'green' if it's natural. We're in the Green Lands, we draw energy from nature ... so ... you are *literally* green energy."

He rolled his eyes in disappointment. "You were always boring and whiny when you were drugged. Anyway... Oh yeah. Why are you here? Because, good news for you, you're not nearly as much of a pathetic weakling as you thought. Just like any other weed girl out there, you're a D battery to our double- or triple-A. It's doing *astonishing* things for our War Vines, which just so happen to be *shredding* up your borders as we speak."

"But no one can take our energy without our permission," she shot back.

He squinted at her. "Now, that was not a question. But I feel like you want a response. Do you? Okay, yeah, we're deducting a question for that. Things are rarely as cut-and-dried as people make them out to be. Can I just walk up, touch your hand," he did just that, stroking her hand, "and use your energy? No. Can I access it through enough contact with your blood?" He smiled. "Apparently, that's a yes."

She remembered both times he'd brought her through a rift, cutting her wrists in the process and acting apologetic about it. She was sick to her stomach—that she had ever believed him, that she'd given him the chance to do this to her, that her pain was causing suffering to her own people.

"That leaves you with two more."

Rachel hadn't prepared for a Q&A session, and doubted he'd be completely forthcoming, anyway. She had held out the tiniest of hope that things weren't as bad as they seemed—but they were. Her heart hollow from the pull of the War Vines, she had nothing left. "Did you ever even care about me at all?"

"Yeah, of course," he professed adamantly, before pausing. "Well, wait. I guess that depends on your definition. I think we know how much I appreciated the physical attention you gave me over the years. And you're as pretty as any human," he waved his hand around, "as long as you don't go all green-eyed."

She fought the urge to vomit.

"But when it comes down to it, I think the cat *always* enjoys hunting the mouse and playing with it a little bit." He grinned without an ounce of remorse.

She closed her eyes, willing herself to not cry. Not that she cared one iota about his opinion anymore, but it hurt nonetheless.

"Come on. Don't cry on me. What did you really expect me to say?" After no response, he spoke again. "One last question, then I've got to be on my way."

"Have you ever been honest with me about *anything*?"

"That is a fair question." He squinted at the ceiling, as if searching his memories. "There were tons of technicalities, like some of my favorite foods, but I sense you don't mean that. Oh, I know. I *do* want to end this war, just maybe not the way I was letting on. And I *was* honest about there being a group of dissenter scum out there. But they're a tiny nuisance that'll be taken care of soon enough."

He took a deep breath. "There, I feel better. It's kind of nice to just get it all out there, isn't it? Here's a bonus one to cheer you up. I lied when I said you gave yourself away as a Seeder. We had you pegged *way* before that." He smirked. "But I won't spoil the fun—someone else will share that story with you at another time."

He crouched down in front of her. "Now, I have one question I need you to answer for me. Just one. I feel like that's a fair exchange for what I just gave you." He surveyed Rachel's face. "Do you know where Meg is?"

Rachel's heart sank. He really *was* after Meg. Just like his lie about the rebellion, he had put a spin on that truth to lure Rachel in. While he'd chastised her for being irrational about his inquiry back home, she was now glad she'd stuck to her guns and hadn't told him anything about Meg and Eric's breakup—in case it somehow mattered. Meg *had* to be one of her sisters, right? Another Seeder girl to strap in a chair just like this.

"So?" he asked.

Rachel scowled. "How would I know? I don't know where anyone is, outside of this room."

He closed one eye skeptically. "You're sure? Girls talk. Maybe something she said was inconsequential to you, but it means something to me."

"Even if I knew, why would I tell you?"

He gently placed his hands on her knees. "Hmm. I could give you some incentive. How about a full night's sleep? You're going to miss those."

She glared and kept her mouth shut. All she knew about Meg was that she'd been distant since the breakup. Rachel didn't have anything useful, and even if she did, there was nothing he could do to coax it out of her.

"Well, if you remember anything or get to the point that you feel like you'd rather die than stay here, let a guard or nurse know you're ready to talk, okay?"

He stood. "You know, one last offer." He wore a menacing smile. "None of the other girls have gotten these generous options. But I'd even be willing to let you have an *entire* day out of this chair, if you wanted to spend it with me in my chambers."

"You're sick. Screw you!"

"Well..."

"Piss off."

He let out a frustrated sigh. "Fine. But it's a limited-time offer, because I don't want you when you're all pathetic and useless. You still have some spunk right now."

He approached the side of her chair, moving her hair to one side. Rachel tried to lean away from him, but she barely had any mobility. He gently caressed her neck and then kissed her on the lips. Despite her refusing to kiss back, he forced his tongue into her mouth.

"Come on, once for old times' sake," he begged, pulling back. "A nice goodbye. Unless you'd prefer something else." His eyes explored her body as he smiled.

As her chest rose and fell with rapid breaths, she dreaded his advances again. "I'll kiss you."

He took great pleasure at her acceptance, moaning and playfully pressing his lips against hers, ever so gently, his hands supporting her head.

Rachel clamped down on his lower lip. His warm, metallic blood pooled in her mouth. He grunted in pain, and a leaf tip burrowed into her forehead. When the searing pain was too much, she finally released his lip with a bloodcurdling scream.

"You bitch!" he belted while backing up.

She spat his own blood at him as he touched his lip. Blood trickled down her face, stinging as some of it reached her eye.

"Shit, Rachel! What am I supposed to tell my fiancée?" He kept touching his lip to see how badly it was bleeding.

Her voice trembled through her clenched teeth. "Don't ever touch me again!"

He glared at her. "Next time I visit, you'll be plenty medicated. It would be a pity to die a virgin. We'll see how you feel about things then."

He turned his head. "Take care of this for me and send someone back to stitch her up. No numbing tonight," he ordered a nurse who had apparently been in a corner of the room for the entire duration of their exchange.

"Yes, Your Highness. Follow me, please."

Leaving with the woman, he slammed the door on his way out. Another nurse appeared shortly after his departure and stitched up Rachel's forehead without an ounce of mercy or compassion. Other than sparing a few words to scold Rachel for flinching, the nurse said nothing. Rachel's head throbbed with each beat of her heart for the rest of the night. She became increasingly painfully aware of each and every leaf puncturing her arms, sitting in agony for hours, all alone.

Chapter 17

By the time Saff, Devin, and Simon arrived in the human world, Rachel and David had been missing for over a week. Saff wasn't really sure what to expect—this type of investigation wasn't something any of them had done before. They interviewed Samantha and Rob, then split up, each taking on specific assignments, hoping to get to the bottom of the situation.

While Seeders often made friends in high places for the purposes of faked identities and deaths, and other disappearance cover stories, they'd still needed to call the local human authorities. Someone was bound to report the teens missing, and they wouldn't want suspicion to fall on Samantha and Rob. The trail died when the police found the known address for David now vacant. After an anonymous tip came in, they discovered David's studio apartment, complete with a letter that the two had run off together. Being seventeen or older, neither of them faced legal repercussions as runaways. Which was all well and good, as it meant the human authorities were keeping their noses out anyway, the Seeders decided.

Samantha and Rob refused to believe Rachel would run away like that—no warning, not taking anything. It didn't make any sense. Given her vulnerable situation as a Seeder and David's apparent lack of parents, they knew something more disturbing had happened. He'd been vetted years ago, as had his parents. But Seeders knew Ivies crafted just as good of covers as Seeder family networks did.

Saff couldn't help but feel like they were being watched. She tried to shake away her anxieties, tried to shake away the memories of Ivy attacks on her and her family a few years prior in the human world. In this same town.

Jeff had caught a breeze after a couple of days without any word, leaving to report to his family and get help from the village. Rob couldn't handle just sitting there and doing nothing. He took his car and left, searching for signs of Rachel and

David, trying to check every place he knew them to have gone for dates or hangouts. He'd left the day after Jeff.

And he hadn't come back. After just one day, Rob's phone went to voicemail and texts remained unanswered.

Meg hadn't been seen by anyone since before prom, nor had her parents. A letter was found saying they took an impromptu trip to Cancun—return date undetermined.

Eric was almost as much of a wreck as Samantha was. He was clearly still in love with Meg and didn't buy the random Cancun story; having her go missing was a huge blow. Either he was a great actor, or he also really cared about Rachel and David, even after the breakup. He was terrified out of his mind when Devin and Simon essentially kidnapped and interrogated him. Once they were satisfied he really was in the dark, they promised they'd let him know if there were any updates. He was still seemingly clueless about the green-folk side of the equation.

Saff followed Ben's advice, meeting up with the Seeder girls in Rachel's family. Immediately following Rachel's disappearance, all of her sisters had been pulled from their host homes and taken to a nearby undisclosed location. Rachel still had three sisters remaining in the human world; two had gone through their bloom and were left without a trainer after Jeff's departure. Saff trained with them from morning to night for three days straight. She did everything she could to get them ready to catch a breeze; they needed to be prepared to evacuate as soon as possible.

Samantha remained at home, available for questions from the police on the case of her now-missing husband. Devin and Simon did as much legwork as they could, tearing up David's apartment floor-to-ceiling, and even breaking into and searching around Meg's place.

There was some satisfaction on Saff's part about being able to train Rachel's sisters, as Ben had recommended. But the rest of it was pure frustration. They'd be leaving with more questions than they'd arrived with, their investigation not giving them any direction.

Saff was nearly ready to turn in for the night before heading home to the Green Lands. They were confident enough in one of the girls' progress that Saff would guide her through a rift the next night. Devin and Simon would return once Saff sent Jeff or one of his brothers back to work with the last two sisters.

While trying to help Samantha out by washing the dishes, Saff was startled when the doorbell rang. She looked through the peephole at an unfamiliar man in his twenties. Preparing for the worst, she opened the door.

"Hi. Uh, are you ... Samantha?" he asked.

"She's not available. Can I help you?"

"Well, I've been doing rideshare for a month now and this is the first time someone paid me to transport a letter." He pulled a small envelope from his hoodie. "But instructions said I could only hand it to someone named Samantha."

"Let me go get her." Saff closed the door, bolting it, and then roused Samantha, who had passed out on the couch.

Groggy and puffy-eyed, Samantha opened the door, and he gave her the envelope. The driver turned to leave.

"Wait! Don't leave yet," Saff ordered.

He held up his hands. "I'm not in the courier service, ya know? The instructions said I'd get a good tip as long as I gave her the envelope and left. I don't know anything else."

"But who gave it to you?"

He shrugged. "No one. The pick-up instructions told me where it was tucked away at a bus stop." He started to look concerned. "Excuse me, but I'm going to take off. I didn't sign up for this double-o-seven nonsense, and I'm starting to think it wasn't worth the promised tip."

Samantha closed the door and tore open the envelope, while Saff spared a quick glance out of a small window by the door to see that he'd returned to his car.

"She'll be in the Neutral Woods. At sunrise, one mile west and two days after the blue fireworks."

Saff called Devin right away, and the men came back to look.

"It's talking about Rachel, right?" Saff asked. "It doesn't say her name, but it has to be. What's it supposed to mean? It doesn't mention a ransom, threats, or demands."

Samantha was in hysterics. "Does this mean she's alive? It doesn't say! And what about Rob?"

Simon tried to calm her down, reassuring her this was a good sign—the first lead they'd had since it all began.

"What's this, down at the bottom?" Saff asked.

Devin furrowed his brow. "Unitas." They did a quick search online. "Pronounced oo-knee-tas. It's Latin for 'Unity.'"

"And the symbol? Do you recognize that?" she asked.

Neither Devin nor Simon did. It was an image of a blossom in front of an ivy leaf.

Saff took Devin to the side. "So, what does this mean?"

He rubbed his eyebrow with a knuckle. "It means you and I need to get home and look for fireworks. And be prepared for an ambush, or..." Devin lowered his voice even more, glancing over at Samantha and Simon. "Or for worse news."

Chapter 18

After hours of painful solitude, guards and a nurse arrived to extract Rachel from the energy-draining chair and take her back to the room she'd originally woken up in. They pumped her full of IV fluids and the nurse tended to her wounds. Rachel was able to eat and use the restroom, then was handcuffed to the bed and allowed to sleep for five hours before the torture started up again.

The War Vines had already been activated by the queen—apparently, she had no need to revisit, because she never did. Now, it was a simple plug and play. The nurse gave Rachel a strong dose of poison to make the initial insertion of leaf blades tolerable. She rested the War Vines on Rachel's arms and they burrowed into her skin. Every four to five hours, a nurse would drop by, giving Rachel a small dose to keep her in a haze. It was a lot more manageable than the first night when David— Prince Soren—had punished her by forbidding any numbing. Olivia was her nurse a few times, but she seemed too afraid to talk again.

When it was close to dosing time, Rachel would remember what Olivia had said about this being the time to resist. But she couldn't. Even being dizzy and nauseous, she felt better being half out of it than being lucid with the physical and mental pain. She tried once to put all her focus into locking in her energy, keeping it centered in her heart. But she didn't last long—it was like trying to hold back floodwaters with a sieve.

After two more days of this routine—drugs, minimal recuperation time, torture—her vision began clearing and the pain of the process was seeping into the forefront of her awareness. Her neck was limp, her head leaning to one side as she fluttered her eyes at the creak of a door opening.

Olivia crouched down next to her and whispered, "You're going to need to pretend you're more medicated than you are." She wrapped her vines around

Rachel's wrist, but didn't squeeze tight enough to break the skin. "She's good for a few more hours," Olivia reported to the guards as she left.

"She's alert enough to talk?" a familiar male voice asked a few hours later.

Rachel remembered Olivia's warning and closed her eyes, preparing to drawl and stare off into the distance, and also willing herself to not wince at the excruciating pain she was enduring in her current state.

"Yes, Your Grace." It was Olivia again.

The man stood in front of Rachel. She hadn't thought it was possible to hurt more, but her heart shattered. She'd hoped she was wrong about the owner of the familiar voice, but she had guessed right—and it took everything she had to not react as much as she wanted to. Rob. He was dressed in similar attire to what Prince Soren had been wearing.

"There you are. Sorry it took so long to visit," he said. "I'm assuming you're pretty familiar with everything going on around you?"

He raised his eyebrows the same way he had when she got in trouble back home. "Prince Soren told me he's not too fond of you right now."

She wanted to smirk at the memory of his bloody lip, but stayed droopy, as though she were still coming out of a haze from the fresh dose that Olivia *hadn't* given her.

"You're looking good. Useful and properly hopeless, just like any livestock doing its job."

Her blood began to boil. Never in all of his years as her stepfather had he said anything remotely unkind, not like this.

"I won't be here forever," she asserted, perhaps a little too forcefully for her acting job.

"No, I imagine not. But I'm guessing you mean you're leaving this place alive? Who will come for you?" He cocked his head to the side. "Your mother, who can't even enter the Green Lands? Or your boyfriend? Oh wait, we've already discussed his indifference. Perhaps your overworked and incompetent brother, who thinks you're a massive disappointment?" He paused, taking a deep breath. "But what about your best friend, Meg?"

Her heart ached at hearing Meg's name again; she still wasn't sure what had become of her.

He cleared his throat. "Do you remember if Meg told you anything about leaving? Going on vacation, or anything like that, before you left? Her family is really worried about her."

Rachel furrowed her brow in confusion and anger.

"Yeah, you're useless." He crossed his arms. "But what if she comes to save the day for you, right? Dang it, that's still a no. I mean, I'm guessing not, since she was the one poisoning you the whole time."

Rachel couldn't hide the shock on her face. He had to be lying. Meg would *never* do something like that.

He didn't even try to hide his joy at her slipped expression. "I really shouldn't wag my tongue so much, but anonymous artists are cliché. *Everyone* wants credit for their clever plans and hard work." His smile brightened. "Your dear friend Meg—she's one of us. Have you ever heard of microdosing? Just enough to get the job done. A smidgen to weaken your energy, leaving you no alternative but to find your way home with your *knight in shining armor*. All delivered with a piping hot cup and a smile on the bottom."

Rachel cried. Had anyone in her life ever genuinely loved her?

"Well, that's why I ask. We're worried about her, too. Prince Soren wants to know where his sister is, and she just so happens to be missing. So, if you know anything, we'd really appreciate your cooperation."

"Then I hope you find her rotting in a ditch somewhere," Rachel seethed in anger.

His face flushed red. "If you know something you're not telling me, that may be exactly how they find your mother."

"I don't know anything!" she blurted. "Don't hurt her!"

He calmed, adjusting the hem of his shirt. "It's okay. Your mother is perfectly fine. For now. After years over there, you kind of get attached to people. I mean, not you—you're just a filthy weed. But your mother... I kind of liked her. If she weren't a useless human, I definitely would have considered bringing her here." He clasped his hands together. "And just so you feel better, assuming you cooperate and we don't have to hurt her, my lawyer has divorce papers drafted. She'll be free to move on to her next failure of a marriage. There's some incentive."

"Her only failure was trusting a leech like you!"

He glanced at Olivia. "She seems far too alert. Make sure you check back on her more frequently, or adjust her doses."

Olivia bowed, looking at the ground. "Yes, Your Grace. My deepest apologies, Your Grace."

He turned back to Rachel. "I'm sorry I couldn't be the father you wanted. But was I really that bad? Compared to a dad that left you to a naïve stranger, and a dad that left you as a young child without a word? I was good to you. It had a purpose, but still..."

She was determined not to cry more. He was right—she'd had the longest relationship with him out of any of them. Staring at the ground, her eyes glazed over in defeat.

"I know you're hurting, but maybe this will help you find some closure about Brad." Brad, of course, was the dad that had deserted Rachel and her mom before they'd met Rob. "You know what, I'm not all about crushing your hopes and dreams any more than we have to, so I'm going to give you a multiple choice, and you get to choose which one you want to believe. He either left because learning your true nature as a weed was too disturbing for him, or we had him permanently removed from your life, and ... his own life."

He likely accomplished what he was looking for—her eyes stung once more with tears.

Rob's voice deepened, abandoning his flippant mocking. "Just remember how *worthless* your existence is, next time we ask you a question and want an answer, or the next time you remember something about dear Meg and try to forget to tell us. You literally serve *one* function in this life, and you are doing a *fantastic* job at it right now. I'd hate to shorten your usefulness by keeping you attached without any breaks and without medication."

He calmly clasped his hands in front of him once more. "So, I'm going to ask you one more time, where—" He was cut off by a knock at the door.

"My apologies for the interruption, Your Grace. We have news of Princess Kaylah," a man announced after opening the door.

Rob squinted with curiosity, heading to the door and closing it behind him. Rachel tried eavesdropping to see if this 'Princess Kaylah' they were talking about was Meg. Maybe the Seeders had her, and maybe she'd make a good prisoner exchange.

No words filtered through the door, only a gasp, some shuffling, a *thud*, and a *thwack*.

The door burst open.

Olivia stood alert with her head held high. A hooded figure entered, wearing all black and holding a machete dripping with blood. The figure pulled off the hood, and Rachel's eyes grew wide. Her best friend looked back at her. Replacing her usual messy bun was a braided updo. Instead of her warm, casual smile, her face showed fierce determination and blood spatter.

"Jon, gag her," Meg ordered. "Guillen, take care of that." She nodded in the direction of the door.

One of the guards, a brunet in his thirties, quickly approached Rachel, following Meg's orders.

Meg looked Rachel directly in the eyes while wiping at her own face. "I need you to listen to me. If you make noise or fight back, you'll probably die. You need to focus everything you have on healing. Do you understand me?"

Rachel's heart raced. She nodded that she would comply, the gag now in place.

"Jon, stand guard. Olivia, help me cut her loose."

Meg began slicing through the vines restricting Rachel's movement with her machete, and Olivia unwound them, carefully but speedily tugging them from Rachel's skin. Unable to easily slice through the War Vines, they gently wiggled them free. Essentially unmedicated, Rachel was grateful to have the gag to bite down on as embedded razor blades were plucked from her arms, one by one. As Rachel winced, she could make out the sound of something dragging across the floor from over her shoulder, and then a stomach-turning *thwack* and a *clang* as sharp metal hit the stone floor.

"I can only imagine what they told you about me. But if you ever valued our friendship, I need you to trust me right now," Meg said as they finished with the vines. "Take a deep breath. Put everything you have right now into getting enough strength to walk." She turned to the door. "How are we, Jon?"

"Still clear."

"Okay, we're going out the way we came in." Meg surveyed her party. "Me, Rachel, Jon, Olivia. Guillen at the back."

Meg and Olivia helped Rachel to stand. "Let's get a move on."

The men stepped out into the hallway. Meg marched over to what was now a beheaded Rob, giving his corpse a swift, hard kick. She rejoined Olivia to help Rachel walk. They followed Jon. The door clicked behind them and Rachel turned to look. Another hooded figure, the one Meg had called Guillen, joined them.

Walking down a couple of unfamiliar halls, they stepped over guards' bodies along the way. The group filed into a small room with what looked like a stone well;

several giant vines were growing out of it and connecting to other parts of the room.

"We're going down," Meg said. "I can help stabilize you from below with my vines, and Jon from above with his."

They climbed down the chute, barely large enough for one person at a time. Rachel found it hard to climb down the metal rungs, as her knees wanted to buckle. At least once, Jon saved her from falling with his vines wrapped firmly around her upper arm. They reached solid ground in another room, similar to the one at the top of the well, but taller.

Meg turned to Rachel. "You promise you won't scream if I take the gag off?" Rachel nodded.

After Meg removed the gag, Jon carefully peeked out of a door and announced the all-clear. They raced down a corridor, stopping in front of a side door. Meg motioned with her head for Jon to move forward, and they breached the door together, taking out a guard on the other side before he could sound the alarm.

They filed out of the door, and shut it behind them.

"Olivia, you'll come with me." Meg looked Rachel over; she was still in her prom dress. Closing her eyes, Meg shook her head. "Soren," she muttered. Opening her eyes, she sighed, looking at the men. "Get her some new clothes as soon as you're able to."

She now addressed Rachel. "I'm *so* sorry. They're going to take you home. Do as they say. I trust them with my life. And you can trust them, more than you were ever able to trust me."

Chapter 19

The palace horns rang through the damp evening air and Rachel ran as fast as she could in their escape, but her group was separated in no time and she fell behind, still weak from the torture she had been subjected to the last few days. Every muscle in her body throbbed.

She hardly even felt the vine that wrapped her ankle, causing her to lose her footing. Emerging from the host of guards, David appeared. Putting his hand over her mouth, he again dug a razor-sharp leaf into her forehead. Pushed past her pain threshold, Rachel screamed.

Her heart racing, her breathing rapid and forceful, she opened her eyes. She was in a cave. A clean-shaven brunet in his early twenties had his hand over her mouth. She looked up in terror and confusion, eyes warm, no doubt glowing green.

"It's okay. It's okay! It was just a dream," Guillen quickly whispered. "You need to be quiet."

She swallowed and tried to calm her breathing, ripping his hand from her mouth. She felt her forehead with a shaky hand, confirming it was coated in sweat, not blood, and the stitches were still there. Sitting up, she moved further away from the man, cowering against the cold stone wall. She didn't even remember walking in there.

Jon loomed at the entrance of the cave, keeping guard and likely making sure her outburst hadn't drawn any attention.

Guillen watched Rachel, crouching nearby. "You passed out. You're okay. We're safe for now. Just take a second to breathe," he coached.

Her eyes were glued on him, their glow slowly fading. "Meg? Rob? David?"

Jon joined them, still positioned closest to the entrance, sparing an extra glance over his shoulder. "I'm sure the princess is fine. We're not sure where the prince is. And, uh ... Rob, yeah—Duke Nuren is out of the picture."

Rachel had a staring contest with the cave floor, sorting through her thoughts. *Nuren. Rob was Nuren?* She'd actually wondered, in her rare moments of lucidity, if Jeff had gotten the name wrong. That it was Soren, not Nuren, the Seeders were searching for. But it had been Rob...

Her concentration broke when something rustled a few feet away. Guillen approached her with food and a canteen. She eyed it, still on edge about everything that had transpired.

"At least drink some water," he calmly insisted. "That will help with your healing."

She glanced down at her arms; the blood was crusting at each point of leaf insertion. She guzzled down the water, then sat with her head against the wall, her eyes closed.

"So, Meg and David, they're ... really brother and sister?" she asked.

"Yes," Jon answered.

"And Rob, you said Duke?"

"Yes. Their uncle."

"They're all Ivy?"

"Yes."

She looked both of the men over. "And you are both..."

Jon continued to answer. "Ivy as well. But we're friendly."

She quietly scoffed. "Yeah, I've been told that before." She gnawed at her bottom lip. "And me? Why me?"

The men glanced at each other.

"That's a broad question, not sure how to answer that," Jon said.

"Like, I get why they had me hooked up, but why did they pick me? Why am I here right now?"

Guillen spoke up. "We don't know all the details. We mostly just know about the Unitas efforts."

"Unitas?" She studied his face.

"Yeah. The movement Kaylah started."

"Do you mean the rebellion?"

Jon chuckled. "Only the *oppressor* calls those in an opposing movement 'rebels' or 'dissidents.'"

Guillen glanced between the two of them. "But yes. Essentially. And Kaylah made you the priority."

"You should consider yourself lucky," Jon said while cleaning under his fingernails. "You're the last to be taken, the first to be freed."

"How many of my people do they have?"

"At least five others that we're aware of."

She swallowed a lump in her throat. "Kaylah—the princess, right? I know her as Meg? Is it true what Rob said about her? About the role she played in getting me here in the first place?"

Jon looked away.

Guillen pursed his lips. "I don't know what all they told you, but you need to remember she had orders to follow. And that Soren and Nuren often twist the truth to get what they want. When she went missing, they knew she'd defected, and they're desperate to get her back." He stressed, "Focus on what she's doing for you right now."

Rachel hesitantly decided to give the food a go, unwrapping a fruit-and-nut bar from a large grape leaf. The tartness of the dried fruit made her mouth water. "Where are we? What's the plan?"

"This cave is well hidden," Guillen said. "No one in the palace even knows about it. Kaylah and I discovered it as kids. Once you're up to it, we can move on and get you to your borders."

"Am I... Is this a hostage sort of thing? Why are you doing this?" she asked, still not sure they could be trusted.

Jon rolled his eyes. "We're risking our lives to get you home because we've pledged our allegiance to the princess. You'll have to ask her yourself about all the details."

She nodded. This was obviously a rescue, but with every shred of her identity and trust having been defiled, it was hard to know where to draw the line. This could just be another colorful deception, like David and Rob ... and Meg ... were clearly so good at. But when it came down to it, this beat life-sucking torture.

Jon informed her of their plan; there would be several days of walking, and she should get as well-rested as possible, healing up and gaining strength. They would need to be swift once they emerged from the cave. If they left before she was ready, she'd only be a liability.

"Why don't we just go through a rift and take me back to my people?" she asked.

Jon and Guillen exchanged a knowing glance.

"There are a few reasons we can't do that," Jon answered. "One being, we can't actually rift into Seeder territory. You can only rift in and out between the worlds, not within them. And even with your border walls compromised, we've never been able to get past the Neutral Woods. Plus, the princess gave orders about one of the stops we need to take on the way. And," his eyes jumped back to Guillen for a second before returning to Rachel, "there are other reasons. Just know it's not a possibility."

"Okay." She frowned, tilting her head to the side. "I used my energy to boost David, or, uh, Soren, to help get me through one of your rifts. That wouldn't make a difference, would it?"

"No. No rifts." Jon cleared his throat. "How about you finish up that water and see if you can get some more sleep. We'll take turns keeping watch throughout the day. By nightfall, we'll be needing to take off."

"Alright. What time is it? How long was I out earlier?" she asked.

"It's been a few hours," said Guillen. "The sun will be up soon, but this cave's hidden well enough that we're not too worried about them finding it. We'll still have our things ready to go in case we need to leave in a hurry."

Rachel finished off the water, every minute feeling the smallest degree better. The Green Lands were starting to replenish her strength, like an IV, one drop at a time. She lay down and recalled her parting with Meg—Kaylah. Rachel hadn't wanted to go with these two men, having to leave Kaylah and Olivia. Kaylah had firmly insisted that Rachel follow her orders, that she and Olivia would be creating a false trail for the guards to follow, then attending to 'other business.' Then the horns blew—the whole palace had been put on alert.

Another horrifying scene tore through Rachel's dreams, and she woke again, screaming. She quickly made out her surroundings. Jon stood nearby. She woke up faster this time, before he could rush over and muffle the sound. Guillen ran back in to check on things. Her eyes met theirs as she slowed her breathing.

"Sorry," she whispered, closing her eyes. She did her best to suppress any noises, but there was really no way to hide the movement of her whole body shaking as tears slipped between the edges of her eyelids.

The next time she woke, she was still breathing hard, but she was calmer. Sitting up, she spotted more food and water placed next to her. Both of the men were in view, eating a meal and whispering. They stopped chatting and greeted her once they noticed she was up.

Rachel looked at the tracks on her arms and, one by one, slowly ran a glowing finger over each wound, then scratched at it to flake off the dried blood. Once she'd finished, she realized she had an audience.

"That's pretty cool," Jon said with eyebrows lifted.

"Impressive," Guillen added with a smile.

She sized up the men. "Have you guys never seen our powers?"

"You're actually the first Seeder I've ever seen," Guillen shyly confessed.

"I've seen your kind, just never that," Jon said.

"Really? I mean, I guess that makes sense. But you've never seen one of us at all, Guillen?"

He shook his head.

She felt her forehead and finished healing up that last wound.

"So, Jon, you've dealt with Seeders." Her recollection was hazy, but she'd seen him more than once during her time in the palace. "What kind of damage did you cause before joining this 'Unitas'?" she asked casually.

He glared at the accusation. "I've never hurt a Seeder. I made my way up the chain peacefully and did a couple-year stint with the humans. Then I proved I was up to snuff for palace detail. I haven't taken any active roles in this current war."

She sighed. "Well, that's good to know."

"I could have, if I'd wanted to," he stressed. "Getting into palace work is hard; volunteering for the front lines is something *anyone* can do. Remember that, when you question my motives and integrity next. I've destroyed an elite career on the chance it will make a permanent difference."

Biting the insides of her cheeks, she looked down. "Thanks."

He took a deep breath. "Actually, I rightly guessed a Seeder girl at the high school where I was stationed back in my day." He sipped from a canteen. "I, uh, delayed reporting it for too long and she made it home. I told myself my hesitation was because I'd wanted to be certain first, but when I look back, I don't think my heart was really in it."

Rachel gave him a nod of approval. Jon was still in his guard uniform, but Guillen was in less formal combat gear. "If you've never seen a Seeder, what kind of assignment do you have?"

Guillen looked at her, squinting. "Is something on your forehead bugging you?"

"Oh." She had been rubbing her hand over the suture wisps the whole time. "Yeah, stitches. These are going to drive me crazy."

He grabbed something from his bag and approached her. "I can help with that." Unrolling a set of small tools, he grabbed tweezers and a sharp blade. "Just hold still and I can get those out." He drew close to her face, squinting in the shadows of the cave.

Being this close, Rachel could take in his pale-blue eyes and a large scar on his temple. His hair was brown and his breath still smelled of the mint leaves she'd seen him chew on after his meal.

Guillen carefully lifted the stitches away from her skin and cut through the sutures, pulling them out. "Good as new." He smiled.

She rubbed her forehead. "Thanks. You're quite the Boy Scout to have all those tools."

He read her face with a subtle narrowing of the eyes, as if he hadn't understood the reference.

It was more than a smidge unlikely that there would be a 'Boy Scouts of the Ivy Kingdom' troop for him to understand what she'd meant. "Oh, um, that's a human reference to being resourceful, prepared."

A spark of recognition shone in his eyes. "Glad I could be of assistance. Any others you need help with?"

She glanced down again at her arms and legs. "Nope, I only injured the prince enough to earn stitches the one time." She beamed at the memory of his bloody lip.

Guillen grinned. "Good for you."

Chapter 20

uillen rolled up his tools. "That's a pretty dress. What's the occasion?"

Rachel examined the sad thing with rips and dirt disgracing it. She smirked. "Naturally, I got all dolled up to be kidnapped."

He chuckled.

"No, it was for a school dance." She sighed. "It's kind of a big deal back home. And just like saying goodbye to my family, I missed it." She shook her head. "All because I was stupid enough to trust an I—" She pursed her lips. "To trust the prince."

He gave a look acknowledging he knew what she had meant to say before she'd caught herself—'stupid enough to trust an Ivy.'

She was still regaining her strength, and since healing always ate up so much energy, Rachel happily went back to napping while the men took turns keeping a lookout. When she woke next, Jon was in the cave with her and Guillen was out taking a turn at watch. She sat up against the cave wall, sipping on water.

"I think I'm going to go stir-crazy. Any chance I can stretch my legs outside if I stay close?"

Jon looked her over. "I don't think that dress is the best camouflage. But you could explore the cave if you'd like. It's sound, and there's enough light to avoid tripping if you're careful." He pointed with his chin. "Keep to the left—there's some parts where daylight peeks through. Probably old rabbit burrowing holes."

She took his advice and looked around. The stone was brown, slightly reddish. A sapling was trying to make a home for itself in a crack halfway through the tunnel. Following Jon's instructions, she took the path to the left when there was a division; the narrow dark opening to the right appeared more foreboding, anyway. She was particularly intrigued when she came to the end of the cave. Leaning against the wall were a handful of wooden sticks and staves. Nearby, Rachel could just barely discern something carved into the rock in the shadows. Experimenting, she channeled energy to her hand, holding it up to look at the carving.

"That's pretty cool, too."

The break in the silence startled her, and she turned. Guillen was approaching from the main cave chamber. Despite how nice he'd been, she didn't like the feeling of being cornered. She started to back away in the direction of the staves.

Picking up on her body language, he moved back, raising his hands. "Sorry, just switched with Jon and wanted to make sure you were okay back here."

She relaxed a little at his soothing reassurance. "Yeah, doing good, thanks. You said you've been in these caves before? What do these symbols etched into the wall mean?"

He walked closer to get a good look, squinting. "You know, I forgot about those. I'm not sure."

"Hmm ... Now that's going to drive me crazy, not knowing." She continued to stare at the carving. Her glance shifted to the staves. "What about these?"

"Training tools." He grinned. "I'm the one who taught Kaylah how to use that machete of hers."

Rachel's eyes widened. "I, uh ... I guess you're good at what you do?"

He gave a gentle nod. "I'm *very* good at what I do." His expression softened as he searched her face. "But I would never hurt you. And neither would Jon. You're safe with us."

She bit her lip. "He was there—one of the guards that handled my transfers. Did you know that?"

Guillen frowned. "He's been on the right side of things for a while now. We needed help from the inside."

She fidgeted with her hands. "What kinds of weapons do I need to be worried about? I was under the impression green folk relied on their natural abilities for fighting. Why would Meg even need to use a machete?" She glanced at Guillen's belt; he carried his own machete and other knives.

He leaned back against the cave wall. "You're right. Most people around here *do* only focus on training with green folk abilities. Kind of stupid though, isn't it? A bit arrogant, too."

She gave him a half-smile. Something about Guillen was ... refreshing, calming. He was more forthcoming than she'd expected, with him being so quiet earlier. She decided to try and get a better picture of the situation.

"Tell me about the royal family. Princess Kaylah... Prince Soren..."

He obliged without hesitation. "The queen and king have four children. Only one daughter. Soren's the oldest. Kaylah came a year later."

"Ivy society is matriarchal too, right? Like Seeder society?"

"Yes. Kaylah's the crown princess—heir to the throne."

Rachel shook her head. That was ... not the girl she'd had silly sleepovers with, or gawked at cute boys with, or ... consoled on the school bathroom floor after a breakup. And she wasn't just *a* princess. She was *the* princess. "So, you've been friends with the princess for a long time? You used to play here?"

"Yeah. I've known her all her life." He smiled. "She's always been generous and kind," he said with a fondness in his voice.

"That's the Meg I know. Or, I guess I should start to say Kaylah? I noticed you don't call her the princess like Jon does—why is that?"

"She *does* prefer Kaylah over Meg. And... I probably should call her by her title. But we've always been real close. She's my cousin."

Rachel swallowed hard, sizing him up. Cousin... He wasn't just an Ivy. He was royalty, too.

He narrowed his eyes. "No relation to Duke Nuren—he was the king's brother. My mother is the queen's sister. And we don't really have any part in palace life."

She studied Guillen's face. He was much more like the Meg she'd known growing up than the cocky and crass David she had become accustomed to. "So, if you're a member of the royal family, what's your title?"

He crossed his arms. "I think a person's choices and actions matter more than their title. Don't you?"

As she crossed her arms to match him, the light in her hand went out. "I think that's a fair assertion." She grinned. "So, I don't have to curtsy every time you pass?"

He laughed loudly before stifling it. "I won't bow if you won't curtsy."

She smiled wide. "Deal."

"Well, I, uh... I'm going to head back." He nodded in the direction they'd both come from.

"Not a bad idea."

After making their way back to the main chamber of the cave, Guillen suggested she try to get more rest before they headed out in a few hours. Before she drifted off to sleep, Rachel made herself a promise that she was going to see this through. She refused to allow herself to become a cowering victim. She was going to survive this. She was going to see her mom again and be there for her. She was going to help her people, and, if possible, play a part in ending this damned war.

Rachel woke to Guillen gently nudging her shoulder and whispering her name. Her eyes shot right open, but softened once she realized it was him.

"We're going to head out soon. Let's have you fill up on food and water before we slip out."

She snacked on some of the sunflower oatcake rations they provided and shook away the grogginess before they left the safety of the cave. The mountainous area surrounding the palace was heavily forested, which would provide great cover as they traveled. Jeff had once drawn Rachel a map of the Green Lands. The Ivy Kingdom occupied the entire eastern sector, and their palace was pretty far south. That was all he'd really shown her, as neither of them had ever expected to actually step foot in Ivy territory.

When Rachel had been rescued, she hadn't been wearing shoes. Her dress heels were hardly useful, and they hadn't cared to cover her feet in the palace, since they would put in an IV during her limited recuperation hours. Until Jon or Guillen could get her a change of clothes, she had to suck it up and watch her step, as her feet were now wrapped in only a pair of cotton bandanas.

After hours of walking in the dark, Jon announced they'd found their stopping point for the night. Jon did most of the navigating, and Guillen had kindly answered Rachel's questions along the way, including naming unfamiliar flora and fauna. Having reached their camping ground, Rachel happily lay on the forest floor and unwrapped her muddy feet, massaging and healing them. Shortly after, she allowed the crickets to sing her to sleep.

Rachel woke to whispering again. The men offered food and water.

"I've got connections in this area. I'll grab you a change of clothes and some shoes, along with extra provisions," Jon announced once she was up. He looked at Guillen while tightening a strap on his pack. "We're clear on what to do if we get separated?"

"We're set."

Guillen explained that Jon had grown up in this region and knew the lay of the land better, which would help him stay hidden along the way. They had a connection on the edge of the nearest city that could help them get what they needed. For several hours, Rachel entertained Guillen with information about the 'ball' she'd missed and other things unique to the human world. She was surprised how much he didn't seem to know, but then again, he hadn't been deployed as an assassin; maybe Ivies were just extra selective in their education on the human world.

"You never answered my question about what you do for work," she remarked over more sunflower oatcakes for lunch.

He shook his head. "No. I guess I didn't."

She waited with eyebrows lifted. "And...?"

He feigned not having understood she wanted an answer. "Oh, you wanted me to tell you?"

She rolled her eyes and picked up a small pebble, chucking it at him. He caught it with quick reflexes.

She smiled. "Impressive. Do you not need to have a job, being part of the royal family?"

He shook his head. "Not likely. I ... do construction work." He twisted his mouth, looking away.

"That's cool. There's no shame in working with your hands." She furrowed her brow at his reaction. "Do you not like it?"

"Not exactly a highly respected position in these parts. What kind of people have to do construction in the human world?"

"Have to? Well, no one really *has* to. I think..." She glanced at the sky in thought. "I guess people who just like to create and be active, and maybe don't like to go through as much formal schooling. There's a good fit for each person and each job. If you don't like it, why don't you try something new?"

He gave her a half-hearted smile. "That sounds nice, to be able to choose. For now, I try not to focus too much on what I can't have." He stood and brushed himself off. "I'm going to do a quick patrol of the area. Stay here and stay quiet, okay?"

Rachel stayed put, pondering their conversation. She realized how little she really knew about either culture in the Green Lands. Having grown up in a nation where she would have been free to choose her own career, she took that for granted.

Once Guillen returned, he sat and took out a couple of knives, throwing them with astounding precision at a log, and then sharpened them.

"Sorry for bringing up work," she said.

He gave her a polite smile. "No apologies necessary." Guillen wasn't exactly timid ... but he was quiet, and there was something hidden there—something under the surface she wished she knew more about.

"So ... you guys can't go over the nitty-gritty of strategy, but what's the end goal of Kaylah's movement? And what are you personally hoping for?"

"I have hope for old ways and new answers." He wore a genuine smile this time. "Kaylah has actually done a lot of research in the old archives. Things forgotten or hidden from our people. About how our powers work, both Ivy and Seeder. About our similarities. She really has a vision that could end this, once and for all, and make vast improvements for both sides." He sheathed his knives. "I'd give anything to have things the way she envisions them. This cause means a lot to me, personally. And once we expose the lies, take away the ignorance, and embrace the best parts of our pasts and people, no other decent person could reject her plans."

Rachel marveled at his speech. "That's pretty poetic. You're really dedicated, aren't you?"

He met her gaze. "One hundred percent."

"How big is the movement? David ... or ... Soren... I'm not sure if I want to call him either name..." Her stomach hurt just thinking about him.

Guillen chuckled. "There are a lot of less polite words that might fit him better."

She joined in with a laugh. "Amen to that. Anyway, he said, at least after he brought me here, that it's really small ... that there's not much hope."

Guillen hesitantly nodded once. "We're still working on that. But we're gaining strength. We can only do so much on our side without your people's help." He raised his eyebrows. "You're going to be key in that."

Swallowing hard, she nervously wrung her hands. "I, uh..." She took a deep breath. "I'm not exactly a phenomenal specimen for this sort of thing. I'm way behind others in training. They either think I ran away or know I allowed myself to get kidnapped. Not sure what good I can do." She frowned and fought tears. Poisoned to destroy her confidence. Fake relationships. Everything was turned upside down. She was no leader.

He mirrored her frown. "From what Kaylah tells me, you've got more going for you than you give yourself credit for. I don't know what all they did to you, but every time her 'parents' would take her on 'vacation' over the years, she was back here. She always tried to carve out some time to visit with me, and she told me all about her best friend." He made it a point to meet her eyes. "It started out as an assignment, but she was just a kid. You softened her heart. If anything, you made this movement possible. Don't discount that."

Rachel wiped away tears. "Well, now you're going to make me blush." She chuckled. "But that's true? She talked about me?"

"Yeah. She started to get busier as you two got older, so I didn't get to see her as much on account of that. But I know she felt guilty about what she had to do to you."

"Thanks. That means a lot." She sniffled. "So, what do you guys need me to do?"

"We'll have more details by the time we get you back to Seeder borders. For now, stay alive. As long as it doesn't slow you down, I'd recommend focusing as much energy as possible on preparing to catch a breeze back to the human world after we get you home."

Tilting her head, she squinted. "Back to the human world?" He talked about Seeder lands as if they were her home. But wasn't her home really with her mom back in the human world? A place she could no longer survive long-term?

"Yeah. The human world. We'll go over that once we're closer to your borders."

She didn't hate the idea of a visit, even if it couldn't last more than a week. "And you're sure we can't just use a tree rift? I have to *fly* back to the human world?"

He nodded. "Things will work out. Have some faith."

Chapter 21

Jon finally came back to camp with a whistle to announce his return. He was now dressed similarly to Guillen, having ditched his palace guard uniform.

"Thought we'd lost you," Guillen said, then scrunched his face comically, "to the pub."

Jon rolled his eyes. "Next time, maybe *you* get to head into town."

With both his hands and vines, Jon reached into his pack and pulled out clothes and shoes for Rachel. "Here, I tried my best, but they might be a bit big." They were similar to what Kaylah had worn, and to what her travel companions were wearing. All black, combat style.

"Do you want me to get dinner ready, or would you rather I show her the lake?" Guillen asked.

"I'll stay here. I've done enough walking today." Jon grunted as he plopped down on a tree stump. "And I don't need to be poisoned by your cooking."

Guillen shot him a dirty look.

"Oh, uh." Jon looked at Rachel. "That was maybe not the most tactful thing to say, sorry."

She stood, choosing to ignore the insensitive comment. "I'm more than ready to clean up and get rid of the memory of this dress. Let's find that lake."

It was a mere ten-minute hike to the beautiful lake. The shallows were home to a variety of minnows and aquatic plants. Her favorite were the large lily pads with giant vibrant purple blossoms. The central part of the lake was crystal clear.

They first refilled everyone's canteens, and then Guillen showed Rachel the best place to get in, and told her where he'd be waiting so she could have some privacy. The water was frigid, but she discovered she could heat herself up a little by expending some Seeder energy. It felt like heaven to scrub away the dirt and sweat and tears. She took her time soaking, mesmerized by the ripples in the water. She could have stayed there forever, allowing the lake to not only wash away the grime, but all of the hurt, the confusion, the hate. But even in the Green Lands, nature could only do so much.

After grabbing her bandanas and underwear from the bank, she hand-washed them. She hastily toweled off after emerging from the lake, and got dressed in the new clothes, which ended up being a bit baggy for her. The shoes fit decently well—Jon had measured her feet before leaving for town. She returned to where Guillen was waiting, her arms clutching the massacred dress. He was back to tossing a throwing knife with exceptional accuracy at the same spot in the ground over and over.

"Sorry that took so long," she said. "But it felt *so* good."

Picking up his knife, Guillen wiped off any dirt before sheathing it. "Then I'm happy to hear it. We've got nothing else on the agenda tonight. Now, about that dress..."

It was ripped in several places, with dirt and detritus all over it. More than the damage, she hated the memories it brought—a prom she'd never get to have, a horror she wished she'd never endured. Even after allowing her to clean up and use the facilities, she'd been forced to redress in it, per Soren's orders. "Can we burn it?" she asked.

Guillen smirked. "Mmm, best not to. But we do need to lose it. Let's go sink it in the lake."

They headed back to the lake together. Finding an ideal spot with seaweed and lily pads, he rolled up his pant legs, taking off his boots to wade out to it. She tossed him the dress and picked up a couple of large rocks he pointed out to weigh it down. She bent down, self-consciously clutching an arm over her chest, picking the rocks up one at a time. Once he got back out, he dried his legs and feet with a small rag, replacing his boots.

"I'm not going to miss that, or what it represents." She let out a short breathy chuckle. "You know, I could have spent more on it. Rob said I could. I wish I would have taken him for every penny he had. Then again, I'm hoping my mom has access to his money now." Vicious homesickness washed over her as she worried about her mom. Jon and Guillen had confirmed, to the best of their knowledge, her mom was still safe, that Nuren hadn't lied about that. "Do you think she can make a life insurance claim if he died in a different realm?"

Guillen shrugged. "That's way over my head. But I'm sure your people will do everything they can to take good care of her. And ours will, too." He lifted an eyebrow. "Well, when I say 'our' people ... you know, those united in the cause."

She frowned. "Yeah. She's tough. I miss her."

"Just remember." He smiled reassuringly. "Part of your job is to get back there once we return you. There's work to be done, but I'm sure seeing your mother can be part of it."

She smiled at his constant words of encouragement. "Yeah. I'll keep that motivation in mind, thanks."

"All ready to head back and see if Jon is capable of making something edible?"

"Almost ready." She thought of the soggy contents of her pants pockets. "Is there, uh, a discreet place I could hang something to dry?" she asked, avoiding eye contact.

He furrowed his brow. "What would you need to—" He went silent, his mouth opening as his eyes settled on her arms, still clutched across her chest. "Oh."

"Jon only got me new outer clothes." She blushed.

"Yeah, we can find somewhere to let them dry overnight."

They found a nice hidden area by the lake in some bushes, and he told her they'd come back to pick them up and fill their canteens the next day before heading out.

Walking back to their campsite in relative silence, Rachel continued to take in the scenery. The variety of greenery was astounding. Green bananas grew high overhead, and just yards away, huckleberry bushes were bursting, full of fruit. Her brother Jeff had explained that unique aspect of the Green Lands, that plant life intermingled much more here than it did in the human world.

Rachel found it soothing—the chirp and buzz of bugs and birds, the rustle of leaves as little lizards chased each other. The air was crisp and their surroundings untouched by the destruction of modern man.

As they foraged sorrel, mushrooms, nuts, and berries along the way to supplement whatever Jon was preparing, Rachel pondered on another cultural lesson from her brother.

"Your kingdom is really beautiful," she said. "I was taught it's a wasteland."

Guillen met her eyes while plucking a few more berries. "Yeah. We're still close to the palace. It's not all this way."

"Do you live close to the palace?"

Looking back down, Guillen shook his head. "Well, kind of. A few days walk away. I've moved around a bit over the last few years."

With bandanas and pockets full, they approached their small clearing.

"Does your family know you're doing this?" she asked Guillen.

"No," he answered softly.

Scanning his face, she dared to pry a little more. "They wouldn't approve of you helping a Seeder?"

He glanced her way with a smile. "I don't really worry about trying to make them proud. My family's kind of a mixed bag, anyway. We're all individuals, right?"

She nodded as they reached Jon and started unloading the ingredients they'd scavenged.

"Any garlic or onion bulbs?" Jon asked.

"No, sorry," Guillen said.

"We'll make do." Jon finished stirring a stew of some kind.

Apparently, Jon was capable of turning out some decent food with the fresh produce he'd brought back from his side trip. They settled down for the night with full stomachs, waking at first light.

"We're going to risk travel in daylight today," Jon explained, "since these woods aren't likely to be patrolled heavily, and our next stop isn't too far away."

"Rachel and I will go top up the canteens, if you want to clean up the rest of camp?" Guillen offered.

"Works for me," Jon said, organizing his pack.

Once Guillen and Rachel arrived at the lake, he offered to fill their canteens while she picked up her delicates and changed.

She'd just finished putting on her bra when a hand slipped over her mouth and an arm wrapped around her, pulling her down to the ground.

"Shh! Quiet!" Guillen hissed in her ear.

She could've had a heart attack with the way he'd surprised her so unceremoniously. She quickly gathered her thoughts and controlled her breathing. Male voices grew louder past the bushes, approaching the lake. Sure, Guillen was protecting her, but she could have happily spent every day of the rest of her life never having a man cover her mouth like that again. And tackling her half-dressed, to boot.

She pried his hands from her mouth and midriff, turning quietly to face him. Giving him a frustrated look, she indicated she understood the stakes by throwing a glance in the direction of the voices. They stayed on the ground in silence for a while. Several minutes passed before the voices faded away. Guillen's eyes wandered once, then he averted his gaze and blushed. She reached for her shirt and held it over her chest.

"Sorry," he whispered. "I'll go check it out and leave you to finish up here."

She quickly finished getting dressed and reemerged, joining Guillen at the lakeside where he was filling the canteens.

"What about Jon?" She couldn't get herself to make eye contact.

"I'm sure he's fine."

They cautiously snuck back to the campsite, where Jon was nowhere to be seen.

"What if something happened to him? What if they saw him?" she asked.

"He can take care of himself. I'm sure he's just hiding out, or trying to get some intel by following them."

"I thought this area wasn't supposed to be patrolled!"

Guillen tilted his head. "We were bound to run across soldiers at some point. Let's hope it's out of the way now. Either way, we wait here for an hour—if he doesn't show, the plan is to meet up at the next location."

She fidgeted with her hands, still uneasy at the close encounter. "And what happens if *I* get separated like this along the way? I don't know where I'm going."

"I promise you—we won't let that happen."

She sat on a stump. "Then I guess we wait."

A half hour passed in silence; all eyes were trained on the perimeter, looking for Jon's return and any additional trouble.

"How long have you known Jon?" she asked.

"Only a few months. Kaylah made the introduction."

"How do you know he can be trusted? Couldn't he have tipped them off in town to come out here?"

Guillen's voice was firm. "If Kaylah trusts him, I trust him."

Rachel shook her head, her stomach in worried knots. "You might think I'm paranoid, but I earned my right to have trust issues."

"I get it. I really do. Either one of us could deceive you." He quickly added, "Well, not me. I wouldn't." He sighed. "I'm just saying, she handpicked us for a reason. But I'll keep an eye on him, okay? Just to be extra cautious?"

"Thanks." She smiled. "But who will keep an eye on you?"

He grinned. "You can." He winked.

Promptly breaking eye contact, she swallowed a few times. She stared blankly at the ground, wringing her hands. He was flirting. That was just ... too soon, and complicated, and too much to process right now.

"Hey..." he started.

Jon's whistle of return claimed their attention; they went back to surveying the area.

"Took you long enough," Guillen complained.

"Well, I'm glad you're okay, too," Jon said gruffly. "They've moved on. I wasn't able to hear anything worthwhile before I stopped tailing them. But we should get going."

They headed away from the lake, giving the path the soldiers had taken when passing their camp a wide berth. Other than chatter about the movement of troops, the trek was relatively quiet. Rachel avoided Guillen's gaze, walking with Jon between them for the most part. When they settled down to eat lunch, Guillen asked Rachel if they could talk in private for a moment.

They stepped a few yards away, Jon curiously looking after them.

Guillen's hands were in his pockets, his arms rigid. "I just wanted to apologize. I didn't mean anything by that. You've been through a hell of a lot, and that was ... uncalled for. Okay?"

She hugged herself. "It's alright, not a big deal." She looked at his apologetic eyes. "You're really nice. I just ... ya know..." *Went through the realm's worst breakup...*

"Yes. I know." He raised his eyebrows. "I don't know *everything*, and that's fine. You don't have to talk about it if you don't want to. But I know what kind of person Soren is; I'm sorry you had to get wrapped up in all of this. I didn't mean to be insensitive back there."

"Thanks." She wore a soft smile. "It was just a twitch anyway, right?"

He smiled back. "Yep, darn eye." He winked again. "Dang it, I should get that checked out."

She chuckled.

"But really, if you ever want to talk—I'm willing to listen. Jon might know more about our training on manipulation tactics, but I know more about Soren, personally."

"Thanks. I have been wondering... Is it true what Soren said, that he's engaged?"

Guillen winced, rubbing the back of his neck. "Yeah, they announced it as soon as he came back."

"How long has it been in the works?"

He arched an eyebrow. "You're sure you want to know these details?"

She nodded.

"They've dated for years. Sorry if that's hard to hear."

She shook her head. "Don't feel sorry for me. Someday, the fog will clear. And I'll be surrounded by people that are actually honest and care about me. I have to believe that." She wanted to add an extra level of assurance. "I don't pine for David. The only thing I want from him right now is for him to get what he deserves, just like Rob did."

Guillen's voice was gentle. "And he will. Are we good?"

"We're good."

Returning to sit down with Jon, Rachel was grateful the tension had dispersed.

"Plotting my demise?" Jon asked lightheartedly.

"Yep," Guillen said with a straight face.

Rachel tapped her fingertips together menacingly.

Jon casually responded, "Sounds good. Hurry up so we can get moving."

With at least a couple of hours before the sun would even start to set, Jon announced they were approaching their stopping point for the night. Rachel's heart dropped to see a tiny worn-down log cabin—another thing she would happily never have contact with again. *Why did David have to ruin everything?* She glanced around at the trees nearby—a few of them were dead, looking as though they'd been used by an Ivy to form rifts to the human world. She stood back, fidgeting with her hands. Her apprehension was evident, her anxiety plastered on her face.

Jon offered to clear the building. She could inspect from outside with the door open before entering.

"We can't just keep going? I don't mind walking more, getting more distance in tonight," she suggested.

"The princess gave explicit instructions about stopping here."

Hesitantly, Rachel entered the cabin, curious at the insistence on this location. Essentially one small room, it was crowded with abandoned items, looking like it hadn't seen much use over the years. After shutting the door behind them, they all found a place to sit.

"Why did she say we needed to come here?" Rachel asked.

"She didn't say." Jon shrugged. "She just said it would be helpful for you. Does it spark any memories? Anything jump out at you?"

"No." Scrutinizing the room, Rachel tried to figure out why this place would matter. And then she spotted it, tucked behind some dusty books—a coffee cup, from the shop Kaylah used to work at back home.

Rachel wanted to run up and grab it, but instead made sure to not let her eyes linger too long. She didn't understand the need for this cloak-and-dagger approach if Kaylah really trusted these men, but either way, it was clearly meant to be private. She'd wait to get a closer look.

Chapter 22

Rachel took in her dusty surroundings. "How is it you have all these random decrepit cabins in the Neutral Woods?"

"They're from the old days, before our people withdrew and the current boundaries were set in treaty," Jon said. "These are part of the property they abandoned." Their little group had officially left Ivy Kingdom borders a while back and were now in neutral territory.

"Really?" She raised her eyebrows in disbelief. "They're in sad shape, but they've been unoccupied for over two hundred years?"

Guillen shrugged, taking a swig from his canteen.

Jon smirked, balancing his pack on the back edge of a sun-faded love seat. "I forget you haven't really lived in the Green Lands yet. Even if the tree is dead—used for lumber, or paper in books—it doesn't degrade as quickly here. Not like in the human world."

Rachel nodded in approval. "This place is pretty amazing."

She decided to wait until Jon took a turn resting before she would go look at the clue Kaylah had left for her. He encouraged Rachel to try and get some shut-eye as well, so they could be on their way before first light. She told him she would, but she just needed a few minutes to wind down first. Guillen stood at the front window, keeping watch. After Jon's quiet snoring began, Rachel meandered around the room, picking up and examining random items. Reaching the table with the coffee cup, she glanced over her shoulder to make sure Guillen was still focused elsewhere.

Opening the lid, she looked inside—nothing. Flipping it over, she was happy to see a picture of a smiling sun staring back at her. A sweet reminder of back home, she thought, until the fond memory grew tainted with the reminder that her best friend had been poisoning her to screw with her mind. Either way, what was the purpose?

She gave it another look-over, turning and searching for any marks or messages. Scrutinizing the bottom of the cup, she found what she was looking for—one of the rays on the sun was touching the edge of the cup, but it didn't perfectly line up. There was a false bottom.(z)

Picking at it with her fingernail, she popped the bottom off. On the other side of the sun was a message in Kaylah's handwriting. "Memorize. Destroy. Itiner."

Itiner? What's that supposed—

A floorboard creaked behind her, and she quickly folded the note, palming it.

"Find anything fascinating over here?" Guillen whispered, now much closer.

Rachel picked up one of the dusty books. "Just fancied some light reading."

He tilted his head to read the spine of the book. "Recipes? Should we have you take over cooking?"

She set it back down. "I think we'll manage without my attempts. I'm going to turn in."

Noticing the coffee cup, he picked it up, looking at it curiously. "Hmm."

Having stirred up some dust when she'd picked up the book, Rachel fought an oncoming sneeze. Unable to control it, she sneezed into her shoulder. Jon snorted out a loud snore, shifting positions and returning to his quieter breathing.

"Sorry," Rachel whispered.

"Good health," Guillen said, setting the coffee cup down.

Rachel scanned his face. "Good health?"

Guillen studied her face in turn. "Yeah, you sneezed. Do Seeders not ... say that?"

Smiling, Rachel now understood. The way he'd said it, with a curious innocence, was undeniably cute. "Well, I honestly don't know what Seeders say for sneezes, since the only ones I've met were pretending to be human. But where I'm from we say 'Bless you.'"

His eyes narrowed slightly. "Is that a power I've never heard of? Can humans bless others with health?"

She bit the insides of her cheeks to suppress a smile. "No. It's just a saying."

He shyly averted his gaze. "Right. Okay."

"Well, I'm going to go lie down now." She settled onto the lumpy old couch to sleep. Once he went back to the window, she carefully tucked the note in her pocket. Struggling to fall asleep, she racked her brain about what she was supposed to use this for. Finally, not long after Jon and Guillen switched places, she found rest.

She woke up to Jon's hand over her mouth this time, a scream ringing in her ears. The warmth of her own breath was trapped by his large hand. Feeling like she could suffocate, she ripped it from her mouth. "Keep your hands off me. Everyone!"

Jon scowled. "I get you've gone through a lot, but you could show a little gratitude. Or should I just let you scream it out and *hope* soldiers aren't nearby next time you have a bad dream?"

Rachel sat up, pinching the bridge of her nose. She was cranky from too little sleep. And the sleep she *had* gotten had felt like a marathon. All. Night. Long. Running for her life, trying to figure out how to hide her little piece of paper. "I'm sorry," she whispered.

It was still dark out, but since they were all up, Jon recommended they take advantage of the cover of night. "Did you figure out ... why we're here?" he asked.

"You've got your orders, and I've got mine," she replied, securing the strap of her pack closed.

"Spoken like a true covert operative." Jon flung his pack over his shoulder. "We might just make you one of us yet."

<hr>

The further they traveled from the palace, the less dense and lush the woods became. They made it a point to travel at night and find a well-hidden space to rest up during the day. Rachel ingrained Kaylah's message into her brain and carefully tore up the paper, hiding small pieces of it in the dirt as they would go, until it was all gone.

After four more nights of walking due west, Jon announced they would be staying a little longer; he'd swing by a local outpost and pick up more supplies to get them through the rest of their trip to Seeder borders.

Rachel woke midday to a haggard-looking Guillen. The split sleeping schedule was taking its toll on both of the men. Rachel got up, then sat next to Guillen on a fallen tree. "How about I take a turn keeping watch? You're looking worn out. Grab some more sleep before he comes back."

Guillen took a deep breath, rubbing the back of his neck. "No, it's fine."

"Maybe... But if you get more sleep now, maybe he can get more sleep, too, and you will both be the better for it."

He looked hesitant to accept the offer.

"I can handle it. I'm healed up. I'm well rested. I've got these guys down." She extended her Seeder blades, and he eyed them. He hadn't yet seen her transform all the way. "And I can stay right next to you. If there's any noise or problem, I can wake you up right away."

He yawned. "Only for a little while. Don't let me sleep too long. And anything suspicious, get me up right away."

"Okay. I promise."

He curled up nearby and soon drifted off, his breathing slowed. She smiled, watching him peacefully sleep. It suited him with how calming he was. She wished she could sleep that well right now.

While the scenery was beautiful, Rachel's eyes wandered to Guillen's sleeping figure more often than not. He was handsome, and sweet, and innocent, and strong. Unlike Jon, who'd let his beard scruff take over the last few days, Guillen made it a point to do a quick shave with his sharp blades every couple of days.

Probably an hour or more passed and, as promised, she was still sitting next to him, her eyes focused now on his belt and the knives attached to it. The only thing that had stirred during his nap was an adorable chipmunk that scurried past them into a bush.

"Had any training with knives?" Guillen asked, startling her. "Other than your own blades?"

"No."

He sat up. "I could show you a thing or two."

She smirked, sneaking a quick glance back at his belt. "Are you trying to offer to let me ... check out your ... tools?"

His jaw dropped. "You ... just went there. Was that a joke about..."

She giggled, thinking it was only fair after he stole a peek at her chest by the lake. "Sorry. Just having some fun." She cleared her throat. "I'd love to learn more about your mad skills. Anything that would help with defense is good."

Grinning, he scanned her face. "I like seeing you smile more. Real smiles."

She blushed. Despite all the chaos she'd been through, his smiles were something she was enjoying, too.

He unsheathed a knife for each of them, then demonstrated his technique on holding it for best control in fighting, then how to throw it to stick it in the ground where he wanted. He had amazing accuracy. She ... needed practice.

Rachel turned the blade in her hand after a while spent chucking it haphazardly. "How do you know when it's dull enough to need sharpening?" Running her finger along the edge of the blade, she winced as she cut herself.

He held his hand out, and she surrendered the knife. "Well, that's not exactly how I would recommend going about it."

She stared at her finger, oddly entranced. As the blood seeped to the surface, she remembered some of her darkest days. Probably caused by Kaylah, but also ended by her, when she'd caught her with the needle. Rachel moved another finger over the blood and focused on healing it.

"You okay? You had one of your looks, like you left for a while."

She continued to stare at the now-healed finger. "Wouldn't it be nice if I could heal my heart and mind, the same way I can my skin?" Her melancholy tone matched the numbness inside her.

His voice was soft. "Even in the Green Lands, with all of our accelerated healing, we all have scars. Most of them just aren't visible."

Snapping out of her trance, Rachel took her canteen and washed off the blood. "Speaking of, I was curious about trying something. Could I look at your hand?"

"Sure..." He offered both hands.

She selected the one bearing a large scar on the back of it, near the wrist—the scar still seemed fresh; it was pink.

"I don't know if it works for old wounds." She placed a healing touch on the scar, smiling internally at the warmth of his hand. Her mind wandered again to their encounter at the lake, and she fought a grin while focusing on her experiment. She checked it twice before calling it done, feeling a significant drain. She'd expected it to heal faster, like Soren's cut that she'd taken care of, especially with the energy of the Green Lands. But she'd never tried healing something that was technically already healed. After a few minutes, she revealed it. It had faded enough to be noticeable.

"That's impressive." He ran his fingers over it.

She raised her hand to the larger scar on his temple. "If you'd like—"

Guillen intercepted her hand, guiding it down. "Some scars we earn, and they become part of our story." His piercing eyes conveyed the importance this one must hold for him. "Plus, I know that takes a lot out of you. Best to use it on fresh things, not focusing on something from the past."

"Okay."

He knew how to say the right things. He wasn't manipulative or flattering the way David was. His words held genuine kindness and wisdom from what must have been years of introspection.

"Can I practice more?" She glanced down at her hand—he was still holding it after preventing her from healing his scar.

"Are you done trying to filet yourself?" He wore a playful grin.

She scrunched her face in defiance before he handed the knife back to her with a softer smile.

He corrected her technique every so often, and she slowly saw improvement in how well she could aim. He then showed her how to sharpen the knives they'd been practicing with.

"Your skills are pretty impressive," she complimented. "You've obviously dedicated a lot of time to learning."

"Your Seeder skills are pretty impressive, as well," he returned.

She carefully made another pass with a sharpening stone. "Yeah, but yours is a learned skill, on top of any natural botanical powers. The sum of what I can demonstrate is seriously insufficient natural ability."

"I *wish* my practice added to natural abilities." He looked down after their eyes met.

"What do you mean?"

He drew a deep breath and met her gaze. "Have you ever seen my vines?"

She searched her memories. It wasn't like Jon had pulled his out often, but she'd seen them. It wasn't exactly something she had fixated on, but now that she thought about it... "No, I guess I haven't."

"That's because I don't have any."

Chapter 23

Rachel surveyed Guillen, confused. "What do you mean? Don't all Ivies have vines?"

Guillen raised his eyebrows. "Not if you're a stunt."

She narrowed her eyes, never having heard that as green folk terminology. "Like ... 'I do my own stunts'? It's from an injury?"

He shook his head. "No. Kaylah once said humans might classify us as 'disabled'?"

Her eyes widened. "Oh."

"Not something I always bring up." Guillen pressed his lips together.

She bit her lip. "You don't have to talk about it, if you don't want to..."

"It's okay. It's probably better you know the limitations of someone you're working with, anyway. Jon knows. I guess you could call it a birth defect. It's pretty rare, but I can't do anything a normal Ivy can. I'm just," he shrugged, "this. I'm essentially human."

Her mouth hung open. "I ... hadn't thought about something like that."

He smiled, though the warmth didn't reach his eyes. "I wish I didn't have to think about it. Stunts are... Well, let's just say there's not a lot of respect for my kind. They group us together, in our own communities, at the back end of our territories—for our own 'safety.' We don't get the same kind of education, since it's not necessary for us to learn to use vines, or create rifts, or how to blend in with humans." He shifted slightly on the fallen tree he'd been sitting on. "We're tasked with the menial work others in more respectable positions don't want to do—so we can feel 'pride' in contributing to the kingdom. We're even forbidden from having kids so we don't pass on our bad genes."

She frowned. "That's so horrible. I'm sorry."

"Thanks. But I try not to let myself dwell on it too much. I'm pretty lucky, honestly." He rolled up one of his sleeves. While his toned arms were impressive, Rachel immediately spotted what he was trying to show her—a tattoo.

"That's neat."

"That's one way of looking at it."

It was the outline of an ivy leaf, and in the middle was a crown symbol.

"Can I?" she asked as she moved closer, running her thumb over it. "What does it mean to you?"

"The middle symbol permits me to move around undocumented. It allows me to have some semblance of normalcy despite my nature. If you're not close in the royal bloodline like I am, you have a number in the middle of the leaf. That signifies the community you're assigned to."

She looked into his eyes, horrified. As if she'd gotten the wind knocked out of her, she stuttered. "They... They ... tattoo *numbers* on your people, just because they don't have the same powers?!"

He took her hand from his arm and unrolled his sleeve to cover the tattoo. "I don't want you to look at me that way." Shaking his head, he looked away. "I don't like people feeling sorry for me. This is just the way it is for my people. I have no room to complain—I still get a lot of freedom. I get to choose which of the communities I live in." He shrugged. "I got extra tutors and was given the choice to live with my family until I was eighteen."

Her heart ached. "Guillen, I know you didn't learn about human history, but ... this is the kind of thing that was done by one of the *worst* rulers over there. It's despicable!"

He looked slightly confused. "When the only thing that differentiates you from your enemy is a demonstration of powers, how do you ensure they're not infiltrating your land under the guise of being a stunt?"

She crossed her arms, scowling at the ground, pondering his question. "I don't know." She lifted her head to look at him again. "But it's still wrong!"

He studied her face. "There are good and bad people in every society, aren't there? I bet you never thought you'd feel sorry for a group of Ivies."

She sighed at the irony. "I guess you're right. I just can't believe they'd do this to their own people."

Guillen blew out a long puff of air. "That's what hate does to us. It makes us forget how much we have in common, and that we all have our own struggles. But like I said, with my ties to the palace, I'm not treated as much like a pariah as most are. And Kaylah's always been a good cheerleader. And she's pretty impressive with a dagger and machete, from years of sparring with me. I couldn't be a military man, but that didn't mean I wasn't capable of learning new skills."

Rachel smiled, finding herself admiring him more each day. "I'd say 'capable' is an understatement. And honestly, humans live every single day without abilities like we have in the Green Lands. They're blissfully ignorant, living their lives over there. Granted, for them it's normal. I bet you'd love it there, not being treated the way you are in your kingdom."

"I'm sure I would..." he said wistfully.

The conversation lit a light bulb for her. "Do you know ... about *my* people? I haven't heard about this kind of thing before, but I can only imagine some of our people might have a condition like this."

"No. Not a lot of cultural information comes our way from your side. It would be interesting to learn about, though. When you're back there, you'll have to find out."

"I'll do that, for sure." She smiled.

"Great. I expect to see you again someday or get a note all about it."

Her smile widened, then shrank with another question. "What does 'stunt' actually mean?"

"Ah, yes, that. It's short for 'stunted.'"

She'd had a feeling he'd say something like that. It made her sick. "That's not right."

Guillen shrugged. "It's the politest term I've ever heard for us."

Rachel frowned. "Really? You don't have anything else you call yourself?"

He smirked, picking up a pine cone. "I thought you knew—*I* call myself Guillen."

She chuckled. "I think you know that's not what I meant, but I'll take it."

He tossed the pine cone back to the forest floor. "Just do me a favor?"

"What's that?"

"I *really* don't want any pity."

"There's nothing pitiful about you, Guillen." She looked into his stormy eyes, which softened, warming her heart.

She took a sharp breath. "So ... Jon... We're still thinking he's on the up-and-up? Why is he the one that disappears for hours at a time and you get the babysitting duty?"

Guillen chuckled, then took a drink from his canteen. "Honestly, he's become a palace boy. I sense he's not quite as fond of the nomadic camping lifestyle. Signs of civilization seem to keep him sane." He smirked again, holding up his canteen. "So, I suffer, taking on this monumental task, watching this beautiful and kind girl. I just don't know how I'll make it through the next few days."

She flashed him a toothy smile. "I guess we'll just have to make do." She bit her lip. "Honestly, I haven't gone camping since ... Brad." Her high spirits began to deflate. Had Rob been honest about Brad leaving, just because he'd found out she was a Seeder? Or that Rob had killed him? Or was he just trying to get to her? None of the options brought her any comfort.

She tried to stop the mental train wreck in progress. "I need to stretch my legs. I saw a patch of wildflowers growing not that far from here. How about a walk to go take a look?"

<hr>

After Jon returned to camp with fresh supplies, they let him rest up and then pressed on after nightfall. They anticipated at least three more days of travel, and then things would get a little more interesting.

"We don't actually know which village you belong to, or where it's located along the border," Jon said. "But your people should have gotten word about your return with plenty of time to have eyes looking out for the signal."

Over the hours and days of their travels, Rachel had a lot to take in and sort through. The exchange of information, hopes, and dreams between green folk that would usually be enemies was thrilling. Rachel had more than enough time to try and make something out of the jumble of mental chaos that had been inflicted on her. Her healing journey was far from complete, but she had a new resolve, and greater perspective on who she was and who she wanted to be from here on out. The energy of the Green Lands, the understanding companions to talk to, the quiet away from chaos—she reaped the rewards, bit by bit.

Initially, starting the journey back to her ancestral home, she'd been bogged down by despair and pain. Over time, it had transformed into hope, and now, unfortunately, building anxiety. The closer they got to Seeder lands, the more she realized how much pressure would be placed on her, how much things would be changing again. She stressed over how she would be received by her new family and people. The shame she felt for allowing herself to become a victim. And not only that, but one that had helped the enemy in their attack. Not willingly, of course, but the fact that they'd had her in the first place to be able to steal her energy...

She also worried about her role in this war. She was now consigned to this world permanently—Soren and Nuren had taken that choice from her by making sure she'd rooted here. But where does one start a new life when they arrive in the middle of a bloodbath?

And Kaylah. The 'rebellion.' Her expectations were more than cryptic, but nonetheless, she had expectations. The quicker Rachel could get back to the human world, the better. Ignoring the request of your best friend/revolution leader/rescuer/princess was hardly an option on the table. And it was getting late in the season, even for an experienced female Seeder, to catch a breeze to the human world.

Rachel woke one morning to birds chirping in the trees. Rolling onto her stomach, she rested her chin on the back of her hands. Thinking of her mom, she ached. How many people willingly took in someone else's child? And to be betrayed like that, being left by two men. Did her mom even know about Rob's betrayal? Did she think her daughter was dead?

An iridescent beetle strolled by, giving Rachel cause to smile. Guillen and Jon were whispering again. This time, Jon said he'd be off relieving himself past some trees. Rachel reached out, moving a twig out of the beetle's path.

"So, you *are* awake," Guillen said.

Rachel took a deep breath. The crispness of the air and the babble of a nearby brook were enchanting. "Even the bugs are pretty here."

Dirt and gravel crunched under his boots as he drew near. He sat a few feet in front of her, tilting his head to the side with a hint of a smile. "Not afraid of the pretty little bugs?"

She propped herself up on her elbows. "Spiders are different. Unless maybe you have rainbow spiders?"

He grinned. "Not that I'm aware of."

Rachel picked herself up, sitting cross-legged facing Guillen and taking a drink of water from her canteen. "I appreciate you and Jon helping me. And Meg ... Kaylah ... said I could trust the two of you."

"Yes."

Looking down at her hands, Rachel picked at her chipped prom manicure. "But how do I know I can trust *her*?"

Guillen frowned when she looked back up. "I don't know how to convince you. All I can say is that I know you can. Kaylah's been lied to, probably as much as you have been. She hardly knows who to trust, herself."

Rachel's eyes narrowed. "Really?"

He nodded. "From what she told me over the years—and I've never known her to lie to me—this whole thing was Nuren's plan, and Soren volunteered to help. Kaylah was the only one not given the choice."

She studied his face. "Why would the future queen spend her youth in the human world? Wasting so much time on a nobody like me?"

He raised his eyebrows in disapproval. "You're not a nobody."

She shrugged. "But I'm not special."

Smiling, he broke eye contact. "I suppose that depends on how you classify 'special.'" He cleared his throat, picking up a pebble and rolling it across his hand. "But you want to know why the queen and king would ship her off like that?" He shrugged. "Because Nuren had trust issues and wanted a girl he could keep under his thumb to befriend you? He had the queen and king's ear. Supposedly, sending their older kids off on this mission could earn them the pride of the kingdom— examples of successful covert operatives as a notch in their belt."

Guillen sighed. "She was constantly kept in the dark. For the first several years, they lied to her, telling her you were a human. She thought she was brought there to study human society."

Rachel's eyes narrowed again in surprise. "Really?"

"Really. Just ... give her a chance. And cut her a little slack. She's so used to putting on an act that sometimes it can take a while for her to really open up about her struggles."

Rachel wore a contented smile. "I'll think about all of that. Thank you. I'm glad she has someone like you to talk to."

He grinned.

Rachel's mind drifted to the coffee cup clue. "If she trusts the two of you, why did we need to stop at the cabin for me to find something? You don't know what she left for me there?"

Shaking his head, he leaned back with his hands propping him up. "It's best to break up intel. That's one less thing they could torture out of Jon and me if we got caught."

Rachel swallowed hard. "Right."

"Did I miss anything important?" Jon asked as he returned.

Guillen looked up. "Just talking about how Rachel can know whether to trust Kaylah."

Rachel craned her neck to see Jon's face.

He dropped his pack on the ground. "You seem like you possess more than half a brain. I'm sure you'll figure it out."

Choking back a laugh, Rachel put a hand over her heart. "Jon, you are just *so* sweet!"

He rolled his eyes, showing the smallest hint of a smile. "Are we ready to move on?"

Chapter 24

hile the woods between the Ivy palace and neutral territory were somewhat sparse, they grew denser again as Rachel and her escorts approached their target. Despite having more trees for cover, they had to be more alert than ever—this area was crawling with soldiers, most of them Ivy. And with two Ivies accompanying her, it wouldn't be ideal if they were caught by either side at this point.

"This is where we start the final phase," Jon announced. He pulled out some items from his pack and handed them to Rachel. First, a rolled letter, sealed. "That is for you, you can read it when you're ready." Another sealed letter, with a gold ring tied to it. "That is for your people once you're safely on the other side. Guard them with your life."

Guillen spoke up. "The last thing Kaylah needed you to know was 13310 North Maplewood. You'll want to remember that."

Rachel repeated it in her mind until it was permanent, adding it to the other clue. *Itiner. 13310 North Maplewood.*(aa)

"Guillen is going to go tonight. Don't be startled by fireworks in the sky," Jon said.

Rachel's eyes darted to Guillen. "You're going?" Her heart was heavy at having to say goodbye already.

He gave her a gentle smile. "I'll be back. You're not getting rid of me yet."

They found shelter in a densely wooded area that, according to their latest contacts, was not heavily patrolled right now. Guillen snuck out before sundown, leaving Rachel and Jon to silently keep watch. Rachel took the opportunity to open her letter from Kaylah.

I hope you can forgive me. I need you to put everything behind you that David and Rob have ever said or done to you. I'm not without fault, and I'm sorry for that. I wish I could undo so many choices, but that's the past. What I can do now, and what you can do, is work together for our people. This is Unitas, the Unity Movement. Change can happen when enough people learn the truth and question the propaganda. It takes strong people like you to get the job done. I need you to meet with me, to provide an introduction. I can explain more when you come. Stay safe. I look forward to seeing you soon. Love you.

Rachel looked up; Jon was watching. "Do you know what's in here?"

He shook his head. "I don't need to know."

"So, when we part ways, what's next for you and Guillen?"

"Well, now that we took out the duke, I'd say we're pretty set on our paths. We have our orders once you're safely back. We each have our specialties and connections; we'll keep growing the movement."

"Will I have any way of contacting you guys?"

"Not that I know of. This assignment will be over. And you'll have plenty to work on, too."

She frowned. If this had been the human world, she'd happily exchange numbers with both of them, to keep in touch. But there were trade-offs for life in the Green Lands, one of them being the lack of electricity.

At least two hours passed before they heard any noise from outside of their shelter. An explosion tore through the night sky, shattering the silence. Jon confirmed the first sign had been deployed—red fireworks.

While anxiously awaiting Guillen's return, Rachel decided to try and get to know Jon better.

"I'd love to hear more about you, your story." She barely spoke above a whisper. "If you're willing to share." More than wanting to calm her nerves, she knew any witness who could speak for the movement may be helpful.

"My story, huh?"

The moon was bright, the sky clear. Jon's shadowed face darkened in his hesitancy to talk.

"Yeah. Why you decided to make the sacrifice and join Unitas."

He nodded. "Our people don't know what's going on at the palace, you know?"

She furrowed her brow. "Really? You mean what they're doing to my people?"

He nodded again. "That's the main thing. It's against orders to talk about it. Some people in the palace don't even know, like servants in the kitchens." He pulled out a flask and took a swig. "People don't want to know the truth. They want to be told *what* to want, and then told *how* to get it. They don't think for themselves."

There was a reason he didn't talk much about anything other than strategy. There was an altogether different tone to his delivery.

"So," he cleared his throat, "the first girl. That was..." He paused. "Sickening. Unbelievable. Horrifying. Especially as they worked things out. Trying to figure out how to tune things, how to balance giving her breaks." He took another drink from his flask. "My least favorite assignment, by far, having to play any part in that."

The full weight of his story sank in for Rachel as he drew a deep breath. She hadn't been an early guinea pig—it could have been worse.

"So, when they bring a second one around," Jon continued, "I see Princess Kaylah come back for a visit. And we shared a look. You don't get cozy with the royal family; we'd never formally met. So, it was a bit terrifying when she sought me out privately. Thinking I'd be dismissed, or worse, for showing weakness."

He let out a breathy chuckle. "Boy, was I wrong about her. It didn't take much convincing to join her little group. She put me to work almost immediately."

Shifting his position, he settled in with more ease as he talked. "It actually wasn't that hard to do my part. You just happen to accidentally, cautiously, be loose-lipped to the right people. You see what their reaction is about what's happening at the palace, gauge their feelings, see where they fall on the spectrum of potential allies."

"That's really neat," Rachel said. They'd been thinking this out and working on it for some time. Of course, this was all just from when Jon had joined. She didn't know how long Kaylah had actively been working on things.

He sighed. "It doesn't come without a cost. Sometimes, you wish you could go back to being ignorant about what people really think."

She frowned. What had his personal cost been? "Do you have a family?"

He arched an eyebrow. "Everyone has a family."

She picked up a twig, starting to draw in the dirt with it. "You know what I mean."

"No. Not one of my own," he said. "My, uh ... partner, of five years—she's one of those I wish I'd never said anything to. Around the time I realized she wasn't likely to come around, Princess Kaylah was starting to ask more of me. I gave Sheila some crap excuse when I decided to move out."

"I'm sorry." Five years—that was a decent investment. At least Ivies weren't stuck mating for life like Seeders were. "You'll find someone that's better for you someday."

He shook his head. "We'll see. I still love her. If I could just change that *one part*... But I can't blame her. *I'm* the one who changed." He took another deep breath, capping his flask and tucking it away. "Doesn't really matter now, anyway. Once they got you, and the princess reached out... I'm as good as burned."

He chuckled. "You're gone. We left bodies. And I didn't show up for work the next day. I think it's safe to say they might have put two and two together."

"Yeah. I guess you're right." She poked at the ground with her twig, feeling a bit guilty, and still nervous to see Guillen return. "What about Guillen and his kind?"

"Good ol' Guillen," he said. "Never lived near his communities. And his kind do their best to blend in when given permission to visit normal cities, so I can't say I've knowingly met one before."

Rachel stayed silent, feeling protective of Guillen. She found herself frustrated that Jon didn't seem to carry equal passion about that particular domestic agenda.

"I was a little nervous to be working with him. Being without... well, you know. But I was surprised. He's really competent, brings a good mix of skills."

After a moment of silence, she decided she'd rather go back to listening for Guillen's return. "Thanks for sharing all that with me."

"No problem."

The quiet helped her mind wander, helped her worry. "What would we do, if we came across a huge ambush out here?"

"Depends on who it is and how bad," he said. "If it's your kind, we surrender and hope for the best. If it's ours, we fight. If there's too many, you're the priority. We both know that."

Her chest tightened, glancing at the trees surrounding them. "Are you capable of taking Guillen's kind through a rift? Like Soren did with me?"

Jon shook his head. "Only Seeder females can do that trick—the only beings in the Green Lands capable of sharing energy."

She'd worried about that. It wasn't just that Guillen couldn't create his own rift because he didn't have vines. He couldn't rift *at all*. While Jon couldn't rift Rachel safely into Seeder lands, he *could* take her back to the human world to get out of immediate danger, and then try to come back from a new place. Guillen would be left alone.

Every moment Guillen was in these woods escorting Rachel back was one of incredible danger. "I... If we find a good clearing, I should be able to catch a breeze and get home on my own this close to our borders, right?"

"No. We're following the plan. Your people will escort you back safely."

She didn't hate the idea of more time spent with Guillen. A day more, even a second more. But she realized that was beyond selfish. "But it would be safer for ... both of you ... if I went the rest of the way on my own."

"The princess is worried about arrows."

"Wait. I thought Ivies primarily used vines to fight."

With a heavier sigh that seemed to carry frustration, Jon shifted his position again. "As a point of pride and practicality, archers are only stationed at the palace. Your people have projectiles and can fly. We have to be able to combat that. Nuren petitioned the queen for years, saying we ought to send archers into the woods, too. Now that he's dead, the princess wants to be prepared for any unintended consequences."

Rachel left it at that. There was no winning.

Three hours passed without sign of Guillen. The knots in Rachel's stomach grew tighter with the nerve-racking silence.

"He'll be fine. It's likely to take longer to return. He has to avoid being followed, and that thing," he pointed to the night sky where the fireworks had previously lit up, "is drawing a lot of attention right now."

Jon was right—she was able to breathe a sigh of relief not much later as Guillen returned. The next night, it was Jon's turn to go out. It was only an hour or so before green fireworks rained down, another decoy.

On the third night, Guillen took off in a different direction, this time taking three or four hours before brilliant blue sparks lit up the sky.

"The finale," Jon whispered.

It was late into the night before Guillen returned. Jon offered to let him sleep, but Guillen insisted he wasn't tired yet and would take over the watch. Rachel tried her best to get some shut-eye, but her mind was playing every possible scenario that could happen over the next few days. Her eyes met with Guillen's in the moonlight and he moved closer, crouching down in front of her.

"Not able to sleep?"

As she shook her head, a wisp of hair fell in front of her eyes.

He tucked it behind her ear, smiling. "How about I sit here next to you?" He did just that, placing his hand on her shoulder, softly rubbing it. "Just until you fall asleep."

She wore a contented grin. "Then I might choose to never fall asleep."

He met her remark with a gentle squeeze of the shoulder, to which she replied by moving her other hand to meet his, intertwining their fingers. She didn't remember falling asleep, but she did remember having the most peaceful rest she'd had in an insanely long time.

When she woke, Jon was anxiously staring at something outside of their hiding place. Guillen was sleeping on the ground, not far from Rachel. When Jon spotted her gaze, he put a finger to his lips and indicated with a nod that there might be danger nearby. Staying still, she listened quietly. There was a faint rustling of foliage, and then whispering voices. Jon pointed to Guillen. Since Rachel was closer, she would be the one to carefully wake him up. Should they be discovered, they would need to be ready.

She cautiously moved over to him, leaning over and covering his mouth, whispering into his ear, "Guillen. We've got trouble."

He reflexively reached for his belt, but the tension in his face and arms melted away once he realized it was Rachel, who now had a finger to her lips. She slowly removed her hand and nodded at Jon. Guillen quietly sat up and listened. They couldn't give away their position, especially now that the final fireworks had gone out. If they had to move, the location wouldn't be accurate for the Seeders to find Rachel.

While the soldiers passed uncomfortably close, it appeared the Unitas party remained undetected.

As they ate their lunch later in the day, Rachel asked with a cocky smile, "So, how do *you* like it? Waking up with someone's hand on your mouth? Not the best feeling, is it?"

Guillen grinned and did a quick up-down look at her. "I'd be okay waking up seeing *that* every day." He winked.

She blushed, having walked right into that.

The rest of the afternoon passed by in cautious silence. They only had a few hours left before they went their separate ways. All three of them were on edge as they bided their time.

More than once, Rachel caught Guillen's gaze. More than once, he also caught her checking him out. Each time their eyes met, they exchanged a shy smile. But no one talked. She didn't know what to say. And they needed to be vigilant about monitoring their surroundings.

What would they have to say, anyway? What could she and Guillen have even hoped for out of this, on a personal level?

The pain and fear mounted as Jon and Guillen packed up their things. They planned to leave before dark to put a good amount of distance between them and Rachel. White fireworks would go up in the sky that night, and they wouldn't be returning.

Guillen approached her first. "You'll do great things." He handed her one of his knives, smiling. His hand lingered as it touched hers in the exchange. "Because you don't have to just rely on natural abilities, right?" He bit his lip, meeting her gaze. "And maybe it's something you can remember me by."

Rachel's heart was screaming that she didn't need anything to remember him by, not if he stayed with her. He could stay; they could figure things out. She could be happy with him by her side. He could be happy in Seeder lands, not being treated as a nobody.

But she knew she couldn't be selfish. It would risk his life further, and they both had work to do. She wasn't even sure if his kind would be immune to the poison that haunted Seeder lands—being there with her might actually carry a death sentence for an Ivy 'stunt,' a being without powers.

She lunged at him with a hug, squeezing tight. "I'll do my research, as promised. And I expect to see you again, so take care."

He wrapped his arms around her, whispering back, "You too."

Releasing Guillen, she gave him a kiss on the cheek.

Jon snickered. "I see what happens when I leave to get supplies."

She turned to Jon, smiling, and opened her arms for a hug.

He held out his hand for a firm handshake. "It's been my pleasure. Do your best to not need saving again, okay?"

"I'll do what I can."

"And don't let down the princess. Everyone's counting on you."

And with that ominous reminder, they left.

Chapter 25

Minutes ticked by. The hours drew long. Finally, the sign came—a shower of lights in the night sky. Jon and Guillen were still alright, and they were keeping Rachel safe. There was no going back, nowhere to go. Now, she just had to wait.

Rachel stayed alert all night, fidgeting with Guillen's knife and Kaylah's letter for comfort. She rehearsed the clues she'd been given to memorize. She practiced reading and manipulating the surrounding air, something she would need to master quickly to catch a breeze.

Just before the sun rose in the sky, the crack of a twig nearby caught her attention.

"Don't worry, we'll find her," a male voice whispered.

"Rachel?" a female called out in a hushed tone.

Rachel peeked out from her cover. Two sets of glowing green eyes searched the area. She lit hers up to give her position.

"Rachel? Is that you? Are you okay?" the man asked.

She emerged from the bushes. "Yeah."

The strangers reached her, giving her a tight hug.

"We've got everyone out looking for you! My name is Saff. This is my husband, Devin. We're going to take you home."

As they quietly and cautiously made their way through the Neutral Woods to Seeder territory, they ran across two more searchers—one being Jeff. Jeff and Rachel shared an awkward hug before approaching the Outer Wall. Once they made it through the Outer Wall, Devin gave a signal and a trumpet blew, recalling the rest of the search parties.

The first day and night were overwhelming, to say the least, as she was taken to the family she'd never known. It would have been a decent walk back to her village, but Rachel insisted she wanted to catch a breeze to cut down the time. She needed more practice if she was going to do what Kaylah expected of her. She was a bit wobbly, and thoroughly embarrassed by her technique, but the new energy coursing through her—now that she was rooted in the Green Lands—helped her complete the trip without incident.

While flying over Seeder territory, Rachel spotted similar plant life to the lush growth she'd seen near the Ivy palace. But this time, she got to see dozens, even hundreds, of Seeder homes. Footpaths leading to every part of the landscape were covered by people going about their tasks and meeting at outdoor markets. It was beautiful, but bustling. Nervous, part of her didn't want to land, didn't want to be around more new people, didn't want to leave the serenity she'd enjoyed with a couple of kind companions in the Neutral Woods. But land she did.

Her Seeder family's warm reception was filled with tears of relief, though not even half of them were present. Most were fighting or still in the human world. Rachel met one-on-one with her birth mom, Lyza. Lyza was thin, with much darker hair than Rachel. They really didn't look much alike, though Rachel had learned that most Seeders didn't carry a strong family resemblance. Before her true Seeder identity had been revealed, she'd always grown up knowing she was adopted, and had secretly painted a picture in her mind of how her parents looked. She imagined she might have shared their eyes or nose, or something distinct. But Lyza looked like a complete stranger. Rachel still hadn't met her Seeder father, but from the pictures Lyza showed her, she didn't seem to share any jump-out-at-you traits with him either.

During their initial exchange, Lyza shared with Rachel the Seeder name she'd been assigned, as was customary in their family upon a girl's return home. Luckily, Rachel didn't feel pressured to accept it right away.

She found herself increasingly shy as all those able to be present sat down to a picnic in their family lot to celebrate her return. Everyone tiptoed around the topic, asking her how she was, but never addressing the elephant in the room.

A new sister she recognized from her high school sat down next to Rachel, offering her a bowl of blackberries. "We're all really glad you're home safe." She gave a cautious smile.

Rachel picked out a few berries. "Thanks." Surveying her family, she tried to hide a frown. The odd glance was thrown her way now and then, eating at her.

What do they know? Is it public knowledge that I was so stupid to not see the signs, and allowed myself to get taken? Did the power drained from me cause anyone harm, or worse? Do they blame me?

One of her brothers approached, crouching next to Rachel. "Hey there."

She forced a smile. "Hi, um..." She blanked on his name. There were too many new names to keep track of.

He gave an understanding grin. "Patrick."

"Right. Sorry."

He waved a dismissive hand in the air. "No need to apologize. I'm sure there's a lot for you to take in."

Rachel nodded.

"I'm going to head out in a couple hours, to let Samantha know you're back safe. Do you want to write her a letter?"

Rachel choked on her words as she unsuccessfully fought tears. "Yeah, um, definitely."

He frowned, moving his hand up to her shoulder. "No rush. Just let me know when you're ready."

She tried to subtly and quickly wipe the tears from the corners of her eyes. "I, uh... Does she know what all happened?"

He pursed his lips. "I was told you went missing. And your boyfriend, and stepdad, and best friend and her parents. Sounds like everything kinda hit the fan at once." He looked down. "As far as I know, that's what she knows."

Rachel's heart dropped. *She* would have to be the one to break the news to her mom about her husband having betrayed them both.

Patrick met her gaze, seemingly hesitant to speak again. "She, uh... Well, maybe don't take too long to write that letter. They found a note that was supposed to be from you and your boyfriend, that you'd run away together."

Rachel looked down, shaking her head. *Soren.*

"And then another note came, I guess, that apparently led us to you?"

She cracked a tiny smile. *Kaylah.*

"I'm just saying, there was some conflicting information, you know? I think she'd feel a ton better knowing for sure that you *are* actually alive."

Rachel immediately looked up. "Where's some paper?"

After taking time to write her letter, Rachel handed it over to Patrick and walked down the lane with him, watching as he caught a breeze.

That night, she slept soundly in a comfortable bed, safe from harm. The next day, however, would not be so easy.

———————————⊙✹⊙———————————

Rachel was asked to meet with the village council for debriefing. Saff, her welcoming mentor, picked her up in the morning. As they walked down the lane together, Rachel bobbed along in silence.

"How are you doing?" Saff asked.

Rachel shrugged. "Good. It was nice to sleep indoors again and get a proper shower."

As they approached the main lane toward their destination, Rachel's heartbeat quickened at the sight of the crowds. "Do we have to take this path?"

Saff frowned. "It's the fastest way to get there. Plus, I figured it would be nice to give you the grand tour of our home village today."

Rachel stayed silent, still not wanting to go that way.

"And we can grab you some lunch from the vendors on the way. It's not usually this busy, we're just crowded with the..." Saff looked down. "With the Vine attacks."

Swallowing hard, Rachel scanned the street. Yards away, near a vendor's handcart full of oranges and cabbage, a pair of girls around her age huddled as though gossiping. In unison, their gazes reached Rachel, and they continued to chatter.

"I can skip lunch," she said, wanting to be anywhere but there right now. "I don't want to go down this street." Right after she'd said it, a little boy bumped into her, being chased by what was probably a brother. Her breathing picking up, she turned to Saff, pleading. "Please, can we go a different way?"

Saff nodded with a sympathetic frown. "Yeah, let's go down a less busy lane." Wrapping her arm around Rachel's shoulder, she guided her off of the main path. "How about I circle back and bring you some lunch when I come to pick you up from your council meeting?"

"Yeah. Thanks."

Joining the local council at a large oval wooden table in a public meeting room, Rachel was drilled about the locations, tactics, strategies, and really anything she'd picked up from being in Ivy territory. She was grateful no open accusations or shame were being thrown her way. They asked how she'd been kidnapped, how the Ivies had targeted her. She chose not to tell them she *willingly* went with Prince

Soren—she carried enough guilt over the situation. From what she gleaned, the other five girls had probably been kidnapped in different ways.

Rachel handed over the sealed letter Jon had given her. They unrolled it and read it aloud.

To the Honorable Leaders of the Seeder People,

As a gesture of goodwill, and sincerity in extending a hand in friendship, we bring you safely back one of your own and present you with the ring of Duke Nuren. Desiring to forge an alliance as a means of ending the current hostility and pointless bloodshed, I request an audience with a small delegation of leadership. My only requirements are an agreement of peaceful parley, and that Rachel accompany the group, as she knows how to find the location. Understanding the urgency for your people, I guarantee safe and swift passage for any Seeder coming at my invitation, including a prompt return to the Neutral Woods, at our expense, upon the completion of negotiations. In so doing, I denounce the ways of the current Ivy leadership. My goal is peace and equality, the kind our peoples have not seen for centuries.

Kaylah Elonta, Crown Princess of the Mountain Palace and Ivy Kingdom, Leader of the Unitas Movement.

Rachel was ready to go. The Seeders were not. They deliberated for hours. They'd only heard faint rumors of such a rebellion happening on the other side, and even though Kaylah had offered a token with the duke's head on a platter, and Rachel's safe return, they wouldn't budge.

"It's not big enough to waste our time on," they said.

"Maybe when they've proven they can do more," they reasoned.

"We could just as easily be walking into another one of their traps," they warned.

"If you give us her location, we can send some men to check it out ourselves," they tried.

"I don't have an address to give you," Rachel lied. "I'd need to go, too, if you want to find her."

A councilwoman narrowed her eyes. "Why would the princess say you knew how to find her and then not give you any indication of where she would be? Why would it make a difference if you were there?"

Rachel swallowed hard. "The only address I know of is her house in the human world. Maybe she left a clue there that only I would recognize?" Her heart raced. She refused to be cut out of this part of the equation. She wasn't going to send Seeder soldiers to kidnap or kill Kaylah.

The councilwoman gave a polite smile, folding her hands on the table. "I hate to be indelicate, Rachel. But do you know what grooming is? Conditioning?"

Rachel glanced down, her stomach knotting. "I want what's best for our people."

The woman sighed. "I hope that's true. I think it's important to remember who has your best interests at heart. They've prepared you to trust the wrong people from a young age. I understand you might be conflicted."

Looking up and staring at the woman, Rachel remained silent.

"How about we start with a show of trust from our side? We'll dispatch some soldiers to her last known residence in the human world. They'll thoroughly photograph everything and bring it back for you to look at. We'll see if anything comes from that." The woman tilted her head to the side.

Rachel read the faces of those in the room, all focused on her. "Yeah. We can start there. Like I said—I want to help."

Rachel knew she would need to win them over, and she *would* be going.

After being dismissed by the council, she was sent to live with her new family permanently and to take lessons, finding a place to help in village defense. It wasn't that her family wasn't kind, or didn't try, but these people still didn't feel like family. She could hardly even look at Jeff. When she'd originally chosen this life, it was because of the insistence of her human mother, who was now, no doubt, devastated, and a stepfather, who she now knew had orchestrated every moment of her life for the last decade, to lead to her demise. When she had planned on coming here, to be with these people, she'd imagined being part of this wonderful rebellion the prince had painted in her mind, that she could play a part in making things better. And she wouldn't have been alone, like she was now.

Rachel's eighteenth birthday came quickly. Though ... she learned it had never really been her birthday, after all. Technically, the anniversary of her sprouting reveal had already passed—the first day of spring, just like every other Seeder. She sat in bed at the beginning of the day, mulling things over.

No one had even mentioned her 'fake' birthday. Not that she'd expected them to. It was wartime, and the date was just a falsehood created to keep everyone from wondering why a dozen girls in school had the exact same birthday.

Before lessons, she'd be visiting the temple. Before that, she had some extra time to herself.

She'd taken to journaling—trying to process the nightmare she'd just lived through, and trying to find a purpose. Daydreaming of Guillen, she yearned to hear his sweet encouragements. Rachel thought about Kaylah. She hated her. And loved her. She really had to come to terms with her part in all of this. But reason won out. Despite the horrible part Kaylah had played in Rachel's trauma, she couldn't deny that Kaylah had saved her life, that she'd only hurt Rachel because she'd had to.

Rachel frowned. Kaylah had probably remembered it was her birthday, wherever she was. She always did.

Glancing around her new bedroom, Rachel mentally compared her experience thus far to what she'd had described to her. Seeder life was simple, charming. There was a stark contrast between her current surroundings and back home in the human world. Outside, asphalt and cement were replaced with dirt and cobblestones. The plant growth in Seeder territory was nothing short of a paradise. No cars, internet, or any modern technology. The only thing that resembled electricity thus far was the stun gun she'd been subjected to at the palace.

Despite her struggle to feel at home, Rachel was surprised to find how easily she'd transitioned to such a foreign setting. Most Seeder homes were made of wood; they rarely painted anything, instead focusing on the simpler, more natural look of it all. And they weren't a wasteful people—she appreciated that. Her mom might have liked it here. The mom she'd grown up with, at least... The one she'd met upon coming here was nice enough, but still...

Rachel closed her journal with a sigh. She needed to get out of the house. After making her bed, she left her room. In their family housing, the girls and guys each had their own level. Each child had a tiny room, but shared common spaces. It was like a rustic version of dorm rooms. The rest of the house was quiet, everyone off already to fulfill duties, go to classes, spend time with others.

Getting ready for the day, she dressed, then cut a slice of bread off of a fresh loaf one of her sisters had made that morning, slathering it with a honey coconut cream. Grabbing a wooden bowl, Rachel headed outside and walked a few yards to their family garden, then proceeded to pick a mound of raspberries and something a sister had called 'pimple berries'—they were white, sweet, and creamy. Pretty delicious if you could get over their name and the association. She sat at a little outdoor table and did some energy-bathing. A lot of things were tainted, and not ideal at the moment. But the sun was still warm, the air was still fresh, and the energy of the Green Lands was still invigorating.

After enjoying her breakfast, Rachel set out for her daily walk to the temple. She'd been given a certain amount of freedom on things like temple deposits, with her people understanding the trauma she'd been through. But she wanted to do her part—it was worth it.

As she approached the temple, she thought of Guillen again, amidst the heavy traffic of Seeders showing their green eyes and purple hair tips, identifying themselves.

Standing in line, Rachel pondered on the history behind these temples, these walls, this war. Like the current attack, the biological warfare that had poisoned their lands had been a new tactic that took Seeders by surprise. Not only did they lose a whole generation of their women in the Great Poisoning, they'd essentially lost that many men before they'd created the thicket walls in the first place. Fighting had been brutal, and matriarchs from every village had given everything they had to erect these walls, keeping them safe from further attacks. The men had fought valiantly, at a high cost, giving their women the time required to complete such an enormous task.

They were quick thinkers; they were people that had sacrificed so much. Rachel frowned. She wanted to go back and chastise her people for giving up. For settling on the human world as an alternate way to raise half of their kids. Sure, it was a great stopgap. But this had gone on far too long.

She sighed. She had no right to judge them. They'd frozen; they'd just had their way of life ripped from them. They'd done the best they could at the time.

When her turn finally came up, Rachel stood at the jade well, placing her hands on the emerging knotted roots. Closing her eyes, she took a deep breath. Envisioning the energy and warmth in her heart, she pushed it down to her hands to do her part in strengthening the walls. She had to exert extra effort to get the energy to move past her forearms. It initially lingered there, she assumed, probably because of her mind getting distracted. She could only hope that eventually things wouldn't be this hard. That it wasn't just muscle memory, her body remembering the energy should drain to leaves drilled into her arms. She stood straighter, willing the energy to make it all the way down. Feeling it leave her body, she opened her eyes.

Emma, one of her sisters, waved at her from a distance. Rachel joined her, walking in the direction of her classes. Emma was one of the sisters she'd met in the human world with Jeff.

"How are you doing today?" Emma asked.

"About like usual." Rachel gave her a half-smile.

"Did you hear the good news?" Emma asked cheerfully.

Rachel's eyebrows lifted. "No. What?"

"Everyone in the family will finally be back soon! Our last sister is blooming now."

Rachel was a little disappointed it wasn't something bigger. "Cool."

"Then Dad and everyone can be here to help at the borders against the leeches." She smiled.

Rachel bit her tongue. The moment Saff and Devin had guided her home, she'd realized how odd it was for her to be around her own kind. Other than Jeff and a couple of sisters, until arriving at their borders, she'd met significantly more Ivies than Seeders. She'd sworn off using the term 'leeches' for Ivies. Maybe still for people like Soren … but generally speaking, it didn't sit right with her anymore. Not after meeting Guillen, Jon, and Olivia.

Emma was kind, as they all were, in trying to make her feel welcome, trying to lift her spirits. But Rachel started to fear that, even *if* the council came around to joining Unitas, the Seeders might not be willing to reconcile. After generations at war, even *if* they weren't at fault in any way, there was equal hatred. She could only hope that when the time came, her people would be able to welcome peace and show compassion, that they'd stick to their beliefs about wanting to live peacefully, being left alone.

Rachel bolstered her courage. Unlike Jon, she didn't have to carefully tiptoe around with her opinions to help the cause. Even if her fellow Seeders disagreed, no one here would harm her for sympathizing with the Ivies. They might not trust her, and they might ostracize her, but she really didn't care. Even if she wasn't able to fulfill Kaylah's request at the moment, she could be a voice.

"You should stop calling them that," she told Emma. "Let me tell you what I know about how things work over there."

Chapter 26

For now, Rachel focused on lessons with Saff—her assigned welcoming mentor. Like most days, they trained in a small portion of a field near the local Seeder school. The sun was warm, but not nearly as heated as their disagreement.

"I get it, Rachel—I heard about the letter. You've been through a lot and you want to see your mom. But you're going to have to wait until next spring. We need you focusing on healing and fighting, *not* catching a breeze," Saff argued while they took a break.

Rachel shook her head. "You don't get it. One way or another, I'm going. And soon."

Saff shot her hands up, exasperated. "What will you accomplish over there? Can't you see it's just playing into their hands? At best, it's a distraction. At worst, it's a death sentence! What happens if you manage to make it to the human world? It's late in the season—I don't even know that *I* could make it back home!

"But you want to rely on the enemy, who's deceived you before. You have one week before you start to die over there from root rot. *One week*. And that's maybe the merciful route compared to them bringing you back to their lands as a battery in their war machine, all over again." She stared at Rachel, her frustration obviously growing.

Rachel crossed her arms, stone-faced. "If you don't want to train me, that's fine. Even if I have to go by myself, I'm going. I was close enough to catching a breeze before I was brought here. And leaving from here is easier than returning." There was the small detail that Rachel had never been through a Seeder rift. She had no idea how or where to make one ... other than the vague knowledge that Seeders created them in the sky.

Rachel appreciated how much Saff had taught her. She was a great teacher. Not always such a great cheerleader. Saff was beyond stubborn. She was just like the council and every other Seeder Rachel had met thus far.

"Don't be selfish," Saff chastised. "Our people are dying *every day*. We need your help at the temples, as a healer, even in combat," she pleaded.

Rachel was tired of being treated like a foolish child. She'd grown up fast—the harsh realities of this war had hit her just as much as anyone else.

"I'm *trying* to help! Maybe the Ivies are right that *we're* the prideful ones. Not willing to even hear out the princess. I'm willing to risk it, because I believe in this cause. You might not think it's worth it, but you weren't there."

Saff sighed, pausing with a pensive look and tightening her ponytail. "You know how people grow up," she started with a softer tone, "and they have the horror of realizing they just said something that would have come out of their parents' mouths?" She gave a weak smile. "Not my parents, but my brother, Ben. After my cover was compromised, like you, back in the world we grew up in—I took some risks. I put other people in danger, myself in danger. I remember yelling at my brother that we all get to be selfish sometimes. But there are limits. I'll try to carve out some extra time for the training you want, but no one here is going to risk their lives, or yours. Not without more evidence to back up her claims."

Rachel huffed. "What if I'm right? Haven't you ever wished our people tried something different to change things? What if *this* is it?"

Saff gently raised her eyebrows. "Of course I've thought about it. And I'm doing the best I can. We're all doing the best we can. I gave up visiting my human parents this year because of this war, and to help your mom and sisters. I'm trying."

Rachel frowned and nodded, accepting the lean olive twig to possibly train more, taking what she could get.

After another hour of training in energy exercises, Saff dismissed Rachel for the rest of the day. They stretched, and Rachel was the first to walk away. After setting down her water bottle, Saff shook her head, watching Rachel go.

Rachel was brainwashed—plain and simple. She was too naïve to see what the Ivies had done to her. She needed protection, possibly even from herself. This poor girl genuinely trusted the very people who had ruined her life. The proof was right in front of Rachel, but she refused to see the danger. Saff knew that danger—intimately. The Seeders were worn thin. She and her family had experienced Ivy brutality firsthand back in the human world. She wished, more than anything, that she knew how to get through to Rachel.

Having been briefed by the council before being assigned as her mentor, Saff had thought she was up to the challenge of helping this girl find her way. But Rachel was just as stubborn as Saff. The big difference was, Saff hadn't been raised by one of the enemy. She didn't have the blurred lines Rachel did. And Rachel hadn't been here the last year to see the devastation that had fallen on their village, on their entire people. She didn't have a mental tally of the dead running through her mind daily.

Sighing, Saff frowned. She wanted to do right by Rachel. And she knew why she was so protective of her, but couldn't bring herself to mention it. It wasn't just that Rachel was another new return, or because she was from Saff's hometown and home village. The moment Saff had heard that name again—Nuren—she'd realized their fates had been intertwined. In the blur of her own thwarted assassination, one of the attackers had referenced that name. Nuren had been hiding out in her own city the whole time. Saff could have easily been in Rachel's position if her brother, Ben, hadn't saved her.

She had a personal obligation to protect Rachel from further harm.

"Rough day?"

Saff looked to her right, spotting none other than Ben himself. "You could say that."

He crossed the field to join her. "What's up?"

She pointed at Rachel, who was still walking away in the distance, now hugging herself as she approached the crowded lane. "That one will be the death of me."

Ben grinned. "You can handle a classroom full of little boys, but one teenage girl will be your downfall?"

Saff chuckled. "You clearly don't know how much trouble teenage girls are."

He raised both eyebrows, tilting his head to the side. "I was your protector, wasn't I? I think I know *precisely* how much trouble teenage girls can be."

Poking him in the arm, she fought a smile. "But you loved every moment of being my protector!"

Ben busted out laughing. "Whatever you want to believe."

Saff rolled her eyes. "Come on, you. I'm headed home. I assume you're headed that way, too?"

"Yeah, c'mon." He nodded, heading in the direction of their homes. He often dropped her off at her and Devin's cottage on his way to the family home, when their schedules aligned.

Saff snatched up her water bottle from the grass, and followed after him. "You know, she's actually really talented."

"Yeah?"

"Yeah. Then again, she probably had to work at least twice as hard as other Seeder girls have to after they bloom, just to make any progress in her training in the human world."

"I bet." He shuddered. "I can't imagine being poisoned like that."

As they hit the bustling long lane, Saff's anxiety grew. It was so crowded these days.

Ben must have noticed her uneasiness, nudging her arm. "Not exactly the calm path we used to take to skip rocks at Glass Lake, is it?"

Saff looked down, shaking her head. "Why can't things be the way they used to be? Simpler? Happier?" They used to skip rocks and chat all the time, multiple times a week. Even after she'd gotten married.

Wrapping his arm around her as they pressed forward into the sea of bodies, Ben gave her a squeeze. "Things will calm down again. I promise."

Only a few yards down the lane, Ben quietly gasped.

"What?!"

He pointed at a passing purple butterfly. "Do you know what that one's called?" His voice was full of awe.

"No..."

"It's a hope butterfly, Saff. If you smile when one crosses your path, you'll have good luck."

She couldn't resist smiling. "You're such a liar."

He winked. "But it worked."

Graduation was about to happen in the human world. Summer was coming soon. Being deeply rooted in the Green Lands, Seeder women best managed short trips in the spring. Summer was iffy—fall was nigh to impossible—winter had never happened. Not a round trip, at least. But Rachel didn't need a return; she knew she could get back with Ivy help. Assuming she was right, that things were on the up-and-up... For now, she trained and kept her ear to the ground.

After a couple more weeks of intensive one-on-one training with Saff, Rachel was called in again to speak with the war council. They'd already shown her pictures of Kaylah's old place. Unsurprisingly, she didn't have any great revelations they'd found helpful. That was all a bluff on Rachel's part, anyway. All it had done was make Rachel homesick. After further deliberation amongst the senior council members, Rachel was pressed for more details on her time at the palace and her journey back.

Her people didn't completely disregard what she had to offer in the way of ideas and suggestions. Rachel helped, wanting the rest of the girls still held captive at the palace to be freed, but her heart wasn't fully in it. She objected to their proposed strategies, the way they planned to use her information—stressing that her rescue had been facilitated by multiple insiders.

"We may not have an inside man, but we've got the numbers, training, and strategy," the elected war council leader said. "We need to hit them and get our girls back before another one comes to fill Rachel's place. It's our time to take the battle to them. It's our turn to cross the Neutral Woods. We can draw them away from the palace and send in a team to extract them."

With Rachel's protests ignored, her stomach was in knots. Surely they had to know the palace would have added extra security after Nuren's death and Rachel's escape. She remembered the questions posed to her—about her loyalty and priorities, and her own judgment and state of mind. She thought she'd finally seen things clearly after meeting Guillen and Jon. But maybe that had been Kaylah's plan all along, lulling her into another false sense of security.

With more than a little hesitance, Rachel accepted the Seeder council's plan. Not that they cared for her approval. At least the Seeders were finally striking back, not just hiding behind their borders and skulking around in the human world. Even if all they did was get the other girls back from the palace, Rachel could perhaps sleep more peacefully.

<hr>

Another week passed. Battle plans were made and orders issued. As a couple with a female as powerful as Saff, she and Devin could do some damage. But it had been decided that no female Seeders would be approaching the palace for extraction. The possibility of one being captured and falling to the torture they were trying to stop was not a risk the Seeders were willing to take.

Saff had been willing to go. Remembering her high school self—barely surviving Ivy attacks and hardly contributing to her own safety back in the human world—she'd wanted to redeem herself.

With the extraction team being all male, Saff and Devin planned on deploying to the Neutral Woods, especially now that they'd done some recon while collecting Rachel. But plans changed. Saff was asked to manage a triage clinic on the border between their village and the next. They'd just had some new girls return home and she could get them up to speed on healing near the walls. Rachel would join them. Devin was still assigned to the Neutral Woods. Saff's anxiety was through the roof at the thought of Devin working out there without her by his side. But she had to trust her people, and Devin's abilities.

Taking a rare opportunity, Saff and Devin's families gathered for a joint family dinner on Thod and Murial's lot. Their parents were still neighbors and many of the kids had consolidated their spaces, still living in the kids' housing in the back.

Sitting on a picnic blanket next to Devin, Saff surveyed the group of over fifty people. Some of their siblings had brought new spouses or significant others. Her closest sister, Tabatha, winked at Saff from several yards away, then snuck a kiss from her boyfriend. Saff smiled.

While chewing a bite of her buckwheat-and-green-apple salad, Saff's heart swelled at taking in the sight of so many loved ones. Their families had fought off a small army of Ivy assassins that had been after her in high school. Her family and in-laws were capable. They were supportive. They were great. But how long would the statistics swing in their favor, that none of them would be lost?

"You look worried," Devin said, bringing her back from her musings.

She gave him a half-smile. "I'm always worried nowadays."

Frowning sympathetically, he leaned over and gave her a sweet kiss on the cheek. He then whispered in her ear, "Even when we're together?"

She quickly matched his grin. "Together-together? I think I'm sufficiently in the moment for those times."

"Mmm. Then I guess we need more of those times."

Laughing, Saff leaned over and reciprocated with a kiss on his cheek. "With the enormous amounts of free time we have, right?"

Devin frowned again, then spared a glance past Saff. "I wish they'd just get it over with and get married. Then they'd have what you and I get to share."

Turning to look, she knew exactly who he was talking about. Ben and Heather. They sported googly eyes for each other, like any engaged couple would. Saff sighed. At this point, she was starting to agree with Devin. Heather wanted a traditional wedding, not a rushed one. But how long would they have to wait for things to calm down? Finding strength in the council's plans to be more proactive, Saff allowed herself to smile. "Hopefully not long now."

Ben would remain at his post on the Outer Wall. He'd requested to be part of the extraction team. But with older and more experienced Seeders willing to sign up for the elite team, he'd been overlooked. Saff knew how much he wanted to contribute, but she was secretly happy to have him safer, closer to home. Heather would be stationed at the temples—close by for energy deposits and directing traffic, as well as healing.

Every Seeder had a role to play. They were a peaceful people. That was what they'd always wanted. But everyone has their limits, and they had found theirs. The Seeders were ready to end this war.

"It's nice to meet all of you girls. I wish it were under better circumstances," Saff introduced herself to scared girls who had just recently learned their identities and were thrown into a war. The longer the war raged, the more girls were choosing to become human, fearful to commit to something so wholly foreign to them. She couldn't blame them, and probably would have made the same choice if the Green Lands had been in this shape when she'd come of age.

"Knowing how to save a life is not as simple as knowing how to heal. We're going to have a crash course on anatomy, so you'll know what we need to focus on. Don't expend energy and time healing up a flesh wound when someone else is dying from a deep gash or stab. And knowing how to heal is not as important as knowing how to heal *efficiently*."

They dedicated one day in their makeshift clinic made of wood and canvas. There were still wounded trickling in from regular fighting on the borders, so they had some practice, but these girls' lives would never be the same once the real push came.

"Wipe up the blood first, if you can—it'll minimize cleanup time between patients," Saff continued. "Don't put your whole hand on a wound if you can concentrate your energy by covering it with just a finger or two. If they have multiple serious wounds, it's best to let your efforts emanate from a central part of the area. If you're unsure what to do or what the problem is—call for me."

Most of these girls were fresh returns to the Green Lands and had just cancelled their plans to hang out with their besties in the human world for the summer break.

Rachel was visibly stressed. "You're sure we can't convince them to wait a few days, try to at least get extra help or intel from the princess before we make our attack?"

"That defeats the element of surprise. We're doing this on our own."

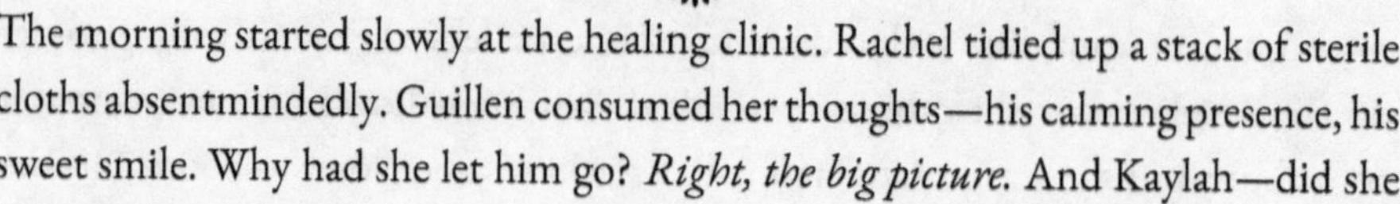

The morning started slowly at the healing clinic. Rachel tidied up a stack of sterile cloths absentmindedly. Guillen consumed her thoughts—his calming presence, his sweet smile. Why had she let him go? *Right, the big picture.* And Kaylah—did she know by now that her request was being denied? Would she extend the same offer after this strike?

Rachel's stomach growled loudly, and she regretted having skipped breakfast. She'd struggled to eat and sleep lately, her anxiety growing as the time was fast approaching for what she considered an ill-prepared Seeder strategy.

Saff scanned the triage tent, packed with cots for the wounded, and several nervous girls. Closing her eyes and taking a deep breath, she tried to prioritize. She couldn't help these girls, couldn't save soldiers' lives, if her mind was out in the Neutral Woods with Devin, was out with all of her family members at their positions. She needed to be here, in the moment.

She didn't have to stew in her thoughts for long. The wounded started to file in, and Saff busied herself with assigning girls to the incoming soldiers. Since the learning clinic was full of new girls, it wasn't the first location for the severely wounded to be sent to. Ideally, women in the woods could heal as needed. But some were brought home and healed at the walls, and once things piled up, the clinic saw more serious cases. Green folk didn't have huge industrial manufacturing plants. They didn't have nuclear bombs. They didn't use planes. But the lack of advanced technology had never stopped a man from taking a life.

The return through neutral territory that had taken Rachel and her companions well over a week could be covered by healthy, trained troops faster. The freshly deployed Seeder troops had no need to get new clothes, or hide to avoid being spotted. They would take out anyone in their path. Those in the woods were starting to draw more and more troops to the Seeder borders.

Saff's heart would only ever calm at night, each time Devin would come home alive. He was out of action for a couple of days at one point, healing after a particularly nasty ambush, but he went back out there fighting for his people as soon as possible. Saff thought fondly of something he'd told her before she'd left his side to return to the Green Lands years ago. 'Nothing is more important to Seeders than family.'

Daily, she counted her blessings, grateful for her family, and that they'd been spared thus far. Many families in her village weren't so lucky. And her dad and brothers were almost all stationed in the woods or at one of the walls—none of them marched on the Ivy palace. With no women allowed to take on the palace, there would be no healing for those men. Those who had signed up knew what the risks were.

To ensure everyone was easily accounted for, and so information could disseminate quickly amongst their families, Saff and Devin's siblings would stop by their parents' houses first, before heading to their individual homes at the end of each day.

Shuffling along in exhaustion, Saff made her way to Thod and Murial's house. It was later than usual and she expected some of her siblings to already have reported in for the night. They were waiting to hear of a triumphant return any time now, to see the War Vines breaching their walls shrink and recede. Every time she twisted that doorknob, she hoped for good news and prayed away the bad.

Saff opened the door at her in-laws' house. Devin's mom and one of his brothers were huddled in a corner. At Saff's arrival, they turned to look at her, revealing Heather—covered in blood, sobbing.

Saff stood frozen in place. "Where's Devin? Where's Ben?"

Devin came bounding from another room.

"Where's Ben?!" Her voice trembled.

No one spoke up.

Devin grabbed her and pulled her in tight; she fought to get out of his arms, thrashing with what little energy she had left.

"No! Where is he? I want to help! I can help!" she screamed while fighting for air.

"It's too late," Devin whispered in her ear. "I'm sorry, Saff. It's too late."

She crumpled to the floor, heaving. "It's a mistake. He's fine. It can't be Ben. He's smart. And strong. And... It can't be."

Devin held her, quietly shedding tears of his own. "I'm so sorry." (bb)

Chapter 27

Saff lay in bed, restless. In shock. Still half expecting Ben and Heather to drop by sometime that week. But that wouldn't happen. It couldn't. Ben was dead. She tried to control her breathing.

He was dead. Nothing could change that. His burial was already scheduled for the next day. More tears wetted her pillow as she dwelled on her memories of him. Meeting him when he was undercover in the human world, pretending to be her foster brother. Him saving her life from Ivy assassins, more than once. Skipping rocks at a local lake after they'd both returned to the Green Lands. His proposal to Heather...

Saff sniffled, struggling not to spiral in a sea of hopelessness. The sun was just starting to rise. Maybe going to work that day would help distract her? But she didn't want to be at that clinic, surrounded by blood, injuries, and death. Her mind lingering on Ben, on his injuries, on her work at the clinic, Saff's thoughts turned to Rachel. What was it Rachel had said about going to meet with the leech princess? 'Haven't you ever wished our people tried something different to change things? What if this is it?'

Wiping away her tears, Saff slipped out of bed, quietly opening a dresser drawer to change.

"What are you doing?" Devin asked, now awake.

She turned to face him after pulling a shirt over her head. "Um... Just going to walk to the clinic."

He frowned, his eyes starting to glow green. "We're allowed to take the day off. I... I think we should spend the day together."

Swallowing hard, she paused. "Yeah, I agree. I just…" She looked away, grabbing a long skirt to change into. "I just want to make sure the girls at the clinic know I won't be there for a couple days."

Devin rolled over in bed to follow her movement as she crossed the room. "Other people can tell them. Come back to bed."

Saff didn't respond as she finished changing. She wasn't accustomed to lying to Devin. After putting her hair up in a ponytail, she sat on the bed next to him, forcing a small smile. "I really need to go for a walk, okay? Alone. Just something to clear my mind. And I'll stop by the temple on the way there." She caressed his face. "I promise. I won't be gone long."

"Okay," he whispered.

Leaning down, she gave him a soft kiss. "I'll be back before you know it. Love you."

"Love you, too."

Leaving the cottage in the direction of the clinic, Saff avoided eye contact with everyone in her path. *This time tomorrow, I'll be getting ready for a … burial.* She'd never been to a funeral in the human world, and had never attended one in the Green Lands of someone so close to her. She picked up the pace, sniffling and wiping away tears as she walked. How was she supposed to handle being at the graveyard? See Ben like that? See their families like that? She didn't think she could bear any of it.

⁕

Rachel scraped herself out of bed and made her way to work for the day. The year-round utopia of the realm was dimmed by the downtrodden spirits of those she passed, and the neglect of aesthetic attention Seeders usually gave to their homes and streets. Yards were unkempt. Flowers—not necessary for food—lay wilted in flowerbeds. This had not been in the brochure. As she arrived at the clinic, it was quieter than usual. Saff was alone, flicking Seeder darts into the wall.

"Where are the other girls?" Rachel asked.

Saff turned, her eyes puffy, jaw clenched.

Rachel tilted her head, worried, nervous. "Did something happen? Is there news from the palace?"

"Do you really trust your friend? That she would still meet with us? That she can guarantee we would get home safely?"

"Yeah… I do. Did the council change their mind?"

"And you realize going could mean a death sentence for us? If we don't come back within a week, we rooted women die in the human world? And we might not be able to come home on our own this late in the year?"

Rachel recalled what she'd been taught about the limitations of Seeder women's powers, their reliance on the energy of the Green Lands. "Yes, I understand how it works."

"And you're sure you know how to find her?"

Scanning Saff's face, Rachel hesitated. Why did it seem like Saff might be willing to help now? What could the council have done to tick her off? Cautiously, she answered, "Yes."

Saff took a deep, shaky breath, then blew it out. "Then go home. Rest up. You and I are going tomorrow."

Rachel's heart lit with hope. But this wasn't exactly how she'd expected it to go. "Just you and me? *None* of the leaders? I know you're respected in our village, but—"

Saff raised her eyebrows. "Do you want to go?"

"Yes."

"Then let's make the introduction. Go home," Saff ordered. "We're leaving at first light. Best to keep this between us for now." She followed Rachel out, walking back to their village together.

Saff hardly slept a wink that night. She and Devin had been given a couple of days off to mourn Ben's loss. She lay in bed with Devin's arm wrapped around her. Exhausted, he slept peacefully.

She mulled over her plan, her promise to Rachel. Saff had gotten to know Rachel plenty over the last few weeks of training and at the healing clinic. Rachel knew more than she was letting on to the council. And Saff had been right about that, with Rachel willingly taking her to the Ivy princess now. Not yet daring to ask herself if this was the wisest decision, Saff had to ask herself if she could even keep her promise.

Rooted Seeder women their age could only manage one round trip to the human world each year, preferably in spring. It seemed like such an arbitrary restriction. After learning from Devin years ago that Seeders didn't understand all of the aspects of their powers, especially rifts, Saff had asked around and done some research. It was true—it was physically impossible for a rooted female Seeder to make a second trip through a rift in a year.

All accounts she'd heard gave the same answer. The women could obviously still catch a breeze all they wanted. They could harness the energy of the realm and fly with ease. They could even *open* a rift. They just couldn't manage to travel through it. Doubting girls tried all the time. All reports followed the same general description. After entering a second rift, the girls experienced a crushing pain, centered in their chests—and instead of emerging in the human world, they just ... kept flying, in a straight path, still in the Green Lands. Time and time again, after each approach, it was the same. They were tied to the Green Lands, the energy that flowed there. No one quite knew how.

The only sliver of hope Saff now held was that she hadn't ever foolishly made a second yearly attempt before. And she wasn't exactly the average Seeder. While she was tired of hearing it, the fact remained—Saff was different. She could harness almost as much energy as a fully-rooted matriarch. Having the extra power, but not the same limitations as a matriarch, maybe, just maybe, she could slip through the crack. Because just like their ties to the energy of the Green Lands, no one had a concrete explanation for Saff's ability to harness that extra power.

Yes, she'd concluded that it had something to do with an immunity to Ivy poison, but there were too many unknowns, too few stories to corroborate.

Rolling over in bed, Saff admired the man she loved. Even if she were *capable* of an impossible feat like this, she had to ask herself if she *should* be doing it. She'd done her best to follow orders in the Green Lands. Her blunders in the human world after her botched bloom had proven that she needed to trust her people. Ben himself had even challenged her to try and keep a few rules, since she'd been such a thorn in his side. But then again, she had been right about her best friend, Zach, being a human. Even if no one else trusted her judgment, she wasn't *completely* off her rocker to entertain this plan.

Devin shifted slightly in bed, still asleep. Saff frowned—he would never approve. He had tried to stop her from her earlier visit to the human world. But he himself had said years ago that he wished they could find a way to end this war— he just didn't know how. And things weren't nearly as bad back then.

Saff moved closer, placing a tender kiss on his lips. He drew a deep breath, barely cracking a smile. He reciprocated with a sweet, sleepy kiss, before letting out a soft moan and wrapping his arm and leg around her. His breathing slowed again as he promptly fell back asleep.

Ben and Heather deserved this. They were some of the best people Saff knew. And Ben shouldn't have died at the Outer Wall. More casualties were expected to tally from those marching on the Ivy palace. The Outer Wall was much more dangerous than the Inner Wall inside their territory, but he still shouldn't have died. Seeders weren't safe anymore—not even in their own lands.

Something had to change.

If Ben had been willing to give his life for Saff, when he came to her rescue more than once in the human world, and for his people, then maybe it was Saff's turn.

And that was what this was. An impossible plan. A suicidal one.

She thought of how mad Ben would be. How livid he had been when they were teenagers in the human world and she would defy his orders, when all he was trying to do was protect her. But she was doing this *for* Ben. She was doing this for all of her brothers and sisters, and for her husband, and Heather, and her village, and everyone. She owed it to them. This much she could do.

What exactly she planned to do if she made it over, she wasn't sure. Maybe this princess could actually help. Maybe it would feel good to kill a leech right now. Maybe the leech princess would make a good bargaining tool.

She could figure things out later. But one thing was certain—Saff knew there would be no coming back for her unless this really paid off. Even if she could make it through a second rift that year, there couldn't possibly be a way back for her on her own. The energy in the human world was significantly weaker. And within a week, fatal root rot would set in. She had a week to live in the human world, maybe less. But Rachel was convinced the princess would keep her promise, helping them return through a rift with minimal energy drain. Even if Saff decided to trust this princess, would it work for Saff? This was all just an experiment. A potentially deadly one.

Setting her resolve, Saff savored Devin's embrace, not allowing herself to drift off again. A couple of hours later, she carefully pried herself from his grasp and got dressed. She penned a letter to him, leaving it on the kitchen table. Her heart heavy, she grabbed one last thing from a ceramic pot—a debit card. All Seeder families kept investments in the human world for visits. For burner phones, food, taxis. Slipping the card into her pants pocket, Saff looked around her cottage, her eyes glazing over. This was her home. Her family. Her people.

Under the light of the moon, Saff quietly closed the door behind her, heading down the dirt lane to meet up with Rachel.

Despite Saff's attempts to make time for Rachel's requests on how to catch a breeze, time and energy had become increasingly limited resources. Rachel approached their agreed-upon meeting spot—a small park nearly halfway between their homes. Rachel hugged herself. She was a bundle of nerves. Excited to visit home, to see Kaylah, to go through her first Seeder rift. Worried she hadn't trained enough, or could be wrong about this decision, or that Saff was somehow setting her up. What if the council had put her up to this as a way to prove that Rachel had been lying about knowing how to contact Kaylah?

Saff was already at the park, pacing. Rachel glanced around in the dark—it appeared they were alone.

"You're ready?" Saff asked.

Rachel nodded. "I don't have a family card yet. I couldn't really ask for one without them knowing I was planning to leave."

"That was smart. We'll be fine with mine." Saff studied Rachel's face. "You promise you know how to get in touch with the princess? Quickly?"

Rachel hesitated. "Yes."

Saff's eyes narrowed slightly. "Because if you don't, you'd better tell me now."

Rachel rolled her eyes. "I know how to. Are you sure you can guide me through? Didn't you already make your yearly trip?"

Saff tucked her hands into her pockets. "Yes. And yes."

"How's that possible? Did they lie to me about that? We can actually go back more often?"

Saff swallowed. "No. But I have a theory."

Rachel's heart dropped. "A theory? I guess I don't really need you to show me around on that side." She glanced at Saff's pockets, thinking of the card. Even if Saff only guided her to their rifting space, Rachel didn't know where to go from there. She didn't know how to find her bearings. And she had no human money. "But it's probably best I don't go alone. What's your theory?"

Saff rubbed her forehead. "Either I'll prove my theory right and we make it, or I'll be wrong and you're left to make yet another plea to the council." She raised her eyebrows. "If you're worried, I could go alone. If you give me the address and information you have."

Rachel shook her head. "We're going together."

"Okay. Let's do this."

Approaching their chosen takeoff location, Saff allowed herself to question her plan once more.

Her mind drifted to the last time she'd seen Ben, their last conversation. She envisioned herself standing in a graveyard later that day. Her knees weakened. She could barely breathe.

She'd made her choice.

Biting her tongue, she attempted to stave off fresh tears. She opened her eyes wide, not daring to wipe at the coating that blurred her eyes, fearing she might draw Rachel's attention.

Once she'd finally regained her composure, she cautioned Rachel. "Whether or not this works, I may get hurt going through this rift. Don't freak out—I'm sure I'll be fine."

Rachel nervously side-eyed her. "Are you sure this is a good idea? Would I somehow be at risk, too?"

Saff thought about it for a moment. "You would only get hurt if I didn't make it through. So, I'll form the rift, then fly through. Hang back. If I just keep flying, then don't go. If I disappear, then it's safe to go through." She hated outright lying to Rachel. There really wasn't any risk of Rachel getting hurt, but Saff wanted to make sure she didn't go alone, should Saff's hopes prove to be in vain.

Rachel cautiously nodded.

Saff had Rachel take off first. She was a pretty shaky beginner, not having been able to train nearly as much as she should have. Some of that was on Saff. But really, the Ivies were the ones to blame.

Saff leapt into the air, also catching a breeze and speeding to catch up. After a long journey to the closest rifting space, Saff gave the signal to Rachel to slow down and hang back. Saff's heart beating a mile a minute, her stomach twisted into knots. Bolstering her courage, she waved her hand in the air; a ripple in the sky signified a rift had been formed. Clenching her jaw in anticipation, she flew into it.

Chapter 28

$\mathcal{S}$aff flew through the rift she'd created. Time passed slower. Panic set in with a telltale pain in her chest. The tether of her rooted energy was trying to keep her in the Green Lands. The crushing pain left her unable to breathe. The pain experienced by rooted females trying to leave too often, more than once a year. The pain felt by any fully-rooted matriarch that tried to leave the Green Lands at all.

Fighting with all she had, Saff pushed extra energy to her heart and ripped through the rift. Gasping, she plummeted.

Realizing she was clutching her chest instead of balancing in the breeze, Saff straightened herself out. Disoriented by the pain, the wind rushing past her, and the turbulence experienced from different energy levels between the worlds, Saff grunted, forcing herself to steady. Before dropping dangerously low, she recovered her trajectory.

Saff flew higher, focusing on her breathing as the pain lingered. The change in scenery and ambient energy was undeniable—she'd made it to the human world again. And she was on borrowed time.

Rachel's anxiety peaked before she approached the rift—her first Seeder rift. Saff had made it through just fine, from what she could tell. The journey had already been difficult on Rachel with so little practice, and it would be harder on the other side without the extra energy boost, but she circled back with resolve to the rift Saff had created.

Making it through with ease, Rachel was immensely grateful to not have an Ivy sucking her life-force to take her through a tree rift. The kind of rifts Seeders made in the air were so easy, as long as you could endure the flight.

Having emerged from the rift, Rachel was jostled about by the difference in energy and the sudden shift in wind direction. She focused and quickly recovered her balance. But there was a problem—Saff was nowhere to be seen.

Rachel's eyes darted around. Saff hadn't risen higher. She hadn't veered off to the side. Looking down, Rachel's eyes grew wide in horror. Saff was dropping in a freefall.

Her breathing rapid, Rachel frantically tried to figure out how to help. But it wasn't like she could catch Saff. Rachel was barely balancing on her own. Slowly and carefully, she shifted her trajectory down, in case she could somehow think of a way to help. Not much later, relief washed over her as Saff balanced herself and slowly climbed. Saff was grimacing, her face red.

Rachel followed Saff's nod for directions, trailing after her.

Between the time difference and extended travel, the sun was just coming down as they landed in a park of their human-world hometown. Rachel's landing was far from graceful—she panicked and thrust energy to her arms and legs to strengthen them, trying to avoid breaking anything. Curling into a ball at the last moment, she tumbled on the ground. Only bruised and a bit shaken, Rachel opened her eyes and scanned the grass for Saff.

Lying on her back with her hands on her chest, Saff was halfway across the park, not moving. Rachel jumped up and ran to her.

Saff was breathing hard, staring up toward the sky.

"Are you okay?" Rachel asked, checking her for injuries.

Saff winced, shifting her weight. "Yeah. Oodles of fun."

"What happened? And how did you even do it? You're sure you're okay?"

Giving her a forced smile, Saff sat up with a groan, then rubbed her chest. "Yeah. Just some bad turbulence."

Rachel raised an eyebrow in disbelief. "Right. Well, I guess mine wasn't so bad, just a few seconds later..." She offered a hand, helping Saff stand.

"Thanks." Saff brushed herself off. "Let's get going. We won't have time to see your mom, but you could call her."

Rachel frowned, hoping they might still be able to carve out time. But she understood the mission.

They entered a nearby gas station and asked for directions to the address Rachel had memorized. With Saff's debit card, they bought a burner phone and called a cab.

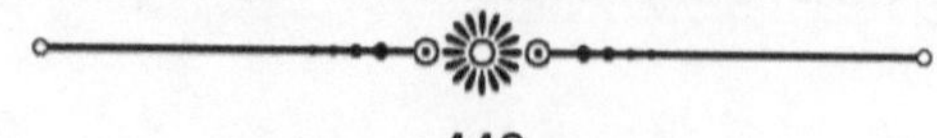

Rachel's palms were sweaty as their cab pulled up to the address she'd provided. The council could be right. This could be a trap.

"Alright, this is us. 13310 North Maplewood," Saff said. "Do you recognize this place?"

It was a standard-looking small house, likely just a couple of bedrooms, on the outskirts of their hometown.

"No. But let's check it out." Rachel swallowed nervously. "Hopefully they don't mind visitors this late at night." She'd never seen this place before and had no idea why Kaylah would have directed her there.

Knocking on the door, they glanced over their shoulders to watch out for suspicious characters. Lights turned on in the house and the door unlocked. A tall man with dark hair, looking to be in his forties, answered. Rachel didn't recognize him, and a momentary glance in Saff's direction confirmed that she didn't either.

"Can I help you?" he asked.

"Yeah, we're looking for a friend." Rachel tried to read his expression.

His face hinted at nothing. "Do you have a name?"

He could have meant Rachel's name or Kaylah's name, but Rachel assumed it had something to do with the coffee cup clue. "Itiner?"

He nodded in recognition. "Come in." Offering them a seat in his front room, he pulled out a small lockbox from a closet. "Will there be any more in your party?"

Rachel was just winging it at this point. "Um … Not with us. Just the people we're coming to meet, if that's what you mean?"

Not looking up, he continued to work on the lock. "Just want to make sure I'm not denying anyone else that trickles in, that should be pointed in that direction."

Rachel shook her head. "No, that was specifically given to me. No one else will be using it that I know of." She surveyed the room while waiting. A set of tall shelves was jam-packed with books. The furniture was a matching set. It felt as cozy as any other home she'd been in; it didn't exude any nefarious vibes.

"Alright." He reached into the lockbox, sorting through small pieces of paper.

❊

"So, we're not meeting anyone here?" Saff asked, itching to get this over with and go home. The aching in her chest had mostly subsided. No matter how much she loved her human parents, she'd never try another trip like this again. Now she just had to see if she'd die from root rot, or if this was all an elaborate trap.

"Afraid not, it's safer for the network to have gatekeepers," he answered.

"And that network is…?" Saff asked.

He looked up, visibly suspicious at Saff's line of questioning.

※

"You can ignore her. She's new," Rachel responded, shooting a look at Saff to shut up. "But I *am* curious. I don't recognize you, are you a..." Rachel hoped he'd fill in the blank.

"A friend in Unitas?" He grinned.

Rachel smiled. "That's enough for me."

He handed Rachel a piece of paper. "Do you have a car?"

"No, but we can call the cab back," Saff replied.

"Okay. Just be prepared—this one's a two-hour drive."

Saff called the cab company again, and the man patiently waited with them until their car arrived. They tried carrying on with painfully awkward small talk, probably all wanting to be aloof given the circumstances. Once the cab pulled up, they bid him farewell, having never even learned the mystery man's name.

"You have to admit, this is kind of cool: secret meetings in the night and whatnot," Rachel remarked as they walked to the car. It felt good to be home, if she could really claim either world as home. She already missed the energy of the Green Lands, but the familiarity of the human world, mingled with adrenaline, was invigorating.

※

"Annoying is more like it." Saff was in no mood for games; she'd missed Ben's burial for this. She was risking her life for this. She remembered how she hadn't been much younger than Rachel when she, too, had found a thrill in covert operations, sneaking away with her boyfriend for training, and to relay information to the Seeder network. Those were different times.

As they ducked into the cab, it registered how her comment had hurt Rachel. Rachel's smile was gone, her posture deflated. She sat back and stared out the window after giving the driver the new address. Saff looked down, rubbing the knee of her jeans. The reality of her choice to come on this mission was starting to settle in. The rifting pain in her heart was replaced by an unwelcome yet familiar one. *Devin. My parents. What did I just do?*

And she'd just lost her job. A job she loved. Not that Seeder career positions were handled the same way they were amongst the humans she'd grown up around. But she was outright disobeying council orders. She was leading one of her mentees into potential danger. No matter what happened with this mission, there would be unpleasant repercussions for Saff. *I'm an idiot.*

But she couldn't allow herself to dwell on doubt and regrets right now. She couldn't take it back. The only way was forward. She glanced at Rachel, who was still frowning at the window. "Sorry."

Without moving a muscle, Rachel whispered, "It's fine."

After two hours of driving through the night, they arrived at the new address. Rachel hopped out of the car first, ready for the next step. This was a much larger off-white house with a two-car garage and a tidy yard—though nothing flashy. It took longer for someone to turn on the lights and answer the door at this house, but it was well worth the wait.

Greeted by a familiar blond, Rachel's jaw dropped. "Eric?!"

"Come in!" He rushed them in and closed the door behind them. "Rachel, it's so good to see you!" He swooped her up in a big hug and spun her around. "Gosh, it's good to see your face! Kaylah hoped you'd be here sooner. I was worried about you."

Rachel beamed. "So, you know? All of it? Her name? Who she is? What we are?" She furrowed her brow. "Wait, what are you?"

He grinned. "Humans can be in Unitas, too, ya know. You'd be surprised."

"So, everything's good with you two? Is she here?"

"No." He pulled a cell from his pocket. "Let me send a text and the network will get word to her that you're here. She's pretty busy."

She waited for him to send it off. "Sorry, let me introduce my travel companion."

He extended his hand to Saff with a smile, and she shook it. "We've met. She was at your mom's place after you and Meg—er, Kaylah went missing, and... Gosh, Rach, I'm sorry about Rob and David. She told me about all that."

Rachel tucked her hands into her pockets. "Thanks. But I'd be happy never hearing those names again."

"Done. You won't hear them from me. Do you guys need something to eat? Or are you ready to rest up? I understand you've got to be tired, and we keep some beds ready at all times."

Rachel looked back to Saff. "I'd love to get caught up first, if that's okay."

Saff stood against the wall, scrutinizing the room. "I don't know how comfortable I'd feel sleeping here. Maybe we should get a hotel room for the night, and we'll come back when you call to tell us she's arrived."

Eric frowned. "You've met me. This is a safe space, a neutral space."

Saff met his frown. "No offense, but we don't know each other *that* well. And I don't know about neutral anything—you or this place. Your girlfriend is the Ivy princess? And who pays the mortgage here?"

He cocked his head to the side. "I care about Kaylah, and I care about Rachel. Maybe you didn't get the memo, but Kaylah's not exactly in the good graces of her parents right now."

Rachel furrowed her brow at Saff. "We came here to meet. Like you said: we can't waste time. We should be here when she arrives, not wasting time finding hotels and calling cabs."

Saff sighed, looking exhausted. "Fine. I'm not letting Rachel out of my sight, so I guess we're staying up for a little while."

Eric gave them a warm smile. "I'm all for it. Let me grab you both some water and get a coffeepot on. Take a seat."

Returning with water, he placed it on the coffee table in the humble living room. A pair of framed nature scene paintings hung on the wall as the only decor in the room. The furniture was a basic matching set that could easily be found at a standard department store. "It's not much, but it's home for now."

"You have to tell me everything, seriously!" Rachel gushed. "You're the *last* person I expected to see."

He laughed. "Is that because I'm human? Or because a princess broke my heart?"

"But you're obviously okay now..."

"Yeah. She wanted to make sure they wouldn't come after me when she went missing. She needed to put some distance between us. When she came back, she explained everything to me. To say it was all a shock is the understatement of the century."

Rachel picked from the millions of questions streaming through her mind. "How was graduation, and what are you doing out here in the middle of nowhere?"

"Can't you tell? I'm *hundreds* of miles away at school right now, taking summer courses." He winked. "If it's important to Kaylah, it's important to me. I can take classes remotely while I help."

Rachel sipped water. "And you said there are humans in the cause? Have you met both of our kind? What about the guy that gave us this address?"

Eric scratched his chin, settling down more comfortably on the couch. "His business is his own, so I can't answer that one. But humans, yeah—you can't send your sons and daughters to be raised and cared for, and then expect us to not care what happens to them. Or, you know, date and befriend us, and expect us to not worry when we learn the truth. We can only do so much on this side, but we're willing to help.

"There are actually several Ivies I've met on this side, too. Like Kaylah's parents. Well, I guess not really her parents, right? Nathan and Ginger. She sent them away for their safety when she went missing, but my understanding is they're actively involved right now. That couple was hand-selected by the queen and king to be her guardians while she lived over here. When she had a change of heart, they followed after her."

The news brought so much renewed hope to Rachel; she prayed it was reaching Saff as well. "So, is that it? You hold down the fort here, for a meeting place?"

Eric shrugged. "That's mostly it for now. It's a safe house for defectors, but Kaylah suspects it might get busier once the alliance is made with your people."

✸

Saff smiled and shook her head.

"What's that about?" he asked.

"Oh, it's just funny. Last time I was in a safe house, I was in high school and a pair of Ivies had just tried to murder me. I never thought I'd see the day where Seeders and Ivies might consider sharing a safe house. And with humans in the loop."

"Sometimes seeing is believing, right?" he said.

"I guess we'll see," Saff replied, still thoroughly uneasy. "How long until she arrives?"

"Sorry, I can't answer that. It can take some time for someone to track her down in the field and for her to get back here."

"Well, maybe we should go to sleep," Rachel offered.

Eric showed them to a room down the hall. "A couple of beds in here for you two. Decoration isn't exactly a priority around here, but the beds are amazing. Humans may be limited in what they can do to help, but they do know how to open their wallets."

The guest room featured a window with blinds and a full-size mirror. The bedspreads were identical navy blue, and the pillows appeared welcoming and fluffy. He gestured to a large built-in wardrobe. "Lots of comfy clothes options, and there's a chute in the bathroom down the hall to the downstairs laundry room." He pointed to another room down the hallway. "That's mine. Wake me up if you need anything at all, day or night—I'm here to help."

"Thanks so much," Rachel said with a smile.

"Yes, thank you," Saff added.

"Sure thing," he said. "Oh yeah, and any toiletries you might need are in the bathroom, and have at anything in the kitchen if you get hungry."

Saff picked out a bed while Rachel gave Eric another huge hug.

Chapter 29

Saff and Rachel had both hoped to see Kaylah first thing in the morning. But they awoke to just the three of them, Eric playing their gracious host.

Saff's patience was growing thin while waiting. Having slept horribly did nothing to help the situation. She refused to admit that she regretted the decision to come already; her whole family had to be worried. And she still didn't know how root rot would affect her on a second trip. So far, she felt pretty much the same as previous trips, but she didn't have any desire to play chicken with an unknown deadline.

"It'll be okay," Rachel said, taking a break from getting caught up with Eric. "She'll be here."

Saff paced the open-concept entryway connecting the living room, kitchen, dining room and hallway. "She does understand we have a timeline, right?"

"She does," Eric assured her. "And I have emergency contacts—human and Ivy. If you needed an Ivy-assisted exit at any time, I could get you one in less than a day."

Saff was somewhat pacified to hear that, from a source she hoped was, at least, benign. And to hear it was a well-coordinated operation was promising. But it wasn't like she was anywhere close to trusting the leech princess. "And if things don't go her way?"

Rachel's tone became less friendly. "Would you calm down? She's been more professional and hospitable than any of *our* kind have been, while extending an olive branch."

Another night and day passed. Saff had tried to go for a walk to ease her anxiety. Had tried to appreciate a ladybug landing on a nearby flower when she spent some time in the backyard. Had tried to take a nap. But nothing helped. She was wound tighter than a clock.

"We have people dying back home that could use our help," Saff complained. "We're not going to wait much longer."

Eric attempted to alleviate the tension. "It should be any time now."

Rachel woke the next morning to Saff sitting on her own bed, ready for the day.

"We're wasting our time," Saff said.

"It's worth waiting for. Maybe we can get Eric to reach out for a better update," Rachel suggested while getting dressed.

Not long after they left their room, Eric came out of his to join them in the dining room. "Coffee's already on. Any requests for breakfast from you lovely ladies? Anything fancier than muffins and yogurt today?"

Rachel yawned. "They're all vegetarians back there. Even the Ivies. I would love you forever if you had bacon and eggs."(cc)

He poked around in the fridge. "I can actually make that happen."

"I love you, Eric. Remind me to kiss your feet."

He chuckled. "Maybe you should start with some coffee; sounds like you could use it."(dd)

❋

Saff poured them each a cup and took a sip, cringing at the bitterness. She'd never really been a fan of the stuff, even if it was half sugar and creamer, and it wasn't likely to calm her nerves...

A shower turned on down the hallway, causing Saff and Rachel to share a glance.

"Is someone else here?" Saff furrowed her brow.

"Yeah, Kaylah got in late last night. We thought it best to let everyone rest. She'll be out in a few." A frying pan sizzled as he cracked eggs into it and got bacon going in another pan. Once the shower turned off, he went into his room for a couple of minutes before reappearing. "She'll just be a few more minutes. I let her know you're both awake."

❋

Eric was making up some toast while Rachel gratefully sipped coffee; Saff had set down her coffee cup, now clutching a glass of water at the table. Eric's bedroom door opened and Kaylah stood in the doorway, pulling her hair into a messy bun like she always used to. It was weird for Rachel to see her looking this way— knowing she was a princess. And the last time she'd seen her, Kaylah had worn all black and carried a blood-covered machete. Kaylah was now dressed in cute and trendy clothes like she always had in high school, her makeup looking sharp.

⁜

Saff's first impression of Kaylah wasn't at all fond. Seeders knew the names and insignias of Ivy royalty, but they'd never known their code names or what they looked like. Save the likeness of the actual queen and king, the rest remained in the shadows, which made sense with how well they had pulled off this kind of operation and attack. Saff looked at Kaylah and saw a ridiculous spoiled teenager.

Kaylah closed her eyes and inhaled deeply, placing her hand over her heart. "There's nothing like bacon to bring people together."

Eric walked up to her, holding a spatula and giving her a kiss. "I'm almost done, then I can make a run to the store if you ladies would like some privacy in your discussions."

Kaylah pulled him in for another kiss. "As long as you're not gone *too* long."

He grinned, returning to the kitchen.

⁜

Rachel wanted to run up and hug her, but Kaylah seemed hesitant, unsure.

"Kaylah, this is Saff. She's from my village. Saff, this is Princess Kaylah."

"Nice to meet you," Kaylah said, nodding with the poise Rachel expected of a princess. "Should we eat some breakfast and talk about how things are going to go today?"

Saff glared. "I think we've wasted enough time already."

Kaylah raised her eyebrows. "Okay... I just figured we were waiting for more of your people to show up?"

"Um..." Rachel's expression was apologetic. "This is going to be it."

Kaylah pressed her lips into a straight line. "I won't lie, I hoped for more. Especially after how poorly your attack on the palace went."

Kaylah's demeanor immediately changed. She was wide-eyed, moving a hand to her pocket, the other wrist being positioned directly in front of her, facing out. She was staring directly at Saff. Rachel looked to Saff to see why Kaylah had reacted that way. Saff was livid—green eyes, yellow hair, blades extended, fists balled up.

Kaylah's nostrils flared, her tone deep and threatening. "I would caution you to watch how you posture yourself. I may not have brought guards on this visit, but I'm not a dainty little palace girl." Kaylah's eyes darted from Saff's face to her hands. "Even if you have something up your sleeve, I wouldn't risk your only shot here."

All green folk knew darts were inherently a male trait, but once a Seeder was old enough and mated, the females gained that lethal weapon as well, with a simple flick of the wrist. And there was no way of knowing who had that ability.

"Can you give us a minute, Kaylah?" Rachel gulped and stood, moving between them.

Kaylah kept her eyes trained on Saff. "Sure. Eric and I would love to take a short stroll."

Eric had quietly stayed in the kitchen. He turned off the stove and strode over to Kaylah, taking her by the hand. Walking behind her, between the women, he escorted her out the front door. "Ten minutes?" he asked over his shoulder.

"Make it fifteen," Rachel said.

Saff kept her eyes on Kaylah as they left.

Rachel turned her frustration on Saff as soon as the door shut. "I knew I should have questioned your motives when you agreed to come, but I didn't really care. But what the hell is wrong with you?"

Saff was seething, pointing at the front door. "Is this a joke? Look at her. How am I supposed to take anything she says seriously? I was right that this would be a waste of time!"

"You've got to be kidding me. Because, what? She's not wearing formal clothes and a flipping tiara? That's what matters here?"

"She kept us waiting while our families could be dying, and she *casually* mentions things are going badly back home? She's a spoiled brat that doesn't give a *shit* about our people!"

Rachel's jaw dropped. She shifted in her seat to face Saff better. "Seriously. What's going on?"

Saff clenched her jaw.

"Is your husband okay? Did you lose someone? Is that what this is about?"

Saff looked as though she would burst into tears.

Rachel frowned. "You should have said something. We could have handled this differently. I'm sorry." She wrapped her arms around Saff.

Saff initially stayed stiff but soon gave into the hug, sobbing. "My brother. He didn't deserve this. He was..." Her shaking whimpers took over.

Rachel held her for a few minutes before speaking again. "I'm sorry. I'm sure he meant a lot to you. But I really believe she's on our side. She wants to stop this from happening. You don't have a lot of reason to trust her, and you don't have a lot of reason to trust my judgment, either. But could you muster enough faith to just try?"

Saff sat back, looking blankly around the room and wiping tears from her cheeks. "I don't know how much more of this I can take. I really don't. They almost got Devin the other day, too. He was in pretty bad shape. I'm just … tired."

Rachel moved her head to get Saff's full attention with eye contact. "Then let's hear her out. A couple of days here could mean we save thousands of lives, even if there's just a small chance of everything working out."

Saff frowned, gesturing at the closed front door. "What is she even offering? She didn't really give us much to go on in her letter."

Rachel was strengthened by remembering Guillen's conviction and commitment to the cause. "I don't know the particulars of her plan. But she killed a high-ranking member of the royal family, her own uncle, just to save me. She's burned her bridges over there. She's taking a lot of risks to try and help."

Saff fidgeted with her hands, her appearance having returned to normal. "Yeah. But from what I understand, she was pretty instrumental in your kidnapping. And you trust her?"

Rachel matched her frown and drew a deep breath. Did she trust her? Seeing Meg—Kaylah—again had rekindled her trust. She could only hope she wasn't being an idiot right now by ignoring the Seeder council's warnings. "I do trust her. I have to live with what they put me through." Horrific flashbacks of the palace played through her mind as she wiped away a tear. "Even then … it's worth giving her a chance. And frankly, we need a different strategy. What we've been doing *isn't working.*"

✻

Saff stood and grabbed a tissue from a box on the kitchen counter, sopping up her tears and blowing her nose. "I'll listen to her. But she's on a short leash until I'm convinced we can really trust her. And the *moment* she starts to act like she has ulterior motives, is the moment her part in this war takes a different role."

"Fair enough. How about you give me some time to talk to her when she gets back? I think you could do with some fresh air."

Saff stared at Rachel, not wanting to leave her alone. She'd been reckless enough by allowing Rachel to come on this dangerous mission. But Saff knew she was shooting herself in the foot already if there was hope for change, and she desperately needed that change. She was going to need to place some trust in Rachel.

"Fine."

Saff was sitting in the living room by herself when the front door opened again. Eric cautiously poked his head in. "Are we, uh ... good?"

Rachel addressed him from the dining room table. "Saff would like to go into town with you to grab a bite, if that works for you."

"There's a great little place nearby with fantastic omelets; I'd be happy to help." He walked in and shot Rachel a questioning glance.

She nodded, indicating it was safe for Kaylah to come in.

Kaylah followed after Eric, keeping her eyes on Saff, though not posturing aggressively. She moved over to allow Saff plenty of space to approach the door.

"Kaylah can contact me when you're ready for us to come back," Eric said while Saff met him and walked out the door.

The door shut, and Kaylah glanced awkwardly at Rachel. "Can I hug you? I'm not really sure where we stand with things right now..."

Rachel stood, opening her arms.

Kaylah squeezed her tight. "Gosh, I missed you. You had me worried sick! I mean, I trusted my men to get you home, but still..."

They sat at the table and Kaylah grabbed a piece of bacon from the pan Rachel had taken off the stove while waiting for them. "What's with her? What's with the delay, and it just being the two of you?"

"Her brother just got killed."

Kaylah gulped. "I'm sorry. I'll keep that in mind." She huffed. "She can take mine in return."

"I think it bothered her you seemed so casual."

Kaylah threw her hands into the air. "A girl just wants to wear comfortable clothes in a safe place. When Eric said there were just two of you, I assumed others were coming and... Well, I assumed." She sighed. "So, where do you and I stand? I don't even know what Soren and my uncle told you—some of it may not be true."

Rachel gnawed on her bottom lip. "Well, I think it's safe to say we both understand your mission was to take out a Seeder, from the moment we met?"

Kaylah frowned, setting the strip of bacon down on a plate. "We were just kids, Rach. I didn't understand everything."

"I get it. Just laying it all out there. And you were the one that recommended I date your brother."

Kaylah nodded, her frown deepening.

"And they said you were poisoning me to weaken me." Rachel shot a quick glance at Kaylah's wrists.

"Yeah," Kaylah whispered. "When they confirmed your bloom, Rob ordered it, so he could ... control you. I'm sorry. I didn't want to do it. For most of our friendship, it was just that—enjoying being your friend."

Rachel shook her head. "I understand you had orders, but you walked out on everyone, just months later. You couldn't have taken a stand earlier? Not done it? Given me a heads-up about Soren so I wouldn't have given him a chance to take me?"

Kaylah huffed. "I did what I had to, and I tried my best. I'm sorry, but there was only so much I could juggle."

She continued to explain. "The poison doses were up and down, helping you feel better when you were with Soren, dragging you down to go back to him when you doubted yourself. Do you know what it's like, having to keep a smile on your face as you betray someone you love? It's a nightmare! And when I found you..." They shared a knowing look about the time Kaylah had caught Rachel hurting herself. "You probably don't remember the timeline, but after I found you that day, that killed me!"

Rachel furrowed her brow. *What timeline?*

"Do you remember what happened a few days later? You started to feel *better*, and then I showed up with a scarf around my neck. That was to cover bruising from my *own brother* strangling me for not doing my job well enough."

Rachel looked down. "Oh."

"And you have to believe me—I had *every* intention of taking you with me before Soren completed the plan. But the sadistic prick took you earlier than he was supposed to. I was gone coordinating Unitas. I did my best. I've had to deceive both sides for a while—I've been homeless for a long time in my heart." She sat back in her chair with a heavy sigh. "We extracted you as soon as we possibly could."

Rachel bit her lip, tears forming in her eyes. "Do you know what he did to me?"

"I... I'm not sure." Kaylah looked down at her lap. "I know what the War Vines do. And Olivia told me about his behavior in your recovery room..."

Rachel remained silent.

"I protested him being assigned to date you from the very beginning. He's ... *literally* the worst person I know. And I tried, in my own way..." She rubbed her forehead, clearly flustered. "It wouldn't have mattered. One of my jobs was to coach him, to make sure you wouldn't dump him, to try and keep him in line."

Rachel envisioned another string in the hands of a puppeteer. That was all she was—a puppet. If it wasn't the Seeder lies of her childhood, it was the Ivy betrayals tugging at her every move. She imagined every conversation she'd had with her best friend about her boyfriend, shared in confidence. Her friend had turned around and told him about them, teaching him what to say, how to act. Rachel was growing increasingly nauseous. "I hate my life. I wish I were human."

Kaylah's face was painted with guilt. "Please don't say that."

Rachel picked at her fingernails. "I'm grateful you saved my life. And I appreciate what you're trying to do. I just... Meg... Kaylah... I almost slept with him, because I didn't know what he really was."

Kaylah's eyes searched Rachel's face. "But you didn't, right?"

"No. But that's not the point."

"I told him I'd have him killed if he slept with you."

Rachel's eyes narrowed as she recalled something Soren had said, about someone getting in his way. "Why would he answer to you? He choked you."

Kaylah shook her head. "He may be my older brother, and he may have been given too much power on this project, but I'm still the heir to the throne." She slid a hand forward on the dining table, reaching toward Rachel. "I had to draw a line somewhere. I couldn't let that happen to you. You never deserved that. That's why I suggested our pact years ago, about sharing with each other if we'd gone all the way, Rach. I'm serious—whether or not you'd wanted it, while you were in this world, if I had found out he'd done it..."

Rachel took a moment to respond. She'd forgotten that the Meg she once knew had been the one to suggest their pact. She could hate Kaylah as much as she did the rest of them. But Kaylah was the only one making amends, and making a difference. "I forgive you."

Kaylah's tough facade broke for the first time as tears rolled down her cheek. "Thank you."

Chapter 30

Kaylah wiped away her tears. "I don't know if it's much consolation, but the fact that Soren took you before I could, might have saved multiple members of your family from the same fate. He acted without my uncle's approval, and your family put all of your known siblings into hiding before the assassin network could get to them."

That comforted Rachel; she hadn't thought about the fact that her stepdad had known some of the other identities and would have naturally gone after them, too.

Taking a cleansing breath, Rachel was ready to move on. This wasn't all about her. This was about their world at war. "Let's not insult Eric by letting this amazing breakfast go to waste." Rachel scooped eggs onto her plate. "Speaking of... I'm happy to see you two together."

Kaylah almost had a glow to her. Not a literal one, of course—Ivies didn't do that. "I don't know what I would do without him, honestly. He's a good man." She poured herself a glass of orange juice. "I really, *really* love him. My visits here keep me sane."

Rachel wore a smirk. "Yeah, you do love him, don't you? Coming out of his bedroom like that—you guys have clearly made up."

Kaylah fought a grin, biting her lip. "We're adults in both worlds, you know. We can make our own choices, thank you very much."

"I'm curious though. Soren and I talked about it... That's not weird or anything? I mean, we're different... Is it races? Species? I don't know the difference, really. But still..."

Kaylah's expression grew even more mischievous. "Neither of us are complaining." She chuckled. "I know your people are even more different from humans than we are, with the whole rooting and giant batch of kids thing, but if you're not focused on reproduction or your weird transfer of powers, there's really no reason you can't have a completely happy relationship with an Ivy or a human."

"That's good to know. And I'm really happy for you guys."

"Why so curious?" Kaylah raised her eyebrows playfully while taking a sip of juice. "Guillen says hi."

Rachel's smile dropped as quickly as her heart did. "You've seen him? How long ago? He's okay?"

Kaylah beamed. "Oh my gosh. Girl, you really did fall for him! He's fine, totally fine."

Rachel drew a deep breath of gratitude.

"He's one of the most capable men I know, and I grew up around elite assassins." Kaylah began to butter some toast. "*And* he has the biggest heart. Those are hard to find." She rolled her eyes. "Especially in *my* family."

Rachel blushed. "Nothing happened. Dating isn't really a priority right now, if you know what I mean."

"You don't need a man to stand on your own two feet. I get that." Kaylah's tone was warm and encouraging. "And we're living through some ugly crap right now. I'm just saying, I give you permission to like him all you want." She pointed at Rachel with the butter knife. "And I'll tell him you said hi when I see him next."

"I'd like that." Rachel bit into a piece of crunchy bacon. Her mouth watered, having missed meat. The vegetarian lifestyle of the Green Lands had been harder to get used to than she'd expected. She savored the salty, smokey bite, barely holding herself back from moaning. "How's Guillen's work going? What's his mission right now?"

"Guillen is out scouting for me. He did want me to ask how your research was going on Seeder people like him."

Rachel frowned, guilt gnawing at her for not having put more focus on it. "I haven't had the time to ask around."

"Well, I recommend putting that high on the list when we get back. I could see myself assigning you two to work with Green Humans." Kaylah grimaced. "Is that a weird label? Ivies don't have any nice ways of referring to them. They're not stunted or disabled, they're just ... unpowered?"

"I don't know. Maybe we'll run the title by them." Rachel huffed. "I really can't believe the way they treat his kind, though. That's horrible. And calling them 'stunts'?"

Kaylah flashed a sympathetic frown. "It's just one of the many things I hope we can fix."

They continued to eat their breakfast and catch up before approaching the reason for the reunion. "So, tell me about what's going on," Kaylah said, pushing away from the table. "Why have your people ignored my offer to meet? Who is this woman you brought with you?"

Rachel shrugged. "I tried—I really did. And honestly, you're lucky *we* even showed up. After the mind games your people have put me through, I'm still kind of waiting for the other shoe to drop."

Kaylah frowned again.

"I say your people, but you know what I mean."

"I know what you mean." Kaylah grabbed their plates, taking them to the kitchen sink. "But the Unitas Movement and Ivy Kingdom aren't mutually exclusive. They're still my people, I'm just trying to ... do the impossible and change things."

Rachel sighed, twisting in her chair to face Kaylah. Even if she hadn't been manipulated for half of her life, she doubted she'd have been ambitious enough to try and end a centuries-old war, taking responsibility for millions of lives. "I'm glad I'm not in your shoes. Anyway, Saff—she's a good ally, she's just worn down, as are all of our people. Her brother's death is still fresh, so be patient with her."

"But what position does she hold? Downstairs, we have a big table set up because I expected maybe a half dozen of you."

"She works at the school, training, right now healing. They say she's possibly the most powerful woman in our village, at least for her age." Rachel flashed back to Saff's miraculous and seemingly perilous entrance into the human world. She'd actually made good on her promise to guide Rachel here. Somehow. Rachel had been too nervous to broach the subject with Saff again, with her being so antsy and grumpy. And Rachel had selfishly enjoyed too much time catching up with Eric, trying to ignore her own worries.

Kaylah turned on the tap, filling the frying pans to soak. "That's impressive, but she's not even on a leadership council? It sounds like this could be a waste of all our time if she can't even represent your people."

Rachel shook her head, at a loss for what more she could have done. "We had to try. It has to start somewhere. Win her over, and just like I made the introduction, she can introduce you to our leaders."

"We'll try. I'd hoped to do this in a more neutral location." Kaylah met her gaze. "If I could do this all on my own, I wouldn't have reached out to your people for help."

Rachel averted her eyes, wishing she could have been more convincing with the Seeder leadership.

Kaylah crossed her arms, leaning her hip against the counter. "How long have you been away? How many days do you have left here before it takes a toll on your health?"

Rachel was already feeling the slight dimming of her energy—the precursor to fatal root rot. "We really should get back as soon as possible. But we can spare a day or two if needed."

"That can be enough to get us started."

Eric came in the squeaky front door and greeted the girls. "She's just taking a minute to herself in the car before she comes in."

Rachel smiled as Kaylah met him at the door, giving him a kiss. "Thank you."

He took a few steps and peeked out the blinds in the living room. "Well, if she takes a while, you could find a way to *really* thank me." He walked back and pulled her close.

Rachel covered her eyes. "No honeymoon with others in the room, please."

Kaylah chuckled, giving him a couple more smooches. "Rain check."

Saff came in after a few minutes, much calmer than before.

Eric grabbed his keys again. "I'll head out and … do something."

"You know what? Stay," Kaylah said, grabbing his hand. "If this is about bringing our people together, we should have a human here for this meeting. Wouldn't you agree, Saff?"

"I think that's a great idea," Saff conceded.

Eric slowly set his keys back down on the entryway ledge, his face clearly expressing his discomfort. No one had to say anything—Rachel knew how he must be feeling. What did a recent high school grad have to say about military strategy or brokering treaties? But this was the first ever meeting of the worlds like this in known history, and he would do fine as a layman representative.

Kaylah recommended they sit in the living room as the downstairs wasn't nearly as comfortable; she and Eric claimed the couch while Saff and Rachel took separate armchairs.

Kaylah first addressed Saff. "I'd like to start by offering my condolences. I'm very sorry for your loss. I'm hoping our working together can prevent more loss of lives."

"Thank you," Saff calmly replied. "But before hearing all your plans, I'd like to be clear on what your end goal looks like. Our people have no need to get caught up in your internal affairs. If you're wanting our help to start your own civil war, or because you have delusions that Seeders will ever recognize the authority of Ivies over them, then this is a wasted meeting."

Kaylah's face showed frustration. "My motives aren't as self-serving as you imagine. Our people used to thrive together, embracing our differences. Imagine not having to use humans and their world as a battleground? Free passage, free commerce, freedom to be who we are without hiding, and fear, and secret identities."

Saff raised her eyebrows. "We're fond of humans—they've always been kind to us. But we don't have much need for Ivies. We're content to keep to ourselves, if your kind could learn to do the same."

Kaylah's lips formed a disingenuous smile. "Then I'd say Seeders are as bad as Ivies at teaching their people history."

Saff scowled. "I don't need to know the particulars, to know when my life is threatened. And I don't have to know every aspect of your culture to recognize you stand to gain a lot with our help, as next in line to be queen."

"I'm talking about things our people have lost—on both sides. Even before the wars. And tell me, Saff, how many years have you studied battle strategy? I didn't get to play with dolls as a child; I moved troops on a battle map!" Kaylah paused. "Your people have numbers and power, but they don't have the organization or tactical preparation. I can help with that. And more.

"I would never assume rulership over your people. And when my time comes, you'd better believe I'm shaking up things on our side as well. Do you think our people like the class system? Do you think they love living in the wastelands?"

"Your people did that to themselves! And I don't give a damn about your lands. I care about us losing good people every day because of something we never provoked!"

Kaylah raised her voice to match Saff's frustration. "I lost good men at the palace in your latest blunder! You got *one* more girl back, congratulations. *One. Of. Five.* How many of your people died in that attempt? How much better could that have gone if you'd had access to the contacts I still have on the inside?

"I'm practically giving you the keys to the kingdom if you'd learn to swallow your pride." Kaylah moved forward in her seat, pointing at Saff. "Don't talk to me about losing people—we've lost on our side, too, by the hand of Ivies *and* Seeders. And by now, our side and your side—they should be the same."

Eric sat silent, not making eye contact with anyone in the room.

Rachel grimaced, adjusting a throw pillow and deciding to take a turn. "I think we can argue about motivation and trust all day. I'd like to hear more concrete plans, and hear how you intend to actually carry them out. We need some validation."

Kaylah gave a heavy sigh. "Fair enough. Aside from my recent actions trying to prove myself, and my inside connections, and years of the best training, there's one more key reason why I'm uniquely qualified to lead this cause."

All eyes focused on her with curiosity.

"Have you never wondered why the royal family would focus three of its own, just for one Seeder? We have troops that can take care of that. We spent *years* preparing for this. Rachel perhaps wasn't ideal because she took longer to bloom than others." She glanced at Rachel. "No offense."

Rachel shrugged, and Kaylah continued.

"First, I think it just started as a way to infiltrate one of your networks. We'd never been able to do that before." Kaylah arched an eyebrow. "We didn't gain as much information as Nuren would have liked. Your people aren't exactly trusting..."

Rachel's lips formed a hint of a smile. No—trusting wasn't exactly high on the list of descriptors for Seeders. They only trusted who they had to. But then again, they *had* been oppressed and hunted for well over a century.

Kaylah continued to address Rachel. "Even when you became a teenager, your Seeder family only doled out the bare minimum needed to your parents, to keep you safe. My uncle only learned about the jade charms you use once they spotted you budding."

Rachel's heart sank. Soren had said as much—that their understanding of the charms was something they'd only recently learned about. If it was true that the Ivies had been in the dark about that tactic until recently, Rachel's family was at fault for endangering her entire species. No doubt, *every* Ivy assassin in the human world was now using that as a method to sort the humans from the blooming Seeders.

She recalled when Soren had asked her other questions, acting as though it were a fascination to learn all about her people. He'd asked if there were other tools they used. And where her family planned to have her catch a breeze to go home. She knew there had to have been other questions. She remembered feeling like her family had kept her in the dark about a lot of that kind of stuff. Which, in retrospect, had been wise. She prayed nothing she'd said had put more Seeders in harm's way.

Realizing the end game hadn't just been to kidnap Rachel, but to infiltrate and gain information, she reflected on the first point of Ivy insertion into her life. "Do you know how they discovered my identity when I was so young? And what ... happened to my dad? Brad?"

Kaylah frowned, shaking her head. "I'm sorry, I don't. They wouldn't tell me."

"I still don't get why the royal family dedicated three people to one Seeder," Saff said.

Kaylah shrugged. "My uncle wanted to make a name for himself. This was a unique opportunity. I just so happened to be dragged into it. As time went on, he wanted to maximize the use of the situation. He had theories; he'd done some perusing in the old archives. Rachel was intended to be the target to test out his brainchild—the War Vines. In a way, his actions will ultimately be the reason we win this. He let the wrong person get too close to his research—he let *me* get involved."

Saff sat up straighter. "Okay, we're listening. What does your research have to do with winning this thing and creating this utopia you're dreaming of?"

Kaylah leaned back in her seat and Eric slid his arm around her shoulder. "Ivies have been lied to for decades about our powers, about our potential. Our people don't realize what they've had stripped from them, how they've been manipulated to benefit the upper class and wage a senseless war. I understand that now."

Still seemingly skeptical and annoyed, Saff scoffed. "I don't see how your people learning they have more powers benefits my people."

"I haven't seen your archives." Kaylah squinted. "But from what I've learned, your people are missing out on some things, too. I know some of the reasons, but not all." She smiled. "We could teach our people together."

Saff rolled her eyes. "That's all well and good, learning more powers. But what does that do for us *right now*? I care more about how I can save lives than finding out I can sprout antennae or something like that."

Kaylah reached for Eric's hand before answering. "Duke Nuren misplaced his focus on what he was researching. What would you say if I told you Seeders would never have to send away their daughters again? And that we could safely bring them all back home, right now? Even the young ones?"

Saff and Rachel glanced at each other. Rachel didn't know all the specifics about Saff's story, and she certainly hadn't told Saff everything about her own, but they knew enough about each other's struggle.

Rachel spoke first. "Then I'd say we're interested in hearing more."

Chapter 31

Saff shook her head, annoyed at Kaylah's overly dramatic delivery. "You'll have to excuse me. I'm just trying to figure out if you're stupid, delusional, or a bad liar. If there were a way to keep our families together, we would have figured it out a long time ago!"

Kaylah glared. "Let's start with getting those back who have bloomed. We can provide instant transport to the Green Lands. They'll be safe from the hunt and able to train better in our realm." She raised her eyebrows. "And able to contribute energy to your borders."

"I guess I'll be experiencing that transportation firsthand? I can see how that could be beneficial," Saff conceded, knowing full well it was probably the only thing able to save her life at this point.

"Then to get the younger ones back ... it'll take a lot more, but I'm confident we can do it. I'll need access to your temples and ancient texts."

Saff arched an eyebrow. "I don't know how much you'll find there. Maybe you're not aware of it—but your people happen to possess stolen knowledge from our archives. And killed off *thousands* of Seeders that might have been old enough to pass down a few tidbits. I think we'd be happy to have those books back. And you want access to even more?"

Kaylah frowned. "I only have part of the equation, but I'm almost there. I'll happily make reparations in regards to things like ancient artifacts and archives when things are righted, but that's not the focus right now. I'm talking about bringing your people home—I know there's a way to open a more permanent rift."

Saff pressed her lips together, reflecting on Ivy rifts and their wastelands. "Speaking of rifts. Even in wartime, we find it objectionable the way your kind destroys nature to punch your way through. What forest are we decimating for this?"

"I said per-ma-nent," Kaylah retorted. "We'll be going back via tree, but in the long run, we won't have to. And I'm not saying it's an overnight solution that just a couple of people can do. But it's been done before and can be done again."

Saff closed her eyes, rubbing her temples. Kaylah was making a lot of vague promises, but Saff had to admit that even the less far-fetched ones could be immensely helpful. She thought back to their trip getting there. Saff had accomplished something she shouldn't have been able to. She definitely *did* want to learn more about Seeder powers, but returning to the human world once more a year wasn't only excruciating—it wasn't all that useful. This was about saving lives. And that was what Kaylah was ultimately promising. Though... "I think we're forgetting something important—even if we can pull it off, where do you expect these young girls to live? You mentioned the unbloomed earlier. Have you forgotten the fact they were taken from our lands in the first place because of the poison? Even if we weren't attacked in the Neutral Woods, we're not that fond of having to give up our homes."

Kaylah acknowledged her words with a triumphant smile. "I think we're at the point I can actually demonstrate something to prove myself. Let's head to the backyard."

They all filed outside, and Kaylah knelt on the grass. Placing her hands on the ground, she extended vines into the soil. Taking in a deep breath, she closed her eyes. Radiating out from her vines, the healthy green grass started to fade, turning brown—a large patch surrounding her all wilted.

Saff wanted to say something, but kept it to herself. *Obviously*, they knew how to poison and destroy things.

❄

Rachel, however, was in awe. And a bit sickened. That kind of poison had laced her drinks for months...

Kaylah took a moment to focus; the grass began to change again. Not only did it grow green again, it grew twice as vibrant and tall. Rachel and Saff stood with their mouths agape. Eric looked proud, like he'd seen this trick before. He helped Kaylah stand up, and everyone went back inside.

"You okay?" he asked as Kaylah sat down on the sofa.

"Yeah, thanks." She smiled.

"The growing thing is hard for her," he explained, clicking on an oscillating fan to help cool the room.

❀

"So, you can really undo the damage to our lands?" Saff asked, still in awe but hesitant. "It's not even a poison we can see. We still have lots of lush plant growth—it's just latent in our soil and water, affecting our girls."

"It can be done. It'll take some training and a lot of help. But it can be done." Kaylah gave another weak smile. "My people don't realize how much they've been lied to, how much they've been weaponized. Our nurses administer crude medication, but good technique can refine how they dose people." She turned her gaze to Rachel. "You remember Olivia? She's learned to administer numbing without *any* of the negative side effects—the nausea, dizziness, all of that."

❀

Rachel pondered if she would have even wanted Olivia to administer only numbing in the palace. Sure, it was to help so the vine insertion wasn't so brutal, and to keep her from resisting, but the haze of the poison they'd administered had helped her pass the time, numbing more than just her body.

Kaylah continued to lay out her plea. "Our abilities aren't just there to hurt others; we're actually capable of a lot of good things for nature and people. It's like nuclear power here in the human world; it can provide electricity, or it can kill without mercy—it's how you use it." She continued with a harder, resentful edge to her voice. "Don't even get me started on how our Mother Vines steal from our own communities. Our people were aiming for progress, instead we got prison. And most of them don't even realize what they've given up."

❀

Saff furrowed her brow in thought. "What's the difference between your 'Mother Vines' and 'War Vines'? Our elders said the new attacks were probably a mutation of your Mother Vines."

Kaylah clicked her tongue. "That, yeah... Mother Vines stretch from our communities to our palace. Their abilities are varied and intended to support the entire kingdom, in theory at least. Only one person has their allegiance—the queen. The War Vines are a similar construction, but a newer experiment. And, well," she looked down, "we all know what their main purpose is, and how they work, right? They also answer only to the queen. My mother created them after my uncle's research and infiltration efforts earned him a position as advisor."

Saff was starting to soften at hearing Kaylah's disdain for the practices of her own people. And now that she'd witnessed a power she hadn't known Ivies possessed, she craved to know more. "You have my attention. Tell me more about these permanent rifts you mentioned."

Kaylah reached for a pad of paper and pen from the coffee table, drawing some symbols. "Have you ever seen anything like this?"

* * *

Rachel cocked her head in recognition. "The cave, by the palace. Guillen said he didn't know what those meant. But you do?"

Saff sat up straighter. "I've seen something like that in our temples, too. Decorative stuff. No one I've asked seems to know what they're supposed to mean."

Kaylah smirked, tossing the pad of paper back on the coffee table. "This is the ancient text of our peoples. This is the key."

Rachel lifted her eyebrows, the intrigue growing.

* * *

Saff was still struggling with diplomacy mode. "So, your people learn more powers." She cleared her throat. "Good ones. And undo what you've done to our lands, and get our girls back home... What's in this for you? And what do you expect from the Seeders?"

"Well, I need access to your temples and archives—so I need safe passage in your lands, and help in my research. Possibly, protection to allow Unitas members to train on new abilities. And when the power changes hands in my kingdom, negotiations for a peaceful resolution. Talk of lands, cooperation, trade."

"You expect our help to protect your little rebellion when we're not even able to protect ourselves?" Saff scoffed. "Seriously, the audacity."

"You'll have more resources to do so!" Kaylah shot back. "Each son and daughter of yours that we bring back helps. Each person that joins our cause from the Ivy side is one less enemy to fight. It will grow—but only if we can agree to unite."

Saff rubbed her eyebrow with a knuckle. "You talk about power changing hands. If you're intending a coup and plan to stop the war and fix society, why don't you just do it yourself? You stormed the castle once already."

"I never said it was a coup."

Saff squinted. "Then what are we even talking about?"

Kaylah sighed. "Your army, my intel—that's how we forge peace. There are a lot of ways we can make this happen, but I refuse to do any of it without trying negotiations first."

"Sounds like a waste of time," Saff said. "Negotiations have never worked before. If they fail, you'd concede to taking the throne and making good on your promises?"

❂

Rachel swallowed a lump in her throat. Was Kaylah really going to have to kill her own parents? That kind of thing had happened throughout human history, and obviously, it would be for the greater good, but still... She tried to read her best friend's face to determine how she felt about it.

Kaylah wore the slightest frown. "One way or another, my mother's power will come to me. My parents may not be as sinister as you think, but... I understand the consequences if we can't find a peaceful resolution with them. Either way, we took out Duke Nuren—that was the first critical move. He's the one that shifted the power; we'll stand a much better chance now that he's out of the picture."

Her gaze moved between the two Seeders. "I get that you've lived your life in societies—both in the human world and Green Lands—that don't involve royalty, but it's not as simple as you're imagining, to just stand up as a new queen and command change. It's easier to kill off a usurper and put someone new in their place, than it is to win over a nation with drastic new ideas." She ran a finger back and forth over the knee of Eric's jeans. "All of my study and planning can be useful. Either as leverage to force my parents to change things, or if we can't get through to them and can't get my people's support to bend their will..." She clasped her hands together, resting them in her lap, then met Saff's gaze. "Then I will take care of it myself. Either way, as long as your people can demonstrate a little trust, we'll be changing the way things are being done."

Rachel was afraid to ask, but needed to speak up. "How will Soren play into your plans, whether or not your parents ... you know?" *Have to die?*

Kaylah grinned. "He doesn't have any say or pull, politically. He's just spoiled and temperamental. Even if he's their favorite, he's not the heir—estranged or not, my opinion matters more; our society and powers dictate that." Her expression grew more serious. "I'll see to it that he pays for what he's done."

Rachel bit the insides of her cheeks, nodding.

❂

Saff blew out a puff of air. "You know I'm not a politician. It sounds like all sorts of crazy plans, but maybe there's something here we can use." She looked down, focusing her thoughts, fighting to trust. Kaylah was still being too vague about what she had to offer. Maybe she was intentionally keeping details back, even if she was being honest about needing access to Seeder information. But this wasn't enough, not yet. If Saff was going to risk her life and defy council orders, she needed more proof that she'd made the right call to come.

Moving her hand up to where her jade charm usually would have rested, Saff considered the necklace. Trying to sneak out quietly, she'd left it in her bedroom at home. But she still wore it most days. She was gutted the Ivies now had another tool in their belt.

She then thought of her high school days. Devin had confessed that they didn't know how Ivy assassins managed to find Seeder networks in the human world. Seeders didn't understand everything about Ivy or Seeder rifting. She looked up. "If you're wanting us to trust you, we need more than campaign promises. I want to know *exactly* how your assassin network does their job. Everything. How do they find our girls?"

"They're not *my* assassins. They're my parents'."

Saff scowled. "Don't give me that shit."

Kaylah pursed her lips more humbly. "You do realize the vulnerable position I'm in, right? This is a give-and-take. Mutually beneficial. If I play all my cards right now, your people have no need to keep me alive."

Warmth grew in Saff's eyes as she tried to control her energy and anger. "Play your cards? I didn't realize this was a game to you. Your assassins are out there right now, fully aware of the most crucial tool we have to keep our girls safe. And you expect us to be okay with that, without anything in return? 'Give-and-take.' If you can't give us that, then *neither* of us are going to take you to a meeting with our council." She glanced at Rachel, daring her to side with Kaylah.

❀

Rachel frowned, digging her fingernails into her palms. She could see both sides. Kaylah was risking everything to change things. She didn't want to just go down as a martyr, not that either side would even think of her that way at this point. But Saff was right. Every second Ivy assassins prowled human high school hallways with the new information was a second Seeder girls were at risk. "She's right, Kaylah."

Kaylah's shoulders dropped, her expression showing her heartache. "I'm not trying to be difficult. I know it's not a game. How do I know I can trust you? That I won't just be tortured, killed, or traded?"

Saff crossed her arms. "If you tell us what we want to know and return us to the Neutral Woods, I'll personally guarantee safe entry to our lands. Whether our people accept your proposals and what you want—that I can't say."

Kaylah slowly nodded. "I've already betrayed my family and kingdom. I hope your people take that into account when they decide whether they'll honor your promise of safety."

Saff glanced at her own hands. "I promised you safe *entry* to our lands, but I can only offer so much. The rest is up to you. Just remember that your ideas and actions are what will be earning you the ability to keep your life."

Kaylah narrowed her eyes in challenge. "*Your* people ignored my request to meet. It's late in the season. I understand that makes it more difficult to catch a breeze home. Just remember, getting home alive is by *my* hand—I hold those cards. I hope you're earnest about getting me in."

Saff flashed green eyes. "You'll get in."

Rachel shifted uncomfortably in her seat. It wasn't like there had been a class in high school on negotiations and confrontation of this sort. She respected Saff, and Saff was one of her kind. But, enemy or not, Kaylah was still her best friend. Witnessing them threatening each other knotted her stomach. Rachel looked down into her lap. Was she just being a pawn again? If push came to shove and Kaylah denied Saff entry back to the Green Lands, would Rachel be spared?

Kaylah sat back on the couch, closing her eyes. She took in a couple of deep breaths. "Ivy assassin networks. Let's talk about it over lunch."

Kaylah offered to order everyone delivery. It felt so odd for Saff, having become used to the Seeder way of life, to just use an app for someone to bring food to you. It also felt off to accept food from an Ivy, but she rested a little easier with the knowledge that they were ordering a family meal—they'd all be sharing the same food. They settled on Chinese, one of Saff's favorites that she missed from her years growing up in the human world.

***

Rachel sat down last with a plate of food; everyone had already reclaimed their seats in the living room. She looked down at her orange chicken and fried rice, stabbing at it with a fork. Eating with Kaylah brought up one of a thousand festering questions. "Are Ivies affected by their own poison? Like Seeders can heal themselves with their own energy?"

Kaylah finished chewing a bite, pointing her chopsticks at Rachel. "Yes. The chemicals are a little different, and you need more of it, but we're affected by our own poison."

Rachel furrowed her brow in thought. "Soren really drank poison when we were together? We shared coffee from you all the time."

Kaylah scoffed. "Not likely. Him, take one for the team? We started you on the coffee routine early, in anticipation of your bloom. That way you'd be conditioned to drinking it."

Rachel felt sick to her stomach, hearing that word again. 'Conditioned.'

"We didn't actually put the poison in until it was pertinent, when you finished your bloom and started training. He either turned down your drinks after that, or only pretended to drink." Kaylah rolled her eyes. "We soak up our poison easier—he barely would have even felt it. And ingestion is especially weak versus direct administration through leaf puncture." Kaylah frowned as Rachel continued to move around the food on her plate. "You really don't think I would have somehow snuck poison into this, do you?" Kaylah pointed her chopsticks at Eric, who'd taken a particularly large bite. "It's much more lethal to humans than Seeders, anyway. You think I'd do that to him?"

Eric swallowed his food, giving Rachel an awkward smile. "Human here. Glad to be of service as the food tester to make sure my girlfriend isn't poisoning people."

Kaylah gave him a playful scowl. "Darn. Now that you know why I've kept you around, I may have to replace you."

He stared into her eyes, stabbing his fork on her plate, stealing one of her pieces of teriyaki chicken.

Rachel grinned and took a bite of her own food. "No. Just lots of questions is all."

✿

"Are Seeders sometimes immune to your poison?" Saff asked, wondering about her own ability.

"Not that I've ever heard of."

Hmm... "Speaking of poison and sharing information, how about those assassins?" Saff prompted.

With a heavy sigh, Kaylah gave information on how the Ivy assassin networks worked, how they hunted out Seeder girls in the human world. A lot of the information was quite nebulous. Traditional assassin networks usually had three to six soldiers, with a general assigned. But that could vary. Kaylah confessed their methods were far from perfect. It really *was* tough work trying to discover a Seeder network. But Seeders kept their border walls too well protected.

That was why this entire strategy had been such a breakthrough, even with so few girls kidnapped and hooked up to the War Vines. Not only could those kidnapped girls not help charge their own border walls, they could significantly amplify the power of the War Vines. It was the perfect one-two punch. Even getting those six Seeder girls in one year was something they'd been proud of. Seeders trusted so little, concealed so well, and always kept the Ivies on their toes because there wasn't just one playbook to look out for—each Seeder family did things their own way.

Saff smiled at that. Her and Devin's families had done something atypical by pairing up. Then again ... that had perhaps done more harm than good, in retrospect. *Barely dodged a dart on that one.* More than three years later, she still occasionally had nightmares about her botched bloom, complete with Ivy assassins who had tried to choke the life out of her.

As they ate and chatted, Saff also pondered on the leaked information of the charms. In hindsight, the elaborate lies to their daughters afforded an extra layer of safety to Seeder family networks—they wouldn't confide in the wrong person about the purpose of the jade charms. But it didn't matter anymore. Seeders hadn't been sure if Ivies knew about them—they hadn't. And now they did. Saff filed it away as one of the first things to let their council know. This information alone could save countless lives. Certainty afforded their families a lifeboat. The girls would still need the charms, but they would need to be absolutely certain to conceal them, and only wear them when necessary, not as mementos when not in use, like Saff had.

Kaylah rounded off her explanation of their hunting tactics. Ivies rifted to a greater variety of destinations, and with relative ease, compared to Seeders. After a century, they'd been able to scope out and map out an approximate area where Seeders were likely to hide their families, based on assumed rifting locations and how far they would be willing to travel within the human world. It was like shooting fish in a barrel. Granted, it was a large barrel. Maybe more like fish in a swimming pool. But it was valuable information, knowing they'd done that work. It could help Seeders strategize better. Assuming ... all this information was true...

Saff reminded herself the Ivies were expert liars. The jury was still out.

"Within those regions, it's just a lot of observation," Kaylah said.

Saff's mind wandered lovingly to Devin. "Is there anything else? I sometimes wonder if, well, it could just be a Seeder thing, but it might be a green folk thing, or maybe I'm just making it up…" She realized she was rambling. "Do you think we can sense the energy within each other?"

She sometimes still wondered if part of her falling in love with Devin in the human world had to do with their energy. There was a rightness, a pull to him. And she'd always felt it was somehow more than a coincidence that one of her attackers had zeroed in on her, and at least one of her sisters. *But maybe not.* That Ivy had tried to get close to both of them before they even began their bloom. Their powers hadn't come in yet at that point.

Kaylah twisted her lips in thought. "I've never really thought about it. Maybe? If that's a thing, maybe it also varies by the person. Like a sense of smell?"

Saff shrugged.

After thorough questioning and no hesitation from Kaylah on the topic, Saff had to admit to herself that Kaylah might be genuine. Or a masterful liar. The sickening thing was that she knew one of those was completely true—but could they both be?

Eric lovingly rubbed Kaylah's arm after they finished eating. Dirty plates piled on the coffee table.

Saff allowed her mind to drift back to her family yet again, and how worried they must all be. Her energy was dimming, a coldness in her roots setting in. She didn't know everything, but she knew enough, and it was time to go home. "When can we leave? You said you could get us quick transportation home?"

✳

Rachel noticed Eric frown; he squeezed Kaylah's hand so tight that his knuckles were white. She loved the two together, but this was bigger than them.

Eric spoke up. "You should leave first thing in the morning. We all saw how much Kaylah's display took out of her earlier."

✳

Saff couldn't bear the thought of wasting any more time. Along with knowing they needed her and Rachel's help back home, Saff's anxiety was growing about root rot. Returning to the human world a second time in one year, she discovered, felt much the same as the first. Their rotting didn't seem to accelerate; perhaps they just needed to take some time to recuperate in the Green Lands between visits. Nonetheless, this was a dangerous experiment; she felt the urgency to return.

"Fine," Saff accepted with great hesitance, wary about how the combined rifting worked, and wanting Kaylah in peak condition to do it. "But I want to talk details. Tell us more about what your people have done in this Unitas. I want numbers. I want to hear a lot more so I can help with the conversations when we get back. Don't leave anything out."

Kaylah nodded. "Okay. I'll set up our return. Let's do this."

Chapter 32

Kaylah excused herself to go make some calls. They would need at least one more Ivy there, so Rachel and Saff both had a personal guide to take them through a rift. Rachel explained how it worked, how it felt, the pain and injury required, so Saff wouldn't be surprised. Once Kaylah returned, they covered more details—approximately where they would appear in the Neutral Woods, where they would go to gain entry, who Saff felt they would need to first seek out.

"Don't be surprised if we gain a significant escort when we approach the Outer Wall... We might even get arrested," Saff warned. "It's not like you can prove your identity. Rachel and I can try to cover with our eye glow, but if they demand to see yours, that's when things will get iffy."

Kaylah slid her phone into her pocket. "I understand. I trust you'll vouch for me and my aide. We're coming at your invitation—we're not infiltrating or attacking."

Rachel wondered who the 'aide' was that would escort them there, if she'd met them. Maybe Jon? She wished it could be Guillen, but rifting wasn't something he could do. Her heart warmed at the thought of him, and she found herself fantasizing about seeing him again, somehow working together in all of this. His knife rested heavily in her pocket, against her leg.

"Saff, do Seeders have children born without powers? I met an Ivy that doesn't have any." Rachel spotted Kaylah smirk knowingly. "How do they prove they're not an enemy, if they can't show the female eye glow, or the male hair?"

✳

Saff was surprised by the turn of conversation, and to hear about Rachel knowing Ivies in such a personal way. They hadn't really talked much about those particulars in their time together.

"Yeah, I learned about that as part of our cultural lessons after I returned to the Green Lands. Of course, my education wasn't put on hold as much as yours is, with the war right now." Saff furrowed her brow, trying to remember a small tidbit of a lesson she'd once heard. "Every race has disabilities, we're not exempt."

※

Rachel cringed at that label. Guillen was perfectly able to do a lot of things others couldn't. He was determined. He was smart, and wise, and sweet, and… Taking a deep breath, she tried to push his handsome face out of her mind.

"Granted, I'm sure it's a drastically different story than the Ivies." Saff threw Kaylah a subtle look of resentment. "It's not common, but sometimes a girl randomly never blooms. Their host family and Seeder father decide whether to tell them their true nature, but I imagine most just keep living life normally as humans in the dark. It would be sad to learn about a life you could have no part in."

"Yeah, of course." Rachel mulled it over. "So, they come here and molt and then … just stay human…" Seeder society was already lopsided when it came to gender representation, because of the poisoned lands. More girls, not returning home.

※

Saff glanced at Kaylah again, trying, somewhat unsuccessfully, not to scowl. "As for the boys, the … defenseless babies, left to root in the Green Lands—it's not promising for them. For the same reason we girls have to leave, they don't stand much of a chance. They're essentially human—they die within our borders."

Kaylah looked down with obvious shame. Eric shyly looked down as well, gently rubbing Kaylah's arm.

※

Rachel observed all the downcast looks in the room. "I hadn't thought of that." At least Guillen had a chance at life. A limited and unfair life, but he made the most of it. Her mind wandered to the times she'd watched him tossing knives, to their conversations full of his reassurances, or his resolve to this cause. *I need to focus.* She wasn't sure why she was starting to obsess over him so much. It wasn't like she'd endlessly pined for him while she was back in Seeder lands, healing people. Maybe it was the distraction and busyness that had kept thoughts of him at bay back there. Maybe it was being in the same room with Kaylah now, or the fact that she'd called Rachel out on her feelings; it made them more real.

※

"I'm sorry for the pain my people have caused," Kaylah offered in a whisper.

Saff surprised herself, and the others in the room. "Thank you. I honestly never thought I'd hear an Ivy say that." She allowed a gentle sigh to escape as she softened. "I'm not so blinded by hate that I can't realize you didn't *personally* start this. And I *am* grateful you brought Rachel back to us."

Rachel's eyes teared up. The Saff she knew was generally kind, definitely kinder than she'd been so far to Kaylah. But always uptight and frustrated, always in survival mode. It was nice to hear that she cared for Rachel personally, despite her failures. And it was good to hear a hint of hope that aligned with the Unitas ideology.

Saff continued, "I remember something else my teacher said. About a small community of that type, for survivors."

Kaylah looked interested; Rachel was all ears.

"After the poisoning, there was a village that carved out a space with naturally defensible borders beyond the tainted soil. If they're strong enough for the journey and it's caught quick enough, there's a chance they can live there."

"I have to go there!" Rachel blurted, frantically looking between Saff and Kaylah. "Kaylah, I promised Guillen I'd learn about his kind in the Seeder world."

"I agree. Once he's done scouting for me, I think your research could benefit those like him in my kingdom." She smirked. "Maybe, if I got word to him of your research, he'd work even faster."

Rachel blushed, glancing at Saff out of the corner of her eye... It looked as though she'd picked up on Kaylah's teasing.

"Rachel, you..." Saff's voice trailed off. "I'd like to talk to Rachel in private. Am I right to assume we can come and go as we please?"

"Yes," Kaylah said. "As long as you don't compromise our safe house location."

Saff got up and stepped out the front door. Rachel followed, stopping at the door and turning back to Kaylah and Eric with a wink. "You two be good."

Saff waited until they were at the end of the long block to talk. "You're a lot like me, you know—impulsive. I'm not sure if you've really realized what we've done."

Rachel resented the condescension. Saff was barely older than her, but talked as if she were some wise old mentor. "Thanks. Everyone likes their flaws and mistakes being rubbed in their faces. We had to come out here to talk about that?"

Saff rolled her eyes. "Rachel, I like you. And I didn't just say it to insult you. But you're talking about some big trip to a remote village, as some kind of social research? We need you helping us back home."

"I'm not planning a vacation, Saff! I *will* be helping. You may not recognize it, but I have a unique position in all of this. I plan to make the most of it to do my part. *Every* Seeder woman can heal; I can do something more." She'd been useless before. In part, because of her naïveté; the other part she was still sorting out. Constant doubt still swirled through her mind. Her entire life—lies. But in her core, she knew who she was. And she knew this was right. Rachel had a position no other Seeder could claim. Ties, trust, having physically been in the palace and Ivy territory.

Saff huffed. "Yeah, but you talk about it like you get to make the calls. First of all, you two talk like she's your leader, like you'll follow her anywhere. We don't even have an alliance yet; this is all tenuous at best. Will you follow her if our leaders don't go along with her plans?"

Rachel stared at the sidewalk, kicking a pebble away. She hadn't asked herself that question, not in so many words. Where did her allegiances really lie? With her people, obviously. But what Kaylah wanted was in the best interests of both peoples, even if they didn't see it.

She wasn't going to tell Saff, but Rachel realized her answer would be 'yes.' She was putting her eggs in Kaylah's basket. She had bought the dream of a new world, not just going back to the way things were before Nuren's plan shook everything up.

Saff continued when Rachel gave no response. "And ... you do realize that coming here could be considered treason, right?"

Rachel's eyes grew wide, just now realizing the severity of the situation.

※

"It's not like our people are going to kill us or anything crazy like that. But, Rachel, we betrayed the trust of our people, of our leaders, of..." Saff frowned, thinking of the note she'd left at home. "My own husband didn't know I was coming here for this. I'm glad you want to play a role in fixing things, but we may not get much choice in what we do after making this move. We may need to toe the line and do as we're told. You'll have to accept the possible consequences."

※

Rachel stared at the ground again, shaking her head. There had been no other way for this to happen, but Saff was right; it didn't mean they were going to get a parade in their honor, welcoming them home.

"And..." Saff continued, "I'm curious about this guy you're mentioning. An Ivy? There's something you're not telling me."

Rachel's cheeks flushed. "It's not a big deal. You're overthinking that one. He's Kaylah's cousin. He helped me escape and get back home. He's a good ally—good with weapons, and connections, and stuff."

Saff furrowed her brow. "You know, you told the council the prince kidnapped you, to get you to the Green Lands. I've always felt that story was missing some detail. Remember, I met your mom; we talked a lot."

Rachel avoided Saff's gaze, her heart sinking in shame.

"I went on a date with an Ivy once," Saff confessed. "Of course, I didn't know what he was back then. When did you first discover your boyfriend was one of their kind?"

Rachel frowned, slowly, intentionally filling and emptying her lungs. "Earlier than anyone knows," she whispered.

✸

Saff had guessed that, with all the focus that had been put on Rachel by the Ivies, and on manipulating her. That was part of why she'd wanted to mentor Rachel, and had been chosen to. They'd both had traumatic experiences at Ivy hands... At Ivy *vines*. Saff knew what a lifeline her Seeder family and community had been to help her through the aftermath of the attacks. "Ivies can be convincing, can't they?"

✸

"Guillen's different," Rachel blurted, shoving her hands in her pockets. "He's nothing like David. He's passionate about the cause." She fought off tears. Yeah, 'David' had pretended to be, too. But Guillen was vulnerable, and thoughtful, and caring... But that was how 'David' had bought her trust, by acting the gentleman, turning down her advances as though he were being chivalrous, by acting like he was giving up *so much* by revealing himself, when he was really just using it as a device to lull her into a false sense of security. But Guillen really *was* different. "I learned my lesson. You don't have to worry about me."

"For all our sakes, I hope you're right. Just remember where your loyalties lie, and that Ivies are fantastic at deception. Your friend back there, I'm giving her a chance, but that doesn't mean I'm sold."

Rachel scowled. "I'm a big girl. I can make my own choices. And we're just friends. I don't need your preaching!" She stopped walking, turning and heading back to the house.

Saff turned to follow her. "Forget that you've demonstrated you're a poor judge of character—you need to realize a lot of choices you're making don't affect just you!"

Clenching her teeth, Rachel fought to keep her energy in check, walking faster to get back to the house. Saff quickened her pace to keep up. Rachel yanked the screen door open and turned back to her. "You may think that you and I have similar stories, just because we've both dated an Ivy, or because we've been personally attacked by them, but don't pretend you actually know me. I'm not as stupid as you think. And you're not as special as you think you are, just because you're more powerful than most, or because you've been back home for longer than me. Just ... get over yourself."

Rachel opened the front door, seething mad. Eric and Kaylah were still on the couch; she was leaning into him, wrapped up in his arms. They looked up at the Seeders, attentive, as if they'd heard some portion of the argument.

Saff entered behind her, shutting the door and glaring at Rachel. "I'm going to go lie down for a while."

Chapter 33

Rachel stood awkwardly by the safe house front door as Saff left down the hallway. She wanted to go somewhere to give the cuddling couple some privacy, but Saff was now in the Seeders' shared room. Rachel considered going back out on a walk by herself...

"Babe, I think I need some time alone with my best friend." Kaylah pressed her forehead against Eric's and they gazed into each other's eyes.

"Mmm, never enough time with you," he said, stealing a kiss.

"But I make our time worthwhile." Kaylah turned and straddled him, wrapping her arms around his neck and voraciously sucking his face.

Rachel scrunched her face in embarrassment, looking away. "I'm going outside."

As Rachel turned the doorknob, Kaylah called out, "I'll be just a minute."

Two or three minutes later, Kaylah joined her, smiling.

Rachel smirked as they began to walk. "You guys are... Well, I'd tell you to get a room, but..."

Kaylah giggled. "Sorry, but I *did* have to watch you all over my brother for two-plus years."

"Yeah..." Rachel cringed. "Thanks for the reminder."

Kaylah frowned. "Sorry." She took a deep breath, a smile reappearing on her face. "I heard you gave him some stitches."

Matching Kaylah's smile, Rachel recalled how livid Soren had been. "It's the least I could do."

"He certainly deserved it. Do you remember a while back, when he got that black eye?"

"Yeah."

Kaylah pointed to herself, beaming.

"What?"

Kaylah held up her hands. "Seriously, the ego on that guy! I was the one who talked you into asking him on a date, right? If his sole purpose in coming here was to date you, why didn't he just ask you out?" She arched an eyebrow.

Rachel shrugged.

"Ego—pure and simple. Well, I think it was partly a test to make sure I was still loyal and would follow orders, that I could convince you. But he'll take anything that strokes his ego. He wanted *you* to come to *him*."

Rachel's stomach churned. "What does that have to do with his black eye?"

"Right. Yeah. The black eye." Kaylah smiled again. "That was what? A couple of days after he revealed himself to you? He was bragging about how he'd ambushed you in the hot tub. It wasn't a heat of the moment thing at all—that was calculated. He knew what he was doing." Kaylah rolled her eyes. "I didn't realize he was going to take things that far. And once I found out... Yeah, he earned that shiner."

Rachel swallowed hard, her heart hurting. "I... I don't know if I want to hear about all the ways I've been manipulated." She looked down at the ground. A sick curiosity ate at her, needing to know every instance, every motivation, every manipulation. But the part of her hanging on by a thread knew she couldn't handle a list of her weaknesses. Not yet.

Kaylah stopped Rachel, pulling her into a hug. "I'm sorry. I'll try not to bring up the sensitive stuff when it's not pertinent, okay?"

Rachel nodded, looking up and continuing their walk. "How did you even end up with Eric? Rob married a human to get to me. But I'm kind of surprised you chose ... or were even allowed ... to date a human."

Kaylah pressed her lips together. "I know how it feels to be used, too. Forget they're my parents—just think about the fact that our queen and king trusted Nuren so much they allowed their only daughter, their heir, to live most of her childhood in another realm."

Rachel furrowed her brow. "I'm not following. You dated Eric to piss off your real parents?"

"No." Kaylah shook her head. "But ... they sent suitors. They would have doubled as security detail if I'd have chosen to really date any of them. I couldn't always be a third wheel as your best friend. And they wanted to make sure I ended up with someone who would fit their agenda. So, when I was back home, or you were busy with Soren... I was trying to get out of an ugly dating game."

Rachel rubbed her forehead. "How is it you lived such a crazy life right under my nose?"

Kaylah blew out a long exhale. "A lot of coordination." She hooked arms with Rachel, and they crossed the street. "Remember Michael, my tutor?"

"Yeah..."

"I'm not dyslexic; he was appointed as a tutor for court business so I was properly trained in politics, culture, and manners."

Rachel just shook her head.

"Anyway, the suitors... They were all idiots. In the end, when I met Eric, I convinced my uncle it was a better cover to date a human. I promised my parents I would focus on an Ivy suitor after I returned for good. After your bloom..."

"But you're staying with Eric?"

Kaylah grinned. "I may not always be here with him physically, but a part of me is always here with him," she said wistfully.

Rachel gave her a half-smile. That had to be hard for them. "I did want to make sure... We're not delaying leaving just so..."

Kaylah gave her the stink eye.

"Okay. Just making sure..."

"Taking Seeders through a rift is not something I've done before, so it's probably for the best I regain my strength. I know I don't go all glowy like you guys do, but our energy can get drained, too."

They turned down a narrow dirt path, running parallel to a ditch. Rachel smiled at a bunny that ran out from a bush ahead of them before scurrying back. "How does that work for you guys, by the way? How do your abilities work? We imagine ours like this chamber of energy in our hearts, when we envision it."

"Hmm. That's pretty cool. I guess when we envision ours, it's in the mind. I mean, it's more like a chemical thing, right? So, I focus on what I want done, then visualize it working its way down through my veins. Through my neck, arms, then vines."

Rachel ducked under a low-hanging tree branch. "That's really cool! What all can you accomplish, if you've been working on refining the poison?"

"So far, I've gotten really good at making people pass out. Gotta have that for fighting. Numbing—there's different focus required for local results without making you go all foggy, as I'm sure you know..."

"Are you capable of doing ... like, more refined medicines? Like, mind-altering stuff?" Rachel shyly asked.

Kaylah lifted an eyebrow. "Are you asking me if I can get people high? Or are you wanting to know more about what I had to do to you?"

Rachel rocked her head back and forth. "Well... I just meant, replacing happy pills, or something like that. But yeah, I guess you might be able to do a lot of good ... and bad ... with the right mix."

Walking silently for a moment, Kaylah pursed her lips in thought. "I don't know if I want to find out. I wouldn't want to push too far. Though, I don't *think* we can make anything that pure, otherwise it would have been exploited already. What I did to you was pretty basic poison." Kaylah sighed. "I'm just happy that, whether it's helping people or it's helping nature, we're starting to explore what we can actually do with our chemical abilities, not just 'poison.'"

"That's pretty neat. I look forward to seeing more of it."

Kaylah threw Rachel a mischievous glance. "Speaking of things we look forward to seeing more of... What about your new love interest?"

Rachel bit her lip. "It's not like that. I don't think, anyway. What did he say?" Kaylah clearly knew something had developed between them, and that knowledge had to have come straight from Guillen. Rachel's stomach fluttered at the thought he'd confided an interest in her.

"You know Guillen; he's not much of a talker. But he sure did blush when he reported how talented and smart he thought you were. I didn't even know he was *capable* of blushing."

Rachel wore a stupid grin. It wasn't like he'd talked nonstop, but he wasn't mute. They'd shared plenty of engaging conversations. She wasn't so sure she could agree with Kaylah's assessment of him not being a talker.

"It's silly to like him. We're so different—our upbringing, being on different sides of the war ... all that stuff. It's not really the time to think about what I want in that way."

"Are you saying I'm selfish for being with Eric?"

"No! I wasn't saying that at all."

Kaylah nudged her arm. "It's not that different, you know. Me and Eric, you and Guillen. We have people who would say we should be apart, other priorities pulling at our attention. But love doesn't wait until life is smooth and perfect. Or at least it shouldn't have to."

Rachel wished it could be that simple. She didn't even know where Guillen was at the moment, and had no way to contact him. "I don't know how you balance all this."

"With lots of desperation, hope, and caffeine." Kaylah laughed. "But..." Her tone dropped to be more serious. "It's all worth it. The sacrifice. The time. The movement. Making things work with Eric."

"But ... how is it really going to work with you guys? He lives in the human world. You're going to be a freaking queen someday; you can't exactly move here to be with him. And aren't you supposed to produce heirs or something?"

Kaylah gnawed on her bottom lip in silence for a few more paces. "We'll figure it out. I have some theories, and hope. Rach, I have to have hope. I love him, and I'm not willing to let him go. And if Guillen is what you want, you'd be lucky to have each other, and you can make it work, too."

"Well, cool your jets on that one. We barely even held hands, kind of." Rachel cleared her throat, her mind drifting back to the lake. "There was that one time I was half-naked in his arms..."

Kaylah's eyes lit up. "Come again? That's it—I need every single detail of your journey back! That's an order!"

Rachel laughed. "It wasn't like that, first of all. And secondly, I'm not sure what the relationship is between you and me. I don't know if I take orders from you."

Kaylah tilted her head, frowning. "Rach, you're still my best friend. And I can promise you, I will *always* be honest with you from now on. I don't have a reason to lie to you anymore."

Rachel nudged Kaylah's arm. "I missed you."

"I missed you too, girl. Now back to my cousin..."

Rachel chuckled. "Okay. But then I want to hear all about what he's doing to help Unitas."

Approaching the house on their return, Kaylah and Rachel took a small detour to the backyard.

"C'mon, two-person hammock!" Kaylah said, running to the patio and lying down.

Rachel joined her with a smile. She was beyond grateful to be back with her best friend. And to see that Kaylah was genuinely the same girl she'd known all along.

They snuggled up in the hammock, and Kaylah grabbed the edges, pulling them together. "Cocoon of love!"

Wrinkling her nose, Rachel glanced at the fabric. "Please tell me you guys haven't had sex on this thing."

Kaylah busted out laughing. "No! But you're giving me ideas." She released the edges of the hammock and wiggled to be able to make eye contact with Rachel. "He's seriously so amazing."

Rachel let out a heavy sigh. "I'm happy you guys are back together, but I really don't need to envision you and Eric in bed."

Kaylah smirked. "While I certainly have my opinions on performance in the bedroom, that's not what I meant. I just... I really appreciate the sacrifices he's willing to make." Her voice softened. "And you, too. That you're willing to give me another chance after all that's gone down."

Rachel scanned Kaylah's face. "What I don't understand is why you're doing this. If this is really you... How can that even be? Why wouldn't you be living with servants pampering you right now? Instead, you're risking your life. Why are you so different from the rest of your family?"

Kaylah met her gaze. "What makes one person or race better than another?"

After a moment of silence, Rachel realized the question hadn't been rhetorical. "Their choices and actions?"

"Hmm. Maybe your answer is better than mine. I was going to say: nothing. If I've learned anything from living so much with humans and being forced to take their history classes, it's that we're all just fools wandering around on this earth. Most of us are just doing the best we can. You. Eric. Guillen. I love the wrong people to be that entitled. And if I'm going to be known as the most disappointing crown princess my kingdom has ever had, I'm going to do everything I can to *earn* that title."

Rachel loved her for her bravery, and for her ability to throw caution to the wind. But Kaylah was making some dangerous moves here. "Are you afraid?"

Kaylah's voice softened once again. "Of course I am. How much do you think we can trust Saff? And your people? Do you think this will actually go somewhere? And it's not just a trap?"

Rachel wiggled a bit, getting a better view of the clouds as they rolled by. "They don't trust my judgment. I'm not sure. I think they'd trust her, though. I hope they do. And I don't think she's setting us up..." She glided her fingers over the teal-and-white striped fabric of the hammock. "I don't know who to trust anymore. I just... I don't know."

"Hey, I get it. But don't give up on yourself. That's the big difference between you and her, you know. You've been hurt, but you still have hope. And you forgive. Some people just get bitter."

Rachel frowned. "That's not fair. She's been through a lot. And we all handle stress differently. And... She's never had a decent experience with an Ivy. I have." Her stomach was tight, her anxiety growing. She hated being in the middle of this. Between Kaylah and Saff. Between the conflicting interests. But, in a very fulfilling way, she was also grateful to be there to hopefully bridge the gap.

They sat in silence for some time, watching the sky. A yellowjacket buzzed around uncomfortably close before heading on its way.

"I wonder how many people died because of me," Rachel whispered.

"What are you talking about? You're not to blame for any of this!"

"If I hadn't fallen for Soren's lies... Been so stupid... I know at least a couple of soldiers had to have lost their lives protecting our walls because of what my energy did for your War Vines. And how many more girls are going to fall to that same fate because your assassins know about our jade charms?"

"Look at me."

Rachel hesitantly turned her head.

Kaylah's eyebrows were raised high. "It's not your fault. It's not even your family's fault. It's *my* family's. Okay?"

Rachel gave a tiny nod. "It's true that our people got one of the girls out? Is she okay?"

"Yeah, they got one out. I'm not sure how she is. But ... from what I understand ... it was kind of a massacre for your people. They didn't realize how our energy barrier protects the palace. They lost the advantage they thought they had."

Rachel's heart ached. "How are we losing so badly? I mean... We can fly, and we have projectiles, and we have twenty-four flipping kids at a time... You'd think we far outnumber your people. How are we losing?"

"You're stronger in a lot of ways—I'll give you that. But our strategies and abilities do a lot to mitigate all that. Your people are split between the worlds, have more limitations, and you're too passive, untrusting, and bad at coordinating."

"Wow, tell me how you really feel." Rachel raised an eyebrow.

"Just telling it like it is. And yeah, you have a lot of kids. You outnumber us. But not as much as you think, from what I'm guessing. Twins and triplets aren't actually that rare for Ivies. And pregnancies are shorter for us than humans. Even then... Do all your Seeder teenagers come back to the Green Lands and look forward to wrestling that many dang kids?"

Rachel chuckled. "Definitely not."

"Maybe not now, because human culture has become such a big part of who you are. But back in the day ... before our people split ways..." Kaylah slowly sat up and Rachel followed suit, wrapping her fingers around the rope holding up the hammock. "Your people used to far outnumber us. I don't exactly love the term, but ... there's a reason my people call yours 'weeds.'"

"Because weeds are trash."

"Yes, and no. Weeds spread. They can grow out of control. They can choke out a garden. Your people are capable of building a *massive* army and obliterating my people."

"But that's not how it happens! I know I've only been over there a few weeks, but really ... not a single one of these people chooses to have kids just to build up some stupid army. Like you said—they're passive. It's a hard choice to have kids at all. And it's not like we can change things... It's zero or twenty-four. We don't get a choice in that!" Rachel furrowed her brow. She hated having to defend herself like she had with Soren. This time she'd actually met other Seeders. They weren't the aggressors in all of this.

"I know," Kaylah answered softly. "I believe you. And... I don't even know what to believe, myself, about history. It's not like either of our recorded or oral histories would be impartial about what happened with the Great Division. I'm just saying... Whether it's true or not, your people have great potential. Fear. Is. Motivating. My people worry."

Rachel looked down, trying to put herself in Ivy shoes.

"Rachel."

Looking up, she met Kaylah's gaze. Kaylah's face was stone-cold sober.

"My people are as tired of this as yours are. They're frustrated. They want it to end. *For good.* This isn't the same war anymore. And it's not just about who lives on the best land anymore, either. My uncle wanted to punish your people. We're talking colonization. We're talking slavery. *Complete* population control. And *every* able-bodied male Ivy is enlisted and ready to be called up for duty. Every last one of them. I *need* your people to see my offer for what it is. I have to believe your councils would prefer to work with me, and maybe even offer some concessions before this goes further. Once my parents have taken down your borders, it's too late. We *need* Unitas to work. We need each other."

Goosebumps covered Rachel's arms as she swallowed hard. "Right. We'll make it happen."

Chapter 34

Saff lay in bed, fuming. Rachel thought Saff was conceited about her extra energy capabilities, but that wasn't true in the slightest. Yes—Saff was different. But it wasn't like she traipsed around their village expecting fanfare. With that extra power, she'd risked her life and relationships to help Rachel, to help their people. With that power, and *a lot* of extra studying and effort, she had been offered the position as a mentor. To mentor someone as ungrateful as Rachel.

Rolling onto her side, Saff angrily punched her pillow into a more comfortable blob, then shoved it back under her head.

Rachel was so ... naïve. She made rash decisions that hurt other people. She was too trusting. She was selfish. She was too much ... like Saff.

Maybe that was why it infuriated her so much. She remembered treating Ben just like Rachel was treating her. He had always tried to keep Saff out of trouble, and she'd never listened. She'd compromised them; she'd gotten people hurt. She was never certain what role she had played in the bloodbath at her parents' house, if she was somehow at fault for that, too. Saff had dealt with her demons and come to terms with her guilt over the last few years. This was all fresh and new for Rachel; she hadn't grown up from it all yet, at least not by Saff's estimation.

And what had Kaylah concretely done to prove she could make good on her promises? She'd killed off a patch of grass and made it grow again. That was hardly proof she could save millions of Seeder lives.

Saff couldn't help but wonder if Ben would still be alive, if just one part of the equation had been altered. If Rachel had never been kidnapped, if the Ivies had never had access to her power; the short amount of time it had pulled away Saff, Devin, and Simon, or the search parties... Could any of that have made a difference? She wasn't directly blaming Rachel for his death, though she couldn't help but wonder, amidst the sea of 'what-ifs,' if he would have still been there with her, if just one minor detail of the past had been changed.

She thought of all the time she had shared with Ben in this world, and their own. She fondly recalled their first Christmas together, before she even knew he was her real brother. Their chats as she'd sorted through major life decisions. They'd grown even closer after returning to the Green Lands—he and Heather would come over often to spend time at Saff and Devin's cottage.

And Saff had promised him she would make up for being a pain when they were in high school, when she'd almost gotten him killed. She'd promised him he'd have his wedding day. And that was a promise she could never fulfill.

Her anger, hurt, and regrets came to a head as she sobbed into her pillow. He wouldn't be coming back. Feelings of hopelessness crowded her mind. She mentally listed the names of her large family, one at a time. It was like throwing a fistful of darts and hoping none of them would stick. Who would she lose next in this war? Whether or not Rachel's mistakes truly had any effect on Ben's outcome, Kaylah's had. Her people's actions had taken Ben. She could have done something differently.

Saff gritted her teeth. She wanted to do what was right, wanted to be able to trust Kaylah like Rachel did. She hated feeling so out of control. But the logical, skeptical, careful side of her kept pulling her back from trusting Kaylah blindly. How was Saff the bad guy in all of this? If Rachel was going to just run off a cliff, shouldn't someone more grounded be there to help weigh the risks? Saff wasn't a pessimist; she was a realist.

After a good long cry, she blew her nose and picked up the cell they'd purchased at the gas station, dialing a number she had memorized a while back.

It only rang twice before being answered. "Hello?"

"Mom?"

"Melody! Is that you?"

Saff burst into tears. "Yeah, Mom. I'm just on another short visit."

"How is that? Are you okay?" Pam, her formerly-Seeder-now-human mom, asked, her voice conveying her concern.

"Yeah, it's complicated. I'm sorry I couldn't visit you and Dad this year." She sniffled, trying to keep her composure.

"Honey, we understand. We're just happy to know you're okay. Is there any chance we'll get to see you this time? You are ... okay, right?"

"Yeah. There's a lot going on. I have a way home; I'm going to be okay."

Pam understood Seeder physiology; the fact that Saff had called during her visit earlier in the year, and was now back in the human world for a second time, and at this late of a season... She knew how impossible it was. And how likely lethal that made it.

"Okay..." Pam hesitantly accepted her daughter's assertion.

"I can't come visit this time either. I'm leaving in the morning. I just needed to hear your voice. And..." She started to ugly cry with all the squeaking and huffing and sniffling that comes with it.

Pam stayed silent on the phone.

Saff's voice trembled. "Mom, Ben's dead."

Pam gasped on the other end of the phone, then stayed silent. While Saff had been raised by Pam and George, Ben had only been in their home as a foster for one year, but they'd treated him like family. He and Heather had even gone to visit them briefly the previous spring.

"I just," Saff choked on her words, "thought you should know."

There was a long silence on the phone. "I'm sorry, honey. He was a good man. Your dad and I are praying for you guys every night."

"Thanks, Mom. I love you guys." Something came to Saff's mind. It seemed massively premature, but it was better to be prepared. Eric's willingness and dedication to Kaylah's cause made her think. "Has anyone approached you guys about us, about our war?"

"Um, no... We haven't talked to anyone in the network since you left, other than you kids visiting us."

"Good." Saff wiped away her tears, sitting up straight on the bed. "Can I trust you with some names and information?"

"I... Yeah. You know you can trust us with anything."

"It's a long shot. But there's a group that might be able to help us stop this war. And I may give them your phone number someday. But only if I know I can trust them, and I'm going to give you a code word so you know you can trust them, too. And... I'm going to give you the names of the other Seeder family hosts from my family and Devin's. I'd rather the information be safe with you instead of giving it to them directly. I trust your and Dad's judgment."

"Oh, honey, that sounds... Are you sure? That's a lot of sensitive information."

"I know. And you might never need it. But if things work out, it could make a world of difference. I just want you to be prepared."

"Alright, let me grab a pen and paper."

Saff listed off her siblings and Devin's, so Pam could try to track down contact information on their human host families. Discreetly, of course, especially in the case of brothers, as their hosts weren't always aware of their true Seeder identities.

Saff had no intention of just handing that information over to Unitas. But if Kaylah could prove herself, it might mean a lot of resources on the human side, if Eric and the gatekeeper they'd met upon their arrival had been right about human involvement in this conflict. No matter what they tried, Saff's people were suffering and slowly losing this war. They needed a new weapon, and this might shift the balance of power, even if Kaylah could only fulfill half of her promises.

Saff couldn't make good on her promise to Ben that he'd get his happily ever after, but she could still keep her promise to give her all, to end this.

"And unless it's Thod, Devin, or Heather, don't trust anyone without the code word, okay? Keep that information safe." Saff thought of a gorgeous flower she'd seen depicted in Seeder art, now believed to be extinct. "The code word is spelled G-u-e-n-j-a-l-i-s. It's pronounced 'gwen-yawl-iss.'"

"Okay. I'll tuck that away in the safe right now. We miss you, honey. I wish I could give you a hug."

"Thanks, Mom." Saff frowned. "I could never repay you and Dad. I'm sorry I was a pain in the butt growing up."

Pam chuckled softly. "You weren't so bad. We're proud of you. I worry about you, but I hope you're still happy with your choice to go. It sounds like you're doing great things for your people."

Saff thought about it. Did she regret her choice? If she had known this was coming, would she have chosen to stay behind and become a human? Either way, the Green Lands was her home now, and she wouldn't change that, even if she could. She would never give up Devin or any member of her family. The sacrifice was worth it.

"I am happy, and I'll be okay. We'll make it out of this stronger. And we'll be happy to see you next spring, okay? Devin says hi." There was a stab of guilt about that last part. He hadn't even known she was returning. But he would have said hi—it felt natural to say it.

"Your dad will be sad he wasn't here to chat, but I'll pass it on. We look forward to seeing you guys." Pam paused. "Honey, I don't know everything that's going on. And I know it's a hard time. I just want to remind you to consider all the options when you're making all of these important choices, okay?"

Saff smirked. Even as a married woman, her mom knew who she was. It was like her mom could read between the lines, knowing Saff's decision to come had been impulsive. "I'll do my best to make you guys proud."

"Stay safe, sweetheart. We love you."

Saff teared up again. "Love you. Bye, Mom."

Saff was still in bed, her emotions wearing her down. A knock on the door caused her to sit up and blow her nose. "Come in."

Rachel stood in the doorway, hesitant. Walking across the room, she gently sat on the other bed. "How are you doing?"

Saff dabbed under her eyes with a chuckle. "Not the most productive nap."

Rachel frowned. "I'm sorry about earlier. I know you just want what's best for our people. And I do, too. I'm just asking you to give me a little credit."

Pursing her lips, Saff took a deep breath.

"You met your husband when he was your protection detail, right?" Rachel asked.

"Yeah."

Rachel cocked her head to the side. "How long were you dating before you found out his identity?"

"A few months."

"I dated the prince for over two years before I found out who he was. What do you think you would have done if it had happened the other way around for you? That Devin was an Ivy, instead of a Seeder?"

Saff furrowed her brow in thought. That would have made things a heck of a lot stickier. "Well, I probably wouldn't be alive. Because he's the one that spotted my bloom in the first place."

"Yeah. Well, mine found out. And you're right; he used me and I probably would have died by his hand at the palace, eventually. But if your husband had told you what David, er, Soren, had told me... If you had shared all of that extra time between you... You don't think you might have made the same stupid mistakes as me?"

Saff looked at the wall and rolled her eyes. "Yeah, I probably would have been just as naï—" She paused. "I probably would have made poor choices."

"But you made your own mistakes, and you learned from them."

"Rachel, I'm sorry. I get what you're saying. And I'm sorry for taking my anger out on you. Everything is a bit ... fresh ... for me right now. And I just want what's best for you."

※

Rachel forced a half-smile. "Thank you. I don't really have a lot of people in my life I can trust, or that trust me, or care about me." She fidgeted with her hands. "Sometimes I feel like I don't have anything or anyone. Not even with my new family back home. My homecoming wasn't exactly a typical celebration."

Saff frowned. "You just have to give it time. It takes a while to acclimate and build those bonds, even if you *had* come home under normal circumstances."

Rachel nodded. "I'll work on it. I haven't given up yet."

"Good. You're a smart girl." Saff picked up her phone, offering it to Rachel. "I know we can't see your mom, and you guys have got to be dying to talk. Why don't you give her a call?"

Rachel eyed the phone with both longing and trepidation. She'd been avoiding it thus far, despite how desperately she'd wanted to hear her mom's voice. "Kaylah and Eric want to talk first. I'll call her before bed, if you're ready to join us."

"Sure."

Rachel stepped out of the room.

"Rachel?" Saff called.

"Yeah?" Rachel poked her head back in.

"I feel like there's something I should tell you."

Rachel's eyes narrowed. "Okay?"

"Duke Nuren."

Rachel frowned. She still had a hard time fully hating him. She recognized her own denial at times, having witnessed a complete one-eighty, just briefly, after years of loving him as her stepdad. "What about him?"

Saff swallowed hard. "I heard his name before, before you were even taken."

Rachel sat down on her bed again. "What?"

"My brother." Saff looked down. "The one that died. He's the one that saved my life, when the Ivy I dated attacked me."

Rachel pressed her lips together. That had to have given them a strong bond.

Saff sniffled. "Anyway, I heard that name—Nuren—in the first attack. We knew there was Ivy royalty there, but we didn't have any other problems after another fight. We killed their general and several others. We ... didn't realize there was another Seeder family across town. And we wondered if maybe I had misheard the name, or if maybe we had actually killed him, or..." She fidgeted with a clean corner of her tissue. "Just, we did you and our people a disservice by not being more open about the possible threat earlier. I'm sorry."

Rachel stared at Saff, her mind running through a myriad of 'what-ifs.' But she couldn't blame Saff's family; they had been taking care of their own. That was how Seeder society worked. And trying to find Rob, with his identity so well concealed—she questioned if it would have even been possible.

Rachel's mind took a darker turn, one she'd been avoiding. She was back in that room in the palace, with Nuren—Rob, her stepdad. She'd wondered if anyone had ever loved her; her closest relationships were all fabricated. Aside from her mom. The woman she feared talking to, the woman she'd brought so much pain upon through her misplaced trust, by her very existence. The woman who had wanted to have more kids, kids of her own, but had been lied to. Rob never could have given her more kids, but hadn't disclosed that when they'd married.

Other than Guillen and Jon, Rachel had struggled to form new relationships. Relationships were hard; they were risky. She'd never been an introvert, but she couldn't deal with the guilt and worry. And that was what this felt like. The looks and actions of her Seeder family—pity. Saff's part in this—guilt.

Rachel cleared her throat. Saff was now looking at her, waiting for a response. "I don't need your help. You don't owe me anything. I don't blame you."

✺

Saff bit her lip, her heart still heavy. She admitted to herself that a lot of her actions regarding Rachel had to do with guilt and a sense of obligation. But she knew that was a dangerous line to toe in relationships. She'd navigated that all with her husband's lies under orders back when she was in high school. Even if it was a motivating factor, she would never admit as much to Rachel.

"I guess I just wanted to say... We have a lot in common. Home towns, raised as only children, dealing with rotten people and experiences. And, maybe I kind of think of you like a little sister." She grinned. "Not that you don't already have plenty of sisters."

✺

Rachel smiled, thinking it over. She was at least grateful Saff had been honest with her about Nuren, that she hadn't held back. "Thanks." Her mind turned to her earlier conversation, Kaylah's eerie warning about where things were going with this war. "You ready to go talk to the others?"

Chapter 35

Rachel walked into the living room, Saff following after her. Eric was giving Kaylah a shoulder massage. She got up from the floor and sat next to him on the couch. Rachel and Saff took their respective armchairs, both ready for more Unitas talk.

"Thanks for joining us again," Kaylah started. "I thought it would be best to discuss the human part of the equation more before we head out, since that wasn't discussed in much detail earlier."

"I'm all ears," Saff said.

"Money isn't a problem," Kaylah said. "We have some generous humans that have joined the cause." She turned to Rachel. "And Ginger and Nathan and I siphoned off a good deal of the royal investments set aside for my upkeep before I sent them away." She looked Rachel squarely in the eye. "They were never part of my uncle's plan. Their job was to keep me safe and ensure I was properly educated. They knew your identity, but never knew any plans until I brought them into mine, okay?"

Rachel nodded, grateful she'd offered another point of clarification. It helped, knowing people she liked and admired actually cared for her, and weren't part of the grand scheme.

Kaylah turned back to Saff. "Anyway... Money, humans. We do want to open up the human network to prepare for any eventuality. We have some Ivy defectors over here, and through a lot of hard work, we've gathered a few human and even a couple of former Seeder host connections, but we need more. Just to be prepared."

"Why do you need more?" Saff asked. "What are you expecting to need them for?"

Kaylah crossed her legs. "Movement, more safe houses. Ivies only ever think of humans as unknowing hosts, as simple pawns, and they mostly ignore them. They don't realize what a huge resource they really are. And, so far ... our movement on this side has done really well, under the radar. But we have to be prepared for negotiations to take a while, and possibly not go the way we're wanting. I imagine the situation could get more aggressive on this side of things. Once they realize we're evacuating your girls, we may need to be prepared for extra hostility."

Kaylah bobbed her head. "I know I said we'll negotiate first. And I have hope with the research I've done, that I can sway things toward a peaceful resolution. But we need to be prepared for every eventuality. Keeping your people and borders safe, winning approval from my people."

"You're talking about them coming after the humans, too?" Saff asked.

Kaylah shrugged. "It's possible. It's not our usual method. But their tactics aren't exactly ethical; they're not above human harm."

Observing silently from her chair, Rachel mentally noted how Kaylah used her words. When she would use 'our' to show she was still an Ivy. And 'their' to disassociate herself from the brutality of the current and past regimes. It didn't sound rehearsed; she sounded genuine.

❁

Saff spoke up with her usual skepticism, but tried to tone down her accusatory attitude of earlier. "So, you're asking for contacts? Realizing that giving away those names may put them in even greater danger, if you or someone in your group betrays us?"

Kaylah slowly nodded once. "Yes. And I understand that's asking a lot."

Saff raised her eyebrows. "I'm glad you have a good grasp on that reality. *If* things pan out, I'm prepared to give you a couple dozen contacts in the human world, some of them still local. Remember that, as we move forward."

Kaylah's eyes widened in obvious shock, as though maybe she had only intended to ask for Saff's parents, or something much smaller. "I would be honored, and would make great use of that information. And I'll be able to prove my worthiness for it."

Saff suppressed a grin, even more glad she had made the call to her mom. It was an extra layer of motivation and insurance. Though her mom's words played back to her: To make sure she was looking at all of her choices. Thinking out the consequences. There was no way Saff would be giving away a single name unless she was beyond convinced this was safe.

✻

Kaylah turned to Rachel. "We've moved your mom to a safe house."

Rachel's heart skipped a beat. "Really? Did they try to hurt her?"

"No. Not yet. But Soren can be vindictive." Kaylah rubbed at her neck. Eric took her hand away from her neck and kissed it.

✻

Eric's attention reminded Saff of Devin, helping her through crushing PTSD as she had healed from Ivy strangulation wounds.

Kaylah snapped out of her trance. "I've arranged for her to join us at our departure point in the morning."

"Really?!" Rachel shrieked, starting to cry. "Thank you, Meg. I mean ... Kaylah!"

Kaylah gave her a reassuring smile. "Of course."

Saff was cautiously starting to warm up to Kaylah. Kaylah was competent, organized, and seemingly caring. Never traits Saff had associated with the enemy. Just like her own discovery of her people and the Green Lands, she realized it might be time to expose herself to a more neutral narrative of the Ivies.

Kaylah's eyes danced between Rachel and Saff. "I ... also need to make sure we're clear on the fact that *no one*—Seeder, Ivy, or human—can know," she paused, "that Eric and I are together."

Eric didn't make eye contact with anyone in the room, but rubbed Kaylah's arm.

"I just ... His location needs to be a secret, and I can't have anyone coming after him to get to me." She lowered her eyes. "It would not bode well for negotiations if my parents knew I was still with him. And... I have to play it safe when it comes to your council. Can you both give me your word that no one will find out?"

"Of course," Rachel said without hesitation.

Saff read Kaylah's face. Every inch of her expression and the inflection in her voice made it clear she was serious, desperate, and determined. It hadn't been wise to use his safe house for this meeting, and to show affection openly. But Saff knew how important it was to have someone you could trust and rely on, to lean on in the hard times. To have someone in your corner. For her, that was Devin. She'd missed him this week; she'd needed him while processing Ben's loss in silence. Sick to her stomach, she imagined how Devin must feel right now, after she'd deserted him.

"You can trust me." Saff smiled, meeting eyes with Eric. "We don't harm humans, especially those that want to help bring peace to green folk."

Eric gave a nod of appreciation.

"Thank you," Kaylah said.

Eric took some time to speak next, explaining the basics of how their network was setting things up and handling it all. Bank accounts, encryptions, codes. It was impressive. It was a shame they were limited to this realm, but they made good use of their resources. Unitas was even hiring hackers to combat the Ivy assassin network's efforts. To help narrow down likely Seeders and coordinate amongst Ivy networks, Nuren had commissioned the creation of an app. Suspected Seeder behavior and spottings data were pooled and run through an algorithm.

"How long have they been that high-tech?" Saff asked, thinking back to her high school days. Nuren had lived across town, and the assassins that came after her and her family hadn't behaved normally.

Kaylah shrugged. "I don't know. It's not like I ever used the app. But I found out about it maybe two or three years ago? It could have been in beta testing for a while."

"Does the name Mel or Melody Walters mean anything to you?" Saff asked.

Kaylah raised her eyebrows. "Nope."

"She went to Franklin High four years ago."

Kaylah shook her head. "Franklin High across town from where Rachel and I grew up? The name still doesn't ring a bell."

"At least ten of your assassins were killed by a pair of Seeder families that year."

"Impressive. What's your point?"

"Melody Walters was my name before I chose the Seeder life. They came after me. They came after my family."

Kaylah looked down, pressing her lips together. "I'm beginning to see how personal this all is for you. I'm sorry."

The logic didn't add up. "But you want me to believe you didn't know a massacre happened across town, with your own people?"

Kaylah cocked her head to the side. "I want you to believe it, because it's true. I was a spy, not an assassin. I was here to ... focus on," she cleared her throat, "to focus on Rachel—gathering intel from her, following orders in regards to her. But in all my 'free' time, I not only had to keep up the appearance of being a normal human teen, I had constant tutoring as the crown princess. I was too busy to associate with anyone deployed in the assassin networks."

Saff had almost started to like Kaylah, but that didn't sit right with her. "Glad to know we were beneath your notice."

Kaylah sighed. "If you're looking for a pity party, I can't offer you that."

Saff glared. "Your pity wouldn't be welcomed. Answers would be. Ten is a lot more than the three to six in a normal network you mentioned."

"I don't know how it all played out, but that sounds like backup. So, they'd obviously made you and considered you guys a threat for some reason."

"They knew my identity for a month before they attacked the second time. Why did they wait?"

"To study you? Study and experimentation were in the scope of what my uncle was doing. Or maybe they were just waiting to unravel your network. If they discover one girl, she could be the first to bloom, or the last. If they can flush out your whole network, they can take down an entire family at once."

It made Saff sick to her stomach, hearing Kaylah discuss it so coolly, so calmly. "But you don't really know. Your uncle was calling all the shots. The one *you* killed. And his secrets died with him."

Kaylah sat up straighter, folding her hands in her lap. "I can't undo the past. And I don't have any regrets about that decision. I'm sorry I can't give you the closure you're looking for, but it's not like it was all for naught. The books and scrolls he gave me access to, when he became so *proud* of me for 'stepping up' to help with his research... I don't think people have set eyes on some of those in decades, maybe centuries. He was selective about his research to benefit his strategy. I studied it *all*. There are some valuable things there that he had access to. And I did, too.

"He's gone. The reading material has been smuggled out of the palace. He can't use that information anymore. No one in the palace can."

Saff took a deep breath, crossing her legs. "I have a knack for learning new things. Especially since some of that is no doubt stolen Seeder information, I'd love access to those resources."

Kaylah gave her a soft smile. "Great. Rachel wants to help and I have a job in mind for her. Glad to hear you're on board and willing to help, too. But I'm not allowing access to those records or sharing any more information about my strategies until I'm safely speaking to your leaders. That's the deal. We get there. We talk. We negotiate with my parents. And then we'll see."

Saff rubbed her forehead. Kaylah was exhausting to work with. This whole ordeal was exhausting. The whole last year had been. "Yeah. Whatever, fine. Let's go over details of what tomorrow morning will look like."

❈

The sun set as the group hashed out final details for their return. Rachel watched Eric and Kaylah, so easily and maturely conversing in each other's arms. Kaylah's hand rested on Eric's thigh as he talked and Eric's arm was slung around her, lovingly drawing a figure eight over and over on Kaylah's shoulder. Before the crap hit the fan, Rachel would have easily voted them the cutest and most compatible couple in their high school. And now, going through all the struggles and real situations they were facing, they couldn't be more perfect. She was happy for them. A little jealous, maybe, but happy.

"Well, I think we should turn in early tonight," Rachel suggested. "We're all a little drained, and the earlier we get to bed, the earlier we can get going."

"You're sure there's nothing else we need to discuss?" Saff questioned. "Especially with you, Eric? We won't so easily have this opportunity to bring human insight into this operation again."

"It's okay. Kaylah knows all of those details and procedures intimately," Eric said with confidence.

Rachel stood up, stretching. "I'm down for going to bed." She was recognizing the warning signs of root rot anyway. Not that she'd ever experienced it before, but she'd been taught about it. Her pool of energy was diminishing by the hour. Good rest and a quick exit were both what the doctor ordered.

After turning in for the night, Saff quickly fell asleep, but Rachel took a while longer. She was proud of herself for her part in these negotiations. While it had mostly been Saff and Kaylah doing the talking, Rachel had been a key piece in, well, keeping the peace. Maybe this could help make up for the shame of her previous failures, assuming it paid off.

Rachel tried to block out the thought of what she knew was happening in the other room, though she couldn't help but wish it was Guillen and her. Not exactly the full intimacy... They were nowhere near that. But just the thought of him being there in that bed, cuddling with her. Those piercing eyes, his muscular arms, his tender touch. Holding hands. Stealing a *real* kiss, not just the one she'd given him on the cheek as they'd parted ways.

She sighed, frowning. They didn't stand a chance. Distance, war, time ... just everything. They had work to do, and even though she had a hint of hope to see him again with Kaylah's plans, she wasn't really sure what that would look like. But she let her mind linger on him. It was helpful to drown out thoughts of Soren and the hurt. She felt guilty, at first, for using the memory of Guillen that way, but in the end justified it. He'd earned her affection by his own merits, not just as a stand-in.

Chapter 36

Guillen wasn't the only person occupying Rachel's thoughts as she struggled to sleep. As an owl's hoot from the backyard pierced the silence of the night, she rehearsed in her head how things would go with her mom in the morning. It was the first time she would get to see her since the kidnapping. What exactly had her mom been told about the circumstances? Rachel would face her in shame—it was her own stupidity that had gotten her kidnapped. Her heart hurt for her mom, knowing she had to be distraught over losing her daughter. That she had been betrayed and left by another man. Rachel sulked at the irony. Like mother, like daughter—they hadn't made the best choices in men.

That had actually been a point of contention with her Seeder mom, Lyza. Lyza had insisted they'd done a *thorough* background check on 'Rob' just like they had 'David.' Rachel didn't know who to believe, and in the end, they couldn't change the past. Assigning blame wouldn't make things better.

Eventually, much later than she would have liked, Rachel found sleep. She woke in the morning to Saff stripping the other bed to be washed.

❁

"Hey, you. How are you doing?" Saff asked.

Rachel groaned. "Just five more minutes? Or five more days?"

"Sorry, doesn't work that way. We've got our lives to preserve and a war to stop. Why don't you hit the shower?" Saff's anxieties were growing as she stared down the barrel of her attempt to return to the Green Lands. She was faced with the question she'd had about leaving for this trip in the first place—could she even do it? If she had failed to get through that second rift a few days ago, she would have just remained back home. If she failed to get through a second one home now... The outcome would be death.

✹

Rachel grunted, pulling her comforter over her face. She didn't want to go back to a war zone, or get out of the pillowy bed so early when she'd gotten such poor sleep. But she also couldn't have any more blood on her hands, and couldn't wait to reunite with her mom. Rolling out of bed, she walked down the hall to the bathroom.

The happy couple only emerged from Eric's room once both Saff and Rachel were out in the dining room. He'd set out muffins for everyone, but didn't leave Kaylah's side to make a special breakfast. Instead of their previous aura of happiness and insatiable lust, their expressions were quieter and more downcast.

No one had to say anything. Rachel had felt just the tip of that iceberg when Guillen had left her in hiding.

✹

Saff even sympathized; she missed Devin like crazy, and knew what it was like to be separated from her love for several months.

After breakfast, they hopped in Eric's car, complete with tinted windows. He held Kaylah's hand the entire way to a nearby forest. The trip went by in almost complete silence. Saff wrung her hands. This would be the first time she'd witness an Ivy rift. To Seeders, the destruction Ivies caused as a means of transportation was a repugnant and vile sin against nature. But this time, it might just save her life. She didn't have a choice.

✹

Rachel bounced her knee excitedly as they pulled up to the meeting point, where another car was already waiting. She tore the door open as soon as Eric parked, running to her mom as she exited the other vehicle.

"Rachel! I'm so sorry, baby. I missed you. Are you okay?" Samantha cried.

"Yeah, Mom. I'm great." Rachel squeezed her tight. "I'm sorry for everything."

"Sweetheart, you have *nothing* to apologize for." Samantha pulled herself away, wiping away one of Rachel's tears. "I'll never forgive myself for bringing Rob into our lives and putting you in harm's way."

Rachel frowned. "Mom, he had everyone fooled. It's not like my birth dad or brothers or anyone else suspected him, either. Don't take the blame for that." Her eyes glazed over for a moment, remembering the bloody scene at her rescue. "I can guarantee you won't ever see him again, and both worlds will be better for it."

✹

Kaylah and Eric smiled in unison, watching the reunion. Eric had his arms wrapped around Kaylah from behind. Saff anxiously stood there until Kaylah made the other introductions.

"Saff, these are my deployment guardians. Ginger and Nathan."

Ginger and Nathan shook hands with Saff, then gave Eric and Kaylah a hug.

❋

Rachel and her mom discussed trying to find a way to pass letters to stay in touch. Being in league with Ivies that could come and go regularly gave Rachel a light at the end of the tunnel—she could stay more connected with her mom. Of course, that was only if things didn't go sideways.

Spotting Ginger and Nathan a few yards to her left, Rachel broke away from her mom and squealed, running up to hug Kaylah's parents. "It's nice to see you guys! I was really touched to hear you guys were part of the cause!"

Ginger smiled wide. "It's good to see you, too. And Unitas is important to us. Just as much as our Kaylah."

"So, you two are..." Saff started.

"We're Ivy," Ginger confirmed. "The warmth of the Green Lands is something green folk hate to live without, but once you live here on assignment for a few years, you start to appreciate the little things of the human world." She playfully swished a finger in the air. "And they don't have beaches like Cancun back there."

"So, are you guys at the safe house my mom's staying at?" Rachel asked. She was too ashamed to admit she was actually uncomfortable at the thought of it. While she loved Kaylah's parents, and they were part of Unitas, they were still Ivies, and her mom had been through a lot at Ivy hands.

"She's been with us, and it's been great getting caught up," Ginger said. "But she'll be relocated again, now that I'm coming with you."

"Okay." Rachel perked up even more. "So, you and Kaylah are our ride home?"

Ginger winked. "You got it."

"I promise we'll take good care of Samantha," Nathan reassured Rachel.

Rachel drew a deep breath and let it out. She could only do so much. She couldn't control everything. Not in her own world, let alone both of them. She'd need to learn to trust people. Out of the corner of her eye, Eric caught her attention. Once their eyes connected, he gave her a signal that he wanted to talk to her in private.

"Hey, babe, why don't you spend a minute with your parents. I've got to talk to Rachel." He kissed Kaylah's cheek and released her, looking like it took every ounce of his resolve to not stay near her.

He and Rachel moved a few feet away, and he started by talking just above a whisper. "I just wanted to ask you to, you know, watch out for her. She's entangled in a lot of dangerous stuff. I can't lose her."

Rachel smirked. "Well, I'm glad to know you care about my safety, too, Eric."

He sighed. "You know what I mean. I love her, Rach. And I can't do a single thing for her on that side. I'm counting on you to help her get through this safely. We're all counting on you."

Rachel pursed her lips. *No pressure, right?* "We'll take care of each other. I'll do everything in my power."

He smiled, grabbing her for a hug. "You're the best."

Glancing past Eric's shoulder, Rachel spotted Kaylah looking at a cell phone. Kaylah's expression dropped, heavier than Rachel had ever seen before. She handed the phone back to Nathan without even looking at him, staring at the ground with a blank face. She glanced up and met Rachel's gaze.

Kaylah's eyes shifted between Rachel and Saff, and she took a deep gulp. Kaylah gave her a tiny nod of the head, as if acknowledging that Rachel knew something was wrong, and asking her to stay silent, to trust her.

Eric released Rachel from the hug and Rachel stood still, her heart racing. Was her loyalty already going to be tested? No one postured threateningly. Other than Nathan, no one else seemed to be in on this big secret. Rachel was a split second away from reciprocating Kaylah's nod, but she couldn't. She wasn't going to walk through a rift blindly, not again. For all she knew, that look Kaylah had just flashed was one of guilt—she'd just gotten word their ambush was prepared on the other side.

"Hey, Kaylah, can we chat for a second?"

Kaylah forced a smile. "Sure, no prob."

They walked away from the group, out of hearing distance.

Rachel looked her in the eyes. "What is it?"

Kaylah frowned. "Just some bad news. It's not going to change our plans."

Rachel squinted. "You know I need more than that. I'm not going through without more than that."

"I promise. I just... Things will be better if we go right now. I'll tell you the second we get over there. I just want you to be safely back there." Kaylah's eyes showed concern.

Rachel continued to study her face, not responding.

"Rach, why would I save you and go through all of this, just to betray you? If *you* won't even trust me, then we don't stand a chance."

There it was again—trust. Rachel closed her eyes, considering the situation. She used to think she was a good judge of character. That delusion was long gone. But why *would* Kaylah have rescued her just to go through all of this? What would her end game be? The logic still fell in Kaylah's favor. If she'd wanted to hurt Rachel, she probably would have done it by now. "Fine. Let's go."

Eric rejoined Kaylah as Rachel made way. He looked lovingly, longingly into her eyes. "You stay safe."

Kaylah smiled through tears. "You, too. I love you."

"I love you, too."

They exchanged a couple of sweet kisses and a long hug. Rachel gave her mom another tight squeeze.

❋

Then Saff took Rachel to the side... "What was that about, between you and Kaylah?"

"Nothing."

Saff narrowed her eyes. "Right..." Her anxiety was too high about her own problems to press further. "I ... might have a problem." She lowered her voice further. "It's going to sound melodramatic, but I don't know if I can go back."

Rachel's mouth hung open. "What do you mean, can't go back?"

"I shouldn't have been able to make this trip in the first place—you knew that."

❋

"I know. You said you had a theory. That panned out." Rachel whispered, "You planned a suicide mission this whole time? You've only got a couple of days before you'd die!" She couldn't imagine Saff being so reckless. Or ... dead.

"I wasn't suicidal. I just ... was a bit ... irrational. I don't know for sure. This might be nothing. I just... In case I don't make it through..." Saff pursed her lips, unsuccessfully fighting back tears.

"Saff, you can't... And we *need* you! The council won't believe me. *Especially* now. A lot of this is riding on you. You should have at least told us earlier. Kaylah's counting on you to make the introduction."

❁

"Then make this trip count. At bare minimum, get home safe and tell them about the charms so our people know to be more vigilant. Tell them everything Kaylah's told us." Saff swallowed hard, her heart breaking. "And if I'm stranded here..." She wiped away tears. "Find Devin. Tell him where you left me. Maybe he could come here in time to say goodbye."

❁

Rachel's heart hurt. "Yeah. I'll do everything I can. But... I still can't believe you did this. Why do you think you might not be able to go back?"

❁

Saff shrugged, at a loss for a concrete answer. She wasn't sure *anyone* had an answer about the limitations of her unique situation. "I'm not drawing from the same energy here. I genuinely don't think I have it in me to catch a breeze back. But you said you barely felt any energy drain going through *their* kind of rift? That it was different?"

"Yes."

Wiping away the rest of her tears, Saff sniffled. "Good. Like I said, I don't know. There are so many variables we don't understand. I just need you to be prepared. I guess we're about to find out."

❁

"Right. I guess so." Rachel's heart was trying to escape her chest. She was dealing with too much. Eric's plea. Kaylah's cryptic secret. Saff's life or death dilemma. *No pressure.*

Kaylah approached them both with raised eyebrows. "Everything okay over here?"

"Yeah. Of course," Saff said. "I just wanted to double check... The girls you kidnapped were all unrooted, but you're sure rooted Seeders can make it through an Ivy rift? Since both of us are rooted now..."

Kaylah nodded. "Yep. Should be just fine according to our research. Otherwise, I would have warned your people in my invite to only send men. We also don't have any seasonal restrictions like you guys do."

❁

That was somewhat calming for Saff. "What about fully-rooted matriarchs? Could the combined rifting work for them? That wasn't in the letter that I'm aware of."

Kaylah furrowed her brow. "No. I chose to leave out something impossible. Your people's mojo is pretty strong. I'm sorry, but I'm fairly certain we still can't help your more mature females go back and forth."

"Right. Makes sense," Saff said.

Kaylah glanced between them. "You look a bit worried. Neither of you is anywhere near old enough to be a matriarch. And I don't know how to assure you any more than I have, that I can be trusted."

Rachel shifted her gaze to Saff. "Well, it's just that Saff is—"

"Too curious for her own good," Saff said. "And shouldn't be wasting our time. Let's go."

Kaylah shared a look with Rachel. "Right. Let's go."

Moving to stand by a pair of healthy trees, Kaylah cleared her throat. "I won't be long-winded, but I feel like I should say something. This is a moment we should all be proud to be a part of. This is Unitas. This is not the cause of the Seeders, or the Ivies, or the humans. This is the cause of all of us, in unity. We're going to create something new together. To hell with the old ways—this is where we start to build a healthy future.

"Saff, which of us would you feel more comfortable taking you through?" she asked.

Saff's anxiety peaked. She never would have fathomed ever giving an Ivy a chance like this. So much could still go wrong. They could show up anywhere on the other side of that tree. Next to the palace, surrounded. Separated from Rachel. And that was if she could even make it at all. "I think I'd like you to take me through."

"Alright," Kaylah accepted. Saff joined her, holding her hand as Kaylah wrapped a vine around her wrist. Every feeling in Saff's body revolted against that vine being there. The last time one had slithered around her, it had been to take her life.

Rachel joined Ginger and followed suit.

"Guess it's you and me, kiddo," Ginger said with a warm smile.

Kaylah and Ginger each ran the end of a vine down the spine of their respective trees, causing shining rifts to open. Saff stared in wonder and terror. Her nerves were strung so tight, she feared one might snap. The other three women looked back for one last glance at the loved ones they'd be leaving behind.

❀

Ginger's vines didn't cling onto Rachel as tightly as Soren's had, only as much as needed to get them both through. The pressure increased once they tried to get the mass of Rachel's body through the rift. The leaves still ended up digging in enough to cut her a little bit.

❈

"This might hurt," Kaylah warned Saff.

Saff prepared for the worst; every muscle in her body tensed.

As soon as Kaylah went through, the pressure of her vine increased around Saff's wrist. Stepping into the rift, Saff winced in anticipation. And then at the pain in her wrist.

But she didn't wince at the pain in her heart—there was none.

Saff gasped on the other side, filling her lungs with the energy coursing through the Green Lands. Kaylah's vine released her and Saff fell to her knees, clutching her chest. She struggled to catch her breath, hardly believing it. Beyond grateful to just be alive. She'd made it back home.

"Are you okay?" Rachel asked, worry in her voice.

Saff stood. "Yes. Just... I am *never* doing that again!"

"That definitely sounds a lot like gratitude, and not at all an overreaction," Kaylah drawled.

Saff shook her head, realizing Kaylah probably assumed she was being a drama queen about accepting Ivy help. "That's not what I meant. Thank you. I mean it." She took a second to survey their surroundings while healing her wrist, remembering that surviving the trip back to their home realm had been only one possible risk.

But it appeared Kaylah had held up her end of the bargain so far, and there wasn't any obvious ambush waiting for them on this side. They were safe. For now.

"Right." Kaylah sighed, stepping back and stealing a glance at Rachel. "Before we get started, I need to let you know something. I just got word that one of your girls at the palace is dead."

509

Chapter 37

Rachel hoped she'd heard wrong. "One of our girls died?" she whispered.

Kaylah frowned. "Yes. I'm sorry."

Rachel looked at Ginger, who also seemed shocked at the news.

"I ... I..." Rachel struggled to breathe. As she began to cry, Ginger put an arm around her. Rachel shook her head as the tears rolled freely down her face.

＊

Saff also teared up, but less from shock, more from anger. "When did it happen?" she demanded. She thought she'd cleared that hurdle, to trust Kaylah.

"I... I don't know the exact details. I just got word."

Saff's eyes glowed. "*Just* got word? This very moment? Not yesterday? Not while you were making us wait?"

Kaylah glared. "No! I just found out a few minutes ago. I haven't been stalling. As you can see," she gestured at the woods around them, "we're here, safe." She stood taller. "I'm sorry about that girl, but I still expect you to keep your end of the bargain. We still have a mission; don't forget that."

Saff was livid. "Right. Just one more of *our* kind dead." Just like Ben. He was just a number to Kaylah. They all were.

"I didn't do it, and I couldn't prevent it!" Kaylah's voice rose.

"You two need to shut it!" Ginger hissed.

Kaylah and Saff shared looks of humbled frustration. Yes, they were in the Green Lands, but they still weren't safe. They were quite literally not out of the (neutral) woods yet.

"We've got an outpost about a quarter of a mile from here," Kaylah said. "There's a map that should be helpful to get us to your borders."

"Then let's go." Saff glanced over at Rachel, who was still being consoled by Ginger.

❋

Rachel dreaded another stupid cabin, but she was barely in the right state of mind to think much of it. Her heart was breaking for that girl and her family. She needed to know more.

They walked quietly for a while, alert to any danger of discovery. Soon enough, they spotted the forgotten abode, carefully checking to make sure it was clear before entering. Ginger led, then the Seeders, and Kaylah hung back, fiddling with something by the door.

❋

"What was that?" Saff asked, on edge. "What you were just doing?"

"I can't endanger my people by permanently stationing them so close to your borders. We have our way of communicating," Kaylah explained.

"Well, I think I should be aware of what kind of signals you're sending, especially if we're cornered in a building, don't you think?"

Kaylah took a breath, doing a better job of trying to restore some shred of proper diplomacy. "You make a fair point. The decorative piece out there—I turned it to indicate that I've safely made it back. That means when my patrols come around, they can get word to those who would need to know. And patrols will pick up more regularly, awaiting my return or other word of developments. Hopefully good news, and soon, after we meet with your council."

Saff was pacified by her explanation, but still watched out of a dirty window to make sure they wouldn't have unexpected visitors, as did Ginger.

❋

Rachel sat on a dusty old chair, staring blankly at the wall. Kaylah crouched down in front of her, holding her hands. "I'm really sorry," she whispered.

Tears still blurred Rachel's vision. "Why did you wait?" she whispered back.

Kaylah frowned. "I didn't think it was fair to your mom to hear that, or see you like this. And..." Her eyes darted to Saff. "I wanted to make sure you got back here safe, even if," she nodded in Saff's direction and lowered her voice even further, "she had lost it over there. I promise—that's all."

Rachel nodded. "Yeah." She tried not to slip back into that place, the place where she didn't care what time of day it was, as long as she was numbed well enough. Jon's words about what he'd witnessed with the first girl haunted her. Rachel didn't deserve to be the one who had been saved.

511

Saff broke her focus from the window regularly to look at Rachel while she recovered from the shock.

Kaylah rested her head sideways in Rachel's lap. "We'll get through this, don't forget how strong you are." She took a breath. "Sometimes it's okay, to not be okay. I'm usually good at hiding it. But I'm..." She paused. "We'll get through this."

Rachel bit the insides of her cheeks. *Right. Strength.* She puffed out a breath of air. She needed to get it together. But she first needed to know one more thing. "How did it happen?"

Kaylah picked her head back up to look into Rachel's eyes. "Exhaustion, from what I understand. I think she was one of the first to be taken there."

Rachel nodded again. She'd assumed as much with how horrifying and draining it was. They hadn't allowed nearly enough time for her to heal and recharge between sessions on the War Vines, and if the girls who had been there for months were enduring the same schedule... It sounded like death would have honestly been a welcome release.

"I..." Kaylah started. "It's more of a slight shade of grey than a silver lining, but that means the Vine attacks will be weaker for now ... and maybe they'll be nicer to them, let them recover more, so it doesn't happen again."

❄

Saff had been straining to overhear their conversation. She couldn't bite her tongue any longer. "Yeah, some benefit. It just means they're going to try harder to get a replacement. As for the others, that just sounds like prolonged torture to me."

"You're right." Kaylah stood, throwing one more sympathetic glance at Rachel, as if apologizing that they didn't have more time to unpack the news. "We need to figure out the next step." Kaylah walked over to an old table and crouched, sticking her head underneath. Emerging with a rolled-up piece of paper, she walked over to Saff.

They studied the map; it took Saff a minute to understand where they were. "Mmm, this is a couple villages over from ours. How far of a walk would it be if we went straight to the nearest border wall?"

"It might take a full day," Kaylah answered.

Saff continued to study the map, disappointed. She would really rather show up at her own village. But the Ivies were more active at night in the Neutral Woods, and *any* amount of time spent in them was risky, day or night. "I think we should just head to the closest point. Once we're in, we can figure it out from there."

"Alright." Kaylah rolled up the paper. "I'm letting you lead on this part." She glanced at the others in the room. "Are we about ready to go?"

※

The question and gazes were really only focused on Rachel. Closing her eyes, she took a couple more deep breaths. She could be strong. She could make a difference. She could fall apart later, but that wasn't a luxury they had right now. Opening her eyes, she stood. "Okay."

Saff pulled her attention from lookout duty again. "Remember, Rachel—you know how to defend yourself, but I have the darts. Keep that in mind; stay close."

"I'd like to remind you this is a *peaceful* delegation," Kaylah added. "But if Ginger's life or mine are in danger, we'll defend ourselves. Everyone here needs to remember to tread lightly, act cautiously. From what I last heard, my part in Unitas isn't officially being recognized by the palace. So, if we come across my people, assuming they're not yet Unitas initiated, they should still follow my orders. They could become allies."

Departing for the wall, they hoped to reach it before it got too dark. The quiet was disconcerting; they barely whispered to coordinate with each other. Saff and Kaylah took the lead, with Ginger and Rachel close behind. After walking for a couple of hours, Kaylah stopped in her tracks, holding up a hand.

Normally, the instinctive reaction would be to hide. But it had been agreed upon that they would face anyone they met—casually, as though they were patrolling the area themselves, on duty. It was a bit far-fetched, but it also depended on which scouts they ran across. If they ran across Seeders, they could show their eye glow and try to vouch for Kaylah and Ginger. Ultimately, their primary concern was just getting past Ivy patrols. Ivy women weren't deployed as soldiers, so their group would naturally be pegged as Seeders if they didn't recognize Kaylah as their princess, or as the leader of Unitas.

Soon enough, the voices grew louder—two men. The women stood in place, prepared for whatever may happen next. The men stopped, taking a defensive stance once they spotted the party. They wore uniforms—Ivy uniforms. What the women didn't know was if they were Unitas initiated. They stared at each other for only a few seconds, but it felt like hours. If the women had actually been soldiers, they'd have identified themselves right away, but they couldn't tip their hand; they were a mixed group, a rogue element. The patrolmen hesitated for some reason, to attack, or to signal or demand identification. They studied the group, seemingly surprised or confused.

"Um, our apologies, Your ... Highness," one said, as they both bowed low.

The Seeders' anxiety grew. Not the side they'd hoped for.

"We just didn't..." The men continued to scrutinize the rest of the party while Kaylah stood tall with perfect posture. It was odd for Rachel to see her friend like this, so regal, demanding attention.

The other man spoke up. "Your Highness, you're alright? We're going to have to ask for identification of your party."

Kaylah furrowed her brow. "You can stand down. My mission is my own concern, and my companions are approved by me."

The men shook their heads; something was clearly wrong. "Sorry, Your Highness. But we need to see vines. Or ... stunt marks?"

The very sound of that demand made Rachel clench her jaw. *You mean friggin' Nazi tattoos?* They didn't even think people like Guillen were capable of being soldiers, anyway.

Ginger stepped forward, her hands up, presenting her vines. "I don't believe the crown princess needs to explain herself to anyone. You two can be on your way."

One of the men extended his vines aggressively, standing tall. "With all due respect, that is not going to happen, until we are satisfied."

"What insubordination is this?" Kaylah demanded.

The other man took a step forward, also challenging with vines. "We have our orders, and this doesn't seem like a difficult task, Your Highness." He squinted, as if trying to understand Kaylah's reaction.

"On whose orders are you to disrespect me?" Kaylah asked.

The men gave each other a look and lunged forward, grabbing with their vines, leaf-tips blunted, at the two closest women—Saff and Ginger.

Saff revealed her blades, slashing in the air, cutting the first attempt short. The Ivy soldier scowled in recognition. Kaylah paired up with Saff, crouching low and trying to grab onto one of his ankles with her vines. He sidestepped and intercepted with a vine to thwart her attempt.

Ginger had vines wrapped around her wrists, but quickly kicked off the ground and twisted to be closer to her attacker. "Rachel!"

Rachel ran over, trying to use her Seeder blades to help with the vines. The other man's eyes widened in surprise as he thrashed about, trying to kick Rachel away while keeping Ginger in his grasp. He attempted to hold Ginger with one arm, releasing one of his vines, and focused on trying to subdue Rachel simultaneously.

He lost his grip and Ginger freed one of her wrists enough to extend her own vine, wrapping it around his arm and piercing his flesh.

Rachel kept his other hand and vine occupied, understanding the strategy. Ginger closed her eyes and took a deep breath as he struggled, then quickly went limp. After he fell to the forest floor, Rachel stood by, ready for him to pop back up, but he didn't. Ginger returned her vines and she and Rachel turned their attention to the others.

Ginger swore. "Did you see where they went to?"

Saff, Kaylah, and the other Ivy were nowhere in sight.

Finding footprints heading in a different direction, they rushed to follow them, swiftly spotting the rest of their group.

Kaylah had vines around the other man, just one of his arms. Saff knelt on his other arm and wrist to pin him down, her Seeder blade extended at his throat.

❀

"Get off him, Saff!" Kaylah ordered as she injected her own poison into the man.

Saff stayed there, contemplating what it would feel like. Revenge—for Ben. She was breathing hard, her Seeder eyes showing.

"GET. OFF!" Kaylah repeated as the man went limp. She swung a leg and kicked Saff off of him. "What part of *peaceful* didn't you understand!"

Saff scowled and stood, dusting herself off. "What part of 'my people will follow my orders' were you delusional about?!"

Kaylah glared at her. "They can't explain themselves if they're dead. And my people have a right to choose a better course, just as much as yours do. Don't do that again!"

"I don't take orders from an Ivy princess!"

"Saff, calm down!" Rachel interjected. "We're all fine."

Saff huffed. "So, what now?"

"They're not ... dead, right?" Rachel asked.

Ginger smirked, sparing a quick glance at the nearest soldier. "Kaylah and I have had a lot of practice refining our poison. Quick and effective, not lethal. They'll be out for a little while."

"And what are we going to do with live Ivies that aren't on your side?" Saff questioned.

"Well, we're not going to kill them!" Kaylah replied. "They'll come with us. We can get information from them, and I can try to bring them into the cause."

"Great. Are we going to *drag* them the rest of the way?" Saff asked.

"You know, sometimes, you have a special talent for being a pain in the ass, don't you?" Kaylah scowled.

Saff rubbed her forehead. Something as stupid as that insult brought fond memories of Ben. "If they stay alive for us to take them, they'll slow us down. If they stay alive and we leave them behind, that could compromise us. You understand this is war, right? Casualties are inevitable."

Kaylah glared. "Like your brother?"

Saff's eyes glowed. "You have *no* right!"

"I have *every* right! Every Seeder is a part of your family, and every Ivy is a part of mine. Misguided or not, they don't deserve to die without a fair chance!"

"Then you're weaker than I thought," Saff replied.

✷

"You don't mean that!" Rachel chastised. "That's not our way."

Saff scratched her head. "Fine! Then what?"

"We'll tie them up, gag them," Kaylah said. "When they come to, we can get more information and find out why they attacked."

Saff scoffed. "I think it's fair to say your cover is blown."

"Any information is good," Kaylah said. "Once they're awake, we can make it to your borders in the dark, or find somewhere safe to camp for the night."

Rachel furrowed her brow. Why had they attacked their own princess? And if Kaylah's part in this was compromised, why hadn't they sharpened their leaf blades in the attack? Rachel decided it was worth voicing an additional concern.

"What if we come across more Ivies? Having two as prisoners won't go over so well."

Kaylah frowned. "Let's hope we don't have to cross that bridge."

Chapter 38

Saff watched in awe as the Ivy women bound the men. Kaylah and Ginger wrapped vines around their wrists, arms, and legs, and gagged their mouths. Each time, they knotted the vines tightly in place before disconnecting.

"How does that work, exactly?" Rachel asked.

Kaylah checked her knots. "The vines? We usually only extend a couple of yards from each arm at a time. And it's not like we have an infinite amount. Like your powers, it can deplete us if we use a ton."

"And why couldn't you just tie them up without putting them to sleep?" Saff asked. "That would have saved us time."

"Because they're physically stronger," Kaylah drawled, obviously annoyed at Saff. "Our poison is an advantage we can offer. Our society dismisses our fighting abilities, overlooking that tool as a weapon."

Saff had understood that, in theory. But her frustration had prompted her to ask the question. They dragged the men under a weeping willow tree and gathered close.

"How long do you think for yours?" Kaylah asked Ginger.

Ginger winced. "I might have gone overboard in the excitement. A couple of hours?"

Kaylah nodded, frowning a little with disappointment. "It's okay." She smiled reassuringly. "Look at you getting some real action in. How about you do a close patrol?"

Saff couldn't bear to sit still and babysit for two whole hours; she volunteered to keep watch as well.

Saff and Ginger walked side by side, agreeing to patrol the area together. Saff wasn't about to let Ginger out of her sight. This whole excursion was a trust exercise, filled with unwelcome twists and turns.

"So, how do you know Rachel?" Ginger broke the ice.

"Mentor? Teacher?"

Ginger raised an eyebrow. "You can't be more than a couple of years older than her."

Saff gave a polite smile. "One of those mysterious Seeder things, I guess." She was just glad to have made it safely back home after her crazy decision to go. And just because Kaylah had shared information with them, didn't mean Saff had to divulge anything to Unitas. About her powers, about Seeders, about anything. She didn't owe them a thing.

But she was curious. "You and your husband raised Kaylah? How does that selection process work?"

Ginger raised both eyebrows this time in emphasized sarcasm. "One of those mysterious Ivy things, I guess."

Saff rolled her eyes. A silent patrol was good enough for her.

Ginger sighed. "My husband and I—the chosen human-world guardians of the heir to the throne." She shoved her hands in her pockets. "We never planned to have kids, honestly. Wasn't really a priority for us. My husband was making his way up the ranks of palace guards. A promising career." She grinned. "I admired him for his hard work. He secretly taught me a lot of moves he'd learned in training, at my request. Not that our women are *forbidden* from fighting. It's just ... looked down on. No one willingly trains us. That whole 'weaker of the sexes' thing."

"I thought Ivies were matriarchal..."

Ginger glanced around. "Domestically, not as much as it used to be. Things changed after the kingdom was formed, after the Mother Vines and queen were established."

Saff considered the cultural difference. Seeder society was complicated. It was a mesh of religions and cultures brought over due to the influence of humans. And women were respected for their extra powers and place in society, but the men still did the majority of the fighting. In part, because healing could only be done by the women, so that task naturally fell to them. In part, because the men had been raised as soldiers to protect their lands and sisters. But Seeder women were never looked down on for volunteering to serve on border patrol.

"When rumors circled amongst the palace guards that an elite project was in the works, Nathan sought it out. His hard work and merit spoke for itself. His dark hair made him a believable candidate to be Kaylah's father. And, of course, we were around the right age to have a child her age." Ginger shrugged. "Bonus points went to us for being married—it was a built-in unit of two protectors who didn't have to pretend to be together."

Ginger ducked under a low-hanging branch, grinning again. "I finally got to train properly." Her face softened. "And I was surprised by how quickly Kaylah became family."

Turning to face Saff, Ginger abruptly stopped, causing Saff to halt in her tracks. Her eyes focused squarely on Saff's. "In every way that matters, she is my daughter. And she'll be my queen. If you or your people have plans to harm her, we have a problem."

Saff studied Ginger's face. She actually admired this woman. Ginger wasn't afraid to go after what she wanted, to be a soldier. And she took her charge seriously. It was intriguing to see such familial loyalty from an enemy hell-bent on destroying what mattered most to Saff, which was also family. But Saff's admiration only stretched so far. It wasn't like venomous snakes were virtuous because they didn't eat their young. Just because Ginger had developed a maternal instinct didn't mean she or Kaylah were saints. A mamma bear could still maul an innocent bystander.

Saff shook her head with a scoff. "You think *we're* the ones planning a trap? She came to *us* for help."

Ginger eyed Saff meaningfully. "Where's the 'us' you speak of? A dozen of your soldiers sent to kill her—that I expected. *One* young girl accompanying Rachel? Not much of an 'us.'"

Saff glared. "You'll have to excuse my people's hesitance. She's not exactly offering up an army of her own. She sounds more like a rebellious teen running away from mommy and daddy at the palace, than a legitimate leader capable of meeting the expectations she's setting."

Ginger shook her head. "You have to start somewhere. Every wildfire needs a spark."

Saff twisted her lips in thought. "I guess we'll soon see if she lights a beacon of hope with that spark, or if it's only a sign that she'll crash and burn."

Rachel and Kaylah sat next to their Ivy prisoners. The men were solidly out.

"Well, that was kinda cool, putting them out so fast like that," Rachel offered, still shaken.

Kaylah chuckled. "Yeah. Family nights for us in the human world consisted of meditation and practice poisoning each other until we learned how to get the right chemicals for different effects."

Rachel stared at her, wide-eyed. "Really?"

"Really."

Rachel shook her head. "Fair enough. My family nights, once I got my powers, involved getting beat up by my brother in training."

Kaylah beamed. "We have such healthy family relationships, don't we?"

They both laughed louder than they should have.

"I feel like there's still a lot I don't understand about your people, your anatomy," Rachel said.

Kaylah arched an eyebrow.

"I mean, like," Rachel blushed, "when our people mate, stuff happens, like an imprint kind of thing, and darts, and eyes, and stuff. What's it like for you guys?"

Kaylah grinned mischievously. "Are you trying to find out what it's like for Eric and me?"

"No!" She looked to the side, somewhat curious. "No. He's human, anyway. I just mean in general, if there's something specific that happens, Ivy to Ivy."

Kaylah waved her hand dismissively in the air. "Not really. You guys are the weird ones. With your whole imprint, root-for-life, have-a-bazillion-kids thing. I'm not aware of any exchange of powers or anything like that with us. Ivy births are different than human ones, but still not as different as your guys'."

Rachel considered Kaylah's assessment of her people. There were some crappy limitations, but some things were equally cool.

"But, uh... If you ever want to have a more detailed birds-and-the-bees talk about the interspecies thing, let me know." Kaylah winked. "And if things work out between you and Guillen, then..."

"For the love, please stop. There is practically no chance of things working out with him." Rachel wished more than anything that she could go there, to that place of hope of being with a great guy like him. But the chances were so slim they didn't even exist.

"Hey." Kaylah nudged her arm. "I'll stop teasing you. Maybe. I'll try. But you know I love you both. I'm just saying, it wouldn't be the worst thing in the world for you two to both be happy."

Rachel grinned, looking down and picking at her nails. "He is pretty great, isn't he?" She swallowed a lump in her throat, guilt washing over her that she had been the one he'd helped save, not the girl who was now dead. "Anyway." She glanced over her shoulder. "Just don't say anything around Saff. She wouldn't approve."

Kaylah rolled her eyes. "Mrs. Stiff over there clings too much to the old ways. She's going to need to change her way of thinking and join the program."

"Just give her some time."

Picking up a stick, Kaylah poked at the dirt by their feet. "I wish we all had that opportunity. To take our time to decide." She glanced at their captives.

Rachel cocked her head to the side. "It's complicated, right?"

Kaylah shrugged. "I guess you could argue that my people have had more than enough time to change things for the better."

"Better late than never?"

Kaylah gave a slight smirk. "That's one way of looking at it."

Rachel thought back to an earlier conversation at the safe house. "You really think your people would turn on you if you took the throne?" She looked over at the men. They'd attacked, knowing the princess's identity...

Pursing her lips, Kaylah drew lines in the dirt with her stick. "My family wasn't the original royal family of the Ivy Kingdom. My great-grandmother claimed the throne after having an entire line of heirs assassinated. Our people had grown tired of old policies. There had been a lot of internal fighting leading up to that."

Rachel fidgeted with her hands, not knowing how to react. Kaylah's people had such a dark past; how could they hope for the changes they dreamed of? "I think ... if anyone could do this, it's you. Look at what you've done already."

Kaylah gave her a forced smile. "Thanks." She paused. "So... Not completely teasing. But I need more dirt on Guillen. I need happy news amidst all of this crazy. When did you first get a thing for him?"

Rachel shifted on the forest floor, sifting through her memories. "I don't know. Maybe when he removed my stitches?"

Kaylah laughed. "That's the most romantic story ever."

"That's unnecessary sarcasm," Rachel defended with a frown. "He was being sweet. And I really got to look into his dreamy eyes, and..." She took a deep breath and sighed. A movement close to her caught her attention. Kaylah's guy was staring at them, looking no less than shocked.

"Well, hello, friend." Rachel smiled.

"I think it's time we find out what's going on." Kaylah pulled out a dagger and the man's eyes filled with terror. "Obey me, and you stay alive. Do you understand?" she asked.

He nodded fervently.

"You don't make any noise. And you only speak to answer my questions," she ordered, and reached over, carefully cutting loose the vines around his mouth.

"Your Highness, what—"

She gave him a stern look, brandishing the dagger.

He bowed his head, shutting up.

"Look at me. Why did you attack?"

He raised his head, his eyes moving from Kaylah to Rachel, and back to Kaylah.

Rachel flashed her glowing eyes. "Aww, I think he just realized we're friends."

Kaylah scolded Rachel with a glance. "Don't antagonize him." She addressed him again. "I asked you a question."

"Your Highness, you're ... with *their* kind? *Willingly?*"

"I'm the one asking questions. Why did you attack?"

He scowled, still visibly confused at the group dynamics. "But they're weeds."

Rachel clenched her jaw.

"You'll refer to them as Seeders," Kaylah calmly corrected.

He swallowed hard. "Yes, Your Highness..."

Saff and Ginger returned.

"Thought we heard voices," Ginger said.

"Well, we're halfway there..." Saff added.

"Why did you attack?" Kaylah repeated herself.

The soldier studied the group again before wiggling to sit up straight. "I'm loyal to my kingdom and ready to die for it. Could you say the same?" He looked away, tight-lipped.

"Then the gag goes back on." Kaylah wrapped him back up, daring Saff with a glare to challenge her. The second soldier behaved in like manner after regaining consciousness.

Having been slowed down by their two captives, the mixed group of Unitas women camped out in the Neutral Woods for the night.

Kaylah tried to pump the men for information, but they wouldn't say a word. She tried to sway them to the cause, but they remained defiant and united with the kingdom for now. She told the group that she still held hope she could work with them individually, once in Seeder territory.

✸

Throughout the night, the women took turns keeping watch—at least one Ivy and one Seeder up at all times. It was a rough night in the open with barely any sustenance—some still-green bananas and a few chestnuts. Everyone was ready to go at first light. Forcing the men to join them, they pushed forward.

"You're sure this is the strategy you want to take?" Saff asked. "I don't really know how it's going to be handled, showing up with four Ivies and only two of them tied up. Maybe we should have the two of you tied up, just to get through?"

Ginger straightened her posture. "We're not entering under those pretenses, or with that disadvantage."

Rachel voiced her opinion. "No, I agree. We may try to fudge things and get Kaylah and Ginger through with us as if they're Seeders, but starting off with them as prisoners is not the right way."

In the far distance, they could finally see the wall. Kaylah stopped the group to finalize their plans. She first turned to Saff. "I've been consistent in proving my intentions as a worthy ally. And you guaranteed us safe entrance into your lands. I need you to remember that."

"I'm doing my part," Saff replied, a little annoyed.

"So far, yes. But I need you to guarantee that these men won't lose their lives when we approach that wall."

"I don't know if I can do that. I can't speak for my people. To us, you and Ginger are a peaceful delegation." She pointed to the men. "They're just soldiers. Who knows how many Seeder lives they've taken!"

Kaylah frowned, looking at the men. One seemed more proud, defiant. The other, more scared at the talk and prospect of being dragged into enemy territory. "You two should be grateful for these Seeders, that they've spared your lives so far. I hope you'll come around."

Kaylah went back to addressing the women. "Whatever happens, I'm going in there and holding my head high. What we want is worth it, and I've sworn an oath to see this through. Ginger is here, risking her life. She's pledged herself to the cause. I need to know what you two really want out of this. Your people are going to ask you, and I need to know where you stand."

✸

Saff and Rachel looked at each other. Rachel had already made her decision, but she hadn't voiced it out loud. She was wary to see Saff's reaction. "I stand with my people. And because I want what's best for them, I'm pledging myself to Unitas."

✺

Hearing Rachel say it was like a punch to the gut for Saff, like Rachel was a traitor to their people. She knew it wasn't that simple. Unitas was about peace, but it wasn't a Seeder movement—not yet. It was headed by an Ivy, run by Ivies and humans. And things hadn't exactly gone smoothly thus far.

Saff frowned, avoiding eye contact while they all stared, waiting for an answer. The goals they talked about, the morals they preached—she agreed with them. But she kept telling herself she wasn't ready to drink the Kool-Aid just yet.

"I don't know what you want me to say. I betrayed my people's trust to parley. I promised you safe entrance. I'm an ambassador, not an initiated member of your cause."

Kaylah frowned. "I understand. But I hope that changes. Just ask yourself why you wouldn't want to join, why you wouldn't want to be numbered as one of us? We don't want to just end this war; we want to end *the* war. All of it. Why wouldn't you want that? Why would you want to go back to shadow wars and being hunted in the human world, just as long as the current surge of attacks calms down?"

Kaylah's eyes narrowed ever so slightly. "Is your hate so strong? Because if that's the case, you're not much better than our prisoners here. Ask yourself why you wouldn't want the same kind of relationship with Ivies that you have with humans. When you can answer those questions for yourself, that's when you can really give me an answer. And hopefully, you can convey that to your people. We need to convince your people of our goals just as much as we do mine." She locked eyes with Saff. "You seem like a person who will do the right thing."

Saff rolled her eyes. "Let's go."

As they moved closer to the Outer Wall, the women gained a better view of the damage being done by the War Vines. Each vine emerging from the woods was as thick as an arm. They converged, bundling and forming a mass that burrowed into the thicket.

The Seeder energy sustaining the wall's protective barrier was generally not something perceptible to the naked eye, but a bright light shone around the penetrating War Vines in the struggle to keep the wall from entirely failing.

Seeders usually caught a breeze over the wall, but today they would be aiming for one of the sporadic stone doors built into the base for transportation and passage of the wounded or dead.

Saff gazed at the wall, sick at the sight of her home under attack. Her energy surged within her. She'd already given so much of herself, sacrificed so much, to try and keep her people safe. Her heart ached as she imagined Ben standing nearby. He'd been stationed at a section of the Outer Wall just like this when he'd died.

❋

Rachel glanced at the War Vines with a frown. This was just one of many places on the Seeder borders that had been fighting such an attack. An attack only made possible by kidnapped girls like herself, by subjecting them to unimaginable torture. She allowed a couple of tears to escape, her mind again turning to the girl who had died. She wouldn't even be afforded a proper Seeder burial in their lands.

The group stopped at the edge of the tree line, pausing to take in the awful sight, hesitant to walk into the clearing where they'd be discovered. Kaylah stood with bunched eyebrows, her eyes focused on the War Vines.

"Is everything okay?" Rachel asked.

Kaylah kept her attention on the War Vines. "Something's different."

"What do you mean?"

"Um... I... I'm not quite sure yet. Let's get going." Kaylah's tone was eerie, disconcerting.

"Wait," Saff said. "Do you hear that?"

Chapter 39

They all stood on edge, listening. A persistent murmur filtered through the trees, slowly growing louder.

A horn sounded in the distance, and Saff's heart dropped. "Crap."

✻

"What?" Rachel looked around, unable to tell which direction the growing murmurs were coming from. But the horn had come from the wall. Not the Outer Wall—it was too faint for that. It had to have come from the Inner Wall, the wall three times as tall, tall enough to get a great view of the Neutral Woods.

"An attack," Saff answered. "We need to get going."

They pushed their captives forward as a closer horn sounded—one from the Outer Wall. Every inch of the Outer Wall had a Seeder soldier at the top now, poised and ready to fly down and meet the enemy head-on. The door they needed to get the Ivies through was right next to the weakened thicket, where the War Vines were, where the Ivy soldiers would be aiming for.

The Unitas party picked up their speed.

"This would be faster without these soldiers..." Saff said, shoving one forward.

Kaylah grunted, looking over her shoulder.

"What if they attack us, thinking we're part of the fight?" Rachel's heart was racing. She glanced behind them. The rustling of trees was more distinct now.

A ways to their right, the first Ivies emerged from the trees. A dozen or more Seeder soldiers took off from the wall.

Saff urged her captive forward again, and he resisted. "That door can take *several* minutes to open. It has multiple locks in place and we still need to negotiate our way in. They're not prepared for incoming wounded if this is just getting started."

Kaylah joined in, pushing one of the soldiers forward.

More soldiers continued to march forward from the woods behind them, rapidly closing in. More Seeders launched from the wall to intercept.

"We need to be *running*," Saff stressed. "These two are dead weight, Kaylah!"

Kaylah's focus was squarely on the War Vines as she pressed forward. "I... I just... I don't get it."

"Don't get what?" Ginger glanced around them. Dozens, maybe even hundreds of Ivies were emerging from the woods. The sky buzzed with an equal deployment of Seeders to meet the enemy. "They're right. We need to go faster."

Rachel was panicking. She *wasn't* a soldier. "Kaylah. They're not worth it if they won't cooperate."

Kaylah stopped in her tracks, her gaze dancing between the War Vines and the approaching soldiers. Her fists were balled, her expression calculating.

"You said something was different. Why are you hesitating?" Rachel asked between quick breaths.

Kaylah whipped out her dagger, facing the soldier who had been the least cooperative. She sliced through the vines that covered his mouth, narrowing her eyes. "Is my mother dead?"

The man clamped his mouth shut, glancing at his fellow troops from the corner of his eye.

Kaylah plunged the dagger into his upper arm, twisting. He groaned.

"Is. She. Dead?"

"Yes," he mumbled between clenched teeth.

"Then your life belongs to me." She yanked out the dagger and moved it to his throat. "Who do you follow?"

He stared defiantly. "No queen of mine would align herself with weeds."

"Wrong answer." She slashed his throat and pushed him over.

Rachel gasped, going pale at all the blood.

❋

Saff's stomach lurched.

The sounds of battle drowned out any remaining noises the soldier made as he bled out. Kaylah cut the vine from the second soldier's mouth.

"I follow you! My life is yours!"

She proceeded to slice off the other vines around his hands and arms, allowing better movement. "Come on!" Kaylah yelled.

Saff glanced behind them. Ivy soldiers were pressing in toward the wall, a few breaking free from fallen Seeders. Seeder soldiers kept coming over the wall.

Recent battle tactics at sections of weakened wall had required a lot more hand-to-hand combat than usual—this was likely to get ugly. She considered whether she ought to let the others move on, and help in the battle with her darts, but they were cutting it too close.

That door. She knew what she needed to do. "Keep running! I'll get the door open!"

Pushing energy to her legs, Saff strengthened her muscles. She bolted forward and kicked off the ground, shifting energy to her core and hands, balancing on the wind. The whistle of air in her ears helped drown out the surrounding chaos of death. Her flight announced she was an incoming friendly.

With all available concentration, she sensed the wind, tugging at it, aiming for her mark as quickly as possible. Swooping low, she launched the energy back to her legs. Dropping down, she landed with extra momentum and barely kept herself from face-planting. A half dozen guards stood by the door.

"I need it open!"

They stared at her, confused. No wounded were being dragged in. "Excuse me?" one asked.

Saff looked behind her. The other four were in a dead sprint. She and Rachel were the only ones who could fly over that wall. She pointed at them, turning back to the guard who'd spoken. "Those four will lead us to the Ivy princess. They need in."

"What?" The man's eyes grew large.

"Yes. Three of them are Ivy. They need to meet with the council. They need in. *Now!*"

The guards exchanged glances. "You're sure?"

"Absolutely. I'd stake my life on it."

He looked up, sending a signal to someone watching from high up on the wall. "This better not be a mistake."

Saff caught her breath. *I hope not.*

She paced, a ball of nervous energy and adrenaline. Her mind danced, deciding if she should join in the battle or maybe even find wounded to heal. But she needed to make sure their group got in. She needed to make sure they hadn't just risked everything for nothing. She needed to make sure Rachel made it back safely.

And she needed answers.

Her heart was still pounding as the group got closer. "They're opening it?"

"Yes. It takes a while. How do you know they can locate the princess?"

Saff swallowed hard. "I'll tell that to the council."

"What village are you from?"

"South Fortinda."

The guards stood firm at their station as more Seeders launched from the top to intercept approaching Ivies. Rachel was in the back of the approaching group, her eyes lit up to full glow.

The group finally reached the wall, panting heavily and clutching their sides. The guards stood defensively, facing the three Ivies.

Kaylah pulled out her dagger, pointing it at the male Ivy. "I have more questions for you."

"Whoa! No way we're letting any of you in with a weapon," a guard protested.

Kaylah chucked the dagger into the battlefield, then pointed at the Ivy again, her hand still covered in blood. "Why did you attack and clam up in the first place?!"

"He was my superior! I had to follow orders."

"The hell he was your superior." She pointed to the soldiers in battle. "I outrank them all put together. *Especially* now."

The man searched Kaylah's face, panicked. "We had orders! We thought you were here against your will. And then when we saw you were working *with* them..."

The large stone door opened behind them.

"Get inside!" a guard ordered. "We need to close this back up."

The Unitas members entered with one of the female guards, and the door closed with a thud behind them. The guard bolted it shut and pushed them forward. Lined with giant stones, the corridor was only lit by quartz-and-jade lightkeepers hung on the walls. After a couple more doors, they emerged on the other side.

While grateful to be alive and safe, it killed Saff that her own people were dying just on the other side of this wall. "How did you know she was dead?"

Kaylah frowned. "As we approached, I just knew."

Saff ground her teeth. "How? That means you're in charge, right? You can stop this!"

The guard explained to other posted soldiers that they'd need extra guards and to fetch members of the council. Letting in Ivies was *definitely* not standard procedure.

Kaylah shook her head at Saff. "I can't explain it. I could sense the change in the Vine's allegiance. That would only happen if…"

"Then that means you're the queen now?" Rachel asked. "You can stop this Vine?" Her eyes shot to the War Vine that had punched through the Outer Wall and was snaking its way to the Inner Wall.

"What?!" the guard said. "You told us they knew how to *find* the princess. This is her?"

Saff pursed her lips. She'd kinda hoped to keep that one under wraps until they met with the council.

❋

"Yes," Kaylah said. She glanced at Rachel. "I don't actually get the title until my coronation. And I can't stop the Vines from here. They have to be retrained at the roots, at the *palace*."

Saff gestured at the wall. "Then stop your troops. They should still recognize your authority. A lot of soldiers out there are going to die. Your family and my family, right?"

Kaylah nervously bit her lip, then turned back to the male Ivy. "You had orders, explain."

He surveyed the group, shrinking from all the eyes on him. "We were told you were kidnapped by the Seeders."

Kaylah's eyes narrowed. "Did my father issue your orders?"

He squinted, shaking his head in obvious confusion. "No. He's dead, too."

Kaylah's shoulders fell. "When and how did they die?"

He glared at all the Seeders around them. "Ask your friends. It happened when they attacked the palace."

"That's a lie!" the guard shouted.

In no time flat, it turned into a screaming match full of pointed fingers.

"Wait!" Kaylah yelled over them. "If they're both dead, who lied about me being kidnapped and issued the orders?"

"His Highness, Prince Soren."

Rachel's chest tightened.

Kaylah covered her face with her hands.

❋

Saff was still a bit sketchy on what it all meant. "So … what now?"

Kaylah sighed. "My brother knows good and well that I wasn't kidnapped. And I never imagined the prick had it in him to do it, but he killed my parents and is pinning it on your people to fan the flames. It's another way to pit my people against yours, if they think you're the aggressor, instead of outing me as a traitor."

Saff was beyond tired of Ivy games and drama. "Then maybe you should set the record straight with the soldiers out there killing each other and go home to claim your throne."

Kaylah rolled her eyes. "Have you ever witnessed an Ivy retreat, Saff? Or even a solo scout doing their job? It takes a *single* soldier and a *single* tree out there for one to slip out, rift to a human-world outpost, and send for reinforcements. The moment they realize I'm in your custody—you're not going to see hundreds out there, you're going to see *thousands*. All dutifully here to 'rescue' me from my captors and not stopping to listen to someone they assume is under duress." She arched her eyebrows. "And if Soren had it in him to kill my parents and issue bogus orders, you'd better believe he's prepared a warm homecoming that includes me being a puppet for him."

Saff huffed, turning to the guard. "How long until we can see the council?"

The guard shrugged.

"Fine. I guess we'll wait to see what they say."

"How about we all calm down and take a seat," the guard said. Shortly after, other guards brought restraining straps for the Ivy wrists to bind their hands and vines.

Kaylah held up her wrists without hesitation. "I've come here to prove myself and propose a peaceful solution. We have no problems complying."

After they were tied up, all sitting on the ground, Ginger leaned against Kaylah. "We'll be okay. It'll be alright."

Kaylah stared straight forward, nodding.

✻

After a few minutes of silence, Rachel glanced at Kaylah with a frown—she looked to be in shock. "I'm sorry about your parents," Rachel offered in a whisper. "I guess negotiations are out the window..."

"It probably had to happen, anyway," she whispered back. "I doubt she would have willingly given up control of the Vines or accepted half of my plans. We've lived with different moral compasses for a long time now."

"But it's still not all bad news, right?" Rachel said. "Sounds like Soren was pretty stupid killing your mom. Doesn't he need a queen to control the War Vines? If he's lost some of his control on the attack..."

"Does that mean you're asking for asylum?" Saff tacked on.

Kaylah shook her head, visibly frustrated. "It means we have work to do. He might have shot himself in the foot, in a way. But he's not a complete idiot. With three girls gone, those War Vines are still primed for new kidnapped Seeders, even without my cooperation. And he trained under Duke Nuren for years." She lowered her voice, her expression somber. "I didn't see this coming. Maybe I should have. But he was the golden child, not me. He was the favorite; my parents were actually proud of him. And now... I'm not really sure what he's capable of. I... I don't know that we're talking about my kingdom's goal being colonization and slavery, anymore. Soren would make offhand comments now and then... I don't think he'd stop there. It would be easier to wipe your people out altogether so you'd never be a threat again."

Rachel was sick to her stomach. The thought of ever having cared for him was revolting, painful. "I know he's a bit ... unhinged and cruel, but you really think he'd go that far?"

Kaylah frowned. "You know firsthand how manipulative he can be. And he has no qualms with taking what he wants and hurting people."

Rachel looked down, visions of her torture back at the palace running through her mind.

"Rach, he's done worse. I'm not trying to minimize what you went through, but honestly—I think part of him genuinely liked you. I'm just saying, we shouldn't underestimate him."

❋

Saff tilted her head to the side. "Guess you should have taken him out, too, when you were rescuing Rachel."

Kaylah glared. "I told you—that was a precision extraction. And he wasn't even at the palace that day."

"So, the plan remains the same?" Saff said. "Negotiate with him, and if it doesn't work, take our armies and claim your throne?"

Kaylah shook her head. "My parents might have been capable of some type of negotiations. Not him. He doesn't feel any sense of obligation to me. Or apparently any of our family or traditions..." Kaylah sighed. "And yes, I still need your armies."

Saff sat up straighter, trying to sort out Kaylah's logic. "He trained under your uncle, just like you. You need our armies while our armies are already fighting ... and losing. Remind me why we just risked everything to bring you here."

Kaylah's jaw clenched. "We might be tit for tat on strategy, though I still think I got the better education. And I told you—my research on our powers has a lot of

532

potential to boost things for your people. We both studied under our uncle, but he was the one chumming around with the assassins. I was the one involved in the research. Our playbooks are bound to be different. It means we need to figure out his game. And we will. It also means your people still need me. We need each other. We need Unitas."

Chapter 40

After an eternity of waiting, a handful of Seeder soldiers arrived to escort the group to the Inner Wall. The full Unitas party stood up.

"How many council members were gathered?" the Outer Wall guard asked.

"Two."

She shook her head. "We'll need a full council now—this one is the princess." She pointed to Kaylah.

The new guard's eyes widened. "Okay."

Saff was desperate to contact her family. "Can a messenger be sent to South Fortinda to let them know we're okay? Our families ... didn't know we were doing this." She and Rachel shared a guilty glance.

The head guard eyed them with disapproval. "Sure... Who do we contact?"

"I'm Saffrona Murialsdotter; my father is Thod. This is Rachel Lyzasdotter; her father, Garrett, is still human-world deployed. We're both near the long lane of the western glen."

"Okay. We'll send someone once we're past the Inner Wall."

Saff blew out a breath of relief. Her stomach was still in knots, not knowing if her family members were all safe, but at least they could stop worrying about her.

Once guided past the Inner Wall, they gained a much more significant escort, additional council members were summoned, and a messenger was sent to Saff and Rachel's homes.

After more waiting, the Ivies were placed under heavy guard as Saff and Rachel went into the council alone to present their pleas. They talked about why they went to the human world without council permission, what they'd witnessed, and what was being proposed. They weren't exactly being offered a parade for a hero's return.

But the intel Kaylah had provided about Ivy assassins was being acted upon immediately. They took a short recess to discuss a course of action. Saff and Rachel were invited outside, where they were greeted by family.

Saff fought tears at the sight of Thod, her Seeder father. Thod had to be a mix of emotions—glad his daughter was back safe, angry she'd defied the council, and still mourning the loss of a son.

✸

Rachel's anxiety grew at seeing her Seeder mom, Lyza. Lyza frowned, shaking her head.

Rachel gave Lyza a shy hug, and Saff took a strong squeeze from Thod.

✸

"Please tell me everyone's okay," Saff pleaded. She needed to know she hadn't lost anyone else she loved during her absence, especially Devin.

Thod's intimidating features and deep voice conveyed no fondness. "Everyone's fine, Saffrona. Physically."

That hurt. She knew she'd have a lot to make up for. But she could breathe, knowing she wasn't looking at another burial in the immediate future.

"How did you even do it?" Thod asked.

Saff fidgeted with her hands. "I, uh... I'm not completely sure."

"*Why* did you do it?" he asked.

She swallowed hard. "That's a longer answer."

He glanced around. "Let's take a walk."

Saff followed after him. "I'm sorry I left the way I did."

Thod didn't respond.

Saff tried again to justify abandoning her family and betraying their leaders' orders. "This wasn't just an impulsive mistake. I've seen what Kaylah can do, and this can legitimately help us."

The lack of response stung.

But Thod finally spoke up. "Not impulsive? Not childish? It was important for you to leave that exact day? Right before your brother's burial? One day would have made a difference?"

She stared at her feet in shame. Of course it had been impulsive. The lectures she'd given Rachel were now falling on her own head.

Saff gathered the courage to defend the decision that she still wasn't sold on herself, remembering Rachel's words back at the safe house. "If this war ends one day earlier, that means one less day of lives lost."

535

Thod shook his head with a sigh. "We're all relieved to hear you're back home safe. That includes Devin."

She was viciously homesick at hearing his name. What she wouldn't do to be home in Devin's arms at that moment.

❋

Rachel and Lyza followed Saff and Thod's example, taking a short stroll in the vicinity.

"How are you doing?" Lyza asked.

"I'm fine." Rachel didn't know what else to say. She'd already struggled to get close to her new Seeder family. Only a couple of her sisters had ever attended school with her. And she'd distanced herself from everyone because of her shame about the kidnapping.

What message was this sending to them now? She hadn't chosen this world, this family. It had been forced on her. And the first chance she got, she ran away from home. That wasn't why she'd done it, but she couldn't help but wonder if that was what they were all thinking.

"Well, we're glad you're safe," Lyza responded.

"And the rest of the family's okay?"

Lyza nodded.

"Good." Rachel wasn't sure if she should mention anything, but she figured she might as well throw it in there. "My mom... Um, I mean, Samantha... She's safe. I think she'll be okay."

Lyza bit her lip, nodding again. "Good."

They continued to walk in silence. There was hurt in Lyza's eyes whenever Rachel would slip and name Samantha as her default mom. Lyza had given Rachel life, had waited for her to come home safely, and was hurt that she'd allowed her childhood friend and 'cousin' to raise her daughter, only to have Samantha misplace that trust and hurt their whole family, their entire nation. Not that Lyza spoke so openly about it, but she wasn't that great at hiding her feelings, and Rachel could read between the lines of their conversations.

It hurt. Rachel loved Samantha. Samantha had made mistakes, so Rachel couldn't fault Lyza. But she loved them both, in different ways. And now she was a point of contention between the two; two women who used to be best friends and could now never really reconcile, being trapped in their own worlds. In a way, it reminded Rachel of being caught between Kaylah and Saff at the safe house. It made her sick.

Rachel was grateful when they eventually recalled the girls and brought Kaylah in to the council meeting. Ginger and the soldier remained in custody elsewhere. Kaylah reiterated her strategies, her plans to help. The council didn't jump at the ideas she shared, but they seemed open enough to hear her out. Their main objection to accepting her invitation to negotiate had been about it being a trap. But since the damage had been done and she'd walked willingly into their custody, they knew they'd be fools to not hear her out now. After talking into the wee hours of the morning, they were to adjourn for sleep, and then deliberate the next day.

Before the regional war council leader called the meeting to a close, he turned again to Rachel and Saff. "Neither of you had position or permission to act in any official capacity," he censured. "Consequences will be discussed. For now, you're free to return to your village, with supervision. The princess will remain here in detention until such time as we deliberate her proposals, and decide what her fate will be, and that of the other Ivies in our custody."

"Your Honor." Rachel spoke up. "We went into this knowing we held no position or permission to do what we did. And we apologize for the offense that may have given our people." She wrung her hands nervously. "But it doesn't require position or permission for someone, anyone, to do the right thing. And that's what we're doing. And I'm here to see it through. I'll be staying with the princess, even if that means I have to be detained as a prisoner."

She glanced at Kaylah, thinking of her promise to Eric back in the human world, to keep Kaylah safe, and fearing what may happen to her friend if she was left alone, should the Seeders decide to go another route other than accepting the Unitas movement.

Kaylah's tired eyes showed a glimmer of gratitude at the gesture.

"You have no right to demand entrance to our meetings, or frankly, to demand *anything*. But if you would like to stay in this village under close guard, we'll allow it for now," he replied. "We may have further questions for you."

The attention of the group focused on Saff, as if to see if she would request the same. She hadn't taken the same oath as Rachel. She wanted nothing more than to be back home with her family, healing, helping, visiting the graveyard Ben now rested in. The council had it under control now, right? She'd done her job. She'd taken Rachel to meet up with Kaylah. She'd gotten them safely through the Outer Wall.

But, thinking of Thod—her dad, who she loved and admired—Saff's mind replayed his accusations of her actions being childish, impulsive. She considered Kaylah's speech as they had approached the Seeder borders, asking Saff if her hatred mattered more than ultimate peace. Kaylah *had* also proven herself when it mattered most, out on that battlefield. Saff's human mom's reminder to consider all of the options sounded in her ears. Last of all, she had to ask herself what Ben would have wanted her to do.

Putting aside her yearning to immediately return home, Saff sighed. "I request to stay as well."

Chapter 41

While they were granted the opportunity to stay, Rachel and Saff were kept separate from Kaylah and the others, despite Rachel's wishes. They were given a room to share for the night. It was basic, but comfortable. Near the border walls, it used to be family housing, but was now used as barracks. A guard was stationed at their door.

Rachel woke from a nightmare, sweating and disoriented. Saff sat on her own bed, chin on her knees.

"You have a lot of nightmares, don't you?"

Rachel sat up, pulling her covers up. "Yeah. Most nights. Sometimes more than once a night." This one had been about Soren and his sadistic perversion. "Have I been waking you up?"

Saff shrugged. "Not a big deal."

Rachel frowned. "Sorry."

"You have nothing to be sorry about. I sometimes get them, too. But I know I haven't been through as much as you. I'm sorry you've had to go through all that."

"Thanks," Rachel whispered, rubbing her face as if she could rub away the haunting visions still dancing in her head. "It's like, even when you try to talk it through with someone, and things start to make sense, you start to feel better ... and then you have a bad day. And it all floods back in. And you question everything. And start all over again. And then the nightmares come, and it's hard to function the whole day when you start off that way."

Saff frowned. "There's no timeline for healing, you know. You just work at it one day at a time." She fiddled with the lace trim of the nightgown she'd been lent. "Some days you dissect it, to rework things for better understanding. Some days, you do your best to bury the feelings, just to get through, or just to allow yourself uninterrupted joy. I don't know if that's wrong, but I think it's okay."

Rachel stared at Saff. It was nice, the friendship they were beginning to build. Shared trauma and risk could do that. It wasn't just her family that Rachel had struggled to connect with since coming 'home.' Rachel hadn't made *any* real friends. No one could relate to the sheer horror she'd been through. Saff obviously still struggled to understand Rachel's mindset, but her mentorship and friendship helped Rachel feel a little less like an island.

Looking down, Rachel tried to shake another recent nightmare from her mind that had just popped up. The vision that haunted her most was that of Duke Nuren—Rob, her stepfather. His lifeless body after revealing himself as the author of this surge in the war. Prince Soren's betrayal was on a different level, and while he was more perverted and unhinged, and the current threat, Nuren had held a different role in her life. Seeing him dispatched so suddenly as she was rescued had given her no time to properly reconcile those feelings. Yes, she was glad he was dead. But she also wanted him to not be the person that he was, in that one hour, compared to the father figure she had known for an entire decade.

"Thanks for staying," Rachel said, forcing herself to focus on the here and now.

"Yeah, well... I think it was the right thing to do. But I hope we don't have to stay long."

"What do you want to do, if they actually let us choose? Whether or not they accept Kaylah's proposals?"

※

Saff considered it for a moment, smoothing out the comforter around her. "Honestly, I just want to go home. And have family nights, and take care of my garden, and go on walks with my husband, and take a *really* long nap." She scrunched her face. "But nothing is going to be that simple."

"It can be, if we work for it."

Shaking her head, Saff let out a long sigh. "You really think this could work, don't you?"

"I do. I think Kaylah has it in her."

Saff reflected on Kaylah's actions since she'd met her. Kaylah was the first Ivy Saff had met that gave her pause, that made her consider things differently. And when it had mattered most, Kaylah had made the hard call out there by taking the life of her own soldier. Saff had to set aside her pain from Ben's death at Ivy hands, and her own trauma from being personally attacked by the Ivy assassin network. She had to focus on the big picture.

"If they don't accept Unitas, I imagine I'll go home and go back to fighting, healing, and training, until we can stop this. And the fact that she's here, that they can't activate any more War Vines to torture our girls and use their energy—that gives me a sliver of hope. And any of my free time will be used trying to repair things with Devin and my family.

"And if we *do* accept Unitas... I don't know. I still want to go home, but I'm open to other tasks that I'm asked to do. I'm willing to do my part." She shifted on her bed, fighting a frown. "I just hope Devin can support me in whatever choices are made."

❋

"You guys are a really cute couple," Rachel offered. Saff smiled in return. "Do you think you guys will decide to have a clutch?" Perhaps that was too personal of a question. "Sorry, you don't have to answer that."

"No, it's okay. Kids... Yeah... That's kind of a huge decision for us Seeders, isn't it?"

"Just a tiny one." Rachel chuckled.

"I don't know about you, but I didn't grow up dreaming of having twenty-four kids at once... Granted, not having a traditional human pregnancy *does* sound appealing if you go the Seeder route. But yeah, we've talked about it. It'll be a few years before we're able to make that choice." Saff twisted her wedding ring. "If things turn out the way Kaylah wants—in a heartbeat. Most of my sisters already know they don't want a clutch of their own, but they'd make great aunts. Growing up as an only child, I always pictured myself having a large family.

"If things go back to normal—that's a lot harder. It's hard to imagine going through what Murial did. But I'd consider it. If this war keeps up like this... I just don't even want to think about it."

Rachel sat up straighter, leaning against the wall. "Yeah. Well, I think we should keep our goal in mind. Plan on a new normal."

Saff pointed at her, smiling. "I don't know about you. You're more of a dreamer than I am. But maybe that's not all bad." She winked. "What about you? Positions and kids?"

"Kids..." Rachel blew out a puff of air. "Well, that one is really up in the air, isn't it? I don't have any romantic interests, no mate to talk with about it." Her mind wandered to Guillen. If somehow, in some way, in some world, they actually

541

worked out—they wouldn't be able to have kids. Seeders, Ivies, and humans didn't have a biocompatibility. "I guess back when I was human, I imagined maybe I'd have one or two. Even if I loved someone like you love Devin, I don't think I could commit to the Seeder way of family life, not in that way. It's just not for me.

"And positions... I don't know. I don't have those family ties dragging me back to our village. I want to make sure Kaylah's okay, and that we have success. And I want to travel, and learn more about our histories and cultures."

Saff slid back down in bed, lying on her side to view Rachel. "I think that—despite our differences, and no matter what others decide—neither of us are the type to just sit here and do nothing."

Rachel smiled.

They didn't have a wake-up call the next morning. When Saff opened the door to check for an update, the guard told her they would have to stay put until they were summoned.

"We should at least be allowed to help. Do some healing or go to the temple," Saff insisted.

He said they'd discuss it at the change of guard, and a few hours later, they were greeted with an escort. They allowed them to make an energy deposit at the local temple well, then returned them to their room. To their relief, the guard reported that the skirmish outside had subsided, and upon further questioning, he shared his opinion that the way it had been done appeared to be in line with normal Ivy tactics. It sounded as though the troops hadn't known about or noticed Kaylah's presence there.

Hours passed before they were finally summoned back to a council meeting. Kaylah again joined them.

"Saff. Rachel. You will both be returning home." The council leader held up his hand before they could protest. "We'll consider your willingness to help with Unitas, and your unique skills, as we move forward with consideration of the princess's recommendations."

That gave Rachel hope. This sounded good... But she hadn't just gone through this nightmare to be cut out of things, and to leave Kaylah hanging. "I want to stay."

He raised an eyebrow. "I understand. And I just made it clear that you will be going."

Anger grew inside her, her heart racing, as she tried to figure out where to go from here. "No one believed me. No one trusted me. Not in my village, not in *any* of the council meetings I've been summoned to. But she's here, because of me. And I'm going to see this through."

Gingerly resting his hands on the table, the council leader sat back in his chair. "You're right. Princess Kaylah is here because of you. After you *lied* about not knowing how to find her. You'll have to forgive us for our hesitation." He glanced at Kaylah. "Trust isn't something easily won, and strong-arming doesn't change this council's decisions, either."

Rachel was fuming. They were all treating her like she was incompetent, like she was brainwashed. But she saw it clearer than anyone. "I don't care what you say. I'm—"

"Rachel," Kaylah interrupted, making eye contact with her. "Go home."

Exchanging a glance with Kaylah, Rachel decided to stay quiet.

"You can choose to go home and be with those you love, contributing to society; or you can stay here, in detainment, being kept from your family, friends, all knowledge of what happens in these deliberations, and any useful contribution to the war effort. Which will it be?" the council leader asked.

Rachel clenched her jaw, shooting another look at Kaylah.

"Go," Kaylah mouthed.

Clamping her mouth shut until she could control her anger enough to not tell them off further, Rachel finally spoke up. "I'll go."

"Wise choice." He continued, "For now, your parents will escort you back and your village leaders will assign you duties."

❁

"Yes, sir," Saff said. She was thrilled to go home, and also to hear they were giving Kaylah a chance. There were a lot of details she wasn't privy to, but it looked promising.

❁

Rachel stayed silent as they were dismissed. Before Saff and Rachel left, they were each given a supervised opportunity to talk with Kaylah.

Rachel frowned. "So, what's next? That's bullshit in there, what they're doing to me. You know that."

Kaylah sighed, putting her hands on Rachel's arms. "You're not doing yourself any favors by fighting back right now. They don't need your approval. And right

543

now, they just see you and I together and imagine I'm controlling you. I don't blame them."

Rachel rolled her eyes. "I'd still rather be helping in *some* way with you."

"One step at a time." Kaylah gave her a gentle smile. "They'll listen and observe as I try to show how my plans can work. I think we'll be okay. This new development just means a different timeframe and order than I'd planned, but we can do it.

"Make amends with your family. Serve with your whole heart. Once they trust me, they'll trust you. And the *moment* they'll let me put you into action, you'll be ready and we'll really get things rolling."

Rachel frowned again, deflated.

"You're so cute with your little temperamental green eyes." Kaylah grinned, pinching Rachel's cheek. "Lit up like an adorable lightning bug."

Rachel crossed her arms. "A bug?"

"Now that I think about it, those bugs glow from their butts, right? And probably not because of emotions. So, never mind." Kaylah flashed pouty lips. "Not a glow-butt bug. Just my favorite Seeder."

Rachel shook her head, chuckling. She loved how Kaylah knew how to build her up and calm her down. "You're sure you can handle this? Please tell me you're not going to head back in there and call the council 'glow-butt bugs.'"

Kaylah wore a toothy grin. "Dang it! That was going to be my first order of business." She winked. "C'mon. I've got this. I know you haven't seen this side of me, but I was tutored in diplomacy. I'll be okay." She bit her lip. "Granted, my people aren't so great at diplomacy... We're kinda more 'you have—me want—me take.'" She rubbed her hands together. "But I feel like I can read a room. Call me crazy, but I think the next appropriate step in negotiations is ... interpretive dance?"

Rachel choked back a laugh, not wanting to give Kaylah the satisfaction of another one. "We're so screwed."

Kaylah gave her a kind smile. "Keep your chin up. We've got this. The millisecond I can manage it, you'll be by my side again." She looked away for a moment, as if calculating her next sentence. "One thing you *can* do, while you're back there, is some research for me. I don't know where your people keep all your old texts, but anything on the history of your village would be helpful."

"Okay, I'll ask. But ours isn't one of the oldest villages," Rachel confessed. She wasn't well-educated on their culture yet, but she still knew some tidbits.

"At the very least, I need you to find out whatever you can about how your village was named."

Rachel furrowed her brow. "South Fortinda? What does the naming have to do with anything?"

Kaylah pursed her lips. "Trust me. It means something. It's important. I have a feeling the name behind *each* of your villages will be an important piece of the puzzle."

They gave each other one last hug before Saff had a word with Kaylah.

❀

"Don't disappoint me," Saff warned.

"I have no intention of that. Thank you for holding up your end of the bargain," Kaylah said with a handshake.

Saff and Rachel walked toward their parents, leaving Kaylah and the council behind.

"You were conveniently silent in there," Rachel chastised.

"You threw enough of a fit for the both of us," Saff mumbled.

"Really? What was the point of all of this?" Rachel scowled. "Right, you didn't *officially* commit to Unitas. Wouldn't want to actually have conviction."

Saff stopped abruptly, a few yards before meeting their parents. "Don't you dare!" Her eyes filled with tears as her fists clenched. "I just risked my life to take you. To bring her here. I walked out on my husband. I missed my brother's burial. Don't you *dare* judge me for wanting to be back home with the people I love!" Tears trickled down her cheeks, her ears warm with anger. "And I want to help, too. If the council approves of her plans and they ask for my help—I'll be there. I want to do my part. But right now, *my* part is back home."

Rachel swallowed hard. "Sorry. Let's go home. Do you want a hug?"

Saff wiped up her tears. "No. I just want to go."

They met Thod and Lyza, who weren't blind to their confrontation and Saff's distress, but tastefully skirted around it while discussing their plans to return to their home village. Seeders could fly with relative ease in the Green Lands, but they didn't do it all the time, considering the necessity and conservation of energy. This time, they'd fly home, crossing the distance to their village to get back significantly faster.

With a short sprint, Thod and Saff lifted into the air. Saff didn't know how to feel. Beyond relieved her family was okay. Beyond terrified about how her husband and family would react to her betrayal. Beyond worried that the war pressed on, despite the risks she'd just taken. She grasped at a ray of hope—the council was working with Kaylah, or at least considering it.

Rachel took off, still wobbly from a lack of practice. Lyza followed after her, catching up and gliding by her side. Out of the corner of her eye, Rachel could see over the border walls—where the skirmish they'd narrowly escaped had taken place. The land below her was beautiful, the lanes crowded. She knew she should appreciate all of that. But going 'home' to be with 'family' felt like a punishment, rather than a victory. She wanted to be helping Kaylah. She wanted to keep Kaylah safe. Every day, every hour, that she waited to hear word from her, would be one filled with worry. Giving Rachel a little hope and forcing a small smile on her face was one of the last things Kaylah had mentioned—that their timeframe and the order of things were going to have to shift. She'd also hinted that Rachel might see Guillen sooner than originally planned.

Kaylah was permitted to watch as they took off. She crossed her arms as Saff lifted into the sky. While Saff was a bundle of energy and sass, Kaylah was grateful she'd made this possible. Observing Rachel catch a breeze brought a smile to Kaylah's face; this was the first time she'd gotten to witness her friend flying.

Kaylah sighed, feeling the weight of the realm on her shoulders. Eric was back in the human world. Her parents were ... dead. Her brother had cut her off from her own kingdom, forcing her to redraft her approach on the fly. And she had to win the Seeders over. She had to fix things for them and her people. She had to claim her throne.

"Alright, please follow me, ma'am," a guard said as the four Seeder bodies shrank in the distant sky.

Kaylah's eyes lingered longer for one last look as she took a cleansing breath. "Right. Let's get to work."

Kaylah's Chronicles

Kaylah lay in bed staring at her ceiling, trying to shake the fresh memory of panic, muffled screaming, and blood. *Lots* of blood. She slid a hand to her stomach, now queasy. The panic had been hers. Well, hers, Guillen's, and the teenage boy's just before she'd murdered him. The muffled screaming and blood had all been his.(ee)

Closing her eyes, she slowly inhaled, then let it go. It didn't work, though she hadn't really expected it to. There was no turning back at this point. It wasn't tantrums and political posturing. She'd officially risen to the level of treason and rebellion. *No.* She swallowed hard. *Words matter. It's revolution. It's reform. It's change.*

Her phone chimed. <Doing anything fun today?>

Kaylah frowned, not responding right away. It was her day to be available to occupy Rachel. But she didn't have it in her. She was too exhausted to spend time with Rachel. Not that Rachel herself was exhausting. Kaylah loved her like the best friend she was. But all of the lies were hard to keep track of, especially when compounded by the lies the royal family wasn't even privy to.

Sighing, Kaylah responded. <Got plans. Fun, though? Not so much :P What about you?> The truth was generally easiest, though ambiguity never hurt.

<Froyo with mom, just figured I'd see if you wanted to hang out.>

<Sounds like fun. Rain check?> Kaylah rolled her eyes. 'Rob' was 'out of town' for 'work,' anyway, and 'David' was 'hanging out with the guys.' They were both visiting the Green Lands—Rachel didn't need to be babysat today to be kept from walking in on some secret meeting.

<Rain check works for me. The offer stands if you end up ditching your other plans!>

Kaylah smiled. How could someone partially raised by a monster like her Uncle Nuren be so sweet and innocent? But she knew that answer. Rachel's human mom, Samantha, was really nice. And Kaylah's uncle had been forced to be kind, otherwise Samantha would have left him long ago, cutting off this experiment and opportunity.

Allowing her phone to drop by her side, Kaylah closed her eyes, taking a couple more deep breaths. She'd known she had been dancing with danger, and that taking a life might become necessary. She just hadn't really anticipated how it would feel. Sure, her mother had ordered people to their deaths, but had never actually done the dirty work of killing someone. At least not that Kaylah knew about.

Abruptly sitting up and rubbing her face, Kaylah let out a frustrated grunt. She needed a distraction. Something happy. Something without strings attached.

A soft knock sounded at her bedroom door.

"Come in."

Ginger appeared with a cheery smile. "How are you doing? Any thoughts on lunch and dinner today?" She paused. "Are you feeling alright? You haven't left your room all morning."

Forcing a smile, Kaylah had no choice but to lie. She wasn't ready to bring Ginger and Nathan into her plans yet. She loved them, but wasn't fully convinced their loyalty could be won. *Full* loyalty. The kind that was severed from her parents, their employers, their queen and king. "I'm fine. I think I'm going to go for a drive and just grab a bite while out. I'll let you know about dinner?"

"Sure thing. Stay in touch and reach out if you need us."

Kaylah swallowed. "Thanks. Will do." The moment Ginger shut the door, Kaylah knew she needed to get up and get out or she would stay in that bedroom for the rest of the day. Tucking her cell into her jeans, she grabbed her keys and left the house.

She was still not sure where she was headed. She'd told Rachel she had plans. The truth was more that she had plans to *make* plans... Traffic was bustling, and once Kaylah left the busier streets, she happily replaced the crowded but smooth asphalt with the calming quiet isolation of an unpaved road.

A large sign ahead brought a genuine smile to her face. She instantly knew what her afternoon was going to look like—the local animal shelter.

Taking a right, the car jostled her a bit with each dip in the dirt path. She'd desperately wanted a puppy or kitten when she was a little girl and had been brought to this realm to 'study humans.' They wouldn't allow her to have one. She had too much to do, to study, to learn. Kaylah frowned, feeling guilty for not inviting Rachel along. Rachel had wanted a pet, too. *Stupid Nuren.* He'd lied and said he was allergic because he didn't want one around. Rachel had been allowed a goldfish as a little girl. After it died, she'd never replaced Mr. Bubbles. Pulling into the shelter's gravel parking lot, where only three other cars sat parked, Kaylah turned off the car and rested her forehead on the steering wheel. Maybe she *should* invite Rachel—she would enjoy it.

Feeling as though she might die of old age before deciding, Kaylah sat up straight and let the idea go. She couldn't be fake with Rachel today, not in person.

This would actually be Kaylah's first time at the shelter, though she'd looked it up before and had considered swinging by. She nervously tucked her hands into her pockets, unsure of what the rules were as she approached the front desk. Muted barks belted out from another room, and a large cage sat behind the receptionist's desk. A tropical bird of some sort, missing several feathers, rested on its perch, eyeing her on her approach. Under the cage swung a label: "My name is Penny."

"Hi, how can I help you?" a woman, likely in her twenties, asked from behind the counter.

"Yeah, I was just wondering if you allow people to volunteer. Like … could I walk a dog today or something?"

The woman smiled. "Sure can. We have regular volunteers if you're interested in doing more, but if you'd just like to give one some fresh air outside, I can get you set up."

Kaylah nodded with a smile of her own. "Yeah, I'd love to. I don't know that I could make a long-term commitment, though."

Waving a dismissive hand in the air, the woman left her station and ushered Kaylah to a hallway. "No problem. Whichever little furry friend you walk today will appreciate the gesture, even if it's only this once."

They first passed by the cat rooms; they were in kennels visible through windows flanking the hallway. Rachel was more of a cat person. Kaylah liked dogs better. The noisy barks had grown louder as she walked down the hallway, but the sound doubled once the employee opened the door to the dog kennels. Kaylah instantly frowned, following the woman in. She'd come here to be happy with cute creatures, and hadn't expected to see them lined up in chain-link prisons. Kaylah's mind turned to Guillen, to the Seeders, to all of the other injustices out there. What had they done to deserve this?

"Do any of these dogs on the right interest you?" the woman asked.

Kaylah took a few steps, surveying the captives. An overgrown black beast barked at her, jumping against the chain-link. A scrawny little thing was curled into a ball, shaking in the back of another kennel. In the next, a wiener dog with wiry fur scratched itself, then licked its privates.

Catching her eye from a kennel on the left was a beautiful medium-sized grey dog, eagerly wagging its tail and letting out a couple of excited barks. She didn't know breeds that well, but she thought it might be a pit bull or something related to that. "Can I walk that one?"

"No, sorry. Only these on this side."

Disappointed, Kaylah turned back and picked the wiener dog. The woman set her up with a leash and guided Kaylah outside to the walking area. More chain-link fences, only four feet tall out here, edged the grass yard, also separating the yard into a few different sections. To the right, a couple and a small child were fawning over a puppy. After getting more instructions on policies and poop bags, Kaylah was all set.

The little dog happily plodded along, stopping randomly now and then to sniff and mark where another dog had likely left its calling card recently. It wobbled a smidge, perhaps a bit too round. One footstep after another, she wondered about the dog's history and how old it was—some of its hairs were randomly white.

This couldn't compare to the warmth of the energy in the Green Lands, but it almost allowed her to leave a fraction of her worries behind, on a nice day with a little dog.

After a few minutes lost in thought, Kaylah spotted another person entering the area, on the other side of one of the fences. Clicking the gate behind him, a tall blond held tight to a leash, walking the very dog she'd wanted to walk in the first place.

Hmm... She was instantly frustrated that she'd been denied. If she were back home in her kingdom, she would never have been denied this kind of request.

Gently coaxing her dog to the fence, she took another glance at the dog on the other side. Yep. It was the one she'd wanted to walk.

"Hi," she said.

The blond turned his attention to her, as did his dog—it yanked on the leash and barked at the one she had been walking. "Hi. Can I help you?"

"I just..." She hesitated, not really sure what she'd planned on saying. "I wanted to walk him, but the lady told me no."

"Sorry. Not just anyone can handle this beast," he said casually, almost even playfully.

Kaylah eyed this guy. He wore dark jeans and a button-up shirt. He was just a pretty boy. His dog pulled on its leash again and her eyes rested on the guy's flexed bicep. Annoyance flared up inside her. A pretty-boy human thinking he was something special, thinking he was so much better and more capable because he was a guy, because he was stronger? If he only knew that she was a princess, a princess with powers, that could manipulate Ivy energy within her body. Having been to the Green Lands so recently, she could easily be stronger than this guy, without even using her vines or poison.

"What? I'm not capable of handling it because...?" She raised her eyebrows. "Because I don't have your bulging biceps? I'm strong enough to handle a bigger, rougher dog."

He instantly grinned, and then laughed. He actually *laughed* at her.

"Never mind. I'm not wasting my time talking to a jerk." She turned to head away. She'd come to relax, not to be mocked.

"Hold on," he said.

She turned to find him still grinning. She narrowed her eyes. "What?"

"I'm not a jerk."

She scoffed. "Could have fooled me."

"You want to know why I can handle this dog and you can't?"

Crossing her arms, she didn't answer, only tilting her head a smidge in response.

"Just..." He pointed at his upper arm. "I find it funny that you noticed my bulging biceps, but not," he drew his finger to his chest, a mere two or three inches over, landing on a metal name badge, "this?"

Kaylah pressed her lips together, reading the name badge. *Eric. Volunteer.* "Oh."

Eric cleared his throat, still sporting a slight smirk. "It has nothing to do with how strong you are. This dog just came in today. If you're not an employee or a trained volunteer, you're not allowed to work with a new animal until its temperament has been proven."

Biting her lip, she nodded. Her posture relaxed as she uncrossed her arms and slid her free hand into her pants pocket. "I just thought maybe it was a breed thing, or?"

Eric wrinkled his nose, changing hands for the leash. "We try not to be breedist."

"Breedist?" She lifted an eyebrow. "Is that an actual word?"

He gave her a handsome smile. "Probably not."

"Right... Well..." Still embarrassed about not having noticed his name tag and for jumping to conclusions, she was ready to move on.

"I'm Eric, though I guess you've figured that out by now." He extended his hand over the chain-link. "What's your name?"

She met his hand, shaking it. "Meg." Her alias was second nature by now, though it still killed her inside each time she had to introduce herself that way.

After releasing her hand, he reached down and scratched his dog's head. "So, if you wanted to walk this guy, are you looking to adopt a bigger dog?"

Kaylah spared a glance at her own dog, which was currently sniffing and marking the fence. "I'd probably be happy with any type of dog, to be honest. But I'm not looking to adopt right now. I'm not allowed."

"Hmm. Against ... college dorm room rules this fall?"

She hid a smile at his possible fishing. School had just released for the year. "I'll be a senior in high school."

He smiled. "Me too. Which school?"

"Lincoln. You?"

He furrowed his brow, his smile growing. "Really? Me too. Are you new?"

"No. You?" For a split second, she was a little nervous at the prospect of a new male student, but that was such a tiny concern that it was practically a nonissue. Even *if* he were a new Seeder brother of Rachel's, it wasn't like he'd suspect a female Ivy assassin, or the crown princess. And, quite frankly, none of them would be wasting time volunteering here, away from sisters and crowds.

"Nope." Eric shook his head. "I've been here since the eighth grade."

They chatted for several minutes about the most popular kids and teachers. About how Mr. Tate was the funniest history teacher, how Mrs. Anderson made math even less enjoyable, and how the student body president had gotten into some sort of college admissions scandal.(ff) Kaylah found herself smiling, easily conversing with him, and even laughing as they walked up and down the fence length a couple of times.

"You said you're not allowed a dog right now. Is that—" He stopped. "Watch out for that—"

She didn't need him to finish the sentence as her sneaker came down into a squishy pile. Closing her eyes, she took a deep breath before glancing down. "That's so awesome."

Eric frowned. "Sorry, should have spotted it sooner."

"No. It's par for the course lately." She sighed, considering her options to scrape off the dog poop.

"Let me go grab some bags." He left, his dog in tow, grabbing a couple of bags and bringing them back.

Kaylah scraped off as much poop as she could into the bags, not able to get into the tread grooves.

"You said this is par for the course?" he asked, watching. "Stepping in a lot of dog poop lately?"

She quietly chuckled, turning a bag inside out and tying it up. "More like it's been a few crappy days."

"Sorry to hear that." His voice was sweet. "Maybe you need something fun to cheer you up. Do you have any plans tonight?"

She threw a quick glance down at her shoe. "Other than burning my shoes?"

Laughing, he leaned against the fence. "I know you said you're too busy for the volunteer program, but if you're not too busy tonight... I'm out of here in a couple hours..."

A smile grew on her face. "What do you have in mind?"

"Unless you'd prefer something else, I was thinking just basic dinner and a movie?"

She bit her lip, looking into his blue eyes. He was undeniably cute and friendly, but she shouldn't be wasting time on a human with everything else she had going on.

Then again... It could potentially save her from having to date more suitors sent by her parents. "That sounds like fun."

Now sporting fresh new shoes, Kaylah stood in front of the mirror in her bedroom, glad to have something to look forward to. She was actually surprised to find herself giddy about this date. She'd gone on plenty of dates, but very few she'd looked forward to. She recognized Ginger's soft knock on her door. "Come in."

"Your date is here," Ginger said, casually leaning against the doorframe. "Taking a breather from your parents' menu?"

Kaylah slid a necklace over her head. "You could say that."

"Have you approved him with your uncle?"

Kaylah gritted her teeth, trying to hide her annoyance. "I just met Eric today, and since my uncle's back home, I suppose I need your approval on this one." She arched an eyebrow.

Ginger pursed her lips. "I know you dislike all the rules. But Nathan and I are here to keep you safe. If he hasn't been properly vetted..."

"Please," Kaylah whispered with a heavy heart. "He's already here. You know I can take care of myself. Can you please trust my judgment on this one?"

Approaching and resting her hands on Kaylah's arms, Ginger frowned. "I trust your judgment. And you know we want you to be happy, right?"

Kaylah hesitantly nodded.

"Enjoy your date. Be careful."

"Thanks!" Kaylah beamed, pulling Ginger into a hug.

Grabbing her purse, Kaylah made her way to the living room, where Nathan was chatting with Eric. She'd almost forgotten how cute he was. Once he spotted her, he also smiled.

"I'm all set," she announced, sliding her hands into her back jeans pockets.

"Great." Eric stood, nodding at Nathan. "It was nice to meet you."

After they got into Eric's car and turned down the music, there was a moment of awkward silence.

"How was the rest of your time at the shelter?" she asked.

He shifted gears. "Good. Always is."

She adjusted her air conditioner vent. "I bet it's a good place to pick up chicks."

He laughed. "Not really. But I don't always have pretty girls objectifying me, so you know, there's that."

Kaylah scoffed. "Objectifying you?"

Grinning, he didn't look away from the road. "Was it my bulky...? No, wait, *bulging* biceps." He threw her a playful glance.

Her cheeks warmed. "Well, that happened..."

Eric cleared his throat. "You look great."

She'd only added the necklace and changed her shoes. "Thanks, I wanted to feel like a real princess. If I learned one thing from Cinderella, it's that a pair of new shoes can do a lot for you."

Eric chuckled.

After hours of dinner, a movie, and ice cream and chatting, they ended the night on Kaylah's front porch.

"I had a lot of fun," Eric said.

Kaylah smiled softly. "Me too." And she genuinely had. She'd forgotten the lies, the pressure, the rules, the murder. All in the company of this sweet, smart, handsome human. The vast majority of people in her kingdom would be appalled, would think that a human was beneath her. Kaylah hadn't thought that way in a long time. But she couldn't deny that this could never work. She couldn't— wouldn't—abandon her kingdom, her cause. Even for someone she enjoyed, for a budding romance.

Eric's hand cautiously grazed hers. She tried to ignore the butterflies in her stomach. They'd made an appearance earlier as well, when he'd gotten the guts to hold her hand in the last twenty minutes of the movie. None of her Ivy suitors would have had the courage to move so quickly with the crown princess.

"What do you say to another date next week?" he asked.

Her heart deflated. No matter the lie—summer camp or traveling—she was always back home in the Green Lands for the summer. "I'll be out of town. I will be for the whole summer." She frowned, having intentionally skirted around that in prior conversations. She didn't get a choice in the matter, and aside from royal obligations and family expectations, she had meetings established with others to try to bring them into her cause.

"Oh." Eric slowly retracted his hand. "Really? Or did this just not go as well as I thought?"

"No! I loved tonight. Really." She raised her eyebrows, making eye contact. "My mom and I fly out to Paris in three days."

"Oh. You don't seem that excited for the most romantic place in the world."

She grinned. "I'm not going there to find romance."

He smiled in return. "Well, then... Three days?"

She nodded.

"Then I may sound like I'm desperate or something, but..." He reached out, holding her hand again. "How busy are you tomorrow? I, uh, well—we could do lunch. Start earlier and see how the day goes?"

Kaylah beamed. "I'd love that. I'm free all day." She and Ginger were really only waiting until Nuren got back to the human world.

"Great." He studied her eyes. "I should head out. How does a hug sound?"

She quickly felt at ease in his arms. Not fearing for her life. Not dreading the dating game and courtly obligations. Just being there, making a genuine connection. It didn't hurt, either, to be embracing someone with strong arms and a strong jawline.

⁂

It was the night before she was set to take off with Ginger for their home realm. Kaylah and Eric slowly walked up to her porch as she reflected on their long day together. A picnic in the park, then bowling, pizza, and capping it off with ice cream with Rachel and 'David.' Soren had returned from the Green Lands before Uncle Nuren. Rachel had given Kaylah a wink of approval after seeing the 'hunk' she'd reeled in.

Standing by the door, Kaylah turned around to face Eric, her heart hurting. She could do this all day, every day—just spending time with him. She'd always feared being unable to connect with someone this way, to have a relationship where she didn't run out of things to say.

"I really enjoyed today," he said.

She nodded, barely able to smile. "Me too."

"It was nice to meet your friends."

A more genuine smile took hold. "Yeah. Rach is great." She lifted a skeptical eyebrow. "You really liked David?"

Eric wrinkled his nose. "Maybe not my cup of tea. But perhaps he'll grow on me."

She smirked, appreciating Eric's good taste.

He set the pizza box he'd been holding down on the porch bench.

"You're sure you don't want to take that?" she asked.

He shrugged, moving closer and holding her hands. "I'm good."

"I'll probably just have one slice of cold pizza in the morning, and then my dad will eat the rest of it."(gg)

He bit his lip. "That's some pretty amazing pizza, and I suppose it wouldn't hurt my chances to have your dad eating it, as long as he associates it with me."

556

She playfully intertwined their fingers, looking down at them. "Hurt your chances, huh?" She looked back up, gazing into his eyes.

He frowned. "You really don't think your parents would budge on their 'no electronics' rule? That's so archaic."

Kaylah matched his frown. That was almost always the story with Rachel, too. That Ginger and Nathan were ridiculously protective of their family time on vacation—electricity and human electronics didn't function in the Green Lands. Sometimes, someone else would be tasked with sending messages to Rachel on Kaylah's behalf, but she loathed that for the lack of privacy and authenticity. "Sorry. Not gonna happen."

Eric pursed his lips. "I guess, just... Don't forget about me?"

She squeezed his hand. "I won't. I'm not going to Paris to fall for anyone."

"I really want to kiss you."

Her heart beat faster. "I really want to say yes."

He searched her face. "Is that a yes? Or a confusing way of saying no?"

Moving his hands to her waist, she smiled wider. "Come a little closer and we'll find out."

Without hesitation, his lips met hers in the sweetest, most perfect first kiss. He pulled back first, but her heart was yearning for more. "I'm going to think of you every day while I'm gone."

"Same." He swallowed. "Is it... I don't know if it's even fair to ask... Not that you have to answer right away, but do you think you'd want to be..."

She gazed into his eyes, loving the feel of his hands on her waist. "Your girlfriend?"

He grinned, confirming they were on the same wavelength. They'd only known each other for less than a week, but they'd spent the bulk of those days together.

"Yeah," he said softly.

Her cheeks were starting to hurt from all the smiling. "I'd love to."

"Great." He bent down, holding her tighter, placing a couple more tender kisses on her lips that made her forget how to breathe entirely. "I guess I should let you go so you're well rested for the airport, huh?"

She nodded. "I'll start counting the days." After a long hug, it hurt to watch him go.

With pizza box in hand, she went inside and trudged up the stairs to the kitchen. She set the box down, filling a glass of water and sipping. Leaning back, she mused on their evening, on his perfect kiss, his perfect everything.

"Interesting choice."

Her mood instantly plummeted from the clouds, as 'David' entered the kitchen.

"I don't know what you're talking about." She took another sip of water.

He raised both eyebrows. "Really? Making out with a human like that."

She narrowed her eyes. "Privacy—ever heard of it? And that was far from making out."

Soren leaned back against the kitchen counter. "But is that idiot approved? I highly doubt that. And I'm sorry if you haven't gotten the memo, but Her Highness doesn't get privacy. None of us do when we're in our own realm—why should you expect it here?"

"Why are you here, Soren?" She set her glass down. "You're an idiot to show up like this. We didn't have a scheduled meeting. What if Eric or Rachel or someone else saw you come by? How would that look?"

He gave her an insincere pouty face. "A big brother can't just drop by to check up on his little sis?"

"No. Not when you're just supposed to be a random dick who's dating my best friend."

He reached out with a vine, lifting the pizza box lid. She slapped his vine away. "Go crawl back where you came from."

"You're not even going to ask how my visit back home went?"

Kaylah rolled her eyes. "How was your visit?"

"It was great. My visits are always good."

She felt nauseous. "Enjoyed your time with some whores, then?"

He smirked. "Nope. Spent most of it with Beata."

Tilting her head to the side, Kaylah flashed a disingenuous smile. "I group her with them."

His lips puckered with rage as his vibrant green eyes turned dark. "Screw you, *Meg*."

Talking about his Ivy girlfriend like that always provoked his anger. The kind of anger she actually feared sometimes. He knew how much Kaylah hated her fake name, and using it was all he could really do as an impotent prick who would someday be subject to the rulings of his little sister. Looking away, she grabbed the pizza box, opening the fridge door and crouching down to make room for it.

"Have you seen Teagan?" Soren asked.

Kaylah froze, her heart pounding. She fought to train her breathing as she recalled the screams, the blood, the awful noises, as Teagan, Soren's assassin buddy, had died by her hand.

"Something wrong?" Soren asked after no response on her part. His voice was innocently curious, though she knew her uncle's minion was rarely innocent.

Snapping out of her episode, she mustered a reply. "Yes, I just realized there's no way this whole box will fit in here." She stood up, closing the door and forcing a smile.

"So have you?"

"What?" she asked while opening a kitchen cupboard.

"Seen Teagan," he drawled with annoyance.

She furrowed her brow, pulling out plasticware for the pizza. "Why would I keep track of Teagan?"

Soren shrugged. "He's gone missing. Can't find him in either world. I checked when I was back there."

"Umm... That sounds less than ideal. Uncle knows?" She tried to add the sound of genuine curiosity and concern to her voice.

Soren nodded.

"I'm sure he'll figure it out. It's not like I'm here to babysit your assassin friends. I don't really give a crap about Teagan or any of the others. Maybe he got tired of working with you and chose the life of a deserter. I know I would."

Glaring, Soren inched closer. "Maybe you should care more."

She turned, challenging him with her hands on her hips. "Maybe you should use your time more wisely. Why would you even waste your time looking for him back home? What if one of Rachel's weed brothers discovered him and took him out? It sounds like you're wasting time looking in the wrong realm, idiot. And if their weed network is on to us..."

Soren studied her face. "You make a good point."

She smiled again. "I know. One of us has to have a brain, right?"

"I love our chats. Just remember, someday when you're coronated as our queen, people will be asking me what it was like growing up as the brother of the beautiful, sweet queen. I'll be able to recount your lovely sentiments about missing teenage assassins with worried parents back home. 'She told me she didn't care whether he was dead or alive. Didn't get active. Didn't try.'"

"You have plenty of your own indiscretions, don't you?" She scowled.

"People won't care as much about that, will they? By the time you become queen, I'll be a nobody." He winked and turned. "Love you. Have a good visit back home." He left out the back door.

Once the door clicked closed, she promptly bolted the lock and let out a shaky breath. Gnawing on her lip, she stared at the closed fridge, analyzing their chat. Had he just been concerned about his friend? Or did Soren know? Did he suspect? Did that mean her uncle or parents knew or suspected her?

"How was your date with that boy?" Nathan said, entering the kitchen.

Kaylah relaxed into a smile, allowing her mind to drift back to Eric. "Good."

Nathan awkwardly cleared his throat. "I imagine so, if you're kissing him."

Kaylah blushed. "I really like him." While she despised Soren's spying, Nathan's had been expected. He was paid to be her protector, her fake father.

"But—"

"I said I'd be his girlfriend." She lifted her chin slightly.

Nathan, however, tilted his head down a bit. "That wasn't the wisest move."

She frowned. "Rachel could bloom any day. You guys know I'm tired of the suitors. And it's stupid to worry about matching me up so seriously. I have a limited amount of time in this world. Just let me be happy."

Nathan sighed. "We want you to be happy. But we don't have much say in that part of things. You know that."

Looking down, she fidgeted with her hands. "Dating a human would be more convincing for my cover, anyway. You could help me convince my uncle..." She looked up after getting no response.

Nathan eyed her, pursing his lips. "Fine. We'll try."

Kaylah beamed, giving him a big hug. "Thank you!"

"You're welcome." He threw a quick glance at the pizza box. "Leftovers before leaving for home?"

"They're for you. From Eric."

He grinned, opening the box with a vine and slipping out a piece with his hand. "Smart boy."

"Did you know Soren was coming over tonight?" she asked.

Nathan shook his head. "He dropped by asking about a friend of his."

Kaylah nodded, considering the risk she was about to take. "Are you a whisper rifter, Nathan?"

His eyes grew wide as he finished chewing. "What?"

"A whisper rifter. The way I look at it, I figure most palace guards are. Hand-picked former assassins, right?"

Nathan cleared his throat again, taking another bite. "Everyone knows they're just a—"

"Don't say myth." She crossed her arms. "I know they're real." Though she'd grown up believing the same as other Ivies, that whisper rifters were as ridiculous as Bigfoot, she now knew better. Her run-in with Teagan had cemented that truth. A truth that her own parents had kept from her, likely a secret only passed down from a paranoid queen to her heir when the time was right.

Setting down his piece of pizza, Nathan grabbed a napkin and wiped his hands. "Even if I believed or knew about such a thing, I suspect you know I couldn't confirm it." He gently raised his eyebrows. "Not even to you, Your Highness."

Her hope deflated. "Don't 'Your Highness' me, Nathan." They only called her that when they were acting as her paid protectors, not her surrogate parents.

His face was stern, or at least as close to stern as it ever got. "Don't put me in that position."

She hesitated, unsure if she should press more. She'd need *a lot* more loyalty than this if she was going to pull everything off. "You know, you and Ginger lied to me for years about Rachel's true identity. I think you owe me."

"That was under orders. You weren't ready to keep that kind of secret, to know that truth."

She analyzed his body language, determination in the set of her jaw. "I'm ready to know this truth. And whether or not you confirm it, I think you are one. And I want to know if you've ever spied on me."

He studied her face in silence. "I've never followed you or watched you without your knowledge." His voice and posture seemed sincere.

Her anxiety grew, knowing it might be now or never, with the way things were falling into place. "Do I have your loyalty, Nathan?"

"Of course you do." He furrowed his brow. "Why would you ask that?"

"If, um..." She stood a little straighter. "Do you know what my uncle has planned for Rachel?"

Nathan gave her a sympathetic frown. "You know we're as fond of her as you are. But sweetheart, she's a Seeder. You've known for a long time that this was the plan."

Narrowing her eyes, she suspected he didn't actually know. "You're talking about intel and death?"

"What else?"

"You don't know what they've started doing at the palace?"

Nathan shook his head, his eyes squinting. "I haven't been privy to palace information in years."

"You said I have your loyalty, but who has it more? Me or my parents?"

He tilted his head with disapproval. "You can't ask that kind of question."

Her heart was pounding, her chest tight. "But I am. And I will. Because some day you're going to have to choose."

Nathan swallowed hard, staring at her. "What is this all about? A human boy? Spies? Rachel?"

"No. It's much more than that. But I..." She took a deep breath. "You can turn me in tonight, and I can only imagine the punishment I would face, or you can help me. Those are the choices. I'm going to... I've already..."

Nathan's face was grim. "What have you done?"

Tears clouded her vision, exhaustion filling her entire being. "I need your help."

He slowly nodded. "Let's go talk this over with Ginger, okay?"

She sniffled, wiping tears away. "Yeah."

Kaylah sat cross-legged on the hotel suite bed, staring at her phone. *I need to get it over with. I shouldn't be wasting time like this.* Years of learning, planning, plotting. And now everything was set in motion. She shouldn't be taking time at the beginning of a revolution for a personal indulgence.

But she couldn't stop herself. He meant too much.

Bolstering her courage, she forced her fingers to type out the words on her new burner phone.

<Please don't say anything. I'm safe. I need to see you. In private. XO> She closed her eyes and sent it off, then waited in agony for a couple of minutes—he should have just gotten home from school.

A text chimed in. <MEG?!? Where have you been?>

She smiled, her heart filling with hope. <Yes. Are you free tomorrow?>

<Yes. All day. What's going on? You guys are back? I can meet at your place.>

<I'll explain everything. Meet me at the mall at 8 a.m.?>

Instead of getting a return text, her phone rang with an incoming call, and she answered.

"What's going on? If you want to talk in private, the mall isn't really the best place to go," he said.

She sighed. "I know this is going to sound crazy, but I need you to pretend you haven't heard from me since our breakup. No one can know we've talked. It's ... dangerous."

Silence.

"Um... Okay? Do you know what happened to Rachel and David? Gosh, and Rachel's stepdad. And then you guys went missing. It's been crazy here, and your family up and goes on vacation in the middle of school?"

She frowned. "I can explain everything. I promise. But I need you to keep it a secret that we've been in touch. Call me at this number when you get to the mall?"

"Sure."

"Okay... Thank you."

It took him a moment to respond. "Yeah. I... I'm glad to hear your voice."

Her heart ached. "You too. See you tomorrow."

Kaylah made her bed and paced the hotel room all morning. A knock came on her door at 8:30 a.m. and she looked through the peephole. Beaming, she unlocked the door and ripped it open. She yanked Eric inside and threw her arms around him. He paused briefly before returning the hug—not a passionate embrace like they used to share.

She'd forgotten. They were broken up. It was all her fault.

Kaylah stepped back, and they shared an awkward half-smile. "Hey, um... sorry if that was weird to have someone else meet you there. Let's sit down."

They moved over to a small table with two chairs. "Yeah. Pretty weird." He pressed his lips together, looking her over. "What's going on?"

She gave him a hesitant smile. He looked sharp and was wearing her favorite cologne. "How are you doing? I missed you."

He looked down, shrugging. "Fine."

The distance between them gutted her. "I still love you."

He met her gaze, the hurt apparent in his eyes. "You have a funny way of showing it."

Kaylah frowned. She deserved that after breaking up with him, and not even giving an explanation. "I'm sorry. I did that to keep you safe." Even meeting with him now wasn't a great idea. And she should have broken up with him earlier, put more time and space between them; but she hadn't been able to bring herself to do it when she should have.

He sighed. "What's going on? This is dangerous? Safety? You know what's going on with Rachel and David running away? Her stepdad going missing? What do you know? Three people I cared about and three of their parents just go missing all in one week, and there wasn't even a mention about it on the news!"

She gazed into his kind eyes, her heart heavy. "Are you dating anyone?"

He raised his eyebrows. "Is that any of your business? You dumped me, remember? And I don't see how that has anything to do with the topic at hand."

She placed her hands on the table, calculating. She couldn't really tell him anything if he wasn't willing to be part of her life.

"No. I'm not dating anyone," Eric volunteered. "You're not that easy to get over."

She blushed. "A girl can hope."

He shifted in his seat. "So?"

She nodded, getting to their reason for meeting. "I reached out because... Well, like I said, you mean a lot to me. And you're one of the few people I trust, Eric. I have a lot of news, a lot of secrets."

He shrugged again. "Shoot."

Taking a deep breath, she bolstered her courage. "Let's go over the facts in phases. Rachel's stepdad, Rob. He was my uncle."

Eric's eyes widened in surprise. "What? Does Rachel know that? Wait, what?"

"My parents aren't my parents. And David's my brother."

He stared at her, blinking a few times. "Why would you say that?"

"Because it's true. It's complicated. I'll explain it."

He narrowed his eyes in apparent disbelief.

This could be going better...

"David is my older brother," she said. "I know that sounds crazy. But it's true. Rob was our uncle. And Ginger and Nathan are my guardians while I live here, but they're not my parents."

"And why would you all be pretending to be something you're not?"

She swallowed hard. "Do you believe in aliens?"

He busted out laughing. "No... Were you abducted? Is that why you're making up crazy stories? Is that where everyone went? Were the guys that interrogated me from the FBI or something?"

She smiled. "No. No aliens. It might be weirder than that." She reached forward, grasping his hands. The warmth of his large hands was reassuring, but the knots in her stomach grew for fear of his denial. She searched his face intently. "I'm not completely human. I don't want you to freak out." She extended vines from her wrists, wrapping them around their joined hands.

Eric froze on the spot, staring down at them. He finally glanced up. "What... What are you?"

She bit her lip. "Rob, David, Ginger, and Nathan are all like this. Rachel's not human either, but she's different."

He blinked, swallowing, but not saying anything.

"My people are called Ivies."

He pressed his lips together, nodding.

She frowned. "Are you freaked out?"

He went back to staring at her vines, his brow furrowed. "Um... I... don't know..."

"Well... It's a great start that you didn't run or scream..."

He shook his head, wide-eyed. "I'm not drugged, right?"

Kaylah frowned again, thinking of Rachel. "No. You're very much awake and lucid."

He kept nodding, processing. "You're not human. You're secretly related or not related to people that have gone missing. I guess I never really knew you at all."

He hadn't said it in a judgmental way, but it pierced deep. She retracted her vines. "You may not have known those sides of me, but in a lot of ways, you know me better than anyone else in my life."

Eric took a deep breath, sitting up straighter. "So, what happened? Why did everyone go missing? Is everyone okay?"

Barely able to look at him, she pinched the bridge of her nose. "There's bad news and good news about all of that. Ginger and Nathan are in hiding for the same reason I broke up with you—so no one would come after you."

"Why would someone come after us?"

"Because I'm in a tight spot. And, um ... as for David and Rachel... He kidnapped her, but I got her out."

"Shit, Meg! You're not joking, are you?"

She shook her head. "You saw my vines. I think it's safe to say I'm not joking about anything today." She cleared her throat. "And my name's not Meg. It's Kaylah." She shyly added, "Most people know me as ... Princess Kaylah."

He cocked his head. "I mean, why not? A princess."

She smiled. "I'm the next ruler after my mother."

He closed his eyes. "Ruling over a kingdom of plant people?"

She stifled a laugh. "Kind of. It's funny when you say it that way. We prefer 'botanical beings.'"

"Oh, well, my apologies, Your Highness." He raised his hands.

She got more serious. "You can call me Meg if you'd like. Though, I do prefer Kaylah."

He nodded guiltily. "Is Rachel okay? When did you help her? She hasn't been back to school."

"She won't be able to come back. She's back home with her people."

"Right. You said she's different? And that covers everyone but her stepdad."

Kaylah wrung her hands. "Right. Yes. And Rob won't be coming back, because he's dead."

Eric's eyes widened in shock. "Seriously?" he whispered.

"My people have been at war with Rachel's for a long time ... like ... a couple of centuries." Kaylah reached out to hold his hands. "How freaked out are you right now? Be honest."

He waited a moment to answer. "I don't even know what to think."

How much could she throw at him in one go? How much could he handle of the truth, period? "I still love you. Do you think you could ever love me again?"

Looking down, he fought a frown. "I never *stopped* loving you."

She knew she should feel hope, even relief. She didn't. "Even now? Now that you know this crazy part of me?"

He took a painfully long amount of time to reply. "I have a million questions. But ... I miss you. I miss us."

She nodded. That might be the best she could get. "It gets worse."

He raised an eyebrow. "Worse than kidnapping and Rob dying in a war?"

She rubbed his hands with her thumbs. If she was going to do this, she needed to be completely honest with Eric. "My people have been on the wrong side of the war. We're not innocent. Rob and David are horrible people. I'm the one who killed Rob."

He snapped his hands back from her grip. "You what?!"

Her heart sank. "They were torturing her, Eric! And other girls just like her. The world is a better place without him."

"Maybe..." He narrowed his eyes. "Are you sure you're the one that gets to make that call? Who lives and who freakin' dies? You murdered someone, Meg!"

She clenched her teeth. "I know! My own uncle. But he has countless lives on his head. War is ugly, Eric. I'm sorry if you don't understand that, living here in the cozy human world, in a nation at peace."

He ran his hands through his hair. "What else? Why do I feel like this conversation is never going to end?"

She was already chin-deep, might as well go all the way. "I will never apologize for executing an evil man. But I will always feel guilty for playing a part in Rachel's kidnapping."

His jaw dropped in disgust. "You're kidding me. She's your best friend!" He shook his head. "I think I've heard enough." He stood up and walked toward the door.

Kaylah hopped up and blocked his exit. "Please. Hear me out."

"You just told me I knew you better than anyone else. *This* isn't the Meg I knew."

Grimacing, she fought back tears. "I never wanted to hurt her. And I got her back. And I'm... I've turned on my family, my people." She reached to hold his hand, and he jerked it back. She hung her head in shame. "Hear me out. If you still hate me when we're done talking, I'll leave you alone."

He scowled. "What if I want to leave right now? Will you kill me? Or kidnap me? Or who knows what else you've done to people?"

Willing to beg, plead, do anything, she looked into his eyes. "I need you in my life. I would never hurt you. And I've never hurt anyone unless I had to. Rachel included."

He rubbed his forehead. "Why are you even telling me any of this?"

"I told you. I love you. I miss you. And I need you to know the truth."

Pursing his lips, he tilted his head to the side. "So, the truth... Your family is messed up. You're a princess plant-person thing... There's a war. You helped kidnap your best friend, killed your uncle, and lied to me about everything. Did I miss anything?"

Kaylah sighed. "Yes. The most important parts. Rachel's safe and alive because of me, despite what I had to do. You can't grant forgiveness on her behalf, Eric. I can only hope she gives me that when I meet with her next. And I'm hoping that'll be soon. I would be convicted of treason for what I'm doing. I'm leading a revolution. I'm coordinating people to fight back. To end the war, the oppression, the death. If you believe everything I've told you so far, then believe me now when

I say I'm doing my best to fix things. I'm planning on approaching the leaders of Rachel's people to try and form an alliance."

He studied her face, still visibly skeptical and upset. "You said you're the next ruler. That means a queen, right? You're saying none of your actions were your fault. Last I checked, the pawn and the queen have very different places on a chessboard."

A faint smile grew on her face. "I appreciate that you understand the difference." Her shoulders dropped. "I've spent a little too much time playing the pawn, and not enough time preparing to rule."

He let out a heavy sigh, walking back to his seat. "I want to hear everything. Start to finish. Don't leave anything out."

She finally allowed herself to hope, joining him at the table.

A good hour later, Kaylah had given Eric a thorough explanation of the Green Lands and details of the nations at war.

He frowned, reaching out his hands. "So, I can't join you there?"

She shook her head. "But I can visit. And maybe, someday... I don't know. I have dreams. But they don't mean much if I'm dead. Right now, my family would do anything to find out where I am. That includes hurting you and other people to get to me. You need to swear to me you won't talk about any of this to others."

Eric smiled. "Wouldn't even if I wanted to. I'd rather not sound crazy."

She chuckled before settling on a look of admiration. "You're amazing."

"How can I help?"

Her heart melted. "You're the best. Do you know that?"

He grinned. "I fell for a pretty ambitious girl. And I know I'm no soldier, but there's got to be something I can do."

She rubbed the back of his hands with her thumbs. "Actually, there is. That is ... if you're willing to move a couple of hours away as soon as graduation is over."

"Name it."

She raised an eyebrow. "Really?"

"Yes."

There were a few things he could do to help Unitas, while staying out of harm's way. "I'm setting up safe houses for meetings and defectors joining the cause. I can't promise it will be completely safe, but—"

"Consider it done."

She cocked her head to the side. "I love you."

He read her face. "You might have said that already. A time or two, or twenty." He winked. "And I love you, too."

She glanced past him to the bed. "How do you feel about cuddling and chatting? You said you have all day free?"

He looked back and then met her eyes. "Cuddle? Is that why you invited me to meet you in a hotel room?" He smirked.

"Hey! I'm meeting you here because it's a safe place out of the public eye." She blushed, then stood up. "Let's start with a hug. I've been needing one of those."

He got up and pulled her in for a tight embrace. "I'm most definitely good with cuddling." He scooted them a few feet to the edge of the bed. "Tiiiiiimber!" He flopped over on the bed with her still in his arms.

Kaylah giggled, snuggling up to him. She couldn't help herself, gazing lovingly at his sweet face. She shifted and gave him a couple of tender kisses. The spark was still there. Eric moved his hand up to the side of her face, leaning over and laying a passionate kiss on her that sent her heart racing.

They'd talked about prom night being their first time together, despite how cliché it was. They'd missed their chance because her focus on Unitas had driven a wedge between them. She didn't want to miss this chance now.

"I leave in the morning." She studied his face, desperation in her eyes. "I... I wish you could go with me. And I wish you could stay the night."

He gave a soft grin. "I wish I could, too. Would be mighty hard explaining to my parents why I didn't come home tonight." He moved closer, caressing her neck with his lips. "But I don't have anything else planned for today. How long is it going to take to discuss this safe house business?"

She smirked. "Not all day."

Kaylah sat impatiently in an Ivy pub smuggler's room—a small back room with a table, chairs, and storage. She shook her head. *This is what my life is reduced to. No palace. No human graduation.* She cursed the timing of Rachel's bloom cutting things short, though she knew that was hardly fair.

The internal door opened, and she gave a forced smile as Guillen joined her.

"Hey. Glad to see you all in one piece," he said.

She let out a long sigh. "You too."

He sat down opposite her. "You certainly *sound* happy to see me."

She cocked her head to the side. "I'm just trying to figure out why you and I are having this debriefing instead of Jon and I..." She raised her eyebrows.

Guillen raised an eyebrow in return. "He checked in, right? He's okay?"

"Yes. But why are you and I having this meeting instead of him coming to see me? What happened?"

Guillen rubbed at a scratch on the edge of the table. "I volunteered to stay back."

Kaylah was unamused. "You both had orders. Why did you not follow them as directed?"

He shrugged. "It wasn't a huge thing. She got home safe. We got home safe."

Kaylah leaned forward. "You were to be the one who left first. Why did you volunteer to hang back? That was reckless."(hh)

He scowled. "I was fine."

"Dammit, Guillen. That's not your call to make! We put a huge arrow pointing to those woods so they'd find her. What would have happened if they'd stumbled upon you?"

"It didn't happen."

"It could have."

He leaned back. "We're going to go there? You of all people? You're going to cite my 'disability'? Why did you ask me to take on the mission if you didn't think I was capable of doing my part?"

She shook her head. "I'll bring up your limitations when they're relevant, yes." She furrowed her brow. He was a proud man and she'd always liked that, but he was never defiant like this. "We use our resources wisely. We play to our strengths. You did your part. She got home safe. It was Jon's part to ensure she was picked up by the right people, and then rift out."

He stared at her for a moment. "It was a risk I was willing to take."

She narrowed her eyes. "Did he ask you to stay?"

"No."

She put a fist to her forehead. "I get that our relationship is different. But you need to look past that and obey my orders. This is serious."

He glared. "I'm pretty sure I understood how serious this was the first time we killed someone. Don't patronize me."

"Then help me understand. It was a simple order. You're one of my best spies. I can't have you taking unnecessary risks." She studied his face. *Why would he put himself in harm's way?* He was usually so organized, so meticulous, so diligent.

He threw his hands up. "I don't know what you want me to say. I just ... needed to know she was okay." He averted his gaze.

Then it clicked. Kaylah studied him, a smile forming on her face. "You like her."

Guillen quickly glanced up, then looked back down. "You know me so well. I risked my life and traipsed around the Green Lands to take advantage of a traumatized teenage girl."

That broke Kaylah's heart. "How is she?"

Guillen rubbed his hands together. "I don't know. She had some ups and downs. Some pretty intense nightmares. She's ... going to struggle for a while." He met Kaylah's gaze. "You haven't seen her yet?"

Kaylah shook her head. "They haven't reached out yet. If it gets too late in the season, I'll have to consider my backup plans. And they're a heck of a lot trickier..." She reached her hand out on the table. "She's pretty. And nice, isn't she?"

He grinned. "Don't you think she's a little young for me?"

Kaylah shrugged. "Five and a half years isn't *that* big of a deal. After Soren, I have a feeling she'd appreciate a more mature man."

Guillen rolled his eyes. "Yeah, well, you weren't the one who had people thinking he was some kind of a perv by taking his kid cousin out into the woods."

That was hard to hear. No doubt Soren had bullied him about it on one of Guillen's visits to the palace. "If they had ever really thought that, we wouldn't have been allowed to slip away for training like we did."

He smiled. "I don't know if she realized how much older I am. She called me a ... Boy Scout?"

Kaylah gave him a soft smile in return. Soren took every chance he could to mock Guillen for his lack of human-world knowledge. Kaylah had always found it endearing. And she appreciated that he felt safe enough to be vulnerable with her about that kind of thing. "A 'Boy Scout' just means she thinks you're capable. It's not necessarily referencing your age. Take it as a compliment."

His smile subtly widened. "Anyway. What else did you need to know from me? She's back home with her family like she should be. Jon and I moved on safely."

"I want to hear more about your time with her. Do you think she'd be up for helping? I don't know how much training she was able to do with my poisoning. Or how much she hates me..."

He shook his head. "I think she understands what you had to do." His cheeks turned pink. "She's pretty talented and smart. And she seems to want to help."

Kaylah smiled at seeing him blush. Guillen was always so private about his life, and love life.

He picked at his fingernails. "You should, uh, ask her about Seeders like me next time you see her. She was going to look into it."

She grinned wider. "She knows?"

"Yeah." He looked at a clock on the wall. "I should get going. Do you have anything to add to my standing orders?"

"No. Do what you're doing. I'll reach out."

Guillen stood. "Great. Stay safe."

Kaylah got up and gave him a hug. "You too, love you."

"You too."

She sat back down at the table; she'd be having a late dinner served soon.

Guillen lingered, looking down at the table. He knocked his knuckles on the wood. "When you, uh, see her... Tell her hi from me."

Kaylah smirked. "I most certainly will."

He met her eyes, unable to hold back a shy grin of his own. "See you later."

UNITAS: TRIO

BOOK 3

Prologue

Kaylah stood in front of the gilded mirror in her chambers, straightening her lace dress. It was striking; she missed getting dolled up, dressing like a princess. She tugged at her itchy sleeve and wiggled a bit. Maybe she didn't miss it as much as she used to. Her human-world, average-teenager clothes were much more comfortable.

But it was still nice to be home. Kind of. The warmth of the Green Lands was always refreshing, but the palace was so cold. At least the people in it were.

A knock at the door claimed her focus.

"It's unlocked."

A woman opened the door and curtsied. "Your Highness, your uncle called for you."

Kaylah bit the insides of her cheeks, forcing herself to not roll her eyes. "Yeah, I'm on my way." *No time to rest. Always about the project.*

After making her way down the quiet palace corridors, she arrived at the entry to the duke's study. She knocked.

"Enter."

Plastering a smile on her face, she opened the door and was greeted by her uncle, and to her surprise, her older brother, Soren.

Daylight bathed the room, backlighting one of dozens, perhaps hundreds, of stained glass inlays in the palace. The room was modest compared to most, but better than her uncle deserved.

"Come on in. We're just discussing our project," Duke Nuren said, running a hand over his bearded chin, sitting at a table with well over a dozen books.

She scowled at Soren. "Why is *he* here?"

Standing next to their uncle, Soren flashed pouty lips. "What kind of a greeting is that? We all missed you so terribly, Your Highness!"

"Not mutual," she drawled.

"That's enough of that." Duke Nuren scolded Kaylah with his eyes. "You two are going to have to learn to get along, because Soren's moving over with us before the next school year begins."

Her jaw dropped. "Why?!"

"To ensure our success," Nuren replied, placing a bookmark and closing one of the books he'd been studying.

She clenched her fists. "I'm doing exactly what I'm supposed to be doing. Why do we need *him*?"

Soren sneered, taunting her.

Duke Nuren set the book on a stack beside him. "We want all angles covered. He'll be dating her."

Kaylah busted out laughing. "Soren? Soren! Dating Rachel?"

Soren glared with cold eyes.

She stifled her laugh. "Sorry, but you're not exactly her type. That would never work."

Nuren raised his voice. "You'll make it work. You're in charge of making sure it does."

"But ... they're nothing alike!" *Because he's horrible!*

Nuren lifted his eyebrows with finality. "Just because you've been away, doesn't mean he hasn't been excelling in his training. That's not your call to make."

She held her tongue while Soren wiggled his eyebrows in triumph. His stupid green eyes teemed with pride.

"I can be charming. I can be whatever she wants me to be."

Kaylah wanted to vomit. "Your precious Beata will be so disappointed."

Soren casually studied his nails. "She won't mind. I'll be back often enough."

"We'll talk later, Soren," Nuren said, dismissing him with a wave of the hand.

Kaylah hung back, giving her latest report. Nothing exciting or big had happened recently in the human world. "What are we even doing?" she asked. She wouldn't get an answer—she never had in the past.

Nuren wagged a finger at her as he stood. "Don't worry about it. You're right. You're doing a great job." He walked to the window, adjusting the curtains. "Just keep her trust. Guide her to Soren. Hopefully she'll bloom early and we can really get things started."

Clamping her mouth shut again, Kaylah forced herself to not reply. All of her protests to her uncle or parents over the years had only earned her their scorn and disappointment.

"That's all," he said. "Enjoy your visit."

She glanced at the table he was now standing over, stacked high with books. "Those look interesting. I'd love to help ... or just learn more?"

He didn't bother to look up. "As long as they don't go missing from this room, I don't mind you perusing. Lots of curious stuff here."

She nodded, planning on coming back soon. Not that she didn't have friends to hang out with, or family to catch up with, but ... she was becoming more distant the longer she was stationed in the human world. "Thank you. I'll see you later."

A week later, Kaylah found herself alone in her uncle's study; his visits were more frequent than hers, but never as long. Sitting sideways in a comfy armchair, she skimmed one of the old books, reading history.

"Your Highness?" a woman called through the partially open door.

"Yes?"

"You have a visitor."

Kaylah instantly beamed. "I'll be right there!"

Saving her place in the book and replacing it on the stack, Kaylah darted down the corridors to the main entrance. Seeing her visitor, she wore a toothy grin.

"Guillen!" she squeaked, giving her cousin a big hug.

"Hey, kiddo! Someone requested that I visit?" He released her and looked her over. "Want to go for a walk?"

She glanced down at her dress. "Yes, let me go get changed!"

Kaylah returned to meet Guillen, now dressed in clothes she didn't have to worry about ruining.

Soren strolled by. "Guillen, so nice of you to visit!" His tone was as arrogant as his grin. "They let you get away from your special people, just to grace us with your presence?"

Guillen glared, then turned to Kaylah. "Ready to go?"

She threw a stink eye at her brother. "Beyond ready."

They walked for quite some time, following their usual path through the dense forest, further into the mountains. They caught up with whispers, always cautious no one followed them to their secret place, a place of refuge.

The cave was chilly; she rubbed her arms as he offered to grab their sparring weapons. Returning from the depths of the cave, Guillen tossed a wooden staff, which she caught.

Without hesitation, Kaylah made the first strike. "I'm so tired of this crap."

He blocked and pushed her off. "Is it so bad?"

She huffed before grazing his arm with another attack. "They're having Soren join me. Like I can't do my job. They're going to make her date him."

"Then I feel sorry for her even more." He landed a blow in her ribs.

She clutched her side, clenching her jaw.

He halted, raising his eyebrows. "Do I need to go easy on you? You're out of practice."

She straightened out. "No."

"Alright. Fight now. Talk later."

They sparred for a good half hour. In the end, they sat on the cool cave floor, catching their breath and wiping their brows.

"Good workout," she said. "Way better than human gym classes."

"Yeah? You talk about it like you hate it there."

She frowned, tucking her knees under her chin. "I kind of hate it everywhere right now."

He matched her frown. "What's going on?"

She shook her head. "She's a nice girl. Sometimes I just want to come out and say everything. I'm delusional to think she'd understand. Who would understand that kind of thing?"

He turned the staff in his hand, inspecting it. "The end goal, right? No matter what the plan is, it won't be good for her. And you're attached."

She stared at the ground. "Yeah."

He took a deep breath. "Teenage drama. Can't say I miss it." He winked once she looked up.

She squinted. "You stopped being a teenager, what? A month ago? You're all older and wiser now?"

He chuckled. "Yep. That's me."

"Then please, wise sage," she bowed her head, "what would *you* do?"

He scratched his chin. "I'd find a way to make them listen. Or, you know, at least do my best to tick them all off."

She let out a breathy chuckle. "Great advice." She sighed. "I just don't get why my parents listen to him so much. Nuren thinks he's the next best thing. And Soren is so much like him."

"I'm always here for you. You know that, right?"

Kaylah smiled. "Definitely my favorite cousin." She stood, extending her hand for his staff.

Walking to the back of the cave, she placed the staves next to the rest of their training weapons they'd hidden away there. She furrowed her brow, studying something on the wall. Something that had always been there, but she'd never made much of. The symbols—they reminded her of something she'd just read. She took a mental photograph, planning to pick that book up after her visit with her cousin.

She couldn't help but wonder... *What if...*

Chapter 1

The Ivy queen and king were dead, assassinated. But the war was far from being won.

Rachel balanced in the breeze with the three others near her, flying home. At least, to the only place she could *call* home anymore. She hadn't chosen this realm, this life—the life of a Seeder in the Green Lands. And if she was going to have to live the rest of her life here, she wanted to make it worthwhile. But the war council wouldn't let her stay and help her best friend, Princess Kaylah. Instead, Rachel was being sent back to her village and had been warned to edit the truth.

Passing over hills and valleys lush with plant growth, wooden rooftops and dirt lanes, Rachel tried to smile. It was gorgeous. People were kind. But her heart wasn't here. Samantha, the human mom she'd grown up with, was in a Unitas safe house back in the human world. Her best friend was back in the village they'd just left, now in custody, where Rachel couldn't do anything to keep her safe. And the only guy she was interested in was an Ivy, one of the enemy. Not technically an enemy—he was a Unitas spy, one of the good guys, but that only made it harder. He was out there, somewhere, possibly in danger.

Rachel shook the memory of Guillen out of her mind. Instead, she tried to commit to memory the lies she'd have to tell people once they landed. Her ex-boyfriend, Prince Soren, had killed his parents and blamed it on the Seeders, adding to the false accusations that they'd also kidnapped his sister Kaylah. That meant the truth of Kaylah being behind Seeder borders and working with their council needed to stay a secret while they sorted things out. The council was giving Kaylah a chance to prove herself, to make an alliance. But trust in an Ivy was hard to come by with Seeders, especially after Kaylah had spent years undercover, with her mission eventually leading to Rachel and others getting hurt. Leading to Seeders getting killed.

A gust of wind hit Rachel from the side, and she shifted the energy in her body to compensate. With the energy in her hands, she pushed back, righting herself. The air had a springiness to it. Compensating when catching a breeze felt a lot like pushing on a trampoline; there was a gentle give.

Flying straighter and glancing at the three others soaring nearby, Rachel took a deep breath, her brown hair flapping in the wind around her. So much in her life was out of her control, but she was going to try and make the most of it. To try to find the positive. She was alive. She could fly and heal. She had a huge Seeder family; she just hadn't given them enough of a chance. And she had hope for helping Kaylah with Unitas, with her movement to end the centuries-old war between their peoples.

✻

Saff communed with the wind, her eyes and heart facing forward, toward her home village of South Fortinda. She yearned to be home, to see the people she loved most. To be reunited with her mother and all twenty-three of her siblings. *No. Twenty-two. Ben is dead, and I missed his burial.* She swallowed hard, trying not to cry. She'd done it again—been impulsive. With her closest brother dead in the war, and at the end of her rope, she'd risked her life to experiment with her powers to take Rachel to the enemy princess. As much as she wanted to hate Kaylah for what her people had done to Seeders for centuries, for what had happened to Rachel, Saff had to admit that Kaylah had done a lot to prove herself already, in the few days she'd come to know her. But now, Kaylah and her fate were in the council's hands.

Saff pondered the meetings they were leaving behind. The intel Kaylah had provided about Ivy assassins was being acted upon immediately. With few formal laws binding Seeder society, most decisions were based on group consensus, tradition, and each family's preferences. But with the war so bleak, and this new information coming to light, the war council had immediately sent out an edict on how families were required to handle the care of blooming girls in the human world. The jade charms were a tool they'd always intended to keep hidden, as they hadn't been sure whether the enemy knew anything about their purpose. The Ivy assassins hadn't. But now they did, and they'd be laser-focused.

Conflicted about the terms of the edict, Saff still knew it was for the best. They couldn't leave it up to family preferences anymore. Before, if a family was careless about their own daughters' protection, they had paid the heartbreaking penalty for it. But now, if they dropped the ball, the price was even worse than assassination—those daughters would be kidnapped and subjected to the same torture as Rachel. The kind of torture that helped the War Vines tear down Seeder border walls.

One wrong move could jeopardize *everyone* in Seeder society now.

Thousands of Seeder girls were hidden in the human world, unable to survive in the poisoned Seeder lands until their powers came in. A lot of lives were about to change abruptly. Most girls bloomed between the ages of fifteen and eighteen, and the majority of the time, human host parents waited to tell them about their heritage until their blooming had been completed with the charm. But now, they would no longer be afforded the luxury of normal teenage lives free from worry of assassins on the hunt, able to spend carefree time with family they loved before moving away forever. *Every* Seeder girl thirteen and up was now to learn the truth. They could be their own advocates when looking for the enemy, spotting early signs of budding, and keeping the jade charms that controlled their changes well-hidden and used consistently.

Saff's heart was heavy. She would have hated losing out on that precious time with her human parents, blissfully unaware. But she also keenly recalled how poorly things had gone for her own family because of her ignorance. Despite that, she didn't blame her family—they'd done the best they could. And there were rarely ideal options in war.

Saff glanced to her right, at Thod, her Seeder dad. He was disappointed. Saff's stomach knotted. She had a lot of family, which meant a lot of people to love, but also meant a lot of people to hurt. She really should have at least waited another day to run away. It had been just a week ago that Ben died, and she'd slipped out before the burial to meet Kaylah in the human world.

Her guilt piled up when her mind turned to Devin, her husband. She wanted nothing more than to be with him, to hold him, to have him hold her. But she'd betrayed him, sneaking away in the dead of night without a word, leaving only a letter. She loved nothing more than her family, and she wanted to end the war, but her needs and wants were at odds, and she'd made a choice. A choice she hoped had been the right one.

She prayed Kaylah wouldn't betray them, and that Saff could make amends.

Approaching a central park good for landing, the four Seeders coasted lower and slower, floating to the ground. Saff had mastered a graceful landing long ago. Rachel's landing was a bit rough, as the least experienced of the group, but she caught herself and landed on her feet. Saff and Rachel had argued before taking off. Saff had wanted to go home; Rachel hadn't. But their hours in the air had allowed them each to do some thinking, and they hugged.

Saff forced a smile. "Maybe, if we're lucky, they'll let us keep working together for now. And hopefully we'll hear from Kaylah soon."

"Yeah. Maybe. Thanks for taking me."

Saff gave her another hug, and they parted ways to their own sections of the village. Saff and Thod walked in silence for a while down the semibusy dirt lane. One of her former students smiled and waved. Soldiers plodded along everywhere.

"Do you want me to drop you off at your cottage?" Thod asked. "Or do you want to stop by and see the family first?"

Both. Neither. She simultaneously wanted to hug everyone, and to shrink from the uncomfortable, but inevitable, meetings all at once. It was still early enough in the day that she figured Devin wouldn't be home yet, and she wasn't sure she could sit all alone in their empty cottage. "Let's go see Mom and the others."

"Okay." After a minute, Thod reached out an arm and slid it around Saff's shoulder, pulling her closer—an olive branch after he'd chastised her back in the village they'd just returned from.

They entered the family cottage, and Murial, Saff's Seeder mom, hugged her within an inch of her life. "You're home. In one piece," she breathed in relief. "Please don't worry us like that again."

Despite Saff's actions, Murial was just happy to have her home safe and sound. Saff's decision to go to the human world to parley with Kaylah had been a dangerous one. It shouldn't have even been possible, according to their understanding of their powers. And the fact that she might have been stranded in the human world in the attempt, had made it a potentially lethal decision. Seeder women's health and powers were tethered to the energy of the Green Lands. Unable to rift back on her own, she could have been dead by now.

A half dozen of Saff's brothers and sisters dropped by during the hour she was back home. Most of them still lived in the kids' housing in the back lot. Things were tense, but she had hope of their relationships bouncing back. None of them seemed to focus on her defiance of council orders. The pain they chiefly expressed was from her walking out before Ben's burial.

"So, how did you even do it?" Tabatha asked, sitting across from her in the cottage living room.

Saff shrugged. "I just ... thought I'd test the limits of my extra capacity with energy."

Tabatha shook her head. "Wow, that's crazy. So, you can make *two* trips to the human world in a year?"

Saff's muscles tensed. She *hadn't* actually made two round trips—not on her own. She probably wouldn't have been able to, and would have died from root rot in the human world, if it hadn't been for Kaylah guiding her home through an Ivy rift.

But they had to edit their story. It might keep Seeders safer, not knowing Kaylah was in their custody, but it made Saff's justification for leaving her family sound a lot more hollow. "Yeah, two round trips. Crazy, right? But I don't plan to ever do it again. It hurt pretty bad. One trip is enough." She rubbed her chest at the echo of intense pain she had endured when she'd punched through the rift into the human world; it had been so bad that she'd almost died just from losing her focus during flight, plummeting in a free fall.

Tabatha frowned. "That would have been cool, to figure out a way to visit the human world more often."

"Yep."

Hesitantly, Tabatha dared to ask the same question the others had. "So, what came of your visit there?"

Saff poked her finger through the open pattern of an afghan.[ii] "Um, unfortunately we didn't actually get to meet the princess. But we found some intel that will be important regarding their assassin networks."

"Oh... Then ... I guess something came out of it. We ... missed you, at Ben's burial."

Saff closed her eyes, trying not to cry, *again*. "I know. I'm sorry."

"Well, I'm just happy you're home now."

After another round of hugs and some food, Saff walked next door to her in-laws' cottage. She was welcomed in by Heather, Ben's fiancée at the time of his death. She wasn't her usual cheery self, not that Saff would have expected her to bounce back so soon.

"I'm so sorry," Saff said as she held Heather tight.

Heather took a while to respond. "I'm glad you're back."

The members of Devin's family who were home acted more casually. One sister even asked questions about how the 'adventure' to meet the princess had gone.

Devin walked in the door, and his eyes focused on Saff. He didn't run to her, instead standing there as if deciding what to do. Seated on the couch, Saff also waited a moment, not sure if he would come to her, or just turn back out the door in anger at her betrayal.

She cautiously stood and walked to him; he grabbed her, closing the gap, and wrapped his arms around her.

"You're really home," he whispered.

She bit her lip. "I'm sorry. I love you. I missed you so much."

They stood there for a while, embracing, and not saying anything more. Not releasing each other. Saff didn't yet know where to go from there; perhaps Devin didn't either. Eventually, he was the first to pull away.

"Just checking in," he told his family.

She wanted to grab his hand, or feel his arm around her, something naturally affectionate. But instead, he was like a stranger, as awkward as when they were teenagers, before dating.

"I think I'm going to head home," she said, hoping he'd follow.

"I'll see you in a little while," he said, looking down. "I'm going to spend some time here."

Saff swallowed a lump in her throat. She could hardly just say she'd changed her mind and hang out there, if he was intentionally staying behind as a way to avoid being with her.

"Okay. I'll see you soon." She frowned and gave him a kiss on the cheek before saying goodbye to the others and heading out the door.

Chapter 2

Saff arrived back at her cottage. It was quiet. Too quiet. She'd only spent a few days apart from Devin, but it felt like months. Perhaps it was the gap she'd forced into their relationship. She'd essentially left for a suicide mission and hadn't had the courage to even tell him to his face.

Passing their wedding portrait and wall of photos in the living room, she stepped into their bedroom. On their dresser sat the note she'd left him, now torn in half.

Her heart ached—she was solely to blame for the wedge in their marriage. She'd made an impulsive decision, had been pushed over the edge with Ben's death. Devin would have stopped her from going to meet Kaylah. She hoped he'd come to understand that she'd had to do it.

By the time Devin returned home, Saff was fast asleep. She woke in the morning to him getting dressed.

"Any chance you could stay and eat breakfast together?" she asked.

"I should get going." He put on his shoes without looking at her.

"You're sure?" She pleaded with her eyes.

"There's work to do." He leaned over and kissed her on the forehead. "I'll see you tonight."

"Yeah," she whispered as he walked out of the room.

After getting ready for the day, she rendezvoused with Rachel to meet with their village council. They were again deposed, individually. Saff couldn't help but wonder if she was taking on the brunt of their anger. She ought to, as Rachel's mentor.

Once they both rejoined the meeting, Saff waited for the hammer to drop, for them to take away her welcoming mentor position and reassign her elsewhere.

They didn't.

"For now, on a *trial* basis, we'll be reassigning you both to the healing clinic you were stationed at before you went AWOL. Standard temple deposits will also be expected," a councilwoman instructed. "Do you think you two can manage that?" There was obvious censure in her tone.

Both girls hung their heads. "Yes, ma'am."

"Good. You're dismissed."

The crunch of gravel under their shoes filled the awkward silence between them as they left the council meeting, headed toward the temple.

"That could have been worse," Rachel timidly encouraged.

"Yeah. I half expected them to order me to the front lines," Saff said wryly.

"You ... do still want to work together, right?"

Saff's eyes shot to Rachel. "Yeah. I just... I guess we'll see what the council makes of our 'trial.'"

Saff was able to leave her work early that first day to visit the graveyard before dark.

She shuffled her tired feet to the edge of town, all alone. She'd only visited the village graveyard a couple of times before, but it hadn't meant as much to her then, as it did now.

Seeder graveyards were one of the most beautiful ways one could witness the Seeders' close ties to nature. In the center of the field rose a giant leafy tree. It stood vibrant, almost glowing. It was said that its roots took the energy from the fallen Seeders and recycled it back into the realm, and that those who came to visit the area could gain comfort and strength from the echoes of their loved ones giving back.

Regret filled her. She didn't even know which plot was her brother's—they didn't mark them. Seeders didn't waste time and money on expensive caskets or anything like that; Seeder funerals were simple, natural, practical.

Sitting on a knotted wooden bench, Saff surveyed the area. There were too many bright flowers. It made her hollow inside to behold such a floral display. Visitors knew that a plot was occupied, and how fresh the burial was, by the flowers that emerged from it. Ben would be under one of the patches of bright purple flowers. The field had several plots of purple flowers, and almost as many with yellow flowers. They would fade as the energy was released, as the bodies decomposed, and then the dirt would be barren, ready for the next.

There was a poetic parallel to human funerals, how people would bring cut flowers to put on the graves as a sign of respect. How over the years those flowers would often stop coming—a mirror of what nature did on its own over here.

Saff tried to talk to Ben, tried to apologize out loud; it felt right. But she choked on her words, instead sobbing.

The snap of a branch down the path announced someone's approach. She wiped at her eyes and turned to see who would be joining her. She wanted it to be Devin, but it wasn't. Heather gave her a sympathetic frown as she approached. Saff scooted over on the bench to make space, and Heather sat down without a word. They both stared over the field. Only the chirp of crickets coming out for the night pierced the stillness.

Heather rested her head against Saff's shoulder. "He's that one, right over there." She pointed at a plot with fresher flowers.

Saff sniffled. "I'm sorry."

"Me too."

Saff leaned her head onto Heather's. They still had a strong bond. They'd still be sisters-in-law, with Heather being Devin's sister. But Heather had lost her fiancé, and Saff her brother. They were close before, and while they had naturally grown closer when Ben proposed to Heather, they were now brought together by something that ached deep in their souls.

Saff realized she hadn't really elaborated on her blanket apology. She was sorry that Heather hurt, that Ben was gone, but also that she'd deserted them before his burial.

"I'm sorry I wasn't here... That I left," she added.

"It's okay," Heather whispered. "He knew you loved him."

"I hope so," Saff squeaked. "I let him down."

"You didn't. No more than I did," Heather reassured her.

Saff sat up, looking over, confused.

Heather continued, "I gave everything I had when he came in. And you know I'm one of the best healers our age, at least in our village." She pursed her lips. "There's only so much we can do."

For work during this onslaught, Heather was often stationed out on the edge of the borders, healing those more severely wounded.

Saff nodded. While she was a talented teacher, training the young girls, she admired Heather. Heather's natural nurturing was something Saff loved about her; she'd always believed it had helped Ben with his temper and rigidity.

"Do you think it will make a difference, what you and your friend did?" Heather asked.

Saff wished more than anything that she could tell Heather about Kaylah and the council's plans. But she'd only been given permission to disclose that to Devin and her parents. "I really hope so. We need something to change. We can't keep going on like this."

Heather gave her a faint smile. "Then I'm glad you went. And if it's something that can end this, I want to help, too."

While surprised by Heather's declaration, Saff appreciated the support.

Heather fidgeted with her hands. "How are you and Devin?"

Saff opened her mouth, unsure of what to say at first. "I don't really know. Maybe someday I'll find out ... if he'll stay in my presence long enough to talk to me."

"He'll come around, you know. You two are strong." Heather tapped her own knee. "But take my advice? Don't waste a day being apart from the one you love."

Saff nodded. She wasn't sure if she should ask what she wanted to. It could be seen as insensitive or impertinent, but she also hated taboos that restricted people from being able to talk about hard things. She hesitated, but took the plunge.

"Do you wish you had gotten married earlier? Knowing he'd be gone so soon?" Being a widow or divorcée in Seeder society was complicated. The mating bond didn't sever just because one of them left or died. Once a Seeder had been mated, a physical relationship wouldn't be the same with future suitors, and they wouldn't be able to have kids with them. In a way, Heather had dodged a dart; she could still find a mate down the road and have a 'normal' life.

Heather didn't answer Saff's question, instead shedding fresh tears. Saff leaned her head against hers again, and held her hand. The two looked out over the field of flowers as all light faded from the sky.

After a while, Saff dropped Heather off at her parents' place and then headed home for the night. Devin was asleep, or pretending to be, by the time Saff got back to their cottage. She slid into bed and cuddled up to him; he didn't react.

Devin's movements in bed woke her in the early morning. She opened her eyes to him studying her face, just inches away.

"Hey, you," she said with a small smile.

"Hey." Instead of returning a smile, he started to get out of bed.

She grabbed his hand. "Just stay for a little while?"

He shook his head, freeing his hand. "I have people counting on me. I need to get to work."

Her heart dropped. Had that been aimed to hurt her? Implying she'd deserted her people, left for a week, when they were counting on her?

She sat up in bed. "Please stay, just for a little while. Don't leave."

He met her gaze with narrowed eyes. "Like you left me?"

Devastated, she looked down. "I know you're mad. I deserve that."

He changed his clothes and continued to get ready, leaving the room.

She followed him to the kitchen. "Please, just talk to me."

He clenched his jaw and sat at the table. His hands were balled into fists. Slowly, he stretched them out onto the wood. "You weren't there when your family needed you the most. I don't know what you expect me to say."

Gripping the back of a kitchen chair, she uttered the only thing she could think to say. "I did what I felt I had to."

"Well, I hope it pans out." He stood as if to leave.

"I want to hear what you have to say. I'm ready."

"Are you really?" he snapped.

Saff swallowed, emboldened by Heather's advice to not waste a day. "Yes."

He scoffed. "I doubt that."

"Try me."

"I don't get to be mad at you. You don't *get* to be mad at someone that just had a family member die!" His glare was piercing. "It doesn't matter that you think you're smarter than the council. Or that he was one of *my* best friends. Or that a lot of people were depending on you for training and healing. Or that *every* family member on both sides felt your absence as they mourned. You get *your* way, and that's *all* you care about!"

His face was growing redder with each offense he spewed out. "And you didn't give a shit about my feelings, enough to even tell me to my face that you were endangering your life. It's like you're a human teenager all over again— inconsiderate and selfish."

Her eyes stung at his assessment of her. She and Devin were only twenty-one. She still had a lot to learn. "I'm not perfect. You knew what I was like when you married me."

"Yeah, well maybe I thought you'd grow out of it."

She pursed her lips, gripping the kitchen chair tighter. They rarely fought, and never like this.

He continued, "It's like you always have to take it too far. You couldn't just find a way to say goodbye to your human best friend—you had to reveal our entire society's secrets to him first. You couldn't just fly off to meet the leech princess, you had to do it before Ben's burial, and without even talking to me. Your husband. Your mate. The person you should be able to talk to and trust the most."

She'd asked for it, but she hadn't prepared herself for his tirade. She was at a loss on how to answer any of it.

When she didn't respond, he finished letting out his frustration. "I don't want to go to more burials, Saff. And as much as Ben's burial hurt, do you know what hurt more?" He paused. "Imagining my wife, signing her own death sentence in the human world. I wouldn't be there to keep you safe. I wouldn't be there for your burial. The person that matters the most to me."

She frowned. "I don't always need protection."

"Then maybe you don't need me." He studied her face. "You healed me once, when I told you not to, and you said that *you* deserved some say in the matter, that you take care of your family. Where did you extend that same courtesy to me?"

He was right. Absolutely right. They were supposed to be a team.

"I need you." She choked on her words as tears fell down her cheeks. "I love you. I won't do it again. I won't leave you again. I'm sorry. I really am." She couldn't yet bring herself to ask for his forgiveness.

Devin closed his eyes, clenching his fists again. "I love you too. I'm going to work." He left without further discussion.

Saff lay down on the couch, sniffling and wondering if she'd done the right thing by pushing Devin to talk. She felt like she'd done the right thing by going to meet with Kaylah. And she still felt guilty about the way she'd done it. But now she wasn't sure if she should have forced him to talk if he wasn't ready.

Either way, it was out in the open, and she'd made a vague promise she hadn't intended to. She'd said she wasn't going to leave again. If Kaylah asked for her to go help with the cause, she wouldn't be joining Unitas. Saff's marriage meant too much to her.

After forcing herself to get up and dress, Saff jogged halfway to work to clear her mind. Rachel was already there, tidying up bandage wraps.

"Hey, stranger. How's it going?" Rachel asked.

Saff set to work helping her. "I've been better."

"Sorry."

Saff managed a tight-lipped smile. "It's not all about us, right?"

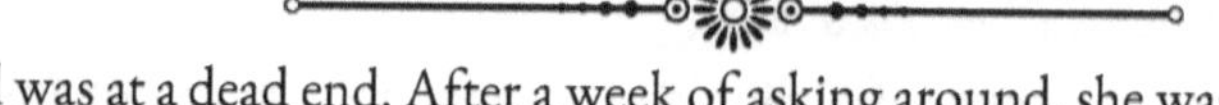

As they worked with the younger girls, healing the wounded as they came in, they would occasionally chat.

"I thought it would be busier, to be honest," Rachel confessed.

"Calm before the storm," Saff replied. "I'm sure the Ivies are building something big to make up for the assassination and kidnapping."

Rachel nodded in agreement. She finished healing a minor head wound on a soldier, and he thanked her. She wasted no time starting on her given assignment from Kaylah. "Saff? Kay—um, *someone* asked me to look into something—the name of our village. Do you know where that came from?"

"No idea." Saff moved over to a newly returned girl who was healing a young soldier. "Not that much. Just enough to heal the immediate area. If you expend that much energy on every scrape, you'll be useless in a couple hours."

"Where do we find the history of our villages?" Rachel asked.

"They keep older relics safely locked away in the temples; there are some interior rooms people don't usually go into. You'd have to ask a temple leader, or a council member."

Rachel welcomed in another wounded soldier, mentally making plans for her time after work. It wasn't like she had friends to hang out with, or a desire to spend copious amounts of time with her Seeder family.

Rachel was at a dead end. After a week of asking around, she was finally allowed to spend some free time perusing old records of their village. But there wasn't much information that seemed pertinent. South Fortinda didn't have much written about its establishment. It was just another village, created as Seeders had spread out over time. From what she could gather, it was fairly identical to the others. And there wasn't really a meaning to the name; it wasn't named after a flower, or a river, or anything like that. She was curious about the fact that it was 'South,' and that other villages shared the same name—there was a North and West Fortinda.

Nothing jumped out as useful, until a certain passage piqued her interest. Rachel sat up straighter, sliding her clear-quartz-and-jade lightkeeper closer to the page. They'd all been named Fortinda because they shared the same rift space. *Hmm...* She sat back in her chair, lightly tapping the tabletop. Seeders were quite different from the Ivies in that regard. Seeders created their rifts to the human world in the air—they could fly. Ivies created their rifts through the sacrifice of trees.

The particularly interesting thing was the precision with which Ivies would travel. Seeders had to prepare for a long strenuous journey, flying for hours to find the right place to cross between realms. Ivies could practically pick any old random tree, and choose whatever destination they wanted in the Green Lands. She'd experienced it herself. She wasn't sure what this meant, but it might mean something to Kaylah. Rachel made a mental note of it so she could report back when, or if, she were to see her friend again.

After she flipped one last page, Rachel's eyes grew wide with curiosity. Intriguing symbols covered the parchment, similar to a type she'd once seen before, carved on a cave wall near the Ivy palace. She jotted them down, knowing that *these*, for certain, meant something.

Chapter 3

A couple of weeks passed without incident. Devin was still cold with Saff, the Ivy attacks were still eerily tame, and no word had come to their village—from or about Kaylah. Saff and Rachel would meet daily for work at the training and healing clinic, passing questioning glances, only to be met with frowns and heads shaking. They were both in the dark.

❋

Rachel hated this. She was grateful they hadn't been punished, as the council had warned about possible 'consequences.' But they probably needed her and Saff healing too much to worry about anything punitive. Maybe, she hoped, they were also not being harder on Saff and Rachel because Kaylah was doing a good job. The part that killed Rachel was that there was no way to know. She'd promised Eric, Kaylah's human boyfriend, that she would watch out for her and keep her safe. She couldn't do that from here.

These weeks were lonely for Rachel. When she'd first met most of her Seeder family, it had been in shame. She'd been stupid enough to trust Prince Soren and had allowed herself to be kidnapped and used as a weapon against her own people. She'd found it hard to talk to her new family about the trauma she'd endured. Weeks later, she'd taken off, running away to go back to meet Princess Kaylah, one of the people at fault for Rachel's kidnapping. And returning to her village now, all she could say was that they'd 'found intel to mitigate the Ivy assassin network's efforts.' It all sounded like Rachel was weak and ungrateful.

She hadn't yet met her Seeder dad—he was still undercover taking care of her last sister in the human world, who was midbloom. Other than Saff, the only confidant Rachel had who knew the truth about Kaylah, was her Seeder mom, Lyza. But their relationship was the touchiest of them all. The tension between her

Seeder and human moms—once best friends, now at odds thanks to Rachel's foolishness—made Rachel feel like she had to walk on eggshells around Lyza. And she wished, more than anything, that she could find some strength in talking with her siblings, even with the edited story. But things hadn't been going well with them, either.

Midafternoon at the clinic one day, Rachel and Saff were slogging through their daily tasks. Rachel collected bloodied rags and threw them in a bucket to be rinsed and boiled. Saff sighed heavily nearby, leaning back against a table, supervising a few trainees while they healed.

"What's up?" Rachel asked, approaching her and leaning against the table as well.

Saff shrugged.

They hadn't really talked about it, but Rachel knew things weren't exactly going well back home for Saff. She'd sometimes talk about spending free time with her family, or going on nature walks, but she never talked about her husband anymore. Rachel dared to ask, "How's Devin?"

Saff wouldn't make eye contact. "He's fine."

Rachel nodded.

"How about your family?" Saff asked.

Rachel grabbed a bar of soap and dipped her hands in a basin of clean water. "They're all safe."

What more could she say? Saff was already struggling with her marriage, and Rachel didn't want to add to that. But things had gone from awkward to silent back home for Rachel. She avoided Lyza more often than not, too ashamed to talk about her human mom and all the trauma Rachel had been through. Her brothers were nice in passing, though often busy fighting at the weakened Seeder border walls, or working other jobs, or dating. Her sisters were plenty occupied, but they all shared a space in their family dormitory; they were in closer proximity to her than anyone else. Rachel had to lie to them, had to keep secrets about Kaylah. The sisters that didn't judge her for her actions had originally tried to be there for her, but that support had died off. She wasn't sure how much of it was them being tired of trying to coax information out of her, or if, with eleven of them, they all assumed someone else had her covered.

But she felt adrift in a sea of pain and memories. She couldn't handle the looks she sometimes got in the mornings after she'd woken from haunting nightmares.

It wasn't often, but it still happened—she'd wake up sweating and moaning or screaming.

The walls were too thin for her mental health. And what was she supposed to say? 'Sorry, just dreaming about my ex-boyfriend attacking me again. Yeah, and then I was strapped to a chair, and they drilled my arms with Ivy leaves to steal my energy?' Or the other nightmares. 'This was the one about my stepdad being the villain, and then being beheaded by my best friend. Did you have any dreams last night? Oh, unicorns—how fun.' She'd *tried* to open up, but it hadn't been easy, and it hadn't helped.

A pair of soldiers entered the clinic, one aiding the other as he limped.

"I've got this one." Rachel dried her hands on a clean rag. She approached the men as the injured one lay down on the stretcher and his helper left. Luckily, it was only a flesh injury. His leg had been sliced, no doubt by sharpened leaves on Ivy vines. One cut was down to the bone. She moved a hand over that one first. She still got a bit queasy at the larger injuries, but was starting to get used to it after so much exposure.

"Sorry," she said as he flinched, and she pinched the skin together, channeling Seeder energy from her heart to her hand. Her hand glowed as the bone, muscle, and skin healed. She preferred this kind of healing to anything internal. Internal was tricky.

Saff and Heather were as well-trained as any fully-rooted matriarch at those techniques. This was a training clinic, so they didn't get the most severely wounded, but when they did get bad ones, it was usually busy enough that the girls were needed for healing elsewhere, and couldn't be spared to train on the worst injuries. But recently, Saff had started to call Rachel over to watch and learn, to study the techniques of deeper healing.

As Rachel finished up on the man, a soldier entered the clinic, and Saff left with him. When Saff returned, she was practically beaming. She spoke to another mentor who had been working with them, and approached Rachel. "Find me outside when you're able to take a dinner break." She left the room again straight away.

Hope swelled in Rachel. It had to be word from Kaylah. Maybe they were being called to action? Though, it was odd they wouldn't have spoken to Rachel, too... What if she had to stay here, forced to work in the drudgery of it all, while Saff was put to work for Unitas? Rachel shook away her doubts. *Any* news that brought a smile to Saff's face was good news.

Finding a lull in healing work, Rachel quickly cleaned up her work area and stepped outside, searching around the wooden building for Saff. She spotted Saff's strawberry blond hair out in the garden. She was giving two girls a private lesson. Rachel hadn't seen these girls before, and something about Saff's instruction seemed ... off. She walked closer to observe. Saff was gesturing, teaching these girls things Rachel had learned from her brother, Jeff. Basics. Like, *really* basic.

✸

Having noticed her spectator, Saff perked up. "Alright, girls, drink lots of water, and you can go grab some dinner, if you're ready."

Rachel strolled up to her. "What's going on?"

"Kaylah." Saff smiled. "They're letting her do it."

"What do you mean? Give me all the details!"

They sat on the ground, watching the new girls from a distance as they collected food and water from a station at the clinic.

"Those girls are sisters from the neighboring village," Saff explained. "The one with long brown hair—she finished blooming just over a month ago. The one with shorter blond hair—they stopped using the jade four days ago."

"Four days!" Rachel blurted, clearly astounded. "So ... they have no training?"

"The one that bloomed earlier has some under her belt, but nowhere near enough to catch a breeze. They were guided home through an Ivy rift." Saff grinned from ear to ear. She was overwhelmed with excitement at seeing some good come from her tumultuous decision.

"Wow," Rachel whispered. "Then it's really happening? We're working with Kaylah?" She stared at the girls for a moment. "Any more information about how things are going? About how Kaylah's doing? When we'll be needed?"

Saff pulled a weed growing near her foot. "No, they only gave me the bare minimum, letting me know these girls would need training in the basics." She thought of Devin. Would he be allowed to train new girls like this with Saff? If he was, would he even accept the responsibility? He'd done a great job of speeding her through learning the basics when she was at that stage.

The girls returned to where Saff and Rachel were sitting, and Saff made the introductions.

✸

"Welcome!" Rachel said. She would have said 'welcome home,' but the Green Lands didn't always feel like home to newly returned girls; it hadn't for her, at least. "You girls are ... really brave to come here. You know everything that's going on?"

Brielle, the one with long hair, seemed jittery, poking at a hole in the knees of her human-world jeans. "They said I would be safe, that I wouldn't have to fight."

Rachel smiled reassuringly. These sisters had bloomed, but not rooted. Technically, either could still choose to go back to the human world and live the rest of their lives there if they wanted to forfeit their powers and home realm. "There's lots you can do within the safety of our borders. Like us—" She gestured to herself and Saff. "We know how to fight, but we help more with healing and training, and energy deposits at the temple wells. We really appreciate you being here."

The short-haired girl, Coral, finished chewing a mouthful of salad, her long dangly earrings swaying. "I hated high school. And that tiny town. This sounded a lot more fun."

Rachel smirked at such a casual description of a life-altering decision. "Adventure of a lifetime."

Saff got up and grabbed dinner for herself and Rachel before rejoining the conversation—the cooks had prepared a thick vegetable stew with rice and salad.

The new girls were itching to talk about their experiences, learning about their identities, and how they'd made their choices to come home. Rachel assumed they'd probably been told to keep quiet about Unitas, like she and Saff had been ordered to, but she couldn't help herself.

"What was it like? Coming through with Ivy help? Do you know the names of the people involved? How many were there?" She poked at a parsnip in her stew, trying to act casual, despite the far-from-casual string of questions she'd just rattled off.

Brielle seemed more nervous to talk about that part. Coral happily obliged.

"I don't know why they think it should be some great secret—there were tons of people there."

"Tons?" Saff raised her eyebrows.

"Well, I mean, you know." She flourished her hand in the air. "There were, I think, like five or six of us girls, so at least that many Ivies to take us through. And then lots of humans and our kind at the forest to make sure things were safe, and to say goodbye."

Saff and Rachel shared a heartfelt glance.

"It was freaky coming to this side. The energy's awesome, but there were like, a thousand guards to escort us through the walls."

"And you don't remember any names? Any of the Ivies or humans?" Rachel asked.

Both girls shook their heads. "No. Sorry," Coral said. "There was a lot going on."

Rachel's heart was light with relief—Kaylah was alive, and the Seeders had decided to work with her! And hopefully, Rachel would soon be requested to help in the Unitas cause.

Saff worked well past sundown training the new girls. She was beyond grateful to know things were progressing, that Kaylah was serving as a beacon of hope in the war.

She caught a breeze straight home, figuring Devin would already be in bed. To her surprise, a lightkeeper still lit up the cottage. She moseyed a bit on her approach to the front door, pondering their relationship. Worse than their fighting was the silence.

Had Devin overreacted? Probably. But as Saff's mate, her husband, her best friend—he knew her better than anyone else. He also had more invested in her than anyone else. Others might think that Saff's impromptu unsanctioned mission with Rachel had been more altruistically motivated than it really was. Devin could see right through that, even if he wasn't empathizing.

Stopping by the front door, Saff checked the pea planters to see if any pods were ready to pick.

Her actions might have brought about some good in the war, but her motivations for leaving in the first place had been primarily about avoiding grieving at Ben's funeral, and seeking revenge for his death.

Then there was the letter she'd left Devin when she snuck out in the middle of the night. Without imagining how hard it would be to stand alone at his best friend's funeral, Saff had scratched out the sorriest of apologies. It hadn't been much more eloquent than 'Sorry. Going to experiment with my life. Please forgive me. Love you.'

Had it been the other way around, she would have been just as devastated to face the funeral alone, having to inform both of their families of Devin's disappearance, defiance of council orders, and general recklessness, all the while worried for his safety, unable to protect him.

None of the pea pods in these planters were quite ready. She sniffed the blossoms, bolstering her courage to head inside. She should stop avoiding the subject, and try apologizing again.

A bundle of daisies greeted her from the kitchen table when she walked inside. Devin was cleaning dishes. He turned around and gave her a hesitant smile.

He glanced over at the kitchen table. "I, uh, I know it's more of a human thing, cutting flowers to bring them inside... I just wanted you to know I was thinking of you."

"Thanks. They're beautiful." She looked into his handsome brown eyes, appreciating the gesture, the shift in tension between them. When she had been sick in high school, going through her bloom before being given her charm, he had shown up with a vase full of daisies. That had been the day they'd first kissed.

"Why don't you sit down?" he said. "Let's talk."

Her chest tightened. "Why?" The flowers were proof she hadn't completely ruined things, right? It wasn't like he was going to move out, right? Seeder divorces were rare, given the strength of the mating bond, but they did happen.

Or maybe someone else close had died? Half of the time, she got bad news— news of the fallen, deaths like Ben's—from Devin.

He read her face. "Nothing's wrong, Saff. I just want to talk."

She swallowed and sat on the soft living room sofa, glancing at him over her shoulder.

"Are you hungry?" he asked. "I made some fruit salad."

"Sure." She pulled off her shoes, tucking them under their wicker coffee table.

He returned with a bowl of mixed fruit—cantaloupe, pomegranate, young coconut, and blueberries.

She smiled. "Thanks." She awkwardly dug in, unsure what was prompting his actions. His sweet treat hit the spot after an exhausting day. He'd always been the better cook between them—he even made a simple bowl of fruit taste amazing.

He sat next to her in silence for a minute. "It was a rough day. We're starting to see more of their soldiers in the woods again." He frowned.

She matched his frown.

"I just..." He rubbed his face with his hands. "I wanted to say I'm sorry for getting so mad at you. And I'm tired of living like this. You and me, just passing each other." He scratched at a spot of dirt on his pants. "Pretending like we're not both hurting. Missing Ben. Coming home drained every day."

She'd lived every day, for *weeks*, riddled with guilt, without her usual confidant to hold, to talk to. Saff grimaced as she fought tears. "I don't want your apology. I just want your forgiveness."

He twisted his wedding ring around his finger. "I don't know if I can say I completely forgive you, yet. I'm not sure if I know what that fully means." He looked up, reaching over to wipe away her tears. "But I know I will. I love you. It might just take more time."

"Okay," she whispered. "I love you too."

He paused, pensive. "I understand you were struggling. I do. And we both could have handled this better." They shared a look of shame. "I just wish you would have been here, that you would have given me the chance to come with you, to be there for you."

"I know."

"And you didn't even *try* talking to the council first, before you ran away like that." His voice was soft as he presented his argument this time.

She opened her mouth to protest. Rachel had never gotten anywhere with her appeals to the council.

He anticipated her response. "Yeah, the council didn't trust Rachel. I don't blame them, considering she's spent years under Ivy influence. But you, Saff—they trusted you to be her mentor. You didn't even *once* suggest this plan to them, or ask to go. They *might* have listened to you. You didn't even give them a chance. Or me."

She sniffled, nodding. Had she been thinking logically, that would have been the right approach. Even if the council had turned her down, like they had Rachel numerous times, Saff still could have absconded during the middle of the night and done as she pleased.

"Come here." He managed a small smile.

Saff put down her bowl and crawled into his arms. "I do love you." After a few minutes wrapped in his embrace, she decided it was her turn to talk about her day.

"I worked with some new girls today." She shifted in his arms to see his face. "They were brought home with Ivy help."

He squeezed her hand. "That's great, love. That's really great. I'm glad to hear things are working out."

"I thought about you. How you trained me in the basics of energy. I wondered if we could work together to train these girls. You were a great trainer for me." She searched his eyes.

Leaning closer, he gave her a kiss on the lips. Since her return, he'd kissed her on the forehead, or on the cheek, but not on the lips. She'd been longing for his touch; the sweet familiarity of it took her breath away.

"Just because I made a decent trainer for you, doesn't mean I'm the best for everyone," he said. "But ... we'll see. You never know."

Saff lightly poked him in the chest. "You're not decent."

He smirked. "I'd like to think I'm a decent person."

She chuckled. "You know what I mean."

He gave her the biggest smile she'd seen in a long time. "I do. Let's get some rest, okay?"

A week down the road, the Ivies made it clear they were taking the war seriously, flooding the Neutral Woods with troops. The Seeders were grateful for the lull they'd been given—time to repair their borders, allowing reinforcement of weak places in the thicket—but they had known it would only last so long.

Rachel was surprised when she and Saff were pulled from training and healing one day to meet with a local council member.

"You're both being asked to report for a special assignment, leaving tomorrow. Our ally has requested assistance in Siqendra."

Rachel was beyond ready to start a new adventure, to help in a different capacity. Siqendra was one of the oldest known Seeder villages, and also one of the more central ones.

"I won't be going." Saff twisted her lips. "I'm needed here."

Rachel furrowed her brow. "Really?"

"You were requested by name," the councilwoman said.

Technically, this was only a request, not an official order. Saff hesitantly answered the question in Rachel's eyes. "I need to be here. For my family. I'm sure someone else can help just as much as I can."

She'd given her word that she would help with Unitas, but she'd also given her word that she wouldn't leave Devin again. If she left her village, she'd be breaking one of those promises.

Rachel bit her lip and nodded slowly. "Don't say no without even asking him."

Saff turned to the councilwoman with a heavy sigh. "I'll discuss it with my family. Can I give you an answer in the morning?"

The woman said that she could. Saff mulled it over during the day and tried to head out from work early that night.

Making it home just before Devin, she paced around their cottage. The moment he came home, she ran up to greet him with a hug.

"Well, I'm happy to see you too!" He let out a soft moan. "Everything okay?"

"Yeah, of course. I just couldn't wait to see you." She smiled. They'd grown closer in the last week, but still had some work to do in their marriage.

He leaned in and placed a lingering kiss on her lips. "I missed you too. I wish we could go back to our old jobs, teaching at the school together."

She searched his eyes; her smile faded as her breathing picked up. If she reported to her assignment, they wouldn't just be a quick flight or a couple of hours of walking apart; they would be several days' walk apart.

"What's wrong?" he asked.

She grabbed his hand and led him to the couch. "I've said no. But ... they wanted me to double-check. I made you a promise."

He cocked his head in confusion.

"The council wants me to go to Siqendra. Kaylah requested help on something. I'd be leaving with Rachel in the morning." She frowned. "I told you I wouldn't leave you." She reached for his other hand. "And I meant that."

He freed his hands and rubbed the back of his neck. "Siqendra? Staying inside the walls? No human-world trips?"

"They didn't give me a lot of details."

He scrunched his face. "You're not sure how long?"

She shook her head.

He nodded. "You should go."

"But ... we've been doing so good. And I need you to know I care about you, that I'm not being impulsive, not ignoring you. Kaylah can find someone else. I don't even know what she wants me for."

He held her hands again. "If the council wants it, it's safe to say you have my blessing. It's not my place to disregard their orders."

She felt a pinch of guilt at that. Though, he'd said it in a kind way, not as though he were rubbing it in that she had done that exact thing—defied council orders while deserting him to meet with the princess.

"Love, it's pretty clear there's something different about you. Your extra energy and second trip make that apparent. And we both know I was first attracted to you because you were the smartest Seeder girl in that stupid human-world trigonometry class of ours."

"None of our siblings were in that class." Saff grinned. "I think it's safe to say I was the *only* Seeder girl in that math class."

He winked. "Either way, you're smart, and you're powerful. And I would never want to stop you from fulfilling your potential, especially when you're capable of doing some amazing things."

Her heart melted at his sweet words.

He smirked. "We've already seen some good things come out of your ... *passionate* ... decision-making, haven't we?"

He was always a giving person, down to calling her defiance 'passionate' instead of 'impulsive.' She couldn't resist smiling.

"You're sure? I mean it—I'll stay. I don't want to ever jeopardize our relationship again."

He looked her straight in the eyes. "I forgive you, Saff. Right now, asking you to stay would only show *my* selfishness." He frowned. "Go. But be safe. Send word when you can?"

"Thank you. You know I will. And I won't be gone a second longer than I need to be." She launched herself onto his lap, giving him a huge hug. "I love you. You're more than I deserve. And definitely more than just a decent man."

He chuckled. "What if I don't want to be decent right now?"

She leaned back, eyebrows raised quizzically.

His handsome dimples made an appearance as he thumbed the collar of his shirt. "We're both pretty decent right now. You're not leaving until the morning?"

Her heart rate doubled as she blushed. "That's right. And I'm not leaving this house a second earlier than I need to tomorrow."

Rachel arrived at their designated meetup point fifteen minutes early, pacing around and imagining what they would be asked to do. The councilwoman greeted her on the hour, and they stood, waiting for Saff.

"She would come to let us know if she turned down the position, right?" the woman asked.

"I'm sure she would. She'll be here." Her words were more confident than she was. As excited as she was to see Kaylah, she didn't want to go it alone. Saff had hesitated to accept the assignment, and her ties to her home were stronger, and touchier still.

Ten minutes later, Saff ran up, a light bag thrown over her shoulder. They couldn't carry things with them when they caught a breeze through rifts, but if experienced, they could carry a bit when flying within the Green Lands. And flying would take days off of their journey.

Rachel was all smiles, taking the bag as a good sign.

"I am *so* sorry!" Saff apologized. "Had to pack everything and talk to my family this morning."

Saff and Rachel didn't talk about such things, but Rachel spotted good news and hid a grin. She scratched at a spot on her lower neck, flashing her eyes neon green at Saff.

Saff slapped her hand to her own neck, blushing and healing a hickey. "So ... what now?"

They were given instructions, and then with a good running leap, took off— soaring to meet Kaylah. Catching a breeze required considerable focus, and it could be hard to hear, so Seeders rarely chatted while traveling. But Saff guided Rachel, letting her know the names of the villages she recognized as they passed. She and Devin had toured a lot of Seeder territory together before their wedding.

After a long day of exhausting travel, they touched down, Rachel still significantly wobblier due to her lack of proper training.

They drank water and caught their breath. "Thanks, Saff. For coming." Rachel smiled. "And I'm glad things are good back home."

Saff blushed again. "Yeah. I got a good one. But that's enough of that for now. Let's get to work."

They'd been instructed on where to meet in the old village, knocking on a door as it got dark. They were greeted by a stranger, a kind elderly gentleman, who showed them to their accommodations.

"Is the princess not here?" Saff asked.

"She'll be here first thing in the morning," the man replied.

Saff and Rachel settled in for the night. Rachel struggled to sleep, wondering what the next day would bring, somewhat comforted by the tossing and turning in Saff's bed as well—at least she wasn't the only one with racing thoughts.

Chapter 4

Kaylah emerged from the rift, straight away sensing the dimmed energy of the human world. She was almost immediately greeted with a warm smile and a strong hug from Nathan, one of her Ivy deployment guardians.

"It's so good to see you," he whispered in her ear.

"You too."

"We all set here?" a voice asked.

Kaylah pulled back from the hug and paid more attention to the large group surrounding her. Nearly a dozen Seeders, Ivies, and humans had gathered for this exchange. At least that was what it felt like—a highly inconvenient prisoner exchange rather than a dignitary on a visit.

"We've got it covered," another answered.

An older Seeder male gave a single nod, then turned and stalked deeper into the woods. He had to be the one assigned to catch a breeze back to the Green Lands to inform their council that she'd arrived at the correct location, that she hadn't deserted them and gone on the run.

Kaylah fought the building bitterness. As if she would have done that. She'd walked willingly into their territory, offering to help. And they were holding her deployment 'mom,' Ginger, hostage, unable to do any work while Kaylah was afforded the rare privilege of visiting the human world. Kaylah wasn't going to just skip out on them all. She'd worked too hard for this.

"Then are we ready to go?" another Seeder asked, all business, no compassion. This time, the question had been aimed at Kaylah.

"Am I allowed *two seconds* to talk to Nathan?" She barely even attempted to hide her frustration.

The Seeder raised her hands. "It's your time. Be our guest."

Kaylah turned her focus back to Nathan, keeping her voice low, keenly aware of all the eyes still on them. "They're treating you okay?"

Nathan wore a soft smile. "I'm perfectly fine. And they've let me chat with Eric a few times."

That gave her at least a little relief. "I'm sorry you haven't been able to see Ginger." She looked down.

"How is she?"

"She's good. Real good."

"I'll be alright, Your Majesty..."

She shook her head. "Don't call me that. No coronation: no title."

He held her hand, squeezing it reassuringly. "By all rights, it should be your title. Formalities or not, you're already our queen."

That only made her feel worse, the weight of her failed strategy digging deeper. "Yeah, well... Maybe if I can manage to turn things around..."

"How are you holding up?"

She forced a half-smile. "Things really are looking up."

Sparing a glance at the group still watching on, Nathan squeezed her hand again. "Well, I know you're not here to visit me, but I'm glad I'm stationed here to see you. And..." He cleared his throat. "Well, I'm sure Ginger's sentiments are the same... Not that we'd presume to fill their places, and now that the undercover gig is up... Just ... if you still ever want to call us 'Mom' and 'Dad,' we'd be more than happy to hear it."

She lunged forward, throwing her arms around him for another hug. "Thanks, Dad." Her words caught in her throat. "I..." She whispered in his ear. "I'm so sorry I told them about you."

He released her, holding her at arm's length. "You did what you had to. If sharing my secret saves lives, especially yours, then don't you dare hold any regrets, okay?"

"Yeah. Okay. Love you."

She pulled out a letter from Ginger and handed it to him. She'd see him the next day and would get another short chance to chat. After a quick goodbye, she was escorted from the woods to a car.

Kaylah sat quietly in the car. Her jaw hurt from clenching it as she mulled over her conversation with Nathan. She shouldn't have needed to share so much with the Seeders, but Soren had disrupted the power dynamics of the entire realm. She'd been at the Seeders' mercy, forced to give more intel than she would have liked. She'd sworn to keep Nathan's secret gift just that—a secret. Now the Seeder council held that information, and his skills, over their heads.

Cracking her neck and sitting up straighter with a sense of satisfaction and a hint of defiance, Kaylah allowed herself to calm. She hadn't given away *all* of her knowledge, her secrets. Some things, she kept only between herself and her closest Unitas followers. Others were only known by herself and Eric.

And some secrets were hers alone.

With each speed bump and pothole on the way to their destination, Kaylah's anger subsided, her anticipation grew. She glanced down at the burner phone in her hands and smiled. She read the message again. He'd given the right code word to assure her things were safe, but her favorite part was the 'XO' he'd included at the end, just like in the good old days.

"You said we're leaving at two tomorrow afternoon?" she asked the pair of Seeder guards in the front seat. With the time zone change and extra transit time, they expected to leave the human world, travel through the Neutral Woods, and make it to Siqendra early the following morning.

"Yes, ma'am."

"No chance that could be pushed back?"

"Not likely," the male drawled.

"Okay." She forced a smile, not quite thrilled with the idea of having less than twenty-four hours with Eric on this visit. But after weeks of proving herself, having not seen him since Rachel and Saff had come to meet at this safe house, she was just grateful to have this much.

Her heart nearly beat out of her chest as they turned down his street, but she waited as patiently as she could while they made a first pass, then came around again to the simple house with the nicely manicured lawn.

The garage door opened on their approach, and the white SUV pulled in. Kaylah followed orders, waiting with one of the guards as the other went in to inspect. She sighed. Seeders were so paranoid. She'd earned their trust, but she was pretty sure their dictionary defined that word differently.

Finally, the all clear was given, and she made every effort to walk into the house calmly, like the dignified almost-queen she was, and not like the giddy teenager that she also was.

Spotting each other, she and Eric instantly beamed, but she kept herself back.

"Thank you for getting her here safely," Eric said.

"Yes," the female Seeder said. "Where will we be staying?"

"Let me show you to your rooms. Have you eaten dinner?"

"We're fine, thanks."

"Okay, great. The fridge is stocked, if you change your mind. Follow me."

Eric led them down the hall to the guest bedrooms. Kaylah's smile grew after the doors clicked and he turned back to her. In no time flat, he was in front of her, pulling her into the tightest possible hug.

"You came back," he breathed.

She squeezed a little more. "I'll always come back."

He was the first to pull away, before quickly leaning in for a kiss. "How are you doing?"

She reached up, feeling his freshly shaven face and the strong jawline she'd missed so much. "A thousand times better now that I'm with you."

His eyes twinkled. "Are you hungry?"

Kaylah bit her lip. "Mmm, maybe later." She took his hand and led him down the hallway, quietly opening his bedroom door and leading him inside.

Once the door closed, she stood tall and held him closer, laying a kiss on him she'd been counting down the days for. She reached for his belt and undid it.

He broke from their kiss. "Alright, you. That can wait two seconds. I want you to see what I did for you."

She glanced around the room.

"Flowers for my favorite girl, and all her favorite snacks."

Kaylah smiled wide. "*You're* my favorite snack." She reached for the top button of his shirt. "Too many of these." She undid the top two.

"Come on, babe. Look, I got a love seat too. Over in the corner."

"Mmm." She undid another button. "I prefer the bed." She kissed him again.

He held her by the arms, frowning. "Kaylah, why don't we talk first? There's plenty of time for that later."

"That also means there's plenty of time for talking later, too."

He raised an eyebrow, giving a disapproving glance.

She knew what he was uptight about, but she didn't want to think about it. She didn't want to think about *anything*, other than him, and her, and them. "Seriously?" She nuzzled his neck. "You don't see me for weeks, and you want to *talk*?" She cocked her head to the side. "I must be wearing too much clothing." She pulled her shirt over her head and dropped it on the ground.

Eric didn't budge. "How are you doing?"

She slid another button out of place, then kissed his exposed chest. "I told you, I'm great."

"Kaylah ... we should get caught up."

"That's what I'm trying to do." She reached for another button, and he grabbed her hand.

"No. Not like this."

She frowned, meeting his gaze. "I told you—I'm fine. I just want to be here with you. Happy."

He read her face. "Don't do this. Don't shut me out."

She swallowed hard, looking down. "The Seeders haven't hurt me. I'm really fine."

"You know that's not what I'm talking about. Sweetheart ... your brother killed your parents."

She met his gaze again. "I don't want to talk about that right now."

"But maybe you should," he said softly. "Come on." He took her hands and led her to the love seat, pulling her onto his lap.

She leaned against him with a sigh. "What do you want me to say, Eric? We knew they probably had to die." No matter how much she knew it, how much she'd repeated the facts to herself—it hadn't actually made it any easier.

"I know. And your relationship was complicated. But you can't pretend you don't feel anything."

"Maybe I don't even *know* how I feel about it," she whispered, staring at his hand on her knee.

"Have you cried?"

Kaylah shook her head. Silence hung in the air.

"It's not like you *have* to cry. Everyone handles things differently. And they didn't exactly win any awards as parents or leaders. But ... how do you feel about Soren being the one to do it?"

She shrugged weakly. "I should thank him. This way I didn't have to do it myself."

"I don't believe that."

She wilted. "Like I said, I don't know. I just wish it meant things were over. But now ... I don't know. It just makes things that much more complicated."

A hesitant smile crept onto his face. "Okay. But you have a solid plan. And you got the Seeders working with you. And a human or two." He poked her knee. "One, I might add, that is madly, hopelessly in love with you."

A genuine smile grew on her face. "Yeah?"

He nodded. "And he worries about you—every day."

"You don't need to worry about me. Now that my entire kingdom is aware of my absence, I get guards wherever I go. I'm safe."

He wrapped his arms around her. "Your physical safety is not all I worry about."

She drew a deep breath. "I know."

"Give me an update. They haven't told me much."

Kaylah reluctantly recounted what she'd had to do to earn Seeder trust. She'd endured endless days introducing her most loyal and available Unitas followers, discussing plans and proposals, divulging information. She had hesitated to share information about Nathan's special gift, even with Eric. It wasn't that particularly helpful or harmful to the human part of the equation, or even the Seeder part of it all. She'd only told the Seeders because they knew how to drive a hard bargain. And her life and hopes to rule her own kingdom had been the trump card she couldn't beat.

She'd originally hoped they could make some headway negotiating with her parents. But then Soren had murdered them and pinned it on the Seeders. And lied about her being kidnapped, so she could no longer meet with her own spies in her own lands, or claim the throne that should be hers. She'd had to pivot. Her knowledge and research were no longer tools to negotiate with; now she had to dig deep and actually use it all to prove herself for this alliance, and to get her throne and end the war.

"It might be slower than you want, but it's going in the right direction," Eric said. "You haven't said anything about Rachel. How's she doing?"

Kaylah pouted. "They haven't allowed me to see her, or really know anything." A faint smile formed. "But that's what I'm excited about for tomorrow. She'll be joining me. And Saff, that other one."

Eric's eyes widened. "Saff? She was a bit of a spitfire. How's that going to work out?"

Kaylah shifted off of his lap, sitting next to him on the love seat. "You know? She really came through at the last moment. I think we'll be okay."

"Good." He rubbed her leg. "What else is bugging you?"

"Why would you think something else is bugging me?" She put on a brave face.

"Because I know you."

She blew out a long breath. "It's up to seven." Her comment required no extra explanation—Eric knew exactly what that meant. That meant her personal body count. Her uncle had been the fifth. The soldier she'd killed in front of Rachel had added to the tally, making it seven.

"I see," he said. "Why did you do it?"

"He... I don't know." She shrugged. "I was mad. And ... he probably would have slowed us down too much. And he refused to join, even though he *knew* my mother was dead."

Eric squeezed her hand. "What did you feel, right before and after?"

They'd done this exercise before. It helped sometimes. Not always. "I don't know. Like I said—mad."

"That doesn't sound like you, just killing someone out of anger. What was happening?"

Her heart beat faster, just like it had that day. "We were close to the border, about to be surrounded by fighting troops. I..." She swallowed hard, her ears pounding with the echo of soldiers closing in on them. "You should have seen Rachel's face."

"So, there was you, and Rachel, and Ginger, and Saff. Imminent danger. One of your own?"

She nodded. "It was frantic. I was panicking. I..."

"Did what you needed to do. And not out of anger. That number could be a thousand and it wouldn't be wrong, if you're doing it for the right reasons."

"I didn't even bother to learn his name." She picked at her fingernails. "What does that say about me?"

"It means you're strong. And having to make decisions no one else in the world is making. And shouldn't judge yourself that way."

She finally found her tears. "I feel like I'm losing myself, Eric. I just... I feel like it's getting easier. And it shouldn't be that way. And I'm just a damned transport half the time, bringing back these Seeder girls instead of helping my people from the palace I have a birthright to be in charge of right now. I'm useless, and I'm sinking, and... I don't know."

"I'm sorry." He pulled her in for another embrace, and she silently shed more tears in his arms.

After several minutes, he sweetly rubbed her back. "It's not possible to lose yourself. Not completely."

She sniffled, sitting back and wiping at her cheeks. "How do you figure that?"

"Well..." He smiled. "You told me a part of your heart was always here with me. And I'm keeping that part safe. So, if you get a little fuzzy on the rest of it, I'm always happy to give you a refresher."

She matched his smile.

"Plus, I think we're each a new version of ourselves, each and every day."

Kaylah took a cleansing breath. "I love you."

He raised her hand, kissing it. "Ditto."

Her stomach growled loud enough for them to both hear.

He chuckled. "Does that mean I should figure out dinner?"

"Nah. Not yet." She stood, taking a peek at the goodies he'd bought for her. A few chocolate bars, jerky, breakfast bars, and her favorite cheese crackers covered the top of the dresser. Opening the box of crackers, she leaned in, sniffing the perfume of the dozen red roses he'd bought for her. He'd been a gentleman from day one.

She took the box back to the love seat, sitting on his lap and crunching into a couple of crackers. "So, all this talk about me. What about you? What have I missed in the last thousand days?"

Eric grabbed a handful of crackers from the box. "Thousand days? I feel like that count might be off."

"*Feels* like a thousand."

He grinned. "Well, I'll have you know it's been as wild and crazy for me as it has been for you."

She arched an eyebrow in disbelief.

"I mean ... if you consider online Economics 101 exams to be as stressful as open war and revolution in a realm of supernatural beings."

Kaylah laughed. "It's probably about the same."

"But, in all seriousness ... mostly quiet here. Nothing big. I keep thinking about enrolling in more classes, but then I get nervous that Unitas will pick up. So..." He shrugged.

She winced. "Sorry."

"We've talked about this. This is my choice. No apologies." He cleared his throat. "And ... I'm a little insulted you didn't notice while you were trying to strip me down—but I've been using my free time to work out more."

Smirking, she set the box of crackers on the floor and dusted her fingers off. "You don't say." She placed a hand on his exposed chest, and he flexed. "Oooh, nice." She threw a glance at the bed. "What do you say we pick up with my original idea and get a little workout together?"

"I might be okay with that." His face softened with hesitance. "Sure there's nothing else you want to talk about first?"

She paused. "I'll be okay. Thank you for making me talk. I needed that." She pressed her lips together. "You know, there *is* one more thing I'd like to get off my chest."

"What's that?"

She couldn't keep a straight face. "This bra. Think you could help with that?"

Looking relieved, he slid his hands to her mostly exposed back. "I think I could manage."

⁕

An hour and a half later, Kaylah sat on Eric's bed in a pair of his boxers and an oversized t-shirt, drinking a tall glass of water. Eric reentered in similar attire, holding a large box of pizza.

"Oooh, I am *starving*." She got up, setting down her glass and approaching him.

Eric held the box high above his head.

Kaylah placed her hands on her hips. "Excuse me? You know I could take that from you with my vines in two seconds flat, right?"

"You wouldn't dare! I'm the one that ordered this. If you want me to share, it's going to come at a cost."

She narrowed her eyes. "Fine. How much per slice?"

"Two kisses."

Her jaw dropped. "That's highway robbery. That's price gouging, and I won't stand for it. One kiss."

He stood firm, shaking his head. "You don't know what kind of pizza this is. It's worth every pucker."

She struggled once again to keep her face straight. "You drive a hard bargain. I will acquiesce this once." Standing on her tiptoes, she gave him two pecks. "We'll start with one slice." She grinned. "Now gimme!"

Eric didn't budge. "Do you want dipping sauce? That'll cost you extra."

She wrinkled her nose. "Now you're just getting greedy."

He chuckled, lowering the box.

Her eyes widened as she read the logo on the top of the box before he opened it.(jj) "Davino's?" She grabbed a slice of meat-lover's pizza and sat on the love seat, tucking her legs under her. "How the heck did you get Davino's all the way out here?!" She bit into it—the cheese pull was nothing short of a masterpiece, and the symphony of sauce and toppings was akin to poetry. She moaned, splaying a hand over her heart as she chewed. "My people don't know what they're missing."

Eric laughed, joining her with a slice of his own. "Careful now, I might get jealous of that pizza if you keep moaning that way."

She finished her bite, giving him a toothy grin. "If you had told me it was Davino's, I would have paid *three* kisses per slice. Lucky for you, the night is young and I am a *very* generous tipper."

He wiggled his eyebrows, taking another bite. "They opened a new branch nearby, and they deliver pretty late."

She peeled open a garlic butter sauce packet, dipping her crust into it. "That's it, I'm petitioning to visit *every* weekend now."

"So, you want me for my body *and* my pizza?"

Kaylah giggled, covering her crust-filled mouth. She finished her slice, grabbing a second. "Add this to my tab."

He winked.

She looked over at the flowers and then back at him. "Thanks for everything, babe. This is perfect. I really do wish it could be every weekend. Every day ... really."

He gave her a half-smile.

"I haven't ... found anything yet. You know..." She hadn't found a way to get a human into the Green Lands. And she didn't know that she ever would. That was the hardest part of being with him. She wanted to be a queen, to be there for her people. But she also wanted to be with Eric.

He picked up a second slice of pizza, meeting her gaze in understanding. "I'm here for the long haul—you know that."

She nodded. "And frankly, I'm too selfish to tell you how foolish it is for you to go along with all of this."

Eric pointed at her with his slice of pizza. "Say what you want. I know I'm the lucky one."

She rolled her eyes, taking another huge bite. "Did you ever suspect Rach was anything other than human?"

He looked taken aback. "What? No... I had no idea she wasn't human until you told me. But I might just be dense. Then again, I didn't know back then that green folk even existed..."

Kaylah bent forward, grabbing a napkin from a little side table. "Yeah, I guess. Just thinking about work stuff, now that they're finally letting me have more say."

She pondered the past, and the hopeful future. "Last time I saw her, I told her she'd see Guillen soon."

"Yeah? How's your cousin doing?"

She smiled, picking up her glass of water. "He's good." She mused on the pair. "I think they'd be good for each other."

"Really? Is she over David, er, Soren?"

Kaylah eyed Eric with adoration. "Sometimes, you just know."

He swooped in and stole a kiss.

She ran her thumb over the bumps in the water glass design. "Plus, they both like each other."

"Good for them. I hope it works out. He sounds like a great guy."

She wore a sad smile. "He really is. You'd like him. I wish you two could meet." Eric couldn't enter the Green Lands realm. Guillen couldn't leave it. "Maybe someday, if I can..."

Eric gently squeezed her knee. "I think we need to talk in terms of 'when' and not 'if.'" He searched her face. "Please."

She swallowed, nodding. "There's no 'if' in how I feel about you."

"Same."

Chapter 5

The housing was comfortable enough, and Rachel slept solidly after finally drifting off. A loud knock on the door woke the two of them in the morning.

Rachel stumbled out of bed and answered it with one eye open. She was practically knocked off her feet as Kaylah lunged forward and hugged her.

"Finally!" Kaylah squealed. "I am so excited for this phase! And that you both came!"

Rachel blinked a few times, still groggy, then returned to her bed and sat down.

Saff pulled herself up in bed. "Hi, Kaylah. How's it going? Why didn't we see you last night?"

"Good. Slow, but good. Last night... I brought another Seeder home this morning. I figured you guys could use a rest after traveling yesterday, so I held off until now."

Unexpected jealousy flared up in Rachel. Had Kaylah put off her departure to spend more time with Eric, back in his safe house in the human world? All of this love around her, and Rachel had no one. A tiny infatuation, perhaps, with a guy she hadn't seen in a while, who she probably meant nothing to, who she was trying to put out of her mind.

"So, what's the plan?" Saff asked.

"We can spare a few minutes to get caught up!" Kaylah insisted. "How are things back in your village?"

Rachel smirked. "Do you remember Jeff, my brother?"

Kaylah nodded.

"He's dating someone."

Kaylah busted out laughing. "Is she as awkward as he is?"

Rachel made a funny face. "Yep. That one's ... unique." She felt kind of bad, but none of them had really taken to Jeff that much in the human world. He was painfully socially awkward, especially around humans. Rachel sometimes wondered if her Seeder parents had been scraping the bottom of the barrel by sending him, out of all of her brothers, to train and protect her. Seeder brothers sent to the human world were *supposed* to blend in seamlessly. But he was a nice guy, and it was wartime ... so...

"How's everyone else?" Rachel asked.

"Good. Jon and Guillen are recruiting. Ginger is helping with bloomed Seeder girl runs. Nathan is helping Unitas in the human world right now."

Rachel smiled at hearing that Ginger and Nathan, Kaylah's Ivy deployment parents, were safe. And that Jon was helping. And at hearing Guillen's name at all.

"And Eric?" Rachel arched an eyebrow.

Kaylah grinned. "Safe, and handsome as ever."

Rachel tried to hide her envy. "When did you get to see him last?"

Kaylah bit her lip. "I had a few hours with him in the human world." She reached into a pack she'd carried in with her. "I haven't seen your mom since we all left together, but Eric gave me these." She handed Rachel a few folded papers.

Guilt for judging Kaylah mingled with pure gratitude for word from her mom in the human world. "Thanks!" She unfolded the pages.

"No prob. Eric helped set up a secure messaging system and wanted to make sure we could keep you two in touch when possible." She sat down next to Rachel on the bed, shoulder to shoulder with her.

✸

As usual, the chitchat was mostly Rachel and Kaylah getting caught up. Saff waited for a good moment to bring them back on task.

"I was happy to start training a couple new girls your people brought back. Thank you."

Kaylah pointed at Saff. "And you doubted me."

"So, what's the plan?" Saff asked again with raised eyebrows.

"Alright," Kaylah drawled. "Getting to business, as usual. Hopefully it won't take us too long before we can move to the next steps of my strategy, but for this part in particular, I wanted *your* help, Saff."

"Okay?"

"A little bird told me you were a good student in high school. I need help with research. And with that research, we're going to change the game. No more needing an Ivy for each Seeder girl we bring home. No more pain in the process. We need to make better use of our resources."

Saff scrunched her face skeptically. "I feel like my high school report cards are *not* that significant here."

Kaylah adjusted her messy bun. "You didn't let me finish." Her tone was friendly. "They granted me access to your archives. And I was able to confirm something. Something that makes you different than other Seeders. And helpful to me."

Saff narrowed her eyes. "Okay. I'm curious."

"Everyone says you're really powerful compared to others your age." She crossed her arms. "You never told me your visit to meet me was a second visit in one year—something that shouldn't have been possible."

Saff grinned. "You'll have to forgive me for not divulging something so sensitive to the enemy princess."

Kaylah smiled in return. "I asked about your story. You didn't go through your whole bloom with the charm on, right?"

"No." Saff rolled her eyes. "I screwed that up and almost got myself and my family killed in the process."

"But ... that's what makes you so powerful."

Saff furrowed her brow. "What? Our theory was that I was born immune to Ivy poison..."

Kaylah chuckled. "I've never heard that one." She extended a short vine tendril from one wrist. "Want to test out that theory?"

Saff eyed the tendril. She definitely wanted to know, but wasn't eager to be stabbed and poisoned. "I'm good. Tell me more about your theory."

Kaylah crossed her legs, sitting further back on Rachel's bed. "Your people use the jade charms to suppress the change so it's hidden and manageable. But it dulls your ultimate potential. Back in the day, before the poisoned lands forced your women into the human world, blooming happened here without them, and you were all stronger."

"Yeah. It was the first generation after the poisoning that showed diminished energy. We assumed it was a lingering effect passed on to the next generations."

Kaylah shook her head. "No. I can understand why you'd draw that conclusion. But if you look *really* hard, and find the exact right scroll, paired with some of the books from my uncle's private collection—it paints a pretty clear picture."

Saff sat speechless. No one had ever been able to explain to her why she was different. She and Devin had just guessed at the poison immunity theory. But this made sense. "But ... Devin told me if we don't wear the charm, the change can be so bad we slip into a coma. What I went through was a nightmare—I wouldn't wish it on anyone."

Kaylah held up a pointer finger with knowing emphasis. "That's because it was done in the *human* world. Once we can heal the land and figure out how to get the unbloomed back, they can change *here,* and it's not like that at all. The saturation of energy here makes it practically seamless, from what the books imply."

"Really?" Saff was still confused. "I can't be the only one that slipped long enough without their charm."

Kaylah shrugged. "I'm sure you're not. Your change must have happened over there at just the right time. They said you were about three-fourths of the way through your change?"

Saff nodded.

"I don't know. Maybe that's far enough along to not fall into the coma that usually lasts until you root, but not so far along that this benefit is lost. There must be a narrow sweet spot. I doubt you're the only one like this, but we don't exactly have social media, and your people kinda keep to themselves."

Saff blinked a few times. 'Sweet spot' didn't feel like an accurate description; nothing about her botched bloom had been sweet. It had been over four years ago, and she could still vividly remember the agony of that day. This, however, was a refreshing discovery. "That's awesome. But ... that's also a ways away, right? Blooming here so they have their full powers? Have you been able to heal the land? Find a way to bring an unbloomed girl through a rift?"

Kaylah frowned. "No, not yet. One thing at a time. Speaking of ... Rachel."

❁

Rachel gave Kaylah her full attention, setting down the letters from her mom that she'd been scanning while listening. She was glad to finally be acknowledged in the plan.

"You researched your village's name and history?"

"Yes! Those symbols you drew back at Eric's, like the ones in the cave near your palace—they were in a book about our history." She pulled out a piece of paper from her pack sitting against the bed. "Here."

"This is brilliant." Kaylah beamed. "We've got homework to do."

❁

The Seeder girls dressed and followed Kaylah out the door. She was still accompanied at all times by at least two Seeder guards. Kaylah led them to the nearest temple and into the old library.

Saff sat down to a pile of books. "I still don't understand why this is a priority when the fighting is picking up, and we still have girls being tortured in your palace, every single day."

"I think about them too," Kaylah said, her voice soft and regretful. "And we'll get them out as soon as we can. But we really need to crack this. We're wasting too much time, with the limited people I have, to keep going back and forth to bring your girls home. Once we can solve this, we can bring back girls faster, easier. *Your* travel time will be significantly faster, too, between realms. And my people can focus on other things—learning to heal the land, protection, finding more to join our cause. Your dads and brothers can help here, too."

"Alright. Then explain what it is we're looking for."

Kaylah rubbed her forehead. "How do you know where to fly, back in your village, to go through a rift? Is it always in the same place?"

Saff searched her memories. "I don't really have to think about it. I mean, I was directed to the general area the first couple times, but I just know when it's time to open it."

"And when you're leaving the human world, is it the same?"

"Yeah..."

"It's intuitive. You feel the pull; there are set locations there for you Seeders, up there, in the sky. I think my people hone in on how it works more naturally, and that's why we can travel so quickly, through a wider variety of rifts."

Rachel looked as lost as Saff was.

Kaylah sighed. "I don't know what to call it. I hesitate to call it magic, or a spell, or anything like that. But the names of your villages—their names match these old symbols, and by knowing the words, you know where the rift is. It's like coordinates. When you know the coordinates and how it works, then you can create more possibilities."

Saff opened one of the books they'd pulled to study. "So, you mean to say, that if I knew a word that connects with my GPS location, I could step outside of this building and form a rift in the sky above, coming out wherever I wanted to on the other side?"

Kaylah rocked her head side to side. "Not that simple ... but along those lines. Your temples and border walls make it so you can't just rift right here, and *we've* never been able to rift into your lands. But further out, we've scouted locations." A giant smile spread across her face. "We're going to open a cave."

"A cave?" Saff and Rachel asked in unison.

"Yeah." Kaylah shifted some papers, revealing a map. She pointed to a location near the mountains in the far north, technically in neutral territory. "It'll be a permanent location. It can be guarded, and a way for Ivy and Seeder alike to travel to that area of the Green Lands. If they know the word, if they know how to do it right."

Rachel cocked her head. "It's been done before. Like the cave by the palace?"

"Yeah," Kaylah said. "I hadn't been able to sort that out. But I'm sure that's what it used to be used for."

The girls pored over old books for hours, jotting down helpful tidbits. The guards had changed shifts once, and a home-cooked meal of lettuce wraps and coconut-carrot juice had been brought to the girls in the temple.

"Alright, I think we have what we need." Kaylah rolled up one last scroll, replacing it on a shelf. "But we can only do so much here. Once we find the right cave, I hope I'll be able to pinpoint the location. And we can make history." She smiled triumphantly. "I know you girls could fly so much faster, but since I'm not able to do that … let's get on the road and start making our way to our next destination."

"What do you mean, next destination?" Saff asked hesitantly. Her excitement over the research had caused her to gloss over the mention of moving their operation to the far north.

"Like I said, we need to be away from the border walls to open a rift like this. We're going to Arcadia, the village where your people without powers live. We've found a prime area over there."

❈

Rachel perked up. She'd been waiting for this. This was where her interests really lay.

"But I…" Saff tucked her hands into her pockets. "I thought we'd be inside the borders. That's what I told Devin."

"Why don't you go check in?" Rachel suggested. "You can take a day to head back, then rest up for a day or two, turn around and join us? By the time you do the back-and-forth, we'll have been able to walk there."

Saff gnawed on her lip. "How many girls have you brought back so far, with Ivy assistance?"

Kaylah shouldered her pack. "A drop in the bucket considering the entire Seeder nation, but I figure forty-seven isn't horrible."

Saff's eyes grew large. "That's a lot of extra womanpower!"

"It's just the beginning." Kaylah's calm and confident voice matched her expression.

"Alright. I'll meet you both there."

Chapter 6

Walking through the vast stretch of Seeder lands was as much a tour for Rachel as it was for Kaylah. Seeders had only one steam engine that crossed their territory, for the purposes of carrying heavier materials and goods across the nation. Its path was less direct than just walking the route to where Rachel and Kaylah were heading, and the train stopped so often for loading and unloading that catching a ride would have been a waste of time.

Instead, they enjoyed rekindling their friendship and discussing the differences between Ivy and Seeder lands. Seeder territory was much greener; homes and property were shared in the communities, usually built out of wood, whereas the Ivy Kingdom mostly built with stone.

Their conversations were perhaps a little surface level, but Rachel wasn't ready to talk about how much she hated it back in South Fortinda, how much she still struggled with her mental health. She was just happy to see her friend and explore along the way.

Each of the girls carried their personal necessities in a pack, weighed down more now with an extra book or two. Rachel glanced at the soldiers walking with them. Each of them had huge backpacks, carrying even more books and scrolls.

"Why aren't there horses in the Green Lands?" Rachel asked. "That would certainly be helpful."(kk)

Kaylah picked up a fresh green pine cone in her path. "Wish I had all the answers. Why don't we have electricity the same way humans do?"

As Rachel pondered that, an echo of pain surged in her body. "When I was held captive at your palace, the nurses ... they would..." Her breathing intensified as she remembered their heartless actions.

Kaylah frowned. "Olivia told me about having to tase you, to keep her cover."

Rachel's eyes moistened as she nodded.

"That's not really electricity, at least not in the way you grew up with. Deep in the mountains by the palace, there are some plants, kinda like cacti. We call them static nettles.(II) Their needles have a bit of a staticky spark, when you get enough of them together. Our scientists have been working with them for decades to see how to propagate them better, how to maybe harness their charge. But the plants are tricky to deal with, and we've never made much progress." She hurled the pine cone into the trunk of a nearby banana tree. "I was *so proud* that they'd decided to put them to use *that* way, out of anything." Kaylah frowned again. "I'm sorry they did that to you."

"You don't have to keep apologizing. I forgave you."

Kaylah linked arms with her. "Doesn't mean I'm not still sorry."

With their soldier escort and no significant hang-ups, Rachel and Kaylah reached the far end of the map. Rachel was apprehensive about stepping outside of the safety of their borders.

Kaylah gave her a reassuring pep talk. "The people who live in the village we're going to are the most vulnerable, but they're safe in there, and we will be too."

After leaving behind the border wall thickets, and making their way through a short stretch of the Neutral Woods, Rachel soon realized why this area was better protected.

"A cliff!" Rachel stared at the rocky landscape before her. It was a *massive* drop from where they stood at the top.

"A canyon, actually. A good natural border, hiding an area that wasn't poisoned."

Swallowing hard, Rachel thought of the Grand Canyon. She'd never been there, but she wondered if this was comparable. This probably wasn't quite as 'grand,' but it was still plenty deep. Stubborn bushes clung to the occasional crack in the almost-sheer grey rock, the canyon snaking its way toward the nearby goliath Outer Rim mountains, taking a sharp turn to the right a few miles from Rachel's current position. "How are we supposed to get there?"

Kaylah chuckled. "Well, you can fly, right? At least you're not the one who has to use hands and vines to make your way down the walls."

Rachel laughed. Catching a breeze was still a novelty for her, not a default she considered naturally. All of her takeoffs thus far had been into the sky, not plunging from a great height. She side-eyed one of the guards. "Do either of you want to go first?"

One smirked. "Sure." He tugged his backpack straps, securing his cargo, and without a speck of hesitation, he jumped into the canyon.

Letting out a little gasp, Rachel watched closely. Other than the eyes on a mated male, nothing on Seeder men glowed, so for the unknowing bystander, he would have looked like he was plummeting to his death with his arms and legs outstretched, his arm blades extended, his hair tips purple. She was actually a bit concerned with how quickly he descended, but after a little while he slowed, and then did a smooth, wide loop in the air. Rachel smiled. "Show-off."

"I expect you to do one of those things on the way down, too," Kaylah kidded.

"Right..." Rachel was pulled back to reality. It was her turn now.

"Wait," Kaylah said. "Um ... have you flown carrying this much weight before?"

Suddenly, Rachel was acutely aware of the straps digging into her shoulders. "You have a point..."

"I can take your extra books," the other guard offered.

She didn't need to be talked into it. Taking off her pack, she opened it and handed her extras to the guard. "You're just worried about the precious books, Kaylah. You've seen how well-trained I am at catching a breeze now, and you want to make sure I don't dirty them if I splat."

Grinning, Kaylah cleared her throat. "I don't know what you're talking about. Smoothest flier I've ever seen."

Rachel matched her grin; they both knew that was a bald-faced lie. Securing her pack again, she prepared for her own leap. Taking a few paces back to ensure she'd safely clear the wall she'd be jumping from, Rachel drew a deep breath, then sprinted and jumped off. At first, it was terrifying. A small scream escaped her mouth before she calmed and almost even enjoyed the fall. Not wanting to build up too much speed, and not being a show-off, she stretched her energy throughout her body, balancing in the wind and coasting.

Approaching the base of the canyon, Rachel now had a clear view of the small river cutting through a millennium of stubborn stone. There was plenty of bank on either side to land on. Squinting to find the first guard, she was thrown off by a bug flying *right* up her nose. Distracted and freaking out, she tried to dislodge it with short forceful bursts of air out of both nostrils. Already struggling to focus as needed on balancing her energy, she quickly moved a finger to her itching nose.

And then she plummeted. Screaming again, she straightened her posture, but it was too late—she smacked into the river in a far-less-than-graceful belly flop.

Startled by how cold the water was, Rachel swiftly found her way to the surface, gasping. Every inch of her exposed skin stung from the impact.

"Are you okay?" The guard on her level came running to her aid.

Moving energy to her arm muscles, Rachel fought the lazy current and swam to the bank, dripping like a drowned rat as she crawled out. "I'm good." She let out one last solid burst of air from her nose, making sure the offending creature had been expelled.

"But the books..." The guard looked at her pack with concern.

Rachel instantly burst into hysterical laughter, still on all fours. Kaylah would love the irony. The guard, however, didn't see the humor in Rachel's casual treatment of precious ancient research literature. She waved a hand dismissively, forcing herself to stop laughing. "They're fine. Totally fine. Your partner has them up there."

He relaxed. "Okay. Well, now we wait."

Rachel picked herself up, still dripping. It would take quite some time for Kaylah to make her way down, so Rachel slung off her bag and found a sunny spot to unpack her belongings for them to air-dry. She also needed a good rest from all the travel, and she certainly wanted to dry off herself, so she lay down with her hands under her head, watching clouds roll by and keeping an eye on where Kaylah would be descending.

Kaylah was astonishingly quick. Then again, she had vines to not only help her securely descend the wall, but also multitask. Two feet, two hands, two vines. At times, as she was nearing the floor of the canyon, she almost even reminded Rachel of a monkey, swinging with an acrobatic flair. Once she was almost to the bottom, probably a couple of hours later, the second guard finally flew down and met her.

Rachel started to repack her things, as Kaylah and the guard had a few dozen yards to walk to meet her. Most of her things had dried, though she was personally still rather soggy.

"Are you okay?" Kaylah's voice came between panting breaths as she ran to Rachel.

"I'm great. Just thought I'd do some laundry," Rachel said, standing up and closing the latch on her pack.

Kaylah dropped her own pack, which was heavy with her books. She opened her arms and hugged Rachel. "Gosh, you had me worried! Samwise here refused to leave my side to go check on you."

Rachel pulled back from the hug, confused. "Samwise?"

Still breathing hard, Kaylah raised a hand. "Never mind."

"She's fine," the guard drawled. "And you know the escort requirements of your agreement with our council."

Rachel realized Kaylah had meant the guard was 'Samwise.' Scrunching her eyebrows, she pointed to the guard. "His name is Cecil, Kaylah."

Kaylah chuckled, wiping sweat from her brow. She was absolutely drenched from descending the wall. Her face was red. Hair wisps were plastered to the back and sides of her neck. "It's from a super long movie Eric made me watch with him once. He thought green folk sounded like flipping hobbits."(mm)

Rachel still didn't get the reference. She shrugged. "Either way, now I feel like I should have joined you. Looks like a good workout." She winked. "And here I was napping the day away."

"Sure. Feel free next time. I'm sure it's even more fun on the way up!" Kaylah stuck out her tongue. "But seriously, what happened? I'm glad we didn't send the books with you."

Rachel whistled. "Bug flew up my nose."

Kaylah grinned. "Yeah, I'd say that too, if I'd biffed it."

"It's the truth!"

Kaylah continued grinning. "If you say so."

"Lovely reunion. Shall we continue?" Cecil asked.

Kaylah glanced at him with subtle annoyance. She had often referred to him as 'the buzzkill' when it was just her and Rachel talking. "Being the one who just exerted the most effort, how about we give me half a second to catch my breath and cool down?" She approached the river, bending down and splashing her face with water.

"You're pretty sweaty. Maybe you should just take a quick swim. Rather refreshing," Rachel kidded.

Kaylah hummed. "Maybe I will." She slipped off her shoes. "Or at least I'll soak my feet for a minute." She waded up to her calves, just below her long shorts.

"I don't think that's going to cut it," Rachel said. "Did you smell yourself? I just hugged you. You do *not* smell like a princess right now."

Kaylah glared playfully. "And for that, you're joining me."

Before Rachel could react, she had vines around her wrists, yanking her back into the river. Emerging from the water, she cleared her nose again. "You are so dead." She grabbed Kaylah's legs, pulling her in the rest of the way.

They screamed and giggled and splashed for a couple of minutes, then pulled themselves back onto dry land. They wrung out their hair as the guards approached where the girls had gotten out after drifting down the river, also carrying the girls' packs. "Just the dignity one would expect from the would-be queen of the Ivy Kingdom," Cecil chastised. "Can we go now?"

Kaylah's smile dropped at his censure. "Yes, we can go."

Rachel glared, snatching her pack from him. "That's uncalled for. Maybe we *should* call you Samwise."

Kaylah did a poor job of stifling a laugh. "Rach, don't use insults you don't understand. You kind of just complimented him." She accepted her own pack from the other guard, slinging it over her shoulder. "Lead the way."

The guards both turned and started walking.

Rachel linked arms with Kaylah, following after them. "But you said it like it was a bad thing," she whispered.

"I'll explain it later."

The guards led the way to a cave—a tunnel—where they were greeted by more Seeders. This was the entrance to Arcadia, the village that gave Seeder boys born without powers a chance at life. Against impassable mountains, tucked away on the floor of a canyon that separated them from the Neutral Woods, the village barely even had any security measures set up.

Once they passed through the tunnel, lit with lightkeepers, they entered a wide clearing. Rachel was in awe at the lush surroundings. Drawing her attention in particular were some beautiful orange flowers she'd spotted before in the Neutral Woods and Ivy Kingdom.

"It's always nice to have guests," an elderly woman greeted them, shaking hands. "I'll show you to your accommodations."

Making Rachel feel a bit like an exhibit in a zoo, eyes of the locals followed them along the way until Kaylah and Rachel were shown to the building with their beds.

The old woman scanned them with a smile. "Would you young ladies like to change before getting a tour?"

"Yes, thank you," Rachel said.

"Alright. I'll be waiting out here."

Kaylah and Rachel went inside the stone building, quickly tossing their packs on a set of beds and stripping out of soggy clothes. Rachel rummaged through her pack to find the driest of her clothes while Kaylah explained the Samwise thing. Apparently, it was from 'Lord of the Rings.' Kaylah also had to clarify that it had nothing to do with a shell and little boys murdering each other. That had been 'Lord of the Flies.'

Rachel sighed, brushing out her wet hair. "Too many lords to keep track of, if you ask me." She'd hated half of the books they deemed mandatory reading in English classes back home... Back in the human world.

Kaylah started braiding her own hair. "By the way, Guillen's on his way here. Not sure how long it will take him to make the trek, but I figured it might give you something to look forward to."

Rachel hid a smile at his name; she didn't want to get her hopes up. And luckily, this time Kaylah wasn't hassling her about him too much. "Good to know."

Kaylah nudged Rachel's arm. "So, be honest, was it really a bug up your nose?"

"Yes!"

"Hmm. Was it a ... glow-butt bug?" She smirked.

Rachel set her jaw, recalling the joke Kaylah had made weeks ago at their parting, comparing Seeders to lightning bugs. She grabbed the damp towel off of her bed, twisting it. "I spent two years on the high school volleyball team. I know how to wield one of these from my time in the locker room."

Matching her game face, Kaylah held out her wrists, inching out vines. "You think you could snap me with that before I could rip it from your hands?"

Changing her strategy, Rachel instead chucked it at Kaylah's face. Kaylah erupted into laughter.

Rachel shrugged. "Strategy, not strength. Come on, let's not keep our tour guide waiting."

They quickly tidied up the room and left the wet clothes draped over drying racks. Rachel loved taking in the sights and interviewing residents. From Kaylah's knowledge of the Ivy population born without powers, the Seeder nation could theoretically hold upwards of one to two thousand male Seeders born without powers, assuming the frequency of the birth defect was equal amongst both races. Just as many female Seeders without powers would likely be in existence, trapped over in the human world.

There were less than three hundred Seeders without powers who resided in this village. Saff's words from their time back in the human-world safe house haunted

Rachel. The 'helpless babies' born without powers were susceptible to the poison in their lands, and only stood a chance if their mothers caught it soon enough, and if they were strong enough for a journey across their lands, and through a small stretch of Neutral Woods to get to the canyon. Rachel's heart ached for these boys and men, and their families. Essentially human, they'd always be susceptible to this poison.

At least half of the people that lived in the village had powers, family members of those born with the rare disability. They considered the sacrifice worth it, to be removed from their kind, to be able to live together. Rachel asked why they couldn't just have girls come to live there, instead of needing to be raised in the human world, but she was reminded that the area was too small, and unable to be expanded, tucked away in stone. Other attempts made by Seeder families to escape their borders and raise their families together in the Neutral Woods had always been met with deadly opposition by Ivy troops occupying what had been penned into the treaty as 'neutral.'

Few children lived in Arcadia. Sometimes only the affected boy and an aunt or uncle lived there, or his mother, with other family raising his brothers in regular Seeder lands. Once the boy's sisters and father returned from the human world, the mother would often leave, since the young boy was a man by that point. They'd visit him often, but he was stuck in a limbo, not able to leave, unless he wanted to find a way to scale the canyon and brave the dangerous Neutral Woods for some reason.

The gender ratio was definitely off as well. Finding a Seeder woman to settle down with wasn't easy for these guys. They had no powers. Unique Seeder physiology meant they could have no kids. And it was out of the way for any woman to come out there. But they weren't completely hopeless; there were always some women sentimental about the simpler 'human' ways of life there.

For Rachel's part, she'd known she would be sad to see the way they had to live as a result of the war, but she was happy to observe the contrast of her people's treatment versus that of the Ivies. Seeders didn't brand them as stunted. They didn't look down on them, or *force* them to live separately. And they didn't require them to do menial work, having little say in their own jobs and industries. The community was its own little capsule oasis, functioning fairly independently, apart from regular society.

After a few hours of talking to some attractive and particularly attentive young men, the women were happy to have Saff finally join them.

❃

"My goodness, this place really is tucked away, isn't it!"

Rachel gave her a hug. "Glad you made it."

"Thanks." Saff scrunched her eyebrows, glancing at a flower garden past Rachel. "Is that Guenjalis over there? Like ... everywhere?"

Rachel looked around. "Um..."

Saff clarified. "Those gorgeous fire-orange flowers? I've only ever seen paintings of them back home. They're kind of like a myth."

"Those?" Rachel asked, doing a double take. "I've seen them past our borders, on my return from the palace."

Kaylah clicked her tongue. "I'd hoped we'd find a few things here. And I think those pretty flowers might be just what we need for one of my theories." She spelled out her meaning. "To heal the land of the poison, we really have to understand better what we're working with. Like you've said before—you can't see the poison. And you guys still have plenty of plant growth in your lands.

"So, I could try to heal the land, but we'd have no way of testing it without putting one of your vulnerable people there and just seeing ... if they got sick." She cringed. "But I'm pretty sure these flowers grow everywhere in the Green Lands, *except* for Seeder territory. Transplanting these, with trial and error—this could save your people." She raised her eyebrows. "You're a floral race, you must share something ... biologically."

Saff and Rachel looked at each other, hope smiling in their eyes. It might take a while before they could figure out the right treatment. And it would take a *ton* of female Ivy power, but in over a hundred years, this was the first time there was a light at the end of the tunnel.

Saff thought of Devin, and how they'd talked about having kids, though it was still years away. But the possibility of raising kids together in the same realm was feasible.

That evening, they ate out over a campfire in the center of the village, sharing time and food with the hospitable residents. Rachel explained to those around her how the Ivy Kingdom treated their citizens without powers. She'd expected more of a reaction, but they weren't as invested as she was. Most Seeders still didn't feel a need to sympathize with Ivies, though they did casually comment on how it sounded like the short end of the stick, having the lack of powers in common.

And none of the men there understood her World War II references, when she compared the Ivy Kingdom to Nazis, requiring those without powers to live in separate communities, not allowed to have kids, and forced to be tattooed with numbers. Whereas Ivies without abilities were *prevented* from taking classes about the human world, the Seeders in this community just didn't feel as much need for that curriculum. Their families generally focused as much education as possible on Seeder-focused history and culture, to help the boys stay connected to their people living in proper Seeder territory.

After a particularly attractive male Seeder asked Rachel if she'd like a refill of her pineapple juice, Saff leaned over and whispered, "A lot of eyes on you."

Rachel's cheeks warmed. "Yeah, on Kaylah, too."

"Yeah, but that's because they don't know what she is."

That rubbed Rachel the wrong way. She and Saff had come a long way, but she still had her annoying moments. "*What* she is, or *who* she is?"

※

"I'm just saying ... if you don't fancy anyone back home, maybe you should give one of these guys a chance." Saff had to admit to herself that Kaylah could be trusted. Even the council thought so. But it was hard to not still worry sometimes, just the smallest amount, that there was deception lurking behind a helpful hand and smiling face. And Rachel was still... Saff had promised herself she wouldn't use the word 'naïve' in regards to Rachel again. But the truth was, dating an Ivy couldn't possibly be good for her. That would dredge up all sorts of pain from her past, even if Rachel didn't realize it. And unless it was for the purpose of kidnap or assassination, there hadn't been a Seeder-Ivy couple in centuries. She admired Rachel's desire for change, but Rachel didn't understand how complicated things were.

※

Rachel rolled her eyes. Saff was obviously bringing up her dislike of Guillen again. "Are you saying that because you think I have a fetish for human men? Or because you'd rather I be with a Seeder without powers, than an Ivy without them?"

Saff stared into the crackling fire. "I'm just saying ... any relationship with a Seeder is less complicated than trying to work it out with an Ivy. Even if he *is* as good as you think he is."

"Again. Guillen and I are not dating. And I appreciate..." Rachel gripped her hands a little more tightly around her empty cup. "No. I don't think I *do* appreciate the advice. I don't consider who I date based on convenience. I don't need you to be a matchmaker." She huffed and stood up, marching over to refill her cup with water.

Leaning against a fence, Rachel surveyed this group of people, this village. It was like a little hideaway—safe, not as much constant talk about the war. It was idyllic in some ways. There wasn't a single overcrowded lane or temple or soldier in sight.

"How does it feel to be the center of attention?" The deep voice startled her.

She snapped her head to the right, taking in a tall muscular figure next to her. "To be honest, it feels like a meat market."

He looked confused.

"Right, sorry. It's ... interesting." The phrase 'meat market' didn't mean much to a Seeder who hadn't had any dealings with the human world—they were all vegetarians here.

He wore a charming smile. "Well, hopefully we don't scare you off too quickly." He stretched out his hand. "I'm Zeus."

Rachel bit her lip, meeting his brown eyes. "Zeus?"

He flashed a look of embarrassment mingled with frustration. "I know. My mom thought it was a great idea; she told me about the human mythology behind it, some super powerful god?"

Rachel shook his hand. She could understand a mother wanting to boost her son's morale, with him being different, having no powers, but it honestly just came off as compensation, and his reaction made it apparent they were on the same page about that. "It's cute. I'm Rachel."

He cleared his throat, running a hand through his light brown hair. "I don't know about that. Most guys aren't hoping for 'cute' names. But I can pretend you meant that about me, and not my name."

She successfully suppressed a laugh; not as successfully, a grin.

"So ... I just wanted to come say hi. I didn't want to seem like a desperate creeper or anything like that. I'm told we'll be working together."

Rachel took a sip of her water. "Well, I didn't think you seemed desperate, or that you were a creeper... We'll be working together?"

"Yeah, I'm one of the master gardeners here." He moved closer, whispering, "They told me about your mission, who that girl is over there." He pointed to Kaylah with a pinky. "And that you're going to do research with some of the flowers?"

He was close enough for the warmth of his skin to radiate onto Rachel's. And it was nice to be able to chat with someone in the know. Most of the time thus far, they'd pretended Kaylah was just another Seeder, for her protection, and plausible deniability.

"Yeah. It's pretty awesome, isn't it?"

"Yeah." He smiled. "Well, it was nice to meet you. I look forward to getting to know more about the girl hand-picked by our leaders for this special project. Do you know how long you'll be here?"

Rachel shook her head. "I'm not too sure."

He looked away, focusing on the dying campfire. "Hopefully long enough that we can get a real breakthrough. But not so long that you miss your boyfriend."

She pursed her lips at his fishing for information. "There's not one to miss."

He flashed flirtatious eyes. "I'll see you in the morning?"

"Sounds like a plan."

After he left her side, Rachel mused on poor Zeus and his name. Yes, that voice and body were certainly heavenly, but his mother hadn't known he'd grow into that when she'd named him. Eventually, Rachel's eyes landed on Saff, who was looking over at her, grinning. Rachel rolled her eyes again. She wasn't there to date or fall in love. She was there to work. And she *especially* didn't want to prove Saff right by falling for one of these men.

A cot was added to their shared room by the end of the day; Kaylah offered to take it so the Seeders could have the beds.

Saff and Kaylah took off together at first light the next morning to scout out a good cave rift location, while Rachel sat outside on a log at the extinguished campfire, drinking a cup of coffee as the sun rose. Zeus gave her a warm smile when he found her, sitting down next to her.

"It's peaceful here," she said wistfully. Compared to the constant noise of her war-torn village of South Fortinda, the silence and wonder of this hideaway made it so serene, like a balm to her soul. Well, it was mostly silent. The blue-breasted, yellow-winged chatterbirds were chirping away rather noisily in a nearby tree.

"It has some redeeming qualities, that's for sure," Zeus said. "Some think it's a nice place to settle down, away from the chaos." He took a sip from his own cup. "How do you like it back in the main villages?"

"I, uh... I don't know." She pictured her mom back in the human world, all alone, moving between safe houses. And her own serious lack of bonding with people back in her home village. "Sometimes I wish I could have just stayed back in the human world, stayed human."

"Why did you decide to come back?" He frowned. "Did you feel pressured into it?"

She grinned and shook her head. "I forget most people don't know much about me. Pressured into it... You could say that."

"Did you leave someone important behind?"

"You mean other than my mom?" She made sure she had eye contact. "Or like a boyfriend?"

He blushed and looked down. "It's not my place to ask. I didn't mean anything by it."

"It's okay." She chuckled. "Zeus, you have no idea. My last boyfriend is the reason I came here."

He pursed his lips.

"It's not like that, trust me. I'm here because he kidnapped me."

His eyes shot back up to meet hers.

"I dated the Ivy prince for almost three years. And he brought me here to use my powers against our people."

Zeus's mouth was agape for a moment as he took in the revelation. "Oh... Uh..."

She set down her coffee cup. "It's okay. You don't have to say anything." She gave a half-hearted smile. "Ready to get to work?"

Chapter 7

Zeus and Rachel left the campfire area to start their research. Seeders rarely wore long sleeves, owing to the impracticality of them when needing their arm blades for fighting or catching a breeze, and the climate was almost always pleasant enough not to need bulky layers. As Zeus strolled alongside Rachel toward his garden, she couldn't help but notice his sleeveless shirt, which put his biceps on full display. Where he lacked Seeder energy to make him strong, it looked as though he compensated with plenty of exercise.

"I just wanted to say, I wasn't judging you back there. I just wasn't quite sure what to say."

She tucked her hands into her pockets. "It's really okay. I don't know what I would expect you to say, to be honest. It's not really something I tell everyone."

He gave her a warm smile. "Then I'm glad you felt you could confide in me."

She returned his smile, but she really wasn't sure *why* she had blurted out her kidnapping and dating history to him. She barely knew the guy. Was it because she felt comfortable with him, like he assumed? Or was it because she was trying to put up an emotional barrier? She reminded herself it mattered little; she wasn't there to date. It was just kind of nice to have someone new to talk to.

They turned a corner, arriving at a community garden bursting at the seams with every possible flower, in every color of the rainbow.

"That's gorgeous!" She stood in awe with her mouth open. She caught his gaze from the corner of her eye; he was beaming with pride.

"Thanks. I'd like to think I have an eye for beautiful things."

She looked back at the flowers, assuming that was just another flirtatious remark. "Honestly, I'm not any better of a gardener than any other Seeder. I feel kind of useless here, being assigned to this project." She didn't want to say as much, but she felt like this was a 'filler' project, just something she could do until Guillen arrived. Kaylah still wouldn't explain what her plans for Rachel and Guillen were, nor did she have a better estimate on his arrival time. It could be days or weeks. Ultimately, working on the poison problem was something Rachel could do to contribute while Kaylah and Saff worked on the trickier, smarter job of locating a rifting cave.

Zeus gave Rachel a gentle nudge. "I'm sure you're better than you're letting on, otherwise they wouldn't have picked you, out of everyone."

Guilt stabbed at her as she suppressed the truth. She'd been picked to go there so she could learn about his way of life, the Seeder equivalent of Guillen. She was trying not to count the days, knowing Guillen was making his way across dangerous territory at that very moment, to meet up with her. And frankly, the only reason she'd been invited on this mission was because she was the princess's best friend.

She tried to change the topic, rubbing the petal of a Guenjalis flower. "So, what's so special about these? Why can't we just have the Ivies try to heal some soil, pluck a few of these up, and transplant them to see if they'll live?"

He shook his head. "They're really delicate, they wouldn't do well being transplanted."

"I guess that makes sense, that they're frail, if they don't survive in our regular villages." She instantly regretted the way she'd phrased that, as if she'd called *him* frail for his human nature, unable to withstand the poison. Luckily, he didn't appear to take offense.

She quickly moved on. "If we can't transplant them, how do we do this? Planting from seed has got to take forever."

"Not if you know what you're doing. You have it in you to accelerate plant growth."

She cocked her head to the side. "Really? No one's told me about that."

"Yeah, it's not something most people train for. The energy of the Green Lands already makes this place, well, green. But it's something you're capable of. It's kind of a hobby, in a way, for some of the women here. It's not like they have a temple well they deposit their energy at on a regular basis."

Her interest was piqued. But why wasn't she working with another Seeder woman who could train her, hands-on? She didn't ask, not wanting to insult him again.

"Alright, what do we do?"

"Let me show you."

They strolled down a dirt path until they reached an area thick with the special flower.

"The seeds are actually best when planted fresh, for what we're doing," he explained. He showed her how to pluck them from the center of the flower. The pollen stained their hands, but he assured her it would easily wash off. The flowers exuded a strong honey and lemon aroma. Once they had gathered a few seeds, he led Rachel to a clearing. "Ironically, these are the easiest for Seeder women to grow with their energy, but the hardest to keep alive. That's kind of where I come in as a master gardener."

They sat down in the clearing.

"We bury them about this deep." He dug up a little soil with a small spade, then replaced it after dropping a seed in. "Add some water." He poured from a watering can. "And this is where you come in." He held his hands up, pointer fingers touching and thumbs meeting, leaving a triangle empty in the middle. "Like this."

She followed along.

"Not too tricky thus far, right?" He moved his hands to demonstrate where hers should go, hovering the triangular opening over where the seed had been planted.

He removed his hands, and she scooched closer, placing hers on the wet soil. She figured it was pretty intuitive, like most Seeder abilities. Imagining energy stretching from her heart down to her hands, Rachel closed her eyes and took a deep breath. Once confident she'd done enough, she opened her eyes and saw … nothing. She frowned.

"It's okay. It doesn't come naturally to everyone," he coached. "Maybe you just need to focus harder."

She nodded and closed her eyes, taking a moment to clear her mind. She tried again, without success. "Yeah, like I said … maybe not the best pick for this."

"Give it another try."

She tried a third time, focusing all she could on that little triangle, trying to coax life into the seed. Large warm hands glided onto hers, weighing them down. She took a sharp breath and opened her eyes. He'd moved closer, looking at her with deep brown eyes.

"I think part of the problem is that you need more pressure on the soil."

"Yeah, okay." She swallowed, her breath irregular. He could have just told her that. He didn't need to get handsy, but he was obviously trying to start something. She allowed his hands to linger while she closed her eyes again, trying not to get distracted. It didn't feel horrible, though, to have someone holding her hands, touching her. She missed that.

"Open your eyes," he prompted moments later.

She did as instructed, and happily admired a sprout popping out of the dirt. Not a fully formed flower by any means, but she had done it—she'd grown something with her energy. Pulling her hands back, Rachel smiled. "Thanks." She scratched an itch on her cheek.

A grin spread across Zeus's face. He reached over and wiped at the spot she'd itched. A quick glance at her hands explained why; they were muddy.

"I don't mean to be forward, Rachel, but I'd like to get to know you better. Do you think you'll have any free time tonight?"

Her cheeks warmed. "I ... don't know. We have a lot going on."

He did a poor job of hiding his disappointment. "Okay."

She tilted her head. "I'll let you know?"

His smile came back. "I'd like that."

They went back to her growing attempts until they were interrupted by a familiar voice, that of a redhead Rachel hadn't seen in weeks.

"Rachel!"

She opened her eyes and hopped up from the ground, running over to Ginger to give her a hug, being careful to not smear her with mud. "I'm so glad to see you! I hear you've been crazy busy!"

"Wouldn't have it any other way," Ginger said. Like Kaylah, she was escorted by a pair of Seeder guards. Ginger rubbed her hands together. "They tell me I'm here to practice killing a sad little flower until I can figure out how to fix it."

Rachel chuckled. "That's a horrible job description. And I'd recommend not letting anyone else hear you say that."

Zeus seemed a little bothered by their new companion, perhaps because she was Ivy, or because she'd intruded on his attempts at flirting. Either way, he formally greeted Ginger and led them to the far edge of the village, where they'd dedicated some space for their experiments.

Ginger knelt and practiced poisoning the ground, trying to only kill off the little flowers, not everything else in the area. Just like when Kaylah had first demonstrated this skill, greenery browned and went limp with Ginger's poison, then recovered with the chemical compound she followed it up with. It was tricky trying to narrow the toxins. She tired quickly, killing off and healing several times. After a few breaks, they decided to call it a night.

Rachel was conflicted when she agreed to spend the rest of the evening with Zeus. He was sweet, giving her options for what she wanted to see and eat. Conversation flowed fairly easily between them. Though, she couldn't help but wonder if she was holding back because of Guillen, or the prince. Or if she was just overthinking it all.

"So, you're keeping your human name?" Zeus asked. They stopped and sat on a wooden bench overlooking a small pond where minnows danced around.

She polished off the last of the pimple berries she'd pulled from a bush while on their stroll. "Yeah. Not all girls make the change." She'd mulled it over a lot since her return. Changing her name, despite it being a common Seeder tradition, felt like it would be severing another tie to her mom back home. Saff—short for Saffrona—was one of those girls who had embraced her new life wholeheartedly. But that wasn't Rachel. That wasn't her story. She hadn't genuinely chosen any of this. "Guess I'm just not really a fan."

"I understand different villages have different traditions about the names. What does your village favor?"

Rachel grinned, fingering a blade of tall ornamental grass swaying next to her in the evening breeze. "The most original—flowers." She looked Zeus dead in the eyes. "But can you believe my dad didn't give it a second thought before he named me *Pansy*? Out of all the flowers available..."

Zeus's eyes grew large as he bit his lip. "I thought my mom had bad taste. But..."

She busted out laughing, putting a hand on his arm. "I am *so* kidding. It's not that bad. It's Mari, for Marigold. Just not my thing."

He relaxed, nodding with a hint of a smile. "That's not so bad. Much better than Pansy."

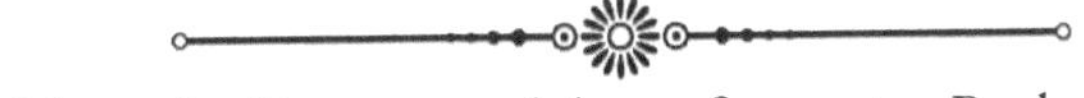

At the end of the night, Zeus stopped short of returning Rachel to her door, where guards were positioned outside. He asked for a hug goodnight, and she obliged. It was nice to be in warm arms, just standing there, not letting go.

She'd forgotten how much she truly missed romantic companionship. How lonely she felt at times, even when surrounded by family and friends.

She wanted to blot out memories of Prince Soren, the last man she'd kissed. She wanted to blot out a lot of things. Stress. Anxiety. Frustration. Guilt.

Releasing Zeus from their hug, she gazed into his eyes. There may not have been instant chemistry, but there could be something there, if she allowed it to grow, if she would stop getting in her own way. Or perhaps a onetime thing with no strings attached could be enough.

She wrapped her hands behind his neck. "You're a nice guy, Zeus." She stood tall, caressing his lips with her own. Her stomach did a somersault. She leaned back to get his reaction.

He looked surprised, but was smiling. "Thanks."

One kiss wasn't enough. She needed more. Rachel leaned closer again, and he took the hint. She kissed him several times, more firmly, more involved with each pass. She wanted to feel something—something new, simple, uncomplicated. She pressed herself against him, and he pulled her in tight. Her heart and lungs kept pace with her lips, but fell short of giving her the spark she was looking for.

She pulled away. There was no warmth in her eyes—they hadn't even changed color.

"I should go to bed," she whispered, studying his face.

He continued to smile. "Yeah, me too." He tucked a strand of hair behind her ear. "I'll see you in the morning." He gave her one more peck and left her to return to her room.

When she entered, Ginger was snoring on a cot, and Kaylah and Saff were sitting in their pajamas, talking about their day.

Saff smirked. "You were out late."

Kaylah dodged eye contact. She had to be making the same assumptions, and disapproving, thinking of Guillen. But Rachel and Guillen were far from being an item. They hadn't made any sort of agreement. She didn't owe him anything.

"I just want to go to bed," Rachel said, heading to the bathroom to get ready for the night. Minutes later, she lay in bed, unable to sleep, beating herself up. *Why didn't that kiss feel better? He didn't seem very experienced.* Then it dawned on her that he may have never had a chance to kiss a girl before. And she'd used him.

She tried to lie to herself, saying it was just a mental block. But the fact was: she didn't feel the same way about him, as he apparently did about her. She stewed in self-hatred. She'd kissed him as a way to forget her previous mistakes, and all she'd done was dig deeper.

Zeus greeted Rachel at her door with a large smile and a coffee in the morning, once her party left the room. She sipped in silence as he sat next to her back at the fire pit. He rested a hand on her back, rubbing as she sat slumped over.

She sat straight up. "Zeus, I'm sorry. I shouldn't have kissed you last night." She stared at the cold black coals.

"It's okay. You took me by surprise." His voice carried a vulnerability that only made her feel worse. "But ... I liked it..."

Knives twisting in her gut, she remained unsure of what else to say. "I just ... don't know if I'm ready for that."

He rubbed her back again. "That's fine, really. I'm still open to spending some time together after work, if you're interested. But no pressure. I just want to get to know you."

She gave him a weak smile. She could do friendship, even if she knew that particular f-word was one no one wanted to hear right after they'd been kissed. "Yeah. If I'm not too busy, I'd like that."

Chapter 8

The next evening, Rachel told Zeus she could only go on a short stroll after dinner. She ended up leaving him with an awkward hug, and going back to her room after their time together. She said she needed more time to coordinate with the others in her party, and then felt guilty, finding she was actually back quite a while before they were.

Saff and Kaylah returned late, clearly exhausted and frustrated.

"Going that well, eh?" Rachel asked, already tucked in for the night.

Saff tossed her pack on her bed. "It feels like we're wasting our time."

"I never said it would be easy," Kaylah snapped back.

Saff rolled her eyes and went to the bathroom.

Rachel lay in uncomfortable silence. *Would it really be Saff and Kaylah in the same room if they weren't bickering about how to get things done?* At least they'd moved past death threats—that had been a real treat in the safe house when they'd first met.

Kaylah explained their predicament to Rachel. "We go out there to find a place with good cover, nicely defensible, but there are a ton of variables. I can sense the location's name, but I'm not sure how close I am. Like, we could be twenty yards to the right, and we don't know it. Or we're not powerful enough between the two of us. I don't know. It could be a million things."

A knock on the door claimed their attention; Kaylah got up to open it.

"Hi, um … is Saff here?" a male voice asked from the door.

Saff came out of the bathroom. "Devin! What are you doing here?" She ran up and squeezed him tight, planting a kiss on him.

"I figured it was worth carving out some time to come all the way out here and see you." He rested his forehead against hers. "I missed you."

She stole another kiss, then looked back at the room of women. "Well..."

"Oh, for the love," Kaylah drawled. "Go ask someone about getting your own room."

Saff blushed. "I'll be ready first thing in the morning." She snatched up her pack.

Kaylah launched herself onto Saff's bed. "Yeah, yeah, yeah. Whatever. I could stand sleeping in."

As soon as Saff and Devin left, Kaylah turned to Rachel. "She had the more comfortable bed, anyway. It's a win-win. Now I get this one."

Rachel let out a half-hearted chuckle. "Then everyone wins." She pulled up her covers. "Almost everyone."

Kaylah gave her no pity. "What's with you and that tall thing? Are you rebounding with him?"

"I feel like such a jerk." Rachel frowned.

"Then don't do it!"

Rachel scowled. "I'm not going to, Mom." She huffed. "I just... I don't know."

"Were you rebounding with Guillen?"

"No! We never even kissed."

Kaylah lifted her eyebrows. "Why was he any different?"

Rachel looked away, aching, longing to see him again. "He just was. I don't want to talk about it." She turned off her lightkeeper. They were both nice guys. But she'd shared an instant chemistry with Guillen. And he was sweet and vulnerable in a different way. But she worried—that she had put him on a pedestal after all this time, that it wasn't the way she remembered. That he could have found some other girl who made him happy. That he wouldn't want a girl like her now, one who took advantage of sweet, innocent men like Zeus.

For the next few days, Rachel occupied herself, avoiding any actions with Zeus that might be misinterpreted. Ginger made progress in her attempts to poison and heal Guenjalis. Saff and Kaylah grew confident they were narrowing in on the right cave location.

Devin returned home to South Fortinda, and with Saff's recommendation and Kaylah's permission, he was going to ask Heather if she would want to join them.

Saff was ecstatic to see her sister-in-law at her arrival. "Thanks so much for coming!"

Heather seemed to be doing somewhat better. She still wasn't her bubbly old self, but she carried herself well. And Saff figured a change of scenery, working far away from where her fiancé had been slain, could only do her good.

"Thanks for inviting me." Heather tucked her hands into her pockets.

The group of Unitas women suspected they needed more energy to create the kind of cave rift they wanted, and while they had plenty of Seeder matriarchs available nearby, Heather had mentioned wanting to help. Heather possessed the average energy-wielding abilities of her peers, but her dedication and focus on learning the ins and outs of healing boosted her knowledge of how to harness it with more finesse.

Ginger and Rachel took a day to join Kaylah, Saff, and Heather—the day they announced they might finally have it. It required three hours of hiking to get to the new location from this village. They'd had to cross the river to find the cave, with a decent path to the top of the canyon. The Seeders easily caught a breeze to avoid getting wet, but Kaylah and Ginger had no choice other than to wade through it.

"I know it, it's got to be right here," Kaylah said. "The location, I can feel it. This is Tonoru. Run that through your minds as we try this."

Kaylah pulled a big book from Saff's pack; the front of it bore the Unitas symbol, a blossom in front of an ivy leaf. "One of my books I smuggled here." She turned a few pages. "This is one of the books where most of the research came from that helped us realize how we could access your powers." She dodged eye contact with Rachel.

"By accessing our blood?" Saff asked.

Kaylah nodded. "Yeah, umm ... that. Anyway..." She found what she'd been searching for and showed everyone the pages pertaining to cave rifts. The instructions were written in the old language Kaylah had educated Rachel and Saff on, but they were hardly fluent. She pointed to a diagram and translated, explaining the gist of what needed to be done.

"But how does this work?" Saff asked. "You guys pull the energy from a tree to do your rifts. We always have to do it in the air. This doesn't make sense."

Kaylah looked exasperated. "Why does everyone expect me to have *all* the answers? I don't know. But this book hasn't been wrong, yet." She set it down on the ground.

"Then I guess we'll find out," Saff said, stretching her arms.

They stood near the opening, afraid of a potential cave-in, not certain how it all worked. Saff and Heather touched hands in the air, sweeping them apart, tracing the outline of the cave opening. Simultaneously, Kaylah and Ginger extended vines, running them on the stone floor, climbing to meet the Seeders' hands.

A ripple formed, a surge of energy. They shared congratulatory smiles. It had *actually* worked. And the realm hadn't come crashing down on them...

"Should we go through?" Rachel asked. "Will it always take this much effort?"

"I really don't know," Kaylah confessed as the shining ripple dimmed. "Maybe we just needed to prime it... Let's step back and see. We need to focus on a specific destination to make this work. I'm going to think of Domiten. That's the closest forest rift I can sense to Eric's safe house."

One of the guards cleared their throat.

Kaylah's face showed frustration—she'd gotten ahead of herself. "Right, sorry. No leaving alone." She added with some sarcasm, "I might up and betray your people after *everything* I've done."

"It's okay, I'll try," Saff said, stepping up to the cave entrance. She ran her hand through the air, opening up a new rift like she had a few times in the past, though this was her first time doing it from the ground. Right before entering, she jerked back, her expression dropping in horror. "Wait! This goes to a forest? Is there someone there to get me back?" She kicked herself for being so reckless. *How could I already forget?* She couldn't catch another breeze back home from the human world this year, and she'd already risked her life once experimenting with their powers.

Kaylah recoiled. "Crap! Wait. You're right, I'm sorry. Got too excited. We need to find a cave or rock formation of some sort on that side to match it, for back-and-forth travel."

Saff took an uneasy breath. They were doing a lot of speculation on brand-new theories, and needed to proceed with more caution. "I, uh... I'm not going to be the guinea pig on this one. I couldn't do that to Devin again."

"I could go with whoever wants to try it," Ginger offered. "We can come back by tree, just experimenting. Then we know we can focus on a match." She looked to the guard, who gave a hesitant nod.

❋

Rachel shrugged. "I could go. I don't have anyone that loves me."

"What?" Kaylah and Saff blurted in unison, both sporting a perturbed look.

Rachel grinned, feeling all the warm fuzzies. "I meant romantically, like Devin."

Kaylah and Saff both mumbled unintelligibly. Rachel was pretty sure Kaylah said something about Guillen, while somewhere in Saff's muttering 'Zeus' could be heard.

Rachel held a hand over her heart. "Wow. So much love *and* annoyance for you both right now."

Heather quietly chuckled. "I should go. I haven't taken a trip yet this year. And Rachel's been a few times. It's probably safest for me."

"Not a bad idea," Kaylah said. "Although, my impression is that it should be safe for *any* of us here to use it. And on a regular basis."

❋

Saff loved the idea of it. All of them did. Regular visits to the human world? Not just once a year? Kaylah had already made it clear in negotiations that this permanent rift still wouldn't support Seeder matriarch travel. And while Saff's powers were near-matriarchal, though technically not fully-rooted, she still couldn't imagine taking the risk.

Saff's rift had timed out. Heather stepped forward, creating one of her own, and with minimal hesitation, walked through it. It closed, then Ginger ran a vine along the floor of the cave, opening her own rift, and stepped through. The others watched on in awe. This was the first time in modern history that a Seeder had created a rift from the ground, and an Ivy through something other than a tree.

Not two minutes later, Heather and Ginger reappeared, a vine around Heather's arm with a minor injury to get her back. They were both beaming.

"Mark this one off the checklist," Heather remarked in a cheery nasal voice Saff recognized. "What's next?"

They took some time to congratulate themselves. With permission and a warning from the guard, Kaylah and Rachel took a trip through the cave; knots in Saff's stomach kept her from even considering it.

They experimented with Ginger and Heather going through again, but the constraint seemed to remain that both races still didn't have enough energy to do more than one roundtrip rift in a day. If an Ivy tried more than once, a rift just wouldn't form. If a Seeder tried more than once, they could form a rift, but not travel through it—they would just continue walking deeper into the cave. Saff rubbed her chest, recalling the price she'd paid to get to the human world just weeks ago. She again declined a trip of her own, even after Kaylah and Ginger offered to have the guards fetch another Unitas Ivy to escort her.

Kaylah then went over the next phase of her plans. "Rachel, I'm going to pull you from flower duty to work on extra training. Saff and Heather, if you two can manage to stay, we could really use your help. Training new girls here, defending the rifting location, and helping me find the cave on the other side.

"Ginger, I'm going to want to get you set up to train here. Bringing some of our women, you can teach them how to better dose, as well as heal the land." She looked at the Seeders. "I've got to talk to your council, though, but everything is looking great!"

Everyone was on a high after their success; they took the rest of the day off after securing the cave with several guards, just in case. After they returned to the village for dinner, they chatted excitedly with the residents about their accomplishment. The Seeders without powers likely still couldn't use it, unable to enter a rift without Green Lands powers, but Kaylah hinted she hoped for something like that down the road.

❁

Knowing her time was short in the village, and with Zeus throwing Rachel sad puppy-dog eyes, she excused herself to go on a walk with him after dinner. They likely wouldn't visit Arcadia often after Kaylah established a training camp on the other side of the canyon.

"It sounds like a big win for you and your posse," he complimented, holding his hands behind his back.

"I was just there for the show, to be honest. But it's pretty cool."

They continued in awkward silence; he slipped his hand into hers. She gave his hand a squeeze and then released, shoving her hands into her pockets. He was definitely more clingy than she'd anticipated, which made it that much worse.

"It really wasn't fair of me to kiss you, Zeus. You're a really nice guy. But I'm confused about a lot of things, and I won't be here for much longer. I'm sorry."

He frowned. "Just do me a favor. Don't completely write me off? I know you're going to go out there, on all these adventures, and I'm ... stuck here..."

She didn't respond right away. Part of her wanted to urge him to learn to fight, to tell him he could be like Guillen and leave the confines designed for his disability. But that wasn't fair. Guillen could freely walk around all of his own kingdom without harm. Zeus was *literally* stuck in his village, with the only alternative being dangerous territory. And he and Guillen were very different people. Guillen was a self-starting fighter. Zeus was comfortable as a gardener.

649

"I won't forget you, Zeus. And who knows, once we get this healing-the-land-thing done, I'd love to see you make the long trek all the way to my village." She smiled.

"Deal." He smiled back, holding out his arms for a hug. She obliged. She still felt crummy about the way she'd treated him, but she was grateful she might leave with a friend.

Upon her return to their room at night, Rachel was happily able to report to Kaylah. "All taken care of."

"Good. You both deserve better."

Rachel threw a pillow at her.

Kaylah caught it, giving her a playful we-both-know-I'm-right look. "Fancy going into the neighboring village with me tomorrow? I need to talk to the local council about approving the training camp and getting support. You and Ginger could do a test on the soil in an originally tainted area."

"Yeah, sure thing."

In the morning, all five women decided to make the trek to regular Seeder territory. Ginger tried healing the soil while Rachel showed Saff and Heather what she'd learned about sprouting the delicate flower using energy. It came with mixed results. She expended a lot of energy trying to sprout the seeds she'd brought, but when they would start to grow, most died quickly in the tainted soil. Ginger kept attempting to fine-tune the chemical composition she would inject into the ground. Worn out, she tried one last time before taking a break. They all watched as the flower bloomed. They stared at it, waiting for it to wilt any second.

Their anticipation rose with each moment that passed, signifying Ginger had properly healed the soil, giving hope for something on a much grander scale.

"Kaylah! Look!" Rachel yelled as Kaylah approached with her guards.

Kaylah rubbed her arm anxiously. "That's brilliant! I'm really proud of you guys." The flower stood tall, but Kaylah's smile didn't.

"What's wrong?" Rachel asked. "Did the council reject your plans?"

"No. That's all great. They're rushing to put it into action. There was just some other news."

Rachel's muscles tensed, and the others also looked at Kaylah with fear in their eyes—they all had someone to lose.

"Saff, you told me once that you could provide Unitas with names to help the network on the other side. I need those."

❋

Saff had been so focused on their work in the Green Lands that she'd hardly given any thought to the humans working hard on their behalf. "Yeah, you've earned it. What happened?"

Kaylah frowned. "There's been an attack. I don't want to freak anyone out. Everyone's fine. It's just the first time they've turned on a human host family."

The Seeder girls stood with mouths wide open.

"Really? They've always left them alone before. It's just..." Heather said.

"Yeah, well, I think Soren's getting impatient. The fact that he hasn't found any new girls to kidnap proves my intel was helpful. But they might have noticed some movement. And opening that cave, there's going to be a lot more movement, and soon. And we need to be prepared to keep our people safe."

"Sure thing, right away," Saff said. "I can give you my mom's number. She was going to look up everyone and see who lived where by now. And I can give you the code word I gave her." Saff grinned. "I told her not to trust anyone without it..."

"That was smart," Kaylah said. "But how about calling her yourself?"

Saff wrung her hands, suddenly feeling warm. Of course she wanted to talk to her human mom again. More than anything. But just thinking about going back to the human world again this year made her anxiety peak. "Maybe Heather should go. I'll give you the password. My parents would love to hear your voice. And I'm sure yours would, too."

Heather gave her a grateful smile. Her parents still didn't know the wedding was off, that her fiancé was dead. "I'd love to."

"Sounds good." Kaylah added with a smile aimed directly at Saff, "And I'll have you know that Unitas has started to pay, to one of those tree-hugger foundations, for each tree we have to sacrifice for our rifts in the human world."

Saff laughed and grabbed Kaylah, pulling her into a hug. She'd always hated the destruction left in the wake of Ivies rifting.

Likely startled, Kaylah awkwardly patted Saff on the back during their first hug.

Chapter 9

The next few days were a whirlwind of action in their tiny corner of neutral territory. Heather and Kaylah briefly popped over to the human world through a cave rift. Saff's human mom gave them their family contacts to grow the safety net for Unitas, and they took a quick look at a cave near Eric's safe house.

Not feeling confident enough to attempt an opening right away, they decided to return for it another day. They still weren't sure how it would affect the Seeder physiology, specifically, making multiple trips in a year like this, so they were going to be cautious.

A decently functioning training camp grew, practically overnight, near the new cave. Trees were cleared to build a defensible barricade, only leaving a few in camp for the purpose of emergency exit rifts for Ivies in the cause.

Rope ladders and a rope bridge were constructed to allow quicker travel across the canyon for Ivies, and Seeders without powers. With dozens of volunteers from Arcadia, and extras assigned by the local Seeder council, they gathered supplies and assembled tents.

Carefully, friendly Ivies made their way to the location—some through the cave, others arriving from the Neutral Woods on foot. With strict screening procedures, one by one, old enemies gathered as allies.

Like Rachel had learned to expand her skill set with growing, the Ivy women also experimented with using their abilities to fertilize. In war, troops needed to be fed. Together, Seeders and Ivies were able to start a garden in camp and make it flourish beautifully. Last, but not least, brave female Seeder teens kept a steady pace in their returns. Saff and others were busier than ever, training at the point of their arrival.

As the commotion of establishing the Unitas camp settled down, Rachel and the others were assigned tents. For now, Saff and Heather shared a tent. Rachel was assigned one all to herself, per her request. She hadn't woken from a screaming nightmare since leaving South Fortinda, likely thanks to less anxiety brought on by so many eyes on her, but she still had nightmares and would sometimes wake up sweating. She didn't want to disturb anyone.

Entering her tent for the first time, she placed her pack in a wooden chest that had been made for her, then sat down on the cot. She ran her hand over the thin blanket that had been donated by their previous hosts in Arcadia. The dirt floor was reddish, speckled with a few pebbles.

She enjoyed being here with Kaylah and Saff, Ginger and Heather, away from the chaotic, noisy border villages. But she also felt useless. She'd handed off her work with the Guenjalis flower to others, so what was she supposed to do now?

Before she had much time to dwell on the question, footsteps thumped outside her tent.

"Rachel?" a woman asked.

"Yes?" Rachel stood, sticking her head out of the tent.

"Please follow me."

The woman turned, and Rachel did as ordered. Just yards away, the woman led her to Kaylah's larger tent, gesturing for Rachel to go inside. Two guards watched on as she entered.

Expecting to just see Kaylah, Rachel was surprised to be met by an additional leader. Sitting in a chair next to Kaylah was Lionel, a grey-haired Seeder councilman who'd been permanently assigned to the Unitas camp to co-lead with Kaylah.

"Hi..." Rachel said nervously.

He smiled. She barely knew the man, so she wasn't sure how genuine the smile was. "Thank you for meeting with us, Rachel. Please take a seat." He gestured to a third chair in the tent.

She sat down.

"You don't need to look so worried, Rach," Kaylah said. "This isn't the principal's office." She winked.

Rachel settled in with more ease.

"But what we're about to discuss should not be taken lightly," Lionel added.

Kaylah sat up straighter in her chair. "Also true."

Lionel scrutinized Rachel. "Her Highness assures me you know how to be discreet? How to keep a secret?"

Rachel looked between them and nodded.

"Good," he said. "Even if you choose not to participate, you will not be allowed to discuss what's shared in this meeting with anyone."

"Okay..." She threw a questioning glance at Kaylah. "Even Saff?"

"No one," Lionel said.

That didn't sit quite right with Rachel, given how much Saff had struggled to trust her and Unitas. But Kaylah nodded.

"Okay. I won't say a word."

Kaylah crossed her legs. "Great. We're here to discuss a mission. It's ... not a small favor." She scanned Rachel's face. "I—I mean *we*—need a, uh, spy." She glanced at Lionel. "Ambassador?"

He nodded. "Ambassador."

Spy? Ambassador? Rachel hadn't exactly been trained as either.

"To do what?"

"You don't have to say yes, but I'd like you to go behind enemy lines, helping in my kingdom," Kaylah said.

Rachel blinked in shock.

Kaylah's lips twisted into a smirk. "With Guillen."

Rachel's stomach knotted as she looked between the two leaders. She wanted to see Guillen, but this wasn't exactly the way she'd imagined it. "Come again? I thought he was coming *here*, to help with research or something..."

Kaylah rested her hands on her knees. "That was the plan before Soren took over. I need your help in a different capacity right now."

"This Guillen, a quote, unquote, Ivy stunt—you've worked with him before?" Lionel asked. "Her Highness seemed to think you would feel comfortable working with him?"

A hint of annoyance flashed across Kaylah's face. "Please stop calling me that. Just call me Kaylah."

"Right, sorry."

Both leaders focused back on Rachel.

"Well, yeah." She wouldn't have phrased it that way. She hadn't so much 'worked' with him, as she'd been *saved* by him, and had developed a tiny, miniscule, kinda huge crush on him. "I trust him. I wouldn't have problems working with him. I just didn't envision myself going behind enemy lines..."

Surely Kaylah wouldn't be so frivolous as to assign a dangerous mission to Rachel just to be a matchmaker, right? "Could I speak to Kaylah alone for a minute?"

Lionel wrinkled his nose. "I think it would be prudent to keep this discussion open between the three of us. If you have any concerns, it's important that I know."

What was Rachel going to say? No? Her best friend—the leader of Unitas, the future queen of the Ivy Kingdom—was asking this of her. And this time, she had the support of the Seeder council. "What do you need me to do?"

"Historically, the disadvantaged population of Ivies without powers has been met with severe punishment for uprisings," Lionel said. "You'll be touring their communities, posing as one of them, to provide a little encouragement."

Kaylah held up her hands. "Nowhere near the palace, I promise. And if Guillen can sneak you out of my kingdom, he can sneak you there and back. Just an ambassador."

"We need more influence from within to weaken Soren's hold," Lionel said. "And to pave the way for Her High— For Kaylah, when we're able to take back the palace to right things."

Rachel didn't immediately respond, pondering the task being asked of her. Part of her yearned to go there—to see what it was like in the Ivy Kingdom, to be there for and with Guillen. But who was she, really? She still wasn't a spy or ambassador.

Kaylah must have read the doubt on her face. "You know, Rach, in the human world, you never once slipped to your best friend that you were a Seeder. And if I hadn't already known your identity, I wouldn't have guessed that you were one— I never spotted any hints of Seeder transformation. No green eyes, yellow hair, any of it. Even when... Well, never."

Rachel picked at her fingernails. That was all true. She'd been so paranoid about discovery that she'd done everything she could to suppress that part of herself. But had that last part Kaylah hinted at really been true? Even when she'd walked in on Rachel hurting herself, not even her eyes had turned green? Seeders often specialized in different powers based on natural skill, or sometimes based on their desire and dedication, like Heather with healing. Perhaps that was one of Rachel's unique gifts, that she was better at concealing Seeder transformations during emotional times.

"And you've been trained to fight and heal, not that we're obviously hoping for any of that," Kaylah added.

That was also true, though so much focus had been placed on healing with Saff at the clinic, Rachel wasn't exactly battle-ready, should she and Guillen meet opposition. "You're sure I'm the best person for this? There's not a soldier or someone else better qualified?"

Lionel didn't have to speak for Rachel to understand his feelings on that topic. He pursed his lips, looking as if he agreed with her. "There *are* definitely other candidates with more impressive résumés."

"We'll train you as much as we can before he gets to camp," Kaylah said. She locked eyes with Rachel. While there was a steady composure to her voice, her eyes reached out in pleading. "We could send someone else, but I want someone I know I can *trust*. With my kingdom. And with Guillen's life."

Rachel read the message loud and clear. Guillen and Kaylah were unfailingly loyal to each other. He was her favorite cousin, one of her best spies. And it made sense that she wanted Rachel with him, out of anyone. The council's cooperation with Kaylah had become increasingly encouraging, but she still wanted to make sure he'd be safe. Some random Seeder going undercover with Guillen wouldn't do. Guillen had once told Rachel that Kaylah herself didn't know who to trust half the time.

"I'll do it."

Relief washed over Kaylah's face. "Thank you," she mouthed.

Lionel drew a deep breath. "Then it's settled. Extra training. We'll brief you more later. And not a word of this to anyone."

"Okay."

After a few more words on the topic, they dismissed Rachel, and she departed Kaylah's tent. Half-dazed, she returned to her own tent and lay down, trying to grasp the reality of what she'd just signed up for. Her heart warmed at the idea of spending time with Guillen, but her stomach knotted at the same time. What if she'd gotten it all wrong when they'd first met? Her brain and nerves protested the mission altogether.

Needing to walk off her jumble of emotions, Rachel got up and strode through camp.

Early afternoon, Saff helped in the camp garden, harvesting moon melons. She'd just sent off her latest pupil to return to her family in proper Seeder lands, and was waiting for a new one to arrive.

Lionel, the camp's councilman, approached her. It was a little surprising to have him single her out to chat, but she'd been friendly with plenty of village elders and council leaders back in South Fortinda.

Her suspicion grew when the topic changed to Rachel.

A request to train a Seeder teenager wasn't new to Saff. However, a request to train *Rachel*, focusing primarily on more advanced fighting techniques, was definitely out of the ordinary.

"Can I ask why fighting?" she asked warily.

"You two come from a border village, right? She may return home soon, and we know she's missed valuable training, so we just want to ensure she's prepared for any eventuality." He wore a politician's smile.

"She's going home? Is this Kaylah's doing?"

He tilted his head to the side. "No. You can ask the girl yourself."

"Yes, of course. I'd be happy to train her."

"Thank you for your services." He gave her a nod.

Saff eyed him with suspicion as he walked away. She asked another Seeder she'd been working with to take care of the melons, and set out to do just that—ask Rachel.

Once she found Rachel, their conversation went nowhere. Rachel shrugged a lot, claiming she was homesick. That couldn't have been further from the truth; she'd seemed so relieved to leave South Fortinda behind. Her anxiety had even seemed to calm a bit with the slower pace of the remote village.

Saff abandoned her line of questioning. She knew who she needed to talk to. This whole thing reeked of Kaylah.

After Saff marched to Kaylah's tent, the guards announced her, and Kaylah let her in. Kaylah sat behind a table covered in research books and scrolls. "Nice of you to visit. How can I help you?" She didn't look up from the table.

"Why am I training Rachel on fighting techniques?"

"Is that what the councilman ordered?" Kaylah drew a line across a page with her finger, still not meeting eyes with Saff. "He said he talked to her and wanted to change her assignment."

"Really?" Saff tucked her hands into her pockets. "And she's going to need those fighting skills back in South Fortinda?"

Kaylah frowned, grasping a pen and jotting something down in a notebook. "It's a pity, really. But she *has* been homesick. I'll miss her."

"*Bull.*" Saff crossed her arms. "What's *really* going on?"

Kaylah finally looked up, leaning back in her chair. She splayed a hand across her chest and opened her mouth as if shocked or offended. "What's this? Are we back to not trusting me again?"

Saff glared.

Kaylah smiled triumphantly. "Funny, because your council finally does. But you know everything, right?"

"No. But I deserve to know what's going on with Rachel."

Kaylah pointed at Saff. "Ya got me. I convinced your council to ship her off to the front lines. We're going to pop some popcorn and see how long she lasts. So you better train her well."

"You're not funny. You know that, right?"

Kaylah shrugged. "I don't know. It seems to me like *you're* the one who can't take a joke."

Saff shook her head, examining Kaylah. She'd spent enough time with her now to recognize when she was deflecting, when she was putting on a facade. "You know, you once told me that I had the talent of being a pain in the ass."

Kaylah grinned.

"You know *your* talents? Being flippant and callous."

Kaylah's grin melted away. Saff had hit a nerve.

"Please, just tell me what's going on," she asked, simply and to the point.

Kaylah kept quiet, closing the book she'd been studying. "You know, Saff. You're a mentor. Not a council member. Not a soldier. Not a politician or strategist of any sort." Kaylah set the book on a large stack next to her desk. "You don't *need* to know."

"Then maybe someone else should train her."

Kaylah sat back down, a small smile crossing her face. "Fine. But *she* wanted you to be the one to train her."

"That's unfortunate. She wants me to train her. I want to know the truth. We don't always get what we want." Saff turned to exit the tent.

"Wait," Kaylah called.

Saff sighed, facing her once more. "Yes?"

Kaylah gestured to an empty seat, and Saff sat. "Do you know why you and Rachel were reassigned to work together after you brought me to your council?"

Saff had assumed it was because the council was too busy with the war, and that they'd needed Saff and Rachel working where they'd already been trained. "I guess maybe not..."

"Rachel vouched for you."

Saff swallowed, guilt washing over her.

"To me, and to your council. And I vouched for the both of you. And I worked my ass off to do my best to ensure you weren't punished to satisfy your council's pride."

"Just tell me," Saff whispered, pleading.

Kaylah buried her face in her hands, mumbling from behind them. "I know you care about her. But why was she assigned the most stubborn Seeder in existence to be her mentor?"

With a measure of satisfaction, Saff let out a breathy chuckle. "I was basically raised a shut-in, only child. Blame it on my human parents." She pictured them in the human world, hoping they were okay. "You earned the council's trust—that's great. But don't I deserve something after trusting you with the names and locations of my family and other human host families in the human world? Plus, after we brought you to our council, I vouched for you too. I may have been hesitant, but I signed up for this."

Kaylah dropped her hands, staring at Saff, seemingly worn down.

Saff pointed to the tent door flap. "No one else out there knows Rachel like I do. They'll buy this 'she was homesick' crap. I know how to keep a secret, if that's what you're all worried about."

After a calculating moment of silence, Kaylah sat up straight again. "If I tell you, you can't speak of it to anyone. I can't even have your council knowing that I told you."

"Done."

"Remember those two guards outside of the tent are not only here to babysit me, but also to protect me, okay?"

Kaylah needing to be protected after disclosing something to Saff? That wasn't at all foreboding. "That sounds like a promising start."

"She'll be working a low-profile mission on the other side of the realm."

"Other side of the realm?" Saff narrowed her eyes. "Why do I have a feeling you don't mean southern Seeder lands?"

"She'll be safe."

Saff's heart dropped. "Like hell she will! What kind of thanks is that for your friend's loyalty? You really are marching her up to death's door."

Kaylah shushed her, pointing to where the guards stood on the other side of the tent door. "She'll be fine. She won't be alone."

"Who will be with her? I can go." Saff's mind flashed to Devin, not sure why she'd volunteered.

"No. She'll be working with one of my best spies."

Saff read Kaylah's face. "Who?"

"Guillen."

"Your cousin? The one she has a thing for?"

Kaylah rolled her eyes. "Yes. Guillen is my cousin. They'll keep each other safe."

"No."

"It's not your choice."

Saff was flabbergasted, unable to believe the council had agreed to this plan. "Even *if* she comes back alive... Do you... Remember how I said you were callous? Hasn't she been through enough? She was lucky to escape your kingdom with her life last time. Don't pretend she came out the same girl you once knew."

Kaylah looked away with a pained expression. "She's doing better. And... Well... She's the best person for the job. It's not up for debate. I've known her since we were little girls. I think she can handle it."

Rachel needed community, and support from people around her, not to be isolated and marching into a den of wolves.

Saff stood, preparing to exit the tent.

"What are you going to do?"

More than she was angry, Saff was disappointed, hurting for Rachel, that she was being used for Kaylah's agenda again. "I'm going to go talk some sense into her."

Rachel ambled to the edge of camp, pensive. She fought her fears of the task ahead of her, choked down the dislike of lying to Saff, and battled her usual onslaught of guilt. Nodding at a couple of Ivies as she passed, she allowed herself to savor the satisfaction of having helped move Unitas forward.

Finding a soft patch of white clover, she sat down. The normal drama played through her head—the hurt her actions had caused others, her own pain from betrayal, attack, and torture. Recently, though, she'd mostly dwelt on the realization that she honestly didn't know whether she was all that likeable.

Tyler, her first kiss, had only kissed her because of spin the bottle. Jeremy, her first date, had probably only asked her out because she'd grown a bra size over the summer break between ninth and tenth grade. David—Prince Soren—had only dated her to use her. And Zeus was only interested because he had limited options, tucked away in that tiny village.

Rachel was no Kaylah. She wasn't a supermodel with full lips and jet-black hair. She wasn't even Saff, with good grades and quick thinking. Rachel was average, at best.

And why did it even matter if Rachel was likeable? Was she not capable of being alone? Of not having a relationship for two seconds? Hadn't that been the reason she didn't dump Soren after he'd attacked her the first time, in a hot tub?

She wasn't even nice. She'd judged her own brother, Jeff, for not having more trendy clothes. *Who does that?* She'd grown up with a princess for a best friend, a prince for a boyfriend, and a duke for a stepdad, all easily affording what they'd wanted thanks to the queen's coffers in the Ivy palace. The palace that still held three Seeder girls hostage, suffering a daily horror Rachel knew too well.

As she fixated on drugged, hazy memories of the palace, her breathing picked up. She couldn't let herself go down that path. She needed to focus on the good. Or better yet, the *possible* good that she could do. She would be far from the palace. She could make a difference.

Plucking one of the clover blooms, Rachel sniffed it and smiled, the vanilla scent reminding her of baking Christmas cookies with her mom, Samantha, back in the human world. Rachel calmed a bit. Her mom was safe. Rachel could help keep Guillen safe on her upcoming mission. She could make a difference.

Saff scoured the Unitas camp to find Rachel again. Luckily, she *wasn't* easy to find. Saff's prolonged search gave her time to calm down, to think through her approach. She wanted to point out how crazy Rachel was to accept this mission, but remembered all too well how that had worked to dissuade her from wanting to defy council orders to meet up with Kaylah in the first place.

Passing a wild red gooseberry bush, Saff finally spotted Rachel, sitting in a patch of white clover.

"Did you know those are edible?"

Rachel looked up, twirling the little blossom in her fingers. "Oh, yeah. I think one of my sisters taught me that."

"Mind if I join you?"

Gesturing to the ground next to her, Rachel popped the clover blossom in her mouth. "Are we starting training tonight?"

Saff sat cross-legged. "I wanted to talk first." She studied Rachel's face. "You're sure you want to leave camp?"

"Yeah, like I said: I want to go home."

"Hmm. You could continue your training back there. I'd love to visit my family. How about we pack up tonight, and I'll take you home?"

Rachel's mouth hung open for a moment. "I... Well, I want to go alone. After I've had more training."

Saff nodded. "Yeah? You don't want Guillen to take you there either? After your mission?"

Rachel's eyes grew wide. "How'd you find—"

"Kaylah."

"Oh..."

"I wish you'd reconsider," Saff said in a soft voice.

Picking another blossom, Rachel shook her head.

"I worry about you."

"I know what I'm doing this time, Saff." Her tone was confident, but not argumentative.

A fluffy bumblebee buzzed around and landed on a nearby blossom.

"After what you went through at the palace, you're the *last* person that should ever have to go back there."

Rachel tucked her knees up under her chin. "Which is why I'll be the last person they'll expect to be there. I don't plan on wearing a t-shirt stamped 'Prince Soren's Ex-Girlfriend.'"

Saff glanced at the garden and tents in the distance. She had about a thousand arguments she could make, but nothing she'd ever tried seemed to get through to Rachel. "Would you be doing this if it weren't with Guillen? If it were with someone else?"

Rachel's nostrils flared. "I'm going to pretend you didn't just ask that."

"It's a valid question."

"No. I don't think I would. Because I know I can trust him, and I wouldn't go over there with someone I didn't know."

Saff rubbed the back of her neck. "What's it going to take to convince you to stay?"

Leaning in, Rachel glanced around, then whispered loudly, "The war to end."

Saff sighed. "What would you do if I didn't train you?"

"I guess I'd ask Heather."

"No, you wouldn't. She's a better healer, but she's *not* a soldier."

Rachel raised her eyebrows. "Then teach me."

"I'm not a soldier, either. I've never actually taken a life." Saff ran a hand over the tops of the clover around her.

"You've taken *every* class offered in our village, and you wouldn't have the position you do if you weren't good. I have faith in you. I wish you'd have a little in me."

Saff frowned. "I believe in you."

Giving her a half-smile, Rachel stood, dusting off her shorts. "Great, then let's train."

"Well, I..." Saff certainly hadn't planned to leave it at that, to just give up so quickly.

"When we first started training, you told me I was a quick learner, didn't you?"

"Yeah, but..." It was true that she'd complimented Rachel about being talented. What with having her powers suppressed in the human world by Kaylah's poison, Rachel had been given no choice but to work twice as hard as others, so now that she was in her home realm and not poisoned, and adding the energy boost that came with rooting in the Green Lands, she wasn't half bad.

"I'm eighteen now," Rachel firmly asserted. "I'm an adult in *both* Green Lands nations, *and* the human world. The moment I next step foot outside of this camp, you'll cease to be my mentor. But I hope we can still be friends."

Hesitantly, Saff stood to join her. "You know what this feels like? Like I'm handing you a bottle of vodka as you sit in the driver's seat."

Rachel slipped her hands into her back pockets. "If you're so worried about my safety, maybe you should look at it as tossing me a life preserver when I'm in the deep end of the pool."

She was right. Saff still wanted to convince her to let someone else go, but perhaps she could do that *while* training her. "Alright, let's get started."

Chapter 10

Rachel woke well-rested one morning, just over a week after starting intensive training with Saff. She sat on a boulder that gave a good vantage point, a place she'd found for a quiet break to think. Saff had used every argument in the book to dissuade her from going. None of it had made a difference in the slightest.

Surveying the area, Rachel could finally smile with real pride and genuine contentment at what they were doing. Unitas—unity between green folk. Growing gardens, eating, and training together. There wasn't a day that went by without at least one new Ivy Unitas member arriving at camp. Her old friend, Jon, had arrived a few days prior, and they'd enjoyed getting caught up.

The sun was barely rising for the day. The air was crisp and quiet. A sea of beige tents stood firm against a slight breeze.

Rachel pondered her mistakes of the past. She saw the evidence of her attempts to make amends. She found purpose. She looked into her future. What Kaylah was asking of her was terrifying in many ways, but she didn't let that feeling win. The challenge made her feel alive; thinking of the success it might bring was exhilarating. And while she'd never admit it to anyone, she couldn't stop smiling, because it would be a mission with Guillen.

Mulling over one of her previous conversations with Kaylah about Guillen, Rachel asked herself why he was different from Zeus, other than the obvious racial difference. She worked herself into a frenzy analyzing the situation and her feelings. Had she just been hypersensitive when she'd met Guillen? Did she like him because she needed fixing, and he was kind? Or because she needed saving, and he was a project? Or was it that he had been key in literally saving her life? Was it just a friendship, and she'd been manipulated for so long in a fake relationship with Prince Soren that she'd assumed too much?

She made herself sick and gave up on it all. None of the answers could be figured out on her own right then, anyway. Guillen would arrive. They'd work together on the mission. She'd see from there if anything developed.

A scraping from her side broke Rachel's concentration. Jon was scaling the rock to join her. This time he was clean-shaven, unlike when he and Guillen had helped save her and escort her to Seeder borders. She stood and gave him a hug, ecstatic to see his familiar face. He stayed rigid, definitely still not comfortable with hugs.

"Well, look at this." He smiled once she let him go, overlooking the area with her.

"This is my special spot." She gestured at the boulder. "You'll have to keep it safe for me." Jon was one of the few people Rachel could talk about her mission with.

"You've got it. For as long as I'm here."

"I knew I could count on you." She nudged him, then they sat down together. "I'm curious—when was the last time you saw Guillen?" She'd tried to slip it in coolly, though she'd done a poor job of it.

"It's been a while. We've been on vastly different missions."

"Okay." She failed to hide the concern in her voice.

"You're worried about him?"

Rachel picked at her fingernails. "No. I'm sure he's fine. I just thought he'd be here by now. Kaylah said she sent for him a while ago."

"Last I heard, he was on the far side of things. He has a cover to worry about, and lots he can accomplish on the way. Plus, he's got to use those two legs of his. He's fine."

She nodded. "You're right." Movement in the camp caught her attention. A couple dozen occupants made their way from the tents and gardens over to a training area at the far end of camp, near the laundry station. "What's going on?"

He watched them as well. "Training exercises."

Rachel furrowed her brow, zeroing in on the movement. "Just the Ivies?"

A grin grew across Jon's face. "Well, now that I think of it, I do remember seeing Guillen more recently."

Her energy pulsated in her chest. "When?"

"Mmm." He scratched his chin. "About fifteen minutes ago at the camp security tent?"

Her eyes grew wide with excitement. Jon chuckled.

Rachel hopped up, about to jump down from the rock to go meet Guillen. Realizing she may not get to see Jon again before leaving camp, she quickly gave him another hug. "Thank you. Again. For everything you've done. Saving my life. And being here, still, for my people." She beamed. "Our people."

He shared a warm smile with her. "The more people talk like that, the better it sounds. Stay safe, kiddo."

Without further delay, she jumped off of the boulder and sprinted across the camp.

A handful of Seeder guards had been stationed at the entrance to the camp security tent, definitely more than normal. They nodded her in without a single word.

Familiar voices and laughter broke through the silence as she pulled back the tent flap. Guillen stood with his arms crossed, sharing a laugh with Olivia, the nurse who had also helped in Rachel's escape from the Ivy palace.

Kaylah entered right behind Rachel. "Look at that, some of my all-time favorite people."

Rachel gave Olivia a tight squeeze. "I never got to say thank you for how you helped me. Thank you. *So much!* I'm really happy to see you doing well." Only the two of them knew how much Olivia had really done to keep Rachel safe. Not only had Olivia helped with her escape from the palace, she'd disrupted Soren's advances, his assault on Rachel. She could never thank Olivia enough for risking her neck.

"Of course." Olivia gave her a bright smile in return.

Guillen wore a handsome smile as well. This was the moment Rachel had been waiting so many weeks for. His pale blue eyes, soft face, and the large scar on his temple were exactly how she'd remembered. His brown hair was neatly trimmed. A little more awkwardly, Rachel extended her arms, and he accepted, bringing her in for a hug. His embrace was like that of a close friend. The kind she *really* wanted to kiss... Apparently, the attraction was genuine still—she could check that fact off of her mental list.

"I..." She wanted to say 'I missed you,' but was worried it might sound too forward. "I'm glad you're safe. And thanks again, for your part in getting me home."

"Any day." He gave her another smile, before breaking eye contact.

"I'm guessing by your arrival at this hour, that you're rested?" Kaylah asked Guillen. "Or did you walk through the night?"

"I'm set to go when everyone else is." Guillen cracked his knuckles.

"Me too," Olivia said. "We had hoped to arrive last night, but we got so tired that we took a nap."

A pang of jealousy coursed through Rachel. Was Olivia coming now, too? Or … were they an item, and she'd just never known?

"Sounds great," Kaylah said. "We could always use some impromptu training for anyone who might recognize Guillen in daylight." She winked, obviously referencing the diversion Rachel had already witnessed with Jon on the boulder. Kaylah poked her head outside of the tent, speaking to one of the guards. "Please have Craig report to my tent."

"Yes, ma'am."

Kaylah looked between Rachel and the new arrivals. "I'm just going to do a debriefing with these two. Join me at my tent in a few?"

Rachel glanced down at her clothes; it was time to get changed, anyway. "Sounds like a plan."

"Fantastic. Then we can get the show on the road."

Rachel made her way to Kaylah's tent, and the guards allowed her entrance.

Kaylah welcomed her and introduced the newcomer, someone Rachel had seen in camp, but hadn't formally met yet. "Craig is one of the official tattoo artists — also an amazing Ivy stunt."

Rachel and Craig exchanged a handshake. Olivia was present, presumably for numbing. Guillen was also there, sitting in a chair.

Rachel eased herself down on the open chair next to Guillen.

Guillen looked at Rachel with a concerned frown. "You're sure you're up for this?"

She smiled reassuringly. "I'm ready. Plus, I hear Olivia's the best Ivy nurse when it comes to refined medicine."

"I heard that rumor too," Guillen acknowledged, nodding at Olivia. Olivia blushed.

Guillen's demeanor again showed worry. "I just remember … how much you're opposed to this."

His sweet concern warmed her heart. "Thanks. It's worth it."

Kaylah stood in the back of the group and winked at Rachel. "Plus, once the mission is done, I'm sure we can saw that chunk of flesh off and Rach can heal it, in like, two seconds flat, right?"

Rachel laughed. "It's great to hear your concern for me. I know my best friend will *always* have my back."

Kaylah chuckled. "Any last words?"

"Let's get this over with."

Olivia approached, wrapping a vine around Rachel's upper arm. "Just a tiny pinch is all."

Rachel winced more than she needed to for the tiny prick. The numbing poison was fast-acting, and, from what she understood, amazing compared to what humans used for numbing when getting tattoos.

Craig got to work, pulling out a bottle of clear liquid, a clean rag, a small vial of black ink, and a stick with a needle embedded at the end. Rachel would be the first Seeder taking this mark.

As an official Ivy Kingdom tattoo artist, Craig was familiar with the work at hand. He poured a little of the clear liquid onto the rag and wiped down Rachel's upper arm and his tools. It was alcohol, by the smell of it. "You'll need to hold still."

Sitting up straight, Rachel rested her hand on her thigh, holding it in place with her other hand. Craig dipped the needle into the ink, and traced a rough outline. Without speaking, or hesitation, Craig held Rachel's arm, dipped for more ink, and plunged the needle in. With quick and precise movements, the needle dug in. Dozens, hundreds, perhaps even thousands of times.

Rachel observed those around her in the completely silent tent. Kaylah stood still, frowning, with arms folded. Olivia stood straight, her gaze traveling between Craig's hands with a look of curiosity, and Rachel's face, checking on her patient. Guillen sat with a pensive frown, his gaze shifting to the ground anytime his eyes would meet Rachel's. She couldn't tell if it was nerves or guilt.

Craig looked to be in his forties, with shoulder-length curly hair. He was laser-focused on the work. She glanced at his arm, wondering what number hid under his sleeve. What his story was. What it felt like to have to do this to teenagers of his own kind. Ivy 'stunts' were taken from their homes at the age of fourteen to be branded and relocated to stunt communities, denied many freedoms Ivies with powers had. This ink meant the rest of their lives would be spent in hard labor.

Just minutes in, the silence was tense; Craig's work, quick. It felt like overkill to have everyone standing around them to watch. Or at least to not talk. But Rachel didn't know what to say herself. The experience thus far hadn't gone exactly how she'd expected it to go. When she'd agreed to get a tattoo, she'd imagined the buzz of modern equipment. But that wasn't what this was.

Rachel finally dared to turn her head to watch. Craig dipped the needle and poked Rachel's arm. In and out. Over and over again.

She observed how her skin gave way. How her arm moved slightly under the pressure, with each intentional injury.

Poke. Poke. Poke.

It was steady, rhythmic, mesmerizing. The needle deposited the ink in her skin without drawing any blood. Especially odd for Rachel because she knew what it was like to shove a needle into her own skin, drawing blood. In and out. Over and over again.

"Craig, let's take a break," Kaylah said.

"Yes, Your Highness," he replied. A moment later, his voice carried concern. "Are you alright?"

Rachel continued to stare at the ink on her skin. Registering his question, she looked up. Craig shyly pursed his lips. She swallowed.

"Do you need more numbing?" Olivia asked with an equally concerned tone and expression.

There was a warmth behind Rachel's eyes; they'd changed. Then it registered that her breathing was a bit quick. Kaylah wore a deeper frown. Rachel didn't dare look at Guillen.

"Let's go get some fresh air," Kaylah said.

Rachel stared at the beige fabric of the tent, wishing she could shrink from all the eyes on her. "Yeah." She stood and exited as quickly as she could, Kaylah following after her.

They walked several paces from the tent. Kaylah faced her. "Are you okay?"

Rachel returned her energy to her core and focused on her breathing. "Of course." She'd been trying so hard, in preparation, to make sure she could control her energy. And she was normally so good at it. She couldn't slip like this.

"I'm so sorry," Kaylah whispered, taking one of Rachel's hands. "I really didn't think this part through."

Unable to make eye contact, Rachel looked down. "I'm fine. My mind just drifted."

"I never should have asked this of you."

Rachel finally met her gaze, frowning. Kaylah's eyes expressed profound guilt.

"I'm fine. It's just different than I thought it would be."

Kaylah shook her head. "No one would think less of you, if you didn't go through with it."

Rachel bit her lip. She'd been trying to be strong. She wanted to prove herself. She wanted to make a difference. "I'll be fine once it's over. I promise. I just won't look at it."

Reading Rachel's eyes, Kaylah slowly nodded. "I can have Olivia leave the tent. The numbing she gave you should be fine for the whole process. And I can dismiss Guillen, too. Would it help to have less of an audience?"

Rachel's heart raced. She fought tears, fought to keep her energy from traveling again. "No. I don't want people to look at me that way." She glanced at the tent. "None of them know, right? You haven't told anyone?" Rachel had never confided in anyone else about hurting herself. Kaylah had walked in on her doing it. And had helped her through that tough time. Kaylah had also been the *cause* of Rachel having turned down that dark path, by poisoning Rachel, causing her to spiral. Their relationship was complex.

"No!" Kaylah said. "I've never told anyone. Not even Eric, and I tell him everything."

Rachel closed her eyes. "Alright. Then let's just walk back in there and get it done. I'll be fine, I promise. This is too important." Before Kaylah could object or question anything else, Rachel took off back to the tent, putting on a smile as she entered. "Sorry, just tired and kind of out of it, I guess."

"Ready to continue?" Craig cautiously asked.

"Of course."

Kaylah reentered the tent.

Avoiding eye contact with her audience, and forcing herself not to look at the needle again, Rachel fixed her eyes on the table of books tucked in the corner of the tent.

Over an hour later, Craig had repeatedly wiped, dipped, and stabbed. He ran over the lines with a second round before packing up his equipment. Rachel's tattoo matched Guillen's, except hers had the number five in the center, where his had a crown. They'd strategized on which community she should be 'assigned' to, had created a backstory for her, forged paperwork, the whole nine yards.

Once everyone agreed that Craig's work was done, Rachel carefully healed the area, making it appear as though she'd had the tattoo for years.

"Well. That's that..." Rachel said. Beyond grateful for this live-time flashback to be over, she now found herself getting nervous about going. "I think I'm going to double-check that I've packed everything I need, and go find Saff."

"Olivia and I have work to do, so we're going to say our goodbyes right now." Kaylah gave Rachel a long, tight hug. "I'm proud of you. Stay safe. Look out for each other." Kaylah had tears in her eyes. "You're amazing, and brave, and one helluva woman." Kaylah gave her one more quick hug, whispering, "And I'm not the only one who knows that." She pulled back with a wink.

Rachel threw her a dirty look. Couldn't let their special moment go without hinting at romance. She internally mused that perhaps that was what it took to pull off this kind of crazy movement—a hopeless romantic.

"You stay safe too. Could you have imagined a year ago that we'd be where we are now?" Rachel let out a breathy chuckle. "Well, I guess you had a better idea of where we'd be. I was thinking about college."

Kaylah laughed. "Right? Ten times better than college." She smiled softly. "I love you. Guillen knows how to send word through the network. I'll keep in touch as much as I can."

Kaylah turned to Guillen, giving him a tight squeeze. "I'm sorry we don't have more time to catch up. I love you."

"You too," he said, not shying away from the hug.

Olivia offered Rachel another hug as well, and she accepted. "So, you're not coming with Guillen and me?" Rachel asked.

Olivia looked confused. "No..."

Rachel was just as confused. She'd obviously misunderstood something earlier. "Well, I'm glad you'll be able to help your women here learn more about your powers."

"Thanks. Stay safe." Olivia and Kaylah left the tent. Craig offered a handshake and followed the others out. Guillen and Rachel were left alone.

Rachel swung her arms with nervous energy.

"I, uh, thought they'd told you it would just be the two of us."

"What? Yeah." She clasped her hands together to stop her fidgeting.

"Okay." He seemed unsure. "But you thought Olivia was coming?"

"Oh. Yeah, I just... No. I know it's just you and me."

It was silent for a moment. Painfully silent.

"You're going to be okay with it just being the two of us?"

Would she be okay with that? Was that question aimed at the butterflies in her stomach?

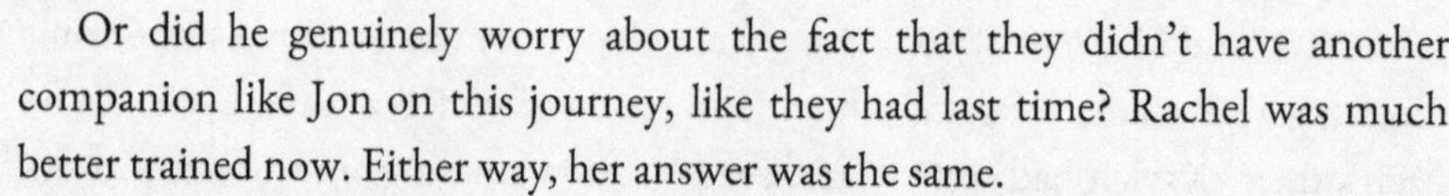

Or did he genuinely worry about the fact that they didn't have another companion like Jon on this journey, like they had last time? Rachel was much better trained now. Either way, her answer was the same.

"I'm fine with it being just you and me."

"Alright."

And then they just stood there again, like two people who hadn't shared hours and days of easy conversation before.

Rachel lifted a hand to her new tattoo. "I'm sorry if that was hard for you to watch. If it brought back any bad memories or anything."

He waved a dismissive hand. "No. Not at all. I'm just really impressed, is all. Can I take a closer look?"

She twisted to show her tattoo. His hand moved up to it, softly rubbing over the fresh ink. His touch took her breath away. She focused on keeping her energy in check, which was pretty silly for something so innocent. She quickly admitted to herself that she *really* hadn't just imagined her attraction to him this whole time. And it would be a long journey with him ... for better or worse.

"It looks just like it should," Guillen said.

She nodded. "Good. Gotta make it look like the real deal, right?" She smiled, noting his hand still on her arm after rubbing at the ink. "Won't just wash or rub off. Like any good waterproof mascara, my mom would say."

He removed his hand, sliding it down her arm as he went. He looked down, pursing his lips.

"What's up?"

He met her gaze with narrowed eyes. "What's mascara?"

She arched an eyebrow. "Makeup? I'm assuming Ivies use it like Seeder girls do." Kaylah certainly did... "More natural stuff, definitely not as good as the commercially sold human kind, but it does the job better than nothing."

"Aha. Yeah. I know what makeup is. I think my sister uses some."

"Sister? I don't remember you talking much about your family when we met before."

Guillen shoved his hands in his pockets. "Yeah. Um ... parents. I'm the oldest. Brother in the middle, then my sister."

Rachel sat back down, and Guillen followed suit. "Are you close?"

Guillen crossed his arms, leaning back. "Mmm ... complicated. I'd say I'm closest to my sister and father."

"I get the good big-brother vibes."

He grinned. "What about your mother? The human one. It sounded like you were pretty close. Did you get to see her?"

Rachel's heart hurt at the mention of Samantha. This mission would take Rachel further from the cave, from the letters she would sporadically get. "I did get to see her. I think she'll be okay."

His smile widened a bit as he stood back up. "Guess I didn't just come here to get caught up. Have you had breakfast? Do you need help packing, or anything like that?"

"I ate, thanks. Did you guys?" Rachel stood to join him.

"Yeah, Olivia and I had plenty of food."

"Okay, great." She pointed to the tent door flap. "Well, if you want, you can wait here while I finish up, or you can keep me company."

"If I won't get in your way, I'd love to join you," he said shyly.

"Sounds great." She smiled. "Follow me."

It was only a few yards to Rachel's small tent. They both ducked inside.

"So, the makeup thing. What was that called again?" he asked.

She brushed her bangs to the side. "Mascara."

"And what does mascara do?"

"Longer, darker, thicker eyelashes."

He squinted, studying her face. "Are you wearing any?"

"No. No makeup since I left my village. Not really worth the hassle."

"I don't think you need any."

Her cheeks warmed as she folded up the blanket on her cot. "Thanks. Every girl could stand to hear that now and again."

"I guess you're right about Ivy girls maybe wearing that stuff, too. At first, I thought it was a human-world reference. But maybe it's just a girl thing."

Rachel chuckled, setting the blanket on the end of the cot. "Pretty sure the vast majority of guys, in either realm, are clueless about cosmetics."

Guillen pulled a folded piece of paper from his pocket. "Kaylah gave me this. A list of observations she's made from being around your people. And in the human world. We'll have time to go over it to help you blend in, so you don't accidentally say the wrong thing in public."

He handed Rachel the paper to look over. "It's not like the residents in stunt communities have never heard things about the human world, but we're just not taught as much, you know. We're more ... isolated ... ignorant..." He pressed his lips together.

Rachel tried to hide a frown. The way they were treated was rotten. Guillen had at least been afforded a more rounded education, having been provided tutors until he was eighteen. But that was considered an extra privilege for someone born without powers in the Ivy Kingdom, a privilege only given to him because he was so close to the Crown in the royal bloodline.

Rachel tucked the note in her pocket. "Take a load off. I shouldn't be too long." She gestured for Guillen to sit on her cot.

He lay down on it. "Nice. You're going to miss something like this as we cross the woods."

She blinked. He was casually stretched out on her bed, his biceps naturally flexed as he crossed his arms under his head for support. She swallowed and turned.

Focus on the mission.

"I'm sure I will. But I'll survive." She rummaged through her packed bag, double-checking she had the most important things with her. She glanced at the folded clothes she'd worn that morning, and then down at the ensemble she'd recently changed into. "How do I look?" She raised her hands and turned full circle.

Guillen wore a soft smile. "I think you look great."

"Good." She turned back to her bag, checking the pockets.

"Does my opinion matter that much?"

She faced him. "Of course it does. Don't get me wrong, I trust whoever smuggled these clothes over here, and Kaylah. But Kaylah's spent most of her life at the palace or in the human world, you know? You'd know better the right fashion for a girl in that region and type of community, right?"

"Right. That." He cleared his throat. "Yeah, you'll blend in great."

She nodded, that much more confident in the success of their mission.

She finished checking her bag. "Then again, I'm asking a guy for fashion advice. Makeup and fashion, all in one day."

He chuckled. "I may not know what all the things are called, but I'm not blind."

"Oh, dang it," she said, pulling her lightkeeper out of the last pocket. "This would be bad if my bag was searched by the wrong people. Definitely not something your kingdom would use."

"What is it?"

Rachel held it in her palm, kneeling next to where he lay on the cot. "Clear quartz on the top, jade stone on the bottom."

"Yeah, I saw some bigger ones out there. What's it do?"

She demonstrated with a touch of a finger at the top of the dome. It lit up, the jade releasing the energy she'd previously deposited into it. "Good as a lamp or flashlight. Would be handy at night, but I guess you guys more commonly use beeswax candles?"

"Yeah," he said, still looking at the lightkeeper. "It's amazing, what your people are capable of."

Rachel ran her hand across the jade to call the energy back. The powers were nice, though they sometimes felt more like a consolation prize since she hadn't been able to actually choose what world she'd live in. She stood, approaching the trunk in the tent. "Yeah. Our guys can turn them on and off, since they can channel energy. But we girls have to initially deposit the energy because they can't share theirs in that way."

After placing the lightkeeper in the wooden chest with the other belongings she was leaving behind, Rachel flung her bag over her shoulder. "Well, I think that's it."

"Rachel?" a deep voice called from outside her tent. She stiffened... *Oh crap.* Zeus had been making the trek to camp from his village on a regular basis. He helped in the garden and often dropped by for a visit.

"I'll be right back," she said to Guillen as she left the tent.

"Hey! They said you're actually taking off today." Zeus held a Guenjalis flower.

"Yeah, just heading out now." She was starting to sweat, wishing he'd talk quieter. "It was nice of you to drop by."

He handed her the flower. "I know it's delicate, so it won't last long like this, but I thought it was fitting."

She gave him a polite smile. "Thanks. That's sweet."

He reached for her hand and raised it, kissing it. "Don't be a stranger."

Her heart sped up as she desperately hoped Guillen wasn't seeing or hearing any of this. She gave Zeus a quick hug. "You keep up the good work. I'm excited to hear how the healing of the land goes! And thanks for everything you taught me."

"Of course. Be safe." He flashed his warm, friendly smile, giving her hand a quick squeeze before taking off.

She turned around, red-faced, nervously tugging on her ear. She then noticed she'd left a gap in the tent door that Guillen could have possibly seen out of, though she wasn't sure he had.

"Well ... um ... a couple more people to see on our way out," she announced after entering the tent.

Guillen hopped up. "Lead the way."

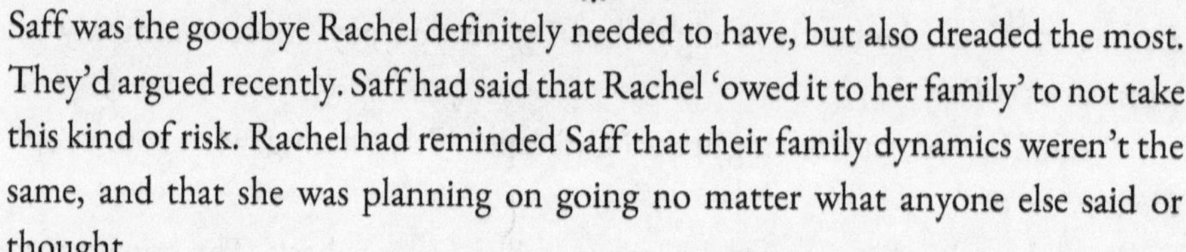

Saff was the goodbye Rachel definitely needed to have, but also dreaded the most. They'd argued recently. Saff had said that Rachel 'owed it to her family' to not take this kind of risk. Rachel had reminded Saff that their family dynamics weren't the same, and that she was planning on going no matter what anyone else said or thought.

But they'd forged a good friendship, and since they'd been the two to open this path, Saff deserved a proper goodbye. Saff had already been up at dawn, training new girls on energy exercises. Rachel stood nearby, hands folded in front of her, waiting for a moment where she wouldn't be interrupting too much. Guillen stood next to her.

Saff spotted her and frowned. "Alright, five minutes, everyone." She strode over to Rachel, offering her arms. "You're sure you know what you're doing?"

Rachel nodded, accepting the hug. "I've never been more sure of anything. In either world."

Saff sighed, surveying her face. "You're crazy, you know. Going back there."

"Yeah, well, I'd say the pair of us have made a lot happen by being a little crazy, haven't we?" Rachel smirked.

Saff cracked a smile. "Yeah, yeah, yeah."

"Do you want to see it?" Rachel twisted, raising her shoulder.

Saff wrinkled her nose. "I guess so..."

Rachel rolled up her sleeve to show the tattoo.

After a momentary glance at it, Saff shifted her focus to Guillen. "You're going to keep her safe?"

He gave her a single nod. "Absolutely."

Saff kept her gaze on him, straight-faced. "If not, I'll hunt you down myself."

Rachel furrowed her brow and unrolled her sleeve. "Okay, Mom."

Guillen chuckled.

"By the way, Saff—this is Guillen. Guillen—this is Saff."

They shared a handshake, and to Rachel's relief, Saff didn't say anything or give any looks that indicated they'd talked about him before.

Saff's attention flickered to the flower Rachel was holding, and she bit her lip.

Don't you dare.

"Is that from Zeus?" Saff smiled. "He's going to miss you."

Rachel's nostrils flared as she considered how to discreetly flash a look of rage, but it was hard with Guillen right there. "He's really *friendly,* isn't he?"

Looking down, Saff ground her shoe into the dirt. "Well, we'll *all* miss you, to be fair." She wrapped her arms around Rachel again, who stood stiff this time.

Saff pulled back, frowning, and added in a more apologetic and sincere tone, "Be safe. Come home soon."

Rachel sighed. "You be safe too. Remember what you promised?" They'd had a good heartfelt conversation recently, and Saff knew exactly what that meant.

Saff adopted a far-off look, rubbing her chin. "Eat my vegetables and wash behind my ears?"

"Right..."

Saff held her by the arms. "I'll do my best to play nice with the other kids."

"Good. Then I'll keep up my end of the deal and stay alive."

Rachel and Guillen headed out of camp, stopping for a hug with Heather as they went. Rachel promised Heather she'd deliver a letter to her family back in South Fortinda, which Kaylah and Lionel had already arranged for someone else to do. Guillen picked up his bag at the entrance, where he'd left it with the guards to search and watch.

As soon as they left camp, the silence was painful. It would be days until they'd reach Ivy territory. Just the two of them, and all the time in the world.

Chapter 11

Not long after watching Rachel and Guillen leave, Saff gave her trainees a longer break. Camp would be terribly lonely without Rachel.

Saff approached Kaylah's tent. Once the guards announced her presence, she was permitted entrance. Kaylah sat at her table, next to a tall stack of books and a jumble of scrolls. She wrote on a piece of paper without looking up. "How can I help you?"

"Um..." Saff hesitated, nervous about how this conversation would go. "How's it going?"

"Everything is dandy." Kaylah set down her pen and blew on the fresh ink. "Just coming to say hi?"

"Well..." Saff shifted her weight from one foot to the other. "No. I mean, I hope things are going alright..."

Not responding, Kaylah grabbed a short candle of golden wax and a striker, lighting the wick and setting the candle upright in a holder as she folded up the paper she'd written on. She removed a ring from her finger, dripped some of the wax onto the folded paper, then pressed her ring into it.

It was cool to watch. Some things still felt foreign in the Green Lands, like the lack of technology. After spending her childhood in the human world, Saff sometimes still patted her pockets for her cell phone when she wanted to know the time.

"If you're too busy, I can come back later."

Kaylah finally looked at Saff, standing and grasping the sealed letter. "You're fine. Just a sec." She crossed the tent and leaned out of the door flap, handing the letter to one of the guards, rattling off some instructions.

"Sorry about that." She returned to her table, giving Saff her full attention.

"Who was that letter to?" Saff asked.

Kaylah studied Saff, looking as if she was deciding how to respond. This time, it wasn't sarcasm or defensiveness about how Saff ought to mind her own business. "Your council."

"Gotcha." She moved her hands awkwardly from her front pants pockets to her back pockets. "But how *are* you doing?"

Kaylah arched an eyebrow. "Me, personally? I'm fine."

This conversation was twice as awkward with Saff still standing. "Mind if I sit?"

"Yeah, sorry." Kaylah gestured to a chair. "Where are my manners?"

Saff sat. "I guess I just wanted to see how you're doing, and if you think they got out of camp without anyone suspecting anything, and, you know, stuff..."

Kaylah nodded. "Hmm. I'll miss her while she's gone. I'm confident they got out cleanly. And ... stuff?"

Saff shyly averted her eyes. "Well, I guess I'm here because of a favor."

"Did she ask you for the same favor she asked me?"

Wait, what? Saff had wanted to ask Kaylah for a personal favor... *Oh...* Rachel had likely tried to prod Kaylah to make peace with Saff as well. "Maybe. Rachel said something about making sure you learned to understand that I'm always right. About everything." She tried to suppress a smile.

Kaylah smirked knowingly. "Funny. I swear she gave me the same talk. But she said that *I'm* the one who's always right."

Saff gave her a genuine smile. "For what it's worth, I'm sorry. You know, you sometimes remind me of one of my sisters that I knew in high school. We didn't always get along. I can ... sometimes be a bit judgmental. Especially in high-stress situations."

"I just wish you'd give me a little credit now and then."

Biting her lip, Saff crossed her legs. "Yeah. Did I mention I grew up as an only child? Well, kind of. And that my parents were overprotective, and kept me in the dark? I just ... don't like being out of the loop."

Kaylah glanced at her table full of books and scrolls. "I can appreciate where you're coming from. But you need to realize you can't control everything, and you don't always know what's best for everyone."

"I know. Though ... that's what you're aiming for, right? As a queen, to have control and decide what's best for everyone?"

Narrowing her eyes, Kaylah changed her tone. "Wow. That's the shortest olive branch I've ever seen. If this is how you put aside our differences," she pointed to the door flap, "then you can—"

"Wait." Saff furrowed her brow, confused. "I genuinely didn't mean that as an insult."

Kaylah crossed her arms, obviously unbelieving.

"I just meant... You still want to be queen, right?"

"Yes."

"That's a lot of power for one person. Have you considered finding a way to reorganize things? Have elections or something?"

Kaylah softened, but only a little. "Show me the perfect form of government, Saff, and I'll consider it. This is my birthright, and the way our Mother Vines work. And once I rightfully sit on my throne, I plan to address the balance of power within my kingdom." She grabbed a water bottle from the floor, unscrewing the cap. "Don't you think your leaders and I have discussed our long-term goals? Concessions?"

Saff blushed as Kaylah took a swig. Of course they had. "For the record, I think you'll make a good queen." The fact that the council had been working side by side with her had genuinely surprised Saff. So far, she was doing a good job.

"Thanks," Kaylah said graciously.

While concerned about how things might work out in the long run, Saff wouldn't dare bring that up. Even if Kaylah could win and keep her kingdom, and fulfill her promises, what would happen if the next ruler just reversed all of their hard work? And who would that next ruler even be? The power of the Mother Vines passed down through the female bloodline. Kaylah loved a human. A man who couldn't enter the Green Lands, and couldn't give her kids.

"How's Eric?" Saff asked.

A twinge of longing flashed across Kaylah's face before she settled on a barely there smile. "He's good. Haven't seen him since you and I paired up, but I sometimes get letters through the cave."

Saff nodded, sorry for her. Kaylah had to be terribly lonely. Politics and leadership galore, but now her best—and locally, only—friend had left. At least Ginger was still here to keep her company. "Why doesn't your dad—well, you know, Nathan—come to camp?"

Kaylah looked down, lining up a few scrolls. "Your council feels he would be more useful on the human-world side of things right now."

Stopping herself from asking more questions like she wanted to, Saff decided it was best to bring up the reason she'd originally come to visit. "So the favor I came here for doesn't have anything to do with Rachel, really."

Kaylah straightened in her chair, taking a deep breath. "Shoot."

"Well, I..." Saff glanced at all the books and scrolls. The stack had grown since her last visit. "I guess, without Rachel, I'm trying to figure out my part. You talked about wanting my help with research, but I haven't done any since we set up camp. And I like training these new girls, but I guess I just..."

The truth was, Saff was a little lost at sea without Rachel. Rachel had been a special assignment for her. And Saff was starting to question a lot about herself and her own path amidst everything happening around them.

"Sorry," Kaylah said. "The research—I haven't had much time, myself. And I'd like to be here to go over it, so I don't want to just hand it off to anyone."

"Right." Saff fidgeted with her hands. She was also homesick. She and Heather got the occasional letter all the way from South Fortinda, but it was so far away. It wasn't fair for Saff to ask for what she wanted, not when Kaylah couldn't be happy in the same way. But she needed to. "I, uh, I understand new people allowed into camp have to be approved by both yourself and Lionel?"

"Yes..."

Saff rubbed at an invisible speck of dirt on her pants. "My husband was a fantastic teacher for me when I first got my powers. I think he'd be great here with me in camp as more girls return through the cave."

Kaylah gave her an understanding smile. "I wouldn't want you to be too exhausted, doing so much on your own. I might be able to do something about that."

Saff's heart somersaulted. "Thank you."

"Sure thing." Kaylah stood. "Is there anything else? I've got a meeting I need to head to."

Saff also stood. "No. That's it."

"You know," Kaylah picked up a pack, swinging it over her shoulder, "I think that me sending for your husband should earn me some forgiveness points for shipping Rachel off to Mordor."

Saff chuckled. "I don't know." She pointed at the ring on Kaylah's finger. "You didn't even send her with anything 'precious.'"

Kaylah busted out laughing. "Are you a Lord of the Rings nerd? Rach totally didn't get a reference I made before."

"My best friend growing up was a guy, so I've seen my fair share of fantasy and sci-fi." She surveyed Kaylah, the picture of traditional femininity. "I'm kinda surprised you're into it."

Kaylah held a hand to her chest. "Judging a book by the cover?" She winked. "Not a superfan, really. Eric made me watch with him once. The *extended* version."

That surprised Saff a little as well. Eric looked more like he ought to be commanding a yacht club or a gym rather than munching popcorn while geeking out on a couch. But then again, Saff barely knew him, and he'd spouted off all sorts of impressive information when she'd met with him and Kaylah back at the human-world safe house. About encryptions, codes, security walls, all of that.

Grabbing her water bottle, Kaylah approached Saff. She had to have read her mind. "He's just the way I like him—sexy and smart."

Saff smiled. She threw one last glance at the books and scrolls. "I need to get back to my girls, too. But let me know when you need help with research?"

"Will do." Kaylah reached for the tent door flap, then paused. "I do," her voice lowered, "have one favor to ask, something you can help me with."

"Okay?"

Kaylah sighed. "Well, there's one pain-in-the-ass Seeder I know who seems to need to control everything." They shared a knowing grin. "But I do understand her predicament, because I struggle with that as well."

"Okay..."

"I used to do the majority of recruiting for Unitas. Ever since Soren cut me off, I've had to rely solely on other Unitas members to take care of that. It just makes me a little uneasy to not know everyone here in camp. Maybe help me keep an eye out for suspicious activity?"

That apprehensive, nerve-filled feeling crept into Saff's mind. Everyone showing up at the cave and Neutral Woods entrance was thoroughly interviewed, but still... "You trust your people, though, right?"

"Of course."

"Yeah, I can help keep an eye out."

Kaylah wrapped an arm around Saff's shoulders, opening up the tent flap. "Fantastic. If we keep up more conversations like this, I might even be able to tolerate you by the time we end this war." She winked again.

Saff chuckled. "I might be able to tolerate you, too."

Chapter 12

A few minutes into the open Neutral Woods, the mumble and rustle of the busy training camp faded, the only sound the crunch of fallen twigs and branches under Rachel and Guillen's feet.

Rachel thought about the time Kaylah had described Guillen as 'not very talkative,' but she really wished he'd be the one to get the conversation started. Glancing in his direction, and with no response, she decided to jump right in. "I guess we'll have lots of time to go over strategy and everything, right? And catch up." She smiled.

He turned and smiled back. "I look forward to it."

They kept walking … awkwardly…

"So, is that a human tradition?" He pointed to the flower Rachel wished she wasn't holding, but hadn't known how to ditch without being disrespectful.

"Yeah, kind of weird, right? Cutting flowers and giving them to someone? I'm assuming you guys don't do it?"

"No. Not an Ivy thing, either." He glanced around, doing a regular check to ensure they were in the clear. "What's it supposed to mean?"

She twirled the flower in her fingers. "Just something nice, and fresh, and pretty. They can mean different things based on what kind of flower it is, or the color."

"What does that one mean?"

She was happy to explain human customs to Guillen, given he'd been denied that education. But this … was uncomfortable. "I actually don't think we have this flower back in the human world. Zeus, the guy that gave it to me—we worked together on the project to help heal the land."

"Sounds like you've kept busy. That's really great." Guillen adjusted his pack. "What about the kissing thing?"

Her eyes grew wide as she stared straight forward, tight-lipped. Had he seen something from the tent? Kaylah wouldn't have dared to mention anything else, right?

"He kissed your hand before you hugged him," he clarified.

She swallowed a couple of times before answering. He had seen the exchange... And ... she couldn't tell if Guillen was genuinely confused, or if he was trying to razz her, or if he was fishing...

"That? You've never seen anyone do that?"

"Or maybe that's a Seeder thing?" He shrugged. "I guess I sometimes don't know where traditions come from, right?"

"A kiss on the hand can mean different things. Just a hello or goodbye. It's kind of old-fashioned." She cleared her throat, glancing out of the corner of her eye to try and read his face.

"Okay."

Rachel stopped, turning to face him. She squinted. "You really haven't seen anyone do that before?" He'd expertly deflected a question about himself before, when they first met in a cave by the palace. "You didn't answer my question. And if I remember right, you're good at that."

His straight face changed into a smirk.

"I knew it!"

He chuckled. She loved the sound of it, and the way his eyes squinted when he laughed. "Sorry. I'm sure your boyfriend will miss you a lot. I'll try to get you back in one piece."

She shook her head. "This flower, as lovely as it is, was a kind gesture. From a *friend*. And not very practical. So, no offense to him, but I think I'll be leaving it here." She bent over and gently placed it on the ground before continuing to walk.

Guillen strolled alongside her again, grinning for another minute.

It was only fair for Rachel to throw something back at him and suss out where he was in relation to the singles arena. "So, you and Olivia arrived together. She's really great. I didn't realize you guys knew each other that well."

"Oh, Olivia? Yeah, she's nice, isn't she? Maybe I should ask her on a date when we get back, do you think?"

Rachel bit her tongue. That was *not* the direction she'd been intending to go at all. But she had no claim on Guillen. They were technically just friends. "Well ... I ... uh... I don't know your type."

"She's not my type," he calmly replied.

Perhaps it was best to leave it at that. They were both single, and she wasn't even the slightest bit mad about it; but she figured she'd give the butterflies in her stomach a rest. "So, what have you been up to lately? What damsels in distress have you been rescuing, and all that?"

"Hmm... No damsels. I did some location scouting. Went through the different stunt communities, getting a feel for who might be on our side, making connections to help us along the way. But I also went back to work for a while."

She raised her eyebrows. "Working construction? Why would you still be doing that?"

"Connections to the palace or not, I only have so much vacation time, especially during an active war."

"They really don't know you're in Unitas yet?" Her mouth hung open. "I figured, when you came to save me, that they'd know..."

"You were kind of out of it at the palace, so you might not have noticed the hood I was wearing at the time. That wasn't just a fashion statement. We'd hoped we could get you out cleanly, and that I wouldn't be identified. And, well, no one ever came for me." Guillen grinned. "Plus, Soren's cocky. He underestimates me." He shrugged. "I'm nothing to him. We have that on our side."

Rachel grinned from ear to ear. "He would, wouldn't he? I, for one, am glad to have you on our side."

They continued to chat, getting caught up and preparing for their mission. Guillen was fascinated to hear how Seeders without powers lived. He was still missing a lot of time from his day job with this campaign, but luckily his supervisor was a sympathizer, so he was able to help with forged paperwork, movement orders, and the like.

Rachel gave Guillen the highlight reel of how things had gone for her since they'd parted ways. Conversation flowed easily between them. She was grateful that if she had to traverse the Green Lands on foot, and go into enemy territory with anyone, that it was with him.

In the early afternoon, Rachel decided to listen to her stomach's complaints. She opened her knapsack and searched through the options she'd packed.

"How about we take a break for lunch?" he suggested.

"That's okay, I can keep walking while we eat."

"Mmm. Yeah, but I want a break."

"Oh. Yeah, sure."

They found a log in a shaded area, and Rachel sat down. Guillen chose to lie on the ground instead, propping his feet up on the log. "You may be all energetic, but I've been walking and sleeping on the ground for days." He closed his eyes and grimaced as he twisted his neck, as if trying to make it pop.

"Sorry, I didn't think about that. Let me know whenever you need a break." She glanced down at his shoes, his elevated feet. "I could help with that, maybe heal a little, so you're not so tired or hurting. Like I healed my feet after our escape, before Jon got me shoes."

"No thanks," he said.

"You're sure? I discovered with Saff that I'm a pretty good masseuse, learning how to incorporate my energy and everything."

"I'm fine."

She raised her eyebrows, unwrapping a granola bar from a dried corn husk. "Do you have gross feet? Are you afraid I'll judge you? I'm not weird about feet."

He shook his head.

She squinted. "Are your feet ticklish?"

He flashed a silly face like he'd been caught in a secret.

"Ooh, now *that* is good to know." She looked him over from head to toe. "Where else are you ticklish?"

"Psh! Like I'd tell you or anyone else." He wiggled his eyebrows. "Unless ... you tell me where *you're* ticklish."

She frowned. "But what if I'm not ticklish at all?"

He crossed his ankles, wearing a knowing grin. "With the sincerity in that face, I'm sure that just *has* to be the case."

She laughed before taking a bite of the granola bar. "How about a shoulder massage? You look like you're in pain." Just in case that was too forward, she added, "I'm not coming on to you. I just figure ... it's a long trip."

He drew a deep breath. "Sure. I'd hate to deprive you of an opportunity to practice your skills."

"Your sacrifice will be remembered."

He moved to sit in front of her, breaking out some food of his own to eat. He leaned back against her legs as she sat on the log. She couldn't help but smile, hoping he was feeling the same way she was. But she wanted to take things slow.

Guillen was special. He wasn't a rebound. She'd worried that, even if she'd been right about them sharing an attraction, she'd have to get to know him all over again. But she was surprised by how quickly they were picking up where they'd left off.

After pulling back his shoulders for better posture, she focused energy into her fingertips, and set to work on his knots. "I'm guessing some of these are from your job, too, aren't they?"

He quietly moaned. "Maybe."

"I remember you not liking your construction job. What would you do if you had a choice?"

"You know, I thought about what you said, and I asked myself that question. But it's hard to imagine a lot of other opportunities here. What kinds of jobs do they have in the human world that they don't here?"

The human world seemed so far away sometimes—something she still longed for, despite the energy of the Green Lands realm. But talking about it with Guillen was a fun walk down memory lane. "Gosh, a lot. I could probably entertain you all day with them." She puckered her lips in thought, staring into the distance. "I'm sure you could do anything you put your mind to, you're obviously a determined person. But right off the top of my head, I'm not sure..." She dug a glowing thumb into a particularly big knot. "You and your knives and machetes, though, that makes me think of something funny. People pay for axe-throwing in the human world. Like, they show up at a building, and pay money to chuck sharp objects at a wall."

He laughed and leaned to the side, twisting to look back at her. "Really? You're not making that up?"

"I kid you not."

He straightened back up. "Hmm. Sounds kind of boring for a job every day, to just watch. What about you? What do you want, when all this is said and done?"

She sat pensively, continuing to work on his shoulders. "I... I honestly don't know. I think my life is kind of the reverse of yours. I started out with all the opportunities at my fingertips, and now I'm here, and the only thing I see in my future is this war."

He reached up and rested a hand on hers before turning to look at her again. "It won't be forever."

She smiled at the gesture. "I hope not. It's exhausting." She glided glowing fingertips up his neck, applying pressure. "I do know one thing for sure—one way or another, I'm getting my GED. Soren stole my graduation from me, but I'm not letting him win on that." Guillen probably had no idea what a GED was. "That's just the formal mark that you've completed your basic education in the human world. My grades were good enough that I still should have been able to apply for graduation, and get a diploma in my absence. If my high school hadn't thought I ran away and dropped out... Anyway, I just figured, since we have the cave for rifting now..."

Guillen tilted his neck to each side; a slight pop followed. "Thanks." He stood, offering his hands to help her up. "That's one of the things I like about you. You're smart. And you're not going to let his crap or anyone else's get in your way."

Chapter 13

Rachel and Guillen walked and talked for hours about jobs in both worlds before stopping for a dinner break. They filled up their canteens and sat on some large boulders by a stream, facing each other.

"You're less scared than I thought you would be," he said.

She sloshed around the water in her canteen, staring at it. "Kaylah assured me there haven't been any Ivy soldier sightings this far north. With that camp and community being secret, and past our borders..."

"She's right. I didn't come across a single soldier on my way here. I guess I was just thinking about the mission as a whole."

"Do you think I should be more scared? I don't know." She met his gaze. She'd been so numb. His comment made her wonder if she was being foolish, or perhaps he really didn't think as highly of her as she'd hoped. "I think a lot of it has to do with being with you. I feel safe with you."

He tossed a peanut down to a happy squirrel. "I don't know that you *should* feel more scared. You're just not as combat trained as others, having been back home for such a short amount of time."

She frowned. Despite all of Saff's training, which had even been supplemented by time with some Seeder soldiers, Rachel still wasn't a soldier. "Do you think this is a mistake? I'm sure we could find someone else to help on the mission."

His expression showed a hint of confusion. "No. I didn't mean that at all. I wouldn't want to do this mission with anyone else." He raised his eyebrows. "I mean it. I don't think I would have gone along with it if Kaylah had made me pick a different Seeder."

She bit her lip. "You picked me? It wasn't just Kaylah's decision?"

His eyes gave off as much warmth as his smile. "I could rally by myself, but we need you to be the face of the Seeder part of this movement. We need to show someone who's passionate, brave, and caring. Kaylah always told me I'd like you, that you were kind. And after meeting you, I couldn't agree more. You're the perfect example of what we're trying to represent."

She blushed, fixating on a scratch on her canteen. She may have been a screwup, but she tried to be a decent person; it had never felt like any sort of extraordinary character trait. "Thanks."

"Hey," he said in a gentle voice, causing her to raise her head. "How are you doing? With everything you've been through?"

She shook her head. "I don't even know how to answer that, to be honest. Did Kaylah warn you I still have nightmares about it? Nothing as bad as before, but we'll need to be careful at night."

"You'll get through this." His voice was as soothing as ever. "And I'll stay close."

"Thank you." She packed up her things before sliding down the boulder.

The rest of the evening, they focused on the work at hand. They talked more about the route they were taking to avoid catching any suspicious eyes, and he filled her in on all things Ivy. They would primarily be going to the stunt communities, but would pass by regular towns. She would need to blend in seamlessly.

"Oh yeah, and you'll be going by Elizabeth."

"Really?" She stepped over a log as the sun began to set in the background. "Is that a normal Ivy name? That sounds very ... human."

"Well, yes and no, and that's kind of the point. It's not what you'd consider a traditional Ivy name, but assassins and generals are notoriously proud of their 'calling' and often try to show it off."

Her stomach churned.

"So they'll use lingo or even name their children more human names to show that off. Not dissimilar from the upper class wearing nicer things." He bent over, picking up a pine cone and crunching it in his hands. "That way, your backstory will make a little more sense if you say too much that would give away your childhood in the human world."

"Oh. Then Elizabeth it is. I suppose we don't need people whispering about a Rachel going around."

"Nope." He glanced at the sun setting in the sky. "You know, we should probably get in a little training before it gets dark. I'd feel better that way."

"Yeah, sure."

While Rachel had trained with her Seeder abilities, they were only to be used as a last resort. Guillen would be rounding off her training with knives.

He picked up a couple of short thick sticks. "Alright, no need to risk it with the real thing." He handed one to her.

"If we had to, you know, kill someone to keep our cover ... wouldn't they suspect a," she still hated saying the word, "stunt? The injuries would obviously be different from Ivy leaf cuts."

"Possibly. More than one murder has been pinned on a stunt because a knife was used." He tossed his stick in the air, then caught it. "Pretty flimsy reasoning, given every regular Ivy has a knife on their person somewhere."

"What? Really? I thought Kaylah did just because of you..."

"Nah." He pointed to the machete on his belt. "She knows how to use one of these, and other weapons, because of me. But it's pretty standard to tuck one in your boot or pocket, but only really as tools, not weapons."

"Oh."

"Think about it this way: Regular Ivies can disconnect their vines internally at the wrist, but once they've used that vine on something, say... to mend a broken fence or as a strap to pull a wagon or something, then they need a way to cut it for some reason, and cutting with a knife is just faster in a lot of cases than using vine leaves. Not to mention most women and children aren't efficiently trained in using their vines as weapons, so they might not have down the rigidity or sharpness required for that kind of cutting."

His explanation painted such a curious picture for Rachel, to imagine Ivy vines being used domestically like a piece of twine, rather than as weapons against her people.

"You look surprised."

"I guess. I dunno, Kaylah just hasn't talked about it that way."

He shrugged, tucking the stick he'd been carrying into his pocket. He then pulled out a smaller pocketknife and approached her. "My favorite servant gifted me this years ago. I've fashioned the others I have in a similar way." He handed Rachel the knife.

She ran her thumbs over the handle. It was made of a pearlescent shell of some type. "It's beautiful." She handed it back, and he slipped it back in place in a pocket. "Did you have many servants growing up?"

He looked embarrassed, rubbing the back of his neck. "Well, my family has money and position, so... Most people don't have any, right? But it's not like I have one now."

"Yeah, of course." She now wished she'd taken more time to ask Kaylah questions about Guillen to avoid making him uncomfortable, but she'd done everything possible to avoid Kaylah's pushing, prodding, and teasing about Rachel's crush on him. "So, um, knife practice before we lose all light?"

"Right, yes."

They only had about a half hour or so before it got dark, but they made good use of that time. He showed her a variety of restraint holds and targets to aim for with a dagger. He was all business, and she tried to be, but it was exceptionally hard at times when he'd have her in a hold for a while, explaining his technique. It was nearly impossible for her mind not to wander with her being so close, being held in his arms, even if it was for such a serious purpose. She could swear he smelled of mint leaves and juniper berries.

After agreeing to resume their training the next day, they walked long past nightfall, hoping to find a well-hidden place to stop for the night. If they could be confident they were tucked away well enough, they could both try to sleep, instead of taking shifts. They were still in the Neutral Woods, where the trees were fairly dense, and they found a spot Guillen was satisfied with.

They tried to get as comfortable as possible, sleeping on the ground under the stars. Lying down, they faced each other.

"So..." He yawned. "Is that your first tattoo?"

"Yep. What about you? Any others?"

"I've got a couple others."

She wished she could see him better, be able to view his face and not just an outline of his body in the dark.

"What are they?" She added playfully, "And *where* are they?" He'd seen her in a lot less clothing than she'd seen him in during their time together before.

"Hmm. Maybe I'll keep that a mystery," he returned in fun.

"Come on." She jabbed a finger in his direction. Meeting his shoulder, she poked a few more times. "I wanna know."

He grabbed her hand, giving it a squeeze. His palm was calloused, but she smiled at his tender touch, then her heart skipped a beat as a pair of lips met the back of her hand.

"Have you ever thought of getting one before? I'm sad this is your first experience with them." He rested his hand on the ground, leaving his palm open, as if letting her choose whether she wanted to keep hers there with his. Not seeing his face, his piercing blue eyes right now, that killed her. She tickled his palm with her fingers.

"I thought about it. My parents, um…" She still had a hard time not calling Duke Nuren one of her parents or her stepdad, but he didn't deserve that title in her life anymore. "My mom definitely wouldn't let me when I was younger. But just something simple, like a cute butterfly, would be fun."

"That suits you," he said in a soft and tired voice. "Just like you. You can both fly. And you're both beautiful."

She stopped drawing on his hand and settled her palm onto his. "Thanks," she whispered.

"Where do you think you would get it?" he asked.

Not that he could see it, but her cheeks had to be red with warmth. She'd just mentally undressed him, searching for his mysterious tattoos. Was he now doing the same? "I don't know. There are a lot of options." She was tempted to ask him where he thought she should get it, but that was pretty intimate, even if he was returning her interest. She gave his hand a gentle rub and then retracted her own. She didn't want to screw this one up. "Good night, Guillen."

His silhouette shifted positions, and he drew a deep breath. "Good night, Rachel."

Rachel woke in the morning to Guillen's face just a couple of feet away; he was peacefully sleeping. She studied him with a contented smile—his eyebrows framing his stunning eyes, the large scar on his temple, his perfectly kissable lips. She looked him over, now that she could see him, and wondered again where he'd placed his tattoos. Her eyes landed on his chest, which moved slowly with each breath he took. His breathing pattern changed, and she looked back at his face. His eyes were now open, his lips upturned in a smile. "How long have you been awake?" he asked.

"Not long. Just wanted to let you get some more sleep."

"Thanks." He shifted into a sitting position, then ran his fingers through his hair.

She followed suit, grabbing a comb from her pack.

"I'd imagine sometime past midday, we'll run into a river and be able to walk near that most of the way back to our borders," he said. They were entering Ivy lands on the opposite end from the palace; this was all new territory for Rachel. Luckily, it wouldn't take them as long to cross the distance as it had months prior, but it was still a couple more days at least. And they were going through areas less patrolled—their odds were good to approach without conflict.

"That sounds great. I'd love to wash up," she said.

"Yeah, I'm sure we can find a good spot for that."

She cleared her throat. "So, I don't have to be worried about what happened last time?" She smirked, referring to the time he'd tackled her when she was half-naked to avoid discovery by enemy troops.

"Hey! That was to keep both of us safe." His unamused face showed he'd taken offense. "I would never just grab you like that if I didn't have to."

"I'm just giving you a hard time. You're obviously a gentleman; that's one of the things I like about you."

He nodded. She then fought a grin. The bra she wore now was the same one he'd seen her in at the lake.

He furrowed his brow. "What?"

She pulled up the collar of her shirt to hide her face below the eyes. "I don't know what you're talking about."

He shook his head. "I hope you can be more convincing than this when we meet some of my people."

She dropped the shirt from her face, giving him a determined look. "I accept that challenge." She flashed her green Seeder eyes.

"I like a girl who's not afraid to take on a challenge." He winked.

Despite his flirtation and attention, Guillen really was a gentleman, and perhaps a bit shyer than Rachel had remembered. He'd probably only dared to hold her hand the night before because it had been dark. He didn't try to make any moves on her the next couple of days, and they had to split the nights to watch out for unexpected visitors. The Seeders described Ivy lands as 'a wasteland,' which was accurate, depending on your definition. Compared to the lush lands near the Ivy palace or Seeder territory, or even neutral lands, there was little plant growth in most of the Ivy Kingdom. They were more vulnerable in this part of the wilderness, closer to the wastelands.

On the last evening of their journey, they stopped early for the night. Taking a late dinner, they sat close to each other as they reviewed what the next day had in store for them.

Rachel rubbed her sore shoulder. "I'll just be glad to sleep indoors again."

"I think that means it's your turn." He invited her over with a nod.

"I don't know. I'm the one with healing hands." She stuck out her tongue.

"Hey now, I'm good with my hands."

She chuckled. "Now *that's* a good pickup line."

He cleared his throat. "I meant, you know, construction and knife work and all that..."

"If you insist." She sat down in front of him, cross-legged.

Guillen gently moved her hair to the side, and the butterflies took flight in her stomach. He started in with his fingers on her neck, then slid them down to her shoulders. She closed her eyes and soaked it all in.

He avoided her bra straps. "Here," she said as she slipped a hand under her collar and pushed the straps down, revealing each shoulder for a moment. Her breathing shuddered as his hands made more contact with her skin. He carefully straightened out her collar and started to massage again.

"Is that better?" he asked.

"It's great, thanks." She took a calming breath. "Speaking of you and your knife work." Reaching into her pocket, she pulled out the knife he'd given her. They had only ever used sticks for their training, for safety.

"You still have it." His smile was audible.

"I always have it with me."

He stopped massaging and glided his hands down her arms, meeting her hands. "Are you keeping it sharp like I taught you?"

She handed him the knife as he leaned forward, setting his chin on her shoulder.

It was intoxicating, being in his arms, having his face so close. "Yeah, I, uh, I've tried to take good care of it."

He checked the blade with his thumb. "Not bad." He slid it back into its sheath, handing it to her and lingering with his arms around her.

Her heart pounded so hard that she feared he might hear or feel it. "I don't think I can ever thank you enough. For this, for saving me that day in the palace, for everything."

"You're welcome," he whispered in her ear.

If she turned her head just a few inches, his lips would be right there. He wanted to kiss too, right? Instead, she panicked. "I owe you my life," she blurted.

He drew a deep breath, moving his hands back up her arms, to her shoulders. He planted a kiss on the top of her head as he shifted back. "You owe me nothing." He continued the shoulder massage.

They sat in silence for another few minutes. She tried to enjoy the vibrant orange-and-purple sunset, as she kicked herself for ruining their moment.

"We should turn in early," he announced.

He would take the first watch and wake her when it was her turn. They'd gotten lucky so far—Rachel hadn't woken up noisily from traumatic nightmares. His calming presence helped. But the stress of entering enemy territory the next day got to her that night, and she woke up, panting in a cold sweat.

"It's okay," Guillen whispered in the dark. He reached out and held her hand. "It's okay."

She focused herself, slowing her breathing and heartbeat.

"Can I do anything to help?" he asked, squeezing her hand.

She swallowed hard. "No. Thanks." She let go of his hand and rolled onto her side, crying. She remembered the look he gave her when she'd found out how poorly he was treated for not having powers. He'd told her he didn't want her pity. That same sentiment ached deeply in her soul right now. She wanted Guillen, but she didn't want him in that way. Not as someone who saw a broken girl to take care of, just because he was nice.

She woke in the wee hours of the morning to birds chirping in the trees above them. She startled and looked around; Guillen stood leaning against a tree. She rose, and he flashed a tired smile. Joining him, she leaned against the other side of the tree.

"You didn't wake me for my turn," she scolded.

"You needed it more." The exhaustion in his eyes begged to disagree.

She sighed. "I don't know about that. How about you try to get some sleep before we pack up?"

"No. I think we should get going. We're so close."

"Okay." She took a breath and decided to ask what was on her mind. "Can I hug you?"

He held his arms open. "Of course."

She wrapped her arms around him, and he pulled her in tighter and tighter. She closed her eyes and melted there. This was the safest place she knew in both worlds. In Guillen's arms.

His breathing matched hers. After what felt like hours, she decided she would finally have to let go, since he wasn't the first to move. She stepped back, glancing at his lips before meeting his heavenly eyes. "Thanks."

He gave his signature roguish grin. "Any time. Are you ready for this?"

Today would be the day she really put on her game face, infiltrating enemy territory. "I'm all in."

Chapter 14

Since a stunt like Guillen had no reason to be in the Neutral Woods, he and Rachel had to take a roundabout path to get into the Ivy Kingdom. Though, even with the war actively raging, the borders were barely patrolled, especially this far from the palace. Eventually, they hit the main path toward the stunt community furthest north.

Guillen had told her how small, and often remote, the communities were, but even still, the symphony of chatter, clangs, and thuds on the approach was deafening after days in the quiet woods. Rachel put extra effort into focusing her energy, tucking it away and calming her nerves. She was an Ivy. One born without powers. She was from Community Five. She worked in a textile workshop. She was visiting her friend Magda here in Community Ten. She was traveling alongside Guillen coincidentally, having met along the way to visit mutual friends.

As they approached the community entrance, a bulky guard stood ready to screen visitors. Guillen went first. He lifted his sleeve, showing his mark. The guard gave him a courteous nod. "Sir."

Rachel was already annoyed. He'd called Guillen 'sir,' and waved him in without travel documents, just because he was royalty, but he was still treated worse than a commoner with powers.

Guillen stopped shortly after entering, watching for Rachel to get through. She handed her forged documents to the guard, smiling as he looked them over. She raised her sleeve, showing her mark. As he read her papers, Rachel studied his face. *Please let this one be the right kind of guard...*

Guards had been front and center in Rachel and Guillen's discussion of culture and potential threats on their mission. The way Guillen had explained it, there were really only two types of guards at the stunt communities. The majority were nothing more than washed-up soldiers looking for an easy paycheck that still boosted their ego. They were also the type that saw the girls without powers in these communities as easy conquests.

The minority of guards were generally there for a good reason, wanting to stand in a place where they recognized an injustice being done. Some of them even had stunt family members they loved, though they'd never be stationed at a community where a family member resided.

The guard squinted, glancing between Rachel and the paperwork. It was taking him a long time to review the papers, and there was something in his eye that forced her to choke down her energy.

Something was wrong.

She looked past the guard, trying to keep her cool. Guillen had his hand subtly ready, concealing a knife, observing.

The guard grasped Rachel's upper arm, extending vines around it. "You're from Five?" He gazed into her eyes in a way that made her uncomfortable. She trained her expression to hide her panic.

"That's what the paperwork and skin say." She shrugged.

He rubbed his thumb over her tattoo. "I think I'd remember a beautiful face like yours—I just transferred from Five last month."

"Oh, really? That's neat." She feigned interest.

In their many hours together, she and Guillen had been able to discuss strategy for this kind of scenario. She likely knew that community better than half of its occupants, without having ever set foot in it.

"Did you work the north or south entrance?" she asked.

"North. Near your job," he replied.

Rachel nodded. "That makes sense. I approach from the other direction. Did you work days?"

"Nights. The schedule is why I transferred."

He was still holding on to her arm. Giving her a line about being beautiful had to mean he was the wrong type of guard... She slid her free hand up, then stroked the back of his hand and looked at him with seductive eyes, licking her lips. "That would be why. I guess I don't get out much. Trust me. I'd recognize you, too, if I had seen you." She winked.

He gave her a lusty grin, glancing at her chest. "I guess it's a shame I left."

"I'll be here a couple of days for my visit." She smiled. "When do you get off work?"

He looked at Guillen out of the corner of his eye. "You're not here with palace boy?"

By this point, she wanted nothing more than to vomit.

She bit her lip. "Acquaintance, at best. The guys in these kinds of places don't exactly do it for me, if you know what I mean."

He released his vines from her arm. "I know *exactly* what you mean. I get off at five. Will I see you at the pub?" He handed back her paperwork.

She tucked it into her back pocket. "I don't know my exact schedule. But if I can sneak away, I know where you'll be."

He nodded her in. As she started to pass, the guard's hand landed on her backside. "Don't lose that paperwork."

Get your hand off me or you'll be losing something much more dear!

"Thanks. I'll see you soon." She forced one last grin while looking back, then moved on.

The moment she turned away, her facade dropped. Her breathing was forced as she focused on controlling her emotions and energy. Guillen walked silently next to her. At the end of the dirt street, they turned the corner and stopped at the community café. They sat down and placed an order—both grateful for fresh, warm food. Once the waitress left, Guillen reached his hand across the table.

"I'm sorry." He frowned.

She shook her head, moving her hand up to his. "We talked about this." Guillen couldn't be seen questioning authority; he couldn't stand up for her. She moved her hand back down; they shouldn't be seen looking too familiar, either.

After an amazing breakfast of warm buckwheat, peppers, and zucchini, Guillen gave Rachel a brief tour. With his unique position, he'd enjoyed significantly more travel opportunities than most stunts. He not only had more freedom of movement, but also in how many vacation days a year he was granted. He'd spent time in every stunt community, and lived in more than one of the communities long-term.

The Ivy Kingdom had four steam engines that traversed their landscape. They had helped him travel between the communities in the past, but for the purposes of this mission, they'd be avoiding them, since they were packed with upper-class citizens, guards, and all the wrong people to avoid suspicion.

Community Ten was a notch or two above bleak. Other than a rare shade tree, there was no plant life to be seen. No yards. No flower gardens. Nothing. People plodded along, fulfilling their daily tasks, with the occasional neighbors stopping to chat with each other. All of the buildings blended together, built of dull grey stone, merging into the background of mountains from whence they were hewn. The air was more stale than in the Neutral Woods or Seeder nation, which wasn't all that shocking considering the lack of plant growth in the vicinity.

One of Guillen and Rachel's last stops was at the blacksmith's.

"This is my old friend, Jacob. He and his wife Magda are going to be hosting us."

Jacob, a man in his late twenties with dark brown hair, wiped his dirty hands on a shop rag, and shook Rachel's hand. "It's a pleasure."

"Thank you. Nice to meet you." Sitting on Jacob's workbench behind him was a basket, plumb-full of arrowheads. Rachel could almost hear Jon's voice from months earlier, when he'd explained how her stepfather had petitioned to issue soldiers in the woods with bows, not just guards at the palace. "How long does it take you to make one of those?"

He glanced behind him, instantly looking perturbed. "Too long, if you ask the folks in charge." Passing another dark, knowing look at Guillen, he added, "And if you ask me, still too long, given the public toilets can't be used until I fix the hardware." He reached into his pocket. "But that's obviously not a priority." He handed Guillen a key. "The place is all yours. Magda should be home in a little while, but she set out some towels and everything so you two can get cleaned up."

Guillen pocketed the key. "Any birthday celebrations tonight?"

Jacob looked at a pendulum clock on the wall, shaking his head. "Not enough time. Tomorrow."

"Alright. Well, it's good to see you." Guillen pointed to the basket of arrowheads. "And good to know about that."

A sinister smile spread across Jacob's face. "It sure would be sad if they went missing after I turned them in." He picked up his hammer to get back to work. "Happy to be the eyes and ears on the eyes and ears."

"You can go first," Guillen said, sitting down on the couch. Rachel willingly took the offer, hopping in the shower. While the materials the shower was built from were different than those she'd grown accustomed to back in South Fortinda, the simple plumbing was similar. She moaned at the refreshing sensation of warm water rushing over her, cleaning her better than the river along the way had.

The hot water didn't last long, which wasn't a huge surprise. Everything in these communities was built economically. Every apartment was a one-bedroom, since they weren't allowed to have kids. Uniform, tiny, boring. She toweled off and got dressed. Planning to warn Guillen he'd have to wait a while for hot water, she headed down the short hallway, then stopped to lean against the wall, grinning. He was fast asleep.

She quietly sat on the living room floor and perused some books on a shelf, flipping through them and looking longingly at Guillen. He was really out.

Not much later, the front doorknob twisted, and a woman with light brown hair entered, presumably Magda, returning from work. Rachel waved and put a finger to her lips, then pointed at Guillen. Magda tiptoed inside and eased the door closed, but the click of the door closing woke him.

He rubbed his eyes. "Gosh. Sorry. Hey, Magda, it's great to see you." He stood and gave her a hug. His voice still groggy, he motioned to Rachel. "This is my friend, Elizabeth."

Magda gave her a cordial smile and handshake. They chatted a while, and Rachel offered to help with dinner as Guillen excused himself to shower. He came out looking fresh and sharp.

After Jacob returned home, the four of them ate a dinner of bean soup and herbed salad, and talked for hours. Jacob and Magda were a cute couple, and Rachel could easily see why Guillen was friends with them. She allowed her mind to wander. How might things be if she and Guillen nurtured their relationship? Would they have friends like this? But ... where would they live? Her mood shifted when she remembered he probably couldn't even come to visit her at her family home in Seeder lands, assuming even Ivies without powers were susceptible to the lingering poison there. Would she be willing to join him in the Ivy Kingdom? That would be a huge commitment. She shook away the thoughts. She was getting ahead of herself.

At the end of the night, Magda pulled out thin pads and blankets for Guillen and Rachel to sleep on in the living room. "Sorry, you know how it is," Magda said.

"Don't we all," Rachel lied, as though she'd experienced the daily discomfort of stunt life. The couch was too short for either of them, but a padded floor was still better than a forest floor.

They wished each other a good night and settled in after all lights were out. Rachel lay on her side, facing away from Guillen.

"Are you warm enough?" he asked.

"Mmm. I'm perfect," she replied, already half-asleep. "Plus, I can warm myself if I get cold."

A moment passed, and she opened her eyes. *Wait a second. After a week of camping in the elements in the Neutral Woods, he asks me if I'm warm now? In a sheltered building? Is he offering ... to cuddle?*

"You know what, it is a bit chilly," she lied.

She smiled as he shuffled behind her. Then he draped another blanket over her. *Stupid chivalry.* "Thanks. Good night."

By the time Rachel woke in the morning, Guillen had folded up his pad and blanket. He sat on the couch, reading a book.

"Good morning, sunshine," he said once she stirred.

After stretching and pulling her shirt back down, she rose from the floor and folded her own bedding, before joining him on the small couch. "Is the book any good?"

He shrugged, setting it down on the floor. "Just passing the time. How did you sleep?"

She had woken up a time or two, and remembered some nightmares, though nothing too intense. "I've had worse."

He gazed into her eyes. "You know you can talk to me about them, right? And anything, if you want, if you're ready."

She scratched her arm. "Thanks. You're sweet." She wasn't ready to talk about it. Especially not with him, no matter how great he was at talking about hard stuff. It was complicated—having a romantic interest in the cousin of your ex-boyfriend who kidnapped, tortured, and assaulted you was *definitely* complicated. "You know what I'd love to hear about?" She reached up, cupping the side of his face and rubbing the scar on his temple. "Of course, only if you want to tell me."

He bit his lip. "That ... is a reminder of the day I learned I needed to stand up for myself, that I couldn't always depend on others. That's when I picked up a blade and decided I was tired of being treated like I was nothing." He leaned into her cradling hand, not breaking eye contact. "My mother had a temper when I was a boy."

She'd expected a story about injuring himself as a little boy, or getting in a fistfight, or something like that. She frowned as a coldness struck her heart. "Your mom did this to you?"

"It's okay. She's calmed down a lot over the years."

Rachel shook her head. "No wonder you're so nice to me. You understand crazy families and how things can get so messed up."

He let out a short breathy chuckle.

She looked down, pulling her hand from his face. "I do worry, sometimes..."

"What?" He moved a hand to caress her cheek, a look of concern on his face.

"I worry that you're nice to me just because you're a nice guy." Her heart raced. "And not because you like me ... the way I like you."

They locked eyes.

In no time flat, Guillen closed the gap, brushing his lips against hers. Smooth, sweet, perfect. He quickly pulled away. "Sorry, I should have aske—"

"Yes."

"Yes?" He lifted his eyebrows.

"Yes." Her smile grew as she leaned in, kissing him back. And he did not disappoint. His hands may have been rough from hard work, but his lips were perfectly soft. He moved his hand to the nape of her neck, drawing her closer.

The click of a door behind Rachel pulled them away from each other.

Guillen hid a sheepish grin behind his fist, looking past Rachel. "Hey, Magda. Good morning."

Rachel wiped her lips off, blushing. Guillen subtly tapped a finger next to his eye.

Crap! She closed her eyes, unable to stop smiling, and focused on bottling up her energy. She reopened them and looked at him. He winked that all was well. They hadn't even told his friends yet that she was a Seeder. They were going to feel out the meeting that night to see when it would be best to divulge that information.

"When Guillen said he was bringing a friend with him, he didn't mention *that* kind of friend," Magda teased as she passed them on the way to the kitchen.

Guillen cleared his throat. "Can I offer a hand in there?"

"No, I'm good. You two ... don't mind me."

Rachel suppressed a laugh. It wasn't like they'd go back to kissing. It was a tiny place, and they were in full view of the kitchen. But they did sit there, holding hands, and chatting with Magda as she made everyone breakfast. Jacob came out of their bedroom and helped set the table as Magda finished up.

"Jacob, our Guillen has been keeping a secret from us," she kidded, and Guillen's face grew pink. Magda whispered loudly, "Elizabeth isn't just a friend." Then it was Rachel's turn to blush.

Jacob raised his eyebrows, smirking. "Really? This is the first time we've met one of Guillen's girlfriends. Why didn't you just say so?"

"It's..." Guillen looked at Rachel. "New."

Trying to stifle a laugh, Rachel instead snorted, which only made her laugh harder. *Right. New. Less-than-an-hour new.*

That garnered her some mixed looks.

"We expect to know all the details," Magda insisted as the group dug into breakfast.

They could hardly share the truth while keeping Rachel's identity a secret.

"We met through family, actually," Guillen offered up.

Rachel pushed around her parsnip hash with a fork, reveling in the ironic truth. They wouldn't have ever met if his cousin hadn't kidnapped her, so … it wasn't a lie.

Magda demanded more information, but Guillen told her they couldn't share too much, that some of their backstory had to do with secret Unitas business. She relented. "Alright, well, you make a cute couple. I hope you know what a great guy you've got here," she told Rachel, pointing at Guillen with a fork.

Rachel smirked. "I know. He is." He rested a hand on her knee under the table, and shivers raced up her spine. She blinked and double-checked that she was controlling her energy.

Chapter 15

Guillen and Rachel offered to clean up the kitchen while Magda and Jacob headed out for work. The meeting they were there for would happen at 7 p.m. They'd have all day in Community Ten.

"Make yourselves at home," Magda said on her way out. "And make sure to show her the garden."

Rachel stood at the sink washing dishes while Guillen wiped down the small dining table. His arms wrapped around her waist from behind, and she took a sudden, deep breath.

"Hey." She beamed.

"Hey back." He planted a kiss on her neck and reached up, removing her hand from the water pump.

Setting down her washcloth, she turned around; he rested his hands on her hips. His bright eyes were mesmerizing.

"I figured we might be able to try that again. Without interruption." His handsome smile lured her in.

"I mean..." She sighed and rolled her eyes. "If you want." She giggled at his stink eye.

He leaned in, taking his time to sweetly graze her lips with his. A fire was burning, radiating from her heart and reaching across her entire body. Her hands grasped the fabric of his shirt, pulling him closer. He matched her enthusiasm by pressing against her; she was snug against the counter now. As she offered more, his breathing picked up; he didn't hold back in the slightest. After a couple of minutes, he pulled back, catching his breath.

She, too, was catching her breath. If he hadn't still been holding her against the counter, she might not be standing at all at that point. *That* was the kind of kiss girls dreamed of.

He gazed into her eyes. "I've waited my whole life for you." He raised a hand, tenderly brushing aside some of her bangs. "How can you be so beautiful both ways?"

His whole life? He was moving ... *fast.* But it also felt completely natural. She looked up; her hair was glowing Seeder-blond, a change that only happened with extreme emotion, much more intense than a simple glow of the eyes.

She swallowed, still catching her breath. "You don't mind the changes?"

"Are you kidding me?" He maintained eye contact. "Not even a little."

She blushed. "I wouldn't change a thing about you."

He responded with a contented grin and gave her a single peck before stepping back. "Let's finish up here."

She nodded and steadied herself, getting back to cleaning the dishes with a perma-smile. He grabbed a hand towel and dried.

When they finished, Rachel leaned against the counter, facing Guillen. "So ... we have all day?"

"Yeah, I can show you around some more. We can grab lunch and dinner before the meeting. Do you have any requests?"

"Would you hate it if we bummed around here for a little while?" she asked.

He raised his eyebrows. "Because...?"

She didn't want him getting the wrong idea, that she was looking to make out all day. "Just to talk, and spend some time where we don't have to pretend to hardly know each other."

He set down his drying rag. "Of course."

They sat down on the couch and held hands, facing each other.

"Jacob said you've never brought a girlfriend around here?"

"That's because none of my previous girlfriends were worth the investment and introduction."

She chuckled. "Yeah. And they weren't here with you as a spy."

He scolded her with his eyes. "I mentioned the reason that mattered."

She rubbed the backs of his hands with her thumbs. "Is that what this is? Am I your girlfriend?"

"If that's what you want." He pursed his lips. "If you think you can get over the guy who gave you the flower. You seemed pretty attached."

She narrowed her eyes at his razzing. "I'll remind you that I know at least one place where you're ticklish."

He shot her a seductive look. "And I'll remind you I'm willing to find out where yours are."

She chuckled again and shook her head. "I like you."

"Come here." He opened his arms, and she snuggled against his chest. He held her close, whispering, "I've liked you for a while now." He gave her a gentle squeeze. "Kaylah would always show me pictures and tell me stories about her best friend. I knew you were beautiful, and that there was something special about you. And I saw that right away when we met."

"In that stupid prom dress."

"Right. That dress." Her body moved with his as he drew a deep breath. "I knew you had just been through a lot, and things were complicated. I didn't want to scare you off. But I thought about you every day after I had to leave you."

"I thought about you a lot, too," she whispered. "I feel safe with you." After a lifetime of lies and manipulation, she needed extra assurances if she was going to put her heart on the line again. "But ... I need to be with someone that will be absolutely honest with me, about everything. Can you promise me that?"

"I can."

Every last muscle she hadn't even realized was tense, relaxed as she molded to his body. "I was so worried about you while you were gone. I'm really glad you're okay."

They sat cuddling for several minutes. He broke the peaceful calm with a whisper. "I know I've already asked, but are you alright? After everything that happened?"

She frowned. "I don't know."

"Have you been able to talk about it with anyone?"

She buried her head deeper into his chest. She had shared details with others, but not in depth, and with liberal censorship. "Not really."

"It helps to talk. I'd be willing to listen."

Her eyes filled with tears. "I'm not ready for that yet."

"That's okay." He hugged her tighter as her tears wetted his shirt.

She stayed in his arms for over an hour. Once she'd finished crying, she rested her eyes and let his body warmth heal her. She shifted in his arms, and he reciprocated with a kiss on her head.

"We should probably go do something, shouldn't we?" she asked.

"If you want to."

Sitting up, she faced him. "Thank you."

He acknowledged her words with a sympathetic smile.

Rachel went to the bathroom to finish getting ready for the day. Guillen took his turn while she perched on the back of the couch, glancing around the kitchen area. Everything was compact and purposeful in these tiny apartments. It wasn't likely she'd see the kitchen of a regular Ivy community home while on this mission, though her curiosity was piqued.

Guillen emerged from the bathroom and rested his hands on her waist. "Are you ready for this?"

She scrunched her face. "I guess."

"What's that about?"

"It's going to be twice as hard pretending I don't care about you, as pretending I'm not a spy."

He grinned and stole a kiss. "I know. But even Jacob and Magda agree it's for the best that we appear unattached. And they don't even understand it all..."

She sighed.

"We'll have tonight, after the meeting." He tucked a strand of hair behind her ear. "How do you feel about ... um ... cuddling tonight?"

She smirked. "To keep me warm? Because there are plenty of blankets here."

He threw his head back and laughed at her calling him out. "Come here, you." He started to kiss her again.

A key turning in the front door brought them back to reality.

"Your eyes," he whispered.

Rachel turned away from the door, toward the hallway, and closed her eyes to get things back in check. This was so hard with Guillen. She wished they would get it over with and tell Magda and Jacob she was a Seeder; they'd find out that night anyway. But he insisted they wait. He knew these people better than Rachel did, and had been a successful spy for quite some time now. He leaned in, covering Rachel more from the front door's immediate field of view.

"Well, hello again," Guillen greeted the intruder.

"Have you two seriously been here the whole time?" Magda's voice conveyed playful surprise.

Rachel gently pushed Guillen back. "Sorry, that's me. I was really tired; I just wanted some more rest. We were literally on our way out."

"She's not lying," he backed her up. "What are you home for at this time of day?"

"I forgot the lunch I packed."

"Well, that won't do. Grab it, and we'll take off with you."

He gave Rachel's hand a last reassuring squeeze before dropping it as they followed Magda out and headed down the street.

For the next few hours, Guillen took Rachel around the community, showing her the pantry, a ruddy little pub, and workshops. Along the way, he introduced her to a few people in the area, most of whom he anticipated being at the meeting that night, though they discussed no such topic in public. He smoothly called her Elizabeth and only a couple of times got a tidbit too close physically for an 'acquaintance.'

As Magda had recommended, they spent a good deal of time in the community garden. Almost all of the food needed for the entire community was grown here. It was as massive and lush as any Seeder family garden, though much larger, as it had to feed hundreds. Honey bees hovered from one squash blossom to another. Small vibrant-red birds landed occasionally to enjoy a buffet of beetles.

As much as Rachel enjoyed, or wanted to enjoy, the brilliant array of colors represented in the wide assortment of produce, her eyes kept landing on something unsettling—Mother Vines.

Propped up on a towering wooden structure in the center of the garden, the Mother Vine threw twisted tendrils into the soil. The tendrils were as thick as her thumb, the main Vine as wide as her arm.

Rachel's stomach physically hurt at the sight of it. Her arms, where leaves of the War Vines had once dug in to drain her of her energy, also ached.

"It's okay," Guillen reassured her, standing close. "They're not trained to do the same thing."

Rachel hugged herself. Kaylah had already explained that to her. The Mother Vines connected the communities in the Ivy Kingdom, distributing nutrients as they were 'trained'—essentially programmed—to do. They also kept a strong protective barrier around the palace. They weren't a weapon; they were central to the Ivy people's powers, their culture. The Mother Vines were a revered piece of every Ivy's identity, and what made a woman in the right bloodline a queen.

She'd have to get used to the sight of them, too. They stretched across the entire kingdom, on structures visible from the main highways, propped up like human power lines, just as this one was propped up.

"I know," Rachel said. Knowing the facts only barely took the edge off of seeing them. They literally couldn't hurt her. The way Kaylah had described them, Mother Vines didn't have sentience, but they did have a strict allegiance. A previous queen had trained them for their task, and without a change in orders, they continued to do their job, even without Kaylah's presence. Her mother's death had passed that allegiance down to Kaylah. She could do as she wished with the Mother Vines, but only by retraining them at the roots, which were dispersed throughout the kingdom, as opposed to the War Vines which were rooted at the palace, and continued to shred through Seeder borders.

"It's illegal to harm them, not that damaging them is even an easy feat," Guillen said. "But you can touch them."

Rachel stood still, considering. They looked *exactly* like the War Vines. Completely indistinguishable. If anything, she wanted to take a few steps back. But perhaps this could be helpful, like one of those therapies where people terrified of snakes force themselves to hold a harmless little garter snake.

She hesitantly stepped forward, bolstered by Guillen's hand on her back. Touching a tendril and a leaf brought flashbacks to when she was with Prince Soren back in the human world. Her trepidation was traded for pain. Crossing her arms, she decided it was enough to be in close proximity to them instead.

"Do you know what they say about the Mother Vines?" Guillen asked.

Rachel shook her head.

"They have eyes and ears."

Rachel side-eyed the Vine, then looked back at Guillen. "What?"

"Well..." He tucked his hands into his pants pockets. "It's just a silly personification, you know? They're plants. Powers or not, they don't actually have eyes and ears. They can't see or hear. But it's a saying." He reached out, running a finger along one of the tendrils. "It's a saying that aims to keep people in line. Across the kingdom, there are royal enforcers, law enforcement. They don't take too kindly to talk that doesn't agree with the royal family and their policies. Some people are superstitious enough to think the Vines have something to do with it. I think they just don't want to imagine their neighbors capable of turning them in."

Recalling something Jacob had said when they'd first met, Rachel furrowed her brow. "Jacob said something about that. Eyes and ears."

Guillen chuckled. "Yeah. 'Happy to be the eyes and ears on the eyes and ears.' Just his way of saying that we can be as secretive as those in power, that we're keeping our eyes on them, and plan to hold them accountable."

They sat down for dinner at the café, chatting about their day. The café was a breath of fresh air, really the only public place in the community with some décor. A little mural of the gardens was painted on one of the walls. In such a small community, with its residents paid so poorly, the café didn't need to be large. There were only eight little square tables.

"There are a lot of nice people here," she said, making sure to speak quietly under the chatter of a dozen other patrons.

Guillen stabbed a chunk of roasted potato with his fork. "You're surprised?"

"Of course not. I just wish people could see each other this way. Without labels and blame."

He smiled and shook his head. "*That* is precisely why you're here."

She sat back and sipped her water. "You know, now that I think about it, *you* are the reason I'm here."

He lifted his eyebrows in question as he brought his fork to his mouth.

She chuckled. "Not just for the," she cleared her throat, "exciting, new reason. But if I hadn't met you and the others," her eyes darted around the dining room, "the way I did ... I would have held just as much prejudice as most others. You're better than me. You came to that conclusion on your own." She bit her lip. "You're the best man I know."

He blushed. "I don't deserve that much credit. Kaylah's an astonishing advocate. And you were her best friend growing up. You play a larger role in this than you allow yourself to believe, so the credit goes back to you." He winked.

She sighed. "How about let's toast to her, then. Without her, none of this would be possible."

They each raised their glass. "To Kaylah."

As they clinked, the elderly waitress returned to refill their glasses. "That's right! To Princess Kaylah, may we get her back from the weeds, sooner than later!" She filled their glasses and moved on.

Rachel had averted her eyes at the woman's pronouncement, stabbing at the last few morsels on her plate. When she looked up, Guillen searched her eyes as though unsure how she'd react to her people being called the filthy nickname. Rachel grinned. "She's right. We all want the princess safe, don't we?"

He stifled a laugh.

They moved on to dessert, a tropical pudding of some sort, as they had time to kill before the meeting.

"You said each of these communities is different based on the industry they provide, but are they all basically like this?" she asked.

"More or less. The closer you get to the palace, the richer people are, so that's why I'm in construction over there. People can afford bigger houses. All the way out here, the woods are still decent; that's why the main industry here is lumber."

She furrowed her brow. "From what you showed me, there's a ton of industry that takes place here. And not that many apartments. How does that balance out?"

"The factories and mills have a private entry for prisoner escorts. Prisons are situated outside of these communities, but they're used for labor as much as my kind."

She shook her head. "Prisoners? And lumber seems like a stretch for this community. The woods are still pretty thin compared to what I've seen. And the community gardens... That garden seemed barely adequate for the people here."

He leaned close so as to not be overheard. "That's one of the things people don't understand. Your temple roots, they transfer energy to your security walls. Our Mother Vines are kind of like that. But since your people aren't the aggressors, we don't focus our resources so much on one place like you do. Instead, the individual communities feed the nutrients from their soil to the palace, and the palace then distributes them as they like. It wasn't always that way. People relinquished their freedoms."

He leaned back, frustration growing on his face. "People blame irresponsible rifting habits for our lack of vegetation, but that's only one factor. Some of it is the Mother Vines. One person calls it progress. Another calls it prison. I think even regular Ivies should have more say over their own communities."

Rachel suppressed a smirk—Kaylah had talked like that once before. Which of the two had first phrased it that way? "So, it's like socialism? Or communism? I guess when I imagine royalty, it's something that's gone back for several centuries. I don't know how it is that people vote on having rulership like that."

He shrugged. "I don't know what those words mean. And honestly, you won't find the truth in what they teach in schools. At least not without a significant spin on it."

Setting her dessert spoon down, she grimaced. "Politics. No thank you... I was kinda surprised, though, that there weren't any jewelry shops, art galleries, museums, libraries—any of it. I mean, these are small communities, but *nothing* beyond the basic necessities? Well, and the pub, I suppose that's not a necessity. But I got the impression Ivies were more ... well ... different and more focused on that kind of stuff, compared to Seeders." She winced at the description. "More materialistic."

Guillen blew out a puff of air, pushing his bowl to the edge of the table. "Well, the pub replaces a good deal of interests. Alcohol can be easily brewed nearby, and booze takes minds off of hard work and hard times. It also makes for loose lips and loose wome—" His mouth hung open for a second. He looked positively mortified.

Rachel's eyes grew wide in shock. She hadn't expected something like that to come from Guillen. "Please, do continue."

"I... You know I'm not like that, right? I don't even drink. It's just ... what people say."

He didn't seem the type, and she considered razzing him a bit for saying it, but decided to let it go. "So, free time consists of cooking and cleaning, drinking and," she raised an eyebrow, "related activities. And time in the garden." He'd already explained how strict stunt rules and restrictions were about possessions and travel; it was all rather ridiculous.

"That's basically it. There's plenty of the rest of it—art, jewelry, libraries— throughout the kingdom. Just not in a stunt community." His voice rarely carried resentment, and now was no exception.

She huffed, then bit down on the insides of her cheeks. These people weren't worth 'wasting' the 'finer things in life' on.

He smiled in appreciation of her silent protest. "We should head out. Let's go change things."

Chapter 16

The secret meeting was held in a community classroom. It wasn't fair to compare these communities to cruel concentration camps, but the stunts who lived there were treated like second-class citizens. Once they were taken from their family homes at the age of fourteen, they were no longer offered formal education; they didn't need school. But each community had a small building. It was multipurpose, helpful if training was needed for a shift in industry, if the guards needed to meet, for celebrations, that sort of thing. It reminded Rachel a lot of Seeder log huts used for education.

Having set everything up, Jacob was the first there. He welcomed Guillen and Rachel in.

Jacob stood at the door, greeting people and introducing them to Guillen and 'Elizabeth' as they trickled in. Magda gave Rachel a huge smile before sitting down. In total, there were just over a dozen new faces for Rachel. They had only invited those they were certain could be trusted, the most outspoken in the community against the treatment of their kind.

Rachel's anxiety bubbled as Guillen invited her to stand next to him at the head of the room. She looked over the crowd, her heart calming at seeing Jacob and Magda holding hands. Jacob was now sitting right next to the door, acting as guard. Magda sat beside him. Guillen had told Rachel how much they wished they could have a child. Just one. But they weren't allowed. This was personal for them.

Being born without powers was a random fluke of nature. But there *had* to be some sort of genetic component to it—if even *one* of the parents was a stunt, the child was also born without powers. The lack of powers was *always* passed down. Many people in society considered stunts inferior simply because they lacked powers, but others plainly saw them as a threat, as a curse. Like Kaylah had once explained about Ivy fears of Seeders overpopulating the Green Lands, Ivies feared losing themselves and their unique abilities if they allowed stunts to mingle with their peers with powers, or to even have kids at all.

Guillen spoke first in the meeting. He had prepared the whole presentation. They'd touched on points Rachel felt comfortable addressing, but he'd give her the green light after feeling out the room.

"Thank you, everyone, for making the sacrifice to be here. I'm honored to stand in this room with like-minded people. People who care about each other, and real equality." He gained some nods from around the room.

"My friend and I are here with a proposal. Something we know for certain will *finally* make a real change for our kind." He paused. "I think we first need to discuss the truth about our former queen and king, and Princess Kaylah."

"Screw them all!" a woman spat. "I hope she rots in enemy hands. Their family has had *decades* to do better!"

Rachel was taken aback by the woman's passion. Did this woman realize Guillen was Kaylah's cousin?

He tilted his head to the side thoughtfully. "You're right. They could have done better. And they will. The first thing you should know is that the queen and king were *not* assassinated by Seeder hands. Prince Soren was behind it."

Looks of confusion and whispers were exchanged around the room.

"I understand most of you don't know me all that well." He lifted his sleeve to show the royal insignia in the middle of his mark. "I'm close enough to know the truth. You can take my word on it." His voice filled the room with strength and authority. Rachel smiled at seeing this new side of him.

"The stories about Princess Kaylah are also false. She's the reason we're here."

Rachel watched the room, checking their expressions for buy-in. It was too early to tell.

"She's perfectly safe. The palace doesn't want our people to know she's turned from their ways. The kind of ways that weaken our lands, that fight senseless wars, that treat people like you and me as though we're only good for labor others don't want to do."

"Do you mean ... the rebellion?" a man near the back cautiously asked.

"Yes. Princess Kaylah is in charge of the rebellion. I don't know what rumors you've heard, but we're here on her behalf. To forge an alliance. She cares deeply about the injustices of our people."

There were a lot of wide eyes and open mouths.

One man scowled. "The rebellion is about the war; I don't see how that has to do with us. If that's true, she's just a weed-lover."

"Please don't use that term," Guillen reproached him, crossing his arms. "And the rebellion has a larger scope to it. Yes, she wants to end this war. She wants to stop wasting our resources and tossing aside the lives of our people. She wants to grant people like us equal opportunities." He paused. "And yes, part of her plan involves the Seeders. I'm sure I've met more Seeders than any of you. They're decent people."

Several heads shook, many of them mumbling. None of them would have ever met a Seeder. Not on the battleground, not in the course of their daily lives.

"You may not want to believe it, but the Seeders care about the treatment in these communities. They want to fight for us, and are asking that we join in the efforts."

"That's the biggest lie I've heard all night!" a bitter-sounding woman yelled. "All they care about is watching out for themselves. This is just empty promises for us to stick our necks out."

Guillen looked at Rachel and nodded.

Rachel cleared her throat and tried to stand tall. "It's not a lie. They do care. I would know." She lit up her eyes to full glow.

The room *erupted*.

"Are you kidding me?!"

"You brought one here?!"

"I didn't sign up for this!"

Rachel choked down a lump in her throat as her heart raced. A lot of angry and skeptical glances swept over her. Jacob stood at attention in front of the door, ensuring no one could exit. His face held a look of contempt, or perhaps betrayal. He clearly didn't appreciate the surprise.

Guillen moved closer to Rachel, placing his hand on her back, brandishing one of his knives in the other hand and pointing it at a couple of aggressive attendees. "Sit down and listen! Don't be fools."

Rachel's eyes rested on Magda, and her heart shattered. Magda looked murderous with rage, her eyes burning a hole right through Rachel.

"You're here to listen, so shut up and listen!" Guillen boomed. "Give her a chance."

The room begrudgingly calmed as everyone sat back down.

"Go ahead," Guillen whispered. Rachel took a step away from him, so his hand was no longer on her back. Magda had been glancing between the two, and by the look she was giving her, she clearly didn't think Rachel was good enough for her friend, not anymore.

Rachel found her voice. "It's true. Everything he says. We didn't kill your queen and king. And Princess Kaylah is fighting for all of our rights, Ivy and Seeder alike. With or without powers. I know. Because I know her. I've worked alongside her in this movement. And I know Prince Soren and Duke Nuren. I was taken from my people and tortured at the palace, personally, at their hands."

Her eyes glowed green, not as part of a show, but as a result of her struggling to deliver the personally gutting speech she'd prepared. Her story softened a few expressions.

"I don't expect you to pity me. Ivies and Seeders, we fight, right? It's war. There are casualties. People get hurt. I don't matter to you. But your people matter to the movement. It's called Unitas. It means Unity. My people, we didn't know your people treated you this way. I was personally enraged when I found out." She and Guillen shared a knowing glance. "And now that we know, we *are* willing to fight for you, too. Seeders have people just like you, and we don't restrict them this way. We just want to live our lives in peace. And we believe you deserve the same rights as anyone else in the Green Lands. We can help each other." She stepped back, silent.

"She volunteered to take a mark; she wasn't forced to," Guillen added. "She walked across the Neutral Woods to come here, endangering her own life. That should hold some weight."

They spent the next hour discussing what Unitas was offering and asking for. Soren overlooked these communities, vastly underestimating the power held there. These people could slow production. Lose supplies. They could reach out to family members in other communities.

The night hadn't gone as smoothly as Rachel and Guillen had hoped, but the participants were more or less pacified and rallied by the end, and interested in their proposals. They reminded the group of their oath of secrecy, and invited them back for another meeting the next night to discuss more.

Only one Ivy approached Rachel at the end and shook her hand, thanking her. The rest filed out. Magda had been one of the first to leave, and Jacob lingered by the door. Guillen and Rachel walked up to him hesitantly.

"I guess that could have gone better," Guillen said.

Jacob's gaze flickered from Guillen to Rachel, then back. He pressed his lips into a thin line. "You could say that. We'll talk."

"Thanks, Jacob. For all you're doing," Rachel offered.

"You guys head back. I'll lock up here. Magda and I are going to take a walk, so we might be a while."

Guillen and Rachel quietly ambled through the dark streets. "We knew our first meeting might be bumpy." He failed to comfort her.

"Yeah," she whispered in defeat.

They got back to the empty apartment, and Guillen locked the door behind them, turning and offering Rachel a hug.

"She hates me," she squeaked into his shoulder.

He rubbed her back. "They just need time. We threw a lot at them."

She knew that. She hadn't expected fanfare in the meeting. But Magda's disapproval in particular pierced her. They had only known each other for a day, but they'd shared an instant connection. One that had corroded in the flash of a Seeder's eye.

Rachel and Guillen sat on the living room floor, opposite the doorway, holding hands. They didn't want to be on the couch with their backs to the entry when Jacob and Magda returned. When a key twisted in the door, Rachel took her hand back and shifted away from Guillen. Magda walked in alone. She glared with contempt at Rachel as she stalked past without a word, slamming her bedroom door behind her.

"It'll be okay," Guillen soothed.

A minute later, Jacob showed up. He poked his head in. "Can we talk?"

Guillen nodded and got up, giving Rachel a reassuring look before shutting the door behind him. Mumbles traveled through the wall, and she was grateful they hadn't walked away. Not that Magda was trained in fighting, and Rachel had her knife and Seeder blades. And she didn't expect Magda to leave her room to try anything, but still...

Guillen came back in after several minutes, his face marred with disappointment. He rejoined Rachel as Jacob entered the apartment and locked the door. Jacob turned to the both of them. "I'm sorry. Good night."

Rachel fidgeted with her hands as Jacob disappeared into his bedroom. "What did he mean by that?"

"They'll still help. We haven't lost them. They just..." He frowned and grabbed her hand. "They're letting us stay the night, but you and I are going to find somewhere else to stay in the morning." He forced a smile. "We'll grab some breakfast and spend the *whole* day together again."

"They're kicking us out?" Tears came to her eyes. "I thought she liked me. I thought she'd understand."

He wiped away some errant tears from her cheek as his own eyes moistened. "I really didn't think she would react that way. But ... that's part of why we were supposed to just be friends, right? Or at least appear that way. Not add more complexities to the issues?"

She nodded. "Did he tell you why she reacted that way?"

"Honestly, this is more about me than you, okay? I have a precarious place in these communities." He held her gaze. "None of their misguided opinions about you, or us, mean anything to me, okay? Just ... asking people who are focused on equality for their own people to start caring about ending a war with the enemy is a huge leap. Then asking them to be okay with a relationship like ours ... it's a lot."

"I know." Her voice betrayed her as she struggled to choke back a fresh batch of tears. "That doesn't mean it doesn't hurt."

They set out their bedding and lay down to sleep. She would have been happy not staying there at all, but with curfew so close and guards patrolling the community, they couldn't risk raising suspicion. Guillen insisted on still sleeping close to her, for safety, but not nearly as close as either would have wanted earlier that same day.

Chapter 17

Back in the training camp on the edge of Seeder lands, the diverse Unitas group was steadily growing in numbers. They'd successfully found a good cave in the human world to link to the one they'd created in the Green Lands. Saff was excited to greet newcomers as more and more Seeder girls could come home safely, now without Ivy escort. The Ivies who had been spending time on transport duty could focus their efforts elsewhere. Brothers and fathers of Seeder girls were able to come home early to help with defense on the home front. Where the Ivy War Vines lacked extra umph in piercing through the border walls, their troops made up for it with increasingly brazen attacks, the soldiers' zeal fueled by Soren's propaganda, as he hid away in the comfort of the Ivy palace.

In the human realm, Saff's contacts and those of other Seeders caused the Unitas network to grow exponentially. Some Seeders decided to pull all family members at once, placing the unbloomed in Unitas safe houses. Tensions rose as Soren ordered extra searches to try to bring back more girls to power the primed War Vines.

Saff and Kaylah sat together one morning, sipping coffee and preparing for the perpetual grind of war.

"Thanks again for requesting Devin's help," Saff said. "It means a lot to me, to have him here."

"No problem." Kaylah's shaky smile was soon replaced by a frown. "I know how hard it is being separated from the one you love."

"I'm sorry you haven't been able to go see Eric. He's really mature for his age. You got a good one."

"Thanks. He knew it might be tough. But he loves me. And sometimes that's enough, right?" Kaylah rubbed her hands together and stood up. "And about your husband... I did have it on good authority that he's great at training your girls on their energy." She gave a more genuine smile.

"He *did* come with some amazing references, didn't he?" Saff chuckled, then became more serious. "Still no word on Rachel?"

Kaylah shook her head. "I don't expect any for a while. They had a lot of travel to get there, but I'm sure they're fine. They're both capable. And he'll take good care of her."

Having Devin there with her had been a balm to Saff's soul, but she still worried about Rachel daily.

She took another sip of her coffee, cringing, wishing she'd made tea instead.

Kaylah sifted through some paperwork, sighing. "I really hope today's briefing is less brutal than yesterday's."

Saff set her mug on the floor, the canvas of the tent whipping behind her in the wind. "Brutal, huh?"

"You didn't hear?" Kaylah's lips puckered in obvious annoyance. "Yeah, well, a few of your people thought they were being *so* clever, expanding on their usual tactics."(nn)

Saff had no idea what that was supposed to mean. "Come again?"

"You know, the jade charms."

"Gonna need more than that."

"You know, the lies they tell their children." Kaylah sat back down. "Well, I guess you don't all use the same playbook. How did your parents convince you to wear your jade charm without telling you the truth about your identity?"

"Actually..." Saff smiled fondly. "They didn't. Devin gave it to me as a gift, and it was our little secret. We were kind of ... sneaking around behind our parents' backs."

Kaylah splayed a hand across her chest, feigning shock. "Our dear Saff, the most upright Seeder, with an impeccable moral compass, a rebellious teenager?" She tutted.

Saff fought a grin. "Anyway, what about the jade charms?"

Kaylah frowned again. "Yeah, that's not a joking matter. Anyway, it sounds like most human host parents play the charm off as a naturopathic healing stone. Once their daughter's bloom starts, they get sick. So the parents say it's a 'healing' stone, and that's how they convince their girls to wear it all the time without worrying them about assassins for a few more months."

"Okay." Saff had never fixated on how other families took care of that particular part of the process. It sounded like a decent plan.

"Right, well, some families weren't too keen on the idea of trusting Unitas safe houses, so they got the bright idea to take to social media about the jade charms instead."

"What?!"

Kaylah held up a finger. "Popularizing *fake* jade charms. Well, it might have been real jade, but not from here. But they went to the lengths of sourcing manufacturers to make the charms, and then paying social media influencers to make them the next fad."

Saff laughed. If Soren's assassins came across a school full of girls wearing jade, they'd completely lose their advantage in the hunt. "That actually sounds brilliant. Now they can't tell who the Seeder girls are anymore."

Kaylah wasn't laughing. She silently nodded. "You're right. It really was a brilliant idea. But I have a feeling the half dozen murdered human girls would beg to disagree."

That sobered Saff up real quick. "What do you mean?"

Kaylah sat straighter in her chair. "I'm sure by now, the assassin networks know they can't just spot a jade charm around a girl's neck and kidnap her. But those first few they tried ... when they didn't bloom, when they couldn't be forced through a rift and taken to the palace to hook up to the War Vines... Yeah, they couldn't have witnesses."

Saff's heart ached for them and their families. Seeders made it a point to try to keep humans safe and out of their affairs as much as possible. These girls wouldn't have even been part of host families, knowingly taking on the risk. They were just teenage girls following a trend.

A male Seeder announced himself and entered the tent. "Princess, we have your morning updates."

Saff stood to leave, still shaken.

"You're fine, stay." Kaylah motioned for her to sit back down.

He looked at a piece of paper with notes. "From the human world, we've been informed there's been more suspicious public news reports."

Saff and Kaylah looked at each other, eyebrows raised.

"What kind of reports?" Kaylah asked.

"Disappearances. Attacks. Nothing giving away specifics of our realm ... but the actions are catching attention."

"Related to yesterday's news?"

He shook his head. "No, ma'am. It all sounded like regular assassin hunting activity. And the disappearances all matched up to families that have fled to Unitas safe houses."

Saff's muscles relaxed a bit. "I'm surprised the assassins aren't being more careful."

Kaylah gave a disingenuous smile. "If Soren wins, and your people are all dead, they have no reason to even go to the human world. The humans aren't exactly able to come here and prosecute my people, are they? It just means he's taking it seriously." She turned to the guard. "As for our part, we'll talk about how we can work on being more discreet while ensuring safety."

"Alright." He looked back down at his paper. "There was another fight last night."

Kaylah rubbed her temples, and Saff could only feel sorry for her. There had been a handful of altercations already in camp. From a brief argument, to a decent fight with injuries that had required healing. "What about?"

"The usual. It was a couple of Seeders and an Ivy, ma'am."

The usual. That was code for: Kaylah couldn't please everyone. Seeders were starting to resent her plans because she wasn't actively taking on the palace, to end the war, to get back their tortured girls. But it wasn't that simple. Security at the palace had been at least doubled or tripled. She insisted they allow more time for Guillen and Rachel, and others, to grow support from inside the kingdom, for a successful takeover.

Some Ivies also found themselves less than dazzled at the camp. The conditions were significantly humbler than they were used to, and some hadn't fully thought out their commitment. Fearing one might change their mind, Kaylah and the Seeder council had decreed that any Ivy who came to the camp (with the exclusion of her most trusted spies and transport help) was required to stay in camp. Bitterness was growing about not being able to leave.

"I don't know what they expect me to do!" Kaylah balled her fists.

Saff grimaced. She and Kaylah had already discussed all of this, but surely there had to be something they could do differently... "You're sure there's no way to speed up your timeline? I know you're working on a way to rift within the Green

Lands, and on how to get the unbloomed back, but those really don't seem like the priority."

Kaylah closed her eyes, breathing deeply. "We need to give you-know-who and the others more time. As we get more progress reports, maybe we can reassess. But we need them. And I'm not giving up on my other goals while we wait."

It wasn't like Kaylah didn't have other spies, in addition to Rachel and Guillen.

Kaylah leaned forward. "The cave—that's crucial. Our Mother Vines ensure we have a border that can't be rifted into, even by our own kind. The War Vines have strengthened that twofold. And just like your people discovered during your last attack on the palace, the Vines make it harder to fly above, too. That border's a much smaller defense than your border walls, but it's right around the palace. And that cave is directly on that border."

The messenger stood there, awkwardly waiting for them to stop talking amongst themselves.

"Was there anything else?" Kaylah asked.

He pursed his lips. "Yes, just the one thing. The Ivy from the fight last night—he's missing."

"What do you mean, missing?" Kaylah shot up from her chair.

Knots twisted in Saff's gut.

"Well, from witness accounts, I don't think the argument was so bad that others would have harmed him ... but he can't be found anywhere. We think he found a way out of camp overnight."

Kaylah pulled on her hair. "We need to find out what happened. Search again. Look for marks of a rift. A gap in the patrol perimeter. And request extra guards. If he's gone back to the Ivy army, and gives up our location ... without the protection of your border walls..."

"Yes, ma'am. I'll talk to our council." He promptly exited the tent.

Kaylah turned back to Saff, who was giving her a sympathetic frown.

"Want to change places?" Kaylah asked.

Saff shook her head. "Not on your life."

It was well past dark when Saff and Devin retired to bed. They shared a wide cot, the soft glow of large lightkeepers in the camp shining through the tent fabric.

Saff snuggled up to Devin, thinking over their time together since joining Unitas, and the still-missing Ivy recruit. "How is it so easy for you to accept this change? They've tried to kill us both."

The rest, she left unspoken. The Ivies had also killed Ben—Devin's best friend and Saff's brother—and left Devin's sister, Heather, hurting. Every time a fight broke out in camp, Saff struggled with hope for their cause.

Devin drew a deep breath. "I figure the council wouldn't be working with Kaylah and letting her have this much freedom if she wasn't really trustworthy."

Perhaps that was true. Lionel wasn't Kaylah's constant companion anymore. A different council member had replaced him, and only visited daily, but didn't stay in camp overnight. "Yeah. I don't know. Definitely took me a while."

Devin gently rubbed Saff's upper arm. "Sometimes, I think you forget I'm a soldier. And not a human soldier. A soldier who didn't always know the difference between play and sparring growing up. I follow the council. I follow orders. It works for me."

She snuggled closer. "Sometimes I wish it was that easy for me."

"I don't know about 'easy.' I'd like to think I'm a *smidge* more complicated. That I have a *few* brain cells to think for myself, and that it's not *all* following orders."

She scoffed. "I'd never describe or imply that. I just wish I knew where to draw the line. And was better at following orders, sometimes. You know me."

"Mmm." He kissed her neck. "I *do* know you."

She smiled.

"That's part of why I love you so much," he said. "You keep me on my toes. You might drive me crazy sometimes, but most of the time, I'm just crazy *about* you."

She chuckled. "Either way, you're crazy. Sounds like I might not be good for you."

He pulled her in tighter, leaving another kiss on her neck. "Oh, you're good for me."

She grinned.

"I'd like to think we're good for each other." His voice softened more. "Why haven't you tried out the cave yet?"

She swallowed, frowning. "Just busy, you know?"

"Hmm. You're sure it's not because of our fight? Because I think you should give it a go. When things calm down, imagine the possibility of being able to visit your human parents more often."

She'd thought about it frequently. "I'm scared," she whispered.

Devin shifted in bed, reaching over and tapping a small lightkeeper by him; it lit up. "Why are you scared?"

She gazed into his eyes. "I could have died. I could have left you and everyone else without a goodbye. And this is still experimental."

He held her hand. "Kaylah's certain it would be safe. You understand your extra power capacity now. Others have taken the risk to prove it works without harm."

She looked away, contemplating it. Her fear wasn't rational; she knew that, too.

Devin tucked her hair behind her ear. "I'd hate to see you paralyzed by fear."

She sighed. She hated the idea of fear holding her back as well.

"What if we went together? There and back? I've always said we're better together."

As she gazed into his warm brown eyes, her hesitancy melted. "I'd like that. With you by my side, I think I could tackle it."

He beamed, scooting closer and nuzzling her neck. "Tackling. I'm a fan. Like football. A full-contact sport. I *like* full contact." He nibbled on her ear, and she slapped a hand to her mouth, quickly stifling a laugh that might wake others in nearby tents.

"Don't you feel guilty?" she asked.

He moved back, propping himself up on his side with an elbow. "For what?"

She rested a hand on his exposed chest. "Being together. Being happy. With all the ugly stuff going on in both worlds?"

Devin took a pensive moment before speaking. "No. I don't. We're not twiddling our thumbs out here. We're working hard, every day. But we still deserve to sleep, and eat, and have *a little* bit of time to recharge. Tomorrow's never promised."

She gave him a soft smile. "You're right. I love you."

He returned the smile. "I love you too. Now are you going to get the hint that we should be naked? Or should I take the hint that I need to try to fall asleep?"

A toothy grin spread across her face. "Turn off that lightkeeper."

Chapter 18

Rachel woke to a pair of lips on her forehead. She smiled and opened her eyes. Guillen smiled back at her. "Hey, beautiful," he whispered. "Let's get going."

Her joy faded as she remembered why they had to quietly pack up and leave so early in the morning. He folded her bedding while she freshened up in the bathroom. She stared at herself in the mirror, flashing her sad eyes green. Did Magda really think she was such a monster because of something as simple as her anatomy? Rachel's natural brown eyes were welcome; but once they glowed green, she became something to hate? They'd been greeted in this little apartment with warmth and love, and in a day's time, it grew cold and they were being turned out without so much as a goodbye.

The streets were still quiet at that early hour. Guillen risked holding her hand as they made their way to the café. They sat, eating pastries on a bench outside.

"Don't worry about tonight. I know exactly where we can stay, and we'll even get a comfortable bed." He tried to cheer her up. "We've got tons of time. How about I take you to a neighboring town? You can check out those art galleries and everything you want."

She shook her head. "It's fine. I can just stay indoors. I don't want to cause any more problems. And I don't want to see that jerk at the entrance again."

"I'll take care of it; we'll go out the other way. I want to show you around. Please?"

"Why can't we just move on to the next community, instead of wasting a whole other day here?" she whined. "I just want to go."

He frowned. "You know we can't do that. We didn't get enough done last night."

"I know." She threw her head back, staring at the cloudy grey sky. "You don't think we'll get rained on, do you?"

"No, we'll be fine. The town I'm thinking of is just over an hour's walk each way; we'll have lots of places we can go to." He lifted her hand, placing a kiss on it. "And we can just be *us*, over there."

She allowed a small smile to spread across her face. They only anticipated spending one or two days at each of the ten stunt communities, depending on when they arrived and when they could rally folks for their meetings. Travel between each community was generally expected to take two to four days on foot with steady speed, and they hoped to cover ground as quickly as possible. But as it was right now, they genuinely didn't have anything to do until the meeting that night. "Alright. I like the sound of that."

He helped her up, and they walked to the opposite end of the community from where they had initially entered.

As soon as she spotted the guard, Rachel grabbed Guillen's arm. "We don't have the paperwork for this. If we show him my papers to leave, he's going to expect me to not return."

"It's okay. Don't take out any paperwork. Let me handle it. Just hang back."

Guillen lifted his sleeve to the guard and was waved through. Instead of moving on, he stood in place and struck up a conversation. He whispered and gestured with his head and hands toward Rachel. The guard shook his head. Guillen reached into his pocket, handing the guard a few things. The guard hesitantly accepted the offer, and Guillen turned to Rachel, winking. "Come on."

She approached, unsure of what to do.

"Let me see your mark," the guard ordered, and she pulled up her sleeve. "Fine. You better be back before my shift is over."

"You know I will be." Guillen grabbed Rachel's hand and guided her out.

"That was too easy," she breathed as they walked down the path, and stashed their belongings in a hedge.

He was beaming. "Sometimes you have to have the right currency."

"It was as simple as bribing him?"

"Not quite. My pockets are lighter, but I also gave him something to hold on to, something he could keep as collateral."

She furrowed her brow. "And that was...?"

"My ring."

Her eyes widened. "Like the one Nuren had? Like the one I've seen Kaylah wear? Isn't that, like, a one-of-a-kind, special thing for royals? I've never even seen you wear it."

He glanced around to make sure they were alone. He stopped and rested his hands on Rachel's waist. "You know I don't care about that stuff. But yes, that kind of ring. I keep it just in case it comes in handy. He knows my word is good— we'll be back for that."

Her very presence had already brought about more problems than solutions. "You're sure it's not going to cause trouble?"

"We will be perfectly fine. It's just a little day trip. Plus," he grinned, "you're the kind of trouble I like."

She fiddled with a button on his shirt, her heart warming. "Thank you. For doing this to cheer me up."

"Anything for you." He gave her a peck on the lips. "Come on. Adventure awaits."

After an hour of walking hand in hand, they approached a much larger town. The area was slightly greener, and the houses larger. Guillen wrapped an arm around her as they entered.

"No guards," she noted. "That's nice."

"Nope. Regular citizens are allowed to come and go at their leisure."

Rachel shook away her annoyance, trying to focus on the adventure of her first time in a standard Ivy city. As she'd already noticed, most structures were stone. Rickshaws and bicycles rode down cobblestone streets. She reminded herself Ivies couldn't fly; they would naturally rely on other forms of transportation that were faster than walking. After a few moments of taking in the view, Rachel made an unnerving observation. Other than little boys and elderly male Ivies, there were no men walking the streets. Only girls and women.

"Where is everyone?" The small community she'd just been in had an equal gender ratio, but none of them were considered competent to enlist in the Ivy army.

Guillen hesitated, facing her more directly. "Kaylah told you all able-bodied males are enlisted, right? Ready to be deployed at any moment?"

Her heart dropped. "Are you kidding me? This is practically a ghost town!" she whispered. "You're telling me they've drained the cities and sent them *all* to war?"

He frowned, holding her hand. "You're surprised? It's not like they all went *willingly*. It doesn't mean every city is like this, either."

The only word that came to Rachel's mind was: *millions*. She imagined the Ivy soldiers in droves. In the human world. Marching on Seeder borders. Soren wasn't holding back.

Her heart raced. "Why are we wasting our time here? We need to let Kaylah know. We need to be doing something. Not just being tourists."

Guillen raised both eyebrows. "You know we're not her only spies. She has plenty of others. Who can rift and get her that kind of intel."

Rachel took her hand back, shoving both of them in her pockets. "Yeah, but we could be doing more. We're asking people in your communities to sabotage things, to steal things. They could get hurt, Guillen. They're not trained for a fight like you and I are. Don't you feel bad about that?"

He crossed his arms. "No. I don't. I know those people, and they need to learn to be their own advocates. They know what the risks are. You and I, we're doing our part. Who else is going to be able to move through those communities without suspicion, spreading Kaylah's message, if you and I get caught sabotaging something?"

She looked down, shaking her head. Guillen gently lifted her head with his hand under her chin. "Please try to enjoy today with me? We're not just being tourists. It's good for you to see this—the empty cities, so we can inform people in the stunt communities, because a lot of them have family they love out here; the culture, so you can blend in better and even share information with your people when this is all over."

Rachel gazed into his eyes, crestfallen.

"Please," he said softly. "Just for today, set aside the noise and worries. And just enjoy it with me."

She nodded, a small smile making its way to her lips. "I'll do my best."

Guillen's face brightened. He wrapped his arm around Rachel again. "Where to first?"

"I'll let you pick."

He didn't know this city well, but he wasn't afraid to ask around. They first found an art gallery. Rachel perked up and took her time admiring the paintings. She wished Saff could be there. Despite all the chaos of war back in their village, Saff had shown Rachel some of her paintings—she was really talented.

"It's amazing, isn't it? Art is a universal language. It speaks to all of us." Rachel stood entranced by a mural with swirls of vibrant blue, green, and yellow, representing the bountiful beauty of the Green Lands.

Guillen held her from behind, resting his chin on her shoulder. "I think you're right. Beauty is universal." He kissed her on the cheek, then swayed back and forth with her.

She let out a small giggle. "You are a *completely* different person."

He stopped swaying. "I... I guess maybe I take a little more than others to open up." He removed his arms from her waist. "Am I making you uncomfortable? Going too fast?"

She faced him, furrowing her brow. "No. I'd let you know." Her face softened into an adoring smile. "I love this version of you."

He grinned and swooped in for a brief kiss. She returned with a hug before moving on to see the rest of the exhibits.

They strolled to a museum nearby. It was interesting to see art and history from an Ivy perspective: The way decades of war were represented. The way her people were depicted. Seeders were often painted with a look of stupor, or monstrous villainy. Ivies were portrayed as heroes, standing triumphant and proud above their enemies. As ridiculous and biased as the paintings seemed, Rachel was curious how they would compare to Seeder art.(oo) Other than what Saff had shown her of her own paintings, Rachel hadn't seen much of Seeder art, hadn't left her family home enough to venture to places like this.

After a while, she caught Guillen admiring her as she was immersed in everything the museum had to offer. They'd never really gone on a 'proper' date, but if they decided to call this outing one, it would have been the perfect one.

"We've only got time for one more stop," he announced after hours spent in beautifully peaceful exploration.

He guided her to a large outdoor market, teeming with bright clothes, fruits and vegetables, home décor, and tons more she couldn't see. Strong spices wafted through the air around them. They walked by a booth that sold jewelry. Unlike mass-produced items in the human world, these items were individually handcrafted. Very few of the gems were precision-cut or sparkling like diamonds. Rachel spotted a fair amount of jade.

She whispered in Guillen's ear so the vendor couldn't hear them. "Does jade mean anything special to your people?"

"I don't think so. I think it's just a common stone in the Green Lands. Is it special to you?"

"Well, to our culture, yeah. It helps harness energy; we get a charm that helps when we bloom."

He smiled. "Let's get you something. Anything you want."

She shook her head. "I'm happy to just look."

"I insist. I want to."

She sighed at his handsome face; he was clearly eager to treat her. "I already have a necklace. What about those cute jade earrings to match?"

He pulled out some money and paid for them.

She put the small studs in her ears as he beamed.

"They were made just for you."

"Yeah, well, when you—" Her voice trailed off, as did her smile. She'd been about to say 'when you come visit *my* home, I get to be the one to treat you.' But her lands were poisoned; they wouldn't be able to share moments like these back in South Fortinda. Sure, they had figured out how to heal the lands, but to do so with their current method would take years, maybe even decades, to cover the expanse of affected land.

"What's wrong?"

She forced a smile, touching her earrings. "Nothing. I love them, thank you."

Guillen took her hand. "You know you're a bad liar, right?" He smirked. "At least you are with me." He gestured with a tilt of the head. "Follow me."

He led her to the center of the market, where a violinist played live music. Lining the town square were tented outdoor cafés. In the exact center was a giant intricately carved water fountain, featuring a stone replica of the Mother Vines snaking around it.(PP)

Guillen stopped, resting one hand on her waist, offering his other hand.

Rachel looked over her shoulder at the passersby. "We can't just dance in the middle of town."

"Says who? No one here knows us. We have the time. And I want to dance with you." A smile tugged at his lips as he dared her to challenge him.

She took his extended hand and let him guide her. Another thing he was surprisingly assertive with was dancing. Not wanting to embarrass him again like she had about having servants, she didn't ask, but she assumed his pedigree probably allowed him the privilege, and possibly even the expectation, of this kind of activity.

"Are you going to tell me what ran through your mind back there, when you lost that sparkle in your eyes?" he asked.

She bit her lip. "I... Does Ivy poison affect you the same way? Like it does with humans, or Seeders, or other Ivies? Kaylah once told me Ivies are affected by their own poison, but it's different than with Seeders. And I know Seeders react different than humans."

He furrowed his brow in thought. "You know, my dear, I don't really know. If I've needed numbing for something, the nurses have always known what I am. But the numbing has some pretty nasty side effects, so I haven't used it often. Why?" His jaw dropped as if he were shocked. "Are you trying to poison me?"

She chuckled. "No. I just wanted to know because, you know ... my home." She gripped his hand tighter. "I kind of imagined me repaying the favor and having you visit. But I don't know that you'd ... be able to." She glanced at the large scar on his temple. Scars were a rare sight amongst Seeders, given their healing abilities. She imagined Ivies might have more, but even then, they had accelerated healing. If his body didn't heal like green folk with powers, he probably couldn't withstand his own people's brand of killer poison.

He gave her a smile, though it didn't reach his eyes. "I'm happy to be with you, one day at a time. Let's not let a mysterious someday steal from our today."

She nodded. "You're right."

He spun her around with a dip as the song came to an end. "Thank you. For a perfect day."

Rachel and Guillen headed out of town, hand in hand, having purchased food from the market to eat on the way. They picked up their pace as they approached the stunt community, fearing the angry clouds darkening overhead. Rachel breathed a sigh of relief when they returned to find the same guard still on duty.

Guillen handed him more money, and the guard returned the ring. "This was a onetime thing," the guard muttered.

"Not a problem. I appreciate your discretion," Guillen remarked. He let go of Rachel's hand long enough to guide her to a row of apartments a few streets down. He had her wait at the street corner while he went to talk to someone.

Returning with keys, he announced they'd be staying the night in room four. It was a clean, minimally furnished studio apartment—the stunts' equivalent of a hotel. These communities were hardly destination locations, but they had a few rooms dedicated for travelers, or visiting family members; just simple accommodations.

"One bed?" She lifted her eyebrows.

Guillen shrugged. "We could get a second room, but I'd feel a lot better if we weren't split up. You can take the bed."

She sat down on it and bounced to check the springiness. It was fairly hard, but the comforter was soft. "We'll make it work. Is it all that different from sleeping on the same floor together?" She lay down. "We have some time, right? I believe you owe me a cuddle session from last night."

He grinned. "We've got some time. I'm a man of my word." He set their packs down, as well as his knives on a side table, and crawled onto the bed next to her. She willingly became the little spoon as his arms enveloped her.

She breathed in the moment, willing time to stop. "Thanks again. For today. I needed it."

"You're welcome. We all need a good distraction sometimes." He squeezed her tight. "You're my favorite mission as a traitor and spy, you know that?"

She shook with laughter. "Oh my gosh. Who says that?"

"Hey, I was just being honest." He chuckled.

"How long until we have to leave for tonight's meeting?"

He drew a deep breath. "I'm... I'm going to this one alone."

A heaviness instantly settled in her chest. "Why?"

"Jacob and I agreed it would be for the best, just to iron things out. They already got to meet you. They understand they have Seeders backing them up now."

She stared at the wall, still in his embrace. "No one wants me there. Why did I even come?"

He let go of her, sitting up. "We need you. Just try to be patient. The next meeting will go much better. I promise."

She didn't look at him or move. Something inside her was bending, breaking.

"Are you mad at me?"

She rolled over to face him, frowning, unsure of what to say. "No. I probably would've done the same thing. Just get done what you need to."

"I won't be out a moment later than I have to." He paused, clearly hesitant. "Do you... Maybe I'll head out now in case everyone gets there early, so I can get back earlier?"

She couldn't muster anything beyond a weak nod.

"Alright. Don't open the door for anyone, okay?" He gave her a quick kiss, then strapped on his knives and patted his pockets. As the door clicked closed behind him, she lay on the bed, frozen.

The first tear hit her pillow as thunder rumbled the building. She wanted more than this. To help. To be with Guillen.

She'd felt so safe with Guillen, so happy. Now she could barely breathe—assaulted by flashbacks, that shining beacon of hope he'd given her dimming. Pain she'd held back for months now flooded in, doubled.

Why did he have to do that?

She sobbed in the empty, lonely room.

Chapter 19

Rachel wiped away her tears, getting out of bed. She blew her nose and grabbed the spare key, making sure she had Ivy money in her pocket. She wasn't going to stay in that room alone. Not alone with her thoughts.

She hadn't expected something so small to trigger her, and she couldn't blame Guillen—he hadn't even realized what he'd done. But her old demons had come calling, and she needed to walk them off. She needed … to try something different.

It took her a moment to orient herself, and she braved asking a stranger for directions. She distracted herself by stabbing her palms with her fingernails. The sky began to spread a mist as she opened the door to the community pub. There couldn't have been more than a dozen patrons, but she wanted to steer clear of them all. Rachel sat at the bar, not completely sure what she was doing. The only alcohol she'd ever had was half a wine cooler. But she was ready to try this, if it could numb the pain.

The bartender came up to her, wiping down the counter. "What'll it be?"

"What's the strongest you have?"

"Vodka usually does the trick."

"I'll take two."

"Your ID?"

She rested her head on the counter, annoyed with herself. She'd forgotten to grab her forged papers. They showed she was of legal age in the Ivy Kingdom. She quietly moaned at the unfairness. *If they're going to let you drink at eighteen, why even check? Especially in such a small community?*

"It's okay, I'll vouch for her."

A hand caressed her lower back, and she bolted upright. The slimy guard from her first day there grinned down at her. "Thought you'd stood me up and skipped town."

She tried to keep a neutral expression and tone. "No. Just got busy."

"I'll have whatever she's having."

"Full strength? For both of you?" The bartender looked between Rachel and the guard.

"Of course," the guard replied.

The bartender returned with four shots, and Rachel tried to tip one back, coughing after the first swallow as it seared down her throat.

The guard chuckled. "Full strength is pretty daring for one of your kind, especially with such a delicate figure." He rested a hand on her thigh.

She ignored him and choked the rest of it down, then moved on to the second as he threw back his first.

"I don't remember your name. Mine's Tony."

"Elizabeth."

"Right. How much longer are you here for?"

"Just tonight."

He smirked. "Then let's make it a good one. Two more for each of us."

Rachel let him talk about himself for what seemed like ages as the buzz set in. He was beyond arrogant, not requiring much from her in return. She tired of his boring small talk, tossing back the next couple of shots, her third and fourth.

After a few minutes, her vision began to blur. She turned to face Tony, wagging a finger at him. "So you, are here. Why aren't you out there? Why guard ... when could be killing weeds?"

His hand rested more heavily on her thigh. "You don't find pretty girls like yourself on the battlefields out there. Do you want another shot?"

She extended her pointer finger, putting it up against her eye.

"Let's get two more for her."

She drank another one.

He gave her a lusty grin. "How about we head back to my place once you finish that last one?"

She closed her eyes, trying to focus as she clung to the counter. "I think. That I'm a *little* tipsy to walk."

He stood and moved behind her, inching his hands and vines between her legs, midthigh. "I can help," he whispered in her ear.

She squeezed her eyelids tighter, shaking her head. The room spun, causing her to grip the counter more firmly.

He quickly removed his hands and vines. "I don't think you were completely honest with me, Elizabeth." His tone was no longer flirtatious.

She registered the change and began to worry.

"I'd say palace boy is more than an acquaintance with the staredown he's giving us."

She turned to look at the entrance. Guillen marched over, disappointment painting his face.

"Mmm. Him." She faced the bar, frowning.

Tony backed up a pace.

Guillen grabbed her wrist, his voice firm. "Come on. You shouldn't be here."

Rachel furrowed her brow and yanked her wrist back. "Maybe I'm not ready." She reached for the other shot, and Guillen pulled it from her hand, slamming it on the counter out of reach.

"You're done."

Tony spoke up. "Hey now, she's free to make her own choices."

Guillen glared at him. "I know your kind. And unless you want to be reassigned to guarding the *Shadows of the Afterworld*, I'd recommend backing off." He put an arm around Rachel. "Please?" he pleaded.

Rachel slid off her stool, Guillen supporting her shaky legs.

She turned back to Tony, waving a finger in his general direction. "Thank you, Toby, fur a luffly evening. And the sshots." She swallowed as stomach acid inched its way up.

Tony plopped down on the stool, scowling. "Yeah. No problem."

Guillen ushered Rachel down the street as fast as her wobbly legs would allow; the earlier trickle of rain had become a full downpour. They were drenched by the time he got her back to their room. He sat her on the edge of the bed and locked the door behind them.

Guillen stood in front of Rachel, arms crossed, his wet hair clinging to his forehead. "Why would you do that?"

She squinted. "Are you jealouss?"

"Was that what you were going for back there?"

She scowled. "No."

"Then what was that about?"

She stared at the ground, her mind still beyond fuzzy.

He huffed. "That was stupid."

She looked back at him, brow furrowed. "I'm not an idjit. I wasn't leaving with him."

"Right." He scoffed. "Because you're clearly in perfect shape to fight off a man twice your size! You were doing a great job *all* by yourself." He shook his head. "And our mission—that was selfish."

"I'm not that drunk!" She pouted. "I wouldn't've said anything."

"Have you ever had hard alcohol before, Rachel? Because I seriously doubt you've had Ivy-distilled. Your people don't handle poison as easily, do they? You wouldn't *have* to say anything! Did you even think about the fact that you might have unknowingly started to glow or something with another shot? You don't know how that stuff affects you!"

She instantly started to ugly cry at his chastisement. "I just didn't want it. I don't wanna be heere. It'ss only abou' my body. They touch it, or they take what they want. But they don't care, 'cause I'm stuuupid. I don't want it. I just wanted you." She licked her salty tears as he frowned. She squeaked out the last part. "I just don't want it."

He sighed softly as his shoulders dropped. "Let's get you to bed. Sleep it off, and we'll talk in the morning."

She pushed herself up and balanced against the wall. Then dropped her pants.

He whipped around. "Why are you stripping?"

She tugged on her shirt sleeve in frustration. "Because. I'm. Wet!"

"Fine. Hurry up and get under the covers."

Her waterlogged shirt fell to the ground with a *splat*. She glanced down at her underwear, deciding not to bother before climbing into bed.

"Are you covered?"

"Maybe."

"Rachel..."

"Yes. Don't know why yur being prude. You've seen me half nak'd before."

He turned, scolding her with his eyes, bending over to pick up her wet clothes and taking them to the bathroom.

"Do you still like me?" She pouted as he returned, her tears threatening to make another appearance.

"Yes," he breathed gently. "You know I do." He grabbed a spare blanket and left the room again, returning with it wrapped around him. A soft *pitter patter* came from the bathroom, where he must have hung their things to drip-dry. "Go to sleep."

"Will you kiss me? I want to cuddle with you." A short candle lit the room, the flame dancing. She craved the warmth of his body next to hers.

He shook his head and sat on the edge of the bed next to her. "No. Not while you're drunk." His blanket dropped, just covering his waist and below. "I'm tucking you in, and we'll talk in the morning."

As he reached over, she grabbed his bicep—the one without the stunt mark. "One of yer tattoos. Is pretty. Whas it mean?"

"It means you should go to sleep. Good night, Rachel."

Chapter 20

Rachel woke, her head screaming like it had been cracked open. She grimaced and placed a hand on her head, moving healing energy to try and help. She forced herself to sit up after feeling hardly any relief.

"Did it help?" Guillen was sitting on the love seat, shirtless, in his spare change of pants. His tone and expression hinted at frustration, but weren't unkind.

She groaned. "Not really."

"Well, it's good to know you can't just zap your way out of all of life's consequences. Drink some of that water on the bedside table."

She reached over, then stopped. The blanket had slipped, revealing her bra. She snapped the covers up to conceal her chest.

"I slept on the floor. Nothing happened."

She frowned. "I'm sorry."

He scratched his knee. "Are you ready to talk?"

She eased the water off the table, guzzling half of it. "I'm guessing you're not going to take 'no' for an answer."

Guillen crossed his arms. "You guessed right. Talk. Why was it so horrible to be left alone for a whole hour and a half? So bad that you had to go drinking?"

"It's not that simple."

"Honestly, Rachel. You acted like a child. I know it hurt, the way Magda and everyone reacted, but I never imagined you'd go out and do something like that. Do you want to go home? Are you going to be able to finish this mission?"

She looked down. "I can do it. I need to do it."

"Why do you *need* to do it?"

She stared at her hands, digging her fingernails in painfully.

"I'm going to grab us some breakfast. You get dressed, and we'll talk more when I get back, okay?" He raised his eyebrows. "Can I trust that you'll be here when I return?"

She rolled her eyes. "Yes."

Guillen threw on a dry shirt and headed out. Once he left, Rachel rifled through her pack. Since they needed to travel light, her only spare clothing, other than the underwear essentials, was a t-shirt with sleeves long enough to conceal her tattoo, and some fairly short shorts. She finished her water and refilled the glass. Sitting on the bed, she rested her pounding head on her knees.

He returned with a couple of pastries and apples. They silently dug in. After a while, he tried again. "I know this is about something deeper. You said you feel safe with me; will you please just talk to me?"

She picked at her pastry. How could she ever share her demons with him? "I don't think you're the right person for this."

"I'm trying to be patient. But I care about you, and I don't want to see you bottling it up anymore and hurting yourself like this." He lifted her chin to make eye contact. "You don't need to worry about sparing my feelings, or me judging you for anything that's happened. I know what that asshole's capable of. Please just let me help you."

She leaned back against the headboard, folding her arms around her legs. Staring at the ceiling, she gathered her courage. "I spent my whole life, happy. Thinking I was something I wasn't. For a short while, I thought I had a loving dad, who I found out either hates me for who I am, or was murdered by Nuren. Nuren acted like he loved me for a decade, just to use me to kill my own people. My best friend poisoned me—for months—to screw with my head and make me feel worthless. I started to hurt myself to deal with it. My boyfriend attacked me in a hot tub and then manipulated me into trusting him." She lowered her head to look at Guillen. "That's all before I was kidnapped. How are we doing so far?"

He gently rubbed her arm. "I'm sorry."

"Me too." Tears filled her eyes, and a whimper escaped her lips. "Because it's *my fault* I ended up here. I didn't get to choose what world I'd live in. He stole that from me! He made me trust him, and then he took me here, and drugged me. And then I was stabbed a thousand times, and all they cared about was my Seeder energy. It felt like ... they drained my soul with it." Her tears flowed freely, carrying with them the rest of the pain she hadn't been able to share with others. "All because I was stupid. And he didn't even rape me, but he," her voice quivered, "he touched me, and I didn't know when he would stop. I couldn't move, and he wouldn't stop!" She bent over, weeping, barely able to breathe.

Guillen wrapped his arms around her. She leaned into him, letting out the hurt that had been pent up. Each tear burned as it rolled down her cheek. They seared with the guilt of each Seeder who had died because of her stupidity in ever trusting Soren, the guilt of her mom's pain at being all alone, the guilt of surviving and being happy to any degree when other kidnapped Seeder girls weren't so lucky.

"It's not your fault. You need to remember that. It's not your fault. And you're not stupid. I shouldn't have said that last night. I'm sorry." He kissed her head. "Don't blame yourself for trusting him. He carries *all* of the blame, and he'll pay for it. I'll make sure of it."

Rachel woke a half hour later, her head on Guillen's lap. Her eyes were puffy, and her headache raged on. She sat up. "Thanks for listening." She couldn't look him in the eyes.

He held her hand. "Any time. Do you feel better?"

She leaned her head on his shoulder. "My head—not so much. My heart—maybe."

"Was the pub all about the human dad thing? Him maybe judging you for being a Seeder? And Magda? Or the other stuff, and Mr. Handsy I-Might-Break-His-Face-Before-We-Leave?"

She grinned before frowning again. "Those are both part of it. But ... I was just so happy with you. You're like that one good part of my life right now. I don't even fit in with my Seeder family. My mom back home is in a Unitas safe house. Everyone in my village thinks I'm brainwashed. And ... you lied to me when you promised you wouldn't."

He leaned away, visibly confused. "I lied to you?"

She sniffled. That had been what sent her over the edge, what had pulled the rug out from underneath her. "You knew I wouldn't be going to the meeting last night, but you didn't tell me until *after* we had a great day. I know you were doing it to make me feel better, but you manipulated my feelings. I don't want that." She fidgeted with her hands. "I just want the truth, even if it's going to hurt."

"I'm sorry." Regret filled his voice. "I never thought of it that way. I swear. I'll do my best to be completely upfront with you, okay?"

"Thank you. I know I'm ... complicated."

"You're worth it." He paused. "What you said, about hurting yourself. Do you ... still have a hard time with that?"

She examined her palms, where she'd been digging her nails in to feel the pain. It wasn't the same as stabbing herself with a needle, but she'd done it in the same spirit. She was too ashamed to look up. "I promised Kaylah I wouldn't. But I don't know if I can keep that promise."

"Would you tell me if you started again?"

She frowned, meeting his soft eyes. "I *want* to say yes. I'll try."

"That's all we can do." He wore a reassuring smile. "We try, learn, and grow, and heal. One day at a time." He cleared his throat. "And I know it's really sensitive, with ... him ... and what he did to you. But please tell me if I do anything, say anything, touch you, in a way you're uncomfortable with. I don't want to be that guy. I want to be with you, but not by hurting you."

She nodded, immensely grateful he was so understanding. "It really doesn't bother you that I dated him?"

He smiled again. "Does it bother you that I've dated other women before you?"

She sighed. "That's hardly the same."

"Maybe not. But I add it to the list of what I admire about you. It just shows you have great taste to ditch a crown, and slum it with the likes of me." He nudged her playfully.

She let out a small sincere laugh.

"There she is." He kissed her shoulder. "Are you ready to pack up and leave this place behind?"

"Can we cuddle for a while longer? Let my headache die down?"

"Sure."

They slipped under the covers, and she rested her head on his chest.

"So, these tattoos—you've been exposed."

"Mmm... It appears so."

"Can I see them?"

"Sure."

She sat up while he pulled off his shirt, then leaned back against him as he lay down. She traced a thin but intricate design on his arm, a band inked on his bicep. "What's the story behind this one?"

"That one has the least meaning, honestly. I just thought it looked cool. And I think I wanted to put something on my body that was by *my* choice. I got it soon after leaving home."

She gently pressed her lips to the tattoo. "Then it means something important." She rolled over, touching his third tattoo, a small one on his chest. "I recognize this one. It's the Unitas symbol, right?"

He grinned. "Yeah. Kaylah was scorched, but it's not like I walk around with my shirt off. And Craig did it for me, anyway. I got it shortly after I pledged my oath to Kaylah. A blossom and an ivy leaf." He held her hand over it. "Keeping what matters most to me, over my heart."

She stared lovingly into his eyes. Scooching up, she placed her head higher on his chest, snuggling again. He kissed the top of her head as her body moved to the rhythm of his lungs.

<hr>

They checked out of their room after a couple of hours. Guillen strode down the street with his arm unashamedly around Rachel. They intentionally left the community from the exit Tony wouldn't be at, despite Guillen wanting to crack his skull open. He didn't want to put Rachel through seeing Tony again, and they couldn't jeopardize their cover any further.

The next community would be a day and a half away if they kept a good pace, so they'd need to find somewhere to stop for the night along the way. Guillen caught Rachel up on what the first group had committed to. Despite the rough first meeting, they'd made great progress the second night. Word was going out to people they trusted, who spread the truth about the cause and about their needs. Sabotage plans were set in place for the Ivy army supply chain.

Wanting to avoid any suspicion, Rachel and Guillen stopped in a regular town to rest for the night instead of trying to find a place on the outskirts of town to camp. Guillen got them a double-bed room, though Rachel would have been happy to share and cuddle. In the end, it was probably for the best that she stuck to her own bed, given how quickly things were developing between them. She didn't want to rush anything too much. She didn't want to screw things up with Guillen.

The next day, they arrived at Community Nine early enough to grab dinner, but too late to call a meeting with their connections. They took their food to-go, back to their room. Like the last community, only single-bed rooms were available.

"This is amazing. You should try some." Rachel covered her mouth while she talked. She'd ordered a salad with a particularly tangy dressing.

Guillen leaned forward and stole a kiss, then licked his lips. "Not bad."

She chuckled. "That's hardly what I meant."

He gave her a toothy smile as she lifted her fork up for him to try a bite.

He opened his mouth and sampled it. "Yeah. It's alright. I liked the first try better."

She shook her head and giggled. She loved this. When they'd been apart and she'd thought of this guy, one of her rescuers, she'd thought fondly of him. But she hadn't really understood what it meant to fall head-over-heels for someone. She'd told Prince Soren she loved him only in reciprocation, after almost three years of dating. Guillen had her heart completely.

They cleared off the bed after eating, and Rachel lay on her side, facing him. "I wish we didn't have to pack so light. It would be nice to have a book or something. Especially without games or a TV."

He flashed a look of confusion.

"It's a box where you can watch entertainment. Like theater."

"Okay." He slipped down on the bed, mirroring her position. "I remember hearing about that now."

He'd continued to teach her more fighting techniques in their free time, but there was only so much they could do in the cramped space of their private rooms.

"I guess I really didn't expect to do so much waiting on this mission," she said.

He flashed pouty lips. "It's pretty rough being stuck with me. Isn't it?"

She gave him a smug grin. "Yep. *Excruciating.*"

"You know, people do other things in rooms like this, if they're bored."

She blushed. "I'm not ready for that."

He shifted a little on the bed. "I meant kissing and cuddling. Naturally."

She bit her lip. "Naturally."

"Can I kiss you?"

She lifted an eyebrow. "Are we going back to asking?"

"When we're lying in bed, yes."

"Come here."

Guillen leaned over, kissing her sweetly. She pulled him in, running her fingers through his hair and nibbling on his lip. He slid closer, some of his weight resting on her as they kissed more passionately than they had before. Every inch of her tingled in waves through her body under his weight. He moved his lips to her neck. She shivered but pulled herself away from the moment.

"Guillen, stop. Please get off."

He jumped back. "I'm sorry. Did I? Was it ... something..."

"Gosh, no!" She rubbed her forehead, having feared this exact thing would happen. "Please. *Please*. Do *not* think about him every time you touch me. I mean it. Sometimes, I just want to take things slower."

Guillen closed his eyes and sighed. "Right." He met her gaze. "I can sleep on the floor again."

"No, that's silly." She smiled softly. "Can you handle being the little spoon?"

He opened his mouth, but nothing came out for a moment. "Well, I... I'm not certain I know what you mean by that."

It was still cute when he'd confess he didn't understand her. She appreciated that he was honest and vulnerable enough to do so. "Spooning?" She cradled her hands together. "Like if they're put away in a drawer together."

He pointed at her hands. "Yeah, but they nestle like that when they're the same size. You said I'd be the *little* spoon?"

She genuinely couldn't tell if he was just trying to pull her leg again, and didn't want to laugh if he was serious. "It's the inside spoon. The one being held."

He continued to look confused. "I just don't understand the logic behind the idiom. I'm larger than you, but I'd be the little spoon?"

"Do you want me to hold you? Or do you want me to stay on my half of the bed?"

He pressed his lips together. "I think I can manage being a little spoon."

Smiling, she blew out the candle on her nightstand, and they settled in for an early night.

Having to logistically explain spooning to her boyfriend had taken away some of the steam from their heated make-out session, but just a whiff of his hair—fresh mint and juniper berries—made her want to kiss his neck. But it wouldn't stop there, and she knew it.

"Do they sell decks of cards around here?" she asked in the dark.

He chuckled, perhaps sharing the same struggle. "I'm sure we can find some."

Chapter 21

uillen gave Rachel the grand tour of Community Nine, introducing people along the way. It was much like Ten—basic, cookie cutter. She was curious, though, about some larger unmarked buildings on the edge of the community.

"What are those?"

"Family homes."

"But ... you're not allowed to have kids."

"Behind them is the orphanage."

She frowned. "How can people be so heartless that they don't even want their own kids? Just because they don't have powers? Is it so hard to live with a human?"

"It's a shame thing. Status. A lot of families, like mine, still raise us. But not everyone."

She couldn't take her eyes off the buildings. "What happens if a couple like Magda and Jacob defy the law and have a kid?"

"They'd be punished, and the baby would end up at one of these, too."

She was relieved they would at least allow the child to live, but still... It went against everything in her family-centered Seeder culture. And any decent society.

He gave her an understanding look. "Not everyone gives up their children. At a young age, or even when they're supposed to, when they're older. Some parents try to conceal the child's condition, but it's impossible to do with our education system. It's a dead giveaway when you're in sparring classes, you know? Then the parents get punished for hiding the truth. Eventually, we all have to come here."

All she could do was shake her head.

"Come on." He wore an understanding half-smile. "Let's go refine our strategy for tonight's meeting."

❖

Finding a quiet place in the community gardens where they wouldn't be overheard, Rachel and Guillen discussed what they would do to make the meeting better this time. They planned to listen more, pose more questions, feel out the concerns and frustrations of the particular group, and then lean into those.

They talked about addressing the Seeder part of the equation much more in depth, earning more attendee trust, not revealing her identity too early. And she wasn't just a representative, a witness bearing testimony. She could demonstrate her people's commitment.

"Are you sure you're okay with that?" Guillen winced. "I know we talked about you possibly offering to heal, but … I just want to make sure you're really okay with it. I think we'd still do alright if you decided not to."

"I want to help. You don't think they'll consider it pandering, do you?"

"No. I'm sure they'll be happy to be healthier. I just … don't want you to feel used." He reached a hand up to her stunt mark.

Her body … yeah… She'd already demonstrated her commitment to the cause, on her own body. The thing she was tired of people using and abusing.

The difference between using her energy to heal, and using it to power a war machine, was her choice in the matter.

She gazed into his eyes. "There's a difference between using someone, and letting them be useful. I'm here to help."

He replied with his signature grin. "Alright."

Their rocky first meeting had taught them a lot. And luckily, reworking their presentation proved successful. The room came together with much more harmony this time. Progress was made. Rachel's heart swelled at the number of people who introduced themselves after knowing what she was, even if it seemed like some did so just out of curiosity. They told the group when they could meet the next morning if they wanted to bring anyone to be healed, as long as they were absolutely sure anyone they brought could be trusted.

Guillen had some acquaintances here as well who offered to let them stay with them, but after the first experience, Rachel preferred the comfort and privacy of having their own place. They lay in bed, facing each other, beaming at the day's success. Rachel hugged herself as they chatted. They were both gushing about how the other had said just the right thing at the right time, connecting with the people. She loved being so united, so in sync.

He traced her curves, tenderly running a couple of fingers from her shoulder down to her hips. His face became pensive. "It really never bothers you? What I am?"

She flashed him a reassuring smile. "Ruggedly handsome and unbelievably kind?"

He blushed. "Yes. That's exactly what I meant."

Her smile grew to a huge grin. "It doesn't. I don't get why it would bother anyone. To me, you're normal. For almost all of my life, every guy I ever met, at least that I knew of, didn't have powers. That's the benefit of growing up in the human world."

He studied her. "That's true. But once you gained powers, can you honestly say you weren't drawn to others who shared them?"

She furrowed her brow in thought. She'd liked the prince *despite* his powers, but that had been complicated, him being the enemy. Not that Guillen wasn't the same race as the enemy... Back in her Seeder village, she had gotten attention, as did all the girls, for being a new arrival. In a society low on females, she was a hot commodity. But she hadn't been drawn to any of the guys. And then Zeus... Well, there was that.

"Think about it like ... well ... *him*." She'd rather not say Soren's name. "Once I realized who he really was, I didn't suddenly think he was better in any way, because he was a prince. Power, whether political or physical—it doesn't change who you really are."

Guillen smiled. "So, you're not just after me for my crown tattoo?"

She chuckled, then lifted an eyebrow. "Wait, is that a thing? I honestly hadn't thought about it that way. Are you a ladies' man and I don't know it? They fling themselves at you? You did once say that you were 'lucky' to have your royal ties." She winked.

He pursed his lips. "It is ... actually kind of a thing. At least in these communities. If I married one of my kind, she'd get the same level of freedom."

"Oh. That kind of sucks. Knowing people might have ulterior motives." She frowned. *Yeah, like the prince dating you, just to use you.* She and Guillen were so different, but at the same time, shared a lot of the same struggles.

She wanted to change the subject away from Soren. "Have you ever dated girls with powers? Or just those like you?"

Guillen shifted his weight. "I've dated both. Do you want to talk about our dating histories?"

Her cheeks warmed. She'd barely turned eighteen when she was back home in her Seeder village, at least according to her human-given birthday. And she'd really only dated the prince in high school. But Guillen was almost twenty-four ... and apparently had women chasing him for status. "Maybe not."

He shrugged with one shoulder. "I don't have anything to hide."

She smiled shyly. "I'm fine. What about me? It doesn't bother you that I'm a Seeder, powers and all? I feel like that's more of a stretch than me being okay with you." She realized ... he might not have always thought fondly of her kind... Or worse yet...

"I mean ... I could assume you like me because I'm a shiny thing, exotic. Maybe a fetish or trophy or something."

His look made his sentiments clear, a 'Really? You're kidding me, right?' kind of face. "Didn't you just say it's about personality and not power?"

Touché. "Yes. And you just clarified that the ladies can't keep their hands off of you, because of your status," she teased with raised eyebrows.

He gently poked her arm. "Before you knew who your brother Jeff was, that either of you were Seeders, you were nice to him. He was awkward and didn't fit in, but you tried hard to make him feel welcome."

She was pulled from the fun of their playful banter, disarmed by his casual mention of Jeff. She searched his face intently. "I don't remember ever mentioning Jeff to you. Or any of that."

He averted his eyes, tracing patterns on the bed between them. "No, you didn't. That was one of the stories Kaylah told me about you."

She'd known Kaylah had talked about her, but it just now dawned on her that she really didn't know to what extent. Rachel felt uneasy, and he must have noticed when he looked back at her.

"I..." He swallowed. "I just feel like I kind of got to know who you were before we met. I might have ... been interested in getting to know you ... but I don't want to come off ... you know..."

She rolled onto her back. Kaylah had never mentioned Guillen in all their years in the human world. And she knew why, aside from the obvious undercover mission. Kaylah had already pushed her into a relationship with Soren. Just like Kaylah had encouraged that romance, she'd been pushing Rachel into Guillen's arms.

Knots formed in Rachel's stomach. She couldn't believe Kaylah had nefarious intentions, but the parallel was sickening.

"I don't know what to say," he whispered. "I'm sorry if that creeped you out. I don't mean to come on too strong."

She stared at the ceiling. "Did Kaylah encourage you to date me?"

He paused far too long. "Not like that. No. Not like a mission."

She couldn't get herself to look at him. If Kaylah could bring people together for the purpose of kidnapping (despite it being under orders), she could certainly manipulate people together for a different cause of her choosing. Rachel despised the thought of possibly being used as a pawn again. And even more, her heart ached at the thought of Guillen innocently being used that way. He might not even realize it. Kaylah could have planned this whole thing, just so the pair of them could rally people to her cause. Not that it wasn't a just cause...

She dared to ask, "When she picked who would help rescue me from the palace..." But she couldn't let herself finish that accusation.

The hurt in his voice was apparent. "I'd like to think I was chosen for an elite mission because I've worked hard for Kaylah, and *earned* her respect, her confidence in me."

She rolled away from him, hiding her face and fighting back tears. *Great. Let's mingle our struggles and personal identities.* She'd just been trying to sort through her own trauma, not realizing what her question had implied. She'd questioned his competence at something intimately personal—at least that was how he'd taken it. The layers of deception and torture in her life were like a rockslide pinning her down. It was too heavy. She may never know what a healthy relationship was.

"I'm sorry," she whispered. "I didn't mean it that way."

After a minute, Guillen blew out his candle. "Good night."

Rachel lay there in the dark, her mood sinking deeper and deeper. And also surprised to find herself getting angry with him. He was textbook perfect in being a considerate boyfriend—soft, kind, understanding, patient. But this once, she wanted him to raise his voice, demand she understand his feelings, make his position clear, *fight* with her, for her.

Chapter 22

Rachel woke in the early morning, having cuddled up to Guillen during the night. He was awake already.

"Sorry," she said as she moved off him.

"Don't be. I'm not." He wore a soft smile. That usual kind, soft smile.

He sat up against the wall, and she followed suit.

She gave him a sincere frown. "I'm sorry about how I asked that last night. I would never question how capable you are. I was just in my head, and it didn't come out right."

He met her gaze. "Thank you. It means a lot to me. Especially because *I* know, that *you* know, that it means a lot to me."

She gave a tiny half-smile of acknowledgement.

"About the rest..." he said.

She looked at him sheepishly. "I don't really want to talk about that right now." He exhaled loudly.

Deciding it was best to just get out of bed and hop in the shower, Rachel started to move. Unexpectedly, he grabbed her hand. "I do."

Owing to the determination on his face, she backed up against the wall, tucking her knees under her chin.

"I'm not trying to rush you through what you're dealing with, but this has to do with me, too, and I deserve to have a say in it."

She didn't even know what to say, but she had a small sense of satisfaction in him standing up for himself, for them.

He continued, "Yes. I knew more about you than you knew about me, before we met. But the chemistry we have, the feelings I have for you, those aren't from pictures and stories."

She blushed and looked away.

"Rachel, I'm not going to patronize you by asking, because I know you. But maybe you need to ask yourself: Would you be here, doing this mission, risking your life every day, if you were with someone else? And if someone other than Kaylah had asked it of you?"

Perhaps he gave her a little too much credit. She'd have been much more hesitant to embark on this mission if it hadn't been with someone she trusted. But in spirit, in morals, Guillen was right. Even if she'd never met him, even if things had happened differently—these people didn't deserve to be treated this way. And her people deserved to stop living in fear. Even before she'd met him, she had wanted to be part of the solution.

"Why do you like me?" he asked.

She searched his face. Wasn't it obvious? "Because you're sweet, and thoughtful, and funny, and smart, and strong, and talented." She bit her lip. "And you're not exactly bad looking, or bad at kissing, or hugging, or really anything." She couldn't look him in the eyes.

"Would you stop dating me if Kaylah ordered you to?"

She furrowed her brow and met his gaze. "No. That's none of her business."

He raised his eyebrows, slightly smirking. "It sounds like you're with me because you actually *want* to be. And I personally know you were picked for this mission because of what you have to offer. And *I'm* here because I've dedicated my life to this, and I'm damned good at it. And I'm with you, because..." He paused with his mouth open. "I think you're amazing ... and I like who I get to be when I'm with you."

Silence hung in the air.

"Guillen, I'm sorry. I really don't know how to do this. I feel like ... I'm always going to be like this. The smallest things, intentional or not, good or bad... They take me back to places and things I'd rather forget. I don't know what I'm doing." Her eyes welled up.

He shifted to face her, leaning his shoulder and head against the wall. "The only way you learn to trust again is by trying. I don't expect you to not have moments like this. Challenge me—I don't have anything to hide. But what you *really* need to do, is challenge yourself. Tell yourself that you've learned, and that you deserve to move on. Because you have, and you do."

She nodded thoughtfully.

"You trust me? You feel safe with me?" he asked.

She drew a deep breath. "Yes." She faced him, also leaning against the wall.

"Do you feel stupid for trusting me?"

She frowned. "Um..."

"Because I could have more training than you think, on manipulation."

She searched his eyes. *No.* Looking back on Soren's behavior, she could now discern where he had molded her the way he'd wanted. She'd never sensed that in Guillen.

"You've slept next to me for, well, weeks now, if we include the first trip with Jon. Have you ever felt like you weren't safe? That I wouldn't respect you?"

She shook her head.

"I have a half dozen weapons within arm's reach right now. And I've had them every single one of those nights. I've killed for this cause. I've killed for Kaylah."

Her eyes grew wider as her heart pumped faster. She'd assumed as much, but they'd never discussed it. The man she knew was the sweetest, most gentle man she'd ever met. He was strong, and competent, and wise. But he was also a successful spy, and she had allowed herself to forget that.

"Why are you telling me this?" she asked.

Guillen searched her eyes. "Because this is who I am. Do you still trust me?"

She closed her eyes. A mix of emotions bombarded her, one of them guilt, for making any of this about her, in her doubts. "I've always trusted you." She fidgeted with her hands. "I know who you are. I'm sorry."

He reached over and took her hands. "I'm not looking for an apology. I'm just asking you to trust yourself more. When you question me, or you, or us, or anything, the only way you're going to move forward is to question your questions, and choose to take a step into the dark."

"Okay," she whispered. "Thank you."

After a moment of silence, he asked, "Can I kiss you?"

She leaned forward, meeting him in the middle. The longer they kissed, the more her worries melted away. She was in that place again, the place she felt safest, with him. She pulled back, grinning. She adored his smile, the piercing look he was giving her, seeing his bare chest rise and fall. She gestured with her head for him to lie back down. She propped up her head, lying on her side. "How about we give this a fresh start?"

"Hmm. What does that entail?"

She straddled him, a mischievous grin spreading across her face. He shifted to accommodate her, matching her smile.

"I think we just have to go back to that first kiss. And maybe it's best if, instead of starting from the beginning, we trace our way back. Just for good measure." She leaned down, getting lost in his eyes before locking lips in a kiss as passionate as any they'd shared.

Her whole body radiated her feelings for him. His strong hands tightly gripped her hips, holding her in place. She pulled back for a moment, catching her breath. She mused at how much her Seeder transformations betrayed her when she shared her affections so freely with him. He didn't need to have any powers to make it clear what he wanted.

"We have lots of time," he said. "Just ... not today."

She smiled sweetly. "I know." She honestly wasn't sure if they were talking about the same thing ... but either way, they were still on the same page. She wasn't ready to go further than this, and they needed to get ready for the day, and focus on their mission.

She sat there, tracing his Unitas tattoo as their breathing calmed down.

"I would kill for you," he whispered.

Taken aback, she met his gaze. His face showed how serious his resolve was, though his soft eyes expressed his vulnerable desperation for her.

"To keep you safe."

She swallowed a lump in her throat. That was a given. They were partners on a mission—that was part of the job description, to keep each other alive. But that was *not* what he was saying. That was the kind of declaration that told her, no matter what, even if this war took a turn for the worse, he planned to be by her side.

"And I'll keep you safe," she whispered back.

The corner of his lip curved up. "We need to move on."

After allowing herself one more moment of pure happiness in the here and now, she slid off him. "Let's go heal some people."

Chapter 23

Only a pair of stunts showed up for minor healing in Community Nine before Rachel and Guillen moved on. Which was good; they didn't want to drain Rachel too much before a long day of travel, and the more people who knew her identity as a Seeder, the riskier it became for them. The handful of people present were in as much shock and awe at her Seeder abilities as Guillen and Jon had been the first time they'd seen her heal herself.

The more heartbreaking of her two patients was a fourteen-year-old boy. For his birthday, he'd been ripped from his family and forced to take the mark, assigned to this community. His arm was still red and sore.

He hadn't even been given the option of numbing like Olivia had provided for Rachel. Or a healer. He looked so confused and scared as he glanced at those around him. They were all strangers to him. She gently placed her hand on his mark, wishing she knew what to say.

He studied her face; this was no doubt the first time he'd ever seen a Seeder. "Why are you doing this?"

"Because you're worth it."

A shy smile appeared on his face, before a frown overtook it. He looked down as Rachel finished healing and removed her hand. "My mom got hurt, when they came to ... well, she ... um..." Tears filled his eyes. "She's in Cassa. Would you be able to go heal her?"

Rachel bit her lip, glancing at Guillen out of the corner of her eye, hoping, praying, that somehow Cassa was a regular city nearby they could stop at.

Guillen's eyes held sadness as he gently shook his head.

They hadn't come to heal. That wasn't their mission. "I'm sorry," Rachel said, her eyes moistening and warming, her heart yearning to do more. "I'm really sorry."

The boy's frown deepened. "Why not? Couldn't you fly there?"

Her chest physically hurt.

"It's Marcus, right?" Guillen asked.

The boy looked at Guillen. "Yeah."

Guillen gestured with a nod to follow him to the front of the room. "Let's chat."

Rachel hung back, standing next to the only other person still in the room—the elderly woman who had been in their meeting the night before, and come this morning, escorting the boy.

"Never gets any easier to see it," the woman muttered, her focus on Guillen and Marcus.

Wiping away tears, Rachel tried to calm herself. "It's so horrible."

The woman slowly nodded. "And you always worry if they'll make it."

Rachel's eyes widened. "What do you mean by that?"

"People can spiral."

Rachel gulped. *Suicide.* "Fourteen is too young to be taken like this."

The woman eased herself down onto a chair. "Is there a better age to have your life stolen from you?"

Rachel's own kidnapping played through her mind; it made her sick to her stomach. "No. I don't suppose there is any sort of ideal for something like this."

Guillen and Marcus sat on a large desk at the front of the room, talking. The boy continued to cry, and Guillen hugged him.

"When did he get here?" Rachel asked.

"His intake was this morning. The rest of today will be his tour and orientation. He'll start work tomorrow."

"So quickly?"

The woman gave a gentle shrug. "If you can walk, you can work. Our people have a lot of labels for our kind. The one I use? Slaves."

"Yeah," Rachel half breathed, crestfallen.

They watched on as Guillen and Marcus chatted. Marcus had wiped away his tears and was putting on a brave face. He even cracked a smile once or twice as Guillen talked to him.

"I'm glad I got to meet the infamous Guillen," the woman said. "He's a good man."

Rachel's heart swelled as she studied him. "Yeah. He's the best kind there is." She knew in that moment that it was love. She didn't even question it. There was no 'maybe' about it.

Less pleasantly, her mind drifted to the first man she'd ever professed her love to. She'd waited for him to say it first. That wasn't going to happen this time. This time she actually meant it.

Guillen lifted his sleeve to show his mark to the boy, then pointed in Rachel's direction. She blushed as Marcus looked at her with a surprised face. She didn't know when she'd tell Guillen how she really felt. She'd wait a little while, making sure it was the right time. They were good together. She promised herself she wouldn't allow doubt to creep in again and screw things up.

Guillen stood, finding a piece of paper and a pen in a drawer of the desk. He handed it to Marcus. While he wrote, Guillen approached the women in the back of the room. "Sorry, we're almost done. I know you have a tight schedule."

The woman waved a dismissive hand in the air. "It's okay. I'll tell them my old, aging body slowed us down if they complain that I took too long to give him the community tour." She winked.

He smiled, then turned to Rachel with a frown. "How are you holding up?"

She gave him a warm smile. "Better." She glanced past him to Marcus, who wiped away another tear as he continued to write. "What's that about?"

Shoving his hands in his pockets, Guillen pressed his lips together. "There's only so much we can do. I didn't want to overpromise." He looked at the woman. "Next time I make a contact that can manage it, we'll get it to his family."

She smiled appreciatively. "That's fantastic. That will make a big difference."

Rachel narrowed her eyes in confusion. "A letter? I thought family could pretty much write or visit whenever they wanted."

"When his mother fought back?" the woman replied.

Rachel's heart deflated. "Yeah, how bad was it?"

Guillen's hand moved as if to reach out and hold hers. Before he touched her, he quickly recoiled and shoved it back in his pocket. "Um ... It's hard to know. It's probably not as bad as he thinks it is. Extractions can be chaotic when the parents fight back. And when they do, visiting and communication privileges are revoked for a while. Depending on how bad it was, it could be a month, could be a year."

Rachel couldn't do anything more than shake her head. The lines blurred between people like Guillen, Soren, and the spectrum in between. How could a society get to this level? She'd never understood it in her human history classes, and she didn't understand it now.

Still at the front of the room, Marcus folded the papers he'd written on. "So, we're finding a way to smuggle it to his mom?" Rachel asked.

Guillen shrugged. "We'll hand it off. But yeah." A smug grin grew on his face. "You'd think by now that I'd learn my lesson on illegal activities. Spy. Smuggler."

Rachel shared his grin. If they had been alone, she would have kissed that smug face and added one more word—sexy.

Heading back to the front of the room, Guillen rejoined Marcus.

Rachel double-checked with the woman to make sure Marcus understood he couldn't speak of this meeting to anyone, and that he'd keep his tattoo covered at all times, as it shouldn't have been that healed for weeks or even months.

Guillen gave Marcus one last hug, handing him something. They approached the women, and Marcus gave Rachel a half-smile. "Thank you."

"You're welcome."

"Alright, come on. We need to hurry," the older woman said, putting an arm around his shoulder and thanking Rachel and Guillen.

After the door shut, Rachel and Guillen were left alone, reading each other's faces.

"You..." she said, unable to form a sentence.

He smiled, his eyes squinting a little. "You."

It only made her smile more.

He finally reached a hand out, intertwining their fingers. "We need to get going. We'll have all day to talk on the road."

She nodded. "But I'm not leaving without at least one kiss."

He pulled her in, giving her the slowest, softest kiss known to mankind or green folk. The kind that literally takes your breath away, that makes you physically weak. He pulled back. It was like torture, leaving it at one.

"I wish we didn't have to hide 'us,'" she said.

A look of longing crossed his face as he squeezed her hand. "I promise you: someday, we won't have to be a secret. And that will be the best day ... ever."

After presenting her exit papers, Rachel safely left Community Nine. A few minutes later, Guillen exited and caught up to her. The back highway was often empty, and therefore their main travel route. It was mostly used by stunts, prison transfers, and unsavory characters with their own agendas.

After ensuring no one was in sight, Rachel took Guillen's hand. Her mind lingered on the boy they'd just left behind. "I still wish I could have done something more."

"I know." Guillen's voice was filled with similar regret. "His family's city is hours out of our way. We'd lose a whole day, at least."

She gave his hand a squeeze. "It is what it is. Better something than nothing." She thought back to the last part of their interaction. "I saw him put something in his pocket. What did you give him?"

A grin formed on Guillen's face, but he kept looking forward. "A birthday present."

She raised her eyebrows. "And that was..."

He cleared his throat. "One of my knives."

She wasn't really sure how she felt about that. What the old woman had said, hinting that some chose to take their own lives, made her uneasy. But it wasn't like stunts weren't allowed kitchen knives. "Isn't he a bit young?"

Guillen looked down, shaking his head. "His childhood is over."

She'd known that, but it was still a punch to the gut. She tried to lighten the mood. "Well, I'm a little jealous now."

He turned his head to face her, an eyebrow raised.

She splayed a hand on her chest. "I thought *I* was the only one special enough to be gifted a Guillen knife."

He chuckled. "Only *very* special people get one of those. I have a few to spare."

"Hmm." She released his hand, moving closer and putting her arm around him. "Hopefully there aren't *too* many special people along the way, or you won't have any weapons by the time we get to Community One."

He chuckled again. "The gentleman I have custom make them is along the way. He knows to have some ready for me."

After just a few more minutes of striding along the path, her mind turned back to Marcus. She didn't know what all they'd talked about, but seeing the relief on his face, after how hard he'd been taking his first morning there... She was an expert witness of how something as simple as a few minutes in conversation with Guillen could make all the difference in the world. "What was it like for you? When they came for you?"

Guillen hesitated. "They *didn't* come for me," he answered softly.

Rachel cocked her head. "I thought you were allowed to live with your family until you were eighteen, as an exception, and then you were forced to go."

He opened his mouth, but nothing came out for a moment. "I had to get my mark at fourteen, just like Marcus. But yeah, eighteen—that was an option for me. An option I didn't actually take." He gave her a quick side-glance. "I still had the tutors, but I left on my own, at sixteen."

Her chest hurt. Moving out at sixteen to go live on his own? And somehow, he'd decided manual labor was preferable to living with his own family. She had a clear view of his scar. "Because of your mom?"

He took a deep breath. "That's the short answer."

"I'm sorry you had to go through that."

He slowly nodded. "Me too." He shrugged. "But then, sometimes I realize I'm not that sorry. You know?"

She lightly kicked away a pebble in her path. "No. I don't know."

"Just..." He stood taller, wearing a pensive look. "If my mother wasn't who she was back then, then I wouldn't be me. And if I wasn't me, I probably wouldn't be that close to Kaylah. And I wouldn't have been as driven to help out. And I never would have met Marcus, or you."

Rachel smiled, her cheeks warming. She could hardly agree that she was somehow okay with his mom being abusive, even if it had eventually brought them together. But she understood what he'd meant by it. "I wish I could say that about my life—that I'm at peace with my past. I mean ... not that I'd obviously give you up."

He grinned, leaning down and planting a kiss on her cheek. "I've had years to process all that. You get a lot of time to think when you're working with your hands on the job. *Your* wounds are still healing."

Her heart full, she stopped walking, turning and gazing into his eyes. "I am *so* lucky. And..." *Is this the right moment?*

Guillen cleared his throat, throwing a sideways glance down the lane. No, this wouldn't be their moment. They quickly moved apart, and she strode forward at a quicker but natural pace while he stayed back, fiddling with his shoe.

Note to self: nowhere public.

She fought resentment as she passed a small group of travelers. They nodded, and she reciprocated. Sometimes, she and Guillen struggled to follow their routine, but they'd agreed to do better—they could only be acquaintances in public.

What were we just saying about life bringing us together?

After a few minutes, Guillen caught up to her, only grabbing her hand again after a few glances to ensure the coast was clear. "Sorry. What were you saying?"

She pursed her lips. "Um … Just that I'm lucky to be here with you."

He gave her hand a double squeeze. "Not as lucky as I am."

Chapter 24

Community eight received Guillen and Rachel well. Rachel was happy to have one of the guards join them for the meeting—one of the guards who served these communities because they actually wanted what was best for these people. Guillen had known him for years. Chatting with the guard gave Rachel a huge boost of confidence. He was able to report how Unitas sentiments were spreading throughout the 'regular' communities, as well. Perhaps not as swiftly—those people weren't as oppressed; they didn't have as much to motivate them. But there were plenty growing tired of splitting up their families and losing people in a war they found themselves decreasingly passionate about.

When Rachel and Guillen made it to Community Seven, they had some time, again, to tour the area before their evening meeting. They stood in front of the family housing and orphanage.

"I know adoption isn't just a magic wand you can wave at couples that can't have kids, but have Magda and Jacob considered it?" she asked.

Guillen pursed his lips, reluctant to answer.

She sighed heavily. "It's never that simple, right?"

"It's a rare defect. Orphanages are positioned in every other stunt community. It's luck of the draw. Magda and Jacob were assigned the wrong place as kids. And we're sometimes allowed to move to a different community for something like work needs, but it's rare. It requires a new tattoo, more paperwork, and a significant reason."

She balled her fists, her jaw clenched. She'd never understood how people grew up thinking themselves so much better than others.

He took her hands, easing them open. "That look you get—when you're indignant, when you're scorched like this—it's one of the reasons I love you."

Her muscles relaxed as she looked into his soft blue eyes. "You love me?"

His mouth hung open. "I guess it wasn't the most romantic way to say it. But yes. Is that too soon?" He gazed into her eyes with a look of hope.

"No." She smiled. "I just kind of hoped I'd say it first."

He grinned. "Then never mind. I retract my statement. I do not love you yet."

She chuckled. "I don't think it works that way." She swallowed. "I love you, Guillen."

"I love you too." He held her hands just a moment longer before letting them go.

They barely had time to grab a quick bite before attending their meeting. It killed her—the glances they exchanged, keeping their distance in public after their moment. They just had to get through their meeting, and then she could be with him.

He closed the door behind them as they returned for the night. Locking it, he turned and leaned back. "That. Went. Great."

"It did." She smiled and fidgeted with her hands. Their propositions in this meeting had been met with minimal resistance, but her mind was already back to the moment they'd shared earlier.

He radiated happiness. "And I'll say it again—I love you."

Her smile widened. "I really love you too. I just don't know that I'm ready ... for some things to change yet."

He stepped forward, setting his key down on the side table next to her. "I didn't say it with expectations. We can take our time."

"Thank you." She blushed, giving him a hug.

After getting ready for the night, they sat on the bed, playing cards they'd picked up. They were different from a standard deck in the human world, and he was teaching her his favorite games.

She thought back to their conversation earlier in the day. "You've said 'scorched' a few times. That means 'pissed,' right?"

His face showed confusion and disgust. "What does being angry have to do with urine?"

She covered her mouth, laughing.

He read her face, bunching his eyebrows. "Is 'piss' not universal with Seeders and humans?"

Rachel struggled to stop laughing, but successfully managed, instead wearing a huge smile. "Yes, I guess you're right. Piss means urine. But when you say you're 'pissed' or 'pissed off,' it means you're upset."

He shook his head. "I still don't get the connection."

"Honestly, I don't even understand that myself." She realized it was her turn, and placed a card down. "Scorched is better."

Guillen studied his hand with a smile. "I guess we'll add that to the list to remember."

"Yeah, I suppose I haven't used that one, since you haven't given me that horrified look until now."

He chuckled. A minute later, he spoke again. "I forgot to tell you—I'll be leaving during the night. We should be getting an update from Kaylah. I made a contact." He played a card. "I know you don't want to be left alone while I head out on official business, but—"

She looked up. "I get it. Sometimes the fewer people involved, the better. Thanks for letting me know so I'm not worried."

"Thanks, honey." He smiled; she grinned back.

"I was wondering ... about the orphans," she started.

"Yeah?"

"When you first explained to me the restrictions on your kind, you sounded like you wanted to have kids." And that was all before she'd seen him with the boy, Marcus.

Guillen shrugged. "Well ... there are a lot of factors involved, aren't there?"

They exchanged a knowing glance. This war, their societies, and physiology. There were a lot of what-ifs. Seeders were incapable of having kids with other races, not even with their own kind without powers.

"Yes. In an ideal world, I think I'd like to have kids," he continued. "If the laws changed. But they haven't yet. And even when they do ... it's not a deal-breaker. I've lived my whole life with the expectation that I couldn't."

Frowning, she set down her playing cards. "But once your people have equality, you shouldn't have to sacrifice that part of yourself. I'm not trying to be presumptuous, but you know what I mean."

He acknowledged his understanding with a lift of the eyebrows. "What about you? Do you want kids?"

Rachel shook her head. "Not the Seeder way. That's way too many kids for me, even if I had closer bonds to my family back there to help out. I always kind of imagined a couple, though. Back when I thought I was human. So, I guess it's all or nothing, for my kind."

He looked back down at his cards.

"Would you ever consider adoption?" she asked. "One of those kids? Or even an Ivy or Seeder with powers, orphaned from this war?"

He read her face. "Yes. I would."

She smirked. "You would make a great dad."

He gave a shy smile, looking down at his hand again. "And anyone in your life is lucky to be there."

They finished the game, and Guillen shuffled the cards. His face looked as though he were lost in thought. "Talking of sacrifices and ... well ... you know, if things..." He twisted his lips. "What about you and your powers?"

She narrowed her eyes. "I'm not following."

"Don't you get another power if you choose to be with one of your own kind?"

"Oh ... that." She hadn't thought about the fact that she'd never get the ability to throw darts if she never paired off with a Seeder. A sinking feeling in her gut brought her gaze down to the bed they were sitting on. She wanted to say that it didn't matter, that it was trivial. But she hesitated. Sometimes, back in the Unitas camp, she'd been paired to train with a male Seeder, and had extended energy for darts. She'd gotten annoyed more than once that all she could do was provide extra power, that she couldn't do the aiming herself, that her part was so passive.

"I don't expect an answer right away," Guillen said. "Or the one you think I want to hear. I want your honesty as much as you want mine."

She glanced up, pressing her lips together, nodding. They continued to play in relative silence. It ate at her. Was she being selfish? He was willing to sacrifice something he wanted and could only get elsewhere, but she wasn't? She tried to shift her perspective. They were talking hypothetically, anyway. In the future. A future where a Seeder and Ivy could actually even be together. A future where they both made it out of the war alive. What could darts do for you when there was no war to fight? Make glorified pushpins?

"I could live without them," she said.

He remained silent as he finished his turn. "You're sure?"

"Yes. You don't have to have everything, to be happy. Look at you—you're amazing with your knife work. You don't need vines."

He looked her in the eye, seemingly skeptical. "Give it some thought. I find people often come to resent crutches, and would usually prefer to have fully functioning legs, if given the choice."

She frowned. "I don't see you that way."

He smiled, but it didn't reach his eyes. "I appreciate that. But my birth defect wasn't a choice. We're talking about you forfeiting potential."

It hurt, the way his truth pierced. But at least he wasn't holding back. She had to ask herself about her checklist of life goals. She obviously hadn't been obsessing over it, and she hadn't even chosen the Seeder life. She could do without darts, but part of her wondered if he was right—that it might nag at her down the road, leaving a box unchecked.

An outsider might just say the easy solution would be to have a quick fling with another Seeder to get those powers. But that wouldn't be fair to a Seeder—he'd be mated to only her for life. Infidelity amongst Seeders was extremely rare; the bond made other romantic and physical relationships unfulfilling. She wouldn't be able to enjoy Guillen the same way afterward.

After finishing another round of their game, she was more confident in her answer. "If I had to choose between you and darts, I'd choose you."

He smiled softly. "Okay."

Rachel opted to stay up late and spend more time together, until Guillen had to leave for his rendezvous, then she promptly passed out in bed.

She woke in the morning to his handsome face resting peacefully. She didn't move, not wanting to wake him, unsure of how long he'd been out.

Her mind drifted to darker times, when she'd woken up in the prince's arms. Someone she'd thought loved her. Someone who, aside from being an evil, warmongering liar, had also cheated on her. He'd dated his fiancée for years behind Rachel's back. Rachel tried to imagine the woman—if she was as horrible as he was, or just naïve, like Rachel had been. Rachel grinned, hoping she'd left him with a nice scar after he'd assaulted her.

Her trust had been violated repeatedly, by several of those closest to her. Why did it come so easily with Guillen? She didn't have an ounce of doubt that he was who he claimed to be. She didn't worry that he'd lost his way during the night and landed in another woman's bed.

"You okay?" His groggy voice pulled her from her memories.

She smiled, breathing in the quiet moment. "I am. Really." She moved closer and gave him a kiss. "So, this is what it's like to wake up to someone you love?"

"Mmm. I guess so."

"How late were you out? What kind of news is there?"

His smile faded, and he broke eye contact. "Not great."

Her heart beat faster. "Just tell me." She sat up, leaning against the wall.

He sat up to join her. "Everyone you and I know is safe. Okay? Let's start there."

"What's that supposed to mean?"

He bit his lip. "Another one of the girls at the palace died."

She wanted to cry, but tears didn't even come. At this point, that kind of news from the palace was exhausting, disappointing, and hopeless. She leaned forward, resting her face in her hands.

He rubbed her back. "I'm so sorry. I wish we could have gotten you all out of there at the same time."

She sat up straight. "You don't get it. It was hell back there, and it was just a few days for me. Those girls have been there for *months*! We need to be doing more!"

"We will. I promise. And there's more. It's not all bad news."

She closed her eyes. "Please at least tell me it doesn't get worse."

"No. I think that's the worst of it."

"What else?"

"Well … Kaylah is safely still at the camp. But … the camp is under siege, and the word will be going out today throughout our kingdom about her part as a traitor. She's been named, as well as accomplices like Jon and Olivia. Kaylah's wanted alive. The others … wanted dead."

Rachel nodded as a couple of tears made their way to the surface. "Do they know about you? About us? Our mission?"

"No. We're still safe, from what we can tell. Barely anyone knows what we're up to."

"Why would Soren finally be changing the story?"

Guillen shrugged. "He's desperate. Losing another girl weakens their attack. Acting like Kaylah was a prisoner wasn't enough. He wants her back. He wants a win."

"He doesn't *seem* desperate." She rolled her eyes. "We're hardly a threat, just letting the rest of the girls rot."

Guillen shook his head. "You know we can't just march there and get them out. I don't mean to sound heartless, but people have to understand the number of lives it would cost to rescue just one of those girls right now, with his fortifications."

She met his eyes. "Would you feel the same way if you'd rescued someone else, instead of me?"

Hurt shone in his eyes. "That's not fair."

She lowered her gaze. "Keep going. I'm assuming there's more."

"Seeders have openly and publicly embraced Unitas," he shared in a more cheerful voice. "Your leaders sent a formal declaration. We're going to do this." He waited a moment. "That's the last of it."

She took a deep breath while he cautiously held her hand. She ought to have felt more triumphant about the success, something she'd been key in, but her heart and mind dwelled on the palace.

"I love you," he said. "I'm going to keep you safe. And we're going to win this. You just keep being your wonderful self. What you and I are doing—we're making a difference."

Her heart was still heavy. "I just wish it was more. I love all the free time with you, and getting to see your lands, but isn't there a way we can move faster?" She wished she could rift from community to community, but catching a breeze in Ivy skies would be a death sentence, even if it were possible to rift within the Green Lands to another location internally. And besides, she didn't know how to rift from the Ivy side; she only vaguely knew the portal locations from Seeder airspace. And Guillen still couldn't rift, even from the ground. "Can't we call earlier meetings, instead of waiting around all day?"

"I know you want to go faster, but it's crucial that our work continues unnoticed. We can't disturb people's work schedules."

She leaned back, faster than she'd intended to, smacking her head against the wall. She winced. "Then let's get going. No more sleeping in. We can travel through the night, sleep outside on the way, if it will get us from place to place faster."

"Okay. We'll see what we can do."

They promptly got up and dressed for the day, setting out for their next destination.

Chapter 25

Saff and Devin departed their tent, walking hand in hand to training practice.

"This should be interesting," he said with a smile.

She nodded with a matching grin. "Who would have thought?" Despite the daily demands on her energy, time, and heart, this was a place where Saff had grown comfortable. She still missed being back home in South Fortinda, where most of her family helped keep the village going and fought to keep their portion of the border safe. But anywhere with Devin was home. And both of them had learned important lessons in trust and forgiveness. Not just with each other, but with the Ivies they associated with on a daily basis.

After a short walk, they met up with their sparring group for advanced training. Twelve Seeders were paired with twelve Ivies, preparing for future tactical teams, when the time would come that they were ready to advance on the palace.

Saff was paired with a female Ivy. While modern Ivy culture usually relegated their women's powers more to nursing roles, Kaylah willingly took volunteers to train in combat. Saff shook hands with her new partner, Flora. Flora's waist-length burgundy hair hung down in braids, and she couldn't have been more than eighteen.

"Let's check out those darts first," Flora said, stepping back and extending a vine from her wrist. She coiled it into a flat disk, holding it out in front of her as a shield.

Saff hesitated. All of her Seeder training thus far had involved dart-throwing at targets, never a living person. "You sure you're ready?"

Flora lowered the shield to reveal her face, wearing a crooked smile. "I'm ready, but maybe you're not?"

Saff accepted the playful taunting. Ivy vines and leaves were less sensitive to pain than even Seeder blades. Her strikes wouldn't physically hurt her partner, as long as they landed in the right place. Saff balled her fist, centering her energy, then flicked her wrist to launch the darts. Three projectiles landed in the coiled vine shield. One made it halfway through, having found its mark between the edges of the vine.

Flora lowered her shield, eyes wide.

Saff grinned. "Keep it tight, or they'll sneak through."

Flora cleared her throat, plucking out the darts. "Right. Yeah. Let's try that a couple more times."

They later moved on to hand-to-hand combat, leaf-tips and blade-edges blunted to avoid any significant damage. Saff snuck a glance in Devin's direction every once in a while to see how he was doing.

Flora was attempting to take Saff down with different vine-wrapping techniques as Saff got distracted by Devin's exercise with his partner. Devin's counterpart had balled up the end of his vine and was swinging it around as a flail. The dulled leaf edges made it less menacing, but Saff had to hand it to the Ivies—Seeders could fly and throw darts, but when determined, Ivies were no less lethal.

In Saff's moment of distraction, Flora tried something new. Saff startled at a couple of quick pricks in each of her forearms, then the surrounding areas went numb—both hands and lower arms quickly lost all feeling.

"Hey!"

Flora reeled in her vines, backing up and folding her arms. "You seemed preoccupied. What can you do now?"

Saff scowled at her, shaking her arms as though that would somehow bring the feeling back. She stood with her mouth agape, realizing how impotent she was at that moment. Numb arms. She couldn't rift, or catch a breeze, extend blades, throw darts ... anything, really. "It's not exactly a fair challenge, though, is it? None of your females will be guarding the palace."

Flora casually studied her nails. "You never know. Either way," she oozed pride, "you have to admit, we have a great teacher."

Saff had to concede she was right. Kaylah, Ginger, and Olivia had not only taught their women in camp how to be more efficient nurses, and how to heal the Seeder lands, but tactics like these—which would be incredibly effective. They didn't need to expend enough poison to make an opponent unconscious; just enough for a simple local numbing could get a lot done.

Saff looked down at her arms again. She had to be able to do *something*... Just like she'd learned to master the separation between her energy and emotions, she surmised she could still force a change, even if she couldn't physically feel it. Focusing on just one arm, she pushed her Seeder energy down. She kept pooling it there, willing it to do what she wanted. Soon enough, her right blade extended, and she glanced up. Flora was ready with a shield and a smirk.

With an uncomfortable lack of feeling and control, Saff swung her arm, striking at Flora and landing a solid slice into her vines. Gaining a little more courage, Saff struck again, cutting through the edge, and leaving a gash in Flora's arm.

Flora flinched, sucking in air through clenched teeth.

Saff gasped. "I'm so sorry! I didn't know it was sharp. I can't really control it while numbed! Let's heal that for you."

Flora instead extended a fresh vine, puncturing herself near the wound. It stopped bleeding, and she poked around it, appearing to no longer be in pain. "We'll heal when we're done. Let's keep going."

After another hour of both experimental and established fighting strategies, Flora and Saff sat down to hydrate and heal.

"You're pretty impressive," Saff said, her glowing hand finishing up the job on Flora's wound.

"Likewise." Flora smiled.

Saff took a swig from her bottle. "If you don't mind me asking ... why did you join Unitas? And why fighting, not just healing the land?"

Flora cracked open a water bottle of her own. "I had *two* boyfriends break up with me, choosing to join a human-world detail." Her tone changed. "Then I had a brother killed in the war."

Saff frowned. They both hurt for brothers who had died on the battlefield, and for all they knew, it could have been in the same battle, against each other. "One of my brothers was killed, too."

Flora nodded. "There's too much of that. It shouldn't be this way. And ... when I learned I could really help, not just sit at home, doing a regular job ... I came with my friend."

Saff smiled. "I appreciate you. I hope someday history will see Kaylah for all she's really done for both sides."

"Same." Flora took a drink.

Saff shifted sitting positions on the hard-packed dirt. "So, how did you learn about Unitas? Who recruited you?"

Flora pointed her water bottle in the direction of some of the others still sparring. "The friend I told you about."

There were dozens of Ivies living in the Unitas camp by now, and Saff hadn't met them all, but she vaguely recognized the girl Flora pointed out. Her friend, a shorter girl with shoulder-length black hair, sparred with a Seeder Saff had spent more time with.

"Her name's Raven," Flora said. "She's actually the one who was initially recruited. I'm just a tagalong."

Devin and his partner joined the girls, both of the guys a little bloody.

Saff gave Devin a disapproving look. "I see neither of you listened about keeping sharp edges to yourselves." She first set to healing the Ivy male's cuts.

Devin smirked. "We decided it wouldn't feel realistic if we weren't actually at risk of getting hurt."

Saff rolled her eyes. "Well, next time, you should pair up with Flora. She's got some surprise moves up her sleeve." She winked at Flora, and Flora chuckled.

The group chatted a bit about the different techniques they'd practiced, while Saff finished healing Devin. Eventually, Raven and her fighting partner also joined them. They all exchanged handshakes before Saff and Devin got up to go.

"I'll walk you to the border?" he offered.

"I'll take it." She straightened her shirt.

He wrapped his arm around her, and they headed to the edge of camp. "Doing alright after all that healing?"

She poked him in the ribs. "You're lucky I have meetings today, so I don't need all of that energy."

"Mmm... I'm glad we get to do this together. I wouldn't have it any other way."

She leaned into his embrace. "Ditto. Better together. Which is why I'm glad they're not holding us women back next time. Or the Ivy women. We need to stop hedging our bets."

He nodded. "There's no doubt about it; you ladies are impressive."

She took a slow, deep breath. "Can you imagine how things could be by the time we're old enough to have a clutch of our own? If the lands were healed enough, or we were allowed more space in the Neutral Woods to raise our kids ... *together*."

"I think about it every day."

Kaylah and her accompanying guards approached to meet up with Saff.

Devin stopped and pulled Saff in for a hug. "Find me for dinner?"

She squeezed him tight, then stole a peck on the lips. "Camp protection detail, right?"

He nodded. "I know. Be safe—I will be. Same goes for you."

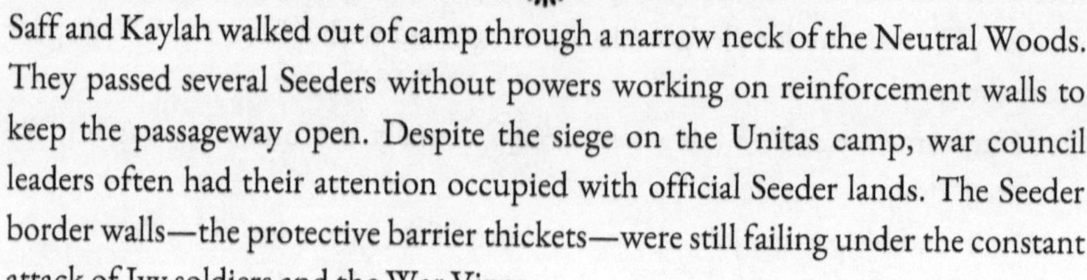

Saff and Kaylah walked out of camp through a narrow neck of the Neutral Woods. They passed several Seeders without powers working on reinforcement walls to keep the passageway open. Despite the siege on the Unitas camp, war council leaders often had their attention occupied with official Seeder lands. The Seeder border walls—the protective barrier thickets—were still failing under the constant attack of Ivy soldiers and the War Vines.

Saff spotted a friendly face. "Zeus, what are you doing out here?"

He lowered a hammer, wiping his brow. "Hey, good to see you. Just doing my part. I'll go back to checking on my cleanup crew soon."

She smiled. "That's great. You guys are doing awesome work." She and Kaylah felt awful for drawing attention to Arcadia, which had previously been undiscovered and untargeted by Ivies. But they had needed to open the cave outside of their border walls, and this rocky terrain afforded them those options. After Unitas's camp location had been compromised, the entire village went to work, helping to build fortifications. In a way, it was good for them to not be so isolated. The goal was to integrate them back into regular Seeder society someday anyway, when enough of the lands were healed.

"Any, uh, word? About," Zeus awkwardly fidgeted with the hammer, "well, in general. People, places, things?"

Saff hid a grin. He was definitely asking about Rachel. "No big news to report, sorry."

He nodded with a half-smile.

"We can't be late for our meeting. But it was good to see you."

He resumed his work while Saff and Kaylah continued on their way.

Saff cleared her throat. "Look at that—he's still interested. And his kind are inching their way into regular society. That makes him even more dateable."

Kaylah laughed. "And I'm sure *many* Seeder women will swoon over that deep voice and those muscles. Rachel will not be one of them."

Saff rolled her eyes. "You're so sure of yourself."

Kaylah grinned. "On some things. I'm good at picking up on what people want and need. That's probably why Eric and I moved so fast. Once I got to know him, I knew he could be the one."

A wave of guilt washed over Saff, that she could be there and have Devin's support while Kaylah and Eric were still separated. "So, I have questions for you."

Kaylah ducked under a tree branch. "Go for it."

"I was just paired up with Flora."

"Ah, yes. That one's a quick learner! Her friend, too."

Saff chuckled, remembering how panicked she'd been with numb arms. "Yeah. You really don't think we'll have female Ivy opposition, even at the palace?"

Kaylah shook her head. "Nope. Guards and soldiers are all male."

"But why? That's pretty stupid. You told us once that Ivies were lied to about their own powers, and that you could teach them. But wouldn't even the palace have a secret stash of competent women with skills like this?"

"Hmm, that is a *very* complicated story."

"Give me the abridged version."

Kaylah linked arms with Saff. "Well, let's first talk about our viewpoints on women. Both of our societies are matriarchal, but how we're treated and how our powers manifest themselves are different. We have the head matriarch, the queen. All of your fully-rooted women are considered matriarchs in their own rights. Let me ask you a question—even without the extra chemical arts, why aren't our women trained as soldiers and assassins, according to what *you* were taught?"

Saff shrugged. "Because you're physically weaker, and your leaves aren't as sharp."

"Yes. The 'weaker' sex. At least some would see it that way. But in a matriarchal society, as in many others, I'm sure, we're also the 'fairer' sex. Some would say we should be revered and protected. So, either way you look at it, people can justify sidelining us. And unlike Seeders, we have pregnancies pretty similar to humans, so we don't just ship women off to war with child."

"Okay. But those that are not pregnant..."

"That's where it gets stickier." Kaylah nodded politely at a group of workers, and they reciprocated. "The hodgepodge of information we're going off of is a collection of your stolen archives and our *hidden* archives. At least that's what I think. I think some of those books were censored, though some may not have been. Either way, I'm fairly certain the general public doesn't have access to those books regarding just my people. My uncle dug those out from some pretty deep vaults."

As gravel crunched under their shoes, Kaylah continued. "The energy your people wield is identical to what we do. Not necessarily the quantity, but the makeup is the same. I think our chemical abilities are more varied, and it's widely accepted that the chemical composition of even our most basic 'poison' varies. That's how true nurses in the profession are sorted out—people prefer their poison to that of others when needing medical help. The main reference I'm teaching these girls and women from was written by Sanath Fulgrum. Do you know what Sanath is known for?"

"Uh ... No..." Saff barely knew anything about the internal workings of Ivy society and its prominent citizens and leaders.

"Publicly—nothing," Kaylah said. "In medical journals—quackery. Someone obviously found it curious enough to store her notes in archives, and for that, we're grateful. Humans used to think they could cure all sorts of sicknesses with bloodletting and, well..."

Saff twisted her lips. They both knew what Kaylah was implying, but Saff wouldn't dare utter it—leeches. She still remembered the last time she let that one slip from her mouth, out of habit. It was undeniable that the term fit in a lot of ways, in relation to Ivies and the ways their powers worked, but that didn't excuse the use of it. And it still stung the way Rachel had censured her. Saff's only experiences with Ivies before Kaylah had been filled with assassins, soldiers, and pain. And she'd never been a racist in the human world. She made a concerted effort after that, to be extra careful.

"Anyway," Kaylah said. "We're always learning more about ourselves. Sanath believed there's a spectrum of powers, that we possess discernable channels for different abilities, and that the crude poison we use is actually a combination of them. It made sense to me when I read it, and I began experimenting. Just like our vines, some things come natural to you guys, like your eye glow, right? But I'm guessing you might have never learned to rift or catch a breeze if no one had taught you."

Saff smiled. "Yeah, that's safe to say. But imagine the first person who realized they could commune with the wind and decided to give it a try!"

Kaylah chuckled.

"So, that's what you meant, by your people being lied to? That some doctor's theories were hidden?"

Kaylah frowned. "I wish it were that simple." They were now just yards away from the Seeder Outer Wall. "Long story short, I can't prove all of my theories. But our people talk about having had extra powers before the wars, and that your people did something to weaken us."

Saff scoffed. "Like what? Our powers don't work that way. We don't know how to do anything to you but physical harm, like—"

"I know. But when you don't have contact with the enemy, it's easy to lie and fashion a scapegoat. Then again, maybe I'm reading into things, and it was a genuine misunderstanding. You yourself misunderstood the reason for your ability to wield extra energy, right?"

Saff nodded. Reaching the stone doorway that led to the other side of the thicket border wall, they waited, surrounded by several more guards.

"Princess." The one in charge gave a polite nod. "Saff."

The women reciprocated.

"Anyway," Kaylah continued, speaking a little quieter. "Do you know how Germans and the Japanese teach their students about World War II?"

Saff shook her head.

"Honestly, me neither. I should have studied that. But we all take unique perspectives. I guess, look at the US. Most people call it the 'Civil War,' while some still call it the 'War of Northern Aggression.'"

Saff rolled her eyes again.

Kaylah shrugged as they opened the door and filed into the stone tunnel lined with lightkeepers. "Your people call what we did 'The Great Poisoning.' Do you know what Ivies call it?"

"No."

"Well, it sounds pretty bad." Kaylah glanced at their guards as they waited for the last locked door to open. She leaned forward, whispering in Saff's ear. "The Great Cleansing."

It churned Saff's stomach. "You mean like racial..."

Kaylah raised her eyebrows. "Kinda. Like I said, it sounds bad. The fact that very few details are taught to the public tells me some things are censored. But we had to have a heck of a lot of poison stored up to be able to poison all of your lands at once. We're talking *vats* of it into your soil and waterways."

Saff gave a polite smile to the guards as they were permitted past the border wall. "Thank you for your service." The daylight was refreshing, as was the whistle of nearby songbirds, but she was still queasy from the conversation.

"Our women stored up that poison for *decades*. If our poison isn't metabolized, it stays potent. The way I've heard it taught, 'The Great Cleansing' was more of a spiritual-type movement. Supposedly, just like your women go to temple wells to deposit energy, ours lined up to 'rid themselves' of the impurities of poison.

Somehow, if they could make regular deposits, they would 'cleanse' themselves, and prove us the superior race. The more vitriolic and potent the poison one could fashion, the better the person became."

Saff scrunched her eyebrows. "Really? And they didn't realize they were just stockpiling a weapon?"

Sighing, Kaylah straightened her bun. "I genuinely don't know. The fact that those deposit sites have all been torn down, and the way it's taught... Not everything lines up for me. Maybe they knew it was a weapon and then dressed it up out of shame. Or the public really didn't know, and there was backlash when they found out, so the truth was buried? Either way, the attack was carried out, and I surmise those who still remembered or tried to use any former channels of chemical arts were silenced. Your people got blamed for us losing nebulous powers." They stopped short of entering the council meeting building. "Maybe we actually did lose our understanding of how to do more, after decades of only being laser-focused on one thing. We'll never know."

Saff frowned. "What will you teach your people after this is all over?"

Kaylah tucked her hands into her pockets. "That's something your leaders and I have discussed, and will continue to discuss. We agree that we hope to both be as truthful as possible. The aftermath of war is just as ugly as the process of being in it."

Saff gave her a fake smile. "On that happy note, let's not keep them waiting."

Kaylah chuckled, throwing an arm around Saff's shoulder. "On that happy note..."

Chapter 26

Saff and Kaylah sat with a dozen Seeder leaders, in a village near the edge of Seeder territory and the Unitas camp. Both women were still utterly exhausted from the efforts just to keep their camp safe. The leaders only looked mildly less worn-out.

"You're really sure there's not a way to stretch your protective borders?" Kaylah asked. "That would allow us to focus our efforts on what we really need."

The head council leader shook her head. "No. It's absolutely out of the question. You know as well as I do that those walls were constructed before The Great Poisoning. We haven't built one in a century. It would require a *massive* amount of energy—energy we don't have to spare. We can't divert our resources like that."

Kaylah rubbed her forehead.

The councilwoman spoke again. "I do still think it would be better to move Saff and Devin's training to be safely behind our borders."

"No," Saff said. "We'll escort the girls home as quickly as we can, but we need to be there to greet them. And the camp needs as many strong people as possible, and we're willing to put in the extra work." They were the new line of defense for the village without powers now, and the cave.

"We still don't even know if the cave strategy has been compromised," the councilwoman reminded them. "We haven't seen any attacks, in either world, trying to use one of the caves."

"Not yet," Kaylah snipped.

"Speaking of caves." The woman stacked some papers on the table. "A lot of your plan hinges on intrarealm rifting between them. How is that coming?"

"I'm almost there. I can feel it. I was going to ask if I could take another look in your old records."

The councilwoman nodded. "Yes, you can be escorted there any time."

"Thank you."

A knock sounded at the door, and a messenger stepped in. "My apologies. You asked for this update the moment it arrived." The messenger handed Kaylah a letter.

She opened it and smiled. "Perfect timing. We could use some good news. It's..." She surveyed the room as if to ensure the information was safe with those in attendance. "It's from Rachel and Guillen."

Saff sat up in her seat.

"They're safe. Still undiscovered. They're picking up speed and doing well. One of our outposts just got a shipment from some of the communities they've already rallied in."

Everyone was happy to hear the news and further details. At the meeting's conclusion, Saff and Kaylah left together.

"I'm glad to hear things are going okay over there. And that she's still in one piece." Saff frowned. "I can only imagine what the news of that last girl at the palace did to her. If things go south, you still think Guillen will be able to keep her safe, without any powers?"

"He will. I wouldn't have sent her over there with anyone I wasn't confident in. They'll keep each other safe."

Saff bobbed her head thoughtfully. "You encouraged her to like him. Knowing what she's been through with your family and people, do you really think that's a good idea? I still ... worry."

Kaylah tilted her head. "I've known them both longer than you. I love them both. They're good for each other." She smirked. "And I'm not usually a matchmaker, but you can't deny I'm good at bringing people together."

Saff laughed. "*That* I will absolutely agree with."

They stopped walking but continued to chat.

"Why is the cave-to-cave strategy so important to you? Are you willing to support an attack if you can't figure it out? Once Guillen and Rachel have made enough progress?"

"We *really* need that element of surprise. If we have to, we could try to send enough of our troops through this cave to the human world, then slingshot them back to that cave. But I haven't been able to get that one to work yet, in any capacity. And it would waste a lot of time and energy. It's not that I'm not open to different ideas, we just need a breakthrough to ensure a quick win once we advance on the palace. I want as few lives lost as possible."

Saff held her hands up. "I'm not the strategist. I'll leave that to you and the council. Why did you request to go back and look at the old records? You really think there's something we missed?"

Kaylah pursed her lips. "I don't know that we were looking for it when we were there last. Do Seeders teach old history?"

"What kind of old history?"

"Like where we come from? Were the Green Lands here first, and those that left became human? Or was it the other way around?"

Saff shook her head. "No. I've never heard that taught. Though Devin and I have speculated before."

"Ivy kids grow up on all sorts of lore and fairy tales. I've sent for some books to be smuggled here for us to review. I think the humans came first. From the way our stories go, a group of people stumbled on the energy of the Green Lands. There are stories of caves, and the ancient language, rifts, travel, transformation and discovery. Even jade is included in the stories, though we don't incorporate it into our powers the way your society does."

"That sounds cool." Saff wished she had more time for studies. She and Kaylah had barely shared any time on research lately. "But that's a lot of hope, basing war strategy on bedtime stories."

Kaylah gestured widely at the sky. "Growing up in the human world, wouldn't this whole place seem like a fantasy to you?"

Saff smiled, sensing the Seeder energy in her heart. "Yeah. It's like a work of fiction."

"And I remember having to read human fairy tales—a lot of those are based in truth. I haven't been wrong yet, have I?"

Saff took a deep breath. "You're pretty clever. I'll give you that. I was a nearly-straight-A student in high school. You must have been one of those five-point-oh students."

Kaylah laughed. "C-average. Not that my real parents knew that. Ginger and Nathan helped me fudge that truth while I focused on learning all of this."

Saff glanced down the path. "Are you heading back to camp?"

"No. I'm going straight to the libraries. Please let Jon and Ginger know. And give everyone my best."

"Will do." Saff hugged Kaylah. "Stay safe, *Princess*." She smirked, having started to annoy Kaylah, addressing her by that title.

Kaylah grinned and rolled her eyes. "Try and keep the camp in one piece until I'm back."

As the sun rose in the sky the next morning, Saff set out from her tent toward the Unitas garden to grab breakfast for herself and Devin; he was on a walk with Heather.

The sunrise was too beautiful to neglect. Pulling her mind from the training ahead, and the murmur of constant battle at camp borders, Saff strolled toward the quietest place she could think of—the canyon's edge.

Detouring from her original destination, she soon found she wasn't the only person with that idea. Kaylah sat on the cliff's edge, her feet dangling over, peering at the painted sky. As usual, two guards accompanied her, standing several paces back.

Saff approached one of them. "Is it okay if I go sit with her?"

The man she'd approached stood tall with crossed arms. "Your Highness, are you—"

"Stop calling me that!" Kaylah snapped.

Okay. Maybe no chat today... "It's fine. I'll go."

Kaylah looked over her shoulder. "Oh." Her tone softened. "Do you need something?"

Maybe it was best to leave Kaylah alone to think in peace, as she was clearly having a rough morning. Then again, maybe she needed someone to talk to. It wasn't like she had a whole lot of personal support now that Rachel was gone. She'd earned loyal followers, but that wasn't the same. Nathan and Eric were still in the human world, and the only other close friend Kaylah had in camp was Ginger.

"Unless you want to be by yourself, I just came to enjoy the sunrise for a minute before getting to work."

Kaylah gestured at the massive expanse of the canyon. "I don't know, it's a bit crowded." She winked.

Saff sat down by her. Oddly, she was still a bit afraid of heights when not flying. It was a little nerve-racking to dangle her legs over the edge. "You okay?"

Leaning back, Kaylah raised her chin to the sky. "Of course I'm okay. I'm always okay."

"Riiiiight…" Saff bit her lip, unsure of what to say. "Why do you hate it so much when people call you by your title now?" Kaylah hadn't seemed to hate it when they'd first met. And she had made it clear she wanted to be queen, but she wouldn't accept people calling her 'Your Majesty,' either. She didn't seem to genuinely mind being called 'Princess,' though, which added to the weirdness. But then again, Saff had never held an official title like that.

"Because it reminds me what I should be, if I'd been brave enough. If I'd had the guts to kill my parents before Soren did, this would all be over, and I could actually be making a difference right now."

Saff frowned. Kaylah was right. If she had assassinated her parents instead of defecting, creating Unitas, trying to negotiate and make an alliance with the Seeders, all of this could be over. Ben might even still be alive right now. "Look at this camp, though. How many hundreds of years has it been since our people occupied a place together and weren't killing each other?"

Kaylah raised a skeptical eyebrow. "Right… This is *wildly* successful. Every other day, there's at least one argument that has to be broken up. We're doing *so* good, just because we're not murdering each other." She glanced over her shoulder again, in the direction of camp. "And I don't sleep all that well, worried when the next betrayal will be."

Picking up a small pebble with jagged edges, Saff turned it in her hand, running her thumbs over the textured surfaces. "Baby steps." She eyed Kaylah. "I don't really know that I've seen suspicious activity. Have you? I mean, I'm always a bit paranoid, but it's not like I've stumbled upon a secret meeting planning Unitas's downfall…"

Kaylah shrugged, gazing across the canyon. "Hard to say. For all I know, *you* might still want me dead, and plan to shove me off this cliffside."

Saff leaned forward, staring down toward the base of the canyon. The river that cut through it was just a thin line from this high up. "I have a feeling I'd fare a lot better, being able to catch a breeze. People might get mad if I shoved off the leader of Unitas."

Kaylah grinned. "I appreciate your forbearance."

After a minute of silence, Saff soaked in the moment—the sky brightening, the faintest of breezes stirring the air. Moving a hint of energy to her bicep, she chucked the pebble as far as she could across the canyon. How much energy would it take for it to actually make it to the other side?

"You know, I've been giving a lot of thought to what I want to do with my life," Saff said.

Reaching to her side, Kaylah also grasped a nearby pebble, studying it. "Yeah? Change of career?"

Saff softly sighed. "I just don't know. I love learning and teaching, but maybe that's not the best use of my time. Maybe I should actually do more fighting, making use of my extra energy abilities."

Kaylah didn't respond. She instead chucked her pebble into the canyon.

"I mean, why not use it to keep our people safe, right?"

"I suppose. I'd kinda hoped that we'd have unlocked more secrets about our powers by understanding your extra abilities."

Saff slowly nodded. She'd been trying to sort through that herself, but on a more personal level. "I'll be honest." She hesitated, not sure if her relationship with Kaylah was at that level yet. "Well, it's like pulling back the curtain and... I don't know... I guess it's petty, but it was a little deflating finding out I'm only special because of a freak accident. Not really all that special."

"Mmm... I would argue that Spiderman is still pretty cool. He didn't sign up for a spider bite."

Saff almost laughed, being compared to a comic book character.

Kaylah twisted her lips. "Your leaders still haven't been able to find any girls your age who can wield as much power as you can."

"Really?" That brought a smile to Saff's face. She didn't expect a fan club, but who didn't want to feel special?

"Yep. Really. By all rights, you should have fallen into a coma and never made it home." She furrowed her brow. "I thought I'd once read something on it that made sense, but the books and scrolls kind of contradict themselves on the topic."

"Hmm."

"Plus." Kaylah shifted, tucking one leg up under the other. "I'd say you're pretty special in Devin's eyes. I see the way he looks at you when you're not watching."

Saff's cheeks burned. "He's better than I deserve."

Kaylah blew out a puff of air, turning to fully face Saff. She crossed her legs, her face more serious. "I don't know what to make of this sometimes."

'This' what?

"When this is over, could you see yourself visiting my kingdom?"

"Ummm..." Saff hadn't really asked herself that question. "Well, no offense, but I doubt it would be safe for a while, right? Unless you're talking about a guarded visit at your palace or something? Not everyone will be on board."

Kaylah pursed her lips, nodding. "Say it's safe—tension has calmed down. You come to visit my kingdom to check out the sights, to do some trading or something."

Unsure what Kaylah was trying to get at, Saff searched her face. "Well, if it's safe, I mean, we have a lot of rebuilding and restructuring of our own society to do. And I don't know how your economic system works, or any of the sights to see, and you still have to fix your own Mother Vines so it's not a wasteland, right?"

Kaylah shook her head, a look of disappointment crossing her face. "You act like you want to be my friend, and we talk about unity, but you can't even fathom crossing the Neutral Woods to be there."

Saff's jaw dropped. "No, it's..." She turned to better face Kaylah. "I'm not outgoing like you." She gestured to the camp. "I couldn't do this like you are. I like working one-on-one with these girls I mentor. I already told you I practically grew up as a shut-in, one that liked just hanging out with family and a small group of friends. It's just ... intimidating." Looking down, she picked up another tiny pebble by her foot, pinching it. "And I'm not as carefree as you are. I like checklists, and prioritizing, and..."

Kaylah continued to stare at her with a calculating expression. "Maybe I could allow for some differences there, but do you know what I really don't get?"

"What?"

"You met Guillen for two seconds, and you still dislike him. It's hard for me to get behind someone who judges the people I love."

Knots of guilt twisted in Saff's stomach. Maybe it wasn't fair how much she worried about Rachel's safety because she was with an Ivy without powers on her mission. Ben could have been twice as strong as Guillen with his Seeder energy, and he'd still been killed in this war.

But it was more than that. "I worry about Rachel. And it's not just that I worry about her physical safety, or even her emotional well-being, because you're right that I don't know him. But..." She choked down her remorse over her own mistakes. "There's more than one way to lose a person."

"What are you talking about?" Kaylah seemed rightfully confused.

When they were making up, Devin had confessed to Saff that he *had* actually considered moving out, even if it was only briefly, when they'd been fighting. She'd abandoned him. In marriage, you didn't just live for yourself. She'd been completely inconsiderate of his grief over Ben's death, and how her actions had made Devin hurt that much more. For the first time since she'd met Devin, she'd had to genuinely face the reality of possibly spending her life without him. During their many heartfelt conversations since making up, they'd promised to be better about communicating with each other.

"I'm not opposed to Rachel being with an Ivy, if that makes her happy. I just see her getting along with more Ivies than Seeders, and I feel like she's pulling away." Just the thought of Saff's few years of living in the Green Lands, of getting to know her family and village, made her long for home. "I love my family, and our village, and so many things about our culture. She's not even giving it a chance."

"Does it matter who she's with, or where she's at, if she's happy?"

Questions like that had made Saff face a lot about herself that she didn't like much lately. Sure, she'd never really liked drama or gossip, but she wasn't exactly a saint. She was slower to forgive than others. She tried to give people the benefit of the doubt, but she also sometimes struggled to put herself in others' shoes. Saff was having to learn all of this the hard way.

Saff rocked her head side to side. "I know. I should trust that she knows better than I do about what would make her happy. But she's also having to figure a lot out right now." She palmed her pebbles and pulled her legs up, hugging them. "It's not like I judge you and Eric for being together. Honestly, sometimes I think about how amazing it is that you discovered cave rifting, and I think of how much closer I could still be with my friend Zach, if we'd had the ability to rift multiple times a year back when I came of age."

Zach was another person she'd lost. Not completely, but he'd faded from her life. And she'd had to let him. She was married now. He was out there dating humans. She couldn't expect him to carry on the rest of his life getting mysterious letters from an old friend he'd once had a crush on, hiding them from future girlfriends or a wife. That wasn't fair. But if they'd had Unitas a few years ago when she first brought Zach into the green-folk equation, he would have been just like Eric, there to help the revolution in a heartbeat.

But he was just another person lost to Saff.

Losing people sucked. Change sucked.

Kaylah continued to eye Saff, not saying anything. Saff wasn't sure what else to say, sensing Kaylah's judgment of her.

"Why am I the bad guy for loving my people?" Saff asked. "I think there's nothing better, in either world, than being married to another Seeder. Genuinely. And I know that sounds bad, but I wouldn't expect you to understand that—no one could that doesn't experience our mating bond. I'm proud of my people's culture and way of life, and ethics. And I feel like you and Rachel judge me for that. What's wrong with enjoying being around people like me?" Loving her own people didn't mean she hated others.

Kaylah gently shook her head. "I think it's great to have national pride. I do. Maybe someday, if you ever visit, you'll come to appreciate our rich culture, our symbiotic relationship to the Mother Vines, all of that." She pressed her lips together. "Obviously, I'm not proud of a lot of things, too. There are more than enough unforgivable things, and a ton of growth that needs to happen. But the majority of my people are just doing their best."

Saff had to concede she was curious, that it could be a fun adventure to learn more about Kaylah's culture someday.

"What I don't understand is how you can be so blind about your own people's shortcomings," Kaylah added. "You're a smart woman. How often do you think a conflict is one hundred percent one side's fault? You don't think your people provoked any of this?"

Saff looked down. It was true that she'd never been taught anything that pointed at Seeder guilt in the 'years of parting.' Seeders were always the victims. But it stood to reason that those stories may have been coated with generalizations.

"Because as much as I know my people are in the wrong," Kaylah continued, "I do believe your people did their fair share to drive my people from their homes. Ivy history lessons may be steeped in lies, half-truths, and propaganda, but *your* people can be pigheaded, intolerant, and difficult."

The souring turn of conversation was unsettling for Saff. This didn't sound like inspirational Unitas ideology.

"So, we're judging our whole nation based on the actions of people hundreds of years ago?" Saff asked.

Kaylah clicked her tongue. "I find it's still relevant if they passed on their mindset to future generations."

Maybe Saff was just being defensive, but this conversation was starting to wear her patience thin. As much as she'd come to like Kaylah, Kaylah was still exhausting to work with at times. Granted, Kaylah probably thought the same of Saff.

Not sure if it would help or hurt, Saff dared to ask a question that had festered for more than two months now. "When we were at the safe house in the human world, you spoke of your parents, but I've never heard you talk about them since your brother killed them."

Kaylah picked at her fingernails. "What about them?"

Kaylah had said that her parents 'probably weren't as sinister' as Saff had thought. "I'm just curious about your relationship with them. What they were like. How you're doing."

Slowly nodding, Kaylah drew a deep breath. "Our relationship was complicated. I lived so many years away from home, and was lied to so much... There's definitely resentment there." She frowned, now examining the ends of her hair. "And every time I'd try to bring up something that matched the Unitas ideals... They were so disappointed."

She looked up, meeting Saff's gaze. "I knew I'd have to take things from a different angle. But truly, in my heart, I don't think they were the worst parents out there. My mother was often absent, but I wouldn't describe her as tyrannical ... exactly... I think my father genuinely loved her, but followed her lead. You always kind of wonder when it comes to relationships of people in positions of power, you know?"

It clicked for Saff as to why Kaylah was so drawn to Eric. Eric was a safe harbor. Human celebrities fell into two categories. They either married other celebrities and became power couples, or they married Average Joes, not having to deal with the complications of how their relationship would be used as a career display piece. What would a royal position, Ivy wealth, and the power that came with it all, do for a human who couldn't even cross into the Green Lands? She didn't have to doubt his motivations. It was sweet.

"So," Saff tried to tread lightly, "maybe they weren't the realm's worst parents. But ... you always attribute the fault with this war to your Uncle Nuren, that he was the mastermind."

Kaylah sat up straighter. "Yes. Without him, things would have continued in the stale old way they used to. Duke is an earned title; as my father's brother, he didn't have any birthright to it." Kaylah spared a glance at the camp. "In private, I used to call him Rasputin."

Saff choked on a laugh. "Like the cartoon villain?"

Kaylah narrowed her eyes slightly. "Seriously? Rasputin was a real person. My uncle would sometimes say that all it took for success was 'lots of work, a touch of luck, and enough charisma to woo the world.'" She rolled her eyes. "Honestly, I know he put in the work studying our archives, learning about psychology, and all of that, but really, I think he just weaseled his way in by catching my mother when she was weak after leaving—" She stopped abruptly, looking away as if she'd said more than intended.

"She was weak after leaving what?"

Standing, Kaylah dusted her pants off. "What? Sorry, I'm just a bit out of sorts today. Rough night's sleep."

Her sudden change of demeanor was discomforting. Saff stood to join her, letting the pebble she'd been holding drop to the ground.

Kaylah cleared her throat, looking at the guards standing a ways away. "We should get going."

"Wait," Saff said. "What was that about?"

Pulling her hair into a ponytail, Kaylah put on a more convincing act. "What? Oh, yeah, crappy night's sleep. Sorry, that's why I was a bit grumpy. Anyway..."

No... That isn't good enough...

"Kaylah..." Saff said, almost in warning.

Glancing past Saff, Kaylah smiled. "Oh look, your husband is coming to collect you. I guess we really do need to go. Thanks for the chat." She took a step toward the guards, but Saff cut her off.

"What are you not telling me?" Saff studied her face intently. "Your uncle, strategy, your mom. You may not be the queen in title, but you are in powers. Are you keeping something from our leaders?"

A smirk overtook Kaylah's face. "A girl's allowed an ounce of privacy now and then. And heaven knows, she's got to keep a secret or two up her sleeve." She winked.

Saff's heart ached as though she'd been betrayed. "*You* asked me to keep an eye on people in camp that were acting suspicious. What's happening right now is about the most suspicious thing I've seen."

Kaylah sighed, putting up her hands. "I'm just saying, some secrets are worth keeping. Ginger has this stroganoff recipe that I'd never divulge in a million years." She did a chef's kiss. "Mind-blowing."

Saff stepped closer. "This isn't a joke," she whispered.

"Hey, Saff," Devin called on his approach. "What are you doing all the way out here?"

Saff glanced over her shoulder; he was quickly closing the gap between them. She turned to Kaylah, urgency in her voice. "Don't do this to me. Don't play mind games. Just tell me what's going on. Don't undo the trust we've been working on."

Kaylah looked genuinely hurt. She locked eyes with Saff. "I have no intentions of hurting you or your people, okay?" she said softly.

Devin's arms slid around Saff's waist from behind. "Good morning, Kaylah."

Kaylah responded with a bright politician's smile. "Right back at you. Thanks for your hard work, both of you." She shot a glance across the canyon. "Sorry I have to go, but I have a meeting with Arcadia's leaders to attend to." She rested a hand on Saff's shoulder. "Thanks again for a good chat. I appreciate you."

As Kaylah and her personal guards walked away in the direction of the rope bridge, Saff's breathing picked up, her eyes glued on Kaylah.

What the heck just happened?

Chapter 27

Devin squeezed Saff tighter, kissing her cheek. "I thought you were going to meet Heather and me back at the tent for breakfast."

"Yeah... It was a pretty sunrise, and I got distracted."

"You ready for breakfast now?"

She stood there in a daze. She hadn't felt this betrayed since she'd discovered her family had lied about her identity all of her life. And the tough thing was that she didn't even know right now if Kaylah *was* betraying her, betraying them.

Was Kaylah just being flippant and callous? What had she genuinely been upset about? What was she hiding? Maybe Saff was being paranoid, but it felt like more than that. Kaylah had gaslit Rachel for years, making Rachel doubt her own reality. Saff had dealt with that as well. Her stomach churned, a bitter taste lingering in her mouth.

"Saff?" Devin said. He was now looking at her from the side, concern painted on his face.

She blinked. "Um... Just..." She shook her head. "Kaylah's acting weird. I think I'll talk about it with the council leader when she comes to visit tomorrow."

"Okay..." He raised an eyebrow. "If you're really this worried, we could catch a breeze and go speak to one now. You look really rattled."

Swallowing, Saff considered it. What did she have to go off of? 'Kaylah said something about her mom being weak and her uncle being evil, and then she clammed up'? Maybe it was just something Kaylah was ashamed of, and Saff had read it all wrong. "No." Saff shook her head again. "I'm probably just losing my mind. I'll bring it up with the councilwoman tomorrow."

Devin smiled. "Okay." He grabbed her hands. "So ... breakfast before work? We're kind of running behind."

Wearing a small smile, Saff nodded. "Yeah, sorry."

They started walking back to their tent, hand in hand.

"Heather got food from the garden after we got back, and I had to come looking for you."

"Sorry. I let the time get away from me."

He squeezed her hand. "No big deal."

"How was the walk with Heather?" Devin had been spending a decent portion of his limited free time with his sister. While Saff didn't always love sharing him, she fully understood their need. Devin was as great of a brother to Heather as Ben had been to Saff. Heather wasn't back to her bubbly old self yet, and no one expected her to be. Walks between brother and sister were uplifting to both Devin and Heather as they worked through their grief.

"Good walk. It was a beautiful sunrise, wasn't it?"

"Yeah, it was."

Devin stopped several yards short of the tent, facing Saff. "I have a proposal."

She slid her hands onto his waist. "Let's hear it."

"You and me, alone time tonight, away from this chaos."

Saff squinted. "You want to go on a date night in the middle of camp being under siege?"

He sighed, reaching up to her neck. His fingers gently dug in, massaging at the knots in it. "We never did get to properly celebrate our one-year anniversary. And you are so tense."

She frowned. "I'd rather be tense, than past tense, if the camp security walls fall." They were both working twelve to sixteen hours a day between training and security detail.

He matched her frown. "Do we or do we not plan to sleep tonight?"

She gazed into his deep brown eyes. "Obviously, we will."

His eyes shot up, looking at the Outer Rim, the mountains beyond the canyon. "It'll take a half hour to catch a breeze. That's all. We'll probably sleep a lot better without the constant noise around here..."

Of all the things she wanted to expend energy on, fighting his sweet notion wasn't one of them. "Okay. I'll let camp security know we'll be gone for the night."

He beamed, giving her a peck on the lips.

Saff surprised herself with how giddy she became throughout the day, the anticipation of their getaway building.

Before dusk, she'd done as required and reported to the camp security that she and Devin would be gone for the night, returning first thing in the morning. A head count was done every night, with each Unitas camp member accounted for.

She'd gotten off work earlier than Devin and had set to packing a few things for the night.

Devin entered the tent, looking utterly exhausted. "You ready for this?"

Saff looked him over. "No blood. That's good." He usually helped with camp security against the Ivy army stationed outside of camp, after his duties as a trainer of newly returned girls.

"Yeah. Mostly hammers and nails today as we worked to rebuild the southern section they keep tearing down. And a little dart action during an attack."

She grasped the hem of his shirt, pulling him in close. "Well, that would definitely explain why there's no blood, but you're worn out."

He puckered his lips expectantly.

She leaned forward, caressing his lips. Deciding she could spare some energy, and that he could definitely use a boost, she pushed Seeder energy from her heart, the warmth traveling through her neck and up to her lips.

Seeder energy kisses, also referred to as love kisses, were utterly intoxicating. They'd learned that lesson quickly with a close call in the intimacy department back in high school when they'd experimented with their first energy kiss.

Devin held her even closer as they kissed, not allowing an inch between them. After a minute, she cut off the energy transfer and leaned back. Her eyes were warm, and his were glowing too.

"I only expected a normal kiss," he said, catching his breath, his hands still holding her tightly.

She smirked, wrapping her arms around his neck. "I figured you could use a top-up before we catch a breeze."

"I can't lie—there are perks to having a mate that has more energy than the average Seeder girl."

"Oh yeah?" she asked playfully. "Is that why you married me? You just want me for my power?"

"It is in fact the *only* reason I married you," he answered coolly.

Saff giggled. "You ready to go? I packed some snacks and blankets."

"Mmm. Give me another kiss like that, and we might as well stay in this tent."

She frowned. "You're the one that talked me into this adventure." She raised her eyebrows in challenge. "And your argument was about getting *sleep*."

His eyes still glowed green. "Do you even know me? Those words will never leave my lips. '*Only* sleep'? There will *always* be hope for more." He wore that look of adoration that always got her. There had never been anyone other than Devin in her heart, not really, not in that way.

Devin stole a quick peck on the lips, his eyes fading to deep brown. "And I will *always* enjoy your company, even if it's *only* sleeping." He winked, and released her.

"Okay." She snatched up the satchels she'd packed, handing one to him. Not wanting to weigh them down, she'd only included the bare necessities. "You know where we're going?"

"Yep." He pulled on his satchel, tightening the straps. "After Kaylah invited me to camp, I talked to some of the families in Arcadia, and asked about the surrounding area. Shouldn't take more than half an hour."

Ready for a change of scenery, and wanting to set out before all light was gone, they headed toward the canyon and caught a breeze out of camp.

It didn't take long to reach the mountainside Devin had been told about. As night fell, they hadn't gotten too much opportunity to take in the scenery, but it was already refreshing to be away from camp. Ivies couldn't fly up there and attack them. No one coughing in a nearby tent would wake them up.

They decided to explore a little in the dark before picking a spot to spend the night. To keep themselves from tripping, they each pulled out a lightkeeper, tapping a finger to the quartz dome and cupping a hand on top to spread the energy out.

Devin led Saff by the hand through a maze of trees and bushes, seemingly knowing where he was going. "I wish I'd been able to bring your paint set from home," he said.

Oh, how she craved to paint. It had always been her favorite thing to do when she was stressed—to step back, retreat from the chaos, and create a world of her own that brought a sense of calm.

After a few minutes, a familiar soft white noise grew louder, but Saff couldn't put a finger on it. "What is that?"

"You'll see."

Soon enough, the source of the noise was within sight. A waterfall, majestically flowing into a quaint little pond. A smile spread across Saff's face.

She took a cleansing breath, allowing the constant stress to pour out of her in an exhale. The light cast by their lightkeepers shimmered across the pond. "It's beautiful. Thank you."

"It really is." Devin nudged her arm. "It might be cold this high up in the mountains, but we could manage that ... if you wanted to skinny-dip." He hummed playfully. "Just like when we were dating and you talked me into it."

Her jaw dropped. "I did not! *You* talked *me* into it!"

"That's *not* the way *I* remember it."

She turned to him, intentionally shifting her blue eyes to bright green. "Then you, sir, remember wrong."

He chuckled. "I vote we agree that we talked *each other* into it."

Devin was still capable of making her blush after four years of dating and marriage, even if no one else was there to overhear the conversation. "Fine. Maybe we talked each other into it." She laughed. "But I am pretty tired, and tomorrow's just another day. I'd rather not take a dip in freezing cold water right now."

"Works for me," he said. "Before we pick a spot to sleep, though, there's a part two to this surprise."

"Okay..."

He held a finger to his lightkeeper. "On three, we'll turn them off."

She followed his instructions, hovering an extended finger next to the lightkeeper she held.

"One. Two. Three."

They both swiped their fingers on the edge of the thin jade disk on the bottom, calling the Seeder energy back into the stone. As the light dimmed, the pond came to life.

Saff stood with her mouth agape. Bioluminescent moss on trees and boulders radiated bright green. A soft pink glow emanated from patches of fungi scattered amidst the trees. Purple pinpricks drifted through the air, winking in and out as they passed between trees.

"The special purple ones," she whispered in awe. Purple lightning bugs were the rarest type in the Green Lands; she'd only seen them once before.

Saff hadn't been the most voracious bookworm back in the human world, but she'd read enough fiction over the years to know that the secret fairy princess *always* felt out of place growing up, which hinted that there was something special about her.

But Saff wasn't a secret fairy princess. She'd felt perfectly at home during her years growing up in the human world. And other than her unique ability to wield extra energy, there wasn't anything spectacular about her. She had twenty-three siblings—just like every other Seeder. She'd sprouted on the first day of spring—just like every other Seeder.

Recalling her prior conversation with Kaylah, the good parts of it, Saff smiled wider. Someone thought Saff was special. What was it Kaylah had said? 'I see the way he looks at you when you're not watching.'

It was too dark to see Devin's face right now, and she didn't want to ruin the wonder of the moment by turning her lightkeeper back on. Saff reached out a hand, finding Devin's waist, and nuzzled up to him. "I love it. And I love you."

"Same, love."

For several more minutes, they stood in quiet contemplation. The Green Lands realm was beautiful, but few places compared to this sight. Beyond its physical beauty, it spoke to her on a higher, more spiritual level. There was a reason most Seeder girls answered the call of their energy once bloomed—it was part of them.

Ivies didn't bloom. They didn't have delayed development of their powers. But even they described the energy of the realm as addictive. Though, Saff surmised, they probably didn't feel it this deeply. After all, Seeder women held the most energy and power in this realm, so much so that it imprisoned them when they reached full maturity. How much more was Saff connected to this place because of her extra energy?

To her left, Devin yawned. "Yeah, I'm beat. Hand me your pack, and I'll set up the blankets over in that clearing we passed."

Devin laid out the thin blankets, and they cuddled up in the dark, watching the purple lightning bugs dance around, whispering as they discussed their days and the latest news via letter from their families back in South Fortinda.

Both worn out, their sleepiness doubled by the soft noise of the waterfall nearby, they quickly gave in to sleep, happily in each other's arms.

Saff woke, a little startled at first, forgetting she wasn't back home in their cottage or in their Unitas tent. Devin wasn't cuddled up to her anymore. Her eyes darted along the horizon, searching for him.

Nearby, a twig snapped, and she twisted to see what had caused it.

"Good morning." It was Devin, holding a mounded handful of burnt-orange sweetberries. "Did I wake you?"

Saff rubbed her eyes, yawning. He rarely woke before her. "No. I'm good."

"Great. I thought I'd supplement what you packed for a proper breakfast before we head out."

She smiled. If they could take a full day here, a week, a month... Maybe someday, when things calmed down.

They dug in, munching on the berries he'd picked, as well as oranges and nuts she'd packed.

Saff eyed Devin with admiration. "Do you know why I love you so much?"

He scratched his chin. "Because I sweep you off your feet and bring you to gorgeous locations?" He chomped down on a berry. "And I bring you tasty things?"

"Nope." She popped an almond into her mouth.

He arched an eyebrow high. "Then it must be my godlike physique. 'Cause we both know—human, Seeder, or Ivy—no one's got anything on this. You got lucky."

She laughed. "Nope."

Devin narrowed his eyes playfully. "Hurtful."

"Do you want me to tell you?"

Holding up a finger, he popped a few more berries into his mouth. "It's because I can cook and garden better than..." He cleared his throat, very clearly implying Saff. "Well, better than some people."

She grinned. "Well, it certainly isn't for your humility."

He chuckled. She'd always loved his confidence. And he wasn't wrong about being handsome, but then again, who didn't think their partner was attractive? Even if they weren't 'conventionally' attractive?

Her face softened. "But I'm serious."

He shifted his seat. "Okay. Tell me why you love me so much."

"Because..." The thought almost instantly brought tears to her eyes. "Because when we were fighting, after I was stupid and left for the human world without you, you were so quick to forgive."

Frowning, Devin shook his head. "We barely talked for *weeks*. I don't know about 'quick to forgive.'"

She wiped away a tear. "Yeah, no, I guess I didn't word that right. What I mean is—you forgave me *before* anything good came from my actions. You didn't forgive me just because you found out Kaylah and her people were doing the right thing."

"Saff," he said softly. "My love for you isn't conditional. Never will be. I gave you all of it, years ago."

How much of that was the Seeder mating bond talking? She'd stopped questioning that a while ago. Did it matter if your attraction was ten percent dimples, thirty percent sense of humor, twenty-five percent shared beliefs, and thirty-five percent natural chemistry? Or any other combination?

"I love you too." She smiled. "And I know I'm lucky to have you." She sighed, picking through the small bag of mixed nuts. "Sometimes I feel sorry for you. Kaylah's helped me to see how much of a control freak I can be."

Not two seconds later, Devin busted out laughing, slapping a hand to his mouth, his eyes wide.

That stung, after their super-sweet moment.

"No, don't take it that way," he blurted, then pleaded with his eyes. "You know I love you the way you are."

It wasn't like he hadn't listed off his reasons for loving her, but it still hurt a little to be laughed at when admitting one of her own flaws.

"It's, um, well ... a Ben thing," Devin explained.

Her heart ached, just hearing his name. Like Heather, Saff had buried herself in work, distracting herself from her grief, but Devin usually found it comforting to share memories of Ben.

"He kind of swore me to secrecy," Devin said.

"What?" What kind of secret would Ben have shared with Devin about Saff?

Devin grinned. "Before your bloom, when you thought he was just a foster brother... Well, it wasn't exactly a secret you two didn't get along."

Saff frowned.

Devin still wore a perma-grin. "He told me you were uptight. He didn't know I had a crush on you. He called you a control freak, and..." Devin pressed his lips together, stifling another laugh.

Saff searched his face. "Just tell me."

"You know how much you hated how he left toothpaste all over the sink?"

She bunched her eyebrows.

"Once he realized how much that annoyed you, he started doing it on purpose."

Her jaw dropped. "What a jerk!" She instantly felt a surge of guilt for speaking ill of the dead, but it quickly subsided. She laughed along with Devin. If Ben had been there to see her face, he would have *lost* it. He would have laughed his head off. Maybe it would do Saff some good to talk more about him, instead of avoiding it.

As they polished off their meal, they shared a few more fond memories of Ben. After packing up their things, Saff dreaded returning to camp. While this little jaunt had been a welcome reprieve from the everyday crazy, it made it that much harder to want to get back to it.

Pausing briefly to take in the daytime scenery, they stood by the pond, watching koi swim. With her mind still on Ben, Saff bent over and picked up a smooth, flat rock. She ran her thumb over it. Skipping rocks had been her favorite activity with Ben after returning to the Green Lands. Raising a hand to her neck, she touched the jade charm she always wore. While it no longer served a purpose with her powers, she still kept the carved sun symbol to her skin like Devin had first instructed her to.

Maybe it was weird, but it might be cool to have Ben's name etched into a rock like this, as some type of memorial, especially since she hadn't been there for his burial.

Turning the grey rock in her hand, she smiled. "Love you, Ben." Taking a step back, she aimed and shot the rock at the pond. It skipped four times. With each skip, her heart felt a little lighter.

Devin kissed her sweetly on the head. "Ready to go?"

"Yeah."

After a few minutes of hiking to the clearing they'd landed in, they communed with the wind, catching a breeze back to camp.

Landing, Saff held out her hand for Devin's pack. "I'll return these to the tent. Would you check in with camp security?"

He handed her the bag. "Yes, ma'am." He kissed her again. "Are you still going to track down the councilwoman on her visit today? To talk to her about Kaylah acting off?"

Saff hesitated. She'd contemplated that exact thing on their half-hour flight back. Hadn't Kaylah proven herself, after all? She'd killed a soldier to get them safely to Seeder borders once. She and her people had helped bring home countless Seeder girls through Ivy rifts and the rifting cave, getting them home quicker and safer than they could do on their own.

But how much of it was an act?

While disappointed in herself for doubting Kaylah after all the work she'd done to try and form a friendship between them, something nagged relentlessly at Saff.

The assassins who tried to kill or kidnap Saff years ago had let Nuren's name slip. But her family had never reported it to a higher council. They hadn't been required to, as nothing about the man ever surfaced. They'd concluded it might have just been a figment of Saff's imagination, the fevered whispers she'd heard while fighting to stay alive, and to not fall into a coma.

But they had been wrong.

What would have happened if Saff's family had taken that threat more seriously? Perhaps there would have been a manhunt and Nuren would have been caught before the War Vines were ever formed, ever activated, ever hurt a single soul.

With her heart and mind at odds, Saff made her decision. Kaylah had probably just had a bad day, and Saff had likely been reading too much into it. But she wouldn't be the weak link.

"Yeah. I'm going to talk to the councilwoman when I can find her. Just ... out of an abundance of caution."

Devin nodded grimly. "Yeah, probably a good idea." He grabbed her hand. "Thanks again, for a perfect night."

Saff grinned. "You didn't even get any action."

"But it was with you. Ergo: perfect." He winked.

She shook her head. "Get out of my face before I kiss yours."

He chuckled, giving her hand a squeeze before releasing it. "I love you. See you after work."

"Love you too."

Chapter 28

The official word hit the Ivy Kingdom with thunderous shock: the princess was a traitor, having taken part in her own parents' murders. She was wanted alive, to answer for her crimes. Circulating rumors about Unitas were being censored—they still sounded like a ragtag, pathetic group of dissenters.

The news was received at Guillen and Rachel's next meeting with mixed results. But overall, it actually seemed to be working in Unitas's favor within the stunt communities.

A small group of Unitas hopefuls gathered in the community room of Six, ready to hear the presentation. Rachel perched on the edge of a table at the front of the meeting room while Guillen began. This group was especially dirty and gruff, having lived hard lives in mines.

"Our people deserve equal rights. That's what we're here to discuss tonight," Guillen said.

"What would *you* know about that?" a man asked, jumping right in.

Guillen raised his eyebrows. "About what?"

The man crossed his arms. "You act like you know how we feel, but do you? Last I checked, your tattoo didn't have a number. How's life without needing documents to travel? What other nice privileges do you get?"

Rachel frowned, glancing at Guillen. He remained silent.

The man continued. "When you're done pretending to be one of us and saving us, do we worship you then? Or do we need to start doing that now?"

Guillen nodded, looking down. Rachel swallowed hard; she'd never seen anything get to him this way. She stood up, addressing the man, not hiding the harshness in her voice. "I'm sorry. Have *you* ever worked your full-time assignment *and* spent all your free time fighting for others' rights? No. You haven't." Guillen worked harder than anyone else she knew.

The man was not impressed. "It's easy to tout superiority when you're born into privilege. I heard he gets loads more free time than we do."

Rachel hesitated. That was true. Guillen had already listed off the crazy restrictions placed on stunts, and also the exceptions his birthright afforded him. He *did* get four times the allotted vacation time that regular stunts did. But he didn't squander it. All of that, in addition to extra time like this, created through the use of bogus orders fabricated by Unitas, had been spent fighting for their rights.

"The question is simple. Do you want more freedoms, equal rights? Or not?" She pointed at the belligerent man. "Because this is your chance to make it happen. It would be a shame to waste the opportunity to make a difference because of your pride. Whether it's a member of the royal family, or the person sitting next to you, or heck ... even a Seeder, why does it matter what they've gone through, if they're willing to help?"

The man rolled his eyes as Guillen cleared his throat. Rachel glanced back at Guillen, and he threw her a quick appreciative look before continuing with his pitch.

The community gathering room cleared out, and Guillen pulled out his keys to lock it up. "You go first, and I'll be a few."

Rachel cocked her head to the side. "Yeah?"

He wore a forced smile. "Just going to take a short stroll, get some fresh air before turning in for the night."

She nodded. "Do you want company?"

"No. You know the drill. Leave separate. Arrive at the room separate."

She hesitated, but gave him a quick peck on the cheek and left the building for their room. She ached on his behalf. She hadn't considered how others might view him with jealousy or anger for his place in the royal family. He wasn't fully accepted in 'regular' society, and even amongst those like him, he didn't always fit in.

Arriving back at their room, Rachel got ready for the night. She sat on the edge of their bed for several minutes, festering over the interaction at the meeting.

Guillen knocked to announce himself, and unlocked the door. She wanted to get up and hug him, but wasn't quite sure what he needed.

He smiled softly. "Hey."

"How are you?" she asked, trying to read his face after he locked the door behind him.

"I'm good. They're on board, after all." He sat down in an armchair.

Rachel got up and sauntered over, sitting down on his lap. "Your condition is rare. How many people in this kingdom have a crown tattoo?"

He met her gaze. "Well ... there's me. And Lewis. Lewis is..." Guillen squinted at the ceiling in thought. "Eighty-something at this point. He lives as far away from the palace as physically possible while still being in our kingdom." Guillen grinned. "That's a perk, too. Once you're too old and broken to work, those of us close enough to the queen in the royal bloodline are graciously allowed to live in *any* community we like."

She gently ran her fingers through his hair. "Just the two of you?"

He shrugged. "That's it right now. We got lucky."

Rachel bit her lip. "That must be hard. Not knowing where you belong."

He wrapped an arm around her. "I know where I belong. With Kaylah in Unitas. And here. With you." He smiled.

Rachel frowned. "You know what I mean. To be part of the royal family," she glanced at the scar on his temple, "but not really being accepted for who you are."

He met her gaze.

"And then to—"

He raised his eyebrows. "To sometimes be rejected by society's rejects?" He rested a hand on her knee. "It comes with the territory. I'm the bastard product of privilege and disappointment."

Her frown deepened. "Don't ever describe yourself that way. That's not who you are."

He sighed. "I've accepted who I am. And I've told you before—I don't want pity. Least of all from you." He shook his head and shifted in his seat. "A lot of people have it worse than me. I can't complain."

She read his face. "Yeah, people have it worse. But there's *always* someone that has it worse. That doesn't mean you're not allowed to feel hurt sometimes." She grabbed his hand. "I love that you make the most of what life has given you, and you try to stay positive. But don't compare yourself that way. Just because someone else hurts worse, doesn't mean you're not hurting. You have a right to your feelings."

Guillen looked down, shaking his head.

Perhaps Guillen wasn't *always* openly expressing how he felt, but she'd started to pick up on his mannerisms. That contemplative look, then a slight shake of the head—she'd even found herself doing it. It was often followed by direct eye contact and a small smile that expressed more than words could. It said 'you get me' or 'how did I get lucky enough to have you in my life?'

"What?" she asked.

He looked up, smiling. "I love you."

She met his smile with one of her own. "I kind of love you a *little* bit, too." She held a hand out, pinching the tiniest bit of air between her thumb and pointer finger.

He narrowed his eyes. "Just a little bit, huh?"

She gave him a toothy smile, widening the gap between her fingers to as wide as they would stretch. "A lot bit."

He squeezed her hand. "How about I get changed and we call it an early night?"

After a quick smooch, she crawled into bed, under the covers, while he got ready. Once he joined her, she slid over to cuddle. A candle still flickered behind him on the nightstand.

"Thanks for having my back tonight," he said.

She planted a soft kiss on his Unitas tattoo, resting a hand on his exposed chest. "I'll always have your back."

"Always?" he whispered.

What kind of promise was she making? She responded with the only thing her heart would allow. "Always."

He pursed his lips. "I, uh, I think that guy got to me so much because ... you know, he was right. It hit close to home. When I first moved away from my family home, I made plenty of mistakes. I wasn't perfect back then." He gently ran a finger across the curve of her shoulder. "Well, not like I'm perfect now, but I learned a lot from my messups."

Rachel furrowed her brow. "You were sixteen when you moved out on your own. No one expects a sixteen-year-old to be perfect."

Guillen raised a skeptical eyebrow. "No? I guess we grew up in different worlds." He let out a breathy chuckle. "I suppose we technically did. But there was plenty of pressure to not disgrace the family name any further. To not make myself a target. To just fade away and be forgotten."

"I'm sorry." A bitterness rose up her throat. "I love that my mom didn't pressure me to get straight-As or anything like that. And neither did Nuren. But why would he care if his stepdaughter was an idiot?" His piercing words still rang in her ears sometimes, the things he'd said as she'd been strapped to a chair, War Vine leaves drilled into her arms, sucking her Seeder energy dry. He'd called her livestock. Why would it matter if a cow had any brain cells before it was sent to slaughter?

Guillen rubbed her shoulder again. "Do you want to talk about it?"

She snapped out of her thoughts. "No. Not tonight. But thanks." She smiled. "I'd like to hear more about your escapades."

His gaze shot to the pendulum clock in the corner. "Yep, it's bedtime."

"Hey!" She scowled playfully. "You've got to give me *something*. It's only fair. You *did* have a jumpstart on getting to know me because of Kaylah."

"Fair enough." He wrinkled his nose. "My messups cover the gambit. Stupid mistakes with girls. Co-workers. Friendships. Guards."

"Uh-oh. Trouble with guards?"

"They don't all treat me the same, right?"

"Yeah, I've noticed that." Some seemed more afraid of Guillen, others resentful, some neutral.

He shifted a bit. "Let's just say Kaylah and I ... conspired... I kind of called in a favor once. In the end, it accomplished what we needed, but came with mixed results. Rumors circulated amongst the stunt community guards. They've got their own little club. Some are terrified of me because they now think I have more pull at the palace than I actually do. Some hate me because of the fallout from what Kaylah and I arranged. Some don't care."

She studied his face. "But you don't want to elaborate on what you did?"

"Um..." Guillen rubbed his face. "It involved an ex-girlfriend."

"I see..." She still wanted to know, but it was obvious he wasn't ready to share, and it wasn't like he'd demanded to know about any of her dating history.

Taking a deep breath, she smiled. "Well, now I know you're not perfect. I think I'll still stick around."

He gave her an appreciative grin.

"After all, there's no such thing as a perfect person." She walked a pair of fingers up his chest, to his lips. "But I do think that every person out there has someone that's perfect *for them*."

They locked eyes.

"Why are you this way?" he whispered.

Even when he said the wrong thing, he could say it the right way. It hadn't been said as an insult. Not with the softness of his voice. Not with the desire in his eyes. Not with the way he swallowed, as if holding back. Sharing a bed, it was no secret he wanted more, but he'd never crossed the line. He knew she needed to heal before taking things to the next step.

But staring into his eyes in this moment... She might be there.

After another swallow, with the silence hanging thick between them, Guillen waved the white flag, breaking eye contact.

"How about I be the little spoon again?"

She fought a smile, her cheeks warming. "I can manage that."

Once they drew closer to Community Five, Guillen rented Rachel a room in a nearby regular community. She couldn't pretend to be a fellow stunt in Five, not with their mark tattooed on her arm. Before Rachel and Guillen embarked on their mission, Guillen had scouted the sentiments of each community. This one seemed to be more hostile toward Seeders; he'd take a different approach here.

He dropped her off before making his way to that night's meeting.

"Remind me why I can't stay here with you?" he asked, before stealing another kiss as they sat on the sofa.

Rachel moaned. "I wish you could." She straddled him and gazed into his eyes. "I love you so much." She nibbled on his ear.

He shifted under her. "Okay. That's my cue. If I don't leave now, then I won't leave at all." He got up and stole one last kiss before heading out. "You have plenty of money, right? And you'll be alright alone?"

"I'll be fine." She smiled softly. "Don't worry about me."

Soon after Guillen took off, Rachel decided to go for a stroll. She mused on what it would be like in the Green Lands when there was peace—how tourism would look, if it ever got to that point. Sure, these communities weren't as beautiful as Seeder lands, but that would change once Kaylah had control. And it held its own kind of charm over here, anyway.

Rachel found a nice little outdoor café to eat dinner before heading back to her room for the night. She expected Guillen to be back pretty late. This town was eerily, though not surprisingly, as empty as the previous 'regular' one she'd toured before. Remembering Guillen's words, Rachel focused on enjoying her chickpea, lentil, and carrot stew. She was halfway through her meal when she overheard a couple of women gossiping behind her.

"I still can't believe it. It's not right."

"But what did you expect him to do? I don't think he can default to the next in line, not until she's out of the picture. It doesn't work that way."

"Yeah, but naming himself king? And his bride, queen? She has *no* power over the Mother Vines. She's not even royal."

"It's just temporary. Once she's dead, I'm sure he'll set things right. We can't be weak without a proper leader while this goes on."

"Yeah. I guess you're right. But it's still weird."

Rachel pushed her wooden bowl aside. It couldn't be interpreted any other way. Soren had gotten married. He'd claimed the throne. He was showing his power-hungry colors.

And that might be just another misstep caused by his pride. If others of his kind shared these girls' sentiments, he may have crossed the line, even by their estimation. Like Kaylah had said—royal birth didn't automatically mean your people would stand behind you. You needed loyalty. And what he considered to be a show of strength...

Rachel wore a smug grin.

"Are you finished here?" her waitress asked.

"Can I get the rest of this to go? And one of your best desserts?" She placed a few more coins on the table to pay for the to-go glass jar and food wrapping.

Rachel took her food back to the room, sorting through her emotions. Yes, she was happy to hear Soren's people disapproving of the 'king' and his latest blunder. But she had so much emotional trauma tied to that man, and his new queen. Rachel knew nothing about the woman, not that she hadn't thought about her. Sometimes Rachel made herself sick thinking about her. But her curiosity always stopped short of asking Kaylah or Guillen. She couldn't unknow that. She didn't want to compare.

Rachel had come to think of Soren's bride as the 'other woman,' but perhaps it was really her that was the other woman, if this new 'queen' was his primary interest. Or maybe it didn't really work that way. Maybe his bride had known about Rachel, and she could only be the 'other woman' if she had been in the dark about his relationship with Rachel on his mission. It mattered little, but Rachel sorted through the complex emotions as best she could.

She had hoped to stay up late enough to see Guillen get back for the night, but realized she'd passed out when the click of the door opening startled her awake.

"Hey, honey. It's just me," he whispered in the dark.

She reached over, her hand feeling and grasping a striker. She lit a beeswax candle, and he sat down on the edge of the bed.

She squinted against the light. "Hey, handsome. How did it go?"

He frowned hesitantly.

"How bad?"

"No, actually, the meeting was surprisingly amazing."

"That's great." She smiled.

"There's just some news that might bother you."

She furrowed her brow. "What?"

"Soren."

"Oh. The whole marriage and calling himself a king thing?"

Guillen raised his eyebrows. "So, you heard? You're taking it better than I thought you would."

She slid her hand into his. "I'm doing great. I gave myself time to process it. And I'm happy he did it. From what I hear, he's shot himself in the foot."

Guillen's face lit up. "Yeah! They were *all* sorts of scorched tonight. If there was a community I was worried about, with the exception of the two closest to the palace, it was this one. We needed this win." He leaned over and stole a kiss.

It warmed her heart to see him so happy. "I'm glad you're back. Did you get a chance to eat?"

"Not much. I'm famished."

"I brought you back some leftovers, just in case. And a dessert to share."

He stole another kiss. "You are going to spoil me."

Rachel got out of bed, giving Guillen a quick hug. "You eat up. I was going to take a shower; that way we can leave first thing in the morning."

By the time she came out, he'd finished eating and was organizing his things.

"I think I'm going to follow your lead before we turn in. Then we'll break into that delicious-looking treat over there?"

A few minutes later, she leaned in the bathroom doorway, brushing her wet hair. He stood at the sink, brushing his teeth, shirtless.

"Was the water cold?" she asked.

He spat out the Green Lands equivalent of toothpaste—crushed, dried mint leaves and a special kind of abrasive fiddlehead fern. "It's fine. I don't mind it that much."

"I love you."

His smile reflected back at her in the mirror. "I love you too."

She sauntered up to him, setting her brush down. Her stomach in knots, she wrapped her arms around his bare midriff. "I ... want to be with you."

His reflection's gaze met hers. "What do you mean by that?"

She blushed. "You know—what I said the other day I wasn't ready for yet. You ... and me ... and ... stuff..." She knew how stupid she sounded, but couldn't bring herself to actually say the words.

He grinned. "And stuff?"

She bit her lip. "Are you going to make me spell it out?"

"No. But I do love watching you squirm." He chuckled. "And you know how to sell it like it's sexy. '*Stuff*.'"

She leaned her head against his shoulder and laughed.

He faced her, holding her by the waist. "Are you sure you're ready for that? I'm not in a rush."

"Well, I ... unless you're not. And if that's the case, I can respect that."

"I'm ready."

She smiled. "I am too."

He took a deep breath. "I know you don't want me asking, but this doesn't have anything to do with today's news, does it?"

She shook her head. "No... I've kinda been wanting to ask you all day."

"Okay." His voice was soft and mesmerizing.

She fidgeted with her hands. "I just, uh... I haven't done this before."

He grinned mischievously. "You say that like it's a bad thing."

She shrugged. "It's just ... you're older, and ... stuff."

He raised his eyebrows. "More stuff, huh?"

She traced his abs while smirking.

"If you're sure, then my answer is yes. And I'll tell you a secret—we'll be figuring this out together."

She looked up and searched his face. "Really?"

It was his turn to blush. "Really."

Rachel pulled Guillen in for a hug, savoring the warmth of his skin. She shuddered as he moved his hand up her shirt and slowly pulled it over her head. He gave her a knowing look—he recognized that bra, the same one he'd accidentally seen her in months before. She embraced him again, more skin now touching as she lingered in his arms. He nuzzled her neck, his soft lips slowly descending.

A loud and quick knock at their door pulled them out of the moment.

"Why?" she whispered. "Why does the universe hate us?"

Their uninvited visitor knocked again with urgency.

"Who knows we're all the way out here?" Her frustration mingled with fear.

"Only William. And he'd only come if it was important. Stay put; I'll check it out." Guillen grabbed a shirt and pulled it on, covering his Unitas tattoo.

Rachel stayed in the bathroom, deflated, as Guillen left her side to open the door.

"William, what's wrong?" he asked.

"It's the princess!" William hissed.

Rachel's eyes shot wide open. She bent down and snatched up her shirt, throwing it on. She brought her energy back in to appear normal. Guillen leaned back to check if she was fit to be seen. "Come inside."

The man named William entered and sat on the couch while Guillen locked the door. Rachel shyly leaned in the bathroom doorway. William, a portly man with greying hair, looked shocked to see someone else in the room.

"Sorry, this is, um..." Guillen blanked, gesturing to Rachel. "Elizabeth. She's safe to talk around. She's close to Kaylah."

Rachel tugged on her sleeve, making sure her tattoo was hidden. Even with a friendly, she wasn't going to risk giving that up in this area.

"She's gone missing."

"What?!" Guillen blurted.

"She just ... went missing from the training camp."

Rachel covered her mouth. "How long has she been gone? We don't know if she's at the palace?"

"No. We haven't been able to confirm yet. And we aren't sure if he'll claim it. He probably wants Unitas to think she's abandoned them."

"Is there doubt?" Guillen asked.

"It's too early to say. There's been tension in camp. Some people are bound to think she's double-crossed us. The royal family is known for elaborate strategies..."

Guillen looked at Rachel. "You know she wouldn't do that, right?"

Rachel shook her head. "No, I know she wouldn't. I just hope she's okay ... and that my people still trust in the cause."

"Is anything being done to get her back?" Guillen asked.

"I don't know; I have very little information. Once she's at the palace ... it's going to be near impossible, with how things stand."

Guillen ran his hands through his hair. "Alright, I'm taking a detour. I know what I need to do." He turned to Rachel. "I can pay for you to stay here for a while. Stay hidden. I'll try and get someone to you soon, to get you out."

She furrowed her brow. "What are you talking about? I'm not just sitting here! Where are you going?"

Guillen glanced at William, then back to Rachel. "Let's talk." He grabbed her wrist and led her outside. "I love you," he whispered. "But I can't take you."

She scowled. "Take me where? I'm not just here as a girlfriend, remember? I'm an initiated member. I've trained enough."

"If Soren has her, he wants her to control the Vines. If she doesn't cooperate, he may just kill her and move on to the next heir."

Wait a second... She looked into his eyes. "The next heir is... How many sisters did the queen have? Kaylah doesn't have any sisters."

He raised his eyebrows, his face grim. "The next queen is my mother. And then my little sister."

Rachel's heart dropped. "Guillen. I don't... I mean..."

"I'm going to go make sure they're okay. Convince them to go into hiding. If they're out of reach, he doesn't have an easy alternative. It'll keep Kaylah safe until we can get her out."

She nodded, still in shock. "But why don't you want me to go?"

"Honey, it's dangerous. And ugly. It's so much closer to the palace. And that's not what you signed up for. I can handle it."

She narrowed her eyes. "That's a shit excuse! I'm coming. I promised Eric I'd watch out for her. I may not have the same training, but I owe her this."

"No!"

Rachel clenched her jaw, fuming. The light of a candle flickered to life in a neighboring apartment at their escalating argument.

"Why can't someone else go?" she whispered. "Someone ... that can rift. They'll go faster."

He shook his head, his voice low. "You don't know my mother like I do. She's not going to easily betray the palace. I need to go. And I need to get going before he realizes what we have. If he hasn't already."

"Unless you tie me up, I'm going with you! We take care of each other."

He stared at her, pursing his lips. "Fine. For now. But if things get dicey, I might take you up on that threat, to tie you up for your own good. I really don't think it's worth the risk."

Chapter 29

Exhausted, having used up her Seeder energy, and having been summoned for a meeting, Saff shuffled across the Unitas camp. *How could this possibly get worse?* She'd never really wanted to be a soldier; she loved teaching. But she was having to take more time from training new girls to help with camp border patrol. With Unitas's location compromised, and the War Vine attacks being significantly weakened on official Seeder territory borders, Soren's army had rerouted an obscene number of troops to take on the camp.

After her and Devin's excursion into the mountains, Saff's worries had mounted about reporting Kaylah's behavior to the council. What if it had really meant nothing, and Saff's words to the council member eroded the trust they held in Kaylah?

But Saff couldn't shake the weight of responsibility to report the behavior. The problem, however, was that the councilwoman assigned to Unitas never showed up for her regular visit that day.

And that night, all hell had broken loose in camp. Kaylah had gone missing, and that was just the half of it.

Saff sighed as she approached her intended destination, Ginger's tent. She pulled back the door flap and cautiously walked in. Ginger sat in a chair, staring at a corner of the tent, pensive and worn out.

"You called for me?" Saff said.

Ginger drew a deep breath. "Yeah. Please sit down. Let's talk."

Saff took a seat facing her. "Talking is about the only thing I'm good for right now."

Ginger frowned. "We need to discuss what's going on. We need answers."

"And you think I have those?" Saff asked, exasperated.

Ginger shrugged. "I don't know what to think anymore."

Saff didn't either. The way Kaylah had gone missing was disturbing. As usual, she'd had guards stationed outside of her tent—two of them. One Ivy, one Seeder. Both were missing. During the surge of aggressive attacks on camp that night, most camp members had been pulled to the borders for fighting. No witnesses had come forward about seeing Kaylah or her guards going missing.

There were, however, plenty of witnesses who had rushed into action when Kaylah's tent, as well as the patch of emergency exit rifting trees, had all lit ablaze.

A few trees remained unharmed, as well as some of the books and scrolls in Kaylah's tent, but many of the ancient books were irreparably lost, reduced to smoke and ash. No bodies had been found.

Ginger pursed her lips, the dark bags under her eyes accentuating her frustration. "My people can't help but worry they're risking their lives for the wrong cause. You can't pretend things aren't suspicious with your leaders and the current circumstances."

Saff's jaw dropped. "You're kidding me. Seeders are somehow at fault? Don't pretend Kaylah hasn't hurt my people before. That she hasn't let people she supposedly cares about get caught in the crosshairs."

Ginger's eyes narrowed, and she stabbed a finger onto the desk she sat at. "Where are your leaders right now? When we need them? *My* people are completely cutoff. *Your* people have made sure of that, haven't they?"

The rifting cave security had been doubled, and the Seeders had chopped down the remaining rifting trees in camp, fearing more betrayal, more deserters.

"We can't exactly rift into your territory for a meeting. *Your* council can send someone through the cave. Or catch a breeze over the troops. But they're *not.* They're ignoring our requests."

Saff sat up straight. "They're a little busy right now!"

Right after Kaylah went missing, a messenger had arrived bearing news from the council. With the War Vines not working as well, missing the energy of the extra kidnapped Seeder girls, Ivies had converged on one weakened point, in the thousands. Maybe even tens of thousands. For the first time in known history, a portion of both the Inner and Outer Walls had fallen, in sickeningly close proximity to Saff and Devin's home village.

It made her physically ill. She had no word from home. From her family. They'd discussed Devin returning to help back home or to at least get an update on their loved ones, but concluded the camp needed him more, and they couldn't justify the time spent traveling.

Ginger shook her head. "They could give us *something*. They've all but abandoned us."

"Abandoned? Their focus is to save lives. And if Soren's people get their hands on even one or two of our fully-rooted matriarchs in their raids, we're screwed." The War Vines weren't as effective as they'd previously been, missing more girls to power their attack, but they continued to break down and weaken the Seeder border thickets. If Soren got his hands on another Seeder girl, especially a powerful matriarch...

Ginger rubbed the back of her neck. "The facts remain. She was supposed to be guarded. We're not getting a lot of help. We're cutoff."

Saff nodded. "The facts *do* remain. Kaylah knows how to take care of herself just fine. And she hasn't really fulfilled her promises, has she?"

"Like your council, she's been a bit busy." Ginger glared. "*My* people aren't blind to the fact that *your* people are impatient, and might consider pivoting their strategy and keeping you out of the loop on that."

Saff crossed her arms, ready to keep going at it. But this was getting them nowhere. "When did we go back to 'your people' and 'my people,' Ginger? This isn't what Kaylah wanted. I know you love her, and I do too." She frowned. "It may have taken me longer to get there, but I believe in this cause. And I know you do too."

There were only three possibilities: Kaylah had double-crossed Unitas and the Seeder people, Seeder leadership had abandoned the cause and double-crossed Kaylah, or Soren's forces had found a way in to take her.

Ginger sighed, studying the ground with a slow nod.

"We've got people searching in both realms, right?" Saff said. "I know things are touchy. I know we all want answers right now. But we need to give them time to find out what really happened."

"Yeah," Ginger whispered. "We should hopefully hear back from palace insiders soon, on whether Soren has her."

Saff fidgeted with her hands. "Hopefully. If we even have any insiders left on our side."

Ginger rubbed her face with her hands. "Business as usual. Protect the camp, the community without powers, the cave. And sit here ... waiting for news. And for something to change..."

"Yeah." Saff's heart was heavy. She *wanted* to believe it had been Soren; she couldn't bear to imagine Kaylah or the council betraying Unitas.

Saff's mind was muddled. Partially from physical exhaustion, partially from the tax on her Seeder energy, and partially from the stress of having taken her first lives. Then again, was it *her* kill, or Devin's, if he had thrown the darts, boosted by Saff's energy?

Splaying her hands on her thighs, Saff tried to think straight. "Can we just go over the logistics again?"

They discussed the events of the night Kaylah had gone missing, both doing their best to not take offense when the loyalty of their people was called into question. They discussed motive and opportunity.

Saff outlined her thinking first. "There could be multiple reasons for Kaylah to turn."

Perhaps Kaylah had found something in her research that didn't sit right with her, prompting her to bail. Or she'd intended to set the camp up to fail from the beginning. Or Soren had snuck in a spy with an offer she couldn't turn down. If she'd abandoned Unitas, it would make sense that she would light fire to her own tent to cause confusion and to destroy the ancient research. The fire would give her a distraction while she and her Ivy guard took out the Seeder guard, disposed of the body in the canyon, and snuck out through a tree rift. But it was odd that they would have set fire to the emergency rifting trees in camp as well. Would Kaylah have been vindictive enough to her own Unitas Ivies to imprison them in camp, knowing they'd fall to either Soren's forces, or the Seeders upon her betrayal?

"None of that is true," Ginger asserted, teeth clenched but her tone civil—barely. "And if she'd discovered anything like that to make her turn on us, she would have discussed it with me, too."

You could cut the tension in camp with a Seeder blade. It was spelled out on everyone's faces. The only reason most of the Unitas Ivies hadn't defected at her departure was likely because they had nowhere to go anymore. They'd staked their lives on this cause. They wouldn't return to their kingdom to be executed as traitors. They couldn't seek refuge in Seeder lands with the existing hostilities. And they couldn't physically leave anyway, with the emergency exit trees now gone, all exits from camp guarded, and the rifting cave well-manned.

The only reason Seeders didn't take on their Ivy counterparts in camp and wipe them out, or detain them, was simply because they were needed in the fighting to keep Soren's forces at bay.

Reluctant or not, begrudgingly or not, both sides of Unitas still needed each other. They didn't know how to deactivate the rifting cave Kaylah had set up, and they couldn't just abandon it to Soren's army. There was nowhere to evacuate the Seeder men without powers to, other than marching them into the mountains somewhere, for some unknown amount of time, with the vines of the Ivy army at their heels.

Unitas was an island in this war right now, and they needed to hold the line and take care of their own while the main Seeder territories managed their weakened borders in the bigger picture.

"So…" Ginger tapped her fingers on the table. "If the Seeder council betrayed Unitas…"

They explored that option as well. Perhaps Kaylah had stumbled upon some darker truths in the history of Seeders that they'd hidden from their people. They'd needed to shut her up. Perhaps they'd been disappointed that she hadn't yet delivered on half of her promises thus far, and were ready to dissolve their alliance. Either way, the same motives for the fires that night loomed as possibilities—destroy evidence, create panic, cut off Unitas Ivies from retreat.

The Ivy guard that night could have been a casualty at the bottom of the canyon somewhere, while the Seeder one had carted Kaylah away, perhaps through the cave, even. But that would have required several guards to look the other way, and would stand to have more witnesses, as the cave was farther to travel to. How many people would have had to conspire for that to happen?

"The logic doesn't hold up," Saff said.

If the Seeders had carried this out, why wouldn't they have sent more troops to protect their own village, and the cave? They could have sent troops in to sweep the camp clean if they'd wanted to end this experiment; they wouldn't have needed to steal Kaylah away in the middle of the night. Then again, their resources were stretched thin with the border walls failing.

Suspicion waxed and waned between Saff's heart and mind, in her attempts to be logical, but in the end, this *didn't* smell of Seeder treachery.

Seeders wouldn't intentionally abandon their sons and brothers without power, and they wouldn't be so heartless and underhanded. Saff could understand Ginger's doubts, though. It wasn't like they'd sat around a campfire singing songs and sharing smiles with council members from the beginning. It had been a rough road. But they'd been giving Kaylah so much more freedom in her strategies, orders, and research.

"It *had* to be Soren's doing, right?" Saff asked.

Kaylah had to have been taken against her will … somehow. But if Soren's forces had found a way to sneak into camp and sneak her out, why hadn't they just wiped out the camp altogether in a bloodbath? It had to have been more stealthy than that. Other than the two missing guards, no one else had gone missing, and it stood to reason that more than one or two guards would have been needed to take her hostage and keep her quiet.

And assuming Soren's people had dragged her back to the palace, how could he even manage that without the cave or on foot? They'd probably used the emergency exit trees, but Ivy rifting wasn't as simple as running a vine down the spine of a tree and shoving someone through. There was a mental component to Ivy rifting. The rifter had to know their destination as they created the rift, and the only being they could pull through one was a female Seeder, not another Ivy. It didn't add up. How could Soren have forced Kaylah to open her own rift to a location of his choosing? No matter her faults, Kaylah was made of tougher stuff than that.

None of it made sense. Which was likely what the culprit had been going for. It was infuriating.

Saff shook her head, trying to clear it. They weren't getting anywhere. "Have you noticed Kaylah acting off lately?"

Ginger leaned back in her seat again. "Off? Not really…"

"Because I did. She clammed up when we were talking about her Uncle Nuren and her mom. Something about a weakness he took advantage of?"

Furrowing her brow, Ginger wore a contemplative look. "No. You mean like a weakness in the queen's powers that would have been passed down to her? Something that would have made her vulnerable to kidnapping?"

Saff stretched her legs out, slumping a bit in the hard chair. "Maybe? Ivies can't rift into this camp because of the coordinates she scouted, but they can rift out. Maybe something … like the royal line has a defect…?"

"Absolutely not."

Something kept tapping Saff in the back of her mind, urging her to keep searching. It tapped. It knocked. It pounded. Her focus shifted to the emergency exit trees time and time again. The culprits could have set more tents on fire if they'd wanted to cause confusion. And they hadn't successfully burned all of the trees down to cut off Unitas Ivy retreats. Maybe they'd just flubbed that part, but that would have been rather sloppy, given how well-timed and silently this had all been carried out.

And then something clicked. Something Kaylah had once brushed off. Something Devin had mentioned after she'd gone missing.

Nathan... Kaylah's Ivy guardian from her mission in the human world. Saff had once asked why he was always in the human world instead of in the Unitas camp, and Kaylah had brushed that question off.

But Devin had seen Nathan in camp shortly after Kaylah's disappearance. According to Devin, Nathan had practically been marched into camp, toward the emergency rifting tree patch, and onlookers had been shooed away. Everything had been chaotic, so they hadn't known what to make of it. But Nathan hadn't stayed in camp. He'd been sent back to the human world again.

Eyeing Ginger, Saff clenched her teeth. "Why isn't your husband here?"

"Because your leaders think he's best suited to working for Unitas in the human world."

Saff narrowed her eyes. "Why? What skills does he have that would justify him being stationed there? I bet you and Kaylah would have loved to have him here in camp for support."

Pressing her fingers to her lips, Ginger averted her gaze.

Saff's stomach knotted. She'd never suspected Ginger and Nathan of malintent. "Why was he in camp right after she went missing?" Her tone was deep and threatening. "Ginger?"

"'Need to know' information, Saff," Ginger said quietly.

"I need to know. Neither of us are leaving this tent until I know the truth." Saff wasn't playing more Ivy games. She wasn't afraid of taking on Ginger, even in her current worn-out state.

Ginger met her gaze, visibly worn down. "If I told you, your leaders would take my life."

Saff's eyes darted, searching Ginger's face. How had the Seeder leaders come into the equation again?

"Why would my people kill you over a secret?" Saff glanced at the closed tent door flap. "If they know whatever secret you're keeping, then I have no reason to tell them. You can trust me."

Ginger kept her mouth closed, barely shaking her head.

"Do you know where Rachel is right now?" Saff asked.

"Of course. She went back to your home village."

It sounded as convincing as any lie Ginger had told before, and in line with the lies Saff had been repeating, to keep Rachel and Guillen's mission a secret.

Kaylah usually brought Ginger or Saff to the council meetings, but they couldn't spare them both. The council now knew that Saff was in on the secret of Rachel and Guillen's mission.

"How about where Rachel's *really* at? And who she's really with? The mission they're on?"

Ginger looked surprised.

"Right. Kaylah entrusted me with that secret, too. Something no one was supposed to know. It's time to bring me into the equation. And I swear, I won't say a thing."

Nervously tapping on the desk, Ginger stared at Saff in silence. Finally, she opened her mouth. "Your leaders keep us separated because if he doesn't do his job, if he lets them down, they've threatened to kill me. It keeps him in line."

That didn't make any sense. He was just guarding the human-world rifting cave right now, or so Saff had thought...

"Doing his job? What's so special about his job?"

"He's a whisper."

That meant nothing to Saff, but before she could ask, Ginger elaborated.

"It's a rare gift. 'Whisper rifters.' Probably our kingdom's best-kept secret."

"And what does a 'whisper' do?"

Ginger was still hesitant to speak, wringing her hands. "It depends who you ask. They're said to be able to hear the whispers of a traitor from miles away, to be able to walk through solid walls, to be able to kidnap your children through a rift, to be able to read your soul, steal your energy, and have five times the strength of a normal Ivy."

Saff's mouth hung open. "Excuse me?" *Some kind of ridiculously overpowered Super Ivy?*

Ginger rolled her eyes. "From what we can tell, the tiniest fraction of that is actually true. That's why they're such a secret, kept even from our own people. That's how the queen and king keep their subjects in line." She blew out a puff of air. "There's a common saying, that 'the Mother Vines have eyes and ears.' It's ridiculous. We have spies planted throughout our cities, reporting to law enforcement about those who would dare oppose the queen and king."

Her heart racing, Saff could only imagine Rachel's situation. "Does Guillen know to look out for them?"

"Yes," Ginger answered confidently. "And he's being careful. The communities they're in aren't managed the same way as regular Ivy society."

That brought little comfort. "So your monarchy spies on your own people. What can whispers actually do, if they can't do all those things?"

Ginger sighed. "It's nebulous. Whispers are steeped in mythology. The rumors and fairy tales that circle the kingdom either lead you to stay in line, because you're paranoid one might come after you, with all of these ridiculous claims about their powers, or you're branded as a fool for believing they even exist. It's the perfect balance for a secret weapon. They're like Bigfoot, or the Loch Ness Monster."

She stood, clasping her hands. "You're either too proud to believe outlandish fairy tales, or too paranoid to be disloyal to your queen."

Saff tried to take it in and make sense of it while Ginger paced the small tent.

"Their powers, as far as we know, can include more energy and strength, as well as reading a tree, and ... third-party rift creation."

"What do those last two mean?"

Ginger pursed her lips. "To read a tree means that a whisper can sense the location a dying tree was used to rift to. It's a way of tracking deserters or anyone else they want, as long as the tree is fresh. It's said they can sense the last whisper of life in that tree as it dies, giving up the coordinates."

"Okay..."

Sitting back down, Ginger crossed her legs. "That's part of why Kaylah and Olivia didn't join Rachel's party after rescuing her from the palace. They rifted out on the palace grounds, hoping they'd be followed, leading their pursuers away, so they wouldn't search for Rachel and the others on foot."

So many questions ran through Saff's mind. "What about that last one you mentioned? Third-party whatever?"

Rubbing her temples, Ginger hesitated. "It's entirely possible that there are a gifted few who can ... open a rift like Seeders do."

Saff furrowed her brow. "In the air?" Could these whispers fly, too?

"No. They can open a tree rift for someone else."

The weight of the truth slammed down on Saff. "Kaylah could have been forced through a rift to any location they wanted, against her will. And if..." She searched to put the pieces together. "If your husband can read a tree, they could have covered their tracks by burning the tree she'd been forced through?"

"Yes," Ginger confessed, a look of defeat overtaking her.

Saff's ears burned. "Why did you waste my time blaming Seeders, when you knew good and well it was an Ivy whisper this whole time!"

Ginger glared. "You're forgetting one key thing here. *Your* people are keeping it a secret, aren't they? But your leaders know some of us Ivies in Unitas know the truth behind the whisper gift, and *your leaders* could have taken her, and burned the tree themselves to incite suspicion."

Saff couldn't believe that. It sounded like the kind of lie you tell yourself when you're in denial. That theory was too much of a stretch, given they'd agreed this was most likely Soren's doing.

But the question remained. Why were the council leaders keeping this ability a secret? Why was Unitas keeping it a secret?

"What are they making your husband do with his gift?"

"He helped Kaylah secure the location for camp. He tried to read the burned trees. And before the cave was primed, he monitored other Unitas Ivies who were running Seeder girls back home, so we could prove our trustworthiness, and so none of them were led through a rift to the palace, should we have a traitor."

That was all great. And understandable. "So he spied on Unitas Ivies to gain Seeder trust. Why hide it? I'm sure they would understand. Seeders would, too. We should be using this gift more, not shoving it under a rock."

Ginger grabbed a water bottle, unscrewing the cap. "Like I said, it's rare. We only have five known whispers within Unitas. And we still know so little about the gift. My husband only divulged his secret to Kaylah and me over a year ago."

Saff recalled the shock of seeing Kaylah's tent half-burned, still smoldering. She'd ached at the years of history they'd lost in the books and scrolls destroyed. "Is the information about whispers in one of the lost books?"

"No." Ginger took a sip of water. "Like I said, whispers are steeped in myth. They're off the record. Men like my husband were picked at a young age, and molded in their education. They didn't even know they had the gift. Because of their gift, and their skill in sparring practices, they were singled out to train as assassins." Ginger puckered her lips. "Once they're in assassin training, their whisper skills are nurtured, in secret. Under the threat of death and the death of those they love, they're not allowed to ever discuss it. Assassin training takes them away from their families. They're privately tutored, not even allowed to know other whispers. It's a burden of isolation, knowing that for the rest of your life, you'll keep this secret, and serve at the beck and call of your queen and king, answering to their every whim, betraying your own people."

Saff could sympathize with Ginger. The levels of deceit within Ivy society rivaled the level of brutality they'd aimed at the Seeders. "I don't get Kaylah. I understand that these men might not easily give up their secrets, but she talked about being honest with her people, about not covering up the ugly truth in history."

Screwing the lid back on her water bottle, Ginger spoke softly. "People can only handle so much at once. She plans to sort out whispers and their exploitation, but you can't bury people in an avalanche of truth all in one go. Because when you do, they stop seeing the person trying to save them. They'd see Kaylah as just another queen in the same family line of manipulators and liars." Ginger's eyes glistened with tears. "I'd rather not have my daughter taken to a guillotine because people couldn't see her for what she is."

Saff's heart went out to Ginger. Sometimes, she forgot that Ginger and Nathan had half raised Kaylah in the human world as her surrogate parents. They loved her. They weren't just regular Unitas members to her.

The two sat in silence, the hopelessness, and grief, and questions still looming. Saff explored the possibilities, the strategies at play. An idea sparked, a glimmer of hope. Even if Unitas only had a handful of whispers...

"Hold on. Kaylah and Olivia rifted away from the palace after rescuing Rachel? Kaylah said the Mother Vines and War Vines restricted rifting within the protective border there."

Ginger waved a dismissive hand. "We can rift out. Just not in."

"Oh." That was disappointing. "I guess the palace barrier isn't *exactly* the same as our thickets."

And then the disturbing reality of the implications crushed Saff. She forgot how to breathe entirely. "Ivies can't rift into our lands because of the protective thickets. I'm guessing not even whispers can...?"

"Correct."

"But if *both* of the walls are compromised... If *both* of them fail..." Saff's eyes blurred in her despair, her mental map dotting with dozens, even hundreds, of rifts opening in the middle of their villages. Raiding whispers could tear away matriarchs left and right, taking them back to the palace to hook up to the War Vines. The War Vines that had done inconceivable damage with just a half dozen teenage Seeder girls, barely rooted. The War Vines that only one person in the realm, in the world, could control—Kaylah.

Unitas had five whole whispers in their pocket. How many did Soren have?

The air had grown cold and thin. Saff panted. This could be catastrophic. Seeders and Unitas were doomed. Looking at Ginger through blurred, warm, glowing eyes, Saff was overcome with rage.

"Why the hell would my leaders keep this a secret? My people deserve to know the threat they're facing! I have family fighting tooth and nail to keep our village safe!" She didn't care if her yelling was too loud, if someone outside of the tent overheard her.

Ginger tried to shush her.

"No! I'm done with this. It's one thing to lie to growing Seeder girls about their identities, so they get to live normal lives while hiding from assassins. It's another to lie to an *entire nation*. They deserve to know." Saff stood, unable to bear this. "I may not be a war strategist, but hiding a massive threat from your own army is the stupidest thing I've ever heard!"

Shooting up from her chair, Ginger crossed the tent in two steps, standing between Saff and the tent door. "Think for one second. Step back for a moment and just look at yourself. You are panicking."

Saff studied her face. *Maybe I wouldn't be panicking if people would just be honest. If my family knew what they might be facing.*

Ginger's voice was firm but quiet. "If your people understood the possible threat posed by whispers, what could they even do about it that they aren't already?" She paused. "Hide all of your women in the human world? Can't do that. Wouldn't even want to, because they're needed for healing and charging your borders. Knowing *this* truth would do nothing but stamp out the barely there hope they cling to. Knowledge of the full threat can be empowering, *if* something can actually be done about it, but we have *nothing* to mitigate this. You are *one* panicking Seeder right now. Do you want millions more to join you?"

Saff's cheeks wetted as she stood there, helpless, her knees threatening to buckle. Never had she been more gutted, more devastated, more hopeless. "I understand."

"Good. Because even if you don't care about *my* life, I don't know that your leaders would take kindly to you knowing something you shouldn't."

"What can I do?" Saff whispered.

Ginger sighed. "Help me keep the peace? Keep a lookout for suspicious activity?" She lightly rested her hands on Saff's shoulders. "We're not even sure that Soren knows the truth about whispers, okay? He may not realize what he has. Kaylah's parents never told her, and she was their heir."

That gave Saff the tiniest speck of hope. Maybe they were overthinking the threat. But the only other alternative was Seeder betrayal or Kaylah deserting them.

"If it was a whisper who took her, they may be someone we're not aware of," Ginger added.

Saff searched Ginger's eyes. "Right... Only one Ivy guard went missing." It wasn't likely that only one traitor had pulled off Kaylah's kidnapping. They might still have a spy in camp. "What whispers do we have on our side, aside from your husband?"

"Three are in my kingdom, undercover. The only other one I'm aware of is Jon, one of the guards who helped in Rachel's rescue. They were all former assassins. All former or current palace guards."

It made sense. *Keep your toolbox close.*

Saff swallowed hard. "Yeah. I'll do everything I can: Keep up morale. Try not to jump to conclusions. Look for odd behavior."

"Good. We just have to hold the line, wait for word, and ... we'll see what we need to do once your council members reach out again."

Saff nodded, dazed.

"And even if Soren has Kaylah..." Ginger pressed her lips together, looking like she might cry. "She wouldn't betray us."

Shoving her hands in her pockets, Saff looked down at her shoes. "I wish I was as confident in that. It's easy for us to imagine we'd be brave in our last moments, or through torture, but no one really knows until they're there." She looked up as tears streamed down Ginger's face.

Saff gave her a hug. "I'm sorry. I shouldn't have said that."

Ginger squeezed her tighter. "But you're right."

After a while, Ginger finally pulled back from the hug. "Thank you," she said with a weak smile.

"Ditto. You and I were here from the start. We need to keep Unitas going."

Ginger nodded. "I'll send word if I get any updates."

"As will I."

Ginger returned to her chair as Saff opened the door flap to leave.

Turning to ask Ginger one last question, Saff hesitated. "I know this isn't the most tactful thing to ask right now, but if we suspect a whisper took Kaylah, are you *absolutely* sure your husb—"

"Don't. You. Dare," Ginger growled. The fire in her eyes matched the fierce redness of her hair.

Saff opened her mouth to elaborate. She understood that Ginger might not want to consider the possibility that Nathan may have betrayed Kaylah. Under duress. Under old orders from Kaylah's real parents that he'd never truly abandoned. After all, he *had* kept this huge secret from his wife for over two decades...

The venomous rage embodied in a single stare caused Saff to close her mouth. She would have sported that look herself, if someone had questioned Devin's integrity that way. She would go to bat for him, just like Ginger was for Nathan, especially after the way Seeder leaders were using Nathan for his gift, dangling Ginger's life in front of him.

"I... I'll see you later." Saff turned and left the tent.(qq)

Walking back to her own tent to rest up and allow her energy reserves to recharge, Saff was lost in thought. She couldn't even risk confiding in Devin this time.

"Hey, stranger. You okay?"

Saff looked to her right. Flora closed the gap to walk alongside her. Gashes covered her arm and face, but she still bore a smile.

Saff frowned. "You look like I feel. Camp protection shift over?"

Flora nodded. "No more fun and games, huh?"

"Something like that."

Flora pursed her lips. "Any updates? What are your thoughts about what's going on?"

Everyone was waiting with bated breath for word from Unitas spies at the palace, as to whether Kaylah had ended up there. "No updates, yet. We need to continue on without her, until we hear more. We have to believe in Unitas. What about you?"

Flora nodded, looking straight forward. "I agree. Maybe it's just selfish thinking, but I can't allow myself to imagine I gave up everything back home to just have your people betray us, or to have *her* betray us."

Saff glanced at Flora's injuries again. She wanted to reach out and heal them. It wouldn't take long. But she'd expended all of her energy on darts.

Flora must have read her mind. "It's fine. I numbed them and got them to stop bleeding. I'm sure I can track down someone around here to help out. Maybe at the far healer station." She smiled. "It's past your tent; that's where you're headed, right?"

Saff nodded. "Yeah. Water and some sleep. If you can't find someone, check back with me in a little while."

Flora put her arm around Saff's shoulders. "Sounds like a deal. I'll drop you off."

This was what Unitas was supposed to be. Normal people, just trying to do their best, and seeing past their differences.

"How's your friend doing?" Saff asked. "What was her name?"

"Raven. She's good. She just finished protection detail a little before me."

Saff smiled. As long as they could keep working together, there was still hope.

Chapter 30

Guillen begrudgingly agreed to have Rachel join him. He wasn't even telling William what their plan was; he wanted to keep this one close to his vest. He told William he'd report his progress with their contacts as he could along the way.

Guillen and Rachel threw their stuff together and set out on the road in the middle of the night. While the trip would normally take several days, if following traditional roads, Guillen would be able to significantly shrink that timeframe. He knew every shortcut, where to find connections along the way, defensible places to rest, where to avoid scrutinizing eyes.

They stopped to rest for short periods, just long enough to allow Rachel to try and heal their aches and pains, take a brief nap, and be on their way. As they got closer to the 'royal region,' as he called it, the scenery became greener, brighter; the homes—bigger.

Splurging on a room for the night, they allowed themselves to finally get a full night's sleep.

Rachel woke the next morning with Guillen's arm around her. While she normally loved his embrace, she couldn't help but be annoyed. Multiple times a day, he was still trying to talk her out of continuing with him. It was pretty much the only thing that cut through the silence between them. The day before, he'd threatened to leave her during the night and go on his own. It hadn't exactly ended in a screaming match, but voices had been raised and less-than-kind sentiments shared.

She rolled her eyes and slid out from underneath his arm, getting out of bed. She took a seat on the couch in their room and stared out the window. When he stirred in bed, she glanced in his direction; he rubbed his eyes and sat up.

"I'm ready to go," she said.

He closed his eyes and shook his head. "Please. For me. Stay."

"I told you I don't like being lied to. And having you withhold things from me. You keep mentioning 'dangerous' and 'messy' and all this other crap, but you won't elaborate. Either you think I'm a liability, or ... what? It's not like this is a girlfriend thing, and you're afraid for me to meet your mom." She huffed. "We're doing a *great* job pretending we're not an item right now, anyway."

"I know you want to help," he replied in the same tone he'd used the last few days, one with a bit of an edge to it. "And it frustrates you that you can't save the realm single-handedly. But this one is on me."

She scowled. "Don't patronize me."

"You want to know why?" His brow furrowed. "My father, while not likely to be home, is not exactly reliable. And my mother... She's always found the Crown's methods distasteful and wasteful. Note that I said 'distasteful'—not 'deplorable,' not 'despicable.'" He ran a hand through his hair. "She's unpredictable. She's lukewarm. She wouldn't be the kind to *plan* to hook you up to the War Vines, but she's loyal to the kingdom, to a fault."

"So, force her to come! Gag her if you have to."

He glared. "I'm sure her loyal guards and servants are going to let us waltz out of there with her tied up. The moment Kaylah's dead, she has the right to the throne. You don't think they've ramped up security at their manor in this chaos?"

Rachel tilted her head. "You think you need to convince her. I'll what? Sour things? Even if she thinks I'm one of you? I can't be there to help keep them safe after you've done the job of leading them away? I can play a lot of roles in this, and you're wanting to dismiss them all."

He clenched his jaw. "She could turn on me. On us."

The way he'd said it gave Rachel pause. She studied him, worried. "You don't think your mom would turn on Kaylah ... do you?"

He rubbed his eyebrow with a knuckle. "No. I don't think so. At least not easily. I think, that if push came to shove, she'd take her place, under Soren's influence. But she's not eager to rule."

"Then it can't be all that bad."

"She's the kind of woman who beat her own son, and hasn't lifted a damn finger to stop this war!"

Rachel frowned. He had to be overreacting, but his feelings were born of pain, and he had a right to them.

He looked at the ground as if ashamed. "And she hates Seeders."

"I won't be going as a Seeder. We've made it through half of the communities without problems, right?"

"I don't care. She's smart. And maybe someone from the palace will recognize you as we get closer. A million things could go wrong."

"You're right. They could. And I signed up for that. And unless you can honestly say to my face that you *genuinely* believe I'm more of a liability than an asset..."

"You're not a liability. I just don't want to have to worry about you at the same time."

She sighed, facing him directly. "I need you to trust me. Believe in me. That when it comes time, I won't let you down. Guillen, I love you. But this is bigger than that."

He gnawed on his bottom lip. "Let's get going. We can be there before nightfall."

<hr>

Guillen's family lived little more than an hour from the palace by train, but Rachel and Guillen still wouldn't risk taking a train, especially in the royal region. Based on reports he'd gotten throughout the last year, his parents and siblings continued to have minimal interaction with the ruling family. Soren had never respected his aunt much, and she wasn't one to interfere.

Guillen prepared Rachel on what to expect. He assumed only his mother and sister would be at their manor, with guards and servants. He described his mother as tall and thin with warm brown hair but none of that warmth in her personality. His little sister was prim and proper, as a lady of her station ought to be. Rachel could tell how much he regretted that he didn't visit more, for her benefit, and how much he loved her, by how he spoke of her.

"She's clever and witty." He smiled. "A bit precocious." He frowned. "She's in a tight spot, having to live with my mother. But she has a good heart."

Rachel looked forward to meeting his little sister. Not so much his mother.

As Rachel and Guillen drew closer to the home he'd grown up in, they talked about strategy and switching up their cover stories. He wanted to keep Rachel's identity a secret, but couldn't come up with a reason for why she'd be there as a co-worker, or a friend, and they certainly wouldn't mention Unitas right out of the gate.

It felt like a frivolous way to spend their time, but Guillen insisted they stop in the nearest city and freshen up with nice new clothes. It was odd for Rachel to wear a fancy dress, but they needed to make a good impression to try to win his mother over.

Rachel chose a cream linen dress with bright embroidery—a much more sophisticated style than the stunt clothes she'd been wearing for their mission. Guillen must have approved, judging by the grin he wore when she came out of the dressing room. She couldn't deny how nice he looked, too, in more formal Green Lands attire—a comfy-looking dark brown linen suit.

Before getting too close to the property, they ditched their travel packs in a bush to reclaim later. Rachel's nerves were all jumbled as they passed several guards at the property entryway. Down a long lane flanked with huge hedges, they finally arrived at the door to the mansion, and Guillen knocked. The butler recognized Guillen right away, bowing. He guided them into a large sitting room. So far, it had gone a lot more smoothly than she'd feared. Her palms were a bit sweaty after passing so many guards, but she and Guillen could handle this.

Rachel caught herself with her jaw down, taking in the exquisite décor of the sitting room. She hadn't seen any fancy rooms in the palace, just basic, tucked-away spaces. As a room meant for audiences, this was the nicest thing she'd seen in the entire Green Lands. Chandeliers and tatted curtains draped from tall ceilings. Wainscoting and murals covered the walls.

Guillen observed her, a small smirk on his face. He took her hand and gave a reassuring squeeze. A cold, hard metal met her skin—he wore his royal ring for the first time. She was intrigued to see him in this environment, even though it hadn't been one of her reasons for coming along.

A rather ill-tempered-looking woman entered the room with a wineglass in her hands. "Guillen, what are you doing here?" Her skin was youthful, but the sour face she wore detracted from her beauty.

"Hi, Mother. Just a short visit."

"Who's this girl?" She sat down without offering a hug to greet her son, instead taking a sip.

He slid his arm around Rachel. "This is Elizabeth, my girlfriend. She's from Community Five. I thought you should meet."

His mother eyed Rachel, scrutinizing her from top to bottom. "I see she must be enjoying your stipend."

Stipend? Money? Did she just assume I'm a gold digger? To a stunt?

Guillen's mother was clearly less than impressed. "A bit foolish to waste your meager week off coming all the way here, and unannounced." She looked at

Rachel, but not really. It was more like looking *past* Rachel. Speaking to her, but in a way that sounded more like she was talking *about* Rachel, rather than *to* her.

She turned her gaze fully on Guillen. "Is she pregnant? I'm not willing to petition Soren for an exception so you can keep that kind of baby, if that's what you're asking."

Rachel bit her tongue and concealed her rage, conscientiously cramming every last speck of her Seeder energy into her heart, locking it up to keep her cover, and hide her true feelings on the discussion at hand.

Guillen replied calmly, as if his mother hadn't just insulted them both, and his kind. "No, Mother. Just a simple visit. I know I don't come around often, but I try to for the important things. And she's important to me. That's all."

"Hmmph. What is it you do, Elizabeth?" The way she said either of their names sounded like their very names were somehow insults.

Rachel forced a smile. "It's nice to meet you, ma'am. I work in textile."

"Hmmph. Wouldn't expect someone like you to do or know any better," she muttered, then drained her glass of wine.

How odd would that feel, if it were true that Rachel actually did work in textiles as a stunt? Her persona could very well be the person who slaved away making some of the ornate fabric in the room, or the very clothes on this woman. The class difference hit Rachel like a punch in the gut. Guillen's mother certainly didn't try to hide her opinion of her guests, and why should she? Rachel was only a gold-digging crown-chaser. But then again, this horrid woman probably didn't care enough about her own son to think that way. She didn't at all give off an air of concern, only ample insults.

"Your father's not around, if you were hoping to see him."

"That's fine." Guillen glanced around the room. "Is Catrina here?"

She stood and poured herself another drink from a carafe on a nearby gilded table. "Yes. I think I saw her running around here somewhere."

"Do you think we could move somewhere more private, perhaps the library, to speak?" he asked.

"This is private enough, I'm sure." She waved her hand, gesturing at the room. "Do you see anyone else here? I'm quite comfortable, thank you." She sat back down.

Guillen tensed.

"Such odd news from the palace, isn't it?" his mother said. "I'm assuming you've heard about Kaylah?"

Rachel's heart skipped a beat.

"It's hard to say," Guillen replied coolly. "One hears a lot of things. What's the most recent news?"

"Well, Betsy's son, Ayden—you remember him, right? He's been promoted at the palace. A good boy—nothing to be embarrassed about with him. He said they've rescued her. Of course, Soren sent out word that she turned on the people, but I can't imagine her doing that. She's such a sweet and capable girl. I'm sure they'll set it right and she'll take her place, putting an end to all of this."

"So, she's at the palace?" Guillen asked.

"Isn't that what I just said?" his mother drawled.

Rachel dared to speak up. "You'd like to end this war, ma'am?"

She furrowed her brow at Rachel. "That's an odd question. All it's doing is disrupting our way of life. We were all quite happy a couple of years ago before my sister let Nuren practically take over, the imbecile." She rolled her eyes. "And all that work, all this fuss, for what? He gets himself killed, and the weeds walk out with a couple of their useless rejects. Stupid idea from the beginning." She shook her head, raising her glass in their direction. "And if you ask me, it's enough to want to take our lands back, but to bring that filth over here, on our soil..."

Every ounce of Rachel's focus went into concealing her energy further, concealing her feelings. She couldn't react. And she'd known ahead of time that this wouldn't be sunshine and daisies, but she hadn't been prepared for a personal attack like that. She was aching to hear Guillen speak up. Just something, *anything*. For him, for her, for her people. Some sort of censure; this vile woman didn't deserve to consider herself so high and mighty.

Guillen reacted calmly. "Has Soren reached out to you throughout all of this?"

"Why should he?" She scoffed. "They messed this up. He and Kaylah can mop up their own mess." She swatted a dismissive hand in the air. "We've obviously attended the funerals, but that's all."

A girl walked in, looking a couple of years younger than Rachel, sharing Guillen's eyes.

"I thought I heard your voice!" She lit up. "What are you doing here?" She ran over to Guillen. He stood and gave her a huge hug.

"Hey, Sis. Just visiting. Stay and chat with us."

"Guillen brought a girlfriend home."

"Elizabeth, this is my sister, Catrina. Catrina, this is my girlfriend."

Catrina raised an eyebrow. "Girlfriend?" She extended a hand to Rachel. "I'll have more questions about that later."

His mom finished her second glass of wine. "He says there's no baby."

Catrina looked back up to Guillen, questioning with a glance.

He finally let out a hint of frustration. "She's not pregnant. It's just a visit."

Catrina sat down opposite them.

With scrutinizing eyes, Guillen's mom addressed him again. "You can't possibly be upset about us drawing that conclusion. You show up unannounced with a girl... And after that whole debacle with your pregnant ex-girlfriend?"

Guillen's jaw dropped.

Rachel couldn't resist the urge to want to hear more about the rumor. It *had* to be a rumor, after all. Guillen had never slept with anyone, and he was *not* the type of guy to have a secret baby out there somewhere.

"How did you even hear about that?" Guillen asked his mother.

Rachel's veins turned cold. *What? It's true?* He'd lied to her...

His mother arched an eyebrow. "You don't think the family hears about your escapades when you drag Kaylah into your shame? When she oversteps her bounds of authority to do you a favor? Her pity has always been wasted on you."

"It wasn't like that," Guillen protested.

Rachel was queasy. Guillen had told her he'd had Kaylah help with an issue that involved an ex-girlfriend, but hadn't elaborated. Rachel hadn't imagined it involving a child... She went to pull her hand out of Guillen's, but he grasped it tighter.

He met her gaze directly. "It's *not* like it sounds," he said emphatically.

What was she supposed to say in that moment, with his mom and sister watching on? She and Guillen weren't there for dating drama.

"So, Guillen..." Catrina shyly spoke up. "What, uh, what brings you on this visit?"

"We were just talking about our dear Kaylah," their mother answered. "Now that she's back home, I was saying, we'll get everything sorted out. And get her properly married off. She may have dawdled on accepting suitors to this point, but it's not right to lead without someone at your side. There's far too much work for it to be done alone."

"I don't know, Mother." Catrina seemed hesitant. "I was talking with Sarah, and I'm really starting to think Kaylah may have done the things they said. Why else would Soren claim the throne, unless he didn't think she'd be fit to lead? She *did* seem kind of soft about the weeds, if I'm honest." She frowned, timidly straightening her dress skirt. "Then again, it doesn't really make sense that he's calling himself that. Maybe he can't bring himself to..."

Her mother threw her a glare. "We've discussed this. I'm not *crawling* to him, asking for the position. If he finds her guilty, then I'm sure he'll do what needs to be done and reach out."

Sitting up straighter, Guillen took a deep breath. "Either way, I don't think we need to know Kaylah's intentions right now. That will sort itself out. But now that you're both here, we need to discuss the real reason for my visit."

He glanced around the room—there were still no guards or servants lurking about. His mother looked thoroughly unamused.

"You two aren't safe," Guillen said. "And I'm here to take you away until things calm down. We need to leave tonight. Quietly."

Catrina shrank back in her chair, visibly concerned, but still skeptical.

"Why would you say something like that?" His mom appeared disbelieving. "No one has a need to hurt us. Should I call for the guards?"

"No!" He paused. "Soren may want to hurt you both."

They both looked shocked.

His mom shook her head. "I know you're bitter that you're not as good as the others, but honestly. Picking up a few knives hardly makes you a valuable army man. Why would anyone confide something like that in you? About your own family, no less."

"I heard it from his own mouth," he lied convincingly.

"Why?" Catrina's voice was filled with worry.

"You know as well as I that he just got married. If he's named Beata as queen, then he intends to kill the downline."

Rachel was surprised he'd brought that up. They thought Soren would be willing to torture and kill his way down the line of heirs to have one be a puppet for him, but this strategy also made sense—he may not intend to place a puppet queen at all, instead wanting to reassign the allegiance of the Mother and War Vines to his bride.

Kaylah had told Rachel how Ivy queens were made, how Vine allegiance could be retrained. Kill the queen and the next five downline heirs, and that unique power could be reassigned. The thought ran shivers down Rachel's spine—Soren and his bride, recognized as legitimate rulers.

Guillen continued. "Let me get you both somewhere safe, and we'll sort things out. We'll be able to go over questions later."

The surly matriarch moved her focus to Rachel. "If your story is true, what's with her? Is she going to knit us a shawl to keep us warm where you're taking us?"

"She has lots of training with blades, too. She's here to help get you out safely."

"Consider me unimpressed," she muttered. "If what you say is actually credible, then all we need to do is alert the guards, and they'll be competent enough to ensure our safety."

"Shut up, Mother!"

Rachel jumped at Guillen's outburst. Catrina sat with her jaw on the floor.

His mother glared. "How dare you!"

"Ma'am." Rachel tried to do some damage control, putting on her best diplomatic tone and resting her hand on Guillen's knee. "I'm sorry, he's just worried about your safety. The reason we can't rely on others is because they may be compromised. Please allow us to see you to somewhere comfortable, to make sure you'll be okay. If it turns out the information is incorrect, we'll return you promptly and ensure no one even knows why you were gone."

She narrowed her eyes at Rachel. "I suppose you do sound *somewhat* competent."

"Mother, please," Catrina pleaded. "We can just go away for a day. You know Guillen wouldn't come around unless it was important."

"Yes, please. Just a day," Guillen echoed. He and Rachel were *definitely* willing to lie to get what they wanted, as long as his mother and sister would come quietly.

"Fine. We'll pack some bags and treat it like a little getaway. We'll discuss it in more detail before we go. And I'm going to need to approve the conditions of the place." Her lip twitched in revulsion, as she looked at Rachel again. "I'm not willing to stay in a substandard hovel, like that awful apartment you have."

Rachel couldn't fathom having to spend any more time with this wretched woman, but it may be the only thing that kept Kaylah alive. She focused on her breathing. In and out. Calmly, smoothly. And hopefully, miraculously, they'd soften this horrible woman's heart and shut her prejudiced mouth enough to make it all tolerable.

"We'll make sure you're well taken care of. Please pack quickly, and quietly."

Chapter 31

Guillen's mother, formally called Lady Vera, and Catrina left the room to go pack a bag each, while Guillen and Rachel stayed in the sitting room.

He gave Rachel a relaxed smile. "I'm sorry. You were right. You did amazing!" he whispered. He leaned in for a kiss, and Rachel moved her head to dodge, crossing her arms.

"What?" he asked.

She huffed, shaking her head. Every glance and insult from that woman had etched deep, on multiple levels. Maybe it was the pent-up energy in Rachel's heart, fighting to get out. Or how tired she was from their journey to get there, or how frustrated she'd been for days about Guillen having dismissed her in this strategy... Rachel's logic wrestled with her emotions, and logic didn't win this time. "You didn't want me to come because you can't stand up to your mom."

Guillen narrowed his eyes. "Are you kidding me? I warned you about her, and I needed her to come willingly."

She rolled her eyes. "It's not like you had to spill your guts, but you couldn't speak up and put her in her place, even once?"

He scowled. "I tried. You saw how well that went. You need to stop taking this so personally."

She was just as frustrated with herself for getting upset, as she was with him. She pursed her lips. Maybe it hadn't been the personal insults. Maybe it had been the implications. She hadn't cared whether or not Guillen was a virgin, but he'd claimed to be. And then the whole pregnant ex-girlfriend bomb... "They both seem to think you're likely to come home after knocking up some random girl. I'm sure that will be interesting to unpack later."

His mouth hung open in obvious contempt. "Really? I shouldn't have to defend myself about that! Kaylah could vouch for every detail of what really happened. Either you love me and trust me, or you trust a self-centered lush that knows practically nothing about me." He stood and strode to the edge of the room.

She instantly regretted the accusation. And hated herself for flying off the handle. She walked up to him. "I'm sorry. I need to not let it get to me." Hadn't she promised to not allow her trust issues to get between them again?

His stare bore a hole right through her. "Integrity means a lot to me; you should know that by now. I don't need you adding to the mess of this. I get attacked enough around here, without someone, who I thought cared about me, making things worse."

"I really am sorry." She reached for his arm, and he shrugged her off.

He shook his head. "I'm patient, aren't I? I understand how it feels to work through crap. But I don't do it at the expense of others. You need to grow up. I'm not a walking mat."

She frowned, holding back her tears and Seeder energy. If she could so easily ruin things with Guillen, the perfectly patient partner, she didn't stand a chance. She shuffled back to the sofa, wilting as she sat down.

"I'm going to make sure they're okay." He walked out.

A few minutes later, he returned with both women.

Rachel surveyed the three of them. "Where are the bags?"

Two men appeared behind them, holding said baggage.

"These are the two guards who will be assisting us. As we go on our short *day trip*," Guillen announced, sharing a look with Rachel. This was not what they had planned.

"I insist," Lady Vera said. "I don't care what you two say. They're coming with us."

"Well, I... Uh..." Rachel grappled to help right the situation.

"Sir, I'd like to briefly discuss security details in private, if that's alright?" one of the men said to Guillen.

"Yes, Richard, of course." Guillen flashed Rachel a glance, as if asking her to carefully watch his mom and sister.

Hair on the back of Rachel's neck stood at attention as she started to panic. It was just supposed to be the four of them. They'd take them away, and if necessary, actually tie them up, until Kaylah could be freed. Taking along two more unpredictable elements might cripple them.

Rachel thought back to when she, Saff, Ginger, and Kaylah had run into Ivy soldiers on their return from meeting in the human world. They had originally spared the soldiers' lives, because they could. While Kaylah had eventually killed one before they made it to Seeder borders, Saff and Rachel had allowed the men to live at Kaylah's request, and because they outnumbered them, and couldn't leave the men to rat them out. Things might not go so smoothly this time; getting just his mom and sister to cooperate was going to be a daunting task on its own.

She ran through different scenarios while waiting for Guillen to return. He was smart—he'd know what to do. But he wasn't the first to return from the discussion.

In fact, he didn't return at all.

The guard reappeared, bloodied and scraped, carrying a dripping knife in his hand.

One of Guillen's knives.

"What did you do to him?!" Rachel screamed. "Where is he?!"

The guard pointed the knife at her. "That traitorous cripple doesn't matter anymore." He barked to the other guard, "These three are coming with us. We're taking them to the palace!"

Rachel threw a panicked glance at Guillen's mom and sister, who looked equally shocked.

"Excuse me!" Lady Vera protested.

The guard next to them extended vines to restrain them when they didn't immediately comply. "M'lady. Miss."

From there, Rachel's next few breaths, her next few moments, all played out in slow motion. Rachel studied the bloodied man, suppressing her Seeder energy, just like she had so desperately trained to do back in the human world when she'd been poisoned.

He still might not know I'm a Seeder.

The man quickly surveyed his injuries; Guillen hadn't gone down without a fight.

Rachel reached for the knife Guillen had once given her, unsheathing it as she slid it out of a pocket in her dress. She pointed it at the man, taking a defensive stance.

He flashed her a look of annoyance, and then amusement. "All of you heaps of compost are the same, aren't you?"

Good. A stunt community guard had once uttered that insult. Guillen's assailant still thought she was an Ivy stunt.

The guard dropped Guillen's knife. With a soft *thud*, Guillen's blood stained the rug at the guard's feet.

Guillen had trained Rachel for this, how to use a knife. But the guard's vines were reaching toward her, and fighting hand-to-hand wasn't her strength with a knife. She didn't have good range for throwing it, and didn't stand a chance of aiming decently with how hard her heart was beating.

But that hadn't been her plan anyway. The knife had done its part.

Jumping back from the man's approaching vine, she held her hands in the air. "I'm sorry. Okay. I'll come. Please don't hurt me!"

"Good. Smarter than your boyfriend."

She fought images of Guillen lying dead somewhere, or bleeding out. Keeping up one hand in surrender, she bent a knee to place the knife on the ground.

As the man stepped forward and wrapped his vine around Rachel's upheld wrist, she stood, concealing her free arm behind her back.

"Come on, your other wrist."

That was never going to happen.

She wasn't the most book smart. She wasn't the strongest. But she'd been poisoned for months. She'd fought tooth and nail to squeeze out any energy during her training in the human world, and if that had done anything for her, it had made her capable of powerful bursts of energy, now that she had no poison hampering her, now that she was rooted in the Green Lands.

Decisively, she thrust her energy into her concealed arm, flaring and sharpening her Seeder blade. Before he knew it, she'd swung her arm forward, slicing clean through the vine restraining her other wrist, and had lunged for him, her eyes now bright green with rage.

A gasp escaped his lips as she barreled into him, her energy strengthening her arms. Off-balance, he fell, taking Rachel down with him as he shot his vines around her body.

Tussling on the ground, he clenched his jaw, reaching his hands up and choking her. The razor-sharp leaves on his vines stabbed her flesh as he pulled her in tighter, limiting the mobility of her arms.

She yanked an arm forward with all the force she could, before his hold would become too tight, fighting to put her blade against his neck. She grunted at the embedded leaves dragging through her flesh. She closed her eyes and focused all of her energy. Her blade now touched his throat. Ignoring her own pain and struggle for air, she pushed.

And kept pushing.

Seeder's blades didn't have as many nerve connections as the rest of their bodies, so she couldn't feel it all, but she could feel enough. She felt the downward movement. She felt the sickening sensation of her blade sinking in. She felt herself hit something bone-hard. And she felt her attacker stop moving.

Rachel peeked to confirm it was over, though she had already known it was. She could breathe, and the vines were looser. She heaved, catching her breath and trying not to vomit on the spot. Behind her, Lady Vera and Catrina had just finished taking down their attacker.

Rachel yanked the embedded leaves from her arms and leapt up, yelling for Guillen. She sprinted in the direction he'd left in. Standing in the front entrance, she looked around. "Guillen!"

No answer.

She darted down the nearest hallway, then turned a corner.

"Guillen!"

Still no response as she ran back to the entry room. His mom and sister now joined her, calling his name.

Maybe they went outside? Her eyes shot to the front door. *No. There are guards stationed out there; there would have been an audience.*

Instantly, she loathed being in such a large house.

Taking a moment to gather herself, she scanned the floor. Droplets of blood, down the hallway.

She dashed back down the hallway, tearing open each and every door. Dizzy and frantic, unsure how many she'd opened, she finally found him.

Guillen lay on the ground, in the middle of a large library. He wasn't moving.

"No! Please, no!" She ran to him, his mom and sister trailing behind her.

She threw herself on the ground next to him. He was still alive. Grimacing, he struggled to breathe, clearly in agony as he clutched his side. Blood pooled around the injury.

Rachel moved his hand and pressed both of her own onto the wound. She put her body weight into it, to help stop the bleeding, and all of the energy she was capable of summoning, into healing him.

"Please, don't leave me. I love you. Stay with me." Her voice shook. "Please!"

Tears poured down her cheeks as she weakened. Having already exerted herself to save her own life, she was struggling to heal him. She reached into her core and accessed every last drop she could. The last thing she saw was his face, as her arms buckled, and she lost consciousness.

The tap of light footsteps on wood accompanied a soft feminine humming as Rachel woke. She opened her eyes, quickly finding her bearings. Catrina paced the room—a bedroom, perhaps a guest room.

"Where is he? Is he okay?"

Catrina startled. She pointed to the wall. A mumble of voices filtered from the other side—one was male.

He was alive. Rachel closed her eyes, starting to cry. Nothing else mattered. He was alive.

Still drained, she forced herself to sit up on the bed, hanging her legs over the edge. "Where am I? What happened?"

"You, uh ... passed out. Saving my brother's life. We're still at our manor."

Rachel shook her head. "That's not safe. We need to go."

"It's okay. They're working something out next door. You just need to recuperate." She pointed to a glass of water on the bedside table. "He said being hydrated helps with your kind's healing and energy like it does ours."

Rachel grabbed the water and drank. "Thank you."

Catrina pressed her lips together, nodding. "Well ... thanks for keeping him alive."

Rachel frowned. The cat was out of the bag now... And the fact that other servants or guards hadn't finished the job already, was a miracle.

"You, uh ... were pretty intense back there," Catrina continued. "We just poisoned our guard until he passed out, but you... That was brutal."

Rachel couldn't hide a resentful scowl. "We don't all have the luxury of poison, do we? And there were two of you; I had to fight on my own."

Catrina shyly shrugged. "I didn't really mean it as an insult. I mean... I can't get that horrible image out of my head. But ... you saved Guillen, and that's what matters."

Rachel was tired of pretenses. These women didn't deserve any courtesies. "Yeah. Well, he wouldn't have needed saving if he wasn't so insistent on protecting you and your horrible mom."

Catrina nodded once more. After a few moments of silence, still pacing the room, she spoke again. "Is it true what you said? That you love him?"

Rachel met Catrina's gaze. "I do."

She pointed to Rachel's arm. "You have our stunt mark. How did you guys even meet? I don't understand why a wee—" She looked away. "Why a Seeder would be over here, pretending to be one of his kind."

"It's a long story." Rachel took another sip of water. "And … you're surprisingly calm about all of this."

Catrina fidgeted with her hands, glancing back at the door. "I'm more like Guillen than my mom. She's a bit crazy."

That's one way of putting it. "Let me guess—she'll come around?"

"Probably not."

Rachel chuckled and then winced in pain. "At least you're honest."

"Is it also true what he said about Kaylah, that she's the leader of the dissenters?"

"I wouldn't put it that way, but yes." Knowing a little about their family dynamics now, Rachel pondered how she could best win Catrina over. She could be a good ally, once properly educated. "How do you feel about Soren?"

Catrina's lip curled. "He's always creeped me out, and he's a real jerk to Guillen. And really, everyone."

"I dated him for almost three years in the human world."

Catrina's eyes widened. "You're *that* girl?"

Rachel narrowed her eyes. Jon had once said that no one outside the palace knew about Duke Nuren's plans. "How long have you and your mom known how Nuren powered the War Vines? A guard told me no one outside of the palace knew about it."

Catrina rested her hands on her hips. "We may not attend many palace functions, but I'd like to think we're not *completely* out of touch. We heard rumors. It was confirmed to my mother at his funeral." A flash of guilt crossed her face as her hands dropped. "I, uh… I don't know *how much* my mother knew about the details. I didn't really understand what all was going on until a few minutes ago. I'm sorry. I just meant, you know, that I knew Soren spent a lot of time in the human world on a mission, dating a Seeder."

Rachel nodded. "Anyway, yes. I'm *that* girl. Alive, thanks to your brother. He's a good man. And Kaylah's amazing. They're not dissenters; they're good people that just want this war to stop. And to give people like Guillen equal rights, like they deserve."

Catrina sat down in an armchair, wringing her hands. "I love Guillen. He's different, but he's family. I'm glad … that…" She forced out the words, as if she spoke against her own will. "That he found … someone … who cares about him.

The way he deserves." She looked down. "I've never heard him talk about a girl the way he does you."

Rachel allowed a smile to cross her face. Catrina had a long way to go, as did most green folk, to accept their kind of relationship. At least she hadn't reacted like Magda. Rachel decided to lean into Catrina's love for her brother.

"He deserves to live a happy life. I'm not stopping until his kind are free to do that."

Catrina returned a warm smile.

The door popped open, and Guillen appeared. He was shirtless, with a bandage wrapped around his midsection. He winced as he strode over to Rachel. She forced herself to stand up, and he gave her a kiss on the forehead. She wanted nothing more than to hug him, but it didn't bode well that he was bandaged up.

"I'm so happy you're okay." His eyes were bloodshot. "Thank you. I love you. I'm so sorry."

She frowned, staring at the bandage. "You're still hurt. Let me see it."

He shook his head. "No. I'll be fine. It's just a flesh wound now, and we need you to focus on healing yourself."

She took his hand. "I'm really sorry about what I said. I know who you are, and it's not those things."

"It's alright. We'll figure it out." He glanced back; his mom lingered in the doorway. Her face still sour, she didn't appear to have softened any, compared to Catrina. Guillen turned back to Rachel. "We need to talk about making a change."

Chapter 32

Guillen asked for some privacy to talk with Rachel. His mom and sister left the room and promised they'd wait in the next room over.

Guillen and Rachel eased themselves down on the edge of the bed, both in rough shape.

Rachel glanced at the large bandage covering his injury. "Let me see it," she demanded.

He took her hand. "It's really not that bad. We had the family nurse finish stitching it up. My body can handle it. I'll be fine on my own."

He was pale, likely from blood loss. She wasn't going to drop it, but she changed the topic for now. "Why are we still here? We need to go. Soren could have people on the way. How can we be sure there aren't more servants or guards that would betray us?"

He replied calmly, "You're right, we need to go. But we have it under control, for now. After you passed out, other servants tied up the other guy. We've addressed the staff and put our own spin on it. It's precarious; but for now, we just need to focus on you getting your energy back."

She found little comfort with all of the variables. At least it was obvious Guillen's family hadn't betrayed him, but their staff's loyalty was clearly unreliable.

He must have sensed her anxiety. "This is the home I grew up in. I know, at least amongst the older staff, who's more on my side. If I'd known my mother was going to insist on guards like that, I would have suggested a different security escort. I have the ones I trust making sure no one leaves."

"Okay."

"I need you to heal. I..." He swallowed hard. "I need you to do something that I can't. I need you to regain your energy enough to take my mother and sister away." He rubbed her hand with his thumb. "I'm asking you to take them to Eric for safekeeping in the human world."

Rachel matched his frown. That had to be a hard request to make. Guillen was a proud man... And now, having been stabbed by his own weapon. Having to ask someone else to use powers he was born without. Having to subject Rachel to close contact with his mother. She could only imagine what was running through his troubled mind and aching heart.

She squeezed his hand. "I'll take them."

Tears coated his eyes. "Thank you."

She tilted her head ever so slightly. "But what will *you* do? I need to know you'll be safe back here."

"I'll be fine. I'll regroup with my contacts. Make sure they know Kaylah's at the palace. We'll get her out as soon as we can, and I'll get word to you as quickly as possible."

She nodded as she processed his request. The whole time, she couldn't shake the dead man's haunting eyes. "I just... Give me some time to rest up. How long can we risk it?"

He kissed her hand. "You'll be fine. Do what you need to. I'm going to walk the perimeter, keep an eye on things, and make sure everything's okay. Try to conserve your energy. If something happens, your knife's right over there." He gestured with his chin to the side table, wearing a far-off look. "Still clean. Guess you didn't need it after all."

The way he'd said it—defeated, as though somehow the knife he'd given her represented his heart, as though somehow any of this was *his* fault—hurt more than any of her physical injuries. "I did need it."

"Right, well, I need to go monitor things. I'll check in in a little while." He kissed her forehead, then clenched his jaw as he stood, clearly still in a great deal of pain. She wished that at the very least, someone like Olivia could be there, someone aptly trained in the Ivies' new numbing methods.

The room fell silent when he left. Rachel finished the glass of water and lay back down. Healing and energy restoration happened a lot faster with proper hydration and rest, but she couldn't fall asleep, despite how thoroughly exhausted she still was. The events played out in her mind as she stared at a small chandelier on the ceiling.

She'd killed a man.

It had been justified. It had been done in self-defense. It had been to save the man she loved, and his family, and Kaylah, and the Unitas movement. Morally, she was in the clear.

But that didn't dull the horror of what she'd just done. She surveyed her arms and hands. They must have cleaned her up a little while she was out; she wasn't completely covered in blood.

She lay there, silently crying. Maybe Guillen had been right—she shouldn't have come. But then again, he'd likely be dead if she hadn't. There was no way to know how it would have played out without her.

She'd taken a life.

She'd been trained to protect herself. This was war. But she'd never had to really fight. She'd been healing, and negotiating, and sharing energy.

Could the man have been turned, convinced to join Unitas? Did he have a family? Her mind shifted to Guillen. Was this whole thing her fault? What could have distracted him so much that he let his guard down? Her stupidity, their argument. He'd almost lost his life because she couldn't keep it together for a single hour. She'd almost had two lives on her conscience, and one of them meant more to her than the world.

Guillen quietly came in after a while to check on her. She rested on her side, staring blankly across the room. He slid a chair over and sat next to her, now wearing a loose shirt.

"You should be sleeping." He rubbed her cheek lovingly.

"Yeah, I can't sleep right now. Sorry."

"How are you feeling?" He frowned.

"I'm getting better."

"How long do you think until you'll be able to guide them through a rift?" he asked, cringing, likely bothered by still having to ask for help.

"I don't think it takes much. I've never felt that drained when being assisted by an Ivy through a tree rift."

He gave her a hesitant smile. "That's good."

She stared at him with an unyielding expression. "But I'm not going until you're completely healed."

He narrowed his eyes slightly. "I told you—I'm fine."

"You're still in pain. Let me see it."

He took off his shirt and carefully removed the bandages. He was out of the woods, as far as she could tell, but it was far from a simple scrape. His family nurse had done a decent job of stitching it up, but that didn't mean he was alright internally.

She moved a hand over to heal it more, but he intercepted her, holding her hand instead.

"No. We can't waste more time. You know this isn't that bad."

She pulled her hand back and hugged herself. The other nicks and bruises he'd sustained in the fight—those she could overlook. Not this giant wound. "I'm not changing my mind."

"I know you love me, and you're worried, but you need to remember this is bigger than us. Think of Kaylah. Look at the big picture."

A dark storm swirled in her mind as she clenched her teeth, and fresh tears formed. She could barely breathe, her chest tight, her anguish choking her. "Right now, all I care about is you. *You* are *my* big picture." She started to dig her fingernails into her arms, simply trying to keep it together. Trying to keep some semblance of self-control. Trying to find some way to just ... make it through this.

"Rachel... I..."

She whimpered, and her voice shook as she cried freely. "I can't leave you again without *knowing* you're okay. I can't handle it."

His mission was dangerous enough. He could get an infection. And she didn't know all the details of how Seeder healing worked. With that serious of a wound ... if he took a tumble, would it rip open? And this was All. Her. Fault. If she hadn't lost her cool earlier, he wouldn't have been distracted, wouldn't have gotten hurt.

Desperation bubbled up inside her. He opened his mouth as if to protest once more.

She whimpered again; she'd never been able to ask for help. Not with this. It was her shame. It was her private torture. It was why she'd turned to the Ivy pub, when she was trying her best to keep her promise to Kaylah about not hurting herself any more.

But she didn't know how to cope, how to manage another moment with him not being safe. Visions flashed before her eyes, of his dying body, lying on the floor in a puddle of blood. She increased the pressure of the grip on her own arms, as if it would somehow help her better grasp on to hope.

Forcing out the words took everything she had. "*I. Can't.*" She sniffled. "*I'm. Not. Okay.*" She stared into his eyes with meaning, with a look that had to be capable of carrying the rest she couldn't say out loud.

I need help.

I'm drowning.

I can't do this on my own.

His brow furrowed, then his gaze landed on her fingers digging into her skin, and his eyes flared wide open. "Okay! Okay!" He carefully removed her hands from her arms and held them. Her own skin and blood were now under her fingernails. He looked terrified. "I'll let you heal me first. Okay?" His eyes welled up. "We'll get through this."

She started to hyperventilate. That had been the hardest thing she'd ever done—calling for help from her personal prison. And he'd understood.

Guillen held their clasped hands in his lap, studying them. He may not have known what to say, but he could be there with her.

Her breathing eventually calmed, and he looked her in the eye. "I love you, Rachel. How can I help?"

She didn't really know. "Just ... buy me some time. And maybe get some more water."

His handsome face was still riddled with concern. "Okay. I promise. We'll be safe long enough to take care of it. If I go get water, will you be alright?"

She searched her mind, and slowly nodded.

"I'll be right back." He left the room and promptly returned with a pitcher of water. A minute after he came back, someone tapped on the door. He got up and thanked whoever it was that handed him a large ceramic bowl and some towels.

He sat down again and asked warily, "Can I clean you up a bit?"

She clenched her jaw and looked down, nodding again. He dipped a towel in the bowl of water and gently wiped at her arms. They still hadn't healed from the Ivy attack; she had only added to the damage. He then took her hands and dipped them in the bowl, one by one, cleaning underneath her fingernails. She hated it, but she loved him more for his kindness.

He dried off her hands and drew in a deep breath. "How is your energy?"

"I have enough to try."

"Alright." He raised his eyebrows. "But if you have to do it in more than one session, that's fine. Don't take yourself too far like you did the first time."

"Okay." She carefully moved a hand to his side. Having somewhat calmed down, she channeled the hints of Seeder energy that had rebuilt. His eyes darted around her face, monitoring how she was doing. She started to get dizzy, but she was *so* close to being done.

"Honey, take a break." He removed her hand.

She closed her eyes and focused on breathing. He was right; she was too close to passing out. That could lose them valuable time. Glancing at the wound, she was frustrated with how close she'd gotten.

He poked near it with his fingers. "It's practically gone." He read her face. "But we can wait, and finish it up."

She averted her eyes, fully knowing her demand was irrational, but grateful he was considering her feelings.

"I'm going to take care of these. You drink some and rest up." He picked up the dirty towels and bowl before leaving.

Rachel balled herself up in the fetal position, still unable to fall asleep. She wished she could be back home, her human home, with her human mom. Samantha would be doting on Rachel like when she'd been sick as a child. Rachel wished she didn't have to ask this of Guillen.

She pushed the swarming chaos away by focusing on the immediate future. She'd take his mom and sister through a rift to Eric. They'd place the women in a safe house. Then she'd return to the Green Lands. Rachel frowned—she couldn't just rift back to the Ivy Kingdom. Whatever Guillen did next, he would be far from her. He would be moving on to more dangerous territory, changing his focus to the palace. She hoped they'd done enough with their mission, having only hit half of the stunt communities. They were far from accomplishing what they'd wanted to, but she knew wars were never tidy. There were always contingency plans. She just hadn't thought of this one.

Not much later, Guillen rejoined her—sitting in the chair again, caressing her hand, simply being there.

"I think your sister might not be horrible," she offered.

He smiled. "She's pretty great. Not perfectly enlightened, but I already see a shift in her from this."

Rachel failed to smile. "I guess *something* good came from all of this, right?"

He squeezed her hand, giving her a look of encouragement.

"Aren't you worried about the rest of your family coming back while we're figuring this out? Where are they?"

"We'll be fine. My brother is plenty busy with the war; I don't think he visits much. And my father... Well... It's not really acceptable for him to get a divorce in his position, but he doesn't stick around here long. If he popped in before we left, I think he'd be okay. He was the reason I was allowed to grow up at home."

Guilt over this whole fiasco weighed her down. "I'm *really* sorry. For treating you like I did. You're the best thing to happen to me, and I don't know why I acted that way."

"I forgive you. I'm sorry I didn't take it well. Let's move past that."

If only it were that easy to dismiss her screwup. "I'm sorry I got you hurt," she whispered.

"What?" He furrowed his brow. "How did you get me hurt?"

"You told me not to come. And I forced you into it. And then I distracted you before you went out to talk with him."

"Rachel..." he scolded lovingly. "No. Don't blame yourself for that. I just... He... It's not your fault. You take the weight of the world on your shoulders, but you shouldn't. Please try to let this one go. It wasn't your fault."

She bit the insides of her cheeks. She wanted to believe him, but he could be lying, or refusing to admit the truth to himself.

"Can I try to finish it?" she asked, throwing a glance at his midsection.

"Have you had enough time?"

"Yeah. It won't take much for what's left."

He nodded, and she set to work again, healing. She got a bit woozy, but stopped once she was satisfied with her work.

"Thank you," he said. "Good as new. I had someone retrieve our packs, so I have my tools to take out the stitches myself. Boy Scout here." He winked.

She cracked a tiny smile. That had been a magical moment for her, too, as a handsome stranger with kind eyes once removed her stitches in the darkness of a cave after he'd helped rescue her from the palace.

"Do you think you could get some sleep?" he asked.

"I haven't been able to."

"Would it help if I lay with you?"

She nodded. "Probably."

Chapter 33

Kaylah woke to a hand covering her mouth, that of one of the guards who was supposed to be keeping her tent secure during the night. Another Ivy stood at the end of her cot, vines wrapped around the neck of a hostage, hands restraining her arms.

"Get up, and stay quiet," the guard ordered.

Still groggy, and now terrified, Kaylah tried to assess the situation. Her guard had already wrapped her wrists tight with his vines, so she couldn't extend her own. The hostage, a girl Kaylah had gotten to know well from training her here in camp, was on the verge of tears. "Please, Your Highness," the girl pleaded.

Kaylah slowly sat up, dazed, starting to panic.

"Let's go have a chat. Scream, and you both die."

He tied a gag around Kaylah's mouth and pulled her up. Her mind raced. *Where are they going to take us? Where's the Seeder guard who was stationed outside?*

Allowing them to push her out of the tent, she bought herself time to plan how to get both herself and the girl out of this mess. They passed tent after tent lit by lightkeepers and flickering candles, but no one was outside, available to give aid. *How late is it?*

Kaylah screamed to get someone's attention, but the gag muffled her voice.

"Shut up," her guard growled, slapping his hand over her mouth to quiet her further.

The shouts of battle on the border of camp were so loud. How could she have slept through that?

As the men marched their hostages forward, Kaylah's mind raced. She kept scanning the horizon for help, but no one was walking around camp at this hour, likely sleeping or in battle at the border.

Assessing the situation, Kaylah was surprised they hadn't even gagged the other hostage. *Why aren't you screaming?* She mentally pleaded for the girl to snap out of her daze, to not be so afraid, to be willing to sound the alarm.

And she'd need to do it soon. As they approached the emergency exit trees, for some reason not guarded at the moment, it clicked as to why they'd brought a hostage. They intended for Kaylah to rift to a new location.

Are the traitors not whispers, then? It stood to reason they had a way of contacting someone on the outside, to confirm Kaylah had rifted to the location they were trying to force her to, and if she didn't, they'd kill this innocent girl.

Kaylah's heart broke. How much was one innocent life worth? One loyal follower sacrificed in the name of keeping Unitas together? Queasy, she accepted the girl's fate. If Kaylah walked through a rift into Soren's clutches, this all would have been a waste. She was *so* close to figuring things out.

They stopped at the trees, and Kaylah desperately tried to catch the girl's eye. *We might survive, if you would just scream!*

"Alright, the rift, hurry it up," one of the men said, glancing around.

They hadn't even told Kaylah where they expected her to rift to, not that she would... Plus, her wrists were still bound.

Instead, they released the hostage, and she reached out a vine, drawing it down a tree trunk. It cracked, opening a rift.

Wait, what?! Perhaps Kaylah was still too dazed from being woken from a deep sleep, or being drugged, or both, but the logic didn't add up. They were sending *both* girls through a rift, with no assurances? When had they even told the girl where they were supposed to rift to?

Kaylah shook her head violently, yelling as loudly as she could through the gag, pleading for the girl to raise the alarm, to not go through, to do *something*.

The girl turned to Kaylah with a somber gaze, stepping back from the tree. "Thank you for the extra training, Your Highness. My apologies." She nodded at the guard holding Kaylah hostage.

Kaylah's eyes grew wide in the split second it took the guard to release his vines and shove her right into the rift.

A rift created by a whisper rifter. Created by a *girl*...

Kaylah stood in the dungeon, shackled to the wall. *How could I be so stupid?* She'd only ever identified a handful of whisper rifters, all palace guards. All former assassins. All men. But a girl? Why had she not even allowed that possibility to cross her mind?

Just as sickening as being held hostage in the dungeon of the palace she ought to be in charge of, was the realization that Unitas had at least two traitors in their midst. Only the solo Ivy guard traitor had created a rift of his own and followed after her.

There wasn't a single chance this was going to end well.

The cell door creaked open, and with zero surprise, Kaylah was greeted by her older brother, Soren. A menacing smile accompanied his green eyes and dark brown hair.

"What did you do to my Seeder guard?" she asked.

"Come on. No 'hello'? That hurts. After the lengths I went through to *save* my little sister." He looked her over from top to bottom. "I'd offer a hug, but you seem a little tied up right now."

"What the *hell* did you do to him?"

Soren rolled his eyes. "You and I both know I have no need for male weeds. Can't milk them for energy on the Vines, can we? And I certainly have no need for witnesses, either."

She had guessed as much.

"I know—you're disappointed. I am too. I would have preferred to nab a female Seeder, as well, while we were at it. I have plenty of use for *them*."

Kaylah huffed. "You were dropped on your head as a child."

He leaned back against the stone wall, crossing his arms. "In fact, I'd prefer to have *several* more female weeds. It's shocking how much we're struggling to get them. How well concealed they are. How many high school students in the human world are going missing."

Kaylah smiled. "Sounds like Uncle would find you a bitter disappointment."

Soren crossed the room, slamming his fist into her gut. She reeled in pain, losing her breath and almost losing her last meal.

He glared, inches from her face. A signature spark of rage rose in his eyes. "I will murder you. Slowly. And with great joy."

She clenched her teeth as she steadied her breathing.

After a minute, he backed up against the wall again, staring her down. "Speaking of Uncle, his study is shockingly empty. Any thoughts on that?"

Kaylah stared right back at him, tight-lipped.

He searched her face. "Yeah, well, none of your spies we've killed have given that one up—yet. So, I guess we'll just keep torturing the staff, one by one, until we find who misplaced those."

She frowned. "What have you done to Kyas and Rian?" If Soren could kill his own parents, she didn't know how far he would be willing to go. They had little brothers, now parentless.

Soren swatted dismissively at the air. "The runts are fine. Servants are taking care of them."

She knew him well enough to actually believe him, for now. "Thank you."

He scoffed. "Don't make me change my mind." He pursed his lips. "How's Rachel? That one hurt a little. You bring a girlfriend home to introduce her to your parents, and then your little sister has to ruin *everything* by stealing her away."

Kaylah scowled. "Somehow, I don't think she saw it the same way." She glanced closer at his lip—there was no scar from where Rachel had bitten him in self-defense. "It's a shame. Someday when I see her again, she'll be disappointed to find out you didn't get a scar. I thought she bit clean through, and there were stitches." She sneered.

He met her challenge with a smile of his own. "Mother loved *one* of us. The one she *wasn't* disappointed in, she granted extra permission to. She let me take a weed off the Vines long enough to recuperate, and then heal me."

"How much did she love you when you murdered her and Father?"

Soren's ever-mercurial temper rose again. "That's on you!"

"How do you figure?"

He jabbed a finger at her. "You're the one who screwed this all up! You messed up the plan. You didn't even understand all of the plan, but you managed to royally screw things up. All you had to do was play your part." Soren shook his head. "If you wanted to roll around in the weed patch and disappoint us all, you could have at least not killed Uncle."

That was a huge relief, in a somewhat-odd way. She had been right in that decision, to make sure and take out Nuren as soon as possible. "I'm not sorry I disappointed you. And I'll continue to. I won't help you with the Vines, and I won't help you find more Seeders. I won't help you with *anything*."

He grinned. "I think you overestimate yourself."

"I won't be a puppet queen."

Soren raised his eyebrows. "Who said anything about you taking your place as queen? Your coronation ship has sailed."

She searched his face. "Then you'll what? Kill me and move to work with Aunt Vera? I doubt that."

He chuckled. "Work with that hag? I don't think even *she* can stand herself. I have no need for her, either."

Kaylah's heart sank. The next in line—Catrina—was a sweet girl. "You'd really take out the line for a succession change? For Beata?" They'd literally announced their engagement the same day he kidnapped Rachel.

He sighed, clasping his hands in front of himself. "You can guess all day and get nowhere. I'm here," he pouted, "for a family reunion." He took a deep breath. "And for answers. I'd like to know how to find weed girls, what you're doing with Uncle's research, and any other little tidbits that can end this thing. I don't want this war to go on any more than you do."

She looked him straight in the eye. "Go screw yourself."

He straightened. "I get that you think I'm the bad guy here. But you lost yourself in the human world. Why else do you think you were kept in the dark? We knew we couldn't really trust you. When you were in the human world, you learned to be weak. You focused on dating airhead humans you met at animal shelters, and making buddies with the weeds." He pointed to himself. "I learned a thing or two, myself. And that includes loyalty, dedication, and pride for my kingdom. And doing what it takes to get the job done. You're no one's hero, Kaylah. Not even for the weeds, anymore."

It hurt—he was right. She hadn't been able to crack as many things as she had wanted. She'd been *so* close on her research. But it hadn't been enough. And certainly wouldn't be from a musty dungeon. Saff had been too busy to help most of the time. Camp was under siege. Rachel was somewhere along the path with Guillen. *And they probably don't even know I'm here.*

Soren glared with a look of genuine contempt. "You've always been ungrateful for what you were given. For the mission you were assigned. Whining to come back home."

She gritted her teeth. "I was a little girl, forced to live in the human world away from my home."

"You were offered the opportunity to prove your worth to your people as a strong leader at the time of a breakthrough." He huffed. "And once I was established with Rachel, you could have come home, but you didn't."

That was also true. She'd finally been allowed to call it quits on her assigned mission in the human world. Her uncle and brother could have handled Rachel without her, though not as easily. *But I couldn't leave Rachel alone.*

Soren pulled Kaylah's dagger from his pocket, using it to clean under his fingernails. "Do you know why we needed someone else to manage Rachel in the first place?"

Kaylah didn't answer. Did the details matter?

"It was enough that you questioned Mother and Father on their policies, but then..." He clicked his tongue. "Words matter, Kaylah. How often did you start calling them 'Seeders' instead of 'weeds'? As the humans say: when you raise a cow for slaughter, you don't give it a name."

What was Kaylah supposed to have done? Not try to change her parents' minds as a girl, and just skip to assassination? And she'd always tried to keep up the ruse of calling Rachel and her family weeds, and every time she scolded Soren for his behavior, warned him about taking things too far with Rachel, it had always been under the guise of his actions jeopardizing the mission.

But it hadn't been enough. *She* hadn't been enough.

A sinister grin overtook his face. "I do very little in life without purpose. Other than ensuring the mission was a success, do you know why I volunteered to be stationed in the human world?"

"Clearly," she drawled, tired of his gloating, "because now you're the one who gets to claim success for infiltrating a Seeder network and establishing the War Vines."

He wrinkled his nose. "Small perk, though appreciated." He pointed Kaylah's dagger at her. "Because I knew Rachel was such a close friend. What an opportunity to screw with you! Every time I touched her, messed with her head, made her feel bad about herself... It hurt you, too. Two for the price of one. The black eye you gave me for attacking her in the hot tub... I'd do it again, ten times over, just to see your reaction."

It took everything Kaylah had not to cry. Everything she'd ever tried to do was wasted, had only hurt those she'd tried to help. Rachel wouldn't be coming to free her from the palace, like Kaylah had done for her just months before. Unitas would fall. No one would be coming.

Curiosity still nagging at her, she studied his face. "How did you even know about whispers? And that girls can be whispers?"

He narrowed his eyes. "That hurts, doesn't it? That I've always been two steps ahead of you in this. That Mother and Father never even told their heir... I'm frankly surprised you even know about whispers at all."

Kaylah was going to be tortured, and was going to die; there was no way around that truth. She probably ought not to fuel Soren's rage, but perhaps it might bring *some* satisfaction before she died.

"I learned about whispers when I made my first kill. Do you know who that was?" she asked.

Soren seemed intrigued. "Do tell."

She wore her own grin now. "I confirmed their existence when I caught one of Uncle's spies following me." She prepared herself for the blow, possibly the end. It had been one of Soren's best friends in the human world, one of his assassin buddies who had gone missing. "You should have heard Teagan *scream* as I slit his throat."

Soren's eyes darkened; his jaw set. And just as quickly as that look came, it passed, giving way to another smirk. "Didn't think you had it in you. I told him to be careful when I sent him to watch you."

Soren won again. She'd always assumed her uncle or parents had sent a spy to make sure she wasn't up to funny business.

"And yeah... Girls as whispers. That's funny you'd assume they couldn't be. The Vines have eyes and ears, after all." He turned the dagger in his hand, examining it. "Like I said, I do very little in life without a purpose. And I do love my women."

Kaylah gaped. "That girl is one of your whores?"

He feigned offense. "Slut shaming? She prefers the term 'lover.' Frankly, I always appreciated Uncle's motto: All you need for success is lots of work, a touch of luck, and enough charisma to woo the world."

Soren flicked at the dagger's edge. "Oh boy, sharp. I bet that means less pain, and definitely less damage." He extended his arm and stabbed the dagger against the stone wall a few times.

Kaylah winced in anticipation with each *clang*.

He reexamined it. "That'll do the job." He approached her again.

Kaylah's heart rate skyrocketed as she eyed the beat-up dagger.

"I want weeds for the Vines, and want to know what's in Uncle's research. Question and answer time."

A half hour later, Kaylah's face was covered in a mix of sweat, tears, and snot. She stared at her arm. Blood dripped from where Soren had carved the word 'traitor' on her forearm. Soren threw her dagger on the floor, on the opposite end of the cell, then stood back to admire his work.

"That was a disappointment," he said, tilting his head. "I've got places to be and things to do, so I guess we'll leave it like this for tonight."

She couldn't say anything; she was still trying to catch her breath.

"How about this? Scream loud enough," he winced, rubbing his own ear, "and the guards will hear you and know you're ready to give us something. Give me information that leads to at least one fresh weed girl, and I'll let her heal you before going on the Vines." His voice was cool, confident, casual. "I consider that more than a fair offer."

"I won't help you," she whispered, her voice shuddering.

He drew a deep breath and let it out. "I think we've learned an important lesson today. You do better when it's other people in harm's way. I can work with that." He glanced down at the dagger with a hint of recognition, then laughed. "Wait a second. That's not standard royal issue, but I thought I recognized the pattern of the handle from somewhere. You got it from that moron cousin you take pity on."

She frowned.

"Carrying around his little knives, compensating." Soren grinned. "What community does the compost pile live in?"

She did her best to steady her breathing. Guillen had been living in Community One. And she didn't know how soon he and Rachel would be there for their campaign.

In the absence of her reply, Soren continued. "That one's easy enough to find out. Until we bring him back, it's a servant a day. Maybe I'll start with the nurses. I knew I should have killed the disobedient nurse who went missing when you took Rachel."

Kaylah struggled not to cry again. She didn't want anyone else hurt on account of her and her failed plans. She hoped camp was at least still intact, and that he wouldn't find Olivia and actually bring her back to torture her to death in front of her.

Soren studied Kaylah in silence, narrowed eyes calculating. "I'll give you till the morning to decide. We could put aside our differences and do what's right for our people—a brother-and-sister team. If you still want to be queen, working with me, then I might really consider it. We can tell our people it was all a misunderstanding, that it was really the weeds who got Mother and Father. But if you can't come to your senses by then, that choice will permanently be gone. And I have a feeling you're going to regret your choice when you find out what comes next."

He looked down at his hands, shaking her blood off, then met her gaze with cold eyes. "One more thing. I owe you this, from high school."

Kaylah flinched, closing her eyes for the inevitable blow. It was swift to follow—the punch to her eye, payback for the shiner she'd given him less than a year ago, when he'd bragged to her about attacking Rachel in the hot tub, just for the fun of it. She kept her eyes closed, only whimpering when the door latched shut.

Soren woke her early in the morning on his promised visit. He beamed. "Hey, you! Did you miss me?"

She swallowed hard, ready for round two. Two of whoever knew how many.

He arched his eyebrows. "Answer time. Queen? Yes or no?"

"Yes. I want to be queen."

He narrowed his eyes. "Really? Okay..."

"When your body is cold and dead."

He put a hand to his heart, smiling. "That's more the Kaylah I know. Glad you haven't lost that can-do spirit. So, no to the queen part. A little disappointing, but that's par for the course, as the humans say. No little tidbits to even earn a healing?"

Kaylah gritted her teeth. "You can torture and kill every servant in this palace, and it wouldn't equal the Seeder lives you'd take by having one of them on the Vines. That's going to be a no from me."

He sighed, gesturing at her. "See, I can't even work with this anymore. I still kinda want the public to go back to liking you for my plans. But then again, I wouldn't have to retract my accusations if they thought you were crazy. And I can still work with crazy."

"Yes, you're crazy."

He smirked. "I love these conversations. But sadly, I'm short on time today. Let's remember the terms before we get started. Weed girls equal healing. Other info might do well, too. Either might save a servant a horrible death." He extended a short vine tendril, sharpening a leaf. "Here's the thing—if we're going to go this route, I'm okay with scars. I think it would actually be kinda cool to do scars. But..." He raised an eyebrow. "They really ought to be nice-looking. So, you should try not to move too much."

Her breathing sped up as he approached her face.

"Oh, yeah, and if you move too much, I might get your eye. I don't see any need for you to be blind."

In no time flat, he'd sliced a diagonal line into each of her cheeks. Her wounds stung once her salty tears seeped down into them.

He examined his work. "Yep. I think it's a good start. You've always been vain, anyway. I was going to rub some mud into it to help it infect and scar," he grimaced, "but your face is already pretty gross from yesterday, so we'll see how this goes."

Soren stood up straight. "Nothing?"

"Go fall in a ravine."

He frowned. "Such harsh words for a groom on his wedding day."

Her eyes widened.

"That's right, I didn't tell you." He beamed. "Today's my big day. Sorry you're not invited. I know that's in bad taste, but you're not really dressed for the occasion." He prodded around her black eye. "Not the right colors."

"Well, congratulations," she said wryly. "You and Beata deserve each other."

"Thanks. That's big of you. I'm crazy about her."

Yep, crazy is definitely one of the words I'd use.

"Anyway, not much time to spare. Obviously, I'm busy."

"Don't let me hold you back."

He winked. "Don't worry, I won't. Since we're congratulating me, you should also congratulate me for becoming king today."

She read his face, not sure how to feel about that. "So, you're killing the downline after all, and naming her queen?"

Soren rolled his eyes. "I didn't say that. I'm only going to say this once, so you should savor it—you were right. Our kingdom should make some changes."

There had to be a catch. There *always* was with Soren.

He sat on the ground, crossing his legs. "Who says we need a queen to lead?"

She stared at him, unamused. "Our laws, traditions, and the dictates of our powers?" It had only ever been named a 'kingdom' to mirror human examples, but Ivy kings had always been consorts to their queens.

He wagged a finger at her. "Yes and no. If one of us is going to change how this kingdom works, anyway, I'm betting our people will more happily follow *my* lead. I learned a thing or two from the humans, just like you did." He shrugged. "Who says power over the Mother Vines means you should be entitled to rule the kingdom? Why couldn't that power and responsibility be relegated to a different title, say ... a priestess? Isn't that great? We can still be a sibling duo and make this work."

Kaylah glared. "You're out of your mind. I don't care what you call it. I still won't help you."

Standing up, he dusted himself off. "I think priestess sounds cool. And it goes with the scar vibes. With how quick we heal, everyone will know they're intentional, ritual. A sign of your penitence. I'll issue a pardon. How many scars you end up with, and how many people die in the process, depends on you. I'm okay with head-to-toe scars. You can even be a slutty priestess, so we maximize the square space. But once your mind goes, from the screaming—that of yourself and others—I have no use for you. I need you to appear lucid in public. If I have to kill you, that would be a shame. But I'd do it, and then take out the old hag, and poor innocent Catrina is next on the list. Choose wisely."

The tiniest slivers of hope Kaylah could cling to were that Unitas could figure out what she hadn't been able to with her research, that they could continue to keep Soren from getting his hands on any more Seeder girls to power the War Vines, and that Soren would make a misstep somewhere, that he'd miscalculated something. Because right now, he had this in the bag.

"You don't understand our people as well as you think you do," she said. "They won't tolerate your brutality for long. They would never accept a king in lieu of a proper queen. Never."

He tucked his hands into his pockets. "No? People forgive heaps of brutality in the name of war. I think when the truth comes to light, people will soften. Sure, you have the rarest gift in the Green Lands. But it's not like I don't have my own gifts."

He really was an arrogant prick. "Stupidity doesn't count as a gift."

He chuckled. "That's a little weak, even for you. Strength comes from loyalty. Take an oppressed and exploited group of people, and give them hope, and you become their savior."

She furrowed her brow. Oppressed and exploited? Stunts would *never* follow Soren's lead willingly. And Rachel and Guillen were already securing their loyalty by explaining her goals to restore their rights. "Sorry to inform you, but stunts hate you."

That garnered a look of confusion. "Who said anything about *them*?" He stuck up a fist, lifting his pointer finger. "Royal birth—check. Strategy—check.

Connections—check." He lifted a finger with each point, ticking off his list. "Unique gift that the majority of the population doesn't possess—check."

Why did he think he was so special? "What gift?"

He looked at her like she was stupid. But maybe she had been, because that last piece snapped into place. "You're a whisper?"

Soren teemed with pride, opening his arms as though he'd just cut the ribbon at a grand opening ceremony, as if presenting himself with an award. "Not the only gifted one in the family."

Crap. That might tip the scales.

Unable to resist patting himself on the back, he breathed in the victory. "Your face tells me you know exactly where this is headed."

And she did. She'd spent enough time talking with Nathan and Jon to understand the plight of whispers, their forced lifelong servitude to their queen and king, betraying their own people as spies. They wanted out. They wanted camaraderie, to be allowed to even discuss their gifts with whom they wanted, to use those powers when *they* wanted to, if at all.

'When the truth comes to light, people will soften.' He had their parents' resources, likely a list of all known whispers in the kingdom.

She had a handful.

"Free them from their shackles," Soren said. "Promise them power, and position, and wealth. Promise them a leader who understands what it's like to be one of them." He reached for the door handle. "I wouldn't even *have* to be one of them. They're so desperate, they'd just need to *think* I was."

Her mouth hung open. "So you're not."

He winked. "I didn't say that. Whether true or not, those words would never come out of my mouth. But it kills you not to know, doesn't it?"

He'd always loved his mind games.

Soren pulled the cell door open. "Oh yeah, normally you gift the bride and groom. But your hands are a little tied up. So, I'll throw you a bone this once. No servant screams today; I think it would put Beata out of the mood. But tomorrow's a new day." He hesitated before leaving. "You *could* offer me a wedding gift, actually. If you led me to Rachel, I'd promise to not even put her on the Vines. I'd just keep her for myself." He smirked.

"You're disgusting. I'm sure your bride would love to hear that on her wedding day."

"What she doesn't know won't hurt her." He winked again. "Plus, kings sometimes have concubines. I think I could wear her down. Love ya, Sis." He exited and closed the door behind him.

Kaylah fell numb, everywhere except the pulsing ache in her arm and eye, and the sting of her fresh wounds. She'd wanted to do right by her people, those with and without powers. She'd wanted to do right by the Seeders, and the humans caught in the crosshairs.

Fresh tears rolled down her cheeks as she thought of Eric. She loved him more than anyone. He was in the human world, and she would never see him again. She would never see *anyone* again. Except for innocent people forced to die in front of her until she broke or Soren ended her.

Staring at the battered knife still on the ground, she wondered if it was even worth it to try to hang on to hope. She'd never follow Soren's stupid plan, but perhaps she should have bided her time. She should have gone about this all a different way—killed Nuren, *and* her parents. But in secret. Then she could have taken her mother's place and *slowly* changed things. But what she could have done, and should have done, were immaterial at this point.

Frowning, she considered Rachel. Despite Soren's declarations, there was a part of him that actually did like Rachel, in his own perverted way. She wasn't just a Seeder. She was a trophy, the one that got away. And if he caught up to Guillen on his mission, he'd also catch up to Rachel. Rachel had already been through enough hell.

Is this what she felt like, captive in this palace—hopeless and alone?

Chapter 34

The man's body went limp, lifeless, under Rachel's weight, and by her hand. She kept her eyes closed for a moment. Panting, she dreaded the next moment. Opening her eyes, she expected to see the guard who'd just attacked her. Instead, she saw the face of the man she loved—dead. She'd just murdered him.

Rachel wailed, pleading for him to come back. She'd made a mistake. She'd killed the wrong man.

"Rachel!"

Her eyes snapped open; a hand gently covered her mouth. Guillen was behind her, lying on the bed, holding her.

"It's okay," he whispered. "It's okay. I'm right here."

He removed his hand from her mouth and stroked her hair. She started to sob as the bedroom door cracked open. Catrina peeked inside, clearly concerned about the screaming. Guillen spoke up again, a little louder, as if addressing both Rachel and Catrina at the same time. "It's okay."

He stayed cuddled up next to Rachel as Catrina left the room, easing the door shut behind her. Rachel had finally been able to find some rest. But the nightmares were back, with a brand-new horror at their disposal. She groaned at the unfairness. Guillen placed a sweet kiss on her head, and she shifted, trying to get herself to fall asleep again.

The next time she woke, it was much less traumatic. Her eyelashes fluttered as she remembered where she was. Her heart warmed at Guillen's touch. They breathed in unison. She didn't want to go, but it was time.

She turned to look at him. Awake, he gazed into her eyes with pure adoration. "I love you."

"I love you too. Thank you. Again."

"You never have to thank me for the pleasure of your company." His lips twitched into a warm smile.

She sighed heavily. "I'm ready to go."

"Are you sure? You're still pretty beat up. We could take them where we were originally planning, and give you another day to heal. Then rift out."

Rachel frowned. "No. You were right. I can't be selfish. And we'll all be safer over there." She paused. "And I'm not waiting until the last minute when there's a dozen soldiers cornering us. I need to know you got out of here cleanly."

He pulled her closer, squeezing tight. "I never want to let you go. But the sooner we take care of this, the sooner I get to see you again."

They slowly got out of bed and made sure she could stand on her own. He held her waist. "I want to be there for you. And I'm sorry we have to rush you like this." He caressed her cheek. "I may not know Eric, but he sounds like a good guy. Can you promise me you'll talk to him ... if you ... need help? And Saff, when you get back to your side?"

Rachel had no idea what she was capable of anymore. But she could try. She nodded.

He held her tight. "I'm going to miss you so much." Finally releasing her, he leaned down and kissed her. It was gentle and sweet, but not just a simple peck. For a fleeting moment, Rachel lost her will to continue in this war. They could run away. They could carve out a space for themselves, a cabin in the Neutral Woods, and be happy and safe—together. They'd both already sacrificed enough.

As their lips parted, she knew it couldn't be that way. She drew a deep breath. "I'm ready."

They walked to the neighboring room. Catrina hopped up from a chair when they entered. Lady Vera sat, looking unimpressed still. "Are we *finally* ready?"

Guillen scowled. "Yes. She's ready to save your selfish life."

Rachel tried to hide a grin of satisfaction. She wanted to say a thing or two, but it would have to wait. The moment they were safe with Unitas, those floodgates might open. But now wasn't the time.

They went out to the lush gardens surrounding the mansion. They were beautifully manicured, their perfume filling the air.

Rachel and the others found some appropriate trees—pines—for Ivy-type rifting. She shared the coordinates they were aiming for in the human world with Guillen's mom and sister. Kaylah had shared the location in her last message to them, so they could quickly reach out to Eric in just such an emergency. The Ivy women easily visualized it. It was briefly discussed who Rachel would be going through with.

She'd rather saw off a leg than be paired with Guillen's mom. The thought of having that woman touch her with vines, puncturing her skin for energy to get them both through... It was visceral, repulsive. But if, heaven forbid, something should go wrong, she should be with the next heir to the throne.

Just before leaving, Guillen gave his sister a hug, then Rachel.

"Here. Give this to Eric when you get there." He handed Rachel a sealed envelope, and she tucked it into her pocket.

She pulled him close, breathing in the moment. They said another round of 'I love yous,' and then he held her at arms-length. A lot could be said or repeated. Nothing was certain, nothing guaranteed.

"I'll stay safe if you will," he said with a grin.

"Deal." She gave him one last kiss before turning and standing next to his mother. Lady Vera glanced at Rachel's arm in disgust as she wrapped a vine around it. The Ivy women each opened a rift; Rachel looked over her shoulder for one last glance at Guillen. He had his hands shoved in his pockets, his face fighting to keep it together, trying to force a smile.

And the women walked through.

The moment they arrived in the human world, the warmth of the Green Lands no longer lingered with Rachel. It was colder here. She would take longer to recharge with less ambient energy. She was on borrowed time until she'd have to return. Catrina and Lady Vera stood still, as they'd been instructed to, looking decently concerned.

"Hold it," one of the guards ordered. There were *a lot* more guards than Rachel had anticipated, though it made sense with Kaylah having gone missing.

Nathan, Kaylah's human-world deployment guardian, bounded up from the line of mixed Unitas guards at the cave. "Rachel?!" He looked both surprised to see her, and horrified at her appearance. She'd only taken a quick glance in the mirror, but she was bruised, sliced, and diced. It wasn't pretty. He cautiously greeted Guillen's mom and sister with a bow.

"Yeah," Rachel said.

A handful of other guards approached, closely following Nathan. Rachel didn't recognize any of the others, and was uneasy about an audience with this mission.

"Could I talk with Nathan in private for a second?"

"No."

Reading the tension in the group, Rachel calculated what to do next. She didn't know who was privy to the details of her and Guillen's mission, she didn't know what details they had about Kaylah's disappearance, and she wanted as few people as possible to know who she was tucking away for safekeeping. "I have details I need to discuss with a member of the council." She wanted someone she could trust on her side. "A member of the council and Nathan. No offense, but the council wouldn't want a dozen guards hearing what I need to report."

The guard eyed her. "Fine. The four of you: follow me."

Nathan, Rachel, Catrina, and Lady Vera all followed after the guard, as the rest fell back to their positions.

After only a few minutes of walking, they reached a small log cabin, and the guard ushered them in. The senior Unitas guard on duty was inside, focused on paperwork. Once the guard who had guided them there left, they all took a seat except for Nathan.

"How can I help you?" the senior officer asked.

Rachel's palms began to sweat. He wasn't a member of the council, at least not one she recognized; she wasn't sure what she was safe to say around him, or what he knew. "I, uh, I was on a mission for Kaylah, for Unitas. It had ... problems."

The senior officer scanned her. "You look it."

"Well, it was classified. Um... Do you know what happened to Kaylah? And are you able to help me put these two women into a safe house?"

The man flipped open a book. "Name?"

"I'm Rachel Lyzasdotter."

He found her name. "Yes, I see you on the list as an anticipated user of the rift cave. And these two?"

A Seeder would obviously be in charge in the human world for Unitas, and it was clear he didn't recognize Lady Vera and Catrina, despite their high station in Ivy society.

"Can't I talk to someone on the council?" Rachel asked.

He was less than thrilled to have his authority questioned. "I have their full authority when in the human world."

She hesitated.

Nathan cleared his throat. "This is Lady Vera, next in line as queen after Kaylah." He gave her another small bow, which she only met with a contemptuous glance. "I don't quite recognize this young lady," he confessed.

"This is Guillen's sister, Catrina," Rachel said.

"You don't say!" Nathan perked up. "I remember you now. You were a little thing when we last met. Before we were stationed here."

Catrina blushed.

Since the cat was out of the bag, Rachel gave the briefest description of her mission with Guillen, and the guards' betrayal at his family manor. "We need to keep them safe. But they're not exactly on board, if you know what I mean. I need Eric—now. And as few people as possible to know about this, even amongst us. But we'll need extra security on-site."

The man nodded and pulled out his phone, stepping outside to make a call.

"Any updates?" Rachel asked Nathan. "On Kaylah, perchance? Last I heard, Soren had her at the palace."

Nathan frowned. "That's the latest I've heard, too. We just got word from one of our remaining spies at the palace."

"How's your wife?" Rachel asked.

"Ginger's good. Worried, of course, but good. She's at the camp, trying to keep everything together."

The man reentered. "Okay. We have someone ready to escort you to a safe house."

"Alright." Rachel stood. "Could it just be Nathan that takes us there?"

"No." He shot a glance at Nathan. "Nathan won't be privy to the location of where you'll be heading."

Rachel frowned. Seeder leadership had been slow to warm to Kaylah, but now they distrusted Nathan? "Why? I trust him more than a stranger I don't know. He wouldn't jeopardize things."

Nathan gave her a tiny downtrodden shake of the head. "Don't worry about me. I'm doing what I need to for Unitas."

Rachel broke the awkward silence of the car ride. "Thank you for the ride."

"No problem," the male Seeder said as he took a right turn on the outskirts of a nearby town. "And always happy to meet new Ivies in the cause."

Lady Vera stared out the window. "Hmmph." She still hadn't deigned to speak to a human or Seeder.

The rest of the ride was fairly quiet. After at least a good half hour, they pulled up to a house Rachel didn't recognize. "I thought we were going to be dropped off at Eric's safe house."

"This is it. After Her Highness went missing, it was best to move his location as well."

Rachel frowned again, but she found a spark of hope in seeing Eric again, and hopefully finding out more about how Unitas was progressing.

As she reached for the door handle, something on the street put her on edge. "There's a guy in that parked car. Just sitting there..."

"You're fine. It's extra security."

She sighed in relief. "Thank you. This is going to make a difference."

He grinned, staying in the car while the others got out. "Unitas."

Rachel guided the women to the front door and didn't even have to knock before Eric pulled it open, ushering them in.

"Let's get them settled, then we can talk," Rachel instructed.

Eric nodded in agreement.

A couple of guards stationed at the safe house appeared from a stairway and guided them up to spare bedrooms. Lady Vera and Catrina were assigned a room with two beds.

Catrina sat down on the far bed, bouncing nervously with tight lips.

Lady Vera surveyed the room disapprovingly. "Intriguing."

With every highbrow mumble and scowl from the woman, Rachel's distaste for her grew. *This* would be that moment she'd waited for. Rachel stood straight. "You are a *horrible* woman! I don't care who you are! You don't deserve to have children, especially not one as great as Guillen. So be grateful for your pathetic life, and shut the hell up!"

Lady Vera glared at her. Catrina stilled, stunned. With them being so close to the Crown, Rachel doubted either had ever had such a candid opinion shared freely. It felt good.

Rachel closed the door, leaving them there, and then turned to Eric. His eyebrows were raised, and it looked like he was fighting a grin. The guards side-eyed her like she'd lost it.

Eric told the guards he'd show Rachel to her room and that they were fine from there. He and Rachel returned downstairs to the living room, where he had a first aid kit ready on the coffee table.

"I know you can heal, but they said you were in pretty rough shape. So, I figured it wouldn't hurt ... as a precaution?"

"Sure. Maybe just some disinfectant until I can regain my strength to finish healing."

He pulled out some alcohol wipes. "It looks like you've had quite an adventure. Bruising on your neck, looks like good old-fashioned strangulation. Not much I can do about that. I recognize the Ivy puncture wounds. What caused this other pattern?" He pointed to the crescent-shaped injuries on her upper arms.

She looked at her arms, disgusted with herself. "I'd rather not talk about it."

"Sorry, yeah. Bad day, obviously." The alcohol stung on her wounds as he cleaned them.

"Thanks. Oh yeah, Guillen gave me a letter for you." She mused at the irony as he opened the envelope. A human and an Ivy, an Ivy and a Seeder. Two relationships that couldn't work. And the men she and Kaylah loved would never be able to meet, both trapped in their own worlds. She studied Eric's face as he read the letter.

"Do you mind if I read it?" she asked, wanting to know what Guillen hadn't told her. Did it disclose his plans?

"I ... think he'd want me to keep this private. Nothing to worry about. Some of it I already knew, like Kaylah."

She couldn't imagine how it would feel to be so isolated here in the human world while everything played out in a completely different realm. "How are you handling it?"

He wore his best brave face. "She'll be okay. I have to believe it."

"I'm sorry I couldn't keep her safe."

He shook his head. "You were on your own mission; I couldn't blame you. And she's strong." He shifted in his seat. "So... Guillen explained why you brought them here. You think it'll keep her safe?"

Rachel rubbed at a dried blood smear on her dress. "I do. It's something. The only thing we can really do until an extraction is worked out. Guillen was brilliant to think of it so quickly."

"Speaking of..." Eric tapped the letter on his leg. "Sounds like Kaylah was right about you two."

Rachel's cheeks warmed. Kaylah had talked about her and Guillen to Eric? Kaylah had no idea how far they'd come in their relationship, but she'd encouraged it... Guillen certainly hadn't written a love note about her to Eric, but maybe he'd mentioned that he loved her and asked Eric to make sure she was safe.

"He's amazing." She smiled, though with longing. Her heart was back there, in a completely different realm right now.

"Then I'm glad you found someone good for you." Eric's eyes darted to the ceiling. "Though, if things work out, it sounds like you might have a rough go of it with your future mother-in-law." He laughed.

"Oh ... gross..." She grimaced. "That never even crossed my mind." She shook her head. "We're far from that. And frankly ... he may forgive her for what she's done, but I never could. After I go back, I'm staying as far away as humanly possible." She paused. "Not that I'm a human... Hmm ... you know, it's funny how sayings change meaning." She chuckled.

Eric met her chuckle with a friendly smile, cleaning up the first aid supplies he'd used. Seeder healing did a fantastic job of repairing damaged bone and tissue, though it wasn't as helpful against infection, so it was for the best they'd gone the extra mile, as she hadn't been able to heal herself right away.

Despite Eric's offer to show Rachel to a room where she could rest and clean up, she wanted to talk more first. They discussed progress with Unitas; there had been a boatload that Rachel hadn't been privy to while on her mission. She'd almost completely forgotten the human side of the equation, how hard Eric and the others had been working on behalf of the green folk from this side of the rifts.

Despite Eric's kindness and dedication, he quietly expressed frustration at the way Seeders were handling things, that they'd even consider that Kaylah, and by association, *he,* might be a traitor.

"Honestly, sometimes I'm not sure if I'm at this new safe house for my protection, or as a hostage."

Rachel's heart ached. "I thought we were doing well. I had so much hope after spending time with Guillen." Granted, Magda and Jacob, and Guillen's family wouldn't exactly become Rachel's BFFs, but she'd met plenty of Ivies who had given her hope along the way.

Eric rubbed his hands together, keeping his voice low. "I get that they're being overly cautious, but your leaders know ... things... It's just as likely that *they* did something with her as it is that Soren had her kidnapped."

The finger-pointing was getting old. So was the war. If Rachel could snap her fingers and make it all go away, she'd do it in half a heartbeat. "What do you mean, our leaders 'know things'?"

Pursing his lips, Eric hesitated. "I can't talk about it, but... Jon, and Nathan..."

Rachel furrowed her brow. "Yeah, what's with Nathan?"

Footsteps creaked above, making their way down the stairs.

Eric and Rachel craned their necks to see.

Catrina timidly poked her head around the corner. "Am I interrupting?"

"No, you're fine. Come on in." Eric offered her a chair.

"This is Guillen's sister, Catrina. Third in line to the throne. Catrina, this is Eric, Kaylah's..." Rachel panicked. What was he by now? Still a boyfriend? Had they made other plans? Lady Vera had mentioned Kaylah should have suitors in the Green Lands...

He acknowledged his precarious position with a glance in Rachel's direction. "I'm the human Kaylah dated in high school. How can we help you?"

"Well... I... Um... Guillen asked a favor before we came. He wanted me to get to know you two." Catrina shrugged. "So... I'm just here to talk, if that's okay."

Eric and Rachel shared a warm smile.

Chapter 35

Catrina shifted uncomfortably in her seat. "That was a car, right? Earlier?"

Rachel's eyes widened. "Right, I forgot. You really haven't been around here. Yeah, that was a car. I imagine there's a lot that's different for you already."

Catrina gave a cautious smile, but sat awkwardly, as if she didn't know what to say.

"I'm going to be blunt, and I hope you're okay with that. 'Cause I'm really tired, but I like you, okay?" It was time Rachel spoke her mind with Catrina, too. She was sweet, but anyone who referred to her people as 'weeds' still needed to learn a thing or two.

"I know you think you're better than us—a human and a Seeder. Just because you're royal, and you're an Ivy. But all that means is we might look different when we transform, that we have different abilities. If you love your brother the way I think you do, you should be able to get over that and realize the Unitas movement is one worth joining."

Rachel paused. "And the humans—sure, they don't have powers, like Guillen ... but that car ride... Wasn't that neat? It would be kind of nice to travel that quickly in the Green Lands, wouldn't it? Different doesn't mean bad."

Catrina looked down into her lap, and Eric sat silent.

Rachel cocked her head to the side. "Sorry. I could be a lot more tactful. But like I said, I'm tired. I should go lie down to heal up and prepare to leave, sooner than later."

"It's okay." Catrina gave a half-hearted smile. "I'm willing to hear anything you have to say. I told Guillen I would."

Rachel loved Guillen more than before, if it was even possible. He couldn't come to the human world, but he was still pushing forward the movement. Where was he that very moment? She refused to worry. He'd be safe. He'd be out there working on getting Kaylah back.

"Just remember I said I liked you first, okay? I'm open to answering questions about anything Seeder, and about how your brother and I met, if you still want to learn more. Maybe in the morning? If you don't have any burning questions, I'm going to head to bed. Eric would be great at explaining Unitas to you."

Catrina said she'd be okay with talking to Eric while Rachel turned in for the night. She stayed in the living room while Eric showed Rachel to a room with a single bed and en suite bathroom, and offered her the necessities.

Going through a rift, she couldn't bring her things with her that she'd been carrying around. Rifts allowed only a limited volume through, in relation to the Seeder or Ivy's body mass. Rachel surveyed her dress and rolled her eyes at the coincidence. The last time she'd been attacked by an Ivy, she had also been in a fancy dress. Neither experience had been worth dressing up for. Perhaps she would never wear a dress again.

"Thanks again, for taking us in," she said before Eric left the room.

"No problem. You know I'm always here for you."

She wrung her hands, figuring she might as well warn Eric. "I ... might have nightmares. I'm sorry if I wake you up." It was going to be hard without Guillen there.

"I'm sorry, Rach. Here, I didn't give you a proper hug." He opened his arms, and she happily obliged.

Rachel frowned as she realized what she'd just done in the living room, that she'd slipped on something she'd promised to keep a secret. "Sorry I told Catrina about you and Kaylah. I promised you two I wouldn't tell anyone you were back together, so you'd be safe."

He shook his head. "No worries. I was technically the one that said it. And Guillen's note said he was certain she could be trusted. And, honestly, the Seeders were half of the concern, anyway, back when we asked you to keep that one under wraps. But I'll let Catrina know to keep that tidbit from her mom." He shrugged. "I guess it's just nice to ... talk about her."

Rachel gave him another long hug. He'd all but given up his family, friends, and foreseeable future plans for Kaylah and Unitas. This had to be immensely difficult for him to trudge through alone.

After a few more minutes of catching up, he left Rachel to the quiet room and the solitude of her thoughts. She appreciated Eric. He was Kaylah's Guillen. She did worry about him, though. Rachel hadn't had someone who loved her that way, when she'd been held captive at the palace. And while Soren's torture wouldn't be the same with his own sister, she had no doubt Kaylah was enduring something at his hand. Eric had to be hiding a world of pain. She also worried how it would affect the network if Kaylah didn't make it out. Eric wasn't the oldest member, but he was pretty central to the human side of Unitas. How long would he stick around if she was gone for good?

Trying to force it out of her mind, Rachel took a shower and lay down, carefully setting her knife and jade earrings on the bedside table. Despite the lack of Green Lands energy, and how cold the empty bed was without Guillen, the comfort of being in the human world afforded her quick rest. The nightmares came, but she didn't seem to disturb anyone during the night. Instead, she woke with sore teeth. She shrugged it off. At least she didn't have to be ashamed in front of the others.

Leaving her room, earrings back in place, dressed in fresh clothes, Rachel was surprised to be the first up. She'd gone to bed first, but it was already pretty late in the morning. A note from Eric on the kitchen table caught her eye.

Stayed up late chatting. Muffins on the counter, juice, anything you want. Save some room for bacon when I wake up.

She poured herself a tall glass of orange juice and sat in the living room, peeking out the blinds. There was a different car parked outside, a change of security detail. After waiting awhile, it was time to do some healing. The self-injuries had to go first; she couldn't handle any more questions. Since the Ivy cuts were in the same area, she cleared them up at the same time. She'd recharged enough that her glowing hands took care of the task without leaving her too drained.

Eric finally got up, clearly wiped out. He stumbled his way to the kitchen, a good host in a comforting refuge. If memory served Rachel right from her experience in a similar safe house months earlier, he wasn't a half-bad cook, either.

"How late did you stay up?" she asked as he reached for a pack of bacon in the fridge.

Eric yawned. "I think around four?"

"Holy crap! Were you talking with Catrina the whole time?"

"Yeah. She's pretty golden." He tore the plastic open. "I think she could be a great ally for Unitas. And she's lived an interesting life. You guys should chat sometime."

"Yeah. Maybe someday when I see her again, we'll have time for that." Rachel pulled out plates to set the table.

As the bacon finished cooking, Catrina emerged from her room.

"Hi, Rachel. You're looking better." She smiled warmly, then turned to Eric. "Is that smell the stuff you were telling me about?" She closed her eyes and breathed deeply.

Eric and Rachel laughed. "It'll blow your mind."

He set a plate of bacon down, and offered to make up anything else he had on hand, but Rachel declined; she'd be fine with anything premade, particularly with how tired he was.

The three of them sat around the kitchen table and munched on the bacon, nibbled on some muffins.

Rachel turned to Eric. "When do you think we could call me a ride to get back to the cave?"

Catrina furrowed her brow. "You're leaving so soon?"

"Yeah. I'm not really very helpful here. I should get back and see how I can help with our camp and Kaylah's rescue."

"I just... I wanted some more time," Catrina confessed.

"With me?" Rachel picked up another piece of bacon. "We can chat a little, and I'm sure we'll be able to talk some other time."

"No. I mean..." Catrina looked at Eric. "I want to go."

Rachel shook her head. "No. You two are meant to stay here. Guillen trusted me to bring you here. Where would you even go?"

"Give me more time today to talk to my mother. She doesn't have to believe in your cause. She just has to be willing to help the right family members, and care enough for her kingdom. She grew up in that palace, before the newest renovations. I think she could help."

Rachel froze, midchew. She hadn't given that a single thought. If nothing else, if Lady Vera was willing to provide insider information ... that could be *immensely* useful. Rachel wasn't a fool. Lady Vera couldn't be trusted, so she'd still need to stay with Eric for safekeeping. But if she could be useful in some way...

"That's a hard sell," Rachel said. "But I can give you a few hours to talk to her. She's still in your room?"

Catrina nodded. "And I know I'm not really useful, but I want to come."

Rachel sighed. That wasn't what Guillen had asked her to do.

Eric raised his eyebrows with a gentle glance at Rachel. "It might be safer to split up the heirs, anyway. Just in case. I understand they've increased camp security since…" He looked down and bobbed his head. "Just … I think your leaders would agree it's for the best."

"Please?" Catrina begged. "I want to help."

Rachel read her expression. Guillen's eyes were framed by Catrina's kind face. Rachel considered her plea to come with her. Eric had a good point.

"If you come, realize you may have a guard escort everywhere," Rachel warned. "Go see if you can reason with your mom, and we'll talk about you coming."

Catrina piled a plate with half of the bacon, and shoved another slice into her mouth, thanking them and bounding up the stairs to her room. It was by far the least ladylike thing Rachel had seen her do thus far.

Eric chuckled. "Should I make more? I forget to make an extra pack when we have bacon virgins in the house."

Rachel pointed at him, equally amused. "You know what, I'd normally turn you down, but I think I could use some extra bacon to make things better. Got any chocolate for breakfast, too?"

"Ooh … chocolate for breakfast." He put up his hands. "I won't judge. I've got hot chocolate, chocolate bars, and chocolate ice cream. What'll it be?"

A flashback to the Ivy pub imparted a bitter taste in her mouth. *'What'll it be?'* Had Guillen been so upset because his mom had a drinking problem? Whether or not that was the case, it had been a stupid mistake.

"Never mind on the chocolate." She forced a smile. "Let's just do the bacon."

While Rachel impatiently waited for Catrina to work her magic, she reflected on the first time she'd been in a safe house like this, with Saff, and how the roles had been reversed in a way. She was in charge this time, instead of Saff.

Catrina was a good egg; Rachel could feel it. If, heaven forbid, Kaylah didn't make it out, Rachel imagined skipping over Lady Vera and forcing Soren out of the palace, then putting in Catrina as their new queen. Of course, it was a little morbid, mentally plotting the imaginary assassination of your love's mother … so Rachel moved on from that line of thinking.

As the day stretched on, Rachel finished off her healing. The huge bruise around her neck would draw unwanted attention. She took some time to call her human mom, Samantha, which was a godsend. She didn't tell her about any of the traumatizing events, or about her mission in any sort of detail, but she told her about the man she loved. It helped. The conversation was only tainted by the reminder that, like Eric, her human mom would never get to meet Guillen. But at least her mom was still safely in Unitas custody, one less person to worry about.

Catrina finally emerged from their room by early evening. "She's ... stubborn. A little more time?"

Rachel shook her head. "I need to go. If she changes her mind, Unitas can reach out to us on the other side."

Catrina looked hesitant. "And me?"

"You really want to go?"

She nodded. "I want to see what it's like, what Guillen is risking his life for. And maybe I could come back and share that with my mother."

Rachel relented. "Alright. Let's do that."

Eric had been kept up-to-date on their cave trials, and shared the details with Rachel while they waited for a Unitas escort to pick the girls up. So far, it seemed neither Seeder nor Ivy had found a way to do more than one round trip a day. They still had energy stores to be able to use their other abilities, but something kept them from being able to expend it all on multiple rift trips in a short amount of time. The effects of fatal root rot on the Seeder women, associated with frequent travel to the human world, were still unknown. Though, as Saff had experienced months prior on her second visit in one year to the human world, it didn't seem cumulative.

Their ride pulled up, and they said their goodbyes. Rachel sat in the back with Catrina. This would be Rachel's first time leaving the human world through a cave. She appreciated the ease of it, and not having to rely on an Ivy.

After a short meeting with the Unitas supervisor, Rachel and Catrina were given permission to return to the Unitas camp, but only through a Seeder-created rift made by one of the guards, to ensure neither of them 'accidentally' rifted somewhere they ought not to.

Catrina was in obvious awe at the concept of cave rifting.

Crossing through the rift, Rachel breathed in the energy of the Green Lands, glad to be free of worry of root rot, glad to be back to work.

With a guard in tow to accompany them, Rachel's first order of business was to find Saff. They made their way up the canyon wall with the rope ladders that had been constructed to aid Ivies, and Seeders without powers, up to camp.

Camp had grown and changed so much since Rachel had last seen it, but Saff's training was in the same place, more or less. Saff immediately dismissed her training class and ran up to hug Rachel.

"You're back! All in one piece!" she breathed in relief.

Devin was working nearby and greeted Rachel as well. She introduced Catrina, and Devin offered to take her on a tour so Rachel and Saff could talk about official business.

There hadn't been any news on Kaylah yet. Unitas was still talking about strategies. Saff broke the news to Rachel that another one of the girls at the palace had died. Rachel hardly reacted. Those girls had to be so drugged up and drained at that point ... they died from exhaustion, and had probably died inside long before that. Unitas didn't just need to rescue the last remaining Seeder girl, or Kaylah, from the palace. They needed a swift and final strike. Especially with the War Vines being weaker now with only one Seeder girl powering them.

"Why don't we just take our armies and march over there?" Rachel asked. "We still have the numbers..."

❀

Saff sighed. "It's ... too risky."

Rachel's shoulders slumped, and Saff had a pretty good guess as to how she felt. Rachel had been one of those girls stuck in the palace, enduring torture every day. And she was unfailingly loyal to Kaylah. But it wasn't that simple. The Mother Vines created a protective border around the expansive palace grounds. Even if the War Vines had never been created, the Mother Vines were a formidable barrier. Add to that the whispers who hardly anyone knew about... Ginger had clarified to Saff that the mythological rumors of possible powers held by whisper rifters had obviously been exaggerated. Even the Seeder leaders balked at the claims that one of those men blessed with the gift could possess the strength of five men. None of the whispers in Unitas were even twice as powerful as their regular Ivy counterparts, but they *did* exhibit more strength. Marching Unitas and a large portion of the Seeder army across the Green Lands would leave the severely damaged Seeder borders too vulnerable.

They needed something more.

Saff pulled Rachel into another hug. "Trust that we're doing our best, okay?"

One thing she would never voice to Rachel, was some of the strategies discussed in meetings Saff had still been permitted to attend on occasion. If they could hold out long enough, and the last Seeder girl in Soren's custody died, a march on the palace would be much more feasible; the War Vines would have no one powering them. But how long would the remaining girl last? And how long would Kaylah?

"Are you going to be staying in camp?" Saff asked, pulling back.

❀

Rachel yearned to be by Guillen's side, but that was a nonstarter. For now, they were on separate paths. She choked down the ache and worry in her heart. "Yeah. How can I help?"

Saff led Rachel to a heavily guarded tent. In the middle was a large table overflowing with all kinds of books and scrolls, in various stages of aging, coated with ashes. Next to the table sat a large chest.

"How do you feel about research?" Saff asked. "Maybe you can make out something useful to figure out Kaylah's plans, or why she went missing. Maybe something we missed." Saff shook her head. "I've spent so much time training... We just..." Her voice was full of regret. "Who knows what we lost for good in the fire? Kaylah and I did a little research, but didn't really have any breakthroughs, and now..." She gestured to the wooden chest. "They just packed it all away in there. Some of the pages are super brittle, and there's no organization. It's like we're starting at square one. *Less* than square one."

Rachel frowned, the singed pages bearing the odor of fire and heartache. "Yeah. I can help."

"Awesome. I'll stop by to join you when I can. Devin and I have limited our training to teaching the newly returned girls to catch a breeze home. They're continuing their training back in their home villages, so when there's a lag in returns through the cave, I've been trying to sort out this mess."

"Do you believe the reports on Soren having her?" Rachel blurted. "You don't think she left Unitas, do you?"

Saff shook her head with certainty. "No. I've spent enough time with her now, to trust her." She bit her lip, looking down. "I've had my doubts—it could've been someone from *our* side that took her."

"Really? You think we'd do that?"

Saff scrunched her eyebrows. "Not really. I was just exploring all the possibilities. Despite any tensions in camp or meetings, I don't think our people would have done it. And the last report was from a palace insider. It doesn't sound like the Ivy people know yet that they have her. Plus, there's... Well, it's just a lot more likely that an Ivy kidnapped her."

No one had been able to explain to Rachel how they'd taken Kaylah. She didn't voice an additional concern that plagued her thoughts, not wanting to stress Saff out further. But what if their sources were all wrong? What if the 'confirmation' that Kaylah was being held at the palace had been intentionally fabricated? What if they had a double agent amongst them? What if Soren had had the foresight to plant that information with Lady Vera as well, knowing someone from Unitas might come for her? "Do you know who the information is being passed to and from?"

Saff shook her head. "Not from inside the palace. But from what I understand, your friend Jon has been doing a lot of back-and-forth with information."

Rachel smiled. He could be such a porcupine on the outside, but she'd come to see the sweet gummy bear hidden in the center.

"Do you trust him?" Saff asked.

"Of course! He and Guillen saved my life."

Saff silently nodded, obviously suspicious. "I just... I promise I've been playing nice with the other kids."

Rachel couldn't help but smile again.

"But he's pretty high on the list of suspects in Kaylah's kidnapping."

He couldn't be. Not after all he'd sacrificed to help Rachel and Kaylah, and Unitas as a whole. "Kaylah and I would trust him with our lives."

❀

Saff didn't respond. When had she and Rachel ever agreed on their suspicions? "Did Kaylah ever say something to you about Ivy queens having a weakness, or your stepdad having some kind of strength or weapon?"

Rachel's face scrunched in confusion. "What? Um..." She looked away, pensive. "No, I... No."

Tucking her hands into her pockets, and shooting another glance at the table full of books, Saff decided to let it go. She didn't even remember the suspicious wording Kaylah had used. Maybe she'd meant nothing by it, despite Saff's hopes that it had meant something that could win this war, that could explain Kaylah's disappearance.

Saff frowned. "Did you hear how many spies we've lost at the palace?"

Rachel shared a frown. "No."

"He's probably dismissed or killed off half of the palace staff, trying to weed out the disloyal ones. We might have the advantage with them struggling to find new girls to put on the Vines, but if we lose our remaining spies in the palace..." She pulled Rachel in for a tight squeeze. "Either way, I'm glad you're back." At least she had one less person to worry about now.

❀

Rachel enjoyed Saff's hug, especially given how stiff and awkward things had been on her departure from camp. She processed the fact that Soren was hunting down their spies, recalling some of their interactions from the years they'd dated. He had a temper. He was ... a bit off. *He's like a spoiled toddler having a tantrum.*

Rachel pulled back from their hug. "I'm glad you guys are okay here. And that camp's doing so well. I ... worried."

Saff swallowed hard. "It's been rough. But once they plugged the main border breach, they sent word and lots of backup." She gave a faint smile. "I'm glad to be back to helping the girls more, and helping with the research."

Rachel looked past Saff. "So, no idea at all how this is organized?"

Saff walked to the table, pointing to a couple of stacks. "I've gone through these already. Granted, that doesn't guarantee I haven't missed something... Kaylah talked about studying our jade charms, and trying to get our cave to open to the one by the palace. I wish she had figured it out before she was taken—we could really use it right now."

"I'll take a look. Maybe some fresh eyes could help. I think Catrina can be trusted; I can keep an eye on her while we work on it."

Saff hesitated. "I don't know her. So that judgment call is up to you and the new council member assigned to camp. Who knows, maybe Catrina could help with Ivy fairy tales." She chuckled.

"What do you mean?"

"Oh." Saff straightened a stack of books. "Something Kaylah said once—that Ivies have more stories about Green Lands origins. She wanted to get some books to compare, but I don't know if any of these are what she was looking for."

Rachel squinted at the stacks. Hopefully Catrina was ready for another late night.

Chapter 36

Saff ended up joining Rachel and Catrina for a late night, poring over the books and scrolls Kaylah had collected and smuggled. Questions bombarded the trio. There were several piles, dozens of bookmarks, but they had no idea where she'd left off.

They asked themselves why jade would matter, what unique properties it held. Seeders used it for energy distribution between their temple wells and border walls, and to dampen and hide their girls' blooms in the human world, to keep the process safer.

Why had they never been able to rift between different locations in the Green Lands? And why wasn't the name of the other cave working?

They studied for hours; exhaustion was setting in. Saff finally retired for the night, and Catrina's energy was waning from her previous long night of chatting with Eric.

Catrina and Rachel claimed a tent for the night. While they couldn't fully obscure Catrina's identity amidst the Ivies in camp, she did her part by styling her hair differently, and wearing Seeder clothes. They hoped she could be mistaken as a doppelganger. Despite how humble the clothing and accommodations were compared to her norm, Catrina graciously followed along with all of it. The primary condition of her permission to stay in the Unitas camp, and to participate in research, was that she would be watched at all times. They surrounded the tent with guards, and both girls slept soundly, safely.

The next morning, Rachel sat on her thinking boulder while Catrina slept in. She breathed in the freshness of the Green Lands. None other than Zeus spotted her and climbed up; she was surprised to have a visitor so early.

He looked as handsome and muscular as ever, armed with a huge smile. "I'm glad you're back! Think you'll be staying long?"

Rachel gave him a soft smile. "I don't know. I hope not. I mean ... no offense."

He chuckled, claiming a spot next to her. "Got a taste of some adventure back home, and back here is too boring now, huh?"

"Something like that. I've just got a lot on my mind."

They sat quietly for a while, side by side.

"I'm guessing you won't have any free time to ... go out anytime soon?"

She fidgeted with her hands. "You're a great guy, Zeus."

"But you're seeing someone?"

She gave him an apologetic frown. "I'm sorry, I am." She considered consoling him, explaining it had nothing to do with his lack of powers. But that kind of explanation would probably have the opposite effect. If she could love an Ivy without powers, why couldn't she a Seeder without them? And she hadn't *officially* been working with Guillen anyway—her cover story still included her spending time away from camp back in her home village, not behind enemy lines.

Zeus pursed his lips, nodding. "I, uh ... thought I saw a guy leaving your tent with you after we hugged goodbye."

"No, he..." She rubbed her face. Both of the guys she'd kissed had had the opportunity to check the other out. *Great.* "Yes. I'm dating that guy. But it wasn't like that at all. We were just friends back then, okay?"

"It's alright." Zeus nudged her. "You're a nice girl. I just didn't get enough time to win you over before you left."

She didn't dare correct him, that he'd never really had a chance with her heart. "How's the progress coming along—clearing the poison behind our borders, growing the flowers?"

"It's incredibly slow, but you have to hand it to them—these Ivy women are working long hours. Before Ivy troops cut off our land access, we'd been able to carve out a path, and a small patch of land, where my kind can survive." He beamed. "The first time in a normal village *in over a century*. A handful of them have been there for over a week without any ill effects."

"That's fantastic! I'm so proud of you guys."

"Thanks. I just kinda wish I'd been trapped over there, instead of over here." He wrinkled his nose. "Feel a bit useless now."

She could empathize, but it was encouraging to hear him stepping out of his comfort zone in his little corner of the realm. "I know they're working on reclaiming that stretch of the woods. We need both you, and more Ivies, over there to help."

After another minute of small talk, she announced that she needed to get on with her day. She stood and offered him a hug.

He accepted, then flashed her one more friendly smile. "Let me know if you need anything with what you're working on. I'm happy to help."

"Sure thing."

As she descended the boulder, she couldn't help but think about Jon. He'd left camp for recon a while back, so she wouldn't get to shoot the breeze with him again as she had before her mission. She smiled as fond memories of Jon replayed in her mind. He'd cracked a smile a time or two after she'd met his callous comments with sarcasm. He'd sacrificed love and a respected career to help Seeders, the enemy.

As much as it annoyed Rachel that Saff and their leaders questioned Ivies like Jon, she could understand that struggle. She herself had once told Guillen that she'd 'earned' her trust issues. Where did one draw the line between caution and paranoia, when they'd been hurt and betrayed?

Several yards before she reached her tent, Rachel ran into Saff.

"Sorry I can't join you," Saff said. "I really need to get back to my girls. But come find me if you need anything, okay?"

"Definitely. No problem."

Saff tilted her head to the side. "Before I head over, I just wanted to see how you're doing. We didn't get to catch up much. You seem different."

Rachel playfully tucked a fist under her chin. "Is that good or bad?"

Saff laughed. "Good. I think. More mature."

"Thanks. I guess. There were some ... uh ... intense moments while I was out there. I'm sure it would help to talk about it, but it's too much to unpack right now."

Saff gave her a warm smile. "I'm here for you, when you're ready."

Rachel scooped her into a hug. "I really appreciate it. It was rough."

✳

"That guy you went with, Guillen. Did he keep up his end of the bargain and keep you safe? Did he treat you right?" Saff released Rachel, eyeing her. Her worries about Rachel had only increased after hearing how much Soren was hunting for spies. And once Kaylah had gone missing, she feared Soren might torture information out of her, like the fact that Rachel was roaming around in his own kingdom.

As far as Rachel was concerned, she still blamed herself for the attack on Guillen and herself. "Yes, he kept me safe." She couldn't hide a longing grin as she felt her earrings, as the weight of his knife rested in her pocket. "He treated me right. He helped a lot."

Saff crossed her arms. "I've seen that look before. I'm guessing Zeus's visit wasn't to rekindle something?"

"No. Definitely not. I know you don't like that Guillen's an Ivy. But I love him."

Saff rocked her head back and forth. "Well, I guess I've done some growing up of my own while you were away. The more time I've spent with decent Ivies, the more I've found myself caring about them. I still need to introduce you to my sparring partner, Flora." Saff poked Rachel in the arm. "But if Guillen's really worthy of you, then I might be okay with you two being together."

Rachel dramatically wiped her brow. "Phew! Now that we have *your* approval, I'll bring him home for dinner sometime."

Saff gave her a wink and headed out.

Rachel returned to her tent.

Catrina sat on her cot, dressed for the day. "I wasn't really sure what to do with you gone, since there are all of those guards outside. And you need to be there for any of the research."

"I'm so sorry! I should have left a note or instructions or something. Are you up to doing more reading?"

Catrina was happy to have something to do. They looked at the stacks of books and each picked one to focus on. Only a few minutes in, Catrina spoke up. "What do you suppose this means? She had a bookmark at this page."

Rachel looked. "Oh, that. The jade charms we use, when we're going through our bloom—they prepare them for us, and it helps so the change isn't so hard in the human world. I guess we don't really need them over here, so maybe someday when the poison is cleared up, and our girls don't have to flee to the other world, they'd be obsolete."

"What do you mean by 'prepare' them? Is that what these symbols mean?"

Rachel furrowed her brow, studying the page. "Maybe. Honestly, I've never asked about how they're prepared. If you think it matters, we could ask."

Catrina shrugged. "I don't know. Doesn't hurt to find out."

"Okay, well…" They could ask the guards outside, but Rachel would rather work with those she knew well. "Let's go ask Devin."

They grabbed the book and headed to Devin's training area. He readily gave them a minute of his attention.

"How do you prepare our charms when you spot our bloom?"

Devin straightened his shirt. "We bring over jade from the Green Lands. I'm not sure if the stuff from the human world would work, too. But we take some of ours, shape it into a smaller stone, and then carve the sun symbol, like the one here." He pointed to a drawing in the book. "You have to place it against your skin for it to work."

"It's just that simple? Carve it and wear it? What about these symbols? Do those mean anything to you?"

He shook his head. "No, sorry. I don't know the old symbols."

Rachel pursed her lips. "Let me see. Kaylah talked a little bit about how to pronounce them. Ex-pe-dee-oh?"

Devin's eyes lit up. "Yeah, expedio. I've heard that referenced. I guess I forgot that part. Before the jade leaves the Green Lands, the matriarchs transfer energy into the stones. That's something they say in the process. I've never seen it done, but I've heard about it."

Rachel loved learning all of the neat tidbits of her Seeder culture, but still didn't see how this helped. "Okay. So … jade. From here. Energy, the right word, the right carving, skin contact. And it controls the energy?"

"Sounds about right."

"What about the other symbol on this page?" It was a swirl. She read the description. "I think this one is labeled 'cogo.'"

He scratched his chin. "I don't know. Sorry. I've never seen it used or heard that word."

Not the breakthrough they'd hoped for. "No problem, thanks for your help." They said goodbye, and the girls started strolling back to the research tent. Rachel stopped, turning to ask one last question. "When you say Seeder matriarch, you're talking about a mother, right? A fully-rooted woman? Not just any of us?"

"Yeah."

Rachel and Catrina returned to the tent. If they were looking for a needle in a haystack, maybe this meant something, even if it was just a small part of the equation.

"Unitas is Latin." Rachel attempted to bring Catrina up to speed. "Maybe cogo is, too. What I wouldn't do for the internet right now."

Catrina gave her the same kind of confused look Guillen sometimes did.

Rachel smiled. "You should spend some time in the human world; it would really open your eyes. The internet is a place to look up information. Anyway, cogo ... and the symbol, it's just a basic sun and swirl."

"Maybe it's as simple as it seems." Catrina drew in the air with a finger. "The sun radiates; the rays shoot out from the center. The swirl keeps it in, so maybe it stops it from leaking?"

Rachel wrinkled her nose, skeptical. "I don't know about that. Everyone talks about the charms we get 'suppressing' or 'dampening' our energy. Doesn't that mean it's keeping it in? Bottled up so it doesn't leak out? That would mean the sun keeps it in."

Catrina plucked up a new scroll, carefully laying it flat on the table. "I could be wrong."

Rachel spent a painful amount of time finishing that book and the next without any seemingly useful clues.

Lunchtime rolled around, and they could both stand to stretch their legs and grab a bite. Rachel and Catrina, accompanied by two guards, strolled to the rudimentary camp kitchen next to the garden. They basked in the sun at a picnic table, munching on a platter of jicama and asparagus with an herb dip.

Catrina people-watched as they munched. Rachel's curiosity got the better of her. Guillen still hadn't talked all that much about his childhood, but he'd obviously felt awkward talking about having grown up with privilege. "What was it like growing up with servants?"

"Umm..." Catrina met her gaze, having just grabbed another jicama stick. "Well, I don't really know what it's like to *not* have them." She dunked her jicama into the herb dip. "Guillen said it was a bit hard to transition to living without them." She looked down shyly, her voice hushed. "Then again, he wasn't treated the same growing up because he wasn't an heir, and because, well, you know. And then when he moved to those communities..."

Trying not to frown, Rachel grabbed another steamed asparagus spear and took a bite. "He loves you."

Catrina gave her a soft smile. "He's a good big brother." After another bite, Catrina hesitantly added, "And what my mother said about, well, back at our manor, the baby thing... It wasn't his." She snapped a jicama stick in half. "You looked pretty shocked when my mother brought that up."

Rachel studied her plate. "Thanks. I believe him." She still felt cruddy for questioning him, for getting jealous, for giving his abuser a second of credibility before allowing him an explanation. She still didn't know the whole story, but Guillen had honestly been the slower one to open up about his past struggles in detail. If she couldn't trust him, who could she?

For the rest of their lunch, they chatted about lighter topics, mostly surrounding new cuisine Rachel had tried in the Ivy Kingdom, and which dishes Catrina thought she ought to try someday. While the textures used in Seeder cuisine were more to Rachel's liking, the spices Ivies used were incredible.

Fully recharged and ready to tackle more books, they moseyed toward the research tent. On their walk back, Rachel couldn't resist the call of a specific tent in the distance, blackened and abandoned.

"Can we take a look at Kaylah's tent?"

The guard shrugged. "Sure."

The closer they walked, the more knives twisted in Rachel's gut. The tan fabric draped from sturdy wooden poles. A third of the fabric had burned away. The guard explained its surprisingly messy state. To put out the flames, dirt had been shoveled onto it. Once they'd extracted the valuable books and scrolls, the remains of the tent had been doused with water for good measure. Mud coated the outside of the tent.

Rachel and Catrina ducked inside. There was a thick layer of dried mud in here, too.

"There's nothing of value in there," the guard said.

Scanning the tent, Rachel easily confirmed that. Kaylah's cot was missing, as well as the table and chest—everything had been removed with the exception of a water bottle and a singed blanket half-stuck in the mud.

"Where's her stuff?" she asked.

"Other than the research, her personal belongings are being kept in Arcadia."

Rachel nodded absentmindedly. "And we're sure—"

"Nothing that would help with your research."

Sighing, she sat on the dirt floor, tucking her knees under her chin. What had run through Kaylah's mind when it all happened? Had she been panicked? Had they started the fire when she was still inside? Was she still alive right now?

Catrina stood with her hands folded in front of her. She surveyed the roof, a good portion of it missing, allowing daylight to fill the area. "It's weird to imagine she's our queen now, and that she was living in a place like this." She reached out and touched the fabric of the tent. "Granted, I'm sure it looked a lot better a few days ago."

Lost in thought, Rachel drew the Unitas symbol in the dirt. That was one of the things she loved about Kaylah, wasn't it? She had her own kingdom, but wasn't above roughing it in a tent. Between her looks, wit, and position, she could have had her pick of *any* suitor in her kingdom, but had fallen in love with a 'lowly' human. Kaylah had become a beacon of hope—not just for Seeders; she was already a woman of the people for Ivies. She'd never be the kind of ruler to harshly dictate and be unrelatable.

But could it be enough? Wistfully, Rachel drew a heart around the Unitas symbol. While her mind jumped to Guillen and his tattoo, her heart actually reached out to his people in that moment. What if Rachel should have gone back to Ivy territory to keep up their campaign? Perhaps she still could... What if their mission could do more than slow Soren's attacks and prepare for a smoother transition when Kaylah took her place on the throne? What if they could get the Ivies to actually revolt and take Soren down? Not a ragtag group of dissenters in Unitas, but the whole kingdom?

It was a wish. A dream. Unitas was already campaigning in regular towns, much like Rachel and Guillen had done in stunt communities. Combatting Soren's propaganda was too tall a task to expect a full-on revolution in time for Kaylah and the last Seeder held captive in the palace to come out of this in one piece.

Resigned to that, Rachel took one last contemplative look around the tent. Wanting a piece of Kaylah with her, no matter how silly it seemed, she grabbed the neglected water bottle and then reached down for the ruined blanket. Perhaps she wouldn't take the blanket back to her tent with her, but tidying up the spot a little felt more respectful.

A good chunk of the blanket was buried in mud. Rachel tugged on it, but it didn't budge. After handing the water bottle to Catrina, Rachel grasped the blanket with both hands, moving energy to her biceps and fingers. She yanked it. The mud resisted giving up its captive, though Rachel was stronger. She had it almost all out when she discovered the real weak point—the blanket itself. With one last pull, the blanket ripped. Before Rachel could react to commune with the wind and catch herself, she landed on her back. Without skipping a beat, she laughed.

"You okay?" Catrina looked down at her, wide-eyed.

Rachel nodded. "Super graceful, right?"

Catrina wore a grin. "Something like that. Maybe you *are* right for Guillen. He was a bit clumsy growing up."

It was hard to imagine that, given his skill level with blades, but Rachel loved hearing anything that had to do with him. She pointed at Catrina. "I like having you around. I expect to hear all of the dirt you can give me." She stood, brushing off her backside. "Speaking of dirt..."

Rachel folded the sad blanket, then knelt down to get a better position for the shred left in the mud. Another quick tug freed it, and to her shock and surprise, it freed something else. Something that had been buried in the corner of the blanket, under inches of soil and mud—a scroll.

"Hey!" Studying it with narrow eyes, Rachel tried to piece together the information on it. Luckily, it had been buried deep enough for the ink to be preserved. The scroll had a few drawings on it. One of those drawings included the sun symbol she and Catrina had been researching earlier. "Hmm."

"What is it?" Catrina asked.

This scroll had modern English on it, making it easier to sift through. It described the blooming process, the different changes the Seeder girls went through in the human world. Rachel hadn't knowingly experienced many of them—her bloom had been completed peacefully with the jade charm on. But a lot of it sounded like it had come right out of Saff's journal. The pain, the surging energy, and the inevitable coma, if the charm wasn't used at all. A diagram showed the human body with wavy lines coming from it. After scouring the entire scroll, Rachel finally realized how the charm worked. It wasn't like she'd imagined. It didn't just bottle up the energy to cloak it.

It's like a balloon.

Not that a Seeder girl would physically pop like a balloon—that was both gruesome and silly to consider. But the intensity and pressure of their powers coming in, the magnified energy, was all too much when blooming in the human world. It caused them to overload. The sun charms slowly 'let out some of the air.' They dispersed some of the energy. Rachel shook her head. Of course it meant that. Kaylah had already explained the trade-off when using those charms in the first place. She'd described the negative side effect as 'dulling their ultimate potential.'

Some of that dispersed energy, once siphoned off to protect them during their bloom, was gone for good.

"You're right," Rachel said, meeting Catrina's gaze. "The sun sends some of the energy out, so the swirl probably keeps it in."

Catrina's lips twitched into a triumphant grin.

"You can say it. 'I told you so.'"

Catrina's smile grew. "That would be undignified of me. I'll just leave it at 'you're welcome.'"

Rachel rolled her eyes, wearing a smile of her own. "Come on, let's get back to work."

Heading back to their study tent with the scroll and water bottle, Rachel found renewed hope.

The swirl keeps energy in. Or... maybe concentrates it? Condenses it? But why would we condense energy?

Ducking back into the tent, she set the new scroll aside and kept searching for clues. By the time dinner approached, Rachel knew exactly what she needed to do, if for no other reason than to shut her curiosity up.

"I know we just got here, but how about we make a super quick trip back to Eric's? You can see if your mom's had a miraculous change of heart."

Catrina was willing to follow Rachel around on the adventure. Nathan and the other guards in the human world were surprised to see them back so soon, and rushed them to Eric's place at Rachel's request.

"What's up?" Eric asked as they sat down in the living room of the safe house. "They didn't give me any updates."

"Nothing yet. But..." Rachel scrunched her face. "I need to ask you some personal questions." She made sure Catrina had already gone upstairs, so she and Lady Vera couldn't overhear.

"Okaaay..." Eric said.

"You and Kaylah. I know she has a lot of grand ideas about what she wants. One includes bringing our unbloomed girls home. They're essentially humans. Has she ever talked about that with you? It's... I just wondered ... what you guys had in mind for your relationship when this is all over..."

"It's a pipe dream." A sad longing tinged his voice. "Their stories talk about humans discovering the Green Lands centuries ago. So, we hoped we could find a way in. But I think that's even more complicated than your unbloomed Seeders, because all of you were at least born with that in your genes—the energy. Or hatched, or whatever, over there."

Rachel sat straighter, silently putting the pieces together. "You're right. Our powers are latent, dormant, we Seeder women. You don't think that..." She asked for his phone and did a quick search. "Cogo. Condense. We might waste some time, or we might make history! Do we always have a human stationed at the cave for security?"

He furrowed his brow in confusion. "Yes. Always, at least one of each of our kinds."

"Great. I'll be in touch." She radiated her excitement.

Their driver prepared to take Rachel and Catrina back to the cave. Unfortunately, Catrina hadn't made much progress with her mom, though they couldn't expect too much. Now that Catrina had been in camp, the Seeder guards at the safe house wouldn't allow her to speak unsupervised with Lady Vera, fearful she might pass secrets to her and they'd somehow make their way to Soren's forces.

As soon as Rachel and Catrina got back to the Green Lands, they went straight to Zeus's garden—he'd been bummed out by not being able to help more right now, and his village wasn't all that much farther from the cave than camp was.

"Well, hello!" he said, setting down some pruning shears.

"Sorry, I'm in a rush, and you said you'd be willing to help if I needed it."

"Yeah, anything."

"I need jade, someone that can carve it, a matriarch, and ... you, if you're willing to try something out." Rachel grinned, her hope building.

Chapter 37

They rapidly put together everything Rachel needed for her experiment. Her mind was running a mile a minute, feverishly connecting the dots, seeing the chain reaction this discovery could cause. Jade was blessed with energy by a Seeder matriarch, using the newer word 'cogo.' The swirl was carved into it. All they had to do was see if Zeus had latent energy—the son of a being with powers, sprouted in a world full of energy.

Rachel brought Zeus and Catrina to the cave entrance the next day, practically bouncing on the balls of her feet. "Okay, I think just holding it will be fine, but hold it tight in your hand, so the symbol makes contact with your skin at all times while you're going through."

"You really think the swirl symbol would work for him?" Catrina asked. "I still think the sun symbol would better fit your theory. If he has hidden energy, wouldn't you want to use the sun one to draw it out? Not make it hide more?"

Rachel sighed, now starting to doubt herself. "I was thinking maybe his energy is already dispersed in his body, and it needs something to pull it together, to make it stronger. Maybe even drawing in external energy?"

Catrina shrugged, and Rachel continued.

"Well, we have this one made, and we came all the way out here. Let's try it first." Her personal blooming necklace was still in South Fortinda where she'd left it, but if this didn't work, Saff would probably loan hers, or they'd get another one made up.

Zeus glanced between the girls warily. "You're really not all that sure what's going to happen?"

"I, uh... Well..." Rachel hesitated. Saff had endured pretty significant pain when experimenting with her powers and rifting. But Saff had also once posed a rather curious question about green-folk abilities—about whether green folk could sense the energy within each other. They'd dismissed the idea a while back, because Saff's close call had been with an Ivy assassin *before* she began her bloom. But Kaylah had commented that maybe some people could sense that hidden energy better. Maybe they were right?

Rachel looked Zeus over. Just like any of the guys with powers, he was once a seedling, one who had sprouted like any other Seeder. But once he grew into more of a standard human form, any uniquely Seeder abilities ceased. He was like any unbloomed girl, but his abilities had been stunted. She cringed just thinking of that label, but there had to be something inside him still.

"I'm confident you'll be fine." She hesitated once more with added guilt. "You'll probably just keep walking, like all the girls that have experimented at this cave, when they've tried to go more than once in a day. None of them experienced anything harmful, but I wouldn't blame you if you didn't want to go."

He puffed out his chest. "I want to go. Just wondering if I should have thought up some clever last words, just in case."

Rachel gave him a smile. "I'll be right behind you."

While Ivies could only form a rift for themselves, or make it large enough to accompany a linked female Seeder, Seeders had always been able to form a rift for more than just themselves. Brothers and fathers accompanying their girls home did it all the time in the air. Rachel surmised that all Zeus needed was this charm and someone else to open the doorway for him. She stepped forward and opened a rift in the air at the cave entrance.

He took a deep breath and walked forward—disappearing from sight.

Rachel squealed, throwing a glance at Catrina. They shared a smile. "I won't say anything undignified," Rachel said.

Catrina giggled and remained with her guards while Rachel quickly followed after Zeus.

Rachel was greeted on the other side by half a dozen guards and an extremely stunned Zeus. She bit her lip and tears came to her eyes. "We did it! We really did it! Zeus: Welcome to the human world!" She jumped up and down and gave him a hug. "I promise you'll get the charm back to go home, but let me try something first."

"Okay…" He handed her the stone, and she asked the guards for a human volunteer. Maybe, just maybe, there was latent energy in these humans no one knew about. They opened a rift at the cave entrance, and the human volunteer walked forward—and kept walking.

She frowned. "Okay. I knew that one might be more of a long shot. Thank you for being willing to try."

She handed the charm back to Zeus and rubbed her temples. Humans couldn't do it. At least not this easily. But Seeders without powers, they could! Bringing back unbloomed girls was still irresponsible—they had nowhere to take them with how slow the poison cleanup was, and they couldn't contribute to their own safety. But this discovery, in and of itself, could win them the war. This was the thing that was going to tip the balance.

She asked to borrow a cell phone and called Eric. Despite the Seeders' caution with Eric after Kaylah went missing, he was still a strong ally. He was tech-savvy and had been one of the first humans in Unitas. His work was monitored more closely by Unitas, but he continued to help with their programming, hacking, and tracking efforts. Eric picked up the phone after a couple of rings.

"Do we have any that have *started* the blooming process," Rachel asked, "that would be ready to go home tonight or tomorrow?"

"Uh ... maybe? Did ... you figure it out? They can't go through that kind of pain by just taking off their charms to finish the change; you know that."

She was still grinning ear to ear. "I haven't figured out humans. But I can get Seeder girls home, without the pain."

He agreed to reach out to his contacts; he'd send someone over to the camp once he could find anyone willing and able.

It was getting late, so Rachel escorted Zeus back home. She asked him to do whatever was necessary to have several more charms just like it made up, ASAP. She needed to run back and talk to Saff and Devin, but before she could go, Zeus grabbed her hands.

"Thank you, Rachel. I know this means a lot to our people, but it means something personal to me, too. It opens a whole new world of possibilities." His eyes and smile were trained on her. "I knew we were meant to meet for a reason."

She squeezed his hands. "Then I'm glad you got the honor of being the first. In this world or that one, you're bound to meet the right girl for you. You've got a lot of potential." She gave him a bear hug.

She ran off to Saff and Devin's tent to share the update, leaving Catrina at their sleeping tent along the way. Both Saff and Devin were excited to hear the news. They realized the implications, if they could actually get partially-bloomed girls back faster. So far, only fully-bloomed girls could rift, even with the new cave rifts. But if they came back earlier... It took almost as much time for a tempered bloom to happen, as it did for them to train and rift. They'd cut their time in half. They could have twice as many girls with energy returning, quickly!

After a few minutes of excited chatter with Saff and Devin, Rachel returned to her tent, apologizing for leaving Catrina alone. Catrina had been supportive, but not exactly giddy about this discovery after Rachel and Zeus returned to the Green Lands. Rachel hadn't expected it to be a big deal for Catrina. It really didn't mean as much to her, personally. But, in a way, it did.

"Do you think it would work for Ivies without powers, too?" Catrina asked.

"I ... don't know. I know some of our stuff works across species, but not everything. Maybe..."

Catrina gave her a hesitant smile. "I'd love for Guillen to be able to go somewhere new. Start fresh. Not have people hate him."

Rachel frowned, an image playing through her mind of Guillen leaving her to follow his dreams of spending time with humans. "Yeah. We'll definitely try it when we get a chance. Let's head to bed."

It took Rachel eons to fall asleep. Between the adrenaline and her thoughts ... it didn't come easy. She thought of Kaylah, praying she was alright, and wishing she could share the news of their accomplishment. She thought of Guillen, and the implications of the discovery she'd just made. Catrina was right—he deserved a chance at human life. Even if the war was won in a day, it would take *years* for his society to alter their ways. He shouldn't have to wait a single day to be treated fairly. And if Magda and Lady Vera were any indication of the way people felt ... they would have a rough go at it, trying to have a relationship publicly.

Rachel's heart sank. He loved her—he would choose Rachel. She couldn't go live with him over in the human world. Nothing in their research had indicated any changes to that knowledge of their limitations. But could she be so selfish as to ask him to stay...

Shortly after she finally found sleep, Rachel was woken by a messenger.

"Sorry, Eric thought you'd want to know right away. He said he'll have two waiting nearby, in the morning."

Excitement entered the tent, while any hopes of sleep exited. She volunteered to help patrol the camp during the night, to keep busy. When it was barely dawn, she went to Saff's tent.

Saff emerged, yawning. "You know, Rachel, I love you, but sometimes a woman just wants to spend some more time with her husband in the morning."

Rachel blushed. She may not be married, but she knew that desire. "Sorry... I've been up all night and couldn't wait."

"Why all night?" Saff scrunched her eyebrows. "You're already worn down from a round trip yesterday. Sit down, crazy woman."

Rachel chuckled. "That's exactly it—I can't go. It hasn't been a full day for me. But I picked up a second charm from the craftsmen, and I need someone to take them through. The girls should be there any time."

Saff smiled warmly. This would be her second trip through the new cave, and the first time alone. "I'd be honored."

Rachel paced impatiently. Catrina joined her at the cave, much calmer than Rachel. "They're probably just taking a while to get there, even with those cars."

Rachel cupped her hands over her mouth once Saff arrived with two girls. The girls' faces were plastered with the usual amazement of first-timers to the Green Lands. They were promptly ushered to camp, where Devin was waiting for them.

The girls sat on a pair of chairs, clearly intimidated to be in a new place, with new people and a growing audience.

❋

"Hi, I'm Devin. We're all excited to get to know you. They told you about the change and everything, right?"

The girls nodded. One had been wearing the charm for a month already, the other, just a few days. Saff was now holding on to their original charms—they'd had to take them off so the new ones would work for a rift. It could take hours for them to really feel sick, as she recalled from her own unfortunate blooming. She prayed they were right about it being different back home in the Green Lands.

Within no time, the girls' eyes, hair, and skin began to glow. The one who had been further along in her blooming changed faster.

"This is how it's supposed to be, right? This is okay?" one asked, fear growing in her eyes.

"You're not hurting?" Devin asked.

"No..."

"Then you're just fine." Devin shared anxious glances with Saff, then offered the girls water to drink, in case it could help. He'd only ever actually seen the change in his wife, midway through the process, and it had been brutal. The fact that these girls were this lit up, so quickly, and feeling *nothing*…

A half hour into the change, the one who was farther along was so bright that the observers were beginning to squint. Almost as quickly as the change started, it faded away. Once she was down to just yellow hair and glowing green eyes, Devin coached her about channeling her energy—from her heart to her hand. A ball of light rested in the palm of her hand. He then asked permission to access it. Devin hovered his hand over the girl's and flicked his wrist at the ground. The darts produced were phenomenal. *Every* Seeder who had gathered to watch now stood with their mouths open.

"Wow," Devin whispered in reverence.

❋

Rachel grinned triumphantly. *Definitely more powerful than Saff, and probably anyone in living generations of matriarchs.* "Give me a couple dozen girls to bloom in the Green Lands, and we'll see how powerful they can make our walls. If that's all they do, from the safety of the temples … how many people can we spare for a march on the palace? How quickly can we end this thing?"

❋

Saff shared a knowing grin. Every risk they'd taken, every sacrifice—it had been worth it. "We need to get the word back to Eric. Let's bring them home. And make a home they can be safe in."

"I'm going to see how those charms are coming along," Rachel said.

"Rachel," Saff scolded. "Sleep."

Rachel smirked. "I'll try. First, charms."

After checking their progress on making more charms, Rachel relented and decided to give sleep another go. Catrina followed her back to their tent, not having much choice in the matter.

"Wasn't that cool?" Rachel exclaimed. "No living Seeders have gotten to see that before, but you got to." Her excitement had her almost bursting at the seams.

Catrina scrunched her face. "Yeah, I guess that was interesting."

"Not easily impressed, huh?" Rachel lay down on her cot.

Catrina fidgeted with her hands. "It … actually kind of worries me."

Rachel sat up. "Why?"

Catrina bobbed her head back and forth, easing herself down onto the edge of her own cot. "Your people are already pretty powerful. Each of our peoples have limitations, but ... what you just showed me, that looked like *a lot* more."

Rachel frowned. "They teach a lot of propaganda in history classes, even Kaylah admits that. I know your people feel like you were wronged, but we're taught differently. What the actual truth is, maybe we'll never really know. Just because we're more powerful, doesn't mean we're going to harm your people or try to take over." She considered something else Kaylah had once said, about their dirty nickname and Ivy fears of Seeder overpopulation. "I think weeds are just plants in unwanted places. That doesn't mean they're bad, or not pretty. Honey bees still like them, right? We just want to be safe and left to live our lives."

Catrina looked at the ground, digging her heel into the packed soil. "It's easy to dream like that, but power corrupts. Look at my brother, his kind. They don't have any, and they're treated like scum."

"Hey." Rachel gave her a half-smile. "I *do* think about your brother. A lot. I'm well aware he doesn't have powers. And I do. And we should be enemies. But what have I done to him or for him, with those powers?"

Catrina nodded. "I wish more people ... were like you."

That melted Rachel's heart. She wanted nothing more than to give Catrina a hug, but she had a feeling Catrina wouldn't be fond of that, not yet. "Have some faith. My people have men like that too, and we don't treat them like Guillen, right? It's not just me."

"You're right. It's actually kind of nice over here. The way people talk to, and about, each other." She threw a glance at a notebook in the corner of their tent. "Anyway, I should let you sleep. I'll quietly look over our notes again."

Rachel lay back down. "Thanks for the chat. I like you too, remember that." Her smile faded. "One last thing... We probably shouldn't mention this development to your mom. I don't imagine she'd take the 'more power' thing well."

Catrina pursed her lips, flipping open the notebook. "No. I don't imagine she would."

Rachel added that to her to-do list—make sure the new girls remained a secret. They'd already made an irresponsible display today. What if a spy let Soren know about these new girls? Even without Kaylah's help, the War Vines were primed and awaiting replacement girls to power Soren's now-shrinking advantage. He would lust after that energy. He would do anything to have it.

Chapter 38

Partially-bloomed Seeder girls trickled into the Unitas camp with increasing speed. Councils met. Plans were formed. There was finally hope on the horizon, and not just to end the last hellish year.

This would be the one to end it all.

Rachel found it hard to hear the various strategies discussed in meetings she, Saff, and Ginger were invited to, but they had to be prepared for anything. What if Kaylah didn't survive? Seeders would no longer be content to slink back to the human world with split families. And Lady Vera didn't seem like a suitable replacement once Soren was out of the picture.

They did discuss occupation, as a last resort—to do what they had to, just until peace could be organized. They talked about what they would do if Kaylah had indeed betrayed them. Either intentionally, or under duress. Her life hung in the balance.

While they couldn't implement many of the battle tactics she'd previously shared, in case they had been tortured out of her, her ideals were still on the table. They would rescue Kaylah, the Unitas leader, and continue to work with her to heal their lands and societies. The remaining Seeder girl in the palace would be saved, the War Vines destroyed.

But no matter what the results were, the means weren't pretty. The Seeders could fly to the palace, saving themselves several skirmishes along the way. But it would still take some time and require breaks, no matter what part of Seeder territory they left from. Ideally, they could fly and shoot darts, but it was nearly impossible to do so simultaneously. To add to that, despite efforts like Jacob's back in Community Ten, more and more archers were popping up in the Neutral Woods amongst Soren's forces.

Most of the Seeders' options were hand-to-hand. All of them bloody. All possible confrontations ended in significant loss of life to break through Soren's troops protecting the palace, and those crawling throughout the woods. And all it took was one scout and one tree, for Soren's troops to be alerted of Seeder movements.

Rachel stressed the cave strategy, that it gave them the element of surprise, located on the border of protected space around the palace that Kaylah had described—which made Ivy rifting near the palace impossible, and Seeder flight above it, near impossible. They could distract Ivy troops with the main attack, and then send in a smaller team much closer on foot from the cave. The council reminded her that no progress had been made on that account—they couldn't wait forever.

With Soren down from six to just one Seeder hostage powering the massive War Vines, the Seeders would be able to shift some of their focus in training and fighting, spending less time protecting their border walls.

As the council discussions came to a close, a messenger arrived.

The leader of the meeting read the latest update with a grim expression. "Their one hostage will soon turn to four."

Gasps filled the room.

She went on to explain, "One of our safe houses was compromised. They've taken three. We're not sure where they're at right now."

Rachel's jaw dropped. "Is ... you-know-who safe?" *And my mom?*

The leader nodded. Even in camp and on the council, they entrusted very few with the information about Lady Vera and Catrina. Few knew they were even in custody, or their true identities, or where they were being kept. "We're confident on that safe house for now; it's disconnected enough. But we're looking into how this breach happened."

The names of the kidnapped and their Unitas protectors—now dead—were read off. Rachel's mom was still safe. Going by the breath of air that whooshed out of Saff, she didn't recognize the names, either. She had significantly more people to be worried about after giving Unitas her and Devin's host family names to help in the cause.

Rachel could give a sigh of relief, albeit the tiniest of sighs. Though, her anxiety still rose about a breach in their safe houses at all. Soren had seemed barely competent at stepping into his parents' and uncle's shoes. But he'd just reminded Unitas how serious he was.

The leader explained the situation, that the girls were midbloom with charms on. From Rachel's experience, they didn't hook them up to the War Vines until the girls were actually rooted, which could take months ... unless they removed the charms. Her stomach churned at the torture. Could they drag someone in a coma through a rift? Would they be as efficient on the War Vines if they were in a coma?

Unitas prioritized retaking a strip of Neutral Woods between camp and Seeder borders, to allow for passage on foot again.

A quota was set. After a certain number of freshly bloomed girls returned and were trained on the walls, the march would begin. They were done waiting.

Much to Rachel's relief, word had gotten back from Guillen. He was safe—for now. She'd had a horrible nightmare about him again, two nights prior. This time, Eric was in the dream and finally let her read the contents of his private letter. In it, Guillen left her a goodbye note, in case he didn't make it out alive. It soured her whole day, and she almost stormed through the cave, just to rip the letter from Eric's hands to make sure it wasn't true.

But Guillen was safe—for now. He was busy rallying support, still undiscovered. If the cave failed, maybe Guillen could still find a way to help sneak people closer. Either way, they needed a new tactic other than just marching up to the palace. It had been breached twice already; Soren wasn't likely to let anything slip a third time. They needed a new option. They needed the help of someone who grew up in that palace.

"You're sure she won't budge? Honestly, just some kind of map would help," Rachel pleaded with Catrina on behalf of Kaylah, the Seeder girl who had been tortured there for months now, and the three new girls—she was desperate.

"No." Catrina shook her head. "She used to like Kaylah, but she doesn't support her now that she knows what she's fighting for."

Rachel bunched her eyebrows, exasperated. "So, she'd rather have Soren be a fake king?"

"No. She hates that, too."

Rachel threw her hands up in the air. "Then, what? I thought she didn't want to rule."

"Also a no."

"Well, she has to go with one of the three options, doesn't she?"

Catrina bit her lip in thought. "Honestly, I think she'd prefer *I* be queen at this point."

Rachel stopped pacing the research tent. "But doesn't that mean both she and Kaylah would have to die first?"

"No."

Rachel stared her down, eyes wide open. "What do you mean? The queen controls the Mother Vines. When Kaylah's mom died, the control went to her. It follows the matriarchal line, right? How can you skip a generation?"

"The queen can choose," Catrina stated, as though it were common knowledge. "She can abdicate and assign that power to the next in line. It can't be taken from her, and it still has to follow the line. That's why Soren can't just kill Kaylah and have his wife control them." She rocked her head side to side. "If Kaylah *did* die, which I don't want, then it would fall to my mother, but she could give it to me willingly."

Rachel drew a deep breath, more than a tad annoyed. "How is it possible no one ever mentioned that?"

"I doubt you know a lot of things about our royal ways." Catrina gently raised her eyebrows. "And I'm guessing if Kaylah never mentioned it, it's because she intends to rule."

"Would *you* want to rule, if given the choice?"

Catrina shifted in her chair. "When you're this close to the crown, you grow up imagining it. But when you're fourth in line, you know it's not likely. I would do it, but only if Kaylah weren't an option."

An idea sprouted in Rachel's mind. She and Catrina rifted over to the human world again. Catrina waited with the cave's guards while Rachel talked privately with Eric. They strolled the woods near the cave, but only after the on-duty Unitas supervisor gave her a stern and direct order to watch what she discussed with Eric.

"Thanks for coming all the way out here. I just figured it would save us some time, and I wanted to talk in person," Rachel said.

"No problem, seriously. I get stir-crazy in that place." He laughed half-heartedly. "Especially with that high-and-mighty 'guest.'"

"Yeah, sorry. She's a pill."

Eric tapped a tree trunk with his shoe as they passed. "She doesn't hate me as much as Seeders, but she still has *no* respect for a human like me. She's hopeless. I'd recommend transferring her to another safe house if she weren't such a valuable political refugee."

"Speaking of that. You're sure the network is still safe?" Rachel stopped to face him. "Those girls."

He gave her a look of dismay. "Yes. Practically no one knows where Lady Vera is. And we're adding extra security." His nostrils flared. "Plus, now that they don't have to worry about *me* being the leak..."

If that wasn't a kick-'em-when-they're-down moment, Rachel didn't know what was. The woman he loved—the woman he'd sacrificed a normal life for—was missing, probably tortured or dead right now. And *both* the Seeder and Ivy leaders of Unitas (excluding Ginger) had voted to curtail Eric's participation. Having been central in coordinating safe houses from the beginning, he was a prime suspect for the latest girls' kidnappings. Either that, or they were punishing him for the leak because they supposed Kaylah might have given information to Soren under duress, or willingly.

The fact of the matter was—Soren might have just gotten lucky. At least that was what Rachel kept trying to tell herself. It wasn't like his assassins hadn't continued roaming the human world in search of more Seeder girls.

Aching inside, Rachel tried to remember what Guillen had told her about taking too much blame on herself. "Are we doing enough to secure the caves? Could we have a traitor that would bring those girls through, bloom them over there, and then turn them over to Soren?" She'd gone over the possibilities constantly. Either Soren was planning ahead and waiting out their blooms, to force them through a rift like he had with her and the other five... Or he could force their bloom by removing the charms—she cringed at the torture that strategy involved. Or ... maybe their latest bloom discovery was known already by a spy. Maybe he knew their potential, his spies would get their hands on the charms, and they'd go through the caves. Or, worse yet, perhaps they knew by now how to make their own cave rifts.

Rachel was rattling off all of her suspicions, starting to hyperventilate.

"Rachel." Eric stopped her, holding her head in place with both hands, getting her full attention. "Calm down."

She focused on her breathing as his friendly eyes calmed her.

"First of all," he countered, "you can't stop trusting everyone. They could only make a new cave with *two* Seeders *that have their powers,* assuming they even knew how to." He stared into her eyes, as if to emphasize his logic. "And they'd need the new charms, which are *well-guarded.* Remember that Soren's family has been working on this for *years.* He's probably just waiting out their bloom here, okay?"

She swallowed hard, looking at the ground as Eric removed his hands. "They're not holding back on troops. He's serious. And you don't know him like I do. He'd force the change." She huffed and shook her head. "Heck, if they slipped into a coma from the change, then he wouldn't have to waste any poison to subdue them."

She looked up to see him frowning.

"You could be right about that," he said. "But still—we've got the cavalry out looking for them. And I refuse to believe they'd have the added benefit of a Green Lands bloom, okay?"

She nodded, conceding the fact that their cause would have to be riddled with a lot more traitors to pull that off. Soren probably didn't even know taking off their charms early gave them a boost in energy capacity, even when done in the human world, like with Saff. Unless he'd gotten information from Kaylah...

Despite fighting it, Rachel began to cry. "I miss her. I just... I'm done with all of this."

His eyes misted over as well. "Me too." He pulled her in for a hug. "We're in the final stretch; I can feel it. We'll get to see her soon enough."

She stood in Eric's arms for a couple of minutes, grateful her best friend had good taste, that she'd found someone so considerate. Rachel lingered longer—Eric needed this too. It had to be hard to be stoic through all of this, so disconnected and helpless.

When they pulled apart, she sniffled and gave him a reassuring smile. He wiped at a tear on his cheek and shoved his hands in his pockets.

"About Kaylah..." She wrung her hands. "And you... I'm going to have to dive back into sensitive territory."

He chuckled. "At this point, my life is your life. Unitas. Out with it."

"You and Kaylah. What were the plans? If she could figure out a way to get you into our realm? And if she couldn't? Did she discuss abdicating?"

Eric blew out a puff of air. "If we can figure it out, I planned to join her. I don't know what all that looks like, and we know it might be rough. Her people aren't likely to easily accept a king, or whatever I'd be, that's human. Not right away. But I have been taking college courses on politics and economics and stuff."

Rachel smiled. "Does that mean you two are engaged?"

He blushed, his eyes darting around. "Yeah. I asked. She said yes. It's just not public, for obvious reasons."

She beamed. "I'm happy for you. That's *so* great. And I know that it's helping her fight over there."

He flashed a sad smile. "Thanks. That makes me feel better."

She gave him a sympathetic frown. "And ... what were the plans if she couldn't bring you over?"

"I really don't want to think about it," he said, his tone dejected, reaching out to touch a branch on a nearby tree as they passed. "I can't imagine her leaving me, but I also couldn't forgive myself if she turned her back on her people. We toyed with the idea of reorganizing things so she played a much less significant role. So she could spend more time over here."

Rachel nodded thoughtfully before responding. That sucked. That kind of life was no couple's ideal. It was worse than being married to a trucker or pilot, because at least *they* got to enjoy each other's company at a mutual home. Kaylah was to be the queen of half of the Green Lands, and she fiercely loved her people and culture. Eric may never be able to fully be part of it. Rachel ignored the avalanche of guilt headed her way as she wished the charm that worked for Zeus had worked for humans as well.

Shaking away the cascade of negativity, Rachel transitioned to the main reason for her visit. "I brought Catrina today because I think the two of you can get Lady Vera to talk. We need to know how to get inside the palace. Every possible entrance. Especially the ones Soren wouldn't think about."

Eric lifted an eyebrow. "How?"

A grin formed on Rachel's lips. "Let's manipulate that bitch."

He poorly stifled a laugh—Rachel rarely swore.

"Catrina is *certain* that her mom would prefer Catrina ruled, out of the options available, instead of Soren, Kaylah, or even Lady Vera herself. If we can get her to think her daughter will be queen if she helps us ... we're as good as gold. Tell her Kaylah wanted to turn it over. Tell her Kaylah's dead. Tell her we changed our strategy. I don't really care. Just get me those locations."

Eric smiled. "We'll make it happen." They began walking back to their original meetup point. "What if we can't manipulate it out of her? I'm not a soldier, but plenty in Unitas are... What if we needed to ... take it further? Hurt her?"

Rachel's stomach knotted. No one liked Lady Vera, least of all Rachel. But Guillen had forgiven her on some level for her abuse in his childhood. And Eric was asking if they could rough her up? Rachel stared at her feet. "That's not really fair to ask me, you know?" She met his eyes, and he gave an understanding frown. "I'm not the one that calls the shots, though. So ... just... You didn't bring it up with me, okay?"

Eric nodded. "We'll obviously try with Catrina first."

They strolled in silence for a while. Rachel considered his question further. What was one person, compared to the millions in the Green Lands? One *rotten* person, compared to just Kaylah? Wasn't this problem still in existence because Seeders had hedged their bets for so long?

"Unofficially, Eric?"

He glanced her way.

"I didn't say 'no.'"

He nodded again, squinting with determination. "One way or another, we'll get it done."

❖

Rachel went back to Kaylah's books while Eric and Catrina sorted out Lady Vera, hopefully. She felt pulled to Kaylah's notes in particular, trying to pick up where she'd left off. Saff had said Kaylah had thought she was close to a breakthrough.

One paper had columns of names, with the first column listing all of the Seeder village names. They all ended with the same letter; Rachel had only previously thought the trend poetic. But seeing them listed on a piece of paper made it stick out. Fortinda, Siqendra, all of them—they ended with the letter *A*.

There was a column of Ivy rift locations; they ended in a different letter of the alphabet.

A third column listed human-world rift names. Again, they all shared an ending letter.

A fourth column had the names of the newly activated cave locations. Scribbled at the top of the paper were the old symbols Rachel had seen scratched into the cave wall in Ivy territory, near the palace. The translation—it ended in a different letter altogether.

Kaylah had underlined the ending letter.

Highlighted it.

Circled it.

She'd had it at the tips of her fingers, so close. She'd known it had meaning.

If the rift didn't enter or exit a known Seeder, Ivy, or human-world location ... what was the fourth option? Could there be ... another realm?

Rachel shook the idea from her head. No one had ever mentioned anything like that. No stories, no fairy tales, no history books. It had to mean this was the kind of thing they were looking for. The fourth ending meant it was intra–Green Lands. But how to work it? Nothing they'd tried had shown any promise. They'd even tried rifting to the old palace cave using the new swirl charm, hoping that was all it would take since it condensed energy, and maybe they just hadn't put enough energy into their attempted rifts.

Rachel dreaded the thought of having to find another preexisting cave that magically connected to it. Or having to create one, like those they were now using in the human world. There was no time to play around with that.

Rachel woke with a sore neck, having fallen asleep while reading. Catrina had woken her up, teeming with pride. "It took all day, but guess what my mother gave us?" She practically danced around the tent. "Let's get my cousin back!" She opened her eyes wide and added with some drama, "The one who's nice to my brother, and *much* better prepared to lead than the rest of us in the family."

Rachel chuckled, rubbing her neck with a hint of a glow to her fingers. She was beyond grateful that Catrina's 'sweet girl / youngest child / only heir' charms had worked on her mom, and that they hadn't been forced to try anything else. "That's great! Really." She cracked her neck. "Look at this page with me. I'm assuming the council has the palace plans already?"

"Yes. First thing before I came here."

"Great. Now we have to do our part. We're on the clock. This paper's about the cave. And you know Ivy fairy tales…"

Catrina looked it over, and Rachel explained what she'd surmised so far.

"Why did she draw the sun and swirl symbols?" Catrina asked, pointing to the paper.

The old language name had been written on the paper; in front of it was the sun, then a dash. Behind it, a swirl.

"I'm sure she was just doodling while trying to put it together," Rachel said.

Catrina raised her eyebrows, skeptical. "But she didn't seem to know the swirl symbol meant anything."

"You're … right…"

Rachel closed her eyes, reminding herself what that cave looked like. It had been so long ago. And it had been dark. And she'd been traumatized. And distracted by a handsome man, who was starting to distract her all over again as she remembered his distraction… She opened her eyes. "I didn't think anything of them. They were just like doodles on the cave walls. They were smaller and weren't weird like the other symbols, so I just filed them away as nothing special."

Catrina tilted her head to the side. "Anything else you forgot from the cave that you might remember now?"

Rachel tapped her fingers on the table, double-checking her memories. "No. That's it. If there's something else, I didn't notice it."

Saff popped her head in the tent. "How's it going?"

Rachel smiled. "Come join us, Miss Four-Point-Oh."

Saff chuckled, sitting down. "Those grades don't matter in the Green Lands. And my theory about using that swirl charm to get to the other cave didn't pan out. But I'm happy for a breather. What's up?"

They ran through the details with her.

"Okay." Saff nodded thoughtfully. "If the symbols mean something, maybe we just need to think the associated words before and after the location name?"

Catrina wrinkled her nose. "But the words don't mean anything without the jade, right?"

Rachel sighed. "True."

Catrina sat down between them. "You keep asking about fairy tales, our origins. Let's go over those again."

They pulled out a fairly thick book that an Ivy in Unitas had smuggled into camp for Kaylah. It was half burned. Some of the pages were completely lost, but several were partially legible, though not enough to make sense of anything.

Focusing intently on each page, Catrina read out loud the fairy tales and poems, one by one. She had to pause and correct herself several times.

"You really know those well," Rachel remarked. "Especially for having half of the pages missing."

Catrina shyly looked back down at the book. "Yeah, I spent a lot of time in my room reading as a little girl."

Saff wouldn't have known the significance of that, having never met Lady Vera, having never heard how Guillen came by the large scar on his face, but Rachel did. She would have hidden in her room a lot as a child, too, if one of her parents had been like Lady Vera.

✸

Catrina cleared her throat and continued to read the Ivy fairy tales, filling in the gaps.

The one in particular that pulled Saff in wasn't a story about how botanical beings had come to be—despite how fantastical those stories were. It took place before that—how the Green Lands had been discovered in the first place. Or more appropriately, how *rifting* had been discovered. Discovered, not necessarily created. Just like Saff with the story, green folk had been pulled in—literally.

"Green Stone, Green Land, Green Eyes—that was the order, three.
Push and Pull of the earth, like Ebb and Flow of the sea.
Rich Soil and Air shared by Green Folk, all Kin:
The Temptations and Prizes that Pulled them In."

Saff loved poetry thanks to her English classes in high school. Hearing those words, it finally made sense to Saff why normal human electronics didn't work in this realm, and why there was turbulence after passing through a Seeder rift to the human side. She smiled. "That's awesome! I think I get it."

Catrina and Rachel still seemed confused by the mysterious grand revelation.

"Green stone—Jade. It was crucial to the discovery. Like we've used it to get Zeus and our girls back. Push and Pull. The sun symbol disperses, dissipates; it *pushes*. The swirling symbol gathers, collects, concentrates; it *pulls*."

As it clicked for Rachel, a lightkeeper lit in her eyes. "It's like a friggin' magnet!"

Catrina squinted. "Like, we need one of the symbols on the special jade, on each side?"

"I think that's *exactly* it!" Saff could barely contain her excitement. "And if we want to end up at the cave by the palace, to be *pulled* there, we need someone in that cave with the right jade."

Chapter 39

Rachel agreed with Saff's suggestion that they discuss their hypothesis with Ginger, as she'd been left to pick up the pieces after Kaylah's disappearance. Ginger was doing her best to liaise.

Rachel gave Ginger a huge hug once she and Saff entered Ginger's tent. They'd hardly gotten any time to chat in passing.

"How can I help you young ladies?" Ginger asked with an exhausted, forced smile.

Rachel and Saff followed her, sitting down. They explained the need to get someone to the cave.

Ginger nodded thoughtfully. "Guillen's network is all on standby, in close proximity to the area. Once we get him—"

"No!" Rachel blurted. Visions of him lying on the ground, bleeding out, danced on her heartstrings. "Anyone but Guillen."

Ginger sat back. "Why? Kaylah trusted him to get you there and back safely."

Rachel shook her head, her chest caving in. "Your kingdom is empty. Our walls are barely even at risk of a breach again with only one girl left on the Vines. Their attacks have calmed down. Where do you think those soldiers are? Protecting Soren as he cowers in the palace. That cave is inside the ring of protection from rifting. They'll be guarding that whole perimeter he'd have to cross."

Ginger gestured at Rachel with her hands. "Isn't that why we need that cave so badly? Because it'll bypass the vast majority of Soren's defenses?"

"You're assigning him a suicide mission!" Tears pooled in Rachel's eyes. "Anyone but him. I love him."

Ginger scanned Rachel's face. "If it's not him, it's someone else's loved one. And if you love Kaylah, too, you want the best person there to make it happen."

Rachel looked down, sniffling. "He's not invincible. He almost died. I barely healed him in time."

Saff quietly reached over and squeezed one of Rachel's hands.

"Did Kaylah ever tell you when she first dedicated herself wholeheartedly to this movement?" Ginger asked.

Rachel looked up, wiping away tears. "No."

Ginger gave her a soft smile. "Or who her first recruit was? Over four years ago?"

"I have a feeling you're going to say Guillen," Rachel half breathed.

Ginger nodded. "Sometimes, I think they recruited each other. I don't know him well, but when Kaylah finally brought Nathan and me into the loop, we knew he was key in this. Guillen knows those woods and mountains likely better than anyone. He knows the risks. Let him do this."

Fighting more tears, all Rachel could muster was a whisper. "Yeah."

❋

While Saff empathized with Rachel, Ginger's logic *was* a bit of a stretch. "But ... how?" Saff asked. "Guillen's network can't be that huge, that they can bust through a line of Ivy soldiers we ourselves are afraid to take on, just to get inside that cave."

Ginger distracted herself, stacking papers on her desk and straightening them. "Like I said, he knows those mountains."

"But ... how?" Rachel echoed. "He never talked about spending time in those mountains... And when they rescued me, Kaylah made a diversion, and the palace hadn't been expecting the rescue."

Ginger still wouldn't look up. "It'll be fine. Just trust me."

Saff may not have picked up on her parents' lies to her over the years as they'd concealed her true nature as a Seeder, but she'd fine-tuned her lie detector since then. "Ginger." Her tone was threatening. "What are you hiding?"

"You always assume the worst, Saff." Ginger finally met her gaze.

"Maybe I'm just good at detecting BS. Is this something else our council would be shocked to hear if I brought it up in one of our meetings?"

Ginger's countenance turned dark. "Don't shoot yourself in the foot. You know too much already, and the only reason you're permitted into *any* planning meetings is because *I* bring you."

"I'm permitted into meetings because Kaylah started inviting me, because I'm trustworthy."

Leaning forward, Ginger looked Saff squarely in the eyes. "And who sits in Kaylah's stead now?"

"You and Kaylah *promised* you never lied to our council. If you're hiding something from them..."

"We never lied. I never lied about that. That doesn't mean we told them *everything*."

Saff couldn't help but think Kaylah and Ginger played fast and loose with the definition of 'truth.'

"Kaylah's always had a contingency plan. Guillen's working on that right now."

Rachel piped up, her face veiled in disappointment. "Soren said that once, after he... He always had backup plans for his backup plans."

"Rach, don't equate them," Ginger said softly. "They may have been trained by some of the same people, but they're not cut from the same cloth."

"If you can trust anyone, Ginger, it's us," Saff pleaded, gesturing to herself and Rachel.

Ginger shook her head. "I swore an oath." She focused on Rachel. "I can't promise things will work out the way we want, but Guillen will find a way to get that jade charm to the cave for us."

"Or die trying," Rachel whispered, hugging herself.

Ginger gave her a reassuring smile. "Let's give him a chance. And once he has the jade stones, he can make his way to the cave. Once he's safely arrived there, we'll have all the pieces we need." She turned to Saff. "And for once, please let my people carry out part of Kaylah's plans without mucking it up in some way."

The first wave of Seeder troops was already set to head out that morning. Jon, who'd somehow still retained Seeder leadership trust, pocketed the new charms and intel for Guillen, rifting out to take them to Guillen on a regular run for information exchange with spies in the Ivy Kingdom.

And now the Seeders marched. And waited.

Jon returned just over twenty-four hours later. The stones were in Guillen's hands—it was up to him.

Saff, Rachel, Catrina, and Ginger found time to meet. There was still a lot they didn't know. This was a long shot. While they had sent a stone with each kind of symbol, their nearby cave wasn't named with the same letter. For now, at least, it might just be a one-way trip.

They were going to give Guillen three days to make his way to the cave, before trying to rift through from the Unitas camp side. Catrina was transferred behind Seeder border walls for safekeeping; Rachel gave her an awkward hug, promising she'd look out for Guillen.

As a last-minute strategic addition, the Unitas camp was to be emptied of all nonessential occupants; only Seeders well trained in battle would be left behind. They planned to set up their strongest troops to fall back and maintain protection of the cave location and Arcadia. It would free up more hands and draw Ivy troops in for an ambush.

Saff worked to pack up her and Devin's belongings while he helped harvest the camp garden before their retreat.

"Saff?" a familiar voice called outside of her tent.

"Flora? Come on in."

Flora entered, and Saff gave her a smile. Instead of reciprocating, Flora held her hands on her hips. "Do you know what they're making us do?"

Saff stopped folding a blanket. "Um... No? Who's 'they' and 'us'?"

"Your leaders, us Ivies. It's a load of crap!"

The strategy had been discussed at the last meeting Saff had been invited to, so she couldn't pretend she didn't know what Flora meant. The list had been all but decided upon as to who would be allowed to try rifting through the cave. Fearing further deception, and having never discovered who the traitor or traitors were in camp, the Seeder war council had struck most Ivy names from the list. Instead, the male Ivies would be broken up and reassigned to Seeder wall protection duty, closely monitored. Ivy females were all being reassigned to healing Seeder lands while troops marched on the palace.

"It's just a change in strategy, okay? It's not a permanent reassignment," Saff reassured her.

Flora frowned. "Are we giving up on Unitas? Because this is what it feels like to give up."

That hurt to hear, but Saff could see how Flora would read the situation that way. No, they weren't joining together at the cave, storming the castle in a blaze of glory, hand in hand. But they also hadn't given up on their alliance with Kaylah, even if things were shaky. They just couldn't risk their cave strategy, or *any* strategy, making its way to Soren's spies, whoever they may be.

"We're not giving up. I *promise*," Saff said emphatically.

Flora studied her face. "Then at least let me fight with the guys." She crossed her arms. "No offense, because I love that I got to make a new friend, even if it was a weirdo Seeder like you," she grinned for just a moment, "but I didn't come here to make friends. And I didn't come to heal your lands."

"Flor—"

"No." Flora held up her hand. "Hear me out. I will fulfill my queen's promise to your people to come back and help heal your lands when she's on her throne, but that's not why I came. I left my family, my friends, my entire life behind to follow her and to learn. I've sparred with you and others in camp at every available chance. Raven, too. We've both devoted countless hours to fighting our own people at the edge of this camp. We're as good as any of your soldiers, so don't pretend this is fair treatment for all we've done."

Needing to keep her knowledge of whispers a secret, and wanting to not be kicked out, Saff had been rather silent at council meetings lately, even if she didn't agree. But in Flora's shoes, she would have felt the same.

Flora continued, "Look at it my way. What happens if this keeps dragging on? Or your people lose and, well, somehow don't all die."

That was a little bleak and insensitive.

"What would become of us women who joined Unitas? We would be slaves in your lands for the rest of our lives, forced to cure the poison in your soil, one day at a time." She pointed at Saff. "Don't you dare tell me it would happen differently."

Saff didn't skip a beat. "You're right." She held no doubt that, at minimum, Seeder leadership would demand reparations via the Ivy women already working on their behalf, if things went sideways.

"Good. Then we're on the same page. We're not stupid, either. If we're closing up shop here in camp, that means something's changed. And if we're not giving up on Unitas, that means," she raised an eyebrow, as well as her inflection, "special strike teams that some of us have been training for?"

Saff couldn't hold back a hint of a smile. She liked this girl. "I can't discuss strategy, but I'll see if I can be a squeaky wheel about letting you fight instead of being assigned to poison duty, okay?"

Beaming, Flora gave her a hug. "You're my favorite Seeder, by far." She winked. "Make sure *both* Raven and I get reassigned, if you can."

Not a minute after Flora left the tent, Devin returned.

"There's the woman I love." He wrapped his arms around Saff, pulling her onto their cot.

She laughed. "Lying down for a nap is counterproductive right now."

He nuzzled her neck. "Who said I wanted a nap?"

She laughed again. "You have got to be out of your mind."

Devin scoffed. "Who's gonna suspect us of anything in our tent in the middle of the day?"

Saff pulled herself closer, resting her forehead against his. "In the middle of the day? When we're supposed to be evacuating camp? I think someone might come by for a head count when we're not accounted for, and they're not likely to announce themselves before peeking in."

Devin huffed, melodramatically flinging his body back on the cot. "War, always coming between me and my love!"

She grinned. "Yes, I can see how you passed your acting classes with *flying* colors. It is in no way astounding that you were picked to go to the human world as one of my protectors."

He chuckled, then drew a pensive breath. "It's weird, isn't it? Leaving camp?"

It had already been over two months since Saff had seen her home, or other family members. "Yeah, it is. I doubt we'll ever see this place again." Either because they'd be back home in South Fortinda, rebuilding after a successful attack on the palace, or they wouldn't return because they'd been killed in the attempt.

Saff and Devin had made it on the short list for the cave rifting attempt. Devin was as good of a soldier as any Seeder out there, but the crux of the choice had been Saff. Seeder matriarchs couldn't rift anymore, not even through the caves, just like Kaylah had suspected. Aside from the newest Seeder teen returns, who had barely any training, Saff was the most powerful female Seeder in the Green Lands capable of going with this strike team. She could pack a punch, and she was willing. Devin was her husband, her mate.

"What was it you told me in high school? You didn't want to fight with me? You wanted me by your side?"

They shared a warm smile. "Yes." He leaned over and stole a peck on the lips. "And hopefully we do come back to this area. We have a second honeymoon in the mountains on the books, don't we?"

"It's a date." She got lost in his dark brown eyes for just a moment, wishing she could share more about the secrets she'd been entrusted with. But this time, it was her turn to keep a few secrets, to keep those she loved happy, blissfully unaware of the potential danger that lurked around them, a threat they couldn't do anything about, even if they knew the truth.

She broke eye contact. "Well, I need to go see a man about a horse. Do you mind packing the last of our things?"

"Come again?" he said as she stood. "No horse beasts in this realm."

Saff winked, adjusting her jade necklace. "Okay, I need to see an Ivy leader about a squeaky wheel. It won't take long."

Saff found Ginger in her tent, also organizing her things. "How goes the packing?"

"Oh, you know..." Ginger stuffed some clothing into a pack. "Getting there."

"I have a favor to ask."

"Favor, huh? Favors often come with strings attached."

"Nope, not this one. Not really."

"What is it?" Ginger placed her pack into a wooden chest and closed the latch.

"I want you to convince the council to let Flora and Raven come on this mission."

Ginger perched on the chest. "That's going to be a no. We don't know how small that cave is, or if this strategy will even work, and we can't risk one of them leaking that information to a spy."

Saff rubbed her face with her hands. *Why can't we ever agree? Even when I'm advocating for Ivies, I can't win!* Sure, she'd been too busy for a lot of things lately, but she'd kept her promise to Kaylah to keep her eye on other members of camp. Especially after Kaylah went missing, Saff had put extra effort into scrutinizing her peers. These girls didn't have a sketchy bone in their bodies. Not to mention, they had been accounted for the night of Kaylah's disappearance, with witnesses vouching that they'd fought by their side during the Ivy army's attack. And, while they hadn't been paired up with Raven in training, Saff and Devin had broken bread with the friends together. He would have agreed with her judgment call.

"They don't have to understand any of the strategy until we have them in the cave on this side. They won't tell anyone. And we know neither of them is a whisper."

Ginger rolled her eyes. "Of course they're not."

Only men were whisper rifters. Unitas just hadn't been able to identify the one unknown whisper amongst them. Granted, it had probably just been the one Ivy guard who had gone missing the same night Kaylah had, and he'd fled through a rift, too.

"Exactly. They're good fighters; even Kaylah thought so."

"They might be good, but they're young."

"So am I. They're barely younger than me."

Ginger crossed her arms. "You're not a standard Seeder, though, are you? Those girls don't have extra powers or capacity to wield energy like you do."

Saff picked at her fingernails. She'd still been struggling to reconcile the truth about her energy, and about her future, and about who she wanted to become. "You know, I didn't earn this extra energy. I wasn't even born with it." She glanced up. "I only have it because I didn't complain about how sick I was when I hadn't been wearing a piece of energy-infused jewelry for too long, and because my brother saved my life before assassins could take it." She shook her head. "These girls are like me, and Rachel. Right place, right time. Or maybe wrong place, wrong time. But the right skills and motivations."

More than anything, the way that Flora had seamlessly called Kaylah 'my queen' had pierced Saff. "You wouldn't stop Kaylah from going. And frankly, I remember, just hours after meeting me, a certain redhead telling me her story, about how she'd always wanted to learn to fight but no one would train her. And how delighted she was to finally get the opportunity when she became a protector and host parent to her future queen." Saff lifted her eyebrows high. "These girls want to fight for their queen. They've been trained."

Ginger shook her head, wearing a knowing smile. That redhead had been her. "I don't know about you." She pointed at Saff. "I don't know if you're brilliant, or manipulative, or brilliantly manipulative."

Saff tucked her hands into her pockets, shrugging. "You can call me narrow-minded, or whatever you want, but I just feel like honesty can go a long way. They're an asset in a fight. Soren doesn't have any female guards or soldiers. He won't see it coming. They'll diversify our team."

"I'll see what I can do."

"Thank you."

Chapter 40

Seeder troops marched on the palace.

In an unprecedented move, a legion of Seeder fathers and brothers—having still been stationed in the human world to protect their daughters and sisters—rifted home to fight, entrusting their unbloomed girls with human hosts and Unitas safe houses.

The camp ambush proved successful, and all that was left to test was the cave.

According to all of their knowledge, a rift either worked, or it didn't. Green folk didn't experience any accidental misdirects, or serious injury. Their hope, and expectation, was that the new cave strategy would work the same way. If they disappeared through a rift, they'd assume it worked as advertised. They didn't have a way to instantly confirm.

An elite group was assembled for the cave strategy, held back from the main march. If their theory didn't pan out, they'd still be able to get to the palace, but it would set them back, taking at least another day to get where they needed, risking having to sneak the group in closer like Guillen was doing with the charms and a small group of allies.

They gathered at the cave entrance at Tonoru, the rope bridges and ladders cut down, camp abandoned, and Seeder soldiers holding the line at the top of the canyon against Ivy forces.

Saff nervously squeezed Devin's hand as she surveyed the group. While Heather's specialty was healing, she'd devoted herself to further training after Ben's death. Healing *and* fighting.

Ginger, and surprisingly, Jon, were in charge of the Unitas Ivies chosen to be on the elite team. Nathan was still sidelined in the human world, but Jon had apparently earned enough Seeder trust through his loyalty, hard work, and intel.

One more male Ivy who Saff hadn't gotten to know well was permitted to join. The fact that Flora and Raven were also there at the cave made Saff proud. She struggled with a pinch of guilt, because it kind of felt like irresponsibly taking Rachel to the human world to meet Kaylah again. But these girls weren't traumatized, new-to-the-Green-Lands pupils of hers. They were young, but they were soldiers.

Reluctantly, Saff was forced to accept that the council had approved Rachel to go as well. Despite Rachel's raw talent in sparring, and the fact that she was now eighteen, and the fact that Saff *knew* she needed to stop trying to protect Rachel and allow her to make her own choices, it wasn't easy to let it go.

"Hey, love?" Devin whispered in her ear as final instructions were being given at the cave.

Saff pulled her gaze from the group. "Yeah?"

"I might need that hand." He kissed her on the cheek.

She loosened her grip, making sure her energy was in check. "Sorry. Yeah."

❁

Rachel stood at the entrance to the cave, gathered with just under two dozen others, mostly Seeders. Her anxiety peaked. *What if this doesn't even work?* They'd built up their hopes, but they didn't even know when those symbols had been etched into that cave on the other side of the realm. Was it after the palace had been built there, in the mountains? Would the Ivy protective barrier now prohibit even a cave rift? Seeder rifts, Ivy rifts, and the combined cave rifts all worked a little differently. And what if the cave was compromised? What if Kaylah had given it up under torture? One of their safe houses had been compromised... And just as sickening was the thought that it might not work because Guillen had died trying to get the jade stones there.

Staring at the cave entrance, Rachel tried not to let the mounting fear grow, or at the very least, not to show it. She had no way of controlling the tightness in her gut, or the sweat on her palms. *There's only one way to find out if this will work.*

After the briefing, Jon volunteered to be the first to try. Rachel found some comfort in that. He and Guillen had been her escorts, her rescuers, when she'd been tortured at the palace. They'd found refuge in that cave. Now, she hoped and prayed that she, Guillen, and Jon could reunite and find strength there again.

Jon extended a vine, running it along the rocky cave floor. A rift formed. Holding the jade charm, he stepped forward. As he breached the rift, the surrounding air rippled, shimmered, and then took him from their sight.

The group erupted into cheers. Rachel exhaled her relief, and was afforded the honor of going next. It felt different—warmer, thicker—going through this type of rift. She was greeted on the other side by relative darkness. The darkness of a familiar cave.

Jon had moved off to the side, and there were a couple of other men at the back of the cave where she and Jon had emerged, right next to the etched symbols. Rachel gave Jon an excited hug.

Jon even hugged back this time, smiling. "Back where we started, huh?"

Rachel matched his smile.

"Rachel! Jon!" Guillen rounded the corner, swooping Rachel up into a firm squeeze.

She could finally truly breathe again.

"I missed you so much!" Guillen said, his tone echoing her own sentiments. "And you did it! That's amazing!"

She held him tight, not wanting to let go, burying her face in his neck. "I missed you too."

That part of the cave was starting to get crowded as more arrived, so they moved their reunion further out.

Between the Unitas group following Rachel, and the men Guillen had brought with him, there wasn't any privacy. Rachel and Guillen couldn't have cared less. He took her to the side and laid a reunion kiss on her. They were both safe. And they were both about to risk their lives again.

"I can't believe you led everyone to the cave without being detected." She surveyed him. He was *completely* dusty and fairly sweaty, with a bit of a nasty scratch on his forehead and arm, but otherwise without injury. "You really are like a shadow, aren't you?" She held his face between her hands, gazing into his gorgeous blue eyes. He even had a little scruff on his face.

"You doubt my skill?" He raised an eyebrow, wearing the sexiest grin she'd ever seen.

Her heart pounded against her ribs. "Never. But how did you even do it?"

He pulled her into another embrace, whispering in her ear, "Tunnels."

Her eyes grew wide as she pulled back. "Wait, what?"

"When Jon and I rescued you and brought you here, you only ever checked out the *left* chamber of the cave, right?"

She nodded. Jon had told her to.

"The right side is narrower, but it keeps going."

Rachel furrowed her brow. "Seriously? And Kaylah knew that the whole time?" It was actually insulting. She almost punched Guillen in the arm right then and there. "Why have we waited? Why didn't we sneak people in that way, weeks or months ago?"

"It's not like that." His voice was soothing. "There are actually a lot of caves and tunnels like this in the Green Lands, especially in this region. I think they're lava tubes? Not really sure. But she's had people secretly scouring the back mountains for a while now. That's what I've been helping with since you left. The right channel of this cave looked like it experienced a cave-in, so Kaylah hoped we could find the right tunnel and clear it, connecting to here."

"So, you just had to find the right one? How long have you known about them?"

He pursed his lips. "We just got here four hours ago and secured the opening. But yeah, I knew this was in the works for a while."

She couldn't pretend she wasn't disappointed to just now be finding out about this.

He held her by the waist, looking her directly in the eyes. "Do you remember us talking about the coffee cup clue she left you in that cabin? About why Kaylah separated those clues? Why she hadn't just given that code to Jon or me to give you?"

Rachel's shoulders slumped. "Because then it couldn't be tortured out of you."

He gave her a half-smile. "Sometimes, when it comes to strategy, it's best if the left and right hands are a bit out of sync."

Rachel shook her head, admiring Kaylah. She really hadn't lied about being trained on strategy. She'd been working from two angles, not even knowing they would need to come together. "And you just barely discovered the right tunnel?"

"We've been narrowing it down, but it's slow work, with more than one cave-in. We'd been working in teams for safety. When we got word of this deadline, we worked through the night and had to split up. We couldn't play it safe."

"Is... Is everyone okay?"

Guillen winced. "There's still half a dozen of us unaccounted for." He moved a hand up, tucking a strand of her hair behind her ear. "But let's stay positive. They might still find their way out and join us before we know it."

She could only imagine what it would feel like to be lost in the depths of a tunnel or cave all alone, or to suffer a slow death crushed by a cave-in. She prayed that his optimism came to fruition, that they'd all find their way here safely.

After hugging Guillen once more, Rachel didn't leave his side as they introduced each other to different people, everyone discussing their training and expertise. Basic plans had been made ahead of time, but final strategy would be hammered out in the cave between the two groups.

A bit of a shocker to Rachel, and apparently a large portion of the group, was news of the existence of a group of Ivies known as 'whisper rifters.' The Unitas party was warned to watch out for each other, and to anticipate that many of the guards at the palace might be stronger than they would normally expect of a regular soldier.

"Okay," Guillen whispered in her ear, "*Now*, I'm not keeping anything from you, and I won't ever again."

She couldn't even be mad. She just leaned her head on his shoulder, savoring his warmth. Most of the others in the cave were too busy with their own preparations to pay them any attention, but a couple of people from the Seeder side did a double take.

Jon, Ginger, and a pair of experienced Seeder generals led the discussions. Anyone with experience in the palace gathered into one group, reviewing drawings of the place. It was tight quarters, so Rachel didn't at all feel guilty about being in Guillen's arms as they discussed such important matters. It gave her strength and calmed her nerves.

Unitas took their time planning. They wouldn't attack until it was dark outside, and they wanted to make sure they weren't missing anything important. Their latest update had the earliest deployed Seeder troops engaged in battle nearby. They could provide backup to hold the palace after the strike teams secured their targets.

As the main Seeder march seemed to already be pulling more Ivy troops from the palace, Unitas decided to take the palace in two groups. Having a couple dozen people there, they would split their infiltration attempts between two entrances. They aimed for one that seemed more structurally vulnerable, and one they only knew about from their new insider knowledge. The second attempted entrance was in a neglected part of the palace that even Jon had never seen.

They broke for lunch, dispersing a smidge. Rachel sat on Guillen's lap as they ate sunflower oatcakes.

Guillen was chuffed that his sister and, unknowingly, his mother, had been helpful with this part of the mission.

"Thank you for taking care of them," he said. "And I'm really happy to hear Catrina came around so quickly. I thought she might."

Rachel smiled. "You should be proud of her. She made a lot happen that we couldn't on our own."

There was an awkward silence between them as they sat there. What did you say to the person you loved, when you were both about to put yourselves in mortal danger?

Rachel's eyes rested fondly on Saff and Devin. Everyone was at risk, but she was sure these two could cause some damage. Devin had years of combat training under his belt, and Saff had come far, and was so powerful.

✻

Saff's heart hung heavy. This was the first time she would be in the middle of a battle. Even at camp, she'd fought with darts, not in hand-to-hand combat. And while they prayed for a quick and stealthy win, there were no guarantees. But she was happy to have her husband by her side. She leaned into him, squeezing his hand.

She exchanged a smile with Flora. During a break in planning conversations, they'd stolen a moment to chat. Flora was understandably jittery, but excited. She confessed that Raven was a lot more nervous. Not wanting someone that might chicken out at the last minute, Saff had suggested that Raven stay behind in the cave to guard it instead. After Flora returned to discuss it with Raven, Saff decided perhaps that hadn't been the best advice to offer. Raven glared at Saff, no doubt resenting the suggestion. If looks could kill...

Saff glanced over at the other team. Heather was in conversation with a male Seeder she'd be working with. Both Devin and Saff had had a hard time accepting Heather coming on the mission, but she was determined.

"What are you thinking?" Devin asked.

"Mmm." She leaned into him more. "Just nervous. What's new?"

He rubbed her back. "We'll be okay."

Maybe it was just the calm before the storm, or the adrenaline pumping, but her mind didn't reject that.

"I know." She turned to him, smiling. "Tell me something about yourself that I don't know."

"Something you don't know?" He held her hand, playfully intertwining their fingers, tickling her palm. "I don't know, love. Um..."

He took another moment to mull it over. "Okay... I ... still think about how I almost lost you in high school. Every day." Regret filled his voice. "I don't know if

I'll ever fully forgive myself for letting you get hurt. I could have said something. I should have."

Her heart went out to him. She'd only asked as a fun distraction as they waited for their attack. "I forgave you years ago, as well as my parents. You know that."

He bobbed his head back and forth. "I know. Sometimes it's easier to forgive others than yourself."

She didn't know what to say to that. "I love you, no matter what."

He cracked a reassuring smile. "In this cave, that palace, or anywhere, in any world, I've got your back."

She squeezed his hand. "Ditto."

Devin shifted on the cool stone floor. "Your turn. What don't I know about you?"

She hadn't prepared anything ahead of time, but it came to her quicker than she'd expected. Unable to stop herself, she actually let out a soft chuckle.

"Oooh, a good one."

A couple of soldiers looked at them, and she blushed.

"No, it's stupid."

He poked her in the ribs, and she squirmed a little. His voice was playful. "No, no, no. Now you have to tell me."

She bit her lip, trying to think of a new one, but she couldn't. "Fine. It's *really* stupid. But, since you mentioned our high school days..." She couldn't look him in the eye. "I know you, and my human parents... I *know* you were picture-perfect in giving me space to choose which world I'd live in, and ... between you and Zach." Her mouth opened and closed like a guppy gasping for a cool drink as she tried to form words. "I just... I never blamed you for not being willing to sacrifice your identity as a Seeder, especially after moving here and meeting our families. I get it. But part of me was always kind of ... hurt ... that you never once *actually* asked me to give everything up, to choose you."

His reaction was spot-on with what she'd anticipated. "You're kidding me, right?" He lifted his eyebrows, his voice quiet enough to not disturb others. "Girls are impossible to please sometimes!"

Her cheeks grew warm. "That's why I never said anything. I know it's silly, or vain, or ... too romanticized."

Scratching his chin, he shook his head. "I was never subtle. I was *pretty* dang clear that I wanted to be with you."

She felt that much more stupid. Why would she have brought up such a silly girlish notion in such a serious moment? "I know. Sorry." That was like a human girl getting a dozen long-stemmed roses and then saying 'Sorry, but I think sunflowers are better.' *Take the stupid roses and appreciate the gesture.*

Perhaps she shouldn't have brought up Zach vying for her heart back in the human world, either. Devin really wasn't normally the jealous type, and he'd thoroughly apologized for what he'd said when they were arguing, about her revealing green-folk secrets to Zach. She could understand why he'd done it, that sometimes people lashed out when they were caught up in their emotions, but maybe the mention of Zach at all during this particularly tense situation had been the wrong move.

Frustrated with herself more than Devin seemed to be with her, Saff reached into her pocket, opening a small satchel of mixed nuts. "Want one?"

"No, I'm good." He focused on the cave wall, a contemplative look painted on his face.

"Are you mad?"

He gave her a half-smile. "Of course not. Just thinking."

She kicked herself even more, shoving a couple of cashews in her mouth. After chewing in silence, surrounded by chattering co-conspirators and allies, she swallowed, then picked up a hazelnut.

"Saff?" Devin finally said, studying her face.

"Yeah?" She set the hazelnut back down.

His face was sober and vulnerable in a way she rarely saw, almost like on the day he'd proposed, but this time his expression carried something more akin to hurt, rather than nerves. "Choose me."

Something within her knew right away what he meant. He wasn't mad about Zach, or about a petty girlish dream. He wasn't mad at all.

Her heart sank instantly to her abdomen. Hadn't she *always* chosen him? She'd moved to the Green Lands. She'd waited for him to return. She'd married him, chosen him as her lifelong mate. She'd built a life with him. And she chose him every single day.

But the hint of hurt, or perhaps fear, in his eyes reminded her that she *hadn't* always chosen him. Not when it had mattered most. Not when she'd left him to risk her life to go to the human world on a dangerous, unsanctioned mission. Not when his best friend and brother-in-law had been killed. She'd left him in the lurch, all alone.

Tears came to her eyes. They were about to march into the palace, outnumbered, outmanned, and *she* was his fighting partner. *She* would be the one to have his back. And while he'd forgiven her for her betrayal, she realized in that moment that forgiveness didn't equate to trust, and perhaps they had more work to do on the latter.

When you made a vow to share your life with someone, to spend it with them, you no longer belonged to just yourself. That was why they called it 'spending' your life together—you were invested, wholeheartedly.

As they stared into each other's eyes, she held his hands and squeezed. She would *never* abandon him again. Pushing out the word with all the emphasis she could muster, she responded. "Always."

He gave her a tiny nod, then pulled her into his arms.

"Always," she repeated. "I promise."

"Thank you," he whispered.

In the warmth of his arms, nothing more needed to be said. As long as they got through this attack, this battle, they could get through anything.

As they sat in silence, Saff people-watched some more. Ginger and Jon, with their Seeder general counterparts, were the most active, gesturing around the cave, shaking and nodding heads, pointing at maps and blueprints. This hodgepodge little group was far from perfect, but it was the best they would have, and they had to believe it would be enough. Once Soren was deposed, they could stop the battles, stop the war. If they could do this quickly, Soren's people wouldn't have time to flee or move Kaylah elsewhere.

Saff's gaze eventually rested on Rachel and Guillen. She'd never seen Rachel with that kind of smile, that kind of confidence in her expression.

✻

Rachel felt Saff's gaze. They locked eyes, having a silent discussion across the room. First, they shared a quick half-hearted smile. Then Saff lifted her eyebrows—questioning, urging. Rachel's face became more stern. She mouthed the word "No."

"What's up?" Guillen asked, having picked up on their exchange.

Rachel took a deep breath. "I'm not staying in this cave."

He bit his lip and looked down.

"I know I haven't been in the parts of the palace that we're expecting to go into. And I don't have as much training as some of the others. But I'm not just staying here to guard the cave. We already have volunteers for that, and that's not why I came. I've trained enough."

He grinned and caressed her cheek. "I can't win this argument, you know. If I tell you not to go ... we've seen how that goes. And you'll feel like I'm not supporting you. If I don't fight you, then I'm not being honest with *either* of us about how much I care about you."

She stared into his concerned eyes, a slight smile forming on her lips.

He sighed, gently rubbing her knee. "So, I'll say it once. I don't want you going in."

"You know my answer."

He nodded, lips pressed tightly. "I love you."

Rachel's words caught in her throat. She'd never once hesitated to reciprocate that, not with him. But the way he'd said it, the way it felt—it felt like a goodbye. A 'just in case.'

She swallowed hard. "I love you too. Today. Tomorrow. Always." She forced a smile and gave him a sweet peck on the lips.

Soren had done a significant purge of the guard staff, realizing there were traitors amongst them. The few left still loyal to Kaylah worked to ensure the strike teams and backup would have an easier time reaching the palace, but they had no hope of help on the inside.(rr)

Guillen, Rachel, and Heather would be in the smaller group, taking on the unfamiliar entrance, entering first and hoping to get closer to the dungeons where Kaylah was believed to be held.

Saff and Devin were part of the larger group, led by Jon, that would be taking on the more guarded entrance, drawing attention away from the dungeons, and then hoping to take Soren. Based on their last reports, Soren, his wife, and Kaylah were all still on the premises.

Guillen guided his group quietly from the cave under the cover of darkness. They'd be approaching via a different route than he'd previously taken when rescuing Rachel, but he knew the area well enough to get them through swiftly.

The target entrance was an old ground cellar. They cleared debris from the cellar door and shimmed the rusted padlocks open. Guillen slowly undid the squeaky old latches and parted the swollen wooden doors. Clearing cobwebs away, he used a lightkeeper Heather had pocketed to look inside.

Once he confirmed it was safe to enter, they filed in. From what they'd been told, this wing was once used for storage and servants' quarters. It had been abandoned long ago when newer additions were built, grander and closer to the throne room.

Rachel shivered in the cold of the damp corridor. There were only seven Unitas members at this entrance. Guillen headed the group; she was in the middle of the pack. The longer they walked in the dark, the more nervous she became. She pictured the palace layout, envisioning where the remaining Seeder girl was being held, powering the War Vines. Were the three missing girls about to join her? Rachel ached to find them, to free them, to make that as much of a priority as freeing Kaylah, but that wasn't the mission.

This wasn't an extraction.

This was a takeover.

❊

Having given Guillen's group ample time to breach the palace stealthily, Saff's team started to make their way out. Jon was coordinating Saff and Devin's team, though he wouldn't be at the front. The Seeders intended to use every tool in their arsenal.

Walking most of the way to the intended entrance, the large group broke up. Four Seeder couples, Saff and Devin included, took flight, soaring to strategic locations, to have an advantage from above. They made sure not to fly too high, or too far out, where the protective barrier caused flight problems. And while traditional human weapons were rarely used by green folk, the palace employed archers—a wise move when your enemy could fly. Completely suppressing your glow while flying was no easy feat, but it was doable, and necessary, to land undetected.

Landing softly on a lower stone balcony, Saff and Devin crouched, carefully making their way to a narrow ledge that led to their target. Not wanting to risk giving away positions earlier than necessary, they had to rely on the others to be in place before they moved next. Two guards were stationed at the door they were aiming for, and two archers on the level directly above. If they could take out those on the ground without noise, they might avoid having to deal with the others.

Devin extended a balled fist, putting his other hand behind his back, helping to conceal the light Saff was pushing to her hand. He quickly flashed his green eyes. Three sets of eyes did the same. He accessed Saff's energy, and flicked his wrist at their target below.

Large darts sliced through the air, biting into a wooden door, and the two guards stationed on the ground. The pounding of the darts against the wood rang through the air, briefly followed by the muffled thud of bodies crumpling to the ground. Unitas Ivies rushed forward to remove the bodies while the Seeders surveyed from above to ensure they hadn't been heard.

The night was still. So far, so good.

✻

Guillen's group finally reached the end of the long corridor, stopping at a large wooden door. It was locked, and since they expected guards to be close on the other side, they planned to open it by force, instead of risking the noise of slowly and carefully prying it open. They anticipated six guards in the immediate area. Two by their door, two further down a hallway lined with cells, and two in the stairwell that led up further into the palace. If they could take the six down, especially before those at the stairs alerted anyone, they could accomplish their goal and get Kaylah out, independent of any commotion the other group might cause.

Guillen stood to the side of the door as three Ivies wrapped their vines around the handle, ready to tug. He held two throwing knives ready. He gave Rachel one last pleading look, asking her to stay back. She shook her head, brandishing her own knife. She and Heather hung back, there for emergency healing, as well as fighting if needed. The others would go first.

Guillen directed the group with hand signals and then motioned for those with their vines on the handle to give it all they had.

✻

The larger party slipped into the palace. The Seeders up above quietly landed, entering the same door. A pair stayed there to hold the position, while the others barreled down a small hallway to the right. When they turned the corner, they were met by a handful of surprised guards. Several Unitas Ivies advanced, tackling those closest, while the Seeders used their darts for those further away.

It worked.

Miraculously, they'd overpowered the first group of soldiers without them raising the alarm.

And then a bloodcurdling scream rang out from behind Saff. "SOREN!"

Saff whipped around, as did the rest of the strike team.

Raven. Clutching her hands to her stomach, wide-eyed.

What?!

She wasn't hurt.

933

Everyone jerked their heads about, trying to locate the target or threat she'd called out. A couple of Unitas members shushed her.

It wasn't like 'King' Soren was standing right there, though.

Saff eyed Raven. She should have stayed back in the cave if she was going to lose it and give up their position. She looked absolutely terrified.

Raven took a few steps back, almost stumbling in her retreat.

And then it clicked.

It took only seconds for the team to put the pieces together, but it was seconds too late.

Raven wasn't calling out a danger. She *was* the danger.

The danger *Saff* had begged to bring with them.

Faster than those around her could react, Raven turned to Flora. "Sorry."

Darting down a tiny hallway in the opposite direction, she screamed Soren's name once more. One of the Seeder pairs bolted after her.

Shit. The element of surprise was beyond gone.

Devin pulled Saff back to their mission before she could even gauge Flora's reaction. "Saff, come on."

Traitor or not, Raven didn't matter. Their strike teams had never intended to take on the entire palace staff—nor could they. They needed Soren, his wife, and Kaylah. Once they had them in their custody, this was over.

Saff squared her shoulders and set her jaw.

More guards rushed down the hallway to meet Unitas. Saff and Devin, along with another Seeder pair, Jon, and another Ivy, broke from the group, hoping to climb a nearby stairwell before the guards cut them off. They darted to the base of the stairs as an enemy vine caught Devin's ankle, yanking him to the ground.

Saff had already bounded up a few stairs. She turned and dashed back down, hacking through the vine while a Unitas Ivy covered them, taking on the offending guard. Now free, they climbed the stairs.

They were met by a pair of guards at the landing of the next level, quickly dispatched by the other Seeder couple. Advancing one more level, they anticipated finding the long hallway that would lead to the sleeping quarters of the 'king.'

❀

Near the dungeons, the Ivy men tugged at the locked door with all their might. The first pull loosened it, but not enough. They yanked again, and the wood splintered. They retracted their vines as a couple of them moved forward and kicked in the door.

One of the Ivy Unitas men rushed through the doorway, and was swept off his feet by a pair of vines, the closest guard having had some warning from the noise of the door breaking down. Guillen crossed the threshold, planting a throwing knife in the throat of another approaching guard. He pulled out his machete and severed the vines binding his Unitas companion, then took down his assailant.

The rest of the group poured into the new room. The three other Unitas Ivies ran to the stairs, hoping to detain the guards there before they alerted those above. Guillen, the Seeder women, and a Seeder male advanced down the hallway, taking on a pair of guards running toward them.

Guillen stopped, back to the wall, as Rachel extended energy to the male Seeder. He shot darts, taking down one of the guards, but the other continued after another round. Guillen met him as Rachel spotted two more coming from the same direction.

✺

As they reached the right level, Jon and the other Unitas Ivy pulled down one of the guards at the edge of the stairwell, then Saff and Devin dispatched them with their blades. Jon indicated he and the other Seeder couple would hold the stairs while Saff, Devin, and the other Ivy rushed down the hallway.

They met the two guards positioned outside of the royal chambers, tussling. More guards sprinted toward them from the opposite end of the hallway. Saff and Devin took one out together, then Devin turned to help the Ivy with the guard he was binding. Saff glanced behind her as a handful of Unitas members emerged from the stairwell as backup against the fast-approaching surge coming her way. The opening was narrow.

But she would never leave Devin.

"Come on, Devin!"

He quickly surveyed the situation, jumping up to join her.

Saff focused energy into her shoulder as she threw her weight against the door, bursting into the queen and king's chambers.

✺

Rachel prepared to extend more energy, but a call for backup came from the men in the stairwell. She motioned for Heather to stay and help in the hallway while Rachel went back to assist.

As she turned the corner, three more guards bounded down the stairs. She settled into a defensive stance, Seeder blades and knife at the ready. The closest guard whipped out a vine, and she allowed it to wrap around her extended wrist.

Moving energy to her surrounding skin, muscles, and bone, she secured the Ivy leaves in place, embedded in her skin. She yanked the vine and turned, reeling the enemy in, planting her knife in his heart. As his vines released, she struggled to steady her breathing.

She assessed the situation in front of her, counting the guards and her allies at the stairs.

Ripping the offending leaves from her wrist, she shot a glance back down to the end of the hallway to see which group needed her more.

In that split second of indecision, a vine wrapped around her throat. It tugged at her, yanking her off her feet, slamming the back of her head into the unforgiving corner of the stone wall.

With the wind knocked out of her, she screamed only internally at the searing pain, barely hearing Guillen shout *Heather's* name, before all Rachel knew was blackness.

Chapter 41

Saff burst into the queen and king's chambers. Had she not used her Seeder energy, her shoulder would've no doubt been dislocated, but she'd strengthened those bones and muscles in anticipation.

With Devin right behind her, she was greeted by a half dozen soldiers.

Devin grabbed her hand. In a fluid, perfectly synced motion, Saff pushed energy to it and he flicked his wrist, dispatching one guard with darts. They separated, extending their Seeder blades, to take on the two closest who had rushed at them, shooting out vines.

After cutting the guard's vines short, Saff made her first solo kill with a blade to his throat.

Luckily, the closest Unitas Ivy from outside came into the room, slamming the door shut. He threw vines at the legs of a nearby settee and dragged it in front of the door. "That'll keep 'em out for a little while."

Now it was an even match. With two Seeders and an Ivy against three Ivies, they could manage this.

With each slice, kick, punch, and dodge, Saff sized up the guards and the room. Soren wasn't even in here.

The stone floors slick with blood, the Unitas members sweaty and nicked from head to toe, they caught their breath. Shouted orders continued to filter in from the hallway; thuds of bodies, grunts and groans.

The three in the queen and king's chambers split up to explore every inch of it—the en suite bathroom, the large closets, under the bed. Soren and his 'queen' were nowhere to be found.

Saff tightened her ponytail. "Of course they wouldn't be here. Not with our forces advancing. Not with Raven sounding the alarm."

The Unitas Ivy wiped his brow. "Is that what that stupid girl's name is?"

"Yeah," Devin answered, squeezing Saff's shoulder.

"So what's next?" Saff asked, choking down any emotion that wouldn't help in the moment.

They could go back out and keep searching, keep fighting. Where would Soren have gone?

Saff folded her arms, trying to recall the palace blueprints they'd studied.

"Why are all the guards outside, though?" Devin asked, right before a loud bang shook the door. The settee moved a few inches.

The Ivy ran to it, pushing it back against the door, holding it in place with his hands, and exerting extra pressure with his vines directly against the door. He dug in his heels with a wide stance, being jostled with each huge pound against the door.

"Need a hand?" Devin started toward the door.

"I've got it. See if you can find some other way out of here!"

"We're sure those aren't our people?" Saff asked.

The Ivy belted out a designated code word. No acknowledgement came from the other side. He shook his head grimly.

Great. And now we're cornered in here. They'd been hoping for stealth and speed. None of that was falling into place.

Devin rubbed the back of his neck. "But why would they be so focused on this room if Soren and his wife weren't in here?"

Why were they? *Six guards in here, too...*

"The White House," Saff said. "Buckingham Palace. The Capitol Building. Probably every castle has them too, right?"

"What are you talking about, Saff?" Devin asked.

"Tunnels."

Both men looked thoroughly confused.

"The tunnel in the cave?" the Ivy asked.

Good gravy. Saff pinched the bridge of her nose. Neither of these men grew up in the human world. Seeders didn't have such large and important structures for lifelong dignitaries. Ivies were secretive about everything.

"No. Humans sometimes build trapdoors or escape tunnels for important people. We need to check under the rugs, look for a fake panel in the wall or something."

"Oh," the Ivy remarked. "Like a pub's smuggling room."

"Uh…" Saff set to work, scouring the walls. "Sure?" She'd never heard of Ivy pubs or smugglers, but why not?

Devin started pulling up the corners of the rugs, pushing dead bodies out of the way.

The banging at the door grew louder, more violent. The Ivy lost his grip and slipped. He quickly jumped up and slammed the settee back in place. "I'm not going to be able to hold this for long by myself."

Saff and Devin feverishly undressed the room. Maybe she was wrong.

The door slammed so hard it nearly buckled, knocking the Ivy a couple of feet away. He scrambled to his feet, thrusting the settee back. Saff rushed to his side, Seeder energy strengthening her as she helped.

At this point, it almost didn't matter if Soren had been in here to escape through a tunnel. They just needed one to get out of here, to be able to search elsewhere. She continued to study the room from her new vantage point.

Devin searched the gaudy wall panels in a far corner of the room. He tilted his head to the side. A sconce was slightly askew.

He went to straighten it, but was met with resistance. He jiggled it, and a loud click followed.

Devin grinned at Saff. "Don't forget I fell in love with you because you're brilliant."

She chuckled. "Not the time. Hurry up." Her muscles ached, and she was expending more energy than she'd like just to hold a door rather than healing or fighting with it.

Devin found a couple of metal ornamental inlays and tugged on the wall panel. It slid to the side. "You're right. Dark tunnel, several yards down from what I can see. Looks like our way out of—"

Devin whipped his arm up, swinging it forward, fist balled.

The moment a handful of darts launched from his fingertips, an arrow slammed into his chest.

"Devin!" Saff screamed.

He didn't answer. But he didn't crumple to the floor, either.

Saff wanted to run to him, but the moment she left her position, that room would be overrun with Soren's extra-strong guards. And she couldn't see into the tunnel; Devin was blocking it as his balance teetered.

"Devin?" she pleaded.

He stood rigid, still facing the tunnel. Her healer training kicked in as she stared at him. Given his skills with Seeder energy, he was capable of surviving that kind of wound, as long as he hadn't been shot through the heart.

"I'll be fine," he forced out with the breath of a single functioning lung. His heart hadn't been pierced. "Go get the bastard," he groaned. "He ran away."

"Okay." Her heart was pounding as hard as the door she was holding in place. She turned to the Ivy. "Take him inside the tunnel. I'll follow you."

The Ivy shook his head. "You can't hold this on your own."

"Trust me. I'm stronger and faster than you. Please."

He sized her up, then nodded. "On three?"

On three, Saff dug in, her jaw clenched, and the Ivy bolted to Devin, helping him inside the tunnel.

"Is there a way to close it?" she asked, sweating profusely, her skin even glowing.

"Um... It looks like it just clicks into place if we slide it back. There's a handle, but I don't see a lock from this side."

It would have to be good enough. She'd have to be fast enough to make it and close that door before the guards on the other side busted in and saw their hiding space. They might not know about the secret passage. It stood to reason knowledge of its existence would only be entrusted to the highest level of guards, and they likely wouldn't be busting down the door if they assumed Soren had already escaped through a tunnel.

"You're both clear of the entry? Ready to close it?"

"Yes."

Faster than she'd ever sprinted before, Saff dashed across the room, straight for the secret passage. The second before she crossed the threshold, she held out her hands, grasping the sconce with a death grip strengthened with Seeder energy. Her momentum carried her as she ripped off the sconce. Needing speed, she hadn't pumped the brakes. She threw her arms up to shield her face, and slammed into a stone wall, the broken sconce falling to the floor with a *clank*, right as the doorway behind her banged shut and the door of the other room crashed to the floor.

She fought a scream at the pain and exhaustion, listening intently, catching her breath.

All three froze in place.

Hopefully, damaging the passageway's entrance lever had disabled it, and wouldn't draw attention to it...

Guards barked orders from the other side of the panel. "Where did they go?"

That was a good sign.

Saff looked for Devin, barely able to see anything now that the door was closed. She silently joined him, lighting her hand enough to assess his wound. It wasn't bleeding yet. The arrow was still lodged in his chest, sticking out the other side—a nasty broadhead. "How are you holding up?"

"I'm fine," Devin whispered, clearly straining to keep his composure. He was capable of freezing a single lung, of surviving with just one side. For a little while. "Go after him. He's getting away."

Saff opened her mouth to speak. She wasn't going to leave Devin.

Devin's gaze was set on her. "Go. I can manage this for now. Hurry up."

She trusted that he could. He was amazing with his energy. He stood still enough, obviously flooding his chest and lungs with energy, clenching the arrow in place, forcing himself to breathe through his undamaged side.

"You ready?" the Ivy asked.

Making sure not to bump the arrow, Saff leaned in and gave Devin a kiss. Not a passionate kiss—there was no time for that. And this wasn't a goodbye kiss, either.

This was the kind of kiss only a Seeder woman could give. One that transferred a portion of her energy to him. Healing him would be useless with the arrow in there, but this could help him hold out longer.

She was already weak, and might end up too weak to properly heal him before this ordeal was over, but healing did no good if he exhausted his own stores and drowned in his own blood before she returned.

Their lips parted. "I love you." She faced the Ivy. "Okay."

With their way dimly lit by the glow of her hand, Saff and the Ivy raced down the corridor together. They took a sharp left at the end, having no idea where they were going. The tunnels might be woven into a complex labyrinth for all they knew.

Saff tripped over something on the floor, almost face-planting onto the ground.

The bow. Hopefully that was the only one, and Soren had given up on it, preferring a swifter exit without the extra weight.

Eventually, the tunnel did branch out, and they had to pick which route to take in their search. Each short offshoot led to a door just like the one they'd ducked through. They listened for a second at each door, assessing whether it was worth the danger to open it to search the room Soren might have left through.

Finally, they got lucky.

A screech came from the closest offshoot, and they slowed their pace to quiet the thump of their footsteps.

And there he was, just around the corner, tugging on a stuck door with his vines and hands.

Saff and the Ivy rushed him, tackling him to the ground, but he didn't go down easily.

The Unitas Ivy entangled Soren's legs with vines, while Saff fought off Soren's attack. With his legs secured, they needed to disconnect his vines.

"Help me pin him down," she said.

The Ivy did as ordered, and the two of them barely kept Soren down. He was strong. Then again, he hadn't been fighting for his life until now.

Saff aimed her sharpened arm blade at a narrow target on Soren's upper wrist, a move Ben had taught her in high school. A move she'd seen Ben and Devin use on an Ivy general when they'd saved her life. She cut deep, and Soren grunted, but barely bled. His vine from that wrist went limp, disconnected. She quickly repeated the move on the other wrist, then ordered the Ivy to bind Soren.

Soren yelled a colorful string of expletives and threats against the two, until they shoved some of his own vines into his mouth to muffle the sound.

No one came barging through the jammed door for him. It likely led to an empty room, perfect to escape through.

Saff caught her breath, her mind racing as to what to do next.

"We're sure this is him?" the Ivy asked.

She pointed at their captive. "What? That's Soren... Right?" She and Devin would recognize the prince better than almost any other Seeders would; they'd seen pictures when they went to the human world to search for him and Rachel when he'd kidnapped Rachel months earlier, after all. But an Ivy ought to recognize their own prince...

The Ivy shrugged, scrutinizing their captive further. "Yeah. It's probably him. Just wanted to make sure. I, uh, generally steer clear of government officials." He grinned. "More of a fringe kind of guy."

"Okay..." She was a bit on edge. "What's that supposed to mean?"

"Well..." He shrugged again. "Government officials tend to dislike those who illicitly transport items of intrinsic value."

"You're a thief?"

He was visibly offended. "Smuggler. Thief? That's debatable."

Soren continued to fight against the restraining vines and yell through the gag. The Unitas Ivy delivered a swift kick right to Soren's gut. "Shut up!"

Saff was stunned. She could get behind that kind of behavior.

But there was no time for that. The corridors were still quiet, so they might be lucky enough to be able to hide there for a bit to gather their strength and assess the situation, but Saff needed to get back to Devin ASAP.

She hesitated. That meant leaving this Ivy alone with Prince Soren. So much could go wrong. This man had only joined the team with Guillen; he'd never been with them in the Unitas camp. "What's your name again?"

He evaluated the injuries on his arms. "Arlo."

"Saff." She tried not to wonder about the rest of the Unitas team, but she couldn't stop thinking about Flora and Raven. Flora had been recruited by Raven. Raven had apparently been recruited by Soren... "Who brought you into Unitas?"

Arlo massaged his wrists. "Jon—the former guard leading our team. He was like a big brother growing up."

Saff still hadn't gotten to know Jon well at all. But everyone, including Kaylah, had trusted him. It would have to be enough. "I need to go help my husband. Can you watch over this idiot here until I get back?"

"Yeah. I've got him."

"Okay. I'll hurry." She looked down at Soren again. "I'm all for kicking him if you need to, but try not to injure him too bad. We need him alive, and I'm not going to have a lot of healing energy to spare."

Arlo smirked. "I can manage that."

Without hesitation, Saff ran back to where they'd left Devin, though she almost got turned around at one point.

When she rounded the last corner, confident she'd found their starting point, she panicked.

Devin wasn't there.

Did I take a wrong turn? Did they find him?

No... She was sure this was where they'd left him. The hidden doorway was still closed, and a few voices mumbled from behind, but it sounded like they'd given up on searching, and the ransacking had stopped.

A raspy cough came from the hallway behind her. She ran toward it, finding Devin in the closest offshoot. He leaned his shoulder against the stone wall, coughing up blood.

"Crap. Okay. Hold on." His Seeder energy was running out, if it hadn't already.

She desperately wished Arlo could be there to help get the arrow out, but dragging Soren back would have wasted far too much time. "Okay. Hold still." She gazed into Devin's eyes, which were glowing a faint green in his struggle to breathe and keep himself upright. "This is going to hurt." What she wouldn't do for Flora or Ginger right now to numb him at least.

With both hands, she grasped the portion of the arrow sticking out of his chest and, trying to move it as little as possible, exerted precious energy to snap off the end. Devin groaned in obvious agony.

Now she could pull it out without causing further injury. She yanked it out from the other end and immediately jammed her thumbs into the holes in his back and chest, pouring healing energy into them. She winced as he moaned and coughed, struggling to keep it together.

As she sensed the internal tissue healing, she changed hand positions, her fingertips surrounding the holes. As her energy drained, his grimace relaxed.

She couldn't afford to pass out or use up every last drop. "Are you going to be alright if I stop now?"

Devin took a couple of test breaths. "Yes."

Depending on how much blood had leaked into his lung, he might still face further complications, but the important thing was that the bleeding had stopped.

"Okay." She wiped her bloodied hands on her pants, scanning his face. He was still in no shape to run out or get back into the fight. They needed a game plan.

"You stay here. Arlo and I have Soren tied up. We'll bring him back."

Devin nodded. "Thank you."

She smiled weakly, giving him a normal peck on the lips—no Seeder energy this time. "Love you."

"Love you."

Worn out, she did her quickest jog back through the dark corridors, almost tripping over the bow again.

Arlo and Soren remained where she'd left them. Arlo's ear was cupped to the door Soren had been trying to escape through.

"Is someone in there?" she whispered.

"Oh, no. Just making sure," Arlo answered. "Is your husband okay?"

"Yeah, not in any fighting shape, but I think he'll make it." She surveyed Soren. Arlo had added some extra vines around Soren's wrists, which had been wise. It usually took at least an hour for vines severed the way she'd done it to start regrowing.

"What's the plan?" Arlo asked.

Only in that moment did the aches and pains and drain set in. Devin wasn't in fighting shape, and right now, she wasn't either. "How are you doing?"

Arlo's exposed arms, neck, and face had just as many cuts as hers from the fighting. He let out a long exhale. "Gonna be honest. I'm not used to using this much vine at once. If we can take a minute, that'll help."

"Yeah, of course. Let's regroup with Devin. Help me drag this waste of space back?"

"Yes, ma'am." Arlo extended vines toward Soren.

"Hold on." She eyed Soren. "A couple of things first." Fueled by anger, but not backed with precious Seeder energy, she delivered a swift kick to Soren's side. "That's for shooting my husband." He breathed hard, his nostrils flaring, his eyes a bright natural green.

She kicked him again. "That one is for Rachel." And she decided a third might feel nice, but this time she balled her fist and aimed for his face. "And you know what? I like Kaylah, too."

Even if they all died during this battle, at least that had felt good.

Saff and Arlo dragged Soren all the way back to where Devin was recuperating. He was still coughing a lot. They'd checked out the crossbow Soren had ditched, but there were no other arrows with it.

Now, the three Unitas members needed to take a breather to allow their energy stores to recover, even if only minimally. And they needed a plan.

They had the usurper, but not his wife or Kaylah. Other Unitas members might have them in their custody, but they had no way of knowing, and they were worn out and injured.

They agreed to take a few more minutes and then assess the situation.

Saff sat next to Devin on the cool stone floor as Arlo paced the area. Devin's breathing was raspy.

She held Devin's hand. "You know, wasn't it you in the cave just a little bit ago that said girls are impossible to please?"

Devin showed a hint of confusion.

"I mean ... I kiss you during a battle, but listen to you—one kiss is *never* enough for guys, is it?"

Devin laughed, and then winced and coughed. She grimaced.

"Yeah... I was curious about that," Arlo added. "This is my first time meeting Seeders. Do your lips always ... do that?"

Saff furrowed her brow. "Do we kiss with our lips?"

Arlo pointed to his mouth. "The glowing thing."

Saff stifled a laugh, then explained how Seeder women could transfer energy that way, not just by extending it for darts or for healing.

He nodded. "That's hot." His eyes shot to Devin. "Well, I mean, not your wife." He looked at Saff. "Well, I didn't mean..."

Saff grinned, fixing her ponytail, which was now a tangled mess. "No worries."

Arlo swung his arms with nervous energy, continuing to pace their little offshoot. "The last thing an Ivy girl gave me when I kissed her was a slap in the face." He rubbed his cheek.

Shaking her head, Saff fought another smile. Arlo certainly hadn't been a chatterbox back in the cave, but his pumping adrenaline was likely a factor here. While giving off more of a player vibe than her human friend Zach ever had, Arlo kind of reminded her of him. She asked Arlo more about himself as they recuperated. He was an interesting character. Then again, she'd never met a smuggler before.

Feeling marginally better, their energy stores having had a chance to recharge, they had to make a decision. The best choice would be to take Soren back out in the open with a blade to his throat, and demand that all of his people surrender. Even without Soren's wife or Kaylah, it might work. But they could easily be overpowered still. When they took the gag out of Soren's mouth for a brief moment, he refused to surrender, swearing they'd never find his wife, and he would never help.

Not having much choice in the matter, they prepared to step out and demand the guards surrender. They needed to try to preserve the lives of any Unitas members who might still be fighting.

Devin was really in no shape to fight, but he could stand straight, and he refused to leave Saff's side.

The three Unitas members pulled Soren up and dragged him down the secret corridor, searching for a doorway that sounded as though no one would be on the other side.

Finding a suitable door, they filed through it into a closet of some sort. Saff held the tip of the arrow that had pierced Devin to Soren's neck.

Arlo opened the door, and they stepped out into a hallway. They took a left, following the loudest fighting. Only as they reached a staircase did they find guards.

Soren shouted louder and fought harder against his restraints. Saff pushed the arrowhead harder against his skin. "You're going to walk in front of us if you want him to live," she ordered the guards.

After a shared glance, the guards held up their hands.

"Where is your queen?" she asked. "And the *real* one, Kaylah?"

The guards kept looking to Soren for guidance, and Soren kept fighting and yelling, but he was tightly secured and well gagged.

Finally, one of the guards answered. "I don't know where Queen Beata is. The traitor is locked up where she should be."

"Take us to Kaylah," Saff demanded.

The men started to move as ordered, down the stairwell, and they collected a couple more on the way. Saff tried to remember the palace blueprint, but her mind was all jumbled, and she grew wary with each step.

After one more level of stairs, they were met by a surprise. A large one. The stairway led into a grand room, full of guards.

Now to see how this works out... Maybe they shouldn't have worried about the other Unitas members. Maybe they should have stayed in hiding until the outside troops had breached the palace.

This time Arlo barked out a command for them to all stand down, in his most authoritative voice. Devin ordered the guards they'd picked up on the way to join the others.

No one moved.

Saff panicked. They could try to book it and hide again, but they'd have dozens of guards on their heels in no time. Unitas couldn't actually kill Soren—they needed information from him, and if he died, they'd have no bargaining chip.

A guard at the bottom of the stairs shouted an order toward an exit. "Call the archers."

Oh crap. They couldn't handle more arrows.

"I'll kill him," Saff said, flaring an arm blade, resting it against Soren's throat. "Stand down." She lit her eyes, hoping that added some level of intimidation, but it likely didn't mitigate her now shaky voice.

It was a stalemate. Until the archers would arrive.

Devin coughed again. That didn't exactly add to their intimidation factor, either.

"So..." Arlo whispered. "Running away again?"

Retreat might be their best option without backup, cooperation, or Kaylah in the same room. If Saff's party decided to kill Soren, the guards' actions would be unpredictable. Had Soren set up someone to take his place? He didn't have a legal right to the throne in the first place. If Saff killed him, they'd lose valuable information, but he'd no longer be a threat... And it might cause enough confusion?

She couldn't risk it. As a Hail Mary, she tried to think of what Kaylah would do, other than tower over the guards with an authority they might actually recognize. Most of these guards were probably whispers, manipulated most of their lives and forced into their line of work. They wanted freedom, right?

Swallowing hard, her heart thumping in her chest, Saff squared her shoulders. "We know most of you are whisper rifters." She surveyed the room; there were subtle looks of acknowledgement and surprise. "We know you don't always get a choice in what you do, and that you're not allowed to share the truth about who you are and what you're capable of. Kaylah wants to stop that, not keep exploiting you. What has *Soren* ever done for you?"[ss]

The guards' eyes focused on Soren, almost in unison. Once they looked back at Saff, their expressions grew darker, more menacing. *That should have worked, right?* Why were they acting like she'd just given them a motivational speech on why they *shouldn't* surrender?

Devin leaned closer. "I think—"

Their time was up. A dozen archers ran into the large room at the base of the stairwell, raising their bows, aiming at the Unitas party.

Saff, Devin, and Arlo stepped back.

"I think it's time to get the hell out of here," Arlo said, only a hint of fear in his voice.

Saff looked over her shoulder, and her hope fell to the floor. Of course they'd sent guards to cut them off. There was nowhere to retreat to now.

"Kaylah cares about you and your loved ones. Soren's not a real king!" Saff shouted, her voice almost pleading. Sweat dripped down her neck and back. "Soren just cares about himself!"

The only movement from the guards was that of the archers as they took aim. Arlo curled his vines in front of himself as a shield, but it wouldn't do much against a dozen archers. Saff stood partially behind Soren, and Devin stepped to cover her more. "Any other ideas?"

Glancing back over her shoulder, she eyed the guards blocking their retreat. There were a half dozen of them, so the three of them stood a better chance attempting to retreat, rather than engaging with the guards and archers at the base of the stairs, but still... *Where's the rest of our strike team?* Were they all dead by now?

Shouts came from the exits of the grand room. Guards barked orders, and half of them ran out of the room.

That was good. Not good enough. *Should we surrender? Would that buy more time?* All of the archers had stayed behind, as well as over a dozen guards.

The yelling and fighting grew louder in the hallway.

No one at the bottom of the stairs gave orders to shoot the Unitas members, but the arrows were still aimed up. The guards on their level didn't rush at them.

Fifty heartbeats pumped in the blink of an eye. Each minute was an hour.

Then the fight poured into the grand room down below. The archers turned their weapons on the intruders—not Unitas members, but Seeder soldiers, the front line of their nation's cumulative force.

Saff's breath hitched with cautious hope, as Seeder soldiers pressed in. She didn't know what the fighting looked like outside, or how many had breached the palace. And Soren's forces had not yet surrendered.

Devin shouted to their troops below that they had Soren.

Saff glanced over her shoulder once more. Three of the six guards decided they didn't like their odds and ran off in the opposite direction. The other three, however, looked like they had made up their minds to take back their king. They charged Saff's group.

Throwing Soren to the floor, Saff blocked the first vine attack with her blades. Devin and Arlo stood their ground, also fighting. Three-on-three wasn't bad odds, especially with a Seeder as powerful as Saff, but that didn't matter with Devin hurt and all of them depleted, especially if these guards were fresh, especially if they had extra strength as whispers.

The rest of the battle was a whirlwind of chaos as Saff's party fought tooth and nail to keep Soren out of reach.

Saff nearly collapsed from exhaustion by the time the remaining palace guards finally announced their surrender, overpowered by Seeder soldiers. She and Devin leaned against each other, both panting. "We should still take him somewhere else until the entire palace is secured," she said.

Devin and Arlo agreed, and they all groaned as they shoved Soren along, back to the nearest room they could find. They shut the door behind them, and Devin slid down a nearby wall, wincing, bloody from head to toe, hacking up more blood.

It killed her, knowing there wasn't much more she could do at that point. Seeder healing repaired damaged tissue, but it didn't miraculously suck excess fluid out of lungs. Still, she moved a hand to his exposed chest where the arrow had pierced, expending additional energy in an attempt to heal it just a *little* more.

Almost instantly, she felt queasy and had to stop.

"I'll be fine." His inhale was more of a gurgle than anything.

She frowned, kneeling next to him, laying her forehead on his chest. She knew what she needed to do next, but before she could force herself to say it, Devin did. "Do you have it in you to go check on the others? See how ... well, how everyone else on the team is?"

He didn't even have to say that he mostly meant his sister, Heather. "Yeah, I'll send some soldiers back to help you two. I'll go check it out."

She grunted as she forced herself to stand and balance.

"Don't worry." Arlo nodded to Devin and a thoroughly disheveled Soren. "They'll take good care of me." He grinned.

Saff cracked a tired smile. He was probably just as worn out, energy-wise, as Saff and Devin, but less severely wounded.

She ambled out of the room, closing the door behind her, praying she didn't meet any resistance. Thankfully, the palace was flooded with Seeder soldiers by now. Saff asked a group of soldiers to go up to the room to help guard Soren, and to heal the Unitas members if they could spare the energy.

Less than an hour later, Saff and Heather sat on the floor in one of the dungeon cells. The walkthrough of the palace to get there had been devastating. Saff had found Flora, and Rachel, and Kaylah, as well as others.

So many bodies. So many lost.

The stone floor Saff and Heather now sat on was covered in as much blood as they were. Saff was sick to her stomach. From hunger. From physical and energy exhaustion. From the horrors she'd just witnessed. She wiped her bloody hands on her pants, but they didn't come away any cleaner.

"Those are some pretty bad gashes," Heather commented.

Still dazed, Saff examined her forearms. It didn't really matter. Neither of them had energy to heal more right now. Or enough to stand. Or do anything. "I'll survive."

Heather frowned. "Are you okay?"

Saff looked at her hands. "I don't know." Her eyes filled with tears. "I can't believe ... she's dead. I should have—"

"Don't," Heather reprimanded. "We did the best we could. We *all* did the best we could."

Saff sniffled, still in shock from the faces of the fallen she'd seen on her way to the dungeon.

And just like her brother, Ben—her friend was gone.

Chapter 42

She didn't hear anything significant when she woke. But she did wake. Rachel opened her eyes, disoriented, not sure where she was. She lay on a soft bed, blinking at the ornate ceiling. She studied the room. This wasn't Seeder style, but it was familiar. This was ... exactly like the room in the palace she'd woken up to after she'd been kidnapped.

She started to breathe heavily. A quick visual sweep of the room told her she was all alone. This time, there wasn't a nurse in the room. She had an IV in her foot, but her arms and legs were free, not handcuffed to the bed. She wanted to get up, but her body ached, especially her head.

The door clicked open, and a nurse came in. Spotting Rachel awake and alert, the nurse called through the still-open doorway. "Let him know she's awake! Right away!"

Rachel swallowed hard. She froze, not sure what to ask first. Who was 'him'? Had they been successful? Was she about to go through a fresh batch of hell? Who had made it out?

Her heart soared when Guillen appeared at the door. He was wide-eyed, relief written all over his face, as he rushed to her side. He crouched and grabbed her hand. "We thought we'd lost you!" he breathed. "How do you feel?"

She blinked. "I... What..." She closed her eyes, trying to focus. "Did it work?"

"Yes. You're okay. Kaylah's okay. Unitas has the palace secured." He kissed her hand.

She bit her lip and started to cry. "Good. Is everyone...?"

He frowned. "We got pretty beat up. But a few of us in the raid made it out alive." He whispered, "We lost Jon."

Rachel's tears flowed freely as she mourned her friend, whose loyalty she'd once questioned. He'd given up so much, too much. Guillen shared the names of the others who had fallen. She wondered how Saff was taking the news of her training partner's passing. Rachel hadn't had much of a chance to get to know her, but Flora had seemed like someone Rachel would have liked.

"And the kidnapped girls?"

Guillen looked down at their hands, rubbing hers with his thumbs. "We got the last one away from the Vines ... but ... she ... um, she's not responding. We don't know about the three who were taken from the safe house. They weren't here, but we'll keep searching."

He looked up with an apologetic frown and wiped at her tears with his thumb. "But how are you feeling? You've been out for almost two weeks. With our combination of medication and your people's healing, we were really worried with how long it was taking."

She closed her eyes again, mentally assessing her aches and pains. The biggest one was her head. She moved a hand up and felt a divot in the back of her skull. "I think I can move everything ... and I think ... I'm okay..."

"Sorry to interrupt," the nurse said cautiously. "I can remove the IV and leave you two in privacy?"

Rachel nodded. "Thank you."

The nurse completed her task and opened the door to leave. "I'll be elsewhere in this hallway, if I'm needed."

After the door clicked shut, Guillen turned his focus back to Rachel. He searched her face with his stormy blue eyes. "I love you. I've been checking on you constantly." He looked as though he might cry. "I was so worried."

"I love you too."

"Is there anything you need? Something the nurse could do? Or something I could do?"

"Stay with me?" she asked.

Guillen pulled up a chair and held her hands while she regained her strength. He went over their victory. They'd gotten to Kaylah; they'd been right about her location. She was currently awaiting her formal coronation, but had already been declared the rightful queen. Between Unitas campaigning and Kaylah having previously been beloved by her people, the transition wasn't being met with too much resistance.

Soren had been clever, but hadn't paced himself well. He'd stretched his soldiers and assassins too thin, and his grandiose plan—his bargaining chip—as 'leader of the whispers' seemed to have been more of a pipe dream than anything. There hadn't been a whisper uprising.

But there *had* been a stunt uprising.

And as much as the Ivy Kingdom was discontent and bitter, the Mother Vines were the lifeblood of their cities and towns—Soren had been far too confident in his chances of winning his people over.

The Vines didn't just protect the palace or distribute nutrients throughout the kingdom; they were the veins and arteries of the Ivy people's sense of community, so much of their identity, their spirit and pride.

Once, smaller Family Vines had been controlled by a matriarch in each Ivy family. When they'd banded together to form their own kingdom, that power had been pooled, sacrificed, willingly given, by *every* family in the kingdom. In an attempt to unite their people and gain strength, they'd assigned it to one matriarch—the queen.

It would have taken a lot more than what Soren had offered for the Ivy people to truly turn from their queen.

Rachel had known that their win was all but inevitable, or at least had convinced herself there was no other option on the table, but now that it was actually reality, it was all so crazy to imagine, hard to grasp. Kaylah was the person she wanted to see next, out of everyone, though she figured it may take a while—a queen in wartime surely had a busy schedule.

Guillen went on to explain how Unitas was guarding the palace. The Seeder army was still out in force, continually fighting with rogue groups that refused to accept the change in power, the absolute shift away from a centuries-old war. There was still a ton of work to be done, but he assured Rachel they could rest safely. Enough had been done ahead of time, and since the win, that he was confident green folk would be able to move forward with hope in a different future.

The good news was invigorating.

Finally.

Their people could glimpse normalcy.

Finally.

And people like Guillen... They could live a normal life now.

Rachel focused on the hands holding hers. Guillen wore a ring she'd never seen him wear before, carved from green stone.

"Is that ... jade?"

He grinned. "Yes. It is."

The victory somehow felt more hollow. "Does that mean...?"

"Yes. It does." He slipped it off, showing her the tiny swirl symbol carved on the inside, then replaced it, the symbol permanently resting against his skin. "Specially commissioned by the queen herself."

She rubbed his hands lovingly. "I'm happy for you. Did you get to be the first Ivy to test it?"

"No. I wanted to wait to share my first time with someone I love." He winked.

"I think you should go." Her voice lacked true conviction.

He raised his eyebrows. "Without you? That's crazy talk. I can wait as long as you need, to be up to full strength. I want to go with you."

She removed her hands from his. "I want you to go." She looked down, unable to keep eye contact. "And I don't mean for a couple of days. Take a break from all of this and explore if it's the right future for you over there. You deserve to find out if a life with humans will make you happy."

"Why would you say that?" His voice conveyed as much confusion as it did hurt.

She pursed her lips. "I love you. But me expecting you to stay is like you asking me not to go into battle. Sometimes we just have to allow those we love to take a chance, to figure out what's best for them."

"I know what's best for me. And that's you. Why are you trying to push me away?"

She fought back tears. Couldn't he see how messed up she'd become?

"Let's," he breathed calmly, "talk about this once you've rested a little more. You just woke up from something pretty rough."

"Yeah... Maybe..."

"I'll stay with you?"

She scooched over, making room for him on the bed, and gestured for him to cuddle up next to her. She loved the warmth of his touch, the scent of fresh mint and juniper berries, but was tortured by it at the same time. They lay in bed for more than an hour. Rachel mulled things over, unable to fall asleep again, her thoughts cycling through everything with each tick of a clock in the corner.

A quiet knock came at the door, and she smiled as Guillen carefully tried to unwrap himself and get out of bed without disturbing her.

Catrina opened the door and cautiously peeked in. Rachel had a good view of her and smiled wider.

Scowling in Guillen's direction, Catrina pointed at Rachel. "She's already awake."

He sighed. "Yeah, well, she needs rest. You should have waited."

Rachel rolled over. "She's fine. I was awake. I'm happy to have another visitor." She started to force herself into a sitting position, and Guillen moved to help her.

Catrina strolled over, sitting in the chair next to the bed. "I'd offer you a hug, but maybe I'll wait until you're feeling a little better."

"Thanks."

"So ... you guys have talked?" Catrina asked, her eyes darting between Rachel and Guillen.

"Not about *everything*," Guillen snipped.

Rachel glanced back at him, surprised by his reproach. Then again, she hadn't seen *that* much interaction between the siblings.

Catrina stubbornly pursed her lips, her nostrils flaring back at him. She turned her focus to Rachel, smiling. "Well, I'm glad you're doing better. We all are."

Rachel smirked. "Even your mom?"

Catrina let out a small chuckle. "Well ... I'm sorry to say I don't think there will be a lot of invitations for holidays."

Rachel's smirk remained. "Yeah..."

"It's nice to be home. Well ... back in our lands," Catrina offered. "For now, we're staying at the palace until things calm down."

Catrina glanced back at Guillen before addressing Rachel again. "Well, I'm going to go. I was just really happy to hear you were up. And thank you, for everything."

"Of course. Let's talk soon."

Rachel watched Catrina leave—she really liked her. She swallowed a lump in her throat as Catrina closed the door, leaving the room to just the two of them now.

Guillen shifted in bed, sitting cross-legged to face her. "She had lots of great things to say about you."

Rachel nodded. "She's a good kid. I'm glad I got to meet her."

"Yeah." He smoothed the comforter. "So..."

"What haven't you told me?" Rachel frowned, waiting for the rest of the bad news.

His eyebrows scrunched in confusion. "I gave you all of the big stuff. It'll take a while for things to calm down, but I promise—everything's fine."

She cocked her head, then straightened. That gesture still caused her head to scream. "Then what is it you two were just talking about?" Her heart sank a little. The tension between Catrina and Guillen must have been about his ring, if there wasn't more bad news. Catrina wished for him to explore the human world, to make a new life for himself.

"I know I'm not alone in thinking you should spend time with humans, give yourself a fair chance to find out if it's right for you." She rubbed the silky bedsheet. "I couldn't forgive myself if you didn't at least give it a try."

Guillen opened his mouth as if to protest.

"Look me in the eye and tell me you didn't join Unitas *knowing* this was one of Kaylah's goals. That not even a small part of you didn't hope for this day to come."

They'd spent *countless* hours on their mission together discussing their cultures. He'd been just as enthralled learning about human culture, as she'd been learning about Ivy culture. Yes, he'd also been intrigued by Seeder society, but a lot more of his questions had centered on humans. It was only natural for a stunt to relate to humans.

Guillen broke eye contact, swallowing. "I promised I'd never lie to you." He shook his head, determination in the set of his jaw. "But I'm not taking the coward's way out by running away from my problems."

She raised her eyebrows in challenge. "That's really what you think of all those people we met together? Just for taking an opportunity at a better life? You think they're cowards?"

He wilted. "No."

"I didn't think so. You once admitted yourself that it was a dream you had."

"Dreams change. You're not getting rid of me that easily."

She weakly gestured at him with an open hand. "*You* once told me to not worry about our future, to take things one day at a time. But … we're here now. You may think you know what you want, but I don't. I don't know what I'm going to do with my life."

She finally allowed herself to think about life beyond the war. Maybe they'd ask for more help on research with the frequent Seeder rifts, or intrarealm rifting. There was so much they still didn't know about cave rifting and the health risks they faced now that they could rift more than once a year.

Perhaps she needed to spend more time trying to bond with her family back home and helping piece Seeder society back together.

Guillen gnawed on his lip, his face turning pinker. "I wish you'd stop taking things I've said and trying to use them against me."

She rolled her eyes. "Just... We could use some space. You figure out what you want. I figure out what I want."

He ran his fingers through his hair. "Dammit, Rachel! No." His eyes narrowed in frustration. "I mean." He rubbed his face with his hands, exasperated. "I know what I want. Stop trying to talk me out of it! And you might be confused about what you want, but I know what that is, too."

"And what's that?"

Chapter 43

Quillen searched Rachel's eyes. "You want to be with someone you can trust, who cares about you. You want to do things that make a difference. We want the same thing."

Magda's death glare flashed through her mind. "There are people out there still fighting against this change. How could we be together right now?"

"I don't care about them." He flopped back on the bed, staring at the ceiling. "And we could start things off right here. We have an offer to stay here, in the palace, as advisors. We could both be happy, continuing to help Kaylah out."

Her eyes widened in surprise. Kaylah had already made more plans for her, for them, than Rachel had imagined for herself at the end of the war. They'd never talked about things that far out.

He sat back up, his eyes piercing her with determination. "I'd throw away this ring, if that's what it took to prove how serious I am. You're trying to break up with me, and all I'm hearing are objections about wildly hypothetical futures and technicalities. But not once have you told me that you want me to leave you alone, because you don't love me anymore."

She couldn't lie. "That's because I *do* love you."

He stared at her. "Great. And I love you. So..."

She studied her hands.

"Or is this about the darts?" His voice was softer. "Because ... maybe if you'd had them in the fight... And now you're..."

She was on the verge of tears. "No. That's not it at all!"

"Then why are you doing this?"

She thought about her head injury, but wasn't sure if she could say it.

When she didn't respond, he puffed out a breath. "Maybe I should let you recuperate more."

"I'm perfectly lucid. But maybe that's really the problem." Her biggest concern finally came to the surface. "I have *so* much that I need to work through. And I don't want to use you. I need to learn to be strong on my own." She couldn't look him in the eyes. "You know what a mess I was, and that was before I'd taken lives. I've got a long road to health, and *not* just with my body. I can't ask you to stand by my side. That's not fair."

"No." His voice was confident, firm. "How is it *using* me, if I want to be there? Working through hard stuff, that's what people do together, when they love each other."

She leaned her head back, gently resting it against the headboard. Closing her eyes, she sifted through her thoughts. It was all a jumbled mess. A tornado swirled with pictures of torture, betrayal, death, and all kinds of hurt, fear, and anxiety. The one light that emerged from it all—clear, untainted—was her love for him.

She opened her eyes. "It's not that I *want* you to leave me. Even if we figured out all of my problems, I couldn't forgive myself if you didn't at least step back and consider what you'd give up, okay? What if you realize you want to start an Ivy family of your own someday, but you miss your opportunity because we're trying to make things work out? You need to be open to the idea of things changing."

He reached for her hands. "I *do* want things to change. But I plan to have you there with me. Nothing has changed for me, not about you."

She was out of excuses. Thinking of Catrina, she rolled her eyes. "She might pull a Magda, you know?"

Guillen squinted, clearly confused.

"Your sister. If I stayed here, if we stayed here together. She... I don't think she'd like me so much after that. I know how much she wants you to go to the human world."

His whole face scrunched with further confusion. "What are you talking about?"

"That's what that exchange was about, between you two, right? Your ring. The human world."

His jaw dropped. After a moment, he closed his mouth, his lips forming a smirk. "You know, we're not good at having these moments at the right time."

It was Rachel's turn to show confusion.

Leaning to the side, he reached into his pocket. "She was bugging me to see if we'd had *this* conversation." He pulled out a tiny decorative bag. "I ... had actually hoped to complete your collection. You have the matching necklace and earrings. But I'd hoped ... that if you still loved me ... that you'd consider adding this." He pulled out a ring. It was set with a jade stone intricately carved into a butterfly. "She was urging me to bring up *this* ring."

Rachel gazed at the beautiful craftsmanship, and then her eyes shot back up to his. "What's this supposed to mean?" She could hardly breathe.

"Well, um..." He cleared his throat. "Kaylah said they make them a little different where you grew up, but I thought this fit you better. I... Rachel, life is complicated and messy. Love doesn't change that. It just means you have someone by your side to walk through it with you. Every kind of future I'd want, has you in it. I'm ... asking you to take a leap of faith. Marry me."

She swallowed hard, stunned.

He flashed an embarrassed smile. "Not that her opinion matters much in our decisions, but Catrina wants to add you to the family."

Rachel smiled and stared at the ring, entranced by it, considering the what-ifs. She'd given him options; she'd offered to set him free. It wasn't something she'd wanted—it was something she'd felt she needed to do. She remembered every happy moment together, and even the rough times, all that they'd worked through. She imagined them taking in little ones of his kind.

After a while with no answer, he continued. "I know I've moved fast, and we never even talked about this. I'm not sure if marriage is even important to you. I guess, you know, what you said in the cave really rang true for me. That you loved me. Today, tomorrow, always. That's how I feel about you. If you need more time, I just really... I just..."

She allowed her walls of hesitancy to crumble as she asked herself what mattered most to her. She wanted a place she could call home. That could never be the human world again. It may not ever be South Fortinda. But a person could be a home, and Guillen was hers. Her eyes welled up with tears. "Yes."

They both looked up, locking eyes.

"Yes?" He searched her face.

She pursed her lips. "Yes."(tt)

He cautiously smiled. "Okay, you're sure?"

She nodded.

His mouth hung open. "Great. I... I love you. I... um..." He blinked. "Kaylah said guys in the human world kneel, or something?" He started to shift on the bed awkwardly.

She tried to stifle a laugh at his sweet attempts to follow Kaylah's overreaching coaching about human customs. "No. Please. Just come here."

She bit her lip as he scooched closer, slipping the ring on her finger. He gently kissed her on the lips.

Leaning back, he scanned her face with nervous eyes. "You're really sure? I don't expect you to turn your back on your people. Until I could safely visit, or move over there, and until Kaylah doesn't need my help as much, it could be complicated. But ... I'm willing to make it work, however you want."

She answered, more clarity and courage in her heart. "We can accomplish a lot of good, no matter where we are. I don't plan on pulling you away from your people." They had plenty of Seeders back in their lands who could research and rebuild without her. "This kingdom needs us more right now, anyway."

He beamed. "One day at a time. As long as it's together."

Her heart content, she slid back down on the bed, under the covers. She admired the ring on her finger. "There is one problem, though." Her comment was met with concerned blue eyes. "That was a pretty weak kiss for a proposal." She grinned.

He glared at her playfully. "You're still recuperating."

She stuck out her tongue. "I'm stronger than you think. I'll let you know if I'm hurting."

He slid down next to her. Turning onto his side, he gazed lovingly into her eyes. "You *are* strong. Don't forget that." He moved in closer, caressing her lips with a tender kiss, then slowly expressing more, following her cues.

It took two full days before Kaylah was able to make a visit, though she'd sent word amidst her onslaught of meetings. In the meanwhile, Rachel happily gained her strength with Guillen at her side, when he didn't have his own meetings to attend. Once Kaylah showed up, Guillen excused himself to allow them some privacy.

Rachel carefully got up from the bed, and Kaylah gave her a tight hug.

"Sorry it took so long!" Kaylah said.

Rachel chuckled. "You should be! I expect a queen to dote on me."

Kaylah smiled warmly.

"You look amazing, by the way," Rachel said as she perched on the edge of the bed. "Gorgeous dress, all the bling. Just saying... I've never been bitter that you look like a supermodel, but I did *not* look this nice after being kidnapped."

Kaylah laughed, flourishing a hand in the air. "That is because I. Am. Amazing." Her smile faded as she sat down in an armchair. "And I didn't take before-and-after pictures from the time of my rescue, to the time Heather and Saff and the nurses were finished healing me. If you know what I mean."

Rachel frowned, positively miserable. She'd just offered the most insensitive compliment possible. "Sorry. Yeah."

Kaylah smoothed out the silky dusty-rose fabric of her dress. "It's okay, you know. We'll always have someone to talk to who understands, right?" Kaylah winked. "Group therapy, on the house."

Rachel grinned. "I love you. I missed you."

"Ditto, of course." Kaylah hummed playfully. "And I understand there's more love in the air, and I *totally* approve."

Rachel raised her eyebrows. "I guess I really need to care about your approval now, don't I? If you're going to be my employer?"

Kaylah grimaced. "Gross. Don't think of it that way."

Kaylah stayed for a while. They caught up on how everything had proceeded and what was to come. Rachel was surprised to hear they hadn't severed the War Vines once they released the last Seeder girl. They instead realized they were a fantastic opportunity. They'd never had something so strong that it could reach all the way across the Green Lands. The Vines were currently inert, but Unitas was going to try to use them—instead of as a way to puncture the Seeder barrier thickets, they'd try to deliver the cure for the poisoned lands. Kaylah expected it to be significantly more efficient than healing the lands by hand, provided they could figure out how to do it.

As for the Mother Vines, the more local ones that had been established for decades, Kaylah would be turning greater control of them over to the communities. She'd formed a council for local representatives to gather and discuss it. As for the stunt communities, she'd formally asked Guillen to step in as a representative. His people hadn't been granted leadership in the past, a voice of their own. They needed the right person to help sort through changes that were to come. Rachel would be appointed to help him and work as a liaison with Seeders born without powers.

It was still in preliminary discussions, but Kaylah and Seeder leaders were already considering redrawing old boundaries. They proposed taking some of the Neutral Woods and designating those places for green folk without powers, Seeder or Ivy, should they want to live there. It wouldn't be compulsory, but it would provide new options for those in the Ivy Kingdom who'd been oppressed, and for the Seeder population that had been forced to live with such drastic limitations.

The last thing Kaylah hesitantly wanted to discuss, before getting back to meetings, was Soren.

"His execution is scheduled. It's set to be public." She pursed her lips pensively. "I ... never thought I'd have to do something like that. But it's what our people need to establish order. It's going to be held next week."

Rachel processed the news in silence. Even now, after all he had put Kaylah through, she gracefully discussed her brother's execution as a necessity for healing, for justice, and not as a hateful, vengeful act.

"This is my suggestion, though you get complete freedom to choose." Kaylah paused. "I think you should be gone. Take Guillen away, try out that ring of his. But before you go, if you want to say your piece, you can. If you never want to see Soren again, I completely understand, and you don't have to."

Rachel nodded. "Thanks for giving me the choice. I'll think about it."

Kaylah gave her another hug. Before leaving, she added one more thing. "We all have demons we need to slay. And while he's hurt both of us, a lot of us, I feel like... What I'm trying to say is ... if you came out of that cell, and he didn't make it to the public execution, I wouldn't fault you. We would make it work."

Chapter 44

Guillen held Rachel's waist. "You're sure you want to do this? You don't have to."

"I need to. But thank you." She kissed him. "I won't be long." She drew a deep breath, forcing herself not to fixate on the bloodstained wall down the hall. Her blood. Her near miss.

She'd mentally prepared herself for this meeting. No matter what Soren said, she wasn't going to let him get to her. The guards opened the cell door, and she stepped in, alone. He was chained to a chair, his arms and legs restrained. He looked a little roughed up, but not nearly as much as he deserved.

He grinned at her. "I knew you'd miss me. Conjugal visit?"

She pulled out her knife, coolly. "That would be hard if I castrated you." She smirked as he tensed up.

She continued, "We still haven't found your wife. But we will."

"Screw you," he spat. "She and I will still put an end to Kaylah's idiocy, and get back what's ours."

Rachel nodded thoughtfully. He was truly unhinged, delusional. He'd never really been the author of any brilliant plan. He'd taken advantage of his mentor and co-conspirator's death, carrying the torch. "You go ahead and think that. I'm not exactly concerned. I'd be more worried about your execution, if I were you."

He scowled.

"My apologies, I won't be there. I'll be on my honeymoon."

He narrowed his eyes.

She turned the knife in her hand, admiring the pearlescent handle. "I'd introduce you, but you've met. His sister is going to be one of the witnesses. Catrina is such a sweet girl!"

Soren laughed. "You fell for that compost heap?"

Her eyes flashed green as she gripped her knife, putting it to his throat. "He is ten times the man you could ever be." She'd told herself she wouldn't let anything he said get to her, but hadn't prepared herself enough for that.

His eyes gleamed with defiance. "You're pathetic. You couldn't turn in an Ivy in the human world, and you couldn't hurt me now."

She pushed the knife tighter against his skin. "You wouldn't be the first Ivy life I've taken since then. Or even the second."

His Adam's apple scraped under the knife as his cocky expression melted to fear.

Rachel had already made the decision as to whether she'd take Soren's life herself. She'd thought about what Kaylah had said, about having demons to slay. When it came down to it, Soren *was* a demon, but not Rachel's. The voice that always told her she wasn't enough—that she was a screwup, that she was beyond redemption because of her mistakes—had never been his voice, not really. It hadn't even been her stepdad's voice. The voice that truly hurt was her own, after years of accepting their lies and falling prey to their manipulation.

Her demon was the mess of self-talk in her head. Killing Soren wouldn't slay that.

Though, she'd decided she might not be opposed to torture. They still needed answers, and he deserved more punishment than a simple death would allow.

She removed the blade from his neck, turning it once more in her hand. "I came up with this fantastic idea. You see, I think the punishment should fit the crime. If I said the number sixty, does that mean anything to you?" She didn't wait long for him to respond. "Sixty is an estimation. That's how many cuts I estimate were made in my skin, between restraints, drugging, and War Vine insertions. Each day. So I think it's only right that you understand how that feels. Sixty cuts, for each day I was hooked up. And sixty more, for *every* day each of the other girls was hooked up. Double for the girls that died in your custody."

She furrowed her brow. "It's only fair. And the beauty is, we can keep doing it and just heal you, so we can ensure you'll survive to the end of the punishment. Unlike our girls."

He stared at her, a subtle glare in his expression, but chose to stay silent.

"I'm not going to waste all of *my* time; we've got others that will gladly help. We could even have you looking perfect for the formal execution, isn't that great?"

She raised her knife, touching the tip to his forehead. "Should we start with one here? Symbolically, for the time you stabbed me right there?"

She looked into his cold eyes and realized how similar they were at that moment. She'd been tortured by her mistakes, but it was mostly self-inflicted by a guilt-ridden mind. He'd just epically lost a war, one blunder after another. Unlike Rachel, his pride would cause his judgment to be carried out by others.

Lowering the knife, she instead crouched down. "I might ask them to spare you some pain, if you can answer one question for me." She tapped his knee with the flat of her knife. "Where are our three missing girls that were taken from the safe house?"

His lips curled into a grin; he remained silent.

She sheathed the knife. "Well, just remember, when you're ready for the pain to stop, to just move on to the merciful death part, let us know you're ready to talk." She glared, standing up. "Good luck with the rest of your life." She crossed the cell, grasping the door handle.

"Wait."

She stopped and turned.

Soren searched her face. "My wife is carrying my child. If you find her, could you live with yourself, executing a pregnant woman?"

Rachel's eyes grew wide. Out of all the scenarios she'd planned for in this encounter, this wasn't one she'd thought of. She studied his expression. He wasn't smug or desperate. He'd said it matter-of-factly. She had to remind herself how fantastic a liar he was. Kaylah still wasn't sure if he actually was a whisper rifter, or if he was a charlatan.

It dawned on Rachel how he must feel at that moment. His wife had fled the palace, leaving him to die alone. Rachel almost even felt sorry for him. She considered his question. "Even if I believed you, that's not my call to make."

He pressed his lips together, nodding. "You know what it's like to not grow up with a real dad. What if I'm not lying? Could you deprive a child of a father?"

She swallowed hard, clenching her teeth. She also hadn't prepared for him to open that wound. Or to be so desperate as to make up such a lie. "*No child* would benefit from having you in their life. You're not a father. You're a monster."

She gripped the door handle, ready to move on.

"I'm sorry!" Soren blurted. "I was stupid. I love you. I've always loved you." His voice was full of remorse, his expression conveying regret.

She stood silently as he rattled off excuse after excuse—about how he hadn't known better, about how he deserved another chance, about all sorts of crap that she half tuned out, lost in her own thoughts.

Was I really ever so weak that he genuinely thinks I'd forgive him? That I'd fall for him? Try to save his life right now?

How many chances had she given him when they'd dated, when he'd lost his temper, or had treated her like she was stupid, or had knowingly pushed her past her comfort zone in their relationship?

It hurt to realize that a year ago, she *might* have actually considered trying to fix him, trying to help him, trying to rehabilitate him. But she wasn't that girl anymore. The curtain had been pulled back, and the unstable, selfish puppeteer was now exposed.

And frankly, his death sentence had nothing to do with her. It had to do with millions of other people.

"Please," Soren pleaded, his handsome green eyes glistening. "I can change. I could make you so happy."

"You could never make me happy," she said calmly. "Guillen does. And I..." If she didn't quite believe it yet, she was close. "I deserve to be happy." Yanking the door open, she promptly left the cell, only breathing again once the door slammed closed, once the guards secured the latch.

The next day, Guillen was off at official meetings when an unexpected knock at Rachel's guest room door pulled her focus from a journal. She opened the door, and a palace guard bowed.

"Please follow me."

Rachel bit her lip, still wary about being in the palace. "Is something wrong?"

"No, ma'am. The queen requested your presence."

She reluctantly followed him, winding through corridors and climbing stairs. "Where are we going?"

"She's waiting for you in the tower."

Rachel still hadn't taken Kaylah's staff up on the offer of an extensive tour of the giant building, and it wasn't exactly a tour they were on, but they covered a lot of ground. The higher the floor level, the more ornate the décor. As they reached the highest levels, real ivy vines ran along the top of the walls almost like crown molding. Something felt different as she got higher in the palace. It wasn't exactly eerie, but quiet ... and not just because there were fewer people there.

They were met by another guard at the base of a short stairwell. The escort had Rachel go up the narrow winding stairs first. Two more guards stood at the top landing, on either side of the only door at the highest level.

Rachel scrutinized the tiny space. Several more ivy vines converged at the landing. She was both oddly calm, and also nervous, to be surrounded by so many muscled guards.

"She's expecting you right inside." A guard opened the door.

Rachel was floored at the sight beyond the open door. Nearly every inch of the walls and ceiling was covered with vines. It was a rather small area, with a massive window at the other end of the room. A border of stained glass surrounded the window; under it sat a padded bench. Facing the window was a throne.

The guard ushered Rachel in as she picked her jaw up from the floor. The moment she passed the threshold and the guard closed the door behind her, a wave of calmness hit Rachel.

"Come sit down." Kaylah's melancholy voice came from the throne.

Rachel strode past the throne and gently perched on the only other place to sit, on the bench under the window. From this angle, she also spotted a large bookshelf inside the room, near the door. Constructed of dark metal, the shelves were closed off with latticework. The latches were busted, looking like they'd been pried open.

She shifted her focus back to Kaylah. "Hey. How are you doing?"

Kaylah sat with her legs tucked up under her, gazing out the window. Her long dress flowed down to the floor. "Not sure."

Something was still off here, and that something included Kaylah. "Pretty cool room," Rachel said. "How long have you been hiding away up here?"

Kaylah continued to look out the window. "Since I got up."

Rachel pursed her lips. It was already early afternoon.

"This is the Queen's Room," Kaylah said, still dazed. "By law, anyone entering without the queen's presence and express invitation, takes upon themselves a death sentence."

Rachel almost smirked at the absurdity of such a law, but Kaylah's face remained completely sober. "You're serious?"

Kaylah's eyes finally met Rachel's. "Yes."

Wow. "Well ... thanks for inviting me, then... I'm guessing not a lot of people get the privilege."

Kaylah cracked a smile and shook her head. "My mother only brought me up maybe a handful of times that I can remember, over the years. Though she spent plenty of time here. And it feels completely different now." She sat up straighter. "And I'd bet the kingdom you're the first Seeder to ever be allowed up here."

"I'd say that's a safe bet. Thanks again, for the honor. On the topic of it feeling different ... am I going crazy, or does it feel, like ... really weird in here?"

Kaylah pointed in Rachel's direction. "This window faces the kingdom. This room is where the Mother Vines end."

Rachel looked around again. She'd never seen a room so overtaken with plant growth—it wasn't like it was a greenhouse. "And how does that work?"

Kaylah drew a deep breath. "What does it feel like to you?"

Rachel bobbed her head back and forth. It felt like a nice place to meditate, honestly. A good place to sort out your thoughts. She could see the appeal—it was quiet, secluded. She shrugged. "It feels nice. Really peaceful. Is that something the Vines do?"

"Yeah. It used to feel that way for me, too."

Used to? "But how does it feel now?"

"I can feel their power. This is where a lot of decisions are made."

Rachel slowly nodded. This ... wasn't the Kaylah she knew. It might be that Kaylah was still sorting through her trauma, and feeling the weight of an entire kingdom on her shoulders. But it felt like something more. Rachel was becoming nervous, and it didn't feel right to outright ask 'Why did you send for me?' Instead, she skirted around her growing suspicions. "You've said the Vines answer to the queen. What does that feel like? Do you actually hear voices or something?"

Kaylah let out a short breathy chuckle. "No. It's not like that. But it's feelings, impressions."

"Your Mother Vines... They're a major cause of nutrient depletion in your kingdom, right? You said you were going to turn them back to the people?"

Kaylah's lip quivered, a look of despair covering her face. "I murdered my uncle here. My parents were killed here. The irony's not lost on me that my brother sits in the dungeon and I'm up here, when a few weeks ago it was the other way around."

"He broke your laws," Rachel replied softly. "They all hurt a lot of people. But I know it's still hard."

Kaylah's eyes filled with tears. "What if I'm wrong? I want to do things right. But this is my legacy ... and I'm destroying it. I love a human. I won't have kids. I have no family. I'm throwing away tradition."

If the crown princess had only been in this room a handful of times, it wasn't likely Catrina had actually ever been there, but perhaps she knew about it as a downline heir. It had been Catrina who voiced concern about power corrupting when they were back at the Unitas camp.

Rachel wrung her hands, not wanting to say the wrong thing. "You have family. Guillen will always be there for you. And Catrina. Ginger and Nathan. And Eric..." That one was a tricky subject she perhaps ought to have omitted. "And me. You're my sister. I'll never leave you."

Kaylah sniffled, wiping away tears.

Rachel cleared her throat, cautiously curious about a sensitive but related subject. "Guillen told me you have two younger brothers. I still haven't met them."

Kaylah looked down. "Yeah. They're in the care of people I trust right now. This is all pretty confusing for them."

Rachel left it at that. After conversations with Catrina, she'd learned more about their family dynamics. Kaylah's younger brothers were only eight and ten. Kaylah hadn't known them well with all of her time away, and now she was going to be something of a mother figure for them. To add to it, Catrina had confessed she wondered if having the younger kids had been an attempt by the former queen and king to produce a second heir, a replacement heir. Rachel wouldn't touch that with a ten-foot pole. The hurt implied by those assumptions could cut incredibly deep.

"As for traditions." Rachel shrugged. "Not all traditions are created equal. Save the best of them. Make new ones. For your kingdom to come to this point, they chose to lay aside even older traditions—remember that." She side-eyed the jungle of vines surrounding them. "You've made a heck of a lot of good decisions without this room. What would happen if these vines were removed? That's what's going to happen soon, right?"

"It's not that simple. I'll be touring the communities. That'll give me an opportunity to meet the people more, and retrain the Vines at the roots."

Rachel squinted at the half answer, adjusting her seat on the bench. "Will the Vines in this room go back to the communities?"

Kaylah frowned, barely speaking above a whisper. "I'm afraid I'll lose that connection to my people."

Rachel opened her mouth, pausing. "I ... couldn't even pretend to understand how your powers work. Or try to tell you what all the right answers are. But I know you'll do the right thing. And I think you need to ask yourself if it's *connection* that you're afraid of losing, or *control*?" Rachel tilted her head, only a slight pain accompanying the movement. "You have a lot of good people in your kingdom; I've met them. They just need a strong leader. And that's you. Not this room."

Kaylah gnawed on her bottom lip.

Rachel touched one of the leaves on a nearby vine. "Are there any other laws I should know about? So I don't accidentally get myself killed?"

Kaylah grinned. "Best friends get immunity. Just try not to murder me?"

Rachel chuckled. "Deal." She stood, running her hand across the leaf-covered wall. The vines clinging to the wall were large, bumpy, and tan, interwoven across a canvas of stone. The leaves rustled, cool and soft against her skin. "Can you tell them apart? If they connect you to the communities, do you know which is which?"

From the throne, Kaylah's eyes followed Rachel's movements. "I can. I couldn't when I was younger, but now I can."

"If Guillen weren't closely related to you, which community would he have been forced to have inked on his arm?"

Kaylah frowned, standing up, surveying the wall. She touched a vine. "This one."

Rachel walked over to meet her. She cautiously grasped the vine, waiting to see if Kaylah would stop her. When she didn't, Rachel slowly tugged it free from the wall. It entered the room through one of several openings near the ceiling. Kaylah didn't stop her, so she proceeded to reach into her pocket, pulling out her knife. "What would happen if I cut it off?"

Kaylah's eyes locked with hers. "It'll regrow, until I retrain them on-site. But I won't be able to feel that connection from here until it regrows over the next few weeks."

Rachel stood on her tiptoes, trying to reach as much of the vine as possible. She held the knife to the vine. "But the people will have less drain on their resources? Sounds like a promising start before your tour to meet the people as their new queen."

Kaylah nodded, mulling it over. "The Vines also help with our rifting barrier, keeping a protective perimeter around the palace." She furrowed her brow in thought. "But just trimming the parts in this room wouldn't weaken that."

Rachel waited for her approval, still holding her knife up to the vine. "Okay. So...?"

"Do it." Her tone landed somewhere between resolve and surrender.

The vine was tough, but with enough force and a little sawing, Rachel cut it loose. These Vines had much smaller tendrils than those she'd seen on her travels thus far. She handed the severed vine to Kaylah. Kaylah ran her fingers over it.

"I wonder what these walls look like under all this," Rachel said.

Kaylah let out a long, slow, measured exhale, gingerly laying the vine over the throne. Then she reached for her own dagger, pulling it from a sheath under the skirt of her dress. "Let's do this."

Rachel smiled as they both picked a new vine.

After a good half hour, the walls were bare, but marred from smaller roots having found cracks to expand. The best friends sat on the bench together, and Rachel wrapped her arm around Kaylah. The energy of the room had dissipated. Now, a *natural* calm was taking its place.

Kaylah laid her head on Rachel's shoulder. "Thanks. I don't think I could have done that alone."

"Any time. I'm honestly surprised you had the wherewithal to tell the guards to bring me. You were pretty out of it."

"I didn't," Kaylah whispered.

"What? The guards came to get me on their own?" That didn't seem consistent with such a strict edict about who was permitted into the Queen's Room.

"I was afraid," Kaylah confessed. "I told them to get you if I was in here too long. I didn't want to become like my mother, at least not the side of her I saw when she'd spent too much time here. And especially not susceptible to anyone else's influence." She picked at her fingernails. "I've never even told Eric."

Rachel rested her head against Kaylah's. Perhaps Seeders and Ivies really did have more in common than they'd previously thought. The most powerful members of their races could also become the most vulnerable, given the right circumstances. And from her own experience, it took great strength to ask for help, to admit that you needed it.

Hadn't Saff asked about this very thing? About the Ivy queen having a weakness?

"You know..." A smile grew on Rachel's face. "I'm not eligible to vote in your kingdom, and you don't even vote for the queen. But you'd have mine."

Kaylah chuckled. "Thanks. I'll take all the votes I can get right now, especially if they're votes of confidence."

Sighing, Rachel examined the marred walls. "Maybe you should commission Saff, or some other artist, to do a mural up here. Something bright that reminds you of your vision for the future, since that's where we're headed anyway." She squinted, looking closer at the junction of the wall and ceiling.

Rachel stood back up, using her knife to push aside bushy stumps of detached vines. "Maybe don't paint the trim. Call me crazy, but I think that's jade."

Kaylah rose, scrutinizing it as well. "Huh ... yeah. I guess there's more I could learn about how that works."

Rachel smirked. "Pretty cool. Catrina recited a poem that said all green folk are kin."

Kaylah gave her a hug. "I'm glad you're staying."

Rachel squeezed her tight. "You're family."

"Well, we've got a lot of work to do. Fixing this mess of a realm is going to be one heck of a marathon."

Rachel pulled back, holding Kaylah's shoulders. "Then I guess we better get to it."

Kaylah frowned, nodding.

"Would it cheer you up if I let you call me a lightning bug?"

A grin grew on Kaylah's face. She slung her arm around Rachel's shoulders. "You'll always be my favorite glow-butt bug."

Rachel laughed as they opened the door and exited the Queen's Room. "You only get to call me that in private."

Chapter 45

Saff and Devin lay down for the night in the massive palace chambers they'd been assigned, in the softest bed she'd ever slept on, holding each other under satin sheets.

The next thing Saff knew, she plodded down a stone corridor, the crispness of her vision veiled in memories. She'd just left a bound-and-gagged Soren with an injured Devin, and an almost-as-ragged Arlo.

The palace air was cold around her as she made her way through the hallways, as her heartbeat slowed, as sweat stung her eyes and wounds. She feared a guard might slip their restraints, might come out of a hiding place and attack her. She was spent.

Despite the soldiers and captives and chaos all around her, the moment seemed muted, foggy, off. Her legs were twice as heavy as they ought to be. She kept plodding forward, searching, *needing* to know who else in the Unitas strike teams had made it out alive.

There were bodies everywhere, but it was especially heartbreaking when she ran across her first Unitas victim, a Seeder. She backtracked to where they'd initially come in. The last time she'd seen Jon was a few flights up, at the top of a set of stairs.

Shock from the battle gave way to tears as she found his body at the base. She double-checked and confirmed Jon was gone. Green folk weren't invincible, not even whispers. She dreaded returning to tell Arlo.

Saff didn't have to search long before her heart completely shattered. Flora lay on her back, her hair a cascade of burgundy braids. Saff dropped to her knees by Flora's side, feeling for a pulse, but there was none. She sobbed, guilt washing over her. Flora had been so promising, so strong, so talented, so young. But her fighting partner had abandoned her, had betrayed them all.

Saff couldn't move. She just knelt there, holding Flora's still-warm hand, crying. She wasn't capable of moving, of seeing anyone else she cared about dead. She couldn't fathom making her way to the dungeons now to discover what had become of Rachel, Heather, and Kaylah.

"Saff?" Ginger's tired voice made Saff look up.

She sniffled, relieved to see a familiar face, even if it was as mangled as Saff's was.

Ginger gave her a sympathetic frown. "Is Devin...?"

Saff sniffled again. "He's okay for now."

Ginger forced a smile. "Good. Have you heard about the other team?"

Saff's stomach knotted. The team taking on the dungeon was much smaller. That wasn't promising. "No. I was going to head down there to see."

Nodding, Ginger held out a hand. "Let's go together."

Forcing herself to stand and join Ginger, Saff couldn't stop thinking about Flora. She'd never get that image out of her mind. As they walked down a long corridor, away from Flora's body, the palace no longer felt cold.

Saff's face and ears grew warm as she thought about Raven and what she'd cost Unitas. Saff didn't care to count how many she'd killed in this war, but none of those kills had been in revenge. Until this point.

If someone hadn't already gotten to the girl, Saff would. And this time, no one would be holding her back.

She balled her fists, trying in vain to contain her anger and hurt. Needing to take out some of the building aggression, she shifted a wisp of energy to her arm, and slammed it into the wall next to her.

"Saff!" Devin groaned, winded. "Oww!"

Her eyes shot open. Her fists were still balled, but it only took a second to realize what she'd done.

She frowned, devastated, as Devin wheezed. "How bad?" she asked.

He lay on his side, clenching his jaw, holding his ribs with his hands. "Why do you have to be so strong?" he muttered through his teeth. "I'll be fine."

"Come on, let me see." She moved his hands and healed him. While he was doing significantly better with his recovery after two-plus weeks, he still had a ways to go. Getting beat up by her certainly wouldn't help.

"Sorry," she said as she removed her hand.

"You're fine," he said, snuggling up next to her. "I'll be fine."

She sighed, kissing him on the forehead. She'd had vivid nightmares after Ivy assassins had tried to kill her twice in the human world, though never as bad as Rachel had them. Saff was definitely having vivid dreams again now, and while she never woke up screaming, she *had* woken up hitting or kicking Devin more than once now.

Saff had suggested she sleep on the couch in the suite they'd been assigned, but Devin wouldn't have it. As guilty as she felt for hurting him and interrupting his sleep, being together was something they both needed.

"You're right. We'll both be okay," she said, holding him tighter.

Closing her eyes, she tried to fall back asleep, but couldn't. Instead, she savored Devin's body warmth while replaying her nightmare, and how everything that day had gone. She analyzed how they could have done things differently, but it wasn't like it could make a difference now. The fog of the nightmare had lifted, but the scene in her mind was as clear now as the day she'd experienced it.

When she and Ginger arrived at the dungeon, a dozen soldiers had just opened the doors and cleared the area. Saff's feet barely moved as she was permitted entrance; it was like trudging through a marsh, her feet hesitant to walk down the stairs and find the rest of their group.

The first truly familiar face was Kaylah's. "Saff!" Kaylah's face and arms were in rough shape, red with cuts and infection. Two Seeder soldiers helped her walk toward the stairs Saff was descending. Ginger ran down the stairs and helped.

Saff and Kaylah shared exhausted but mutually relieved smiles. "I'm glad you're okay." Saff wanted to give her a hug, but Kaylah didn't look to be in a state where that was a good idea.

"You too. How's camp, and everyone else?"

Saff fought back fresh tears. She couldn't answer that. She couldn't make a list of the dead yet. "I think Devin will be okay."

Kaylah frowned.

Almost tripping over a body at the bottom of the stairs, Saff stepped back to allow space for Ginger and the soldiers to help Kaylah up.

The stillness of the area weighed on Saff's heart and nerves. "What about Rachel and Heather?"

Now Kaylah's eyes filled with tears. Saff's heart stopped beating entirely.

"They're down the hall with Guillen."

Saff forced herself to breathe. *Would she word it that way if they were dead?* As Kaylah was escorted up the dungeon stairs, Saff crossed the landing to the hallway. To her right, all she could see were fallen guards and an open cell door.

To her left was a busted old wooden door; that was the direction Kaylah had been led from. Saff crossed the threshold. A Seeder soldier stood facing an opening several yards down.

Saff willed her legs to move faster, and peeked inside once she got there. Rachel lay unconscious on the floor, her head and neck soaked in blood. A Seeder matriarch cradled the back of Rachel's skull with glowing hands. Guillen knelt next to Rachel, squeezing her hand, his face the picture of desperation and concern.

Heather sat against the wall, hugging her legs, despondently staring at Rachel. Heather didn't look to have any injuries of her own, but she was drenched in almost as much blood as she had been when Saff found her right after Ben had died.

They'd saved Kaylah. They'd caught Soren. But at what cost?

"Can ... I help?" Saff offered, not that there was much she could do.

The healer shook her head, continuing her work. Heather finally looked up, meeting Saff's gaze. She frowned and started to cry.

Saff sat next to Heather, and in silence, everyone watched the healer do her work. After several minutes, someone arrived with a stretcher. Saff, Guillen, and Heather stepped into the hallway so the others could carefully lift Rachel onto the stretcher.

Guillen followed Rachel, thanking Heather before leaving down the hallway. Only then did Saff give Heather a tight hug.

"Is he okay?" Heather asked.

"Yeah, Devin will be fine."

"Please tell me it's over," Heather begged in a soft voice.

Was it? Taking the palace back didn't mean the war had officially ended. Saff had to have hope, or at the very least, had to give Heather some. "Yeah. It's over."

Heather sniffled in her arms for a minute. Everyone else had left the dungeon area except for a few guards who were sweeping and clearing each and every room.

The prospect of climbing back up a short staircase felt akin to climbing one of the impossibly tall mountains on the realm's Outer Rim. Not up to it quite yet, Saff instead focused on the open cell door down the hallway. "That's where Kaylah was being kept?"

Heather had her arm around Saff, Saff's arm around her. "Yeah."

Curiosity called Saff closer. They stepped over pools of blood and a few bodies of guards to reach it.

The cell was disgusting, the floors covered in dirt and dried blood. Something glimmered from the corner of the cell—a knife she'd seen Kaylah use before. Saff picked it up and examined it. The tip was bent, the blade covered in nicks.

After looking the room over, the sisters-in-law stared at each other, neither of them speaking. Nothing needed to be said. They weren't lifelong soldiers. Nothing was guaranteed right now. They both desperately needed healing, showers, naps, willow bark, and a gallon of water each. Probably chocolate, too. None of those were options right now. Maybe the water, once they gained the strength to tackle those stairs...

Saff slumped to the floor of the cell, and Heather followed suit. Resting her face in her hands, Saff breathed deeply. "Just a few minutes."

Saff turned in bed, blowing out a long breath. By the time she had finally gotten around to hunting down Raven, someone else had already taken her out. Never before had Saff been that livid, but it had likely been a blessing in disguise that she couldn't kill Raven herself. Now that she had a clearer mind, she was grateful fate hadn't afforded her that opportunity, that choice. She wasn't sure what a revenge killing would do to her, and if she could ever be the same person after that.

That scared her.

In the two-plus weeks since they'd been there, Kaylah had ordered the palace searched. Every inch was scoured for information Soren wouldn't give up, like where the kidnapped Seeder girls were located. Nothing was found on their account, but Kaylah had discovered information about whisper rifters, and she'd confirmed rather quickly that Raven had been the whisper who helped in her kidnapping.

As much as Saff hated Raven, new information helped her understand Raven's plight. Like 'Queen' Beata *supposedly* was, Raven had been hiding a pregnancy.

Saff admittedly hadn't always been great at putting herself in other people's shoes. But how would that have felt, to have your powers used against you from a young age, to have an attractive, charismatic, powerful man seek you out, to think he loved you, to think you shared something rare and special, and to have him be the father of your unborn child? What lengths would a mother go to for her child and the man she loved?

Kaylah shared with Saff that Soren had callously admitted since his capture that he'd known Raven was pregnant, and still sent her as a spy, still allowed her to die in battle. When Kaylah had informed him of Raven's demise, he'd remarked, with the warmth of a sociopath, 'That's a shame. I kind of liked that one.'

It felt wrong to pity the traitor. What she'd done was unforgivable, yet somehow, understandable.

Saff rolled onto her back, sighing again.

"Not able to fall back asleep either?" Devin asked.

"Nope."

Later that same day, Kaylah escorted Saff, Devin, Rachel, and Guillen out to the burial grounds to pay their respects. Saff's feet were heavy as she walked with Devin's arm around her shoulder. It was too nice of a day to go to a graveyard. The sky should have been dark and stormy, rainy and depressing. It didn't have a right to be filled with warm sunshine and songbirds. Nature hadn't gotten the memo.

Kaylah first showed them the Seeder burial yard. She'd consulted with a Seeder council member about how to respectfully handle their dead. With battles still being fought, and it being several days' walk across the Neutral Woods, they'd settled on a plot of land next to the Ivy royal burial grounds, so they could be buried as heroes.

Devin rubbed Saff's upper arm as they gazed on the soil; yellow flowers emerged from some spots, purple flowers from others. The area had been set up with a picket fence and guards to ensure it was safe and the graves wouldn't be desecrated.

Saff pondered on the site and the names of those she'd gotten to know. She was conflicted. This wasn't one of their traditional burial grounds. It wasn't surrounded by dozens of loved ones from their families and villages. It didn't have the large central tree with soothing energy that she knew from back home. But each of these Seeders had known what they were up against, what they were willing to sacrifice. She hadn't previously thought about where she and Devin would have been buried if they hadn't made it out alive, but it would have been here. It didn't feel as wrong as it should have, to have their fallen comrades so far from their homelands, given family meant so much. It still didn't feel right, though—how could *any* untimely death be?

After a little while, they walked with Kaylah to the Ivy royal burial grounds. A mat of intertwining vines covered the ground. Unsurprisingly, the graveyard was filled with tons of large ornate tombs. The larger the stone, the more important the person. This was the final resting place of Ivy queens and kings, and their families. Passing one, Kaylah shook her head. Rachel and Guillen trailed behind her. Rachel's head lowered as they walked by. Saff's stomach knotted when she read the name on the offending gravestone—Nuren. It was sickening to have his body in a place of honor. She wished she could cover it with a black cloth, or something—a mark of shame. But he had made his mark on history, and *that* mark would bear his shame.

Kaylah hesitated at a much larger set of tombstones—her parents. Rachel and Guillen wrapped their arms around Kaylah. Saff frowned. That had to be hard. Saff had grown up as Mel, a girl with two loving human parents, and then added two loving Seeder parents. Kaylah's family was a mess, and she was rightfully conflicted. Saff and Kaylah had shared some good conversations since Kaylah's liberation, and had *finally* put to rest all of their differences.

Though they weren't technically Ivy royalty, Kaylah had still chosen to bury the Ivy Unitas fallen in a far corner of these grounds. This one was harder for both Saff and Rachel. Saff and Devin strolled over to Flora's grave. Devin held her tighter as the tears came. Flora had been so young, so full of life, and had had so much life still left to live. But she had lived her days with conviction; she was an example Saff would never forget.

"It's not fair, you know?" Saff whispered.

"I know," Devin replied.

Saff had experienced firsthand how impressive Flora was in a fight. But when Flora was forced to take three enemies on by herself, even *she* couldn't win. Saff sighed. If she'd been a Seeder, she might have been able to heal her own wounds ... perhaps could have lived. But not everyone was born with the same abilities and advantages.

Saff still struggled with guilt. She knew she shouldn't. *She* hadn't killed Flora. Saff and Devin had been paired on the strike team—their job had been to move swiftly and seek out Soren as soon as possible. But for every point of logic she held, a counterpoint of grief and guilt contradicted her.

Saff glanced over at Rachel and Guillen, standing by Jon's gravestone. Jon had given off that 'strong but silent' aura. He'd been key in Kaylah's first real move to stop this, when she'd freed Rachel and killed Nuren. Jon had sacrificed a lot to join Unitas.

Arlo had taken the news hard that his childhood buddy hadn't made it out. He'd demanded to bury Jon himself. He'd left for home a few days after the palace takeover, to inform Jon's family of the loss. Saff hoped they'd see Arlo again someday to properly thank him for helping out.

Despite the sadness of Jon's demise, a small smile crept onto Saff's face as Rachel bent over and placed a sunflower on his grave. Green folk didn't do that—they didn't cut flowers for decorations or gifts or memorials. It was very human, very nostalgic and sweet.(uu)

After a few more moments, the group shared hugs and began the walk back to the palace. Saff continued to watch and think about Rachel. Guillen's arm was firmly around her, as Devin's was around Saff. Rachel leaned her head against Guillen's arm. If they made each other happy, then they couldn't be wrong for each other. Happiness was what Rachel deserved.

Saff frowned, her mind momentarily drifting to her sister-in-law, Heather. She hadn't gotten her happily ever after with Ben, but she'd saved Rachel's life that day, down in the dungeons.

Heather was another great example for Saff, on pivoting when life changed your plans. After she'd lost her fiancé, Heather had wanted to throw herself into Unitas and help. Saff and Devin couldn't be more proud. Heather had already returned home to Seeder lands. They still didn't know how their families fared—they had several family members likely still fighting in the war.

"How are you doing?" Devin dared to break the silence with a whisper.

Saff stood straighter. "Ready to go home." They were staying for the coronation, then going back to South Fortinda.

"Me too." He kissed her cheek. "How are you feeling about coming home one short?"

She knew he meant the fact Rachel was staying behind. Like with a lot of things, Saff was conflicted. It wouldn't be a walk in the park for those two, but Rachel had always been on a different path from Saff. She hadn't ever settled in back home with Seeders. But she'd found a home; she'd made one.

Saff and Guillen had shared a couple of good private conversations while Rachel was unconscious. The only thing Saff could find to disapprove of was the fact that being with Guillen would most certainly mean Rachel was truly giving up her Seeder culture. Guillen wouldn't even allow Saff that point; he'd promised to try to urge Rachel to give her family and people a chance, to try to visit often when things calmed down.

"I'm happy for her," Saff finally answered Devin, though it didn't mean her heart didn't hurt. She'd mentored several students, but had only risked her life with one. Had only felt fiercely protective of this one—and she was growing up and walking away. She didn't need Saff anymore. "We all have to learn to let go and move on, right?"

Devin gave Saff another squeeze.

Chapter 46

The next day, Kaylah lent Rachel one of her gowns. Rachel chose a simple yet elegant cornflower-blue one from Kaylah's enormous closet.

It had actually been Rachel's idea to have the ceremony so quickly. Guillen hadn't planned on popping the question right away while she was still recovering, but Catrina had all but forced his hand.

Rachel and Guillen knew what they wanted. While they could have waited for things to calm down, or to organize something bigger, they'd decided to start a new chapter before they were thrown into the hectic demands of their new positions. Perhaps someday, they'd have a ceremony that involved more of those they loved.

Rachel sat in front of a beautiful vanity decorated with carved and gilded nature-themed filigree, as one of Kaylah's maids braided her hair. A soft knock rattled the door.

"Come in."

Saff popped her head in. "Just wanted to see how you were doing."

Rachel grinned, sparing a glance at her new ring. "I'm good."

Saff entered, shutting the door behind her. She crossed the room and sat in a nearby chair.

Rachel drew a deep breath, imagining all of Saff's objections. "I appreciate you and Devin attending the wedding."

"It's an honor. We're happy to be here for it."

"But..." Rachel ran her thumb over the soft bristles of a hairbrush she held in her lap. "I'm young. And we haven't dated long. And my family hasn't even met him, and they don't know I'm doing this. And that I'll be living over here for who-knows-how-long."

Saff crossed her legs, straightening a dress she'd also borrowed. "Why are you telling *me* all of that? Are you having second thoughts?"

Rachel bit her lip. She was anxious, but none of it was centered on whether she was meant to be with Guillen. "No. I could never be happier with someone else. I just ... know this won't make everyone happy."

Saff shrugged. "Marriage isn't about making *other* people happy. And I'm not one to talk. I married young. Devin was my first boyfriend."

Rachel narrowed her eyes. "And you're still happy with your choice?"

"Every day," Saff answered confidently. "Sometimes, you just know."

Rachel nodded as the maid finished up and excused herself from the room.

Saff gently tugged at creases in the yellow fabric of the dress she wore, smoothing them out. "Family is important. But not all families look the same."

"Thanks. I really appreciate you."

Saff stood, resting her hands on Rachel's shoulders. They looked into the beautiful gilded mirror together. "Ditto," Saff said.

"You guys are going back to Seeder territory soon?"

Saff tucked a piece of baby's breath a little tighter in Rachel's braid.(vv) "That's where we belong, but we'll be in touch. We're still working with the council and Kaylah. We're just a rift or two away." She smirked. "I had a queen approach me about a painting."

Rachel met her smile. "Do tell."

Saff pursed her lips. "I'm flattered. But I'm not a pro. And I feel that project would be more appropriate assigned to an Ivy. I told Kaylah I'll work on something a little smaller as a coronation gift, when I can grab some free time."

Rachel thought back to her museum tour with Guillen. Someday, when the dust settled, they could have artists from both sides working together. They could exchange work in exhibits between the nations. Someday.

Saff straightened the chain of the necklace Rachel wore. "Well, things are about to start. I shouldn't be bugging you. Anything I can do for the bride?"

Rachel cocked her head. "I think I'm good. Any advice for a soon-to-be-newlywed?"

Saff looked at the wall, pondering. "Fight for your marriage as much as you did for Unitas."

Rachel beamed. "I will." Her thoughts turned pensive. She and Saff had chatted a bit during her recovery, but there was still so much unknown about their futures. "Going back to mentoring in South Fortinda?"

Saff crossed her arms, wrinkling her nose. "I don't know."

"Hmm." Rachel twisted her lips, nodding. "Yeah, I'd be hesitant too. It's kind of like when humans have their last kid and they call it quits. They know they can't turn out anything superior after that one, so they stop while they're ahead."

Saff chuckled. "You weren't my last Seeder girl to mentor."

Rachel pointed at her. "Last full-time assignment."

"You have a point. But ... I've had this conversation with my sisters before. Human parents only stop at the last child because they realize things are going downhill and they can't handle it anymore." She winked, and Rachel stuck out her tongue.(ww)

"But in all seriousness, I don't know," Saff confessed. "That scares me. Sometimes I don't like options. Someday, who knows how soon, we won't need all these soldiers, or training in covert ops in the human world. Maybe I'll focus on my paintings, or help with education in other ways." Saff scratched her arm. "I wish I knew."

Rachel stood and gave her a hug. "You'll do great, no matter what you pick." She squeezed a little tighter.

Another knock sounded at the door, and Kaylah peeked her head in. "Hugging without me?"

Rachel and Saff chuckled. Kaylah sauntered over, every bit the queen in a dark plum gown, and gave them each a hug. "Are we ready?"

Rachel gathered another breath, standing tall. "Absolutely."

In a beautiful room at the palace, Kaylah officiated Rachel and Guillen's wedding, with a half dozen witnesses. Saff and Devin held hands, smiling wide. Catrina was just a hair short of giddy. Catrina and Guillen's father, who Rachel finally got to meet, stood next to Catrina, peace in his expression. Ginger and Nathan were happily reunited, ever supportive as they'd been in the human world.

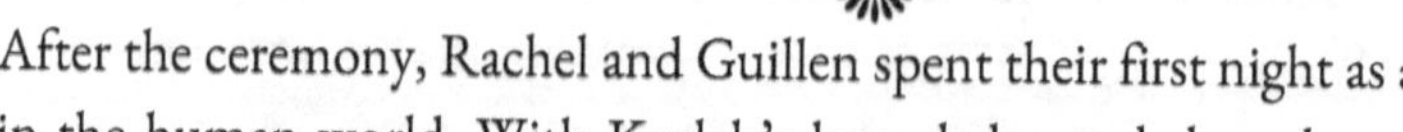

After the ceremony, Rachel and Guillen spent their first night as a married couple in the human world. With Kaylah's knowledge and the other girls' discoveries, Kaylah now had the cave near the palace primed to travel there, too. Taking Kaylah's suggestion, Rachel and Guillen planned to be gone for Soren's execution, but would return in plenty of time for Rachel to not be in danger of root rot. The official coronation would take place the day after they planned to return.

As always, the lack of Green Lands energy made it feel colder in the human world, but the crisp autumn air made Rachel feel it even more. Having spared no expense, they honeymooned in an extravagant hotel—at least, the nicest one that wasn't too far from one of their caves.

It was the middle of the night; Rachel sat out on the balcony, lost in her thoughts and wrapped in a blanket. The sliding glass door opened, and Guillen strolled out to join her, also wrapped up. She scooched over on the bench she'd claimed, making room for him.

He kissed her on the forehead. "You okay?"

She smiled warmly, her heart full. "I'm perfect. Just woke up and couldn't fall back asleep. Figured I'd take in the view."

He tugged on his blanket. "It really is colder over here. This is supposed to be the same season as back home? How is it you're not freezing?"

She nodded. "I'm alright. I'm tempted to seek out some hot cocoa, but for now, this blanket and my Seeder warmth have me covered."

Guillen nudged her shoulder. "Just remember, it's okay to ask for help. I would not be at all opposed to helping you keep warm." He gave her a seductive grin.

She giggled. "Offering to warm me up back in bed?"

He bit his lip.

She tried to keep a straight face. "Or were you offering me another blanket?"

He pursed his lips. "You're never going to let me forget that, are you?"

She gave him a toothy smile. "Nope. Never." She leaned over and placed a tender kiss on his lips.

He moaned as she moved to whisper in his ear. "I love you." She shifted and left a trail of kisses down his neck.

"Are you ready to come inside?" he asked, wanting in his voice.

"Just give me a couple more minutes."

He took a deep breath and stood. "Okay. If you're still having trouble sleeping, I don't mind staying up. And if you're *sure* you want to get a matching Unitas tattoo, I *really* don't mind helping you determine where on your body you want to get it." He winked before leaning down for one more smooch.

Her whole body tingled at his touch; she wanted to jump into his arms right then, but remained seated. She couldn't stop grinning as she watched him go back inside. She was elated to be with the man she loved. To have won the war. To have a safe place back home in the Green Lands, a position where she could make a difference.

But everything was still a bit grey. Every day was a struggle, and it would continue to be. Yet, she could confidently smile—things would never be the same.

Her sense of safety had been ripped from her in her childhood. But as a woman, she was now surrounded by those who really did love her. And would support her, be there for her, as much as she would be for them.

She thought of Saff. Saff and Devin wanted to have a clutch someday. Rachel couldn't help but think how crazy they must be to want that many kids. But she was also ecstatic for them, that their lands were being healed, and Seeder borders expanded past the tainted soil into the Neutral Woods. Their families would no longer have to be separated.

Rachel was at peace, looking forward to their plans for the next day. She'd finally be able to introduce Guillen to her human mom, Samantha. And ... to her human dad, Brad.

It was something of a wedding gift from Guillen and Eric, though they'd never anticipated it that way. Guillen had picked up on how much it gutted Rachel to not know what had happened to the dad who had disappeared from her life when she was a little girl. He'd sent a request to Eric in a letter, to try to find out—the letter she herself had delivered when she brought Guillen's mom and sister there for safekeeping.

Eric had used some Unitas funds to hire a private investigator to find out what had happened with Brad's mysterious disappearance. In typical fashion, Nuren had told a truth, peppered with lies. Brad was alive and well. And he *had* actually freaked out when his wife finally shared their daughter's nonhuman identity, two years into their marriage.

But he hadn't abandoned them willingly. Not sure how to process the news all those years ago, he'd confided in the wrong man—a co-worker named Rob. Rob—Duke Nuren, Kaylah's uncle—had been serving as a lowly assassin general in the human world at the time. He'd latched on to the opportunity to infiltrate a Seeder family network and learn their secrets, gaining him a position with his brother, the king, in the palace as an advisor. Nuren had threatened Rachel and Samantha's lives, and Brad had left the picture. Brad had looked them up every year, but kept his distance, seeing that 'Rob' was still there, a looming threat.

Apparently, Brad and Samantha had already been reunited. Rachel hoped for her mom's sake that they could pick things back up, and was over the moon that Samantha might have some confidence in love again. Brad had always made her mom happy, and happiness was what she deserved.

All that aside, it would be an awkward conversation the next day. It had taken *one* man in shock, taking a revelation from his wife poorly, to start all of this. To lead to the pain and deaths of so many, his own adopted daughter included in the host of those harmed. Rachel didn't harbor any ill will against him. She couldn't. Had he never done that, the war would still probably be carrying on back in the Green Lands, and here in the human world as well, hidden in the shadows, always locked in a stalemate.

Rachel took one last cleansing breath and spotted a falling star in the night sky. She watched it glide from view, not wishing for a single thing, before returning to bed.(xx)

After five blissful days in the human world, Rachel and Guillen drove back to the cave. He'd absolutely loved it there, able to walk around so casually with people just like him. The couple agreed to carve out vacations to make sure he'd get to enjoy plenty more experiences, even starting a list of what they wanted to do.

Rachel couldn't contain her excitement at seeing a familiar face at the cave entrance. She jumped out of the car and ran to give Eric a hug.

"Congratulations!" he said.

Guillen walked up and extended a hand. "It's nice to finally meet you. Thank you for all you've done."

Eric gave him a hearty handshake. "My thoughts exactly. Thanks for *your* part in all of this." He pulled Guillen into a brotherly hug. "I mean it. And I'm happy for you and Rach."

She beamed, her eyes glistening with gratitude. But then her joy faded. Eric hadn't been able to attend the wedding. He wasn't able to be with the one he loved. She and Saff hadn't been able to figure that one out.

Eric stayed by their side, and Rachel gave him another hug. He smirked.

"What?" she asked.

"I'm not here to say goodbye. I'm here to escort you two back." He pointed out a ring of his own.

Rachel grabbed his hand. "How did you get it to work?!"

"Nuren would be *livid* to know how much he's done for us. He discovered he could make the War Vines work for him by accessing Seeder blood. But *any* regular Seeder or Ivy blood can be used, with the right symbol, and right words, to make this work. Just like with Guillen's ring, there are a lot of restrictions right now on how the jade is being distributed."

She stared in awe at the ring, shaking her head. Kaylah hadn't divulged how close she was to figuring this one out. "How did she even find the time with all she's doing right now?"

"They said your mentor helped."

Rachel's heart warmed. Saff and Devin were still at the palace, and of course she would have her nose in a book, eager to help and discover more lost secrets of the Green Lands.

"Its use is limited, until they can sort it all out," Eric continued, a grin plastered on his face as he turned the ring. "But I'm kinda lucky, being the fiancé of the queen and all."

Rachel surveyed his face. "We still don't know how you'll be affected. It might not be safe."

Eric shrugged. "The first human to test it made a trip without any harm."

Rachel shook her head. "We still don't really know much about our origins, our evolution process. How our people and powers changed over time. We think humans came over first and *became* green folk.(yy) So much could go wrong. Have you really thought this through?"

"Well ... your ancestors might have been drinking primordial soup for a century before they went botanical, for all we know. And to me, Kaylah's worth the risk. I'd even drink the soup for her."

Rachel let her worries go. Kaylah needed as much support as she could get in her corner right now. She needed Eric at this pivotal point in her life. They needed each other.

"Take good care of her," Guillen said. "She deserves the best."

Rachel and Guillen walked through her rift first, followed by Eric, in shock and awe. Once they left the cave, he was even more dumbstruck.

"It's so ... *green!*"

They laughed at his observation. The Green Lands were called such because of the lush and rich atmosphere, and the botanical beings who lived there. But apparently, to the naked human eye, there was *actually* a tint to it as well—like a slightly green photo filter.

Rachel and Guillen got to be present for the first moments of Kaylah and Eric's reunion. It was beautiful. Kaylah even cried, and probably squeezed Eric half to death.

The next day at Kaylah's coronation, the throne room was filled to overflowing. Afforded special positions at the front were the usual suspects—those closest to her, the honored members of Unitas. Representatives from across the Ivy Kingdom were in attendance, as well as Seeder leaders.

Kaylah commanded everyone's attention as she entered in a breathtaking gown, which glistened as though beaded with emeralds. As she made her vows of loyalty to her kingdom, she made promises, she gave assurances, she planted hope. She pronounced the end of Unitas as a war movement, and designated it as a new way of life. The official Unitas symbol would also change. It wouldn't just be a flower and an ivy leaf. Behind them both was now a handprint: the sign of the third group, the easily forgotten ally that had stepped up to help end a war in a realm they'd never previously set eyes on—the humans.

Epilogue

Saff ran around their family cottage, tidying things up for the special visit. She threw an extra glance at the corner of the family room where her canvas and painting supplies resided. It was a bit untidy, but she wasn't sure she had the time...

"They're here!" Devin called out.

Squealing, she bolted out the door. She almost bowled George over as she hugged him tight, and then turned to give her love to Pam. "Mom! Dad! We're so excited you could make it again!"

A crowd was gathering around them. "Come inside."

"I'll be in in a few," George said.

"I'll hang back and make sure they don't tackle the old man," Devin razzed.

George gave him a playful stink eye.

Pam and Saff snuck inside while Saff and Devin's kids were busy chasing each other and jumping all over 'Human Grandpa.'

Saff took a relaxing breath as she sat down. "Sorry they're so crazy; usually they're so well behaved. They're just *really* excited to see you guys!"

Pam pointed at Saff. "Never apologize for my grandkids." She sat down and crossed her legs. "How are things going? What's new and exciting?"

Saff thought about where to start. Visits from her human parents were rare, and now that she'd reached full maturity, her rooting had her permanently stuck in the Green Lands—that limitation had never changed, not even with the caves. Though, they *had* discovered matriarchs could actually cave rift intrarealm. The equal energy on both sides of the rift still allowed that.(zz)

"Things are good." Saff smiled. "The kids are growing so fast. We love helping with the local education board. Everything's just ... really great. And you guys?"

"I'm glad to hear it. We're doing just fine."

A pair of Saff and Devin's kids dashing past the open doorway caught Saff's attention, and her eyes grew wide. "Benjamin!"

A little boy returned to view, scowling.

"Come here!" she ordered with a stern maternal voice.

Pam covered her mouth with a hand, poorly concealing a smile.

"What did I tell you?" Saff asked firmly.

"She started it!" Little Benjamin looked down at his bare feet, wiggling his toes.

Saff's eyebrows lowered as she gently lifted his chin to make him look at her. "I don't care. It's not safe, and it's not fair. If I see you chasing your sister with your blades out again, there will be *serious* consequences."

"Fine." He pouted.

Saff sighed. "Give Grandma a hug and then go out to Dad."

Little Benjamin got a warm snuggle from Pam before leaving.

After he left the room, Saff shook her head. "Seriously, that one. The irony of his defiance!"

Pam smiled warmly. "He looks a lot like his namesake, doesn't he? Especially when he's grumpy."

They both had a good laugh.

"Right?" Saff said. "But he'll be in for a serious awakening the day those girls' powers come in and they're ready for payback!"

Not five minutes later, a little girl came into the room, crying. Her lip quivered as she showed Saff a skinned elbow.

Saff gave her a kiss on the forehead and healed her injury before sending her on her way.

"Really, I swear, it's not always like this." Saff chuckled. "We normally have a ton of family help, everyone's just off doing other things so we could have more time alone with you guys before tonight's picnic." Saff was used to the chaos of large numbers by now, though it might be overwhelming for her aging human parents at a combined family picnic—all of Saff's and Devin's Seeder parents and their kids and grandkids had been invited. It would be a madhouse. The kind of madhouse Saff loved.

She shifted in her seat. "Which, by the way, Heather and her husband—they're hoping they can still have a clutch. They're thinking next spring will be her last chance. Either way, they look like they're doing real well."

"I'm glad to hear it," Pam said. "She deserved to find someone good for her, and live her life. Ben would have wanted her to be happy."

Saff wiped away a tear. Sometimes it still got to her, how much she missed him. Especially with how much she owed him. He hadn't just helped save her life in high school; he'd been the one to give her her extra power, extra energy-wielding ability. At least that was what she and Kaylah had surmised years ago. The timing of his intervention during the assassination attempt on her—during her botched bloom—had been perfect. Theoretically, she should have slipped into a coma, and by the time she'd woken up, her rooting would have likely passed. But instinctively, he'd accessed her energy to fight off their attackers, using just enough to keep the two of them safe, and, apparently, to keep her from losing consciousness, instead allowing her to reap the benefit of additional power for the rest of her life. He'd died never knowing that.

Pam gave her an understanding smile, then slapped her hand to her own forehead. "I almost forgot to tell you about the debacle at the cave on our way here!"

Saff was all ears.

Pam picked a piece of lint off her shirt. "I was *mortified*. Your dad and I went to pass through the cave rift, but it didn't work."

"What?" Saff scrunched her eyebrows.

Pam huffed. "Your dad and I had switched our tokens."

Saff chuckled. "Don't be embarrassed. I'm sure the cave workers see that happen all the time."

That was another awesome discovery Saff had had the pleasure of taking part in with her studies after the war. She still usually called Pam her 'human mom.' But strictly speaking, biologically—Pam *wasn't* human. In a way, they'd always kind of known that. If a Seeder girl didn't go back to the Green Lands by the time of her initial rooting, her powers died out, and she 'reverted' to her 'human form.' But she'd started out a seedling just like her sisters. And like any other green folk, Seeder girls, even those who had forfeited their powers, couldn't have kids with humans.

When they'd expanded their cave rifting trials to try to allow some of these girls to return home to the Green Lands, the kind of charms (or tokens, as a lot of people called them now) that humans like King Eric used, didn't work for them. They finally realized Seeder girls who had given up their powers still had residual Seeder energy in them somewhere. Just like Guillen and others who had been born without powers, they were technically Bomen. 'Bomen' was an agreed-upon title green folk without powers from both nations had taken for themselves—Botanical Humans. Bomen and humans had to use different tokens to rift.

"I'm sure they do have people goof like that often enough," Pam admitted. "I guess I was just too excited about this trip when I pulled them from my pocket."

Saff perked up. "Right! I got your riftmail. You said you were able to learn something exciting?"

"Yes!" Pam leaned forward in her seat, beaming. "We've discovered what village I'm from. My parents are gone, but I have some siblings still in the area. We're going to meet them!"

Saff smiled from ear to ear. Pam had admitted years ago that she'd regretted so casually forfeiting her powers, and the Seeder way of life. "That's so exciting for you! You'll have to tell me all about it. And get me their information—I'd love to meet more family."

"I will! Their village is in the far northwest, so it's not too close to here."

"Will you be taking the caves? Do you need help figuring anything out?"

Pam settled into her chair more comfortably. "No. With your dad retired, we have all the time in the world. And the Seeder council graciously extended our visa long enough for us to take our time making our way there. We're going to enjoy ourselves, taking in the sights." Pam started to choke up. "Finally making my trek home."

Rachel gave Guillen a huge hug. After a moment, he released her, gazing into her eyes. "I'm going to miss you."

He moved closer, leaning against her, her back against the wall. Sliding his hands to her waist, he stole a kiss.

"Ugh! *Gross!* Hurry up, Dad, they're here."

Rachel and Guillen chuckled in unison.

"Fine," Guillen called over his shoulder. "Make sure you and your brother have everything you need."

Rachel gave him one more peck on the lips. "That's a good sign, right? When you can still gross out your kids?"

He leaned in for another kiss. "I'm a firm believer in that."

She pulled back after a short smooch. "Alright, handsome. Let's go greet them."

He pouted. "I just got back from the northern council and you're already shipping me off!"

She stroked his chest with a finger, right above the place his Unitas tattoo was inked. "Yeah, well, I think you guys will somehow manage on a boys' weekend at the palace." She poked him in the ribs, and he grabbed her hand.

"Alright. But you and I have a date night when we're back." He walked with her outside. Wrapping his arms around her from behind, they stood and watched as the guards marched down their lane.

To their left was the teenager who had interrupted them; down the lane, their preteen son ran out to meet the approaching entourage.(aaa)

"Make sure you both behave," Rachel reminded their eldest. "Uncle Eric will let us know if you were any trouble."

He rolled his eyes. "We'll be good, Mom."

Once Kaylah and Catrina were in sight, Rachel broke free from Guillen's arms and ran to hug them. Eventually, the group gathered at Rachel and Guillen's front door, accompanied by several guards. Guillen and their sons also exchanged hugs with his cousin and sister before taking off with a few guards.

"Come on in!" Rachel welcomed in her sister-in-law and the queen.

The three women sat down in the family room.

Rachel grimaced. "I'm sorry I don't really have good places for all of your guards to stay the night... Guillen didn't build this place with this kind of visit in mind."

Kaylah waved her hand while taking a sip of tea. "That's their job. They'll survive camping out there." She took in the room. "I'm glad I finally get to see the place all finished. It's stunning!"

"He always did take pride in his work, didn't he?" Catrina added with a smile.

"Yeah." Rachel grinned, savoring the warmth of the cup in her hands. "Took long enough to finish it, but he wanted something of his own." She set her tea down, making an animated face at Catrina. "Of course, it would have been done sooner, if our boss didn't work us to death."

Kaylah gasped. "How *dare* you! Off with your head!"

The room erupted with laughter. Rachel stood, offering to give the women a full tour of their house. Guillen had built it from the ground up, but it had taken him several years with all of his duties in Ivy government that he balanced. Rachel's favorite part was the unique zebrawood paneling in the living room.

After their walkthrough, the group of friends settled back down to catch up.

Catrina shook her head. "I still can't believe how tall those boys are getting. Did you guys decide on what Tobias is doing for school next year?"

Rachel sat straighter in her chair. She still couldn't believe it herself. She had a *teenager*. Adopting a five-year-old and an infant when she was so young had *never* been on her list. The circumstances surrounding that decision had been filled with chaos and pain and struggle. Frankly, her and Guillen's first year of marriage could have been described that way as they tried to settle into a 'new normal.' In the end, the timing was right, Rachel and Guillen's little family was perfect, and the day they'd adopted the boys felt like it was just a week ago.

"Yes," she answered Catrina's question. "Tobias is definitely doing a foreign exchange year. I tried to talk him into doing it in Seeder schools, but he was *adamant* that he wanted to do it in the human world." She shrugged. "What can I say? Anything far away from his parents. And of course, the allure of humans is pretty exciting for their kind."

"You're not worried about him being so far away?" Kaylah asked. "It's been a couple of years now since your permanent change, right?"

"Yeah," Rachel said, trying to hide her longing for the world she'd grown up in, the world she'd never be able to step foot in again. "But my parents are hosting him back there, and Guillen can always go check on him. Tobias will be alright." She held up a finger. "Oh yeah, and since he didn't choose a Seeder exchange, we're going to spend some time visiting Seeder family this summer."

Kaylah smiled. "Tell Saff and Devin hi for me. It's been way too long since I've seen them both."

"Will do." Rachel turned her focus to Catrina. "So ... what's this I hear about a suitor?"

Catrina giggled. "Is that what we're calling him?" She took a deep breath and continued more seriously, unable to hide her smile. "He's a good man. And the right kind." She shared a knowing look with Kaylah. "When the time is right, for things to change."

Kaylah cleared her throat. "He *is* good, isn't he? Who was it that made the introduction, again?"

Rachel chuckled. "Always the matchmaker."

Kaylah gestured with her hands innocently. "What can I say? I'm good with people."

A lightkeeper lit up in Rachel's mind as she jumped forward in her seat. "I almost forgot! You'll never believe this. Not to bring up work, but Guillen just got back and discovered the *craziest* thing!"

Catrina cocked her head to the side, and Kaylah bent forward.

"He was doing a regular visit out at the far Bomen colony. He met a couple—a male Boman, from the Seeders, married to a female Boman, from our Ivies." She paused. "They're pregnant..."

Both Kaylah and Catrina's eyes grew large.

"I didn't think that was possible," Kaylah said.

Rachel smirked. "Well ... I guess it is."

Catrina rested her chin on a fist, leaning back in her chair. "I mean ... it would be an Ivy birth. I'm assuming the child would just be an Ivy Boman, right?"

Rachel shrugged. "I don't know. Maybe the latent energy from them both will produce something more ... a mixing of the races, something new? It's something we'll be monitoring closely."

Kaylah arched an eyebrow. "You never know. Every day is a new adventure."

"How's your husband's new job?" Kaylah asked the guard stationed directly outside of the Queen's Room.

"Oh, he *loves* it," she replied. "Thank you for the recommendation, Your Majesty."

Kaylah gave her a smile. "Good. It sounded like a perfect fit."

The guard opened the door, and Kaylah stepped inside. It was quiet and calm, one of her favorite places to hide away in the palace. It looked nothing like the room she'd seen as a little girl, or even as a brand-new queen. The ivy-damaged walls had been smoothed out and painted. She adored the bright mural on one of the walls, the style bearing a similarity to works by Monet or Van Gogh.

The throne had been moved a little to accommodate a love seat, and a new bookcase had long ago replaced the one her brother and his wife had damaged as they'd desecrated the sanctuary in their search for information that would help them win the war.

Kaylah strode to the bookshelf, running her hand along the edge of a hammered metalwork shelf. They'd lost so much ancient information in the old war. So many secrets had likely gone to the grave with Soren and their parents.

Some of the books here were ancient, others more modern. *None* of them were in her possession to hide secrets from her own people. She touched the spine of one that she often questioned whether she ought to have kept. It had been found in her parents' old chambers, which Soren had claimed as his own. The book contained names and details of known whisper rifters from back in those days.

It was an odd memento to keep. That information did nothing for her now. Whispers, just like Bomen, had equal rights, the same as everyone else in the kingdom now.

Sighing, Kaylah couldn't resist pulling out the book, making sure a few loose pages in the front didn't fall out. The loose pages had been torn out, kept separately—Soren's targets, or at least some of them. One of the names always left a bitter taste in Kaylah's mouth—Raven.

Of all things, Raven had been training to be a *schoolteacher*. She'd helped teach little kids. That trend popped up a lot in this little black book. Kaylah's parents, or those they'd entrusted who reported back to them, had a system all worked out to identify whispers. Based on observations and data collection, their pool of whispers to target had been narrowed down to two main categories—the assassins, and the spies. Male Ivies who showed more strength, and had already been identified by the Crown as a whisper, were singled out for assassin training, and after their days as assassins, they made it onto a priority list for palace guard duty.

Female Ivies, however, who were identified as whispers, were the true spies. Schoolteachers could report back to officials when little kids, oft missing filters, would blab about things they'd overheard their parents say, things the Crown might find disagreeable. Teachers could also ensure the right agenda and propaganda were taught in those impressionable years.

But the real reason behind having these Ivy whispers in the schools had been to detect the future generation of whispers, to identify them in the first place. Buried in the mythology of whispers was the truth. One of the ridiculous claims that circulated in Ivy society was that whispers were able to 'read your soul, and steal your energy.' That actually wasn't far from the truth.

Under order of the queen, for generations, Ivy children at the tender age of five had been required to rift for their first time. Their teachers trained them on the mental process, how to use their energy with their vines, where they would go to— an established location in the human world—and then return. It was a terrifying prospect for many kids, though they were conditioned to hide that fear, and show excitement. The event was massively hyped up.

What no one had known was that those very teachers were able to read not only a tree's last whisper after it had been used for a rift, but a person's energy—their gift—when they first learned to rift. In interviews following the war, whisper teachers had described to Kaylah how it worked. They had an extrasensory ability at that initial interaction to detect the gifted. They could also read it in the subtle difference in the children's reactions to opening their own portal. These women who had been forced into becoming spies, had also been required to handpick their own future replacements.

Kaylah shelved the book again. Maybe she kept it out of shame, as a reminder of the lengths her progenitors had gone to, or the shame that still lingered for her having made the assumption in the first place that whispers could only be men.

As she straightened the loose pages that stuck out the top, she was reminded of the most likely reason she kept the book. It still held secrets, and she hated secrets she couldn't solve. More pages had been ripped out than they'd found. She could only assume Soren had destroyed them for some reason. His wife, Beata, who to this day had never been found, wasn't listed in the book. Soren himself wasn't listed, but their parents may have chosen to omit him in the first place. Of course, that was assuming he actually *had been* a whisper.

Soren's staunch whisper supporters swore up and down that he'd proven himself to be one of them, but Kaylah wasn't sure they could be trusted. They couldn't really force Soren to demonstrate anything, and he'd needed to die so the realm could move on.

Kaylah frowned. As much as she wanted to believe her brother had only been a charlatan, the truth remained that she would never know for certain.

A soft knock on the door broke her from her train of thought. Eric poked his head in. "Mind if I join you?"

She pointed at him. "You know you never have to ask that."

"I know, but you might want some quiet time to yourself."

Shrugging, she glanced back at the bookshelf. She reached for the second-largest tome and pulled it out.

"Hmm, one of the big ones, huh?" he asked, sliding his arms around her waist. "Planning on staying up here all night?"

"Nah ... just perusing."

Still holding her, he pulled her back and sat down on the love seat, situating her on his lap. She smiled. While she loved her larger statement-piece gowns, she usually wore her thinner dresses around the palace and to less formal affairs. They were more convenient, and made it more comfortable to snuggle when she and Eric were able to sneak some time together.

"How was your meeting?" she asked.

"Blech." Eric wrinkled his nose. "Governor Channing can be so long-winded... Especially when it comes to human visitation laws."

Kaylah snuck a kiss. "Well, my dear, I don't think you will ever *not* be a novelty for these people."

"I don't know..." he said skeptically. "I woke up to some growths today... I think I might be going botanical."

She eyed him, knowing full well there was a punch line. There always was. Other than when he'd been devastated to be the first to find a grey hair, he hadn't ever noticed any changes as a human living full-time in the Green Lands.

He raised a hand to his chest. "Cross my heart." He then rubbed his chin. "A *ton* of growths."

She rolled her eyes. "Growing whiskers is something you do *every* day, babe. And if anything, it implies you're transforming into a cat, not a botanical being."

He chuckled. Eric had officially reached the dad joke phase a few years ago, not that they were parents. They'd never wanted kids, and while Kaylah should have technically produced heirs, she and Eric weren't capable of that. Adoption wouldn't have given a daughter the power of the Mother Vines, nor the legal right to succeed Kaylah. And Kaylah flat-out refused the idea of a relationship with anyone who could 'sire' an heir for her.

If anything, once things had finally settled in the realm and they'd felt safe sharing their relationship, the Seeders had warmed up to Kaylah even more. They'd always been fond of humans.

Kaylah couldn't live forever, nor would she want to. But she and Eric had a plan for the future of the kingdom.

Would it really be Kaylah, if she didn't have a plan?

Eric held her tight, and she nestled in more comfortably. He rested his chin on her shoulder. "So, more fairy tales?"

She balanced the large book on her lap with one hand, interlacing their fingers with the other hand. "You know me. Always searching for something I may have missed. Especially with that report of the mixed-race Bomen couple getting pregnant."

Eric groaned quietly. "But come on... We all know that's not possible, and what it's going to turn out to be... Right?"

Of course she knew it was statistically impossible... Ivy Bomen women could get pregnant by Ivy men—Boman or otherwise. But they *couldn't* conceive with humans, or Seeders—Boman or otherwise. The woman's claims that she was pregnant with her Seeder Boman husband's child was more than likely a sad attempt to explain infidelity.

Maybe Kaylah would ask Saff on her next visit, which would hopefully be soon. Saff had only missed visiting the palace once in the last dozen years.

"I know what you're thinking. But between you, me, and that mural..." Kaylah shook her head while extending a vine from her wrist, that hand occupied holding Eric's at the moment. With the vine, she flipped open the front cover of the book. "*This* queen will never openly accuse one of our subjects of that. We'll see how it plays out."

"You're right." He nuzzled her neck. "I suppose crazier things have happened."

She grinned, an Ivy queen sitting on her human husband's lap, in a realm filled with unique energy, with so many secrets to their past still hidden, so much of their future to be enjoyed.

Using her vine, she flipped through more pages of poetry, myths, and fairy tales. "Crazier things have happened."(bbb)

Annotations

Seeder Shadow Wars

Symbol	Page #	Annotation
a	1	Murial is a name I initially made up because I simply thought it sounded pretty. To ensure I'm not accidentally naming a character something with an unintended connection or meaning, I always look it up. I thought it was rather fitting once I did, learning the Latin-based meaning on a baby name site. If you happen to look it up, you'll find a good clue about which Seeder region Murial is from!
b	2	This scene was the inspiration for the entire Seeder Wars series. I had a dream about dandelion fluffs flying away, and a sense of foreboding, like they were being hunted. Wanting something different than the usual fantasy beings, I soon created Seeders and Ivies.
c	2	Bichons are the sweetest little fluffy white dogs, bred solely for companionship. At the time I wrote the first five novels in this series, I also had a bichon–mini poodle fur baby cuddled up with me for every step of the process. ♥
d	7	A loving nod to my Houser grandparents, who had a turquoise house for years because Grandma liked it so much.
e	11	My dad always made fun of his own age when I was growing up, mentioning he had a pet T. rex as a kid.
f	54	We'll see this callback a couple more times in the series.
g	67	We'll get to see this (the Grand Sea) in a later book as part of Thod & Murial's love story!
h	80	I broke my ankle in high school, requiring surgery. 10/10 do not recommend.
i	104	I hadn't solidly decided on Mel's/Saff's hair color until I decided on her Seeder name. I wanted something floral since Seeders are based on dandelions. I have a culinary arts degree, so that factored in, too. I thought it was fun to go with saffron (Saffrona), the most expensive spice, each bit hand-plucked from the center of a flower.
j	113	This is definitely a childhood memory for me. I had no fear of catching grasshoppers or hunting for earthworms.
k	178	I may or may not have helped my friend Bonnie cheat on a spelling test in the first grade. And the teacher may or may not have caught us and torn our tests... I don't recall ever cheating again after that!

The Return & Question

Symbol	Page #	Annotation
l	245	*Seeder Shadow Wars* was originally written as a standalone book, simply one Seeder girl's journey to stay alive, learn her powers, and choose her destiny. When my mind kept working and wanting more, I came up with the rest of the central trilogy. I knew there would be a gap in the timeline between books 1 & 2, and readers would be sad to miss important moments like these. Originally written as a preorder bonus for *Trouble in the Green Lands*, these 2 scenes are a sweet addition to connect the two books!

Symbol	Page #	Annotation
m	246	There's a crazy selection of plant life in the Green Lands—fruits and vegetables that just aren't found next to each other in the real world. There are pine trees next to pineapple trees, fresh spring produce harvested at the same time as typically fall crops. While I gave a lot more thought to an intricate hard magic system, I definitely threw caution to the wind to have fun in a whimsical perpetually spring realm filled with magic & plant people!
n	248	Sadly, we don't get to witness a traditional Seeder wedding ceremony in this central trilogy, but we will in Thod's book!
o	250	Sprout reveal day is HUGE for Seeders. It's what started these books in the first place. We get to see the tiniest bit of it in the prologue of *Seeder Shadow Wars*, but we'll get to see it more in-depth in at least one more book!
p	250	Thod's book is more of a romance and family story than the rest of this series, but I love the dynamic we get to see of Seeder life before Mel/Saff was ever in the picture.
q	251	While these 2 scenes were short, I think they're the perfect bridge between books 1 & 2. I realized we needed to expand the world, the cast, and the conflict, and these two set the scene quite a bit. We understand Saff and Devin and their families are safe, and despite her initial struggles to embrace her Seeder heritage, she's settled in and loves it.

Trouble in the Green Lands

Symbol	Page #	Annotation
r	258	Naming conventions for Seeders and Ivies—both given names and family names—are outlined in *Seeder Stories*. Information about Ivy royalty & titles can also be found there. Seeder family names are matronymic—since Seeder culture is matriarchal, the children take on the mother's given name plus either 'son' or 'dotter' as their last/family name.
s	259	Tatting is a kind of knotted lace made by hand with a small shuttle. It's not the most commonplace talent, so I run the risk of people misreading this as 'tattered.' Tatted is vastly different from tattered! It's a charming technique I've seen videos of and would love to learn myself one day.
t	263	We'll get to see this in Thod & Murial's book!
u	268	*Seeder Shadow Wars* was originally written as a standalone, and Saff's attackers were all regular ol' lackey assassins. Once I explored the Green Lands universe more, I connected the dots, and Nuren found a place. Luckily, I'd drafted the entire trilogy before publishing book 1, so I was able to add him in smoothly!
v	269	*Trouble in the Green Lands* gives us the fun opportunity to see a wider scope of Seeder family network techniques. Rachel's family is definitely different than Mel's, and we get a little more insight into how some of the human host families are scouted!
w	325	I had fun expanding both Seeder and Ivy powers. This is the first time we learn how they rift differently. We learn even more about Ivy tree rifting in the heir's duology spinoff!
x	338	I love to mirror themes within a book or series, especially to provide contrast. There's another shooting star scene in *Unitas: Trio* specifically meant to pair with this one.
y	347	We really don't get to know Murial in this trilogy, but we'll get much more acquainted with her in Thod's book.

Symbol	Page #	Annotation
z	395	I've believed for a while that I like the mystery and clues I weave into stories (and that my target audience would be on the same page) in part because I love escape rooms. I've participated in several and even designed a few with friends.
aa	407	Most (if not all) street names in this series are tree names. Just a fun & fitting trend for plant people.
bb	431	I get pretty deep into my emotions when I write. I cry as I write and edit—through the happy and the sad. I had a roommate in the room when I wrote this scene. She got worried when she noticed I was crying. I'm fairly certain she thought I was nuts for crying over a fictional death once I explained, lol!
cc	448	Simply for fun, I decided to mention 2 things in each book in this series—bacon and dancing.
dd	448	Different from the regular 'scene break' symbol we've seen throughout the story, we now run across 'POV shift' symbols. Otherwise known as 'head hopping,' POV shifts allow us to see into multiple points of view within a given scene. Head hopping is generally frowned upon by the literary community, but I'm in the school of thought that once you understand a rule, you can learn how to properly break it. It was important to me that we could smoothly and intentionally shift between our main characters' heads within some scenes. It helps balance the narrative and keeps us close to both when they're at odds. While this writing style isn't for everyone, it was necessary for this story, and I'm grateful for a fantastic editor who helped me navigate how to make the shifts smooth and clear.

Kaylah's Chronicles

Symbol	Page #	Annotation
ee	547	Guillen's story in the *Spy's Duology* will give an additional insight into scenes and events like this!
ff	552	I did have a wonderful high school history teacher named Mr. Tate. The Mrs. Anderson mentioned doesn't represent an actual person, though.
gg	556	Yes, this is the same brand of pizza mentioned in book 3. It might just end up as a recipe in my Green Lands cookbook someday, too...
hh	570	A sweet insight into Guillen and his mission—Rachel doesn't realize he hid and watched after leaving her, ensuring Saff & Devin found her safely...

Unitas: Trio

Symbol	Page #	Annotation
ii	584	I love learning about other cultures and languages. One of my readers from New Zealand messaged me, and we had a good laugh about my use of the word 'afghan.' While Afghan can mean a native or inhabitant of the country Afghanistan, it can also mean a knitted or crocheted blanket, which was my intended meaning. Apparently, in New Zealand they also have a traditional cookie/biscuit called an afghan.
jj	614	See symbol (gg) above!

Symbol	Page #	Annotation
kk	624	Why *aren't* there horses and larger animals in the Green Lands? I honestly don't remember why I made that decision. I think the biggest reason is it felt weird to have plant people eating animals. It's more of a special treat for them in the human world, though… It creates a fun environment where they rely on flight, walking, bicycles, rickshaws, and the occasional train. I think it's also charming and unique to be in a place with a different biodiversity than you're used to. It was hard to wrap my mind around the lack of dangerous snakes and spiders, and any major predators when I visited New Zealand. Why not have a place without bigger animals altogether?
ll	625	Electricity really doesn't work in the Green Lands realm, and the creation of static nettles was a bit of an accident on my part. I didn't want Rachel's torture to involve blood, so we had her shocked. But then I had to consider how that was possible. Static nettles may have been created for the plot, but that doesn't mean we don't learn more about these magical plants in future books…
mm	628	One of my beta readers told me Seeders made her think of Hobbits. I had a good laugh about that, but she's not wrong. They love nature and gardening, and are pacifists who prefer to keep to themselves… I added this as a fun nod to her comment.
nn	722	While editing *Trouble in the Green Lands*, my editor commented on this strategy. It really is brilliant, and I considered it, but decided it would probably have some downsides. She recognized how I used her feedback and then turned it on its head. We had fun with that. Sorry for raining on your parade, Nia!
oo	732	Art can tell us so much about our view on the world, and I was grateful for a chance to explore that here. Would the painter have focused on certain colors and shading to make their propaganda-fueled paintings darker? Did they mix uncomplementary colors to make the Seeders' skin appear unappealing? Did they—intentionally or not—misrepresent their attributes? Are the Ivies painted with more detail? With conventionally attractive attributes and more muscles? With lighter colors because they're enlightened?
pp	733	Several aspects of Ivy society were influenced by my experiences living in Poland. I intend no commentary or connection about the virtues and vices between the actual country and the Ivy Kingdom. But it was a loving nod. Magda and Beata are both common Polish women's names. Polish town squares (ryneks) are often astoundingly beautiful, full of vibrant colors and industry. The buildings, statues, and fountains are ornate, the flower and food vendors lively. I don't remember much live music in the ryneks, but it was fitting for the scene. This scene is depicted in my *Green Lands Fantasy Coloring Book*, where you can see the described fountain and everything!
qq	827	Whisper rifting wasn't originally built into the magic system when I started writing this series. It wasn't actually added until much later in the beta reading process of *Unitas: Trio*. Beta readers asked me how Kaylah went missing, because my earlier drafts were rather vague about that. I also kept asking myself how the Ivies are able to oppress Seeders when Seeders seem to have more powers and numbers. In the end, I enjoy the possibilities it opens up, and we'll learn even more about whispers in future books. Whereas Seeders are unnaturally and predictably consistent and homogenous in their powers and genetics, Ivies are quite a bit more complex.

Symbol	Page #	Annotation
rr	931	Authors are never able to spell out everything. We're not given every character's point of view, and the plot would slow down too much if we were. That said, I try not to have too many plot conveniences. I've had to ask myself more than once why Jon wouldn't have taken the charms to the remaining palace spies to sneak into the cave from within the protective barrier. Ultimately, Soren was far too paranoid at this point, and everyone in the palace was under intense scrutiny. Passing information is a lot easier than having something on your person and finding a way to wander around on the property without drawing unwanted attention to a cave that needed to stay secret.
ss	948	It's such a poetic and unfortunate irony that she really is giving them a peptalk, fueling the exact opposite of what she wants. At this point, Kaylah knows of Soren's claims as a whisper and a leader of the whispers, having made promises to them, but Saff has no way of knowing that.
tt	961	I like to include the occasional echo or callback. If you analyze Soren and Kaylah's relationship in contrast to Saff and Ben's, there are intentional comparisons. In this instance, this is an echo to their first kiss—Guillen's hesitance to believe her acceptance.
uu	982	Identity is subtly interwoven into this series. Our unique experiences mold how we see ourselves, what we call ourselves, and where we call home. Rachel never truly chose the Seeder life or felt accepted. She rejects her Seeder name, still clings to human customs, and doesn't shy away from an expat's life. I admire Saff for wholeheartedly accepting her heritage, but I also love Rachel for making the most of her choices on a path she hadn't planned for. In a lot of ways, Kaylah also struggles with her identity, titles, and role.
vv	985	My mom used to tuck baby's breath into my braids when I was a little girl. She would braid my hair into a crown and tuck them in for church. I always felt special when she did that.
ww	986	This is a joke my siblings and I have made more than once. I'm the youngest child, so *naturally* my parents decided I would be the last because they couldn't do better after me. My siblings, of course, had it all wrong...
xx	989	Mirrors symbol (x) for contrast.
yy	990	I knew very little about the Green Lands and green folk when I wrote book 1. Only as I delved into the rest of the trilogy did I seriously ask myself more about their powers and history. We get a taste of them here, but we'll get to dive into more of the realm's history in a future book, and I'm excited for that!
zz	992	That had to be a punch to the gut when they realized that... Matriarchs taking on the palace could have saved lives. That reveal would have the same bitter taste as when Kaylah realized her assumptions on whispers had landed her in hot water.
aaa	996	We know so little about their sons from this prologue, especially the unnamed preteen, but this scene speaks volumes and will matter down the road...
bbb	1002	Sometimes, I intricately plan out little clues I sprinkle into the story. Other times, I plant open-ended possibilities without concrete plans for them. Did I have a plot in mind when I established this rumor about the species mixing? I'll let you guess on that...

Don't forget to leave a review!

★★★★★

On Amazon, Goodreads, StoryGraph and/or anywhere else this book can be found.

Don't forget to sign up for J. Houser's newsletter for publishing updates, promotions, and bonus content!

JHouserWrites.com

Also, connect with the author here:

On YouTube, TikTok, Facebook, and Instagram under:

JHouserWrites

About the Author

J. Houser has spent most of her life in the Pacific Northwest of the United States. Her writing philosophy aligns with 'write what you want to read' and 'let the characters be who they are.' While her life is not nearly as exciting as that of her characters (and luckily less heartbreaking), she enjoys the journey, the thought process, the romance and relationships.

Also by J. Houser

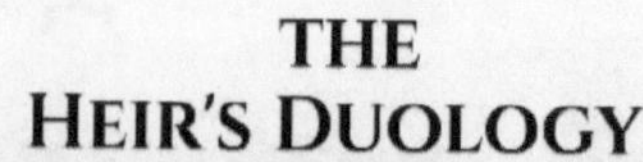

THE SEEDER WARS TRILOGY

THE HEIR'S DUOLOGY

ALSO AVAILABLE
IN THE
SEEDER WARS
WORLD!

Magic in the Match

A SERIES OF STANDALONE
ADULT FAIRY TALE
SWEET ROMANCES

A SELECTION OF PREMIUM BOOK JOURNALS.
EACH ACCOMMODATES ENTRIES FOR 250 BOOKS
AND HAS INDIVIDUAL AESTHETIC TOUCHES

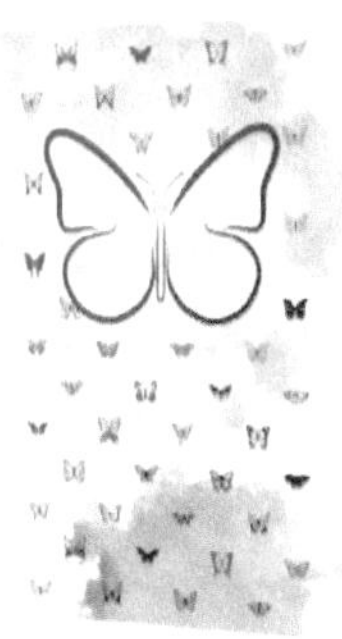

NOTEBOOKS
&
WRITER
RESOURCES

www.ingramcontent.com/pod-product-compliance
Lightning Source LLC
Chambersburg PA
CBHW021221220726
48287CB00016B/2618